THE GRASS CROWN

By Colleen McCullough

The First Man in Rome
The Grass Crown
Fortune's Favorites
Caesar's Women
Caesar

Tim
The Ladies of Missalonghi
A Creed for the Third Millennium
An Indecent Obsession
The Thorn Birds

COLLEEN McCULLOUGH

THE GRASS CROWN

AVON

An Imprint of HarperCollins*Publishers*

First William Morrow hardcover printing: October 1991
First Avon A trade paperback printing: November 2008

HarperCollins books may be purchased for educational, business, or sales promo-
tional use. For information please write: Special Markets Department, Harper-
Collins Publishers, 10 East 53rd Street, New York, NY 10022.

FIRST EDITION

Library of Congress Cataloging-in-Publication Data is available upon request.

ISBN 978-0-06-158239-4

09   10   11   12   13   WBC/RRD   10   9   8   7   6   5   4   3   2

*For Frank Esposito with love,
thanks, admiration and respect.*

A note to the reader: to shed light on the world of ancient Rome, several maps and illustrations have been included throughout this book. Their locations are noted on page vii. A list of the main characters begins on page xiii. An author's note appears on pages 1035–1036. If you would like to know more about the historical background of *The Grass Crown*, turn to pages 1037–1038 for a list of consuls holding office during this period and to page 1039 for a glossary explaining some Latin words and unfamiliar terms.

LIST OF MAPS
AND ILLUSTRATIONS

ITALIA

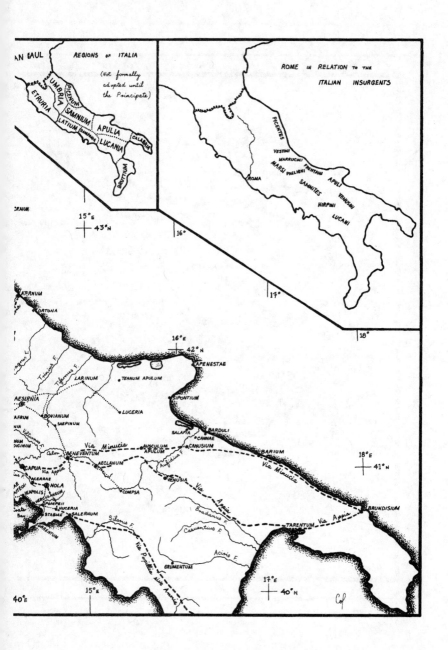

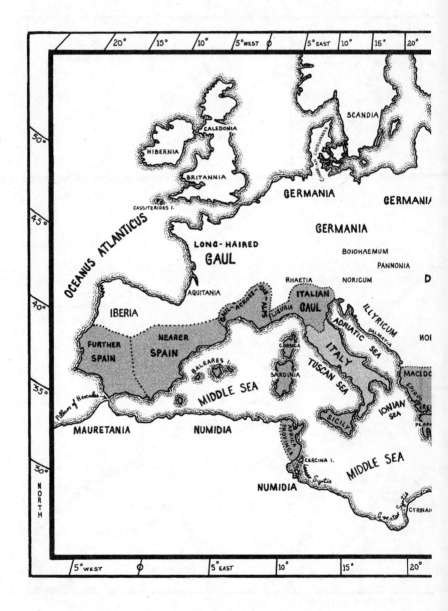

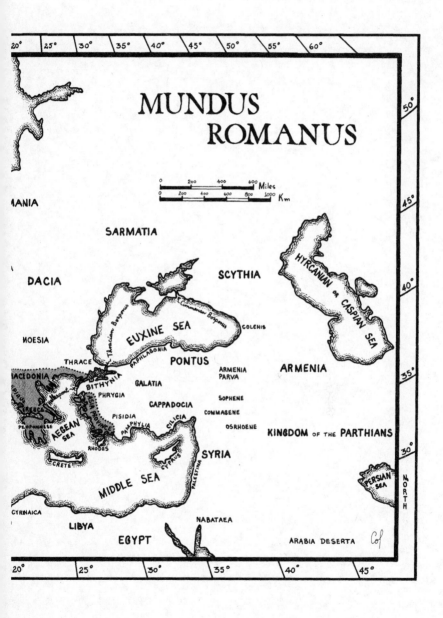

THE MAIN CHARACTERS

NOTE: Parentheses contain biographical information; brackets contain the character's name or diminutive as used in this book. All dates are B.C.

Caepio

Quintus Servilius Caepio [Caepio]
Livia Drusa, his wife (sister of Marcus Livius Drusus)
Quintus Servilius Caepio Junior [Young Caepio], his son
Servilia Major [Servilia], his elder daughter
Servilia Minor [Lilla], his younger daughter
Quintus Servilius Caepio (consul 106), his father, of Gold of Tolosa fame
Servilia Caepionis, his sister

Caesar

Gaius Julius Caesar
Aurelia, his wife (daughter of Rutilia, niece of Publius Rutilius Rufus)
Gaius Julius Caesar Junior [Young Caesar], his son
Julia Major [Lia], his older daughter
Julia Minor [Ju-ju], his younger daughter
Gaius Julius Caesar [Caesar Grandfather], his father
Julia, his sister
Julilla, his sister
Sextus Julius Caesar, his older brother
Claudia, Sextus's wife

Drusus

Marcus Livius Drusus
Servilia Caepionis, his wife (sister of Caepio)
Marcus Livius Drusus Nero Claudianus, his adopted son
Cornelia Scipionis, his mother
Livia Drusa, his sister (wife of Caepio)
Mamercus Aemilius Lepidus Livianus, his blood brother, adopted out

Marius

Gaius Marius
Julia, his wife (sister of Gaius Julius Caesar)
Gaius Marius Junior [Young Marius], his son

Metellus

Quintus Caecilius Metellus Pius [the Piglet]
Quintus Caecilius Metellus Numidicus [Piggle-wiggle] (consul 109, censor 102), his father

Pompeius

Gnaeus Pompeius Strabo [Pompey Strabo]
Gnaeus Pompeius [Young Pompey], his son
Quintus Pompeius Rufus, his remote cousin

Rutilius Rufus

Publius Rutilius Rufus (consul 105)

Scaurus

Marcus Aemilius Scaurus Princeps Senatus (consul 115, censor 109)
Caecilia Metella Dalmatica [Dalmatica], his second wife

Sulla

Lucius Cornelius Sulla
Julilla, his first wife (sister of Gaius Julius Caesar)
Aelia, his second wife
Lucius Cornelius Sulla Junior [Young Sulla], his son (by Julilla)
Cornelia Sulla, his daughter (by Julilla)

Bithynia

Nicomedes II, King of Bithynia
Nicomedes III, his older son, King of Bithynia
Socrates, his younger son

Pontus

Mithridates VI Eupator, King of Pontus
Laodice, his sister and wife, first Queen of Pontus (d. 99)
Nysa, his wife, second Queen of Pontus (daughter of Gordius of Cappadocia)
Ariarathes VII Philometor, his nephew, King of Cappadocia
Ariarathes VIII Eusebes Philopator, his son, King of Cappadocia
Ariarathes X, his son, King of Cappadocia

PART I

GAIUS MARIUS

The most exciting thing that's happened during the last fifteen months," said Gaius Marius, "is the elephant Gaius Claudius showed at the *ludi Romani*."

Aelia's face lit up. "Wasn't it wonderful?" she asked, leaning forward in her chair to reach the dish of huge green olives imported from Further Spain. "To be able to stand on its back legs and walk! And dance on all four legs! And sit on a couch and feed itself with its trunk!"

Turning a contemptuous face to his wife, Lucius Cornelius Sulla said very coldly, "Why is it people are charmed to see animals aping men? The elephant is the noblest creature in the world. Gaius Claudius Pulcher's beast I found a double travesty—of man and elephant both."

The pause which followed was infinitesimal, though everyone present in the dining room was uncomfortably aware of it; then Julia diverted all eyes from the blighted Aelia by laughing merrily. "Oh, come, Lucius Cornelius, it was the absolute favorite of the whole crowd!" she said. "I know I admired it—so clever and busy!—and when it lifted its trunk and trumpeted in time to the drum—amazing! Besides," she added, "no one *hurt* it."

"Well, I liked its color," said Aurelia, thinking it wise to contribute her mite. "Pink!"

All of which Lucius Cornelius Sulla ignored by swiveling on his elbow and talking to Publius Rutilius Rufus.

Eyes sad, Julia sighed. "I think, Gaius Marius," she said to her husband, "that it's time we women withdrew and let you men enjoy your wine. Would you excuse us?"

Out went Marius's hand across the narrow table between his couch and Julia's chair; she lifted her own hand to clasp it warmly, and tried not to feel even sadder at the sight of his warped smile. So long now! Yet still his face bore the evidence of that insidious stroke. But what the loyal and loving wife could not admit, even to herself, was that the stroke had wrought a tiny havoc within Gaius Marius's mind; the temper that now flared too easily, the increased emphasis he placed upon largely imagined slights, a hardening in his attitude toward his enemies.

She rose, disengaged her hand from Marius's with a very special smile for him, and put the hand upon Aelia's shoulder. "Come, my dear," she said, "we'll go down to the nursery."

Aelia got up. So did Aurelia. The three men did not, though their conversation ceased until the women had gone from the room. A gesture from Marius sent the servants scurrying to clear the women's chairs from the dining room after which they too vanished. Now only the three couches remained, forming a U; to make conversation easier, Sulla shifted from where he had lain beside Marius to the vacant couch facing Rutilius Rufus. Both of them were then able to see Marius as well as they could each other.

"So Piggle-wiggle is to come home at last," said Lucius Cornelius Sulla when he was sure his detested second wife was out of earshot.

Marius shifted restlessly on the middle couch, frowning, but less direfully than of yore, for the lingering paralysis gave the left half of the grimace a mournful quality.

"What do you want to hear from me by way of answer, Lucius Cornelius?" Marius asked finally.

Sulla laughed shortly. "Why should I want anything but an honest answer? Though, you know, I did not phrase what I said as a question, Gaius Marius."

"I realize that. But it required an answer nonetheless."

"True," said Sulla. "All right, I'll rephrase it. How do you feel about Piggle-wiggle's being recalled from exile?"

"Well, I'm not singing paeans of joy," said Marius, and gave Sulla a piercing glance. "Are *you*?"

They have drifted subtly apart, thought Publius Rutilius Rufus, reclining on the second couch. Three years ago—or even two years ago—they could not have had such a tensely wary conversation. What *happened*? And whose fault is it?

"Yes and no, Gaius Marius." Sulla stared down into his wine cup. "I'm bored!" he said then through clenched teeth. "At least when Piggle-wiggle returns to the Senate, things might take an interesting turn. I miss those titanic battles you and he used to have."

"In which case, Lucius Cornelius you're going to be disappointed. I'm not going to be here when Piggle-wiggle arrives in Rome."

Both Sulla and Rutilius Rufus sat up.

"Not going to be in Rome?" asked Rutilius Rufus, squeaking.

"Not going to be in Rome," said Marius again, and grinned in sour satisfaction. "I've just remembered a vow I made to the Great Goddess before I beat the Germans. That if I won, I'd make a pilgrimage to her sanctuary at Pessinus."

"Gaius Marius, you can't *do* that!" said Rutilius Rufus.

"Publius Rutilius, I can! And I will!"

Sulla flopped on his back, laughing. "Shades of Lucius Gavius Stichus!" he said.

"Who?" asked Rutilius Rufus, always ready to be sidetracked if there was a possibility of gossip.

"My late lamented stepmother's late lamented nephew," said Sulla, still grinning. "Many years ago he moved into my house—it belonged to my late lamented stepmother then. His aim was to get rid of me by destroying Clitumna's fondness for me, and his thinking was that if the two of us were there together in Clitumna's house, he'd show me up. So I went away. Right away from Rome. With the result that he had nobody to show up except himself—which he did very effectively. Clitumna was fed up in no time." He rolled over, belly down now. "He died not long afterward," Sulla said reflectively, and heaved a stagey sigh through the middle of his smile. "I ruined all his plans!"

"Here's hoping then that Quintus Caecilius Metellus Numidicus Piggle-wiggle finds his return a hollow victory," said Marius.

"I'll drink to that," said Sulla, and did.

A silence fell that was not easy to break, for the old accord was missing, and Sulla's answer had not brought it back. Perhaps, thought Publius Rutilius Rufus, that old accord was a matter of expedience and the battlefield, rather than a truly deep-seated friendship. Only how can they forget all those years when together they fought Rome's foreign enemies? How can they let this Rome-induced discontent blot out all that's gone before? The tribunate of Saturninus was the end of the old life. Saturninus, who had wanted to be king of Rome—and that unfortunate stroke of Marius's. Then, said he to himself, Nonsense, Publius Rutilius Rufus! They're both men who have to be up and doing important things, they're just not the sort to like sitting at home—and being out of office when they are at home. Give them another war to fight together, or a Saturninus inciting revolution, and they'd be purring like a pair of cats washing each other's faces.

Time got away, of course. He and Gaius Marius were in their sixtieth year, and Lucius Cornelius Sulla was forty-two. Not being addicted to peering into the uneven depths of a mirror, Publius Rutilius Rufus wasn't sure how he himself had weathered the vicissitudes of age, but there was nothing wrong with his eyes at the distance from which he now viewed Gaius Marius and Lucius Cornelius Sulla.

Gaius Marius was sufficiently heavier these days to warrant the making of new togas; a big man always—but a fit and well-proportioned one—his extra weight was distributed on shoulders, back, hips and thighs as well as a rather muscular-looking paunch; and to some extent this additional burden he carried had smoothed out his face, which was bigger, rounder, higher in the forehead thanks to receding hair. Deliberately Rutilius Rufus ignored the left-sided paresis, dwelt instead upon those amazing eyebrows, as huge and bushy and undisciplined as ever. Oh, what storms of artistic consternation Gaius Marius's brows had raised in many a sculptor's breast! Commissioned to take the Marian portrait in stone for some town or guild or vacant plot just crying for a statue, those sculptors who lived in Rome or Italy knew before they set eyes on Gaius Marius what they had to contend with. But the look of horror on the face of some much-vaunted Greek sent by Athens or Alexandria to do a likeness of the most sculpted man since Scipio Africanus when he saw the Marian brows—! Each artist did what he could; yet even painted on a piece of board or linen, Gaius Marius's face ended up as mere background for his eyebrows.

Whereas the best portrait of his old friend that Rutilius Rufus had ever seen had been a crude drawing in some black substance upon the outside wall of Rutilius Rufus's own house. Just a few lines was all—a single voluptuous curve to suggest that full lower lip, a sort of glitter for the eyes—how could whoever did it make black seem a glitter?—and no more than ten lines for each eyebrow. Yet it was Gaius Marius to the life, with all the pride, the intelligence, the indomitability, the sheer *character*. Only how did one describe it, that form of art? *Vultum in peius fingere* . . . A face fashioned out of malice. But so good that the malice had turned into truth. Alas, before Rutilius Rufus could work out how he might remove the piece of plaster without its crumbling into a thousand fragments, there had been a heavy fall of rain, and Gaius Marius's best likeness was no more.

No backstreet scrawler upon walls could ever do that to Lucius Cornelius Sulla, however. Without the magic of color, Sulla could have been any of a thousand fairly handsome men. Regular face, regular features, a proper Romanness about him that Gaius Marius could never own. Yet seen in color, he was unique. At forty-two he showed no signs of thinning hair—such hair! Neither red, nor gold. Thick, waving, worn perhaps a little too long. And eyes like the ice in a glacier, the palest of blues, ringed around with a blue as dark as a thundercloud. Tonight his thin, upcurving brows were a good brown, as were his long thick lashes. But Publius Rutilius Rufus had seen him in more urgent circumstances, and knew that tonight, as was his wont, he had applied *stibium* to them; for in reality, Sulla's brows and lashes were so fair they only showed at all because his skin was a pallid, almost unpigmented white.

Women lost sanity, virtue, judgment over Sulla. They threw caution to the winds, outraged their husbands and fathers and brothers, gushed and giggled if he so much as glanced at them in passing. Such an able, intelligent man! A superlative soldier, an efficient administrator, brave as any man could hope to be, little short of perfection at organizing himself or others. And yet women were his downfall. Or so thought Publius Rutilius Rufus, whose nice but homely face and ordinary mousy coloring had never distinguished him from a myriad other men. Not that Sulla was a philanderer, or even an occasional ladykiller; as far as Rutilius Rufus knew, he behaved with admirable rectitude. But there was no doubt that a man who hungered to reach the top of the Roman political ladder stood a much better chance of doing so if he did not have a face like Apollo's; handsome men who were enormously attractive to women were generally mistrusted by their peers, dismissed as lightweights, or as effeminate fellows, or as potential cuckolders.

Last year, thought Rutilius Rufus, his reminiscences meandering on, Sulla had run for election as a praetor. Everything seemed to be in his favor. His war record was splendid—and well advertised, for Gaius Marius had made sure the electors knew how invaluable Sulla had been to him, as quaestor, tribune, and finally legate. Even Catulus Caesar (who had no real cause to love Sulla, the author of his embarrassment in Italian Gaul, when Sulla, by instigating a mutiny, had saved Catulus Caesar's army from annihilation) had come forth and praised his services in Italian Gaul, the year the German Cimbri had been defeated. Then, during the few short days when Lucius Appuleius Saturninus had threatened the State, it had been Sulla, tirelessly energetic and efficient, who had enabled Gaius Marius to put an end to the business. For when Gaius Marius had issued an order, it had been Sulla who implemented it. Quintus Caecilius Metellus Numidicus—he whom Marius, Sulla and Rutilius Rufus called Piggle-wiggle—had been assiduous before he went into exile in explaining to everyone he knew that in his opinion, the successful conclusion of the war in Africa against King Jugurtha was entirely due to Sulla, that Marius had claimed the credit unfairly. For it had been thanks to Sulla's solo efforts that Jugurtha himself had been captured, and everyone knew that until Jugurtha was captured, the war in Africa would drag on. When Catulus Caesar and some of the other ultra-conservative leaders in the Senate agreed with Piggle-wiggle that the credit for the Jugurthine War should by rights go to Sulla, Sulla's star seemed sure to rise, his election as one of the six praetors a certainty. To all of which had to be added Sulla's own conduct in the matter—admirably modest, deprecating, fair-minded. Until the very end of the electoral campaign, he had insisted that his capture of Jugurtha must be attributed to Marius, as he himself had only been acting under Marius's orders. This kind of conduct the voters usually appreciated; loyalty to one's commander in the field or the Forum was highly prized.

And yet, when the Centuriate electors assembled in the *saepta* on the Campus Martius and the Centuries one by one gave their choices, the name of Lucius Cornelius Sulla—so aristocratic and acceptable in itself—was not among the six successful candidates; to add insult to injury, some of the men who were elected were as mediocre in achievement as in their ability to show the proper ancestors.

Why? Immediately after polling day, that was the question everyone attached to Sulla asked, though he said nothing. However, he knew why; a little later, Rutilius Rufus and Marius learned what Sulla already knew. The reason for his failure had a name, and was not physically very large. Caecilia Metella Dalmatica. Barely nineteen years old. And the wife of Marcus Aemilius Scaurus Princeps Senatus, he who had been consul in the year the Germans first appeared, censor in the year Metellus Numidicus Piggle-wiggle had gone off to Africa to fight Jugurtha, and Leader of the House since his consulship, now seventeen years in the past. It had been Scaurus's son who was contracted to marry Dalmatica, but he had killed himself after Catulus Caesar's retreat from Tridentum, a self-confessed coward. And Metellus Numidicus Pigglewiggle, guardian of his seventeen-year-old niece, promptly gave her in marriage to Scaurus himself, though there were forty years between husband and wife.

No one, of course, had asked Dalmatica how she felt about the union, and at first she hadn't been very sure herself. A little dazzled by the immense *auctoritas* and *dignitas* her new husband possessed, she was also glad to be free of her uncle Metellus Numidicus's stormy household, which at that time contained his sister, a woman whose sexual proclivities and hysterical behavior had made her a torment to live with. Dalmatica became pregnant at once (a fact which increased Scaurus's *auctoritas* and *dignitas* even more), and bore Scaurus a daughter. But in the meantime she had met Sulla at a dinner party given by her husband, and the attraction between them had been powerful, mutual, distressing.

Aware of the danger she presented, Sulla had made no attempt to pursue an acquaintance with Scaurus's young wife. She, however, had different ideas. And after the shattered bodies of Saturninus and his friends were burned with all the honor their properly Roman status decreed, and Sulla began to go about the Forum and the city making himself known as part of his campaign to win a praetorship, Dalmatica too began to go about the Forum and the city. Wherever Sulla went, there too would be Dalmatica, all muffled in draperies, hiding behind a plinth or a column, sure that no one noticed her.

Very quickly Sulla learned to avoid places like the Porticus Margaritaria, where indeed a woman of a noble house might be expected to haunt the jeweler's shops, and could claim innocent presence. That reduced her chances of actually speaking to him, but to Sulla her conduct was a resurrection of an old and awful nightmare—of the days when Julilla had buried him beneath an avalanche of love letters she or her girl had slipped into the sinus of his toga at every opportunity, in circumstances where he didn't dare draw attention to their actions. Well, that had ended in a marriage, a virtually indissoluble *confarreatio* union which had lasted— bitter, importunate, humiliating—until her death by suicide, yet one more terrible episode in an endless procession of women hungry to tame him.

So Sulla had gone into the mean and stinking, crowded alleys of the Subura, and confided in the only friend he owned with the detachment he needed so desperately at that moment—Aurelia, sister-in-law of his dead wife, Julilla.

"What can I do?" he had cried to her. "I'm trapped, Aurelia; it's Julilla all over again! I can't be rid of her!"

"The trouble is, they have so little to do with their time," said Aurelia, looking grim. "Nursemaids for their babies, little parties with their friends chiefly distinguished by the amount of gossip they exchange, looms they have no intention of using, and heads too empty to find solace in a book. Most of them feel nothing for their husbands because their marriages are made for convenience— their fathers need extra political clout, or their husbands the dowries or the extra nobility. A year down the road, and they're ripe for the mischief of a love affair." She sighed. "After all, Lucius Cornelius, in the matter of love they can exercise free choice, and in how many areas can they do that? The wiser among them content themselves with slaves. But the most foolish are those who fall in love. And that, unfortunately, is what has happened here. This poor silly child Dalmatica is quite out of her mind! And you are the cause of it."

He chewed his lip, hid his thoughts by staring at his hands. "Not a willing cause," he said.

"*I* know that! But does Marcus Aemilius Scaurus?"

"Ye gods, I hope he knows nothing!"

Aurelia snorted. "I'd say he knows plenty."

"Then why hasn't he come to see me? Ought I to see him?"

"I'm thinking about that," said the landlady of an insula apartment building, the confidante of many, the mother of three children, the lonely wife, the busy soul who was never a busybody.

She was sitting side-on to her work table, a large area completely covered by rolls of paper, single sheets of paper, and book buckets; but there was no disorder, only the evidence of many business matters and much work.

If she could not help him, Sulla thought, no one could, for the only other person to whom he might have gone was not reliable in this situation. Aurelia was purely friend; Metrobius was also lover, with all the emotional complications that role meant, as well as the further complication of his male sex. When he had seen Metrobius the day before, the young Greek actor had made an acid remark about Dalmatica. Shocked, Sulla had only then realized that all of Rome must be talking about him and Dalmatica, for the world of Metrobius was far removed from the world Sulla now moved in.

"Ought I see Marcus Aemilius Scaurus?" Sulla asked again.

"I'd prefer that you saw Dalmatica, but I don't see how you possibly can," said Aurelia, lips pursed.

Sulla looked eager. "Could you perhaps invite her here?"

"Certainly not!" said Aurelia, scandalized. "Lucius Cornelius, for a particularly hard-headed man, sometimes you don't seem to have the sense you were surely born with! Don't you understand? Marcus Aemilius Scaurus is undoubtedly having his wife watched. All that's saved your white hide so far is lack of evidence to support his suspicions."

His long canines showed, but not in a smile; for an unwary moment Sulla dropped his mask, and Aurelia caught a glimpse of someone she didn't know. Yet—was that really true? Better to say, someone she had sensed lived there inside him, but never before had seen. Someone devoid of human qualities, a naked clawed monster fit only to scream at the moon. And for the first time in her life, she felt terrible fear.

Her visible shiver banished the monster; Sulla put up his mask, and groaned.

"Then what do I do, Aurelia? What *can* I do?"

"The last time you talked about her—admittedly that was two years ago—you said you were in love with her, though you'd only met her that once. It's very like Julilla, isn't it? And that makes it more unbearable by far. Of course, *she* knows nothing of Julilla beyond the fact that in the past you had a wife who killed herself— exactly the sort of fact to enhance your attractiveness. It suggests you're dangerous for a woman to know, to love. What a challenge! No, I very much fear poor little Dalmatica is hopelessly caught in your toils, however unintentionally you may have thrown them."

She thought for a moment in silence, then held his eyes. "Say nothing, Lucius Cornelius, and do nothing. Wait until Marcus Aemilius Scaurus comes to you. That way, you look utterly innocent. But make *sure* he can find no evidence of infidelity, even of the most circumstantial nature. Forbid your wife to be out of your house when you are at home, in case Dalmatica bribes one of your servants to let her in. The trouble is, you neither understand women, nor like them very much. So you don't know how to deal with their worst excesses—and they bring out the worst in you. Her husband must come to you. But be kind to him, I beg you! He will find his visit galling, an old man with a young wife. Not a cuckold, but only because of your disinterest. Therefore you must do everything in your power to keep his pride intact. After all, his clout is only equaled by Gaius Marius's." She smiled. "I know that's one comparison he wouldn't agree with, but it's true. If you want to be praetor, you can't afford to offend him."

Sulla took her advice, but unfortunately not all of it; and made a bad enemy because he was not kind, not helpful, did not strive to keep Scaurus's pride intact.

For sixteen days after his interview with Aurelia, nothing happened, except that now he searched for Scaurus's watchers, and he took every precaution to give Scaurus no evidence of infidelity. There were furtive winks and covert grins among Scaurus's friends, and among his own; no doubt they had always been there to see, but he had closed his eyes to them.

The worst of it was that he still wanted Dalmatica—or loved her—or was obsessed by her—or all three. Julilla once more. The pain, the hatred, the hunger to lash out in any direction at anyone who got in his way. From a dream about making love to Dalmatica, he would pass in a flash to a dream about breaking her neck and seeing her dance insanely across a patch of moonlit grass in Circei— no, no, that was how he had killed his stepmother! He began frequently to open the secret drawer in the cupboard which housed the mask of his ancestor Publius Cornelius Sulla Rufinus Flamen Dialis, take from it his little bottles of poisons and the box containing white foundry powder—that was how he had killed Lucius Gavius Stichus and Hercules Atlas the strongman. Mushrooms? That was how he had killed his mistress—eat these, Dalmatica!

But time and experience had accumulated since Julilla died, and he knew himself better; he couldn't kill Dalmatica any more than he had been able to kill Julilla. With the women of noble and ancient houses, there was no other alternative than to see the business out to its last and bitterest flicker. One day—some day—he and Caecilia Metella Dalmatica would finish what he at this moment did not dare to start.

Then Marcus Aemilius Scaurus came knocking on his door, that same door which had felt the hands of many ghosts, and oozed a drop of malice from out of its woody cells. The act of touching it contaminated Scaurus, who thought only that this interview was going to be even harder than he had envisioned.

Seated in Sulla's client's chair, the doughty old man eyed his host's fair countenance sourly through clear green orbs which gave the lie to the lines upon his face, the hairlessness of his skull. And wished, wished, wished that he could have stayed away, that he didn't have to beggar his pride to deal with this hideously farcical situation.

"I imagine you know why I'm here, Lucius Cornelius," said Scaurus, chin up, eyes direct.

"I believe I do," said Sulla, and said no more.

"I have come to apologize for the conduct of my wife, and to assure you that, having spoken to you, I will proceed to make it impossible for my wife to embarrass you further." There! It was out. And he was still alive, hadn't died of shame. But at the back of Sulla's calm dispassionate gaze he fancied he discerned a faint contempt; imaginary, perhaps, but it was that which turned Scaurus into Sulla's enemy.

"I'm very sorry, Marcus Aemilius." *Say* something, Sulla! Make it easier for the old fool! Don't leave him sitting there with his pride in tatters! Remember what Aurelia said! But the words refused to come out. They milled inchoate within his mind and left his tongue a thing of stone, silent.

"It will be better for everyone concerned if you leave Rome. Take yourself off to Spain," Scaurus said finally. "I hear that Lucius Cornelius Dolabella can do with competent help."

Sulla blinked with exaggerated surprise. "*Can* he? I hadn't realized things were so serious! However, Marcus Aemilius, it isn't possible for me to uproot myself and go to Further Spain. I've been in the Senate now for nine years, it's time I sought election as a praetor."

Scaurus swallowed, but strove to continue seeming pleasant. "Not this year, Lucius Cornelius," he said gently. "Next year, or the year after. This year you must leave Rome."

"Marcus Aemilius, *I* have done nothing wrong!" Yes, you have,

Sulla! What you are doing at this very moment is wrong, you're treading all over him! "I am three years past the age for a praetor, my time grows short. I shall stand this year, which means I must stay in Rome."

"Reconsider, please," said Scaurus, rising to his feet.

"I cannot, Marcus Aemilius."

"If you stand, Lucius Cornelius, I assure you, you won't get in. Nor will you get in next year, or the year after that, or the year after that," said Scaurus evenly. "So much I promise you. Believe my promise! Leave Rome."

"I repeat, Marcus Aemilius, I am very sorry. But remain in Rome to stand for praetor, I must," said Sulla.

And so it had all fallen out. Injured in both *auctoritas* and *dignitas* though he may have been, Marcus Aemilius Scaurus Princeps Senatus was still able to marshal more than enough influence to ensure that Sulla was not elected a praetor. Other, lesser men saw their names entered on the *fasti*; nonentities, mediocrities, fools. But praetors nonetheless.

It was from his niece Aurelia that Publius Rutilius Rufus learned the true story, and he in turn had passed the true story on to Gaius Marius. That Scaurus Princeps Senatus had set his face against Sulla's becoming a praetor was obvious to everyone; the reason why was less obvious. Some maintained it was because of Dalmatica's pathetic crush on Sulla, but after much discussion, it was generally felt this was too slight an explanation. Having given her ample time to see the error of her ways for herself (he said), Scaurus then dealt with the girl (kindly yet firmly, he said), and made no secret of it among his friends and in the Forum.

"Poor little thing, it was bound to happen," he said warmly to several senators, making sure there were plenty more drifting in the background well within hearing distance. "I could wish she had picked someone other than a mere creature of Gaius Marius's, but . . . He's a pretty fellow, I suppose."

It was very well done, so well done that the Forum experts and the members of the Senate decided the real reason behind Scaurus's opposition to Sulla's candidacy lay in Sulla's known association with Gaius Marius. For Gaius Marius, having been consul an unprecedented six times, was in eclipse. His best days were in the past, he couldn't even gather sufficient support to stand for election as censor. Which meant that Gaius Marius, the so-called Third Founder of Rome, would never join the ranks of the most exalted consulars, all of whom had been censors. Gaius Marius was a spent force in Rome's scheme of things, a curiosity more than a threat, a man who wasn't cheered by anyone higher than the Third Class.

Rutilius Rufus poured himself more wine. "Do you really intend to go to Pessinus?" he asked of Marius.

"Why not?"

"Why so? I mean, I could understand Delphi, or Olympia, or even Dodona. But *Pessinus*? Stuck out there in the middle of Anatolia—in *Phrygia*! The most backward, superstition-riddled, uncomfortable hole on earth! Not a decent drop of wine or a road better than a bridle track for hundreds of miles! Uncouth shepherds to right and to left, wild men from Galatia milling on the border! Really, Gaius Marius! Is it Battaces you're anxious to see in his cloth-of-gold outfit with the jewels in his beard? Summon him to Rome again! I'm sure he'd be only too delighted to renew his acquaintance with some of our more modern matrons—they haven't stopped weeping since he left."

Marius and Sulla were both laughing long before Rutilius Rufus reached the end of this impassioned speech; and suddenly the constraint of the evening was gone, they were at ease with each other and in perfect accord.

"You're going to have a look at King Mithridates," said Sulla, and didn't make it a question.

The eyebrows writhed; Marius grinned. "What an extraordinary thing to say! Now why would you think that, Lucius Cornelius?"

"Because I know you, Gaius Marius. You're an irreligious old fart! The only vows I've ever heard you make were all to do with kicking legionaries up the arse, or conceited tribunes of the soldiers up the same. There's only one reason why you'd want to drag your

fat old carcass to the Anatolian wilderness, and that's to see for
yourself what's going on in Cappadocia, and just how much King
Mithridates has to do with it," said Sulla, smiling more happily
than he had in many months.

Marius turned to Rutilius Rufus, startled. "I hope I'm not so
transparent to everyone as I am to Lucius Cornelius!"

It was Rutilius Rufus's turn to smile. "I very much doubt that
anyone else will even guess," he said. "I for one believed you—you
irreligious old fart!"

Without volition (or so it seemed to Rutilius Rufus), Marius's
head turned to Sulla, and back they were discussing some grand
new strategy. "The trouble is, our sources of information are completely unreliable," Marius said eagerly. "I mean, who of any worth
or ability has been out in that part of the world in years? New Men
scrambled up as far as praetor—no one *I'd* rely on to make an accurate report. What do we really know?"

"Very little," said Sulla, utterly absorbed. "There have been
some inroads into Galatia by King Nicomedes of Bithynia on the
west and Mithridates on the east. Then a few years ago old Nicomedes married the mother of the little King of Cappadocia—she
was the regent at the time, I think. And Nicomedes started calling
himself King of Cappadocia."

"That he did," said Marius. "I suppose he thought it unfortunate when Mithridates instigated her murder and put the child
back on the throne." He laughed softly. "No more King Nicomedes of Cappadocia! I don't know how he thought Mithridates would
let him get away with it, considering that the murdered Queen was
the sister of Mithridates!"

"And her son rules there still, as—oh, they have such exotic
names! An Ariarathes?" asked Sulla.

"The seventh Ariarathes, to be exact," said Marius.

"What do you think is going on?" asked Sulla, his curiosity
whetted by Marius's evident knowledge of these tortuous eastern
relationships.

"I'm not sure. Probably nothing, beyond the normal squabbling
between Nicomedes of Bithynia and Mithridates of Pontus. But I

fancy he's a most interesting fellow, young King Mithridates of Pontus. I'd like to meet him. After all, Lucius Cornelius, he's not much more than thirty years of age, yet he's gone from having no territory other than Pontus itself to owning the best part of the lands around the Euxine Sea. My skin is crawling. I have a feeling he's going to mean trouble for Rome," said Marius.

Deeming it high time he entered the conversation, Publius Rutilius Rufus put his empty wine cup down on the table in front of his couch with a loud bang, and seized his opportunity. "I suppose you mean Mithridates has his eye on our Roman Asia Province," he said, nodding wisely. "Why wouldn't he want it? So enormously rich! And the most civilized place on earth—well, it's been Greek since before the Greeks were Greek! *Homer* lived and worked in our Asia Province, can you imagine it?"

"I'd probably find it easier to imagine it if you started to accompany yourself on a lyre," said Sulla, laughing.

"Now be serious, Lucius Cornelius! I doubt King Mithridates thinks of our Roman Asia Province as a joke—nor must we, even in jest." Joke—jest; Rutilius Rufus paused to admire his verbal virtuosity, and lost his chance to dominate the conversation.

"I don't think there can be any doubt that Mithridates is slavering at the thought of owning our Asia Province," said Marius.

"But he's an oriental," said Sulla positively. "All the oriental kings are terrified of Rome—even Jugurtha, who was far more exposed to Rome than any eastern king, was terrified of Rome. Look at the insults and indignities Jugurtha put up with before he went to war against us. We literally forced him to war."

"Oh, I think Jugurtha always intended to go to war against us," said Rutilius Rufus.

"I disagree," said Sulla, frowning. "I think he *dreamed* of going to war against us, but understood it could be nothing but a dream. It was we who forced the war upon him when Aulus Albinus entered Numidia looking for loot. In fact, that's how our wars usually begin! Some gold-greedy commander who shouldn't be let lead a parade of children is given Roman legions to lead, and off he goes looking for loot—not for Rome's sake, but for the sake of his own purse. Carbo and the Germans, Caepio and the Germans, Silanus and the Germans—the list is endless."

"You're getting away from the point, Lucius Cornelius," said Marius gently.

"Sorry, so I am!" Unabashed, Sulla grinned at his old commander affectionately. "Anyway, I think the situation in the east is very similar to the situation in Africa as it was before Jugurtha went to war against us. We all know that Bithynia and Pontus are traditional enemies, and we all know that both King Nicomedes and King Mithridates would love to expand, at least within Anatolia. And in Anatolia there are two wonderfully rich lands which make their royal mouths water—Cappadocia, and our Roman Asia Province. Ownership of Cappadocia gives a king swift access to Cilicia, and fabulously rich growing soil. Ownership of our Roman Asia Province gives a king unparalleled coastal access onto the Middle Sea, half a hundred superb seaports, *and* a fabulously rich hinterland. A king wouldn't be human if he didn't hunger after both lands."

"Well, Nicomedes of Bithynia I don't worry about," said Marius, interrupting. "He's tied hand and foot to Rome, and he knows it. Nor do I think that—for the present, at any rate—our Roman Asia Province is in any danger. It's Cappadocia."

Sulla nodded. "Exactly. Asia Province is Roman. And I don't think King Mithridates is so different from the rest of his oriental colleagues that he's shed his fear of Rome enough to attempt to invade our Asia Province, misgoverned shambles though it might be. But Cappadocia *isn't* Roman. Though it does fall within our sphere, it seems to me that both Nicomedes and young Mithridates have assumed Cappadocia is a little too remote and a little too unimportant for Rome to go to war about. On the other hand, they move like thieves to steal it, concealing their motive behind puppets and relatives."

There came a grunt from Marius. "I wouldn't call old King Nicomedes's marrying the Queen Regent of Cappadocia furtive!"

"Yes, but that situation didn't last long, did it? King Mithridates was outraged enough to murder his own sister! He had her son back on the Cappadocian throne quicker than you can say Lucius Tiddlypuss."

"Unfortunately it's Nicomedes is our official Friend and Ally, not Mithridates," said Marius. "It's a pity I wasn't in Rome when all that was going on."

"Oh, come now!" said Rutilius Rufus indignantly. "The kings of Bithynia have been officially entitled Friend and Ally for over fifty years! During our last war against Carthage, so too was the King of Pontus an official Friend and Ally. But this Mithridates's father destroyed the possibility of friendship with Rome when he bought Phrygia from Manius Aquillius's father. Rome hasn't had relations with Pontus since. Besides which, it's impossible to grant the status of Friend and Ally to two kings at loggerheads with each other unless that status prevents war between them. In the case of Bithynia and Pontus, the Senate decided awarding Friend and Ally status to both kings would only make matters worse between them. And that in turn meant rewarding Nicomedes of Bithynia because the record of Bithynia is better than Pontus."

"Oh, Nicomedes is a silly old fowl!" said Marius impatiently. "He's been ruling for over fifty years, and he wasn't a child when he eliminated his *tata* from the throne, either. I'd guess his age at over eighty. And he exacerbates the Anatolian situation!"

"By behaving like a silly old fowl, I presume is what you mean." The retort was accompanied by a near-purple look from Rutilius Rufus's eyes, very like his niece Aurelia's, and just as direct, if a little softer. "Do you not think, Gaius Marius, that you and I are very nearly of an age to be called silly old fowls?"

"Come, come, no ruffled feathers, now!" said Sulla, grinning. "I know what you mean, Gaius Marius. Nicomedes is well into his senescence, whether he's capable of ruling or not—and one must presume he *is* capable of ruling. It's the most Hellenized of all the oriental courts, but it's still oriental. Which means if he dribbled on his shoes just once, his son would have him off the throne. There-fore he has retained his watchfulness and his cunning. However, he's querulous and he's grudging. Whereas across the border in Pontus is a man hardly thirty—vigorous, intelligent, aggressive and cocksure. No, Nicomedes can hardly be expected to give Mithridates his due, can he?"

"Hardly," agreed Marius. "I think we can be justified in assuming that if they do come to open blows, it will be an unequal contest. Nicomedes has only just managed to hang on to what he had at the beginning of his reign, while Mithridates is a conqueror. Oh yes, Lucius Cornelius, I must see this Mithridates!" He lay back on his left elbow and gazed at Sulla anxiously. "Come with me, Lucius Cornelius, do! What's the alternative? Another boring year in Rome, especially with Piggle-wiggle prating in the Senate, while the Piglet takes all the credit for bringing his *tata* home."

But Sulla shook his head. "No, Gaius Marius."

"I hear," said Rutilius Rufus, nibbling the side of his fingernail idly, "that the official letter recalling Quintus Caecilius Metellus Numidicus Piggle-wiggle from his exile in Rhodes is signed by the senior consul, Metellus Nepos, and none other than the Piglet, if you please! Of the tribune of the plebs Quintus Calidius, who obtained the recall decree, not a mention! Signed by a very junior senator who is a *privatus* into the bargain!"

Marius laughed. "Poor Quintus Calidius! I hope the Piglet paid him handsomely for doing all the work." He looked at Rutilius Rufus. "They don't change much over the years, do they, the clan Caecilius Metellus? When I was a tribune of the plebs, they treated me like dirt too."

"Deservedly," said Rutilius Rufus. "All you did was to make life hard for every Caecilius Metellus in politics at that time! *And* after they thought they had you in their toils, at that! Oh, how angry was Dalmaticus!"

At the sound of that name Sulla flinched, was conscious of a flush mounting to his cheeks. Her father, Piggle-wiggle's dead older brother. How was she, Dalmatica? What had Scaurus done to her? From the day Scaurus had come to see him at his home, Sulla had never set eyes on her. Rumor had it she was forbidden ever to leave Scaurus's house again. "By the way," he said loudly, "I heard from an impeccable source that there's going to be a marriage of great convenience for the Piglet."

Reminiscences stopped at once.

"*I* haven't heard about it!" said Rutilius Rufus, a little put out; he considered his sources the best in Rome.

"It's true nevertheless, Publius Rutilius."

"So tell me!"

Sulla popped an almond into his mouth and munched for a moment before speaking. "Good wine, Gaius Marius," he said, filling his cup from the flagon placed close at hand when the servants had been dismissed. Slowly Sulla added water to the wine.

"Oh, put him out of his misery, Lucius Cornelius, do!" sighed Marius. "Publius Rutilius is the biggest old gossip in the Senate."

"I agree that he is, but you must admit it made for highly entertaining letters while we were in Africa and Gaul," said Sulla, smiling.

"*Who?*" cried Rutilius Rufus, not about to be deflected.

"Licinia Minor, younger daughter of none other than our urban praetor, Lucius Licinius Crassus Orator himself."

"You're joking!" gasped Rutilius Rufus.

"No, I'm not."

"But she can't be old enough!"

"Sixteen the day before the wedding, I hear."

"Abominable!" growled Marius, eyebrows interlocked.

"Oh really, it's getting beyond all justification!" said Rutilius Rufus, genuinely concerned. "Eighteen is the proper age, and not a day before should it be! We're *Romans,* not oriental cradle snatchers!"

"Well, at least the Piglet is only in his early thirties," said Sulla casually. "What about Scaurus's wife?"

"The least said about that, the better!" snapped Publius Rutilius Rufus. His temper died. "Mind you, one has to admire Crassus Orator. There's no shortage of money for dowries in that family, but just the same, he's done very well with his girls. The older one gone to Scipio Nasica, no less, and now the younger one to the Piglet, only son and heir of. I thought *that* Licinia was bad enough, at seventeen married to a brute like Scipio Nasica. She's pregnant, you know."

Marius clapped his hands for the steward. "Go home, both of you! When the conversation degenerates to nothing more than old women's gossipy tidbits, we've exhausted all other avenues. Pregnant! You ought to be down in the nursery with the women, Publius Rutilius!"

All the children had been brought to Marius's house for this dinner, and all were asleep when the party broke up. Only Young Marius remained where he was; the others had to be taken home by their parents. Two big litters stood outside in the lane, one to accommodate Sulla's children, Cornelia Sulla and Young Sulla, the other for Aurelia's three, Julia Major called Lia, Julia Minor called Ju-ju, and Young Caesar. While the adult men and women stood talking low-voiced in the atrium, a team of servants carried the sleeping children out to the litters and placed them carefully inside.

The man carrying Young Caesar looked unfamiliar to Julia, automatically counting; then she stiffened, clutched Aurelia by the arm convulsively.

"That's Lucius Decumius!" she gasped.

"Of course it is," said Aurelia, surprised.

"Aurelia, you really shouldn't!"

"Nonsense, Julia. Lucius Decumius is a tower of strength to me. I don't have a nice respectable journey home, as you well know. I go through the middle of a den of thieves, footpads, the gods know what—for even after seven years, I don't! It isn't often that I'm lured out of my own home, but when I am, Lucius Decumius and a couple of his brothers always come to bring me home. And Young Caesar isn't a heavy sleeper. Yet when Lucius Decumius picks him up, he never stirs."

"A couple of his *brothers*?" whispered Julia, horrified. "Do you mean to say that there are more at home like Lucius Decumius?"

"No!" said Aurelia scornfully. "I mean his brothers in the crossroads college—his minions, Julia." She looked cross. "Oh, I don't know why I come to these family dinners on the rare occasions when I do come! Why is it that you never seem to understand that I have my life very nicely under control, and don't need all this fussing and clucking?"

Julia said no more until she and Gaius Marius went to bed, having settled the household down, banished the slaves to their quarters, locked the door onto the street, and made an offering to the trio of gods who looked after every Roman home—Vesta of the hearth, the Di Penates of the storage cupboards, and the Lar Familiaris of the family.

"Aurelia was very difficult today," she said then.

Marius was tired, a sensation he experienced a great deal more often these days than of yore, and one which shamed him. So rather than do what he longed to do—namely to roll over on his left side and go to sleep—he lay on his back, settled his wife within his left arm, and resigned himself to a chat about women and domestic problems. "Oh?" he asked.

"Can't you bring Gaius Julius home? Aurelia is growing into an old retired Vestal Virgin, all—I don't know! Sour. Crabby. *Juiceless!* Yes, that's the right word, juiceless," said Julia. "And that child is wearing her out."

"Which child?" mumbled Marius.

"Her twenty-two-month-old son, Young Caesar. Oh, Gaius Marius, he is astonishing! I know such children are born occasionally, but I've certainly never met one before, nor even heard of one among our friends. I mean, all we mothers are happy if our sons know what *dignitas* and *auctoritas* are after their fathers have taken them for their first trip to the Forum at age seven! Yet this little mite knows already, though he's never even *met* his father! I tell you, husband, Young Caesar is truly an astonishing child."

She was warming up; another thought occurred to her, of sufficient moment to make her wriggle, bounce up and down. "Ah! I was talking to Crassus Orator's wife, Mucia, yesterday, and she was saying that Crassus Orator is boasting of having a client with a son like Young Caesar." She dug Marius in the ribs. "You must know the family, Gaius Marius, because they come from Arpinum."

He hadn't really followed any of this, but the elbow had completed what the wriggle and bounce had begun, and he was now awake enough to say, "Arpinum? Who?" Arpinum was his home, there lay the lands of his ancestors.

"Marcus Tullius Cicero. Crassus Orator's client and the son have the same name."

"Unfortunately I do indeed know the family. They're some sort of cousins. Litigious-minded lot! Stole a bit of our land about a hundred years ago, won the court case. We haven't really spoken to them since." His eyelids fell.

"I see." Julia cuddled closer. "Anyway, the boy is eight now, and so brilliant he's going to study in the Forum. Crassus Orator is predicting that he'll create quite a stir. I suppose when Young Caesar is eight, he'll create quite a stir too."

"Huh!" said Marius, yawning hugely.

She dug her elbow in again. "You, Gaius Marius, are going off to sleep! Wake up!"

His eyes flew open, he made a rumbling noise in the back of his throat. "Care to race me round the Capitol?" he asked.

Giggling, she settled down once more. "Well, I haven't met this Cicero boy, but I have met my nephew, little Gaius Julius Caesar, and I can tell you, he isn't . . . *normal.* I know we mostly reserve that word for people who are mentally defective, but I don't see why it can't mean the opposite as well."

"The older you get, Julia, the more talkative you get," complained the weary husband.

Julia ignored this. "Young Caesar isn't two years old yet, but he's about a hundred! Big words and properly phrased sentences—and he knows what the big words mean too!"

And suddenly Marius was wide awake, no longer tired. He lifted himself up to look at his wife, her serene face softly delineated by the little flame of a night lamp. Her *nephew!* Her nephew named Gaius! The Syrian Martha's prophecy, revealed to him the first time he ever saw the crone, in Gauda's palace at Carthage. She had predicted that he would be the First Man in Rome, and that he would be consul seven times. But, she had added, he would not be the greatest of all Romans. *His wife's nephew named Gaius would be!* And he had said to himself at the time, Over my dead body. No one is going to eclipse me. Now here was the child, a living fact.

He lay back again, his tiredness translated to aching limbs. Too much time, too much energy, too much passion had he put into his battle to become the First Man in Rome, to stand by tamely and see the luster of his name dimmed by a precocious aristocrat who would come into his own when he, Gaius Marius, was too old or too dead to oppose him. Greatly though he loved his wife, humbly though he admitted that it was *her* aristocratic name which had procured him that first consulship, still he would not willingly see her nephew, blood of her blood, rise higher than he himself had.

Of consulships he had won six, which meant there was a seventh yet to come. No one in Roman public life seriously believed that Gaius Marius could ever regain his past glory, those halcyon years when the Centuries had voted him in, three times *in absentia,* as a pledge of their conviction that he, Gaius Marius, was the only man who could save Rome from the Germans. Well, he had saved them. And what thanks had he got? A landslide of opposition, disapproval, destructiveness. The ongoing enmity of Quintus Lutatius Catulus Caesar, of Metellus Numidicus Piggle-wiggle, of a huge and powerful senatorial faction united in no other way than to bring down Gaius Marius. Little men with big names, appalled at the idea that their beloved Rome had been saved by a despised New Man—an Italian hayseed with no Greek, as Metellus Numidicus Piggle-wiggle had put it many years before.

Well, it wasn't over yet. Stroke or no stroke, Gaius Marius would be consul a seventh time—*and* go down in the history books as the greatest Roman the Republic had ever known. Nor was he going to let some beautiful, golden-haired descendant of the goddess Venus step into the history books ahead of himself—the patrician Gaius Marius was not, the *Roman* Gaius Marius was not.

"I'll fix you, boy!" he said aloud, and squeezed Julia.

"What was that?" she asked.

"In a few days we're leaving for Pessinus, you and I and our son," he said.

She sat up. "Oh, Gaius Marius! Really! How wonderful! Are you sure you want to take us with you?"

"I'm sure, wife. I don't care a rush what the conventions say.

We're going to be away for two or three years, and that's too long a time at my age to spend without seeing my wife and son. If I were a younger man, perhaps. And, since I'm journeying as a *privatus*, there's no official obstacle to my taking my family along with me." He chuckled. "I'm footing the bill myself."

"Oh, Gaius Marius!" She could find nothing else to say.

"We'll have a look at Athens, Smyrna, Pergamum, Nicomedia, a hundred other places."

"Tarsus?" she asked eagerly. "Oh, I've always wanted to travel the world!"

He still ached, but the sleepiness surged back overwhelmingly. Down went his eyelids; his lower jaw sagged.

For a few more moments Julia chattered on, then ran out of superlatives, and sat hugging her knees happily. She turned to Gaius Marius, smiling tenderly. "Dear love, I don't suppose . . . ?" she asked delicately.

Her answer was his first snore. Good wife of twelve years that she was, she shook her head gently, still smiling, and turned him onto his right side.

 Having stamped out every last ember of the slave revolt in Sicily, Manius Aquillius had come home, if not in triumph, at least in high enough standing to have been awarded an ovation by the Senate. That he could not ask for a triumph was due to the nature of the enemy, who, being enslaved civilians, could not claim to be the soldiers of an enemy nation; civil wars and slave wars occupied a special niche in the Roman military code. To be commissioned by the Senate to put down a civil uprising was no less an honor and no less an undertaking than dealing with a foreign army and enemy, but the general's right to claim a triumph was nonetheless denied. The triumph was the way the People of Rome were physically shown the rewards of war—the prisoners, the captured money, plunder of all descriptions from golden nails in once-kingly doors to packets of cinnamon and frankincense. For everything taken enriched the coffers of Rome, and the People could see with their own eyes how profitable a business war was—if you were Roman, that is, and being Roman, won. But in civil and slave uprisings there were no profits to be made, only losses to be endured. Property looted by the enemy and recaptured had to be returned to its rightful owners; the State could demand no percentage of it.

Thus the ovation was invented. Like the triumph, it consisted of a procession along the same route; however, the general didn't ride in the antique triumphal chariot, did not paint his face, did not wear triumphal garb; no trumpets sounded, only the less inspirational tweetling of flutes; and rather than a bull, the Great God received a sheep, thereby sharing the lesser status of the ceremony with the general.

His ovation had well satisfied Manius Aquillius. Having celebrated it, he took his place in the Senate once more, and as a consular—an ex-consul—was asked to give his opinion ahead of a consular of equal standing but who had not celebrated a triumph or ovation. Tainted with the lingering odium of his parent, another Manius Aquillius, he had originally despaired of reaching the consulship. Some facts were hard to live down if a man's family was only moderately noble; and the fact was that Manius Aquillius's father had, in the aftermath of the wars following the death of King Attalus III of Pergamum, sold more than half the territory of Phrygia to the father of the present King Mithridates of Pontus for a sum of gold he had popped into his own purse. By rights the territory should have gone, together with the rest of King Attalus's possessions, into the formation of the Roman Asia Province, as King Attalus had willed his kingdom to Rome. Backward, owning a populace so ignorant they made poor slaves, Phrygia hadn't seemed to the elder Manius Aquillius like much of a loss for Rome. But the men in Senate and Forum with real clout had not forgiven the elder, nor forgotten the incident when the younger Manius Aquillius entered the political arena.

To attain the praetorship had been a struggle, and had cost most of what was left of that Pontic gold, for the father had been neither thrifty nor prudent. So when the younger Manius Aquillius's own golden opportunity had come, he seized it very quickly. After the Germans had defeated that ghastly pair Caepio and Mallius Maximus in Gaul-across-the-Alps—and looked set to pour down the Rhodanus Valley and into Italy—it had been the praetor Manius Aquillius who had proposed that Gaius Marius be elected consul *in absentia* in order to have the requisite imperium to deal with the menace. His action put Gaius Marius under an obligation to him—an obligation Gaius Marius was only too happy to discharge.

As a result, Manius Aquillius had served as Marius's legate and been instrumental in defeating the Teutones at Aquae Sextiae. Bearing the news of that much-needed victory to Rome, he had been elected junior consul in conjunction with Marius's fifth term. And after the year of his consulship was over, he had taken two of his general's superbly trained veteran legions to Sicily, there to cauterize the festering sore of a slave revolt which had been going on for several years at great peril to Rome's grain supply.

Home again, treated to an ovation, he had hoped to stand for election as censor when it came time to vote a new pair in. But the leaders with the real clout in Senate and Forum had only been biding their time. Gaius Marius himself had fallen in the aftermath of Lucius Appuleius Saturninus's attempt to take over Rome, and Manius Aquillius found himself without protection. He was haled into the extortion court by a tribune of the plebs with plenty of clout and powerful friends among the knights who served both as jurors and presidents of the major courts—the tribune of the plebs Publius Servilius Vatia. Not one of the patrician Servilii, admittedly, Vatia came nonetheless from an important plebeian noble family. And he intended to go far.

The trial took place in an uneasy Forum; several events had helped render it so, starting with the days of Saturninus, though everyone had hoped after *his* death that there would be no more Forum violence, no more murders of magistrates. Yet there had been violence, there had been murder; chiefly as the result of the efforts of Metellus Numidicus Piggle-wiggle's son, the Piglet, to bring some of his vindicated father's enemies to account. Out of the Piglet's strenuous fight to bring his father home, he had earned a more worthy cognomen than the Piglet—he was now Quintus Caecilius Metellus Pius—Pius meaning the Dutiful One. And with that fight successfully concluded, the Piglet Metellus Pius was determined Piggle-wiggle's enemies would suffer. Including Manius Aquillius, so obviously Gaius Marius's man.

Attendance in the Plebeian Assembly was down, so a poor audience surrounded the spot in the lower Forum Romanum where the extortion court had been directed by the Plebeian Assembly to set up its tribunal.

"This whole business is manifestly ridiculous," said Publius Rutilius Rufus to Gaius Marius when they arrived to hear the proceedings of the last day of Manius Aquillius's trial. "It was a slave war! I doubt there were any pickings to be had from Lilybaeum clear to Syracuse—and you can't tell me that all those greedy Sicilian grain farmers didn't keep a strict eye on Manius Aquillius! He wouldn't have had the chance to palm a bronze coin!"

"This is the Piglet's way of getting at me," said Marius, shrugging. "Manius Aquillius knows that. He's just paying the penalty for supporting me."

"*And* paying the penalty for his father's selling most of Phrygia," said Rutilius Rufus.

"True."

The proceedings had been conducted in the new manner laid down by the dead Gaius Servilius Glaucia when he legislated to give the courts back to the knights, thereby excluding the Senate from them save as defendants. Over the preceding days the jury of fifty-one of Rome's most outstanding businessmen had been nominated, challenged and chosen, the prosecution and the defense had given their preliminary addresses, and the witnesses had been heard. Now on this last day the prosecution would speak for two hours, the defense for three, and the jury would then deliver its verdict immediately.

Servilius Vatia had done well for the State, Vatia himself being no mean advocate, and his helpers good; but there was no doubt that the audience, larger by far on this last day, had gathered to hear the heavy artillery—the advocates leading Manius Aquillius's defense.

Cross-eyed Caesar Strabo spoke first, young and vicious, superbly well trained and gifted by nature with a fine turn of rhetorical phrase. He was followed by a man so able he had won the extra cognomen of Orator—Lucius Licinius Crassus Orator. And Crassus Orator gave way to another man who had won the cognomen Orator—Marcus Antonius Orator. To have acquired this cognomen, Orator, was not merely because of consummate public speaking; it rested too upon an unparalleled knowledge of the procedures of rhetoric—the proper, defined steps which had to be adhered to. Crassus Orator had the finer background in law, but Antonius Orator was the finer speaker.

"By a whisker only," said Rutilius Rufus after Crassus Orator ended and Antonius Orator began.

A grunt was his only answer; Marius was concentrating upon Antonius Orator's speech, wanting to be sure he got his money's worth. For of course Manius Aquillius wasn't paying for advocates of this quality, and everyone knew it. Gaius Marius was funding the defense. According to law and custom, an advocate could not solicit a fee; he could, however, accept a gift tendered as a token of appreciation for a job well done. And, as the Republic grew from middle into elderly age, it became generally accepted that advocates be given gifts. At first these had been works of art or furniture; but if the advocate was needy, he then had to dispose of the work of art or piece of furniture given to him. So in the end it had come down to outright gifts of money. Naturally nobody spoke about it, and everybody pretended it didn't happen.

"How short your memories are, gentlemen of the jury!" cried Antonius Orator. "Come now, cast your minds back a few short years in time, to those impoverished Head Count crowds in our beloved Forum Romanum, their bellies as empty as their granaries. Do you not remember how some of you"—there were inevitably half a dozen grain lords on the panel—"could put no less than fifty sesterces a *modius* upon what little wheat your private granaries contained? And the crowds of Head Count gathered day after day, and looked at us, and growled in their throats. For Sicily, our breadbasket, was a ruin, a very Iliad of woes—"

Rutilius Rufus clutched at Marius's arm and emitted a squawk of outraged horror. "There *he* goes! Oh, may every last one of these verbal thieves come down with worm-eaten sores! That's *my* little epigram! A very Iliad of woes, indeed! Don't you remember, Gaius Marius, how I wrote that selfsame phrase to you in Gaul years ago? And had to suffer Scaurus's stealing it! And now what happens? It's passed into general usage, with Scaurus's name on it!"

"Tace!" said Marius, anxious to hear Marcus Antonius Orator.

"—made more woeful by a monumental maladministration! Now we all know who the monumental maladministrator was, don't we?" The keen reddish eye rested upon a particularly vacant face in the second row of the jury. "No? Ah—let me refresh your memories! The young Brothers Lucullus brought him to account, sent him into a citizenless exile. I refer of course to Gaius Servilius Augur. No crops had been gathered in Sicily for four years when the loyal consul Manius Aquillius arrived. And I would remind you that Sicily is the source of over half our grain."

Sulla slid up, nodded to Marius, then bent his attention upon the still simmering Rutilius Rufus. "How goes the trial?"

Rutilius Rufus snorted. "Oh, concerning Manius Aquillius, who knows? The jury wants to find any excuse to convict him, so I daresay it will. He's to be an object lesson for any imprudent fellows who might contemplate supporting Gaius Marius."

"Tace!" growled Marius again.

Rutilius Rufus moved out of earshot, tugging at Sulla to follow. "You're not nearly so quick to support Gaius Marius yourself these days, are you, Lucius Cornelius?"

"I have a career to advance, Publius Rutilius, and I doubt I can do so by supporting Gaius Marius."

Rutilius Rufus acknowledged the truth of this with a nod. "Yes, that's understandable. But, my friend, he doesn't deserve it! He deserves that those of us who know him and hold him in regard should stand by him."

That cut; Sulla hunched his shoulders, hissed his pain. "It's all very well for you to talk! You're a consular, you've had your day! I haven't! You can call me traitor if you like, but I swear to you, Publius Rutilius, that I *will* have my day! And the gods help those who oppose me."

"Including Gaius Marius?"

"Including him."

Rutilius Rufus said no more, only shook his head in despair.

Sulla too was silent for a while, then said, "I hear the Celtiberians are proving more than our current governor in Nearer Spain can bear. Dolabella in Further Spain is so tied down by the Lusitani that he can't move to assist. It looks as if Titus Didius is going to have to go to Nearer Spain during his consulship."

"That's a pity," said Rutilius Rufus. "I like Titus Didius's style, New Man though he may be. Sensible laws for a change—*and* out of the consul's chair."

Sulla grinned. "What, you don't think our beloved senior consul Metellus Nepos thought the laws up?"

"No more than you do, Lucius Cornelius. What Caecilius Metellus ever born was more concerned with improving the machinery of government than his own standing? Those two little laws of Titus Didius's are as important as beneficial. No more rushing bills through the Assemblies, because now three full *nundinae* days must elapse between promulgation and ratification. And no more tacking unrelated matters together to make a law that's as confusing as unwieldy. Yes, if nothing else good has happened this year in Senate or Comitia, at least we can claim Titus Didius's laws," said Rutilius Rufus with satisfaction.

But Sulla wasn't interested in Titus Didius's laws. "All fine and fair, Publius Rutilius, but you're missing my point! If Titus Didius goes to Nearer Spain to put down the Celtiberians, I'm going with him as his senior legate. I've already had a word with him, and he's more than agreeable. It's going to be a long and nasty war, so there'll be booty to share in, and reputations to be made. Who knows? I might even get to command an army."

"You already have a military reputation, Lucius Cornelius."

"But look at all the *cacat* between then and now!" cried Sulla angrily. "They've forgotten, all these voting idiots with more money than sense! So what happens? Catulus Caesar would prefer I was dead in case I ever open my mouth about a mutiny, and Scaurus punishes me for something I didn't do." He showed his teeth. "They ought to worry, that pair! Because if the day ever comes when I decide they've kept me out of the ivory chair forever, I'll make them wish they were never born!"

And I believe him! thought Rutilius Rufus, conscious of a coldness in his bones. Oh, this is a dangerous man! Better that he absents himself. "Then go to Spain with Didius," he said. "You're right, it's the best way to the praetorship. A fresh start, a new reputation. But what a pity you can't manage election as curule aedile. You're such a showman you'd put on wonderful games! After that, you'd be a landslide praetor."

"I don't have the money for curule aedile."

"Gaius Marius would give it to you."

"I won't ask. Whatever I have, at least I can say I got it for myself. No one *gave* it to me—I *took* it."

Words which caused Rutilius Rufus to remember the rumor Scaurus had circulated about Sulla during his campaign to be elected a praetor; that in order to obtain enough money to qualify as a knight, he had murdered his mistress, and then to obtain a senatorial census, he had murdered his stepmother. Rutilius Rufus's inclination had been to dismiss the rumor along with all the other usual rubbish about carnal knowledge of mothers and sisters and daughters, interfering sexually with little boys, and making meals out of excrement. But sometimes Sulla said such things! And then—one wondered . . .

There was a stir on the tribunal; Marcus Antonius Orator was coming to an end.

"Here before you is no ordinary man!" he shouted. "Here before you is a Roman of the Romans, a soldier—and a gallant one!—a patriot, a believer in Rome's greatness! Why should a man like this pilfer pewter plate from peasants, steal sorrel soup from servants and bad bread from bakers? I ask you, gentlemen of the jury! Have you heard any stories of gargantuan peculations, of murder and rape and misappropriation? No! You've had to sit and listen to a shady collection of mean little men, all sniveling at the loss of ten bronze coins, or a book, or a catch of fish!"

He drew a breath and made himself look even bigger, blessed with the wonderful physique of all the Antonians, the curly auburn hair, the reassuringly unintellectual face. Every last member of the jury was fascinated by him.

"He's got them," said Rutilius Rufus placidly.

"I'm more interested in what he intends to do with them," said Sulla, looking alert.

There was a gasp, a cry of amazement. Antonius Orator strode up to Manius Aquillius and assaulted him! He ripped the toga away, then took the neck of Aquillius's tunic in both hands, tore it as easily as if it had been tacked together, and left Manius Aquillius standing on the tribunal clad in nothing more than a loincloth.

"Look!" thundered Antonius. "Is this the lily-white, plucked hide of a *saltatrix tonsa*? Do you see the flab and paunch of a stay-at-home glutton? No! What you see are *scars*. War scars, dozens of them. This is the body of a *soldier*, a brave and very gallant man, a Roman of the Romans, a commander so trusted by Gaius Marius that he was given the task of going behind enemy lines and attacking from the rear! This is the body of one who didn't stagger screaming off the battlefield when a sword nicked him, or a spear skinned his thigh, or a stone knocked the wind out of him! This is the body of one who bound up serious wounds as mere nuisances and got on with the job of killing enemy!" The advocate's hands waved in the air, flopped down limply. "Enough. That's enough. Give me your verdict," he said curtly.

They gave their verdict. *ABSOLVO.*

"Poseurs!" sniffed Rutilius Rufus. "How can the jurors fall for it? His tunic shreds like paper, and there he stands in a *loincloth,* for Jupiter's sake! What does that tell you?"

"That Aquillius and Antonius cooked it up beforehand," said Marius, smiling broadly.

"It tells me that Aquillius doesn't have enough to risk standing there *without* a loincloth," said Sulla.

After the laugh which followed, Rutilius Rufus said to Marius, "Lucius Cornelius says he's going to Nearer Spain with Titus Didius. What do you think?"

"I think it's the best thing Lucius Cornelius can do," said Marius calmly. "Quintus Sertorius is standing for election as a tribune of the soldiers, so I daresay he'll go to Spain as well."

"You don't sound very surprised," said Sulla.

"I'm not. The news about Spain will be general knowledge tomorrow anyway. There's a meeting of the Senate called for the temple of Bellona. And we'll give Titus Didius the war against the Celtiberians," said Marius. "He's a good man. A sound soldier and a general of some talent, I think. Especially when he's up against Gauls of one description or another. Yes, Lucius Cornelius, it will do you more good in the elections to go to Spain as a legate than to rattle all over Anatolia with a *privatus*."

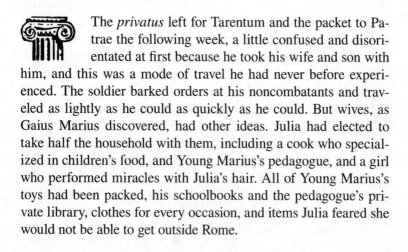

The *privatus* left for Tarentum and the packet to Patrae the following week, a little confused and disorientated at first because he took his wife and son with him, and this was a mode of travel he had never before experienced. The soldier barked orders at his noncombatants and traveled as lightly as he could as quickly as he could. But wives, as Gaius Marius discovered, had other ideas. Julia had elected to take half the household with them, including a cook who specialized in children's food, and Young Marius's pedagogue, and a girl who performed miracles with Julia's hair. All of Young Marius's toys had been packed, his schoolbooks and the pedagogue's private library, clothes for every occasion, and items Julia feared she would not be able to get outside Rome.

"The three of us have more baggage and attendants than the King of the Parthians moving from Seleuceia-on-Tigris to Ecbatana for the summer," Marius growled after three days on the Via Latina saw them no further along than Anagnia.

However, he put up with it until some three weeks later they arrived in Venusia on the Via Appia, prostrated by the heat and unable to find an inn large enough to accommodate all their servants and baggage.

"I'll have an end to it!" roared Marius after the less needed servants and baggage had been sent to another hostelry, and he and Julia were as alone as a busy posting-house on the Via Appia permitted. "Either you streamline your operation, Julia, or you and Young Marius can go back to Cumae, spend the summer there. We are not going to be in uncivilized parts for months to come, so there's no need for half this clutter! And no need for so many people! A cook for Young Marius! I ask you!"

Julia was hot, exhausted, and close to tears; the wonderful holiday was a nightmare from which she could not awaken. Upon hearing the ultimatum, her first instinct was to seize upon the chance to go back to Cumae; then she thought about the years during which she would not see Marius, the years during which he would not see his son. And the possibility that, somewhere unsafe and strange, he might suffer another stroke.

"Gaius Marius, I have never traveled before, except to our villas at Cumae and Arpinum. And when Young Marius and I go to Cumae or Arpinum, we go in the same state as we are now. I see your point. And I wish I could oblige you." She put her head on her hand, furtively brushed at a tear. "The trouble is, I do not have the faintest idea how to go about it."

Never had Marius thought to hear his wife admit something was beyond her! Understanding how hard it was for her to say it, he gathered her into a hug, and kissed the top of her head. "Never mind, I'll do it," he said. "But if I do, there's one thing I shall have to insist upon."

"Anything, Gaius Marius, anything!"

"Whatever you find you need but I've thrown out, whomever you find you need but I've sent home, not a word, Julia! Not—one—word. Understood?"

Sighing with pleasure and squeezing him hard, Julia closed her eyes. "Understood," she said.

After that they got along speedily and well, with, as Julia discovered, surprising comfort. Where possible the Roman nobility on the road stayed in privately owned villas, either belonging to friends or opened by a letter of introduction; it was a form of hospitality sure to be repaid, and therefore not felt to be an imposition. But beyond Beneventum they had mostly to avail themselves of inns, none of which, Julia now realized, could have accommodated them in their old state.

The heat continued remorselessly, for the southern end of the peninsula was dry and largely lacking in shade along the main roads, but the quicker pace at which the party traveled at least varied the monotony and offered a watery solace more often—a swimming hole in a river, or some flat-roofed, mud-brick town with sufficient business acumen to offer baths.

So the Greek-colonized fertility of the coastal plains around Tarentum was very welcome, Tarentum even more so. It was still a town more Greek than Roman, of less importance than of yore, when it had been the terminus of the Via Appia. Now most traffic went to Brundisium, the main point of departure between Italy and Macedonia. Whitewashed and austere, a dazzling contrast to the blue of sea and sky, the green of fields and forests, the rusts and greys of mountain crags, Tarentum professed itself delighted to greet the great Gaius Marius. They stayed in the comfortable coolness of the house of the chief *ethnarch*, though these days he was a Roman citizen, and pretended he was more at ease being called a *duumvir* than an *ethnarch*.

As at many other places along the Via Appia, Marius and the town's more important men gathered to speak of Rome, and of Italy, and of the strained relations at present existing between Rome and her Italian Allies. Tarentum was a Latin Rights colony, its senior magistrates—the two men called *duumviri*—entitled to assume the full Roman citizenship for themselves and their posterity. But its roots were Greek, it was as old or older than Rome; it had been an outpost of Sparta, and in culture and habits, the old Spartan mores persisted still.

There was, Marius discovered, much resentment of the newer Brundisium, and this in turn had led to a great deal of sympathy for the Italian Allied citizens within the lower strata of the town.

"Too many Italian Allied soldiers have died serving in Roman armies commanded by military imbeciles," said the *ethnarch* heatedly to Marius. "Their farms are untended, their sons unsired. And there's an end to money in Lucania, in Samnium, in Apulia! The Italian Allies are obliged to equip their legions of auxiliaries, and then pay to keep them in the field on Rome's behalf! For what, Gaius Marius? So that Rome can keep a road between Italian Gaul and Spain open? What use is that to an Apulian or a Lucanian? When is he ever likely to use it? So that Rome can bring wheat from Africa and Sicily to feed Roman mouths? How much grain in time of famine is put into a Samnite mouth? It is many years since a Roman in Italy paid any kind of direct tax to Rome. But we of Apulia and Calabria, Lucania and Bruttium, never cease to pay Roman taxes! I suppose we should thank Rome for the Via Appia— or Brundisium should, at any rate. But how often does Rome appoint a curator of the Via Appia who keeps it in any sort of decent fettle? There's one section—you must have passed over it—where a flash flood washed out the very roadbed *twenty years ago*! But has it been repaired? No! And will it be repaired? No! Yet Rome tithes us and taxes us, and takes our young men from us to fight in her foreign wars, and they die, and the next thing we know, some Roman landlord has his foot in our door, and our lands are being gobbled up. He brings slaves in to tend his huge flocks, chains them to work, locks them in barracks to sleep, and buys more when they die. Nothing does he spend with us, nothing does he invest with us. We don't see one sestertius of the money he rakes in, nor does he use our people as employees. He decreases our prosperity rather than increases it. The time has come, Gaius Marius, for Rome to be more generous to us, or let us go!"

Marius had listened impassively to this long and very emotional speech, a more articulate version of the same theme he had heard everywhere along the Via Appia.

"I will do what I can, Marcus Porcius Cleonymus," he said gravely. "Indeed, I've been trying to do something for a number of years. That I've had little success is mostly due to the fact that many members of the Senate, those in senior government in Rome, neither travel the way I do, nor speak to local people—nor, Apollo help them!—use their eyes to see. You do certainly know that I have spoken up time and time again about the unforgivable wastage of lives in our Roman armies. And it would seem, I think, that the days when our armies were commanded by military imbeciles are largely over. If no one else taught the Senate of Rome that, *I* did. Since Gaius Marius the New Man showed all those noble Roman amateurs what generalship is all about, I notice that the Senate is more eager these days to give Rome's armies to New Men of proven military worth."

"All well and good, Gaius Marius," said Cleonymus gently, "but it cannot raise the dead from their ashes, nor put sons on our neglected farms."

"I know."

And as their ship put out to sea and spread its big square sail, Gaius Marius leaned on the rail watching Tarentum and its inlet disappear to a blue smudge, and then a nothing. And thought again about the predicament of the Italian Allies. Was it because he had so often been called an Italian—a non-Roman? Or was it because, for all his faults and weaknesses, he did own a sense of justice? Or was it rather that he simply couldn't bear the bungling inefficiency behind it all? One thing of which he was utterly convinced: the day would come when Rome's Italian Allies would demand a reckoning. Would demand the full Roman citizenship for every last man of the whole Italian peninsula, and maybe even Italian Gaul as well.

A shout of laughter broke into his thoughts; he lifted himself off the rail and turned to find his son demonstrating that he was a good sailor, for the ship was moving in the teeth of a stiff breeze, and a poor sailor would by now have been retching miserably. Julia too was looking well and confident.

"Most of my family settle down at sea," she said when Marius joined her. "My brother Sextus is the only poor sailor, probably because of his wheezes."

The packet to Patrae plied that same route permanently, and made as much money from passengers as from cargo, so could offer Marius a cabin of sorts on deck; there was no doubt, however, that when Julia disembarked in Patrae, she was glad to do so. As Marius intended to sail down the Gulf of Corinth too, she refused to budge from Patrae until they had journeyed overland to make a pilgrimage to Olympia.

"It's so odd," she said, riding a donkey, "that the world's greatest sanctuary of Zeus should be tucked away in a backwater of the Peloponnese. I don't know why, but I always used to think Olympia was at the foot of Mount Olympus."

"That's the Greeks for you," said Marius, who itched to get to Asia Province as quickly as possible, but didn't have the heart to deny Julia these obviously welcome treats. Traveling with a woman was not his idea of an enjoyable time.

In Corinth, however, he brightened up. When Mummius had sacked it fifty years earlier, all its treasures had been spirited back to Rome. The town itself had never recovered. Huddled around the base of the mighty rock called the Acrocorinth, many of its houses lay abandoned and crumbling, doors flapping eerily.

"This is one of the places I had intended to settle my veterans," Marius said a little grimly as they walked Corinth's dilapidated streets. "Look at it! Crying for new citizens! Plenty of land fit for growing, a port on the Aegean side and a port on the Ionian side, all the prerequisites of a thriving emporium. And what did they do to me? They invalidated my land bill."

"Because Saturninus had passed it," said Young Marius.

"Exactly. And because those fools in the Senate failed to see how important it is to give Head Count soldiers a bit of land when they retire. Never forget, young Marius, that the Head Count have absolutely no money or property! I opened our armies to the Head Count, I gave Rome fresh blood in the form of a class of citizens who never before had been of real use. And the soldiers of the Head Count went on to prove their worth—in Numidia, at Aquae Sextiae, at Vercellae. They fought as well as or better than the old style of soldier, man of substance though he was. But they can't be discharged and let go back to the stews of Rome! They have to be settled on land. I knew the First Class and the Second Class would never countenance my settling them on Roman public lands within Italy, so I enacted laws to settle them in places like this, hungry for new citizens. Here they would have brought Rome to our provinces, and made us friends in the fullness of time. Unfortunately, the leaders of the House and the leaders of the knights consider Rome to be exclusive, her customs and her way of life not to be disseminated throughout the world."

"Quintus Caecilius Metellus Numidicus," said Young Marius in tones of loathing; he had grown up in a house where that name had never been spoken of with love or liking, and usually with the tag Piggle-wiggle attached to it. However, Young Marius knew better than to add the tag in the presence of his mother, who would have been horrified to hear him using such language—Piggle-wiggle was nursery slang for a little girl's genitalia.

"Who else?" asked Marius.

"Marcus Aemilius Scaurus Princeps Senatus, and Gnaeus Domitius Ahenobarbus Pontifex Maximus, and Quintus Lutatius Catulus Caesar, and Publius Cornelius Scipio Nasica . . ."

"Very good, enough. They marshaled their clients and they organized a faction too powerful even for me. And then, last year, they took most of Saturninus's laws off the tablets."

"His grain law and his land bills," said Young Marius, who was getting on very well with his father now they were emancipated from Rome, and liked to be praised.

"Except the first land bill, the one to settle my soldiers of the Head Count on the African islands," said Marius.

"Which reminds me, husband, of something I wanted to say to you," Julia interrupted.

Marius cast a significant glance down at Young Marius's head, but Julia sailed on serenely.

"How long do you intend to keep Gaius Julius Caesar on that island? Could he not come home?" she asked. "For the sake of Aurelia and the children, he ought to come home."

"I need him on Cercina," said Marius tersely. "A leader of men he is not, but no commissioner ever worked harder or better on any agrarian project than Gaius Julius. As long as he's there on Cercina, the work goes forward, the complaints are minimal, and the results are splendid."

"But it's been so long!" Julia protested. "Three years!"

"And likely to be three more years." Marius was not about to give in. "You know how slow land commissions are—there's so much to do, between surveying, interviewing, compensating, sorting out endless confusions—and overcoming local resistance. Gaius Julius does the work with consummate skill. No, Julia! Not one word more! Gaius Julius stays right where he is until the job is finished."

"I pity his wife and children, then."

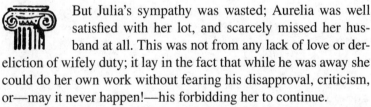 But Julia's sympathy was wasted; Aurelia was well satisfied with her lot, and scarcely missed her husband at all. This was not from any lack of love or dereliction of wifely duty; it lay in the fact that while he was away she could do her own work without fearing his disapproval, criticism, or—may it never happen!—his forbidding her to continue.

When they had married and moved into the larger of the two ground floor apartments within the insula apartment building that was her dowry, Aurelia had discovered that her husband expected her to lead exactly the kind of life she would have led had they lived in a private *domus* on the Palatine. Gracious, elite, and rather pointless. The kind of life she had criticized so tellingly in talking to Lucius Cornelius Sulla. So boring and devoid of challenge that a love affair became irresistible. Appalled and frustrated, Aurelia had learned that Caesar disapproved of her having anything to do with the many tenants who occupied her nine floors of apartments, preferred her to use agents to collect the rents, and expected her to dwell exclusively within the walls of a rather cramped domain.

But Gaius Julius Caesar was a nobleman of an ancient and aristocratic house, and had his own duties. Tied to Gaius Marius by marriage and lack of money, Caesar had begun his public career in Gaius Marius's service, as a tribune of the soldiers and then a military tribune in his armies, and finally, after a quaestorship and admission to the Senate, as the land commissioner deputed to settle Gaius Marius's African Head Count veterans on the island of Cercina in the African Lesser Syrtis. All of these duties had taken him away from Rome, the first of them not long after his marriage to Aurelia. It had been a love match and was blessed by two daughters and a son, none of whom their father had seen born, or progress through infancy. A quick visit home that resulted in a pregnancy, then he was off again for months, sometimes years.

At the time the great Gaius Marius had married Caesar's sister Julia, the house of Julius Caesar had arrived at the end of its money. A providential adoption of the eldest son had given the other and senior branch the funds to ensure its remaining two sons could reach the consulship; that had been the adoption of the son whose new name was Quintus Lutatius Catulus Caesar. But Caesar's father (Caesar Grandfather as he was known these days, long after his death) had two sons and two daughters to provide for, and money enough to provide for only one son out of the four. Until, that is, he had a brainwave and invited the enormously rich, disgracefully lowborn Gaius Marius to take his choice of the two daughters. It had been Gaius Marius's money which dowered the girls and gave Caesar his six hundred *iugera* of land near Bovillae, more than enough income to qualify for the senatorial census. It had been Gaius Marius's money which smoothed every obstacle from the path of the junior branch—Caesar Grandfather's branch—of the house of Julius Caesar.

Caesar himself had summoned up the grace and fairness of mind to be sincerely grateful, though his older brother Sextus had writhed, and moved slowly away from the rest of the family after he married. Without Marius's money, Caesar knew well that he would not even have been eligible for the Senate, and could have hoped for little for his children when they arrived. Indeed, had it not been for Gaius Marius's money, Caesar would never have been permitted to marry the beautiful Aurelia, daughter of a noble and wealthy house, desired by many.

Undoubtedly had Marius been pressed, a private dwelling on the Palatine or Carinae would have been forthcoming for Caesar and his wife; indeed, Aurelia's uncle and stepfather Marcus Aurelius Cotta had begged to use some of her large dowry to purchase this private dwelling. But the young couple had elected to follow Caesar Grandfather's advice, and abandon the luxury of living in complete seclusion. Aurelia's dowry had been invested in an insula, an apartment building in which the young couple could live until Caesar's advancing career enabled him to buy a *domus* in a better part of town. A better part of town would not have been hard to find, for Aurelia's insula lay in the heart of the Subura, Rome's most heavily populated and poorest district, wedged into the declivity between the Esquiline Mount and the Viminal Hill—a seething mass of people of all races and creeds, with Romans of the Fourth and Fifth Classes and the Head Count mingled among it.

Yet Aurelia had found her metier, there in the Suburan insula. And the moment Caesar was gone and her first pregnancy over, she plunged with heart and mind into the business of being a landlady. The agents were dismissed, the books her own to keep, the tenants soon friends as well as clients. She dealt competently, sensibly and fearlessly with everything from murder to vandalism, and even compelled the crossroads college housed within her premises to behave itself. This club, formed of local men, was supposed—with the official sanction of the urban praetor—to care for the religious welfare and facilities of the big crossroads which lay beyond the apex of Aurelia's triangular apartment building—its fountain, its roadbed and sidewalks, its shrine to the Lares of the Crossroads. The custodian of the college and the leader of its denizens was one Lucius Decumius, a Roman of the Romans, though only of the Fourth Class. When Aurelia took over the management of her insula, she discovered that Lucius Decumius and his minions ran a protection agency on the side, terrorizing shopkeepers and caretakers for a mile around. But that she put a stop to; and in the process made a friend of Lucius Decumius.

Lacking milk, she had farmed out her children to the women of her insula, and opened the doors of a world to those impeccably aristocratic little patricians that under more normal circumstances they would never have dreamed existed. With the result that long before they could be expected to commence their formal schooling, the three of them spoke several different grades of Greek, Hebrew, Syrian, several Gallics, and three kinds of Latin—that of their ancestors, that of the lower Classes, and the argot peculiar only to the Subura. They had seen with their own eyes how the people of Rome's stews lived and eaten all sorts of meals foreigners called good food, and were on first-name terms with the evil fellows of Lucius Decumius's crossroads college tavern and officially sanctioned sodality.

All of which, Aurelia was convinced, could do them no real harm. She was not, however, an iconoclast or a reformer, and she held sternly to the tenets of her origins. But alongside all that, there lay in her a genuine love of proper work, and an abiding curiosity about and interest in humanity. Whereas in her sheltered youth she had clung to the example of Cornelia the Mother of the Gracchi, deeming that heroic and star-crossed lady the greatest Roman woman who ever lived, now in her growing maturity she clung to something more tangible and valuable—her mine of good sound common sense. So she saw nothing wrong in the polyglot chatter of her three little impeccably aristocratic patricians, and thought it excellent training for them to have to learn to cope with the fact that those they mixed with could never know or hope to know the heights of distinction theirs by birthright.

What Aurelia dreaded was the return of Gaius Julius Caesar, the husband and father who had never actually been either husband or father. Familiarity would have bred some degree of expertise in these two roles, but Gaius Julius Caesar had never grown at ease, let alone familiar. A Roman of her class, Aurelia neither

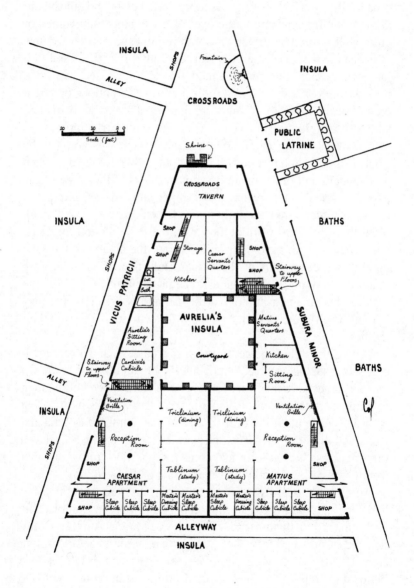

INSULA

ALLEY

SHOPS

Fountain

CROSS ROADS

INSULA

PUBLIC LATRINE

Shrine

CROSSROADS TAVERN

INSULA

BATHS

Shop

Shop

Storage

Caesar Servants' Quarters

Shop

Shop

VICUS PATRICII

SHOPS

Kitchen

Lat. Bath

Stairway to upper Floors

AURELIA'S INSULA

Matius Servants' Quarters

SUBURA MINOR

BATHS

Aurelia's Sitting Room

Courtyard

Kitchen

Stairway to upper Floors

Cardixa's Cubicle

Sitting Room

Ventilation Grille

ALLEY

Triclinium (dining)

Triclinium (dining)

Ventilation Grille

Cal

INSULA

Reception Room

Reception Room

SHOPS

Tablinum (study)

Tablinum (study)

SHOP

CAESAR APARTMENT

MATIUS APARTMENT

SHOP

SHOP

Sleep Cubicle

Sleep Cubicle

Sleep Cubicle

Master's Dressing Cubicle

Master's Sleep Cubicle

Master's Sleep Cubicle

Master's Dressing Cubicle

Sleep Cubicle

Sleep Cubicle

Sleep Cubicle

SHOP

ALLEYWAY

INSULA

20 10 5 0
Scale (feet)

knew nor much cared about the women he undoubtedly used from time to time to rid himself of his more basic needs, though she did know from her exposure to the lives of her tenants that women of other walks could be driven to screaming fits and murder for love of or jealousy of their men. To Aurelia, rather inexplicable. But a fact nonetheless. She just thanked the gods that she had been brought up to know better, and discipline her emotions better; it did not occur to her that there were many women of her own class who also suffered terrible torments of jealousy or frustration.

No, when Caesar came home for good there was going to be trouble. Aurelia had no doubt of it. But put it aside for the day when it happened, and in the meantime enjoyed herself thoroughly, and didn't worry about her three little impeccably aristocratic patricians, or which language they fancied speaking today. After all, didn't the same sort of thing occur on the Palatine and the Carinae, when women gave their children into the charge of nursery-maids from every part of the globe? Only then the results were ignored, swept under the edge of some piece of furniture; even the children became conspirators at the art, and concealed what they felt for the girls and women they knew far better than they did their mothers.

Baby Gaius Julius, however, was a special case, and a very difficult one; even the capable Aurelia felt the breath of some unknown menace upon the back of her neck whenever she stopped long enough to think about this only son, about his qualities and his future. That he drove her to the brink of madness she had admitted to Julia and Aelia at Julia's dinner party, and now was glad she had displayed this weakness, for out of it had come a suggestion from Aelia that Young Caesar be placed in the charge of a pedagogue.

Aurelia had heard of extremely bright children, naturally, but had long ago assumed that they came from poorer, humbler circumstances than the senatorial order; it was Marcus Aurelius Cotta, her uncle and stepfather, their parents had come to see, to solicit from him the wherewithal to give their extremely bright child a better start in life than they could afford—and in return to pledge themselves and their child as clients in his service for the rest of their lives. Cotta had always been pleased to oblige them, happy to think that when the child grew up, he and his sons would be able to avail themselves of the services of someone superlatively gifted. However, Cotta was also a practical and sensible man, so, as Aurelia had heard him say to his wife, Rutilia, one day,

"Unfortunately they don't always live up to their promise, these children. Either their early flame burns too brightly, and they grow dark and cold and inert, or else they become too conceited or too confident, and come crashing down. But a few turn out to be of great use. And when they're useful, they're great treasures. That's why I always agree to help the parents."

What Cotta and Rutilia (who was Aurelia's mother) thought of their extremely gifted grandchild Young Caesar, Aurelia didn't know, for she had hidden her son's precociousness from them as much as she could by not exposing him to them. In fact, she tried to hide Young Caesar from everyone. On one level his brilliance thrilled her, inspired her with all kinds of dreams for his future. But on most levels he depressed her deeply. Had she known his weaknesses and his flaws, she could have coped with him more easily; but who—even a mother—could possibly know the innate character weaknesses and flaws of a child not yet two years old? Before she held him up to satisfy the curiosity of the world, she wanted to feel more securely informed about him, more comfortable with him. And ever at the back of her mind there loomed the dread that he would not contain the strength and the detachment to deal with what a freak of nature had given him.

He was sensitive, she knew that; to crush him was easy. But he bounced back, possessed of some alien and therefore incomprehensible joyousness of being that she herself had never known. His enthusiasm was boundless, his mental processes so thirsty for information that he gobbled up knowledge like some vast fish the contents of its sea. What worried her most was his trustfulness, his anxiety to make friends of everyone, his impatience with her cautions to stop and think, that he not take it for granted that the whole world was there to serve his ends, that he understand the world contained many destructive people.

Yet—how ridiculous, such heart searchings on behalf of a baby! Just because the mental processes were huge did not mean the experience matched it. For the moment, Young Caesar was simply a sponge soaking up whatever he found fluid enough to sink in, and what was not fluid enough, he proceeded to squeeze and pound to make it so. There *were* weaknesses and flaws, but his mother did not know whether they were permanent, or merely the passing phases of an enormous learning process. He was—for instance—utterly charming, and knew it, and played upon it, and bent people to his will. As he did with his Aunt Julia, peculiarly prone to fall for his ploys.

She didn't want to raise a boy who relied upon such dark techniques as charm. Aurelia herself had no charm at all and despised those who had it, for she had seen how easily they got what they wanted, and how little they valued it once they had it. Charm was the mark of a lightweight, not a leader of men. Young Caesar would have to abandon it, for it would do him no good with those men and in those areas where seriousness and all the proper Roman virtues mattered most. He was also very pretty—another undesirable quality. Only how could one iron beauty out of a face, especially when both his parents had plenty of it?

As a result of all this worry nothing but time would answer, she had got into the habit of being hard on the little boy, of finding far less excuse for his mistakes than for the transgressions of his sisters, of rubbing salt into his wounds instead of balm, of being very quick to criticize or scold him. As everyone else he knew tended to make much of him, and his sisters and cousins downright spoiled him, his mother felt *someone* had to play the role of Nasty Stepsister. If it had to be her, his mother, so be it. Cornelia the Mother of the Gracchi would not have hesitated.

The finding of a pedagogue suitable to take charge of a child who ought by rights to have been in the hands of women for years to come was not a task to daunt Aurelia, but rather, just the sort of thing she enjoyed. Sulla's wife Aelia had advised strongly against buying a slave pedagogue, which did make Aurelia's task harder.

Not caring much for Sextus Caesar's wife, Claudia, she did not think of going there for advice. Had Julia's son been in the care of a pedagogue she would certainly have gone to Julia, but Young Marius, an only child, went to school so that he could enjoy the companionship of boys his own age. As, indeed, had been Aurelia's intention with Young Caesar when the time came; she now realized the school alternative was out of the question. Her son would have oscillated between being everyone's butt and everyone's idol, and neither state would be good for him.

So Aurelia went to her mother, Rutilia, and her mother's only brother, Publius Rutilius Rufus. Many times had Uncle Publius been of help to her, even including the subject of her marriage; for it had been he, when the list of her suitors became dauntingly long and august, who had advocated that she be allowed to marry whomsoever she liked. In that way, he had explained, only Aurelia could be blamed for choosing the wrong husband, and perhaps future enmity for her younger brothers could be avoided.

She packed all three of her children off upstairs to the Jewish floor, their favorite asylum in that crowded, noisy home of theirs, and betook herself to her stepfather's house in a litter, accompanied by her Arvernian Gallic maid, Cardixa. Naturally Lucius Decumius and some of his followers would be waiting for her when she emerged from Cotta's house on the Palatine; it would then be coming on for darkness, and the Suburan predators would be prowling.

So successfully had Aurelia's secretiveness hidden her son's extraordinary talents that she found it difficult to convince Cotta, Rutilia and Publius Rutilius Rufus that her little son, not yet two years old, was in urgent need of a pedagogue. But after many patient answers to many incredulous questions, her relatives began to believe her predicament.

"I don't know of a suitable fellow," said Cotta, ruffling his thinning hair. "Your half brothers Gaius and Marcus are in the hands of the rhetors now, and young Lucius goes to school. I would have thought that the best thing to do would be to go to one of the really good vendors of slave pedagogues—Mamilius Malchus or Duronius

Postumus. However, you're set against any but a free man, so I don't know what to tell you."

"Uncle Publius, you've been sitting there saying nothing for the last many moments," said Aurelia.

"So I have!" exclaimed that remarkable man guilelessly.

"Does that mean you know of someone?"

"Perhaps. But first I want to see Young Caesar for myself, and in circumstances where I can form my own opinion. You've kept him mighty dark, niece; and I can't fathom why."

"He's a dear little fellow," said Rutilia sentimentally.

"He's a problem," said his mother without any sentiment.

"Well, I think it's more than time we all went round to see Young Caesar for ourselves," said Cotta, who was growing a little stout, and in consequence breathed noisily.

But Aurelia struck her hands together in dismay, looking from one interested face to another with such trouble and pain in her own that the other three paused, shocked. They had known her since birth, and never before had seen her dealing with a situation she clearly felt beyond her.

"Oh, please!" she cried. "No! Don't you understand? What you propose to do is exactly what I cannot allow to happen! My son must think of himself as *ordinary*! How can he do that if three people descend on him to quiz him—and gush over his answers!—and fill him with false ideas of his own importance?"

A red spot burgeoned in each of Rutilia's cheeks. "My dear girl, he *is* my grandson!" she said, tight-lipped.

"Yes, Mama, I know, and you shall see him and ask him what-ever you wish—*but not yet!* Not as part of a crowd! He—is—so—clever! What any other child of his age wouldn't think to question, he knows the answers to! Let Uncle Publius come on his own for the moment, please!"

Cotta nudged his wife. "Good idea, Aurelia," he said with great affability. "After all, he has his second birthday soon—halfway through Quinctilis, isn't it? Aurelia can invite us to his birthday party, Rutilia, and we'll be able to see for ourselves without the child's suspecting a special motive for our presence."

Swallowing her ire, Rutilia nodded. "As you wish, Marcus Aurelius. Is *that* all right with you, daughter?"

"Yes," said Aurelia gruffly.

Of course Publius Rutilius Rufus succumbed to Young Caesar's ever-increasing mastery of charm, and thought him wonderful, and could hardly wait to tell his mother so.

"I don't know when I've taken such a fancy to anyone since you rejected every servant girl your parents chose for you, and came home yourself with Cardixa," he said, smiling. "I thought then what a pearl beyond price you were! And now I find my pearl has produced—oh, not a moonbeam, but a slice of the sun."

"Stop waxing lyrical, Uncle Publius! This sort of thing is not why I asked you here to see him," said the mother, edgy.

But Publius Rutilius Rufus thought it imperative that she should understand, and sat down with her on a bench in the courtyard at the bottom of the light-well which pierced the center of the insula. It was a delightful spot, as the other ground-floor tenant, the knight Gaius Matius, had a flair for gardening that bordered on perfection. Aurelia called the light-well her hanging gardens of Babylon, for plants trailed over the balconies on every floor, and creepers rooted in the earth of the courtyard had over the years grown all the way to the very top of the shaft. This being summer, the garden itself was redolent with the perfume of roses and wallflowers and violets, and blossoms drooped and reared in every shade of blue, pink, lilac, the year's color scheme.

"My dear little niece," said Publius Rutilius Rufus very seriously, taking both her hands in his, and making her turn to look into his eyes, "you must *try* to see what I see. Rome is no longer young, though by that I do not mean to imply that Rome is in her dotage. Only consider . . . Two hundred and forty-four years of the kings, then four hundred and eleven years of the Republic. Rome has been in existence now for six hundred and fifty-five years, growing ever mightier. But how many of the old families are still producing consuls, Aurelia? The Cornelii. The Servilii. The Valerii. The Postumii. The Claudii. The Aemilii. The Sulpicii. The

Julii haven't produced a consul in nearly four hundred years—
though I think there will be several Julii in the curule chair in this
generation. The Sergii are so poor they've been reduced to finding
money by farming oysters. And the Pinarii are so poor they'll do
virtually anything to enrich themselves. Among the plebeian nobility matters are better than among the patricians. Yet it seems to
me that if we are not careful, Rome will eventually belong to New
Men—men without ancestors, men who can claim no connection
to Rome's beginnings, and therefore will be indifferent to what
kind of place Rome becomes."

The grip on her hands tightened. "Aurelia, your son is of the
oldest and most illustrious lineage. Among the patrician families
still surviving, only the Fabii can compare with the Julii, and the
Fabii have had to adopt for three generations to fill the curule chair.
Those among them who are genuine Fabii are so odd that they
hide themselves away. Yet here in Young Caesar is a member of
the old patriciate with all the energy and intelligence of a New
Man. He is a hope for Rome of a kind I never thought to see. For I
do believe that to grow even greater, Rome *must* be governed by
those of the blood. I could never say this to Gaius Marius—whom
I love, but whom I deplore. In the course of his phenomenal career
Gaius Marius has done Rome more harm than half a hundred
German invasions. The laws that he has tumbled, the traditions he
has destroyed, the precedents he has created—the Brothers Gracchi at least were of the old nobility, and tackled what they saw as
Rome's troubles with some vestige of respect for the *mos maiorum,* the unwritten tenets of our ancestors. Whereas Gaius Marius
has eroded the *mos maiorum* and left Rome prey to many kinds of
wolves, creatures bearing no relationship whatsoever to the kind
old wolf who suckled Romulus and Remus."

So arresting and unusual, her wide and lucent eyes were fixed
on Publius Rutilius Rufus's face almost painfully, and she did not
notice how strongly he held on to her hands. For here at last she
was being offered something to seize hold of, a guidance through
the shadowy realm she trod with Young Caesar.

"You must appreciate Young Caesar's significance, and do everything in your power to put his feet firmly on the path to pre-eminence. You must fill him with a purpose no one save he can accomplish—to preserve the *mos maiorum* and renew the vigor of the old ways, the old blood."

"I understand, Uncle Publius," said Aurelia gravely.

"Good!" He rose to his feet, drawing her up with him. "I shall bring a man to see you tomorrow, at the third hour of the day. Have the boy here."

And so it was that the child Gaius Julius Caesar Junior passed into the care of one Marcus Antonius Gnipho. A Gaul from Nem-ausus, his grandfather had been of the tribe Salluvii, and hunted heads with great relish during constant raids upon the settled Hel-lenized folk of coastal Gaul-across-the-Alps until he and his small son were captured by a determined party of Massiliotes. Sold into slavery, the grandfather soon died, whereas the son had been young enough to survive the transition from headhunting barbarian to domestic servant in a Greek household. He had turned out to be a clever fellow, and was still young enough to marry and raise a family when he managed to save enough to buy his freedom. His choice of a bride had fallen upon a Massiliote Greek girl of modest back-ground, and he met with her father's approval despite his alien hugeness and his bright red hair. Thus his son, Gnipho, had grown up in a free man environment, and soon demonstrated that he shared his father's scholarly bent.

When Gnaeus Domitius Ahenobarbus had carved a Roman prov-ince along the coast of Gaul-across-the-Alps lapped by the Middle Sea, he had taken a Marcus Antonius with him as one of his senior legates, and that Marcus Antonius had used the services of Gnipho's father as interpreter and scribe. So when the war against the Arverni was successfully concluded, Marcus Antonius had secured the Ro-man citizenship for Gnipho's father as no mean token of his thanks; the generosity of the Antonii was always lavish. A freedman at the time Marcus Antonius had employed him, Gnipho's father therefore could be absorbed into Antonius's own rural tribe.

The boy Gnipho had early evinced a desire to teach, as well as having an interest in geography, philosophy, mathematics, astronomy, and engineering. So after he assumed the toga of manhood his father put him on a ship and sent him to Alexandria, the intellectual hub of the world. There in the cloisters of the museum library he had studied under the Librarian himself, Diokles.

But the heyday of the library was over, its librarians no longer of the quality of Eratosthenes; and so when Marcus Antonius Gnipho turned twenty-six, he decided to settle in Rome, and there to teach. At first he had taken on the role of *grammaticus,* taught rhetoric to young men; then, a little wearied by the posturings of noble Roman youths, he opened a school for younger boys. From the very first it was a success, and soon he was able to ask the highest fees without discomfort. He had no worries about paying the rent upon two large rooms on the quiet sixth floor of an insula far from the crowded squalor of the Subura, and was also able to afford four rooms one floor higher up in the same Palatine palace for his private living quarters and the housing of his four expensive slaves, two of whom attended to his personal needs, and two of whom assisted him in his dual classrooms.

When Publius Rutilius Rufus had called to see him, he laughed, assuring his visitor that he had no intention of giving up his profitable little venture in order to pander to a baby. Rutilius Rufus then offered him a properly drawn-up contract which included a luxurious apartment in an even better Palatine insula, and more money than his school brought in. Still Marcus Antonius Gnipho laughed a refusal.

"At least come and see the child," said Rutilius Rufus. "If someone dangles a bait the size of this one under your nose, you'd be a fool if you declined to look."

When he met Young Caesar, the teacher changed his mind.

"Not," he said to Publius Rutilius Rufus, "because he is who he is, or even because of his amazing intelligence. I am committing myself to Young Caesar as his tutor because I like him enormously— and I fear for his future."

"That wretched child!" Aurelia said to Lucius Cornelius Sulla when he called in late September to see her. "The family clubbed together to find the money to hire him a magnificent pedagogue, and what happens? The pedagogue has fallen for his charm!"

"Huh," said Sulla, who hadn't called to hear a litany—even of complaint—about any of Aurelia's offspring. Children bored him, no matter how bright and charming; that his own did not bore him was a source of mystery. No, he had called to tell Aurelia he was going away.

"So you're deserting me too," she said, offering him grapes from her courtyard garden.

"Very soon, I'm afraid. Titus Didius wants to ship his troops to Spain by sea, and early winter's the best time of year. However, I'm going ahead by land to prepare for their arrival."

"Tired of Rome?"

"Wouldn't you be, in my shoes?"

"Oh, yes."

He moved restlessly, clenched his fists in frustration. "I am never going to get there, Aurelia!"

But that only provoked a laugh. "Pooh! You've got October Horse written all over you, Lucius Cornelius. One day it will come, you wait and see."

"Not entirely, I hope," he said, laughing too. "I'd like to keep my head on my shoulders—which is more than the poor October Horse ever does! Why *is* that, I wonder? The trouble with all our rituals is that they're so old we don't even understand the language in which we rattle off the prayers, let alone know why we harness war-horses in pairs to chariots, and race them, and then sacrifice the right-hand beast of the winning team. As for fighting over its head—!" So bright was the light that his pupils had contracted to pinpoints and gave him the look of a blinded seer; the eyes he turned on her were filled with a seer's pain—not a pain of past or present, but doomed by knowledge of the future. And he cried out, "Aurelia, Aurelia! Why is it that I never manage to be happy?"

Her heart squeezed itself up, she pressed her nails into her palms. "I don't know, Lucius Cornelius."

"Nor do I."

How horrible to offer him good sense, yet what else could she do? "I think you need to be busy."

He answered her dryly. "Oh, definitely! When I'm busy, I have no time to think."

"So I find it," she said huskily, and then said, "There ought to be more to life than that."

They were sitting in the reception room alongside the low wall of the courtyard garden, one on either side of a table, the grapes, all swollen and purple, in a dish between them. When she finished speaking she continued to look at him, though he had turned his gaze away from her. How attractive he is! she thought, feeling a sudden stab of a private misery she normally kept completely below conscious level. He has a mouth like my husband's, and beautiful it is. Beautiful. Beautiful . . .

Up came Sulla's eyes, straight into hers; Aurelia blushed scarlet. His face changed, exactly how, hard to define—he just seemed to become *more* of himself. Out went his hand to her, a sudden and bewitching smile lighting him.

"Aurelia—"

She put her own hand into his, caught her breath, felt dizzy. "What, Lucius Cornelius?" she managed to ask.

"Have an affair with me!"

Her mouth was dry, she felt she must swallow or lose consciousness, yet could not; and his fingers around hers were like the last threads of a slipping life, she could not leave them go and survive.

How he got himself around the table she never afterward understood, only looked up at his face so close to hers, the sheen on his lips, the layers in his eyes flaked as in the depths of polished marble. Fascinated, she watched a muscle in his right arm move beneath its sheath of skin, and found herself vibrating rather than trembling, as weak, as lost . . .

She closed her eyes and waited, and then when she felt his mouth touch hers, she kissed him as if starved of love for some long eternity, awash with more emotions than she had ever known existed, stunned, terrified, exalted, burned to a cinder.

One moment more and the whole room lay between them, Aurelia flat against a brightly painted wall as if trying to lose a dimension, Sulla by the table drawing in great breaths, with the sun seeding fire through his hair.

"I—*can't!*" she said, a quiet scream.

"Then may you never know another moment's peace!"

Determined even in the midst of this towering rage that he would do nothing she could find laughable or farcical, he dealt magnificently with his toga, abandoned on the floor; then, every footstep telling her he would never come back, he walked out of that place as if *he* were the victor of the field.

But there could be no satisfaction for himself in being the victor of the field—he was too furious at his defeat. Home Sulla walked with such a storm wrapped round him that whole crowds leaped out of his way. How dared she! How dared she sit there with the hunger naked in her eyes, lead him on with a kiss—*such* a kiss!—then tell him she couldn't. As if she hadn't wanted it more than he. He ought to kill her, break her slender neck, see her face puff up from some poison, watch those purple eyes bulge out as his fingers tightened about her throat. Kill her, kill her, kill her, kill her, said the heart he could hear in his ears, said the blood distending the veins of forehead and scalp. Kill her, kill her, *kill her!* And no less a part of that gigantic fury was the knowledge that he couldn't kill her any more than he had been able to kill Julilla, kill Aelia, kill Dalmatica. *Why?* What did these women have that women like Clitumna and Nicopolis did not?

At sight of him when he erupted into the atrium his servants scattered, his wife retreated voiceless to her own room, and his house shrank in upon itself, so huge was its silence. In his study he went straight to the little wooden temple which held the wax mask of his ancestor the *flamen Dialis,* and wrenched open the drawer hidden in its perfect flight of steps. The first object his groping fingers fastened around was a tiny bottle, and there it lay upon his palm, its clear contents lapping sluggishly inside its walls of greenish glass. He looked, and he looked.

The time he spent looking down at what he held in his hand had no measure, nor could his mind now dredge up one single thought; all he owned was rage. Or was it pain? Or was it grief? Or was it just a monumental loneliness? From fire he fell down through warmth to coolness, and finally to ice. Only then could he face this frightful disability, the fact that he, so enamored of murder as a solace as well as a necessity, could not physically perform the deed upon a woman of his own class. With Julilla as with Aelia, he had at least found comfort in witnessing their manifest misery because of him, and with Julilla he had known the satisfaction of *causing* her death; for there could be no doubt that had she not seen his reunion with Metrobius, she would have continued to guzzle her wine and fix her great hollow yellow eyes upon him mournfully in silent, eternal reproach. With Aurelia, however, he could count on no reaction lasting longer than his presence in her house; as soon as he had gone out her front door, no doubt, she had picked up the pieces of a momentary lapse and buried herself in her work. By tomorrow, she would forget him completely. That was Aurelia. May she rot! May she be chewed up by worms! The malignant sow!

In the midst of these futile, age-old curses, he caught himself up and grinned a twisted travesty of amusement. No comfort there. Ridiculous, ludicrous. The gods took no note of human frustrations or desires, and he was not of that kind who could in some awful, mysterious way transfer his destructive thoughts into a death wish which bore fruit. Aurelia still lived within him, he needed to banish her before he went to Spain if he was to bend all his energies to the advancement of his career. He needed a something to replace the ecstasy he would have known in breaching the walls of Aurelia's citadel. The fact that until he surprised the look on her face he had harbored no wish to seduce her was beside the point—the urge had been so powerful, so all-pervasive that he could not shake himself free of it.

Rome, of course. Once he got to Spain it would all go away. *If* he could find some kind of satisfaction now. In the field he never suffered these dreadful frustrations, perhaps because he was too busy, perhaps because death lay all around him, perhaps because he could tell himself he was moving upward. But in Rome—and he had been in Rome now for almost three years—he came eventually to a degree of thwarted boredom which in the past had only dissipated after literal or metaphorical murder.

He fell, ice-cold, into a reverie; faces came and went, of victims and of those he wished were victims. Julilla. Aelia. Dalmatica. Lucius Gavius Stichus. Clitumna. Nicopolis. Catulus Caesar—how nice to wipe that haughty camel's look away forever! Scaurus. Metellus Numidicus Piggle-wiggle. Piggle-wiggle . . . Slowly Sulla got up, slowly closed the secret drawer. But kept the little bottle in his hand.

The water clock said it was the middle of the day. Six hours gone, six hours to go. Drip drip, drip drip. Time enough and more to visit Quintus Caecilius Metellus Numidicus Piggle-wiggle.

Upon his return from exile, Metellus Numidicus had found himself turned into something of a legend. Not nearly old enough to be dead, he told himself exultantly, yet here he was, already become a part of Forum lore. They recounted the story of his Homeric career as censor, the fearless way he had dealt with Lucius Equitius, the beatings he had taken, the courage he displayed in coming back for more; and they gave the story of how he had gone into exile, with his stammering son cuh-cuh-cuh-counting that endless stream of denarii while the sun went down on the Curia Hostilia and Gaius Marius waited to enforce his oath of allegiance to Saturninus's second land bill.

Yes, thought Metellus Numidicus after the last client of the day had been dismissed, I will pass into history as the greatest of a great family, the quintessential Quintus of the Caecilii Metelli. And he swelled with pride in himself, happy with being home again, pleased with his welcome, replete with an enormous satisfaction. Yes, it had been a long war against Gaius Marius! But now it was definitely over. And he had won, Gaius Marius had lost. Never again would Rome suffer the indignity of Gaius Marius.

His steward scratched upon the door to his study.

"Yes?" asked Metellus Numidicus.

"Lucius Cornelius Sulla is asking to see you, *domine.*"

When Sulla came through the door Metellus Numidicus was already on his feet and halfway across the room, his hand stretched out in welcome.

"My dear Lucius Cornelius, what a pleasure to see you," he said, oozing affability.

"Yes, it's more than time I came to pay my personal respects in private," said Sulla, seating himself in the client's chair and assuming an expression of rather charming self-deprecation.

"Some wine?"

"Thank you."

Standing by the console table upon which two flagons and some goblets of very nice Alexandrian glass reposed, Metellus Numidicus turned back toward Sulla, one eyebrow lifted, a slightly quizzical look on his face. "Is this an occasion to merit Chian unadulterated by water?" he asked.

Sulla put on a smile suggesting that he was beginning to feel more at ease. "To water Chian down is a crime," he said.

His host didn't move. "That's a politician's answer, Lucius Cornelius. I didn't think you belonged to the breed."

"Quintus Caecilius, leave the water out of your wine!" cried Sulla. "I come in the hope that we can be good friends," he said, voice sincere.

"In that case, Lucius Cornelius, we will drink our Chian without water."

Back came Metellus Numidicus bearing two of the goblets; he placed one on Sulla's side of the desk, one on his own, then sat down, picked up his glass. "I drink to friendship," he said.

"And I." Sulla sipped a little of his wine, frowned, and looked very directly at Metellus Numidicus. "Quintus Caecilius, I am going as senior legate with Titus Didius to Nearer Spain. I have no idea how long I'm likely to be away, but at this moment it looks as if it could be several years. When I come back, I intend to stand as soon as possible for election as praetor." He cleared his throat, sipped a little more wine. "Do you know the real reason why I was not elected praetor last year?"

A smile played about the corners of Metellus Numidicus's mouth, too faint for Sulla to be able to decide whether it was ironic, malicious, or merely amused.

"Yes, Lucius Cornelius, I do."

"And what do you think?"

"I think you greatly annoyed my dear friend Marcus Aemilius Scaurus in the matter of his wife."

"Ah! *Not* because of my connection to Gaius Marius!"

"Lucius Cornelius, no one with Marcus Aemilius's good sense would suffocate your public career because of a military connection to Gaius Marius. Though I wasn't here myself to see it, I did preserve sufficient contact with Rome to be aware that your relations with Gaius Marius have not been close in some time," said Metellus Numidicus smoothly. "Since you are no longer brothers-in-law, I find that understandable." He sighed. "However, it is unfortunate that, just when you had succeeded in divorcing yourself from Gaius Marius, you should almost provoke a divorce in the household of Marcus Aemilius Scaurus."

"I did nothing dishonorable, Quintus Caecilius," said Sulla stiffly, careful not to let his anger at being patronized show, but moment by moment hardening in his resolve that this conceited mediocrity should die.

"I know you did nothing dishonorable." Metellus Numidicus quaffed the last of his wine. "How sad it is that in the matter of women—particularly wives—even the oldest and wisest heads spin round like tops."

When his host moved to get up Sulla rose quickly to his feet, plucked both goblets from the table, and went to the console to refill them.

"The lady is your niece, Quintus Caecilius," said Sulla, his back turned, the bulk of his toga hiding the table.

"That is the only reason I know the full story."

Having handed one goblet to Metellus Numidicus, Sulla sat down again. "Do you, being the lady's uncle—and being a very good friend of Marcus Aemilius's—consider my treatment fair?"

A shrug, a mouthful of wine, a grimace. "Were you some mushroom, Lucius Cornelius, you would not be sitting here now. But yours is a very old and illustrious name, you are a patrician Cornelius, and you are a man of superior ability." He pulled another face, drank some more wine. "Had I been in Rome at the time my niece developed her fancy for you, I would of course have supported my friend Marcus Aemilius in anything he chose to do to rectify the situation. I gather he asked you to leave Rome, and you refused. Not a prudent thing to do!"

Sulla laughed without amusement. "I suppose I didn't believe Marcus Aemilius would act less honorably than I had."

"Oh, how much a few years in the Forum Romanum as a youth would have improved you!" exclaimed Metellus Numidicus. "You lack *tact,* Lucius Cornelius."

"I daresay you're right," said Sulla, finding this the hardest role his life had yet called upon him to play. "But one cannot go back, and *I* need to go forward."

"Nearer Spain with Titus Didius is definitely a step forward."

Once more Sulla got up, poured two goblets of wine. "I must make at least one good friend in Rome before I go," he said, "and I would—I say it from the heart—very much like that friend to be you. In spite of your niece. In spite of your close ties to Marcus Aemilius Scaurus Princeps Senatus. I am a Cornelian, which means I cannot offer myself to you in the role of a client. Only as a friend. What do you say?"

"I say—stay to dinner, Lucius Cornelius."

And so Lucius Cornelius stayed to dinner, a pleasant and intimate affair, since Metellus Numidicus had originally intended to dine alone that day, a little tired of living up to his new status as a Forum legend. They talked about the indefatigable struggle of his son to end the exile on Rhodes.

"No man was ever blessed with a better boy," said the returned exile, feeling his wine, for his intake had been considerable, and started well before his dinner.

Sulla's smile was charm personified. "I cannot argue with that, Quintus Caecilius. Indeed, I call your son a good friend of mine. My boy is still a child. However, the blind prejudice of fatherhood says my boy is going to be hard to beat."

"He is a Lucius, like you?"

Sulla blinked, surprised. "Of course."

"Odd, that," Metellus Numidicus said, the two words very carefully pronounced. "Isn't Publius the first name of the eldest son in your branch of the Cornelians?"

"My father being dead, Quintus Caecilius, I can't ask him. Certainly I never remember his being sober enough while he was alive to talk about family customs."

"Oh well, doesn't matter." Metellus Numidicus thought for a moment, then said, "On the subject of names, I suppose you know that—that *Italian* always called me Piggle-wiggle?"

"I have heard Gaius Marius use it, Quintus Caecilius," said Sulla gravely, and leaned over to fill both the beautiful glass goblets from an equally beautiful glass flagon; how fortunate that Piggle-wiggle had a penchant for glass!

"Disgusting!" said Metellus Numidicus, slurring the word.

"Absolutely disgusting," agreed Sulla, feeling an enormous sense of well-being flow through him. Piggle-wiggle, Piggle-wiggle.

"It took me a long time to live that name down."

"I'm not surprised, Quintus Caecilius," said Sulla innocently.

"Nursery slang! He couldn't even call me a fully fledged *cunnus,* that—that Italian."

Suddenly Metellus Numidicus struggled to sit up, one hand to his brow, drawing audible breaths. "Oh, so dizzy! Can't—seem to—catch my—breath!"

"Draw some more big deep ones, Quintus Caecilius."

Obediently Metellus Numidicus labored, then gasped, "I—do not—feel well!"

Sulla slid toward the back of his couch, where his shoes lay. "I'll get you a basin, shall I?"

"Servants! Call—servants!" His hands went to his chest, he fell back. "My—lungs!"

By now Sulla had come round to the front of the couch, and leaned across the table before it. "Are you sure it's your lungs, Quintus Caecilius?"

Metellus Numidicus writhed, half-reclining, one hand still

clutching at his chest, the other, fingers curled into claws, crawling across the couch toward Sulla. "So—dizzy! Can't—breathe! Lungs!"

Sulla bellowed, "Help! Quickly, help!"

The room filled with slaves immediately; calmly efficient, he sent several for doctors and set others to propping Metellus Numidicus up on bolsters, for he would not lie down.

"It won't be long, Quintus Caecilius," he said gently as he sat down on the front edge of the couch, kicking the table aside with his shod foot; both the goblets fell to the floor along with the wine and water flagons, and broke into small pieces. "Here," he said to the straining, bright-faced, terrified Metellus Numidicus, "take my hand." And to one dumbfounded servant standing helplessly by, "Clean up that mess, would you? I wouldn't want anyone cut."

He remained holding Metellus Numidicus's hand while the slave removed the shards and splinters from the floor and mopped up the liquid, almost entirely water; and he was still holding Metellus Numidicus's hand when the room filled up with yet more people, doctors and their acolytes; and by the time Metellus Pius the Piglet arrived, Metellus Numidicus would not let go Sulla's hand even to extend it to his indefatigable and beloved son.

So while Sulla held Metellus Numidicus's hand and the Piglet wept inconsolably, the doctors went to work.

"The potion of hydromel with hyssop and crushed caper root," said Apollodorus of Sicily, still reigning supreme on the best side of the Palatine. "I think we will blood him too. Praxis, my lancet, please."

But Metellus Numidicus was too busy breathing to swallow the honeyed potion; his blood when the vein was opened streamed out a vivid scarlet.

"It is a vein, I am sure it is a vein!" said Apollodorus Siculus to himself, then said to the other physicians, "How bright the blood is!"

"He fights us so, Apollodorus, it is no wonder the blood is bright," said Publius Sulpicius Solon the Athenian Greek. "Do you think—a plaster on the chest?"

"Yes, it must be a plaster on the chest," said Apollodorus of Sicily, looking grave, and snapping his fingers imperiously at his chief assistant. "Praxis, the barbatum plaster!"

Still Metellus Numidicus struggled for breath, beat at his chest with his free hand, looked with clouding eyes at his son, refused to lie down, clung to Sulla's hand.

"He is not dark blue in the face," said Apollodorus Siculus in his stilted Greek to Metellus Pius and Sulla, "and that I do not understand! Otherwise, he has all the signs of a morbid acuteness in the lungs." He nodded to where his assistant was smearing a black and sticky mess thickly upon a square of woolen fabric. "This is the best poultice, it will draw the noxious elements out. Scraped verdigris—a properly separated litharge of lead—alum—dried pitch—dried pine resin—all mixed to the right consistency with vinegar and oil. See, it is ready!"

Sure enough, the poultice was finished. Apollodorus of Sicily smoothed it upon the bared chest himself, and stood with praiseworthy calm to watch the barbatum plaster do its work.

But it could not cure, any more than the bloodletting or the potion; slowly Metellus Numidicus relinquished his hold on life, and on Lucius Cornelius Sulla's hand. Face a bright red, eyes no longer capable of seeing, he passed from paralysis to coma, and so died.

As Sulla left the room, he heard the little Sicilian physician say timidly to Metellus Pius, "*Domine,* there should be an autopsy," and heard the devastated Piglet say:

"What, so you Greek incompetents can butcher him as well as kill him? No! My father will go to his pyre unmolested!"

His eyes on Sulla's back, the Piglet pushed between the cluster of doctors and followed Sulla out into the atrium.

"Lucius Cornelius!"

Slowly Sulla turned, his face when he presented it to Metellus Pius a picture of sorrow; the tears welled in his eyes, slipped down his cheeks unchecked. "My dear Quintus Pius!" he said.

Shock still kept the Piglet on his feet, and his own weeping had lessened. "I can't believe it! My father is dead!"

"Very sudden," said Sulla, shaking his head. A sob burst from him. "Very sudden! He was so well, Quintus Pius! I called to pay him my respects and he invited me to dinner. We had such a pleasant time! And then, when dinner was over—this!"

"Oh, why, why, why?" The Piglet's tears began to increase again. "He was just home, he wasn't old!"

Very tenderly Sulla gathered Metellus Pius to him, pressed the jerking head into his left shoulder, his right hand stroking the Piglet's hair. But the eyes looking past that cradled head reflected the washed-out satisfaction following a great and physical emotion. What could he possibly do in the future to equal that amazing experience? For the first time he had inserted himself completely into the extremis of a dying, been much more than merely its perpetrator; he had been its minister as well.

The steward emerged from the *triclinium* to find the son of his dead master being comforted by a man who shone like Apollo. Then he blinked, shook his head. Imagination.

"I ought to go," said Sulla to the steward. "Here, take him. And send for the rest of the family."

Outside on the Clivus Victoriae, Sulla stood for long enough to allow his eyes to get used to the darkness. Laughing softly to himself, he moved off in the direction of the temple of Magna Mater. When he saw the barred maw of a drain he dropped his empty little bottle into its blackness.

"*Vale,* Piggle-wiggle, Piggle-wiggle!" he howled, and raised his hands to clutch at the sullen sky. "Oh, I feel *better!*"

 "Jupiter!" said Gaius Marius, putting Sulla's letter down to stare at his wife.

"What is it?"

"Piggle-wiggle is dead."

The refined Roman matron her son thought would die if she heard anything cruder than *Ecastor!* didn't turn a hair; she had been used to hearing Quintus Caecilius Metellus Numidicus referred to as Piggle-wiggle since the first days of her marriage.

"Oh, that's too bad," she said, not knowing what her husband wanted her to say.

"Too *bad*? It's almost too good—too good to be true!" Marius picked up the scroll again and spread it out to mumble his way through his initial reading. Once he had deciphered its endless scrawl, he read it out more loudly and coherently to Julia, his voice betraying his elation.

The whole of Rome turned out for the funeral, which was the biggest I for one can remember—but then, I was not much interested in funerals when Scipio Aemilianus was popped on his pyre.

The Piglet is beside himself with grief, and has definitely branded himself Pius forevermore by weeping and wailing from one gate of Rome to the next. The Caecilius Metellus ancestors were a homely lot if their *imagines* are anything to go by, which I presume they are. Some of the actors wearing them hopped and skipped and jumped like some sort of peculiar hybrid frog-cricket-deer, and I found myself wondering just where the Caecilii Metelli came from. An odd breeding ground, at any rate.

The Piglet clings to me these days, probably because I was there when Piggle-wiggle died, and—since his dear *tata* wouldn't leave go my hand—the Piglet is convinced all differences between me and Piggle-wiggle were at an end. I didn't tell him my invitation to dinner was a spur of the moment thing. One fact of interest—all through the time his *tata* was dying and even afterward, the Piglet never stammered once. Mind you, he only developed his speech impediment after the battle of Arausio, so one must assume it is a nervous tic of the tongue rather than an innate defect. He says it bothers him most these days when he remembers it, or he has to give a formal speech. I keep visualizing him conducting a religious ceremony! How hard I'd laugh to see everybody shifting from one foot to another while the Piglet tripped over his tongue and was forced to start all over again.

I write this on the eve of departing for Nearer Spain, and what hopefully will be a good war. From the reports, the Celtiberians are absolutely boiling and the Lusitani creating havoc in the Further Province, where my remote Cornelian cousin Dolabella has had a trifling success or two without stamping rebellion out.

The tribunes of the soldiers have been elected, and Quintus Sertorius goes with Titus Didius too. Almost like old times. Except that our leader is a different—and a less outstanding—New Man than Gaius Marius. I shall write whenever there is news, but in return I expect you to write and tell me what sort of man is King Mithridates.

"What was Lucius Cornelius doing, dining with Quintus Caecilius?" asked Julia curiously.

"Currying favor, I suspect," said Marius gruffly.

"Oh, Gaius Marius, no!"

"And why shouldn't he, Julia? I don't blame him. Piggle-wiggle is—was—in high fettle, and his clout is certainly greater than mine these days. Under the circumstances, poor Lucius Cornelius can't attach himself to Scaurus, and I also understand why he has not tried to attach himself to Catulus Caesar." Marius gave a sigh, shook his head. "However, Julia, at some time in the future I predict that Lucius Cornelius will mend all his fences, and stand on excellent terms with the lot of them."

"Then he is no friend to you!"

"Probably not."

"I don't understand it! You and he were so close."

"Yes," said Marius, speaking deliberately. "However, my dear, it wasn't the closeness of two men drawn together by a natural affinity of mind and heart. Old Caesar Grandfather felt much the same about him as I do—one couldn't have a better man at one's side in a tight spot, or when there's work to be done. It's easy to maintain pleasant relations with such a man. But I doubt that Lucius Cornelius will ever enjoy the kind of friendship that I enjoy with Publius Rutilius, for example. You know, when one loves the faults and quirks with the same affection as one does the splendid attributes. Lucius Cornelius hasn't got it in him to sit in silence on a bench with a friend, just relishing being together. That type of behavior is foreign to his nature."

"What *is* his nature, Gaius Marius? I've never known."

But Marius shook his head, laughed. "No one knows. Even after all our years together, I couldn't begin to guess at it."

"Oh, I think you could," said Julia shrewdly, "but I don't think you want to. At least to me." She moved to sit beside him. "If he has a friend at all, it's Aurelia."

"So I've noticed," said Marius dryly.

"Now don't go assuming there's anything between them, because there isn't! It's just that I think if Lucius Cornelius opens his innermost self to anyone, it's to her."

"Huh," said Marius, ending the conversation.

They were in Halicarnassus for the winter, having arrived in Asia Minor too late in the season to attempt the journey overland from the Aegean coast to Pessinus. In Athens they had lingered too long because they loved it so, and from there they went to Delphi to visit Apollo's precinct, though Marius had refused to consult the Pythoness.

Surprised, Julia had asked him why.

"No man can badger the gods," he said. "I've had my share of prophecies. If I ask for more revelations of the future, the gods will turn away from me."

"Couldn't you ask on behalf of Young Marius?"

"No," said Gaius Marius.

They had also visited Epidauros in the near Peloponnese, and there, after dutifully admiring the buildings and the exquisite sculptures of Thrasymedes of Paros, Marius took the sleep diagnosis administered by the priests of Asklepios. He had drunk his potion obediently, then gone to the dormitories lying near the

great temple, and slept the night away. Unfortunately he could remember no dreams, so the best the priests could do was to instruct
him to reduce his weight, take more exercise, and do no stressful
mental work.

"Quacks, if you ask me," said Marius scornfully, having given
the god a costly bejeweled golden goblet as thanks.

"Sensible men, if you ask *me*," said Julia, eyes fixed upon his
expanding waistline.

It was therefore October before they sailed from the Piraeus in
a large ship which plied a regular route between Greece and Ephesus. But hilly Ephesus hadn't pleased Gaius Marius, who huffed
and puffed across its cobbles, and very quickly procured his family room on a ship sailing south to Halicarnassus.

Here, in perhaps the most beautiful of all the Aegean port cities
of the Roman Asia Province, Marius settled down for the winter
in a hired villa, well staffed, and equipped with a heated bath of
seawater; for though the sun shone for much of the time, it was too
cold to bathe. The mighty walls, the towers and the fortresses, the
imposing public buildings all made it seem both safe and rather
Roman, though Rome did not own a structure as wonderful as the
Mausoleum, the tomb his sister-wife Artemisia had erected, in-
consolable in her grief, after King Mausolus died.

Late the following spring, the pilgrimage to Pessinus got under
way, not without protest from Julia and Young Marius, who wanted
to stay on the sea for the summer; that they lost the battle was a
foregone conclusion. From invaders to pilgrims, everyone followed the route along the valley of the Maeander River between
coastal Asia Minor and central Anatolia. As did Marius and his
family, marveling at the prosperity and the sophistication of the
various districts they passed through. After leaving the fascinating crystal formations and mineral spas of Hierapolis, where black
wool was treated and its coveted color fixed by the salts in the
water, they crossed the immensely tall and rugged mountains—still
following the Maeander—into Phrygia's forests and wildernesses.

Pessinus, however, lay at the back of an upland plain devoid of
encroaching woodlands, but green with wheat when they reached

it. Like most of the great religious sanctuaries of inner Anatolia, their guide explained, the temple of the Great Mother at Pessinus owned vast tracts of land and whole armies of slaves, and was rich enough and self-contained enough to function like any other state. The only difference was that the priests governed in the name of the Goddess, and preserved the sanctuary's wealth to entrench the Goddess's power.

Expecting a Delphi situated amid stunning mountains, they were amazed to discover that Pessinus lay below the level of its plain, down in a brilliantly white, chalky, steep-sided gulch. The precinct lay at its northern end, narrower and less fertile than the miles meandering southward, and was built athwart a spring-fed stream which eventually fed into the big river Sangarius. Town and temple and sanctuary buildings oozed antiquity, though the present structures were Greek in style and date, and the great temple, perched on a rise in the valley floor, plunged down at its front abruptly in a three-quarter circle of steps, upon which the pilgrims sat to have their congress with the priests.

"Our navel-stone you have in Rome, Gaius Marius," said the *archigallos* Battaces, "given to you freely in your time of need. For that reason, when Hannibal fled to Asia Minor, he came nowhere near Pessinus."

Remembering Publius Rutilius Rufus's letter about the visit of Battaces and his underlings to Rome at the time when the German invasion threatened, Marius tended to view the man with some amusement, an attitude Battaces was quick to pick up.

"Is it my castrated state makes you smile?" he asked.

Marius blinked. "I didn't think you were, *archigallos*."

"One cannot serve Kubaba Cybele and remain intact, Gaius Marius. Even her consort, Attis, was required to make that great sacrifice," said Battaces.

"I thought Attis was cut because he strayed to another woman," said Marius, feeling he had to say something, and not willing to become enmeshed in a discussion about amputated gonads, though the priest clearly wanted to discuss his condition.

"No!" said Battaces. "That story is a Greek embroidery. Only in Phrygia do we keep our worship pure, and with it, our knowledge of the Goddess. We are her true followers, to us she came from Carchemish aeons ago." He walked from the sunlight into the portico of the great temple, dimming the brilliance of his cloth-of-gold garments, the glitter of his many jewels.

In the Goddess's *cella* they stood, it appeared so Marius could admire her statue.

"Solid gold," said Battaces complacently.

"Sure of that?" asked Marius, remembering how the guide at Olympia had told him about the technique used to make Zeus.

"Absolutely."

Life-sized, it stood upon a high marble plinth, and showed the Goddess seated upon a short bench; to either side of her sat a maneless lion, and her hands rested on their heads. She wore a high, crownlike hat, a thin robe which showed off the beauty of her breasts, and a girdle. Beyond the lion on the left stood two child shepherds, one blowing a set of double pipes, the other plucking a large lyre. To the right of the other lion stood Kubaba Cybele's consort, Attis, leaning on a shepherd's staff, his head covered by the Phrygian cap, a soft conical affair which rose to a rounded point, and flopped over to one side; he was wearing a long-sleeved shirt tied at his neck but open to display a well-muscled belly, and his long trousers were slit up the front of each leg, then held together at intervals with buttons.

"Interesting," said Marius, who didn't consider it at all beautiful, solid gold or not.

"You do not admire it."

"I daresay that's because I'm a Roman, *archigallos*, rather than a Phrygian." Turning away, Marius paced back down the *cella* toward its great bronze doors. "Why is this Asian goddess so concerned with Rome?" he asked.

"She has been for a long time, Gaius Marius. Otherwise, she would never have consented to giving Rome her navel-stone."

"Yes, yes, I know that! But it doesn't answer my question," said Marius, growing testy.

"Kubaba Cybele does not reveal her reasons, even to her

priests," said Battaces, once more a vision to hurt the eyes, for he had moved down to the three-quarter circle of steps, bathed in sun. He sat down, patting the marble slab in an invitation to Marius to be seated. "However, it would seem that she feels Rome will continue to increase in importance throughout the world, and perhaps one day have dominion over Pessinus. You have sheltered her in Rome now for over one hundred years as Magna Mater. Of all her foreign temples, it is her most favored one. The great precinct in the Piraeus of Athens—and the one in Pergamum, for that matter—do not seem to concern her half as much. I think she simply loves Rome."

"Well, good for her!" said Marius heartily.

Battaces winced, closed his eyes. A sigh, a shrug, and then he pointed to where beyond the steps there stood the wall and coping of a round well. "Is there anything you yourself would care to ask the Goddess?"

But Marius shook his head. "What, roar down that thing and wait for some disembodied voice to answer? No."

"It is how she answers all questions put to her."

"No disrespect to Kubaba Cybele, *archigallos*, but the gods have done well by me in the matter of prophecies, and I do not think it wise to ask them more," said Marius.

"Then let us sit here in the sun for a while, Gaius Marius, and listen to the wind," said Battaces, concealing his acute disappointment; he had arranged some important oracular answers.

"I don't suppose," said Marius suddenly after several moments, "that you'd know how best I can contact the King of Pontus? In other words, do you know where he is? I've written to him at Amaseia, but not a sign of a reply have I had, and that was eight months ago. Nor did my second letter reach him."

"He's always moving about, Gaius Marius," said the priest easily. "It's possible he hasn't been in Amaseia this year."

"What, doesn't he have his mail forwarded on?"

"Anatolia is not Rome, or Roman territory," said Battaces. "Even King Mithridates's courts do not know whereabouts he is unless he notifies them. He rarely does so."

"Ye gods!" said Marius blankly. "How does he manage to hold things together?"

"His barons govern in his absence—not an arduous task, as most of the cities of Pontus are Greek states governing themselves. They simply pay Mithridates whatever he asks. As for the rural areas, they are primitive and isolated. Pontus is a land of very high mountains all running parallel to the Euxine Sea, with the result that communications are not good between one part and any other. The King has many fortresses scattered through the ranges, and at least four courts when last I heard—Amaseia, Sinope, Dasteira, and Trapezus. As I say, he moves about constantly, and usually without much state. He also journeys to Galatia, Sophene, Cappadocia, and Commagene. His relatives rule those places."

"I see." Marius leaned forward, linked his hands together between his knees. "What you're saying, I suppose, is that I may never succeed in making contact with him."

"It depends how long you intend to remain in Asia Minor," said Battaces, sounding indifferent.

"I think I must stay until I manage to see the King of Pontus, *archigallos*. In the meantime, I'll pay a visit to King Nicomedes—at least *he* stays put! Then it's back to Halicarnassus for the winter. In the spring I intend to go to Tarsus, and from there I shall venture inland to see King Ariarathes of Cappadocia." Marius rattled all this off casually, then turned the subject to temple banking, in which he professed himself interested.

"There is no point, Gaius Marius, in keeping the Goddess's money mouldering in our vaults," said Battaces gently. "By lending it at good rates of interest, we increase her wealth. However, here at Pessinus we do not seek depositors, as some others among the temple confraternity do."

"It's not an activity one sees in Rome," said Marius, "I suppose because Rome's temples are the property of the Roman People, and administered by the State."

"The Roman State could make money, could it not?"

"It could, but that would lead to an additional bureaucracy, and

Rome doesn't care much for bureaucrats. They tend either to be inert, or too acquisitive. Our banking is private, and in the hands of professional bankers."

"I do assure you, Gaius Marius," said Battaces, "that we temple bankers are highly professional."

"What about Cos?" asked Marius.

"The sanctuary of Asklepios, you mean?"

"I do."

"Ah, a *very* professional operation!" said Battaces, not without envy. "Now there is an institution eminently capable of funding whole wars! They have many depositors, of course."

Marius got up. "I thank you, *archigallos*."

Battaces watched Marius stride down the incline toward the beautiful colonnade built above the spring-fed stream; then, sure Marius would not turn back, the priest hurried to his palace, a small but lovely building within a grove of trees.

Ensconced in his study, he drew writing materials toward him, and proceeded to begin a letter to King Mithridates.

It would appear, Great King, that the Roman consul Gaius Marius is determined to see you. He applied to me for help in tracking you down, and when I gave him no kind of encouragement, he told me that he intends to remain in Asia Minor until he manages to meet you.

Among his plans for the near future are visits to Nicomedes and Ariarathes. One wonders why he would submit himself to the rigors of a journey into Cappadocia, for he is not very young—nor very well, I strongly suspect. But he made it clear that in the spring he goes to Tarsus, and from there he will go to Cappadocia.

I find him a formidable man, Great One. If such as he succeeded in becoming consul of Rome no less than six times—for he is a blunt and rather uncouth individual—then one must not underestimate him. Those noble Romans I have met before were far smoother, more

sophisticated men. A pity perhaps that I did not have
the opportunity to meet Gaius Marius in Rome, when,
contrasting him with his peers, I might have been able
to make more of him than I can here in Pessinus.

In all this, please find me your devoted and ever-loyal
subject, Battaces.

The letter sealed and wrapped in softest leather, then put inside
a wallet, Battaces gave it to one of his junior priests and sent him
posthaste to Sinope, where lay King Mithridates.

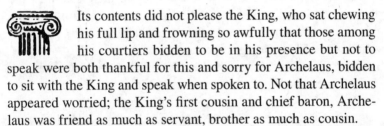 Its contents did not please the King, who sat chewing
his full lip and frowning so awfully that those among
his courtiers bidden to be in his presence but not to
speak were both thankful for this and sorry for Archelaus, bidden
to sit with the King and speak when spoken to. Not that Archelaus
appeared worried; the King's first cousin and chief baron, Archelaus was friend as much as servant, brother as much as cousin.

Beneath his unconcerned exterior, however, Archelaus harbored
the same degree of apprehension for his safety as the rest of those
in attendance on the King; if any man might be excused for thinking he stood high in the King's favor, he had better remember the
fate of the chief baron Diophantus. Diophantus too had been friend
as much as servant, father as much as the uncle he actually was.

However, reflected Archelaus as he sat watching the strong yet
petulant face only feet away, a man really had no choice in the
matter. The King was the King, all others his to command—and
to kill, if such was his pleasure. A state of affairs that sharpened
the wits of those living in close proximity to so much energy, capriciousness, infantilism, brilliance, strength, and timidity. All a
man owned to extricate himself from a thousand perilous situations were his wits. And these perilous situations could blow up
like storms off the Euxine, or simmer like kettles on glowing
coals at the back of the King's mind, or loom out of some unre-

membered sin a decade old. The King never forgot an injury, real or imagined; only put it away for future use.

"I will have to see him, it appears," said Mithridates, then added, "Won't I?"

A trap: what did one answer?

"If you don't choose to, Great King, you don't have to see anyone," said Archelaus easily. "However, I imagine Gaius Marius would be an interesting man to meet."

"Cappadocia, then. In the spring. Let him get the measure of Nicomedes first. If this Gaius Marius is so formidable, he will not be predisposed to like Nicomedes of Bithynia," said the King. "And let him meet Ariarathes first too. Send that little insect word from me that in the spring he will present himself to Gaius Marius in Tarsus, and personally escort the Roman to Cappadocia."

"The army will be mobilized as planned, O Great One?"

"Of course. Is Gordius coming?"

"He should be in Sinope before the winter snows close the passes, my King," said Archelaus.

"Good!" Still frowning, Mithridates returned his attention to the letter from Battaces, and began to chew his lip again. These Romans! Why couldn't they keep their noses out of what was, after all, none of their business? Why was a man as famous as Gaius Marius concerning himself with the doings of peoples in eastern Anatolia? Had Ariarathes already concluded a bargain with the Romans to have Mithridates Eupator off his throne, turn Pontus into a satrapy of Cappadocia?

"The road has been too long and too hard," he said to his cousin Archelaus. "I will not bow down to the Romans!"

Indeed the road had been long and hard, almost from birth, for he had been the younger son of his father, King Mithridates V, and the King's sister-wife, Laodice. Born in the same year Scipio Aemilianus had died so mysteriously, Mithridates called Eupator had had a brother less than two years older than himself, called Mithridates Chrestos because he was the anointed one, the chosen king. The King their father had dreamed of enlarging Pontus at anyone's expense, but preferably at the expense of Bithynia, the oldest enemy—and the most obdurate.

At first it had seemed as if Pontus would retain the title Friend and Ally of the Roman People, earned by the fourth King Mithridates when he assisted the second Attalus of Pergamum in his war against King Prusias of Bithynia. The fifth Mithridates had continued in this alliance with Rome for some time, sending help against Carthage in the third of Rome's Punic wars, and against the successors of the third King Attalus of Pergamum after his will had revealed that he had left his entire kingdom to Rome. But then the fifth Mithridates had acquired Phrygia by paying the Roman proconsul in Asia Minor, Manius Aquillius, a sum of gold into his own purse; the title Friend and Ally had been withdrawn and enmity between Rome and Pontus had persisted ever since, cunningly fostered by King Nicomedes of Bithynia—and by anti-Aquillian senators in Rome.

Roman and Bithynian enmity or no, the fifth Mithridates had continued his expansionist policies, drawing Galatia into his net, and then succeeding in getting himself named heir to most of Paphlagonia. But his sister-wife didn't like the fifth King Mithridates; she had conceived a desire to rule Pontus on her own behalf. When young Mithridates Eupator was nine years old—the court was at Amaseia at the time—Queen Laodice murdered the husband who was also her brother, and put Mithridates Chrestos, aged eleven, on the throne. She, of course, was regent. In return for a guarantee from Bithynia that the borders of Pontus itself would not be breached, the Queen relinquished the claims of Pontus to Paphlagonia, and liberated Galatia.

Not yet ten years old, young Mithridates Eupator fled from Amaseia scant weeks after his mother's coup, convinced that he too would be murdered; for, unlike his slow and biddable brother Chrestos, he reminded his mother of her husband, and she had begun to say so with increasing frequency. Completely alone, the boy fled not to Rome or some neighboring court but into the eastern Pontic mountains, where he made no secret of his identity to the local inhabitants, only begging them to keep his secret. Awed and flattered, predisposed to love a member of the royal house who would choose exile among them, the local people protected Mithridates fanatically. Moving from village to village, the young prince came to know his country as no other scion of the royal house ever had, and penetrated deeply into parts of it where civilization had slowed, or stopped, or never started. In the summers he roamed utterly free, hunting bear and lion to win a reputation for daring among his ignorant subjects, knowing that the bounty of the Pontic forests would yield him food—cherries and hazelnuts, apricots and succulent vegetables, deer and rabbits.

In some ways his life was never again to yield to him so much simple satisfaction—nor any subjects to yield him so much simple adoration—as during the seven years Mithridates Eupator hid in the mountains of eastern Pontus. Slipping silently beneath the eaves of forests brilliant with the pink and lilac of rhododendron, the pendulous cream of acacia, never it seemed without the roar of tumbling white water in his ears, he grew from boy into young man. His first women were the girls of tiny and primitive villages; his first lion a maned beast of huge proportions that he killed, a reincarnation of Herakles, with a club; his first bear a creature far taller than he was.

The Mithridatidae were big people, their origins Germano-Celt from Thrace, but this was admixed with a little Persian blood from the court (if not the loins) of King Darius, and through the two hundred and fifty years the Mithridatidae had ruled Pontus, they had occasionally married into the Syrian Seleucid dynasty, another Germano-Thracian royal house, descended as it was from Alexander the Great's Macedonian general Seleucus. An occasional throwback to the Persian strain provided someone slight and smooth and creamy-dark, but Mithridates Eupator was a true Germano-Celt. So he grew very tall, grew shoulders wide enough to support the carcass of a fully developed male deer, and grew thighs and calves strong enough to scale the crags of a Pontic peak.

At seventeen he felt himself sufficiently a man to make his move; he sent a secret message to his uncle Archelaus, a man he knew to bear no love for Queen Laodice, who was his half sister as well as his sovereign. A plan was evolved through a number of furtive meetings in the hills behind Sinope, where the Queen now lived permanently; one by one, Mithridates met those barons whom Archelaus thought trustworthy, and took their oaths of allegiance.

Everything went exactly according to plan; Sinope fell because the struggle for power went on within its walls, never threatened from without. The Queen and Chrestos and those barons loyal to them were taken bloodlessly; when blood did flow, it gushed out from under an executioner's sword. Several uncles, aunts and cousins perished at once, Chrestos somewhat later, and Queen Laodice last of all. Pious son, Mithridates threw his mother into a dungeon under Sinope's battlements, where—how *could* it have happened?—someone forgot to feed her, and she starved to death. Innocent of matricide, the sixth King Mithridates ruled alone. He was not yet eighteen.

He felt his oats, he itched to make a great name for himself, he burned to see Pontus become more powerful by far than any of its neighbors, he hungered to rule the world; for his huge silver mirror told him he was no ordinary king. Instead of a diadem or a tiara, he took to wearing the skin of a lion, its huge fanged mouth jammed down across his forehead, its head and ears covering his scalp, its paws knotted on his chest. Because his hair was so like Alexander the Great's—the same yellow-gold color, as thick, as loosely curled—he wore it in the same style. Then, wanting to demonstrate his masculinity, he grew not a beard or a moustache (they were beyond the boundaries of Hellenic taste) but long bristling side-whiskers in front of each ear. What a contrast to Nicomedes of Bithynia! Virile, a man entirely for women, huge, lusty, fearsome, powerful. Such were the qualities his silver mirror showed him, and he was well satisfied.

He married his oldest sister, another Laodice, then married anyone else he fancied as well, so that he had a dozen wives and several times that number of concubines; Laodice he appointed his Queen, but—as he told her quite often—that would last only as long as she was loyal. To reinforce this warning, he sent to

Syria for a Seleucid bride of the reigning house, and—there being a plethora of princesses at that moment—he received his Syrian wife, whose name was Antiochis. He also acquired one Nysa, who was the daughter of a Cappadocian prince named Gordius, and gave one of his younger sisters (yet another Laodice!) to the sixth King Ariarathes of Cappadocia.

Marriage alliances, as he quickly found out, were extremely useful things. His father-in-law Gordius conspired with his sister Laodice to murder Laodice's husband, King of Cappadocia; looking smugly at a decade and a half of regency, Queen Laodice put her baby son on the throne as the seventh Ariarathes and held Cappadocia in thrall to her brother Mithridates. Until, that is, she succumbed to the blandishments of old King Nicomedes of Bithynia, for she fancied ruling independently of Mithridates and his Cappadocian watchdog, Gordius. Gordius fled to Pontus, Nicomedes assumed the title King of Cappadocia, but remained in Bithynia and allowed his new wife Laodice to act precisely as she wanted within Cappadocia provided she had nothing friendly to do with Pontus. An arrangement which suited Laodice very well. However, her little son was now nearly ten years of age, and like all the kingly oriental breeds, he had developed autocratic tendencies already; he wanted to rule by himself. A clash with his mother saw his pretensions crushed, but not his convictions. Within a month he presented himself at the court of his uncle Mithridates in Amaseia, and within a month more his uncle Mithridates had installed him alone on his throne in Mazaca, for the army of Pontus was permanently in a state of readiness, that of Cappadocia not. Laodice was put to death, her brother watching impassively; the tenure of Bithynia in Cappadocia was abruptly severed. The only thing which annoyed Mithridates was that the ten-year-old seventh King Ariarathes of Cappadocia refused to allow Gordius to return home, steadily maintaining that he could not play host to his father's murderer.

All this Cappadocian meddling had occupied but a small part of the young King of Pontus's time; during the early years of his reign, his main energies were directed at increasing the manpower and excellence of the Pontic armies, and the wealth in the Pontic treasury. He was a thinker, Mithridates, despite his leonine affectations, his grandiose posturings, and his youth.

With a handful of those barons who were also his close (and Mithridatid) relatives—his uncle Archelaus, his uncle Diophantus, and his cousins Archelaus and Neoptolemus—he took ship in Amisus for a voyage around the eastern shores of the Euxine Sea. The party went in the guise of Greek merchants looking for trade alliances and passed muster everywhere they landed, as the peoples they encountered were neither learned nor sophisticated. Trapezus and Rhizus had long paid tribute to the Kings of Pontus and were nominally a part of the realm; but beyond these two prosperous outlets for the rich silver mines of the interior lay *terra incognita*.

The expedition explored legendary Colchis, where the Phasis River poured into the sea and the peoples who lived along it suspended the fleeces of sheep in its stream to catch the many particles of gold it carried down from the Caucasus; they gaped up at mountains even taller than those of Pontus and Armenia, sides perpetually crusted with snow, and kept a wary eye out for the descendants of the Amazons who had once lived in Pontus where the Thermodon spread its alluvial plain into the sea.

Slowly the Caucasus decreased in height and there began the endless plains of the Scythians and Sarmatians, teeming peoples of almost settled habits who had been somewhat tamed by the Greeks who had set up colonies on the coast—not militarily tamed, but exposed to Greek customs and culture—most alluring, most exotic, most seductive.

Where the delta of the Vardanes River cut up the shoreline, the ship bearing King Mithridates entered into a huge and almost landlocked lake called Maeotis and sailed along its triangular shape, discovering at its apex the mightiest river in the world, the fabled Tanais. They heard the names of other rivers—Rha, Udon, Borysthenes, Hypanis—and tales about the vast sea to the east called Hyrcanus or Caspium.

Wheat was growing everywhere the Greeks had established their trading cities.

"We would grow more, did we have a market," said the *ethnarch* of Sinde. "Liking their first taste of bread, the Scythians have learned to break ground, grow wheat."

"You sold grain to King Masinissa of Numidia a century ago," said Mithridates. "There are still markets. The Romans were willing to pay anything not long ago. Why aren't you actively seeking markets?"

"Perhaps," said the *ethnarch,* "we have grown too isolated from the world of the Middle Sea. And the taxes Bithynia levies for passage through the Hellespont are very heavy."

"I think," said Mithridates to his uncles, "we will have to do what we can to help these excellent people, don't you?"

An inspection of the fabulously fertile near-island called the Tauric Chersonnese by the Greeks and Cimmeria by the Scythians was all the further proof Mithridates needed; these lands were ripe for conquest, and must belong to Pontus.

However, Mithridates was not a good general, and was wise enough to know it. Soldiering intrigued him for short periods, and he was no coward, far from it; but somehow the knowledge of what to do with many thousands of troops evaded him, and that before ever he tried it in practice. Whereas he found that he enjoyed organizing a campaign, assembling armies. Let others better qualified than he lead them.

Pontus yielded troops, of course, but its King was aware that their quality left much to be desired, for the Greeks who inhabited the coastal cities despised warfare—the native peoples, descendants of the Persic strains who had once lived around the south and west of the Hyrcanian Sea, were so backward they were almost impossible to train. So, like most eastern rulers, Mithridates was forced to rely upon mercenaries. Most of these were Syrians, Cilicians, Cypriots, and the hot-blooded citizens of those quarrelsome Semitic states around the Palus Asphaltites in Palestina. They fought very well and very loyally—provided they were paid. If the pay was one day late, they packed up and started to walk home.

But having seen the Scythians and Sarmatians, the King of Pontus decided that from these peoples he would in future obtain his soldiers; he would train them as infantry and arm them like Romans. And with them he would set out to conquer Anatolia. First, however, he had to subjugate them. And for this task he chose his uncle Diophantus, son of his father's blood sister and a baron named Asklepiodorus.

His pretext was a complaint the Greeks of Sinde and the Chersonnesus had made about raiding incursions by the sons of King Scilurus, dead now, but the craftsman of a Scythian state of Cimmeria which had not entirely collapsed after he died. Thanks to the efforts of the Greek outpost at Obia to the west, they were farming Scythians, but they were warlike.

"Send to King Mithridates of Pontus for help," said the false merchant visitor before he left the Tauric Chersonnese. "In fact, I'll carry a letter on your behalf, if you like."

A proven general from the time of the fifth King Mithridates, Diophantus espoused his task with enthusiasm, and took a large and well-trained army to the Tauric Chersonnese in the spring following the visit of Mithridates. The result was a triumph for Pontus; the sons of Scilurus crumbled, as did the inland Kingdom of Cimmeria; within the first year Pontus possessed all of the Tauric Chersonnese, huge Roxolani territory to the west, and the Greek city of Olbia, much reduced by constant Sarmatian-Roxolani incursions. In the second year the Scythians fought back, but by its end Diophantus had subjugated the eastern parts of Lake Maeotis, the inland Sindian Maeotians under their king, Saumacus, and had established two strong fortress towns facing each other across the Cimmerian Bosporus.

Home sailed Diophantus, leaving his son Neoptolemus to settle the affairs of Olbia and the west, and his son Archelaus to regulate the new Pontic empire of the northern Euxine. The job had been splendidly done, the spoils considerable, the manpower for Pontic armies bottomless, the trade possibilities most promising. All this did Diophantus report to his young King in tones of pride; whereupon his young King, jealous and afraid, executed Uncle Diophantus.

The shock waves traveled through every level of the Pontic

court and eventually reached the northern Euxine, where the sons of Diophantus wept in mingled terror and grief, then bent with redoubled energy to finish what their father had started. Down the eastern seaboard of the Euxine marched and sailed Neoptolemus and Archelaus, and one by one the little kingdoms of the Caucasus yielded to Pontus, including gold-rich Colchis and the lands between the Phasis and Pontic Rhizus.

Lesser Armenia—which the Romans called Armenia Parva— was not actually a part of Armenia proper; it lay to the west and on the Pontic side of the vast mountains between the Araxes and the Euphrates Rivers. To Mithridates it was rightfully his, if for no other reason than that its king regarded the Kings of Pontus as his suzerains rather than the Kings of Armenia. As soon as the eastern and northern Euxine belonged to him in fact as well as in name, Mithridates invaded Lesser Armenia, leading his army in person because he was sure nothing more than his presence would be necessary. He was correct. When he rode into the little town of Zimara, which called itself the capital, he was hailed by the whole populace with open arms; King Antipater of Lesser Armenia advanced toward him in the garb of a suppliant. For once in his life Mithridates *felt* like a general, so it was not surprising that he became entranced with Lesser Armenia. He eyed its ranks of snow-clad peaks, its boiling spring-fed torrents, its remoteness and inaccessibility, and decided that here he would house the bulk of his rapidly accumulating treasure. The orders went out immediately; fortress repositories would be built on any insurmountable rock, atop the cliffs of some great alpine wall, on the far banks of murderously swift rivers. For one whole summer he amused himself riding about selecting this chasm, that gorge; by the time the project was finished, over seventy strongholds had come into being, and word of his fabulous wealth had traveled as far as Rome.

Thus it was that, not yet thirty years old but already the owner of a far-flung empire, the custodian of staggering riches, the commander-in-chief of a dozen armies now made up of Scythians, Sarmatians, Celts and Maeotians, and the father of a large brood of sons, the sixth King Mithridates of Pontus sent an embassage to

Rome to ask that he be awarded the title of Friend and Ally of the Roman People. It was the year that Gaius Marius and Quintus Lutatius Catulus Caesar beat the last division of the Germans at Vercellae, so Marius himself had only heard of events second-hand, mostly through the medium of letters from Publius Rutilius Rufus. King Nicomedes of Bithynia had complained at once to the Senate that it was impossible for Rome to name two kings Friend and Ally of the Roman People when those kings were at permanent loggerheads, and pointed out that *he* had never varied in his allegiance to Rome since his assumption of the Bithynian throne over fifty years before. Tribune of the plebs for a second time, Lucius Appuleius Saturninus had sided with Bithynia, and in the end all the money the envoys of Mithridates had paid out to needy senators went for nothing. The Pontic embassage was refused, and sent home.

Mithridates took the news hard. First he had a temper tantrum which saw his court scatter, shaking in terror, while he roared up and down his audience chamber calling down curses and frightful imprecations upon Rome and all things Roman. Then he lapsed into an even more horrifying quiet, and sat for many hours alone on his royal lion seat, brooding. Finally, after a brief instruction to Queen Laodice that she was to rule the kingdom in his absence, he left Sinope, and was not seen again for over a year.

He went first to Amaseia, the original Pontic capital of his ancestors, where all the early kings were buried in tombs hewn from the solid rock of the mountains ringing Amaseia round, and stalked up and down the corridors of the palace for several days, oblivious to the presence of his cowering servants and the seductive pleas of the two wives and eight concubines he kept permanently installed there. Then, as suddenly and completely as a storm was blown away across the mountains, King Mithridates emerged from his furor and settled down to make plans. He did not send back to Sinope for more courtiers, nor ride to Zela, where his nearest army was encamped; instead, he summoned those barons who lived in Amaseia and sent them to choose him a detachment of one thousand crack troops. His instructions were well thought out,

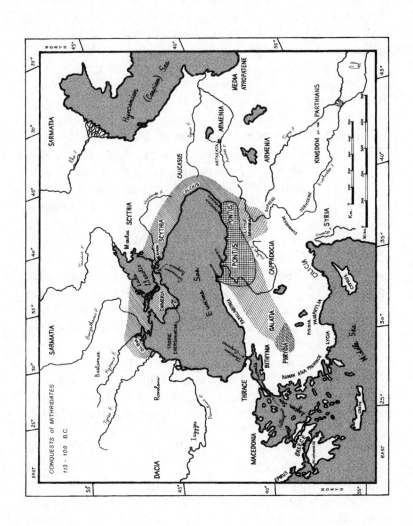

CONQUESTS of MITHRIDATES
113 - 100 B.C.

and issued in tones which brooked neither argument nor defiance. Forth he would go to Ancyra, the biggest town in Galatia, but with a bodyguard only, his soldiers many miles behind. The barons he dispatched ahead of his own progress were under orders to bring every Galatian tribal chieftain to a great congress at Ancyra, where the King of Pontus would have interesting proposals to make.

It was an outlandish place, Galatia, a Celtic outpost in a sub-continent peopled by those of Persic, Syriac, Germanic and Hittite strains; all save the Syriacs tended to be fair, at least of skin, but not fair like these Celtic immigrants descended from the second King Brennus of the Gauls. For almost two hundred years they had occupied their big piece of the Anatolian heartland, a rich place and roomy, and lived the lives of Gauls, heedless of the cultures surrounding them. Their intertribal contacts, even, were tenuous; they owned no overall king, and were not interested in banding together to conquer additional territory. For a while, indeed, they had acknowledged the fifth King Mithridates of Pontus as their suzerain, an empty kind of business that yielded them nothing and the fifth Mithridates the same, for they never produced the tithes and tributes Pontus had demanded, and Pontus died before he could exact retribution. No one tampered with them; they were Gauls, far fiercer than Phrygians, Cappadocians, Pontines, Bithynians, Ionian or Dorian Greeks.

The leaders of the three Galatian tribes and their tribelets came to Ancyra to answer the summons of Mithridates, looking more forward to the great feast they had been promised than to whatever projected campaign of mayhem and booty the sixth Mithridates was undoubtedly going to offer them. And in Ancyra—little more than a village—they found Mithridates waiting for them. He had scoured the countryside all the way from Amaseia for every delicacy and kind of wine money could buy, and spread before the Galatian chiefs a feast grander and more delicious even than their imaginations had conjured up. Already in a state of affable content before they made inroads upon the food and drink, they succumbed blissfully to the twin snares of full bellies and whirling heads.

And while they lay amid the shambles to which they had reduced the feast, snoring and twitching in drunken stupor, the
thousand handpicked soldiers of King Mithridates spilled silently
into the compound, went among them, and killed them. Not until
the last Galatian thane was dead did King Mithridates move from
his lordly chair at the head of the head table, sitting with his leg
thrown over its arm, wagging his foot, his big smooth bland face
displaying a keen interest in the slaughter.

"Burn them," he said at the end, "then spread their ashes on top
of their blood. This place will grow superb wheat next year. Nothing makes soil more fruitful than blood and bone."

He then had himself proclaimed King of Galatia, with no one
left to oppose him save leaderless and scattered Gauls.

And then he suddenly and completely disappeared. Not his
most senior baron knew where he had gone, or what he was up to;
he simply left a letter ordering them to tidy Galatia up, return to
Amaseia, and send to the Queen at Sinope to appoint a satrap for
the new Pontic territory of Galatia.

Clad in the garb of a merchant, astride a mediocre brown horse
and leading a donkey upon which he had placed spare clothing
and a rather stupid young Galatian slave who didn't even know
who his master was, Mithridates rode down the track to Pessinus.
At the precinct of Kubaba Cybele the Great Mother he revealed
his true identity to Battaces and brought the *archigallos* into his
service, obtaining from Battaces much information he would
need. From Pessinus he proceeded into the Roman Asia Province
down the long valley of the Maeander River.

Scarcely one town in Caria did he leave uninvestigated; the big,
curious, slightly-vague-about-his-business eastern merchant rode
from one place to another administering an occasional beating to
his dullard slave, eyes everywhere, mind filing every item of information away. He supped with other merchant travelers at inn
tables, he lingered in the market squares on market days talking to
anyone who looked to have something interesting to impart, he
strolled the quays of Aegean seaports poking his fingers into bales
and sniffing at sealed amphorae, he flirted with village girls and

rewarded them most generously when they gratified his fleshly urges, he listened to tales of the riches in the precinct of Asklepios on Cos, in the Artemisium at Ephesus, the sanctuary of Asklepios at Pergamum, and the fabulous treasures of Rhodes.

From Ephesus he turned north to Smyrna and Sardis, and eventually arrived in Pergamum, capital of the Roman governor, glittering from its mountaintop like a jeweled box. Here for the first time he saw genuine Roman troops, a small guard belonging to the governor; Asia Province was not considered a military risk, so its soldiers were made up of local auxiliaries and militia. Long and hard did Mithridates study the eighty members of the real thing, noting the heaviness of the mailed armor, the short swords and tiny-headed spears, the well-drilled way in which they moved, seconded to soft duty though they were. Here too he saw his first purple-bordered toga upon the person of the governor himself. This worthy, escorted by lictors in crimson tunics, each bearing the bundle of rods upon his left shoulder with the axes inserted because the governor had the power to deal out death, seemed to the watching Mithridates to defer very humbly to a small number of men in plain white togas. These, he discovered, were the *publicani,* executives of the companies which farmed the provincial taxes; from the way they strutted through the exquisitely planned and laid out streets of Pergamum, they seemed to think they owned the province, rather than Rome.

Not, of course, that Mithridates presumed to strike up a conversation with any of these august fellows, they were obviously far too busy and important to take heed of a lone eastern merchant; he simply noted them as they passed by in the midst of their small armies of clerks and scribes, and did his talking to Pergamites across friendly tables in little taverns far beneath the notice of the *publicani.*

"They bleed us dry," he was told so many times he judged it to be the truth rather than the typical grumblings of men who grumbled only to hide their prosperity, as rich farmers and those running monopoly businesses did.

"How so?" he replied at first, and was asked where he had been

since the death of King Attalus thirty years earlier. So he concocted a tale of long wanderings to the north of the Euxine Sea,
secure in the knowledge that should some fellow quiz him on Olbia or Cimmeria, he could indeed speak of these places as one
who had seen them.

"In Rome," he was told, "they have two very high officials they
call censors. They are elected—isn't that odd?—and they must pre-
viously have been consuls, which shows you how important they
are. Now in any decent Greek community, the business of the
State is run by proper civil employees, not men who might last year
have been leading armies! Not so in Rome, where these censors
are complete amateurs in business. Yet they have control of every
kind of State business, and it is their job every five years to let
contracts on behalf of the State."

"Contracts?" asked the oriental despot, frowning.

"Contracts. Like any other contracts, except that these are between companies in business and the Roman State," said the merchant of Pergamum whom Mithridates was entertaining.

"I fear I have been too long in places ruled by kings," said the
King. "Does the Roman State have no servants to ensure its enterprises are properly run?"

"Only the magistrates—consuls and praetors and aediles and
quaestors—and they are solely interested in one thing, that the
Treasury of Rome be full." The Pergamite merchant sniggered.
"Of course, friend, quite often their major concern is that their
own purses be full!"

"Continue. I am fascinated."

"Our plight here is all the fault of Gaius Gracchus."

"One of the Sempronius brothers?"

"The same. The younger one. He legislated to have the taxes of
Asia collected by companies of men specially formed for the purpose. That way, he reasoned, the Roman State could have its share
without actually employing tax-gatherers. Out of his laws the
Asian *publicani* were born, the men who farm the taxes here. The
censors in Rome announce to the bidders for contracts the terms
the State requires. In the case of the taxes of Asia Province, they

announce the sum of money the Treasury wants paid in each year for the next five years—*not* the actual sum of money to be collected in Asia Province. *That* figure is up to the tax companies to decide, as they have to make a profit for themselves before paying the Treasury what they contracted to pay it. So a squadron of accountants sit down with their abacuses and calculate how much it will be possible to squeeze from Asia Province annually for the next five years, and then the bid for the contract is made."

"Forgive me, I must be dense—how can it matter to Rome what amount is bid, if the sum the State wants has already been told to the bidders?"

"Ah! But that figure, my dear fellow, is merely the *minimum* the Treasury is prepared to accept! So what happens is that each company of *publicani* tries to calculate a figure that will be sufficiently higher than the minimum to make the Treasury very happy indeed—and also incorporate in it a fat profit!"

"Oh, I see," said Mithridates, blowing through his nose. "The contract is let to the firm which makes the highest bid."

"Correct."

"But is the figure bid the figure to be paid to the Treasury, or the whole sum including the fat profit?"

The merchant laughed. "Only the sum to be paid to the State, friend! What sort of profit the company expects to make is purely company information, and the censors don't ask any questions, believe me. They open the bids, and whichever firm has offered the Treasury the most is the firm awarded the contract."

"Do the censors ever award the contract to a firm bidding less than the highest figure?"

"Not in my memory, friend."

"And the result of all this? Are the company estimates, for instance, within the bounds of probability, or are they far too optimistic?" Mithridates asked, knowing the answer.

"Well, what do you think? The *publicani* base their estimates, as far as we can tell, on a set of figures obtained from a survey done in the Garden of the Hesperides, not Attalus's Asia Minor!

So when there's a fall in production in the smallest district and in the smallest activity there, all of a sudden the *publicani* panic—the sum they've contracted to pay the Treasury is suddenly more than they're gathering! If only they'd make their bids realistic, everyone would be better off! As it is, unless we have a bumper harvest, don't lose a single sheep in the shearing or the lambing, sell every last link of chain, foot of rope, piece of fabric, hide of cow, amphora of wine and *medimnus* of olives—why, the tax-farmers start squeezing, and everybody suffers," said the merchant bitterly.

"How do they squeeze?" asked Mithridates, wondering where the camps of soldiers were, as he had seen none in his travels.

"They hire Cilician mercenaries from the areas where even wild Cilician sheep starve, and they let them loose. I've seen whole districts sold into slavery, down to the last woman and child, no matter how old or how young. I've seen whole fields dug up and houses pulled down, searching for money. Oh, friend, if I told you everything I've seen the tax-farmers do to squeeze a drop more, you'd weep! Crops confiscated except for just enough to let the farmer and his family eat and plant the next year's crop, flocks halved, shops and stalls rifled—and the worst of it is that it encourages people to lie and cheat—if they don't, they lose the lot."

"And all these tax-farming *publicani* are Romans?"

"Romans or Italians," said the merchant.

"Italians," said Mithridates thoughtfully, wishing that he hadn't spent seven years of his childhood hiding in the Pontic forests; his education, as he had discovered since beginning his journey of exploration, was sadly lacking in geography and economics.

"Well, Romans, really," explained the merchant, who wasn't sure of the distinction either. "They come from special suburbs of Rome called Italy. But beyond that, there's no difference as far as I can see. They all start rolling tides of Latin when they gather together instead of doing the decent thing and keeping what they say in honest Greek, and they all wear frightful unshaped and untailored tunics—the sort of thing a shepherd would be ashamed to wear, not a dart or a tuck in it to make it fit nicely." The merchant plucked at the soft stuff of his own Greek tunic complacently, sure it had been perfectly cut to flatter his rather small and spare figure.

"Do they wear the toga?" Mithridates asked.

"Sometimes. On holidays, and if the governor summonses them," said the merchant.

"Italians too?"

"Don't know," said the merchant, and shrugged. "I daresay."

From conversations like this did Mithridates gather his information, mostly a litany of hate against the *publicani* and their hired minions. There was also another thriving business in Asia Province, again run by Romans; the lending of money at rates of interest no self-respecting borrower would agree to, nor self-respecting lender stipulate. And, learned Mithridates, these moneylenders were usually employees of the tax-farming companies, though the companies had no share in the moneylending. Roman Asia Province, thought Mithridates, is a fat fowl the Romans pluck, they have no other interest in it. They come here from Rome and the suburbs called Italy, they pinch and squeeze and extort, and then they go home again with purses bulging, indifferent to the plight of those they leave behind, the people of Dorian, Aeolian, and Ionian Asia. And they are *hated*!

From Pergamum he journeyed inland to cut off the unimportant triangle called the Troad, and emerged on the southern shore of the Propontis Lake near Cyzicus. From here he rode along the Propontis Lake to Prusa, in Bithynia. Prosperous and growing, it lay in the lap of the vast, snow-covered mountain called Mysian Olympus; pausing only to note that its citizens were uninterested in the machinations of their octogenarian king, he went on to the capital of Nicomedia, where the octogenarian king kept court. It too was a prosperous and fairly large city, dominated by the temple precinct and palace atop a small acropolis, dreaming alongside its wide calm inlet.

This of course was dangerous country for a Mithridatid; it was even possible that on the streets of Nicomedia he might encounter some person who would recognize him, a priest of the far-flung confraternity of Ma or Tyche, or some Sinopean visitor. So he chose to stay in a foul-smelling inn well away from the better parts of the city, and muffled himself closely in the folds of his cloak whenever he ventured out. All he wished to do was to gain a feel of the people, test the temperature of their devotion to King Nicomedes, decide how wholeheartedly they might support their king in a war with— idle speculation though it was, of course—the King of Pontus.

The rest of winter and all of spring he spent wandering from Heracleia on the Bithynian Euxine to the remotest parts of Phrygia and Paphlagonia, observing everything from the state of the roads— more like tracks—to how much of the countryside was cleared for the planting of crops, and how educated the people were.

And thus in early summer he returned to Sinope feeling all-powerful, vindicated, brilliant, to find his sister-wife Laodice shrill-voiced and prone to feverish chatter, and his barons too quiet. His uncles Archelaus and Diophantus were dead and his cousins Neoptolemus and Archelaus were in Cimmeria, a state of affairs which left the King aware of his vulnerability, and that upset his mood of triumph, made him suppress his impulse to sit upon his throne and regale the entire court with every detail of his odyssey to the west. Instead, he dowered everyone with a breezy smile, made love to Laodice until she cried for quarter, visited all his sons and daughters and their mothers, and sat back to see what would happen next. Something was going on, of that he was sure; until he discovered its nature, he resolved to say not a word about where he had been during his long and mysterious absence, nor about his plans for the future.

Then came Gordius his Cappadocian father-in-law to see him in the night marches, a finger upon his lips, a hand indicating that they should meet upon the battlements above the palace as soon as possible. The air was silver-drenched by a great full moon, a wind blew glittering skitters across the surface of the sea, the shadows were blacker than the deepest cave, the light beneath the still orb in the sky a colorless parody of the sun. Sprawled across the neck of land which connected the mainland with the bulbous promontory whereon stood the palace, the town slept easily, dreamlessly; and the dense darkness of the walls enveloping all human habitation loomed stubby-toothed against the sheen of a low-lying cloud bank.

Midway between two watchtowers the King and Gordius met, hunched themselves down below the parapet of the battlements, and murmured too softly for sleeping birds to hear.

"Laodice was convinced that this time you would not come back, Great One," Gordius said.

"Was she?" asked the King, stony-voiced.

"She took a lover three months ago."

"Who?"

"Your cousin Pharnaces, Great One."

Ah! Clever Laodice! Not a nobody lover, but one of the few males of the line who could hope to ascend the Pontic throne without fearing that eventually he would be displaced by one of the King's brood of underaged sons. Pharnaces was the son of the fifth king's brother—and also of the fifth king's sister. The blood was pure on both sides; he was perfect.

"She thinks I won't find out," said Mithridates.

"She thinks those few who know will be too afraid to speak," said Gordius.

"Why then are you speaking?"

Gordius smiled, teeth reflecting the moon. "My King, no one will best you! I have known it from the first time I saw you."

"You will be rewarded, Gordius, I pledge it." The King leaned back against the wall, and thought. Finally he said, "She will try to kill me very soon."

"I agree, Great One."

"How many loyal men have I got in Sinope?"

"More by far, I think, than she has. She is a woman, my King, therefore crueler and more treacherous by far than any man. Who could trust her? Those who follow her have done so for great promotions, but they rely upon Pharnaces to ensure promotion. I think they also rely upon Pharnaces killing her once he's well established on the throne. However, most of the court was proof against their blandishments."

"Good! I leave it to you, Gordius, to alert my loyal people as to what is going on. Tell them to be ready at any hour of the day or night," said the King.

"What are you going to do?"

"Let her try to kill me, the sow! I know her. She's my sister. So it won't be knife or bow and arrow. She'll choose poison. Something really nasty, so I suffer."

"Great One, let me arrest her and Pharnaces at once, please!" whispered Gordius frantically. "Poison is so insidious! What if, in spite of every precaution, she should trick you into swallowing hemlock, or put an adder in your bed? Please, let me arrest them now! It will be easier."

But the King shook his head. "I need proof, Gordius. So let her try to poison me. Let her find whatever noxious plant or mushroom or reptile she thinks will suit her purpose best, and let her administer it to me."

"My King, my King!" quavered Gordius, appalled.

"There's no need to worry, Gordius," said Mithridates, his calm unimpaired, no atom of fear in his voice. "It is not generally known—even to Laodice—that during the seven years when I hid from the vengeance of my mother, I rendered myself immune to every kind of poison known to men—and some no one has yet discovered, except me. I am the world's greatest authority upon the subject of poisons, I can say that with truth. Do you think all these scars I bear are the result of weapons? No! I have scarred myself, Gordius, to make sure that not one of my relatives can succeed in eliminating me by the easiest and least impeachable method we know—by poison."

"So young!" marveled Gordius.

"Better to stay alive to grow old, say I! No one is going to take my throne from me."

"But how did you render yourself immune, Great One?"

"Take the Egyptian asp, for example," said the King, warming to his theme. "You know the creature—big wide hood and little head swaying between its wings. I brought in a box of them in every size, and I started with the little ones, made them bite me.

Then I worked up to the biggest one of all, a monster seven feet long and thick as my arm. By the time I was finished, Gordius, that thing could strike me, and I never even became ill! I did the same with adders and pythons, scorpions and spiders. Then I took a drop of every poison—hemlock, wolfsbane, mandragora, cherry seed pulp, brews of berries and bushes and roots, the Death Cap mushroom and the white-spotted red mushroom—yes, Gordius, I took them all! Increasing the dose a drop at a time until even a cup of any poison had no effect. And I have continued to keep myself immune—I continue to take poison, I continue to let myself be bitten. *And* I take antidotes." Mithridates laughed softly. "Let Laodice do her worst! She can't kill me."

But she tried, during the state banquet she gave to celebrate the King's safe return. As the whole court was invited, the big throne room was cleared and furnished with dozens of couches, the walls and pillars were decked with garlands of flowers, and the floor strewn with perfumed petals. Sinope's best musicians had been summoned, a traveling troupe of Greek actors was commissioned to give a performance of the *Elektra* of Euripedes, and the famous dancer Anais of Nisibis was brought from Amisus, where she was summering on the Euxine.

Though in ancient times the Kings of Pontus had eaten sitting at tables like their Thracian ancestors, they had long espoused the Greek habit of reclining upon couches, and fancied in consequence that they were finished products of Greek culture, genuinely Hellenized monarchs.

How thin that layer of Hellenism was became evident when the courtiers entered the throne room one by one and prostrated themselves flat on the ground before their King; if additional evidence was necessary, it was furnished during the agonizing space of time after Queen Laodice, smiling seductively, offered her Scythian goblet of gold to the King, licking at its rim with her pink tongue.

"Drink from my cup, husband," she commanded, but gently.

Without hesitation Mithridates drank, a good deep draft which halved the goblet's contents; he put it down on the table in front of the couch he shared with Queen Laodice. But the last mouthful of wine he kept in his mouth, rolling it round as he stared with his brown-flecked, grape-green eyes at his sister. Then he frowned, but not direfully; a thoughtful, reminiscent sort of frown that changed in a twinkling to a wide smile.

"Dorycnion!" he said delightedly.

The Queen went white. The court stilled, for he spoke the word loudly, and this welcome-home feast had so far been quiet.

The King turned his head to the left. "Gordius," he said.

"My King?" asked Gordius, sliding quickly from his couch.

"Come here and help me, would you?"

Four years older than her brother, Laodice was very like him—not surprising in a house where brother had married sister often enough down the generations to compound family resemblances. A big but well-proportioned woman, the Queen had taken special care with her appearance; her golden hair was done in Greek style, her greenish-brown eyes ringed with *stibium,* her cheeks daubed with red chalk-powder, her lips carmined, and her hands and feet dark brown from henna. The white ribbon of the diadem bisected her forehead, its tasseled ends straying across her shoulders. She looked every inch the Queen, and such had been her intention.

Now she read her fate in her brother's face, and twisted her body to leave the couch. But not quickly enough; he grasped the hand she used to propel herself backward and yanked her across the bank of cushions she had reclined against until she half lay, half sat within the King's arm. And Gordius was there, kneeling at her other side, his face ugly with a wild triumph; for he knew what reward he was going to ask for—that his daughter Nysa, a minor wife, be elevated to Queen, and that her son, Pharnaces, therefore take precedence over Laodice's son, Machares.

Laodice turned her head helplessly to see four barons march her lover Pharnaces up to the King, who gazed at him impassively. Then the King swung his attention back to her.

"I will not die, Laodice," he said. "In fact, this paltry brew won't even make me sick." He smiled, genuinely amused. "However, there's more than enough left to kill you."

Her nose was nipped between the thumb and forefinger of the King's left hand, he tilted her head back, and she gasped, mouth falling open at once, for terror had taken her breath away, she could not hold it. A little at a time, he poured the contents of her beautiful golden Scythian goblet down her throat, making Gordius clamp her mouth shut between each application, himself stroking her neck voluptuously to make swallowing easier. She did not struggle, deeming it beneath her to do so; a Mithridatid was not afraid to die, especially when there had been a chance to snatch at the throne.

When it was done and the goblet was empty, Mithridates laid his sister full-length upon the couch, there before the horrified eyes of her lover.

"Don't try to vomit it up, Laodice," the King said pleasantly. "If you do, I'll only make you drink it a second time."

Those in the room waited, silent, still, terrified. How long a wait it was no one afterward could tell, except (had they asked him, which they did not) the King.

He turned to his courtiers, male and female, and began to address them in much the same tones as a teacher of philosophy might have used in imparting his expertise to new students. For everyone there the King's knowledge of poisons came as a revelation, a side to the King that was to circulate swifter than rumor from one end of Pontus to the other, and from there to the outside world; Gordius added his additional information, and the words Mithridates and poison became linked together in legend forever.

"The Queen," said the King, "could not have chosen better than *dorycnion,* which the Egyptians call *trychnos.* Alexander the Great's general, Ptolemy who later became King of Egypt, brought the plant back from India, where it grows, they say, to the height of a tree, though in Egypt it remains the height of a woody bush, with leaves akin to those of our common sage. Next to *aconiton* it is the best of all poisons—very sure! You will notice as the Queen dies that consciousness is not lost until the last breath is drawn— indeed, from personal experience I can assure you that all one's perceptions are exquisitely heightened, one looks out at a world more important and visionary than the normal state of being could ever suggest. Cousin Pharnaces, I must tell you that every heart-beat you suffer, the least flutter of your eyelids, your gasps as you feel her pain, she will take inside her as never, never before. A pity, perhaps, that she can take no more of you inside her, eh?" He glanced at his sister, nodded. "Watch now, it's beginning to happen."

Laodice's gaze was fixed on Pharnaces, who stood between his guardians staring doggedly at the floor, the look in her eyes something no one in the room ever forgot, though many tried; pain and horror, exaltation and sorrow, a rich and ever-changing gamut of emotions. She said nothing, it became obvious because she could not, for slowly her lips stretched away from her big yellow teeth, and slowly her neck curved and her spine arched so that the back of her head strained to meet the backs of her knees. Then came fine and rhythmic tremors which slowly increased in size as they decreased in frequency, until they turned into massive jerks of head and body and all four limbs.

"She's having a fit!" cried Gordius shrilly.

"Of course she is," said Mithridates rather scornfully. "It's the fit will kill her, wait and see." He watched her with a genuine clinical interest, having suffered minor variations of this himself, but never in front of his big silver mirror. "It is my ambition," he remarked to the people in the room as Laodice's convulsions dragged on and on and on without let, "to develop a universal antidote, a magic elixir to cure the effect of any poison, be it a poison of plant or animal or fish or inanimate substance. As it is, every day I must sip a concoction composed of no less than one hundred different poisons, otherwise I will lose my immunity. And after that, I must sip a concoction composed of no less than one hundred antidotes." Said he in an aside to Gordius, "If I don't take the antidotes, I confess I feel a little unwell."

"Understandable, Great One," croaked Gordius, trembling so violently he dreaded the King's noticing.

"Not long now," said Mithridates.

Nor was it. Laodice's jerks grew grosser and sloppier as her body literally wore itself out. But still her eyes held feeling, awareness, and only closed tiredly at the moment she died. Not once did she look at her brother; though that may have been because she was looking at Pharnaces when the rigors clamped down, and after that, even the muscles controlling the direction of her eyes would not answer their devastated owner.

"Excellent!" cried the King heartily, and nodded at Pharnaces. "Kill him," he said.

No one had the courage to ask how, with the result that Pharnaces met his death more prosaically than poor Laodice, beneath the blade of a sword. And everyone who had seen the Queen die absorbed the lesson; there would be no more attempts upon the life of the sixth King Mithridates for a long time to come.

Bithynia, as Marius discovered when he journeyed overland from Pessinus to Nicomedia, was very rich. Like all of Asia Minor, it was mountainous, but except for the massif of Mysian Olympus at Prusa, the Bithynian ranges were somewhat lower, rounder, less forbidding than the Taurus. A multitude of rivers watered the countryside, which had been cleared and settled for a long time. Sufficient wheat was grown to feed the people and the army, with enough left over to fetch the price of Bithynia's tribute to Rome. Pulses grew well, and sheep thrived. There were vegetables and fruit aplenty. The people, Marius noted, looked well fed, content, healthy; each village Marius and his family passed through seemed populous and prosperous.

Such, however, was not the story he got from the second King Nicomedes when he arrived in Nicomedia, and was installed in the palace as the King's honored guest. As palaces went, this one was fairly small, but, Julia was quick to inform Marius, the art works were immensely valuable, and the materials of which the building was constructed were of the very best, the architecture brilliant.

"King Nicomedes is far from a poor man," Julia said.

"Alas!" sighed King Nicomedes, "I am a very poor man, Gaius

Marius! As I rule a poor country, that is to be expected, I suppose. But Rome doesn't make it easy, either."

They were sitting on a balcony overlooking the city on its inlet, the water so calm that everything from mountains to shoreline structures was reflected as perfectly as in a mirror; it made Nicomedia seem, thought the fascinated Marius, suspended in midair, as if a world went on beneath it as much as above it, from a parade of donkeys walking upside down to the clouds which floated in the sky-blue middle of the inlet.

"How do you mean, King?" asked Marius.

"Well, take that disgraceful business with Lucius Licinius Lucullus only five years ago," said Nicomedes. "He came in the early spring demanding two legions of auxiliaries to fight a war against slaves in Sicily, he said." The King's voice grew petulant. "I explained to him that I had no troops to give him, thanks to the activities of the Roman tax-farmers, who carry off my people as slaves. 'Free my enslaved people according to the decree of the Senate freeing all slaves of Allied status throughout all Roman territories!' I said to him. 'Then I will have an army again, and my country will know prosperity again.' But do you know what he answered? That the Senate's decree was directed at slaves of *Italian* Allied status!"

"He was right," said Marius, stretching out his legs. "Had the decree covered slaves of nations owning a Friend and Ally of the Roman People treaty, you would have received official notification of the fact from the Senate." He directed a keen glance at the King from beneath his brows. "As I remember, you did find the troops for Lucius Licinius Lucullus."

"Not as many as he wanted, but yes, I did find him men. Or rather, he found the men for himself," said Nicomedes. "After I told him there were no men available, he rode out of Nicomedia into the countryside, and came back some days later to tell me that he could see no shortage of men. I tried to tell him that the men he had seen were farmers, not soldiers, but all he said was that farmers made excellent soldiers, so they would do nicely. Thus were my troubles compounded, for he took seven thousand of the very men I needed to keep my kingdom solvent!"

"You got them back a year later," said Marius, "and they came back with money in their purses, at that."

"A year during which not enough was grown," said the King stubbornly. "A year of low production, Gaius Marius, under the system of tribute Rome levies, sets us back a decade."

"What I want to know is why there are tax-gatherers in Bithynia at all," said Marius, aware the King was finding it harder and harder to prove his contentions. "Bithynia is not a part of the Roman Asia Province."

Nicomedes wriggled. "The trouble is, Gaius Marius, that some of my subjects have borrowed money from the Roman *publicani* of Asia Province. Times are difficult."

"*Why* are times difficult, King?" Marius persisted. "I would have thought that—certainly since the Sicilian slave war broke out—you must be enjoying increasing prosperity. You grow plenty of grain. You could grow more. Rome's agents were buying grain for inflated prices for a number of years, especially in this part of the world. In fact, neither you nor Asia Province could provide half the quantity our agents were commissioned to buy. The bulk of it, I understand, came from lands under the rule of King Mithridates of Pontus."

Ah, that was it! Marius's remorseless probing finally lifted the crust on top of Bithynia's festering sore; out came all the poison in a rush.

"Mithridates!" the King spat, rearing back in his chair. "Yes, Gaius Marius, there you have the adder in my backyard! There you have the cause of Bithynia's fading prosperity! It cost me one hundred talents of gold I could ill afford to buy support in Rome when *he* applied to be made a Friend and Ally of the Roman People! It costs me many times more than that each and every year to police my outlands against his sly incursions! I am forced to keep a standing army because of Mithridates, and *no* country can afford the expense of that! Look at what he did in Galatia only three years ago! Mass slaughter at a *feast*! Four hundred thanes perished at the congress in Ancyra, and now he rules every nation around me—Phrygia, Galatia, coastal Paphlagonia. I tell you plainly, Gaius Marius, that unless Mithridates is stopped now, even Rome will rue the day she did nothing!"

"So I think too," said Marius. "However, Anatolia is a long way from Rome, and I very much doubt anyone in Rome is fully aware of what might happen here. Except perhaps Marcus Aemilius Scaurus Princeps Senatus, and he's growing old. It is my intent to meet this King Mithridates, and warn him. Perhaps when I return to Rome, I can persuade the Senate to take Pontus more seriously."

"Let us dine," said Nicomedes, rising. "We can continue our talk later. Oh, it is good to speak to someone who cares!"

To Julia, this sojourn in an oriental court was a completely new experience; we Roman women should agitate to travel more, she thought, for I see now how narrow we are, how ignorant of the rest of the world. And it must tell in the way we raise our children. Particularly our sons.

The first regnant individual she had ever met, the second Nicomedes was a revelation, for naturally she had assumed all kings were something like a patrician Roman of consular status—haughty, erudite, stately, magnificent. Un-Roman Catulus Caesars, or even un-Roman Scaurus Princeps Senatuses; there was no denying that Scaurus Princeps Senatus, despite his small stature and shiny bald pate, conducted himself right royally.

What a revelation indeed was this second Nicomedes! Very tall, he had obviously once been heavily built, but extreme old age had taken its toll of height and weight, so that, at well over eighty, he was skinny and bent and hobbling, with empty dewlaps beneath his chin and sagging cheeks. Every tooth was gone from his head, and most of its hair as well. These, however, were purely physical states, and might be seen too on any octogenarian Roman consular. Scaevola Augur, for example. The difference lay in bearing and inner resources, thought Julia. For one thing, King Nicomedes was so effeminate she longed to laugh; he affected long, flowing garments of gauzy wool in truly exquisite colors; for meals he wore a golden wig of sausage-like curls, and was never without enormous jeweled earrings; his face was painted like a cheap whore's, and he kept his voice in the falsetto range. Of majesty he had none, and yet he had ruled Bithynia for over fifty years—ruled it with an iron hand, and successfully evaded every plot by either of his sons to dethrone him. Looking at him—and knowing that at all stages of his life from puberty onward he must have presented this same shrill, womanish personage to the world—it was extremely difficult for Julia to believe, for example, that he had efficiently disposed of his own father; or that he could preserve the loyalty and affection of his subjects.

His sons were both in attendance at court, though no wife remained; his queen had died years earlier (she was the mother of his elder son, another Nicomedes), and so had his minor wife (she was the mother of the younger son, named Socrates). Neither the younger Nicomedes nor Socrates could be called youthful; the younger Nicomedes was sixty-two years of age, and Socrates was fifty-four. Though both were married, both sons were as effeminate as their father. The wife of Socrates was a mouselike little creature who hid in corners and scurried when she moved, but the wife of the younger Nicomedes was a big, strapping, hearty woman much addicted to practical jokes and booming gusts of laughter; she had borne the younger Nicomedes a girl, Nysa, who was now perilously close to being too old for marriage, yet had never married; the wife of Socrates was childless, as indeed was he.

"Mind you, that's to be expected," said a young male slave to Julia as he tidied up the sitting room she had been given for her exclusive use. "I don't think Socrates has ever managed to succeed in penetrating a *woman*! As for Nysa, she's inclined the other way—likes fillies, though that's not surprising—she's got a face like a horse."

"You are impertinent," said Julia in freezing tones, and waved the young man out of the room, disgusted.

The palace overflowed with handsome young men, most of slave status, a few it seemed free men in service to the King or his sons; there were also dozens of little page boys, even prettier than the young men. What their chief duty was, Julia tried to put out of her mind, especially when she thought of Young Marius, so attractive and friendly and outgoing, almost ready to enter the initial stages of puberty.

"Gaius Marius, you *will* keep an eye on our son, won't you?" she asked her husband delicately.

"What, with all these mincing flowers prancing around?" Marius laughed. "You needn't be afraid on his behalf, *mea vita*. He's awake, he knows a pansy from a side of pork."

"I thank you for the reassurance—and the metaphor," said Julia, smiling. "You don't grow any more verbally graceful with the passing of the years, do you, Gaius Marius?"

"Quite the opposite," he said, unperturbed.

"That *was* what I was trying to say."

"Were you? Oh."

"Have you seen enough here?" she asked, rather abruptly.

"We've scarcely been in residence eight days," he said, surprised. "Does it oppress you, all this circus atmosphere?"

"Yes, I think it does. I always wanted to know how kings lived, but if Bithynia is any example, I'd much prefer a Roman existence. It isn't the homosexuality, it's the gossip and the airs and affectations. The servants are a disgrace. And the royal women are not women with whom I have anything in common. Oradaltis is so loud I want to cover my ears, and Musa—how well named she is in Latin, if you think of *mus* the mouse rather than *musa* the muse! Yes, Gaius Marius, as soon as you feel you can move on, I would be grateful," said Julia the austere Roman matron.

"Then we'll move on at once," said Marius cheerfully, taking a scroll from the sinus of his toga. "Having followed us all the way from Halicarnassus, this has finally found me. A letter from Publius Rutilius Rufus, and guess where he is?"

"Asia Province?"

"Pergamum, to be exact. Quintus Mucius Scaevola is the governor this year, and Publius Rutilius is with him as his legate." Marius waved the letter gleefully. "I also gather that governor and legate would be absolutely delighted to see us. Months ago, as this was intended to reach us in the spring. By now, they'll be starved for company, I imagine."

"Aside from his reputation as an advocate," said Julia, "I don't know Quintus Mucius Scaevola at all."

"I don't know him well myself. And *of* him, little more than the fact that he and his first cousin Crassus Orator are inseparable. Not surprising I don't know him, really. He's barely forty."

Under the impression that his guests would remain with him for at least a month, old Nicomedes was reluctant to let them go, but Marius was more than a match for an anxious, rather silly antique like the second Nicomedes. They left with the King's wails piercing their ears, and sailed down through the narrow straits of the Hellespont into the Aegean Sea, the winds and currents with them.

At the mouth of the Caicus River their ship turned into it, and so they came to Pergamum, a few miles inland, by exactly that route which showed the city to best advantage, high on its acropolis, and surrounded by tall mountains.

Quintus Mucius Scaevola and Publius Rutilius Rufus were both in residence, but Marius and Julia were fated not to get to know Scaevola better, for he was just about to leave for Rome.

"Oh, what company you would have been during this last summer, Gaius Marius!" said Scaevola with a sigh. "As it is, I must reach Rome before the season makes traveling by sea too risky." He smiled. "Publius Rutilius will tell you all."

Marius and Rutilius Rufus went down to wave Scaevola off, leaving Julia to settle into a palace she liked far more than the menage at Nicomedia, even if feminine company was just as scarce.

Of course Marius didn't think of Julia's lack of feminine companionship; he left her to her own devices, and settled down to hear the news from his oldest and dearest friend. "Rome first," he said eagerly.

"I'll give you the really excellent news first, then," said Publius Rutilius Rufus, smiling in pure pleasure; how good it was to meet Gaius Marius so far from home! "Gaius Servilius Augur died in exile at the end of last year, and of course there had to be an election to fill his place in the College of Augurs. And you, Gaius Marius, were elected."

Marius gaped. *"I?"*

"None other."

"I never thought—why me?"

"You still have a lot of support among the voters in Rome, in spite of the worst Catulus Caesar and his like can do, Gaius Marius. And I think the voters felt you deserved this distinction. Your name was put up by a panel of knights, and—there being no rule against election *in absentia*—you won. I can't say your victory was well received by the Piglet and company, but it was very well received by Rome at large."

Marius heaved a sigh of sheer satisfaction. "Well, that's good news, all right! An augur! Me! It means my son will be priest or augur in his turn, and his sons after him. It means I did it, Publius Rutilius! I managed to get inside the heart of Rome, Italian hayseed with no Greek though I may be."

"Oh, hardly anyone says that sort of thing about you anymore. The death of Piggle-wiggle was a milestone of sorts, you know. Had he still been alive, I doubt you could have won any election," said Rutilius Rufus deliberately. "It wasn't that his *auctoritas* was so much greater than anyone else's, or even his following. His *dignitas*, however, had become enormous after those battles in the Forum while he was censor—love him or hate him, everyone admits his courage was supreme. But I think his most important function was that he formed a nucleus around which too many others could clot, and after he returned from Rhodes, he exerted all his energies to pull you down. I mean, what other task was left for him to do? All that power and influence was directed at destroying you. His death came as a terrific shock, you know. He looked so well when he came home! I for one thought he'd be with us for many years to come. And then—he was dead."

"Why was Lucius Cornelius there with him?" Marius asked.

"No one seems to know. They hadn't been thick, so much is sure. Lucius Cornelius simply said his presence was an accident, that he hadn't intended to dine with Piggle-wiggle at all. It's really very odd. What perturbs me most, I suppose, is that the Piglet seems to find nothing strange in Lucius Cornelius's presence there. And that indicates to me that Lucius Cornelius was making a move to join Piggle-wiggle's faction." Rutilius Rufus frowned. "He and Aurelia have had a severe falling out."

"Lucius Cornelius and Aurelia, you mean?"

"Yes."

"Where did you hear that?"

"From Aurelia."

"Didn't she say why?"

"No. Just said that Lucius Cornelius wouldn't be welcome in her house again," Rutilius Rufus said. "Anyway, he went off to Nearer Spain not long after Piggle-wiggle died, and it wasn't until he was gone that Aurelia told me. I think she was afraid I'd tax him with it if he was still in Rome. All in all, an odd business, Gaius Marius."

Not very interested in personal differences, Marius pulled a face and shrugged. "Well, it's *their* business, however odd it may be. What else has happened?"

Rutilius Rufus laughed. "Our consuls have passed a new law, forbidding human sacrifice."

"They *what*?"

"They passed a law forbidding human sacrifice."

"That's ridiculous! How long is it since human sacrifice was a part of Roman life, public or private?" asked Marius, looking disgusted. "What rubbish!"

"Well, I believe they did sacrifice two Greeks and two Gauls when Hannibal was marching up and down Italy. But I doubt that had anything to do with the new *lex Cornelia Licinia*."

"What did, then?"

"As you know, Gaius Marius, sometimes we Romans decide to point up a new aspect of public life by rather bizarre means. I think this law falls into that category. I think it's meant to inform the Forum Romanum that there is to be no more violence, no more deaths, no more imprisonment of magistrates, no more illegal activity of any kind," said Rutilius Rufus.

"Didn't Gnaeus Cornelius Lentulus and Publius Licinius Crassus explain?" asked Marius.

"No. They just promulgated their law, and the People passed it."

"Tchah!" said Marius, and passed on. "What else?"

"The younger brother of our Pontifex Maximus, a praetor this year, was sent to Sicily to govern there. We'd had rumors of yet another slave insurrection, if you'd believe that."

"Do we treat our slaves in Sicily so badly?"

"Yes—and no," said Rutilius Rufus thoughtfully. "There are too many Greek slaves there, for one thing. A master doesn't need to ill-treat them to have trouble on his hands, they're very independent. And I gather that all the pirates Marcus Antonius Orator captured were put to work in Sicily as grain slaves. Not work to their liking, I'd say. Marcus Antonius, by the way," Rutilius Rufus announced, "has adorned the rostra with the beak of the biggest ship he destroyed during his campaign against the pirates. Most imposing-looking thing."

"I wouldn't have thought that there was room. The rostra's stuffed with ship's beaks from this sea battle and that," said Marius. "Anyway, do get on with it, Publius Rutilius! What else has happened?"

"Well, our praetor Lucius Ahenobarbus has created havoc in Sicily, so we hear, even in Asia Province. He's gone through the place like a high wind. Apparently he hadn't been in Sicily long enough to get his land legs when he issued a decree that no one in the whole country was to own a sword or other weapon, save for soldiers and the militia under arms. Of course no one took the slightest notice."

Marius grinned. "Knowing the Domitii Ahenobarbi, I would say that was a mistake."

"It was indeed. Lucius Domitius cracked down unmercifully when his decree was ignored. All of Sicily is smarting. And I very much doubt there'll be any uprisings, servile or free."

"Well, they're a crude lot, the Domitii Ahenobarbi, but they do get results," said Marius. "And is that the end of the news?"

"Just about, save only that we have new censors in office, and that they've announced they intend to take the most thorough census of all Roman citizens anywhere in many decades."

"About time. Who are they?"

"Marcus Antonius Orator and your consular colleague, Lucius Valerius Flaccus." Rutilius Rufus rose to his feet. "Shall we take a walk, old friend?"

Pergamum was perhaps the most carefully planned and built city in the world; Marius had heard that, and now saw it for himself. Even in the lower town sprawled around the base of the acropolis there were no narrow alleyways or tumbledown blocks of apartments, for everything was obviously subject to a rigid system of surveys and building codes. Vast drains and sewers underlay all areas of human habitation, and running water was piped everywhere. Marble seemed to be the material of choice. The pillared colonnades were many and magnificent, the agora was huge and filled with superb statuary, and a great theater plunged down the slope of the rock.

And yet, an air of dilapidation clung to town and citadel both; things were not being kept up in the way they had been during the reigns of the Attalids who had conceived and cared for Pergamum, their capital. Nor did the people look content; some, noted Marius, looked hungry, surprising in a rich country.

"Our Roman tax-farmers are responsible for what you see," said Publius Rutilius Rufus grimly. "Gaius Marius, you have no idea what Quintus Mucius and I found when we got here! The whole of Asia Province has been exploited and oppressed for years, due to the greed of these idiot *publicani*! To begin with, the sums Rome asks for the Treasury are too high; then the *publicani* bid too much on top of that—with the result that in order to make a profit, they have to wring Asia Province out drier than a dishrag! It's a typical money-hungry enterprise. Instead of concentrating upon settling Rome's poor on public land and funding the buying of that public land from the taxes of Asia Province, Gaius Gracchus would have done better to have first sent a team of investigators to Asia Province to assess exactly what the taxes ought to be. But Gaius Gracchus did not do that. Nor has anyone since. The only estimates available in Rome are estimates plucked out of thin air by the commission which came here just after King Attalus died—and that is thirty-five years ago!"

"A pity I wasn't aware of any of this when I was consul," said Marius sadly.

"My dear Gaius Marius, you had the Germans to worry about! Asia Province was the last place on earth anyone in Rome thought of during those years. But you are right. A Marian-administered commission sent here would quickly have determined realistic figures—and disciplined the *publicani*! As it is, the *publicani* have been allowed to become insufferably arrogant. They rule Asia Province, not Rome's governors!"

Marius laughed. "I'll bet the *publicani* got a shock this year, with Quintus Mucius and Publius Rutilius in Pergamum."

"They certainly did," said Rutilius Rufus with a reminiscent grin. "You could have heard them squeal in Alexandria. Rome has certainly heard them squeal—which is why, between you and me, Quintus Mucius has gone home early."

"What exactly have you been doing here?"

"Oh, just regulating the province and its taxes," said Rutilius Rufus blandly.

"To the detriment of the Treasury *and* the tax-farmers."

"True." Rutilius Rufus shrugged, turned into the great agora. He waved his hand at an empty plinth. "We've stopped this kind of thing, for a start. There used to be an equestrian statue of Alexander the Great up there—the work of no less than Lysippus, and held to be the finest portrait he ever did of Alexander. Do you know where it is now? In the peristyle of none other than Sextus Perquitienus, Rome's richest and most vulgar knight! Your close neighbor on the Capitol. He took it as payment of tax arrears, if you please. A work of art worth a thousand times the sum in question. But what could the local people do? They just didn't have the money. So when Sextus Perquitienus pointed his wand at the statue, it was taken down and given to him."

"It will have to be given back," said Marius.

"Small hope," said Rutilius Rufus, sniffing scornfully.

"Is that what Quintus Mucius has gone home to do?"

"One might wish! No, he's gone home to stop the *publicani* lobby in Rome having him and me prosecuted."

Marius stopped walking. "You're joking!"

"No, Gaius Marius, I am not joking! The tax-farmers of Asia wield enormous power in Rome, especially among the Senate. And Quintus Mucius and I have mortally offended them by putting the affairs of Asia Province on a proper footing," said Publius Rutilius Rufus. He grimaced. "Not only have we mortally offended the *publicani,* we have also mortally offended the Treasury. There are those in the Senate who might be of a mind to ignore the tax-farming companies when they start squealing, but ignore the Roman Treasury they will not. As far as they can see things, any governor who reduces the Treasury's income is a traitor. I tell you, Gaius Marius, the last letter Quintus Mucius received from his cousin Crassus Orator caused him to go the same color as his toga! He was informed there was a movement under way to have him stripped of his proconsular imperium, and prosecuted for extortion *and* treason. So off he went home in a hurry, leaving me here to govern until next year's appointee arrives."

Thus it was that on their way back to the governor's palace Gaius Marius took note of the way Publius Rutilius Rufus was greeted by everyone who passed by—warmly, with obvious affection.

"They love you here," he said, not really surprised.

"Even more do they love Quintus Mucius. We've made a very big difference to their lives, Gaius Marius, and for the first time they have seen true Romans at work. I for one cannot find it in me to blame them for the hatred they cherish for Rome and Romans. They have been our victims, and we have used them abominably. So when Quintus Mucius reduced the taxes to what we had estimated as a fair figure, and put a stop to the extortionate brand of usury some of the local representatives of the *publicani* have been practising, why—they danced in the streets, quite literally! Pergamum has voted an annual festival in honor of Quintus Mucius, and so I believe has Smyrna, and Ephesus. At first they kept sending us gifts—extremely valuable things too—works of art, jewels, tapestries. And when we sent them back with our thanks, they were returned to us. In the end, we had to refuse to let them come inside the palace door."

"Can Quintus Mucius convince the Senate that he—and not the *publicani*—is in the right?" asked Marius.

"What do you think?"

Marius pondered, wishing he had spent more of his public career in Rome, rather than in the field. "I believe he will succeed," he said finally. "His reputation is peerless, and that will sway a lot of the backbenchers who might otherwise be tempted to support the *publicani*—or the Treasury. And he'll deliver a superb speech in the House. Crassus Orator will speak in his support, and do even better."

"So I think too. But he was sorry to have to leave Asia Province, you know. I don't think he'll ever have another job he can enjoy the way he has this one. He has such a meticulous, precise mind, and his organization is unparalleled. It was my task to gather information from every district in the province, his to make firm decisions from the facts I gave him. With the result that, thirty-five years down the road, Asia Province has a realistic estimate of taxes at last, and the Treasury no excuse to demand more."

"Of course, unless the consul arrives, within the province the governor's imperium can override any directive from Rome," said Marius. "However, you've flouted the censors as well as the Treasury, and the *publicani* can claim to have legal contracts, as can the Treasury. With new censors in, new contracts will have been let—did you manage to transmit your findings to Rome in time to influence the sums demanded in the new contracts?"

"Unfortunately, no," said Rutilius Rufus. "That's yet another reason why Quintus Mucius had to go home now. He feels he can influence this pair of censors sufficiently to cause them to recall the Asia Province contracts, and reissue them."

"Well, that shouldn't irritate the *publicani*—provided the Treasury agrees to the cut in its revenues," said Marius. "I predict that Quintus Mucius will have more trouble with the Treasury than with the tax-farmers. After all, the *publicani* will be in a better position to make a nice profit if they don't have to pay unrealistic sums to the Treasury, not so?"

"Exactly," nodded Rutilius Rufus. "It's on that we pin our hopes, once Quintus Mucius gets it through the thick heads of the Senate and the tribunes of the Treasury that Rome *cannot* expect what she expects from Asia Province."

"Who do you think is going to squeal the loudest?"

"Sextus Perquitienus, for one. He'll make a nice profit, but there won't be any more priceless works of art taken in default if the local people can afford to pay their taxes. Some of the leaders of the House who are heavily committed to knight lobbies—and who might have been acquiring an occasional priceless work of art themselves. Gnaeus Domitius Ahenobarbus Pontifex Maximus, for one. Catulus Caesar. The Piglet, I imagine. Scipio Nasica. Some of the Licinii Crassi, but not the Orator."

"What about our Leader of the House?"

"I think Scaurus will support Quintus Mucius. Or so both of us hope, Gaius Marius. Give Scaurus his due, he's an upright Roman of the old kind." Rutilius Rufus giggled. "Besides, his clients are all in Italian Gaul, so he's not *personally* interested in Asia Province, he just likes to dabble in king-making and similar exercises. But tax-gathering? Sordid stuff! Nor is he a collector of priceless works of art."

Leaving a much happier Publius Rutilius Rufus to rattle around the governor's palace on his own (for he refused to desert his post), Gaius Marius took his family south to Halicarnassus and their villa, and spent a very pleasant winter there, breaking the monotony with a trip to Rhodes.

That they were able to sail from Halicarnassus to Tarsus was thanks solely to the efforts of Marcus Antonius Orator, who had put paid—at least for the time being—to the activities of the pirates of Pamphylia and Cilicia. Before the campaign of Antonius Orator, the very thought of a sea journey would have been the height of foolhardiness, as no captured cargo was more appreciated by the pirates than a Roman senator, particularly one of Gaius Marius's importance; they would have been able to put a ransom of twenty or thirty silver talents upon his person.

The ship hugged the coast, and the journey took over a month. The cities of Lycia played host to Marius and his family gladly, as did the big city of Attaleia in Pamphylia. Never had they seen such mountains in close proximity to the sea, even, said Marius, on his coastal march to far Gaul; their snow-covered heads scraped the sky, and their feet paddled in the water.

The pine forests of the region were magnificent, never having been logged; Cyprus, only a short distance away, had more than enough timber to supply the needs of the entire area, including Egypt. But, thought Marius as the days went by and the Cilician coast unfolded, no wonder piracy had thrived here; every twist in the mighty mountains produced almost perfectly concealed little coves and harbors. Coracesium, which had been the pirate capital, was so right for this role it must have seemed a gift from the gods, with its towering fortress-crowned spur almost surrounded by the sea. It had fallen to Antonius by treachery from within; gazing up at its stark sides, Marius exercised his brain by working out a way to capture it.

And then finally came Tarsus, a few miles up the placid stream of the Cydnus, and therefore sheltered from the open sea but able to function as a port. It was a walled and powerful city, and of course the palace was made available to these august visitors. Spring in this part of Asia Minor was early, so Tarsus was already hot; Julia began to drop hints that she wouldn't welcome being left in such a furnace when Marius began his journey inland to Cappadocia.

A letter had come to Halicarnassus late in winter from the Cappadocian King, the seventh Ariarathes; it promised that he himself would be in Tarsus by the end of March, and would be very pleased and proud to escort Gaius Marius personally from Tarsus to Eusebeia Mazaca. Knowing the young King would be waiting, Marius had chafed when the voyage took so long, yet was reluctant to destroy Julia's pleasure in treats like disembarking in some enchanted cove to stretch her legs and swim. But when they did

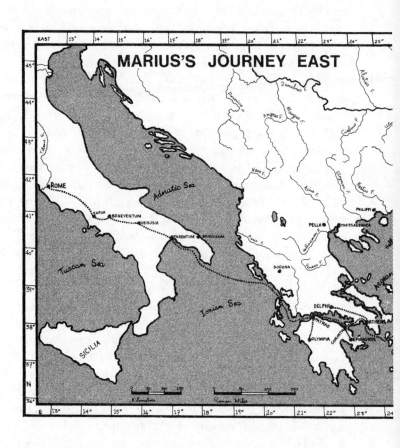

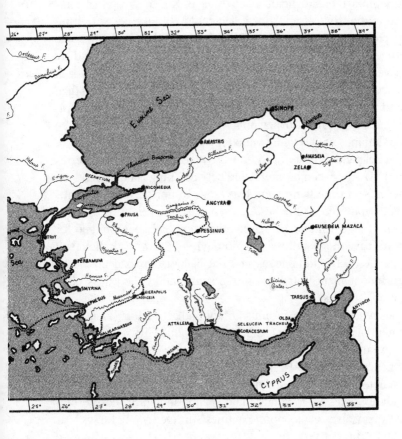

arrive in Tarsus halfway through April, the little King was not there, and no word had come from him.

Several couriered letters to Mazaca failed to provide an answer; indeed, none of the couriers came back. And Marius began to worry. This he concealed from Julia and Young Marius, but it made his dilemma more difficult when Julia began to press to be included in the trip to Cappadocia. He could not take her with him, so much was apparent, nor could he leave her behind to become prostrated by the summer heat. Her plight was compounded by Cilicia's unenviably ambivalent position in that part of the world. Once an Egyptian possession, Cilicia had passed to Syria and then entered a period of neglect; during this time the pirate confederations had gradually usurped much of the power, even over the fertile flatlands called Pedia which lay to the east of Tarsus.

The Seleucid dynasty of Syria was wearing itself out in a series of civil wars between brothers, and between kings and pretenders; at the present time there were two kings in northern Syria, Antiochus Grypus and Antiochus Cyzicenus, so busy fighting for possession of Antioch and Damascus that they had been obliged for years to leave the rest of the kingdom lying fallow. With the result that the Jews, the Idumaeans and the Nabataeans had all established independent kingdoms in the south, and Cilicia was quite forgotten.

Thus when Marcus Antonius Orator had arrived in Tarsus with the intent of using the city as his base, he found Cilicia ripe for the picking, and—endowed with full imperium—declared Cilicia a province answering to Rome. But when he departed no governor was sent to replace him, and once more Cilicia entered into limbo. The Greek cities large enough and secure enough to have established themselves as economic entities survived well; Tarsus was one such. But between these centers were whole tracts where no one governed in anyone's name, or local tyrants held sway, or the people simply said they belonged now to Rome. Marius had very quickly come to the conclusion that not many years would go by before the pirates moved back in force. In the meantime, the local magistrates seemed happy to welcome the man they assumed was the new Roman governor.

The longer he waited to hear from little King Ariarathes, the more apparent it became to Marius that he might be called upon to do something desperate in Cappadocia, or something requiring a lengthy stretch of time. His wife and son had become Marius's greatest worry. Now I know why we leave them safely at home! he thought, grinding his teeth. To leave them in Tarsus, a prey to summer diseases, was out of the question; so too was taking them to Cappadocia; and whenever he decided to consign them to a sea voyage back to Halicarnassus, the image of Coracesium's unreduced fortress loomed, peopled in his imagination by the followers of a new pirate king. What to do, what to do? We know nothing about this part of the world, he thought, but it is clear to me that we must learn; the eastern end of the Middle Sea is rudderless, and some tempest is going to wreck it.

When May was almost half over and there was still no word from King Ariarathes, Marius made up his mind.

"Pack up," he said to Julia more curtly than was his wont. "I'm taking you and Young Marius with me, but not to Mazaca. As soon as we're high enough for the weather to be cooler and hopefully healthier, I intend to leave the pair of you with whatever people I can find, and go on alone into Cappadocia."

She wanted to argue, but she didn't; though she had never seen Gaius Marius in the field, she often picked up echoes of his military autocracy; now too she caught faint echoes of some problem preying upon him. Something to do with Cappadocia.

Two days later they moved out, escorted by a band of local militia commanded by a young Tarsian Greek to whom Marius had taken a strong fancy. So had Julia. Which was just as well, as things turned out. On this journey no one walked, for the way lay through the mountain pass called the Cilician Gates, and it was steep and hard. Perched sidesaddle on a donkey, Julia found the beauty of the climb worth its discomfort, for they plodded over thin tracks amid vast mountains, and the higher they climbed, the heavier the snow lying on them became. It was almost impossible to believe that only three days before, she had been panting from the coastal heat; now she dug into her boxes for warm wraps. The weather remained calm and sunny, but when the pine forests enveloped them they were chilled to the bone, and looked forward to those parts of the journey when pine forests gave way to sheer cliffs, and turbulent streams fed into a roaring river which dashed itself in great foaming waves against rocks and precipices.

Four days out of Tarsus, the climb was more or less over. In a narrow valley Marius found an encampment of local people who had accompanied their flocks of sheep up from the plains for summer grazing, and here he left Julia and Young Marius behind, together with his escort of militia. The young Tarsian Greek, whose name was Morsimus, was instructed to care for them and protect them. A generous gift of money purchased immense good will from the nomads, and Julia found herself the owner of one of their big brown leather tents.

"Once I get used to the smell, I'll be comfortable enough," she said to Marius before he departed. "Inside the tent is warm, and I gather some of the nomads have gone somewhere or other to buy extra grain and provisions. Off you go, and don't worry about me. Or Young Marius, who is planning to become a shepherd, I gather. Morsimus will care for us beautifully. I'm only sorry that we've become a burden to you, dearest husband."

And so Gaius Marius rode off, accompanied only by two of his own slaves and a guide furnished by Morsimus, who looked as if he would rather have been traveling with Marius than staying behind. As far as Marius could gather, these inland valley bottoms and the occasional wider uplands he rode across lay at about five and a half thousand feet—not quite high enough to cause dizziness and headache, but quite high enough to make staying in the saddle hard work. They still had a long way to go to reach Eusebeia Mazaca, which, his guide told him, was the only urban settlement of any kind within Cappadocia.

The sun had gone in the moment he crested the watershed between those rivers which flowed down to Pedian Cilicia and those rivers which contributed to the enormous length and volume of the Halys, and he found himself riding through sleet-showers, fog, and occasional rain. Cold, saddlesore, aching with fatigue, he endured the long hours of jogging along with his legs dangling uselessly, and could only be thankful that the skin of his inner thighs was tough enough not to break down under the constant chafing.

On the third day the sun came out again. The ever-widening plains looked a perfect place for sheep and cattle, as they were grassy, relatively free of forests; Cappadocia, his guide told him, did not have the right kind of soil or climate for extensive woodlands, but it grew excellent wheat when the soil was tilled.

"Why isn't it tilled, then?" asked Marius.

The guide shrugged. "Not enough people. They grow what they need, plus a little to sell along the Halys, where some barges come to buy. But they cannot sell produce in Cilicia, the road is too difficult. And why should they bother? They eat well. They are content."

That was almost the only conversation between Marius and his guide while they rode; even when they sought shelter at night within the brown leather tents of nomad shepherds, or within a mud-brick house belonging to some tiny village, they talked little. The mountains marched, now closer, now further away, but never seemed to grow smaller, or less green, or less snowy.

And then, when the guide announced that Mazaca was only four hundred *stades* away (and Marius had translated this into fifty Roman miles), they entered a region so bizarre that Marius wished Julia could see it. The rolling plains persisted, but were broken up by twisting ravines filled with rounded, tapering towers which looked as if they had been carefully shaped out of multicolored clays, a vast toyland built by some demented giant child; in some areas the towers were all topped by huge flat rocks Marius fancied swayed, so precariously were they perched on the skinny necks of these round towers. And—wonder of wonders!—his eyes began to distinguish windows and doors in some of these unnatural natural structures.

"That's why you don't see any more villages," said the guide. "It's cold up here, and the season is short. So the people of this area cut themselves dwellings inside the rock towers. In the summer they are cool. In the winter they are warm. Why should they build houses, when the Great Goddess Ma has already done so?"

"How long have they been living inside the rocks?" asked Marius, fascinated.

But the guide didn't know. "Since men were," he said vaguely. "At least that long. In Cilicia we say that the very first men came from Cappadocia, and lived then in the same way."

They were still riding round these ravines of clay towers when Marius began to notice the mountain; it stood almost alone, the mightiest mountain he had ever seen, higher than Mount Olympus in Greece, higher even than the massifs hedging Italian Gaul around. Its main bulk was cone-shaped, but there were smaller cones on its flanks, and it was solidly white with snow, a brilliant presence against a cloudless sky. He knew which mountain it had to be, of course; Mount Argaeus, described by the Greeks, seen only by a handful of men out of the west. And at its foot, he knew, lay Eusebeia Mazaca, the only city in Cappadocia. The seat of the King.

Unfortunately coming from Cilicia meant that Marius approached the mountain from the wrong direction; Mazaca lay on its north side, closest to the Halys, the great red river of central Anatolia, as the Halys represented Mazaca's best contact with the world.

Thus it was just after noon when Marius saw the shapes of many buildings clustered together beneath Mount Argaeus, and was in the midst of a sigh of relief when he suddenly realized he was entering a battlefield. The most extraordinary sensation! To ride where men had fought and perished in their thousands not many days before, yet to have neither knowledge of the battle, nor a vested interest in it. For the first time in his life, he, Gaius Marius, the conqueror of Numidia and the Germans, was on a battlefield in the role of a tourist.

He itched, he prickled, he burned; but on he rode toward the small city, looking about him no more than he had to. No effort of any kind had been made to tidy things up; bloated corpses denuded of armor and clothing lay decomposing everywhere, only spared flies in plague proportions by the inhospitably icy air, which also cut the stench of necrotic flesh to a bearable level. His guide was weeping, his two slaves were being sick, but Gaius Marius rode on as if he saw nothing untoward, his eyes busy searching for something far more ominous; the camp of a living, victorious army. And it was there, two miles away to the northeast, a huge collection of brown leather tents beneath a thin blue pall of smoke from many fires.

Mithridates. It could be no one else. And Gaius Marius did not make the mistake of thinking that the army of dead men belonged to Mithridates. No, his was the living, victorious army; the field Marius rode across was strewn with Cappadocians. Poor rock-dwellers, nomad shepherds—and probably, he told himself, his practical streak reviving, the bodies of many Syrian and Greek mercenaries as well. Where was the little King? No need to ask. He hadn't come to Tarsus and he hadn't answered any of the couriered letters because he was dead. So too, no doubt, were the couriers.

Perhaps another man would have turned his horse around and ridden away hoping his approach hadn't been detected; but not Gaius Marius. He had run King Mithridates Eupator to earth at last, though not on his own earth. And he actually kicked his tired mount in its trembling sides, urging it on to the meeting.

When he realized that no one was watching—that no one had remarked his progress—that no one noticed him even when he rode through the main gate into the town, Gaius Marius was amazed. How secure the King of Pontus must feel! Pulling his sweating beast to a halt, he scanned the rising tiers of streets in search of an acropolis or citadel of some kind, and saw what he presumed to be the palace lying on the mountain flank at the rear of the city. It was evidently built of some soft or lightweight stone not fit to take the brunt of the local winter winds, for it had been plastered, and painted then in a rich deep blue, with red columns blazing, and Ionic capitals of a deeper red picked out in a glittering gold.

There! thought Marius. He'll be there! He turned his horse up one of the sloping narrow streets, navigating his way by sight to the palace, which was hedged around by a blue-painted wall, and lay within chilly bare gardens. Spring comes late to Cappadocia, he thought, and regretted that it would never come at all for young King Ariarathes. The people of Mazaca had apparently gone into hiding, for the streets were utterly deserted, and when he arrived at the gate opening into the palace precinct, Marius found it unguarded. How secure indeed, King Mithridates!

He left his horse and attendants at the foot of the flight of steps leading up to the main door, a double affair in chased bronze adorned with reliefs depicting, in dauntingly graphic detail, the rape of Persephone by Hades; Marius had plenty of time to absorb these repellent antics as he stood there waiting for someone to answer his thunderous knock. Finally the door creaked, groaned, and one leaf came hesitantly open.

"Yes, yes, I heard you! What do you want?" asked an old, old man, in Greek.

Somewhere inside Marius a dreadful urge to laugh was growing, very difficult to suppress, so when he spoke, his voice, was shaky, squeaky, unimpressive. "I am Gaius Marius, consul of Rome. Is King Mithridates about?" he asked.

"No," said the old, old man.

"Are you expecting him?"

"Before dark, yes."

"Good!" Marius pushed the door open and stepped into the vastness of what was obviously a throne room or main reception room, beckoning his three attendants to follow. "I need accommodation for myself and these three men. Our horses are outside and should be stabled. For myself, a hot bath. At once."

When word came that the King was approaching, a togate Marius walked out into the portico of the palace and stood on the top step unattended. Up through the streets of the town he could see a troop of cavalry proceeding at a walk, all well mounted and well armed; their round shields were red, emblazoned with a white crescent moon embracing a white eight-pointed star, they wore red cloaks over plain silver cuirasses, and conical helmets crested not with feathers or horsehair, but with golden crescent moons embracing golden stars.

The King was not leading the troop, and was impossible to distinguish among those several hundred men. He may not care that the palace is unguarded during his absence, thought Marius, but he takes fine care of his person, so much is clear. The squadron came through the gate and pattered up to the steps with the curious sound unshod hooves in large numbers made—which told Marius that Pontus was not sufficiently endowed with smiths to shoe horses. Of course Marius was highly visible as he stood majestically enfolded in his purple-bordered toga many feet above the horsemen.

The troopers parted. King Mithridates Eupator rode out from their midst on a big bay horse. His cloak was purple and the shield borne by his squire was purple also, though it displayed the same insignia of crescent moon and star. However, the King wore no helmet; instead, his head was wrapped in the skin of a lion, its two long front fangs actually pressing into his brow, its ears standing up stiffly, the cavities where its eyes had been now dim black pools. A skirt and sleeves of gold-plated chain mail showed beneath the King's ornate golden cuirass and pterygoid kilt, and on his feet he wore beautifully made Greek boots of lion skin laced with gold and finished with overhanging tongues in the form of golden-maned lion heads.

Mithridates slid from his horse and stood at the foot of the steps looking up at Marius, an inferior position which clearly did not please him. Yet he was too clever to ascend the steps at once. About the size I used to be myself, thought Marius, and equally tall. A handsome man he was not, though his face was pleasant enough, large and rather square, and having a prominent round chin and a long, large, slightly bumpy nose. He was fair in coloring, glints of golden hair and side-whiskers showing beneath the lion's head, and hazel eyes; a small mouth with full, extremely red lips suggested that the King was both short-tempered and petulant.

Now where have you seen a man in the *toga praetexta* before? asked Marius silently, running what he knew of the King's history through his mind, and finding no time when the King might have seen a *toga praetexta*—or even a *toga alba*. For the King did not betray any hesitation in identifying a Roman consular, of that Marius was positive, and experience told him those who hadn't seen the garb before were always fascinated, even if it had been well described to them. Where have you *seen* one of us?

King Mithridates Eupator mounted the steps in a leisurely manner, and at the top held out his right hand in the universal gesture of peaceful intent. They shook hands, each too intelligent to turn the ceremony into a duel of strength.

"Gaius Marius," the King said, his Greek owning the same accent as Marius's did, "this is an unexpected pleasure."

"King Mithridates, I wish I could say the same."

"Come in, come in!" said the King heartily, throwing an arm about Marius's shoulders and propelling him in the direction of the door, now fully open. "I hope the staff here have made you comfortable?"

"Quite, thank you."

A dozen of the King's guards spilled into the throne room ahead of Marius and the King, a dozen more behind; every nook and cranny of the chamber was searched, then half of them went off to search the rest of the palace, while half remained to keep an eye on Mithridates, who walked straight to the purple-cushioned marble throne and seated himself upon it, snapping his fingers to command that a chair be set beside it for Gaius Marius.

"Have you been offered refreshments?" the King asked.

"I chose a bath instead," said Marius.

"Shall we dine, then?"

"If you like. But why move, unless you want more company than mine? I don't mind sitting to eat."

So a table was placed between them, wine was brought, and then a simple meal of salad vegetables, yogurt mixed with garlic and cucumber, and some savory balls of broiled minced lamb. The King made no comment upon the meal's simplicity, merely proceeded to eat ravenously—as indeed did Marius, hungry from his journey.

Only when the repast was finished and the dishes taken away did the two big men settle down to speak. Outside an indigo twilight lingered dreamily, but inside the throne room it had grown completely dark; terrified servants crept from lamp to lamp like shadows, and pools of illumination melted until they touched, each little tongue of flame flickering smokily because the quality of the oil was poor.

"Where is the seventh King Ariarathes?" Marius asked.

"Dead," said Mithridates, picking his teeth with a golden wire. "Died two months ago."

"How?"

Closer proximity than a flight of separating steps had revealed to Marius that the King's eyes were quite green, and that the brown in them took the form of little specks, unusual enough to be judged remarkable. The eyes now glazed, slid away and then returned looking wide open and guileless; he will lie to me, thought Marius immediately.

"A terminal illness," said the King, and heaved a sad sigh. "Died here in the palace, I believe. I wasn't here then."

"You fought a battle outside the city," said Marius.

"Had to," said Mithridates briefly.

"For what reason?"

"The throne had been claimed by a Syrian pretender—some sort of Seleucid cousin. There's a lot of Seleucid blood in the Cappadocian royal family," the King explained smoothly.

"How does this concern you?"

"Well, my father-in-law—one of my fathers-in-law, that is—is Cappadocian. Prince Gordius. And my sister was the mother of the dead seventh Ariarathes and his little brother, who is still very much alive. This younger son is now, of course, the rightful king, and I am pledged to see that the rightful kings rule Cappadocia," said Mithridates.

"I wasn't aware that the seventh Ariarathes has a younger brother, King," said Marius mildly.

"Oh, yes. Indubitably."

"You must tell me exactly what happened."

"Well, a plea for help came to me at Dasteira during the month of Boedromion, so naturally I mobilized my army and marched for Eusebeia Mazaca. There was no one here, and the King was dead. His little brother had fled into the troglodyte country. I occupied the city. And then the Syrian pretender turned up with his army."

"What was this Syrian pretender's name?"

"Seleucus," said Mithridates promptly.

"Well, that's certainly a good name for a Syrian pretender!" Marius remarked.

But the blatant irony was lost on Mithridates, who definitely did not possess a Roman or Greek attitude to words, and probably hardly ever laughed. He is more alien by far than Jugurtha of Numidia, Marius thought; perhaps not as intelligent, but far more dangerous. Jugurtha killed many of his close blood relatives, but always in the knowledge that the gods might call upon him to answer for it. Whereas Mithridates deems himself a god, and knows neither shame nor guilt. I wish I knew more about him, and about the Kingdom of Pontus. The little bit Nicomedes told me is hollow; he might fancy he knows this man, but he does not.

"I gather then that you fought a battle and defeated Seleucus the Syrian pretender," said Marius.

"I did." The King snorted. "Poor stuff! We slaughtered them almost to the last man."

"So I noticed," said Marius dryly, and leaned forward in his chair. "Tell me, King Mithridates, is it not a Pontic habit to clean up a battlefield?"

The King blinked, understanding that Marius was not being complimentary. "At this time of year?" he asked. "Why? By summer they'll have melted."

"I see." Spine straight because this was the posture of all Romans seated in chairs, the toga not a garment tolerating much disturbance, Marius laid his hands on the chair arms. "I would like to see the eighth King Ariarathes, if such be his title. Is that possible, King?"

"Of course, of course!" said the King genially, and clapped his hands. "Send for the King and Prince Gordius," he ordered when the old, old man came. Then, to Marius, "I found my nephew and Prince Gordius safe with the troglodytes ten days ago."

"How fortunate," said Marius.

Prince Gordius came leading a child about ten years old by the hand, himself a man in his fifties; both were clad in Greek dress, and stood obediently at the foot of the dais whereon Marius and Mithridates were seated.

"Well, young man, and how are you?" asked Marius.

"Good, thank you, Gaius Marius," said the child, so like King Mithridates that he might have posed for a portrait of Mithridates as a boy of the same age.

"Your brother is dead, I believe?"

"Yes, Gaius Marius. He died of a terminal illness here in the palace two months ago," said the little talking bird.

"And you are now the King of Cappadocia."

"Yes, Gaius Marius."

"Does that please you?"

"Yes, Gaius Marius."

"Are you old enough to rule?"

"Grandfather Gordius will help me."

"Grandfather?"

Gordius smiled, not a pretty sight. "I am grandfather to the whole world, Gaius Marius," he said, and sighed.

"I see. Thank you for this audience, King Ariarathes."

Boy and elderly man exited, bowing gracefully.

"Good boy, my Ariarathes," said Mithridates in tones of great satisfaction.

"Your Ariarathes?"

"Metaphorically, Gaius Marius."

"He's very like you to look at."

"His mother was my sister."

"And your line is much intermarried, I know." Marius's eyebrows wriggled, but what would have been a message plain to Lucius Cornelius Sulla was lost on King Mithridates. "Well, it seems the affairs of Cappadocia have been settled nicely," he said jovially. "That means, of course, that you are taking your army home again to Pontus."

The King started. "I think not, Gaius Marius. Cappadocia is still rumbling, and this boy is the last of his line. It will be better if I keep my army here."

"It will be better if you take your army home!"

"I can't do that."

"You can, you know."

The King began to swell, his cuirass to creak. "You can't tell *me* what to do, Gaius Marius!"

"Oh yes, I can," said Marius strongly, his calm preserved. "Rome isn't *terribly* interested in this part of the world, but if you start keeping armies of occupation in countries which don't belong to you, King, I can assure you Rome's interest in this part of the world will just mushroom. Roman legions are composed of Romans, not Cappadocian peasants or Syrian mercenaries. I'm sure you wouldn't want to see Roman legions in this part of the world! But unless you go home and take your army with you, King Mithridates, Roman legions you will see. I guarantee it."

"You can't say that, you're not in office!"

"I am a Roman consular. I can say it. And I do say it."

The King's anger was growing; but, Marius noticed with interest, he was also growing afraid. We can always do it to them! he thought jubilantly. They're just like those timid animals which make a great show of aggression; call their bluff, and they run away yelping, tails clipped between their legs.

"I am needed here, and so is my army!"

"You are not. *Go home*, King Mithridates!"

The King jumped to his feet, hand on his sword, and the dozen guards still in the room grew nearer, waiting for orders. "I could kill you here and now, Gaius Marius! In fact, I think I will! I could kill you, and no one would ever know what had happened to you. I could send your ashes home in a great golden jar with a letter of apology explaining that you died of a terminal illness here in the palace of Mazaca."

"Like the seventh King Ariarathes?" asked Marius gently, sitting upright in his chair, unafraid, unruffled. He leaned forward. "Calm down, King! Sit down and be sensible. You know perfectly well you cannot kill Gaius Marius! If you did, there would be Roman legions in Pontus and Cappadocia as fast as ships could fetch them here." He cleared his throat and went on conversationally. "You know, we haven't had a really decent war to sink our teeth into since we defeated three quarters of a million German barbarians. Now *there* was an enemy! But not nearly as rich an enemy as Pontus. The spoils we'd carry home from this part of the world would make a war highly desirable. So why provoke it, King Mithridates? *Go home!*"

And suddenly Marius was alone; the King was gone, his guards with him. Thoughtfully Gaius Marius rose to his feet and strolled out of the room, making for his quarters, his belly full of good plain food, just as he liked, and his head full of interesting questions. That Mithridates would take his army home, he had no doubt; but where had he seen togate Romans? And where had he seen a Roman in a purple-bordered toga? The King's assumption that he was Gaius Marius might have been because the old, old man sent word to him; but Marius doubted it. No, the King had received both the letters sent to Amaseia, and had been trying ever since to avoid this confrontation. Which meant that Battaces the *archigallos* of Pessinus was a Mithridatid spy.

Up early though he was the next morning, anxious to be on his way back to Cilicia as soon as possible, he was still too late to catch the King of Pontus. The King of Pontus, said the old, old man, had left to take his army back to his own country.

"And little Ariarathes Eusebes Philopator? Did he go with King Mithridates, or is he still here?"

"He is here, Gaius Marius. His father has made him the King of Cappadocia, so here he must stay."

"His father?" asked Marius sharply.

"King Mithridates," said the old, old man innocently.

So that was it! No son of the sixth Ariarathes at all, but a son of Mithridates. Clever. But not clever enough.

Gordius saw him off the premises, all smiles and bows; of the boy king there was no sign.

"So you'll be acting as regent," said Marius, standing by a new horse, much grander than the beast which had carried him all the way from Tarsus; his servants too were now better mounted.

"Until King Ariarathes Eusebes Philopator becomes old enough to rule alone, Gaius Marius."

"Philopator," said Marius in musing tones. "It means father-loving. Will he miss his father, do you think?"

Gordius opened his eyes wide. "Miss his father? His poor father has been dead since he was a baby."

"No, the sixth Ariarathes has been dead too long to have fathered *this* boy," said Marius. "I am not a fool, Prince Gordius. Relay that message to your master, Mithridates, as well. Tell him I know whose son the new King of Cappadocia is. And that I will be watching." He accepted a leg up onto his horse. "You, I imagine, are the boy's actual grandfather, rather than grandfather to the world. The only reason I decided to leave matters as they are is because the boy's mother at least is a Cappadocian—your daughter, I presume."

Even this creature belonging utterly to Mithridates could see no point in further dissimulation; instead, he nodded. "My daughter is the *Queen* of Pontus, and her oldest son will succeed King Mithridates. So it pleases me that this boy will rule my own land. He is the last of the line—or rather, his mother is."

"You're not a royal prince, Gordius," said Marius scornfully. "Cappadocian you might be, but I imagine you gave yourself the title of prince. Which doesn't make your daughter the last of the line. Relay my message to King Mithridates."

"I will, Gaius Marius," said Gordius, betraying no offense.

Marius turned his horse, then stopped and looked back. "Oh, one final matter! Clean up the battlefield, Gordius! If you eastern-ers want to earn the respect of civilized men, conduct yourselves like civilized men. You don't leave several thousand corpses lying around to rot after a fight, even if they are the enemy, and you de-spise them. It's not good military technique, it's the mark of barbarians. And as far as I can see, that's precisely what your master Mithridates is—a barbarian. Good day to you." And off he trotted, followed by his attendants.

It was not in Gordius to admire Marius's audacity, but nor did he truly admire Mithridates. So it was with considerable pleasure that he ordered his own horse brought round, and set off to catch the King before he left Mazaca. Every word would he report! And watch the sting of them sink in. His daughter was indeed the new Queen of Pontus, his grandson Phamaces the heir to the throne of Pontus. Yes, the times were good for Gordius, who, as Marius had shrewdly guessed, was not a prince of the old Cappadocian royal house. When the boy king who was the son of Mithridates asserted his right to rule alone—no doubt supported by his father—Gordius intended to make sure that he was given the temple kingdom of Ma at that Comana in a Cappadocian valley between the upper Sarus and the upper Pyramus Rivers. There, priest and king in one, he would be safe, secure, prosperous and exceedingly powerful.

He found Mithridates the next day, encamped on the banks of the Halys River not far from Mazaca. And reported what Gaius Marius had said—but not word for word. Gordius limited his tale to cleaning up the battlefield—the rest, he had decided, was too risky to his own person to mention. The King was very angry, but made no comment, only stared with his eyes slightly bulging, his hands clenching and unclenching.

"And have you cleaned up the battlefield?" the King demanded.

Gordius swallowed, not knowing which answer the King wanted to hear, and so guessed wrongly. "Of course not, Great One."

"Then what are you doing here? Clean it up!"

"Great King, Divine Majesty—he called you a barbarian!"

"According to his lights, I see that I am," said the King, voice hard. "He will not get the chance again. If it is the mark of civilized men to waste their energies on such things when the time of year does not make it necessary, then so be it. We too will waste our energies. No one deeming himself a civilized man will find anything in my conduct to deem me a barbarian!"

Until your temper flies away with you, thought Gordius, but did not say it aloud; Gaius Marius is right, O Great One. You are a barbarian.

And so the battlefield outside Eusebeia Mazaca was attended to, the piles of bodies burned, and the ashes buried beneath a huge tumulus mound which dwindled to insignificance when seen against the bulk of Mount Argaeus, its backdrop. But King Mithridates did not remain to see his orders carried out; he sent his army home to Pontus, while he himself set out for Armenia, traveling in unusual state. Almost the whole of his court went with him, including ten wives, thirty concubines, and half a dozen of his eldest children, and his entourage extended for a full mile of horses, ox-drawn wagons, litters, carriages and pack mules. He moved at a relative snail's pace, covering no more than ten or fifteen miles in a day, but he moved constantly, deaf to all the pleadings of some of his frailer women for a day or two of rest. A thousand picked cavalry troops escorted him, exactly the right number for a kingly embassage.

For this was indeed an embassage; Armenia had a new king. The news had reached Mithridates just as he had begun his campaign in Cappadocia, and he responded quickly, sending to Dasteira for stipulated women and children, stipulated barons, stipulated gifts, stipulated clothing and baggage. It had taken almost two months for the caravan to reach the Halys near Mazaca, and it had arrived at almost the same moment as Gaius Marius; when Marius had found the King absent, the King was visiting his traveling court beside the Halys to make sure all had been done as he wanted it.

As yet, Mithridates knew no more about the new King of Armenia than that he was young, a legitimate son of the old king, Artavasdes, that his name was Tigranes, and that he had been held as a hostage by the King of the Parthians since his early boyhood. A ruler of my own age! thought Mithridates exultantly, a ruler of a powerful eastern realm with no commitments whatsoever to Rome, a ruler who might join Pontus against Rome!

Armenia lay amid the vast mountains around Ararat and stretched eastward to the Caspian or Hyrcanian Sea; it was closely bound by tradition and geography to the Kingdom of the Parthians, whose rulers had never evinced interest in what lay to the west of the Euphrates River.

The easiest route lay along the Halys to its sources, then across the watershed to Mithridates's little realm called Lesser Armenia and the upper Euphrates, then across another watershed to the sources of the Araxes, and so down to Artaxata, the city on the Araxes serving as Armenia's capital. In winter, the journey would have been impossible, so high was the lowest land, but in early summer it could not have been more pleasant, the cavalcade trundling along through valleys filled with wildflowers—the blue of chicory, the yellow of primroses and buttercups, the stunning crimson of poppies. Forests did not exist, only carefully tended plantations of trees cultivated for firewood and to serve as windbreaks; so short was the growing season that the poplars and birches were still bare of leaves, though the month was June.

There were no towns save Carana, and very few villages of any kind; even the brown tents of nomads were scanty. This meant the embassage had to carry grain with it, forage for fruit and vegetables, and rely upon encountering shepherds for meat. Mithridates, however, was wise, for he bought what he could not obtain by gathering it in the wild, and so lived in the dazzled memories of those simple people he came across as truly a god, scattering undreamed -of largesse.

In Quinctilis they reached the Araxes River and wended their way through its frowning valley, Mithridates scrupulous in his compensations to farmers for whatever damage his caravan did, all such business conducted now in sign language, for those who knew a little Greek were left behind with the Euphrates. He had sent a party ahead to Artaxata to announce his coming, and approached the city wreathed in smiles, for in his heart he knew that this long and wearisome pilgrimage would not be wasted.

Tigranes of Armenia came in person to greet Mithridates of Pontus on the road outside the walls, escorted by his guards, all clad in chain mail from head to foot and carrying long lances before them, their shields across their backs; fascinated, King

Mithridates studied their big horses, which were also completely clad in chain mail. And what a sight was their King, riding standing up in a small-wheeled golden car drawn by six pairs of white oxen and shaded by a fringed parasol! A vision in tiered and tasseled skirt of embroidered flame and saffron, a short-sleeved coat upon his upper body, and on his head a towerlike tiara tied round with the white ribbon of the diadem.

Clad in golden armor and his lion skin, with his Greek boots upon his feet and his jeweled sword on its jeweled baldric flashing in the sun, Mithridates slid off his big bay horse and walked down the road toward Tigranes, his hands held out. Tigranes descended from his four-wheeled car and held out his hands. And so their hands met; dark eyes looked into green eyes, and a friendship was formed that did not entirely depend upon liking. Each recognized in the other an ally, and each immediately began to assess his needs in relation to the other. They turned together and began to walk through the dust of the road toward the city.

Tigranes was fair-skinned but dark of hair and eye, his hair and beard worn long and intricately curled, then entwined with golden threads. Mithridates had expected Tigranes to look like a Hellenized monarch; but Tigranes wasn't Hellenized at all, he was Parthianized, hence the hair, the beard, the long dress. Fortunately, however, he spoke excellent Greek, as did two or three of his most senior nobles. The rest of the court, like the populace, spoke a Median dialect.

"Even in places as Parthian as Ecbatana and Susia, to speak Greek is the mark of a properly educated man," said King Tigranes when they settled in two kingly chairs to one side of the golden Armenian throne. "I will not insult you by taking a seat above yours," Tigranes had said.

"I come to seek a treaty of friendship and alliance with Armenia," Mithridates explained.

The discussion proceeded delicately for two such arrogant and autocratic men, an indication of how necessary both men viewed a comfortable concord. Mithridates of course was the more powerful ruler, for he owned no suzerain and ruled a far larger realm—and was a great deal wealthier besides.

"My father was very like the King of the Parthians in many ways," said Tigranes. "The sons he kept with him in Armenia he killed one by one; that I escaped was because I had been sent as hostage to the King of the Parthians when eight years old. So when my father became ill, the only son he had left was I. The Armenian council negotiated with King Mithridates of Parthia to secure my release. But the price of my release was heavy. Seventy Armenian valleys, all seventy along the boundary between Armenia and Median Atropatene, which meant that my country lost some of its most fertile land. Also, the valleys contained gold-bearing rivers, fine lapis lazuli, turquoise, and black onyx. Now I have vowed that Armenia will recover those seventy valleys, and that I will find a better place to build a better capital than this cold hole of Artaxata."

"Didn't Hannibal help to design Artaxata?" asked Mithridates.

"So they say," said Tigranes shortly, and went back to his dreams of empire. "It is my ambition to extend Armenia southward to Egypt and westward to Cilicia. I want access to the Middle Sea, I want trade routes, I want warmer lands for growing grain, I want to hear every citizen of my kingdom speaking Greek." He stopped, wet his lips. "How does that sit with you, Mithridates?"

"It sits well, Tigranes," said the King of Pontus easily. "I will guarantee to give you support and soldiers to achieve your aims—if you will support me when I move westward to take the Roman province of Asia Minor away from the Romans. You may have Syria, Commagene, Osrhoene, Sophene, Gordyene, Palestina, and Nabataea. I will take all Anatolia, including Cilicia."

Tigranes didn't hesitate. "When?" he asked eagerly.

Mithridates smiled, sat back in his chair. "When the Romans are too busy to take much notice of us," he said. "We're young, Tigranes, we can afford to wait. I know Rome. Sooner or later Rome will become embroiled in a western war, or in Africa. And then we will move."

To seal their pact Mithridates produced his eldest daughter by his dead queen, Laodice, a fifteen-year-old child named Cleopatra, and offered her to Tigranes as his wife. As yet Armenia had no queen, so he seized upon the match avidly; Cleopatra would become Queen of Armenia, a pledge of great significance, as it meant a grandson of Mithridates would fall heir to the throne of Armenia. When the golden-haired, golden-eyed child set eyes upon her husband-to-be, she wept in terror at his alien appearance; Tigranes made an enormous concession for one brought up in a claustrophobic oriental court of beards—real and artificial—and of curls—real and artificial—by shaving off his beard and cutting his long hair. His bride discovered that he was after all a handsome fellow, and put her hand in his, and smiled. Dazzled by so much fairness, Tigranes thought himself very lucky; it was perhaps the last time in his life he was to feel anything akin to humility.

 Gaius Marius was profoundly glad to find his wife and son and their little Tarsian escort safe and well, and happily espousing the life of nomad shepherds; Young Marius had even learned quite a few words of the strange-sounding tongue the nomads spoke, and had become very expert with his sheep.

"Look, *tata!*" he said when he had brought his father to the place where his small collection of animals was grazing, close-fitting coats of kidskin covering the wool from the elements and burrs. Picking up a small stone, he threw it accurately just to one side of the leading beast; the whole flock stopped grazing at once, and obediently lay down. "See? They know that's the signal to lie down. Isn't it clever?"

"It certainly is," said Marius, and looked down at his boy, so strong and attractive and brown. "Are you ready to go, my son?"

Dismay filled the big grey eyes. "Go?"

"We have to leave for Tarsus at once."

Young Marius blinked to stem the tears, gazed adoringly at his sheep, sighed. "I'm ready, *tata,*" he said.

Julia edged her donkey alongside Marius's tall Cappadocian horse as soon as she could after they got under way. "Can you tell me yet what was worrying you so?" she asked. "And why have you sent Morsimus ahead of us now in such a hurry?"

"Cappadocia has been the victim of a coup," said Marius. "King Mithridates has installed his own son on the throne, with his father-in-law as the boy's regent. The little Cappadocian lad who was the king is dead, I suspect killed by Mithridates. However, there's not much I or Rome can do about it, more's the pity."

"Did you see the proper king before he died?"

"No. I saw Mithridates."

Julia shivered, glanced at her husband's set face. "He was there in Mazaca? How did you escape?"

Marius's expression changed to surprise. "Escape? It wasn't necessary to escape, Julia. Mithridates might be the ruler of the whole of the eastern half of the Euxine Sea, but he'd never dare to harm Gaius Marius!"

"Then why are we moving so fast?" asked Julia shrewdly.

"To give him no opportunity to start haboring ideas of harming Gaius Marius," her husband said, grinning.

"And Morsimus?"

"Very prosaic, I'm afraid, *meum mel.* Tarsus will be even hotter now, so I've sent him to find us a ship. The moment we get to Tarsus we sail. But in a leisurely manner. We'll spend a lovely summer exploring the Cilician and Pamphylian coasts, take that trip up into the mountains to visit Olba. I know I hustled you past Seleuceia Trachea on our way to Tarsus, but there's no hurry now. As you're a descendant of Aeneas, it's fitting you should say hello to the descendants of Teucer. And they say there are several glorious lakes in the high Taurus above Attaleia, so we'll visit them too. Is that to your satisfaction?"

"Oh, yes!"

This program being faithfully carried out, Gaius Marius and his family did not reach Halicarnassus until January, having pottered happily along a coastline renowned for its beauty and isolation. Of pirates they saw none, even at Coracesium, where Marius had the pleasure of climbing the mountainous spur on which stood the old pirate fortress, and finally worked out how to take it.

Halicarnassus seemed like home to Julia and Young Marius, who no sooner disembarked than were walking about the city re-acquainting themselves with its delights. Marius himself sat down to decipher two letters, one from Lucius Cornelius Sulla in Nearer Spain, the other from Publius Rutilius Rufus in Rome.

When Julia came into his study, she found Marius frowning direfully.

"Bad news?" she asked.

The frown was replaced by a slightly wicked twinkle, then Marius composed his face to an expression of bland innocence. "I wouldn't say *bad* news."

"Is there any *good* news?"

"Absolutely splendid tidings from Lucius Cornelius! Our lad Quintus Sertorius has won the Grass Crown."

Julia gasped. "Oh, Gaius Marius, how wonderful!"

"Twenty-eight years old . . . He's a Marian, of course."

"How did he win it?" Julia asked, smiling.

"By saving an army from annihilation, of course. That's the only way one can win the *corona obsidionalis*."

"Don't be smart, Gaius Marius! You know what I mean."

Marius relented. "Last winter he and the legion he commands were sent to Castulo to garrison the place, along with a legion seconded from Publius Licinius Crassus in Further Spain. Crassus's troops got out of hand, with the result that Celtiberian forces penetrated the city's defenses. And our dear lad covered himself in glory! Saved the city, saved both legions, won the Grass Crown."

"I shall have to write him my congratulations. I wonder does his mother know? Do you think he would have told her?"

"Probably not. He's too modest. You write to Ria."

"I shall. What else does Lucius Cornelius have to say?"

"Not much." A growl rumbled out of Marius. "He's not happy. But then, he never is! His praise of Quintus Sertorius is generous, yet I think he'd rather have won the Grass Crown himself. Titus Didius won't let him command in the field."

"Oh, poor Lucius Cornelius! Whyever not?"

"Too valuable," said Marius laconically. "He's a planner."

"Does he say anything about Quintus Sertorius's German wife?"

"He does, as a matter of fact. She and the child are living in a big Celtiberian fortress town called Osca."

"What about his own German wife, those twin boys she had?"

Marius shrugged. "Who knows? He never speaks of them."

A little silence fell; Julia gazed out the window. Then she said, "I wish he did speak of them. It isn't natural, somehow. I know they're not Roman, that he can't possibly bring them to Rome. And yet—surely he must have some feeling for them!"

Marius chose not to comment. "Publius Rutilius's letter is very long and newsy," he said provocatively.

"Is it fit for my ears to hear?"

Marius chuckled. "Eminently! Especially the conclusion."

"Then read, Gaius Marius, read!"

"Greetings from Rome, Gaius Marius. I write this in the New Year, having been promised a very quick trip for my missive by none other than Quintus Granius of Puteoli. Hopefully it will find you in Halicarnassus, but if it does not, it will find you sooner or later.

"You will be pleased to know that Quintus Mucius staved off threat of prosecution, largely thanks to his eloquence in the Senate, and to supporting speeches by his cousin Crassus Orator and none other than Scaurus Princeps Senatus, who finds himself in agreement with everything Quintus Mucius and I did in Asia Province. As we expected, it was harder to deal with the Treasury than with the *publicani;* give a Roman businessman his due, he can always see commercial sense, and our new arrangements for Asia Province make sound commercial sense. It was chiefly the art collectors who wailed, Sextus Perquitienus in particular. The statue of Alexander he took from Pergamum has mysteriously disappeared from his peristyle, perhaps because Scaurus Princeps Senatus used his filching it as one of the most telling points in his address to the House. Anyway, the Treasury eventually subsided, muttering, and the censors recalled the Asian contracts. From now on, the taxes of Asia Province will be based upon the figures Quintus Mucius and I produced. However, I do not want to give you the impression that all is forgiven, even by the *publicani*. A well-regulated province is difficult to exploit, and there are plenty among the tax-farmers who would still like to exploit Asia Province. The Senate has agreed to send more distinguished men to govern there, which will help keep the *publicani* down.

"We have new consuls. None other than Lucius Licinius Crassus Orator and my own dear Quintus Mucius Scaevola. Our urban praetor is Lucius Julius Caesar, who has replaced that extraordinary New Man, Marcus Herennius. I've never seen anyone with more voter appeal than Marcus Herennius, though why escapes me. But all they have to do is see Herennius, and they start crying out to vote for him. A fact which did not please that slimy piece of work you had working for you when he was a tribune of the plebs—I mean Lucius Marcius Philippus. When all the votes for praetor were counted a year ago, there was Herennius at the top of the poll and Philippus at the very bottom. Of the six who got in, I mean. Oh, the wails and whines and whimpers! This year's lot are not nearly as interesting. Last year's *praetor peregrinus*, Gaius Flaccus, drew attention to himself by giving the full Roman citizenship to a priestess of Ceres in Velia, one Calliphana. All Rome is still *dying* to know why—but we all can guess!

"Our censors Antonius Orator and Lucius Flaccus,

having finished the letting of the contracts (complicated by the activities of two people in Asia Province,
which slowed them down quite a bit!), then scanned the
senatorial rolls and found no one reprehensible, after
which they scrutinized the knights, same result. Now
they are moving toward a full census of the Roman
People everywhere in the world, they say. No Roman
citizen will escape their net, they say.

"With that laudable purpose in mind, they have set
up their booth on the Campus Martius to do Rome. To
do Italy, they have assembled an amazingly well organized force of clerks whose duty will be to go to every
town in the peninsula and take a proper census. I approve, though there are many who do not; the old way—
of having rural citizens go through the *duumviri* of
their municipality and provincial citizens go through
the governor—should be good enough. But Antonius
and Flaccus insist their way will be better, so their way
it is. I gather, however, that the provincial citizens will
still have to go through their various governors. The
fogies of course are predicting that the results will be
the same as they always are.

"And a little provincial news, since you are in that
neck of the world, but may not have heard. The eighth
Antiochus of Syria, nicknamed Grypus Hook-nose, has
been murdered by his cousin—or is it his uncle?—or
his half brother?—the ninth Antiochus of Syria, nicknamed Cyzicenus. Whereupon the wife of Grypus,
Cleopatra Selene of Egypt, promptly married his murderer, Cyzicenus! I wonder how much weeping she did
between being widowed and remarried? However, this
news does at least mean that for the moment northern
Syria is under the rule of a single king.

"Of more interest to Rome is the death of one of the
Ptolemies. Ptolemy Apion, bastard son of horrible old
Ptolemy Gross Belly of Egypt, has just died in Cyrene.

He was, you may recollect, the King of Cyrenaica. But he died without an heir. And you'll never guess! He willed the Kingdom of Cyrenaica to Rome! Old Attalus of Pergamum has started a fashion. What a nice way to end up ruling the world, Gaius Marius. Left everything in a will.

"I do hope you decide to come home this year! Rome is a very lonely place without you, and I don't even have Piggle-wiggle to complain about. There is the most peculiar rumor going around, incidentally—that Piggle-wiggle died as the result of being *poisoned*! The originator of the rumor is none other than that fashionable physician practitioner on the Palatine, Apollodorus Siculus. When Piggle-wiggle took ill, Apollodorus was summoned. Apparently he wasn't happy about the death, so he asked for an autopsy. The Piglet refused, his *tata* Piggle-wiggle was burned, and his ashes put in a hideously ornate tomb, and all that was many moons ago. But our little Greek from Sicily has been doing some research, and now he insists that Piggle-wiggle drank a very nasty brew decocted from crushed peach seeds! The Piglet rightly says that no one had a motive, and has threatened to haul Apollodorus into court if he doesn't stop going around saying Piggle-wiggle was poisoned. No one—even I!—thinks for one moment that the Piglet did his *tata* in, and who else is there, I ask you?

"One final delicious snippet, and I will leave you in peace. Family gossip, though it's become the talk of Rome. Her husband having come home from abroad and seen the bright red hair of his new son, my niece has been divorced for adultery!

"Further details of this will be forthcoming when I see you in Rome. I will make an offering to the Lares Permarini for your safe return."

Putting the letter down as if it burned, Marius looked at his wife. "Well, what do you think of that little bit of news?" he asked. "Your brother Gaius has divorced Aurelia for adultery! Apparently she's had another boy—a boy with bright red hair! Oh ho ho ho! Three guesses who's the father, eh?"

Julia was gaping, literally unable to find anything to say. A bright tide of red flooded into the skin of neck and head, her lips thinned. Then she began to shake her head, and went on shaking it until finally she found words. "It's not true! It *can't* be true! I don't believe it!"

"Well, her uncle's the one telling us. Here," said Marius, and thrust the last part of Rutilius Rufus's letter at Julia.

She took the scroll from him and began to work on separating the endless row of continuous letters into words, her voice sounding hollow, unnatural. Over and over she read the brief message, then put the letter down.

"It is not Aurelia," she said firmly. "I will never believe it is Aurelia!"

"Who else could it be? Bright red hair, Julia! That's the brand marked Lucius Cornelius Sulla, not Gaius Julius Caesar!"

"Publius Rutilius has other nieces," said Julia stubbornly.

"On close terms with Lucius Cornelius? Living all alone in Rome's worst slum?"

"How would we know? It's possible."

"So are flying pigs to a Pisidian," said Marius.

"What's living all alone in Rome's worst slum got to do with it, anyway?" Julia demanded.

"Easy to carry on an affair undetected," said Marius, who was highly amused. "At least until you produce a little red-haired cuckoo in the family nest!"

"Oh, stop *wallowing*!" cried Julia, disgusted. "I do not believe it, I will not believe it." Another idea occurred to her. "Besides, it can't be my brother Gaius. He isn't due to come home yet, and if he had come home, you would have heard. It's your work he's doing." She looked at Marius with a minatory eye. "Well? Isn't that true, husband?"

"He probably wrote to me in Rome," said Marius feebly.

"After I wrote to tell him we'd be away for three years? And giving him our approximate whereabouts? Oh, come now, Gaius Marius, admit it's highly unlikely to be Aurelia!"

"I'll admit anything you want me to admit," said Marius, and began to laugh. "All the same, Julia, it *is* Aurelia!"

"I am going home," said Julia, rising to her feet.

"I thought you wanted to go to Egypt?"

"I am going home," Julia repeated. "I don't care where you go, Gaius Marius, though I would prefer it be the Land of the Hyperboreans. *I* am going home."

PART II

LIVIA DRUSA

"I'm going to Smyrna to bring back my fortune," said Quintus Servilius Caepio to his brother-in-law, Marcus Livius Drusus, as they walked home from the Forum Romanum.

Drusus stopped, one pointed black eyebrow flying upward. "Oh! Do you think that's wise?" he asked, then could have bitten off his tactless tongue.

"What do you mean, wise?" Caepio asked, looking pugnacious.

Out went Drusus's hand to grip Caepio's right arm. "Just what I said, Quintus. I am *not* implying that your fortune in Smyrna is the Gold of Tolosa—nor for that matter that your father stole the Gold of Tolosa! But the fact remains that almost all of Rome *does* believe your father guilty, and also believes that the fortune in your name in Smyrna is really the Gold of Tolosa. In the old days, to have brought it back might have earned you nothing more harmful than black looks and a degree of odium you would have found a nuisance in your public career. But nowadays there is a *lex Servilia Glaucia de repetundis* on the tablets, don't forget. Gone is the time when a governor could peculate or extort and see his loot safe because he put it in someone else's name. Glaucia's law specifically provides for the recovery of illegally acquired monies from their ultimate recipients as well as from the guilty party. Using Uncle Lucius Tiddlypuss doesn't work anymore."

"I remind you that Glaucia's law is not retroactive," said Caepio stiffly.

"All it will take is one tribune of the plebs in a mood of vengeance, a quick appeal to the Plebeian Assembly to invalidate that particular loophole, and you'll find the *lex Servilia Glaucia* is retroactive," said Drusus firmly. "Truly, brother Quintus, think about it! I don't want to see my sister and her children deprived of both *paterfamilias* and fortune, nor do I want to see you sitting out the years as an exile in Smyrna."

"Why did it have to be my father they picked on?" demanded Caepio angrily. "Look at Metellus Numidicus! Home again just covered in glory, while my poor father died in permanent exile!"

"We both know why," said Drusus patiently, wishing for the

thousandth time at least that Caepio was brighter. "The men who run the Plebeian Assembly can forgive a high nobleman anything— especially after a little time goes by. But the Gold of Tolosa was unique. *And* it disappeared while in your father's custody. More gold than Rome has in her Treasury! Once people here made up their minds your father took it, they conceived a hatred for him that has nothing to do with right, justice, or patriotism." He started walking again, and Caepio followed. "Think it out properly, Quintus, please! If the sums you bring home total anything like ten percent of the value of the Gold of Tolosa, you'll have the whole of Rome saying your father *did* take it, and you inherited it."

Caepio began to laugh. "They won't," he said positively. "I have already thought everything out properly, Marcus. It's taken me all these years to solve the problem, but solve it, I have. Truly!"

"How?" asked Drusus skeptically.

"First of all, none except you will know where I've really gone and what I'm really doing. As far as Rome will know—as Livia Drusa and Servilia Caepionis will know—I'm in Italian Gaul-across-the-Padus, looking into property. I've been talking about doing so for months; no one will be surprised or bother to query it. Why should they, when I've deliberately harangued people with my plans to set up whole towns full of foundries geared to make anything from ploughshares to chain mail? And as it's the property side of the project I'm interested in, no one can criticize my senatorial integrity. Let others run the foundries—I'm happy to own the towns!"

Caepio sounded so eager that Drusus (who had hardly heard his brother-in-law on the subject because he had hardly listened) stared at him now in surprise.

"You sound as if you mean to do it," Drusus said.

"Oh, I do. The foundry towns represent just one of many things in which I intend to invest my money from Smyrna. As I'm going to keep my investments in Roman territories rather than in Rome herself, there will be no new amounts of my money coming into city financial institutions. Nor do I think the Treasury will be clever enough—or have time enough—to look into who, what, and how much I am investing in business enterprises far from the city of Rome," said Caepio.

Drusus's expression had changed to amazement. "Quintus Servilius, I am staggered! I didn't think you had so much guile in you," he said.

"I thought you might be staggered," said Caepio smugly, then spoiled the effect by adding, "though I must admit I had a letter from my father not long before he died, telling me what I must do. There's an *enormous* amount of money in Smyrna."

"Yes, I imagine there is," said Drusus dryly.

"No, it is *not* the Gold of Tolosa!" cried Caepio, throwing his hands out. "There's my mother's fortune as well as my father's! He was clever enough to move his money before he was prosecuted, in spite of that conceited *cunnus* Norbanus's measures to prevent his doing so, like throwing my father in prison between trial and exile. Some of the money has been gradually returned to Rome over the years, but not sufficient to draw attention. Which is why— as you yourself have cause to know!—I still live modestly."

"I do certainly have cause to know," said Drusus, who had been housing his brother-in-law and his brother-in-law's family since the elder Caepio had been convicted. "One thing does puzzle me, however. Why not just leave your fortune in Smyrna?"

"Can't," said Caepio quickly. "My father said it wouldn't be safe forever in Smyrna—or any other city in Asia Province with the right banking facilities, like Cos—or even Rhodes, he said. He said Asia Province will revolt against Rome. He said that the tax-farmers there have made everyone hate Rome. He said sooner or later the whole province will rise up."

"If it did, we'd soon get it back," said Drusus.

"Yes, I know that! But in the meantime, do you think all the gold and silver and coins and treasures on deposit in Asia Province would just sit there safe and sound? My father said the first thing the revolutionaries would do would be to pillage the temples and the banks," said Caepio.

Drusus nodded. "He's probably right. So you're going to move your money. But to *Italian Gaul*?"

"Only some, only some. Some of it will go to Campania. And some to Umbria. And some to Etruria. Then there are places like Massilia, Utica, and Gades—some will go to them. All up the western end of the Middle Sea."

"Why don't you admit the truth, Quintus—at least to me, your brother-in-law twice over?" asked Drusus a little wearily. "Your sister is my wife, and my sister is your wife. We are so tied together we can never be free of each other. So admit it, at least to me! It *is* the Gold of Tolosa."

"It is not the Gold of Tolosa," said Quintus Servilius Caepio stubbornly.

Thick, thought Marcus Livius Drusus, leading the way into the peristyle-garden of his house, the finest mansion in Rome; he is as thick as porridge which has boiled too long. And yet . . . There he is, sitting on fifteen thousand talents of gold his father smuggled from Spain to Smyrna eight years ago, after pretending it was stolen en route from Tolosa to Narbo. A cohort of good Roman troops perished guarding that wagon train of gold, but does he care? Did his father—who must have organized their massacre—care? Of course not! All they care about is their precious gold. They're Servilii Caepiones, the Midases of Rome, can't be jolted out of their intellectually moribund state unless someone whispers the word *"Gold!"*

It was January of the year Gnaeus Cornelius Lentulus and Publius Licinius Crassus were consuls, and the lotus trees in the Livius Drusus garden were bare, though the magnificent pool and its statues and fountains by Myron still played, thanks to piped warm water. The paintings by Apelles, Zeuxis, Timanthes, and others had been removed from the back walls of the colonnade and put into storage earlier in the year, after Caepio's two daughters had been caught daubing them with pigments taken from two artists who were restoring the atrium frescoes at the time. Both little girls had been beaten thoroughly, but Drusus had judged it prudent to remove temptation; as the daubs were still fresh, they were able to be removed, yet—who was to say it wouldn't happen all over again when his own small boy grew a little larger, and more mischievous? Priceless collections of art were best not displayed in houses containing children. He didn't think Servilia and Servililla would do anything like it again, but there were bound to be more offspring.

His own family was finally started, though not in the way he had hoped for; somehow he and Servilia Caepionis couldn't seem to make babies. Two years ago they had adopted the youngest son of Tiberius Claudius Nero, a man as impoverished as most of the Claudii of all branches, and delighted to hand over his new child to become heir to the Livius Drusus wealth. It was more usual to adopt the eldest boy of a family, so that the family adopting might be sure the child they took on was sane, healthy, nice-natured and reasonably intelligent; but Servilia Caepionis, starved for a baby, had insisted upon adopting a baby. And Marcus Livius Drusus— who had learned to love his wife dearly, though he had loved her not at all when they married—allowed her to have her way. His own misgivings he placated by making a generous offering to Mater Matuta, enlisting the goddess's support to ensure that the baby would prove satisfactory when he grew into his wits.

The women were together in Servilia Caepionis's sitting room just next door to the nursery, and came to greet their men with every evidence of pleasure. Though they were only sisters-in-law, they looked more like real sisters, for both were short, very dark of hair and eye, and owned small, regular features. Livia Drusa— who was Caepio's wife—was the prettier of the two, as she had escaped the family affliction of stumpy legs, and had the better figure; into the bargain, she fulfilled the criteria of beauty in a woman, for her eyes were very large, well spaced and well opened, and her mouth was tiny, folded like a flower. The nose in between was a little too small to please the connoisseurs, but it escaped the additional disadvantage of straightness by ending in a little knob. Her skin was thick and creamy, her waist was trim, her breasts and hips well curved and ample. Servilia Caepionis—who was Drusus's wife—was a thinner version of the same; however, her skin had a tendency to produce pimples around chin and nose and her legs were too short for her trunk, her neck too short as well.

Yet it was Marcus Livius Drusus who loved his less pretty wife, Quintus Servilius Caepio who did not love the beautiful one. At the time of their joint marriage eight years earlier, it had been the other way around. Though neither man realized it, the difference lay in the two women; Livia Drusa had loathed Caepio and had been forced to marry him, whereas Servilia Caepionis had been in love with Drusus since childhood. Members of Rome's highest nobility, both women were model wives of the old kind—obedient, subservient, even-tempered, unfailingly respectful. Then as the years went by and a certain degree of knowledge and familiarity crept into each marriage, Marcus Livius Drusus's indifference melted in the steady glow of his wife's affection, an increasing ardor she displayed in their bed, a shared grief because there were no children; whereas Quintus Servilius Caepio's inarticulate adoration was suffocated by his wife's unspoken dislike, an increasing coolness she displayed in their bed, a resentment because their children were both girls and none had followed.

A visit to the nursery was mandatory, of course. Drusus made much of his chubby, dark-visaged little boy, who was known as Drusus Nero, and was now almost two years old. Caepio merely nodded to his daughters, who flattened themselves in awe against the wall and said nothing. They were miniature copies of their mother—as dark, as big-eyed, as bud-mouthed—and had all the charm of little girls, had their father only bothered to look. Servilia was almost seven years old, and had learned a great deal from her beating after she decided to improve Apelles's horse and Zeuxis's bunch of grapes. She had never been beaten before, and had found the experience more humiliating than painful, more galling than instructive. Lilla on the other hand was an uncomplicated bundle of mischief—irrepressible, strong-willed, aggressive and direct. The beating she had received was promptly forgotten, save that it served to endow her with a healthy respect for her father.

The four adults repaired to the *triclinium,* there to dine.

"Is Quintus Poppaedius not joining us, Cratippus?" asked Drusus of his steward.

"I have had no word that he isn't, *domine.*"

"In which case, we'll wait," said Drusus, deliberately ignoring the hostile look he got from Caepio.

Caepio, however, was not about to be ignored. "Why do you put up with that frightful fellow, Marcus Livius?" he asked.

The eyes Drusus turned upon his brother-in-law were stony. "There are some, Quintus Servilius, who ask me that question of you," he said levelly.

Livia Drusa gasped, choked back a nervous giggle; but, as Drusus expected, the criticism went over Caepio's head.

"Well, isn't that what I said?" asked Caepio. "Why do you put up with him?"

"Because he's my friend."

"Your leech, more like!" snorted Caepio. "Truly, Marcus Livius, he battens on you. Always arriving without any notice, always with favors to ask, always complaining about us Romans. Who does he think he is?"

"He thinks he's an Italian of the Marsi," said a cheerful voice. "Sorry I'm late, Marcus Livius, but you should start your meal without me, as I've said before. My excuse for tardiness is impeccable—I've been standing very still while Catulus Caesar subjected me to a long lecture on the perfidies of Italians."

Silo sat on the back edge of the couch upon which Drusus reclined and allowed a slave to remove his boots and wash his feet, then cover them with a pair of socks. When he twisted lightly and lithely onto the couch, he occupied the *locus consularis*, the place of honor to Drusus's left; Caepio was reclining upon the couch at right angles to Drusus's, a less honored position because he was part of the family rather than Drusus's guest.

"Complaining about me again, Quintus Servilius?" asked Silo without concern, lifting one thin brow at Drusus, and winking.

Drusus grinned, his eyes resting upon Quintus Poppaedius Silo with a great deal more affection in them than they held whenever he looked at Caepio. "My brother-in-law is always complaining about something, Quintus Poppaedius. Take no notice."

"I don't," said Silo, inclining his head in a greeting to the two women, seated on chairs opposite their husbands' couches.

* * *

They had met on the battlefield of Arausio, Drusus and Silo, after the battle was over and eighty thousand Roman and Italian Allied troops lay dead—thanks mainly to Caepio's father. Forged in unforgettable circumstances, their friendship had grown with the years; and with the bond of a mutual concern for the fate of the Italian Allies, a cause to which both men were pledged. They were an unlikely combination, Silo and Drusus, but no amount of complaining on Caepio's part—or lecturing on the part of some of the Senate's senior members—had so far managed to drive a wedge between them.

The Italian Silo looked more Roman, the Roman Drusus looked more Italian. Silo had the right kind of nose, the right kind of middling coloring, the right kind of bearing; a tall man and well built, he was a fine-looking fellow save for his eyes, which were a yellowish green—and thus were unseemly, a trifle snakelike because he rarely blinked; however, this was not remarkable in a Marsian, as the Marsi were snake-worshippers and had trained themselves not to blink more than absolutely necessary. Silo's father had been the leading man of the Marsi, and after his death the son took his place, despite his youth. Moneyed and highly educated, Silo ought by rights to have commanded a great deal of respect from just those Romans who—if they did not blatantly cut him—looked down their noses at him and stooped to patronize him. For Quintus Poppaedius was not a Roman, nor even a holder of the Latin Rights; Quintus Poppaedius Silo was an Italian, and therefore an inferior being.

He came from the rich highlands of the central Italian peninsula, not so very many miles from Rome, where the great Fucine Lake rose and fell in mysterious cycles having nothing to do with rivers or precipitation, and the chain of the Apennines divided to hedge the lands of the Marsi around. Of all Italian peoples, the Marsi were the most prosperous and the most numerous. For centuries they had been Rome's loyalest allies; it was the proudest boast of the Marsi that no Roman general had ever triumphed without Marsi in his army, nor triumphed over Marsi. Yet even after the passing of so many centuries, the Marsi—like the other Italian nationals—were regarded as unworthy of the full Roman citizenship. In consequence, they could not bid for Roman State contracts, or marry Roman citizens, or appeal to Roman justice in the event of any conviction on a capital charge. They could be flogged within an inch of their lives, they could have their crops or their products or their women stolen without redress at law—if the thief was a Roman.

Had Rome left the Marsi to their own devices in their fertile highlands, all these injustices might have been less intrusive, but—as was true in every part of the peninsula that did not belong outright to Rome—the lands of the Marsi had a Roman implant in their midst in the guise of the Latin Rights colony called Alba Fucentia. And, of course, the town of Alba Fucentia became a city, then the biggest settlement in the whole region, for it had a nucleus of full Roman citizens able to conduct business freely with Rome, and the rest of its population held the Latin Rights, a kind of second-class Roman citizenship allowing most privileges belonging to the full citizenship, save only that those with the *ius Latii* could not vote in any Roman election; the city's magistrates automatically inherited the full citizenship for themselves and all their direct descendants when they assumed office. Thus had Alba Fucentia grown at the expense of the old Marsic capital, Marruvium, and sat there as a perpetual reminder of the differences between the Roman and the Italian.

In olden days all of Italy had aspired to eventual owning of Latin Rights and then the full citizenship, for Rome under the doughty and brilliant leadership of men like Appius Claudius Caecus had been conscious of the necessity of change, the prudence in seeing all Italy eventually become properly Roman. But then after some Italian nations had sided with Hannibal during the years when he had marched up and down the Italian peninsula, the attitude of Rome hardened, and the awarding of the full citizenship or even the *ius Latii* ceased.

One reason had been the swelling immigration of Italians into Roman and Latin towns—and also into Rome herself. Protracted residence in these places brought with it a sharing in the Latin Rights, and even in the full Roman citizenship. The Paeligni had complained of the loss of four thousand of their people to the Latin town of Fregellae, and used this as an excuse not to furnish Rome with soldiers when she demanded them.

From time to time Rome attempted to do something about the problem of mass immigration; these efforts had culminated in a law of the tribune of the plebs Marcus Junius Pennus the year before Fregellae revolted. Pennus expelled every non-citizen from the city of Rome and her colony towns, and in so doing uncovered a scandal which rocked the Roman nobility to its foundations. The consul of four years before, Marcus Perperna, was discovered to be an Italian who had never held the Roman citizenship!

A wave of reaction inside the ranks of those who governed Rome had immediately occurred; one of the leading opponents of Italian advancement was Drusus's father, Marcus Livius Drusus the Censor, who had connived at the disgrace of Gaius Gracchus and the tearing down of Gaius Gracchus's laws.

No one could have predicted that the Censor's son, Drusus—who came young into the role of *paterfamilias* when his father died in office as censor—would forsake the attitudes and precepts of Drusus the Censor. Of impeccable plebeian-noble ancestry, a member of the College of Pontifices, enormously wealthy, connected by blood and marriage to the patrician houses of Servilius Caepio, Cornelius Scipio and Aemilius Lepidus, young Marcus Livius Drusus ought to have evolved into a pillar of the ultra-conservative faction which controlled the Senate—and therefore controlled Rome. That this had not happened was pure chance; Drusus had been present as a tribune of the soldiers at the battle of Arausio, when the patrician consular Quintus Servilius Caepio had refused to co-operate with the New Man Gaius Mallius Maximus, and in consequence the legions of Rome and her Italian Allies had been annihilated by the Germans in Gaul-across-the-Alps.

When Drusus had returned from Gaul-across-the-Alps, he cherished two new factors in his life; one, the friendship of the

Marsian nobleman Quintus Poppaedius Silo, and the other, the knowledge that the men of his own class and background—in particular his father-in-law Caepio—had no appreciation of or respect for the efforts of the soldiers who died at Arausio, be they noble Romans, or Italian auxiliaries, or Roman *capite censi.*

This was not to say, however, that young Marcus Livius Drusus immediately espoused the aims and aspirations of a true reformer; he was too much a product of his class. But he—like other Roman noblemen before him—had been exposed to an experience which made him *think.* It was said that the fate of the Brothers Gracchi had been decided when the elder, Tiberius Sempronius Gracchus— a scion of the highest nobility in Rome—had journeyed as a young man through Etruria and seen the public lands of Rome in the control of a mere handful of rich Roman men who grazed it using chain gangs of slaves locked up each night in the infamous barracks known as *ergastula.* Where, Tiberius Gracchus had asked himself, were the smallholder Romans who ought to be in possession of these lands, earning a fruitful living and breeding sons for the army? Product of his class though he was, Tiberius Gracchus had begun to think—and, being a product of his class, he was endowed with a strong sense of right as well as an overwhelming love for Rome.

Seven years had gone by since the battle of Arausio, seven years during which Drusus had entered the Senate, served as quaestor in Asia Province, been forced to house his brother-in-law and his brother-in-law's family after the disgrace of the father Caepio, become a priest of the State religion, productively gardened his personal fortune, seen and heard the disastrous events which led to the murder of Saturninus and his colleagues, and fought on the side of the Senate against Saturninus when he attempted to make himself King of Rome. Seven years during which Drusus had played host to Quintus Poppaedius Silo many times, listened to him talk—and continued himself to think. It was his ardent ambition to solve the vexed question of the Italians in a way properly

Roman, entirely peaceful, and pleasing to both sides; to this end he quietly devoted his energies, unwilling to make his intentions public until he had found that ideal solution.

The Marsian Silo was the only man who knew the direction Drusus's mind was taking, and Silo trod with exquisite delicacy, too shrewd and too prudent to commit the mistake of pushing Drusus, of becoming too articulate about his own point of view, which was somewhat different from Drusus's. The six thousand men of the legion Silo had commanded at Arausio had died almost to the last noncombatant, and they had been Marsians, not Romans; it was the Marsi had sired them, the Marsi had armed them, the Marsi had paid for their upkeep in the field. An investment in humanity, time, and money that Rome had neither acknowledged afterward, nor offered compensation for.

Whereas Drusus dreamed of a general enfranchisement for the whole of Italy, Silo dreamed of secession from Rome, of a completely independent and united nation composed of all Italy that was not in the hands of the Romans—Italia. And when Italia came into existence—as Silo had vowed it would—the Italian peoples who comprised it would go to war against Rome and win, absorb Rome and the Romans into this new nation, together with all of Rome's territories abroad.

Silo was not alone, and he knew he was not alone. During the past seven years he had journeyed all over Italy and even into Italian Gaul, sniffing out men of like mind and discovering that they were not thin on the ground. They were all leaders of their nations or peoples, and of two different kinds; those who—like Marius Egnatius, Gaius Papius Mutilus, and Pontius Telesinus—came from ancient noble families prominent in their nations; and those who—like Marcus Lamponius, Publius Vettius Scato, Gaius Vidacilius, and Titus Lafrenius—were relative New Men of present importance. In Italian dining rooms and Italian studies the talks had proceeded, and the fact that almost all the talking was done in Latin was not felt to be sufficient reason to forgive Rome her crimes.

The concept of a united Italian nation was not perhaps a novel one, but certainly it had never before been discussed as a viable alternative by the various Italian leaders. In the past, all hopes had been pinned upon gaining the full Roman franchise, becoming a part of a Rome which stretched undivided along the whole length and breadth of Italy; so senior was Rome in her partnership with her Italian Allies that they had thought along Roman lines—wanted to espouse Roman institutions, wanted to see their blood, their fortunes, their lands become a full and equal part of Rome.

Some of those who participated in the talks blamed Arausio, but there were those who blamed the mounting lack of support for the Italian cause among the Latin Rights communities, who now were beginning to regard themselves as a cut above mere Italians. Those blaming the Latin Rights communities could point with truth to an ever-increasing enjoyment of Latin Rights exclusivity, a need in the Latin Rights people to keep one segment of the peninsular populace inferior to themselves.

Arausio of course had been the culmination of decades of a soldier mortality which had seen the entire peninsula grow shorter and shorter of men, with all the concomitant evils of farms and businesses abandoned or sold for debt, and too few children and men young enough to work hard. But that soldier mortality had equally affected Romans and Latins too, so could not bear the entire blame. There were festering resentments against Roman landlords—the rich men who lived in Rome and farmed vast tracts called *latifundia* using only slave labor. There were too many cases of Roman citizens blatantly abusing Italians—employing their power and influence to flog the undeserving, take women who did not belong to them, and confiscate smallholdings to swell their own lands.

Just what had swayed the majority of those talking Italian secession away from wanting to force Rome to give them full citizenship and toward the formation of a separate and independent nation was unclear, even to Silo. His own conviction that secession was the only way had sprung out of Arausio, but those with whom he talked had not been at Arausio. Perhaps, he thought, this new determination to break away from Rome stemmed from sheer tiredness, a rooted feeling that the days when Rome gave away her precious citizenship were over, that the situation as it was at the moment was the way things were always going to be in the future. Insult had piled on top of injury to a point where life under Rome looked to an Italian unbearable, intolerable.

In Gaius Papius Mutilus, the leader of the Samnite nation, Silo found a man who seized upon the possibility of secession almost frantically. For himself, Silo did not hate Rome or Romans, only his own people's predicament; but Gaius Papius Mutilus belonged to a people who had been Rome's most obdurate and implacable foes since the tiny Roman community athwart the salt route of the Tiber had first begun to show its teeth. Mutilus hated Rome and Romans with every string that tied his heart, with every thought that grew to consciousness—and every thought that lay below it. He was a true Samnite, yearning to see every Roman ever born obliterated from the pages of history. Silo was Rome's adversary. Mutilus was Rome's enemy.

Like all congresses where the common cause was great enough to override every objection and every practical consideration, the Italian men who gathered at first merely to see if anything could be done quickly decided there was only one thing to be done— secede. However, every one of them knew Rome better than to think Italia could come into being without a war; for that reason, no one contemplated making any kind of declaration of independence for some years to come. Instead, the leaders of the Italian Allies concentrated upon preparing to make war upon Rome. It would require an enormous effort, huge sums of money—and more men than the years immediately after Arausio could possibly provide. A firm date was neither set nor mentioned; for the time being, while the Italian boy-children grew up, every atom of energy and money available was to go into the making of arms and armor, the stockpiling of sufficient quantities of war materials to make war with Rome—and a successful outcome—feasible.

Not much was ready to hand. Almost all the Italian soldier casualties had occurred far from Italy itself, and their arms and armor never seemed to reach home again, chiefly because it was

Rome picked them up from the battlefield whenever possible—and naturally Rome forgot to label them "Allied." Some arms could be legitimately purchased, but not nearly enough to equip the hundred thousand men Silo and Mutilus thought the new Italia would need to beat Rome. Therefore arming was a surreptitious business, and proceeded very slowly. Years would have to go by before the target could be met.

To make things more difficult, every undertaking had to be carried out beneath the noses of many people who would, did they learn what was going on, report immediately to someone Roman, or directly to Rome. The Latin Rights colonies clearly could not be trusted, any more than could wandering Roman citizens. So centers of activity and caches of equipment were concentrated in poor and remote areas far from Roman roads and travelers, far from Roman or Latin colonies. Every way the Italian leaders turned, they encountered mountainous difficulties and dangers. Yet the work of arming went on, and recently the work of training new soldiers had been added to it; for some Italian lads were growing up.

All of this secret knowledge Quintus Poppaedius Silo harbored as he slid easily into the mealtime conversation, and felt neither guilt nor anxiety because of it—who knew? Perhaps in the end it would be Marcus Livius Drusus who came up with the solution, peaceably and efficiently. Stranger things had happened!

"Quintus Servilius is leaving us for some months," said Drusus to the others in general; it was a good change of subject.

Was that a flash of joy in Livia Drusa's eyes? wondered Silo, who thought her a thoroughly nice woman, but had never been able to make up his mind what sort of woman she was—did she like her life, did she like Caepio, did she like living in her brother's house? Instinct told him no to all those questions, but he could not be sure. And then he forgot all about Livia Drusa, for Caepio was talking about what he was going to do.

". . . around Patavium and Aquileia especially," Caepio was saying. "Iron from Noricum—I shall try to acquire the Noricum iron concessions—can supply foundries built around Patavium and Aquileia. The most important thing is that these areas of eastern Italian Gaul are very close to huge forests of mixed trees ideal for making charcoal. There are whole stands of beech and elm ready to be coppiced, my agents tell me."

"Surely it's the availability of iron dictates the location of foundries," said Silo, now listening eagerly. "That's why Pisae and Populonia grew into foundry towns, isn't it? Because of the iron shipped directly from Ilva?"

"A fallacy," said Caepio, waxing articulate for once. "In actual fact, it's the availability of good charcoal-making trees makes Pisae and Populonia so desirable as foundry towns. The same will hold true in eastern Italian Gaul. The making of charcoal is a manufacturing process, and ironworks gulp down ten times the amount of charcoal they do of metal. That's why my project in eastern Italian Gaul is as much to do with establishing towns of charcoal-makers as it is towns of steel-makers. I shall buy land suitable for the building of houses and workshops, then persuade smiths and charcoal-makers to settle in my little towns. Work will go on much easier among a number of similar little businesses than where a man is surrounded by many unrelated businesses."

"But won't the competition between all these similar little businesses be deadly, and buyers too hard to find?" asked Silo, concealing his mounting excitement.

"I don't see why," said Caepio, who really had studied his subject, and had made surprising headway in it. "If, for instance, a *praefectus fabrum* belonging to an army is looking for—say, ten thousand shirts of mail, ten thousand helmets, ten thousand swords and daggers, and ten thousand spears—isn't he going to head for places where he can go from one foundry to another without needing to search a hundred back streets to find every single one? And won't it be easier for a man owning a nice little foundry with—say, ten free men and ten slaves working for him—to sell what he produces without crying his wares all over town, because his clients know where to go?"

"You're right, Quintus Servilius," said Drusus thoughtfully.

"The armies of the present do indeed require ten thousand steel thises and thats, and always in a hurry. It was different in the old days, when soldiers were men of property. On a lad's seventeenth birthday his *tata* gave him his mail-shirt, his helmet, his sword, his dagger, his shield and his spears; his mama gave him his *caligae*, the cover for his shield, his kitbag, his horsehair plume and his *sagum;* and his sisters knitted him warm socks and wove him six or seven tunics. For the rest of his life he kept his gear—and in most cases, when his own campaigning days were over, he passed his gear on to his son or his grandson. But since Gaius Marius enlisted the Head Count in our armies, nine out of every ten recruits can't even afford the price of a scarf to tie around their necks to prevent their mail-shirts from chafing—let alone have mothers and fathers and sisters able to fit them out like proper soldiers. All of a sudden we have whole armies of recruits as naked of military equipment as the least noncombatant in the old days. The demand has outstripped the supply—yet from somewhere it must be found! We cannot possibly send our legionaries into battle without the proper gear."

"This answers a question," said Silo. "I wondered why so many retired veterans were coming to me begging for loans to set themselves up in business as smiths! You are absolutely right, Quintus Servilius. It will be near enough to a generation before these projected steel centers of yours will have to start looking for something other than military gear to make. In fact, as leader of my people, I am scratching my head as to where to find arms and armor for the legions I have no doubt we'll be asked to furnish for Rome in the not far distant future. The same must be true for the Samnites—and probably for the other Italian peoples too."

"You should think of Spain," said Drusus to Caepio. "I imagine there must still be forests near the iron mines."

"In Further Spain, yes," said Caepio, grinning delightedly because he was suddenly the center of respectful attention, a novel experience for him. "The old Carthaginian mines of the Orospeda have long exhausted their timber resources, but all the new mines are in well-forested areas."

"How long will it be before your towns start producing?" asked Silo casually.

"In Italian Gaul, hopefully within two years. Of course," added Caepio quickly, "I have nothing to do with the *businesses* or the goods they produce. I wouldn't do anything which would incur displeasure from the censors. All I personally intend to do is to build the towns and then collect the rents—quite, quite proper for a senator."

"Laudable of you," said Silo ironically. "I hope you're going to situate your towns on good waterways as well as in close proximity to forests."

"I shall choose sites on navigable rivers," said Caepio.

"The Gauls are good smiths," said Drusus.

"But not organized enough to prosper as they ought," said Caepio, and looked smug, an expression he was beginning to produce regularly. "Once I organize them, they'll do much better."

"Commerce is your forte, Quintus Servilius, I see it clearly," said Silo. "You should abandon the Senate, become a knight. That way, you could own the foundries and charcoal works too."

"What, and have to deal with *people*?" asked Caepio, appalled. "No, no! Let others do that!"

"Won't you be collecting the rents in person?" asked Silo slyly, eyes directed at the floor.

"Certainly not!" cried Caepio, rising to the bait. "I am establishing a nice little company of agents in Placentia to do all *that*. It might be considered permissible for your cousin Aurelia to collect her own rents, Marcus Livius," he said to Drusus, "but personally I consider it in very poor taste."

There had been a time when the mere mention of Aurelia's name would have twisted Drusus's heart, for he had been one of the most ardent suitors for her hand; but these days, secure in the knowledge that he loved his wife, he could grin at his brother-in-law and say, carelessly, "Aurelia is impossible to measure by any standards other than her own. I think her taste impeccable."

All through this, the women had sat on their chairs without offering a single contribution to the conversation—not because they

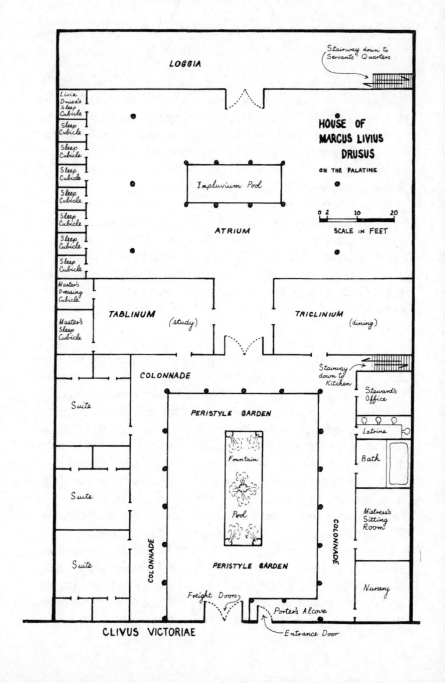

had nothing to say, but rather because their participation was not encouraged. They were used to sitting in silence.

After dinner Livia Drusa excused herself, pleading work which would not wait, and left her sister-in-law Servilia Caepionis in the nursery with little Drusus Nero. It was very dark and very cold, so Livia Drusa instructed a servant to bring her a wrap, swaddled herself in it, and walked through the atrium onto the loggia, where no one would think to look for her and she could enjoy an hour of peace. Alone. Wonderfully, thankfully alone.

So he was going away! At last he was going away! Even when he served as a quaestor he had chosen duty inside Rome, and never once in the three years his father had lived in exile before he died had Caepio ventured to Smyrna to see him. Save for that short period during the first year of their marriage when he had served as a tribune of the soldiers and survived the battle of Arausio suspiciously unscathed, Quintus Servilius Caepio had never been away from his wife.

What gnat was whining around in his mind at the moment Livia Drusa did not know—nor did she care, provided the gnat drove him to travel. Presumably his financial circumstances had finally become pinched enough to prod him into doing something to improve them, though many times through the years Livia Drusa had privately wondered whether her husband was truly as poor as he said he was. How her brother had put up with them, she did not know. Not only was his house not his own; he had even been obliged to take down his peerless collection of paintings. How horrified their father would have been! For their father had built this huge *domus* purely to display his works of art fittingly. *Oh, Marcus Livius, why did you force me to marry him?*

Eight years of marriage and two children hadn't reconciled Livia Drusa to her fate. The early years of the marriage, however, had been the worst, a descent into the slough of despond; once she reached its bottom she learned to cope better with her unhappiness, and she never had forgotten her brother's words to her when he had finally succeeded in breaking her:

"I expect you to behave toward Quintus Servilius as any young woman would who welcomed her marriage. You will let him know that you are pleased, and you will treat him with unfailing deference, respect, interest, and concern. At no time—even in the privacy of your bedroom after you are married—will you give Quintus Servilius the slightest indication that he is not the husband of your choice."

Drusus had marched her to the shrine in the atrium where the family gods were honored—Vesta of the hearth, the Di Penates of the pantry, and the Lar Familiaris—and made her swear a terrible oath that she would do as he had told her. The time when she had hated her brother for his action had long passed, of course. Maturity had done that, and constant exposure to a side of Drusus she had not known existed.

The Drusus of her childhood and adolescence was stern, aloof, indifferent to her—how afraid of him she had been! Only after the fall and exile of her father-in-law did she come to know what Drusus was really like. Or perhaps, she reasoned (for she too had that cool Livius Drusus head), Drusus had changed after the battle of Arausio—and after he grew fond of his wife. Certainly he had softened, become more approachable, though he never mentioned his forcing her to marry Caepio, nor unbound her from that frightful oath. Most of all, she admired him for his steadfast loyalty to her, his sister, and to Caepio, his brother-in-law—he never complained by word or look about their presence in his house. Which was why she had nearly choked this evening when Drusus had actually come back at Caepio for criticizing Quintus Poppaedius Silo.

How articulate Caepio had been tonight! Warmed to his theme, explained what he was doing quite logically and enthusiastically, seemed so far to have proceeded in a practical and businesslike way. Maybe Silo was right—maybe Caepio was by nature a commercial person, a knight businessman. What he planned to do sounded exciting. And profitable. Oh, how wonderful to live in our own house! thought Livia Drusa, who longed for it.

A huge burst of laughter erupted from the maw of the staircase leading from the loggia down to the servants' crowded quarters below; Livia Drusa started, shivered, squeezed herself very small in case the noise meant slaves would suddenly come scurrying across the loggia to the atrium door. Sure enough, up came a little group of men, still chuckling among themselves as they chattered away in Greek, some patois they spoke so rapidly Livia Drusa had no idea what the joke could be. They were so happy! Why? What did they possess she did not? Answer: a chance at freedom, the Roman citizenship, and the right to lead their own lives. They were paid, she was not; they were rich in friends and companionship, she was not; they could form intimate relationships among themselves without criticism or interference, she could not. That this answer was not quite accurate concerned Livia Drusa not at all; in her mind, it was the truth.

They didn't see her. Livia Drusa relaxed again. A gibbous moon, just waning from the full, had risen high enough now to illuminate the depths of the city of Rome. She turned on her marble bench, put her arms on the balustrade, and looked at the Forum Romanum. Drusus's house was right on the corner of the Germalus of the Palatine where the Clivus Victoriae turned at right angles to run along the length of the Forum Romanum, so it possessed a wonderful view; in earlier days the view had extended to the left into the Velabrum when the vacant space of the *area Flacciana* had existed next door, but now the huge porticus Quintus Lutatius Catulus Caesar had erected on it reared columns skyward, and blocked that old lookout. For the rest, nothing had changed. The house of Gnaeus Domitius Ahenobarbus Pontifex Maximus still jutted further forward below Drusus's house, affording her sight of its loggia.

This was Rome without her daytime vividness, the rich colors in which everything was painted bled to greys and glitters. Not that the city was quiet; torches flickered everywhere in dark alleys, the rumblings of carts and the bellowing of oxen drifted up to her ears because many of Rome's shops and tradesmen took advantage of the lack of crowds night afforded, and had their goods delivered then. A group of drunken men weaved across the open space of the lower Forum, singing a popular ditty about—what else?—love. Quite a large escort of slaves shepherded a carefully closed litter between the Basilica Sempronia and the temple of Castor and Pollux—some important lady going home after a dinner party, no doubt. A tomcat on the prowl squalled his come-hithers at the moon and a dozen dogs began to bark, all of which amused the drunks so much that one of them lost his footing as they skirted the round black well of the Comitia, and tumbled down its tiers amid shouts of mirth from his friends.

Livia Drusa's eyes strayed back to the loggia of the Domitius Ahenobarbus house below, and rested upon its vacant expanse wistfully. A long time ago, it seemed—before her marriage, at any rate—she had been cut off from all companionship, even of girls her own age, and had filled her empty life with books; and fallen in love with someone, someone she had no hope of meeting. In those days she used to sit here during the hours of sunlight and watch that balcony beneath for the tall, red-haired young man who had so strongly attracted her that she wove whole fantasies around him, pretending he was King Odysseus of Ithaca and she was his faithful Queen Penelope, waiting for him to come home. For years the very infrequent glimpses she caught of him—for he was not a frequent visitor, she decided—were sufficient to fuel this private, tormenting enchantment, a state of mind that had persisted after her marriage, and only served to increase her misery. His identity eluded her, though she knew he was not a Domitius Ahenobarbus, for that was a squat family, albeit red-haired; all the Famous Families had a look about them, and he did not look like an Ahenobarbus.

Never would she forget the day of her disillusionment; it had been the day her father-in-law was convicted of treason in the Plebeian Assembly; the day her brother's steward, Cratippus, had hurried across to the other side of the Palatine and plucked her and baby Servilia out of the Servilius Caepio house, brought them here for safety. Quite a day, that one had been! For the first time, watching Servilia Caepionis with Drusus, she saw how a wife could play up to her husband; for the first time she realized women were not always excluded from serious family discussions; for the first time she had tasted unwatered wine. And then, when all the upheavals had seemed over and done with, Servilia Caepionis had supplied the tall, red-haired Odysseus on the loggia below with a name. Marcus Porcius Cato Salonianus. No king, he! Not even a true nobleman, but the grandson of a Tusculan peasant on one side and the great-grandson of a Celtiberian slave on the other.

In that moment, Livia Drusa had grown up.

"There you are!" said Caepio's voice sharply. "What are you doing out here in the freezing cold, woman? Come inside!"

Obediently Livia Drusa rose and went to her hateful bed.

 At the end of February, Quintus Servilius Caepio left on his journey, having told Livia Drusa that she must not expect him back for at least a year, perhaps longer. That had surprised her until he explained that it was essential, having sunk all his money into this venture in Italian Gaul, that he stay there to supervise every aspect of it. His sexual attentions had been many and prolonged, for—he said—he wanted a son, and it would keep her occupied in his absence if she became pregnant. During the earlier years of her marriage these intimacies had distressed her greatly, but after she learned the name of her adored red-haired King Odysseus, Caepio's lovemaking had simply become a boring inconvenience unattended by revulsion. Saying nothing to her husband of her own plans to fill in the time while he was away, she waved him off; she then waited one market interval of eight days before seeking an interview with her brother.

"Marcus Livius, I have a great favor to ask," she began, seated in his client's chair; she looked surprised, laughed. "Ye gods! Do you know this is the first time I've sat here since the day you persuaded me to marry Quintus Servilius?"

Drusus's olive skin darkened. He looked down at his hands, folded on his desk. "Eight years ago," he said neutrally.

"Yes, it was," she said, then laughed again. "However, I did not sit myself here today to talk about what happened eight years ago, brother. I'm here to ask a favor."

"If I can grant it, Livia Drusa, I would be very pleased," he said, grateful that she was letting him off so lightly.

Many times he had longed to apologize to her, beg her to forgive him for that dreadful mistake; her constant unhappiness had not been lost on him, and it was he who had had to admit to himself that hers had been the true reading of Caepio's dreary character. But pride had stoppered up his mouth, and always at the back of his mind had lurked the conviction that, in marrying her to Caepio, he had at least averted any possibility she might turn out like her mother. That frightful woman had embarrassed him for years by turning up—in conversation, at least—as someone's butt after a particularly sordid love affair had foundered, as they always, always did.

"Well?" he prompted when Livia Drusa did not go on.

Frowning, she licked her lips, then raised her lovely eyes to look directly at him. "Marcus Livius, for a very long time I have been aware that my husband and I have outstayed our welcome."

"You're wrong," he countered quickly, "but if in any way I have inadvertently given you that impression, then I apologize. Truly, sister, you have always been welcome—and you always will be welcome in my house."

"I thank you. However, what I said is a fact. You and Servilia Caepionis have never had a chance to be alone, which may be one reason why she has failed to conceive."

He winced. "I doubt it."

"I do not." She leaned forward earnestly. "Times are tranquil at the moment, Marcus Livius. You have no office in the government and you have had little Drusus Nero long enough to make the possibility of a child of your own much greater. So the old women say—and I believe them."

Finding all this painful, he said, "Get to the point, do!"

"The point is that while Quintus Servilius is away, I would very much like to remove myself and my children to the country," said Livia Drusa. "You have a little villa near Tusculum, which isn't more than half a day's journey from Rome. No one has lived in the house for years. Please, Marcus Livius, give it to me for a while! Let me live on my own!"

His eyes searched her face, looking for any evidence that she was planning some indiscretion. But he could find none.

"Did you ask Quintus Servilius?"

Keeping her eyes looking into his, Livia Drusa said steadily, "Of course I did."

"He didn't mention it to me."

"How extraordinary!" She smiled. "But how like him!"

That provoked a laugh. "Well, sister, I can't see why not, since Quintus Servilius said yes. As you say, Tusculum isn't very far from Rome. I can keep an eye on you."

Face transfigured, Livia Drusa thanked her brother profusely.

"When do you want to go?"

She rose to her feet. "At once. May I ask Cratippus to organize everything?"

"Of course." He cleared his throat. "Actually, Livia Drusa, you'll be missed. So will your daughters."

"After putting an extra tail on the horse and changing the bunch of grapes to rather lurid apples?"

"It could as easily have been Drusus Nero in a couple of years' time," he said. "If you think about it, we were lucky. The paint was still wet, no harm was done. Father's works of art are quite safe in the cellar, and there they'll stay until the last child is fully grown."

He rose too; they walked together down the colonnade to the mistress's sitting room, where Servilia Caepionis was busy on her loom, weaving blankets for little Drusus Nero's new bed.

"Our sister wants to leave us," said Drusus, entering.

There could be no mistaking his wife's dismay—nor her guilty pleasure. "Oh, Marcus Livius, that's too bad! Why?"

But Drusus beat a quick retreat, leaving his sister to do her own explaining.

"I'm taking the girls to the villa at Tusculum. We're going to live there until Quintus Servilius comes home again."

"The villa at Tusculum?" asked Servilia Caepionis blankly. "But my dear Livia Drusa, it's a tumbledown wreck of a place! It belonged to the first Livius, I believe. There's no bath or latrine, no decent kitchen, and it won't be big enough."

"I don't care," said Livia Drusa. She lifted her sister-in-law's hand and held it to her cheek. "Dear lady of this house, I would live in a hovel for the chance to be the lady of a house! I don't say that to hurt you, nor is it a reproach. From the day your brother and I moved in here, you have been graciousness itself. But you must understand my position. I want my own house. I want servants who don't call me *dominilla* and take no notice of anything I say because they've known me since I was a baby. I want a bit of land to walk on, a bit of freedom from the crush of this dreadful city. Oh, please, Servilia Caepionis, understand!"

Two tears rolled down the cheeks of the lady of the house, and her lip quivered. "I do understand," she said.

"Don't grieve, be happy for me!"

They embraced, in full accord.

"I shall find Marcus Livius and Cratippus at once," said Servilia Caepionis briskly, putting away her work and covering the loom against dust. "I insist that builders be hired to turn that antique villa into something comfortably livable for you."

But Livia Drusa would not wait. Three days later she had packed up her daughters, her many buckets of books, Caepio's very few servants, and set out for the farm at Tusculum.

Though she hadn't visited it since childhood, she found it quite unchanged—a small plastered house painted a bilious yellow, with no garden to speak of, no proper facilities, very little air or light inside, and no peristyle. However, her brother had not wasted time; the place already teemed with the employees of a local builder, who was there in person to greet her, and promised that within two months the house would be livable.

Thus Livia Drusa installed herself amid a controlled chaos—plaster dust, the noise of hammers and mallets and saws, a constant volley of instructions and queries shouted in the broad Latin of Tusculans who might live only fifteen miles from Rome, but rarely if ever went there. Her daughters reacted typically; half-past-four-year-old Lilla was entranced, whereas that composed and secretive child Servilia all too obviously loathed the house, the building activity, and her mother, not necessarily in that order. However, Servilia's mood was unobtrusive; Lilla's boisterous participation in everything only added to the chaos.

Having placed her daughters under the charge of their nurse and Servilia's dour old tutor, Livia Drusa set out the next morning to walk through the peace and beauty of the deep winter countryside, hardly able to believe that she had thrown off the shackles of a long imprisonment.

Though the calendar said it was spring, deep winter it was. Gnaeus Domitius Ahenobarbus Pontifex Maximus had not prodded the College of Pontifices he headed to do their duty and keep the shorter calendar year in time with the seasons. Not that Rome and her environs had endured a harsh winter that year; of snow there had been little, and the Tiber hadn't frozen over at all. Thus the temperature was well above freezing, the wind was no more than an occasional breath, and there was good grass underfoot.

Happier than she had ever been in all her life, Livia Drusa wandered across the home field, clambered over a low stone wall, walked carefully around the perimeter of a field already under the plough, climbed another stone wall, and entered a place of grass and sheep. All bound up in their leather coats, the silly creatures galloped away from her when she tried to call them to her; shrugging and smiling, she walked on.

Beyond that field she found a boundary stone painted white, and beside it a little towered shrine, the ground before it still marked with the blood of some sacrifice. In the lowest branches of an overhanging tree there bobbed little woolen dolls, little woolen balls, and heads of garlic, all looking weatherworn and drab. Beyond the shrine was a clay pot turned upside down; curiously Livia Drusa lifted it, then dropped it back in a hurry; under it lay the decomposing body of a big toad.

Too citified to understand that if she went any further she would be trespassing—and that she was now on the land of someone scrupulous in his attentions to the gods of the soil and of boundaries—Livia Drusa strolled on. When she found the first crocus she knelt to look at its vivid yellow flower, rose again to gaze into the naked branches of the trees with an appreciation so new that trees might have been invented just for her.

An orchard of apples and pears came next, some of the pears still unpicked, a temptation to which Livia Drusa happily succumbed, finding her pear so sweet and juicy her hands became a sticky mess. Somewhere she could hear water running, so she walked through the carefully tended trees in the direction of the sound until she came upon a little brook. Its water was icy, but she didn't care; she dabbled her hands and laughed softly to herself as she shook them dry in the sun, now high enough to have warmed the air. Off came her *palla* wrap; still kneeling beside the stream, she spread the huge piece of cloth out and folded it into a rectangle she could carry, then rose to her feet. And saw him.

He had been reading. The scroll was in his left hand, curled up again because he had quite forgotten it, so fixedly was he staring at this invader of his orchard. King Odysseus of Ithaca! Encountering his eyes, Livia Drusa caught her breath, for they were the very eyes of King Odysseus, large and grey and beautiful.

"Hello," she called, smiling at him without shyness or any kind of discomfort. Having watched him for so many years from her balcony, he seemed indeed the wanderer returned at this moment, a man she knew at least as well as Queen Penelope had known her King Odysseus. So she threw the folded *palla* over her arm and began to walk toward him, still smiling, still talking.

"I stole a pear," she said. "It was delicious! I didn't know pears hung so long on trees. Whenever I go out of Rome, I go to the seaside in summer, and it isn't the same."

He said nothing, just followed her approach with those grey and luminous eyes.

I still love you, she was saying within herself. I still love you!

I don't care if you're the progeny of a slave and a peasant. I love you. Like Penelope, I had forgotten love. But here you are again after so many years, and I still love you.

When she stopped, she was too close to him for this to be the chance encounter of two strangers; he could feel the warmth radiating from her body, and the big dark eyes looking now into his own were filled with recognition. With love. With welcome. It therefore seemed absolutely natural to step a very few inches closer to her, to put his arms around her. She put her face up and her arms about his neck, and both of them were smiling as they kissed. Old friends, old lovers, a husband and wife who had not seen each other for twenty years, torn apart by the machinations of others, divine and human. Triumphant in this reunion.

The sure strong touch of his hands was a recognition, she had no need to tell him where to go, what was fitting; he was the king of her heart, and always had been. As gravely as a child placed in charge of some precious treasure, she bared and offered him her breasts, went about him taking his clothes while he spread out her wrap upon the ground, then lay down beside him. Trembling her pleasure, she kissed his neck and sucked the lobe of his ear, held his face between her hands and found his mouth once more, caressed his body blissfully, mumbled a thousand endearments against his tongue.

Fruit, sweet and sticky—thin bare twigs tangled amid a bluest sky—the jerky pain of hair caught too tight—a tiny bird with stilled wings glued to the tendrils of a webby cloud—a huge lump of packed-down exultation struggling to be born, then suddenly soaring free, free—oh, in such an ecstasy!

They lay together on their clothing for hours, keeping each other warm with skin on skin, smiling foolishly at each other, amazed at finding each other, innocent of transgression, enmeshed in the deliciousness of all kinds of discoveries.

They talked too. He was married, she learned—to one Cuspia, daughter of a *publicanus,* and his sister was married to Lucius Domitius Ahenobarbus, the younger brother of the Pontifex Maximus; dowering his sister had been a staggering expense, one he had only managed to achieve by marrying his Cuspia, whose father was enormously wealthy. There were as yet no children, for he too could find nothing to admire or love in his spouse—she was, he said, already complaining to her father that he neglected her.

When Livia Drusa told him who she was, Marcus Porcius Cato Salonianus grew very still.

"Are you angry?" she asked, lifting herself up to look down on him anxiously.

He smiled, shook his head. "How can I be angry when the gods have answered me? They set you down here on the lands of my forefathers *for me*. The moment I saw you at the stream, I knew it. And if you are connected to so many powerful families, it must be yet another sign that I am indeed favored."

"Did you truly not have any idea who I am?"

"None at all," he said, not quite happily. "I've never seen you in my life."

"Not even once? Did you never walk out onto Gnaeus Domitius's balcony and see me on my brother's balcony above?"

"Never," he said.

She sighed. "I saw you many times over many years."

"I'm profoundly glad you liked what you saw."

She cuddled into his shoulder. "I fell in love with you when I was sixteen years old," she said.

"How perverse the gods are!" he said. "Had I looked up and seen you, I wouldn't have rested until I married you. And we would have many children, and neither of us would be in this awful situation now."

To turn and cling together was instinctive, a mixture of pleasure and pain.

"Oh, it will be terrible if they find out!" she cried.

"Yes."

"It isn't fair."

"No."

"Then they must never find out, Marcus Porcius."

He writhed. "We should be together with honor, Livia Drusa, not guiltily."

"There is honor," she said gravely. "It's only our present circumstances make it seem otherwise. I am not ashamed."

He sat up, hugged his knees. "Nor I," he said, and took her back into his arms and held her until she protested, for she wanted to look at him, so beautifully put together, long-armed and long-legged, skin cream and hairless, his scant body hair the same fiery color as on his head. His body was well knit and muscular, his face bony. Truly King Odysseus. Or *her* King Odysseus, anyway.

It was late afternoon when she left him, having arranged that they would meet at the same place and time on the morrow, and they took so long making their farewells that by the time she reached Drusus's house, the builders had done with their work for the day. Her steward, Mopsus, was on the point of marshaling everyone to start looking for her. So happy and uplifted was she that realities of this nature hadn't even occurred to her; standing in the fading light blinking stupidly at Mopsus, she had not the wits to think of reason or excuse.

Her appearance was appalling. The hair hung down her back in a tangle liberally larded with bits of twig and grass, great smears of mud marred her clothes, the sensible closed shoes she had worn now dangled by their straps from her hand, her face and arms were dirty, her feet covered in mud.

"*Domina, domina*, what happened?" cried the steward. "Have you had a fall?"

Her wits returned. "Indeed I have, Mopsus," she answered cheerily. "In fact, I fell about as far as I could, and live."

Surrounded by clucking servants, she was swept into the house. An old bronze tub was produced, put in her sitting room, filled with warm water. Lilla, who had been crying because Mama was missing, trotted off now in the wake of her nurse to eat a delayed dinner, but Servilia followed her mother unobtrusively and stood in the shadows while a girl unfastened the clasps of Livia Drusa's gown, clicking her tongue at the state of Livia Drusa's body, dirtier than her clothes.

When the girl turned away to see that the water was the right temperature, Livia Drusa, naked and unashamed, stretched her arms above her head so slowly and voluptuously that the unnoticed little girl beside the door understood the meaning of the gesture on some utterly primitive, atavistic level only time would elucidate. Down came the arms, up went their hands to cup the full but lovely breasts; Livia Drusa's thumbs played with her nipples for a moment, while Livia Drusa's mouth smiled and smiled and smiled. Then she stepped into her bath, turned so her girl could trickle water down her back from a sponge, and so didn't see Servilia open the door and slip out.

At dinner—which Servilia was allowed to share with her mother—Livia Drusa chattered away happily about the pear she had eaten, the first crocus, the dolls in the tree above the boundary shrine, the little brook she had found, even details of an imaginary fall many feet down a steep and muddy bank. Servilia sat, eating daintily, her expression neutral. An outsider looking at them would have judged the mother's face that of a happy child, and the child's face that of a troubled mother.

"Does my happiness puzzle you, Servilia?" the mother asked.

"It's very odd, yes," said the child composedly.

Livia Drusa leaned forward across the small table at which both of them sat and tucked a strand of black hair out of her daughter's face, genuinely interested for the first time in this miniature reproduction of herself. Back rushed the past, her own desolate childhood.

"When I was your age," Livia Drusa said, "my mother never took any notice of me. It was Rome responsible. And just recently I realized Rome was having the same effect on me. That's why I moved us to the country. That's why we're going to be living on our own until *tata* comes home. I'm happy because I'm free, Servilia! I can forget Rome."

"I like Rome," said Servilia, sticking out her tongue at the various plates of food. "Uncle Marcus has a better cook."

"We'll find a cook to please you, if that's your worst complaint. *Is* it your worst complaint?"

"No. The builders are."

"Well, they'll be gone in a month or two, then things will be more peaceful. Tomorrow"—she remembered, shook her head, smiled—"no, the next day—we'll go walking together."

"Why not tomorrow?" asked Servilia.

"Because I have to have one more day all to myself."

Servilia slipped from her chair. "I'm tired, Mama. May I go to bed now, please?"

And so began the happiest year of Livia Drusa's life, a time when nothing really mattered save love, and love was called Marcus Porcius Cato Salonianus, with a little bit left over for Servilia and Lilla.

Very quickly they settled into a pattern, for of course Cato didn't spend much time on his Tusculan farm—or hadn't, until he met Livia Drusa. It was necessary that they find a more secure rendezvous, one where they wouldn't be seen by a farm worker or a wandering shepherd, and one where Livia Drusa could keep herself clean, tidy, presentable. This Cato solved by evicting a family who lived in a tiny secluded cottage on his estate, and announcing to his world that he would use it as a retreat, as he wanted to write a book. The book became his excuse for everything, especially for protracted absences from Rome and his wife; following in the footsteps of his grandfather, this opus was to be an extremely detailed compendium about Roman rural life, and would incorporate every kind of country spell, rite, prayer, superstition, and custom of a religious nature, then would go on to explain modern farming techniques and activities. No one in Rome found its genesis at all surprising, given Cato's family and background.

Whenever he could be in Tusculum they met at the same hour each morning, for Livia Drusa had established this as her own private and personal time because the children were doing their lessons, and they parted—an emotional business—at noon. Even when Marcus Livius Drusus came down to see how his sister was faring and how the renovations to the farmhouse were proceeding, Livia Drusa continued her "walks." Of course she was so obviously happy in such a simple and artless way that Drusus could only applaud his sister for her good sense in relocating; had she displayed signs of nervousness or guilt, he might have wondered. But she never did, because she thought of her relationship with Cato as just, right, proper—deserved and deserving.

Naturally there were awkwardnesses, especially in the beginning. To Livia Drusa, the chief one was her beloved's dubious ancestry. This no longer worried her to the extent it had when Servilia Caepionis had first explained who he was, but it did niggle at her still. Luckily she was too intelligent to tax him with it openly. Instead, she sought ways to bring the subject up that would not give him reason to think she looked down on him—though of course she did look down on him. Oh, not with patronization or malice! Only with a regret founded in the security of her own impeccable ancestry; a wish that he too could participate in this most Roman of all securities.

His grandfather was the illustrious Marcus Porcius Cato Censorius—Cato the Censor. Of wealthy Latin stock, the Porcii Prisci had been sufficiently prominent to have held the Public Horse of Roman knighthood for several generations when Cato the Censor was born; however, though they enjoyed the full citizenship and knight's status, they lived in Tusculum rather than in Rome, and had harbored no aspirations of a public nature.

Her beloved, she quickly discovered, did not consider his ancestry dubious at all, for, as he said to her,

"The whole myth originated in my grandfather's character—he masqueraded as a peasant after some rarefied patrician sneered at him when he was a seventeen-year-old cadet, early in Hannibal's war. The peasant pose delighted him so much he never changed it—and we think he was quite right to do so, if for no other reason than that New Men come and go and are forgotten, but who could ever forget Cato the Censor?"

"The same might be said of Gaius Marius," Livia Drusa ventured diffidently.

Her beloved reared back as if she had bitten him. "*That* man?

Now he's a genuine New Man—an outright peasant! My grandfather had *ancestors*! He was only a New Man in that he was the first of his family to sit in the Senate."

"How can you know your grandfather only posed as a peasant?"

"From his private letters. We still have them."

"Doesn't the other branch of your family have his papers? After all, it's the senior branch."

"The Liciniani? Don't even mention them!" said Cato in tones of disgust. "It is *our* branch, the Saloniani, who will shine the brighter when the historians of tomorrow write about the Rome of our time. *We* are the true heirs of Cato the Censor! *We* put on no airs and graces, *we* honor the kind of man Cato the Censor was—a great man, Livia Drusa!"

"Yet masqueraded as a peasant."

"Indeed! Rough, bluff, outspoken, full of the old ways, a real Roman," said Cato, eyes shining. "Do you know, he drank the same wine his slaves drank? He never plastered his farmsteads or his country villas, he wouldn't have a piece of tapestry or purple cloth in his Roman house, and he never paid more than six thousand sesterces for a slave. We of the Saloniani have continued in his tradition, we live the same way."

"Oh, dear!" said Livia Drusa.

But he didn't notice this evidence of dismay, he was too involved in explaining to his little Livian love how wonderful a man Cato the Censor had been. "How could he really have been a peasant when he became the best friend of a Valerius Flaccus—and upon moving to Rome, was the best orator and advocate of his or any other time? To this day, even overrated experts like Crassus Orator and old Mucius Scaevola the Augur admit that his rhetoric was peerless, that no one has ever used aphorism and hyperbole better! And look at his written words! Superb! My grandfather was educated in the grand manner, and spoke and wrote a Latin so well thought out that he never needed to draft."

"I can see I must read him," said Livia Drusa, ever so slightly dryly; her tutor had deemed Cato the Censor beneath her attention.

"Do!" said Cato eagerly, putting his arms around her, drawing her body between his legs. "Start with his *Carmen de Moribus*, it will give you an idea of how moral a man he was, how properly Roman. Of course, he was the first Porcius to bear the cognomen Cato—until then, the Porcii had been cognominated Priscus—and doesn't that tell you how ancient our stock is, that it was *called* Ancient? Why, my grandfather's grandfather was paid the price of *five* Public Horses killed under him while fighting for Rome!"

"It's the Salonianus concerns me, not the Priscus or the Cato. Salonius was a Celtiberian slave, was he not? Whereas the senior branch can claim descent from a noble Licinia, and from the third daughter of the great Aemilius Paullus and Scipio's eldest Cornelia."

He was frowning now; this statement definitely smacked of Livian snobbishness. But she was gazing up at him wide-eyed and adoring, and he was so very much in love with her; it wasn't her poor little fault that she had not been properly informed about the Porcii Catones. It was up to him to convert her.

"Surely you know the story of Cato the Censor and Salonia," he said, resting his chin on her shoulder.

"No, I don't, *meum mel*. Tell me, please."

"Well, my grandfather didn't marry for the first time until he was forty-two. By then he had been consul, won a great victory in Further Spain, and celebrated a triumph—*he* wasn't greedy! *He* never took a share of the spoils or sold the captured prisoners for his own pocket! *He* gave everything to his soldiers, and their descendants still love him for it," said Cato, so enamored of his grandfather that he had forgotten the point of his story.

She proceeded to remind him. "So it was at the age of forty-two that he married the noble Licinia."

"That's right. He had one child by her, his son Marcus Licinianus, though it seems he was very attached to Licinia. I don't know why there weren't more children. Anyway, Licinia died when my grandfather was seventy-seven years old. After her death he took one of the household slave girls into his bed and kept her there. His son Licinianus and his son's wife, the high-born lady you've already referred to, were living in his house, naturally. And they were outraged by his action. It appears he made no secret of it, and permitted the slave to strut around as if she owned the place. Soon all of Rome knew what was going on, because Marcus Licinianus and Aemilia Tertia told everybody. Everybody, that is, except Cato the Censor. But of course he found out what they were saying all over the city, and instead of asking them why they had said nothing to *him* of their outrage, my grandfather quietly dismissed the slave girl very early one morning, and set off for the Forum without telling them the girl was gone."

"How very odd!" said Livia Drusa.

Cato chose not to comment upon her comment, but went on. "Now Cato the Censor had a freedman client named Salonius, a Celtiberian from Salo who had been one of his slave scribes.

" 'Ho there, Salonius!' said my grandfather when he reached the Forum. 'Have you found a husband for that pretty daughter of yours yet?'

" 'Why, no, *domine,*' said Salonius, 'but rest assured when I do find a good man for her, I shall bring him to you and ask for your judgment and consent.'

" 'There's no need to look any further,' said my grandfather. 'I have a good husband for her—a prince of fellows! Comfortable fortune, stainless reputation, excellent family—everything desirable! Except—well, I'm afraid he's a bit long in the tooth. Healthy, mind you! But even the most charitably inclined would have to say he's a very old man.'

" '*Domine,* if he is your choice, how can he do otherwise than please me?' Salonius asked. 'My daughter was born while I was your slave, and her mother was your slave too. When you put the cap of liberty on my head, you were kind enough to free my whole family. But my daughter is still your dependent—as I am, and my wife, and my son. Have no fear, Salonia is a good girl. She will marry any man you've taken the time and trouble to find for her, no matter what his age.'

" 'Oh, terrific, Salonius!' cried my grandfather, clapping him on the back. 'He's me!' "

Livia Drusa stirred. "That's bad grammar," she said. "I thought Cato the Censor's Latin was perfect?"

"*Mea vita, mea vita,* have you no sense of humor at all?" asked Cato, staring. "He was joking! He wanted to make light of it, is all! Salonius was flabbergasted, of course. He couldn't believe he was being offered a marriage alliance with a noble house which could boast a censor and a triumph!"

"I'm not surprised he was flabbergasted," said Livia Drusa.

Cato hurried on. "My grandfather assured Salonius that he was absolutely serious, the girl Salonia was fetched, and she and my grandfather were married at once, as the day was auspicious.

"But when Marcus Licinianus heard of it an hour or two later—the word flew round Rome!—he gathered a host of his friends, and they went en masse to Cato the Censor.

" 'Is it because we disapproved of your slave girl mistress that you disgrace our house still further by offering me such a step-mother?' asked Licinianus, very angry.

" 'How can I disgrace you, my son, when I am about to prove what a formidable man I am by siring more sons at my advanced age?' asked my grandfather, his manner lordly. 'Would you have me marry a noblewoman when I am closer to eighty than I am to seventy? An alliance like that would not be appropriate. In marrying the daughter of my freedman, I am making a marriage suitable to my age and needs.' "

"What an extraordinary thing to do!" said Livia Drusa. "He did it to vex Licinianus and Aemilia Tertia, of course."

"So we Saloniani think," said Cato.

"And did they all continue to live in the same house?"

"Certainly. Marcus Licinianus died not long afterward, however—most people thought he suffered a broken heart. And that left Aemilia Tertia alone in the house with her father-in-law and his new wife, Salonia, a fate she richly deserved, in my opinion. Her father being dead, she couldn't go home, you see."

"Salonia, I gather, bore your father," said Livia Drusa.

"She did indeed," said Cato Salonianus.

"But don't you feel it keenly, being the grandson of a woman who was born a *slave*?" asked Livia Drusa.

Cato blinked. "What's to feel so keenly?" he asked. "All of us have had to start somewhere! And it seems the censors agreed with my grandfather Cato the Censor, who maintained that his blood was noble enough to sanctify the blood of any slave. They've never tried to exclude the Saloniani from the Senate. Salonius came from good Gallic stock. If he had been Greek, now—*that* was something my grandfather would never have done! He hated Greeks."

"Have you plastered the farmsteads?" asked Livia Drusa, beginning to move her hips against Cato.

"Of course not," he answered, breathing quickening.

"And now I know why we have to drink such dreadful wine."

"*Tace*, Livia Drusa!" said Cato, and turned her around.

To exist in the midst of a love so great its participants think it perfect usually leads to indiscretions, to careless remarks and eventual discovery; but Livia Drusa and Cato Salonianus pursued their affair with extraordinarily efficient secrecy. Had they been in Rome, of course, things would have been different; luckily sleepy Tusculum remained oblivious to the juicy scandal going on beneath its nose.

Within four weeks Livia Drusa knew she was pregnant, and knew too that the child was not Caepio's. The very day on which Caepio had left Rome, she had menstruated. Two weeks later she was lying in the arms of Marcus Porcius Cato Salonianus; and when the time came due, no period arrived. Two previous pregnancies had acquainted her with other signs that she was gravid, and now she was prey to them all. She was going to have the child of her lover, Cato, not the child of her husband, Caepio.

In a philosophical spirit, Livia Drusa decided to make no secret of her condition, relieved that the close proximity of Caepio to Cato in the time reference would protect her. What if she hadn't fallen so quickly? Oh, best not to think of that!

Drusus professed himself quite delighted, as did Servilia Caepionis; Lilla thought a baby brother would be tremendous fun, whereas Servilia just looked even more wooden than usual.

Of course Cato had to be told—only how much, exactly what? The cool Livius Drusus head came to the fore; Livia Drusa sat down to think things out. Terrible to cheat Cato of his child if it were a boy. And yet . . . And yet . . . The baby would undoubtedly be born before Caepio returned, and all the world would assume the baby belonged to Caepio. And if Cato's child were a boy, he would—did he bear the name Quintus Servilius Caepio—fall heir to the Gold of Tolosa. All fifteen thousand talents of it. He would be the richest man in Rome, and own a glorious name. More glorious by far than Cato Salonianus.

"I'm going to have a baby, Marcus Porcius," she said to Cato when next they met in the two-roomed cottage she had come to regard as her true home.

Alarmed rather than overjoyed, he stared at her fixedly. "Is it mine, or is it your husband's?" he asked.

"I don't know," said Livia Drusa. "Honestly, I don't know. I doubt if I will when he's finally born."

"He?"

"I'm carrying a boy."

Cato leaned back against the bedhead, closed his eyes, compressed his beautiful mouth. "Mine," he said.

"I don't know," she said.

"So you'll let everyone believe he's your husband's."

"I don't see what other choice I have."

His eyes opened, he turned his head to look at her, his face sad. "None, I know. I can't afford to marry you, even if you did have the opportunity to divorce. Which you won't, unless your husband comes home sooner than you expect. I doubt that. There's a pattern in all this. The gods are laughing their hardest."

"Let them! In the end, it's we men and women who win, not the gods," said Livia Drusa, and pushed herself up in the bed to kiss him. "I love you, Marcus Porcius. I hope he's yours."

"I hope he's not," said Cato.

* * *

Livia Drusa's condition made no difference to her routine; she continued to go for her morning walks, and Cato Salonianus continued to spend far more time on his grandfather's old place near Tusculum than ever before. They made love passionately and without any consideration for the foetus curled up in her womb, Livia Drusa maintaining whenever Cato demurred that so much love could never harm her baby.

"Do you still prefer Rome to Tusculum?" she asked her little daughter Servilia on an idyllic day in late October.

"Oh, yes," said Servilia, who had proven a hard nut to crack over the months—never forthcoming, never initiating a conversation, and answering her mother's questions so briefly that the dinner hour was largely a solo effort on Livia Drusa's part.

"Why, Servilia?"

Servilia eyed her mother's belly, which was huge. "For one thing, there are good doctors and midwives there," she said.

"Oh, don't worry about the baby!" cried Livia Drusa, and laughed. "He's very content. When his time comes, he'll be easy. I have at least a month to go."

"Why do you keep saying 'he,' Mama?"

"Because I know he's a boy."

"No one can really know until the baby comes out."

"What a little cynic you are," said Livia Drusa, amused. "I knew you were a girl and I knew Lilla was a girl. Why should I not be right this time too? I'm carrying him differently, and he talks to me differently."

"Talks to you?"

"Yes. You all talked to me while you were inside me."

The look Livia Drusa got was derisive. "Truly, Mama, you are queer! And getting queerer. How can a baby talk to you from the inside when babies don't talk for at least a year after they're born?"

"You're just like your father," said Livia Drusa, and pulled a hideous face.

"So you don't like *tata*! I didn't think you did," said Servilia, her tone more detached than accusatory.

She was seven now; old enough, thought her mother, for some hard facts. Oh, not couched in a way which would prejudice her against her father, but . . . Wouldn't it be lovely to make a real friend of this oldest child?

"No," said Livia Drusa deliberately, "I don't like *tata*. Do you want to know why?"

Servilia shrugged. "I daresay I'm going to be told why."

"Well, do *you* like him?"

"Yes, yes! He's the best person in the world!"

"Oh . . . Then I have to tell you why I don't like him. If I don't, you'll resent the way I feel. I have justification."

"No doubt you think so."

"Darling, I never wanted to marry *tata*. Your Uncle Marcus forced me to marry him. And that's a bad start."

"You must have had a choice," said Servilia.

"None at all. We rarely do."

"I think you ought to have accepted the fact that Uncle Marcus knows better than you about everything. I find nothing wrong with his choice of husband for you," said the seven-year-old judge.

"Oh, dear!" Livia Drusa stared at her daughter in despair. "Servilia, we can't always dictate whom we like and whom we dislike. I happened to dislike *tata*. I always had disliked him, from the time I was your age. But our fathers had arranged that we would marry, and Uncle Marcus saw nothing wrong in it. I couldn't make him understand that lack of love need not imperil a marriage, whereas dislike must ruin it from the beginning."

"I think you're stupid," said Servilia disdainfully.

Stubborn little mule! Livia Drusa labored on. "Marriage is a very intimate affair, child. To dislike one's husband or wife is a frightful burden to carry. There's a lot of touching in marriage. And when you dislike someone, you don't want them to touch you. Can you understand *that*?"

"I don't like anyone to touch me," said Servilia.

Her mother smiled. "Hopefully that will change! Anyway, I was made to marry a man I don't like to touch me. A man I dislike.

I still dislike him. And yet, some sort of feeling does grow. I love you, and I love Lilla. How then can I not love *tata* with at least a part of me, when he helped make you and Lilla?"

A look of distaste spread across Servilia's face. "Oh, really, Mama, you are stupid! First you say you dislike *tata,* then you say you love him. That's nonsense!"

"No, it's human, Servilia. Loving and liking are two utterly different emotions."

"Well, I intend to like and love the husband my *tata* chooses for me," Servilia announced in tones of great superiority.

"I hope time proves you right," said Livia Drusa, and tried to shift the emphasis of this uncomfortable conversation. "I am very happy at the moment. Do you know why?"

The black head went over to one side as Servilia considered, then she shook it while she nodded it. "I know why, but I don't know why you ought. You're happy because you're living in this awful place, and you're going to have a baby." The dark eyes gleamed. "And . . . I think you have a friend."

A look of terrible fear came into Livia Drusa's face, a look so alive and haunted that the child shivered in sudden excitement, in surprise; for the shaft had not been aimed in earnest, it was pure instinct arising out of her own keenly felt lack of a friend.

"Of course I have a friend!" cried the mother, wiping all fear from her face. She smiled. "He talks to me from inside."

"He won't be *my* friend," said Servilia.

"Oh, Servilia, don't say such things! He will be the best friend you ever have—a brother is, believe me!"

"Uncle Marcus is your brother, but he forced you to marry my *tata* when you didn't like him."

"A fact which doesn't make him any less my friend. Brothers and sisters grow up together. They know each other better than they ever know anyone else, and they learn to like each other," said Livia Drusa warmly.

"You can't learn to like someone you dislike."

"And there you're wrong. You can if you try."

Servilia produced a rude noise. "In that case, why haven't you learned to like *tata*?"

"He's not my brother!" cried Livia Drusa, wondering where she could go next. Why wouldn't this child cooperate? Why did she persist in being so obdurate, so obtuse? Because, the mother answered herself, she's her father's daughter. Oh, she is like him! Only cleverer by far. More cunning.

She said, "*Porcella*, all I want for you is that you be happy. And I promise you that I'll never let your *tata* marry you to someone you dislike."

"You mightn't be here when I marry," said the child.

"Why shouldn't I be?"

"Well, your mother wasn't, was she?"

"My mother is a different case entirely," said Livia Drusa, looking sorrowful. "She isn't dead, you know."

"I know *that*. She lives with Uncle Mamercus, but we don't talk to her. She's a loose woman," said Servilia.

"Where did you hear that?"

"From *tata*."

"You don't even know what a loose woman is!"

"I do so. She's a woman who forgets she's patrician."

Livia Drusa suppressed a smile. "That's an interesting definition, Servilia. Do you think you'll ever forget you're a patrician?"

"Never!" said the child scornfully. "I shall grow up to be everything my *tata* wants me to be."

"I didn't know you'd talked to *tata* so much!"

"We talked together all the time," lied Servilia, so well that her mother did not detect the lie. Ignored by both her parents, Servilia had aligned herself with her father early in her little life, as he seemed to her more powerful, more necessary than Livia Drusa. So her childish daydreams all revolved around enjoying a degree of intimacy with her father that common sense said would never happen; her father deemed daughters a nuisance, wanted a son. How did she know this? Because she slid like a wraith around her Uncle Marcus's house, listening to everyone from hidden corners, and hearing much she ought not have heard. And always, it had seemed to Servilia, it was her father who spoke like a true Roman, not her Uncle Marcus—and certainly not that Italian nobody Silo. Missing her father desperately, the child now feared the inevitable— that when her mother produced a boy, all hope of becoming her father's favorite would be over.

"Well, Servilia," said Livia Drusa briskly, "I am very glad that you can like your *tata*. But you'll have to display a little maturity when he comes home and you talk together again. What I've told you about my own dislike of him is a confidence. Our secret."

"Why? Doesn't he already know?"

Livia Drusa frowned, puzzled. "If you talk to your father so much, Servilia, you surely know he has not the slightest idea I dislike him. Your *tata* is not a perceptive kind of man. If he were, I may not have disliked him."

"Oh, well, we never waste time discussing *you*," said Servilia contemptuously. "We talk about important things."

"For a seven-year-old, you're very good at hurting people."

"I'd never hurt my *tata*," said the seven-year-old.

"Good for you! Remember what I said, however. What I've told you—or tried to tell you—today is our secret. I've honored you with a confidence, and I expect you to treat that confidence as a Roman patrician woman would—with respect."

When Lucius Valerius Flaccus and Marcus Antonius Orator were elected censors in April, Quintus Poppaedius Silo arrived at Drusus's house in a mood of great excitement.

"Oh, how wonderful to be able to talk without Quintus Servilius around!" exclaimed Silo with a grin; he never made any bones about his antipathy toward Caepio, any more than Caepio disguised his own antipathy.

Understanding this—and secretly agreeing with Silo even if family loyalties prevented his saying so—Drusus ignored the remark. "What's brought you to the boil?" he asked.

"Our censors! They're planning the most comprehensive cen-

sus ever taken, *and* they're going to change the way it's taken."
Silo raised his arms above his head exultantly. "Oh, Marcus Livius,
you have no idea how pessimistic I had become about the Italian
situation! I had begun to see no other way out of our dilemma than
secession and war with Rome."

This being the first Drusus had heard of Silo's fears, he sat very
straight in his chair and looked at Silo in alarm. "Secession?
War?" he asked. "Quintus Poppaedius, how can you even *say* such
words? Truly, the Italian situation will be solved by peaceful
means—I am dedicated to that end!"

"I know you are, my friend, and you must believe me when I say
that secession and war are far from what I want. Italy doesn't need
these alternatives any more than Rome does. The cost in money
and men would cripple our nations for decades afterward, no matter which side won. There are no spoils in civil wars."

"Don't even think of it!"

Silo wriggled on his chair, put his arms on Drusus's desk and
leaned forward eagerly. "That's just it, I'm not thinking of it! Because I've suddenly seen a way to enfranchise enough Italians to
make a big difference in how Rome feels about us."

"You mean a mass enfranchisement?"

"Not total enfranchisement, that would be impossible. But great
enough that once the thing is done, total enfranchisement will follow," said Silo.

"How?" asked Drusus, feeling a little cheated; he had always
thought of himself as ahead of Silo in the planning of full Roman
citizenship for the Italians, but it now appeared his complacence
had been mistaken.

"Well, as you know, the censors have always cared more about
discovering who and what live inside Rome than anything else.
The rural and provincial censuses have been tardy and completely
voluntary. A rural man wanting to register has had to go to the
duumviri of his municipality or town, or else journey to the nearest
place with municipal status. And in the provinces, a man has had
to go to the governor, which can be a long journey. Those who care

make the trip. Those who don't promise themselves they'll do it next time and simply trust that the clerks of the census transfer their names from the old rolls to the new—which mostly they do."

"I am quite aware of all this," said Drusus gently.

"It doesn't matter, I think you must hear it again right now. Our new censors, Marcus Livius, are a curious pair. I've never thought of Antonius Orator as particularly efficient, yet I suppose when you think about the kind of campaign he had to wage against the pirates, he must be. As for Lucius Valerius, *flamen Martialis* and consular, all I remember about him is what a mess he made of Saturninus's last year in office, when Gaius Marius was too ill to govern. However, they do say that there's no man born without a talent of some kind! Now it turns out that Lucius Valerius has a talent for— I suppose you'd have to call it logistics. I came in through the Colline Gate today, and I was walking across the lower Forum when Lucius Valerius appeared." Silo opened his strange eyes wide, and heaved a theatrical gasp. "Imagine my surprise when he hailed *me*, asked *me* if I had any time to talk! An Italian! Naturally I said I was entirely his to command. Turns out he wanted me to recommend him the names of some Roman citizen Marsi who would be willing to take a census of citizens and Latin Rights citizens in Marsic territory. By dint of looking stupid, in the end I got the whole story out of him. They—he and Antonius Orator, that is— intend to employ a special staff of what they're calling census clerks, and send them all over Italy and Italian Gaul late this year and early next year to conduct a census in the rural fastnesses. According to Lucius Valerius, your new censors are worried that the system as it has always been practised overlooks a large group of rural citizens and Latins who are unwilling to bestir themselves to register. What do you think of that?"

"What ought I to think?" asked Drusus blankly.

"First of all, that it's clear thinking, Marcus Livius."

"Certainly! Businesslike too. But what special virtue does it possess to have you wagging your tail so hard?"

"My dear Drusus, if we Italians can get at these so-called census clerks, we'll be able to ensure that they register large numbers of deserving Italians as Roman citizens! Not rabble, but men who ought by rights to have been Roman citizens years and years ago," said Silo persuasively.

"You can't do that," said Drusus, his dark face stern. "It's as unethical as it is illegal."

"It's morally right!"

"Morality is not at issue, Quintus Poppaedius. The law is. Every spurious citizen entered on the Roman rolls would be an illegal citizen. I couldn't countenance that, any more than you should. No, say no more! Think about it, and you'll see I'm right," said Drusus firmly.

For a long moment Silo studied his friend's expression, then flung his hands up in exasperation. "Oh, curse you, Marcus Livius! It would be so *easy!*"

"And just as easy to unravel once the deed was done. In registering these false citizens, you expose them to all the fury of Roman law—a flogging, their names inscribed on a blacklist, heavy fines," said Drusus.

A sigh, a shrug. "Very well then, I do see your point," said Silo grudgingly. "But it was a good idea."

"No, it was a bad idea." And from that stand, Marcus Livius Drusus would not be budged.

Silo said no more, but when the house—emptier these days— was stilled for the duration of the night, he took an example from the absent Livia Drusa without being aware he did, by going to sit outside on the balustrade of the loggia.

It had not occurred to him for one moment that Drusus would fail to see matters in the same way he did; had it, he would never have brought the subject up to Drusus. Perhaps, thought Silo sadly, this is one of the reasons why so many Romans say we Italians can never be Romans. I didn't understand Drusus's mind.

His position was now invidious, for he had advertised his intentions; he saw that he could not rely upon Drusus's silence. Would Drusus go to Lucius Valerius Flaccus and Marcus Antonius Orator on the morrow, tell them what had been said?

His only alternative was to wait and see. And he would have to work very hard—but very subtly!—to convince Drusus that what had been said was a bright idea conceived between the Forum and the lip of the Palatine, something foolish and unworthy that a night's sleep had squashed flat.

For he had no intention of abandoning his plan. Rather, its simplicity and finality only made its attractions grow. The censors *expected* many thousands of additional citizens to register! Why then should they query a markedly increased rural enrollment? He must travel at once to Bovianum to see Gaius Papius Mutilus the Samnite, then they must both travel to see the other Italian Ally leaders. By the time that the censors started seriously looking for their small army of clerks, the men who led the Italian Allies must be ready to act. To bribe clerks, to put clerks in office prepared to work secretly for the Italian cause, to alter or add to any rolls made available to them. The city of Rome he couldn't tamper with, nor did he particularly want to. Non-citizens of Italian status within the city of Rome were not worth having; they had migrated from the lands of their fathers to live more meanly or more fatly within the environs of a huge metropolis, they were seduced beyond redemption.

For a long time he sat on the loggia, thoughts chasing across his mind, ways and means and ends to achieve the ultimate end—equality for every man within Italy.

And in the morning he set out to erase that indiscreet talk from Drusus's mind, suitably penitent yet cheerful with it, as if it didn't really matter in the least to him now that Drusus had shown him the error of his ways.

"I was misguided," he said to Drusus, but in light tones. "A night's sleep told me you are absolutely right."

"Good!" said Drusus, smiling.

 Quintus Servilius Caepio did not come home until autumn of the following year, having traveled from Smyrna in Asia Province to Italian Gaul, then to

Utica in Africa Province, to Gades in Further Spain, and finally back to Italian Gaul. Scattering great prosperity in his wake. But gathering even more prosperity unto himself. And slowly, slowly, the Gold of Tolosa became translated into other things; big tracts of rich land along the Baetis River in Further Spain, apartment buildings in Gades, Utica, Corduba, Hispalis, Old Carthage and New Carthage, Cirta, Nemausus, Arelate, and every major town in Italian Gaul and the Italian peninsula; the little steel and charcoal towns he created in Italian Gaul were joined by textile towns; and wherever the farmlands were superlative, Quintus Servilius Caepio bought. He used Italian banks rather than Roman, Italian companies rather than Roman. And nothing of his fortune did he leave in Roman Asia Minor.

When he arrived at the house of Marcus Livius Drusus in Rome, his coming was unheralded. In consequence, he discovered that his wife and daughters were absent.

"Where are they?" he demanded of his sister.

"Where you said they could be," answered Servilia Caepionis, looking bewildered.

"What do you mean, I said?"

"They're still living on Marcus Livius's Tusculan farm," she said, wishing Drusus would come home.

"Why on earth are they living there?"

"For peace and quiet." Servilia Caepionis put her hand to her head. "Oh dear, I must have got it all muddled up! I was so sure Marcus Livius told me you had agreed to it."

"I didn't agree to anything," said Caepio angrily. "I've been away for over a year and a half, I come home expecting to be welcomed by my wife and children, and I find them absent! This is ridiculous! What are they doing in Tusculum?"

One of the virtues the men of the Servilii Caepiones most prided themselves upon was sexual continence allied to marital fidelity; in all his time away, Caepio had not availed himself of a woman. Consequently, the closer he got to Rome, the more urgent his expectations of his wife had become.

"Livia Drusa was tired of Rome and went to live in the old

Livius Drusus villa at Tusculum," said Servilia Caepionis, her heart beating fast. "Truly, I thought you had given your consent! But in all events, it has certainly done Livia Drusa no harm. I've never seen her look better. Or so happy." She smiled at her only brother. "You have a little son, Quintus Servilius. He was born last December, on the Kalends."

That was good news indeed, but not news capable of dispelling Caepio's annoyance at discovering his wife absent, his own satiation postponed.

"Send someone to bring them back at once," he said.

Drusus came in not long afterward to find his brother-in-law sitting stiffly in the study, no book in his hand, nor anything on his mind beyond Livia Drusa's delinquency.

"What's all this about Livia Drusa?" he demanded as Drusus came in, ignoring the outstretched hand and avoiding the brotherly salutation of a kiss.

Warned by his wife, Drusus took this calmly, simply went round his desk and sat down.

"Livia Drusa moved to my Tusculan farm while you were away," said Drusus. "There's nothing untoward in it, Quintus Servilius. She was tired of the city, is all. Certainly the move has benefited her, she's very well indeed. And you have a son."

"My sister said she was under the impression I had given my permission for this relocation," said Caepio, and blew through his nose. "Well, I certainly didn't!"

"Yes, Livia Drusa did say you'd given your permission," said Drusus, unruffled. "However, that's a minor thing. I daresay she didn't think of it until after you'd gone, and saved herself a great deal of difficulty by telling us you had consented. When you see her, I think you'll understand that she acted for the best. Her health and state of mind are better than I've ever known. Clearly, country life suits her."

"She will have to be disciplined."

Drusus raised one pointed brow. "That, Quintus Servilius, is none of my business. I don't want to know about it. What I do want to know about is your trip away."

* * *

When the servant escort arrived at Drusus's farm late in the afternoon of that same day, Livia Drusa was on hand to greet them. She betrayed no dismay, simply nodded and said she would be ready to travel to Rome at noon tomorrow, then summoned Mopsus and gave him instructions.

The ancient Tusculan farmstead was now something more like a country villa, equipped with a peristyle-garden and all hygienic conveniences; Livia Drusa hurried through its gracious proportions to her sitting room, closed the door and the shutters, threw herself on the couch and wept. It was all over; Quintus Servilius was home, and home to Quintus Servilius was the city. She would never be allowed to so much as visit Tusculum again. No doubt he now knew of her lie about obtaining his permission to move here—and that alone, given his temperament, would put Tusculum permanently out of bounds for her.

Cato Salonianus was not at his country villa because the Senate was in full session in Rome; it had been several weeks since Livia Drusa had last seen him. Tears over, she went to sit at her worktable, drew forward a sheet of paper, found her pen and ink, and wrote to him.

> My husband is home, and I am sent for. By the time you read this, I will be back within the walls of my brother's house in Rome, and under everyone's eye. How and when and where we may ever meet again, I do not know.
>
> Only how can I live without you? Oh, my most beloved, my dearest one, how will I survive? Not to see you—not to feel your arms, your hands, your lips—I cannot bear it! But he will hedge me round with so many restrictions, and Rome is such a public place—I despair of ever seeing you again! I love you more than I can tell. Remember that. I love you.

In the morning she went for her walk as always, informing her household that she would be back before noon, when all was to be ready for the journey to Rome. Usually she hurried to her rendez-vous, but this morning she dawdled, drinking in the beauty of the autumn countryside, committing every tree and rock and bush to memory for the lonely years to come. And when she reached the tiny whitewashed two-room house in which she and Cato had met for twenty-one months now, she drifted from one wall to another, touching everything with tenderness, sadness. Against hope she had hoped he would be there, but he was not; so she left the note lying in open view on their bed, knowing no one would dare enter the house.

And then it was off to Rome, being bounced and thrown about in the closed two-wheeled *carpentum* Caepio considered appropri-ate transportation for his wife. At first Livia Drusa had insisted upon having Little Caepio—as everyone called her son—inside the vehicle with her, but after two of the fifteen miles had been cov-ered, she gave the baby to a strong male slave and commanded that he be carried on foot. Servililla remained with her a little longer, then her stomach revolted against the rough journey and she had to be held out the carriage window so often that she too was bidden walk. Nothing would Livia Drusa have liked better than to join the pedestrians, but when she asked to do this, she was informed firmly that the master's instructions were clear on one point—she must ride inside the *carpentum* with windows covered.

Servilia, unlike Lilla, possessed a cast-iron digestion, so she too remained in the carriage; offered the chance to walk, she had an-nounced loftily that patrician women didn't walk. It was easy to see, thought Livia Drusa, that the child was very excited, though only liv-ing in close proximity to her for so long had given her mother this insight. Of external evidence there was little, just an extra glitter in the dark eyes and two creases in the corners of the small full mouth.

"I'm very glad you're looking forward to seeing *tata*," said Livia Drusa, hanging on to a strap for dear life when the *carpen-tum* lurched precariously.

"Well, I know you're not," said Servilia nastily.

"Try to understand!" cried the mother. "I so loved living in Tusculum, is all! I loathe Rome!"

"Hah," said Servilia.

And that was the end of the conversation.

Five hours after starting out, the *carpentum* and its big escort arrived at the house of Marcus Livius Drusus.

"I could have walked faster!" said Livia Drusa tartly to the *carpentarius* as he prepared to drive his hired vehicle away.

Caepio was waiting in the suite of rooms they had always lived in. When his wife walked through the door he nodded to her aloofly, and when she shepherded his two daughters in after her so that they might say hello to *tata* before going to the nursery, they too were dowered with an aloof, disinterested nod. Even when Servilia gave him her widest, shiest smile, he did not unbend.

"Off you go, and ask Nurse to bring little Quintus," said Livia Drusa, pushing the girls out the door.

But Nurse was already waiting. Livia Drusa took the baby from her and carried him into the sitting room herself.

"There, Quintus Servilius!" she said, smiling. "Meet your son. Isn't he beautiful?"

That was a mother's exaggeration, as Little Caepio was not a beautiful child. Nor, however, was he ugly. At ten months of age he sat very straight in Livia Drusa's arms and looked at his audience as directly as he did soberly; not a smiling or charming child. The ample mop of straight, lank hair on his head was a most aggressive shade of red, his eyes were a light hazel-brown, his physique long of limb, thin of face.

"Jupiter!" said Caepio, gazing at his son in astonishment. "Where did he get red hair from?"

"My mother's family, so Marcus Livius says," Livia Drusa answered composedly.

"Oh!" said Caepio, relieved; not because he suspected his wife of infidelity, but because he liked all the ends neatly tied and tucked away. Never an affectionate man, he did not attempt to hold the baby, and had to be prompted before he chucked Little Caepio under the chin and talked to him like a proper *tata*.

Finally, "Good," said Caepio. "Give him back to his nurse. It's time you and I were alone, wife."

"But it's dinnertime," said Livia Drusa as she carried the baby back to the door and handed him through it to Nurse. "In fact," she said, heart beginning to knock at the prospect of what had to come, "dinner's late. We can't possibly delay it further."

He was closing the shutters and bolting the door. "I'm not hungry," he said, starting to unwind his toga, "and if you are, that's too bad. No dinner for you tonight, wife!"

Though he was not a sensitive or perceptive man, Quintus Servilius Caepio could not but be aware of the change in Livia Drusa the moment he climbed into bed beside her and pulled her urgently against him. Tense. Utterly unresponsive.

"What's the matter with you?" he cried, disappointed.

"Like all women, I'm beginning to dislike this business," she said. "After we have two or three children we lose interest."

"Well," said Caepio, growing angry, "you'd better grow some interest back! The men of my family are continent and moral, we are famous for sleeping only with our wives." It came out sounding pompous, ridiculous, as if learned by rote.

Thus the night could be called a successful reunion only on the most basic level; even after repeated sexual assaults by Caepio, Livia Drusa remained cold, apathetic, then offended her husband mightily by going to sleep in the middle of his last effort, and *snoring.* He shook her viciously awake.

"How do you expect us to have another son?" he asked, his fingers digging painfully into her shoulders.

"I don't want any more children," she said.

"If you're not careful," he mumbled, coming to his climax, "I'll divorce you."

"If divorce meant I could go back to Tusculum to live," she said above the groans of his climax, "I wouldn't mind it in the least. I hate Rome. And I hate this." She wriggled out from under him. "Now may I go to sleep?"

Tired himself, he let this go, but in the morning he resumed the subject the moment he woke, his anger grown greater.

"I am your husband," he said to her as she slid out of bed, "and I expect my wife to be a proper wife."

"I told you, I've lost interest in the whole business!" she said tartly. "If that doesn't suit you, Quintus Servilius, then I suggest you divorce me."

But Caepio's brain had grasped the fact that she wanted a divorce, though as yet had not thought of infidelity. "There will be no divorce, wife."

"I can divorce you, you know."

"I doubt your brother would allow it. Not that it makes any difference. There will be no divorce. Instead, you will flog a little interest—or rather, I will." He picked up his leather belt and folded it double, tugging at it to make it snap.

Livia Drusa stared at him in simple amazement. "Oh, do stop posturing!" she said. "I'm not a child!"

"You're behaving like one."

"You wouldn't dare touch me!"

For answer, he grabbed her arm, twisted it deftly behind her back and pulled her nightgown up to hold it in his same hand. The belt curled with a loud crack against her flank, then against her thigh, her buttock, her calf. At first she tried to struggle free, then understood that he was capable of breaking her arm if he had to. Each time he struck her the pain increased, a fierce fire going deeper than skin; her gasps became sobs, then cries of fear. When she sank to her knees and tried to cradle her head in her arms he let her go, took the belt in both hands and flogged her huddled body in a frenzy of rage.

Her screams began to go through him like a glorious paean of joy; he ripped her gown completely away and wielded his belt until his arms were so tired he couldn't raise them.

The belt fell, was kicked away. Hand locked in her hair, Caepio dragged his wife to her feet and back to the airless sleeping cubicle, sour and stinking from the night.

"Now we'll see!" he panted, grasping his huge erection in one hand. "Obedience, wife! Otherwise there'll be more!" And, mounting her, he truly thought that her leaping flinches, the feeble beating of her fists, her anguished cries, were excitement.

The noises emanating from the Caepio suite had not gone unnoticed. Sidling along the colonnade to see if her beloved *tata* was awake, little Servilia heard it all, as did some of the house servants. Drusus and Servilia Caepionis did not hear, nor were they informed; no one knew how to tell them.

After bathing her mistress, Livia Drusa's maid reported the extent of the damage in the slave quarters, face terrified.

"Covered in huge red welts!" she said to the steward, Cratippus. "*Bleeding!* And the bed covered in blood! Poor thing, poor thing!"

Cratippus wept desolately, powerless to help himself—but did not weep alone, for there were many among the household servants who had known Livia Drusa since early childhood, had always pitied her, cared about her. And when these old retainers set eyes upon her that morning they wept again; she moved at the pace of a snail, and looked as if she wanted to die. But Caepio had been cunning, even in the midst of his engorged fury. Not a mark showed on arms, face, neck, feet.

For two months the situation continued unchanged, save that Caepio's beatings—administered at intervals of about five days—altered in pattern; he would concentrate upon one specific area of his wife's body, thus permitting other areas time to heal. The sexual stimulus he found irresistible, the sense of power fantastic; at last he understood the wisdom of the old ways, the reasons behind the *paterfamilias*. The true purpose of women.

Livia Drusa said nothing to anyone, even the maidservant who bathed her—and now dressed her wounds as well. The change in her was patent, and worried Drusus and his wife a great deal; all they could put it down to was her return to Rome, though Drusus, remembering how she had resisted marriage to Caepio, also found himself wondering whether it was the presence of Caepio at base of her dragging footsteps, her haggard face, her utter quietness.

Inside herself, Livia Drusa felt hardly anything beyond the physical agony of the beatings and their aftermath. Perhaps, she would find herself wondering dully, this was a punishment; or perhaps in so much actual pain the loss of her beloved Cato was made bearable; or perhaps the gods were really being kind to her, for she had lost the three-month child Caepio would certainly have known he hadn't fathered. In the shock of Caepio's sudden return that complication hadn't risen to the surface of her mind before it ceased to be a complication. Yes, that must be it. The gods were being kind. Sooner or later she would die, when her husband forgot to stop. And death was infinitely preferable to life with Quintus Servilius Caepio.

The entire atmosphere within the house had changed, a fact Drusus for one fretted about; what should have occupied his thoughts was his wife's pregnancy, a most unexpected and joyous gift they had long despaired of receiving. Yet Servilia Caepionis fretted too, as blighted by this inexplicable pall of darkness as was Drusus. What was the matter? Could one unhappy wife truly generate so much general gloom? His servants were so silent and serious, for one thing. Normally their noisy progress about his house was a perpetual minor irritation, and he had been used since childhood to being wakened occasionally by a huge burst of hilarity from the quarters below the atrium. No more. They all crept round with long faces, answered in monosyllables, dusted and polished and scrubbed as if to tire themselves out because they couldn't sleep. Nor was that veritable tower of strong composure, Cratippus, acting like himself.

As dawn broke at the end of the old year, Drusus caught his steward before Cratippus could instruct the door warden to admit the master's clients from the street.

"Just a moment," said Drusus, pointing toward his study. "I want to see you."

But after he closed the room to all other comers, he found himself unable to broach the subject, and walked up and down, up and down, while Cratippus stood in one place and looked steadfastly at the floor. Finally Drusus stopped, faced his steward.

"Cratippus, what is the matter?" he asked, his hand extended. "Have I offended you in some way? Why are the servants so unhappy? Is there some terribly important thing I have overlooked in my treatment of you? If there is, please tell me. I wouldn't have any slave of mine rendered miserable through my fault, or the fault of anyone else among my family. But especially I wouldn't want *you* made miserable. Without you, the house would fall down!"

To his horror, Cratippus burst into tears; Drusus stood for a moment without the slightest idea what to do, then instinct took over and he found himself seated with his steward on the couch, his arm about the heaving shoulders, his handkerchief put into service. But the kinder Drusus became, the harder Cratippus wept. Close to tears himself, Drusus got up to fetch wine, persuaded Cratippus to drink, soothed and hushed and rocked until finally his steward's distress began to die down.

"Oh, Marcus Livius, it has been such a burden!"

"What has, Cratippus?"

"The beatings!"

"The beatings?"

"The way she screams, so quietly!" Cratippus wept anew.

"My sister, you mean?" asked Drusus sharply.

"Yes."

Drusus could feel his heart accelerating, his face grow dark with blood, his hands begin to tremble. "Tell me! In the name of our household gods, I command you to tell me!"

"Quintus Servilius. He will end in killing her."

The trembling had become visible shaking, it was necessary to draw a huge breath. "My sister's husband is beating her?"

"Yes, *domine*, yes!" The steward struggled to compose himself. "I know it is not my place to comment, and I swear I would not have! But you asked me with such kindness, such concern—I—I—"

"Calm yourself, Cratippus, I am not angry with you," said Drusus evenly. "I assure you, I am intensely grateful to be informed of this." He got to his feet, and helped Cratippus up gently. "Go to the door warden now, and have him make my excuses to my clients. They will not be admitted today, I have other things to do. Then I want you to ask my wife to go to the nursery and remain there with the children because I have need to send every servant down to the cellar to do some special work for me. You will make sure that every servant goes to quarters, and you will then do so yourself. But before you leave, make your last task a request to Quintus Servilius and my sister to come here to my study."

In the moments Drusus had to himself, he disciplined his body to stillness and his anger to detachment, for he told himself that perhaps Cratippus was overreacting, that things might not be as bad as the servants obviously thought.

One unblinkered look at Livia Drusa told him no one had exaggerated, that it was all true. She came through the door first, and he saw the pain, the depression, the fear, an unhappiness so deep it had no end. He saw the deadness in her. Caepio entered in her wake, more intrigued than worried.

Standing himself, Drusus asked no one to sit down. Instead, he stared at his brother-in-law with loathing, and said, "It has come to my attention, Quintus Servilius, that you are physically assaulting my sister."

It was Livia Drusa who gasped. Caepio braced himself and assumed an expression of truculent contempt.

"What I do to my wife, Marcus Livius, is no one's business except my own," he said.

"I disagree," said Drusus as calmly as he could. "Your wife is my sister, a member of a great and powerful family. No one in this house beat her before she was married. I will not permit you or anyone else to beat her now."

"She is my wife. Which means she is in my hand, not yours, Marcus Livius! I will do with her whatever I will."

"Your connections to Livia Drusa are by marriage," said Drusus, face hardening. "My connections are blood. And blood matters. I will not permit you to beat my sister!"

"You *said* you didn't want to know about my methods of disciplining her! And you were right. It's none of your business."

"Wife-beating is everybody's business. The lowest of the low." Drusus looked at his sister. "Please remove your clothes, Livia Drusa. I want to see what this wife-beater has done."

"You will not, wife!" cried Caepio in righteous indignation. "Display yourself to one not your husband? You will not!"

"Take off your clothes, Livia Drusa," said Drusus.

Livia Drusa made no move to obey, did not speak.

"My dear, you must do this thing," said Drusus gently, and went to her side. "I have to see."

When he put his arm about her she cried out, pulling away; keeping his touch as light as possible, Drusus unfastened her robe at its shoulders.

No greater contempt did a man of senatorial class have than for a wife-beater. Yet, knowing this, Caepio found himself without the courage to stop Drusus unveiling his work. Then the gown was hanging below Livia Drusa's breasts, and there, marring their beauty, were scores of old welts, lividly purple, sulphurously yellow. Drusus untied the girdle. Both gown and undergarment fell about his sister's feet. Her thighs had taken the most recent assault and were still swollen, the flesh scarlet, crimson, broken. Tenderly Drusus pulled dress and undergarment up, lifted her nerveless hands, placed their fingers around her clothes. He turned to Caepio.

"Get out of my house," he said, face rigidly controlled.

"My wife is my property," said Caepio. "I am entitled at law to treat her in any way I deem necessary. I can even kill her."

"Your wife is my sister, and I will not see a Livius Drusus abused as I would not abuse the most stupid and intractable of my farm animals," said Drusus. "Get out of my house!"

"If I go, she goes with me," said Caepio.

"She remains with me. Now leave, wife-beater!"

Then a shrill little voice screamed from behind them in venomous outrage: "She deserves it! She deserves it!" The child Servilia went straight to her father's side and looked up at him. "Don't beat her, Father! *Kill her!*"

"Go back to the nursery, Servilia," said Drusus wearily.

But she clutched at Caepio's hand and stood defying Drusus with feet apart, eyes flashing. "She deserves to be killed!" the child shrieked. "*I* know why she liked living in Tusculum! *I* know what she did in Tusculum! *I* know why the boy is red!"

Caepio let go her hand as if it burned, enlightenment dawning.

"What do you mean, Servilia?" He shook her mercilessly. "Go on, girl, say what you mean!"

"She had a lover—and I know what a lover is!" cried his daughter, lips peeled back from her teeth. "My mother had a lover! A red man. They met every single morning in a house on his estate. *I* know—I followed her! *I* saw what they did together on the bed! And *I* know his name! Marcus Porcius Cato Salonianus! The descendant of a *slave*! I know, because I asked Aunt Servilia Caepionis!" She turned to gaze up at her father, face transformed from hatred to adoration. "*Tata,* if you won't kill her, leave her here! She's not good enough for you! She doesn't deserve you! Who is she, after all? Only a plebeian—not patrician like you and me! If you leave her here, I'll look after you, I promise!"

Drusus and Caepio stood turned to stone, whereas Livia Drusa came at last to life. She fastened her gown and her girdle, and confronted her daughter.

"Little one, it isn't as you think," she said, very gently, and reached out to touch her daughter's cheek.

The hand was struck away fiercely; Servilia flattened herself against her father. "I know what to think! I don't need *you* to tell me! You dishonored our name—my father's name! You deserve to die! And that boy isn't my father's!"

"Little Quintus *is* your father's," said Livia Drusa. "He is your brother."

"He belongs to the red man, he's the son of a slave!" She plucked at Caepio's tunic. "*Tata,* take me away, please!"

For answer, Caepio took hold of the child and pushed her away from him so roughly that she fell. "What a fool I've been," he said, low-voiced. "The girl is right, you deserve to die. A pity I didn't use my belt harder and more often." Fists clenched, he rushed from the room with his daughter running after him calling for him to wait for her, howling noisy tears.

Drusus and his sister were alone.

His legs didn't seem to want to hold him up; he went to his chair, sat down heavily. Livia Drusa! Blood of his blood! His only sister! Adultress, *meretrix*. Yet until this hideous interview he had not understood how much she meant to him; nor could he have known how deeply her plight would touch him, how responsible he felt.

"It's my fault," he said, lip quivering.

She sank down on the couch. "No, my fault," she said.

"It's true? You do have a lover?"

"I *had* a lover, Marcus Livius. The first, the only one. I haven't seen or heard from him since I left Tusculum."

"But that wasn't why Caepio beat you."

"No."

"Why, then?"

"After Marcus Porcius, I just couldn't keep up the pretense," said Livia Drusa. "My indifference angered him, so he beat me. And then he discovered he liked beating me. It—it excited him."

For a brief moment Drusus looked as if he would vomit; then he lifted his arms and shook them impotently. "Ye gods, what a world we live in!" he cried. "I have wronged you, Livia Drusa."

She came to sit in the client's chair. "You acted according to your lights," she said gently. "Truly, Marcus Livius, I came to understand that years ago. Your many kindnesses to me since then have made me love you—and Servilia Caepionis."

"My wife!" Drusus exclaimed. "What might this do to her?"

"We must keep as much as possible from her," said Livia Drusa. "She's enjoying a comfortable pregnancy, we can't jeopardize it."

Drusus was already on his feet. "Stay there," he said, moving to the door. "I want to make sure her brother doesn't say anything to upset her. Drink some wine. I'll be back."

But Caepio hadn't even thought of his sister. From Drusus's study he had rushed to his own suite of rooms, his daughter crying and clinging to his waist until he slapped her across the face and locked her in his bedroom. There Drusus found her huddled on the floor in a corner, still sobbing.

The servants had been summoned back to duty, so Drusus helped the little girl up and ushered her outside to where one of the nurserymaids hovered doubtfully in the distance. "Calm down now, Servilia. Let Stratonice wash your face and give you breakfast."

"I want my *tata*!"

"Your *tata* has left my house, child, but don't despair. I'm sure that as soon as he's organized his affairs he'll send for you," Drusus said, not sure whether he was thankful Servilia had blurted out all the truth or whether he disliked her for it.

She cheered up at once. "He will send for me, he will," she said, walking with her uncle onto the colonnade.

"Now go with Stratonice," said Drusus, and added sternly, "Try to be discreet, Servilia. For your aunt's sake as well as your father's—yes, your father's!—you cannot say a word about what has transpired here this morning."

"How can my talking hurt him? He's the victim."

"No man enjoys the humbling of his pride, Servilia. Take my word for it, your father won't thank you if you chatter."

Servilia shrugged, went off with her nursemaid; Drusus went then to visit his wife, and told her as much as he thought she needed to know. To his surprise, she took the news tranquilly.

"I'm just glad we know now what the matter is," she said, remaining wrapped round by the bloom of her pregnancy. "Poor Livia Drusa! I am afraid, Marcus Livius, that I do not like my brother very much. The older he becomes, the more intractable he seems to get. Though I remember that when we were children, he used to torment the slaves' children."

Back to Livia Drusa, who was still sitting in the client's chair, apparently composed.

He sat down again. "What a morning! Little did I know what I was unleashing when I asked Cratippus why he and the servants were so unhappy."

"Were they unhappy?" asked Livia Drusa, puzzled.

"Yes. Because of you, my dear. They had heard Caepio beating you. You mustn't forget they've known you all your life. They're extremely fond of you, Livia Drusa."

"Oh, how nice! I had no idea."

"Nor did I, I confess. Ye gods, I've been dense! And I am very, very sorry for this mess."

"Don't be." She sighed. "Did he take Servilia?"

Drusus grimaced. "No. He locked her in your room."

"Oh, poor little thing! She adores him so!"

"I gathered *that*. I just can't understand it."

"What happens now, Marcus Livius?"

He shrugged. "To be honest, I haven't the faintest inkling! Perhaps the best thing all of us can do is to behave as normally as possible under the circumstances, and wait to hear from—" He nearly said Caepio, as he had been doing all morning, but forced himself back to the old courtesy, and said, "Quintus Servilius."

"And if he divorces me, as I imagine he will?"

"Then you're well rid of him, I'd say."

Livia Drusa's major preoccupation now surfaced; she said anxiously, "What about Marcus Porcius Cato?"

"This man matters a great deal to you, doesn't he?"

"Yes, he matters."

"Is the boy his, Livia Drusa?"

How often she had worked at this in her mind! What would she say when some member of the family queried her son's coloring, or his growing likeness to Marcus Porcius Cato? It seemed to her that Caepio owed her something in return for the years of patient servitude, her model behavior—and those beatings. Her son had a name. If she declared that Cato was his sire, he lost that name—and, given that he had been born under that name, he could not escape the taint of illegitimacy did she deny it to him. The date of his birth did not exclude Caepio as his father; she was the only person who knew beyond any doubt that Caepio was not his father.

"No, Marcus Livius, my son is Quintus Servilius's child," she said firmly. "My liaison with Marcus Porcius began after I knew I was pregnant."

"It is a pity then that he has red hair," said Drusus, no expression on his face.

Livia Drusa smiled wryly. "Have you never noticed the tricks Fortune delights in playing upon us mortals?" she asked. "From the time I met Marcus Porcius, I had a feeling Fortune was plotting cleverly. So when little Quintus came out with red hair, I was not at all surprised—though I am aware no one will believe me."

"I will stand by you, sister," said Drusus. "Through thick and thin, I will lend you every iota of support I can."

Tears gathered in Livia Drusa's eyes. "Oh, Marcus Livius, I do thank you for that!"

"It is the least I can do." He cleared his throat. "As for Servilia Caepionis, you may rest assured she will support me—and therefore you."

Caepio sent the divorce notification later that day, and followed it up with a private letter to Drusus that had Drusus metaphorically winded.

"Do you know what that insect says?" he demanded of his sister, who had been seen by several physicians, and was now relegated to her bed.

As she was lying on her stomach while two medical acolytes plastered the back of her from shoulders to ankles with bruise-drawing poultices, it was difficult for her to see Drusus's face; she had to twist her neck until she could glimpse him out of the corners of her eyes. "What does he say?" she asked.

"First of all, he denies paternity for *every one* of his three children! He refuses to return your dowry, and he accuses you of multiple infidelities. Nor will he repay me for the expense of housing him and his for the last seven and more years—his grounds, it appears, are that you were never his wife and your children are not his, but other men's."

Livia Drusa dropped her head into the pillow. "*Ecastor!* Marcus Livius, how can he do this to his daughters, if not to his son? Little Quintus is understandable, but Servilia and Lilla? This will break Servilia's heart."

"Oh, he has more to say than that!" said Drusus, waving the letter. "He is going to change his will to disinherit his three children. And *then* he has the gall to demand back from me 'his' ring! *His* ring!"

Livia Drusa knew which ring her brother referred to at once. An heirloom which had belonged to their father and his father before him, and said to be a seal-ring of Alexander the Great. From the time as a lad Quintus Servilius Caepio had become friends with Marcus Livius Drusus he had coveted the ring, watched it transferred from Drusus the Censor's dead finger to Drusus's living one, and finally, leaving for Smyrna and Italian Gaul, he had begged of Drusus that he be allowed to wear the ring as a good-luck charm. Drusus had not wanted to let his ring go, but felt churlish, and in the end handed it over. However, the moment Caepio returned, Drusus asked for his ring. At first Caepio had tried to find some reason why he ought to be allowed to keep it, but eventually took it off and gave it back, saying with a laugh which rang hollow,

"Oh, very well, very well! But the next time I go away, Marcus Livius, you must give it back to me—it's a lucky gem."

"How dare he!" snarled Drusus, clutching at his finger as if he expected Caepio to materialize at his elbow and snatch the ring, which was too small for any but the little finger, yet was too large for that; Alexander the Great had been a very small man.

"Take no notice, Marcus Livius," Livia Drusa comforted, then turned her head again to look at him as best she could. "What will happen to my children?" she asked. "Can he do this thing?"

"Not after I've dealt with him," said Drusus grimly. "Did he send you a letter too?"

"No. Just the bill of divorcement."

"Then rest and get well, my dear."

"What shall I tell the children?"

"Nothing, until I finish with their father."

Back to his study went Marcus Livius Drusus, there to take a length of best-quality Pergamum parchment (he wanted what he wrote to stand the test of time), and reply to Caepio.

> You are of course at liberty to deny the paternity of your three children, Quintus Servilius. But I am at liberty to swear that indeed they are your offspring, and so

I will swear if it should come to that. In a court of law.
You ate my bread and drank my wine from April in the
year that Gaius Marius was consul for the third time
until you left for abroad twenty-three months ago, and I
then continued to feed, clothe, and shelter your wife and
family while you were away. I defy you to find any evidence of infidelity on the part of my sister during the
years in which you and she lived in this house. And if
you examine the birth records of your son, you will see
that he too must have been conceived in my house.

I would strongly suggest that you abandon any and
all intentions to disinherit your three children. If you
persist in your present attitude, I will undertake to conduct in a court of law a suit against you on behalf of
your children. During my address to the jury I will make
very free of certain information I have concerning the
aurum Tolosanum, the whereabouts of huge sums of
money you have removed from deposit in Smyrna and
invested in banking houses, property and unsenatorial
trade practices throughout the western end of the Middle Sea. Among the witnesses I would find myself
forced to call would be several of Rome's most prestigious doctors, all of whom can attest to the potentially
maiming nature of the beatings you inflicted upon my
sister. Further to this, I would be fully prepared to call
my sister as a witness, and my steward, who heard
what he heard.

As regards my sister's dowry, the hundreds of thousands of sesterces you owe me for supporting you and
yours—I will not soil my hands with repayment. Keep
the money. It will do you no good.

Finally, there is the matter of my ring. Its status as a
Livian family heirloom is so much a fact of public record that you would be wise to cease and desist from
claiming it.

The letter was sealed and a servant dispatched at once to carry it to Caepio's new lair, the house of Lucius Marcius Philippus. Having been kicked sprawling, his servant limped back to inform Drusus that there would be no reply. Smiling a little, Drusus bestowed ten denarii upon his injured slave, then sat back in his chair, closed his eyes, and amused himself by imagining Caepio's thwarted rage. There would be no lawsuit, he knew. And no matter whose son little Quintus really was, officially he was going to remain Caepio's. The heir to the Gold of Tolosa. His smile enlarging, Drusus found himself wanting badly to believe that little Quintus would turn out to be a long-necked, big-nosed, red-haired cuckoo in the Servilius Caepio nest. How delicious a retribution that would be for a wife-beater!

He went shortly thereafter to the nursery and called his niece Servilia out into the garden. Until today he hadn't ever really noticed her save to smile at her in passing, or pat her on the head, or give her a gift at the appropriate time, or reflect that she was a surly little wretch, never smiled. How can Caepio deny her? he wondered; she was her father through and through, vengeful little beast. Drusus believed children should be neither seen nor heard when it came to adult affairs, and her behavior that morning had horrified him. Tattle-telling, malicious child! It would have served *her* right if Caepio had been allowed to do what he intended, and disown her.

Following on these thoughts, his face when Servilia came out of the nursery and down the path to the peristyle fountain was flinty, and his eyes were cold.

"Servilia, since you made yourself privy to the congress of your elders this morning, I thought it best to inform you myself that your father has seen fit to divorce your mother."

"Oh, good!" said Servilia, honor satisfied. "I'll pack my things and go to him now."

"You will not," said Drusus, enunciating very clearly. "He doesn't want you."

The child went so pale that under normal circumstances Drusus would have feared for her, and laid her down; as it was, he simply stood watching her rock. But she didn't faint, she righted herself instead, and her color flowed back dark red.

"I do not believe you," she said. "My *tata* wouldn't do that to me, I know he wouldn't!"

Drusus shrugged. "If you don't believe me, go and see him yourself," he said. "He's not far away, just a few doors down at the house of Lucius Marcius Philippus. Go to him and ask him."

"I will," said Servilia hardily, and off she marched, her nurserymaid hurrying after her.

"Let her go, Stratonice," said Drusus. "Just keep her company and make sure she comes back."

How unhappy they all are, thought Drusus, staying where he was by the fountain. And how unhappy I would be were it not for my beloved Servilia Caepionis and our little son—and the child in her womb, settling down so cosily. His mood of contrition was wearing off, replaced by this urge to lash out at Servilia, since he couldn't reach her father. And then, as the weak sun warmed his bones and some of the stirrings of the day subsided, his sense of fairness and justice righted itself; he became once more Marcus Livius Drusus, advocate of those who had been wronged. But never advocate of Quintus Servilius Caepio, wronged though he might be.

When Servilia reappeared he was still sitting by the sunny silvered stream of water gushing out of a scaly dolphin's mouth, his eyes shut, his face its normal serene self.

"Uncle Marcus!" she said sharply.

He opened his eyes and managed a smile. "Hello," he said. "What happened?"

"He doesn't want me, he says I'm not his, he says I'm the daughter of someone else," said the child, closed tight.

"Well, you wouldn't believe me."

"Why should I? You're on *her* side."

"Servilia, you can't remain unsympathetic toward your mother. It's she who is wronged, not your father."

"How can you say that? She had a lover!"

"If your father had been kinder to her, she wouldn't have found a lover. No man can find excuse for beating his wife."

"He should have killed her, not beaten her. I would have."

Drusus gave up. "Oh, go away, you horrible girl!"

And hopefully, Drusus thought, closing his eyes again, Servilia would benefit from her father's rejection. As time went on, she would draw closer to her mother. It was natural.

Finding himself hungry, he ate bread and olives and hard-boiled eggs with his wife shortly thereafter, and acquainted her more fully with what had happened. Since he knew her to have the Servilius Caepio sense of fitness and standing, he wasn't sure how she would react to the news that her sister-in-law had been divorced because of an involvement with a man of servile origins. But— though the identity of Livia Drusa's lover did disappoint her— Servilia Caepionis was too much in love with Drusus ever to go against him; long ago she had discovered that families always meant divided loyalties, so had elected to leave all her loyalty with Drusus. The years of sharing her house with Caepio had not endeared him to her, for the insecure inferiority of childhood had quite gone and she had lived with Drusus for long enough to have received some of his courage.

So they had an enjoyable meal together despite the situation, and Drusus felt more capable of dealing with whatever else the day might bring. Which was just as well; early afternoon brought him fresh trouble in the shape of Marcus Porcius Cato Salonianus.

Inviting Cato to join him in a stroll about the colonnade, Drusus prepared himself for the worst.

"What do you know about all this?" he asked calmly.

"I had a visit from Quintus Servilius Caepio and Lucius Marcius Philippus not so many moments ago," said Cato, his tones as level and unemotional as Drusus's.

"Both of them, eh? I presume Philippus's role was that of a witness," said Drusus.

"Yes."

"And?"

"Caepio simply informed me that he had divorced his wife on the grounds of her adultery with me."

"Nothing else?"

Cato frowned. "What else is there? However, he said it in front of my wife, who has gone to her father."

"Ye gods, it goes on and on!" cried Drusus, throwing his hands in the air. "Sit down, Marcus Porcius. I had better tell you all of it. The divorce is only the beginning."

All of it had Cato angrier than Drusus had been; the Porcii Catones put on a grand front of imperturbable coolness, but to the last man—and woman—they were renowned for their tempers. It took Drusus a long time and many reasonable words to persuade Cato that if he went to find Caepio and killed him—or even half killed him—matters would only be worse for Livia Drusa than they already were. After he was sure Cato's temper was well mended, Drusus took him to Livia Drusa; any doubts he might have harbored as to the depth of the feeling between them were allayed in that first look which passed between them. Yes, this was a love for life. Poor things!

"Cratippus," he said to his steward after he had left the lovers together, "I am hungry again, and I intend to eat dinner immediately. Inform the lady Servilia Caepionis, would you?"

But the lady Servilia Caepionis elected to eat in the nursery, where Servilia had laid herself on her bed and announced that no morsel of food nor drop of water would pass her lips, and that when her father heard she was dead, he would be sorry.

Off went Drusus alone to the dining room, wishing the day would end and that his allotted span on earth did not contain another such. Sighing gratefully, he settled himself in solitary state upon his couch to await the *gustatio*.

"What's this I hear?" cried a voice from the door.

"Uncle Publius!"

"Well, what's the real story?" Publius Rutilius Rufus demanded, kicking off his shoes and waving the servant away who wanted to wash his feet. He clambered onto the couch beside Drusus and leaned on his left elbow, his perky homely face alight with curiosity, luckily salved by an accompanying sympathy and concern. "Rome is absolutely buzzing with garbled versions of a dozen different kinds—divorce, adultery, slave lovers, wife-beating, nasty children—where does it all come from, and so quickly?"

Drusus, however, was not able to tell him, for this last invasion was too much; he lay back on his bolster and literally cried with laughter.

Publius Rutilius Rufus was right, all of Rome was buzzing; two and two were cleverly added together and mostly totaled the correct figure, considerably aided by the fact that the youngest of the divorced wife's three children had a thatch of bright red hair—and that Marcus Porcius Cato Salonianus's hugely rich but vulgar wife, Cuspia, had also served her husband with divorce papers. That inseparable pair, Quintus Servilius Caepio and Marcus Livius Drusus, were now not on speaking terms, though Caepio for one kept insisting it had nothing to do with divorced wives, but was on account of the fact that Drusus had stolen his ring.

There were those with sufficient intelligence and sense of rightness who noticed that all the best people were siding with Drusus and his sister. Others of less admirable character—like Lucius Marcius Philippus and Publius Cornelius Scipio Nasica—were siding with Caepio, as were those sycophantic knights who browsed in the same commercial fields as Gnaeus Cuspius Buteo, Cato's wronged wife's father, nicknamed "The Vulture." Then there were those who sided with no one, finding the whole sensation exquisitely funny; among these was Marcus Aemilius Scaurus Princeps Senatus, just beginning to surface again after several years of extreme quietness following the disgrace of his wife's falling in love with Sulla; he felt he could afford to laugh, since young Dalmatica's crush had been unrequited, and she was now beginning to swell with a child Scaurus knew full well could be no one's save his own. Publius Rutilius Rufus was another who laughed, in spite of his position as the adultress's uncle.

Yet as things turned out in the end, neither of the guilty participants in the affair suffered the way Marcus Livius Drusus was made to suffer.

"Or perhaps it would be better to say," Drusus grumbled to Silo not long after the new consuls entered office, "that, as usual, I seem to wind up being responsible for everybody's baby! If I had all the money which that wretched boor Caepio has cost me over the years in one way or another, I'd be considerably better off! My new brother-in-law, Cato Salonianus, has been left without a feather to fly with—he's strapped by dowry payments to Lucius Domitius Ahenobarbus on behalf of his sister—and of course his wife's fortune has been withdrawn, along with the support of her social-climbing father. So not only have I had to pay Lucius Domitius out, but I am—as usual!—expected to house my sister, her husband, and her rapidly expanding family—she's increasing *again*!"

Though he knew he was offering scant comfort to Drusus, Silo too joined the ranks of those who saw the funny side, and laughed until he hurt. "Oh, Marcus Livius, never was a Roman nobleman abused as you are!"

"Stop it," said Drusus, grinning. "I could wish that life—or Fortune, or whoever it is—treated me with a little more of the respect I deserve. But whatever my life might have been like before Arausio—or had there never been an Arausio!—is now utterly beyond me. All I know is that I cannot abandon my poor sister—and that, though I tried not to, I like my new brother-in-law a great deal better than I liked my old one. Salonianus may be the grandson of a girl born in slavery, but he's a true gentleman nonetheless, and my house is the happier for sheltering him. I even approve of the way he treats Livia Drusa, and I must say he's won my wife over—she was inclined to think him quite unacceptable coming from that particular brood, but now she likes him very well."

"It pleases me that your poor little sister is happy at last," said Silo. "I always had the feeling she existed in some deep misery, but she concealed her predicament with the will of a true Livius Drusus. However, it's a pity you can't free yourself of pensioners—I take it you'll have to finance Salonianus's career?"

"Of course," said Drusus, displaying no chagrin. "Luckily my father left me with more money than I can ever spend, so I'm not reduced to penury yet. Think of how annoyed Caepio will be when I push a Cato Salonianus up the *cursus honorum*!"

"Do you mind if I change the subject?" asked Silo abruptly.

"Not at all," said Drusus, surprised. "Hopefully the new subject is going to contain a detailed description of your doings over the past few months—I haven't seen you in nearly a year, Quintus Poppaedius."

"Is it that long?" Silo did some calculations, and nodded. "You're right. Where does time go?" He shrugged. "Nothing very much, actually. My business ventures have benefited, is all."

"I don't trust you when you're cagey," said Drusus, delighted to see this friend of his heart. "However, I daresay you have no intention of telling me what you've really been up to, so I won't make it hard for you by pressing. What was the subject you wanted to bring up, then?"

"The new consuls," said Silo.

"Good ones, for a change," said Drusus happily. "I don't know when we've elected such a solid pair—Crassus Orator and Scaevola! I'm expecting great things."

"Are you? I wish I could say the same. I'm expecting trouble."

"On the Italian front? Why?"

"Oh, rumor as yet. I hope unfounded, though somehow I doubt that, Marcus Livius." Silo scowled. "The censors have gone to the consuls with the registers of Roman citizens throughout Italy, and I hear are concerned about the vast number of new names on the rolls. Idiots! One moment they're prating about how their new census methods will reveal many more citizens than the old way did, the next moment they're saying there are too many new citizens!"

"So that's why you've not been to Rome in months!" cried Drusus. "Oh, Quintus Poppaedius, I warned you! No, no, please don't lie to me! If you do we can't continue to be friends, and I for one would be the poorer! You doctored the rolls."

"Yes."

"Quintus Poppaedius, I *told* you! Oh, what a mess!" For some time Drusus sat with his head in his hands, while Silo, feeling more uncomfortable than he had expected to, sat saying nothing and thinking hard. Finally Drusus lifted his head.

"Well, there's no point in repining, I suppose." He got to his feet, shaking his head at Silo in patient exasperation. "You had better go home—don't show your face in this city for a long time to come, Quintus Poppaedius. We can't afford to tickle the interest of some particularly bright member of the anti-Italian faction by having you on prominent display. I'll do what I can in the Senate, but unfortunately I'm still a junior, I won't be called upon to speak. Among those who can speak, your friends are going to be few, alas."

Silo was standing too. "Marcus Livius, it will come to war," he said. "I'll go home because you're right, someone will start wondering if they see my face. But, if nothing else, this shows there is no peaceful way to gain enfranchisement for Italy."

"There is a way. There must be a way," Drusus said. "Now go, Quintus Poppaedius, as unobtrusively as you can. And if you plan to use the Colline Gate, detour around the Forum, please."

Drusus himself didn't detour around the Forum; he went straight there, togate and looking for familiar faces. There was no meeting of Senate or Comitia, but a man could be fairly sure of seeing people in the general area of the lower Forum. And luckily the first valuable man Drusus spied was his uncle, Publius Rutilius Rufus, wandering toward the Carinae and his house.

"This is one time I could wish Gaius Marius was here," said Drusus as they found a quiet place in the sun just to one side of the ancient Forum trees.

"Yes, I'm afraid there won't be much support in the Senate for your Italian friends," said Rutilius Rufus.

"I think there could be—if only there was a powerful man present to urge a little thought. But with Gaius Marius still away in the east, who is there? Unless, Uncle, you—?"

"No," said Rutilius Rufus firmly. "I am sympathetic to the Italian cause, but a power in the Senate I am not. If anything, I've lost *auctoritas* since my return from Asia Minor—the tax-farmers are still screaming for my head. Quintus Mucius they know they can't get, he's too important. But an old and humble consular like me, who never had a famous reputation in the law courts or was a famous orator or led a famous army to victory? No, I haven't enough clout, truly."

"So you're saying there's little can be done."

"That's what I'm saying, Marcus Livius."

On the other side of popular opinion there was much being done, however. Quintus Servilius Caepio sought an interview with the consuls, Crassus Orator and Mucius Scaevola, and the censors, Antonius Orator and Valerius Flaccus. What he had to say interested the four men enormously.

"Marcus Livius Drusus is to blame for this," said Caepio. "In my hearing he has said many times that the Italians must be given the full citizenship, that there can be no difference between any men within Italy. And he has powerful Italian friends—the leader of the Marsi, Quintus Poppaedius Silo, and the leader of the Samnites, Gaius Papius Mutilus. From the things I overheard in Marcus Livius's house, I would be prepared to swear formally that Marcus Livius Drusus allied himself with those two Italians and concocted a plan to tamper with the census."

"Quintus Servilius, have you other evidence to substantiate your accusation?" asked Crassus Orator.

Whereupon Caepio drew himself up with immense dignity, and looked suitably offended. "I am a Servilius Caepio, Lucius Licinius! I do not lie." Offense became angry indignation. "Evidence to substantiate my accusation? I do not accuse! I simply state the facts. Nor do I need 'evidence' to substantiate anything! I repeat—*I* am a Servilius Caepio!"

"I don't care if he's Romulus," said Marcus Livius Drusus when the consuls and the censors came to see him. "If you can't see that these 'facts' he says he's simply stating are part of Quintus Servilius Caepio's current persecution of me and mine, then you're not the men I think you are! Ridiculous nonsense! Why should I plot against the interests of Rome? No son of my father could do such a thing. For Silo and Mutilus I cannot speak. Mutilus has never been inside my house, as a matter of fact, and Silo comes only as my friend. That I believe the franchise should be extended to every man in Italy is a matter of record, I make no secret of it. But the citizenship I would see extended to the Latins and the Italians must be legal, given freely by the Senate and People of Rome. To falsify the census in any way—be it by physically altering the rolls or by men testifying to a citizenship they do not own entitlement to—is something I could not condone, no matter how right I believe the cause behind it to be." He threw his arms wide, then up in the air. "Take it or leave it, *Quirites*, that's all I have to say. If you believe me, then come and drink a cup of wine with me. If you believe that unconscionable liar Caepio, then leave my house and don't come back."

Laughing softly, Quintus Mucius Scaevola linked his arm through Drusus's. "I for one, Marcus Livius, would be very pleased to drink a cup of wine with you."

"And I," said Crassus Orator.

The censors elected to drink wine too.

"But what worries me," said Drusus in the dining room later that afternoon, "is how Quintus Servilius got hold of his so-called information. Only one conversation occurred between me and Quintus Poppaedius on this subject, and that was many moons ago, when the censors were first elected."

"What transpired, Marcus Livius?" asked Cato Salonianus.

"Oh, Silo had some wild scheme to enroll illegal citizens, but I dissuaded him. Or thought I did. That was the end of it as far as I was concerned. Why, I hadn't even seen Quintus Poppaedius until recently! Yet—how did Caepio get his information?"

"Perhaps he did overhear you, perhaps he wasn't out," said Cato, who didn't honestly approve of Drusus's attitude about the Italians, but was in no case to criticize; one of the more distressing aspects of being Drusus's pensioner.

"Oh, he was definitely out," said Drusus dryly. "He was out of Italy at the time, and he certainly didn't sneak back for one day in order to eavesdrop on a conversation I didn't know I was going to have until it happened."

"Then—how indeed?" asked Cato. "Something you'd written he might have been able to find?"

Drusus shook his head so positively he left his audience in no doubt. "I have written nothing. Absolutely nothing."

"Why are you so sure Quintus Servilius had help in framing his accusations?" asked Livia Drusa.

"Because he accused me of falsifying the enrollment of new citizens, and lumped me with Quintus Poppaedius."

"Could he not have plucked that out of thin air?"

"Perhaps, except for one really worrying aspect—he gave a third name. Gaius Papius Mutilus of the Samnites. *Where* did he learn that particular name? I knew of it only because I knew Quintus Poppaedius had grown very friendly with Papius Mutilus. The thing is, I'm certain both Quintus Poppaedius and Papius Mutilus did falsify the rolls. But how did Caepio know it?"

Livia Drusa got to her feet. "I cannot promise anything, Marcus Livius, but it's possible I can provide an answer. Will you excuse me for a moment?"

Drusus, Cato Salonianus, and Servilia Caepionis waited out the moment, hardly curious; what could Livia Drusa produce to answer such a mysterious question, when the real answer was probably that Caepio had made a lucky guess?

Back came Livia Drusa marching her daughter Servilia in front of her, one hand digging into the child's shoulder.

"Stand right here, Servilia. I want to ask you something," said Livia Drusa sternly. "Have you been visiting your father?"

The girl's small face was so still, so expressionless that it struck those who observed it as a guilty face, guarded.

"I require a truthful answer, Servilia," said Livia Drusa. "Have you been visiting your father? And before you speak, I would remind you that if you answer in the negative, I will make enquiries in the nursery of Stratonice and the others."

"Yes, I visit him," said Servilia.

Drusus sat up straight, so did Cato; Servilia Caepionis sank lower in her chair, shielding her face with her hand.

"What did you tell your father about your Uncle Marcus and his friend, Quintus Poppaedius?"

"The truth," said Servilia, still expressionless.

"What truth?"

"That they have conspired to put Italians on the roll of Roman citizens."

"How could you do that, Servilia, when it isn't the truth?" asked Drusus, growing angry.

"It is the truth!" cried the child shrilly. "I saw letters in the Marsian man's room not many days ago!"

"You entered a guest's room without his knowledge?" asked Cato Salonianus incredulously. "That's despicable, girl!"

"Who are you to judge me?" asked Servilia, rounding on him. "You're the descendant of a slave and a peasant!"

Lips thin, Cato swallowed. "I might be all of that, Servilia, but even slaves can own principles too high to invade the sacred privacy of a guest."

"*I* am a patrician Servilius," said the child hardily, "whereas that man is just an Italian. He was behaving treasonously—and so was Uncle Marcus!"

"What letters did you see, Servilia?" asked Drusus.

"Letters from a Samnite named Gaius Papius Mutilus."

"But not letters from Marcus Livius Drusus."

"I didn't need to. You're so thick with the Italians that everyone knows you do what they want, and conspire with them."

"It's as well for Rome that you're female, Servilia," said Drusus, forcing his face and voice to appear amused. "If you entered the law courts armed with such arguments, you'd soon make a public fool of yourself." He slid off his couch and came round it to stand directly in front of her. "You are an idiot and an ingrate, my child. Deceitful and—as your stepfather said—despicable. If you were older, I would lock you out of my house. As it is, I will do the opposite. You will be locked inside my house, free to go wherever you like within its walls provided there is someone with you. But outside its walls you will not go at all for any reason. You will not visit your father or anyone else. Nor will you send him notes. If he sends demanding that you go to live with him, I will let you go gladly. But if that should happen, I will never admit you to my house again, even to see your mother. While your father refuses custody of you, I am your *paterfamilias*. You will accept my word as law because such is the law. Everyone in my house will be instructed to do as I command concerning you and the life you will lead in my house. Is that understood?"

The girl betrayed no trace of shame or fear; dark eyes full of fire, she stood her ground indomitably. "I am a patrician Servilius," she said. "No matter what you do to me, you cannot alter the fact that I am better than all of you put together. What might be wrong for my inferiors is no more than my duty. I uncovered a plot against Rome and informed my father. As was my duty. You can punish me in any way you choose, Marcus Livius. I don't care if you lock me inside one room forever, or beat me, or kill me. *I* know I did my duty."

"Oh, take her away, get her out of my sight!" cried Drusus to his sister.

"Shall I have her beaten?" asked Livia Drusa, quite as angry as Drusus.

He flinched. "No! There will be no more beatings in my house, Livia Drusa. Just do with her as I've ordered. If she ventures outside the nursery or her schoolroom, she must have an escort. And though she is now old enough to be moved from the nursery to her own sleeping cubicle, I will not allow it. Let her suffer lack of privacy, since she accords none to my guests. All this will be punishment enough as the years go on. Ten more of them before she has any hope of leaving here—*if* her father then takes enough interest in her to make a match for her. If he doesn't, I will—and not to a patrician! I'll marry her to some peasant country bumpkin!"

Cato Salonianus laughed. "No, not a country bumpkin, Marcus Livius. Marry her to a truly wonderful freedman, a natural nobleman without the slightest hope of ever becoming one. Then perhaps she will discover that slaves and ex-slaves can be better than patricians."

"I hate you!" screamed Servilia as her mother hustled her away. "I hate you all! I curse you, I curse you! May every last one of you be dead before I am old enough to marry!"

Then the child was forgotten; Servilia Caepionis slid from her chair to the floor. Drusus gathered her up, terrified, and carried her to their bedroom, where burning feathers held under her nose brought her back to consciousness. She wept desolately.

"Oh, Marcus Livius, you have had no luck since you allied yourself to my family," she sniffled, while he sat on the edge of the bed and held her close, praying that her baby weathered this.

"I have, you know," he said, kissing her brow, wiping her tears tenderly. "Don't make yourself ill, *mea vita,* the girl isn't worth it. Don't give her the satisfaction, please."

"I love you, Marcus Livius. I always have, I always will."

"Good! I love you too, Servilia Caepionis. A little more each and every day we spend together. Now calm yourself, don't forget our baby. He's growing so nicely," he said, with a pat for her enlarging belly.

Servilia Caepionis died in childbirth the day before Lucius Licinius Crassus Orator and Quintus Mucius Scaevola promulgated a new law about the Italian situation to the members of the Senate, with the result that the Marcus Livius Drusus who dragged himself to the meeting to hear the nature of the bill was in no fit state to lend the matter the attention it warranted.

No one in the Drusus household had been prepared; Servilia Caepionis had been very well, her pregnancy proceeding snugly and without incident. So sudden was her labor that even she had felt no warning; within two hours she was dead of a massive haemorrhage no amount of packing and elevation served to staunch. Out of the house when it happened, Drusus rushed back in time to be with her, but she passed from terrible pain to a dreamy, carefree euphoria, and died without knowing that Drusus held her hand, or understanding that she was dying. A merciful end for her

but a horrifying one for Drusus, who received from her no words
of love, or comfort, or even acknowledgment of his presence. All
her years of trying for that elusive child had come to a finish; she
just dwindled to a bloodless, oblivious white effigy in a bed saturated with her life force. When she died the child had not so much
as entered the birth canal; the doctors and midwives beseeched
Drusus to let them cut the baby out of his wife, but he refused.

"Let her go still wrapping it round," he said. "Let her have that
consolation. If it lived, I couldn't love it."

And so he hauled himself to the Curia Hostilia no more than
half-alive himself, and took his place among the middle ranks
to listen, his priesthood allowing him a position more prominent
than his actual senatorial status warranted. His servant situated
his folding chair and literally lowered his master down onto it,
while those around him murmured their condolences and he nodded, nodded, nodded his thanks, face almost as white as hers had
been. Before he was ready for it, he caught sight of Caepio in the
back row of the opposite tiers, and managed to go whiter still.
Caepio! Who had sent back word when notified of his sister's
death that he was leaving Rome immediately after this meeting,
and would not in consequence be able to attend the funeral of Servilia Caepionis.

Indeed, Drusus's view of proceedings and the House was virtually unimpeded, as he sat near the end of the left-hand tiers, where
the great bronze doors of the *curia* built centuries before by King
Tullus Hostilius stood open to permit those crowded in the portico
to hear. For this, the consuls decided, must be a fully public meeting. No one save the senators and their single attendants was permitted inside, but a public meeting meant that anyone else could
cluster just outside the open doors to listen.

At the other end of the chamber, flanked on either side by the
three tiers of steps upon which the House placed their folding
stools, stood the raised podium of the curule magistrates, in front
of it the long wooden bench upon which the ten tribunes of the
plebs perched. The beautiful carved ivory curule chairs of the two
consuls were positioned at the front of the platform, those belong-

ing to the six praetors behind, and the ivory curule chairs of the two curule aediles behind them again. Those senators permitted to speak because of sheer accumulation of years or curule office occupied the bottom tier on either side, the middle tier went to those who held priesthoods or augurships, or had served as tribunes of the plebs, or were priests of the minor colleges, while the top tier was reserved for the *pedarii*—the backbenchers—whose only privilege in the House was to vote.

After the prayers and offerings and omens were declared all satisfactory, Lucius Licinius Crassus Orator, the senior of the two consuls, rose to his feet.

"Princeps Senatus, Pontifex Maximus, fellow curule magistrates, members of this august body, the House has been talking for some time about the illegal enrollment of Italian nationals as Roman citizens during this present census," he said, a document curled in his left hand. "Though our distinguished colleagues the censors, Marcus Antonius and Lucius Valerius, had expected to see several thousand new names added to the rolls, they did not expect to see very many thousands of new names. But that is what happened. The census in Italy has seen an unprecedented rise in those claiming to be Roman citizens, and testimony has been made to us that most of these new names are those of men of Italian Allied status who have absolutely no right to the Roman citizenship. Testimony has been made to us that the leaders of the Italian nations connived at having their people enroll as Roman citizens virtually en masse. Two names have been put forward: Quintus Poppaedius Silo, leader of the Marsi, and Gaius Papius Mutilus, leader of the Samnites."

Fingers snapped imperiously; the consul stopped, bowed toward the middle of the front row on his right. "Gaius Marius, I welcome you back to this House. You have a question?"

"I do indeed, Lucius Licinius," said Marius, rising to his feet looking very brown and fit. "These two men, Silo and Mutilus. Are *their* names on our rolls?"

"No, Gaius Marius, they are not."

"Then, testimony aside, what evidence do you have?"

"Of evidence, none," said Crassus Orator coolly. "I mention

their names only because of testimony to the effect that they personally incited the citizens of their nations to apply for enrollment in huge numbers."

"Surely then, Lucius Licinius, the testimony to which you refer is entirely suspect?"

"Possibly," said Crassus Orator, unruffled. He bowed again, with a great flourish. "If, Gaius Marius, you would permit me to proceed with my speech, I will make all clear in time."

Grinning, Marius returned the bow, and sat down.

"To proceed then, Conscript Fathers! As Gaius Marius so perceptively observes, testimony unsupported by solid evidence is questionable. It is not the intent of your consuls or your censors to ignore this aspect. However, the man who testified before us is prestigious, and his testimony does tend to confirm our own observations," said Crassus Orator.

"Who is this prestigious person?" asked Publius Rutilius Rufus, without rising.

"Due to a certain danger involved, he requested that his name not be divulged," said Crassus Orator.

"I can tell you, Uncle!" said Drusus loudly. "His name is Quintus Servilius Caepio Wife-beater! He also accused me!"

"Marcus Livius, you are out of order," said the consul.

"Well, and so I did accuse him! He's as guilty as Silo and Mutilus!" shouted Caepio from the back row.

"Quintus Servilius, you are out of order. Sit down."

"Not until you add the name of Marcus Livius Drusus to my charge!" shouted Caepio, even louder.

"The consuls and the censors have satisfied themselves that Marcus Livius Drusus is not implicated in this business," said Crassus Orator, beginning to look annoyed. "You would be wise— as would all *pedarii*!—to remember that this House has not yet accorded you the freedom to speak! Now sit down and keep your tongue where it belongs—inside your shut mouth! This House will hear no more from men involved in a personal feud, and this House will pay attention to me!"

Silence followed. Crassus Orator listened to it reverently for some moments, then cleared his throat and began again.

"For whatever reason—and at whoever's instigation—there are suddenly far too many names upon our census rolls. The assumption that many men have illegally usurped the citizenship is a fair one to make given the circumstances. It is the intention of your consuls to rectify this situation, not to pursue false trails or apportion blame without evidence. We are interested in one thing only: the knowledge that unless we do something, we are going to be faced with a surplus of citizens—all claiming to be members of the thirty-one rural tribes!—who will within a generation be able to cast more votes in the tribal elections than we bona fide citizens, and may possibly also be able to influence voting in the Centuriate Classes."

"Then I sincerely hope we *are* going to do something, Lucius Licinius," said Scaurus Princeps Senatus from his seat in the middle of the right-hand front row, next to Gaius Marius.

"Quintus Mucius and I have drafted a new law," said Crassus Orator, not taking offense at this particular interruption. "Its intent is to remove all false citizens from the rolls of Rome. It concerns itself with nothing else. It is not an act of expulsion, it will not call for a mass exodus of non-citizens from the city of Rome or from any other center of Romans or Latins within Italy. Its concern is to uncover those who have been entered on the rolls as citizens who are not citizens at all. To effect this, the act proposes that the Italian peninsula be divided into ten parts—Umbria, Etruria, Picenum, Latium, Samnium, Campania, Apulia, Lucania, Calabria, and Bruttium. Each of the ten parts will be provided with a special court of enquiry empowered to investigate the citizen status of all those whose names appear on the census for the first time. The act proposes that these *quaestiones* be staffed by judges rather than juries, and that the judges be members of the Senate of Rome—each court president will be of consular status, and he will be assisted by two junior senators. A number of steps are incorporated to serve as guidelines for the courts of enquiry, and each man arraigned before them will have to answer—with proof!—the questions included within each step of the guidelines. These protocols will be too strict for any false citizen to escape detection, so much we do assure you for the moment. At a later *contio* meeting we will of course read out the text of the *lex Licinia Mucia* in full, but I am never of the opinion that the first *contio* on any bill should mire itself in detailed legalities."

Scaurus Princeps Senatus rose to his feet. "If I may, Lucius Licinius, I would like to ask if you propose to set up one of your special *quaestiones* in the city of Rome herself, and if so, whether this *quaestio* will function as the one investigating Latium as well as Rome?"

Crassus Orator looked solemn. "Rome herself will constitute the eleventh *quaestio*," he answered. "Latium will be dealt with separately. With regard to Rome, however, I would like to say that the rolls of the city have not revealed any mass declarations of new citizens we believe to be spurious. Despite this, we believe it will be worth setting up a court of enquiry within Rome, as the city probably contains many enrolled citizens who—if the enquiries are taken far enough—will be proven ineligible."

"Thank you, Lucius Licinius," said Scaurus, sitting down.

Crassus Orator was now thoroughly put out. All hopes he might have cherished to work up to some of his finer rhetorical periods were now utterly destroyed; what had started out as a speech had turned into a questions-and-answers exercise.

Before he could resume his address, Quintus Lutatius Catulus Caesar got up, confirming the senior consul's suspicions that the House was just not in the mood to listen to magnificent speeches.

"May I venture a question?" asked Catulus Caesar demurely.

Crassus Orator sighed. "Everyone else is, Quintus Lutatius, even those not entitled to speak! Feel free. Do not hesitate. Be my guest. Avail yourself of the opportunity, do!"

"Is the *lex Licinia Mucia* going to prescribe or specify particular penalties, or is punishment going to be left up to the discretion of the judges, working from existing statutes?"

"Believe it or not, Quintus Lutatius, I *was* coming to that!" said

Crassus Orator with visibly fraying patience. "The new law specifies definite penalties. First and foremost, all spurious citizens who have declared themselves to be citizens during this last census will incur the full wrath of the courts. A flogging will be administered with the knouted lash. The guilty man's name will be entered upon a list barring him and all his descendants in perpetuity from acquiring the citizenship. A fine of forty thousand sesterces will be levied. If the spurious citizen has taken up residence within any Latin Rights or Roman city, town, or municipality, he and his relations will be deprived of residence and will have to return to the place of his ancestors. In that respect only is this a law of expulsion. Those who do not possess the citizenship but who did not falsify their status will not be affected, they may remain where currently domiciled."

"What about those who falsified their status on an earlier census than this last one?" asked Scipio Nasica the elder.

"They will not be flogged, Publius Cornelius, nor will they be fined. But they will be entered on the list and they will be expelled from any Latin or Roman center of habitation."

"What if a man can't pay the fine?" asked Gnaeus Domitius Ahenobarbus Pontifex Maximus.

"Then he will be sold into debt bondage to the State of Rome for a period of not less than seven years."

Up clambered Gaius Marius. "May I speak, Lucius Licinius?"

Crassus Orator threw his hands in the air. "Oh, why not, Gaius Marius? That is, if you *can* speak without being interrupted by all the world and his uncle!"

Drusus watched Marius walk from the place where his stool sat to the center of the floor. His heart, that organ he had thought to have died inside him when his wife died, was beating fast. Herein lay the only chance. Oh, Gaius Marius, little though I like you as a man, Drusus said within himself, say now what I would say, did I only have the right to speak! For if you do not, no one will. No one.

"I can see," said Marius strongly, "that this is a carefully planned piece of legislation. As one would expect from two of our finest legal draftsmen. It requires but one more thing to make it watertight, and that is a clause paying a reward to any man who comes forward as an informant. Yes, an admirable piece of legislation! But is it a just law? Ought we not to concern ourselves with that aspect above all others? And, even more to the point, do we genuinely consider ourselves powerful enough, arrogant enough— *dim-witted* enough!—to administer the penalties this law carries? From the tenor of Lucius Licinius's speech—not one of his better ones, I add!—there are tens of thousands of these alleged false citizens, scattered from the border of Italian Gaul all the way to Bruttium and Calabria. Men who feel themselves entitled to full participation in the internal affairs and governance of Rome— otherwise, why run the risk of making a false declaration of citizenship? Everyone in Italy knows what such a declaration involves if it is discovered. The flogging, the disbarment, the fine— though usually all three are not levied upon the same man."

He turned from the right side of the House to the left side, and continued. "But now, Conscript Fathers, it seems we are to visit the full force of retribution upon each and every one of these tens of thousands of men—*and* their families! We are to flog them. Fine them more than many of them can afford. Put them upon a blacklist. Evict them from their homes if their homes happen to be situated within a Roman or a Latin place."

Down the length of the House he walked to the open doors, and turned there to face both sides. "Tens of thousands, Conscript Fathers! Not one or two or three or four men, but tens of thousands! And families of sons, daughters, wives, mothers, aunts, uncles, cousins, all adding up to tens of thousands more. They will have friends—even perhaps have friends among those who do legally possess the Roman citizenship or the Latin Rights. Outside the Roman and Latin towns, their own kind will be in the majority. And we, the senators who are chosen—by lot, do you think?—to man these boards of enquiry, are going to listen to the evidence, follow the guidelines for the inquisition of those brought before us, *and* follow the letter of the *lex Licinia Mucia* in sentencing those discovered spurious. I applaud those among us brave enough to do our duty—though I, for one, will be pleading another stroke! Or is the *lex Licinia Mucia* going to provide for armed detachments of militiamen to be in constant attendance upon each and every one of these *quaestiones*?"

He began to walk slowly down the floor, continuing to speak as he did so. "Is it really such a crime? To want to be a Roman? It is not much of an exaggeration to say that we rule all of the world that matters. We are accorded every respect, we are deferred to when we travel abroad—even kings back down when we issue orders. The very least man who can call himself a Roman, albeit a member of the Head Count, is better than any other kind of man. Too poor to own a single slave though he may be, he is still and yet a member of the people who rule the world. It endows him with a precious exclusivity no other word than Roman can bestow. Even as he does the menial work his lack of that single slave dictates, still and yet he can say to himself, 'I am a Roman, I am better than the rest of mankind!' "

Almost upon the tribunician bench, he turned to face the open doors. "Here within the bounds of Italy, we dwell cheek by jowl with men and women who are racially akin to us, even racially the same in many instances. Men and women who have fed us troops and tribute for four hundred years at least, who participate with us in our wars as paying partners. Oh yes, from time to time some of them have rebelled, or aided our enemies, or spoken out against our policies. But for those crimes *they have already been punished*! Under Roman law we cannot punish them all over again. Can they be blamed for wanting to be Roman? That is the question. Not *why* they want to be Roman, nor what prompted this recent onslaught of false declarations. Can they truly be blamed?"

"Yes!" shouted Quintus Servilius Caepio. "Yes! They are our inferiors! Our subjects, not our equals!"

"Quintus Servilius, you are out of order! Sit down and be silent, or leave this meeting!" thundered Crassus Orator.

At a pace which enabled him to preserve physical dignity, Gaius Marius rotated to look about him through a full circle, his face deformed further by a bitter grin. "You think you know what I'm going to say, don't you?" he asked the House. Then he laughed aloud. "Gaius Marius the Italian, you are thinking, is going to recommend Rome forget the *lex Licinia Mucia,* leave those tens of thousands of extra citizens on the rolls." Up flew the brows. "Well, Conscript Fathers, you're wrong! That is not what I advocate. Like you, I do not believe that our suffrage can be demeaned by allowing men to retain registration who lacked the principles to reject illegal enrollment as Romans. What I advocate is that the *lex Licinia Mucia* proceed with its courts of enquiry as its eminent engineers have outlined—but only up to a certain point. Beyond that point we dare not go further! Every false citizen must be struck from our rolls and ejected from our tribes. That—and nothing else. *Nothing* else! For I give you solemn warning, Conscript Fathers, *Quirites* listening at the doors, that the moment you inflict penalties upon these spurious citizens that consist of defilement of their bodies, their homes, their purses, their future progeny, you will sow a crop of hatred and revenge the like of which will give pause to the dragon's teeth! You will reap death, blood, impoverishment, and a loathing which will last for millennia to come! Do not condone what the Italians have tried to do. But do not punish them for trying to do it!"

Oh, well said, Gaius Marius! thought Drusus, and applauded. Some others applauded too. But most did not, and from outside the doors came rumbles indicating that those who heard in the Forum did not agree with so much clemency.

Marcus Aemilius Scaurus got up. "May I speak?"

"You may, Leader of the House," said Crassus Orator.

Though he and Gaius Marius were the same age, Scaurus Princeps Senatus had not retained the same illusion of youth, despite his symmetrical face. The lines which seamed it ate into the flesh, and his hairless dome was anciently wrinkled too. But his beautiful green eyes were young, keen, healthy, sparkling. And formidably intelligent. His much-admired and much-anecdoted sense of humor was not to the fore today, however, even in the creases at the corners of his mouth; today those corners turned right down.

He too strolled across the floor to the doors, but then he turned away from the House to face the crowds outside.

"Conscript Fathers of the Senate of Rome, I am your leader, duly reappointed by our present censors. I have been your leader since the year of my consulship, exactly twenty years ago. I am a consular who has been censor. I have led armies and concluded treaties with our enemies, and with those who came asking to be our friends. I am a patrician of the *gens* Aemilia. But more important by far than any of those things, laudable and prestigious though they may be, *I am a Roman!*

"It sits oddly with me to have to agree with Gaius Marius, who called himself an Italian. But let me tell you over again the things he said at the beginning of his address. Is it really such a crime? To want to be a Roman? To want to be a member of the race which rules all of the world that matters? To want to be a member of the race which can issue orders to kings and see those orders obeyed? Like Gaius Marius, I say it is no crime to want to be a Roman. But where we differ is on the emphasis in that statement. It is no crime to *want*. It is a crime to *do*. And I cannot permit anyone hearing Gaius Marius to fall into the trap he has laid. This House is not here today to commiserate with those who want what they do not have. This House is not here today to wrestle with ideals, dreams, hungers, aspirations. We are here today to deal with a reality—the illegal usurpation of our Roman citizenship by tens of thousands of men who are *not* Roman, and therefore not entitled to say they are Roman. Whether they *want* to be Roman is beside the point. The point is that a great crime has been committed by tens of thousands of men, and we who guard our Roman heritage cannot possibly treat that great crime as something minor deserving no more than a metaphorical slap on the wrist."

Now he turned to face the House. "Conscript Fathers, I, the Leader of the House, appeal to you as a genuine Roman to enact this law with every ounce of power and authority you can give it! Once and for all this Italian passion to be Roman must cease, be crushed out of existence. The *lex Licinia Mucia* must contain the harshest penalties ever put upon our tablets! Not only that! I think we should adopt both of Gaius Marius's suggestions, amend this law to contain them. I say that the first amendment must offer a reward for information leading to the exposure of a false Roman— four thousand sesterces, ten percent of the fine. That way our Treasury doesn't have to find a farthing—it all comes out of the purses of the guilty. And I say that the second amendment must provide a detachment of armed militia to accompany each and every panel of judges as they go about the business of their courts. The money to pay these temporary soldiers can also be found out of the fines levied. It is therefore with great sincerity that I thank Gaius Marius for his suggestions."

No one afterward was ever sure whether this was the conclusion of Scaurus's speech, for Publius Rutilius Rufus was on his feet, crying, "Let me speak! I must speak!," and Scaurus was tired enough to sit down, nodding to the Chair.

"He's past it, poor old Scaurus," said Lucius Marcius Philippus to his neighbors on either side. "It's not like him to have to seize upon another man's speech to make one of his own."

"I found nothing to quarrel with in it," said his left-hand neighbor, Lucius Sempronius Asellio.

"He's past it," Philippus repeated.

"*Tace,* Lucius Marcius!" said Marcus Herennius, his right-hand neighbor. "I'd like to hear Publius Rutilius."

"You would!" snarled Philippus, but said no more.

Publius Rutilius Rufus made no attempt to stride about the floor of the House; he simply stood beside his little folding stool and spoke.

"Conscript Fathers, *Quirites* listening at the doors, hear me, I implore you!" He shrugged his shoulders, pulled a face. "I have no real confidence in your good sense, so I do not expect to succeed in turning you away from Marcus Aemilius's opinion, which is the opinion of most here today. However, what I say must be said—and must be heard to have been said when the future reveals its prudence and rightness. As the future will, I do assure you."

He cleared his throat, then shouted, "Gaius Marius is correct!

Nothing must be done beyond taking every false citizen off our rolls and out of our tribes. Though I am aware most of you—and I think including me!—regard the Italian nationals as a distinct cut below true Romans, I hope we all have sufficient judgment left to understand that this by no means makes barbarians out of the Italian nationals. They are sophisticated, their leading men are extremely well educated, and basically they live the same kinds of lives as we Romans do. Therefore they *cannot* be treated like barbarians! Their treaties with us go back centuries, their collaborations with us go back centuries. They are our close blood kindred, just as Gaius Marius said."

"Well, Gaius Marius's close blood kindred, at any rate," drawled Lucius Marcius Philippus.

Rutilius Rufus turned to stare at the ex-praetor, speckled brows lifting. "How perceptive of you to make a distinction," he said sweetly, "between close blood kindred and the sort of kinship forged by money! Now if you hadn't made that distinction, you'd have to stick to Gaius Marius like a suckerfish, wouldn't you, Lucius Marcius? Because where money is concerned, Gaius Marius stands closer to you than your own *tata* does! For I swear that once you begged more money from Gaius Marius than your own *tata* ever had to give you! If money were like blood, you too would be the object of Italian slurs, am I not right?"

The House roared with laughter, clapped and whistled, while Philippus turned a dull red and tried to disappear.

Rutilius Rufus returned to the subject. "Let us look at the penal provisions of the *lex Licinia Mucia* more seriously, I beg you! How can we flog people with whom we must coexist, upon whom we levy soldiers and money? If certain dissolute members of this House can cast aspersions upon other members of this House as to their blood origins, how different *are* we from the Italians? That is what I am saying, that is what you must consider. It is a bad father brings up his son on a regimen consisting of nothing save daily beatings—when that son grows up he loathes his father, he doesn't love or admire him. If we flog our Italian kindred of this peninsula, we will have to coexist with people who loathe us for our cruelty. If we prevent their attaining our citizenship, we will have to coexist with people who loathe us for our snobbery. If we impoverish them through outrageous fines, we will have to coexist with people who loathe us for our cupidity. If we evict them from their homes, we will have to coexist with people who loathe us for our callousness. How much loathing does that total? More by far, Conscript Fathers, *Quirites*, than we can afford to incur from people who live in the same lands we do ourselves."

"Put them down even further, then," said Catulus Caesar wearily. "Put them down so far they have no feelings whatsoever left. It is what they deserve for stealing the most precious gift Rome can offer."

"Quintus Lutatius, *try* to understand!" pleaded Rutilius Rufus. "They stole because we would not give! When a man steals what he regards as rightly belonging to him, he does not call it stealing. He calls it repossession."

"How can he repossess what wasn't his in the first place?"

Rutilius Rufus gave up. "All right, I have tried to make you see the foolishness of inflicting truly frightful penalties upon people among whom we live, who flank our roads, form the majority of the populace in the areas where we site our country villas and have our estates, who quite often farm our lands if we are not modern enough to employ slave-labor. I say no more about the consequences to us of punishing the Italians."

"Thank *all* the gods for that!" sighed Scipio Nasica.

"I move now to the amendments suggested by our Princeps Senatus—*not* by Gaius Marius!" said Rutilius Rufus, ignoring this remark. "And may I say, Princeps Senatus, that to take another man's irony and turn it into your own literality is *not* good rhetoric! If you're not more careful, people will begin to say you're past it. However, I understand it must have been difficult to find moving and powerful words to describe something your heart isn't in— am I not right, Marcus Aemilius?"

Scaurus said nothing, but had flushed a trifle red.

"It is not Roman practice to employ paid informers any more

than it is Roman practice to employ bodyguards," said Rutilius Rufus. "If we start to do so under the provisions of the *lex Licinia Mucia*, we will be demonstrating to our Italian co-dwellers that we fear them. We will be demonstrating to our Italian co-dwellers that the *lex Licinia Mucia* is not intended to punish wrongdoing, but to crush a potential menace—none other than our Italian co-dwellers! In an inverted way, we will be demonstrating to our Italian co-dwellers that we think they can swallow us far more effectively than we have ever been able to swallow them! Such stringent measures and such un-Roman tools as paid informers and bodyguards indicate an enormous fear and dread—we are displaying *weakness*, Conscript Fathers, *Quirites*, not strength! A man who feels truly secure does not walk about escorted by ex-gladiators, nor glance over his shoulder every few paces. A man who feels truly secure does not offer rewards for information about his enemies."

"Rubbish!" said Scaurus Princeps Senatus scornfully. "To employ paid informants is plain common sense. It will lighten the Herculean task before these special courts, which will have to wade through tens of thousands of transgressors. *Any* tool capable of shortening and lightening the process is desirable! As for the armed escorts, they are also plain common sense. They will discourage demonstrations and prevent riots."

"Hear, hear! Hear, hear!" came from every part of the House, sprinkled with scattered applause.

Rutilius Rufus shrugged. "I can see I'm talking to ears turned to stone—what a pity so few of you can read lips! I will conclude then by saying only one more thing. If we employ paid informers, we will let loose a disease upon our beloved homeland that will enervate it for decades to come. A disease of spies, petty blackmailers, haunting doubts of friends and even relatives—for there are some in every community who will do *anything* for money—am I not right, Lucius Marcius Philippus? We will unleash that shabby brigade which slinks about the corridors of the palaces of foreign kings—which always appears out of the woodwork whenever fear rules a people, or repressive legislation is enacted. I beg you, do not unleash this shabby brigade! Let us be what we have always been—*Romans*! Emancipated from fear, above the ploys of foreign kings." He sat down. "That is all, Lucius Licinius."

No one applauded, though there were stirs and whispers, and Gaius Marius was grinning.

And that, thought Marcus Livius Drusus as the House wound up its session, was that. Scaurus Princeps Senatus had clearly won, and Rome would be the loser. How could they listen to Rutilius Rufus with ears turned to stone? Gaius Marius and Rutilius Rufus had spoken eminent good sense—good sense so clear it was almost blinding. How had Gaius Marius put it? A harvest of death and blood that would give pause to the dragon's teeth. The trouble is, hardly one of them knows an Italian beyond some business deal or uneasy boundary sharing. They don't even have the faintest idea, thought Drusus sadly, that inside each Italian is a seed of hatred and revenge just waiting to germinate. And I would never have known any of this either, had I not met Quintus Poppaedius Silo upon a battlefield.

His brother-in-law Marcus Porcius Cato Salonianus was seated on the top tier not far away; he threaded a path down to Drusus, put his hand upon Drusus's shoulder.

"Will you walk home with me, Marcus Livius?"

Drusus looked up from where he still sat, mouth slightly open, eyes dull. "Go on without me, Marcus Porcius," he said. "I'm very tired, I want to collect my thoughts."

He waited until the last of the senators were disappearing through the doors, then signed to his servant to pick up his stool and go home ahead of his master. Drusus walked slowly down to the black and white flagging of the floor. As he left the building, the Curia Hostilia slaves were already beginning to sweep the tiers, pick up a few bits of rubbish; when they were done with their cleaning, they would lock the doors against the encroaching hordes of the Subura just up the road, and go back to the public slaves' quarters behind the three State Houses of the major flaminate priests.

Head down, Drusus dragged himself through the ranks of the portico columns, wondering how long it would take Silo and Mutilus to hear of today's events, sure in his heart that the *lex Licinia Mucia* would go—complete with Scaurus's amendments—through the process from promulgation to ratification in the prescribed minimum time limit of three market days and two intervals; just seventeen days from now, Rome would have a new law upon its tablets, and all hope of a peaceful reconciliation with the Italian Allied nations would be at an end.

When he bumped into Gaius Marius, it was entirely unexpected. And literal. Stumbling backward, the apology died on his lips at the look on Marius's fierce face. Behind Marius lurked Publius Rutilius Rufus.

"Walk home with your uncle and me, Marcus Livius, and drink a cup of my excellent wine," said Marius.

Not with all the accumulated wisdom of his sixty-two years could Marius have predicted Drusus's reaction to this kindly tendered invitation; the taut dark Livian face already starting to display lines crumpled, tears flooded from beneath the eyelids. Pulling his toga over his head to hide this unmanliness, Drusus wept as if his life was over, while Marius and Rutilius Rufus drew close to him and tried to soothe him, mumbling awkwardly, patting him on the back, clucking and shushing. Then Marius had a bright idea, dug in the sinus of his toga, found his handkerchief, and thrust it below the hem of Drusus's impromptu hood.

Some time elapsed before Drusus composed himself, let the toga fall, and turned to face his audience.

"My wife died yesterday," he said, hiccoughing.

"We know, Marcus Livius," said Marius gently.

"I thought I was all right! But this today is too much. I'm sorry I made such an exhibition of myself."

"What you need is a long draft of the best Falernian," said Marius, leading the way down the steps.

And indeed, a long draft of the best Falernian did much to restore Drusus to some semblance of normality. Marius had drawn an extra chair up to his desk, at which the three men sat, the wine flagon and the water pitcher handy.

"Well, we tried," said Rutilius Rufus, sighing.

"We may as well not have bothered," rumbled Marius.

"I disagree, Gaius Marius," said Drusus. "The meeting was recorded word for word. I saw Quintus Mucius issue the instructions, and the clerks scribbled as busily while you two were talking as they did while Scaurus and Crassus Orator talked. So at some time in the future, when events have shown who is right and who is wrong, someone will read what you said, and posterity will not consider all Romans to be arrogant fools."

"I suppose that's some consolation, though I would rather have seen everyone turn away from the last clauses of the *lex Licinia Mucia*," said Rutilius Rufus. "The trouble is, they all live among Italians—but they know nothing about Italians!"

"Quite so," said Drusus dryly. He put his cup down on the desk and allowed Marius to refill it. "There will be war," he said.

"No, not war!" said Rutilius Rufus quickly.

"Yes, war. Unless I or someone else can succeed in blocking the ongoing work of the *lex Licinia Mucia,* and gain universal suffrage for all Italy." Drusus sipped his wine. "On the body of my dead wife," he said, eyes filling with tears he resolutely blinked away, "I swear that I had nothing to do with the false registration of these Italian citizens. But it was done, and I no sooner heard about it than I knew who was responsible. The high leaders of *all* the Italian nations, not merely my friend Silo and his friend Mutilus. I don't think for one moment that they truly thought they could get away with it. I think it was done in an effort to make Rome see how desperately universal suffrage is needed in Italy. For I tell you, nothing short of it can possibly avoid war!"

"They don't have the organization to make war," said Marius.

"You might be unpleasantly surprised," said Drusus. "If I am to believe Silo's chance remarks—and I think I must—they have been talking war for some years. Certainly since Arausio. I have no evidence, simply knowledge of what sort of man Quintus Poppaedius Silo is. But knowing what sort of man he is, I think they are already physically preparing for war. The male children are growing up and they're training them as soon as they reach seventeen. Why should they not? Who can accuse them of anything beyond wanting to be sure their young men are ready against the day Rome wants them? Who can argue with them if they insist the arms and equipment they're gathering are being gathered against the day Rome demands legions of auxiliaries from them?"

Marius leaned his elbows on the desk and grunted. "Very true, Marcus Livius. I hope you're wrong. Because it's one thing to fight barbarians or foreigners with Roman legions—but if we have to fight the Italians, we're fighting men who are as warlike and Romanly trained as we are ourselves. The Italians would be our most formidable enemies, as they have been in the distant past. Look at how often the Samnites used to beat us! We won in the end—but Samnium is only a *part* of Italy! A war against a united Italy may well kill us."

"So I think," said Drusus.

"Then we had better start lobbying in earnest for peaceful integration of the Italians within the Roman fold," said Rutilius Rufus with decision. "If that's what they want, then that's what they must have. I've never been a wholehearted advocate of universal enfranchisement for Italy, but I am a sensible man. As a Roman I may not approve. But as a patriot I must approve. A civil war would ruin us."

"You're absolutely sure of what you say?" asked Marius of Drusus, his voice somber.

"I am absolutely sure, Gaius Marius."

"I think, then, that you should journey to see Quintus Silo and Gaius Mutilus as soon as possible," said Marius, forming ideas aloud. "Try to persuade them—and through them, the other Italian leaders—that in spite of the *lex Licinia Mucia,* the door to a general citizenship is not irrevocably closed. If they're already preparing for war, you won't be able to dissuade them from continuing preparations. But you may be able to convince them that war is so horrific a last resort that they would do well to wait. And wait. And wait. In the meantime, we must demonstrate in the Senate and the Comitia that a group of us is determined to see enfranchisement for Italy. And sooner or later, Marcus Livius, we will have to find a tribune of the plebs willing to put his life on the line and legislate to make all Italy Roman."

"I will be that tribune of the plebs," said Drusus firmly.

"Good! Good! No one will be able to accuse *you* of being a demagogue, or of wooing the Third and Fourth Classes. You will be well above the usual age for a tribune of the plebs, therefore will present as someone mature, responsible. You are the son of a most conservative censor, and the only liberal tendency you have is your well-known sympathy for the Italians," said Marius, pleased.

"But not yet," said Rutilius Rufus strongly. "We must wait, Gaius Marius! We must lobby, we must secure support in every sector of the Roman community first—and that is going to take several years. I don't know whether you noticed it, but the crowds outside the Curia Hostilia today proved to me what I have always suspected—that opposition to Italian enfranchisement is not limited to the top. It's one of those odd issues where Rome is united from the top all the way down to the *capite censi* Head Count—and where, unless I'm mistaken, the Latin Rights citizens are also on Rome's side."

"Exclusivity," said Marius, nodding. "Everyone *likes* being better than the Italians. I think it's very possible that this sense of superiority is more entrenched among the lower Classes than it is among the elite. We'll have to enlist Lucius Decumius."

"Lucius Decumius?" asked Drusus, knitting his brows.

"A very low fellow I am acquainted with," said Marius, grinning. "However, he has a great deal of clout in his low way. And as he is utterly devoted to my sister-in-law Aurelia, I shall endeavor to enlist her so she in turn can enlist him."

Drusus's frown grew darker. "I doubt you'll have much luck with Aurelia," he said. "Didn't you see her older brother, Lucius Aurelius Cotta, up there on the praetors' part of the platform? He was cheering and clapping with the rest. And so was his uncle, Marcus Aurelius Cotta."

"Rest easy, Marcus Livius, she's not nearly as hidebound as her male relatives," said Rutilius Rufus, looking besotted. "That young woman has a mind of her own, and she's tied by marriage to the most unorthodox and radical branch of the Julii Caesares. We will enlist Aurelia, never fear. And, through her, we will also enlist Lucius Decumius."

There was a light knock on the door; Julia floated in, surrounded by the gauziest of linen draperies, purchased on Cos. Like Marius, she looked splendidly brown and fit.

"Marcus Livius, my dear fellow," she said, coming to slip her arms about him as she stood behind his chair and leaned her head down to kiss his cheek. "I shan't unman you by being too maudlin, I just want you to know how very sorry I am, and to tell you that there is always a warm welcome for you here."

And, so soothing was her presence, so strong her radiated sympathy, that Drusus found himself exquisitely comforted, and felt revived rather than cast down by her condolences. He reached up to take her hand, and kissed it. "I thank you, Julia."

She sat in the chair Rutilius Rufus brought for her and accepted a cup of lightly watered wine, absolutely sure of her welcome in this male group, though it must have been obvious to her as she came in that the discussion had been deep and serious.

"The *lex Licinia Mucia,*" she said.

"Quite right, *mel,*" said Marius, gazing at her adoringly, more in love with her now than he had been when he married her. "However, we've gone as far as we can at the moment. Though I shall need you. I'll talk to you about that later on."

"I shall do whatever I can," she said, clasped Drusus on the forearm and shook it, beginning to laugh. "You, Marcus Livius, indirectly broke up our holiday!"

"How could I possibly have done that?" asked Drusus, smiling.

"Blame me," said Rutilius Rufus with a wicked chuckle.

"I do!" said Julia, darting a fierce look at him. "Your uncle, Marcus Livius, wrote to us in Halicarnassus last January and told us that his niece had just been divorced for adultery, having given birth to a red-haired son!"

"It's all true," said Drusus, his smile growing.

"Yes, but the trouble is, he has another niece—Aurelia! And, though you may not know it, there was a little gossip in the family about her friendship with a certain red-haired man who is now serving as senior legate to Titus Didius in Nearer Spain. So when we read your uncle's cryptic comment, my husband assumed he was talking about Aurelia. And I insisted on coming home because I would have offered my life as a bet that Aurelia would not involve herself with Lucius Cornelius Sulla beyond simple friendship. When we got here, I learned that we had been worried about the wrong niece! Publius Rutilius tricked us brilliantly." She laughed again.

"I was missing you," said Rutilius Rufus impenitently.

"Families," said Drusus, "can be a dreadful nuisance. But I must admit that Marcus Porcius Cato Salonianus is a more likable man by far than Quintus Servilius Caepio. And Livia Drusa is happy."

"Then all's well," said Julia.

"Yes," said Drusus. "All is well."

Quintus Poppaedius Silo was traveling from place to place during the days which intervened between the first discussion of the *lex Licinia Mucia* and its passage into law by a virtually unanimous vote of the tribes in the Assembly of the Whole People. So it was from Gaius Papius Mutilus that Silo learned of the new law, when he arrived in Bovianum.

"Then it's war," he said to Mutilus, face set.

"I am afraid so, Quintus Poppaedius."

"We must call a council of all the national leaders."

"It is already in train."

"Whereabouts?"

"Where the Romans will never think of looking," said Papius Mutilus. "In Grumentum, ten days from now."

"Excellent!" cried Silo. "Inland Lucania is a place no Roman ever thinks of for any reason. There aren't any Roman landlords or *latifundia* within a day's ride of Grumentum."

"Nor any resident Roman citizens, more importantly."

"How will we get rid of visiting Romans, should any turn up?" asked Silo, frowning.

"Marcus Lamponius has it all worked out," said Mutilus with a faint smile. "Lucania is brigand territory. So any visiting Romans will be captured by brigands. After the council is over, Marcus

Lamponius will cover himself in glory by securing their release without payment of ransom."

"Clever! When do you yourself intend to start out?"

"Four days from now." Mutilus linked his arm through Silo's and strolled with him into the peristyle-garden of his large and elegant house; for, like Silo, Mutilus was a man of property, taste, education. "Tell me what happened during this trip of yours to Italian Gaul, Quintus Poppaedius."

"I found things pretty much as Quintus Servilius Caepio led me to believe two and a half years ago," said Silo contentedly. "A whole series of neat-looking little towns scattered up the River Medoacus beyond Patavium, and up both the Sontius and the Natiso above Aquileia. The iron is shipped overland from that part of Noricum near Noreia, but most of its journey is by water—down an arm of the Dravus, then it's portaged across the watershed to the Sontius and the Tiliaventus, where it goes the rest of the way by water also. The settlements highest up the rivers are devoted to the production of charcoal, which is sent down to the steel settlements by water. I posed as a Roman *praefectus fabrum* when I visited the area—and I paid in cash, which everyone grabbed at. Sufficient cash, I add, to ensure that they'll work madly to complete my order. And, as I turned out to be the first serious client they had seen, they're very happy to go on making arms and armaments exclusively for me."

Mutilus looked apprehensive. "Are you sure it was wise to pose as a Roman *praefectus fabrum*?" he asked. "What happens if a real Roman *praefectus fabrum* walks in? He'll know you're not what you purported to be—and notify Rome."

"Rest easy, Gaius Papius, I covered my tracks very well," said Silo, unperturbed. "You must understand that because of me it is not necessary for these new settlements to search for business. Roman orders go to established places like Pisae and Populonia. Whereas shipping from Patavium and Aquileia, our armaments can be transported down the Adriatic to Italian ports the Romans don't use. No Roman will get a whiff of our cargoes, let alone learn that eastern Italian Gaul is in the armaments business. Roman activity lies in the west, on the Tuscan Sea."

"Can eastern Italian Gaul take on more business?"

"Definitely! The busier the area becomes, the more smiths it will attract. I'll say this for Quintus Servilius Caepio, he's got a wonderful little scheme going."

"What about Caepio? He's no friend to the Italians!"

"But cagey," said Silo, grinning. "It's no part of his plans to advertise his business ventures inside Rome—he's just trying to hide the Gold of Tolosa in out-of-the-way corners. And he works well shielded from senatorial scrutiny, which means he's not going to be vetting anything beyond the account books too thoroughly. Nor visiting his investments too often. It surprised me when he demonstrated a talent for this sort of thing—his blood is much higher quality than his thinking apparatus under every other circumstance. No, we don't need to worry too much about Quintus Servilius Caepio! As long as the sesterces keep tinkling into his moneybags, he'll stay very quiet and very happy."

"Then what we have to do is concentrate upon finding more money," said Mutilus, and ground his teeth together. "By all our old Italian gods, Quintus Poppaedius, it would afford me and mine enormous satisfaction to stamp Rome and Romans out of existence!"

But the next day Mutilus was made to suffer the presence of a Roman, for Marcus Livius Drusus arrived in Bovianum, hot on the trail of Silo, and full of news.

"The Senate is busy drawing lots to empanel judges for these special courts right now," said Drusus, uneasy because he was inside a chronic hotbed of insurrection like Bovianum, and hoping he had not been seen coming here.

"Do they really intend to enforce the provisions of the *lex Licinia Mucia*?" asked Silo, still hardly able to believe it.

"They do," said Drusus grimly. "I'm here to tell you that you have about six market intervals to do what you can to cushion the blow. By seasonal summer the *quaestiones* will be in session, and every place where a *quaestio* sits will be plastered with posters advertising the joys and financial rewards of laying information. There'll be many a nasty type raring to earn four or eight or twelve thousand sesterces—and some will make their fortunes, I predict. It's a disgrace, I agree, but the Whole People—yes, patricians as well as plebeians!—passed that wretched law well-nigh unanimously."

"Where will the closest court to me be situated?" asked Mutilus, his face ugly.

"Aesernia. In every case the regional *quaestio* will sit in a Roman or Latin Rights colony."

"They wouldn't be game to sit anywhere else."

A silence fell. Neither Mutilus nor Silo said anything about war, which alarmed Drusus more than if they had talked of it openly. He knew he had intruded upon the hatching of many plots, but he was caught in a cleft stick; too loyal a Roman not to lodge information about any plots, he was too loyal a friend to Silo to want to learn about any plots. So he held his tongue and concentrated upon doing what he could without impugning his patriotism.

"What do you suggest we do?" asked Mutilus of Drusus.

"As I said, what you can to cushion the blow. Convince those living in Roman or Latin colonies or municipalities that they must flee immediately if they put their names down as Roman citizens without entitlement. They won't want to move, but you must persuade them to move. If they stay, they'll be flogged, fined, disbarred, and evicted," said Drusus.

"They can't do it!" cried Silo, hands clawing at nothing. "Marcus Livius, there are just too many of these so-called spurious citizens! Surely Rome has to see the sheer volume of enemies she'll make if she enforces this law! It's one thing to flog an Italian here and an Italian there, but to flog whole villages and towns of them? Insanity! The country won't lie down under it, I swear it won't!"

Drusus put his hands over his ears, shaking his head. "No, Quintus Poppaedius, don't say it! I beg you, don't say a word I could construe as treason! I am still a Roman! Truly, I am only here to help you as best I can. Don't involve me in things I sincerely hope will never bear fruit, please! Get your false citizens out of any place where to stay will lead to discovery. And do it now, while they can at least salvage something of their investments in living among Romans or Latins. It doesn't matter that everyone will know why they're leaving as long as they go far enough away to make apprehension difficult. The armed militiamen will be too few and too busy guarding their judges to voyage far afield in search of culprits. One thing you can always rely on—the traditional reluctance of the Senate to spend money. In this situation, it's your friend. Get your people out! And make sure the full Italian tributes are paid. Don't let anyone refuse to pay because of a Roman citizenship that isn't a true one."

"It will be done," said Mutilus, who as a Samnite knew how remorseless Roman vengeance could be. "We will bring our people home, and we will look after them."

"Good," said Drusus. "That alone will reduce the number of victims." He fidgeted restlessly. "I cannot stay here, I must be off before noon and reach Casinum before nightfall—a more logical place to find a Livius Drusus than Bovianum. I have land at Casinum."

"Then go, go!" said Silo nervously. "I wouldn't have you charged with treason for all the world, Marcus Livius. You've been a genuine friend to us, and we appreciate it."

"I'll go in a moment," said Drusus, finding it in him to smile. "First, I want your word that you will not seek recourse in war until there is absolutely no other alternative. I have not given up hope of a peaceful solution, and I now have some powerful allies in the Senate. Gaius Marius is back from abroad and my uncle Publius Rutilius Rufus is also working on your behalf. I swear to you that before too many years have gone by, I will seek office as a tribune of the plebs—and I will then force a general enfranchisement for the whole of Italy though the Plebeian Assembly. But it cannot be done now. We must first gain support for the idea within Rome and among our peers. Especially among the knights. The *lex Licinia Mucia* may well turn out to be more your friend than your enemy. We think that when its effects are seen, many Romans will shift their sympathy toward the Italian nationals. I am sorry that it will create heroes for your cause in the most painful and costly way—but heroes they will be, and eventually Romans will weep at their plight. So I vow it to you."

Silo accompanied him to his horse, a fresh beast from the stables of Mutilus, and discovered he was quite unattended.

"Marcus Livius, it's dangerous to ride alone!" said Silo.

"It's more dangerous to bring someone with me, even a slave. People talk, and I can't afford to give Caepio an opportunity to accuse me of being in Bovianum plotting treason," said Drusus, accepting a leg up.

"Even though none of us leaders registered as citizens, I dare not venture into Rome," said Silo, gazing up at his friend, head haloed from the sun.

"Definitely do not," said Drusus, and grimaced. "For one thing, we have an informant in our house."

"Jupiter! I hope you crucified him!"

"Unfortunately I must bear with this informant, Quintus Poppaedius. She's my nine-year-old niece Servilia, who is Caepio's daughter—and his creature." Shadowed though his face was, it became discernibly red. "We discovered that she invaded your room during your last visit—which is why Caepio was able to name Gaius Papius as one of the innovators of mass registration, in case you wondered. You may tell him this news, so that he too will know how divided this issue makes all of us who live in Italy. Times have changed. It isn't Samnium against Rome anymore, truly. What we have to achieve is a peaceful union of all the peoples of this peninsula. Otherwise Rome cannot advance any more than the Italian nations can."

"Can't you pack the brat off to her father?" Silo asked.

"He doesn't want her at any price, even the betrayal of my house guests—though I think she thought he would," said Drusus. "I have her muzzled and tethered, but there's always the chance that she'll slip her leash and get to him. So don't come near Rome or my house. If you need to see me urgently, send a message to me and I'll meet you in some out-of-the-way place."

"Agreed." Hand raised to slap Drusus's horse on the flank, Silo stayed it for one last message. "Give my warmest regards to Livia Drusa, Marcus Porcius, and of course dear Servilia Caepionis."

Pain washed over Drusus's face just as Silo's hand came down and the horse jolted into motion. "She died not long ago!" he called back over his shoulder. "Oh, I miss her!"

The *quaestiones* provided for by the *lex Licinia Mucia* were set up in Rome, Spoletium, Cosa, Firmum Picenum, Aesernia, Alba Fucentia, Capua, Rhegium, Luceria, Paestum, and Brundisium, with provision that as soon as those parts of each region had been scoured, the respective court would move to a fresh location. Only Latium ended in not having a court; the lands of the Marsi were felt to be more important, so to Alba Fucentia was the tenth place given.

But on the whole, the Italian leaders who met at Grumentum seven days after Drusus visited Silo and Mutilus at Bovianum had succeeded in removing their spurious citizens from all those Roman and Latin colony towns. Of course there were some who refused to believe they would suffer, as well as some who perhaps did believe but were just too well entrenched to consider fleeing. And upon these men the full wrath of the *quaestiones* fell.

As well as its consular president and two other senators as judges, each court had a staff of clerks, twelve lictors (the president had been empowered with a proconsular imperium) and an armed mounted escort of a hundred militiamen culled from the ranks of retired cavalry troopers and those ex-gladiators who could ride well enough to turn a horse at the gallop.

The judges had been chosen by lots. Neither Gaius Marius nor Publius Rutilius Rufus drew a lot, no surprise—most likely their wooden marbles hadn't even been put inside the closed jar of water—so how, when the jar was spun like a top, could their marbles possibly have popped out of the little side spout?

Quintus Lutatius Catulus Caesar drew Aesernia, and Gnaeus Domitius Ahenobarbus Pontifex Maximus drew Alba Fucentia; Scaurus Princeps Senatus wasn't chosen but Gnaeus Cornelius Scipio Nasica was, drawing Brundisium, a location which didn't please him in the least. Metellus Pius the Piglet and Quintus Servilius Caepio were among the junior judges, as was Drusus's brother-in-law, Marcus Porcius Cato Salonianus. Drusus himself didn't draw a lot, a result pleasing him profoundly, as he would have had to announce to the Senate that his conscience would not permit of his serving.

"Someone blundered," said Marius to him afterward. "If they had the sense they were presumably born with, they would have ensured that you draw a lot, thus forcing you to declare your feelings very publicly. Not good for you in this present climate!"

"Then I'm glad they don't have the sense they were presumably born with," said Drusus thankfully.

Marcus Antonius Orator the censor had drawn the lot for the presidency of the *quaestio* inside the city of Rome. This delighted him, as he knew his transgressors would be more difficult to find than the mass registrants of the country, and he enjoyed conundrums. Also, he could look forward to earning millions of sesterces in fines thanks to the efforts of informers, already milling eagerly with long lists of names.

The catch varied considerably from place to place. Aesernia failed to please Catulus Caesar one little bit; the town was situated in the middle of Samnium, Mutilus had succeeded in persuading all but a handful of the guilty to leave, and the Roman citizen and Latin residents had no information to offer—nor could the Samnites be subverted into betraying their own for any amount of money. However, those who remained were summarily dealt with in an exemplary manner (at least according to Catulus Caesar's lights), the President of the court having found a particularly brutal fellow among his escort to perform the floggings. The days were boring nonetheless, the procedure calling for the reading out of every citizen name new to the rolls; it took time to discover that each name when read off was no longer resident within Aesernia. Perhaps once every three or four days a name would produce a man, and these encounters Catulus Caesar looked forward to eagerly. Never lacking in courage, he ignored the rumbles of outrage, the boos and hisses with which he was greeted wherever he went, the furtive little sabotages which plagued not only him but his two more junior judges, the clerks and lictors, even the troopers of his escort. Girths snapped on saddles and riders went crashing to the ground, water had a habit of becoming mysteriously fouled, every insect and spider in Italy had seemingly been rounded up and put in their quarters, snakes slid out of chests and cupboards and bedclothes, little togate dolls all smeared with blood and feathers were found everywhere, as were dead cockerels and cats, and episodes of food poisoning became so rife the President of the court was obliged in the end to force-feed slaves some hours before every meal as well as putting guards to watch the food constantly.

Oddly enough, Gnaeus Domitius Ahenobarbus Pontifex Maximus in Alba Fucentia proved a heartening President; like Aesernia, most of the guilty were long gone, so it took the court six days of sessions to unearth its first victim. No one informed, but the man was well off enough to afford to pay his fine, and stood with head held high while Ahenobarbus Pontifex Maximus ordered the immediate confiscation of all his property within Alba Fucentia. The trooper deputed to administer the lash enjoyed his task too much; white-faced, the President of the court ordered the flogging stopped when blood began to spatter everyone within ten paces of the hapless victim. When the next culprit came to light, a different man plied the knout so delicately that the guilty back showed scarcely a laceration. Ahenobarbus Pontifex Maximus also found in himself an unsuspected distaste for informers, of whom there were not many, but who were—perhaps in consequence—particularly loathsome. There was nothing he could do save pay the reward, but he then would turn around and subject an informer to such a lengthy and unpleasant inquisition about his own citizen status that informers ceased to present themselves. On one occasion when the accused false citizen was revealed to have three deformed and retarded children, Ahenobarbus secretly paid the fine himself and firmly refused to allow the man to be ejected from the town, in which his poor children fared better than they would have in the country.

So whereas the Samnites spat contemptuously at the mere mention of Catulus Caesar, Ahenobarbus Pontifex Maximus grew to be quite well liked in Alba Fucentia, and the Marsi were treated more gently than the Samnites. As for the rest of the courts, some presidents were ruthless, some steered a middle course, and some emulated Ahenobarbus. But the hatred grew, and the victims of this persecution were enough in number to steel the Italian nationals in their determination to be rid of the Roman yoke if they died trying. Not one of the courts found itself with the backbone to send its militiamen into the rural fastnesses in search of those who had fled the towns.

The only judge who got himself into legal trouble was Quintus Servilius Caepio, who had been seconded to the court at Brundisium, under the presidency of Gnaeus Scipio Nasica. That sweltering and dusty seaport pleased Gnaeus Scipio Nasica so little after he actually arrived there that a minor illness (later discovered to be haemorrhoids, much to the mirth of the local people) caused him to scurry back to Rome for treatment. His *quaestio* he left under the aegis of Caepio as President, assisted by none other than Metellus Pius the Piglet. As in most places, the guilty had fled before the court went into session, and informers were scarce. The list of names was read out, the men could not be found, and the days went by fruitlessly—until an informer produced what seemed like ironclad evidence against one of Brundisium's most respected Roman citizens. He was not of course a part of the concerted mass enrollment, the informer testifying that his illegal usurpation of the citizenship went back over twenty years. As industrious as a dog unearthing rotting meat, Caepio went about making an example of this man, even to the extent that he ordered his questioning under torture. When Metellus Pius grew afraid and protested, Caepio refused to listen, so sure was he that this ostensible pillar of the community was guilty. But then evidence was brought forward proving beyond any shadow of a doubt that the man was what he purported to be—a Roman citizen in high standing. And the moment he was vindicated, he sued Caepio. It took a hasty trip to Rome and an inspired speech by Crassus Orator to secure Caepio's acquittal, but clearly he could not return to Brundisium. A snarling Gnaeus Scipio Nasica was obliged to go in his stead, mouthing imprecations against all Servilii Caepiones. As for Crassus Orator, obliged to undertake the defense of a man he disliked heartily, the fact that he won the case was scant comfort.

"There are times, Quintus Mucius," he told his cousin and boon companion Scaevola, "that I wish anyone but us had been consuls in this hideous year!"

Publius Rutilius Rufus was writing these days to Lucius Cornelius Sulla in Nearer Spain, having received a missive from that news-starved senior legate begging for a regular diary of Roman events; Rutilius Rufus seized upon the invitation eagerly.

> For I swear, Lucius Cornelius, that there is no one abroad among my friends to whom I can be bothered penning a single line. To be writing to you is wonderful, and I promise I will keep you well informed of the goings-on.
>
> To start with, the special *quaestiones* of the most famous law in many years, the *lex Licinia Mucia*. So unpopular and perilous to those conducting them did they become by the end of this summer that not one person connected to them did not long for any excuse to wind their enquiries down. And then luckily an excuse popped up out of nowhere. The Salassi, the Brenni, and the Rhaeti began to raid Italian Gaul on the far side of the Padus River, and created some slight degree of havoc between Lake Benacus and the Vale of the Salassi—middle and western Italian Gaul-across-the-Padus, in other words. Quick as you can say Lucius Tiddlypuss, the Senate declared a state of emergency and wound down the legal operations against the illegal Italian citizens. All the special judges flocked back to Rome, intensely grateful for the respite. And—perhaps in retaliation—voted to send none other than poor Crassus Orator to Italian Gaul with an army to put down the rebellious tribes—or at least eject them from civilized parts. This Crassus Orator did most effectively in a campaign lasting less than two months.
>
> Not many days ago Crassus Orator arrived back in

Rome and put his army into camp on the Campus Martius because, he said, his troops had hailed him as *imperator* on the field, and he wanted to celebrate a triumph. Cousin Quintus Mucius Scaevola, left to govern Rome, received the encamped general's petition and called a meeting of the Senate in the temple of Bellona immediately. But there was no discussion about the requested triumph!

"Rubbish!" said Scaevola roundly. "Ridiculous rubbish! A piddling campaign against several thousand disorganized savages, worthy of a *triumph*? Not while I'm in the consul's curule chair, it's not! How can we award a single shared triumph to two generals of the caliber of Gaius Marius and Quintus Lutatius Catulus Caesar, then turn round and award an unshared triumph to a man who didn't even wage a war, let alone win a proper battle? No! He can't have his triumph! Chief lictor, go and tell Lucius Licinius to dismiss his troops back to their Capuan barracks and get his fat carcass back inside the *pomerium,* where he can at least make himself useful for a change!"

Ow, ow, ow! I daresay Scaevola had fallen out of the wrong side of the bed—or his wife had kicked him out of it, which amounts to the same thing, I suppose. Anyway, Crassus Orator dismissed his troops and hustled his fat carcass back across the *pomerium,* but not to make himself useful for a change! All that concerned him was to give Cousin Scaevola a piece of his mind. But he got short shrift.

"Rubbish!" said Scaevola roundly. You know, Lucius Cornelius, there are definitely times when Scaevola reminds me irresistibly of the younger Scaurus Princeps Senatus! "Dear and all to me though you might be, Lucius Licinius," Scaevola went on to say, "I will not condone quasi-triumphs."

The result of this brouhaha is that the cousins have

ceased to speak. Which is making life in the Senate rather difficult these days, as they are fellow consuls. Still, I have known fellow consuls who were on far worse terms with each other than Crassus Orator and Scaevola could ever be. It will all blow over in time. Personally I consider it a great pity that they didn't stop speaking to each other *before* they dreamed up the *lex Licinia Mucia*!

And, having narrated that bit of nonsense, I have run out of Roman news! Very inert these days, the Forum is.

However, I think you ought to know that we hear great things of *you* in Rome. Titus Didius—an honorable man, I have always known—mentions you in glowing terms every time he sends a dispatch to the Senate.

Therefore, I would strongly suggest that you think seriously about returning to Rome toward the end of next year, in time to stand for the praetorian elections. As Metellus Numidicus Piggle-wiggle has been dead for some years now, and Catulus Caesar and Scipio Nasica and Scaurus Princeps Senatus are terribly involved in keeping the *lex Licinia Mucia* alive despite the trouble it has generated, no one is very interested in Gaius Marius—or who, or what might have happened in the past concerning him. The electors are in the right mood to vote for good men, as there seems to be a dearth of them at the moment. Lucius Julius Caesar had no trouble getting in as *praetor urbanus* this year, and Aurelia's half brother Lucius Cotta was *praetor peregrinus*. I think your public standing is higher than that of either of those two men, I truly do. Nor do I think Titus Didius would block your return, for you have given him longer than most senior legates give their commanders—it will be four years by autumn of next year, a good stint.

Anyway, think about it, Lucius Cornelius. I have talked to Gaius Marius, and he applauds the idea, as does—believe it or not!—none other than Marcus Aemilius Scaurus Princeps Senatus! The birth of a son the living image of him has quite turned the old boy's head. Though why I call a man my own age an old boy, I do not quite know.

Sitting in his office in Tarraco, Sulla digested his breezy correspondent's words slowly. The news that Caecilia Metella Dalmatica had given Scaurus a son occupied his mind first, and to the complete exclusion of Rutilius Rufus's other, more important news and opinions until Sulla had smiled sourly for long enough to scotch the memory of Dalmatica. Then he turned his mind to the idea of standing for praetor, and decided that Rutilius Rufus was right. Next year was the time—there would never be a better time. That Titus Didius would not oppose his going, he did not doubt; and Titus Didius would give him letters of recommendation that would greatly enhance his chances. No, he hadn't won a Grass Crown in Spain; it had fallen to Quintus Sertorius's lot to do that. But he hadn't done too badly, either.

Was it a dream? A little spiteful arrow shot from Fortune's bow through the medium of poor dead Julilla, who had woven a crown for him out of Palatine grass and put it on his head, not knowing the military significance of what she did. Or had Julilla seen clearly? Was the Grass Crown still waiting to be won? In what war? Nothing serious enough was going on, nothing serious loomed anywhere. Oh, Spain still boiled in both provinces, but Sulla's duties were not of the kind to permit the winning of a *corona graminea*. He was Titus Didius's much-valued chief of logistics, supplies, arms, strategy, but Titus Didius didn't care to use him to command armies. After he was praetor Sulla would get his chance, and dreamed of relieving Titus Didius in Nearer Spain. A rich and fruitful governorship, that was what he needed!

Sulla needed *money*. He was well aware of it. At forty-five his time was running out rapidly; soon it would be too late to make a bid for the consulship, no matter what people said to him about Gaius Marius. Gaius Marius was a special case. He had no like, not even Lucius Cornelius Sulla. To Sulla, money was the harbinger of power—and that had been true for Gaius Marius as well. If he hadn't had the fortune he had won for himself while praetorian governor of Further Spain, old Caesar Grandfather would never have considered him as a husband for Julia—and if he hadn't married Julia, he could never have secured the consulship, difficult though that had been. Money. Sulla *had* to have money! So to Rome he would go to seek election as praetor, then back to Spain he would come to make money.

Wrote Publius Rutilius Rufus in August of the following year, after a long silence:

> I have been ill, Lucius Cornelius, but am now fully recovered. The doctors called my malady all manner of abstruse things, but my own private diagnosis was boredom. However, I have thrown off both malady and ennui, for things in Rome are more promising.
>
> First off, your candidacy for praetor is already being bruited about. Reactions among the electors are excellent, you will be pleased to know. Scaurus continues to be supportive of you—a circumscribed way of saying he did not find you at fault in that old matter of his wife, I imagine. Stiff-necked old fool! He should have been big enough to have admitted it openly at the time instead of virtually forcing you into what I always think of as an exile. But at least Spain has done the trick! Had Gaius Marius only obtained the kind of support from Piggle-wiggle that you are receiving from Titus Didius, his task would have been both easier and more direct.
>
> Now to the international news. Old Nicomedes of Bithynia has died at last, aged, we believe, somewhere

in the vicinity of ninety-three. His long-dead Queen's son—now no chicken himself at sixty-five—has succeeded to the throne. But a younger son—aged fifty-seven—by name of Socrates (the elder's name is Nicomedes, and he will rule as the third of that name), has lodged a complaint with the Senate in Rome demanding that Nicomedes the Third be deposed, and himself elevated. The Senate is deliberating the matter with extreme turgidity, deeming foreign affairs unimportant. There has also been a little bit of a stir in Cappadocia, where the Cappadocians apparently have haled their boy-king off his throne and replaced him with a fellow whom they call the ninth Ariarathes. But the ninth Ariarathes died recently in suspicious circumstances, so we are told; the boy-king and his regent, Gordius, are back in control—not without some aid from Mithridates of Pontus and a Pontic army.

When Gaius Marius came back from that part of the world he made a speech to the House warning us that King Mithridates of Pontus is a dangerous young man, but those who bothered to turn up to that particular meeting contented themselves with dozing all the way through Gaius Marius's statement, and then Scaurus Princeps Senatus got up and said he thought Gaius Marius was exaggerating. It appears that the young King of Pontus has been wooing Scaurus with a spate of terrifically polite letters written in immaculate Greek and absolutely larded with quotations from Homer, Hesiod, Aeschylus, Sophocles, and Euripides—not to mention Menander and Pindar. Therefore Scaurus has concluded he must be a nice change from your average oriental potentate, keener on reading the Classics than on driving a spike up through his grandmother's posterior fundamental orifice. Whereas Gaius Marius contends that

this sixth Mithridates—called Eupator, of all things!—
starved his mother to death, killed the brother who
was King under the mother's regency, killed several
of his uncles and cousins, and then finished things off
by poisoning the sister to whom he was married! A
nice sort of fellow, you perceive, *very* up on the Classics!

Politically Rome is saturated with lotus-eaters, for I
swear nothing happens. On the court front things have
been more interesting. For the second year in a row
the Senate sent out its special courts to enquire into
the illegal mass enrollment of Italian nationals, and—
as was the case last year—found it impossible to trace
most of the men who had put down their names. However, there have been several hundred victories, which
means several hundred poor bleeding wretches have
been entered against Rome's debit account. I tell you,
Lucius Cornelius, one gets a chill on the back of the
neck if one is stranded without a dozen stout fellows
at one's back in any Italian locality! Never have I encountered such looks, such—I suppose the word is
passive—lack of co-operation from the Italians. It is
probably many years since they loved us at all, but
since these courts were established and began their
dirty work of flogging and dispossessing, the Italians
have learned to hate us. The one cheering factor is that
the Treasury is starting to bleat because the fines levied
haven't even begun to cover the cost of sending ten lots
of expensive senators out of Rome. Gaius Marius and I
intend to move a motion in the House toward the end of
the year, to the effect that the *quaestiones* of the *lex
Licinia Mucia* be abandoned as futile and far too costly
to the State.

A very new and very young sprig of the plebeian
house Sulpicius, one Publius Sulpicius Rufus, actually
had the gall to prosecute Gaius Norbanus in the treason

court for unlawfully driving Quintus Servilius Caepio of *aurum Tolosanum* and Arausio fame into exile. The charge, alleged Sulpicius, was inadmissible in the Plebeian Assembly; it should have been tried in the treason court. This young Sulpicius, I add, is a constant companion of the present Caepio's, which shows extremely poor taste on his part. Anyway, Antonius Orator acted for the defense—and made, I personally think, the finest speech of his entire career. With the result that the jury voted solidly for absolution and Norbanus thumbed his nose at Sulpicius and Caepio. I enclose a copy of Antonius Orator's speech for your delectation. You will enjoy it.

Concerning the other Orator, Lucius Licinius Crassus, the husbands of his two daughters have fared oppositely in the nursery. Scipio Nasica's son, Scipio Nasica, now has a son, called Scipio Nasica. *His* Licinia is breeding superbly, as there is already a daughter. But the Licinia who married Metellus Pius the Piglet has had no luck at all. The Piglet nursery is full of echoes because Licinia Piglet is not full. And my niece Livia Drusa had a girl toward the end of last year—a Porcia, of course, and boasting a head of hair that would set six haystacks on fire. Livia Drusa continues to be besotted by Cato Salonianus, whom I find a really pleasant sort of fellow, actually. Now in Livia Drusa, Rome really has a breeder!

I wander about, but what does it matter? Our aediles this year are curiously linked. My nephew Marcus Livius is one of the plebeian aediles, his colleague a fabulously rich nonentity named Remmius, whereas his brother-in-law Cato Salonianus is a curule aedile. Their games will be splendid.

Family news. Poor Aurelia is still living alone in the Subura, but we hope to see Gaius Julius home at last next year—or the year after, at the latest. His brother

Sextus is a praetor this year, and it will soon be Gaius Julius's turn. Of course Gaius Marius will honor his promise, bribe heavily if he has to. Aurelia and Gaius Julius have the most remarkable son. Young Caesar, as they call him, is now five years old, and can already read and write. What is more, he reads *immediately*! Give him a piece of gibberish you wrote down yourself not moments before and he rattles it off without pausing for breath! I have never known a grown man who could do that—yet there he stands, all of five years old, making fools of the best of us. A stunning-looking child too. But not spoiled. Aurelia is too hard on him, I think.

I can think of nothing else, Lucius Cornelius. Make sure you hurry home. I know in my bones that there is a praetor's curule chair waiting for you.

Lucius Cornelius Sulla hurried home as bidden, half of him alight with hope, the other half convinced something would happen to mar his chances. Though he longed with every cord that tied his heart to visit his lover of many years, Metrobius, he did not, nor was he at home to Metrobius when that star of the tragic theater came as a client to call. This was his year. If he failed, the goddess Fortune had turned her face away forever, so he would do nothing to annoy that lady; she was especially prone to dislike it when her favorites engaged in love affairs which mattered too much. Goodbye, Metrobius.

He did, however, call upon Aurelia as soon as he had spent a little time with his children, who had grown up so much that he wanted to weep; four years of their little lives stolen from him by a foolish girl he still hankered after! Cornelia Sulla was thirteen years old, and had enough of her dead mother's fragile beauty to turn heads already, allied as it was to Sulla's richly waving red-gold hair. She was regularly menstruating, so Aelia said, and the budding breasts beneath her plain gown confirmed. The sight of her made Sulla feel old, a sensation entirely new and most unwelcome; but then she gave him Julilla's bewitching smile and ran into his arms and stood almost on his level to cover his face with kisses. His son was twelve, an almost pure Caesar in physical type—golden hair and blue eyes, long face, long bumpy nose, tall and slender yet well muscled.

And in the boy Sulla found at last the friend he had never owned; a love so perfect, pure, innocent, heart-whole, that he found himself thinking of nothing and no one else when he should have been concentrating upon charming the electors. Young Sulla—though still in the purple-bordered toga of childhood and wearing the magical talisman of the *bulla* around his neck on a chain to ward off the Evil Eye—accompanied his father everywhere, standing gravely off to one side and listening intently to whatever was said between Sulla and his acquaintances. Then when they went home they sat together in Sulla's study and talked about the day, the people, the mood in the Forum.

But Sulla did not take his son with him to the Subura; he walked alone, surprised when every now and then someone in the crowd greeted him, or clapped him on the shoulder; at last he was beginning to be known! Taking these encounters as a good omen, he knocked on Aurelia's door with greater optimism than he had experienced as he left the Palatine. And, sure enough, Eutychus the steward admitted him immediately. Possessing no sense of shame, he felt at no disadvantage as he waited in the reception room; when he saw her emerge from her workroom he simply held out his hand with a smile. A smile she returned.

How little she had changed. How much she had changed. What was her age now? Twenty-nine? Thirty? Helen of Troy, yield up your laurels, he thought; here is beauty personified. The purple eyes were larger, their black lashes as dense, the skin as thick and creamy as ever, that indefinable air of immense dignity and composure more marked.

"Am I forgiven?" he asked, taking her hand and squeezing it.

"Of course you are, Lucius Cornelius! How could I continue to blame you for a weakness in myself?"

"Shall I try again?" he asked irrepressibly.

"No, thank you," she said, taking a seat. "Some wine?"

"Please." He looked around. "Still alone, Aurelia?"

"Still alone. And perfectly happy, I do assure you."

"You are the most self-sufficient person I have ever met. If it hadn't been for that one little episode, I'd be tempted to think you inhuman—or superhuman!—so I'm glad it happened. One could not maintain a friendship with a genuine goddess, could one?"

"Or a genuine demon, Lucius Cornelius," she countered.

He laughed. "All right, I yield!"

The wine came, was poured. Sipping at his cup, he looked at her across its brim, her face rayed by the fizzing little purple bubbles the slightly effervescent wine gave off. Perhaps it was the peace and contentment of his new friendship with his son allowed his eyes an extra measure of vision, pierced the lucent windows of her mind and dived into the depths beyond, there to discover layer upon layer of complexities, contingencies, conundrums, all logically put away in carefully sorted categories.

"Oh!" he said, blinking, "There isn't a facade to you at all! You are exactly what you seem to be."

"I hope so," she said, smiling.

"We mostly aren't, Aurelia."

"Certainly *you* aren't."

"So what do you think exists behind my facade?"

But she shook her head emphatically. "Whatever I think, Lucius Cornelius, I shall keep to myself. Something tells me it is safer."

"*Safer?*"

She shrugged. "Why that word? I don't honestly know. A premonition? Or something from long ago, more likely. I don't have premonitions, I'm not giddy enough."

"How are your children?" he asked, changing the subject to something *safer.*

"Would you like to see for yourself?"

"Why not? My own have surprised me, that much I can tell you. I confess I shall find it hard to be civil to Marcus Aemilius Scaurus. Four years, Aurelia! They're almost grown up, and I was not here to see it happen."

"Few Roman men of our class are, Lucius Cornelius," she said placidly. "In all likelihood you would have gone away even had that business with Dalmatica never happened. Just enjoy your children while you can; and don't think harshly of what cannot now be altered."

The fine fair brows he darkened artificially lifted quizzically. "There is so much about my life that I would change! That's the trouble, Aurelia. So much I regret."

"Regret it if you must, but don't let it color today or tomorrow," she said, not mystically, but practically. "If you do, Lucius Cornelius, the past will haunt you forever. And—as I have told you several times before—you still have a long course to run. The race has hardly commenced."

"You feel that?"

"Completely."

And in trooped her three children, Caesars all. Julia Major called Lia was ten years old and Julia Minor called Ju-ju was almost eight. Both girls were tall, slender, graceful; they looked like Sulla's dead Julilla, save that their eyes were blue. Young Caesar was six. Quite how he contrived to give the impression that his beauty was greater than that of his sisters, Sulla didn't know, only felt it. A totally Roman beauty, of course; the Caesars were totally Roman. This was the boy, he remembered, who Publius Rutilius Rufus had said could read at a glance. That indicated an extraordinary degree of intelligence. But many things might happen to Young Caesar to damp down the fires of his mind.

"Children, this is Lucius Cornelius Sulla," said Aurelia.

The girls murmured shy greetings, whereas Young Caesar turned on a smile which caught at Sulla's breath, stirred him in a way he hadn't felt since his first meeting with Metrobius. The eyes looking directly at him were very like his own—palest blue surrounded by a dark ring. They blazed intelligence. Here am I as I might have been had I known a mother like the wonderful Aurelia and never known a drunkard like my father, thought Sulla. A face to set Athens on fire, and a mind too.

"They tell me, boy," said Sulla, "that you're very clever."

The smile became a laugh. "Then you haven't been talking to Marcus Antonius Gnipho," Young Caesar said.

"Who's he?"

"My tutor, Lucius Cornelius."

"Can't your mother teach you for two or three more years?"

"I think I must have driven her mad with my questions when I was a little boy. So she got a tutor for me."

"Little boy? You're still that."

"Litt*ler*," said Young Caesar, not at all daunted.

"Precocious," said Sulla dismissively.

"Not that word, please!"

"Why not, Young Caesar? What do you know, at six, about the nuances in a word?"

"About that one, enough to know that it's almost always applied to haughty little girls who sound exactly like their grandmothers," said Young Caesar sturdily.

"Ahah!" said Sulla, looking more interested. "That's not got out of a book, is it? So you have eyes which feed your clever mind with information, and from it you make deductions."

"Naturally," said Young Caesar, surprised.

"Enough. Go away now, all of you," said Aurelia.

The children went, Young Caesar smiling at Sulla over his shoulder until he caught his mother's eye.

"If he doesn't burn out, he'll either be an adornment to his class or a thorn in its paw," said Sulla.

"Hopefully an adornment," said Aurelia.

"I wonder?" And Sulla laughed.

"You're standing for praetor," said Aurelia, changing the subject, sure Sulla had had enough of children.

"Yes."

"Uncle Publius says you'll get in."

"Let us hope he's more like Teiresias than Cassandra, then!"

He was like Teiresias; when the votes were counted, not only was Sulla a praetor, but—as he was returned at the top of the poll—he was also *praetor urbanus*. Though under normal circumstances the urban praetor's duties were almost entirely involved with the courts and with those petitioning for litigation, he was empowered (if both the consuls were absent or unfit to govern) to act *in loco consularis*—to defend Rome and command its armies in case of attack, to promulgate laws, to direct the Treasury.

The news that he was to be urban praetor dismayed Sulla greatly. The urban praetor could not be away from Rome for more than ten days at a time; the office denied Sulla a bolt-hole, he was forced to remain inside Rome among all the temptations of his old life and in the same house as a woman he despised. However, he now had a form of support never before so much as imagined, in the person of his son. Young Sulla would be his friend, Young Sulla would be in attendance on him in the Forum, Young Sulla would be at home each evening to talk to, to laugh with. How like his first cousin Young Caesar he was! To look at, anyway. And the lad had a good mind, even if not in Young Caesar's class. Sulla had a strong feeling that he wouldn't have liked his son nearly as much were he as clever as Young Caesar.

The elections had produced a bigger shock than Sulla's topping the praetors' poll, a shock not without its amusing side for those not directly affected. Lucius Marcius Philippus had announced his candidacy for consul, convinced he was the jewel in an uninspiring field. But first place went to the younger brother of the censor Lucius Valerius Flaccus, one Gaius Valerius Flaccus. That was all right, perhaps; at least a Valerius Flaccus was a patrician, his family influential! But the junior consul was none other than that ghastly New Man, Marcus Herennius! Philippus's howls of outrage could be heard in Carseoli, vowed the Forum frequenters, chuckling. Everyone knew where the fault lay, including Philippus—in those remarks of Publius Rutilius Rufus during his speech advocating a kinder *lex Licinia Mucia*. Until then, the world had forgotten how Gaius Marius had bought Philippus after he had been elected a tribune of the plebs. But insufficient time had elapsed between that speech and Philippus's consular candidacy for people to forget all over again.

"I'll get Rutilius Rufus for this!" vowed Philippus to Caepio.
"We'll both get him," said Caepio, also smarting.

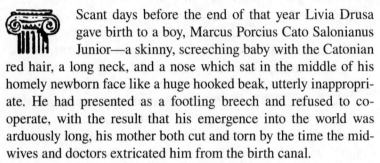 Scant days before the end of that year Livia Drusa
gave birth to a boy, Marcus Porcius Cato Salonianus
Junior—a skinny, screeching baby with the Catonian
red hair, a long neck, and a nose which sat in the middle of his
homely newborn face like a huge hooked beak, utterly inappropriate. He had presented as a footling breech and refused to co-
operate, with the result that his emergence into the world was
arduously long, his mother both cut and torn by the time the midwives and doctors extricated him from the birth canal.

"But, *domina,*" said Apollodorus Siculus, "he is quite without
harm—no bruises, no swellings, no blueness." A slight smile
crossed the little Greek physician's face. "If his behavior at birth is
anything to go by, *domina,* be warned! He will grow up to be a
difficult man."

Too exhausted to do more than smile wanly, Livia Drusa found
herself hoping she would have no more children; this was the first
time she had suffered enough during labor to feel negative afterward.

It was some days before her other children were permitted to
see her, days during which Cratippus was obliged to administer
the household unaided, as Livia Drusa was now its mistress.

Servilia predictably came no further than the door, refusing to
acknowledge her new half brother. Lilla—sternly indoctrinated
these days by her elder sister—tried to stay aloof, but succumbed
to her mother's coaxing and ended in kissing the thin, wriggling
mite tucked into Livia Drusa's arm. Porcia called Porcella was too
young at fourteen months to be invited to this puerperal visit, but
Young Caepio, now turned three, was. His reaction was ecstatic.
He couldn't get enough of this new baby brother, demanding to
hold him, to cuddle him, to kiss him.

"He's going to be *mine*," said Young Caepio, digging his heels in as his nursemaid attempted to drag him away.

"I give him to you, little Quintus," said Livia Drusa, enormously grateful that one of Young Cato's siblings had taken to him wholeheartedly. "You shall have full charge of him."

Though she hadn't come into the room, Servilia lingered in the doorway until Lilla and Young Caepio were removed, then edged just a few feet closer to the bed. Her eyes rested upon her mother derisively, her sore spirit finding satisfaction in Livia Drusa's haggard face, weary look.

"You're going to die," Servilia said, looking smug.

Livia Drusa's breath caught. "Nonsense!" she said sharply.

"You will die," the ten-year-old insisted. "I have wished it to happen, so it will. It did to Aunt Servilia Caepionis when I wished *her* dead!"

"To say things like that is as silly as it is unkind," said the mother, heart knocking frantically. "Wishes cannot make things happen, Servilia. If they do happen and you have wished, it is a coincidence, no more. Fate and Fortune are responsible, not you! You are just not important enough to engage the attention of Fate and Fortune."

"It's no use, you can't convince me! *I* have the Evil Eye! When I ill-wish people, they die," said the child gleefully, and disappeared.

Livia Drusa lay silent, eyes closed. She didn't feel well; she hadn't felt well since Young Cato was born. Yet believe that Servilia was responsible, she could not. Or so she told herself.

But over the next few days, Livia Drusa's condition deteriorated alarmingly. A wet-nurse had to be found for Young Cato, who was removed from his mother's room, whereupon Young Caepio pounced and took charge of him.

Apollodorus Siculus clucked. "I fear for her life, Marcus Livius," he said to Drusus. "The bleeding is not profuse, but it is remorseless, and nothing seems to help. She has a fever, and there is a foul discharge mixed with the blood."

"Oh, what is the matter with my life?" cried Drusus, rubbing the tears out of his eyes. "Why is everyone dying?"

A question of course that could not be answered; nor did Drusus take credence of Servilia's ill-wishing when Cratippus, who loathed the child, reported it to him. Nevertheless, Livia Drusa's condition continued to deteriorate.

The worst thing, thought Drusus, was that there was no other woman in the house of higher status than slaves. Cato Salonianus was with his wife as much as possible, but Servilia had to be kept away, and it seemed to both Drusus and Cato that Livia Drusa looked for something or someone who was not there. Servilia Caepionis, probably. Drusus wept. And made up his mind what to do.

On the following day he went to visit a house into which he had never stepped; the house of Mamercus Aemilius Lepidus Livianus. His brother. Though his father had told him Mamercus was no son of his. So long ago! Would he be received?

"I want to speak to Cornelia Scipionis," he said.

The door warden, whose mouth had been open to say that the master of the house was not home, shut it, nodded instead. Drusus was conducted to the atrium, and there waited a short time.

He literally did not recognize the elderly woman who stumped in, grey hair pulled back in an unflattering bun, clothes drab and chosen without regard for color schemes, body stout, face scrubbed and rather ugly; she looked, he thought, very like the busts of Scipio Africanus which dotted the Forum. Which was not surprising, given that she was closely related to him.

"Marcus Livius?" she asked in a lovely mellow deep voice.

"Yes," he said, completely at a loss how to proceed.

"How like your father you are!" she said, but without evidence of dislike. She sat down on the edge of a couch, and indicated a chair opposite. "Seat yourself, my son."

"I suppose you're wondering what brings me here," he said, and felt a huge lump grow in his throat. His face worked, he struggled desperately to preserve his composure.

"Something very serious," she said, "so much is obvious."

"It's my sister. She's dying."

A change came over her, she got immediately to her feet. "Then we have no time to waste, Marcus Livius. Let me only tell my daughter-in-law what's amiss, then we'll go."

He didn't even know that she had a daughter-in-law; nor might she know his wife was dead. His brother Mamercus he knew slightly from seeing him around the Forum, but they never spoke; the ten years between them meant that Mamercus was not yet old enough to enter the Senate. But, it seemed, he was married.

"You have a daughter-in-law," he said to his mother as they left the house.

"Just recently," said Cornelia Scipionis, beautiful voice suddenly colorless. "Mamercus married one of the sisters of Appius Claudius Pulcher last year."

"My wife died," he said abruptly.

"Yes, I heard that. I'm sorry now I didn't come to see you. But I didn't honestly think I'd be a welcome face in time of grief, and I have a great deal of pride. Too much pride, I know."

"I take it I was supposed to come to you."

"Something like that."

"I didn't think of it."

Her face twisted. "That's understandable," she said evenly. "It's interesting that you'd climb down for the sake of your sister, but not for yourself."

"That's the way of the world. Or our world, at any rate."

"How long has my daughter got?"

"We don't know. The doctors think very little time now, but she's fighting it. Yet she has some great fear too. I don't know what, or why. Romans are not afraid of dying."

"Or so we tell ourselves, Marcus Livius. But beneath the show of fearlessness, there's always a terror of the unknown."

"Death isn't an unknown."

"Do you not think so? Perhaps it's rather that life is sweet."

"Sometimes."

She cleared her throat. "Can you not call me Mama?"

"Why should I? You left home when I was just ten years old, and my sister five."

"I couldn't live with that man a moment longer."

"I'm not surprised," he said dryly. "He wasn't the sort of person to put up with a cuckoo in his nest."

"Your brother Mamercus, you mean?"

"Who else?"

"He is your full brother, Marcus Livius."

"That's what my sister keeps telling her daughter about her son," said Drusus. "But one look at Young Caepio is enough to tell the biggest fool whose son he really is."

"Then I suggest you look more closely at Mamercus. He's a Livius Drusus to the life, not a Cornelius Scipio." She paused, added, "Or an Aemilius Lepidus."

They had come to the house of Drusus. After the door warden admitted them, Cornelia Scipionis gazed about her in awe.

"I never saw this house," she said. "Your father had truly wonderful taste."

"It's a pity he didn't have a truly wonderful warmth," said Drusus bitterly.

The mother glanced sideways at him, but said nothing.

Whether the passionately unhappy curse of Servilia had any influence with Fate and Fortune or not, Livia Drusa grew to believe it had. For she had come to realize that she was dying, and could find no other reason for it. Four children had she brought into the world without a single complication; why should a fifth change that pattern? Everyone knew they got easier to bear.

When the stout little elderly lady appeared in the doorway of her room, Livia Drusa simply stared, wondering who was wasting her ebbing energy on a stranger. The stranger walked inside, her hands outstretched.

"I'm your mother, Livia Drusa," the stranger said, sat down on the edge of the bed, and took her girl into her arms.

They both wept, as much for the unexpectedness of this reunion as for the lost years, then Cornelia Scipionis made her daughter comfortable, and sat on a chair drawn up close.

The already clouding eyes drank in that plain Scipionic face, the matronly garb, the unadorned hair, wondering.

"I thought you'd be very beautiful, Mama," she said.

"A typical eater of men, you mean."

"Father—even my brother—"

Cornelia Scipionis patted the hand she held, smiling. "Oh, they're Livii Drusi—what more can one say on that subject? I love life, girl! I always, always did. I like to laugh, I don't take the world seriously enough. My friends numbered as many men as women. Just friends! But in Rome a woman cannot have men friends without half the world at least assuming she has more on her mind than intellectual conversation. Including, as it turned out, your father. My husband. Yet I felt myself entitled to see my friends—men as well as women—whenever I wanted. But I certainly didn't appreciate the gossip, nor the way your father always believed what the gossipers said ahead of his wife. He never once took *my* side!"

"So you never did have lovers!" Livia Drusa said.

"Not in the days when I lived with your father, no. I was more maligned than maligning. Even so, I came to realize that if I stayed with your father, I would die. So after Mamercus was born I allowed your father to think that he was the child of old Mamercus Aemilius Lepidus, who was one of my dearest friends. But no more my lover than any other of my men friends. When old Mamercus asked to adopt my baby, your father agreed at once—provided I would go too. But he never divorced me, isn't that odd? Old Mamercus was a widower, and was very glad to welcome the mother of his new adopted son. I went to a much happier house, Livia Drusa, and lived with old Mamercus as his wife until he died."

Livia Drusa managed to lift herself off her pillows. "But I thought you had many love affairs!" she said.

"Oh, I did, dear girl. *After* old Mamercus died. For a while, dozens of them. But love affairs pall, you know. They're only a way of exploring human nature if a strong attachment is lacking, which it mostly is. One looks for something, always hoping to find it. But then one day a realization dawns—that love affairs are more trouble than they're worth, that the elusive something cannot be found in this way. It's some years now since I've had a lover, actually. I'm happier simply living with my son Mamercus and enjoying my friends. Or I was until Mamercus married." She pulled a face. "I don't like my daughter-in-law."

"Mama, I'm dying! I'll never know you now!"

"Better the little we have than nothing, Livia Drusa. It isn't *all* your brother's fault," said Cornelia Scipionis, facing the truth without flinching. "Once I left your father, I made no attempt to try to see you or your brother Marcus. I could have. I didn't." She squared her shoulders, adopted a cheerful mien. "Anyway, who says you're dying? It's almost two months since you had your baby. Too long for him to make you die."

"It isn't his fault I'm dying," said Livia Drusa. "I've been cursed. I have the Evil Eye."

Cornelia Scipionis stared, astonished: "The Evil Eye? Oh, Livia Drusa, what rubbish! It doesn't exist."

"Yes, it does."

"Child, it does not! And who is there to hate you enough for that, anyway? Your ex-husband?"

"No, he doesn't even think about me."

"Who, then?"

But Livia Drusa shivered, wouldn't answer.

"Tell me!" her mother commanded, sounding every inch a Scipio.

"Servilia." It came out as a whisper.

"Servilia?" Brows knitted, Cornelia Scipionis worked the name out. "You mean a daughter by your first husband?"

"Yes."

"I see." She patted Livia Drusa's hand. "I won't insult you by telling you this is all your imagination, my dear, but you must overcome your feelings. Don't give the girl the satisfaction."

A shadow fell across her; Cornelia Scipionis turned around to see a tall, red-haired man in the doorway, and smiled at him. "You must be Marcus Porcius," she said, getting up. "I'm your mother-in-law, and I've just had a wonderful reunion with Livia Drusa. Look after her now. I must find her brother."

Out to the colonnade she went, eyes darting about fiercely until she saw her older son sitting by the fountain.

"Marcus Livius!" she said sharply when she reached him. "Did you know that your sister believes herself ill-wished?"

Drusus looked shocked. "She doesn't!"

"Oh yes she does! By a daughter called Servilia."

His lips thinned. "I see."

"Now you're *not* surprised, my son."

"Anything but. That child is a menace. Having her in my house is like playing host to the Sphinx—a monster capable of organized thought."

"Is it possible Livia Drusa is dying because she does believe herself cursed?"

Drusus shook his head positively. "Mama," he said, the word slipping out without his noticing it, "Livia Drusa is dying from an injury sustained during the birth of her last child. The doctors say it, and I believe them. Instead of healing, the injury has broken down. Haven't you noticed the smell in her room?"

"Of course. But I still think *she* believes she's cursed."

"I'll get the girl," said Drusus, getting up.

"I confess I'd like to see her," said Cornelia Scipionis, and settled back to wait by filling her mind with that slipped "Mama."

Small. Very dark. Mysteriously pretty. Enigmatic. Yet so filled with fire and power that she reminded her grandmother of a house built upon a stoppered-up fumarole. One day the shutters would burst open, the roof would fly off, and there she would stand revealed for all the world to see. A seething mass of poisons and scorching gales. What on earth could have made her so unhappy?

"Servilia, this is your grandmother, Cornelia Scipionis," said Drusus, not leaving go of his niece's shoulder.

Servilia sniffed, said nothing.

"I've just been to visit your mother," said Cornelia Scipionis gently. "Did you know that she believes you've cursed her?"

"Does she? Good," said Servilia. "I did curse her."

"Oh, well, thank you," said the grandmother, and waved her away without any expression on her face. "Back to the nursery!"

When he returned, Drusus was grinning widely. "That was brilliant!" he said, sitting down. "You squashed her flat."

"No one will ever squash Servilia flat," said Cornelia Scipionis, then added thoughtfully, "Unless it's a man."

"Her father has done it already."

"Oh, I see. . . . I did hear that he refuses to acknowledge any of his children."

"That is correct. The others were too young to be affected. But Servilia was heartbroken at the time—or I *think* she was. It's hard to tell, Mama. She's as sly as she is dangerous."

"Poor little thing."

"Hah!" said Drusus.

Cratippus came at that moment, ushering Mamercus Aemilius Lepidus Livianus.

Very like Drusus to look at, he yet lacked the power everyone sensed in Drusus. Twenty-seven to Drusus's thirty-seven, no brilliant career as a young advocate in the courts had been forthcoming, no brilliant political future was predicted for him, as it always had been for Drusus. Even so, he had a certain phlegmatic strength his older brother lacked, and the things poor Drusus had had to learn unaided after the battle of Arausio had been offered to Mamercus from birth, thanks to the presence of his mother, a true Cornelian of the Scipionic branch—broad-minded, educated, intellectually curious.

Cornelia Scipionis shifted up on her seat to make room for Mamercus, who hung back a little shyly when Drusus made no move to welcome him, just gazed at him searchingly.

"Be of good cheer, Marcus Livius," their mother said. "You are full brothers. And you must become good friends."

"I never thought we weren't full brothers," said Mamercus.

"I did," said Drusus grimly. "What is the truth of it, Mama? What you've said to me today, or what you told my father?"

"What I've said today. What I told your father enabled me to escape. I make no excuses for my conduct—I was probably all you thought me and more, Marcus Livius, even if for different reasons." She shrugged. "I don't have the temperament to repine, I live in the present and the future, never the past."

Drusus held out his right hand to his brother, and smiled. "Welcome to my house, Mamercus Aemilius," he said.

Mamercus took the hand, then moved forward and kissed his brother on the lips. "Mamercus," he said shakily. "Just Mamercus. I'm the only Roman with that name, so call me Mamercus."

"Our sister is dying," said Drusus, not releasing Mamercus's hand when he sat down, his brother next to him.

"Oh . . . I'm sorry. I didn't know."

"Didn't Claudia tell you?" asked their mother, scowling. "I gave her a detailed message for you."

"No, she just said you'd rushed off with Marcus Livius."

Cornelia Scipionis made up her mind; another escape was necessary. "Marcus Livius," she said, looking at him with tears in her eyes, "I have given all of myself to your brother for the last twenty-seven years." She winked the tears away. "My daughter I will never get to know. But you and Marcus Porcius are going to be left with six children to care for and no woman in the house—unless you plan to marry again?"

Drusus shook his head emphatically. "No, Mama, I don't."

"Then if you wish it I will come here to live, and look after the children."

"I wish it," said Drusus, and turned to his brother with a new smile. "It is good to know I have more family."

On Young Cato's two-month anniversary, Livia Drusa died. In some ways it was a happy death, as she had known its imminence, and striven to do everything in her power to make her passing easier for those she left behind. The presence of her mother she found an enormous comfort, knowing her children would be cared for with love and family feeling. Taking strength from Cornelia Scipionis (who excluded Servilia from all sight of Livia Drusa), she came to terms with her dying and thought no more of curses, of Evil Eyes. More important by far was the fate of those destined to live.

There were many words of love and consolation for Cato Salonianus, many instructions and desires, and his was the face her dimming eyes rested upon at the last, his was the hand she clung to, his the love she felt wash her away into oblivion. For her brother Drusus there were words of love and encouragement too, and words of consolation. The only child she asked to see was Young Caepio.

"Take care of your little brother Cato," she mumbled, and kissed him with lips fiery from fever.

"Take care of my children," she said to her mother.

And to Cato Salonianus she said, "I never realized Penelope died before Odysseus." They were her last words.

PART III

PUBLIUS RUTILIUS RUFUS

Though his experience in the law courts was nonexistent and his knowledge of Roman law minimal, Sulla enjoyed being the *praetor urbanus*. For one thing, he had common sense; for another, he surrounded himself with good assistants whom he was never afraid to ask on those occasions when he needed advice; and, by no means least, he had the right kind of mind for the job. What he chiefly enjoyed was what he privately thought of as his autonomy—no more being lumped with Gaius Marius! Finally he was beginning to be known for himself, as a distinct and separate entity. His tiny retinue of clients increased, and his habit of taking his son with him everywhere was deemed charming; his son, vowed Sulla, would have every conceivable advantage, including a youthful career in the law courts and the right commanders in the army.

The lad not only looked like a Caesar, but had some of the Julian brand of attractiveness as well, so that he made friends easily, and those he made, he tended to keep, thanks to a turn of mind as sympathetic as it was fair. Chief among his friends was a lad some five months older than Sulla's son, a scrawny boy with an enormous cranium rather than head, named Marcus Tullius Cicero. Oddly enough, he came from Gaius Marius's home town of Arpinum; his grandfather had been the brother-in-law of Gaius Marius's brother, Marcus, both being married to Gratidia sisters. All of this Sulla was not put to discover, for when Young Sulla brought Cicero home, Sulla found himself buried beneath a huge landslide of information; Cicero was a talker.

There was, for instance, no need to ask what the boy from Arpinum was doing in Rome—Sulla was quickly told.

"My father is a good friend of Marcus Aemilius Scaurus, the Princeps Senatus," said young Cicero importantly, "and also a good friend of Quintus Mucius Scaevola the Augur. *And* he is the client of Lucius Licinius Crassus Orator! So when Father realized I was just too gifted and intelligent to remain in Arpinum, he moved us to Rome. That was last year. We have a nice house on the Carinae, next door to the temple of Tellus—Publius Rutilius Rufus lives on the other side of the temple. I am studying with both Quintus Mucius Augur and Lucius Crassus Orator, though more with Lucius Crassus Orator, because Quintus Mucius Augur is so old. We've been coming to Rome for years, of course—I started my Forum studies when I was only eight. We're not country bumpkins, Lucius Cornelius! *Much* better stock than Gaius Marius!"

Hugely amused, Sulla sat and let the thirteen-year-old rattle on, privately wondering when the inevitable was going to happen; when that great melon of a head would snap itself off its too-slender stem, go crashing to the ground and roll away, still talking. It nodded so, it heaved itself up and down and sideways, it burdened its owner in ways obviously uncomfortable, precarious.

"Do you know," Cicero asked artlessly, "that I already have an audience when I give my exercises in rhetoric? There's no argument my preceptors can set me that I can't win!"

"I gather, then, that you're planning a career as an advocate?" Sulla asked, sneaking a few words in edgeways.

"Oh, certainly! But not like the great Aculeo—*my* blood is good enough to seek the consulship! Well, the Senate first, naturally. I shall have a great public career. *Everyone* says so!" Cicero's head flopped forward. "In *my* experience, Lucius Cornelius, a legal exposure to the electorate is much more effective than that tired old grandmother, the army."

Gazing at him with a fascinated eye, Sulla said gently, "I managed to get where I am on my tired old granny's back, Marcus Tullius. I never had a legal career, yet here I am, urban praetor."

Cicero brushed this aside. "Yes, but you didn't have *my* advantages, Lucius Cornelius. *I* shall be praetor in my fortieth year, as is correct and proper."

Sulla gave up. "I'm positive you will, Marcus Tullius."

"Yes, *tata*," said Young Sulla later, when he was alone with his father, and therefore at liberty to revert to the childhood diminutive of *tata*, "I know he's a bit of a terrible wart, but I do rather like him anyway. Don't you?"

"I think young Cicero is frightful, my son, but I agree that he's likable. Is he really as good as people say?"

"Hear him, and judge for yourself, *tata*."

Sulla shook his head emphatically. "No, thank you! I wouldn't give him the satisfaction, presumptuous little Arpinate mushroom!"

"Scaurus Princeps Senatus is terrifically impressed with him," said Young Sulla, leaning against his father with an ease and familiarity that poor young Cicero would never know; poor young Cicero was already discovering that his father was too much the country squire to impress Roman nobles, and was generally dismissed as some sort of relative of Gaius Marius's. Anathema! The result was that young Cicero was rapidly withdrawing from his father, too aware that to be labeled with Gaius Marius was a disadvantage he didn't need in his pursuit of high office.

"Scaurus Princeps Senatus," said Sulla to his son with some satisfaction, "has too much on his plate at the moment to worry about young Marcus Tullius Cicero."

It was a fair comment. As Leader of the House, Marcus Aemilius Scaurus normally attended to foreign embassages and those aspects of foreign relations not considered likely to lead to a war. Few senators honestly considered any foreign nation not a province of Rome's important enough to occupy their time, so the Leader of the House was always scratching to find members for any committee which didn't carry the perquisite of a trip abroad at State expense, and they were scant. Thus it was that the senatorial answer to the aggrieved Socrates, younger son of the deceased King of Bithynia, took ten months to formulate before the courier left for Nicomedia. It was not an answer likely to please Socrates, as it confirmed the third King Nicomedes in his tenure of the throne, and dismissed the claim of Socrates emphatically.

Then before that matter was resolved, Scaurus Princeps Senatus inherited yet another squabble concerning a foreign throne. Queen Laodice and King Ariobarzanes of Cappadocia arrived in Rome, refugees from King Tigranes of Armenia and his father-in-law, King Mithridates of Pontus. Fed up with being ruled by a son of Mithridates and the grandson of his Pontic puppet, Gordius, the Cappadocians had been trying ever since Gaius Marius departed from Mazaca to find a truly Cappadocian king. Their Syrian choice had died, rumored by poison at the hand of Gordius, so the Cappadocians dug deeply into their genealogical records and came up with a Cappadocian baron who definitely had royal blood in his veins, one Ariobarzanes. His mother—inevitably named Laodice—was a cousin of the last King Ariarathes who could honestly be called Cappadocian. Off the throne came the boy-king Ariarathes Eusebes and his grandfather Gordius, who fled at once to Pontus. But, aware that thanks to Gaius Marius Rome was looking his way, Mithridates did not act directly; he employed Tigranes of Armenia as his agent. Thus it was Tigranes who invaded Cappadocia, Tigranes who selected the new Cappadocian king. Not a son of Mithridates of Pontus this time. Pontus and Armenia in conference had agreed that no child could sit comfortably on that throne. The new King of Cappadocia was Gordius himself.

But Laodice and Ariobarzanes got away, and duly appeared in Rome in the early spring of the year Sulla was urban praetor. Their presence was a great difficulty for Scaurus, who had been heard (and read, in letters) often enough to say that the fate of Cappadocia must be left in the hands of its people. His advocacy of King Mithridates of Pontus was now an embarrassment, though the accusation of Laodice and Ariobarzanes that Mithridates was behind the invasion of Tigranes of Armenia could not be proven.

"You'll have to go and see for yourself," said Sulla to Scaurus as they left the poorly attended meeting of the Senate that had debated the matter of Cappadocia.

"Wretched nuisance!" Scaurus grumbled. "I can't afford to leave Rome at the moment."

"Then you'll have to appoint someone else," said Sulla.

But Scaurus drew his meager frame upward, chin especially, and assumed the burden. "No, Lucius Cornelius, I'll go."

And go he did, a whirlwind visit not to Cappadocia but to see King Mithridates at his court in Amaseia. Wined and dined, feted and applauded, Marcus Aemilius Scaurus Princeps Senatus had a wonderful time in Pontus. As the King's guest, he went hunting lion and bear; as the King's guest, he went fishing on the Euxine for fighting tunny and dolphin; as the King's guest, he went exploring some of the more famous beauty spots—waterfalls, ravines, towering peaks; as the King's guest, he feasted on cherries, the most delicious fruit he had ever tasted.

Assured that Pontus harbored no desire to rule Cappadocia, the conduct of Tigranes was deplored and deprecated. And having found the Pontic court gracefully Hellenized and entirely Greek-speaking, Marcus Aemilius Scaurus Princeps Senatus packed up and went home in one of the King's ships.

"He fell for it," said Mithridates to his cousin Archelaus, smiling broadly.

"I think in great measure due to your letters to him during the past two years," said Archelaus. "Keep writing to him, Great One! It's a splendid investment."

"So was the bag of gold I gave him."

"Very true!"

From the outset of his term as *praetor urbanus,* Sulla began to intrigue for one of the two governorships of the Spains, thus his cultivation of Scaurus Princeps Senatus—and, through Scaurus, of the other Senate leaders. Catulus Caesar he doubted he could ever win over entirely, due to events along the Athesis River when the Cimbric Germans had invaded Italian Gaul. But on the whole he did well, and by the beginning of June he felt himself assured of Further Spain, the better Spain to govern when it came to a man's making plenty of extra money.

But Fortune, who loved him so well, put on the guise of a strumpet, and seemed yet again to betray him. Titus Didius had come home from Nearer Spain to celebrate a triumph, leaving his quaestor to govern until the end of the year. And two days after Titus Didius, Publius Licinius Crassus celebrated a triumph for his victories in Further Spain; his quaestor was also left behind to govern until the end of the year. Titus Didius had ensured all was quiet in Nearer Spain before he departed, having waged a thorough war and utterly exhausted the Celtiberian natives. But Publius Crassus had hustled himself from his province early without the same precautions; he had collared the tin concessions, and wanted to co-ordinate his activities within some companies in which he owned sleeping partnerships. Voyaging to the Cassiterides—the fabled Tin Isles—he had overawed all who met him with the magnificence of his Romanness, offered better terms and guaranteed firmer delivery on the shores of the Middle Sea for every pound of tin the miners could produce. The father of three sons, he had used his time in Further Spain to line his own nest, and had left a province far from subjugated.

Not two market intervals after Publius Crassus celebrated his triumph the day before the Ides of June, word came that the Lusitani had erupted with renewed vigor and determination. The praetor Publius Cornelius Scipio Nasica, sent to Further Spain as a relief governor, settled down to acquit himself so well that many talked of proroguing his command into the following year; his was a very powerful family, and naturally the Senate wished to please him. Which meant Sulla could no longer hope for Further Spain.

Nearer Spain was removed from him too, in October, when the quaestor left to govern after Titus Didius's departure sent an urgent message for help; from the Vascones to the Cantabrians to the Illergetes, Nearer Spain was also in revolt. Being urban praetor, Sulla could not volunteer to go, and had to watch from the praetor's tribunal while the consul, Gaius Valerius Flaccus, was hastily equipped and sent to govern Nearer Spain.

Where else was left? Macedonia? It was a consular province, rarely if ever given to a praetor, yet only that year it had been given to last year's urban praetor, the New Man Gaius Sentius. Who had promptly demonstrated that he was brilliant, thus was not likely to be replaced halfway through a campaign he had mounted with his equally capable legate, Quintus Bruttius Sura. Asia? That province, Sulla knew, was already promised to another Lucius Valerius Flaccus. Africa? A backwater these days, a nothing. Sicily? A backwater, a nothing. Sardinia, together with Corsica? Another backwater, another nothing.

Desperate for money, Sulla was forced to watch every avenue to a lucrative governorship blocked one by one, while he was confined to Rome and the courts. The consulship was only two years away in time, and among his fellow praetors were Publius Scipio Nasica and the Lucius Flaccus who had enough influence to have already ensured he would be governor of Asia Province the following year. Both men with the money to bribe heavily. Another praetor, Publius Rutilius Lupus, was even richer. Unless he could make a fortune abroad, Sulla knew he had no hope.

Only the company of his son kept him sane, kept him from doing something stupid even though he knew it would ruin his chances forever. Metrobius was there in the same city, but thanks to Young Sulla he managed to resist his overwhelming impulse to seek Metrobius out. The urban praetor was very well known by sight to everyone in Rome by the end of his year in office—and Sulla was, into the bargain, a striking-looking man. The presence of his children negated his using his own house for a rendezvous, and that apartment out on the Caelian Hill where Metrobius lived was impossible. Goodbye, Metrobius.

To make matters worse, Aurelia was not available either; Gaius Julius Caesar had finally come home that summer, and poor Aurelia's freedom had come to an abrupt end. He had called once, to find a stiff welcome from a stiff lady, who formally asked him not to call again. No information was imparted that gave him any idea exactly what the trouble was, but he had no trouble imagining its nature. Gaius Julius Caesar would be contesting the praetorian elections in November, Gaius Marius would be throwing a still considerable weight behind him, and Caesar's wife would be one of the most watched women in Rome, even though she dwelt in the Subura. No one had told Sulla of the furor he had inadvertently caused among the vacationing Gaius Mariuses, but Sextus Caesar's wife, Claudia, had told the story as a good joke to Aurelia's husband at his welcome-home party. Though everyone passed it off as just that, a good joke, Caesar himself was not amused.

Oh, thank every god there was for Young Sulla! Only with Young Sulla was there any solace at all. Foiled at every turn, the

Sulla who would have erupted in some potentially lethal way was magically soothed, put back to sleep. Not for every piece of gold or silver in the world would Sulla have lowered himself in the eyes of his beloved son.

And so as the year wore down toward its end, Sulla watched his chances disappear, endured being deprived of Metrobius and Aurelia, listened patiently to the pretentious prating of the young Cicero, and loved his son more and more and more. Details of his life before the death of his stepmother that Sulla had never thought to divulge to anyone of his own class were freely imparted to this wonderfully understanding and forgiving boy, who drank in the stories because they painted a picture of a life and a person Young Sulla would never know. The only facet of himself Sulla did not reveal was the naked clawed monster fit only to howl at the moon. That thing, he told himself, was gone forever.

When the Senate apportioned the provinces out—which it did at the end of November that year—everything fell as Sulla had expected. Gaius Sentius was prorogued in Macedonia, Gaius Valerius Flaccus in Nearer Spain, Publius Scipio Nasica in Further Spain, while Asia Province went to Lucius Valerius Flaccus. Offered his choice of Africa, Sicily, or Sardinia and Corsica, Sulla gracefully declined. Better no governorship at all than to be relegated to a backwater. When the consular elections two years in the future came along, the voters would check up whereabouts the candidates had gone as praetorian governors, and the answer of Africa, Sicily, or Sardinia and Corsica would not impress one little bit.

And then Fortune dropped her guise, stood revealed in all the blazing glory of her love for Sulla. In December there came a frantic letter from King Nicomedes of Bithynia, accusing King Mithridates of designs on all Asia Minor, but especially Bithynia. At almost the same moment, word came from Tarsus that Mithridates had invaded Cappadocia at the head of a large army, and was not stopping until all of Cilicia and Syria also lay within his fief. Expressing amazement, Scaurus Princeps Senatus advocated that a governor should be sent to Cilicia; troops Rome did not have to spare, but the governor should go well funded, and if necessary raise local troops. He was a hardheaded Roman, Scaurus, something Mithridates hadn't understood, deeming him comfortably under his control forever thanks to a packet of letters and a bag of gold. But Scaurus was quite capable of burning a packet of letters when a threat to Rome of this magnitude presented itself; Cilicia was vulnerable—and important. Though governors were not routinely sent there, Rome had come to regard Cilicia as hers.

"Send Lucius Cornelius Sulla to Cilicia," said Gaius Marius when consulted. "He's a good man in a tight corner. He can train troops, equip them, and command them well. If anyone can salvage the situation, Lucius Cornelius can."

"I've got a governorship!" said Sulla to his son when he came home from the meeting of the Senate in the temple of Bellona.

"No! Where?" Young Sulla asked eagerly.

"Cilicia. To contain King Mithridates of Pontus."

"Oh, *tata,* that's wonderful!" Then the boy realized that this would mean a separation. For an infinitely small space of time his eyes betrayed grief, pain, then he drew a sobbing breath, and gazed at his father with that unbelievable respect and trust Sulla always found so touching, so hard to live up to. "I shall miss you, of course, but I am so very glad for you, Father." There. That was the adult emerging; Sulla was now father, not *tata.*

Bright with unshed tears, the pale cold eyes of Lucius Cornelius Sulla looked upon his son, as respectful, as trusting, as the boy's had been. Then he smiled a smile of total love. "Ah! What's all this missing business?" he asked. "You don't think I'd go away without you, do you? You're coming with me."

Another sobbing breath, a transformation into utter joy; Young Sulla's smile was enormous. "*Tata!* Do you mean it?"

"I've never meant anything more, boy. We go together, or I don't go. And I'm going!"

They left for the East early in January, which as the seasons went was still autumnal enough to make sailing feasible. With him Sulla took a small entourage of lictors (twelve, as his imperium was proconsular), clerks, scribes, and public slaves—his son, wild with excitement—and Ariobarzanes of Cappadocia, together with his mother, Laodice. His war chest was respectably filled, thanks to the efforts of Scaurus Princeps Senatus, and his mind was well primed, thanks to a long conversation with Gaius Marius.

They crossed from Tarentum to Patrae in Greece, caught ship for Corinth, went overland to the Piraeus of Athens, and there bought passage on another ship bound for Rhodes. From Rhodes to Tarsus, Sulla was obliged to hire a ship, as the season was drawing on into winter, and commercial traffic had ceased. Thus it was that by the end of January the party arrived safely in Tarsus, having seen nothing en route save a few seaports and shipyards, and a great deal of sea.

Nothing had changed in Tarsus since the visit of Marius three and a half years before, nor in Cilicia, still unhappily dwelling in limbo. The arrival of an official governor sat well with both Tarsus and Cilicia, and Sulla had no sooner taken up residence in the palace than he found himself inundated with helpful people, many of whom were not averse to the thought of some good army pay.

However, Sulla knew the man he was after, and found it significant that he had not appeared to curry favor with the new Roman governor, but rather went about his normal business, which was to command the Tarsian militia. His name was Morsimus, and he had been recommended to Sulla by Gaius Marius.

"As of now, you are relieved of your command," said Sulla in a friendly way to Morsimus when he came in answer to the governor's summons. "I need a local man to help me recruit, equip, and train four good legions of auxiliaries before the spring thaws open the passes to the interior. Gaius Marius says you're the man for this job. Do you think you are?"

"I know I am," said Morsimus immediately.

"The weather's good here, that's one thing," said Sulla briskly. "We can knock our soldiers into military condition all through the winter—provided, that is, that we can get the right material to train, and enough equipment to arm the right material no less adequately than the troops of Mithridates. Is it possible?"

"Definitely," said Morsimus. "You'll find more thousands of eager recruits than you'll need. The army is a good provider for the young, and there hasn't really been an army here for—oh, many years! If Cappadocia had had less internal strife and less interference from Pontus and Armenia, she might have invaded and conquered us anytime. Luckily, Syria has been equally beleaguered. So here we've existed by sheer good luck."

"Fortune," said Sulla, grinning his most feral grin, and threw his arm around his son's shoulders. "Fortune favors me, Morsimus. One day I shall call myself Felix." He gave Young Sulla a hug. "However, there's one extremely important thing I have to do before another day of sun goes by, even if it is winter sun."

The Tarsian Greek looked puzzled. "Is it something I can assist you with, Lucius Cornelius?"

"I imagine so. You can tell me whereabouts I can buy a good shady hat which won't fall apart in ten days," said Sulla.

"Father, if you mean me to wear a hat, I won't," said Young Sulla as he walked with Sulla to the marketplace. "A *hat*! Only old farmers sucking straws wear hats."

"And I," said Sulla, smiling.

"You?"

"When I'm on campaign, Young Sulla, I wear a big shady hat. Gaius Marius advised me to do so years ago, when we first went to Africa to fight King Jugurtha of Numidia. Wear it and don't take any notice of the jeers, he said—or words to that effect. After a while, everyone ceases to notice. I took his advice, because my skin is so fair I burn and burn and burn. In fact, after I made my reputation in Numidia, my hat became famous."

"I've never seen you wear one in Rome," said his son.

"In Rome I try to stay out of the sun. That's why I had a canopy erected over my praetor's tribunal last year."

A silence fell; the narrow alley through which they were walking suddenly opened out into a huge irregular square shaded by many trees, and filled with many booths and stalls.

"Father?" asked a small voice.

Sulla glanced sideways, surprised to find there was very little between his height and his son's; the Caesar blood was winning, Young Sulla would be tall.

"Yes, my son?" he asked.

"Please, may I have a hat too?"

 When King Mithridates heard that a Roman governor had been sent to Cilicia and was busy raising and training local troops, he stared in blank amazement at his informant, Gordius, the new King of Cappadocia.

"Who is this Lucius Cornelius Sulla?" he asked.

"None of us knows anything about him, Great One, except that last year he was chief magistrate of the city of Rome, and that he has been a legate to several famous Roman generals—Gaius Marius in Africa against King Jugurtha, Quintus Lutatius Catulus Caesar in Italian Gaul against the Germans, and Titus Didius in Spain against the local savages," said Gordius, rattling off all this information in tones which indicated the names save for Gaius Marius meant little or nothing to him.

They meant little or nothing to Mithridates too, yet one more time when the King of Pontus found himself regretting his lack of a geographical and historical education. It was left to Archelaus to expand the King's horizons.

"He's no Gaius Marius, this Lucius Cornelius Sulla," said Archelaus thoughtfully, "but his experience is formidable, and we ought not underestimate him just because his name is one we don't know. Most of his time since he entered the Senate of Rome has been spent with the armies of Rome, though I do not think he has ever commanded an army in the field."

"His name is Cornelius," said the King, chest swelling, "but is he a Scipio? What is this 'Sulla' business?"

"Not a Scipio, Almighty King," said Archelaus. "However, he is a patrician Cornelius, rather than what the Romans call a New Man, a nobody. He is said to be—difficult."

"Difficult?"

Archelaus swallowed; he had come to the end of his information, and had no idea what Sulla's difficulty consisted of. So he guessed. "Not easy in negotiation, Great One. Not willing to see any side of things except his own."

They were at the court in Sinope, the King's favorite city at any time, but in winter especially. Things had been fairly peaceful for some years; no courtiers or relatives had bitten the dust, Gordius's daughter Nysa had proven so satisfactory a consort that her father had found himself elevated to the throne of Cappadocia after the intervention of Tigranes, the King's brigade of sons were growing up, and Pontus's possessions along the Euxine on the east and north were prospering.

But the memory of Gaius Marius was fading, and the King of Pontus was looking once more to the south and west; his ploy of using Tigranes in Cappadocia had worked, and Gordius was still king there, despite Scaurus's visit. All of benefit to Rome that the visit of Scaurus had achieved was the withdrawal of the army of Armenia from Cappadocia—always the intention of Mithridates anyway. Now at last it seemed as if Bithynia might fall into his grasp, for a year before, Socrates had come bleating to beg for asylum in Pontus, and had turned himself so thoroughly into a Mithridatic creature that the King decided he might safely be installed upon the Bithynian throne as a measure preliminary to outright invasion. This last Mithridates had intended to start in the spring, marching so swiftly westward that King Nicomedes the Third would find himself completely lost.

The news now brought by Gordius gave him pause; dare he move to annex Bithynia or even seat Socrates upon its throne when not one, but two, Roman governors dwelt nearby? Four legions in Cilicia! It was said that Rome could beat the world with four good legions. Admittedly these were Cilician auxiliaries, not Roman soldiers, but the Cilicians were warlike and proud—had they not been, Syria would have retained possession of the place, weakened condition and all. Four legions numbered about twenty thousand actual fighting men. Whereas Pontus could field two hundred thousand. Numerically, no contest. Yet—yet—yet . . . Who *was* this

Lucius Cornelius Sulla? No one had heard of Gaius Sentius or his legate Quintus Bruttius Sura either, yet the two of them were sweeping the Macedonian border from Illyricum in the west to the Hellespont in the east, a devastating campaign which had the Celts and the Thracians reeling. No one was even sure anymore that the Romans would stay out of the lands of the Danubius River; this worried Mithridates, who planned to move down the western shores of the Euxine into the lands of the Danubius. The thought of finding Rome there when he arrived was not welcome.

Who was Lucius Cornelius Sulla? Another Roman general of Sentius's caliber? Why send this particular man to garrison Cilicia when they had Gaius Marius and Catulus Caesar at home, two men who had beaten the Germans? One—Marius—had appeared alone and unarmed in Cappadocia, speaking words which had indicated he would be back in Rome keeping his eyes and ears on the doings of Pontus. So why wasn't it Gaius Marius in Cilicia? Why was it this unknown Lucius Cornelius Sulla? Rome seemed always to be able to produce a brilliant general. Was Sulla even more brilliant than Marius? Though armies aplenty did Pontus possess, brilliant generals he did not. After doing so well against the barbarians at the top of the Euxine Sea, Archelaus itched to try his luck against more formidable foes. But Archelaus was a cousin, he had the Blood Royal, he was a potential rival. The same could be said of his brother Neoptolemus and his cousin Leonippus. And what king could be sure of his sons? Their mothers hungered after power, their mothers were all potential enemies; so too were they when they reached an age to covet their father's throne of their own volition.

If only he had been gifted with generalship! thought King Mithridates to himself, while his brown-flecked grape-green eyes roamed unseeingly over the faces of the men around him. But in that area, the heroic talents passed down to him from his ancestor Herakles had failed. Or had they? Come to think of it, Herakles had not been a general! Herakles had worked alone—against lions and bears, usurping kings, gods and goddesses, chthonic dogs, all manner of monsters. The sort of adversaries Mithridates himself might welcome. In the days of Herakles, generals had not been invented; warriors banded together, met other bands of warriors, got down from the chariots they seemed to tool everywhere, and fought hand-to-hand duels. Now *that* was the kind of war the King felt himself qualified to wage! But those days were gone forever, just like the chariots. Modern times were army times; generals were demigods who sat or stood somewhere elevated above the field and pointed, and gave orders, and nibbled reflectively at a hangnail while their eyes were busy, busy, overseeing each and every movement below. Generals seemed instinctively to know where the line was about to flag or fall back, where the Enemy was going to concentrate for a mass assault—and generals were *born* already understanding flanks, maneuvers, sieges, artillery, relief columns, formations, deployments, rank from file. All things Mithridates could not cope with, had no feeling for, interest in, talent at.

And while his eyes roved sightlessly, everyone who watched the King watched him more closely than a hovering falcon the mouse in the grass below—not feeling like the falcon, but like the mouse. There he sat upon his chair of solid gold inlaid with a million pearls and rubies, clad (since this was a war council) in lion skin and a shirt of the softest, most flexible mail, every knitted link plated with gold. Glittering. Striking fear into every heart. No one stood against the King, no one knew how he stood with the King. Complete ruler of men, complex mixture of coward and hero, braggart and groveler, savior and destroyer. In Rome, no one would have believed him, and everyone would have laughed. In Sinope, everyone believed him, and no one laughed.

Finally the King spoke. "Whoever this Lucius Cornelius Sulla is, the Romans have sent him without an army to garrison a strange land and employ troops unfamiliar to him. Therefore I must assume this Lucius Cornelius Sulla is a worthy foe." He let his eyes rest upon Gordius. "How many of my soldiers did I send to your kingdom of Cappadocia in the autumn?"

"Fifty thousand, Great King," said Gordius.

"In the early spring I will come to Eusebeia Mazaca myself,

with a further fifty thousand. Neoptolemus will come with me as my general. Archelaus, you will go to Galatia with fifty thousand more men and garrison that place on its western border, in case the Romans are actually planning to invade Pontus on two fronts. My Queen will govern from Amaseia, but her sons will remain here in Sinope under guard, hostages against her good behavior. If she should plan anything treasonous, all her sons will be executed immediately," said King Mithridates.

"My daughter does not dream of such things!" cried Gordius, aghast, worried that one of the King's minor wives would manufacture a treason which would see his grandsons dead before the truth could be established.

"I have no reason to suppose she does," said the King. "It is a precaution I always take these days. When I am out of my own lands, the children of each of my wives are taken to a different city, and held against each wife's conduct in my absence. Women are odd cattle," the King went on thoughtfully. "They always seem to prize their children ahead of themselves."

"You had better guard yourself against the one who does not," said a thin and simpering voice which emanated from a fat and simpering person.

"I do, Socrates, I do," said Mithridates with a grin. He had developed a liking for this repellent client from Bithynia, if for no other reason than he could point with pride to the fact that no brother of his so repellent could possibly have survived into his late fifties. That no brother of his had survived to see twenty, repellent or not, was something he never bothered to think about. A soft lot, the Bithynians. If it hadn't been for Rome and Roman protection, Bithynia would have been gulped into the maw of Pontus a generation ago. Rome, Rome, Rome! Always it came back to Rome. Why couldn't Rome find a terrible war at the other end of the Middle Sea to keep her occupied for a decade or so? Then, by the time she managed to turn her eyes eastward again, Pontus would reign supreme, and Rome would have no choice but to confine her attentions to the west. The setting sun.

"Gordius, I leave it to you to watch how this Lucius Cornelius

Sulla goes about things in Cilicia. Keep me informed about every last detail! Nothing must escape you. Is that clear?"

Gordius shivered. "Yes, Almighty One."

"Good!" The King yawned. "I'm hungry. We'll eat." But when Gordius moved to accompany the group to the dining room, the King balked. "Not you!" he said sharply. "You go back to Mazaca. At once. Cappadocia must be seen to have a king."

Unfortunately for Mithridates, the spring weather favored Sulla. The pass through the Cilician Gates was lower and the snow less deep than the series of three passes through which Mithridates had to move those extra fifty thousand men from their camp outside Zela to the foot of Mount Argaeus. Gordius had already sent word all the way to Sinope that Sulla and his army were moving before the King could hope to traverse his mountainous barriers. So when further word came as the King was setting out from Zela that Sulla had arrived in Cappadocia and was putting his men into camp some four hundred *stades* south of Mazaca and four hundred *stades* west of Cappadocian Comana—and seemed content to be doing this—the King breathed easier.

Even so, he hustled his army through the treacherous terrain, indifferent to the plight of men and animals, his officers ready with the lash to goad the driven on, equally ready with the boot to shove the hopeless out of the way. Couriers had already gone east to Armenian Artaxata and the King's son-in-law Tigranes, warning him that Cilicia was now garrisoned by the Romans, and that a Roman governor was on the prowl in Cappadocia. Alarmed, Tigranes thought it best to notify his Parthian masters of this fact and wait for orders from Seleuceia-on-Tigris before he did anything at all. Mithridates hadn't asked for aid, but Tigranes had got his measure long since, and wasn't sure *he* wanted to face Rome, whether Mithridates did or not.

When the King of Pontus reached the Halys, crossed it, and put his fifty thousand men into camp alongside the fifty thousand who already occupied Mazaca, he was met by Gordius, big with the most extraordinary news.

"The Roman is busy building a *road*!"

The King stopped, absolutely still. "A road?"

"Through the pass of the Cilician Gates, O Great One."

"But there's a road already," said Mithridates.

"I know, I know!"

"Then why build another?"

"I don't know!"

The full red lips enclosing the small mouth pursed smaller, curled outward, worked inward, giving Mithridates, had he known it (or had some had the courage to tell him, which no one ever did), a distinct resemblance to a fish; this activity continued for some moments, then the King shrugged. "They love building roads," he said in tones of puzzled wonder. "I suppose it might be a way to fill in time." His face became ugly. "After all, he got here a lot faster than I did!"

"About the road, Great King," said Neoptolemus delicately.

"What about it?"

"I think it may turn out to be that Lucius Cornelius Sulla is *improving* the road. The better the road, the quicker he can move his troops. That's why the Romans build good roads."

"But he marched up the existing road without changing it then—why build it anew after he's traveled it?" cried Mithridates, who did not begin to understand; men were expendable, the lash got them there as long as there was some kind of track. Why bother to make the way as easy as a stroll through town?

"I imagine," said Neoptolemus with exquisite patience, "that, having experienced the condition of the existing road, the Roman decided to improve it in case he ever has to use it again."

That penetrated. The King's eyes bulged. "Well, he's due for a surprise! After I've thrown him and his Cilician mercenaries out of Cappadocia, I won't bother to tear up his new road—I'll tear the mountains down on top of it instead!"

"Splendidly expressed, Great One," fawned Gordius.

The King grunted contemptuously. He moved toward his horse, stepped upon a kneeling slave's back, and settled himself in the saddle. Without waiting to see who was ready to follow, he kicked the animal in its sides, and galloped off. Gordius scrambled into his own saddle and pursued the King, bleating, leaving Neoptolemus standing watching them recede into the distance.

Very difficult getting foreign ideas into the King's head, thought Neoptolemus. Has he grasped the point of the road? Why does he not see it? I do! We're both Pontines, neither of us was educated abroad, our backgrounds are similar as far as blood goes. In actual fact, his is the richer exposure to various places. Yet he can be so blind to the significance of some things I see at once. Though other things he sees more quickly than I do. Different minds, I suppose. Different ways of thinking. Perhaps when a man is a complete autocrat, his mind shifts in some way? He is no fool, my cousin Mithridates. A pity then that he understands the Romans so little. Much as he would deny the charge vigorously, he isn't even interested in understanding the Romans. Most of his conclusions about them are based on his bizarre adventures in Asia Province, and that is not the excellent background he thinks it is. How can the rest of us make him see what we see?

The King's stay in the blue palace at Eusebeia Mazaca was brief; on the day following his arrival he led his army out in Sulla's direction, all hundred thousand soldiers. No need to worry about roads here! Though there was an occasional hill to climb and the outlandish gorges of tufa towers to skirt round, the way was easy for men on the march. Mithridates was satisfied with his progress, one hundred and sixty *stades* in the day; not unless he had seen it through his own eyes would he have believed that a Roman army marching across the same roadless terrain could have covered over twice that distance without being really extended.

But Sulla didn't move. His camp lay in the midst of a huge expanse of flat ground and he had used his time in fortifying it formidably, despite the fact that the Cappadocian lack of forests had meant fetching the timber from the Cilician Gates. Thus when Mithridates came over the horizon he saw a structure, perfectly square, enclosing a space some thirty-two square *stades* in area within massive embankments, topped by a spiked palisade ten feet high, and having in front of its walls three ditches, the outermost twenty feet wide and filled with water, the middle one fifteen feet wide and filled with sharpened stakes, and the innermost twenty feet wide and filled with water. There were, his scouts informed him, four paths across the ditches, one to each of the four gates, which were placed in the center of each side of the square.

It was the first time in his life that Mithridates had seen a Roman camp. He wanted to gape, but could not because there were too many eyes upon him. That he could take it he was sure—but at enormous cost. So he sat his vast army down and rode out himself to look at Sulla's fortress at close quarters.

"My lord King, a herald from the Romans," said one of his officers, coming to find him as he rode slowly along one side of Sulla's admirably engineered stronghold.

"What do they want?" asked Mithridates, frowning at the wall and the palisade, the tall watchtowers which marched along it at frequent intervals.

"The proconsul Lucius Cornelius Sulla requests a parley."

"I agree to that. Where, and when?"

"On the path leading to the Roman camp's front gate—that path to your right, Great King. Just you and he, the herald says."

"When?"

"Now, Great One."

The King kicked his horse to the right, eager to see this Lucius Cornelius Sulla, and not at all afraid; nothing he had heard about Romans suggested the kind of treachery that would, under a truce, fell him with a spear as he walked unguarded to a rendezvous. So when he reached the path he slid down from his horse without thinking things through, and stopped, annoyed at his own obtuseness. He mustn't let a Roman do to him again what Gaius Marius had done to him—look down on him! Back onto the horse he climbed. *He* would look down on Lucius Cornelius Sulla! But the horse refused to tread this roadway, eyes rolling white at sight of the perilous ditches on either side. For a moment the King fought the animal, then decided this would harm his image even more. Back he came, back off the horse he slid, and now he walked alone to its middle, where the ditches literally stuffed with sharpened pointed stakes yawned like mouths full of teeth.

The gate opened, a man slid round it and walked toward him. Quite a little fellow compared to his own splendid height, the King was pleased to see—but very well put together. The Roman was clad in a plain steel cuirass shaped to his torso, wore the double kilt of leather straps called *pteryges,* a scarlet tunic, and, flowing out behind him, a scarlet cape. Bareheaded, his red-gold hair blazed in the sun, stirred by a little wind. King Mithridates couldn't take his eyes off it, for in all his life he had never seen hair that color, even on the Celtic Galatians. Nor such ice-white skin, visible between the hem just above the Roman's knees and his sturdy unornamented boots midway up impressively muscled calves, visible down the length of his arms, visible on neck and face too. *Ice*-white! No atom of color in it!

And then Lucius Cornelius Sulla was close enough for the King to see his face, and then he was close enough for the King to see his eyes. The King literally shivered. *Apollo!* Apollo in the guise of a *Roman!* The face was so strong, so godlike, so awful in its majesty—no smooth-faced simpering Greek statue, this, but the god as the god must surely be, so long after his creation. A man-god in the prime of his life, full of power. A Roman. *A Roman!*

Sulla had gone out to this meeting completely sure of himself, for he had listened to Gaius Marius describe his own encounter with the King of Pontus; between the two of them, they had got his measure. It hadn't occurred to him that his very appearance would throw the King off balance—nor did he, seeing this was so, understand exactly why. Exactly why didn't matter. He simply resolved to use this unexpected advantage.

"What are you doing in Cappadocia, King Mithridates?" he asked.

"Cappadocia belongs to me," the King said, but not in the roaring voice he had originally intended to use before he set eyes on the Roman

Apollo; it came out rather small and weak, and he knew it, and he hated himself for it.

"Cappadocia belongs to the Cappadocians."

"The Cappadocians are the same people as the Pontines."

"How can that be, when they have had their own line of kings for as many hundreds of years as the Pontines?"

"Their kings have been foreigners, not Cappadocians."

"In what way?"

"They are Seleucids from Syria."

Sulla shrugged. "Odd, then, King Mithridates, that the Cappadocian king I have inside these camp walls behind me doesn't look a scrap like a Seleucid from Syria. Or like you! Nor is his genealogy Syrian, Seleucid or otherwise. King Ariobarzanes is a Cappadocian, and chosen by his own people in place of your son Ariarathes Eusebes."

Mithridates started. Gordius had never told him Marius found out who was father to King Ariarathes Eusebes; Sulla's statement seemed to him prescient, unnatural. Yet one more evidence of the Roman Apollo.

"King Ariarathes Eusebes is dead, he died during the invasion of the Armenians," said Mithridates, still in that small meek voice. "The Cappadocians now have a Cappadocian king. His name is Gordius, and I am here to ensure he remains king."

"Gordius is your creature, King Mithridates, as is only to be expected in a father-in-law whose daughter is the Queen of Pontus," said Sulla evenly. "Gordius is not the king chosen by the Cappadocians. He is the king *you* chose through the agency of your son-in-law Tigranes. Ariobarzanes is the rightful king."

Yet more inside knowledge! Who was this Lucius Cornelius Sulla, if not Apollo? "Ariobarzanes is a pretender!"

"Not according to the Senate and People of Rome," said Sulla, pressing his advantage. "I am here on commission from the Senate and People of Rome to ensure that King Ariobarzanes is reinstated, and that Pontus—*and* Armenia!—stay out of Cappadocian lands."

"It is no business of Rome's!" cried the King, gathering courage as his temper frayed.

"Everything in the world is Rome's business," said Sulla, and gauged the time right to strike. "Go home, King Mithridates."

"Cappadocia is as much my home as Pontus!"

"No, it is not. Go home to Pontus."

"And are you going to make me, with your pathetic little army?" sneered the King, angry now indeed. "Look out there, Lucius Cornelius Sulla! A hundred thousand men!"

"A hundred thousand barbarians," said Sulla scornfully. "I'll eat them."

"I'll fight! I warn you, I'll fight!"

Sulla turned his shoulder, preparing to walk away, and said over it, "Oh, stop posturing and go home!" And walked away. At the gate he turned back and said more loudly, "Go home, King Mithridates. Eight days from now I march to Eusebeia Mazaca to put King Ariobarzanes back on his throne. If you oppose me, I'll annihilate your army and kill you. Not twice the number of men I can see would stop me."

"You don't even have Roman soldiers!" shouted the King.

Sulla smiled dreadfully. "Roman enough," he said. "They have been equipped and trained by a Roman—and they will fight like Romans, so much I promise you. Go home!"

Back to his imperial tent stormed the King, in such a fury that no one dared speak to him, even Neoptolemus. Once inside he didn't pause, but went straight to his private room at the back, and there sat upon a kingly seat, his purple cloak thrown over his head. No, Sulla *wasn't* Apollo! He was just a Roman. But what sort of men were Romans, that they could look like Apollo? Or, like Gaius Marius, bulk so large and so kingly that they never doubted their power, their authority? Romans he had seen in Asia Province, even—in the distance—the governor; they had seemed, though arrogant, ordinary men. But two Romans only had he met, Gaius Marius and Lucius Cornelius Sulla. Which kind of Roman was the real Roman? His common sense said the Asia Province Roman. Whereas his bones said, Marius and Sulla. After all, he was a great king, descended from Herakles, and from Darius of Persia. Therefore those who came against him were bound to be great.

Why couldn't he command an army in person? Why couldn't he understand the art? Why did he have to leave it to men like his cousins Archelaus and Neoptolemus? There were some sons with promise—but they had ambitious mothers. Where could he turn and be *sure*? How could he deal with the great Romans, the ones who beat hundreds of thousands of soldiers?

Rage dissolved into tears; the King wept vainly until his despair passed into resignation, moods alien to his nature. Accept he must that the great Romans could not be beaten. And his own ambitions could not in turn come to pass—unless the gods smiled on Pontus by giving the great Romans something to do much closer to Rome than Cappadocia. If the day should come when the only Romans sent against Pontus were ordinary men, then Mithridates would move. Until then, Cappadocia, Bithynia and Macedonia would have to wait. He threw off his purple cloak, got to his feet.

Gordius and Neoptolemus were waiting in the outer room of the tent; when the King appeared in the aperture leading to his private domain, the two men leaped up from their chairs.

"Move the army," said Mithridates curtly. "We go back to Pontus. Let the Roman put Ariobarzanes back on the Cappadocian throne! I am young. I have time. I will wait until Rome is occupied elsewhere, and then I will march into the west."

"But what about me?" wailed Gordius.

The King bit his forefinger, staring at Gordius fixedly. "I think it's time I was rid of you, father-in-law," he said, lifted his chin and shouted, "Guards! Inside!"

In they spilled.

"Take him away and kill him," said the King, waving at the cringing Gordius, then turned to Neoptolemus, standing white-faced and trembling. "What are you waiting for?" he asked. "Move the army! *Now!*"

* * *

"Well, well!" said Sulla to Young Sulla. "He's packing up."

They were standing atop the watchtower by the main gate, which looked north to the camp of Mithridates.

One part of Young Sulla was sorry, but the larger part was very glad. "It's better this way, Father, isn't it?"

"At this stage, I think so."

"We *couldn't* have beaten him, could we?"

"Yes, of course we could have!" said Sulla heartily. "Would I bring my son on campaign with me if I didn't think I'd win? He's packing up and leaving for one reason only—because he knows we would have won. A bit of a backwoods hayseed our Mithridates might be, but he can recognize military excellence and a better man when he sees them, even though it is for the first time. It's lucky for us, actually, that he has been so isolated. The only role-model these eastern potentates have is Alexander the Great, who by Roman military standards is hopelessly outdated."

"What was the King of Pontus like?" asked the son curiously.

"Like?" Sulla thought for a moment before replying. "Do you know, I am hard put to say! Very unsure of himself, certainly, and therefore capable of being manipulated. He wouldn't cut an imposing figure in the Forum, but that's his foreignness. Like any tyrant, used to getting his own way—and I include brats in the nursery. I suppose if I had to sum him up in one word, I'd call him a yokel. But he's king of all he surveys, he's dangerous, and he's quite capable of learning. Just as well he didn't have Jugurtha's exposure to Rome and Romans at an early age—or Hannibal's sophistication, come to that. Until he met Gaius Marius—and me—I imagine he was satisfied with himself. Today he isn't. But that won't sit well with friend Mithridates! He'll set out to look for ways to best us at our own game, is my prediction. He's very proud. And very conceited. He won't rest until he's tested his mettle against Rome. But he won't run the risk of doing that until he's absolutely sure he can win. Today he isn't sure. A wise decision on his part to withdraw, Young Sulla! I would have taken him and his army to pieces."

Young Sulla rolled a fascinated eye at his father, amazed at his father's sureness, his conviction he was right. "So *many*?"

"Numbers mean nothing, my son," said Sulla, turning to leave the watchtower. "There are at least a dozen ways I could have rolled him up. He thinks in numbers. But he hasn't yet arrived at the real answer, which is to use what you have as one single unit. If he had decided to fight and I had humored him by leading my forces out to face him, he would simply have ordered a charge. Everyone in his army would have rushed at us together. That's so easy to deal with! As for his taking my camp—impossible! But he's dangerous. Do you know why I say that, Young Sulla?"

"No," said his son, all at sea.

"Because he decided to go home," said Sulla. "He will get home and worry the business over and over in his mind until he begins to grasp what he ought to have done. Five years, boy! I give him five years. Then I think Rome will have great trouble with King Mithridates."

Morsimus met them at the bottom of the tower, looking much as Young Sulla had looked—glad and sorry simultaneously. "What do we do now, Lucius Cornelius?" he asked.

"Exactly what I said to Mithridates. Eight days hence we march for Mazaca, and we pop Ariobarzanes back on his throne. For the time being he'll be all right. I don't think Mithridates will come back to Cappadocia for some years, because I'm not done yet."

"Not done yet?"

"I mean I'm not done with *him* yet. We're not returning to Tarsus," said Sulla, smiling nastily.

Morsimus gasped. "You're not marching on Pontus!"

Sulla laughed. "No! I'm going to march on Tigranes."

"Tigranes? Tigranes of *Armenia*?"

"The very one."

"But why, Lucius Cornelius?"

Two pairs of eyes were riveted upon Sulla's face, waiting to hear his answer; neither son nor legate had any idea why.

"I've never seen the Euphrates," said Sulla, looking wistful.

An answer neither listener had expected; but it was Young

Sulla, who knew his father very well, who began to giggle. Morsimus went off scratching his head.

Of course Sulla had an inspiration. There was going to be no
trouble in Cappadocia, so much was sure; Mithridates would stay
in Pontus for the time being. But he needed a little extra deterrent.
And as far as Sulla was concerned, no battle had been fought, no
opportunity to acquire gold or treasure had been forthcoming. Nor
did Sulla think that the Kingdom of Cappadocia itself was rich
enough to donate him anything. What riches might once have
lived in Eusebeia Mazaca had long since gone into the coffers of
Mithridates—unless he mistook his King of Pontus, which Sulla
didn't think he had.

His orders were specific. Evict Mithridates and Tigranes from
Cappadocia, place Ariobarzanes on the throne, then cease any
further activity without the borders of Cilicia. As a mere praetor—
proconsular imperium or not—he had little choice except to obey.
However . . . Of Tigranes there had been no sign; he had not joined
with the King of Pontus on this particular invasion. Which meant
he was still dwelling within the mountain fastnesses of Armenia,
ignorant of Rome's wishes, uncowed by Rome because he had
never set eyes upon a Roman.

No one might rely upon Rome's wishes being transmitted with
accuracy to Tigranes if the only messenger were Mithridates. Thus
it behooved the governor of Cilicia to find Tigranes for himself and
issue Rome's directives in person, did it not? And who knew?
Maybe somewhere along the way to Armenia, a bag of gold would
fall at Sulla's feet. A bag of gold he needed desperately. Provided
that the bag of gold meant for the personal use of the governor was
accompanied by another bag of gold for the Treasury of Rome, it
was not considered inappropriate for the governor to accept such
largesse; charges of extortion or treason or bribery were only levied
when the Treasury saw nothing, or—in the case of Manius Aquillius's father—the governor sold something belonging to the State
and popped the proceeds into his own purse. Like Phrygia.

At the end of the eight-day waiting period Sulla marched his four legions out of the fortress camp he had built, leaving it sitting abandoned on the plateau; one day it might come in handy, as he doubted it would occur to Mithridates to pull it down should he return to Cappadocia. To Mazaca he went with his son and his army, and stood in the palace reception room to watch Ariobarzanes mount his throne, the King's mother and Young Sulla beaming. That the Cappadocians were delighted was obvious; out they came from their houses to cheer their king.

"If you're wise, King, you'll start recruiting and training an army immediately," said Sulla as he was preparing to leave. "Rome might not always be in a position to intervene."

The King promised fervently to do this; Sulla had his doubts. For one thing, there was very little money in Cappadocia, and for another, the Cappadocians were not martial people by nature. A Roman farmer made a wonderful soldier. A Cappadocian shepherd did not. Still, the advice had been tendered, and heard. More than that, Sulla knew, he could not accomplish.

Mithridates, his scouts informed him, had crossed the big red Halys River and was already negotiating the first of the Pontic passes en route to Zela. What no scout could tell him, of course, was whether Mithridates had sent a message to Tigranes of Armenia. Not that it mattered. What Mithridates would say would not show Mithridates in a bad light; the truth would only come out when Tigranes personally encountered Sulla.

So from Mazaca, Sulla led his neat little army due east across the rolling highlands of Cappadocia, heading for the Euphrates River at the Melitene crossing to Tomisa. The season was now advanced into high spring, and, Sulla was informed, all the passes except the ones around Ararat were open. Should he wish to skirt Ararat, however, those passes would also be open by the time he reached the area. Sulla nodded, said nothing, even to his son or to Morsimus; he had little idea as yet exactly where he was going, intent only upon reaching the Euphrates.

Between Mazaca and Dalanda lay the Anti-Taurus mountains, not as difficult to cross as Sulla had imagined; though the peaks were high, the pass itself was a fairly low one, and clear of snow and landslides. They marched then through a series of vividly colored rocky gorges, in the floors of which ran torn white rivers, and farmers tilled the rich alluvium through the short growing season. These were ancient peoples, largely left alone as the ages advanced, never inducted into armies nor uplifted from their lands, too insignificant to covet. Sulla marched courteously, bought and paid for whatever he needed by way of supplies, and strung his men out to leave the fields untouched; it was magnificent ambush country, but his scouts were extremely active, and he had no premonition that Tigranes had mobilized and was lying in wait for him this side of the Euphrates.

Melitene was just an area, it had no town of any size, but the countryside was flat and rich—a part of the Euphrates plain, quite wide between its flanking mountains. Here the people were more numerous but hardly more sophisticated, and clearly they were unused to seeing armies on the march; even Alexander the Great in his tortuous wandering had not visited Melitene. Nor, Sulla learned, had Tigranes on his way to Cappadocia; he had preferred to take the northern route along the headwaters of the Euphrates, in a straighter line from Artaxata than Sulla's present position was.

And there at last was the mighty river confined between clifflike banks, not as wide as the lower Rhodanus, but flowing much faster. Sulla eyed its racing waters pensively, amazed by their color, a haunting and milky blue-green. His arm tightened about his son, whom he was loving more and more. Such perfect company!

"Can we cross it?" he asked Morsimus.

But the Cilician from Tarsus was no wiser than he, and could only shake his head dubiously. "Perhaps later in the year, after all the snows have melted—if they ever do, Lucius Cornelius. The local people say the Euphrates is deeper than it is wide, which must make it the mightiest river in the world."

"Does it have no bridges across it?" Sulla asked fretfully.

"This far up, no. To bridge it here would call for better engineering skills than any in this part of the world possess. I know Alexander the

Great bridged it, but much lower down its course, and later in the year."

"It needs Romans."

"Yes."

Sulla sighed, shrugged. "Well, I don't have engineers with me, and I don't have the time. We have to get wherever it is we are going before the snows close the passes and prevent our getting back. Though I think we'll go back through northern Syria and the Amanus mountains."

"Where *are* we going, Father? Now that you've seen the mighty Euphrates?" Young Sulla asked, smiling.

"Oh, I haven't seen nearly enough of the Euphrates yet! That is why we're going to march south along this bank until we find a crossing safe enough," said Sulla.

At Samosata the river was still too strong, though the locals offered bargelike boats; after inspecting them, Sulla declined.

"We'll continue south," he said.

The next ford, he was informed, lay at Zeugma, across the border in Syria.

"How settled is Syria now that Grypus is dead and Cyzicenus reigns alone?" Sulla asked of a local who could speak Greek.

"I do not know, lord Roman."

And then, the army packed up and ready to move out, the great river calmed down. Sulla made up his mind.

"We'll cross here by boat while it's possible," he said.

Once on the far side he breathed easier, though it was not lost upon him that his troops were more fearful—as if they had crossed some metaphorical Styx, and were now wandering the lands of the Underworld. His officers were summoned and given a lecture on how to keep troops happy. Young Sulla listened too.

"We're not going home yet," said Sulla, "so everyone had better settle down and enjoy himself. I doubt there's an army capable of defeating us within several hundred miles—if there is one at all. Tell them that they are being led by Lucius Cornelius Sulla, a far greater general than Tigranes or some Parthian Surenas. Tell them that we are the first Roman army east of the Euphrates, and that alone is a protection."

With summer coming on, it was no part of Sulla's plan to descend to the Syrian and Mesopotamian plains; the heat and the monotony would demoralize his soldiers faster by far than braving the unknown. So from Samosata he struck east again, heading for Amida on the Tigris. These were the borderlands between Armenia to the north and the Kingdom of the Parthians to the south and east, but of garrisons and troops there were none. Sulla's army tramped through fields of crimson poppies, watching its provisions carefully, for though the land was sometimes under cultivation, the people seemed to have little in their granaries to sell.

There were minor kingdoms hereabouts, Sophene, Gordyene, Osrhoene, and Commagene, each hedged in by vast snowcapped peaks, but the going was easy because it was not necessary to travel through the mountains. In Amida, a black-walled town on the banks of the Tigris, Sulla met the King of Commagene and the King of Osrhoene, who journeyed to see him when news of this strange, peacefully inclined Roman force reached them.

Their names Sulla found unpronounceable, but each produced a Greek epithet to glorify his name, so Sulla called Commagene, Epiphanes, and Osrhoene, Philoromaios.

"Honored Roman, you are in Armenia," said Commagene very seriously. "The mighty King Tigranes will assume you invade."

"And he is not far away," said Osrhoene, equally seriously.

Sulla looked alert rather than afraid. "Not far away?" he asked eagerly. "Where?"

"He wants to build a new capital city for southern Armenia, and he has settled upon a site," said Osrhoene. "He plans to call the city Tigranocerta."

"Where?"

"To the east of Amida and slightly to the north, perhaps five hundred *stades* away," said Commagene.

Quickly Sulla divided by eight. "About sixty miles."

"You do not intend to go there, surely?"

"Why not?" asked Sulla. "I haven't killed anybody, nor looted a temple, nor stolen provisions. I come in peace to talk to King Tigranes. In fact, I would ask a favor of you—send messages to King Tigranes at Tigranocerta and tell him I'm coming—in peace!"

The messages went out and found Tigranes already well aware of Sulla's advance, yet very reluctant to block his progress. What was Rome doing east of the Euphrates? Of course Tigranes didn't trust the peaceful intent, but the size of Sulla's army did not indicate a serious Roman invasion. The important question was whether or not he should attack—like Mithridates, Tigranes feared the name, Rome, enormously. Therefore, he resolved, he would not attack until he was attacked. And in the meantime he would go with his army to meet this Roman, Lucius Cornelius Sulla.

He had heard from Mithridates, of course. A defensive and sullen letter, informing him briefly that Gordius was dead and Cappadocia once more under the thumb of the Roman puppet, King Ariobarzanes. A Roman army had come up from Cilicia and its leader (not named) had warned him to go home. For the time being, had said the King of Pontus, he had judged it prudent to abandon his plan to invade Cilicia after subduing Cappadocia once and for all. In consequence he had urged Tigranes to abandon his plan to march west into Syria and meet his father-in-law on the fertile alluvial plains of Cilicia Pedia.

Neither of the Kings had dreamed for one moment that, his mission in Cappadocia successfully completed, the Roman Lucius Cornelius Sulla would go anywhere save back to Tarsus; and by the time Tigranes believed what his spies told him—that Sulla was on the Euphrates looking for a crossing—his messages to Mithridates in Sinope had no hope of reaching their recipient before Sulla appeared on the Armenian doorstep. Therefore Tigranes had sent word of Sulla's advent to his Parthian suzerains in Seleuceia-on-Tigris; their journey, though long, was an easy one.

The King of Armenia met Sulla on the Tigris some miles west of the site of his new capital; when Sulla arrived on the west bank, he faced the camp of Tigranes on the east bank. Compared to the Euphrates, the Tigris was a creek, running shallower and more sluggishly, brownish in color, perhaps half as wide. It rose, of course, on the wrong side of the Anti-Taurus, and received not one tenth of the tributaries the Euphrates did, nor the bulk of the melting snows and permanent springs. Almost a thousand miles to the south in the area around Babylon and Ctesiphon and Seleuceia-on-Tigris, the two rivers ran only forty miles apart; canals had been dug from the Euphrates to the Tigris to help the latter stream find its way to the Persian Sea.

Who goes to whom? asked Sulla of himself, smiling perversely as he put his army into a strongly fortified camp and sat down on the western bank to see who would give in first and take the trip across the river. Tigranes did, not motivated by aggression or fear, but by curiosity. As the days had gone by without Sulla's showing himself, the King just couldn't wait any longer. Out came the royal barge, a gilded, flat-bottomed affair guided by poles rather than oars, shielded from the heat of the sun by a gold and purple canopy fringed with bullion, under which, on a dais, stood one of the King's minor thrones, a magnificent contraption worked in gold, ivory, and gems galore.

The King came down to the wooden jetty in a four-wheeled golden car which hurt the eyes of the watchers on the west bank, it flashed and glittered so, a slave standing behind the King in the car holding a golden, gem-studded parasol above the royal head.

"Now how is he going to manage this?" asked Sulla of his son from their hiding place behind a wall of shields.

"What do you mean, Father?"

"Dignity!" Sulla exclaimed, grinning. "I can't believe he will soil his feet on that wooden wharf, yet they haven't spread a carpet for him to walk on."

The conundrum solved itself. Two brawny slaves shoved the parasol-holder aside as they stepped up into the car with the little wheels; there they linked arms and waited. Delicately the King

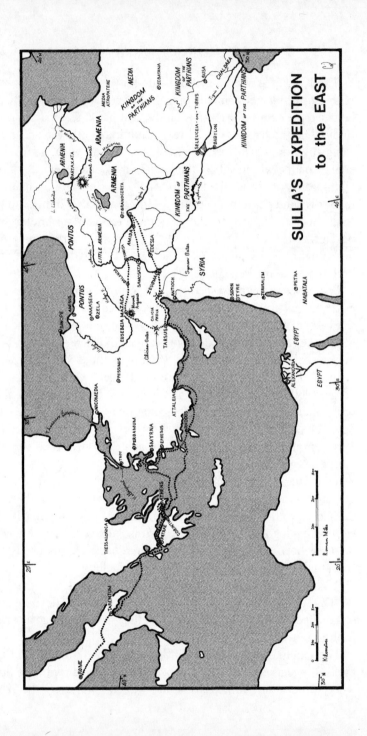

SULLA'S EXPEDITION to the EAST

lowered the royal posterior onto their arms, and was carried to the barge, deposited gently upon the throne. While the languid vessel plied its way across the languid river the King sat immobile, not seeming to see the throng on the western bank. The barge bumped into the sloping earth, as there was no jetty on this side, and the whole process was repeated. The slaves picked the King up and stood off to one side while the throne was carried to a high flat-topped rock, deposited upon it, and the royal parasol-holder clambered up to shade the chair. Only then was the King transported to his resting place, quite a struggle for the slaves.

"Oh, well done!" cried Sulla.

"Well done?" asked Young Sulla, learning avidly.

"He's got me by the balls, Young Sulla! No matter what *I* sit on—or even if I stand—he's going to tower above me."

"What can you do?"

Well concealed even from the King at his new height, Sulla snapped his fingers for his body-slave. "Help me get this off," he said curtly, struggling with the straps on his cuirass.

Divested of armor, he removed his leather under-dress as well, changed scarlet tunic for a coarsely woven oatmeal one, belted it with a cord, threw a dun-colored peasant cloak about his shoulders, and put on his wide-brimmed straw peasant's hat.

"When in the company of the sun," he said to Young Sulla with a grin, "be a cavern."

Thus it was that when he emerged from between his guard and strolled down to the spot where Tigranes sat like a statue upon his throne, Sulla looked like one of the local lowly. The King, in fact, discounted him as anyone of importance, and continued to stare, frowning, into the massed ranks of Sulla's army.

"Greetings, King Tigranes, I am Lucius Cornelius Sulla," said Sulla in Greek, arriving at the base of the rock where the King's chair perched. He swept off his hat and looked upward, his pale eyes wide because the King's parasol was between him and the sun.

The King gaped, first at sight of that hair, then at sight of those eyes. To one used to seeing no eyes save brown—and who considered his Queen's yellow orbs unique—Sulla's were horrifying, patches punched out of a doomsday sky.

"This army is yours, Roman?" asked Tigranes.

"It is."

"What is it doing in my lands?"

"Journeying to see you, King Tigranes."

"You perceive me. What now?"

"Not a thing!" said Sulla airily, brows climbing, horrible eyes dancing. "I came to see you, King Tigranes, and I have seen you. Once I have told you what I am ordered to tell you, I shall turn my army round and go back to Tarsus."

"What are you ordered to tell me, Roman?"

"The Senate and People of Rome require you to stay within your own boundaries, King. Armenia does not concern Rome. But to venture into Cappadocia, Syria, or Cilicia will offend Rome. And Rome is mighty—mistress of all the lands around the Middle Sea, a greater domain by far than Armenia. Rome's armies are undefeated, and many in number. Therefore, King, stay in your own ward."

"I am *in* my own ward," the King pointed out, thrown off balance by this direct talk. "Rome is the trespasser."

"Only to carry out my orders, King. I'm simply a messenger," said Sulla, uncowed. "I trust you've listened well."

"Huh!" said the King, raising one hand. His brawny slaves linked arms and stepped upward, the King sat himself down, and was duly enthroned once more upon his barge. With his back to Sulla. And off poled the boat across the turgid stream, Tigranes unmoving.

"Well, well!" said Sulla to his son, rubbing his hands together gleefully. "An odd lot, these eastern kings, my boy. Mountebanks all. Full of importance, as prickable as a bladder." He looked about, and called, "Morsimus!"

"Here, Lucius Cornelius."

"Pack up. We're going home."

"Which way?"

"To Zeugma. I doubt we'll encounter any more trouble from

Cyzicenus of Syria than from the conceited heap of rubbish you can see disappearing across the water. Much and all as they dislike the sensation, they are all afraid of Rome. That pleases me." Sulla snorted. "A pity I couldn't maneuver him into a situation where he has to look up at me."

Sulla's reasons for heading southwest to Zeugma were not entirely because it was the shorter route—and a less mountainous one—to Cilicia Pedia; provisions were low, and the crops of the highlands still green. Whereas in the lowlands of upper Mesopotamia he might hope to find ripe grain to buy. His men were growing very tired of the fruits and vegetables they had been living on since leaving Cappadocia; they craved bread. Therefore they must endure the heat of the Syrian plains.

Sure enough, when he came down from the crags south of Amida onto the plains of Osrhoene he found the harvests in, and bread aplenty as a result. In Edessa he visited Philoromaios the King, and found Osrhoene only too pleased to give this strange Roman whatever he wanted. And to impart some rather alarming news.

"Lucius Cornelius, I am afraid that King Tigranes has gathered his army and is following you," said King Philoromaios.

"I know," said Sulla, unruffled.

"But he will attack you! And attack me!"

"Keep your army disbanded, King, and your people out of his way. It's my presence worries him. Once he's sure I really am going back to Tarsus, he'll hie himself back to Tigranocerta."

This calm confidence did much to quieten the King of Osrhoene, who sped Sulla on his way with a bounty of wheat and an object Sulla had despaired of ever seeing—a big bag of golden coins, stamped not with Osrhoene's features, but with the face of none other than King Tigranes.

Tigranes tracked Sulla all the way to the Euphrates at Zeugma, but too far in his rear to warrant Sulla's halting and readying for battle; this was clearly a precautionary rather than an aggressive measure. But then after Sulla had got his troops over the river at Zeugma—an easier business by far than at Samosata—he was visited by a party of fifty dignitaries, all clad in garb of a style strange to any Roman—high round little hats studded with pearls and golden beads, neck-choking spiral collars of gold wire descending to their chests, gold-embroidered coats, long stiff gold-embroidered skirts reaching their gold-shod feet.

When he learned the group was an embassage from the King of the Parthians, Sulla was not surprised; only Parthians had so much gold to wear. Exciting! And a vindication for this unprojected, unauthorized trip east of the Euphrates. Tigranes of Armenia was subject to the Parthians, that much he knew; perhaps he could convince the Parthians to muzzle Tigranes, prevent his yielding to the blandishments of Mithridates.

This time he wasn't going to look up at Tigranes—nor look up at the Parthians, for that matter.

"I will meet with those Parthians who speak Greek—and with King Tigranes—the day after tomorrow, on the banks of the Euphrates at a spot to which the dignitaries will be conducted by my men," said Sulla to Morsimus. The members of the embassage had not yet set eyes upon him, though he had managed to inspect them; since it had not escaped him that both Mithridates and Tigranes had been amazed by his appearance—and very much intimidated by it—Sulla had resolved that he would burst upon the Parthians also.

Born actor that he was, he set his stage with scrupulous attention to every fine detail. A huge tall dais was constructed out of some polished slabs of white marble he borrowed from the temple of Zeus in Zeugma. Then upon the dais he constructed another dais just large enough to hold a curule chair, a good foot taller than the rest of the platform, and faced with a plummy purple marble which had formed the plinth of the statue of Zeus. Fine marble seats with arms and backs of griffins and lions, sphinxes and eagles, were pillaged from all over town, and these were placed upon the main dais, a group of six to one side, and a single, splendid specimen formed by the backs of two winged lions off to the other side for Tigranes. Upon the purple marble smaller dais he placed his ivory curule chair, a thin and spindly, chaste-looking seat compared to those below it. And over the top of the whole structure he erected an awning made from the gold and purple tapestry which had curtained off the sanctuary behind Zeus in his temple.

Shortly after dawn on the appointed day, a guard of his men escorted six of the Parthian ambassadors to the dais and placed them in the six chairs forming a group; the rest of the embassage remained upon the ground, suitably seated and shaded. Tigranes wanted to mount the purple podium, of course, but was firmly yet courteously placed upon his royal seat at the opposite end of the semicircle the chairs made. The Parthians looked at Tigranes—he looked at them—and everybody looked up at the purple podium.

Then when all were seated came Lucius Cornelius Sulla, clad in his purple-bordered *toga praetexta* and carrying the plain ivory wand which was his staff of office, one end nestling in his palm, its foot-long stick resting upon his forearm, its other end nestling into the hollow of his elbow. Hair blazing even after he had passed out of the sun, he walked without turning his head to left or to right up the steps to the dais, then up another step to his ivory curule chair, and seated himself, rod-straight, spine unsupported, one foot forward and the other back in the classic pose. A Roman of the Romans.

They were not amused, especially Tigranes, but there was little they could do about it, having been jockeyed into their present positions with such dignity that to start insisting upon being seated at the same height as the curule chair would have done nothing to enhance dignity.

"My lords the representatives of the King of the Parthians, and King Tigranes, I welcome you to this parley," said Sulla from his paramount position, and taking great delight in unsettling them with his strange light eyes.

"This is not your parley, Roman!" snapped Tigranes. "*I* summoned my suzerains!"

"I beg your pardon, King, but this is my parley," said Sulla with a smile. "You have come to my place, at my invitation." And then, not giving Tigranes time to reply, he turned slightly toward the

Parthians and gave them the full benefit of his most feral grin, long canines well bared. "Who among you, my lords of Parthia, is the leader of this delegation?"

Predictably, the elderly man seated in the first of the chairs nodded his head regally. "I am, Lucius Cornelius Sulla. My name is Orobazus, and I am satrap of Seleuceia-on-Tigris. I answer only to the King of Kings, Mithridates of the Parthians, who regrets that time and distance do not permit him to be here today."

"In his summer palace at Ecbatana, eh?" asked Sulla.

Orobazus blinked. "You are well informed, Lucius Cornelius Sulla. I was not aware our movements are so well known in Rome."

"Lucius Cornelius will do, Lord Orobazus," said Sulla. He leaned forward a little, still keeping his spine absolutely straight, his pose in the chair a perfect fusion of grace and power, as befitted a Roman conducting an audience of magnitude. "We make history here today, Lord Orobazus. This is the first time that the ambassadors of the Kingdom of the Parthians have met with an ambassador of Rome. That it takes place upon the river which forms the boundary between our two worlds is fitting."

"Indeed, my lord Lucius Cornelius," said Orobazus.

"Not 'my lord,' just plain Lucius Cornelius," said Sulla. "In Rome there are no lords and no kings."

"We had heard it was so, but we find it strange. You do follow the Greek way, then. How is it that Rome has grown so great, when no king heads the government? The Greeks one can understand. They were never very great because they had no High King—they fragmented themselves into a myriad little states and then went to war against each other. Whereas Rome acts as if there *was* a High King. How can your lack of any kind of king permit such power, Lucius Cornelius?" asked Orobazus.

"Rome is our king, Lord Orobazus, though we give Rome the feminine form, Roma, and speak of Rome as 'her' and 'she.' The Greeks subordinated themselves to an ideal. You subordinate yourselves to one man, your king. But we Romans subordinate ourselves to Rome, and only to Rome. We bend the knee to no one human, Lord Orobazus, any more than we bend it to the abstraction of an ideal. Rome is our god, our king, our very lives. And though each Roman strives to enhance his own reputation, strives to be great in the eyes of his fellow Romans, in the long run it is all done to enhance Rome, and Rome's greatness. We worship a place, Lord Orobazus. Not a man. Not an ideal. Men come and go, their terms on earth are fleeting. And ideals shift and sway with every philosophical wind. But a place can be eternal as long as those who live in that place care for it, nurture it, make it even greater. I, Lucius Cornelius Sulla, am a great Roman. But at the end of my life, whatever I have done will have gone to swell the might and majesty of my place—Rome. I am here today not on my own behalf, nor on behalf of any other man. I am here today on behalf of my place—*Rome!* If we strike a treaty, it will be deposited in the temple of Jupiter Feretrius, the oldest temple in Rome, and there it will remain—not my property, nor even bearing my name. A testament to the might of Rome."

He spoke well, for his Greek was Attic and beautiful, better by far than the Greek of the Parthians or Tigranes. And they were listening, fascinated, obviously wrestling to understand a concept utterly alien. A place greater than a man? A place greater than the mental product of a man?

"But a place, Lucius Cornelius," said Orobazus, "is just a collection of objects! If it is a town, a collection of buildings. If it is a sanctuary, a collection of temples. If it is countryside, a collection of trees and rocks and fields. How can a place generate such feeling, such nobility? You look at a collection of buildings—for I know Rome is a great city—and do what you all do for the sake of those buildings?"

Sulla extended his ivory wand. "This is Rome, Lord Orobazus." He touched the muscular snow-white forearm behind it. "This is Rome, Lord Orobazus." He swept aside the folds of his toga to display the carved curved X of his chair's legs. "This is Rome, Lord Orobazus." He held out his left arm, weighed down by fold upon fold of toga, and pinched the woolen stuff. "This is Rome, Lord Orobazus." And then he paused to look into every pair of eyes raised to him on high, and at the end of the pause he said, "*I* am Rome, Lord Orobazus. So is every single man who calls himself a Roman. Rome is a pageant stretching back a thousand years, to the time when a Trojan refugee named Aeneas set foot upon the shores of Latium and founded a race who founded, six hundred and sixty-two years ago, a place called Rome. And for a while Rome was actually ruled by kings, until the men of Rome rejected the concept that a man could be mightier than the place which bred him. No man must ever consider himself greater than the place which bred him. No Roman man is greater than Rome. Rome is the place which breeds great men. But what they are— what they do—is for *her* glory. Their contributions to her ongoing pageant. And I tell you, Lord Orobazus, that Rome will last as long as Romans hold Rome dearer than themselves, dearer than their children, dearer than their own reputations and achievements." He paused again, drew a long breath. "As long as Romans hold Rome dearer than an ideal, or a single man."

"But the King is the manifestation of everything you say, Lucius Cornelius," Orobazus objected.

"A king cannot be," said Sulla. "A king is concerned first with himself, a king believes he is closer to the gods than all other men. Some kings believe they are gods. All personal, Lord Orobazus. Kings use their countries to fuel themselves. Rome uses Romans to fuel herself."

Orobazus lifted his hands in the age-old gesture of surrender. "I cannot understand what you say, Lucius Cornelius."

"Then let us pass to our reasons for being here today, Lord Orobazus. It is an historic occasion. On behalf of Rome, I extend you a proposition. That what lies to the east of the river Euphrates remain solely your concern, the business of the King of the Parthians. And that what lies to the west of the river Euphrates become Rome's concern, the business of those men who act in the name of Rome."

Orobazus raised his feathery greying brows. "Do you mean, Lucius Cornelius, that Rome wishes to rule every land west of the Euphrates River? That Rome intends to dethrone the Kings of

Syria and Pontus, Cappadocia and Commagene, many other lands?"

"Not at all, Lord Orobazus. Rather, that Rome wants to ensure the stability of lands west of the Euphrates, prevent some kings expanding at the expense of others, prevent national borders shrinking or expanding. Do you, for instance, Lord Orobazus, know precisely why I am here today?"

"Not precisely, Lucius Cornelius. We received word from our subject king, Tigranes of Armenia, that you were marching on him with an army. So far I have not been able to obtain a reason from King Tigranes as to why your army has made no aggressive move. You were well to the east of the Euphrates. Now you appear to be traveling west again. What did bring you here, why did you take your army into Armenia? And why, having done so, did you not make an aggressive move?"

Sulla turned his head to look down at Tigranes, discovering that the toothed margin of his tiara, decorated on either side above the diadem with an eight-pointed star and a crescent formed by two eagles, was hollow, and that the King was going very bald. Clearly detesting his inferior position, Tigranes lifted his chin to glare angrily up at Sulla.

"What, King, not told your master?" Sulla asked. Failing to receive an answer, he turned back to Orobazus and the other Greek-speaking Parthians. "Rome is seriously concerned, Lord Orobazus, that *some* kings at the eastern end of the Middle Sea do not become so great that they can expunge other kings. Rome is well content with the status quo in Asia Minor. But King Mithridates of Pontus has designs on the Kingdom of Cappadocia, and on other parts of Anatolia as well. Including Cilicia, which has voluntarily placed itself in Rome's hands now that the King of Syria is not powerful enough to look after it. But your subject king, Tigranes here, has supported Mithridates—and upon one occasion not long ago, actually invaded Cappadocia."

"I heard something of that," said Orobazus woodenly.

"I imagine little escapes the attention of the King of the Parthians and his satraps, Lord Orobazus! However, having done Pontus's dirty work for him, King Tigranes returned to Armenia, and has not stirred west of the Euphrates since." Sulla cleared his throat. "It has been my melancholy duty to eject the King of Pontus yet again from Cappadocia, a commission from the Senate and People of Rome that I concluded earlier in the year. However, it occurred to me that my task would not be finished conclusively until I journeyed to have speech with King Tigranes. So I set off from Eusebeia Mazaca to look for him."

"With your army, Lucius Cornelius?" asked Orobazus.

Up went the pointed brows. "Certainly! This is not exactly a part of the world I know, Lord Orobazus. So—purely as a precaution!—I took my army with me. It and I have behaved with perfect decorum, as I am sure you know—we have not raided, looted, sacked, or even trodden down crops in the field. What we needed, we bought. And we continue to do so. You must think of my army as a very large bodyguard. I am an important man, Lord Orobazus! My tenure of government in Rome has not yet reached its zenith, I will rise even higher. Therefore it behooves me—and Rome!—to look after Lucius Cornelius Sulla."

Orobazus signed to Sulla to stop. "One moment, Lucius Cornelius. I have with me a certain Chaldaean, the Nabopolassar, who comes not from Babylon but from Chaldaea proper, where the Euphrates delta runs into the Persian Sea. He serves me as my seer as well as my astrologer, and his brother serves none other than King Mithridates of the Parthians himself. We—all of us here today from Seleuceia-on-Tigris—believe in what he says. Would you permit him to look into your palm, and into your face? We would like to find out for ourselves if you are truly the great man you say you are."

Sulla shrugged, looked indifferent. "It makes no odds to me, Lord Orobazus. Have your fellow poke his nose into the lines on my palm and in my face to your entire satisfaction! Is he here? Do you want him to do it now? Or must I go somewhere more seemly?"

"Stay where you are, Lucius Cornelius. The Nabopolassar will come to you." Orobazus snapped his fingers and said something to the little crowd of Parthian observers seated on the ground.

Out of their ranks stepped one who looked exactly the same as all the others, with his little round pearl-studded hat, and his spiral necklace, and his golden garments. Hands tucked into his sleeves, he trotted to the dais steps, hopped up them nimbly, and then stood on the step halfway between Sulla's podium and the main floor of the platform. Out came one hand, snatching at Sulla's extended right hand; and for a long time he mumbled his way from one line to another, then dropped the hand and peered at Sulla's face. A little bow, and he backed off the step, backed across the dais to Orobazus, only then turning his front away from Sulla.

The report took some time to give; Orobazus and the others listened gravely, faces impassive. At the end he turned back to Sulla, bowed down to the ground in Sulla's direction, and got himself off the platform without ever presenting more than the top of his head to Sulla, an extraordinary obeisance.

Sulla's heart had leaped, had begun to thud a hasty tattoo as the Nabopolassar gave his verdict, leaped again joyously as the Chaldaean seer wormed his way off the platform and back to his place among the little crowd on the ground. Whatever he had said, he had clearly confirmed Sulla's own words, that he, Sulla, was a great man. And he had bowed down to Sulla as he would have bowed down to his King.

"The Nabopolassar says, Lucius Cornelius, that you are the greatest man in the world, that no one in your lifetime will rival you from the River Indus to the River of Ocean in the far west. We must believe him, for he has by default included our own King Mithridates among your inferiors, and thereby placed his head in jeopardy," said Orobazus, a new note in his voice.

Even Tigranes, Sulla noticed, now gazed at him in awe.

"May we resume our parley?" asked Sulla, not varying his pose, his expression, or his tone from normal.

"Please, Lucius Cornelius."

"Very well, then. I have arrived at that point in my account, I think, where my army's presence has been explained, but not what I came to say to King Tigranes. Briefly, I instructed him to remain on his own side of the Euphrates River, and warned him that he was not to assist his father-in-law of Pontus in attaining Pontus's ambitions—be they with regard to Cappadocia, Cilicia, or Bithynia. And, having told him, I turned back."

"Do you think, Lucius Cornelius, that the King of Pontus has even grander designs than Anatolia?"

"I think his designs encompass the world, Lord Orobazus! He is already the complete master of the eastern Euxine from Olbia on the Hypanis to Colchis on the Phasis. He secured Galatia by the mass murder of its chieftains, and has murdered at least one of the Cappadocian kings. I am very sure he masterminded the invasion of Cappadocia undertaken by King Tigranes here. And, further to the point of our meeting"—Sulla leaned forward, his strange light eyes blazing—"the distance between Pontus and the Kingdom of the Parthians is considerably less than the distance between Pontus and Rome. Therefore I consider that the King of the Parthians should look to his boundaries while ever the King of Pontus is in an expansive mood. As well as keep a stern eye on his subject, King Tigranes of Armenia." Sulla produced a charming smile, canines well hidden. "That, Lord Orobazus, is all I have to say."

"You have spoken well, Lucius Cornelius," said Orobazus. "You may have your treaty. All to the west of the Euphrates to be the concern of Rome. All to the east of the Euphrates to be the concern of the King of the Parthians."

"This means, I trust, no more western incursions by Armenia?"

"It most certainly does," said Orobazus, with a glare at the angry and disappointed Tigranes.

At last, thought Sulla as he waited for the Parthian envoys to file off the dais—followed by a Tigranes who looked nowhere save at the white marble floor—at last I know how Gaius Marius must have felt when Martha the Syrian prophetess foretold that he would be consul of Rome seven times, and be called the Third Founder of Rome. But Gaius Marius is still alive! Yet *I* have been called the greatest man in the world! The *whole* world, from India to Oceanus Atlanticus!

Not one tiny hint of his jubilation did he display to any other man during the succeeding days; his son, who had been let watch proceedings from a distance, knew only what his eyes had seen, as his ears were beyond hearing distance; in fact, no member of Sulla's own people had been within hearing distance. All Sulla reported was the treaty.

This agreement was to be drawn up on a tall stone monument Orobazus planned to place at the spot where Sulla's platform had stood, for it was now dismantled, its precious materials returned from whence they came. The stone was a four-sided obelisk and the terms were inscribed in Latin, Greek, Parthian, and Median, one language upon each side. Two copies were made on Pergamum parchment, for Sulla to take to Rome and Orobazus to take to Seleuceia-on-Tigris, where, Orobazus predicted, King Mithridates of the Parthians would be well pleased.

Tigranes had slunk off with the mien of a whipped cur the moment he could secure leave from his suzerains, returned to where his new city of Tigranocerta was having its streets surveyed. His first logical step was to write to Mithridates of Pontus, but he did not for some time. When he did, it was at least with some private satisfaction emerging from the news he had received from a friend at court in Seleuceia-on-Tigris.

> Take heed of this Roman, Lucius Cornelius Sulla, my valued and mighty father-in-law. At Zeugma on the Euphrates he did conclude a treaty of friendship with the satrap Orobazus of Seleuceia-on-Tigris, acting on behalf of my suzerain, King Mithridates of the Parthians.
>
> Between them, they have tied my hands, beloved King of Pontus. Under the terms of the treaty they concluded, I am bound to remain to the east of the Euphrates, and I dare not disobey—not while that merciless old tyrant your namesake sits upon the throne of the Parthians. Seventy valleys my kingdom paid for my return. Did I disobey, seventy more valleys would be taken from me.

Yet we must not despair. As I have heard you say, we are still young men, we have the time to be patient. This treaty of Rome and the Kingdom of the Parthians has made up my mind. I will expand Armenia. You must look to those domains you named—Cappadocia, Paphlagonia, Asia Province, Cilicia, Bithynia, and Macedonia. I will look south to Syria, Arabia, and Egypt. Not to mention to the Kingdom of the Parthians. For one day soon old Mithradates the King of the Parthians will die. And I predict that there will then be a war of succession, for he has sat on his sons as he sits on me, and favors none above the others, and torments them with threats of death, and even occasionally does kill one to watch the others hop. So there has been no ascendancy of one son above any of the others, and that is dangerous when an old king dies. This much I do swear to you, honored and esteemed father-in-law—that the moment there is internal war between the sons of the King of the Parthians, I will seize my chance and strike out for Syria, Arabia, Egypt, Mesopotamia. Until then, I will continue my work of building Tigranocerta.

One further thing I must report to you about the meeting between Orobazus and Lucius Cornelius Sulla. Orobazus told the Chaldaean seer, the Nabopolassar, to scan the palm and face of the Roman. Now I know the work of this Nabopolassar, whose brother is seer to the King of Kings himself. And I tell you, great and wise father-in-law, that the Chaldaean is a true seer, never wrong. When he had done with the hand and face of Lucius Cornelius Sulla he fell upon his stomach and humbled himself to the Roman as he humbles himself to the King of Kings and no other. Then he told Orobazus that Lucius Cornelius Sulla was the greatest man in the world! From the River Indus to the River of Ocean, he did say. And I was very afraid. So too was Oroba-

zus. With good reason. When he and the others got
back to Seleuceia-on-Tigris they found the King of the
Parthians in residence there, so Orobazus reported
what had happened immediately. Including details the
Roman had given him about our own activity, mighty
father-in-law. And including the Roman's warning that
you might look toward the Kingdom of the Parthians to
conquer it. King Mithridates took heed. I am strapped
with watchers. But—the only news which cheers me—
he executed Orobazus and the Nabopolassar for making more of a Roman than their king. Yet he has decided
to honor the treaty, and has written to Rome to this effect. It seems the old man is sorry he never set eyes on
Lucius Cornelius Sulla. I suspect had he, he would
have employed his executioner. A pity then that he was
in Ecbatana.

Only the future can show us our fates, my dearest
and most admired father-in-law. It may be that Lucius
Cornelius Sulla comes no more to the east, that his
greatness will be aimed at the west. And it may be too
that one day it is *I* who assume the title, King of Kings.
This means nothing to you, I know. But to one brought
up at the courts in Ecbatana and Susia and Seleuceia-
on-Tigris, it means everything.

My dear wife, your daughter, is very well. Our children are well. Would that I could inform you our plans
were going well. That is not to be. For the moment.

Ten days after the parley on the platform, Lucius Cornelius
Sulla received his copy of the treaty, and was invited to be present
at the unveiling of the monument beside the great milky blue
river. He went clad in his *toga praetexta,* trying to ignore the fact
that the summer sun was wreaking havoc upon the skin of his
face; this was one occasion upon which he could not wear his hat.
All he could do was oil himself and hope the many hours in the
sun would not burn him too deeply.

Of course they did, a lesson his son absorbed, vowing he too would always wear his hat. His father's misery was acute. He blistered, peeled, blistered again, peeled again, oozed precious water from the healing layers, and scratched, and suppurated. But by the time he and his little army reached Tarsus some forty days later, Sulla's skin was finally beginning to heal and he no longer itched. Morsimus had found some sweet-smelling cream in a market along the Pyramus River; from the time he first anointed himself with it, his skin ceased to plague him. And it healed without a blemish, a fact which pleased Sulla, who was vain.

Like the prediction of the Nabopolassar, he told no one, even his son, about the bags of gold. The one he had been given by the King of Osrhoene had been joined by five others, the gift of the Parthian Orobazus. These coins were emblazoned with the profile of the second King Mithridates of the Parthians, a short-necked old man with a nose suitable for catching fish, carefully curled hair and pointed beard, and on his head the little round brimless hat his ambassadors had worn, except that his boasted the ribbon of the diadem and had ear-flaps and neck-shield.

In Tarsus Sulla changed his golden coins for good Roman denarii, and found to his amazement that he was the richer by ten million denarii—forty million sesterces. He had more than doubled his fortune! Of course he didn't haul bags and bags of Roman coins away from the Tarsian banking house; he availed himself of *permutatio* and tucked a little roll of Pergamum parchment into his toga instead.

The year had worn down, autumn was well under way, and it was time to be thinking of going home. His job was done—and done well. Those in the Treasury at Rome who had dowered his war chest would not complain; for there had been ten more bags of gold—two from Tigranes of Armenia, five from the King of the Parthians, one from the King of Commagene, and two from none other than the King of Pontus. This meant Sulla could pay his army out and give Morsimus a generous bonus, then put more than two thirds of it into his war chest, now far richer than it had been when he started out. Yes, a good year! His reputation in

Rome would rise, and he now had the money to stand for the consulship.

His trunks were packed and the ship he had hired was riding at anchor on the Cydnus when he had a letter from Publius Rutilius Rufus, dated in September.

I hope, Lucius Cornelius, that this catches you in time. And I hope yours has been a better year than mine. But more of that anon.

I do so love writing to those far away about the goings-on in Rome. How I shall miss it! And who will write to me? But more of that anon.

In April we elected ourselves a new pair of censors. Gnaeus Domitius Ahenobarbus Pontifex Maximus and Lucius Licinius Crassus Orator. An ill-assorted pair, you perceive. The irascible allied to the immutable— Hades and Zeus—the succinct coupling with the verbose—a harpy and a muse. All of Rome is trying to find the perfect description of the world's most imperfect duo. It should of course have been Crassus Orator and my dear Quintus Mucius Scaevola, but it wasn't. Scaevola refused to run. He says he's too busy. Too wary, more like! After the fuss the last censors created—and the *lex Licinia Mucia* to cap it—I daresay Scaevola thought himself well out of the business.

Of course the special courts provided for by the *lex Licinia Mucia* are now defunct. Gaius Marius and I succeeded in having them disbanded early in the year, on the grounds that they were a financial burden the returns could not justify. Luckily everyone agreed. The amendment was passed without incident in both Senate and Comitia. But the scars linger, Lucius Cornelius, in truly terrible ways. Two of the more obnoxious judges, Gnaeus Scipio Nasica and Catulus Caesar, have had farmsteads and villas they own burned to the ground; and others have had crops destroyed, vineyards torn apart, water cisterns poisoned. There is a new nocturnal sport up and down the country—find a Roman citizen and beat him half to death. Not, naturally, that anyone—even Catulus Caesar—will admit that the *lex Licinia Mucia* has anything to do with all these private disasters.

That revolting young man, Quintus Servilius Caepio, actually had the effrontery to charge Scaurus Princeps Senatus in the extortion court, the charge being that he had accepted an enormous bribe from King Mithridates of Pontus. You can imagine what happened. Scaurus turned up at the spot where the court had gathered in the lower Forum, but *not* to answer any charges! He walked straight up to Caepio and smacked him on the left cheek, then the right cheek—snap, snap! Somehow at such moments I swear Scaurus grows two feet. He seemed to tower over Caepio, whereas in fact they are much the same height.

"How *dare* you!" he barked. "How dare you, you slimy, miserable little worm! Withdraw this ridiculous charge at once, or you'll wish you'd never been born! You, a Servilius Caepio, a member of a family famous for its love of gold, dare to accuse *me*, Marcus Aemilius Scaurus, Princeps Senatus, of taking gold? I piss on you, Caepio!"

And off he marched across the Forum, escorted by huge cheers, applause, whistles, all of which he ignored. Caepio was left standing with the marks of Scaurus's hand on both sides of his face, trying not to look at the panel of knights who had been ordered to appear for jury selection. But after Scaurus's little scene, Caepio could have produced ironclad evidence to prove his case, and the jury still would have acquitted Scaurus.

"I withdraw my charge," said Caepio, and scurried home.

Thus perish all who would indict Marcus Aemilius Scaurus, showman without peer, poseur, and prince of good fellows! I admit that I, for one, was delighted. Caepio has been making life miserable for Marcus Livius Drusus for so long now it is a Forum fact. Apparently Caepio felt that my nephew should have taken his side when my niece was discovered in her affair with Cato Salonianus, and when things didn't turn out that way, Caepio reacted downright viciously. He's still carrying on about that ring!

But enough of Caepio, grubby subject for a letter that he is. We have another useful little law upon the tablets, thanks to the tribune of the plebs Gnaeus Papirius Carbo. Now there is a family has had no luck since its members decided to forsake their patrician status! Two suicides in the last generation, and now a group of young Papirian men who just itch to make trouble. Anyway, Carbo called a *contio* in the Plebeian Assembly some months ago—early spring, actually—how time does get away! Crassus Orator and Ahenobarbus Pontifex Maximus had just declared themselves candidates for the censorship. What Carbo was trying to do was to push an updated version of Saturninus's grain law through the Plebs. But the meeting got so out of hand that a couple of ex-gladiators were killed, some senators were molested, and a riot suspended the proceedings. Crassus Orator was caught in the midst of it, thanks to his electoral campaigning, got his toga dirty, and was absolutely livid. The result is that he promulgated a decree in the Senate to the effect that the entire responsibility for keeping order during a meeting rests squarely upon the shoulders of the magistrate convoking it. The decree was hailed as a brilliant piece of lawmaking, went to the Assembly of the Whole People, and was passed. Had Carbo's meeting taken place under the auspices of Crassus Orator's new law, he could have been charged with inciting violence, and been heavily fined.

Now I come to the most delicious bit of news.

We no longer have censors!

But Publius Rutilius, what happened? I hear you cry. Well, I shall tell you. At first we thought they would manage to deal together fairly well, despite their manifest differences of character. They let the State contracts, perused the rolls of the senators and then the knights, and then followed this up with a decree expelling all save an unimpeachable handful of teachers of rhetoric from Rome. Their chief fury fell upon the teachers of Latin rhetoric, but those teaching in Greek didn't fare too well either. You know the kind of fellows, Lucius Cornelius. For a few sesterces a day they guarantee to turn the sons of impecunious but social-climbing Third or Fourth Classers into lawyers, who then solicit business tirelessly up and down the Forum, preying upon our gullible but litigious-minded populace. Most don't bother to teach in Greek, as the due process of the law is conducted in Latin. And—as everyone admits!—these so-called teachers of rhetoric drag the law and lawyers down, prey upon the uninformed and the underprivileged, trick them out of what little money they have, and do not glorify our Forum. Out they all went, bag and baggage! Calling down curses upon the heads of Crassus Orator and Ahenobarbus Pontifex Maximus, but to no avail. Out they all went. Only those teachers of rhetoric with pristine reputations and a proper clientele have been permitted to stay.

It looked good. Everyone sang the praises of the censors, who might therefore have been thought to get on somewhat better together. Instead, they began to fight. Oh, the arguments! In public! Culminating in an acrimonious exchange of incivilities heard by at least half of Rome, that half (I am a part of it, I admit it freely!) which took to lingering in the vicinity of the censors' booth to hear what it could hear.

Now you may or may not know that Crassus Orator

has taken to farming fish, this now being regarded as a kind of trade practice in keeping with senatorial rank. So he has installed vast ponds on his country estates and is making a fortune selling freshwater eels, pike, carp, and so forth to—for instance—the college of *epulones* before all the big public feasts. Little did we know what we were in for when Lucius Sergius Orata started farming oysters down in the Baiae lakes! It is but a small step from oysters to eels, dear Lucius Cornelius.

Oh, how much I will miss this kind of deliciously Roman furor! But more of that anon. Back to Crassus Orator and his fish-farming. On his country estates it is purely a commercial activity. But, being Crassus Orator, he rather fell in love with his fish. So he extended the size of the pond in his peristyle right here in Rome and filled it with some more exotic and expensive piscine denizens. He sits on the wall of the pool, tickles the water with his finger, and up they swim for their crumbed bread, little shrimps, all manner of delicacies. Especially this one carp, a huge creature the color of well-cared-for pewter with quite a lovely face, as fish go. It was so tame it would come buzzing to the edge of the water the moment Crassus Orator entered his garden. And I really don't blame him for growing fond of the thing, I really don't.

Anyway, the fish died, and Crassus Orator was brokenhearted. For one whole market interval no one saw him; those who ventured to call at his house were told he was prostrate with grief. Eventually he reappeared in public, face very cast down, and joined his colleague the Pontifex Maximus at their booth in the Forum— they were, I add, about to move their booth out to the Campus Martius to take a much-needed new census of the general populace.

"Hah!" said Ahenobarbus Pontifex Maximus when

Crassus Orator appeared. "What, no *toga pulla*? No formal mourning garb, Lucius Licinius? I am amazed! Why, I heard that when you cremated your fish, you hired an actor to don its wax mask and made him swim all the way to the temple of Venus Libitina! I also hear that you have had a cupboard made for the fish's mask and intend to parade it at all future Licinius Crassus funerals as a part of the family!"

Crassus Orator drew himself up majestically—well, like all the Licinii Crassi, he has the bulk for it!—and looked down his considerable nose at his fellow censor.

"It is true, Gnaeus Domitius," said Crassus Orator haughtily, "that I have wept for my dead fish. Which makes me a far better kind of man than you! You've had three wives die so far, and wept not a single tear for any of them!"

So that, Lucius Cornelius, was the end of the censorship of Lucius Licinius Crassus Orator and Gnaeus Domitius Ahenobarbus Pontifex Maximus.

A pity, I suppose, that we will not now obtain a true census of the populace for another four years. No one plans to have new censors elected.

And now I come to the bad news. I write this on the eve of my departure for Smyrna, where I am going into exile. Yes, I see you start in surprise! Publius Rutilius Rufus, the most harmless and upright of men, sentenced to exile? It is true. Certain people in Rome have never forgotten the splendid job Quintus Mucius Scaevola and I did in Asia Province—men like Sextus Perquitienus, who can no longer confiscate priceless works of art in lieu of unpaid taxes. And since I am the uncle of Marcus Livius Drusus, I have also incurred the enmity of that ghastly individual, Quintus Servilius Caepio. And through him, of such human excrement as Lucius Marcius Philippus, still trying to get himself elected consul. Of course no one tried to get Scaevola,

he's too powerful. So they decided to get me. Which
they did. In the extortion court, where they produced
blatantly fabricated evidence that I—*I!*—obtained
money from the hapless citizens of Asia Province. The
prosecutor was one Apicius, a creature who boasts of
being Philippus's client. Oh, I had many outraged offers
of defense counsel—Scaevola, for one, and Crassus
Orator, and Antonius Orator, and even ninety-two-year-
old Scaevola the Augur, if you please. That hideously
precocious boy they all drag round the Forum with
them—Marcus Tullius Cicero, from Arpinum—offered
to speak up for me too.

But, Lucius Cornelius, I could see it would all be in
vain. The jury was paid a fortune (Gold of Tolosa?) to
convict me. So I refused all offers and defended myself. With grace and dignity, I flatter myself. Calmly.
My only assistant was my beloved nephew, Gaius Aurelius Cotta, the eldest of Marcus Cotta's three boys,
and my dear Aurelia's half brother. Her half brother on
the other side, Lucius Cotta, who was praetor in the
year of the *lex Licinia Mucia,* actually had the effrontery to assist the prosecution! His uncle Marcus Cotta
isn't speaking to him anymore, nor is his half sister.

The outcome was inevitable, as I have said. I was
found guilty of extortion, stripped of my citizenship,
and sentenced to exile not closer to Rome than five
hundred miles. I was not, however, stripped of my
property—I think they knew that any move in *that* direction might have seen them lynched. My last words
to the court were to the effect that I would go into exile
among the people on whose behalf I was convicted—the
citizens of Asia Province—and in particular, Smyrna.

I will never go home, Lucius Cornelius. And I do not
say that in a spirit of umbrage, or injured pride. I do not
want ever to set eyes again upon a city and a people who
could consent to such a manifest injustice. Three quarters

of Rome is going about weeping at the manifest injustice, but that doesn't alter the fact that I, its victim, am no longer a Roman citizen, and must go into exile. Well, I will not demean myself or gratify them, those who convicted me, by subjecting the Senate to a barrage of petitions to have my sentence repealed, my citizenship restored. I will prove myself a true Roman. I will lie down obediently, good Roman dog that I am, under the sentence of a legally appointed Roman court.

I have already had a letter from the *ethnarch* of Smyrna—wild with joy, it seems, at the prospect of having a new citizen named Publius Rutilius Rufus. It appears they are organizing a festival in my honor, to be celebrated the moment I arrive. Strange people, to react in this way to the advent of one who allegedly plundered them piecemeal!

Do not pity me too much, Lucius Cornelius. I will be well looked after, it seems. Smyrna has even voted me a most generous pension, and a house, and good servants. There are enough Rutilii left in Rome to make a nuisance of our clan—my son, my nephews, and my cousins of the branch Rutilius Lupus. But I will don the Greek *chlamys* and Greek slippers, for I am no longer entitled to wear the toga. On your way home, Lucius Cornelius, if you can possibly spare the time, would you call in to Smyrna to see me? I anticipate that no friend of mine at the eastern end of the Middle Sea will *not* call in to Smyrna to see me! A little solace for an exile.

I have decided to begin to write seriously. No more compendiums of military logistics, tactics, strategy. Instead, I shall become a biographer. I plan to start with a biography of Metellus Numidicus Piggle-wiggle, incorporating some juicy stuff which will have the Piglet gnashing his tusks in rage. Then I shall pass on to Catulus Caesar, and mention certain mutinous events which took place on the Athesis in the days when the

Germans were milling around Tridentum. Oh, what
fun I shall have! So do come and see me, Lucius Cornelius! I need information only you can give me!

Sulla had never thought himself particularly fond of Publius
Rutilius Rufus, yet when he laid the fat scroll down he found his
eyes full of tears. And he made a vow to himself: that one day
when he—the greatest man in the world—was fully established as
the First Man in Rome, he would visit retribution upon men like
Caepio and Philippus. And upon that vast equestrian toad, Sextus
Perquitienus.

However, when Young Sulla came in with Morsimus, Sulla was
dry-eyed and calm.

"I'm ready," he said to Morsimus. "But remind me, would you,
to tell the captain that we sail first to Smyrna? I have to see an old
friend there and promise him that I'll keep him abreast of events
in Rome."

PART IV

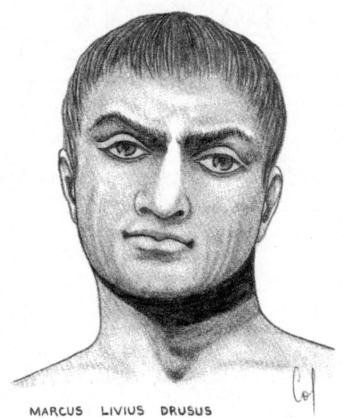

MARCUS   LIVIUS   DRUSUS

While Lucius Cornelius Sulla was away in the east, Gaius Marius and Publius Rutilius Rufus succeeded in legislating to suspend the proceedings of the special courts commissioned by the *lex Licinia Mucia*. And Marcus Livius Drusus took heart.

"That settles it, I think," he said to Marius and Rutilius Rufus shortly after the measure went through. "At the end of this year, I shall stand for the tribunate of the plebs. And at the beginning of next year I shall force a law through the Plebeian Assembly enfranchising every man in Italy."

Both Marius and Rutilius Rufus looked doubtful, though neither voiced opposition; Drusus was right in that there was nothing to lose by trying, and no reason to assume that additional time would soften Rome more. With the suspension of the special courts, there would be no more lacerated backs. No more visible reminders of the inhumanity of Rome.

"Marcus Livius, you have already been aedile. You could stand for election as a praetor," said Rutilius Rufus. "Are you *sure* you wish to espouse the tribunate of the plebs? Quintus Servilius Caepio is seeking election as a praetor, so you'll be doing battle in the Senate with an enemy who has imperium. Not only that, but Philippus is standing yet again for the consulship, and if he gets in—as he probably will because the voters are so tired of seeing him in the *toga candida* year after year—you have a consul allied to a praetor in Philippus and Caepio. They would make life as a tribune of the plebs very difficult for you."

"I know," said Drusus firmly. "However, I intend to stand for the tribunate of the plebs. Only please don't tell anyone. I have a special plan to gain election that necessitates people think I decided at the last moment."

The conviction and exile of Publius Rutilius Rufus early in September was a great blow to Drusus, who had deemed his uncle's support in the Senate invaluable. Now it would be left entirely to Gaius Marius, not a man Drusus stood on very close terms with, nor admired wholeheartedly. No substitute for a blood relative, at any rate. This also meant Drusus had no one left to talk to within the bosom of his family; his brother Mamercus had become a friend, but his politics inclined toward Catulus Caesar and the Piglet. Drusus had never broached the delicate subject of enfranchisement for Italy with him—nor did he want to. And Cato Salonianus was dead. A busy praetorship in charge of the murder and embezzlement courts, as well as those of fraud and usury, had sustained Cato after the death of Livia Drusa; but when the seething unrest in the Spains had decided the Senate to send a special governor to Gaul-across-the-Alps early in this present year, Cato Salonianus had seized eagerly upon it as a way of keeping busy. Off he went, leaving his mother-in-law Cornelia Scipionis and his brother-in-law Drusus to care for his children. Word had come during the summer that Cato Salonianus had fallen from his horse, sustaining a head injury which hadn't at the time seemed serious. Then had come an epileptic fit, a paralysis, a coma, and an end to life. Peaceful and oblivious. To Drusus the news had come like the closing of a door. All left to him now of his sister were her children.

It was therefore understandable that Drusus should write to Quintus Poppaedius Silo after his uncle's exile, and invite Silo to stay with him in Rome. The special courts of the *lex Licinia Mucia* were out of action, and the Senate in tacit agreement had decided that the massive enrollment of the Antonius-Flaccus census in Italy should simply be ignored until the next census came along. No reason then why Silo should not come to Rome. And Drusus badly wanted to talk to someone he could trust about his tribunate.

Three and a half years had gone by since last they met on that memorable day in Bovianum.

"There is only Caepio left alive," said Drusus to Silo as they sat in his study waiting for dinner to be announced, "and he refuses to see the children who are legitimately his, even now. Of the two who are Porcii Catones Saloniani, I need say no more than that they are orphans. Luckily they don't remember their mother at all, and the little girl, Porcia, remembers her father in only the vaguest terms. In this dreadful and stormy sea the poor children are perpetually tossed upon, my mother is their anchor. Cato Salonianus had no fortune to leave, of course. Just his property at Tusculum, and an estate in Lucania. I shall ensure that the boy has enough to enter the Senate when his time comes, and that the girl is suitably dowered. I gather Lucius Domitius Ahenobarbus, who is married to the girl's aunt—Cato Salonianus's sister—is very seriously thinking of my little Porcia for *his* son, Lucius. My will is made. So, I have ensured, is Caepio's will. Whether he likes it or not, Quintus Poppaedius, he cannot disinherit them. Nor can he disown them in any other way, apart from refusing to see them. Cur!"

"Poor little things," said Silo, who was a father himself. "For tiny Cato, neither mother nor father, even in memory."

Drusus smiled wryly. "Oh, he's a strange one! Thin as a stick, with an enormously long neck and the most amazingly beaky nose I have ever seen on such a small boy. He reminds me for all the world of a plucked vulture. Nor can I like him, no matter how hard I try. He's not quite two years old, but he stumps around the house with his neck craning his head forward, and that nose pointed—or part of it, anyway!—at the ground. Hollering! No, not weeping. Just yelling. He cannot say anything in a normal tone of voice. He shouts. And hectors without mercy. I see him coming, and much as I pity him, I flee!"

"What about the one who spied—Servilia?"

"Oh, very quiet, very self-contained, very obedient. But do not trust her, Quintis Poppaedius, whatever you do. Another one of the brood I dislike," said Drusus a little sadly.

Silo gave him a keen glance out of yellowish eyes. "Are there any you do like?" he asked.

"My son, Drusus Nero. A dear little boy. Not so little these days, actually. He's eight. Unfortunately his intelligence is not the equal of his good nature. I tried to tell my wife it was imprudent to adopt a baby, but she had her heart set on a baby, and that was that. I like Young Caepio very much too, though I *cannot* credit he's Caepio's son! He's the image of Cato Salonianus, and very like little Cato in the nursery. Lilla is all right. So is Porcia. Though girl-children are a mystery to me, really."

"Be of good cheer, Marcus Livius!" said Silo, smiling. "One day they all turn into men and women, and one can at least dislike them on merit then. Why don't you take me to see them? I admit I'm curious to see the plucked vulture and the spy-girl. How chastening, that it is the imperfect one finds most interesting."

The rest of that first day was spent in social congress, so it was the following day which saw Drusus and Silo settle to talk about the Italian situation.

"I intend to stand for election as a tribune of the plebs at the beginning of November, Quintus Poppaedius," said Drusus.

Silo blinked, unusual for a Marsian. "After being aedile?" he asked. "You must be due for praetor."

"I could stand for praetor now," said Drusus calmly.

"Then why? *Tribune of the plebs?* Surely you can't be thinking of trying to give Italy the citizenship!"

"That's exactly what I'm thinking of doing. I have waited patiently, Quintus Poppaedius—the gods be my witnesses, I have been patient! If the time is ever going to be right, it is now, while the *lex Licinia Mucia* is still fresh in all men's minds. And name me a man in the Senate of the appropriate age who can possibly summon up the *dignitas* and *auctoritas* as a tribune of the plebs that I can? I've been in the Senate for ten long years, I've been the *paterfamilias* of my family for almost twenty years, my reputation is stainless, and the only tic I have ever had is full enfranchisement for the men of Italy. I've been plebeian aedile, and given great games. My fortune is immense, I have a crowd of clients, I am known and respected everywhere in Rome. So when I stand for the tribunate of the plebs instead of the praetorship, everyone is going to know that my reasons must be compelling ones. I was famous as an advocate, I am famous as an orator. Yet for ten years my voice has been silent in the House, I have yet to speak. In the law courts the mention of my name is enough to draw big crowds. Truly, Quintus Poppaedius, when I choose to stand for the tribunate of the plebs, everyone in Rome from highest to lowest will know my reasons must be as cogent as they are deserving."

"It will certainly create a sensation," said Silo, puffing out his cheeks. "But I don't think you have a chance of succeeding. I think you'd use your time more wisely if you became praetor, and consul two years from now."

"I cannot succeed in the consul's chair," said Drusus strongly. "This is the kind of legislation that must come from the Plebeian Assembly, promulgated by a tribune of the plebs. If I were to try to pass it as consul, it would be vetoed immediately. But as a tribune of the plebs myself, I can control my colleagues in ways the consul cannot. And I have authority over the consul by virtue of my veto. If necessary, I can trade this off for that. Gaius Gracchus flattered himself he used the tribunate of the plebs brilliantly. But I tell you, Quintus Poppaedius, *no one* will equal me! I have the age, the wisdom, the clients and the clout. I also have a program of legislation worked out that will go much further than merely the citizenship for all of Italy. I intend to reshape Rome's public affairs."

"May the great light-bearing Snake protect and guide you, Marcus Livius, is all I can say."

Eyes unwavering, demeanor suggesting that he believed in himself and what he was saying implicitly, Drusus leaned forward. "Quintus Poppaedius, it is time. I cannot allow a state of war between Rome and Italy, and I suspect you and your friends are planning war. If you go to war, you will lose. And so will Rome, even though I believe she will win. Rome has never lost a war, my friend. Battles, yes. And perhaps in the early days of a war, Italy would do much better than anyone in Rome save I suspects. But Rome will win! Because Rome always wins. Yet—what a hollow victory! The economic consequences alone are appalling. You know the old adage as well as I do—never fight a war on your own home ground—let it be someone else's property which suffers."

Out went Drusus's hand across the desk top to clasp Silo around the forearm. "Let me do it my way, Quintus Poppaedius, please! The peaceful way, the logical way, the only way it can possibly work."

There was no constraint in the nodding of Silo's head, nor doubt in his eyes. "My dear Marcus Livius, you have my wholehearted support! Do it! The fact I don't think it can be done is beside the point. Unless someone of your caliber tries, how can Italy ever know the exact extent of Rome's opposition to a general enfranchisement? In hindsight, I agree with you that to tamper with the census was a stupidity. I don't think any of us thought it would work—or could work. It was more a way of telling the Senate and People of Rome how strongly we Italians feel. Yet—it set us back. It set you back. So do it! Anything Italy can do to help you, Italy will. You have my solemn word on it."

"I would rather have all of Italy as a client," said Drusus ruefully, and laughed. "Once I succeed in giving every Italian the vote, if every Italian then regarded himself as my client, he would have to vote as I want him to vote. I could work my will on Rome with impunity!"

"Of course you could, Marcus Livius," said Silo. "All of Italy *would* be in your clientele."

Drusus pursed his lips, striving to overcome the jubilation leaping within him. "In theory, yes. In practice—impossible to enforce."

"No, easy!" cried Silo quickly. "All it requires is that I and Gaius Papius Mutilus and the others who lead Italy demand an oath of every Italian man. To the effect that, should you succeed in winning general enfranchisement, he is your man through thick and thin, and to the death."

Wondering, Drusus stared at Silo with mouth open. "An oath? But would they be prepared to swear?"

"They would, provided the oath didn't extend to their progeny or your progeny," said Silo steadily.

"Inclusion of progeny isn't necessary," said Drusus slowly. "All I need is time and massive support. After me, it will be done." All Italy in his clientele! The dream of every Roman nobleman who ever lived, to have clients enough to populate whole armies. Did he have all of Italy in his clientele, nothing would be impossible.

"An oath will be forthcoming, Marcus Livius," said Silo briskly. "You're quite right to want all Italy your clients. For general enfranchisement should only be the beginning." Silo laughed, a high, slightly ragged sound. "What a triumph! To see a man become the

First Man in Rome—no, the First Man in Italy!—through the good offices of those who at the moment have no influence whatsoever in Rome's affairs." Silo released his forearm from Drusus's grip gently. "Now tell me how you intend to go about it."

But Drusus couldn't collect his thoughts; the implications were too big, too overwhelming. All Italy in his clientele!

How to do it? *How?* Only Gaius Marius among the important men in the Senate would stand with him, and Drusus knew Marius's support would not be enough. He needed Crassus Orator, Scaevola, Antonius Orator and Scaurus Princeps Senatus. As the tribunician elections loomed closer, Drusus came close to despair; he kept waiting for the right moment, and the right moment never seemed to come. His candidature for the tribunate of the plebs remained a secret known only to Silo and Marius, and his powerful quarry kept eluding him.

Then very early one morning at the end of October, Drusus encountered Scaurus Princeps Senatus, Crassus Orator, Scaevola, Antonius Orator and Ahenobarbus Pontifex Maximus clustered together by the Comitia well; that they were talking about the loss of Publius Rutilius Rufus was obvious.

"Marcus Livius, join us," said Scaurus, opening a gap in the circle. "We were just discussing how best to go about wresting the courts off the Ordo Equester. To convict Publius Rutilius was absolutely criminal. The knights have abrogated their right to run any Roman court!"

"I agree," said Drusus, joining them. He looked at Scaevola. "It was you they really wanted, of course, not Publius Rutilius."

"In which case, why didn't they go after me?" asked Scaevola, who was still very upset.

"You have too many friends, Quintus Mucius."

"And Publius Rutilius not enough. That is a disgrace. I tell you, we cannot afford to lose Publius Rutilius! He was his own man, always, and that is rare," said Scaurus angrily.

"I do not think," said Drusus, speaking very carefully, "that we will ever succeed in wresting the courts completely away from the knights. If the law of Caepio the Consul didn't stay on the tablets—and it didn't—then I don't see how any other law returning the courts to the Senate can. The Ordo Equester is used to running the courts, it's had them now for over thirty years. The knights like the power it gives them over the Senate. Not only that, the knights feel inviolate. The law of Gaius Gracchus does not specifically say that a knight-staffed jury is culpable in the matter of taking bribes. The knights insist that the *lex Sempronia* says they cannot be prosecuted for taking bribes when serving as jurors."

Crassus Orator was staring at Drusus in alarm. "Marcus Livius, you are by far the best man of praetorian age!" he exclaimed. "If *you* say such things, what chance does the Senate have?"

"I didn't say the Senate should abandon hope, Lucius Licinius," said Drusus. "I just said that the knights would refuse to let the courts go. However, what if we maneuver them into a situation in which they have no choice but to share the courts with the Senate? The plutocrats do not run Rome yet, and they're well aware of it. So why not put in the thin end of the wedge? Why not have someone propose a new law to regulate the major courts, incorporating a half-and-half membership between Senate and Ordo Equester?"

Scaevola drew in a breath. "The thin end of the wedge! It would be very difficult for the knights to find convincing reasons to decline—to them, it would seem like a senatorial olive branch. What could be fairer than half-and-half? The Senate cannot possibly be accused of trying to wrest control of the courts away from the Ordo Equester, can it?"

"Ha, ha!" said Crassus Orator, grinning. "Within the Senate the ranks are closed, Quintus Mucius. But, as all we senators know, there are always a few knights on any jury with ambitions to dwell within the Curia Hostilia. If the jury is entirely knight, they don't matter. But if the jury is only fifty percent knight, they can sway the balance. Very clever, Marcus Livius!"

"We can plead," said Ahenobarbus Pontifex Maximus, "that we senators possess such valuable legal expertise that the courts will be the richer for our presence. And that, after all, we did have exclusive control of the courts for nearly four hundred years! In our modern times, we can say, such exclusivity cannot be allowed to happen. But nor, we can argue, ought the Senate be excluded." For Ahenobarbus Pontifex Maximus, this was a reasonable argument; he had mellowed somewhat since his experiences as a judge in Alba Fucentia during the days of the *lex Licinia Mucia,* though Crassus Orator did bring out the worst in him. Yet here they stood together, united in respect of class and its privileges.

"Good thinking," said Antonius Orator, beaming.

"I agree," said Scaurus. He turned to face Drusus fully. "Do you intend to do this as a praetor, Marcus Livius? Or do you intend that someone else should do it?"

"I shall do it myself, Princeps Senatus, but not as a praetor," said Drusus. "I intend to run for the tribunate of the plebs."

Everyone gasped, and the circle swung to focus on Drusus.

"At your age?" asked Scaurus.

"My age is a distinct advantage," said Drusus calmly. "Though old enough to be praetor, I seek the tribunate of the plebs. No one can accuse me of youth, inexperience, hotheadedness, a desire to woo the crowds, or any of the usual reasons a man might want the tribunate of the plebs."

"Then, why do you want to be a tribune of the plebs?" asked Crassus Orator shrewdly.

"I have some laws to promulgate," said Drusus, still seeming calm and composed.

"You can promulgate laws as a praetor," said Scaurus.

"Yes, but not with the ease and acceptance a tribune of the plebs possesses. Over the course of the Republic, the passage of laws has become the province of the tribune of the plebs. And the Plebeian Assembly *likes* its role as lawmaker. Why disturb the status quo, Princeps Senatus?" asked Drusus.

"You have other laws in mind," said Scaevola softly.

"I do indeed, Quintus Mucius."

"Give us an idea of what you propose to legislate."

"I want to double the size of the Senate," said Drusus.

Another collective gasp; this one accompanied by a collective tensing of bodies.

"Marcus Livius, you begin to sound like Gaius Gracchus," said Scaevola warily.

"I can see why you might think so, Quintus Mucius. But the fact remains that I want to strengthen the influence of the Senate in our government, and I am broad-minded enough to use the ideas of Gaius Gracchus if they suit my purposes."

"How can filling the Senate with knights suit any proponent of senatorial dominance?" asked Crassus Orator.

"That was what Gaius Gracchus proposed to do, certainly," said Drusus. "I propose something slightly different. For one thing, I don't see how you can argue against the fact that the Senate *isn't* big enough anymore. Too few come to meetings, all too often we can't even form a quorum. If we are to staff juries, how many of us will be forever wearied by constant impaneling? Admit it, Lucius Licinius, a good half or more senators refused jury duty in the days when we entirely staffed the courts. Whereas Gaius Gracchus wanted to fill the Senate with knights, I want to fill it with men of our own senatorial order—plus some knights to keep them happy. All of us have uncles or cousins or even younger brothers who would like to be in the Senate and have the money to qualify, but who cannot belong because the Senate is full. These men I would see admitted ahead of any knights. And what better way to have certain knights who are opposed to the Senate transformed into supporters of the Senate than to make them senators? It is the censors admit new senators, and their choices cannot be argued with." He cleared his throat. "I know at the moment we have no censors, but we can elect a pair next April, or the April after."

"I like this idea," said Antonius Orator.

"And what other laws do you propose promulgating?" asked Ahenobarbus Pontifex Maximus, ignoring the reference to himself and Crassus Orator, who ought by rights still to be censors.

But now Drusus looked vague, and said only, "As yet I do not know, Gnaeus Domitius."

The Pontifex Maximus snorted. "In my eye you don't!"

Drusus smiled with innocent sweetness. "Well, perhaps I do,

Gnaeus Domitius, but not certainly enough to want to mention them in such august company as this. Rest assured, you will be given an opportunity to have your say about them."

"Huh," said Ahenobarbus Pontifex Maximus, looking skeptical.

"What I'd like to know, Marcus Livius, is how long you've known you would be seeking the tribunate of the plebs?" asked Scaurus Princeps Senatus. "I wondered why, having been elected a plebeian aedile, you made no move to speak in the House. But you were saving your maiden speech for something better even then, weren't you?"

Drusus opened his eye wide. "Marcus Aemilius, how can you say such things? As aedile, one has nothing to speak about!"

"Huh," said Scaurus, then shrugged. "You have my support, Marcus Livius. I like your style."

"And my support," said Crassus Orator.

Everyone else agreed to support Drusus as well.

Drusus did not announce his candidacy for the tribunate of the plebs until the morning of the elections, normally a foolhardy ploy—yet, in his case, a brilliant one. It saved his having to answer awkward questions during the pre-electoral period, and it made it look as if, having seen the quality of the tribunician candidates, he simply threw his hands in the air in exasperation, and impulsively declared his own candidacy to improve the standard. The best names the other candidates could produce were Sestius, Saufeius, and Minicius—none of them noble, let alone wonderful. Drusus announced himself only after the other twenty-two had done so.

It was a quiet election, a poor turnout of the electors. Some two thousand voters appeared, a minute percentage of those entitled to cast a ballot. As the well of the Comitia could hold twice that number comfortably, there was no need to shift the venue to a bigger location, such as the Circus Flaminius. The candidates all having declared themselves, the President of the outgoing College of the Tribunes of the Plebs began the voting procedure by calling for the electors to separate into their tribes; the consul Marcus Perperna, a

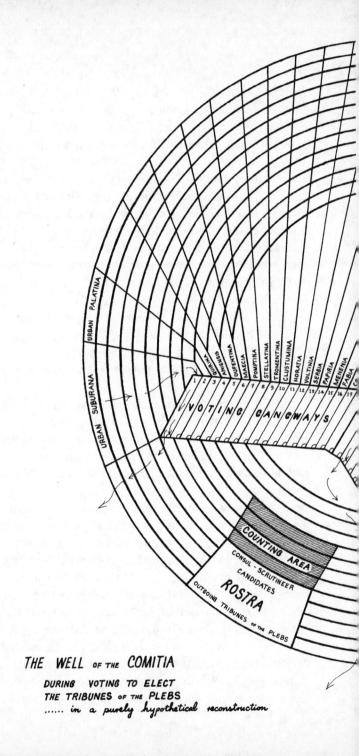

THE WELL OF THE COMITIA

DURING VOTING TO ELECT
THE TRIBUNES OF THE PLEBS
...... in a purely hypothetical reconstruction

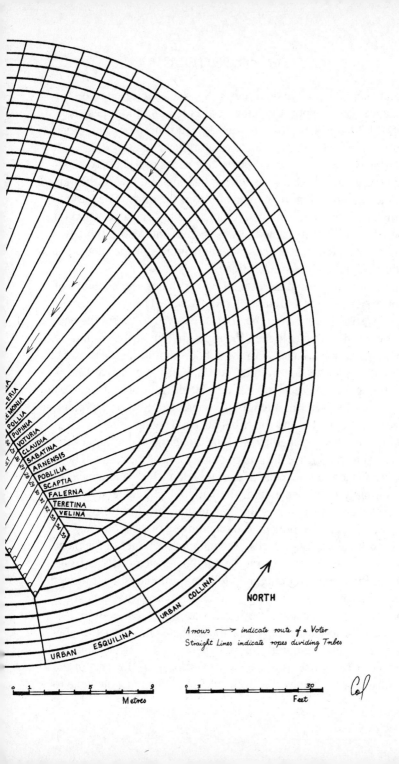

ERIA
EMONIA
POLLIA
PUPINIA
VOTURIA
CLAUDIA
SABATINA
ARNENSIS
POBLILIA
SCAPTIA
FALERNA
TERETINA
VELINA

URBAN ESQUILINA   URBAN COLLINA

↑
NORTH

Arrows ——→ indicate route of a Voter
Straight Lines indicate ropes dividing Tribes

0   1   5   9
Metres

0   3   30
Feet

Col

plebeian, kept a stern eye on things in his role as scrutineer. As the
attendance was so poor, the public slaves holding the ropes separating tribe from tribe had no need to send the more numerous
tribes to rope enclosures outside the Comitia well.

As this was an election, all thirty-five tribes cast their votes simultaneously, rather than—as for the passing of a law or the verdict in a trial—casting their votes one after the other. The baskets
in which the inscribed wax ballot tablets were deposited stood on
a temporary platform below the well-side of the rostra; the latter
remained the province of the outgoing tribunes of the plebs, the
candidates, and the consul-scrutineer.

The temporary wooden addition curved along the contours of
the lower tiers of the Comitia well, hiding them. Thirty-five narrow
gangways rose steeply from the floor of the well to where the baskets stood some six feet higher, the ropes dividing tribe from tribe
extending like pie wedges across the floor and up the tiers of the
well on the opposite side from the rostra. Each voter arrived at his
ascending gangway, received his wax tablet from one of the *custodes,* paused to inscribe it with his stylus, then trod up the plank
bridge and dropped it into the tribal basket. Having done his electoral duty, he then escaped by walking along the upper tiers of the
well until he could leave the scene at either end of the rostra. Those
who had found the interest and energy to don a toga and appear to
vote normally didn't leave until the ballots had been counted, so
once they were finished, they lingered in the lower Forum chatting,
eating snacks, and keeping an eye on progress in the Comitia.

All through this long process, the outgoing tribunes of the plebs
stood to the back of the rostra, the candidates nearer to its front,
while the President of the outgoing College and the consul-scrutineer
sat on a bench right at the front, well able to see what was going
on below them in the actual voting arena.

Some tribes—particularly the four urban ones—on this day
contained several hundred voters, whereas other tribes had far
fewer, perhaps as few as a dozen or two dozen in the case of the
more distant rural tribes. Yet each tribe really had just one vote to

cast, that of the majority of its members; which gave the distant rural tribes a disproportionately high effectiveness.

As the baskets only held about a hundred tablets, they were removed for counting the moment they were filled, empty baskets put in their place. The counting was kept in his central vision by the consul-scrutineer the whole time; it went on at a large table on the top tier just below him, thirty-five *custodes* and their assistants as busy as the numbers in their tribes demanded.

And when it was all done about two hours before sunset, the consul-scrutineer read out the results to those voters who had lingered to hear, now standing in the ropeless Comitia well again. He also authorized the publication of the results upon a sheet of parchment pinned to the back (Forum) wall of the rostra, where any Forum frequenter could read it during the succeeding days.

Marcus Livius Drusus was the new President of the College, having polled the most tribes—in fact, all thirty-five tribes had voted for him, an unusual phenomenon. The Minicius, the Sestius, and the Saufeius were also elected, and six more with names so unknown and uninspiring that hardly anyone remembered them— nor had cause to remember them, as they did nothing during their year in office, which began on the tenth day of December, about thirty days hence. Drusus of course was glad he had no formidable opponents.

The College of the Tribunes of the Plebs had its headquarters inside the Basilica Porcia, on the ground floor at the end nearest to the Senate House. This consisted of an open space of floor, a few tables and folding backless chairs, and was grossly encumbered by a number of big pillars; the Basilica Porcia being the oldest of the basilicas, it was also the most awkwardly constructed. Here, on days when the Comitia could not meet or when no meeting had been called, the tribunes of the plebs seated themselves to listen to those who approached them with problems, complaints, suggestions.

Drusus found himself looking forward to this new exercise, and to the delivering of his maiden speech in the Senate. Opposition from the senior magistrates in the Senate was certain, as Philippus had been returned as junior consul behind Sextus Julius Caesar— the first Julian to sit in the consul's chair in four hundred years. Caepio had been returned as a praetor, though one of eight men rather than the normal six; some years the Senate felt six praetors would not be enough, and recommended the election of eight. This was one such year.

It had been Drusus's intention to start legislating ahead of any of his fellow tribunes of the plebs, but when the new college was inducted on the tenth day of December, that boor Minicius rushed forward the moment the ceremonies were over and announced in a shrill voice that he was calling his first *contio* to discuss a much-needed new law. In the past, cried Minicius, the children of a marriage between a Roman citizen and a non-citizen were accorded the status of their father. Too easy! cried Minicius. Too many hybrid Romans! cried Minicius. To wall up this undesirable breach in the citizen citadel, cried Minicius, he announced the promulgation of a new law forbidding the Roman citizenship to *all* children of a mixed marriage, even when the father was the Roman half.

This *lex Minicia de liberis* came as a disappointing surprise to Drusus, for it was hailed in the Comitia with shouts of approval, thereby demonstrating that the bulk of the tribal electors at any rate still felt the Roman citizenship must be withheld from all those considered inferior: in other words, the rest of mankind.

Of course Caepio supported the measure, but wished nonetheless that it had never been promulgated; he had recently befriended a new senator, a client of Ahenobarbus Pontifex Maximus's whom (while he was censor) he had added to the senatorial rolls. Very rich—largely at the expense of his fellow Spaniards—Caepio's new friend had an imposing name: Quintus Varius Severus Hybrida Sucronensis. Understandably, however, he preferred to be known simply as Quintus Varius; the Severus he had earned because of his cruelty rather than a gravity he could not claim, the Hybrida was evidence of one parent's non-citizen status, and the Sucronensis indicated that he had been born and brought up in the town of Sucro, in Nearer Spain. Barely a Roman, more foreign than any Italian national, Quintus Varius was determined he would become one of Rome's greatest men, and was not fussy about how he might achieve this exalted status.

Introduced to Caepio, Varius attached himself to Caepio more firmly than a barnacle to a barge bottom, an adept at flattery, untiring in his attentions and little services—and more successful than he might otherwise have been because, without knowing it, he elevated Caepio to the level upon which Caepio used to put Drusus in the old days.

Not all of Caepio's other friends welcomed Quintus Varius, though Lucius Marcius Philippus did, as Varius was ever-ready to extend a distressed consular aspirant some financial help, and quick to waive repayment. Quintus Caecilius Metellus Pius the Piglet loathed Varius from the moment he met him.

"Quintus Servilius, how do you stomach that vile creature?" the Piglet was heard to ask Caepio without a single stammer. "I tell you, if Varius had been in Rome at the time my father died, I would have believed Apollodorus the physician, and known exactly who poisoned the great Metellus Numidicus!"

Said the Piglet to Ahenobarbus Pontifex Maximus, "Why is it that your top clients are such a lot of turds? Truly, they are! Between the plebeian Servilii of the Augur's family and this Varius character, you're making a name for yourself as the patron of pimps, shits, butcher's scraps, and maggots!"

A comment which left Ahenobarbus Pontifex Maximus openmouthed, bereft of the power to reply.

Not all eyes saw Quintus Varius so clearly; to the gullible and the uninformed he presented as a wonderful kind of man. For one thing, he was extremely good-looking in a very masculine way— tall, well built, dark but not swarthy, fiery of eye, pleasing of features. He was also plausible, but on a personal level only. His oratory left much to be desired and would always be marred by his very thick Spanish accent, but he was working hard at it, upon Caepio's advice. And while he did, the arguments raged about the sort of man he truly was.

"He's that rare man, a reasonable man," said Caepio.

"He's a parasite and a panderer," said Drusus.

"He's a most generous, charming man," said Philippus.

"He's as slippery as a gobbet of spit," said the Piglet.

"He's a worthy client," said Ahenobarbus Pontifex Maximus.

"He's no Roman," said Scaurus Princeps Senatus scornfully.

Naturally the charming, reasonable, worthy Quintus Varius was rendered uncomfortable by the new *lex Minicia de liberis*. It called his citizen status into question. Unfortunately he only now discovered how obtuse Caepio could be; nothing he could say would persuade Caepio to withdraw his support for the law of Minicius.

"Don't worry about it, Quintus Varius," said Caepio, "it's not a retroactive law, you know."

Drusus was more daunted by the law than anyone else, of that there could be no doubt, though none knew he was daunted. It was a strong indication that feeling—within Rome at least—was still heavily against giving away the citizenship.

"I shall have to reorganize my program of legislation," he said to Silo during one of Silo's visits, just before the end of the year. "General suffrage will have to be postponed until the end of my tribunate. I had hoped to start with it, but I cannot."

"You will never succeed, Marcus Livius," said Silo, shaking his head. "They won't let you succeed."

"I will get there because they *will* let me," said Drusus, more determined than ever.

"Well, I can offer you one crumb of comfort," said Silo with a pleased smile. "I've talked to the other Italian leaders, and to the last man they feel the way I do—that if you can bring us into the Roman fold, you deserve to be the patron of every Italian so enfranchised. We've drawn up a form of oath, and we'll be administering it between now and the end of next summer. So perhaps it's for the best that you can't start your tribunate off with your law of general suffrage."

Drusus flushed, hardly able to believe it. Not merely an army of clients, but nations of clients!

He plunged into his program of laws by promulgating the measure to share the major courts between Senate and Ordo Equester, and followed that up with a separate bill to enlarge the Senate. His first audience, however, was not the Plebeian Assembly; he introduced his measures in the House, requesting that the House empower him to take them to the Plebeian Assembly for ratification adorned with a senatorial decree of approval.

"I am not a demagogue," he said to the hushed rows of togate senators inside the Curia Hostilia. "In me, you see the tribune of the plebs of the future—a man old enough in years and in experience to recognize that the old ways are indeed the right and proper ways—a man who will safeguard the *auctoritas* of the Senate to his last breath. Nothing I do in the Comitia will come as a surprise to the members of this House, for I will introduce it here first, seeking your mandate. Nothing I will ask of you is unworthy of you, nothing I will ask of myself is unworthy of me. For I am the son of a tribune of the plebs who felt about his duties as I do, I am the son of a man who was consul and also censor, I am the son of a man who repulsed the Scordisci in Macedonia so soundly that he was awarded a triumph. I am descendant of Aemilius Paullus, of Scipio Africanus, of Livius Salinator. I am old in name. And I am old in years for this office I presently hold.

"Here, Conscript Fathers, in this building, in this assemblage of ancient and glorious names, lie the wellsprings of Roman law, of Roman government, of Roman administration. It is to this assemblage, in this building, that I will speak first, hoping that you have the wisdom and foresight to see that everything I propose has logic, reason, necessity."

At the end of his speech the House applauded with a thankfulness which could only be experienced by men who had witnessed with their own eyes the tribunate doings of Saturninus. Here was a very different kind of tribune of the plebs—first a senator, and only after that, a servant of the plebs.

The consuls of course were the outgoing pair, both fairly liberal in their ideas and ideals, and the outgoing praetors were also independent-minded. It was therefore with little opposition that Drusus got his mandate from the Senate endorsing his two laws.

Though the incoming consuls were not so promising, Sextus Caesar was in support of the measures, and Philippus remarkably subdued; only Caepio spoke in condemnation; since everybody knew how Caepio felt about his erstwhile brother-in-law, nobody took any notice. The Plebeian Assembly—in which the knights were very strong—was where Drusus expected opposition, but he encountered very little. Perhaps, he thought, this was because he had introduced both his bills at the same *contio,* enabling a certain group of knights to see the bait dangled in the second bill. The chance to sit in the Senate, denied this same certain group of knights due to the small size of the senior governing body, was a powerful inducement. Besides, half-and-half seemed a very fair sort of jury, as the odd man out—the fifty-first juror—would be a knight, in return for which the president of the court would be a senator. Honor was definitely satisfied.

Drusus's entire thrust was in the direction of a concord between the two great orders, senatorial and equestrian—an appeal to each side to pull together for a change. At one and the same time, Drusus deplored the actions of Gaius Sempronius Gracchus in driving an artificial wedge between the orders.

"It was Gaius Gracchus who separated the two orders in the first place, an artificial kind of social distinction at best—for what is a non-senatorial member of a senatorial family, even now, but a knight? If he possesses enough money to qualify as a knight at the census, he is enrolled as a knight. Because there are too many members of his family in the Senate already. Knights and senators both belong to the First Class! One family may have many members of both orders, yet, thanks to Gaius Gracchus, we suffer an *artificial* separation. The only difference rests with the censors. Once a man enters the Senate, he cannot engage in commercial pursuits having nothing to do with land. And that has always been so," said Drusus in the Plebeian Assembly, with most of the Senate listening as well.

"Men like Gaius Gracchus may not be admired or their actions approved," he went on, "but there is nothing wrong with my taking what is admirable and worth approving out of his bag of tricks! It was Gaius Gracchus who first suggested that the Senate be enlarged. However, because of the general atmosphere at that time—the opposition of my father—and the less ideal parts of the Gracchan program—nothing came of it. I revive it now, son of my father though I am, because I see how useful and beneficial this law is *in our time*! Rome is growing. The public duties demanded of each man in public life are growing. Whereas the pool from which our public men are fished out is stagnant, turgid, unrefreshed. Both Senate and Ordo Equester need new swimmers in their pool. My measures are designed to help both sides, the two different kinds of fish in the pool."

The laws were passed midway through January of the New Year, despite Philippus as junior consul and Caepio as one of the Rome-based praetors. And Drusus could sit back with a sigh of relief, well launched. So far he hadn't actually alienated anyone! Too much to hope perhaps that this state of affairs would continue, yet better than he had expected by a long way.

At the beginning of March he spoke in the Senate about the *ager publicus,* aware that his mask was sure to slip, that some of the ultra-conservatives would suddenly see how dangerous this son of one of their own was going to be. But Drusus had confided in Scaurus Princeps Senatus, in Crassus Orator, and in Scaevola, and brought them round to his way of thinking. And if he could do that, then he had a chance to win over the whole Senate, so much was sure.

He got up to speak with a certain change in his demeanor that warned everyone something special was coming. Never had he seemed so self-contained, so wrought, so immaculate in manner and garb.

"There is an evil in our midst," Drusus said, speaking from the center of the floor down by the great bronze doors—which he had requested be closed. And paused, his eyes passing slowly from one part of the House to another, using that trick he had of making each and every man believe he looked at and spoke to him alone.

"There is an evil in our midst. A great evil. An evil we have brought upon ourselves! For we created it! Thinking—as is so often the way—that what we were doing was admirable, a good and proper thing. Because I am aware of this, and have nothing but respect for our ancestors, I do not criticize the creators of this evil in our midst, nor cast the slightest slur upon those who inhabited this august building in earlier times.

"But what is this evil in our midst?" Drusus asked rhetorically, pointed brows raised even as he dropped his voice. "It is the *ager publicus,* Conscript Fathers. The *ager publicus.* The evil in our midst. Yes, it is an evil! We took the best land from our Italian, our Sicilian, and our foreign enemies and we made it our own, and called it the *ager publicus* of Rome. Convinced that we were adding to the common wealth of Rome, that we would reap the benefits of so much good soil, so much extra prosperity. But it has not turned out that way, has it? Instead of keeping the confiscated land in its original small parcels, we expanded the size of the blocks we rented out—all in order to lessen the workload upon our civil servants, and keep Roman government from becoming a Greek bureaucracy. Thus we rendered our *ager publicus* unattractive to the farmers who had cultivated it, daunted them by the size of the allotments, and removed all hope of their continuing to use it by the size of the rents. The *ager publicus* became the province of the wealthy—those who can afford the rent and turn the land to the kind of activities its sheer size dictates. Where once these lands contributed greatly to the feeding of Italy, now they can only produce things to wear. Where once these lands were well settled and properly farmed, now they are huge, sparse, quite often neglected."

The faces he looked at were setting; Drusus's heart seemed to slow and labor within his chest, he could feel his breath growing short, he had to struggle to maintain his air of calm, his stern tones. No one had interjected. They hadn't had enough of him yet. Therefore he must plough on as if he hadn't noticed the change.

"But that, Conscript Fathers, was only the beginning of the evil. That was what Tiberius Gracchus saw when he rode through the *latifundia* of Etruria and found that the work was being done by foreign slaves rather than the good men of Italy and of Rome. That was what Gaius Gracchus saw when he took up his dead brother's task ten years later. I see it too. But I am not a Sempronius Gracchus. I do not regard the reasons of the Brothers Gracchi as big enough to disturb the *mos maiorum,* our customs and traditions. In the day of the Brothers Gracchi, I would have sided with my father."

He stopped to use his trick with his eyes, now blazing his absolute sincerity. "I mean that, Conscript Fathers! In the day of Tiberius Gracchus, in the day of Gaius Gracchus, I would have sided with my father. He was in the right of it. But times have changed. Other factors have evolved that swell the evil attached to the *ager publicus.* First, I mention the troubles in our Asia Province—started by Gaius Gracchus when he legislated to provide for the farming of the tithes and taxes there by private companies. The taxes of Italy have been farmed for longer by far, but were never so significant. As a result of this shelving of our senatorial responsibilities and the increasing role in public government of factions within the Ordo Equester, we have seen a model Asia Province administration lobbied against, attacked vitriolically—and finally, in the trial of our esteemed consular Publius Rutilius Rufus, have been given to understand by these knight factions that we—the members of the Senate of Rome!—had better not dare again to graze upon their turf. Well, I have begun the cessation of that kind of intimidation by making the Ordo Equester share its control of these courts equally with the Senate, and palliated knightly injury by expanding the size of the Senate. But the evil is still there."

Some of the faces were not quite so set; mention of his dear uncle, Publius Rutilius Rufus, had worked in his favor—and so, he saw, did his reference to Quintus Mucius Scaevola's administration of Asia Province as a model one.

"It has been joined, Conscript Fathers, by a new evil. How many of you know what this new evil is? Very few, I would think. I am referring to an evil created by Gaius Marius—though I acquit that eminent sextuple consular of acting in any knowledge of what he was starting. That is the trouble! At the time the evil begins it is not an evil at all! It is a result of change, of need, of shifting balances within our systems of government and within our armies. We had run out of soldiers. And why had we run out of soldiers? Among the many reasons is one which cannot be separated from the *ager publicus*. I mean that creation of the *ager publicus* threw the smallholding farmers off their land, and they ceased to breed so many sons, and so could not fuel the army. Gaius Marius did the only thing he could do, looking back on it from this point in time. He enlisted the *capite censi* in the army. He made soldiers out of the Head Count masses who did not have the money to buy their gear, did not come from landowning families—did not, in effect, have two sesterces to jingle together."

When he spoke on his voice was hushed; every head craned forward, every ear was cocked.

"Army pay is little. The spoils from our defeat of the Germans were pitiful. Gaius Marius and his successors, including his legates, had taught the Head Count how to fight, to know one end of a sword from the other, to experience a sense of worth, of dignity as Roman men. And I happen to agree with Gaius Marius! We cannot just throw them back into their mean urban back lanes, into their mean rural hovels. To do that would be to breed an entirely new kind of evil, a mass of well-trained men with nothing in their purses, time on their hands, and a growing sense of injury at their treatment by men of our class. Gaius Marius's answer—which started while he was still in Africa fighting King Jugurtha—was to settle these retired army veterans of no means upon *foreign* public land. It was the long and praiseworthy task of last year's urban praetor, Gaius Julius Caesar, to do this upon the islands in the African Lesser Syrtis. I am of the opinion—and I urge you strongly, fellow members of this House, to consider what I say as no more than a safeguard against *our* future!—I am of the opinion that Gaius Marius was right, and that we should continue to settle these Head Count veterans on foreign *ager publicus*."

From the beginning Drusus had not moved from his original place. Nor did he move now. There were those whose faces had hardened again at the mere mention of Gaius Marius's name, but Marius himself continued to sit upon his chair in the forefront of the consulars with great dignity and an impassive face. On the middle tier opposite Marius's central position sat the ex-praetor Lucius Cornelius Sulla, returned now from his governorship of Cilicia, and very interested in what Drusus was saying.

"All this, however, does not deal with the most brooding and immediate evil, the *ager publicus* of Italy and Sicily. Something must be done! For while ever we have this evil on our hands, Conscript Fathers, it is going to eat into our morals, our ethics, our sense of fitness, the *mos maiorum* itself. At the moment the Italian *ager publicus* belongs to those among ourselves and the First Class knights who are interested in *latifundia* grazing. The *ager publicus* of Sicily belongs to certain large-scale wheat growers who mostly live here in Rome and leave their Sicilian undertakings to overseers and slaves. A stable situation, you think? Then consider this! Ever since Tiberius and Gaius Sempronius Gracchus put the idea into our minds, the *ager publicus* of Italy and Sicily sits there just waiting to be sliced up and grabbed for this or that. How honorable will the generals of the future be? Will they, like Gaius Marius, be content to settle their veterans upon foreign public lands—or will they woo their veteran troops with promises of Italian land? How honorable will the tribunes of the plebs be in future years? Isn't it possible that another Saturninus might arise, woo the lowly with promises of land allotments in Etruria, in Campania, in Umbria, in Sicily? How honorable will the plutocrats of the future be? Might it not come about that the public lands are extended in the size of their allotments even more, until one or two or three men own half of Italy, half of Sicily? For what is the point of saying that the *ager publicus* is the property of the State, when the State leases it out, and when the men who run the State can legislate to do whatever they like with it?"

Drusus drew a great breath, straddled his legs wide apart, and launched into his peroration.

"*Get rid of the lot,* I say! Blot the so-called public lands of Italy and Sicily out of existence! Let us gather the courage here and now to do what must be done—slice up the whole of our public lands and donate them to the poor, the deserving, soldier veterans, any and all comers! Start with the richest and most aristocratic among us—give each man sitting here today his ten *iugera* out of our *ager publicus*—give every Roman citizen there is his ten little *iugera*! To some of us, not worth spitting upon. To others, more precious than all they own. Give it away, I say! Give every last iota of it away! Leave nothing for the pernicious men of the future to use to destroy us, our class, our wealth. Leave nothing for them to fiddle with save *caelum aut caenum*—sky and scum! I have sworn to do it, Conscript Fathers, and do it I will! I will leave nothing in the Roman *ager publicus* below the sky that is not the scum on top of useless swamp! Not because I care about the poor and deserving! Not because I worry about the fates of our Head Count veterans! Not because I grudge you of this House and our more pastoral knights the leasehold of these lands! Because—and this is my only reason!—because the public lands of Rome represent future disaster, lying there for some general to eye as a pension for his troops, lying there for some demagogic tribune of the plebs to eye as his ticket to First Man in Rome, lying there for two or three plutocrats to eye as their road to the ownership of all Italy or Sicily!"

The House heard and the House was moved to think, so much did Drusus achieve; Philippus said nothing, and when Caepio asked to speak, Sextus Caesar denied him, saying curtly that enough had been said, the session would resume on the morrow.

"You did well, Marcus Livius," said Marius, passing by on his way out. "Continue your program in this spirit, and you may be the first tribune of the plebs in history to carry the Senate."

But, much to Drusus's surprise—he hardly knew the man—it was Lucius Cornelius Sulla who battened onto him outside, and asked for further speech without delay.

"I've only just returned from the East, Marcus Livius, and I want to hear every detail. I want to know about the two laws you've already passed, as well as every single thought you own about the *ager publicus*," said that strange man, looking a little more weatherbeaten in the face than he had been before going east.

Sulla was indeed interested, as he was one of the very few men listening who had sufficient intelligence and understanding to discern the fact that Drusus was not a radical, not a true reformer, but rather an intensely conservative man chiefly concerned to preserve the rights and privileges of his class, keep Rome as Rome had always been.

They got no further than the well of the Comitia, where they were sheltered from the winds of winter, and there Sulla soaked in all of Drusus's opinions. From time to time he asked a question, but it was Drusus who spoke at length, grateful that at least one patrician Cornelius was disposed to listen to what most of the patrician Cornelii regarded as a betrayal. At the end Sulla held out his hand, smiling, and thanked Drusus sincerely.

"I shall vote for you in the Senate, even if I can't vote for you in the Plebeian Assembly," he said.

They walked back to the Palatine together, but neither evinced any interest in repairing to a warm study and a full flagon of wine; the kind of liking which would have produced such an invitation was not present on either side. At Drusus's house Sulla clapped him on the back and went straight on down the hill of the Clivus Victoriae to the spot where the alley in which his house lay branched off it. He was anxious to talk to his son, whose counsel he was coming to value more and more, though of mature wisdom there was none, a fact Sulla understood. Young Sulla was a partisan sounding board. To one who had few clients and scant chance of assembling armies of them, Young Sulla was a treasure beyond price.

But it was not to be a happy homecoming. Young Sulla, said Aelia, had come down with a bad cold. There was a client to see him who had insisted upon waiting, purporting to be the bearer of urgent news. The mere mention of malaise in Young Sulla was enough to drive the client temporarily out of Sulla's head, however; he hurried not toward his study, but toward the comfortable sitting room where Aelia had established this cherished son, feeling that his airless, lightless sleeping cubicle was not a proper place for the invalid. There was a fever, a sore throat, sniffles from a runny nose, a slightly rheumy-eyed look of adoration; Sulla relaxed, kissed his son, comforted him by saying,

"If you look after this affliction, my boy, it will last two market intervals—and if you do not, it will last sixteen days. Let Aelia look after you, is my advice."

Then he went to his study, frowning as to who or what was waiting for him; his clients were not of a kind to worry about him so much, for he was not a generous man, therefore did not distribute largesse. They mostly consisted of soldiers and centurions, provincial and rural nobodies who at one time or another had encountered him, been helped by him, and asked to become his clients. Few of what few there were had addresses in the city of Rome herself.

It was Metrobius. He ought to have known, though he hadn't even guessed. A mark of how successful his mental campaign to keep Metrobius out of memory had been. How old was he now? In his early thirties, perhaps thirty-two or thirty-three. Where did the years go? Into oblivion. But Metrobius was still Metrobius—and still, the kiss told him, his to command. Then Sulla shivered; the last time Metrobius had come to call on him at his house, Julilla had died. He didn't bring luck, even if he deemed love a substitute for luck. To Sulla, love was no substitute at all. He moved resolutely away from Metrobius's vicinity, seated himself behind his desk.

"You should not be here," he said, quite curtly.

Metrobius sighed, slid gracefully into the client's chair, and leaned his folded arms on the desk, his beautiful dark eyes sad. "I know I should not, Lucius Cornelius, but I *am* your client! You procured the citizenship for me without freedman status—I am legitimately Lucius Cornelius Metrobius, of the tribe Cornelia. If anything, I imagine your steward is more worried by the infrequency of my appearances here, rather than the other way around. Truly, I do or say *nothing* to imperil your precious reputation! Not to my friends and colleagues in the theater, not to my lovers, not to your staff. Please, credit me where credit is due!"

Sulla's eyes filled with tears, hastily blinked away. "I know,

Metrobius. And I do thank you." He sighed, got up, went to the console where the wine was kept. "A cup?"

"Thank you."

Sulla deposited the silver goblet on the desk in front of Metrobius, then slipped his arms around Metrobius's shoulders, and stood behind him to lean his cheek on the dense black hair. But before Metrobius could do more than lift his hands to clasp at Sulla's arms, Sulla was gone again, seated at his desk.

"What's this urgent matter?" he asked.

"Do you know a fellow called Censorinus?"

"Which Censorinus? Nasty young Gaius Marcius Censorinus, or that Censorinus who is a Forum frequenter of easy means with amusing senatorial aspirations?"

"The second specimen. I didn't think you knew your fellow Romans so well, Lucius Cornelius."

"Since I last saw you, I've been urban praetor. That job filled in a lot of gaps in my knowledge."

"I suppose it did."

"What about this second specimen of Censorinus?"

"He's going to lay charges against you in the treason court, alleging that you took a huge bribe from the Parthians in return for betraying Rome's interests in the East."

Sulla blinked. "Ye gods! I didn't think there was anyone in Rome with so much awareness of what happened to me in the East! I have received no encouragement even to report my adventures in full to the Senate. Censorinus? How would he know what went on east of the Forum Romanum, let alone east of the Euphrates? And how did you find out, when I've heard no whisper of this elsewhere?"

"He's a theater buff, and his chief recreation is the giving of parties at which actors strut round—the more tragic the actor, the better. So I go to his parties regularly," said Metrobius, smiling without any admiration for Censorinus. "No, Lucius Cornelius, the man is *not* one of my lovers! I despise him. But I do adore parties. None are ever as good as the ones you used to throw in the old days, alas. But Censorinus's efforts are bearable. And one meets the usual crowd at them—people I know well, am fond of. The man serves good food and good wine." Metrobius pursed his red lips, looked thoughtful. "However, it has not escaped me that in the past few months Censorinus has had some odd people at his flings. And is sporting a quizzing-glass made from a single flawless emerald—the sort of gem he could never have afforded to buy, even if he does have enough money for the senatorial census. I mean, that emerald quizzing-glass is a gem fit for a Ptolemy of Egypt, not a Forum frequenter!"

Sulla sipped at his wine, smiling slowly. "How fascinating! I can see I must cultivate this Censorinus—after my trial, if not before. Have you any ideas?"

"I think he's an agent for—I don't know! Perhaps the Parthians, or some other eastern lot. His peculiar party guests are definitely orientals of some kind—embroidered robes flashing gold, jewels all over the place, plenty of money to drop into every eagerly outstretched Roman hand."

"Not the Parthians," said Sulla positively. "They are not concerned about what happens west of the Euphrates, I know that for a fact. It's Mithridates. Or Tigranes of Armenia. But I'll settle for Mithridates of Pontus. Well, well!" He rubbed his hands together gleefully. "So Gaius Marius and I have Pontus really worried, do we? And, it seems, more Sulla than Marius! That's because I've had speech with Tigranes and concluded a treaty with the satraps of the King of the Parthians. Well, well!"

"What can you do?" asked Metrobius anxiously.

"Oh, don't worry about me," said Sulla cheerfully, getting up to nudge the shutter flaps on his windows completely closed. "Forewarned is definitely forearmed. I'll bide my time, wait for Censorinus to make his move. And then . . ."

"And then—what?"

Sulla's teeth showed nastily. "Why, I'll make him wish he had never been born." He passed to the atrium door to shoot its bolt, and from there he went to the door opening onto the peristyle colonnade, bolted it. "In the meantime, the best love of my life apart from my son, you're here and the damage is done. I can't allow you to leave without touching you."

"Nor would I go until you did."

They stood embraced, chins on each other's shoulders.

"Do you remember, all those years ago?" asked Metrobius dreamily, eyes closed, smiling.

"You in that absurd yellow skirt, with the dye running down the insides of your thighs?" Sulla smiled too, one hand sliding through the crisp head of hair, the other sliding down the straight hard back voluptuously.

"And you wearing that wig of living little snakes."

"Well, I *was* Medusa!"

"Believe me, you looked the part."

"You talk too much," said Sulla.

It was over an hour later before Metrobius departed; no one had evinced any interest in his visit, though Sulla did say to the ever-warm, always-loving Aelia that he had just been given news of an impending prosecution in the treason court.

She gasped, fluttered. "Oh, Lucius Cornelius!"

"Don't worry, my dear," said Sulla lightly. "It will come to nothing, I promise you."

She looked anxious. "Are you feeling well?"

"Believe me, wife, I haven't felt so well in years—or so in the mood to make passionate love to you," said Sulla, his arm about her waist. "Now come to bed."

There was no need for Sulla to ask further questions about Censorinus, for the next day Censorinus struck. He appeared at the tribunal of the urban praetor, the Picentine Quintus Pompeius Rufus, and demanded to prosecute Lucius Cornelius Sulla in the treason court for accepting a bribe from the Parthians to betray Rome.

"Do you have proof?" asked Pompeius Rufus sternly.

"I have proof."

"Then give me the gist of it."

"I will not, Quintus Pompeius. In the court I will do all that is necessary. This is a capital charge. I am not appealing for the lodgment of a fine, nor am I obliged under the law to divulge my case to you," said Censorinus, fingering the gem inside his toga, too precious to be left at home, but too noticeable to be displayed in public.

"Very well," said Pompeius Rufus stiffly, "I will tell the President of the *quaestio de maiestate* to assemble his court by the Pool of Curtius, three days hence."

Pompeius Rufus watched Censorinus almost skip across the lower Forum toward the Argiletum, then snapped his fingers to his assistant, a junior senator of the Fannius family. "Mind the shop," he said, getting to his feet. "I have an errand to run."

He located Lucius Cornelius Sulla in a tavern on the Via Nova, not such an arduous task as it might have seemed; he knew whom to ask, as any good urban praetor did. Sulla's drinking companion was none other than Scaurus Princeps Senatus, one of the few in the Senate who was interested in what Sulla had accomplished in the East. They were at a small table at the back of the tavern, which was a popular meeting place for those august enough to belong to the Senate, yet the proprietor's eyes bulged when a third *toga praetexta* walked in—the Princeps Senatus and two urban praetors, no less! Wait until his friends heard about this!

"Wine and water, Cloatius," said Pompeius Rufus briefly as he passed the counter, "and make it a *good* vintage!"

"The wine or the water?" asked Publius Cloatius innocently.

"Both, you pile of rubbish, or I'll hale you into court," said Pompeius Rufus with a grin as he joined the other two.

"Censorinus," said Sulla to Pompeius Rufus.

"Right in one," said the urban praetor. "You must have better sources than I do, for I swear it came as a complete surprise to me."

"I do have good sources," said Sulla, smiling; he liked the man from Picenum. "Treason, is it?"

"Treason. He *says* he has proof."

"So did those who convicted Publius Rutilius Rufus."

"Well, I for one will believe it when the streets of Barduli are paved with gold," said Scaurus, picking the poorest town in all of Italy as his example.

"So will I," said Sulla.

"Is there anything I can do to help?" asked Pompeius Rufus, taking an empty cup from the tavern keeper and splashing wine and water into it. He grimaced, looked up. "They're *both* terrible vintages!" he cried. "Worm!"

"Try and find better anywhere else on the Via Nova," said Publius Cloatius without umbrage, and slid off regretfully to a spot where he couldn't hear what was said.

"I can deal with it," said Sulla, who didn't seem disturbed.

"I've set the hearing for three days hence, by the Pool of Curtius. Luckily we're now under the *lex Livia,* so you'll have half a jury of senators—which is very much better than a jury composed entirely of knights. How they hate the idea of a senator getting rich at other people's expense! All right for them to do it, however," said Pompeius Rufus, disgusted.

"Why the treason court rather than the bribery court?" asked Scaurus. "If he alleges you took a bribe, then it's bribery."

"Censorinus alleges that the bribe was taken as payment for betrayal of our intentions and movements in the East," said the urban praetor.

"I brought back a treaty," said Sulla to Pompeius Rufus.

"That he did! An enormously impressive feat," said Scaurus with great warmth.

"Is the Senate ever going to acknowledge it?" asked Sulla.

"The Senate will, Lucius Cornelius, you have the word of an Aemilius Scaurus on it."

"I heard you forced both the Parthians and the King of Armenia to sit lower than you did," chuckled the urban praetor. "Good for you, Lucius Cornelius! Those eastern potentates need putting down!"

"Oh, I believe Lucius Cornelius intends to follow in the footsteps of Popillius Laenas," said Scaurus, smiling. "The next thing, he'll be drawing circles round their feet too." He frowned. "What I want to know is, where could Censorinus have obtained information about anything that happened on the Euphrates?"

Sulla shifted uneasily, not quite sure whether Scaurus was still of the opinion that Mithridates of Pontus was harmless. "I think he's acting as an agent for one of the eastern kings."

"Mithridates of Pontus," said Scaurus immediately.

"What, are you disillusioned?" asked Sulla, grinning.

"I like to believe the best of everybody, Lucius Cornelius. But a fool I am not," said Scaurus, getting up. He threw a denarius at the proprietor, who fielded it deftly. "Give them some more of your brilliant vintages, Cloatius!"

"If it's all that bad, why aren't you at home drinking your Chian and your Falernian?" yelled Publius Cloatius after Scaurus's vanishing back, his humor unimpaired.

His only answer was Scaurus's finger poking holes in the air, which made Cloatius laugh hilariously. "Awful old geezer!" he said, bringing more wine to the table. "What would we do without him?"

Sulla and Pompeius Rufus settled deeper into their chairs.

"Aren't you on your tribunal today?" asked Sulla.

"I've left young Fannius in charge; it will do him good to battle the litigious-minded populace of Rome," said Pompeius Rufus.

They sipped their wine (which really was not poor quality, as everyone knew) in silence for a few moments, not feeling awkward—more that when Scaurus left any group, it suffered.

Finally Pompeius Rufus said, "Are you hoping to stand for the consulship at the end of this year, Lucius Cornelius?"

"I don't think so," said Sulla, looking serious. "I *had* hoped to, in the belief that the presentation to Rome of a formal treaty binding the King of the Parthians in an agreement of great benefit to Rome would create quite a stir here! Instead—not a ripple on the Forum puddle, let alone the Senate cesspool! I may as well have stayed in Rome and taken lessons in lascivious dancing—it would have created more talk about me! So it has become a decision as to whether I think I stand a chance to get in if I bribe the electorate.

I'm inclined to think I'd be wasting my money. People like Rutilius Lupus can offer ten times as much to our wonderful little lot of
voters."

"I want to be consul," said Pompeius Rufus, equally seriously,
"but I doubt my chances, being a Picentine."

Sulla opened his eyes wide. "They voted you in at the top of the
praetors' poll, Quintus Pompeius! That usually counts for something, you know!"

"You were voted in at the top of the same poll two years
ago," said Pompeius Rufus, "yet you don't consider your chances
good, do you? And if a patrician Cornelius who has been *praetor urbanus* rates his chances nonexistent, what do you think
are the chances of—well, not a New Man, precisely—a man
from Picenum?"

"True, I am a patrician Cornelius. But my last name isn't Scipio,
and Aemilius Paullus wasn't my granddad. I was never a great
speaker, and until I became urban praetor, the Forum frequenters
didn't know me from a Magna Mater eunuch. I pinned all my
hopes on that historic treaty with the Parthians and the fact that I
led Rome's first army ever to cross the Euphrates. Only to find the
whole Forum far more fascinated with the doings of Drusus."

"*He'll* be consul when he decides to run."

"He couldn't miss if they set Scipio Africanus and Scipio Aemilianus up against him. Mind you, Quintus Pompeius, I find
myself fascinated with what he's doing."

"So am I, Lucius Cornelius."

"Do you think he's right?"

"Yes."

"Good! So do I."

Another silence fell, broken only by the noise of Publius Cloatius
serving four newcomers, who eyed the purple-bordered togas in
the far corner with awe.

"How about," began Pompeius Rufus, turning his pewter cup
slowly between his hands, and looking down into it, "your waiting
a couple more years, and running in tandem with me? We're both
urban praetors, we both have good army records, we're both senior

in years, we're both able to do a little bribing, at least. . . . The voters like a pair standing together, it bodes well for consular relations during the year. Together, I think we stand a better chance than either of us does alone. What do you say, Lucius Cornelius?"

Sulla's eyes rested upon Pompeius Rufus's ruddy face, his bright blue eyes, his regular and slightly Celtic features, his shock of curling red hair. "I say," he said deliberately, "that we'd make a prime pair! Two red-heads from opposite ends of the senatorial array, impressive to look at—a matching pair! You know, we'd appeal to those whimsical, cantankerous *mentulae*! They love a good joke, and what better joke than two red-haired consuls of the same height and the same build, yet out of totally different stables?" He held out his hand. "We'll do it, my friend! Luckily neither of us has a grey hair to spoil the effect, nor is either of us balding!"

Eager to show his pleasure, Pompeius Rufus squeezed Sulla's hand, beaming. "It's a deal, Lucius Cornelius!"

"It's a deal, Quintus Pompeius!" Sulla blinked, visited with an inspiration evoked by Pompeius Rufus's enormous wealth. "Do you have a son?" he asked.

"I do."

"How old is he?"

"Twenty-one this year."

"Contracted to a marriage?"

"No, not yet."

"I have a daughter. Patrician on both sides. She'll be eighteen the June after we stand for our joint consulships. Would you consent to a marriage between my daughter and your son in Quinctilis, three years from now?"

"I would indeed, Lucius Cornelius!"

"She's well dowered. Her grandfather transferred her mother's fortune to her before he died, some forty talents of silver. A bit over a million sesterces. Is that satisfactory?"

Pompeius Rufus nodded, well pleased. "We'll start talking in the Forum about our joint candidature now, shall we?"

"An excellent idea! Best to get the electors so used to us that when the time comes they'll vote for us automatically."

"Ahah!" rumbled a voice from the door.

In walked Gaius Marius, sweeping past the gaping drinkers at a table near the counter without acknowledging their existence.

"Our revered Princeps Senatus said I'd find you here, Lucius Cornelius," Marius said, sitting down. He turned his head toward Cloatius, hovering nearby. "Your usual vinegar will do, Cloatius."

"So I should think," said Publius Cloatius, discovering that the wine jug on the table was almost empty. "What do Italians know about wine, anyway?"

Marius grinned. "I piss on you, Cloatius! Mind your manners— and your tongue."

The pleasantries disposed of, Marius settled to business, rather glad Pompeius Rufus was there.

"I want to find out how each of you stands on Marcus Livius's new batch of laws," he said.

"We're both of the same opinion," said Sulla, who had called to see Marius several times since his return, only to find the Great Man unavailable. He had no reason to suppose this treatment was purposive—indeed, common sense said it was not, that he had simply chosen his times badly. Yet he had gone away on the last occasion vowing he would not call again. Thus he had not told Marius what had happened in the East.

"And that opinion is?" asked Marius, apparently unaware he had offended Sulla.

"He's right."

"Good." Marius leaned back to permit Publius Cloatius access to the table. "He needs every iota of support he can get for the land bill, and I've pledged myself to canvass on his behalf."

"You'll help," said Sulla, and could find nothing else to say.

Marius now turned to Pompeius Rufus. "You're a good urban praetor, Quintus Pompeius. When are you going to stand for consul?"

Pompeius Rufus looked excited. "That's what Lucius Cornelius and I have just been talking about!" he cried. "We intend to stand together three years from now."

"Clever!" said Marius appreciatively, seeing the point at once.

"A perfect pair!" He laughed. "Keep that resolution, don't dissolve your partnership. You'll both get in easily."

"We believe so," said Pompeius Rufus contentedly. "In fact, we've sealed it with a marriage contract."

Up went Marius's right eyebrow. "Oh?"

"My daughter, his son," said Sulla, a little defensively; why was it that Marius could unsettle him, when no one else had that power? Was it the man's character, or his own insecurities?

Out came a huge sigh of relief. "Oh, splendid! Oh, well done!" Marius roared. "That solves the family dilemma superbly! From Julia through Aelia to Aurelia, they'll be pleased."

Sulla's fine brows knitted. "What on earth do you mean?"

"My son and your daughter," said Marius, tactless as ever. "It appears they like each other too much. But old dead Caesar said none of the cousins should marry—and I must say I agree with him. Which hasn't stopped my son and your daughter making all sorts of absurd promises to each other."

This was a shock to Sulla, who had never dreamed of such a union, and associated so little with his daughter that she had found no opportunity to talk to him about Young Marius. "Oho! I am away too much, Gaius Marius, I've been saying it for years."

Pompeius Rufus listened to this exchange in some dismay, and now cleared his throat. "If there's any difficulty, Lucius Cornelius, don't worry about my son," he said diffidently.

"No difficulty at all, Quintus Pompeius," said Sulla firmly. "They're first cousins and they've grown up together, no more than that. As you may have gathered from Gaius Marius, it was never our intention to see that particular match. The agreement I've made with you today scotches it nicely. Don't you concur, Gaius Marius?"

"Indeed, Lucius Cornelius. Too much patrician blood, and first cousins into the bargain. Old dead Caesar said no."

"Do you have a wife in mind for Young Marius?" asked Sulla curiously.

"I think so. Quintus Mucius Scaevola has a daughter who will come of age in four or five years. I've made overtures, and he isn't averse." Marius laughed irrepressibly. "I may be an Italian hay-seed with no Greek, Lucius Cornelius, but it's a rare Roman aristocrat who can resist the size of the fortune Young Marius will inherit one day!"

"Too true!" said Sulla, laughing just as hard. "So it only remains for me to find a wife for Young Sulla—and *not* one of Aurelia's daughters!"

"How about one of Caepio's daughters?" asked Marius, full of mischief. "Think of all that gold!"

"It's a thought, Gaius Marius. There are two of them, aren't there? Living with Marcus Livius?"

"That's right. Julia was rather keen on the elder one for Young Marius, but I'm of the opinion that a Mucia will be much better for him politically." For once in his life, Marius dredged up a morsel of diplomacy. "You're differently situated, Lucius Cornelius. A Servilia Caepionis would be ideal."

"I agree, she would. I'll see to it."

But the question of a wife for Young Sulla did not remain in Sulla's mind beyond the moment in which he informed his daughter that she was to be betrothed to the son of Quintus Pompeius Rufus. Cornelia Sulla demonstrated only too clearly that she was Julilla's child by opening her mouth and screaming, and going on screaming.

"Screech all you like," said Sulla coldly, "it won't make any difference, my girl. You'll do as you're told and marry whomsoever I say you'll marry."

"Go away, Lucius Cornelius!" cried Aelia, wringing her hands. "Your son is asking to see you. Leave me to deal with Cornelia Sulla, please!"

So Sulla went to see his son, still angry.

Young Sulla's cold had not improved; the boy was still in bed, still plagued by aches and pains, still coughing up muck.

"This has got to stop, lad," said Sulla lightly, sitting on the edge of the bed and kissing his son's hot brow. "I know the weather is cold, but this room isn't."

"Who's screaming?" asked Young Sulla, breath rasping.

"Your sister, Mormolyce take her!"

"Why?" asked Young Sulla, who was very fond of Cornelia Sulla.

"I've just told her that she's to marry the son of Quintus Pompeius Rufus. But it appears she thought she was going to marry her cousin Young Marius."

"Oh! We *all* thought she was going to marry Young Marius!" exclaimed Sulla's son, shocked.

"No one ever suggested it, no one ever wanted it. Your *avus* Caesar was against marriage between any of you. Gaius Marius agrees. And so do I agree." Sulla frowned. "Does this mean you have ideas of marrying one of the Julias?"

"What, Lia or Ju-ju?" Young Sulla laughed merrily until the activity provoked a bout of coughing only assuaged when he brought up a mass of foul-smelling sputum. "No, *tata*," he said when he could, "I can't think of anything worse! Whom am I to marry?"

"I don't know, my son. One thing I promise you, however. I will ask you first if you like her," said Sulla.

"You didn't ask Cornelia."

Sulla shrugged. "She's a girl. Girls don't get offered choices or favors. They just do as they're told. The only reason a *paterfamilias* puts up with the expense of girls is so that he can use them to advance his own career, or his son's. Otherwise, why feed and clothe them for eighteen years? They have to be well dowered, yet nothing comes back to the father's family. No, my son, a girl's only use is for advantage. Though, listening to your sister scream, I'm not sure we didn't do things better in the old days, when we just chucked girl-babies in the Tiber."

"It doesn't seem fair, *tata*."

"Why?" asked *tata*, surprised at his son's continuing obtuseness. "Females are inferiors, young Lucius Cornelius. They weave their patterns in fabrics, not on the loom of time. They don't have any importance in the world. They don't make history. They don't govern. We look after them because it is our duty. We shield them from worry, from poverty, from responsibility—that's why, provided they don't die in childbirth, they all live longer than we men do. In return, we demand obedience and respect from them."

"I see," said Young Sulla, accepting this explanation in the light it was tendered—a simple statement of pure fact.

"And now I must go. I have something to do," said Sulla, getting up. "Are you eating?"

"A little, but it's hard to keep food down."

"I'll be back later."

"Don't forget, *tata*. I won't be asleep."

First he had to behave normally, go off with Aelia to dinner at the house of Quintus Pompeius Rufus, very eager to commence friendly relations. Luckily Sulla had not indicated he would bring Cornelia Sulla along to meet the son; she had ceased her screaming, but, said Aelia, looking flustered, she had retired to her bed and announced she wouldn't eat.

Nothing else poor Cornelia Sulla might have thought to do in protest could have affected Sulla the way that news did; the eyes he turned on Aelia were like bitter stars, blazing ice.

"That will stop!" he snapped, and was gone before Aelia could prevent him, down to Cornelia Sulla's sleeping cubicle.

He came through the door and hauled the weeping girl out of her narrow bed in the same stride, heedless of her fear, dragging her up from the floor onto her toes with his fingers locked in her hair. Again and again his hand cracked across her face. She didn't scream, she emitted shrieks so high-pitched they were scarcely audible, more terrified by the look on her father's face than by his physical abuse. Perhaps twelve times he struck her, then threw her away like a stuffed doll, so angry he didn't care if the violence of his thrust killed her.

"Don't do it, girl," he said then, very softly. "Don't you try to bluff me with starvation! As far as I'm concerned, it would be good riddance! Your mother almost died because she wouldn't eat. But let me tell you, *you* won't do it to me! Starve yourself to death, or choke on the food I'll have forced down your throat with a lot less consideration than a farmer gives to his goose! You will marry young Quintus Pompeius Rufus, and you'll do it with a smile on your face and a song on your lips, or I'll kill you. Do you hear me? I will kill you, Cornelia."

Her face was on fire, her eyes blackened, her lips swollen and split, her nose running blood, but the pain in her heart was far, far worse. In all her life she hadn't known this kind of rage existed, or feared her father, or worried for her own safety. "I hear you, Father," she whispered.

Aelia was waiting outside the door, tears running down her cheeks, but when she went to enter Sulla grabbed her cruelly by one arm, and pulled her away.

"Please, Lucius Cornelius, please!" Aelia moaned, the wife in her terrified, the mother in her anguished.

"Leave her alone," he said.

"I must go to her! She needs me!"

"She'll stay where she is, and no one will go to her."

"Then let me stay home, please!" Try though she did to stem her tears, she was weeping harder.

Sulla's towering rage toppled, he could hear his heart beating, tears were close to the surface in him too—tears of reaction, not tears of grief. "All right, then stay home," he said harshly, and drew a quivering breath. "I shall represent the family joy at the prospect of this marriage. But don't go to her, Aelia, or I'll deal with you as I've dealt with her."

Thus he went alone to the house of Quintus Pompeius Rufus, on the Palatine, but overlooking the Forum Romanum; and made a good impression upon the delighted Pompeius Rufus family, including its women, who were tickled at the thought that young Quintus would be marrying a patrician Julio-Cornelian. Young Quintus was a handsome fellow, green-eyed and auburn-haired, tall and graceful, but it didn't take Sulla long to estimate his intelligence at about half that of his father. Which was all to the good; he would fill the consulship because his father had, he would breed red-haired children with Cornelia Sulla, and he would be a good husband, as faithful as considerate. In fact, thought Sulla, smiling in private amusement, little though his daughter would admit it did she know, young Quintus Pompeius Rufus would be far pleasanter and more tractable to live with than that spoiled and arrogant pup Gaius Marius had spawned.

Since the Pompeii Rufi were still at heart country folk, the dinner was well over before darkness fell, even though Rome was in the depths of seasonal winter. Knowing he had one more task to perform before he went home, Sulla stood atop the Ringmakers' Steps leading down to the Via Nova and the Forum Romanum, and looked into the distance frowningly. Too far to walk out to see Metrobius, and too dangerous too. Where else might he fill in an hour or so?

The answer came the moment his eyes rested upon the smoky declivity of the Subura—Aurelia, of course. Gaius Julius Caesar was off again governing Asia Province. Provided he made sure Aurelia was adequately chaperoned, why shouldn't he pay her a visit? He ran down the steps with the ease and suppleness of a man far junior to himself in years, and strode off toward the Clivus Orbius, the quickest way to the Subura Minor and that triangular insula of Aurelia's.

Eutychus admitted him, but a little reluctantly; Aurelia's manner was much the same.

"Are your children up?" Sulla asked.

She smiled wryly. "Unfortunately, yes. I seem to have bred owls, not larks. They hate to go to bed, and they hate to get up."

"Then give them a treat," he said, sitting down on a well-padded and comfortable couch. "Invite them to join us, Aurelia. There are no better chaperones than one's children."

Her face lightened. "You are quite right, Lucius Cornelius."

So their mother settled the children in a far corner of the room, the two girls grown tall because they were nearing puberty, and the boy grown tall because that was his fate, always to be much taller than the rest.

"It's good to see you," Sulla said, ignoring the wine the steward put at his elbow.

"And good to see you."

"Better than last time, eh?"

She laughed. "Oh, that! I was in serious trouble with my husband, Lucius Cornelius."

"I understood *that*! Why? No loyaler or chaster wife ever lived than you, as I have good cause to know."

"Oh, he didn't think I had been disloyal, any more than he believed I had been unchaste. The trouble between Gaius Julius and me is more—theoretical," said Aurelia.

"Theoretical?" asked Sulla, smiling broadly.

"He doesn't like the neighborhood. He doesn't like my acting as a landlady. He doesn't like Lucius Decumius. And he doesn't like the way I'm raising our children, who can all speak the local cant as well as they can speak Palatine Latin. They also speak about three different kinds of Greek, plus Aramaic, Hebrew, Arvernian Gallic, Aeduan Gallic, Tolosan Gallic, and Lycian."

"Lycian?"

"We have a Lycian family on the third floor these days, you see. The children go wherever they like, not to mention that they pick up languages the way you or I might pick up pebbles on a beach. I didn't realize the Lycians had a language of their own, and incredibly antique too. It's akin to Pisidian."

"Did you have a *very* bad argument with Gaius Julius?"

She shrugged, pulled her mouth down. "Bad enough."

"Made worse by the fact that you stood up for yourself in a most unladylike, un–Roman-woman way," said Sulla tenderly, fresh from assaulting his own daughter for doing exactly that. But Aurelia was Aurelia, she couldn't be measured by any standards save her own—as many people said, with admiration rather than condemnation, so strong was her spell.

"I'm afraid I did stand up for myself," she said, not seeming very sorry. "In fact, I stood up for myself so well that my husband lost." Her eyes were suddenly sorrowful. "And that, as I'm sure you will appreciate, Lucius Cornelius, was the worst part about our difference of opinion. No man of his status likes losing a fight with his wife. So he retreated into a kind of aloof disinterest and wouldn't even consider a re-match, for all my prodding. Oh, dear!"

"Has he fallen out of love with you?"

"I don't think so. I wish he had! It would make life a great deal easier for him when he's here," she said.

"So you wear the toga these days."

"I am afraid so. Purple border and all."

His lips thinned, he nodded wisely. "You should have been a man, Aurelia. I never saw it until now, but it's a truth."

"You're right, Lucius Cornelius."

"So he was glad to go away to Asia Province, and you were glad to see him go, eh?"

"You're right again, Lucius Cornelius."

He passed then to his trip to the East, and gained one more auditor; Young Caesar scrambled up beside his mother on her couch, and listened avidly as Sulla recounted the story of his meetings with Mithridates, Tigranes, and the Parthian envoys.

The boy was almost nine years old. And more beautiful than ever, Sulla noted, unable to take his eyes off that fair face. So like Young Sulla! Yet not like Young Sulla at all. He had emerged from his questioning phase and passed into his listening phase, and sat leaning against Aurelia, eyes shining, lips parted, his face a constantly changing panorama reflecting his mind, his body still.

At the end he had questions to ask, asking them with more intelligence than Scaurus, more education than Marius, more interest than either. How does he know all this? asked Sulla of himself, finding himself speaking with an eight-year-old on precisely the same level as he had with Scaurus and Marius.

"What do you think will happen?" Sulla asked, not because he patronized, but because he was intrigued.

"War with Mithridates and Tigranes," said Young Caesar.

"Not war with the Parthians?"

"Not for a long time to come. But if we win a war against Mithridates and Tigranes, it brings Pontus and Armenia within our fold, and then the Parthians will start to worry about Rome the way Mithridates and Tigranes do at the moment."

Sulla nodded. "Quite right, Young Caesar."

For a further hour they talked, then Sulla rose to go, ruffling Young Caesar's hair in farewell. Aurelia walked with him to the door, shaking her head slightly to the hovering Eutychus, who began to shepherd children bedward.

"How is everyone?" Aurelia asked, allowing Sulla to open the door onto the Vicus Patricius, still thronged with people, even though darkness had long fallen.

"Young Sulla has a bad cold, and Cornelia Sulla a very sore face," he said, unconcerned.

"Young Sulla I understand, but what happened to your girl?"

"I walloped her."

"Oh, I see! For what crime, Lucius Cornelius?"

"It appears she and Young Marius had decided they would marry when the time came. But I've just promised her to the son of Quintus Pompeius Rufus. She decided to show her independence by starving herself to death."

"*Ecastor!* I suppose the poor child didn't even know about her mother's efforts in that direction?"

"No."

"But she knows now."

"She certainly does."

"Well, I know the young man slightly, and I'm sure she'll be a lot happier with him than she would with Young Marius!"

Sulla laughed. "My thoughts exactly."

"What about Gaius Marius?"

"Oh, he didn't want the match either." Sulla's top lip curled up to show his teeth. "He's after Scaevola's daughter."

"He'll get her without too much trouble—*ave,* Turpillia." This last was said to a passing crone, who promptly stopped walking and stood looking as if she wanted to talk.

Sulla took his leave, while Aurelia leaned against the doorframe and looked attentive as Turpillia started to speak.

It never worried Sulla to traverse the Subura after dark, any more than it worried Aurelia to see him disappear into the night. No one molested Lucius Cornelius Sulla. The moment he entered them, he had the stews of Rome written all over him. If anything about his conduct might have puzzled Aurelia, it was the fact that he walked off up the Vicus Patricius instead of down it toward the Forum Romanum and the Palatine.

He was going to see Censorinus, who lived on the upper Viminal in the street which led to the Punic apple tree. A respectable knightly neighborhood, but not nearly imposing enough to house one who sported an emerald quizzing-glass.

At first it seemed as if Censorinus's steward was going to deny him entry, but Sulla could always deal with that; he simply looked nasty, and something in the steward's mind clattered a warning so strong that he automatically held the door wide open. Still smiling nastily, Sulla walked through the narrow passage which led from the front door to the reception room of the ground-floor insula apartment, and stood looking about him while the steward pattered off to find his master.

Oh, yes, very nice! The frescoes on the walls were newly done, and in the latest style, rich red panels depicting the events which led to the yielding up of Briseis to Agamemnon by the Prince of Phthia, Achilles; they were framed in beautifully painted artificial agate-stones which merged into a splendid dark green dado, also painted rather than the real thing. The floor was a colored mosaic, the drapes were a purple so black it was definitely Tyrian, and the couches were covered with gold and purple tapestry of the best workmanship. Not bad for a middling member of the Ordo Equester, thought Sulla.

An angry Censorinus emerged from the passage to his inner rooms, baffled by the conduct of his steward, who did not appear.

"Well, what do you want?" Censorinus demanded.

"Your emerald quizzing-glass," said Sulla gently.

"My what?"

"You know, Censorinus, the one given to you by the agents of King Mithridates."

"King Mithridates? I don't know what you mean! I have no such object as an emerald quizzing-glass."

"Nonsense, of course you do. Give it to me."

Censorinus choked, face purple, then pallid.

"Do give me your emerald quizzing-glass, Censorinus!"

"I'll give you nothing except conviction and exile!"

Before Censorinus could move, Sulla was standing so close to him that it might have passed to an onlooker as a farcical embrace; and then Sulla's hands were on his shoulders, but not like a lover's. They bit, they hurt, they were iron claws.

"Listen, you contemptible maggot, I've killed better men by far than you," said Sulla very softly, his tones actually amorous. "Stay out of court, or you'll be dead. I mean it! Abandon this ridiculous prosecution of me, or you'll be dead. As dead as a legendary strongman named Hercules Atlas. As dead as a woman with a broken neck below the cliffs of Circei. As dead as a thousand Germans. As dead as anyone is who threatens me and mine. As dead as Mithridates will be, if I decide he must die. You can tell him that when you see him. He'll believe you! He clipped his tail between his legs and fled Cappadocia when I told him to go. Because he knew. Now you know, don't you?"

There was no reply, nor did Censorinus attempt to struggle free of that cruel hold. Still and quiet save for his breathing, he gazed at Sulla's too-close face as if he had never seen this man before, and did not know what to do.

One of Sulla's hands left Censorinus's shoulder to slip inside his tunic, its fingers reaching for what was on the end of a stout leather cord; the other of Sulla's hands slipped from Censorinus's other shoulder and clamped around his scrotum, and crushed it. While Censorinus screamed as shrilly as a dog when the wheels of a wagon pass over it, Sulla ripped the leather thong apart with the fingers of one hand as easily as if it had been made of wool, then put the flashing green thing dangling from it inside his toga. No one came running to see who screamed. Sulla turned on his heel and walked out without hurrying.

"Oh, I feel *better*!" he cried as he opened the door, and laughed so long that only its closing shut the sound from out of Censorinus's ears.

Rage and frustration at the conduct of Cornelia Sulla vanished, home Sulla went with footsteps as light as a child's, face a picture of happiness. Happiness wiped away in the thinnest sliver of time when he opened his own front door and discovered, instead of the hushed, dimly lit peace of sleeping tenants, a blaze of light from every lamp, a huddle of strange young men, a steward wiping tears from his streaming eyes.

"What is it?" Sulla asked, gasping.

"Your son, Lucius Cornelius!" cried the steward.

Sulla waited to hear no more, but ran to the room off the peristyle-garden where Aelia had put the boy to get over his cold. She was standing outside its door, wrapped in a shawl.

"What is it?" Sulla asked again, grabbing at her.

"Young Sulla is very ill," she whispered. "I called the doctors two hours ago."

Pushing the doctors aside, Sulla appeared beside his son's bed looking benevolent and relaxed.

"What is this, Young Sulla, giving everybody such a fright?"

"Father!" Young Sulla cried, smiling.

"What's the matter?"

"So cold, Father! Do you mind if I call you *tata* in front of strangers?"

"Of course not."

"The pain, it's terrible!"

"Whereabouts, my son?"

"Behind my breast-bone, *tata*. So cold!"

He breathed shallowly, loudly, with obvious distress; to Sulla it seemed a parody of Metellus Numidicus Piggle-wiggle's death scene, which perhaps was why Sulla could not believe in this as a death scene. Yet Young Sulla looked as if he were dying. Impossible!

"Don't talk, my son. Can you lie down?" This, because the doctors had propped him into a sitting position.

"Can't breathe, lying down." The eyes, ringed with what looked like black bruises, looked up at him piteously. "*Tata,* please don't go away, will you?"

"I'm here, Lucius. I won't go away for a moment."

But as soon as possible Sulla did draw Apollodorus Siculus out of earshot to ask him what the matter was.

"An inflammation of the lungs, Lucius Cornelius, difficult to deal with at any time, but more difficult in your son's case."

"Why more difficult?"

"The heart is involved, I fear. We do not quite know what is the significance of the heart, though I believe that it assists the liver. Young Lucius Cornelius's lungs are swollen, and have transmitted some of their fluids to the envelope wrapping up the heart. It is being squashed." Apollodorus Siculus looked frightened; the price he paid for his fame was paid on occasions like this, when he had to tell some august Roman that the patient was beyond the skills of any physician. "The prognosis is grave, Lucius Cornelius. I fear there is nothing I or any other doctor can do."

Sulla took it well outwardly, and had besides a reasonable streak which told him the physician was completely sincere—that, if he could, he would cure. A *good* physician, though most were quacks—look at the way he had investigated the death of Pigglewiggle. But every body was subject to storms of such magnitude the doctors were rendered helpless, despite their lancets, their clysters, their poultices, their potions, their magical herbs. It was luck. And Sulla saw now that his beloved son did not have luck. The goddess Fortune did not care for him.

Back he went to the bed, pushed the heaped pillows aside and took their place, holding his son within his arms.

"Oh, *tata,* that does feel better! Don't leave me!"

"I won't budge, my son. I love you more than the world."

For many hours he sat holding his lad up, his cheek on the dulled wet hair, listening to the labored breathing, the staccato gasps which were evidence of that remorseless pain. The boy could not be persuaded to cough anymore, the agony of it was too much to bear, nor could he be persuaded to drink, his lips encrusted with fever sores, his tongue furred and dark. Occasionally he spoke, always to his father, in a voice growing gradually weaker, more mumbling, the words he said ever less lucid, less sensible, until he wandered without logic or reason in a world too strange to comprehend.

Thirty hours later he died in his father's numbed arms. Not once had Sulla moved, except at the boy's request; he had not eaten or drunk, had not relieved bladder or bowels, yet knew no discomfort whatsoever, so important was it that he be there for his son. It might have been a comfort for the father had Young Sulla acknowledged him at the moment of death, but Young Sulla had moved far from the room where he lay, the arms in which he lay, and died unknowing.

Everyone feared Lucius Cornelius Sulla. So it was in breathless fear that four physicians loosened Sulla's arms from about his breathless son, helped Sulla to his feet and held him on them, laid the boy out on his bed. But Sulla said or did nothing to inspire this fear; he behaved like the sanest, most admirable man. When he regained the use of his spasmed muscles, he helped them wash the boy and clothe him in the purple-bordered toga of childhood; in December of this year, on the feast of Juventas, he would have become a man. To allow weeping slaves to change the bed, he picked up his son's limp grey form and held it in his arms, then laid him down on the fresh clean sheets, tucked his arms along his sides, put the coins on his eyelids to keep them closed, and slipped the coin into his mouth to pay Charon the price of that last lonely voyage.

Nor had Aelia moved from the doorway during all those terrible hours; now Sulla took her by the shoulders and guided her to a chair beside the bed, sat her down so she could look at the boy she had reared from his nursery days, and thought of as her own. Cornelia Sulla was there, face frightful from punishment; and Julia, and Gaius Marius, and Aurelia.

Sulla greeted them like a sane man, accepted their tearful condolences, even smiled a little, and answered their hesitant questions in a firm clear voice.

"I must bathe and change," he said then. "It's dawn of the day I stand my trial in the treason court. Though my son's death would serve as a legitimate excuse, I will not give Censorinus the satisfaction. Gaius Marius, will you accompany me as soon as I'm ready to go?"

"Gladly, Lucius Cornelius," said Marius gruffly, wiping the tears from his eyes. He had never admired Sulla more.

But first Sulla went to his house's modest latrine, and found no one, slave or free, inside it. His bowels loosened at last, he sat alone in that place, with its four shaped seats in the marble bench, listening to the deep sound of running water below, his hands fiddling with the disordered folds of his toga, which he had not thought to remove before settling to that last vigil with his son. His fingers encountered an object, wondering; he drew it forth to look at it in the growing light, only recognizing it from some huge distance, as if it belonged to another life. The emerald quizzing-glass of Censorinus! When he was done and had tidied himself, he turned to face the marble bench, and dropped the priceless thing down into the void. The water ran too loudly to hear its splash.

As he appeared in the atrium to join Gaius Marius, walk down to the Forum Romanum, some strange agency had given him back every atom of the beauty of his youth, so that he shone, and everyone who saw him gasped.

He and Gaius Marius trod in silence all the way to the Pool of Curtius, where several hundred knights had gathered to offer themselves for jury duty, and the court officials were readying the jars to draw the lots; eighty-one would be chosen, but fifteen would be removed at the request of the prosecution, and fifteen at the request of the defense, leaving fifty-one—twenty-six knights, and twenty-five senators. That extra knight was the price the Senate had paid to put the courts under senatorial presidency.

Time wore on. The jurors were chosen. And when Censorinus had not appeared, the defense, led by Crassus Orator and Scaevola, was permitted to remove its fifteen jurors. Still Censorinus did not come. At noon, the entire court restless, and now in possession of the knowledge that the defendant had come straight from his only son's deathbed, the President sent a messenger to Censorinus's house to find out where he was. Long moments later, the clerk returned with the news that Censorinus had packed up his portable belongings the day before and left for an unknown destination abroad.

"This court is dismissed," said the President. "Lucius Cornelius, you have our profound apologies as well as our condolences."

"I'll walk with you, Lucius Cornelius," said Marius. "An odd situation, this! What happened to him?"

"Thank you, Gaius Marius, I would prefer to be alone," said Sulla calmly. "As for Censorinus, I imagine he's gone to seek asylum with King Mithridates." There came a hideous grin. "I had a little word with him, you see."

From the Forum Romanum, Sulla walked swiftly in the direction of the Esquiline Gate. Almost completely covering the Campus Esquilinus outside the Servian Walls lay Rome's necropolis, a veritable city of tombs—some humble, some splendid, most in between—housing the ashes of Rome's inhabitants, citizens and non-citizens, slaves and free, native and foreign.

On the eastern side of a great crossroads some hundreds of paces from the Servian Walls stood the temple of Venus Libitina, she who ruled the extinction of the life force. Surrounded by a large grove of cypresses, it was a beautiful building, painted a rich green with purple columns, their Ionic capitals picked out in gold and red, and a yellow roof to its portico. The many steps were paved with a deep pink terrazzo, and the pediment portrayed the gods and goddesses of the Underworld in vivid colors; atop the peak of the temple roof was a wonderful gilded statue of Venus Libitina herself, riding in a car drawn by mice, harbingers of death.

Here amid the cypress grove the Guild of Undertakers set up their stalls and touted for business, not a doleful or sad or hushed activity. Prospective customers were grabbed at, harangued, coaxed, badgered, cajoled, prodded and pushed and pulled, for undertaking was a business like any other, and this was the marketplace of the servants of death. Sulla passed like a ghost among the booths, his uncanny knack of repelling people keeping even the most importunate at bay until he came to the firm which buried the Cornelii, and made his arrangements.

The actors would be sent to his house for instructions on the following day, and all would be splendidly readied for the funeral, to be held on the third day; a Cornelius, Young Sulla would be inhumed rather than cremated, as was the family tradition. Sulla paid in full with a promissory note for twenty silver talents at his bank, the price of a funeral Rome would talk about for days, and did not count the cost, he who normally squeezed every sestertius so carefully, so ungenerously.

At home again, he sent Aelia and Cornelia Sulla out of the room where Young Sulla lay and sat in Aelia's chair, staring at his devastated son. He didn't know what he felt, how he felt. The grief, the loss, the finality of it all sat within him like a huge lead boulder; to carry the burden was as much as he could manage, he had nothing left over with which to explore his feelings. There before him lay the ruin of his house, there lay all that was left of his dearest friend, the companion of his old age, the heir to his name, his fortune, his reputation, his public career. Vanished in the space of thirty hours, a decision of no god, not even a whim of fate. The cold had worsened, the lungs had become inflamed, and the heart squeezed dry of animation. The story of a thousand illnesses. No one's fault, no one's design. An accident. For the boy, who could know nothing, feel nothing, it was simply the end of life, suffered to conclusion. For those left behind, knowing all, feeling all, it was the prelude to an emptiness in the midst of life that would not cease until life was over. His son was dead. His friend was gone forever.

When Aelia came back two hours later he went to his study, and sat to write a note to Metrobius.

> My son is dead. The last time you came to my house, my wife died. Given your trade, you ought to be precursor of joy, the *deus ex machina* of the play. Instead, you are the veiled one, precursor of sorrow.
>
> Never come to my house again. I see now that my patroness, Fortuna, does not permit rivals. For I have loved you with that same space inside me she regards as exclusively her own. I have set you up like an idol. To me, you have become the personification of perfect

love. But *she* demands to be that. And she is female, both beginning and end of every man.

If a day should come when Fortune finishes with me, I shall call to you. Until that day, nothing. My son was a good son, a fitting and proper son. A Roman. Now he is dead, and I am alone. I do not want you.

He sealed it carefully, summoned his steward, and instructed him as to whereabouts it was to be sent. Then stared at the wall whereon—how strange life was!—Achilles sat on the edge of a bier, holding Patroclus within his arms. Obviously influenced by the tragic masks of the great plays, the artist had put a look of gape-mouthed agony upon the face of Achilles that seemed to Sulla utterly wrong, a presumptuous incursion into a world of private pain never to be shown to the motley. He clapped his hands, and when his steward returned, said,

"Tomorrow, find someone to remove that painting there."

"Lucius Cornelius, the undertakers have been. The *lectus funebris* is set up in the atrium ready to receive your son for his lying in state," said the steward, weeping.

Inspecting the bier, which was beautifully carved and gilded, with black cloth and black pillows upon it, Sulla nodded his approval. He carried his son to it himself, feeling the beginning of the rigor of death; the pillows were piled up and the boy placed in a sitting position, his arms held up by more pillows. Here in the atrium he would remain until eight black-clad bearers picked up the *lectus funebris* and carried it in the funeral procession. Its head was aligned with the door to the peristyle-garden, its foot with the outside door, on the street side of which cypress branches were fixed.

On the third day, the funeral of Young Sulla took place. As a mark of courtesy toward one who had been *praetor urbanus* and would in all likelihood be consul, public business in the Forum Romanum had been suspended; those who would have been engaged in it waited instead for the cortege to appear, all clad in the *toga pulla,* the black toga of mourning. Because of the chariots, the procession originating at Sulla's house wended its way down the Clivus Victoriae to the Velabrum, turned into the Vicus Tuscus, and entered the Forum Romanum between the temple of Castor and Pollux and the Basilica Sempronia. First came two undertakers in black togas, then came black-clad musicians playing straight military trumpets, curved horns, and flutes made from the shinbones of Roman enemies slain in battle. The dirges were solemn, owning little melody or grace. With the musicians came the black-clad women who earned their livings as proper professional mourners, keening their own dirges and beating their breasts, every last one of them weeping genuine tears. A group of dancers followed, twisting and turning in ritual movements older than Rome herself, waving cypress branches. And after them came the actors wearing the five wax masks of Sulla's ancestors, each riding in a black chariot drawn by two black horses; then came the bier, held on high by eight black-garbed freedmen who had once belonged to Sulla's stepmother, Clitumna, and had passed into Sulla's clientele when she freed them in her will. Sulla walked in the rear of the *lectus funebris,* his black toga pulled up to veil his head; with him walked his nephew, Lucius Nonius, Gaius Marius, Sextus Julius Caesar, Quintus Lutatius Caesar and his two brothers, Lucius Julius Caesar and Gaius Julius Caesar Strabo, all with their heads veiled; and behind the men walked the women, dressed in black but bareheaded, hair in disarray.

At the rostra the musicians, professional mourners, dancers, and undertakers assembled in the Forum below the back wall, while the actors wearing the wax masks were guided by attendants up the steps to the top of the rostra and seated upon ivory curule chairs. They wore the purple-bordered toga of Sulla's ancestors' high rank, that Sulla who had been *flamen Dialis* robed in his priestly garments. The bier was put upon the rostra, and the mourning relatives—all save Lucius Nonius and Aelia attached in some way to the Julian house—ascended it to stand and hear the eulogy. Sulla delivered it himself, very briefly.

"Today I bury my only son," he said to the silent crowd which had gathered. "He was a member of the *gens* Cornelia, of a branch two hundred and more years old, containing consuls and priests, most venerable men. In December he too would have become a Cornelian man. But it was not to be. At the time of his death, he was almost fifteen years old."

He turned to look at the family mourners, Young Marius in a black toga with his head veiled, for he had put on the toga of manhood; his new status placed him well away from Cornelia Sulla, who gazed at him sorrowfully from out of a torn and swollen face. Aurelia was there, and Julia, but while Julia wept and physically supported Aelia, Aurelia stood erect and tearless, looking more grim than sad.

"My son was a beautiful fellow, well loved and well cared for. His mother died when he was very young, but his stepmother has been all that his real mother might have been. Had he lived, he would have proven a true scion of a noble patrician house, for he was educated, intelligent, interested, courageous. When I traveled to the East to interview the Kings of Pontus and Armenia, he went with me, and survived all the dangers foreign places entail. He saw my meeting with the Parthian envoys, and would have been the logical man of his generation for Rome to send to deal with them. He was my best companion, my loyalest follower. That illness should cut him down inside Rome was his fate. Rome will be the poorer, as I and all my family are the poorer. I bury him now with great love and greater sorrow, and offer you gladiators for his funeral games."

The ceremonies on the rostra were now concluded; everyone got up, the cortege reassembled to wend its way toward the Capena Gate, for Sulla had procured his son a tomb upon the Via Appia, where most of the Cornelii were buried. At the door of the tomb Young Sulla was lifted by his father from his funeral couch, and placed inside a marble sarcophagus mounted upon skids. The lid was levered into position, it was pushed into the tomb by the freedmen who had carried the boy's bier, and the skids removed. Sulla closed the great bronze door. And closed a part of himself inside as well. His son was gone. Nothing could ever be the same again.

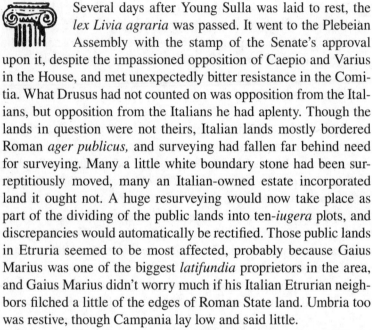 Several days after Young Sulla was laid to rest, the *lex Livia agraria* was passed. It went to the Plebeian Assembly with the stamp of the Senate's approval upon it, despite the impassioned opposition of Caepio and Varius in the House, and met unexpectedly bitter resistance in the Comitia. What Drusus had not counted on was opposition from the Italians, but opposition from the Italians he had aplenty. Though the lands in question were not theirs, Italian lands mostly bordered Roman *ager publicus,* and surveying had fallen far behind need for surveying. Many a little white boundary stone had been surreptitiously moved, many an Italian-owned estate incorporated land it ought not. A huge resurveying would now take place as part of the dividing of the public lands into ten-*iugera* plots, and discrepancies would automatically be rectified. Those public lands in Etruria seemed to be most affected, probably because Gaius Marius was one of the biggest *latifundia* proprietors in the area, and Gaius Marius didn't worry much if his Italian Etrurian neighbors filched a little of the edges of Roman State land. Umbria too was restive, though Campania lay low and said little.

Drusus, however, was very pleased, and could write to Silo in Marruvium that all was looking good; Scaurus, Marius, and even Catulus Caesar had been impressed by Drusus's reasoning about the *ager publicus,* and between them managed to persuade the junior consul, Philippus, to be quiet. No one could shut Caepio up, but his words fell on largely deaf ears, partly due to his minimal skill as an orator, and partly due to a highly effective whispering campaign about people who inherited masses of gold—no one in Rome would ever forgive the Servilii Caepiones for that.

So please, Quintus Poppaedius, see what you can do to persuade the Etrurians and the Umbrians to cease com-

plaining. The last thing I need is a fuss from those who
originally owned the lands I am trying to give away.

Silo's answer was not encouraging.

Unfortunately, Marcus Livius, I have little clout either
in Umbria or Etruria. They're an odd lot in both places,
you know—very convinced of their own autonomy,
and wary of Marsi. Be prepared for two incidents. One
is fairly publicly bruited in the north. The other I heard
of by sheer chance, and am far more concerned about.

The first incident first. The larger Etrurian and Umbrian landowners are planning to march in deputation
to Rome, to protest the breaking up of the Roman *ager
publicus*. Their excuse (of course they cannot admit
they've been tampering with the boundaries!) is that
the Roman *ager publicus* of Etruria and Umbria has
been in existence now for so long that it has altered
both the economy and the populace. To suffer an influx of smallholders, they argue, will ruin Etruria and
Umbria. The towns, they argue, do not now contain
the kind of shops and markets smallholders would
patronize—the shops have become warehouses because *latifundia* owners and managers buy in bulk.
Also, they argue, the *latifundia* proprietors would simply free their slave workers without bothering about the
consequences. With the result that thousands of liberated slaves would be wandering the regions getting
into trouble, perhaps robbing and marauding. Thus,
they argue, it would be Etruria and Umbria would have
to foot the bill to ship these slaves home. And on, and
on, and on. Be prepared for the deputation!

The second incident is potentially more dangerous.
Some of our hotheads from Samnium have decided
there is no hope of either citizenship or peace with
Rome, and are going to show Rome the depth of their

discontent during the celebration of the festival of Jupiter Latiaris on the Alban Mount. They plan to murder the consuls Sextus Caesar and Philippus. The scheme is well worked out—they will fall upon the consuls as they return to Rome from Bovillae, in sufficient numbers to overcome all the celebrants on this peaceful journey.

You had better do what you can to calm down the Umbrian and Etrurian landowners, and crush the assassination attempt before it can possibly take place. More cheering news is that everyone I have approached to swear the oath of personal allegiance to you has done so with great good will. The pool of potential clients for Marcus Livius Drusus grows ever wider.

That at least *was* good news! Frowning, Drusus bent his mind to the less entrancing contents of Silo's letter. About the Italians from Etruria and Umbria he could do little save compose a stunning speech for use upon their advent in the Forum. About the plan to assassinate the consuls, he had no choice but to warn the consuls. Who would then press him as to the source of his information, and not be pleased at evasive answers— especially Philippus.

Consequently Drusus decided to see Sextus Caesar rather than Philippus, and make no secret of his sources.

"I have had a letter from my friend Quintus Poppaedius Silo, the Marsian from Marruvium," he said to Sextus Caesar. "It seems a band of Samnite malcontents have decided that the only way Rome will ever listen to reason about citizenship for all Italy is to demonstrate to Rome how determined all Italy is—through violence. You and Lucius Marcius will be attacked by a large and well-armed number of Samnites somewhere between Bovillae and Rome as you return from the Latin Festival along the Via Appia."

This was not one of Sextus Caesar's good days; his wheezing breaths were quite audible, his lips and earlobes faintly blued. However, he was inured to his affliction and had managed to reach the consulship in spite of it—and ahead of his cousin Lucius Caesar, who had been praetor before him.

"I shall accord you a vote of thanks in the House, Marcus Livius," the senior consul said, "and make sure our Princeps Senatus writes to thank Quintus Poppaedius Silo on behalf of the House."

"Sextus Julius, I would so much rather you didn't adopt that course!" said Drusus quickly. "Surely it would be better to say nothing to anyone, borrow a few cohorts of good troops from Capua, and try to trap and capture the Samnites? Otherwise, they will be warned that their plot is discovered, they will not carry it out, and Lucius Marcius your fellow consul is one who will disbelieve there ever was a plot. To safeguard my reputation, I would much rather see the Samnite malcontents apprehended in the act. That way, we can teach Italy a lesson by flogging and executing every last one in the gang. Telling Italy that violence will go nowhere."

"I see your point, Marcus Livius, and will act accordingly," said Sextus Julius Caesar.

Thus in the midst of angry Italian landowners and Samnites bent on assassination did Drusus continue his work. The Etrurians and Umbrians came, luckily so truculent and overbearing that they irritated men they might otherwise have wooed, and were dispatched home again with a flea in the ear and scant sympathy from anyone. Sextus Caesar acted exactly as Drusus had requested in respect of the assassination plan, with the result that when the Samnites attacked the peaceful-looking procession outside Bovillae, they were routed by some cohorts of legionaries concealed behind the tombs on the far side of the Via Appia; some died fighting, but many more were taken alive, flogged, executed.

What concerned Drusus was that—predictably, he supposed—his *lex agraria* had gone into law providing that every single Roman citizen man be allocated ten *iugera* from the public lands. The Senate and the rest of the First Class were to receive their parcels first, and the *capite censi* Head Count last of all. Though all told there were millions of *iugera* of public land in Italy, Drusus very much doubted that by the time the allocating of it got down as low as the Head Count, there would be much land left. And, as everyone knew, it was not wise to antagonize the Head Count. They would have to receive some other compensation in lieu of land. Only one compensation was possible—public grain at a reduced price made stable even during times of famine. Oh, what a battle it would be in the Senate to have a *lex frumentaria* sanctioned allowing permanently cheap grain to the Head Count!

To compound his troubles, the assassination attempt during the Latin Festival had alarmed Philippus to the point where he began to make enquiries from what friends he had throughout Italy; in May he stood up in the House and announced that Italy was restive, and some men talked of war with Rome. His demeanor was not that of a frightened man, but rather a man who felt the Italians must be given a well-deserved fright. He therefore proposed that two praetors should be deputed to travel—one to the south of Rome, the other to the north of Rome—and discover on behalf of the Senate and People of Rome just what was going on.

Catulus Caesar, who had suffered so in Aesernia during the days when he had chaired his special court of enquiry under the *lex Licinia Mucia,* thought this was an excellent idea. Of course senators who might not otherwise have been impressed immediately hailed Philippus's suggestion as an excellent idea. In short order the praetor Servius Sulpicius Galba was instructed to make enquiries south of Rome, and the praetor Quintus Servilius of the Augur's family was instructed to make enquiries north of Rome. Both men were allowed to choose a legate, they were endowed with a proconsular imperium, and given the money to travel in appropriate state, even to a small force of hired ex-gladiators to serve as bodyguards.

The news that the Senate had deputed two praetors to enquire into what Catulus Caesar insisted on calling "the Italian question" did not please Silo one little bit. Mutilus in Samnium, smarting already because of the flogging and execution of two hundred brave men on the Via Appia, was inclined to call this new indignity an act of war. Frantically Drusus wrote letter after letter to both men, pleading with them to give him a chance, to sit back and wait.

In the meantime he girded his loins for battle, and proceeded to tell the Senate of his plans to issue a cheaper grain dole. Like the allocation of the *ager publicus*, cheap grain could never be confined to the lowly. Any Roman citizen prepared to join the long line at the aediles' booth in the Porticus Minucia could obtain his official chit entitling him to five *modii* of public wheat, then trek to the State granaries beneath the Aventine cliffs, present his chit, and cart his grain home. There were some, even of great wealth and prestige, who actually did avail themselves of this citizen privilege—about half because they were incurable misers, about half on principle. But on the whole, most men who could afford to drop some coins into the steward's hand and tell him to buy grain from the privately owned granaries along the Vicus Tuscus were not prone to seek a chit in person just to have cheap grain. Compared to the costs of other aspects of living in the city of Rome—like rent, which was always relatively astronomical—the sum of fifty or a hundred sesterces a month per person for privately vended grain was minute. Thus it was that the vast majority of those who did queue to receive their chits were the needful citizens of the Fifth Class, and the Head Count.

"The land just will not extend to all of them by any means," said Drusus in the House, "but we must not forget them, or give them reason to assume they have been overlooked yet again. Rome's manger is sufficiently large, Conscript Fathers, to permit *all* of Rome's mouths to feed at it! If we cannot give the Head Count land, then we have to give them cheap grain. At a flat price of five sesterces per *modius* year in and year out, irrespective of times of shortage or times of surplus. This in itself will make the financial burden somewhat easier for our Treasury to bear—when times see a surplus of wheat, the Treasury buys it for between two and four sesterces the *modius*. Thus by selling at five, it will still be possible for the Treasury to make a small profit, which will bolster the Treasury's task during years of scarcity. For that reason, I suggest that a separate account be maintained within the

Treasury that can only be used to purchase wheat. We must not make the mistake of dipping into the general revenues to fund this law."

"And how, Marcus Livius, do you propose to pay for this magnificent largesse?" drawled Lucius Marcius Philippus.

Drusus smiled. "I have it all worked out, Lucius Marcius. As one part of my law, I intend to devalue some of our normal issues of currency."

The House stirred, murmured; no one liked to hear the word "devaluation" mentioned, for most were intensely conservative when it came to the *fiscus*. It was not Roman policy to debase the coinage, the device being condemned as a Greek trick. Only during the first and second Punic wars against Carthage had it been resorted to, and then much of it was due to attempts to standardize coin weight. Radical though he was in other ways, Gaius Gracchus had increased the value of silver currency.

Nothing daunted, Drusus went on to explain. "One in every eight denarii will be cast of bronze mixed with a drop of lead to make the weight the same as a silver coin, then silver-plated. I have worked out my calculations in the most ultra-conservative way—namely, I have presumed we will have five poor grain years to every two good ones—which, as you all know, is far too pessimistic. In fact, we enjoy more good years than we do bad. However, one cannot exclude another period of famine like that we endured thanks to the Sicilian slave war. Also, there is more work involved in silver-plating a coin than there is in stamping out pure silver. Consequently I costed my program out at one in every eight denarii, whereas the true figure is more likely to be one in every ten. The Treasury, you perceive, cannot lose. Nor will the measure be burdensome to businessmen who negotiate with paper. The major load will fall upon those limited to using coins, and—the most important factor of all, in my opinion—it avoids the odium of a form of direct taxation."

"Why go to the trouble of plating one in every eight coins in each issue when you could simply plate one in every eight issues?" asked the praetor Lucius Lucilius, who was (like all his family) very clever with words, but an absolute dunce at arithmetic and practicalities.

"Because," said Drusus patiently, "it is, I think, vital that most of those using coins not be able to tell the real from the plated. If a whole issue were to be cast in bronze, no one would be willing to spend them."

Miraculous though it seemed, Drusus got his *lex frumentaria.* Lobbied by the Treasury (which had done its sums and come out with the same answers Drusus produced, and seen how profitable this debasement might be), the Senate sanctioned its promulgation in the Plebeian Assembly. In that body the most powerful knights were quick to understand how little it would bother them in all transactions not requiring cash. Of course everyone knew it affected everyone, that the distinction between real money and pieces of paper was at best specious; but they were pragmatists, and knew full well that the only true value money of *any* kind had was the faith of the people who used it, in it.

By the end of June the law was on the tablets. The public grain in all future years was to be sold at five sesterces the *modius,* and the quaestors attached to the Treasury were planning their first issue of debased coins, as were the *viri monetales* who would supervise the actual minting. It would take a little time, of course, but the concerned officials estimated that by September one in every eight new denarii would be silver-plated. There were grumblings. Caepio never ceased to shout his protests, the knights were not entirely happy with the way Drusus was heading, and Rome's lowly suspected that they were being fobbed off in some way their rulers had not divulged. But Drusus was no Saturninus, and the Senate was grateful for it. When he held a *contio* in the Plebeian Assembly, he insisted upon decorum and legality; if either became at risk, he suspended his meeting at once. Nor did he fly in the face of the augurs, or employ strong-arm tactics.

The end of June saw an enforced cessation in Drusus's program, as official summer had arrived; the Senate broke off its meetings, as did the Comitia. Glad of the respite—he found himself increasingly fatigued by less and less activity—Drusus too quit Rome. His mother and the six children in her care he sent to his sumptuous villa on the sea at Misenum, while he traveled first to see Silo, then Mutilus, and accompanied both of them all over Italy.

He couldn't help but notice that the Italian nations of the central peninsula were ready to put themselves on a war footing; as he rode down some dusty track with Silo and Mutilus, he saw whole legions of well-equipped troops engaged in training maneuvers far from Roman or Latin settlements. But he said nothing, asked no questions, believing implicitly that none of this martial practice would be needed. In an unprecedented spate of legislation, he had succeeded in convincing the Senate and the Plebeian Assembly that reform was necessary in the major law courts, the Senate, the *ager publicus,* and the grain dole. No one—not Tiberius Gracchus, Gaius Gracchus, Gaius Marius, or Saturninus—had done what he had done, introduce so much contentious legislation without violence, senatorial opposition, knight rejection. Because they believed him, they respected him, they trusted him. He knew now that when he made his intentions public about general enfranchisement for Italy, they would let him lead them, even if they did not precisely follow him. It *would* be done! And as a consequence he, Marcus Livius Drusus, would hold one quarter of the population of the Roman world as his clients, for the oath of personal allegiance to him had been sworn from one end of the Italian peninsula to the other, even in Umbria and Etruria.

About eight days before the Senate reconvened on the Kalends of September, Drusus arrived at his villa in Misenum to enjoy a little rest before the hardest work began. His mother, he had discovered, was as great a joy to him as she was a comfort—witty, clever, well read, easygoing, almost masculine in her appreciation of what was, after all, a man's world. She took a keen interest in politics, and had followed Drusus's program of laws with pride and pleasure. Her liberal Cornelian background predisposed her to a certain radicalism, yet the essential conservatism of that same Cornelian background approved of her son's masterly grasp on the realities of Senate and People. No force or violence, no battering ram of threats, no other weapons than a golden voice and a silver tongue. That was what great politicians should be! That was how Marcus Livius Drusus was, and she congratulated herself that he never got it from his pigheaded, stiff-necked, misunderstanding father. No, he got it from *her.*

"Well, you've dealt brilliantly with the law, the land, and the lowly," she said neatly. "What next, if anything?"

He drew a breath, looked at her directly, sternly. "I will legislate the full Roman citizenship for every last man in Italy."

Paler than her bone-colored dress, she cried, "Oh, Marcus Livius! They've let you have your way so far, but they won't let you have your way in this!"

"Why not?" he asked, surprised; he had got quite used to thinking these days that he could do what no one else could do.

"The guarding of the citizenship has become a task given to Rome by the gods," she said, still pallid. "Not if Quirinus himself appeared in the middle of the Forum and ordered them to dole it out to everyone, would they consent!" Out went her hand to grasp his arm. "Marcus Livius, Marcus Livius, give it up! Don't try!" She shivered. "I *beg* you, don't try!"

"I have sworn to do it, Mama—and do it I will!"

For a long moment she searched his dark eyes, her own less remarkable orbs filled with fear for him. Then she sighed, shrugged. "Well, I won't talk you out of it, I can see that. You're not the great-grandnephew of Scipio Africanus for nothing. Oh, my son, my son, they'll kill you!"

One peaked brow went up. "Why should they, Mama? I am no Gaius Gracchus, no Saturninus. I proceed absolutely within the law—I threaten neither man nor *mos maiorum.*"

Too upset to continue this particular conversation, she got up quickly. "Come and see the children, they've missed you."

If that was an exaggeration, it wasn't a large one. Drusus had achieved a measure of popularity among the children.

That a quarrel was in progress became obvious as they neared the children's playroom.

"I'm going to kill you, Young Cato!" the two adults heard Servilia say as they entered.

"Enough of that, Servilia!" Drusus said sharply, sensing something serious in the girl's tone. "Young Cato is your half brother, and inviolate."

"Not if I get him alone for long enough, he isn't," said Servilia ominously.

"You won't ever get him alone, Miss Knobby-nose!" said Young Caepio, pushing himself in front of Young Cato.

"I do not have a knobby nose!" said Servilia angrily.

"You do so too!" said Young Caepio. "It's a horrible little nose with a horrible little knob on the end, ugh, erk, brrh!"

"Be quiet!" cried Drusus. "Do you ever do anything save fight?"

"Yes!" said Young Cato loudly. "We argue!"

"How can we not, with *him* here?" asked Drusus Nero.

"You shut up, Nero Black-face!" said Young Caepio, leaping to Young Cato's defense.

"I am not a black-face!"

"Are, are, are!" shouted Young Cato, fists clenched.

"You're no Servilius Caepio!" said Servilia to Young Caepio. "You're the descendant of a red-haired Gallic slave, you were foisted on us Servilii Caepiones!"

"Knobby nose, knobby nose, ugly horrible knobby nose!"

"*Tacete!*" yelled Drusus.

"Son of a slave!" hissed Servilia.

"Daughter of a dullard!" cried Porcia.

"Freckledy-face porky!" said Lilla.

"Sit down over here, my son," said Cornelia Scipionis, quite unruffled by this nursery brawl. "When they've finished, they'll pay attention to us."

"Do they always bring up ancestry?" asked Drusus above the cries and shouts.

"With Servilia here, of course," said their *avia*.

The girl Servilia, figure formed at thirteen and blessed with a lovely, secretive face, ought to have been segregated from the younger children two or three years earlier, but had not been, as part of her punishment. After witnessing some of the contents of this quarrel, Drusus found himself wondering if he had been wrong to keep her in the nursery.

Servililla-Lilla, now just turned twelve, was also maturing fast. Prettier than Servilia yet not as attractive, her dark and roguish, open face told everyone what sort of person she was. The third member of the senior group, and very much aligned with them against the junior group, was Drusus's adopted son, Marcus Livius Drusus Nero Claudianus; nine years old, handsome in the mould of the Claudii—who were dark and dour—he was not a clever boy, alas, but he was pleasant and docile.

Then came Cato's brood, for Drusus could never think of Young Caepio as Caepio's child, no matter how Livia Drusa had insisted. He was so like Cato Salonianus—the same slenderly muscular build, the promise of tall stature, the shape of his head and ears, the long neck, long limbs—and the bright red hair. Though his eyes were light brown, they were not Caepio's eyes, for they were widely spaced, well opened, and deeply set within their bony orbits. Of all six children, Young Caepio was Drusus's favorite. There was a strength about him, a need to shoulder responsibility, and this appealed to Drusus; now aged three quarters past five, the child would converse with Drusus like an old, tremendously wise man. His voice was very deep, the expression in his reddish eyes always serious and thoughtful. Of smiles he produced few, save when his little brother, Young Cato, did something he found amusing or touching; his affection for Young Cato was so strong it amounted to outright paternalism, and he would not be separated from him.

Porcia called Porcella was almost due to turn four. A homely child, she was just beginning to develop freckles everywhere, big splotchy brown freckles which made her the object of contemptuous teasing from her older half sisters, who disliked her intensely, and made her poor little life a secret misery of sly pinches, kicks, bites, scratches, slaps. The Catonian beak of a nose ill became her, but she did have a beautiful pair of dark grey eyes, and by nature she was a nice person.

Young Cato was three quarters past two, a veritable monster both in looks and essence. His nose seemed to grow faster than the rest of him, beaked with a Roman bump rather than a Semitic hook, and was out of keeping with the rest of his face, which was strikingly good-looking—exquisite mouth, lovely luminous and large light grey eyes, high cheekbones, good chin. Though broad shoulders hinted that he might develop a nice body later on, he was painfully thin because he evinced absolutely no interest in food. By nature he was obnoxiously intrusive, with the kind of mentality Drusus, for one, abominated most; a lucid and reasonable answer to one of his loud and hectoring questions only provoked more questions, indicating that Young Cato was either dense, or too stubborn to see another point of view. His most endearing characteristic—and he needed an endearing characteristic!—was his utter devotion to Young Caepio, from whom he refused to be parted, day or night; when he became absolutely intolerable, a threat to take his brother away from him produced immediate docility.

Not long after Young Cato's second birthday, Silo had paid his last visit to Drusus; Drusus was now a tribune of the plebs, and Silo had felt it unwise to show Rome that their friendship was as strong as ever. A father himself, Silo had always liked to see the children whenever he was a guest in Drusus's house. So he had paid attention to the little spy, Servilia, and flattered her, yet could be detached enough to laugh at her contempt for him, a mere Italian. The four middle children he loved, played with them, joked with them. But Young Cato he loathed, though he was hard put to give Drusus a logical reason for detesting a two-year-old.

"I feel like a mindless animal when I'm with him," said Silo to Drusus. "My senses and instincts tell me he is an enemy."

It was the child's Spartan endurance got under his skin, admirable trait though Spartan endurance was. When he saw the tiny little fellow stand tearless and firm-jawed after a nasty injury, physical or mental, Silo found his hackles rising along with his temper. Why is this so? he would ask himself, and could never arrive at an answer that satisfied him. Perhaps it was because Young

Cato never bothered to hide his contempt for mere Italians. That of course was the malign influence of Servilia. Yet when he encountered the same sort of treatment from her, he could brush it off. Young Cato, he concluded, was just not the sort of person anyone would ever be able to brush off.

One day, goaded beyond endurance by Young Cato's harsh and badgering questions to Drusus—and his lack of appreciation for Drusus's patience and kindness—Silo picked the child up and held him out the window above a rock garden full of sharp stones.

"Be reasonable, Young Cato, or I'll drop you!" Silo said.

Young Cato hung there doggedly silent, as defiant and in control of his fate as ever; no amount of shaking, pretended dropping, or other threats served to loosen the child's tongue or determination. In the end Silo put him down, the loser of the battle, shaking his head at Drusus.

"Just as well Young Cato is a baby," he said. "If he were a grown man, Italy would never persuade the Romans!"

On another occasion, Silo asked Young Cato whom he loved.

"My brother," said Young Cato.

"And who next after him?" Silo asked.

"My brother."

"But who next-best after your brother?"

"My brother."

Silo turned to Drusus. "Does he love no one else? Not you? Not his *avia,* your mother?"

Drusus shrugged. "Apparently, Quintus Poppaedius, he loves no one but his brother."

Silo's reaction to Young Cato was very much the reaction of most people; certainly Young Cato did not provoke fondness.

The children had permanently polarized into two groups, the seniors allied against Cato Salonianus's brood, and the nursery resounded perpetually to the cries and screeches of battle. It might logically have been presumed that the Servilian-Livians outweighed, outranked and outdid the much smaller Catonians, but from the time Young Cato turned two years old and could add his minuscule bulk to the fray, the Catonians gained the ascendancy. No one could cope with Young Cato, who couldn't be pummeled into submission, shouted into submission, argued into submission. A slow learner when it came to facts Young Cato might be, but he was the absolute quintessence of a natural enemy—indefatigable, constant, carping, loud, remorseless, monstrous.

"Mama," said Drusus to his mother, summing the nursery up, "we have gathered together every disadvantage Rome possesses."

Other men than Drusus and the Italian leaders had also worked through that summer; Caepio had lobbied the knights assiduously, Varius and Caepio combined had managed to harden Comitial resistance to Drusus, and Philippus, his tastes always outrunning his purse, allowed himself to be bought by a group of knights and senators whose *latifundia* holdings represented the major part of their assets.

Of course no one knew what was coming, but the House knew that Drusus had lodged a request to speak at the meeting on the Kalends of September, and was consumed with curiosity. Many among the senators, carried away by the force of Drusus's oratory earlier in the year, were now wishing Drusus had talked less well; the initial flush of senatorial supportive enlightenment had dissipated, so that the men who gathered in the Curia Hostilia on the first day of September were resolved to close their ears to Drusus's magic.

Sextus Julius Caesar was in the chair, September being one of the months during which he held the *fasces,* which meant the preliminary rites were scrupulously observed. The House sat and rustled restlessly while the omens were consulted, the prayers said, the sacrificial mess cleared away. And when the House finally settled down to business, everything taking precedence over a speech from a tribune of the plebs was dealt with extremely quickly.

Time. It was time. Drusus rose from the tribunician bench below the dais on which sat the consuls, the praetors and the curule aediles, and walked to his usual spot up by the great bronze doors, which—as on previous occasions—he had asked be shut.

"Revered fathers of our country, members of the Senate of Rome," he began softly, "several months ago I spoke in this House of a great evil in our midst—the evil of the *ager publicus*. Today I intend to speak about a much greater evil than the *ager publicus*. One which, unless crushed, will see the end of us. The end of Rome.

"I mean, of course, the people who dwell side by side with us in this peninsula. I mean the people we call Italians."

A wave of sound passed through the white ranks on either side of the House, more like a rising wind in trees than human voices, or like a swarm of wasps in the distance. Drusus heard it, understood its import, continued regardless.

"We treat them, these thousands upon thousands of people, like third-class citizens. Literally! The first-class citizen is the Roman. The second-class citizen holds the Latin Rights. And the third-class citizen is the Italian. He who is considered unworthy of any right to participate in our Roman congress. He who is taxed, flogged, fined, evicted, plundered, exploited. He whose sons are not safe from us, he whose women are not safe from us, he whose property is not safe from us. He who is called upon to fight in our wars and fund the troops he donates us, yet is expected to consent to his troops being commanded by us. He who, if we had lived up to our promises, would not have to endure the Roman and Latin colonies in his midst—for we promised full autonomy to the Italian nations in return for troops and taxes, then tricked them by seeding our colonies within their borders—thus taking the best of their world off them, as well as withholding our world from them."

The noise was increasing, though as yet it did not obscure what Drusus was saying; a storm coming closer, a swarm coming closer. Drusus found his mouth dry, had to pause to lick and swallow in the most natural manner he could summon. There must be no obvious nervousness. He pressed on.

"We of Rome have no king. Yet within Italy, every last one of us acts like a king. Because we like the sensation it gives us, we like to see our inferiors crawl about under our regal noses. We *like* to play at kings! Were the people of Italy genuinely our inferiors, there might be some excuse for it. But the truth is that the Italians are not inferior to us in any natural way. They are blood of our blood. If they were not, how could anyone in this House cast aspersions upon another member of this House for his 'Italian blood'? I have heard the great and glorious Gaius Marius called an Italian. Yet he conquered the Germans! I have heard the noble Lucius Calpurnius Piso called an Insubrian. Yet his father died gallantly at Burdigala! I have heard the great Marcus Antonius Orator condemned because he took the daughter of an Italian as his second wife. Yet he overcame the pirates, and was a censor!"

"He was indeed a censor," said Philippus, "and while he was a censor, he permitted thousands and thousands of Italians to enroll themselves as Roman citizens!"

"Do you mean to imply, Lucius Marcius, that I connived at it?" asked Antonius Orator in a dangerous voice.

"I most certainly do, Marcus Antonius!"

Antonius Orator rose to his feet, big and burly. "Step outside, Philippus, and repeat that!" he cried.

"Order! Marcus Livius has the floor!" said Sextus Caesar, beginning to wheeze audibly. "Lucius Marcius and Marcus Antonius, you are both out of order! Sit down and be silent!"

Drusus resumed. "I repeat. The Italians are blood of our blood. They have been no mean part of our successes, both within Italy and abroad. They are no mean soldiers. They are no mean farmers. They are no mean businessmen. They have riches. They have a nobility as old as ours, leading men as educated as ours are, women as cultured and refined as ours are. They live in the same kind of houses as we do. They eat the same kind of food as we do. They have as many connoisseurs of wine as we do. They look like us."

"Rubbish!" cried Catulus Caesar scornfully, and pointed at Gnaeus Pompeius Strabo from Picenum. "See him? Snub nose and hair the color of sand! Romans may be red, Romans may be yellow, Romans may be white, but Romans are not sandy! He's a

Gaul, not a Roman! And if I had my way, he and all the rest of the un-Roman mushrooms glowing in the dark of our beloved Curia Hostilia would be pulled up and thrown out! Gaius Marius, Lucius Calpurnius Piso, Quintus Varius, Marcus Antonius for marrying beneath him, every Pompeius who ever marched down from Picenum with a straw between his teeth, every Didius from Campania, every Pedius from Campania, every Saufeius and Labienus and Appuleius—get rid of the lot, I say!"

The House was in an uproar. Either by name or by inference, Catulus Caesar had managed to insult a good third of its members; but what he said sat very well with the other two thirds, if only because Catulus Caesar had reminded them of their superiority. Caepio alone did not beam quite as widely as he ought—Catulus Caesar had singled out Quintus Varius.

"I will be heard!" Drusus shouted. "If we sit here until darkness falls, I will be heard!"

"Not by me, you won't!" yelled Philippus.

"Nor by me!" shrieked Caepio.

"Marcus Livius has the floor! Those who refuse to allow him to speak will be ejected!" cried Sextus Caesar. "Clerk, go outside and bring in my lictors!"

Off scurried the head clerk, in marched Sextus Caesar's twelve lictors in their white togas, *fasces* shouldered.

"Stand here on the back of the curule dais," said Sextus Caesar loudly. "We have an unruly meeting, and I may ask you to eject certain men." He nodded to Drusus. "Continue."

"I intend to bring a bill before the *concilium plebis* giving the full Roman citizenship to every man from the Arnus to Rhegium, from the Rubico to Vereium, from the Tuscan Sea to the Adriatic Sea!" said Drusus, shouting now to make himself heard. "It is time we rid ourselves of this frightful evil—that one man in Italy is deemed better than another man—that we of Rome can keep ourselves exclusive! Conscript Fathers, Rome *is* Italy! And Italy is Rome! Let us once and for all admit that fact, and put every man in Italy upon the same footing!"

The House boiled into madness, men shouting "No, no, no!,"

feet stamping, roars of outrage, boos and hisses, stools flying to crash on the floor around Drusus, fists shaking at Drusus from every tier on either side.

But Drusus stood unmoving and uncowed. "I will do it!" he screamed. "I—will—do—it!"

"Over my dead body!" howled Caepio from the dais.

Now Drusus moved, swung to face Caepio. "If necessary, it will be over your dead body, you overbred cretin! When have you ever had speech or congress with Italians, to know what sort of men they are?" Drusus yelled, trembling with anger.

"In your house, Drusus, *in your house*! Talking sedition! A nest of them, all dirty Italians! Silo and Mutilus, Egnatius and Vidacilius, Lamponius and Duronius!"

"Never in my house, and *never* sedition!"

Caepio was on his feet, face purple. "You're a traitor, Drusus! A blight on your family, an ulcer on the fair face of Rome! I'll bring you to trial for this!"

"No, you festering scab, it's I who will bring you to trial! What happened to all that gold from Tolosa, Caepio? Tell this House that! Tell this House how enormous and prosperous your business enterprises are, and how unsenatorial!" Drusus shouted.

"Are you going to let him get away with this?" roared Caepio, turning from one side of the chamber to the other, hands outstretched imploringly. "*He's* the traitor! *He's* the viper!"

Through all of this exchange Sextus Caesar and Scaurus Princeps Senatus had been calling for order; Sextus Caesar now gave up. Snapping his fingers at his lictors, he adjusted his toga and stalked out of the meeting behind his escort, looking neither to left nor to right. Some of the praetors followed him, but Quintus Pompeius Rufus leaped from the dais in the direction of Catulus Caesar at precisely the same moment as Gnaeus Pompeius Strabo came at Catulus from the far side of the House. Both meant murder, fists doubled, faces ugly. However, before either Pompeius could reach the sneering, haughty Catulus Caesar, Gaius Marius stepped into the fray. Shaking his fierce old head, he grabbed at Pompey Strabo's wrists and bore them down, while Crassus Orator restrained the furious Pompeius Rufus. The Pompeii were hauled unceremoniously from the chamber, Marius gathering in Drusus as he went, Antonius Orator helping. Catulus Caesar remained standing beside his stool, smiling.

"They didn't take that too well," said Drusus, drawing in big deep breaths.

The group had sought the bottom of the Comitia well wherein to shelter and compose itself; within moments a small crowd of angry and indignant partisans had joined it.

"How dared Catulus Caesar say that about us Pompeians!" yelled Pompey Strabo, clutching at his remote cousin Pompeius Rufus as if at a spar in a tempestuous sea. "If I had to put a color on *his* hair, I'd call it sandy!"

"*Quin tacetis,* the lot of you!" said Marius, eyes seeking Sulla in vain; until today, at any rate, Sulla had been one of Drusus's most enthusiastic supporters, hadn't missed a single meeting during which Drusus had spoken. Where was he now? Had today's events put him off? Was he perhaps bowing and scraping to Catulus Caesar? Common sense said that was unlikely, but even Marius had not expected such a violent House. And where was Scaurus Princeps Senatus?

"How dared that licentious ingrate Philippus imply that I fiddled the census?" demanded Antonius Orator, ruddy face a richer red. "He backed down soon enough when I invited him to say the same thing outside, the worm!"

"When he accused you, Marcus Antonius, he also accused me!" said Lucius Valerius Flaccus, lifted out of his normal torpor. "He will pay for that, I swear he will!"

"They didn't take it at all well," said Drusus, his mind not able to deviate from its beaten track.

"You surely didn't expect them to, Marcus Livius," said the voice of Scaurus from behind the group.

"Are *you* still with me, Princeps Senatus?" Drusus asked when Scaurus elbowed his way to the center of the group.

"Yes, yes!" cried Scaurus, flapping his hands. "I agree it's time we did the logical thing, if only to avert a war," he said. "Unfortunately most people refuse to believe the Italians could ever mount a war against Rome."

"They'll find out how wrong they are," said Drusus.

"They will that," said Marius. He looked about again. "Where is Lucius Cornelius Sulla?"

"Gone off on his own," said Scaurus.

"Not to one of the opposition?"

"No, just off on his own," said Scaurus with a sigh. "I very much fear he hasn't been terribly enthusiastic about anything since his poor little son died."

"That's true," said Marius, relieved. "Still, I did think this fuss might have stimulated him."

"Nothing can, save time," said Scaurus, who had also lost a son, in many ways more painfully than Sulla.

"Where do you go from this, Marcus Livius?" asked Marius.

"To the Plebeian Assembly," said Drusus. "I'll call a *contio* for three days hence."

"You'll be opposed more strongly still," said Crassus Orator.

"I don't care," said Drusus stubbornly. "I have sworn to get this legislation through—and get it through I will!"

"In the meantime, Marcus Livius," said Scaurus soothingly, "the rest of us will keep working on the Senate."

"You ought to do better among those Catulus Caesar insulted, at least," said Drusus with a faint smile.

"Unfortunately, many of them will be the most obdurately against giving the citizenship away," said Pompeius Rufus, grinning. "They would all have to speak to their Italian aunties and cousins again, after pretending they don't have any."

"*You* seem to have recovered from the insult!" snapped Pompey Strabo, who clearly hadn't.

"No, I haven't recovered at all," said Pompeius Rufus, still grinning. "I've just tucked it away to take out on those who caused it. There's no point taking my anger out on these good fellows."

Drusus held his *contio* on the fourth day of September. The Plebs gathered eagerly, looking forward to a rousing meeting, yet feeling safe to gather; with Drusus in charge, there would be no violence. However, Drusus had only just launched into his opening remarks when Lucius Marcius Philippus appeared, escorted by his lictors and followed by a large group of young knights and sons of senators.

"This assembly is illegal! I hereby demand that it be broken up!" cried Philippus, shoving through the crowd behind his lictors. "Move along, everybody! I order you to disperse!"

"You have no authority in a legally convened meeting of the Plebs," said Drusus calmly, looking unruffled. "Now go about your proper business, junior consul."

"I am a plebeian, I am entitled to be here," said Philippus.

Drusus smiled sweetly. "In which case, Lucius Marcius, kindly conduct yourself like a plebeian, not a consul! Stand and listen with the rest of the plebeians."

"This meeting is illegal!" Philippus persisted.

"The omens have been declared auspicious, I have adhered to the letter of every law in convoking my *contio,* and you are simply taking up this meeting's valuable time," said Drusus, to an accompaniment of loud cheers from his audience, which may have come to oppose what Drusus wished to talk about, but resented Philippus's interference.

That was the signal for the young men around Philippus to start pushing and shoving the crowd, ordering it to go home at the same moment as they pulled cudgels from beneath their togas.

Seeing the cudgels, Drusus acted. "This *contio* is concluded!" he cried from the rostra. "I will not permit anyone to make a shambles out of what should be an orderly meeting!"

But that didn't suit the rest of the gathering; a few men began pushing and shoving back, a cudgel was swung, and it took Drusus himself, leaping down from the rostra, to make sure no blows were struck, persuade people to go peacefully home.

At which point a bitterly disappointed Italian client of Gaius Marius's saw red. Before anyone could stop him—including the junior consul's cluster of apathetic lictors—he had walked straight up to Philippus and walloped him on the nose; then he was gone too quickly to be apprehended, leaving Philippus trying to cope with a pulped nose pouring fountains of blood all over his snowy toga.

"Serves you right," said Drusus, grinning again, and departed.

"Well done, Marcus Livius," said Scaurus Princeps Senatus, who had watched from the Senate steps. "What now?"

"Back to the House," said Drusus.

When he went back to the House on the seventh day of September, Drusus met with a better reception, much to his surprise; his consular allies had lobbied to considerable effect.

"What the Senate and People of Rome *must* realize," said Drusus in a loud, firm, impressively serious voice, "is that if we go on denying our citizenship to the people of Italy, there will be war. I do not say so lightly, believe me! And before any of you start ridiculing the idea of the people of Italy as a formidable enemy, I would remind you that for four hundred years they have been participating with us in our wars—or, in some cases, warring against us. They *know* us as a people at war—they know how we war, and it is the same way they war themselves. In the past, Rome has been stretched to her very limits to beat one or two of the Italian nations—is there anyone here who has forgotten the Caudine Forks? That was inflicted upon us by *one* Italian nation, Samnium. Until Arausio, the worst defeats sustained by Rome all involved the Samnites. So if, in this day and age, the various nations of Italy decide to unite and go to war against us united, the question I ask of myself—and of all of you!—is—*can* Rome beat them?"

A wave of restlessness passed through the white ranks on either side of the floor where Drusus stood, like wind through a forest of feathery trees; and with it, a sigh like wind.

"I know the vast majority of you sitting here today believe that war is absolutely impossible. For two reasons. The first, because you do not believe the Italian Allies could ever find enough in common to unite against a common enemy. The second, because you will not believe any nation in Italy save Rome is prepared for war. Even among those who support me actively, there are men who *cannot* believe the Italian Allies are ready for war. Indeed, it might not be inaccurate if I said none of those who support me actively can credit that Italy is ready for war. Where are the arms and armor? they ask. Where the equipment, where the soldiers? And *I* say, *there!* Ready and waiting. Italy is ready. If we do not grant Italy the citizenship, Italy will destroy us in war."

He paused, threw his arms out. "Surely, Conscript Fathers of our Senate, you can see that war between Rome and Italy would be *civil* war? A conflict between brothers. A conflict upon the soil we call our own, and they call their own. How can we justify to our grandchildren the ruination of their wealth, their inheritances, on grounds as flimsy as these I hear from this assembly every time it meets? There is no victor in civil war. No spoils. No slaves to sell. Think about what I am asking you to do with a care and a detachment greater than any you have ever summoned! This is not a matter for emotions. Not a matter for prejudices. Not a matter for lightness. All I am really trying to do is to save my beloved Rome from the horrors of civil war."

This time the House really listened. Drusus began to hope. Even Philippus, who sat looking angry and muttered under his breath from time to time, did not interject. Nor—perhaps more significantly—did the vociferous and malignant Caepio. Unless, of course, these were new tactics they had dreamed up during the six intervening days. It might even be that Caepio didn't want a nose as hugely swollen and sore as Philippus's.

After Drusus was finished, Scaurus Princeps Senatus, Crassus Orator, Antonius Orator, and Scaevola all spoke in support of Drusus. And the House listened.

But when Gaius Marius rose to speak, the peace shattered. At precisely that moment when Drusus had decided the cause was won. Afterward, Drusus was forced to conclude that Philippus and Caepio had planned it this way all along.

Philippus jumped to his feet. "Enough!" he screamed, jumping off the curule dais. "It is enough, I say! Who are you, Marcus Livius Drusus, to corrupt the minds and the principles of men as great as our Princeps Senatus? That the Italian Marius is on your side I find inevitable, but the Leader of the House? My ears, my ears! Do they truly hear what some of our most revered consulars have said today?"

"Your nose, your nose! Does it truly smell how you smell, Philippus?" mocked Antonius Orator.

"*Tace*, Italian-lover!" shouted Philippus. "Shut your vile mouth, pull in your Italian-loving head!"

As this last was a reference to a part of the male anatomy not mentioned in the House, Antonius Orator was up from his stool the moment the insult was uttered. Marius on one side of him and Crassus Orator on the other were ready, however, and pulled him back before he could attack Philippus.

"I will be heard!" Philippus yelled. "Wake up to what is being put to you, you senatorial sheep! *War?* How can there possibly be war? The Italians have no arms and no men! They could hardly go to war with a flock of sheep—even sheep like you!"

Sextus Caesar and Scaurus Princeps Senatus had been calling for order ever since Philippus had inserted himself into the proceedings; Sextus Caesar now beckoned to his lictors, kept inside today as a precaution. But before they could advance upon Philippus, standing in the middle of the floor, he had ripped the purple-bordered toga from his body, and thrown it at Scaurus.

"Keep it, Scaurus, you traitor! Keep it, all of you! I am going into Rome to find another government!"

"And I," cried Caepio, leaving the dais, "am going to the Comitia to assemble all the People, patrician and plebeian!"

The House dissolved into chaos, backbencher senators milling without purpose, Scaurus and Sextus Caesar calling again and again for order, and most of those in the front and middle rows streaming out of the doors in the wake of Philippus and Caepio.

The lower end of the Forum Romanum was crowded with those who waited to hear how the Senate felt at the end of this session. Caepio went straight to the rostra, shouting for the Whole People to assemble in their tribes. Not bothering with formalities—or with the fact that the Senate had not been legally dismissed, which meant no Comitia could be convoked—he launched into a diatribe against Drusus, who now stood beside him on the rostra.

"Look at him, the traitor!" howled Caepio. "He's busy giving away our citizenship to every dirty Italian in this peninsula, to every flea-bitten Samnite shepherd, to every mentally incompetent Picentine rustic, to every stinking brigand in Lucania and Bruttium! And such is the caliber of our *idiot* Senate that it is actually about to let this traitor have his way! But I won't let them, and I won't let him!"

Drusus turned to his nine fellow tribunes of the plebs, who had followed him onto the rostra; they were not pleased at the presumption of the patrician Caepio, no matter how they felt about Drusus's proposal. Caepio had called the Whole People, it was true, but he had done so before the Senate had been dismissed, and he had usurped the territory of the tribunes of the plebs in the most cavalier fashion; even Minicius was annoyed.

"I am going to break this farce up," said Drusus, tight-lipped. "Are you all with me?"

"We're with you," said Saufeius, who was Drusus's man.

Drusus stepped to the front of the rostra. "This is an illegally convened meeting, and I veto its continuance!"

"Get out of my meeting, traitor!" shouted Caepio.

Drusus ignored him. "Go home, people of this city! I have interposed my veto against this meeting because it is not legal! The Senate is still officially in session!"

"Traitor! People of Rome, are you going to let yourselves be ordered about by a man who wants to give away your most precious possession?" shrieked Caepio.

Drusus lost his patience at last. "Arrest this lout, fellow tribunes of the plebs!" he cried, gesturing to Saufeius.

Nine men surrounded Caepio and took hold of him, quelling his struggles easily; Philippus, who was standing on the floor of the well looking up at the rostra, suddenly thought of urgent business elsewhere, and fled.

"I have had enough, Quintus Servilius Caepio!" said Drusus in a voice which could be heard throughout the lower Forum. "I am a tribune of the plebs, and you have obstructed me in the execution of my duties! Take heed, for this is my only warning. Cease and desist at once, or I will have you thrown from the Tarpeian Rock!"

The Comitia well was Drusus's fief, and Caepio, seeing the look in Drusus's eyes, understood; the old rancor between patrician and plebeian was being called into effect. If Drusus did instruct the members of his college to take Caepio and throw him from the Tarpeian Rock, Drusus would be obeyed.

"You haven't won yet!" Caepio yelled as he pulled free of the restraining hands and stormed off after the vanished Philippus.

"I wonder," said Drusus to Saufeius as they watched the graceless exit of Caepio, "if Philippus is tired of his house guest yet?"

"I'm tired of both of them," said Saufeius, and sighed sadly. "You realize, I hope, Marcus Livius, that had the Senate meeting continued, you would have secured your mandate?"

"Of course I do. Why do you think Philippus suddenly went into that manic temper tantrum? What a terrible actor he is!" said Drusus, and laughed. "Throwing his toga away! What next?"

"Aren't you disappointed?"

"Almost to death. But I will not be stopped. Not until I have no breath left in my body."

The Senate resumed its deliberations on the Ides, officially a day of rest, and therefore not a day upon which the Comitia could meet. Caepio would have no excuse to quit the session.

Sextus Caesar was looking worn out, his breathing audible throughout the House, but he saw the initial ceremonies to their conclusion, then rose to speak.

"I will tolerate no more of these disgraceful goings-on," he said, voice clear and carrying. "As for the fact that the chief source of the disruptions emanates from the curule podium—I regard that as an additional humiliation. Lucius Marcius and Quintus Servilius Caepio, you will conduct yourselves as befits your office—which, I take leave to inform you, neither of you adorns! You demean it, both of you! If your lawlessness and sacrilegious conduct continue, I will send the *fasces* to the temple of Venus

Libitina, and refer matters to the electors in their Centuries." He nodded to Philippus. "You now have the floor, Lucius Marcius. But heed me well! I have had enough. So has the Leader of the House."

"I do not thank you, Sextus Julius, any more than I thank the Leader of the House, and all the other members who are masquerading as patriots," said Philippus impudently. "How can a man claim to be a Roman patriot, and want to give our citizenship away? The answer is that he cannot be the one and do the other! The Roman citizenship is for Romans. It should *not* be given to anyone who is not by family, by ancestry, and by legal writ entitled to it. We are the children of Quirinus. The Italians are not. And that, senior consul, is all I have to say. There is no more to be said."

"There is much more to be said!" Drusus countered. "That we are the children of Quirinus is inarguable. Yet Quirinus is not a Roman god! He is a god of the Sabines, which is why he lives on the Quirinal, where the city of the Sabines once stood. In other words, Lucius Marcius, Quirinus is an *Italian* god! Romulus took him into our fold, Romulus made him Roman. But Quirinus belongs equally to the people of Italy. How can we betray Rome by making her mightier? For that is what we will be doing when we give the citizenship to all of Italy. Rome will be Italy, and mighty. Italy will be Rome, and mighty. What as the descendants of Romulus we retain will be ours forever, exclusively. That can never belong to anyone else. But what Romulus gave us is not the citizenship! That, we have already given to many who cannot claim to be the children of Romulus, the natives of the city of Rome. If Romanness is at issue, why is Quintus Varius Severus Hybrida Sucronensis sitting in this august body? His is a name, Quintus Servilius Caepio, that I note you have refrained from mentioning whenever you and Lucius Marcius have sought to impugn the Romanness of certain members of this House! Yet Quintus Varius is truly not a Roman! He never laid eyes on this city nor spoke Latin in normal congress until he was in his twenties! Yet—here he sits by the grace of Quirinus in the Senate of Rome—a man less Roman by far in his thoughts, in his speech, in his way of looking at things, than *any* Italian! If we are to do as Lucius Marcius Philippus wants, and confine the citizenship of Rome to those among us who can claim family, ancestry, and legal writ, then the first man to have to leave both this House and the city of Rome would be Quintus Varius Severus Hybrida Sucronensis! *He* is the foreigner!"

That of course brought Varius cursing to his feet, despite the fact that, as a *pedarius,* he was not allowed to speak.

Sextus Caesar summoned all his paucity of breath, and roared for order so loudly that order was restored. "Marcus Aemilius, Leader of this House, I see you wish to speak. You have the floor."

Scaurus was angry. "I will not see this House degenerate to the level of a cock-pit because we are disgraced by curule magistrates of a quality not fit to clean vomit off the streets! Nor will I make reference to the right of *any* man to sit in this august body! All I want to say is that if this House is to survive—and if Rome is to survive—we must be as liberal to the Italians in the matter of our citizenship as we have been to certain men sitting in this House today."

But Philippus was on his feet. "Sextus Julius, when you gave the Leader of the House permission to speak, you did not acknowledge that *I* wished to speak. As consul, I am entitled to speak first."

Sextus Caesar blinked. "I thought you had done, Lucius Marcius. Are you not done, then?"

"No."

"Then please, will you get whatever it is you have to say over with? Do you mind waiting until the junior consul has his say, Leader of the House?"

"Of course not," said Scaurus affably, and sat down.

"I propose," said Philippus weightily, "that this House strike each and every one of the laws of Marcus Livius Drusus off the tablets. None has been passed legally."

"Arrant nonsense!" said Scaurus indignantly. "Never in the history of the Senate has any tribune of the plebs gone about his legislating with more scrupulous attention to the laws of procedure than Marcus Livius Drusus!"

"Nonetheless, his laws are not valid," said Philippus, whose nose was apparently beginning to throb greatly, for he began to pant, fingers fluttering around the shapeless blob in the middle of his face. "The gods have indicated their displeasure."

"My meetings met with the approval of the gods too," said Drusus flatly.

"They are sacrilegious, as the events throughout Italy over the past ten months clearly demonstrate," said Philippus. "I say that the whole of Italy has been torn apart by manifestations of divine and godly wrath!"

"Oh, really, Lucius Marcius! Italy is *always* being torn apart by manifestations of divine and godly wrath," said Scaurus wearily.

"Not the way it has been this year!" Philippus drew a breath. "I move that this House recommend to the Assembly of the Whole People that the laws of Marcus Livius Drusus be annulled, on the grounds that the gods have demonstrated marked displeasure. And, Sextus Julius, I will see a division. Now."

Scaurus and Marius were both frowning, sensing in this something as yet hidden, but unable to see what it was. That Philippus would be defeated was certain. So why, after such a brief and uninspiring address, was he insisting upon a division?

The House divided. Philippus lost by a large majority. He then lost his temper, screaming and ranting until he spat; the urban praetor, Quintus Pompeius Rufus, near him on the dais, pulled his toga ostentatiously over his head to ward off the saliva rain.

"Greedy ingrates! Monumental fools! Sheep! Insects! Offal! Butcher's scraps! Maggots! Pederasts! Fellators! Violators of little girls! Dead flesh! Whirlpools of avarice!" were but some of the names Philippus hurled at his fellow senators.

Sextus Caesar allowed him sufficient time to run down, then had his chief lictor pound the bundle of rods on the floor until the rafters boomed.

"Enough!" he shouted. "Sit down and be quiet, Lucius Marcius, or I will have you ejected from this meeting!"

Philippus sat down, chest heaving, nose beginning to drip a straw-colored fluid. "Sacrilege!" he howled, drawing the word out eerily. After which he did sit quietly.

"What *is* he up to?" whispered Scaurus to Marius.

"I don't know. But I wish I did!" growled Marius.

Crassus Orator rose. "May I speak, Sextus Julius?"

"You may, Lucius Licinius."

"I do not wish to talk about the Italians, or our cherished Roman citizenship, or the laws of Marcus Livius," Crassus Orator said in his beautiful, mellifluous voice. "I am going to talk about the office of consul, and I will preface my remarks with an observation—that never in all my years in this House have I seen and heard the office of consul abused, abashed, *abased* as it has been in these last days by Lucius Marcius Philippus. No man who has treated his office—the highest in the land!—the way Lucius Marcius Philippus has, ought to be allowed to continue in it! However, when the electors put a man in office he is not bound by any code save those of his own intelligence and good manners, and the many examples offered him by the *mos maiorum.*

"To be consul of Rome is to be elevated to a level just a little below our gods, and higher by far than any king. The office of consul is freely given and does not rest upon threats or the power of retribution. For the space of one year, the consul is supreme. His imperium outranks that of any governor. He is the commander-in-chief of the armies, he is the leader of the government, he is the head of the Treasury—and he is the figurehead of every last thing the Republic of Rome has come to mean! Be he patrician or be he New Man, be he fabulously rich or relatively poor, he is the consul. Only one man is his equal, and that man is the other consul. Their names are inscribed upon the consular *fasti,* there to glitter for all time.

"I have been consul. Perhaps thirty men sitting here today have been consuls, and some of them have been censors as well. I shall ask them how they feel at this moment—how *do* you feel at this moment, gentlemen consulars, after listening to Lucius Marcius Philippus since the beginning of this month? Do you feel as I feel? Unclean? Disgraced? Humiliated? Do you think it right that this third-time-lucky occupant of our office should go uncensured? You do not? Good! Nor, gentlemen consulars, do I!"

Crassus Orator turned from the front rows to glare fiercely at Philippus on the curule dais. "Lucius Marcius Philippus, you are the worst consul I have ever seen! Were I sitting in Sextus Julius's chair, I would not be one tenth as patient as he! How dare you swish round the *vici* of our beloved city preceded by your twelve-lictor escort, calling yourself a consul? You are *not* a consul! You are not fit to lick a consul's boots! In fact, if I may borrow a phrase from our Leader, you are not fit to clean vomit off the streets! Instead of being a model of exemplary behavior to your juniors in this assemblage and to those outside in the Forum, you conduct yourself like the worst demagogue who ever prated from the rostra, like the most foul-mouthed heckler who ever stood at the back of any Forum crowd! How dare you take advantage of your office to hurl vituperations at the members of this House? How dare you imply that *other* men have acted illegally?" He pointed his finger at Philippus, drew a breath, and roared, "I have put up with you long enough, Lucius Marcius Philippus! Either conduct yourself like a consul, or stay at home!"

When Crassus Orator resumed his place the House applauded strenuously; Philippus sat looking at the ground with head at an angle preventing anyone from seeing his face, while Caepio glared indignantly at Crassus Orator.

Sextus Caesar cleared his throat. "Thank you, Lucius Licinius, for reminding me and all who hold this office who and what the consul is. I take as much heed of your words as I hope Lucius Marcius has. And, since it seems none of us can conduct ourselves decently in this present atmosphere, I am concluding this meeting. The House will sit again eight days from now. We are in the midst of the *ludi Romani,* and I for one think it behooves us to find a more fitting way to salute Rome and Romulus than acrimonious and ill-mannered meetings of the Senate. Have a good holiday, Conscript Fathers, and enjoy the games."

Scaurus Princeps Senatus, Drusus, Crassus Orator, Scaevola, Antonius Orator and Quintus Pompeius Rufus repaired to the house of Gaius Marius, there to drink wine and talk over the day's events.

"Oh, Lucius Licinius, you squashed Philippus beautifully!" said Scaurus happily, gulping at his wine thirstily.

"Memorable," said Antonius Orator.

"And I thank you too, Lucius Licinius," said Drusus, smiling.

Crassus Orator accepted all this approval with becoming modesty, only saying, "Yes, well, he asked for it, the fool!"

Since Rome was still very hot, everyone had doffed his toga on entering Marius's house and repaired to the cool fresh air of the garden, there to loll comfortably.

"What I want to know," said Marius, seated on the coping of his peristyle pool, "is what Philippus is up to."

"So do I," said Scaurus.

"Why should he be up to anything?" asked Pompeius Rufus. "He's just a bad-mannered lout. He's never been any different."

"No, there's something working in the back of his grubby mind," said Marius. "For a moment there today, I thought I'd grasped it. But then it went, and I can't seem to remember."

Scaurus sighed. "Well, Gaius Marius, of one thing you can be sure—we'll find out! Probably at the next meeting."

"It should be an interesting one," said Crassus Orator, and winced, massaged his left shoulder. "Oh, why am I so tired and full of aches and pains these days? I didn't give a very long speech today. But I was angry, that's true."

The night was to prove that Crassus Orator paid a higher price for his speech than he would have cared to, had he been asked. His wife, the younger Mucia of Scaevola the Augur, woke up at dawn quite chilled; cuddling against her husband for warmth, she discovered him horribly cold. He had died some hours earlier, at the height of his career and the zenith of his fame.

To Drusus, Marius, Scaurus, Scaevola, and those of similar ideas, his death was a catastrophe; to Philippus and Caepio, it was a judgment in their favor. With renewed enthusiasm Philippus and Caepio moved among the *pedarii* of the Senate, talking, persuading, coaxing. And felt themselves in excellent case when the Senate reconvened after the *ludi Romani* were over.

"I intend to ask again for a division upon the question as to whether the laws of Marcus Livius Drusus should be kept on the tablets," said Philippus in a cooing voice, apparently determined to conduct himself like a model consul. "I do understand how tired of all this opposition to the laws of Marcus Livius many of you must be, and I am aware that most of you are convinced that the laws of Marcus Livius are absolutely valid. Now I am not arguing that the religious auspices were not observed, that the Comitial proceedings were not conducted legally, and that the consent of the Senate was not obtained before any move in the Comitia was made."

He stepped to the very front of the dais, and spoke more loudly. "However, there *is* a religious impediment in existence! A religious impediment so large and so foreboding that we in all conscience cannot possibly ignore it. Why the gods should play such tricks is beyond me, I am no expert. But the fact remains that while the auguries and the omens were interpreted favorably before each and every meeting of the Plebeian Assembly held by Marcus Livius, up and down Italy were godly signs indicating a huge degree of divine wrath. I am an augur myself, Conscript Fathers. And it is very clear to me that sacrilege has been done."

One hand went out; Philippus's clerk filled it with a scroll Philippus peeled apart.

"On the fourteenth day before the Kalends of January—the day Marcus Livius promulgated his law regulating the courts and his law enlarging the Senate in the Senate—the public slaves went to the temple of Saturn to ready it for the next day's festivities—the next day, if you remember, was the opening day of the Saturnalia. And they found the woolen bonds swaddling the wooden statue of Saturnus soaked with oil, a puddle of oil upon the floor, and the interior of the statue dry. The freshness of this leakage was not in doubt. Saturnus, everyone agreed at the time, was displeased about *something*!

"On the day that Marcus Livius Drusus passed his laws on the courts and the size of the Senate in the Plebeian Assembly, the slave-priest of Nemi was murdered by another slave, who, according to the custom there, became the new slave-priest. But the level of the water in the sacred lake at Nemi suddenly fell by a whole hand, and the new slave-priest died without doing battle, a terrible omen.

"On the day that Marcus Livius Drusus promulgated in the Senate his law disposing of the *ager publicus,* there was a bloody rain on the *ager Campanus,* and a huge plague of frogs on the *ager publicus* of Etruria.

"On the day that the *lex Livia agraria* was passed in the Plebeian Assembly, the priests of Lanuvium discovered that the sacred shields had been gnawed by mice—a most dreadful portent, and immediately lodged with our College of Pontifices in Rome.

"On the day that the tribune of the plebs Saufeius's Board of Five was convened to commence parceling out the *ager publicus* of Italy and Sicily, the temple of Pietas on the Campus Martius near the Flaminian Circus was struck by lightning, and badly damaged.

"On the day the grain law of Marcus Livius Drusus was passed in the Plebeian Assembly, the statue of Diva Angerona was discovered to have sweated profusely. The bandage sealing her mouth had slipped down around her neck, and there were those who swore that they had heard her whispering the secret name of Rome, delighted that she could speak at last.

"On the Kalends of September, the day upon which Marcus Livius Drusus introduced in this House his proposed bill to give the Italians our precious citizenship, a frightful earthquake utterly destroyed the town of Mutina in Italian Gaul. This portent the seer Publius Cornelius Culleolus has interpreted as meaning that the whole of Italian Gaul is angry that it too is not to be rewarded with the citizenship. An indication, Conscript Fathers, that if we award the citizenship to peninsular Italy, all our other possessions will want it too.

"On the day that he publicly chastised me in this House, the eminent consular Lucius Licinius Crassus Orator died mysteriously in his bed, and was ice-cold in the morning.

"There are many more portents, Conscript Fathers," said Philippus, hardly needing to raise his voice, so hushed was the chamber.

"I have cited only those which actually occurred on the selfsame day as one of Marcus Livius Drusus's laws was either promulgated or ratified, but I give you now a further list.

"A bolt of lightning damaged the statue of Jupiter Latiaris on the Alban Mount, a frightful omen. On the last day of the *ludi Romani* just concluded, a bloody rain fell on the temple of Quirinus, but nowhere else—and how great a sign of godly wrath is that! The sacred spears of Mars moved. An earth tremor felled the temple of Mars in Capua. The sacred spring of Hercules in Ancona dried up for the first time on record, and there is no drought. A huge gulch of fire opened up in one of the streets of Puteoli. Every gate in the walls of the city of Pompeii suddenly and mysteriously swung shut.

"And there are more, Conscript Fathers, *many* more! I will have the full list posted on the rostra, so that everyone in Rome can see for himself how adamantly the gods condemn these laws of Marcus Livius Drusus. For they do! Look at the gods chiefly concerned! Pietas, who rules our loyalty and our family duties. Quirinus, the god of the assembly of *Roman* men. Jupiter Latiaris, who is the Latin Jupiter. Hercules, the protector of Roman military might and the patron of the Roman general. Mars, who is the god of war. Vulcan, who controls the lakes of fire beneath all Italy. Diva Angerona, who knows the secret name of Rome—which, if spoken, can ruin Rome. Saturnus, who keeps the wealth of Rome intact, and rules our stay in time."

"On the other hand," said Scaurus Princeps Senatus slowly, "all these omens could well be indicating how terrible matters will be for Italy and Rome if the laws of Marcus Livius Drusus are *not* kept on the tablets."

Philippus ignored him, handing the scroll back to his clerk. "Post it on the rostra at once," he said. He stepped down from the curule dais and stood in front of the tribunician bench. "I will see a division of this House. All those in favor of declaring the laws of Marcus Livius Drusus invalid will stand on my right. All those in favor of keeping the laws of Marcus Livius Drusus on the tablets will stand to my left. Now, if you please."

"I will take the lead, Lucius Marcius," said Ahenobarbus Pontifex Maximus, getting to his feet. "As Pontifex Maximus, you have convinced me beyond a shadow of a doubt."

A silent House filed down from its tiers, many of the faces as white as the togas beneath; all but a handful of the senators stood on Philippus's right, their eyes fixed upon the flagging.

"The division is conclusive," said Sextus Caesar. "This House has moved that the laws of the tribunate of Marcus Livius Drusus be removed from our archives and the tablets destroyed. I shall convoke the Assembly of the Whole People to that effect three days from now."

Drusus was the last man to leave the floor. When he did walk the short distance from Philippus's left to his end of the tribunician bench, he kept his head up.

"You are, of course, entitled to interpose your veto, Marcus Livius," said Philippus graciously as Drusus crossed in front of him; the senators all stopped in their tracks.

Drusus, his face quite blank, looked at Philippus blindly. "Oh, no, Lucius Marcius, I couldn't do that," he said gently. "I am *not* a demagogue! My duties as a tribune of the plebs are always undertaken with the consent of this assemblage, and my peers in this assemblage have declared my laws null and void. As is my duty, I will abide by the decision of my peers."

"Which rather left," said Scaurus proudly to Scaevola as the meeting broke up, "our dear Marcus Livius wearing the laurels!"

"It did indeed," said Scaevola, and twitched his shoulders unhappily. "What do you *really* think about those omens?"

"Two things. The first, that in no other year has anyone ever bothered to collect natural disasters so assiduously. The second, that to me, if the omens suggest anything, it is that war with Italy will ensue if Marcus Livius's laws are not upheld."

Scaevola had of course voted with Scaurus and the other supporters of Drusus; he could not have done otherwise and continued to keep his friends. But he was clearly troubled, and said now, demurring, "Yes, but . . ."

"Quintus Mucius, you *believe*!" said Marius incredulously.

"No, no, I'm not saying that!" said Scaevola crossly, his common sense warring with his Roman superstition. "Yet—how does one account for Diva Angerona's sweating, and losing her gag?" His eyes filled with tears. "Or for the death of my first cousin Crassus, my dearest friend?"

"Quintus Mucius," said Drusus, who had caught up to the group, "I think Marcus Aemilius is right. All those omens are a sign of what will happen if my laws are invalidated."

"Quintus Mucius, you are a member of the College of Pontifices," said Scaurus Princeps Senatus patiently. "It all began with the only believable phenomenon, the loss of the oil out of the wooden statue of Saturnus. But we have been expecting that to happen for years! That's why the statue is swaddled in the first place! As for Diva Angerona—what easier than to sneak into her little shrine, yank down her bandage and give her a bath of some sticky substance guaranteed to leave drops behind? We are all aware that lightning tends to strike the highest point in an area, and you well know that the temple of Pietas was small in every way but one—*height*! As for earthquakes and gulches of fire and bloody rains and plagues of frogs—tchah! I refuse even to discuss them! Lucius Licinius died in his bed. We should all hope for such a pleasant end!"

"Yes, but—" Scaevola protested, still unconvinced.

"Look at him!" Scaurus exclaimed to Marius and Drusus. "If *he* can be gulled, how can we possibly blame the rest of those superstition-riddled idiots?"

"Do you not believe in the gods, Marcus Aemilius?" asked Scaevola, awestruck.

"Yes, yes, yes, of course I do! What I do *not* believe in, Quintus Mucius, are the machinations and interpretations of men who claim to be acting in the name of the gods! I never met an omen or a prophecy that couldn't be interpreted in two diametrically opposite ways! And what makes Philippus such an expert? The fact that he's an augur? He wouldn't know a genuine omen if he tripped over it and it sat up and bit him on his pulverized nose! As for old Publius Cornelius Culleolus—he's just what his name says he is,

Walnut Balls! I would be prepared to take a very large bet with you, Quintus Mucius, that if some clever fellow had chased up the natural disasters and so-called unnatural events which occurred during the year of Saturninus's second tribunate, he could have produced a list equally imposing! Grow up! Bring some of that healthy courtroom skepticism of yours into this situation, I beg of you!"

"I must say Philippus surprised me," said Marius gloomily. "I bought him once. But I never realized how crafty the *cunnus* was."

"Oh, he's clever," said Scaevola eagerly, anxious to divert Scaurus from his shortcomings. "I imagine he thought of this some time ago." He laughed. "One thing we can be sure of—this wasn't Caepio's brilliant idea!"

"How do you feel, Marcus Livius?" asked Marius.

"How do I feel?" Drusus looked pinched about the mouth, and very tired. "Oh, Gaius Marius, I don't honestly know anymore. It was a clever piece of work, that's all."

"You should have interposed your veto," said Marius.

"In my shoes, you would have—and I wouldn't have blamed you," said Drusus. "But I cannot retract what I said at the beginning of my tribunate, please try to understand that. I promised then that I would heed the wishes of my peers in the Senate."

"There won't be any enfranchisement now," said Scaurus.

"Whyever not?" asked Drusus, genuinely astonished.

"Marcus Livius, they've canceled all your laws! Or they will!"

"What difference can that make? Enfranchisement hasn't gone to the Plebeian Assembly yet, I merely put it before the House. Which has voted not to recommend it to the Plebs. But I never promised the House that I wouldn't take a law to the Plebs if they *didn't* recommend it—I said I would seek their mandate first. I have acquitted myself of that promise. But I cannot stop now, just because the Senate said no. The process is not complete. The Plebs must say no first. But I shall try to persuade the Plebs to say yes," said Drusus, smiling.

"Ye gods, Marcus Livius, you *deserve* to win!" said Scaurus.

"So I think too," Drusus said. "Would you excuse me? I have some letters to write to my Italian friends. I must persuade them not to go to war, that the battle isn't over yet."

"Nonsense, it isn't possible!" exclaimed Scaevola. "If the Italians really do mean war should we refuse them the franchise—and I believe you there, Marcus Livius, I really do, otherwise I would have put myself on Philippus's right—it will take years for them to prepare for war!"

"And there, Quintus Mucius, you're wrong. They are already on a war footing. Better prepared for war than Rome is."

 That the Marsi at any rate were prepared for war was brought home to the Senate and the People of Rome some days later, when word came that Quintus Poppaedius Silo was leading two full-strength legions of Marsi, properly equipped and armed, down the Via Valeria toward Rome. A startled Princeps Senatus summoned the Senate to an urgent meeting, only to find that a mere handful of senators were willing to attend; neither Philippus nor Caepio was there, nor had sent any message as to why. Drusus had also refused to come, but had sent word that he felt he could not be present while his peers contended with a threat of war from such an old personal friend as Quintus Poppaedius Silo.

"The rabbits!" said Scaurus to Marius, eyeing the empty tiers. "They've bolted into their burrows, apparently on the theory that if they stay there, the nasty men will go away."

But Scaurus didn't think the Marsi meant war, and managed to convince his meager audience that the best way to deal with this "invasion" was by peaceful methods.

"Gnaeus Domitius," he said to Ahenobarbus Pontifex Maximus, "you are an eminent consular, you have been censor, and you are Pontifex Maximus. Would you be willing to travel out to meet this army like a Popillius Laenas, accompanied only by lictors? You were the *iudex* in the special court of the *lex Licinia Mucia* set up in Alba Fucentia a few years ago, so the Marsi know you—and I hear they respect you greatly, thanks to your clemency. Find out why this army is on the march, and what the Marsi want of us."

"Very well, Princeps Senatus, I will be another Popillius Laenas," said Ahenobarbus, "provided that you endow me with a full proconsular imperium. Otherwise I won't be able to say or do what I might think necessary at the moment. I also want the axes put into my *fasces*, please."

"You shall have both," said Scaurus.

"The Marsi will reach the outskirts of Rome tomorrow," said Marius, grimacing. "You realize, I hope, what day it is?"

"I do," said Ahenobarbus. "The day before the Nones of October—the anniversary of the battle of Arausio, at which the Marsi lost a whole legion."

"They planned it this way," said Sextus Caesar, quite enjoying this meeting, despite its gloomy atmosphere; no Philippus, no Caepio, and only those senators present whom he privately deemed patriots.

"That's why, Conscript Fathers, I do not think they mean this as an act of war," said Scaurus.

"Clerk, go summon the lictors of the thirty *curiae*," said Sextus Caesar. "You will have your proconsular imperium, Gnaeus Domitius, as soon as the lictors of the thirty *curiae* get here. And will you report back to us in a special session the day after tomorrow?" he asked.

"On the *Nones*?" asked Ahenobarbus incredulously.

"In this emergency, Gnaeus Domitius, we will meet on the Nones," said Sextus Caesar firmly. "Hopefully it will be a better attended meeting! What is Rome coming to, that a genuine emergency produces no more than a handful of concerned men?"

"Oh, I know why, Sextus Julius," said Marius. "They didn't come because they didn't believe the summonses. They all decided this was a manufactured crisis."

On the Nones of October the House was fuller, yet by no means full. Drusus was present, but Philippus and Caepio were not, having decided that their absence would show the senators what they thought of this "invasion."

"Tell us what happened, Gnaeus Domitius," said the only consul present, Sextus Caesar.

"Well, I met Quintus Poppaedius Silo not far from the Colline Gate," said Ahenobarbus Pontifex Maximus. "He was marching at the head of an army. Two legions would be about right—at least ten thousand actual soldiers, the appropriate number of noncombatants, eight pieces of excellent field artillery, and a squad of cavalry. Silo himself was on foot, as were his officers. I could see no sign of a baggage train, so I presume he had brought his men in light marching order." He sighed. "They were a magnificent sight, Conscript Fathers! Beautifully turned out, in superb condition, well disciplined. While Silo and I talked, they stood to attention in the sun without speaking, and no one broke ranks."

"Could you tell, Pontifex Maximus, if their mail shirts and other arms were new?" asked Drusus anxiously.

"Yes, Marcus Livius, easily. Everything was new, and of the highest quality manufacture," said Ahenobarbus.

"Thank you."

"Continue, Gnaeus Domitius," said Sextus Caesar.

"We stopped within hailing distance, I and my lictors, Quintus Poppaedius Silo and his legions. Then Silo and I walked out alone to talk, where we could not be overheard.

" 'Why this martial expedition, Quintus Poppaedius?' I asked him, very courteously and calmly.

" 'We come to Rome because we have been summoned by the tribunes of the plebs,' said Silo, with equal courtesy.

" '*The* tribunes of the plebs?' I asked him then. 'Not *a* tribune of the plebs? Not Marcus Livius Drusus?'

" '*The* tribunes of the plebs,' he said.

" 'All of them, you mean?' I asked, wanting to be sure.

" 'All of them,' he said.

" 'Why should the tribunes of the plebs summon you?' I asked.

" 'To assume the Roman citizenship, and to see that every Italian is awarded the Roman citizenship,' he said.

"I drew back from him a little, and raised my brows, looking beyond him at his legions. 'By threat of arms?' I asked.

" 'If necessary,' he said.

"So I employed my proconsular imperium to make a statement I could not otherwise have made, given the tenor of the recent sessions in this House. A statement, Conscript Fathers, that I considered the situation required. I said to Silo, 'Force of arms will not prove necessary, Quintus Poppaedius.'

"His answer was a scornful laugh. 'Oh, come, Gnaeus Domitius!' he said. 'Do you honestly expect me to believe that? We of Italy have waited literal generations for the citizenship without taking up arms, and for our patience, have seen our chances dwindle away to nothing! Today we have come to understand that our only chance to gain the citizenship is by force.'

"Naturally that upset me greatly, Conscript Fathers. I struck my hands together and cried, 'Quintus Poppaedius, Quintus Poppaedius, I assure you, the time is very close! Please, I beg of you, disband this force, put up your swords, go home to the lands of the Marsi! I give you my solemn promise that the Senate and People of Rome will grant every Italian the Roman citizenship.'

"He looked at me for a long time without speaking, then he said, 'Very well, Gnaeus Domitius, I will take my army away from here—but only far enough and for long enough to see whether you speak the truth. For I tell you straight and fair, Pontifex Maximus, that if the Senate and People of Rome do not grant Italy the full Roman citizenship during the term of this present College of the Tribunes of the Plebs, I will march on Rome again. And all of Italy will be marching with me. Mark that well! *All* of Italy will unite to destroy Rome.'

"Whereupon he turned and walked away. His troops about-faced, showing me how well trained they were, and marched off. I returned to Rome. And all night, Conscript Fathers, I thought. You know me well. You know me of old. My reputation is not that of a patient man, nor even that of an understanding man. But I am quite capable of telling the difference between a radish and a bull! And I tell you plainly, my fellow senators, that yesterday I saw a bull. A bull with hay wrapped round both horns, and fire trickling from his nostrils. It was not an empty promise I made to Quintus Poppaedius Silo! I will do everything in my power to see that the Senate and People of Rome grant the franchise to all of Italy."

The House was humming; many eyes gazed at Ahenobarbus Pontifex Maximus in wonder, and many minds took note of this remarkable change in attitude by one famous for his intractable and intolerant nature.

"We will meet again tomorrow," said Sextus Caesar, looking pleased. "It is time we searched for the answer to this question yet again. The two praetors who have been traveling Italy at the instigation of Lucius Marcius"—Sextus Caesar bowed to Philippus's empty seat gravely—"have not come up with any kind of answer so far. We must debate the issue again. But first, I want to see the people here to listen who have not bothered to listen lately—my fellow consul and the praetor Quintus Servilius Caepio, in particular."

They were there on the morrow, both of them, obviously familiar with every detail of Ahenobarbus's report; yet not, it seemed to Drusus, Scaurus Princeps Senatus and the others who wanted so badly to see that pair back down, worried or even concerned. Gaius Marius, his heart inexplicably heavy, let his eyes roam across the faces of those present. Sulla hadn't missed one meeting since Drusus had become a tribune of the plebs, but nor had he been helpful; the death of his son had removed him from any normal congress with all men, even his proposed colleague in that future consulship, Quintus Pompeius Rufus. He sat and listened, face impassive, then left each meeting the moment it was over, and may as well have disappeared from the face of the earth. Significantly, he had voted to keep the laws of Drusus on the tablets, so Marius presumed he was still in their camp. But speech with him was something no one had known. Catulus Caesar looked a little uncomfortable today, probably as a result of the defection of his hitherto staunch ally, Ahenobarbus Pontifex Maximus.

There was a stir; Marius returned his attention to the House. Philippus of course held the *fasces* for the month of October, so today it was he in the chair, not Sextus Caesar. He had another document with him, one he had not entrusted to his clerk this time. When the formalities were over he rose to speak first.

"Marcus Livius Drusus," Philippus said clearly and coldly, "I wish to read something to the House of far greater import than a quasi-invasion by your best friend, Quintus Poppaedius Silo. But before I read it, I want every senator to hear you say you are present and will listen."

"I am present, Lucius Marcius, and I will listen," said Drusus, equally clearly and coldly.

Drusus looked, thought the watching Gaius Marius, terribly tired. As if he had long since outrun his strength, and carried on now purely by the power of his will. In recent weeks he had lost a great deal of weight, his cheeks had fallen in, his eyes sunk back in his head and circled with dark grey shadows.

Why do I feel as if I'm a slave in a treadmill? wondered Marius. Why am I so on edge, so desperately anxious and apprehensive? Drusus does not have my sinews, nor does he have my unshakable conviction that I am right. He is too fair, he is too reasonable, he is too inclined to see both sides. They will kill him, mentally if not physically. Why did I never see how dangerous is this Philippus? Why did I never see how brilliant he is?

Philippus unrolled his single sheet of paper and held it out at arm's length between his right hand and his left. "I shall not preface this by any comment, Conscript Fathers," he said. "I shall simply read, and let you draw your own conclusions. The text goes as follows:

" 'I swear by Jupiter Optimus Maximus, by Vesta, by Mars, by Sol Indiges, by Terra and by Tellus, by the gods and heroes who founded and assisted the people of Italy in their struggles, that I will hold as my friends and foes those whom Marcus Livius Drusus holds as his friends and foes. I swear that I will work for the welfare and benefit of Marcus Livius Drusus and all those others who take this oath, even at the cost of my life, my children, my parents, and my property. If through the law of Marcus Livius Drusus I become a citizen of Rome, I swear that I will worship

Rome as my only nation, and that I will bind myself to Marcus Livius Drusus as his client. This oath I take upon myself to pass on to as many other Italians as I can. I swear faithfully, in the knowledge that my faith will bring its just rewards. And if I am forsworn, may my life, my children, my parents and my property be taken from me. So be it. So do I swear.' "

Never had the House been so still. Philippus looked from Scaurus with mouth agape to Marius grinning savagely, from Scaevola with lips pressed together to Ahenobarbus purpling in the cheeks, from Catulus Caesar's horror to Sextus Caesar's grief, from Metellus Pius the Piglet's dismayed consternation to Caepio's naked joy.

Then he let his left hand go from the paper, which recoiled with a loud snap; half the House jumped.

"That, Conscript Fathers, is the oath which thousands upon thousands of Italians have sworn over the course of the past year. And that, Conscript Fathers, is why Marcus Livius Drusus has worked so hard, so unflaggingly, so *enthusiastically,* to see his friends of Italy awarded the priceless gift of our Roman citizenship!" He shook his head wearily. "Not because he cares one iota about their dirty Italian hides! Not because he believes in justice— even a justice so perverted! Not because he dreams of a career so luminous it will put him in the history books! But because, fellow members of this body, because he holds an oath of clientship with most of Italy! Were we to give Italy the franchise, Italy would belong to Marcus Livius Drusus! Imagine it! A clientele stretching from the Arnus to Rhegium, from the Tuscan Sea to the Adriatic! Oh, I do congratulate you, Marcus Livius! *What* a prize! What a reason to work so indefatigably! A clientele bigger than a hundred armies!"

Philippus turned then, stepped down from the curule dais, and walked with measured steps around its corner to the end of the long wooden tribunician bench where Drusus sat.

"Marcus Livius Drusus, is it true that all of Italy has sworn this oath?" asked Philippus. "Is it true that in return for this oath, you have sworn to secure the citizenship for all of Italy?"

Face whiter than his toga, Drusus stumbled to his feet, one

hand outstretched, whether imploring or fending off, no one could tell. And then, even as his mouth worked at a reply, Drusus pitched full length upon the old black and white flags which formed the tesselated floor. Philippus stepped back and out of the way fastidiously, but Marius and Scaurus were both on their knees beside Drusus almost as quickly as he had fallen.

"Is he dead?" asked Scaurus against the background noise of Philippus dismissing the meeting until the morrow.

Listening with ear to Drusus's chest, Marius shook his head. "A severe collapse, but not death," he said, leaning back on his heels and drawing in a deep breath of relief.

The syncope lasted so long that Drusus began to mottle and grey in the face; his arms and legs moved, jerked colossally several times while he emitted dreadful and frightening sounds.

"He's having a fit!" cried Scaurus.

"No, I don't think so," said the militarily experienced Marius, who had seen in the field almost everything at one time or another. "When a man passes out for so long, he often starts to jerk around, but at the end of it. He'll revive soon."

Philippus paused on his way out to look down from far enough away to ensure that if Drusus should vomit, his toga would not wear it. "Take the cur out of here!" he said contemptuously. "If he's dying, let him die on unhallowed ground."

Marius lifted his head. *"Mentulam caco, cunne!"* he said to Philippus loudly enough for everyone in the vicinity to hear.

Philippus walked on, rather more quickly; if there was any man in the world he feared, that man was Gaius Marius.

Those who cared enough to linger waited a long time for Drusus to come round; enormously pleased, Marius saw that among them was Lucius Cornelius Sulla.

When Drusus did return to consciousness, he seemed not to know where he was, what had happened.

"I've sent for Julia's litter," said Marius to Scaurus. "Let him lie here until it arrives." He was minus his toga, sacrificed as a pillow for Drusus's head and a blanket for his poor cold limbs.

"I'm absolutely confounded!" said Scaurus, perching on the

edge of the curule dais, and so short that his feet swung clear of the ground. "Truly, I would never have believed it of *this* man!"

Marius blew a derisive noise. "Rubbish, Marcus Aemilius! Not believe it of a Roman nobleman? I'd not be prepared to believe the contrary! Jupiter, how you do fool yourselves!"

The bright green eyes began to dance. "Jupiter, you Italian bumpkin, how you do shine a light on our weaknesses!" Scaurus said, shoulders heaving.

"It's just as well someone does, you attenuated heap of old bones," said Marius affably, seating himself beside the Princeps Senatus and looking at the only three men who remained—Scaevola, Antonius Orator, and Lucius Cornelius Sulla. "Well, gentlemen," he said, thrusting his legs out and waggling his feet, "what do we do next?"

"Nothing," said Scaevola curtly.

"Oh, Quintus Mucius, Quintus Mucius, forgive our poor inanimate tribune of the plebs his very Roman weakness, do!" cried Marius, now laughing as hard as Scaurus was.

Scaevola took umbrage. "It *may* be a Roman weakness, Gaius Marius, but it is not one I own!" he snapped.

"No, probably not—which is why you'll never be *his* equal, my friend," said Marius, pointing one foot at Drusus on the floor.

Scaevola screwed up his face in disgust. "You know, Gaius Marius, you really are impossible! And as for you, Princeps Senatus, pray stop regarding this as a laughing matter!"

"None of us has yet answered Gaius Marius's original query," said Antonius Orator pacifically. "What do we do next?"

"It isn't up to us," said Sulla, speaking for the first time. "It's up to him, of course."

"Well said, Lucius Cornelius!" cried Marius, getting up because the familiar face of his wife's chief litter bearer had poked itself timidly around one great bronze door. "Come on, my squeamish friends, let's get this poor fellow home."

The poor fellow still wandered deliriously through some strange world when he was delivered into the care of his mother, who very sensibly declined to call in the doctors.

"They'll only bleed him and purge him, and they're the last things he needs," she said firmly. "He hasn't been eating, that's all. Once he comes out of his shock, I'll feed him some hot honeyed wine, and he'll be himself again. Especially after a sleep."

Cornelia Scipionis got her son into his bed and made him drink a full cup of the promised hot honeyed wine.

"Philippus!" he cried, trying to sit up.

"Don't worry about that insect until you feel stronger."

He drank again and did manage to sit up, pushing his fingers through his short black hair. "Oh, Mama! Such a terrible difficulty! Philippus found out about the oath."

Scaurus had apprised her of the situation, so she had no need to question him; instead, she nodded wisely. "Surely you didn't think Philippus or some other wouldn't ask?"

"It's been so long that I'd forgotten the wretched oath!"

"Marcus Livius, it isn't important," she said, and drew her chair closer to the bed, took his hand. "*What* you do is far more significant than *why* you do it—that's a fact of life! *Why* you do a thing is solely balm for the self, *why* you do a thing cannot affect its outcome. The *what* is all that matters, and I'm sure that a sane and healthy self-regard is the best way to get *what* done properly. So do cheer up, my son! Your brother is here, and very anxious about you. Cheer up!"

"They will hate me for this."

"Some will, that's true. Mostly out of envy. Others will be utterly consumed with admiration," said the mother. "It certainly doesn't seem to have deterred the friends who brought you home."

"Who?" he asked eagerly.

"Marcus Aemilius, Marcus Antonius, Quintus Mucius, Gaius Marius," she said. "Oh, and that *fascinating* man, Lucius Cornelius Sulla! Now if I were only younger—"

Knowledge of her had softened the impact of such remarks, no longer offensive to him; he was able therefore to smile at this whimsy. "How odd that you like him! Mind you, he does seem very interested in my ideas."

"So I gathered. His only son died earlier this year, not so?"

"Yes."

"It shows in him," said Cornelia Scipionis, getting up. "Now, Marcus Livius, I shall send your brother in to you, and you must make up your mind to eat. There is nothing wrong with you that good food won't remedy. I'll have the kitchen prepare something as tasty as it is nourishing, and Mamercus and I will sit here until you eat it."

Thus it was that darkness had fallen before he was left alone with his thoughts. He did feel much better, it was true, but the dreadful weariness would not go away, and he seemed no more inclined to sleep after his meal, even after so much mulled wine. How long had it been since he last slept deeply, satisfyingly? Months.

Philippus had found out. Inevitable that somebody would, inevitable that whoever did would go either to him, Drusus, or to Philippus. Or Caepio. Interesting, that Philippus hadn't told his dear friend Caepio! If he had, Caepio would have pushed in, tried to take over, unwilling that Philippus should have all the victory. Which was, no doubt, why Philippus had kept it to himself. All will not be peace and amity in the house of Philippus tonight! thought Drusus, smiling in spite of himself.

And now that the knowledge of discovery had sunk into his conscious mind, Drusus found himself at rest. His mother was right. Publication of the oath couldn't affect what he was doing; it could only affect his own pride. If people chose to believe he did what he had done because of the enormous clientele the deed would bring him, what did it really matter? Why should he want them to believe his motives were entirely altruistic? It would not be Roman to abrogate personal advantages, and he *was* Roman! In any other instance, he could see now very clearly, the implications of a clientele in one man's giving the citizenship to several hundred thousand men would have screamed at his fellow senators, at the leaders of the Plebs, and probably at most of lowly Rome. That no one had seen the implications until Philippus actually read out the oath was symptomatic of how emotional this issue was, how lacking in reason—it provoked a storm of feeling so powerful it clouded every practical aspect. Why had he expected people to see the logic in what he was trying to do, when they were so enormously involved emotionally that they hadn't even seen the client side of it? If they couldn't see the clients, then they had no hope of seeing the logic, so much was sure.

His eyelids lowered, and he slept. Deeply, satisfyingly.

When he went to the Curia Hostilia at dawn the next morning, Drusus felt his old self, and quite equal to dealing with the likes of Philippus and Caepio.

In the chair, Philippus ignored any other business, including the march of the Marsi; he got straight down to Drusus and the oath sworn by the Italians.

"Is the text of what I read out yesterday correct, Marcus Livius?" Philippus asked.

"To the best of my knowledge, Lucius Marcius, yes, though I have never heard the oath, nor seen it written down."

"But you knew of it."

Drusus blinked, face the picture of surprise. "Of course I *knew* of it, junior consul! How could a man not know about something so advantageous to himself, as well as to Rome? If you had been the advocate of general enfranchisement for all of Italy, wouldn't *you* have known?"

This was attacking with a vengeance; Philippus had to pause, thrown off balance.

"You'd never catch me advocating anything for the Italians beyond a good flogging!" he said haughtily.

"Then more fool you!" cried Drusus. "Here is something well worth doing on every level, Conscript Fathers! To rectify an injustice which has persisted for generations—to bring all of our country into an hegemony as real as it is desirable—to destroy some of the more appalling barriers between men of different Classes—to remove the threat of an imminent war—and it *is* imminent, I warn you!—and to see every one of these new Roman citizens bound by oath to Rome and to a Roman of the Romans! That last is *vitally* important! It means every one of these new citizens will be guided properly and Romanly, it means they will know how to vote and who to vote for, it means they will be led to elect *genuine* Romans rather than men from their own Italian nations!"

That was a consideration; Drusus could see it register on the faces of those who listened intently, and everyone was listening intently. He knew well the chief fear of all his fellow senators—that an overwhelming number of new Roman citizens spread across the whole thirty-five tribes would markedly decrease the Roman content of the elections, would see Italians contest the polls for consul, praetor, aedile, tribune of the plebs, and quaestor, would see Italians in huge numbers enter the Senate, all determined to wrest control of the Senate away from the Romans and into the hands of Italy. Not to mention the various comitia. But if these new Romans were bound by an oath—and it was a frightful oath—both to Rome and to a Roman of the Romans, they were honor-bound to vote as they were told to vote, like any other group of clients.

"The Italians are men of honor, as are we," said Drusus. "By the very swearing of this oath, they have shown it! In return for the gift of our citizenship, they will abide by the wishes of true Romans. *True* Romans!"

"You mean they will abide by your wishes!" said Caepio with venom. "The rest of us *true* Romans will simply have appointed ourselves an unofficial dictator!"

"Nonsense, Quintus Servilius! When in the conduct of my tribunate of the plebs have I shown myself anything less than completely conforming to the will of the Senate? When have I shown myself more concerned with my own welfare than with the welfare of the Senate? When have I shown myself indifferent to the wants of every level throughout the People of Rome? What better patron could the men of Italy have than I, the son of my father, a Roman of the Romans, a truly thoughtful and essentially conservative man?"

Drusus turned from one side of the House to the other, his hands outstretched. "Whom would you rather have as patron to so many new citizens, Conscript Fathers? Marcus Livius Drusus, or

Lucius Marcius Philippus? Marcus Livius Drusus, or Quintus Servilius Caepio? Marcus Livius Drusus, or Quintus Varius Severus Hybrida Sucronensis? For you had better make up your minds to it, members of the Senate of Rome—the men of Italy *will* be enfranchised! I have sworn to do it—*and do it I will!* You have taken my laws off the tablets, you have stripped my tribunate of the plebs of its purpose and its achievements. But my year in office is not yet over, and I have honorably acquitted myself in respect of my treatment of you, my fellow senators! On the day after tomorrow, I will take my case for the general enfranchisement of Italy to the Plebeian Assembly, and I will have the matter discussed in *contio* after *contio,* always religiously correct, always conducted with due attention to the law, always in a peaceful and orderly manner. For, other oaths aside, I swear to all of you that I will not pass out of my tribunate of the plebs without seeing one *lex Livia* on the tablets—a law providing that every man from the Arnus to Rhegium, from the Rubico to Vereium, from the Tuscan to the Adriatic, shall be a full citizen of Rome! If the men of Italy have sworn an oath to me, I also swore an oath to them—that during my time in office, I would see them enfranchised. And I will! Believe me, I will!"

He had carried the day, everyone knew it.

"The most brilliant thing about it," said Antonius Orator, "is that now he has them thinking of general citizenship as inevitable. They're used to seeing men break, not being broken. But Drusus has broken them, Princeps Senatus, I guarantee he has!"

"I agree," said Scaurus, who looked quite lit up from within. "You know, Marcus Antonius, I used to think that nothing in Roman government could surprise me—that it has all been done before—and usually done better. But Marcus Livius is unique. Rome has never seen his like. Nor will again, I suspect."

Drusus was as true as his word. He took his case for the enfranchisement of Italy to the *concilium plebis,* surrounded by an aura of indomitability every man present could not but admire. His fame had grown and spread, he was talked about at every level of society; that solid conservatism, that iron determination to do things properly and legally, now turned him into a novel kind of hero. All of Rome was essentially conservative, including the Head Count, capable of espousing a Saturninus yet not willing to kill its betters for a Saturninus. The *mos maiorum*—all those traditions and customs piled up by centuries of time—would always matter, even to the Head Count. And here at last was a man to whom the *mos maiorum* mattered as much as justice did. Marcus Livius Drusus began to assume the mantle of a demigod; and that in turn meant people started to believe that anything he wanted must be right.

Helplessly Philippus, Caepio, Catulus Caesar, and their followers, with Metellus Pius the Piglet hovering indecisively on the outskirts, watched Drusus conduct his *contiones* all through the last half of October, and into November. At first the meetings tended to be stormy, a condition Drusus dealt with beautifully, permitting every man a hearing, and even permitting massed voices, yet never succumbing to the tyranny or the seduction of the crowd. When a gathering grew too heated, he disbanded it. In the beginning, Caepio had tried to break the meetings up with violence, but that formerly tried and true technique of the Comitia didn't work with Drusus, who seemed to have an inbuilt instinct as to when violence was likely to erupt, and again, dismissed his meeting before it could erupt.

Six *contiones*, seven, eight . . . And each one quieter than the last, each one seeing an audience more reconciled to the inevitability of this piece of legislation. Water on stone, Drusus wore his opponents down with unfailing grace and dignity, admirable good temper, ever-present reasonableness. He made his enemies look crass, ill-mannered, oafish.

"It is the only way," he said to Scaurus Princeps Senatus after the eighth *contio,* standing with him on the steps of the House, from which vantage point Scaurus had watched. "What the noble Roman politician lacks is patience. Luckily that is a quality I possess in abundance. I cope with them, all those who come to listen, and they like that. They like *me*! I have been patient with them, and they have grown to trust me."

"You're the first man since Gaius Marius whom they have genuinely liked," said Scaurus reminiscently.

"With good reason," said Drusus. "Gaius Marius is another man they feel they can trust. He appeals to them because of his quite wonderful directness, his strength, his air of being one of them rather than a Roman nobleman. I don't have his natural advantages—I cannot be other than I am, a Roman nobleman. But patience has won out, Marcus Aemilius. They have *learned* to trust me."

"And you really think the time has come for a vote?"

"I do."

"Shall I gather the others? We can dine at my house."

"Today above all days, I think we should dine at my house," said Drusus. "Tomorrow will seal my fate, one way or the other."

Scaurus hurried off to find Marius, Scaevola, and Antonius Orator. When he saw Sulla, he waved to him as well. "I'm bearing an invitation from Marcus Livius. Dinner at his house, Lucius Cornelius?" And, seeing the look of antisocial reluctance appear on Sulla's face, he added impulsively, "Oh, *do* come! There will be no one there to poke or pry, Lucius Cornelius!"

The look vanished. Sulla actually produced a smile. "All right then, Marcus Aemilius, I'll come."

At the beginning of September the six men would have had the walk to themselves, for though Drusus had many clients, it was not normal practice for the clients to follow their patron home at the end of business in the Forum. Dawn was when they gathered at the patron's house. Yet on this day of the eighth *contio,* Drusus's following in the Comitia had grown so hugely that he and his five noble companions were the center of an excited crowd some two hundred strong. The escort was not comprised of important men, or wealthy men. Of the Third and Fourth Classes, even some of the Head Count, they had come to admire, wanting to honor this steadfast, indomitable, integral man. Since his second *contio* they had gathered to escort him home in ever-increasing numbers, and were particularly eager to do so today because the morrow would see the vote.

"So it's for tomorrow," said Sulla to Drusus as they walked.

"Yes, Lucius Cornelius. They have learned to know me and to trust me, from the knights with the plebeian power to all these small men surrounding us now. I can see no point in postponing the vote any longer. There's a kind of fulcrum involved. If I am to succeed, I will succeed tomorrow."

"There's no doubt you will succeed, Marcus Livius," said Marius contentedly. "And I for one will be voting for you."

It was a very short walk; across the lower Forum to the Vestal Steps, a right turn onto the Clivus Victoriae, and Drusus's house was upon them.

"Come in, come in, my friends!" Drusus said cheerily to the crowd. "Go through to the atrium, and I will take my leave of you there." To Scaurus he said very quietly, "Take the rest to my study and wait. I shan't be long, but it's courtesy to speak to them before I dismiss them."

While Scaurus and the other four noblemen hastened ahead to the study, Drusus shepherded his straggling escort through the vast peristyle-garden to the great double doors on the back wall of the colonnade at its far end. Beyond them lay the atrium, a lovely room vivid with colors, but dim now because the sun had gone down. For some time he stood in the middle of his admirers, joking and laughing, exhorting them to vote the right way on the morrow; in small groups they began to take their leave of him, those men about him dwindling away until only a few were left. The brief twilight was fading, and the shadows of that moment just before the lamps were lighted turned the recesses behind the pillars and in the many alcoves into impenetrable darkness.

Oh, wonderful! The last few were turning to go. One of the men brushed hard against Drusus in the gloom, he felt the sinus of his toga yanked down, experienced a sharp and burning pain in his right groin, and bit back the noise he almost made because, though they were his admirers, these men were strangers nonetheless.

Now they were hurrying, exclaiming at the way the light had suddenly gone, and anxious to get themselves home before night transformed the alleys of Rome into defiles boiling with dangers.

Half-blinded by pain, Drusus stood in the doorway looking along the garden, his left arm raised, encumbered by the multiple folds of his toga; he watched until the door warden at the far end of the peristyle had let the men out into the street, then turned to walk to his study, where his friends waited. But the moment he moved, that inexplicable and dazzling pain exploded into fury. He could not stifle this scream, it ripped its way out of him with as little mercy as a harpy. Something warm and liquid was suddenly pouring down his right leg. *Frightening!*

When Scaurus and the others burst out of the study, Drusus was standing with legs already buckling, his hand clasped against his right hip; he took the hand away and gazed at it in astonishment, for it was covered in blood. His blood. Down on his knees, he subsided slowly to the floor like a billowing sack with the air trapped beneath it, and lay, eyes wide open, gasping in growing pain.

It was Marius, not Scaurus, who took control. He freed the right hip from folds of toga until the hilt of a knife protruding from the upper part of Drusus's groin became visible, an answer to the mystery.

"Lucius Cornelius, Quintus Mucius, Marcus Antonius, each of you go for a different doctor," Marius said crisply. "Princeps Senatus, have the lamps lit immediately—all of them!"

Without warning Drusus screamed again, a horrifying noise which rose to the starry painted sky of his atrium ceiling and lingered there like some audible bat blundering from beam to beam; and the atrium came to life, slaves flying everywhere crying out, Cratippus the steward helping Scaurus light the lamps, Cornelia Scipionis running into the room with all six children in her wake, rushing to her son's side, kneeling on a floor now awash with blood.

"Assassin," said Marius tersely.

"I must send for his brother," said the mother, getting to her feet with the skirt of her gown soaked in blood.

No one noticed the six children, who crept up behind Marius and gaped at the scene on the floor, enormous eyes taking in the spreading sheet of blood, their uncle's awful twisted face, the dirty stubby thing growing out of his lower belly. He screamed now continuously, the pain growing as the internal bleeding compressed the great nerve-trunks feeding the leg; at each new cry of agony the children jumped, flinched, whimpered, until Young Caepio recollected himself enough to take his scrawny little brother Cato within his arm and push Cato's quivering head against his chest, cutting off the sight of Uncle Marcus from little Cato's bulging eyes.

Only when Cornelia Scipionis returned were the children seen, banished under the escort of a weeping and shivering nurserymaid; the mother knelt again opposite Marius, as helpless as he.

Sulla appeared at that moment, almost literally carrying Apollodorous Siculus, whom he threw to the ground beside Marius. "The cold-hearted *mentula* didn't want to leave his dinner."

"He must be taken to his bed before I can examine him," said the Sicilian Greek physician, still breathless from Sulla's assault.

So Marius, Sulla, Cratippus and two other servants lifted the shrieking Drusus from the floor, dragging a broad trail of bright red blood behind them from the soaked toga as they carried him to his big bed, where he and Servilia Caepionis had tried vainly for so many years to make children. The room, a small one, had been so stuffed with lamps it seemed as bright as day to those who dumped Drusus down.

Other doctors were arriving; Marius and Sulla left them to it, joining the others in the atrium, from which place they could still hear Drusus screaming, screaming. When Mamercus ran in, Marius pointed toward the master's bedroom, but made no move to follow.

"We can't leave," said Scaurus, looking very old.

"No, we can't," said Marius, feeling very old.

"Then let's move back to the study. We'll be less in the way," said Sulla, trembling from a combination of shock and the effort of dragging a reluctant doctor away from his dinner couch.

"Jupiter, I don't believe it!" cried Antonius Orator.

"Caepio?" asked Scaevola, shivering.

"I'd pick Varius the Spaniard cur," said Sulla, teeth showing.

They settled in the study feeling useless, impotent, as men do who are used to directing things, their ears still assaulted by those terrible cries emanating from the bedroom. But they hadn't been in the study long when they discovered that Cornelia Scipionis was a true member of her formidable clan, for even in the midst of this ordeal she found the time to have wine and food sent to them, and gave them the services of a slave.

When the doctors finally managed to remove the knife, it turned out to be ideal for the purpose upon which it had been employed; a wicked little wide-bladed, curved-bladed shoemaker's knife.

"It has been twisted completely around inside the wound," said Apollodorus Siculus to Mamercus above the remorseless racket of Drusus's cries.

"What does that mean?" asked Mamercus, sweating in the heat of so many tiny tongues of flame, incapable yet of appreciating any of the implications, let alone all of them.

"Everything is torn beyond repair, Mamercus Aemilius. The blood vessels, the nerves, the bladder, even, I think, the bowel."

"Can't you give him something for the pain?"

"I have already administered syrup of poppies, but I will give him more. Unfortunately I do not think it will help."

"What *will* help?" demanded Mamercus.

"Nothing."

"Are you saying my son is going to *die*?" asked Cornelia Scipionis incredulously.

"Yes, *domina*," said the doctor with dignity. "Marcus Livius is bleeding both internally and externally, and we have not the skill to stop either. He must die."

"In such pain? Can you do nothing for that?" asked the mother.

"There is no more effective drug in our pharmacopoeia than

syrup of Anatolian poppies, *domina*. If that does not help him, nothing will."

All through the long night Drusus lay on his bed screaming, screaming, screaming. The sound of his agony penetrated into every last inch of that fabulous house, reached the ears of the six children huddled together in the nursery for company and comfort, little Cato's head still buried in his brother's arms, all of them weeping and whimpering, the memory of Uncle Marcus on the floor burning their minds and spoiling their lives, already spoiled from so much tragedy.

But Young Caepio cradled his little brother Cato fiercely, kissing his hair. "See, I am here! Nothing can hurt you!"

On the Clivus Victoriae people kept gathering until the crowd stretched for three hundred paces in either direction; even out there the sound of Drusus's screaming was audible, echoed by sighs and sobs, smaller cries of smaller yet no less real pain.

Inside, the Senate had gathered in the atrium, though Caepio did not come, nor Philippus, a prudent decision; and nor, noted Lucius Cornelius Sulla, poking his head round the door of the study, had Quintus Varius. Something moved in a pool of darkness near the exit to the loggia; Sulla slid silently around and out to see. A girl, perhaps thirteen or fourteen, dark and pretty.

"What do you want?" he asked, suddenly materializing in front of her, a lamp directly behind him.

She gasped as she looked up at the fiery halo of red-gold hair, thinking for a moment that she looked at the dead Cato Salonianus; her eyes blazed hate, then died down. "And who are you to ask *me* that?" she snapped with huge hauteur.

"Lucius Cornelius Sulla. Who are you?"

"Servilia."

"Back to bed, young lady. This is no place for you."

"I'm looking for my father," she said.

"Quintus Servilius Caepio?"

"Yes, yes, my father!"

Sulla laughed, not caring enough about her to spare her. "Why would he be here, silly child, when half the world suspects him of having Marcus Livius murdered?"

Her eyes lit up again, this time with joy. "Is he truly going to die? Truly?"

"Yes."

"Good!" she said savagely, opened a door, and disappeared.

Sulla shrugged, went back to the study.

Shortly after dawn, Cratippus appeared. "Marcus Aemilius, Gaius Marius, Marcus Antonius, Lucius Cornelius, Quintus Mucius, the master is asking to see you."

The screams had died down to sporadic, gurgling moans; the men in the study understood the meaning of this, and made haste behind the steward, pushing through the clusters of senators waiting in the atrium.

Drusus lay, his skin as white as the sheets, his face no more than a mask in which someone diabolical had inserted a brilliant, vital, beautiful pair of great dark eyes. To one side of him stood Cornelia Scipionis, tearless and rigid; to the other side stood Mamercus Aemilius Lepidus Livianus, tearless and rigid. The doctors had all gone.

"My friends, I must depart," said Drusus.

"We understand," Scaurus said gently.

"My work will not be done now."

"No, it will not," said Marius.

"But to stop me, they had to do this." He cried out in pain, but softly, worn out.

"Who was it?" asked Sulla.

"Any of seven men. I don't know them. Ordinary men. Of the Third Class, I would say. Not Head Count."

"Have you received any threats?" asked Scaevola.

"None." He moaned again.

"We will find the assassin," said Antonius Orator.

"Or the man who paid the assassin," said Sulla.

They stood around the foot of the bed in silence then, not wanting to waste any more of what little life Drusus had left. But at the very end, when he was gasping with the effort of breathing and the pain had died down to something he could bear, Drusus struggled to sit up, looking at them out of clouding eyes.

"Ecquandone?" he asked, loudly, strongly. *"Ecquandone similem mei civem habebit res publica?* Who will ever be able to succor the Republic in my like?"

The work of the little film creeping across those splendid eyes became complete; they glazed to an opaque gold. Drusus died.

"No one, Marcus Livius," said Sulla. "No one."

PART V

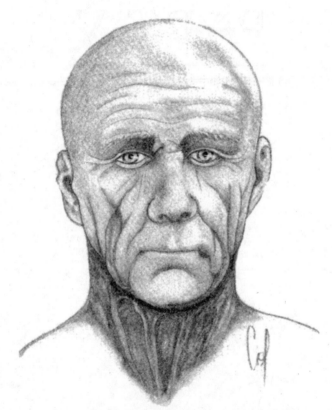

MARCUS AEMILIUS SCAURUS

Quintus Poppaedius Silo received the news of Drusus's death in a letter written by Cornelia Scipionis; it reached him in Marruvium not two days after the disaster, yet one more testament to the remarkable fortitude and presence of mind the mother of Drusus owned. Having promised her son she would tell Silo before he could learn the news in a roundabout way, she did not forget.

Silo wept, but without surprise or genuine shock. Afterward, he found himself lighter, full of new purpose; the time of waiting and wondering was over at last. With the death of Marcus Livius Drusus, any hope of peacefully attaining Italian enfranchisement had evaporated.

Off went letters to Gaius Papius Mutilus of the Samnites, Herius Asinius of the Marrucini, Publius Praesenteius of the Paeligni, Gaius Vidacilius of the Picentines, Gaius Pontidius of the Frentani, Titus Lafrenius of the Vestini, and whoever was currently leading the Hirpini, a nation famous for changing its praetors frequently. Only where to meet? All the Italian nations were acutely aware of the two Roman praetors trundling around the peninsula enquiring into "the Italian question," and suspicious of any place having Roman or Latin status. Somewhere central to the majority and off the Roman track, yet on a good road—a Roman road, that is. The answer loomed in Silo's mind almost immediately, rocky and forbidding, fortified with high walls, nestling in the lap of the central Apennines and with access to unfailing water. Corfinium on the Via Valeria and the river Aternus, a city of the Paeligni adjoining the lands of the Marrucini.

There in Corfinium they met only days after the death of Drusus, the leaders of eight Italian nations, and many of their followers—the Marsi, the Samnites, the Marrucini, the Vestini, the Paeligni, the Frentani, the Picentes, and the Hirpini. Excited and determined.

"It's war," said Mutilus in the council, almost the first words to be spoken. "It must be war, fellow Italians! Rome refuses to accord us the dignity and standing our deeds and our might have earned us. We will forge for ourselves an independent country

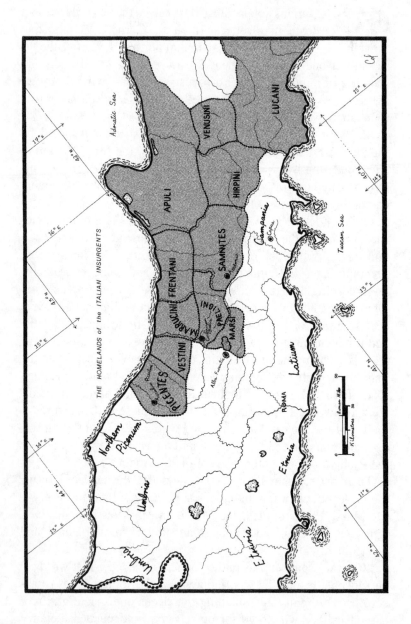

THE HOMELANDS of the ITALIAN INSURGENTS

having no truck with Rome or Romans, we will take back the Roman and Latin colonies founded within our borders, we will find our own destiny with our own men and our own money!"

Cheers and stamping feet greeted this militant declaration, a reaction Mutilus found exhilarating and Silo found heartening; for the one was consumed with hatred of Rome, and the other was devoid of faith in Rome.

"No more taxes for Rome! No more soldiers for Rome! No more lands for Rome! No more Italian backs bared for Roman lashes! No more debt-bondage to Rome! No more bowing and scraping and saluting and groveling to Rome!" Mutilus shouted. "We will be a power unto ourselves! We will *replace* Rome! For Rome, fellow Italians, will be in ashes!"

This meeting took place in Corfinium's public marketplace, as Corfinium had no hall or forum great enough to hold the two thousand men who congregated there; so the cheers which greeted the second part of Mutilus's short speech rose into the air and floated out over the city walls in a huge wave of sound that frightened birds and awed the populace.

And it is done, thought Silo, listening. All the decisions have been taken.

But there were many decisions yet to be taken. First, a new name for the new country.

"Italia!" cried Mutilus.

Then, a name for Italia's new capital, hitherto Corfinium.

"Italica!" cried Mutilus.

After that, a government.

"A council of five hundred men, drawn equally from all the nations which join Italia," said Silo, to whom Mutilus had yielded willingly; Mutilus was Italia's heart, Silo was Italia's brain. "All our civil regulations, including our constitution, will be drawn up and administered by this *concilium Italiae*, which will be permanently based here in our new capital of Italica. But, as you all know very well, we must war with Rome before Italia can come into real existence. Therefore, until the war with Rome is concluded successfully—as it will be!—Italia will have an inner or war council consisting of twelve praetors and two consuls. Roman names, I know, but they will do, for simplicity's sake if for no other. Always acting with the knowledge and consent of the *concilium Italiae* itself, this war council will be responsible for the conduct of our war against Rome."

"No one in Rome will believe it!" shouted Titus Lafrenius of the Vestini. "Two names? That's all we have to offer! A name for a nonexistent country and a new name for an old city!"

"Rome will believe it," said Silo steadily, "when we start issuing coins and calling for architects to design the nucleus of a magnificent city! Our first currency will show the eight founding nations symbolized by eight men with drawn swords about to sacrifice the pig, Rome, and on the other side, the face of a new goddess in the Italian pantheon—Italia herself! For our animal, we will take the Samnite bull. For our patron god, we will take Liber Pater, the Father of Freedom, and he will lead a panther on a string, for that is how tame we will make Rome! And before a year is out, our new capital city of Italica will have a forum as large as that in Rome, a council house big enough for five hundred men, a temple to Italia grander than the temple of Ceres in Rome, and a temple to Jupiter Italiae greater than the temple of Jupiter Optimus Maximus in Rome! We will owe Rome nothing, as Rome will quickly see!"

The cheering broke out anew; Silo stood on the tribunal and waited, smiling fiercely, until quiet descended again.

"Rome will *not* find us divided!" he said. "So much do I swear to every man here, and to every man in a free Italia. We will pool our every resource, from men to money, from food to goods! And those who conduct the war against Rome in Italia's name will work together more closely than any commanders in the history of war! All over Italia our soldiers are waiting for the call to arms! We have one hundred thousand men ready to take the field within days—and more will come, many more!" He paused, laughed aloud. "Within two years, my fellow Italians, I pledge you that it is Romans who will be crying out to become enfranchised citizens of Italia!"

Because the cause was as just as it was deserving, as longed for as it was needed, there was virtually no skirmishing for the positions of power, and no internal strife; the council of five hundred buckled down to its civic duties that very day, while the inner council sat down to talk war.

The magistrates of the inner council had been elected by the simple Greek show of hands, and even included two praetors from nations as yet to join Italia, so sure were the electors that the Lucani and the Venusini would be with them.

The two consuls were Gaius Papius Mutilus of the Samnites and Quintus Poppaedius Silo of the Marsi. Among the praetors were Herius Asinius of the Marrucini, Publius Vettius Scato of the Marsi, Publius Praesenteius of the Paeligni, Gaius Vidacilius of the Picentes, Marius Egnatius of the Samnites, Titus Lafrenius of the Vestini, Titus Herennius of the Picentes, Gaius Pontidius of the Frentani, Lucius Afranius of the Venusini, and Marcus Lamponius of the Lucani.

The war council, sitting inside the small meeting chamber of Corfinium/Italica, got down to business immediately also.

"We *must* enlist the Etrurians and the Umbrians," said Mutilus. "Unless they join us, we will never be able to isolate Rome from the north. And if we can't isolate Rome from the north, she will be able to continue using the resources of Italian Gaul."

"The Etrurians and the Umbrians are a peculiar lot," said the Marsian Scato. "They never have regarded themselves as Italian in the way we do ourselves—and the way Rome regards them, the fools!"

"They did march in force to protest the breaking up of the *ager publicus*," said Herius Asinius. "Surely that indicates they will stand with us?"

"I think it indicates they won't," said Silo, frowning. "Of all the Italian nations, the Etrurians are the most closely tied to Rome, and the Umbrians just blindly follow the Etrurians. Whom do we know among them by name, for instance? No one! The trouble is that the Apennines have always shut them off from the rest of us to the east, Italian Gaul lies to their north, and Rome and Latium bound them to the south. They sell their pine and their pigs to Rome, not to other Italian nations."

"The pine I can see, but what do a few pigs matter?" asked the Picentine, Vidacilius.

Silo grinned. "There are pigs and pigs, Gaius Vidacilius! Some pigs go oink-oink. Other pigs make wonderful mail-shirts."

"Pisae and Populonia!" said Vidacilius. "I take your point."

"Well, Etruria and Umbria are for the future," said Marius Egnatius. "I suggest we depute the most persuasive among our five hundred councillors outside to go and see their leaders, while we get down to what is more properly our business. War. How do we want to begin this war?"

"Quintus Poppaedius, what do you say?" asked Mutilus.

"We call our soldiers to arms. But while we're doing that, I suggest that we lull Rome a little by sending a deputation to the Senate of Rome, asking again to be granted the citizenship."

Marius Egnatius snorted. "Let them use their citizenship the way a Greek uses a pretty boy!"

"Oh, certainly," said Silo pleasantly. "However, there's no need to let them know that until we can provide them with a tool to ram it home in the person of our armies. We're ready, yes, but it will take us at least a month to mobilize. I know for a fact that almost everybody in Rome thinks we're years off being able to march. Therefore, why disillusion them? Another deputation will make it seem as if they're right about our state of preparedness."

"I agree, Quintus Poppaedius," said Mutilus.

"Good. Then I suggest we pick a second lot of persuasive talkers from the five hundred councillors outside, to go to Rome. Led by at least one of the war council, I think."

"One thing I'm sure of," said Vidacilius, "is that if we are to win this war, we must do it quickly. We have to hit the Romans hard and fast, on as many fronts as possible. We have wonderfully trained troops, and we're well supplied with all the materials of war. We have superb centurions." He paused, looking very dour. "However, we don't have any generals."

"I disagree!" said Silo strongly. "If you mean by that we don't have a Gaius Marius ready to hand, then you're right. But he's an old man now, and who else do the Romans have? Quintus Lutatius Catulus Caesar, he who prates that he beat the Cimbric Germans in Italian Gaul, when we all know it was Gaius Marius? They have Titus Didius, but he's no Marius. More importantly, they have his legions in camp in Capua—four of them, and all veterans. Their best generals currently fighting are Sentius and Bruttius Sura in Macedonia, but no one would dare bring them home, they're too busy."

"Before Rome will see herself conquered by the likes of us," said Mutilus bitterly, "she'll throw every province she has to the four winds and bring the lot home to fight. *That* is why we have to win this war in a hurry!"

"I have one further thing to say about the subject of generals," said Silo patiently. "It doesn't really matter whom Rome has in her general's cupboard, you know. Because Rome will behave as Rome always does—the consuls of the year will be the commanders in the field. I think we can discount Sextus Julius Caesar and Lucius Marcius Philippus—their terms are almost over. Who next year's consuls are likely to be, I don't know. However, they must surely have elected someone by now. Which is why I disagree with you, Gaius Vidacilius, and with you, Gaius Papius. We in this room have all done as much military service as any of the current crop of consular candidates in Rome. I for one have seen several major actions—and been privileged to see Rome lose horribly at Arausio! My praetor Scato, you yourself, Gaius Vidacilius, Gaius Papius, Herius Asinius, Marius Egnatius—why, there isn't a man in this room who hasn't served in his six campaigns! We know the command routines at least as well as whomsoever the Romans will field, both legates and commanders."

"We also have a great advantage," said Praesenteius. "We know the country better than the Romans do. We've been training men up and down Italy for years now. Roman military experience is abroad, not in Italy. Once the legionaries are out of their recruit schools in Capua, they're gone. It's a pity Didius's troops haven't been shipped out yet, but those four legions of veterans are just about all the troops Rome has at her disposal, short of bringing overseas legions home."

"Didn't Publius Crassus bring home troops from Further Spain when he celebrated his triumph?" asked Herius Asinius.

"He did, but they were shipped back again when the Spains revolted as usual," said Mutilus, in best situation to know what was going on in Capua. "Titus Didius's four were kept in case they were needed in Asia Province and Macedonia."

At that moment a messenger came in from the marketplace with a note from the councillors; Mutilus took it, muttered his way through it several times, then laughed harshly.

"Well, generals of the war council, it appears our friends out there in the public square are as determined as we are to see this thing done! I have here a document informing us that all the members of the *concilium Italiae* have agreed that every major town in Italia will pair itself with a town of like size in a different Italian state, and the two will exchange hostages—fifty children from all walks of life, no less!"

"I'd call that evidence of mistrust," said Silo.

"I suppose it is. Nonetheless, it's also physical proof of dedication and determination. I'd prefer to call it an act of faith, that every town in Italia is willing to put the lives of fifty of its children at risk," said Mutilus. "The fifty from my town of Bovianum are to go to Marruvium, while Marruvium's fifty go to my town of Bovianum. I see several more exchanges have already been decided—Asculum Picentum and Sulmo—Teate and Saepinum. Good!"

Silo and Mutilus walked outside to confer with the grand council, and came back some time later to discover their fellow members of the war council had been talking strategy in their absence.

"We march on Rome first," said Titus Lafrenius.

"Yes, but we don't commit all our forces to it," said Mutilus, sitting down. "If we proceed on the assumption that we'll get no co-operation from Etruria and Umbria—and I think we must—then we can do nothing to the north of Rome for the moment. And we can't allow ourselves to forget that northern Picenum is too firmly under the control of the Roman Pompeii to aid us either. Do you agree, Gaius Vidacilius, Titus Herennius?"

"We must agree," said Vidacilius heavily. "Northern Picenum is Roman. Pompey Strabo owns more than half of it personally—and what he doesn't own, Pompeius Rufus does. We have a wedge between Sentinum and Camerinum, no more."

"Very well, we'll have to abandon the north almost entirely," said Mutilus. "East of Rome, we're in much better condition, of course, once the Apennines start rising. And in the south of the peninsula we've an excellent chance of cutting Rome off completely from Tarentum and Brundisium. If Marcus Lamponius brings Lucania into Italia—and I'm sure he will—then we'll also be able to isolate Rome from Rhegium." He stopped to grimace. "However, there remain the lowlands of Campania, extending through Samnium to the Apulian Adriatic. And it's here we must strike hardest at Rome, for several reasons. Chiefly because Rome thinks Campania is a spent force, undeniably Roman at last. But that is not true, gentlemen! They may hang on to Capua, they may hang on to Puteoli. But I think we can take the rest of Campania off Rome! And if we do that, we take their best seaports near to Rome, we cut their access to the big and vital seaports of the far south, we deprive them of their best local growing lands—and we isolate Capua. Once we have Rome fighting defensively, Etruria and Umbria will scramble to throw in their lots with us. We have to control every road into Rome on her east and her south, and we have to make a bid to control the Via Flaminia and the Via Cassia as well. Once Etruria comes in on our side, of course, we'll own every last Roman road. If necessary, we can then starve Rome out."

"There, Gaius Vidacilius, you see?" asked Silo triumphantly. "Who says we don't have any generals?"

Vidacilius lifted his hands in surrender. "I take your point, Quintus Poppaedius! In Gaius Papius, we have a general."

"I think you'll find," said Mutilus, "that we have a dozen good generals without going outside this room."

 On the same day that the new nation of Italia was formed and its most prominent men settled down in the new capital city of Italica to deliberate, the praetor Quintus Servilius of the Augur's family commenced to ride along the Via Salaria from the port city of Firmum Picenum, going in the direction of Rome at last. Since June he had patrolled the lands north of Rome, heading up through the fertile rolling hills of Etruria to the river Arnus, which formed the boundary of Italian Gaul; from there he went east into Umbria, thence south into Picenum, and down the Adriatic coast. He had, he felt, acquitted himself very well. No Italian stone had gone unturned—and if he had discovered no deep-laid plots, that was because there *were* no deep-laid plots, he was sure of it.

His progress had been royal in all save name. Dowered with a proconsular imperium, he enjoyed the sumptuous panoply of riding behind twelve crimson-clad, black-and-brass-belted lictors bearing the axes in their bundles of rods. Ambling along on a snow-white palfrey, clad in silver-plated armor with a purple tunic underneath, Quintus Servilius of the Augur's family had unconsciously borrowed from King Tigranes of Armenia by ordering that a slave travel beside him holding a parasol to shade him from the sun. Had Lucius Cornelius Sulla only seen him, that strange man would have laughed himself sick. And probably proceeded to haul Quintus Servilius off his demure little lady's mount and rub his face in the dust.

Each day a group of Quintus Servilius's servants rushed ahead of him to find the best accommodation available, usually in some local magnate's or magistrate's villa; that he was indifferent as to how the rest of his entourage fared was typical of him. As well as his lictors and a large party of slaves, he was escorted by twenty heavily armed and beautifully mounted troopers. With him for much-needed company on this leisurely progress he took as his legate one Fonteius, a rich nonentity who had just purchased himself a small share of glory by donating (along with a huge dowry) his daughter, Fonteia, aged seven, to the College of Vestal Virgins.

It seemed to Quintus Servilius of the Augur's family that much senatorial fuss had been made about nothing in Rome, but he was disinclined to complain, having seen more of Italy than he had ever thought to see, and under circumstances of unparalleled deliciousness. Wherever he went, he was feted and feasted; his money chest was still more than half full due to the generosity of his hosts and the awesome power of a proconsular imperium, which meant he would finish the year of his praetorship nicely plump in the purse—and at the expense of the State.

The Via Salaria of course was the Old Salt Road, Rome's original key to prosperity in the days before the kings, when the salt mined from the flats at Ostia had been disseminated along this road by Latin merchant-soldiers. However, in these modern times the Via Salaria had dwindled in importance to the point where its roadbed was not kept up by a negligent State, as Quintus Servilius discovered shortly after he left Firmum Picenum. Washouts due to past flooding plagued him every few miles, there was not a scrap of surface left atop the rounded stones of the foundations—and, to cap everything, when he entered the pass to the next town of any importance, Asculum Picentum, he found his passage barred by a landslide. It took his men a day and a half to clear a safe path, time which poor Quintus Servilius was obliged to spend at the site of the landslide in conditions of acute discomfort.

The journey from the coast was steeply uphill, for the eastern littoral was narrow, the spine of the Apennines looming close and very tall. Yet inland Asculum Picentum was the largest and most important town in all southern Picenum, surrounded by a daunting circumference of high stone walls which echoed the daunting peaks of the mountains also encircling the city. The river Truentius flowed nearby, little more than a string of waterholes at this time of the year, but the clever Asculans had tapped their water supply from a layer of gravel well below the riverbed.

His advance guard of servants had done their work, Quintus Servilius discovered when he reached the main gates of Asculum Picentum at last; there he was welcomed by a small gathering of obviously prosperous merchants who spoke Latin instead of Greek, and all wore the togas of Roman citizenship.

Quintus Servilius dismounted from his snow-white lady's horse, hitched his purple cloak across his left shoulder, and received his welcoming committee with gracious condescension.

"This isn't a Roman or Latin colony, is it?" he asked vaguely, his knowledge of such things not as good as it ought have been, especially given that he was a Roman praetor traveling Italy.

"No, Quintus Servilius, but there are about a hundred of us Roman businessmen living here," said the leader of the deputation, whose name was Publius Fabricius.

"Then where are the leading Picentines?" demanded Quintus Servilius indignantly. "I expect to be met by the natives too!"

Fabricius looked apologetic. "The Picentines have been avoiding us Romans for months, Quintus Servilius. Why, I don't know! However, they seem to be harboring a lot of ill feeling toward us. And today is a local festival in honor of Picus."

"Picus?" Quintus Servilius blinked. "They have a festival in honor of a *woodpecker*?"

They were walking through the gates into a small square festooned with garlands of autumn flowers, its cobbles strewn with rose petals and tiny daisies.

"Hereabouts, Picus is a kind of Picentine Mars," said Fabricius. "He was the King of Old Italy, they believe, and he led the Picentes from their original Sabine lands across the mountains to what we call Picenum. When they got here, Picus transformed himself into a woodpecker, and marked out their boundaries by drilling the trees."

"Oh," said Quintus Servilius, losing interest.

Fabricius conducted Quintus Servilius and his legate Fonteius to his own splendid mansion on the highest point within the city, having arranged that lictors and troopers be quartered nearby in appropriate comfort, and having managed to accommodate the party's slaves within his own slave quarters. Quintus Servilius began to expand under this deferential and luxurious treatment, especially after he saw his room, quite the best in a very nice house.

The day was hot, the sun still overhead; the two Romans bathed, then joined their host on the loggia overlooking the city, its impressive walls, and the more impressive mountains beyond, a grander view than most city houses anywhere owned.

"If you would like, Quintus Servilius," said Fabricius when his guests appeared, "we could go to the theater this afternoon. They're playing Plautus's *Bacchides*."

"That sounds delightful," said Quintus Servilius, sitting in a shady, cushioned chair. "I haven't been to see a play since I left Rome." He sighed voluptuously. "Flowers everywhere, I noticed, yet hardly a person on the streets. Is that because of this woodpecker's festival?"

Fabricius frowned. "No. Apparently it has something to do with a peculiar new policy the Italians have adopted. Fifty Asculan children—all Italians—were sent off to Sulmo early this morning, and Asculum is waiting to receive fifty of Sulmo's children in place of their own."

"How extraordinary! If one didn't know better, one might be excused for presuming they're exchanging hostages," said Quintus Servilius comfortably. "Are the Picentes thinking of going to war against the Marrucini? That's what it seems like, doesn't it?"

"I haven't heard of any rumors of war," said Fabricius.

"Well, they've sent fifty Asculan children off to a town of the Marrucini and they're expecting fifty Marrucine children in their place, so it certainly suggests uneasy relations between the Picentes and the Marrucini, to say the least." Quintus Servilius giggled. "Oh, wouldn't it be wonderful if they started fighting each other? It would certainly keep their minds off acquiring our citizenship, not so?" He sipped his wine and looked up, startled. "My dear Publius Fabricius! *Chilled* wine?"

"A nice conceit, isn't it?" asked Fabricius, pleased that he could actually astonish a Roman praetor with a name as old and famous and patrician as Servilius. "I send an expedition to the snows every second day, and have enough snow brought down to chill my wine all through summer and autumn."

"Delicious," said Quintus Servilius, leaning back in his chair. "What's your line?" he asked abruptly.

"I have an exclusive contract with most of the orchardists hereabouts," said Publius Fabricius. "I buy all their apples and pears and quinces. The best of them I ship straight to Rome for sale as fresh fruit. The rest I make into jam in my little factory, then I send the jam to Rome. I've also got a contract for chick-pea."

"Oh, very nice!"

"Yes, I must say I've done very well," said Fabricius in tones of distinct self-congratulation. "Mind you, it's typical of the Italians that once they see a man with the Roman citizenship start living better than they are, they begin to carp about monopolies and unfair trade practices and all the rest of that idler's rubbish. The truth is, they don't want to work, and those who do don't have business heads! If it were left to them, their fruit and produce would rot on the ground. I didn't come to this cold and desolate hole to steal their businesses, I came here to *establish* a business! When I first started, they couldn't do enough for me, they were so grateful. Now, I'm *persona non grata* with every Italian in Asculum. And my Roman friends here all tell the same story, Quintus Servilius."

"It's a story I've heard before, from Saturnia to Ariminum," said the praetor delegated to look into "the Italian question."

When the sun was about a third of the way down the western sky and the heat was beginning in that cool mountain air to diminish, Publius Fabricius and his distinguished guests walked to the theater, a temporary wooden structure built against the city wall so that the audience was shaded while the sun still lit up the *scaena* upon which the play would be performed. Perhaps five thousand Picentines were already installed, though not in the two front rows of the semicircular building; those seats were reserved for the Romans.

Fabricius had made some last-minute alterations to the center of the very first row, where he had erected a pleasant dais shaded by a canopy. It contained enough room for the curule chair of Quintus Servilius, a chair for his legate Fonteius, and a third chair for Fabricius himself. That the structure obscured the view of those in the rows immediately behind didn't worry him at all. His guest was a Roman praetor with a proconsular imperium—far more important than a lot of Italians.

The party entered the auditorium through a tunnel beneath the curving *cavea,* and emerged on an aisle perhaps twelve rows from the dais, which fronted on to the orchestra, an unoccupied half circle of space between audience and stage. First came the strutting lictors shouldering their *axed fasces,* then came the praetor and his legate with a beaming Fabricius trotting beside them, and behind came the twenty troopers. Fabricius's wife—to whom the Roman visitors had not been introduced—sat with her friends to the right of the dais, but in the row behind; the front row was reserved exclusively for Roman citizen men.

As the party appeared, a great murmur ran through the rows upon rows of Picentines, who leaned forward, craning their necks to see; the murmur grew to a growl, a roar, a howl, larded with boos and hisses. Though secretly astonished and dismayed at this hostile reception, Quintus Servilius of the Augur's family stalked, nose in air, onto the dais, and placed himself regally in his ivory seat, looking for all the world like the patrician Servilius he was not. Fonteius and Fabricius followed, while the lictors and troopers filed into the front-row seats on either side of and adjacent to the dais, tucking spears and *fasces* between their bare knees.

The play began, one of Plautus's finest and funniest—and one of his most delightfully musical. The cast was a strolling one, but good, of mixed origins in that some were Roman, some were Latin, and some were Italian; of Greeks there were none, as this company specialized in Latin comedy theater. The festival of Picus in Asculum Picentum was one of their regular stops each year, but this year the mood was different; the undercurrents of anti-Roman feeling running through the Picentine audience were entirely new. So the actors threw themselves into their routines with redoubled vigor, broadened the funny lines with additional nuances of walk and gesture, and determined that before the performance was over, they would have succeeded in jollying the Picentines out of their ill humor.

Unfortunately the ranks were split between the players too; while a pair of Romans acted shamelessly to the men on the dais, the Latins and the Italians concentrated upon the native Asculans. After the prologue came the establishment of the plot, some hilarious exchanges between the major characters, and a pretty duet sung against the warbling of a flute. Then came the first *canticum,* a glorious tenor aria sung to the accompaniment of a lyre. The singer, an Italian from Samnium as famous for his ability to alter the playwright's lines as for his voice, stepped to the front of the stage and played directly to the dais of honor.

> "All hail to thee, praetor of Rome!
> All hail to thee, and get thee home!
> What need have we at this Picalia
> To blinded be by Rome's regalia?
> Look at him raised to haughty height
> Never amazed by any sight!
> It is not fair, men of Asc'lum
> That he should share our ergast'lum!
> Come one come all, let's toss him out!
> Let's see him fall, the filthy lout!
> He sits too tall on his iv'ry seat—
> Just got one ball and it's dead meat!
> Give him a kick, the Roman prick,
> Make him real sick with ours to lick!"

He got no further with his invented song. One of Quintus Servilius's bodyguards disengaged his spear from between his knees, and without even bothering to get up, threw it; the Samnite tenor fell dead, the spear protruding hideously through back and front, his face still wearing its look of utter contempt.

A profound silence descended, the Picentine audience not able to believe what had happened, no one sure what to do. And as they sat numbed, the Latin actor Saunio, a favorite of the crowd, bounded to the far side of the stage and began feverishly to talk while four of his fellows dragged the body away and the two Roman actors disappeared in a hurry.

"Dear Picentes, I am not a Roman!" Saunio cried, clinging like an ape to one of the pillars and jigging up and down, his mask dangling from the fingers of one hand. "Do not, I implore you, lump me in with those fellows there!" He pointed to the Roman dais. "I am a mere Latin, dear Picentes, I too suffer the *fasces* marching up and down our beloved Italy, I too deplore the acts of these arrogant Roman predators!"

At which point Quintus Servilius rose from his ivory curule chair, stepped down from the dais, walked across the orchestra space, and mounted the stage.

"If you don't want a spear through *your* chest, actor, get yourself off!" said Quintus Servilius to Saunio. "Never in my life have I had to put up with such insults! Think yourselves lucky, you Italian scum, that I don't order my men to kill the lot of you!"

He turned from Saunio to the audience, the acoustics so good he was able to speak in a normal voice and be heard at the very top of the *cavea*. "I shall not forget what was said here!" he snapped. "Roman *auctoritas* has been mortally offended! The citizens of this Italian dungheap will pay dearly, so much I promise you!"

What happened next happened so quickly that no one afterward quite understood its mechanics; the whole five thousand Picentines in the audience descended in one screaming, flailing mass upon the two Roman front rows, leaping to the vacant half circle of the orchestra and turning there to fall upon troopers and lictors and togate Roman citizens in a solid wall of moving bodies and plucking, pulling, pinching hands. Not one spear was raised, not one sword was drawn, not one axe was detached from its surrounding bundle of rods; troopers and lictors, togate men and their ornamented women, all were literally torn apart. The front of the theater became a welter of blood, bits of bodies were thrown like balls from one side of the orchestra to the other. The crowd shrieked and squealed shrilly, wept with joy and hate, and reduced forty Roman officials and two hundred Roman businessmen and their women to chunks of bleeding meat. Fonteius and Fabricius perished among the first.

Nor did Quintus Servilius of the Augur's family escape. Some of the crowd jumped onto the stage before he could think of moving, and took exquisite pleasure in tearing off his ears, twisting his nose until it came away, gouging out his eyes, ripping his fingers off all cruelly bitten by their rings, and then, as he screamed without pause, they lifted him at feet and hands and head, and pulled him effortlessly into six heaving pieces.

When it was finished the Picentines of Asculum cheered and danced, heaped the various bits of every Roman slain in the theater upon a pile in the forum, and ran through the streets dragging those Romans who had not gone to see the play to their deaths. By nightfall, no Roman citizen or relative of a Roman citizen remained alive within Asculum Picentum. The town shut its massive gates and began to discuss how it would both provision itself and survive. No one regretted the madness of a moment; it was rather as if the action had finally lanced a huge festering abscess of hate within them, and now they could enjoy that hate, vow never again to tolerate Rome.

Four days after the events at Asculum Picentum, the news of them reached Rome. The two Roman actors had escaped the stage and hidden, shivering in terror, watching the ghastly slaughter in the theater, then had fled the city just before the gates were closed. It took them four days to get to Rome, walking part of the way, begging seats in mule carts and pillion rides on horses, too terrified to say a word about Asculum Picentum until they reached safety. As they were actors, the tale lost nothing in its retelling; all of Rome recoiled in incredulous horror, the Senate donned mourning for its lost praetor, and the

Vestal Virgins made an offering for Fonteius, the father of their newest little acquisition.

If anything about the massacre could be termed fortunate, it was perhaps that the elections in Rome had already taken place, thus sparing the Senate at least the ordeal of having to cope with Philippus unaided. Lucius Julius Caesar and Publius Rutilius Lupus were the new consuls, a good man in Caesar tied by economic necessity to a conceited but rich inadequacy like Lupus. It was another eight-praetor year, with the usual mixture of patrician and plebeian, competent and incompetent, getting in; the new consul Lucius Julius Caesar's cross-eyed younger brother, Caesar Strabo, was a curule aedile. The quaestors included none other than Quintus Sertorius, whose winning of the Grass Crown in Spain would procure him any and every office. Gaius Marius, the cousin of his mother, had already ensured that Sertorius possessed the senatorial census; when a new pair of censors were elected, he was sure to be admitted to the Senate. Of law courts he may have seen little, but for such a young man, his name was quite famous, and he had that magical appeal to the general populace Gaius Marius also possessed.

Among an unusually impressive collection of tribunes of the plebs was one hideous name—Quintus Varius Severus Hybrida Sucronensis, already vowing that the moment the new college entered office, he would see that those who had supported citizenship for Italy would pay, from the highest to the lowest. When the news of the massacre at Asculum Picentum arrived, it provided Varius with wonderful ammunition; not yet in office, he canvassed tirelessly among the knights and Forum frequenters for support of his program of vengeance in the Plebeian Assembly. For the Senate, exasperated by the harping reproaches of Philippus and Caepio, the old year could not wind down quickly enough.

Then hard on the heels of the news from Asculum Picentum came a deputation of twenty Italian noblemen from the new capital of Italica, though they said nothing about Italica or Italia; they simply demanded an audience with the Senate on the matter of granting the franchise to every man south of—not the Arnus and the Rubico, but—the Padus in Italian Gaul! That new boundary had been shrewdly calculated to antagonize everyone in Rome from Senate to Head Count, for the leaders of the new nation Italia no longer wanted to be enfranchised. They wanted war.

Closeted with the delegation in the Senaculum, a little building adjacent to the temple of Concord, Marcus Aemilius Scaurus Princeps Senatus attempted to deal with this piece of blatant impudence. A loyal supporter of Drusus, after the death of Drusus he saw no point in continuing to press for a general enfranchisement; he liked being alive.

"You may tell your masters that nothing can be negotiated until full reparation for Asculum Picentum has been made," said Scaurus disdainfully. "The Senate will not see you."

"Asculum Picentum is simply steely evidence of how strongly all Italy feels," said the leader of the delegation, Publius Vettius Scato of the Marsi. "It is not in our power to demand anything of Asculum Picentum, anyway. That decision belongs to the Picentes."

"That decision," said Scaurus harshly, "belongs to Rome."

"We ask again that the Senate see us," said Scato.

"The Senate will not see you," said Scaurus, adamant.

Whereupon the twenty men turned to leave, none looking at all downcast, Scaurus noted. Last to go, Scato slipped a rolled document into Scaurus's hand. "Please take this, Marcus Aemilius, on behalf of the Marsi," he said.

Scaurus didn't open the document until he got home, when his scribe, to whom he had entrusted it, gave it back to him. Pulling it apart with some annoyance because he had forgotten it, he began to decipher its contents with growing amazement.

At dawn he summoned a meeting of the Senate, poorly attended because of the short notice; as usual, Philippus and Caepio did not bother to turn up. But Sextus Caesar did, as did the incoming consuls and praetors, all the outgoing tribunes of the plebs and most of the incoming ones—with the conspicuous exception of Varius. The consulars were present; counting heads, Sextus Caesar saw in some relief that he did have a quorum after all.

"I have here," said Scaurus Princeps Senatus, "a document signed by three men of the Marsi—Quintus Poppaedius Silo, who calls himself consul—Publius Vettius Scato, who calls himself praetor—and Lucius Fraucus, who calls himself councillor. I shall read it out to you.

> "To the Senate and People of Rome. We, the elected representatives of the Marsic nation, do hereby on behalf of our people declare that we withdraw from our Allied status with Rome. That we will not pay to Rome any taxes, tithes, duties, or dues which may be demanded of us. That we will not contribute troops to Rome. That we will take back from Rome the town of Alba Fucentia and all its lands. Please regard this as a declaration of war."

The House hummed; Gaius Marius extended his hand for the document, and Scaurus gave it to him. Slowly it went round the ranks of those present, until everyone had seen for himself that it was both genuine and unequivocal.

"It appears that we have a war on our hands," said Marius.

"With the *Marsi*?" asked Ahenobarbus Pontifex Maximus. "I know when I spoke to Silo outside the Colline Gate he *said* it would be war—but the Marsi couldn't defeat us! They don't have enough people to go to war against Rome! Those two legions he had with him would be about as many as the Marsi could scrape up."

"It does seem peculiar," admitted Scaurus.

"Unless," said Sextus Caesar, "there are other Italian nations involved as well."

But that no one would believe, including Marius. The meeting dissolved without any conclusion being reached, save that it would be prudent to keep a closer eye on Italy—only not with another pair of itinerant praetors! Servius Sulpicius Galba, the praetor deputed to investigate "the Italian question" to the south of Rome, had written to say he was on his way back. When he arrived, the

House thought it would be in better case to decide what ought to be done. War with Italy? Perhaps so. But not yet.

"I know that when Marcus Livius was alive, I believed with fervor that war with Italy was just around the corner," said Marius to Scaurus as the meeting broke up, "but now that he's gone, I *cannot* credit it! And I have been asking myself if it was just that way he had. Now—I don't honestly know. Are the Marsi in this alone? Surely they must be! And yet—I never thought of Quintus Poppaedius Silo as a fool."

"I echo everything you have just said, Gaius Marius," Scaurus agreed. "Oh, why didn't I read that paper while Scato was still inside Rome? The gods are toying with us, I feel it in my bones."

Of course the time of year militated against anything outside of Rome occupying senatorial minds, no matter how serious or how puzzling; no one wanted to make decisions when one pair of consuls was almost at the end of their term, and the incoming pair was still feeling their way anent House alliances.

Thus it was that internal affairs preoccupied both Senate and Forum during December; the most trivial incidents, because close at hand and essentially Roman, outweighed the Marsic declaration of war easily. Among the more trivial incidents was the vacant priesthood of Marcus Livius Drusus. Even after so many years, Ahenobarbus Pontifex Maximus still felt he should have been given the place given to Drusus; so he was very quick to put up the name of his elder son, Gnaeus, recently engaged to Cornelia Cinna, the oldest daughter of the patrician Lucius Cornelius Cinna. The pontificate of course belonged to a plebeian, as Drusus had been a plebeian. By the time the nominations were all in, the list of candidates read like a plebeian honor roll. It included Metellus Pius the Piglet, another man existing in a smoldering resentment, as his father's place had gone by election to Gaius Aurelius Cotta. Then at the last moment Scaurus Princeps Senatus stunned everyone by putting up a patrician name—Mamercus Aemilius Lepidus Livianus, the brother of Drusus.

"It's not legal on two counts!" snarled Ahenobarbus Pontifex

Maximus. "Number one, he's a patrician. Number two, he's an Aemilius, and you're already a pontifex, Marcus Aemilius, which means another Aemilius can't belong."

"Rubbish!" said Scaurus roundly. "I'm not nominating him as an adopted Aemilius, but as the blood brother of the dead priest. He's a Livius Drusus, and *I* say he must be nominated."

The College of Pontifices finally agreed that in this situation Mamercus should be accounted a Livius Drusus, and permitted his name to be added to the list of candidates. How fond of Drusus the electors had become was soon obvious; Mamercus carried all seventeen tribes and succeeded to the priesthood of his brother.

More serious—or so it seemed at the time—was the conduct of Quintus Varius Severus Hybrida Sucronensis. When the new College of Tribunes of the Plebs entered office on the tenth day of December, Quintus Varius immediately moved that a law be placed on the tablets to treason-try every man who had been known to support the general enfranchisement of Italy. All nine of his colleagues promptly vetoed even the discussion of such an act. But Varius took his example from Saturninus, filled the Comitia with louts and hirelings, and succeeded in intimidating the rest of the college into withdrawing their vetos. He also succeeded in intimidating all other opposition, with the result that the New Year saw the establishment of a special treason court all of Rome began to call the Varian Commission, empowered to try only those men who had supported enfranchisement of the Italians. Its terms of reference were so vague and flexible that almost anyone could find himself arraigned, its jury composed purely of knights.

"He'll use it to pursue his own enemies—and the enemies of Philippus and Caepio," said Scaurus Princeps Senatus, who made no secret of his opinion. "Wait and see! This is the most disgraceful piece of legislation ever foisted upon us!"

That Scaurus was right Varius demonstrated in the selection of his first victim, the stiff, formal, ultraconservative praetor of five years earlier, Lucius Aurelius Cotta. Half brother of Aurelia on her father's side. Never an ardent proponent of enfranchisement, Cotta had nonetheless swung round to it—along with many others in the Senate—during those days when Drusus had fought so strenuously in the House; one of the most cogent reasons behind Cotta's change of heart was his detestation of Philippus and Caepio. He then made the mistake of cutting Quintus Varius dead.

This oldest Cotta of his generation was an excellent choice for the Varian Commission's first victim; not as high as the consulars, nor as low as the *pedarii*. If Varius gained a conviction, his court would become an instrument of terror for the Senate. The first day's proceedings showed Lucius Cotta all too clearly what his fate was going to be, for the jury impaneled was stuffed with haters of the Senate, and scant notice of the defense's jury challenges was taken by the court president, the enormously powerful knight-plutocrat Titus Pomponius.

"My father is wrong," said young Titus Pomponius, standing in the crowd which had gathered to watch the Varian Commission swing into action.

His auditor was another member of Scaevola the Augur's little band of legal acolytes, Marcus Tullius Cicero, four years his junior in age, forty years his senior in intellect—if not in common sense.

"How do you mean?" asked Cicero, who had gravitated to young Titus Pomponius after the death of Sulla's son. That had been the first real tragedy of Cicero's life; even so many months later, he still found himself mourning and missing his dear dead friend.

"This obsession my father has to get into the Senate," said young Titus Pomponius gloomily. "It eats at him, Marcus Tullius! Not one thing does he do that isn't directed toward the Senate. Including snapping up Quintus Varius's wheedling bait to be president of this court. Of course the invalidation of Marcus Livius Drusus's laws destroyed his certain selection for the Senate, and Quintus Varius has used that to lure him into this. He's been promised that if he does as he's told, he'll get his Senate membership as soon as the new censors are elected."

"But your father's in business," objected Cicero. "He'd have to give it all up except for owning land if he became a senator."

"Oh, don't worry, he would!" said young Titus Pomponius, voice bitter. "Here am I, not quite twenty years old, already doing most of the work in the firm—and scant thanks I get, I can tell you! He's actually *ashamed* of being in business!"

"What has all this got to do with your father's being wrong?" asked Cicero.

"Everything, you dunce!" said young Titus. "He wants to get into the Senate! But he's wrong to want that. He's a knight, and one of Rome's ten most important knights, at that. I can see nothing wrong with being one of Rome's ten most important knights. He has the Public Horse—which he will pass on to me—everyone asks his advice, he's a great power in the Comitia, and a consultant to the tribunes of the Treasury. Yet what does he want? To be a senator! To be one of those fools in the back row who never even get a chance to speak, let alone speak well!"

"You mean he's a social climber," said Cicero. "Well, I can see nothing wrong with that. So am I."

"My father is already socially the best, Marcus Tullius! By birth and by wealth. The Pomponii are very closely related right down the generations to the Caecilii of the Pilius branch, and you can't do better than that without being a patrician." Born to the highest knightly nobility, young Titus went on without realizing how his words would hurt: he said, "I can understand your being a social climber, Marcus Tullius. When you get into the Senate you'll be a New Man, and if you attain the consulship, you'll ennoble your family. Which means you'll have to cultivate every famous man you possibly can, plebeian and patrician. Whereas my father's becoming a *pedarius* senator would actually be a backward step."

"Getting into the Senate is never a backward step!" said Cicero, smarting. Young Titus's words contained additional sting these days; Cicero had come to understand that the moment he said he came from Arpinum, he was immediately smeared with a little of the same ordure reserved for Arpinum's most famous citizen, Gaius Marius. If Gaius Marius was an Italian with no Greek, what else could Marcus Tullius Cicero be than a better-educated version of Gaius Marius? The Tullii Cicerones had never been over-fond of the Marii, despite the occasional marriage between the clans: but since arriving in Rome, young Marcus Tullius Cicero had learned to loathe Gaius Marius. And to loathe his birthplace.

"Anyway," said young Titus Pomponius, "when I am *paterfamilias,* I am going to be perfectly content with my knight's lot. If the censors both get down on their knees to me, they'll beg in vain! For I swear to you, Marcus Tullius, that I will never, never, never enter the Senate!"

In the meantime, Lucius Cotta's despair was becoming more evident. It was therefore no surprise when the court reconvened the next day to learn that Lucius Aurelius Cotta had chosen to go into voluntary exile rather than wait for an inevitable verdict of *CONDEMNO.* This ploy at least enabled a man to gather most of his assets and take them with him into exile; if he waited and was convicted, his assets would be confiscated by the court, and the ensuing exile harder to bear because of lack of funds.

It was a bad time to have to liquidate capital assets, for, while the Senate vacillated in a mood of sheer disbelief and the Comitia were absorbed in the doings of Quintus Varius, the business community sniffed something nasty in the wind, and took appropriate measures. Money went into immediate hiding, shares tottered, the smaller companies held emergency meetings. Manufacturers and importers of luxury goods debated the possibility of strict sumptuary laws should a war ensue, and concocted schemes for switching their lines of goods to war essentials.

Nothing happened to convince the Senate that the Marsic declaration of war was sincere; no word came of an army on the march, no word came of any kind of martial preparations in any Italian nation. The only worrying thing, perhaps, was that Servius Sulpicius Galba, the praetor delegated to look into matters in the south of the peninsula, did not come to Rome. Instead, he had lapsed into complete silence.

The Varian Commission gathered impetus. Lucius Calpurnius

Bestia was convicted and sent into exile, his property confiscated; so was Lucius Memmius, who went to Delos. Halfway through January Antonius Orator was arraigned, but gave such a magnificent speech—and was so cheered by the Forum crowds—that the jury prudently decided to acquit him. Angry at this fickle conduct, Quintus Varius retaliated by charging Marcus Aemilius Scaurus Princeps Senatus with treason.

Scaurus appeared totally unattended to answer the indictment, clad in his *toga praetexta* and positively radiating the awesome aura of his *dignitas* and *auctoritas*. Impassively he listened to Quintus Varius (who was conducting every prosecution himself) reel off the long list of his wrongdoings in regard to the Italians. When Varius finally stopped speaking, Scaurus snorted. He turned not to face the jury, but to face the crowd.

"Did you hear that, *Quirites*?" he thundered. "A half-breed upstart from Sucro in Spain accuses Scaurus, Princeps Senatus, of treason! Scaurus denies the charge! Whom do you believe?"

"Scaurus, Scaurus, Scaurus!" chanted the crowd. Then the jury joined in, and finally left its seats to chair Scaurus on its shoulders in a triumphant parade all around the lower Forum.

"The fool!" said Marius to Scaurus afterward. "Did he really think he could convict *you* of treason? Did the knights think it?"

"After the knights succeeded in convicting poor Publius Rutilius, I imagine they thought they could convict anyone if only they were given the chance," said Scaurus, adjusting his toga, which had become a little disorganized during his ride.

"Varius should have started his campaign against the more formidable consulars with me, not you," said Marius. "When Marcus Antonius got off, there was a strong message in it. A message now well and truly driven home! I predict Varius will suspend his activities for a few weeks, then start again—but with less august victims. Bestia doesn't matter, everyone knows him for a wolfshead. And poor Lucius Cotta didn't have enough clout. Oh, the Aurelii Cottae are powerful, but they don't like Lucius—they like the boys his uncle Marcus Cotta bred from Rutilia." Marius paused, eyebrows dancing wildly. "Of course, Varius's *real* disadvantage is that he's not a Roman. You are. I am. He's not. He doesn't understand."

Scaurus refused to rise to the bait. "Nor do Philippus and Caepio understand," he said scornfully.

The month which Silo and Mutilus had allowed for mobilization was ample. Yet at the end of it, not one Italian army marched. There were two reasons. One, Mutilus could see; the other drove him to the brink of despair. Dickering with the leaders of Etruria and Umbria proceeded at a snail's pace, and nobody in the war council or the grand council wanted to start aggression before they had an idea what the results might be; that, Mutilus could see. But there was also a curious reluctance to be the first to march—not from fear, rather from an ingrained, centuries-old awe of Rome; and that, Mutilus deplored.

"Let us wait until Rome makes the first move," said Silo in the war council.

"Let us wait until Rome makes the first move," said Lucius Fraucus in the grand council.

When he learned that the Marsi had delivered a declaration of war to the Senate, Mutilus had been furious, thinking that Rome would mobilize at once. But Silo had remained unrepentant.

"It's the proper thing to do," he maintained. "There are laws governing war, just as there are laws governing every aspect of men's conduct. Rome cannot say she wasn't warned."

And, following that, nothing Mutilus could say or do served to budge his fellow Italian leaders from their decision that Rome must be seen to be the first aggressor.

"If we marched now, we'd murder them!" Mutilus cried in the war council, even as his deputy Gaius Trebatius was saying the same thing in the grand council. "Surely you can see that the more time we give Rome to ready herself, the less likely we are to win this conflict!

The fact that no one in Rome is taking any notice of us is our greatest advantage! We *must* march! We must march tomorrow! If we delay, we'll lose!"

But all the others solemnly shook their heads save Marius Egnatius, Mutilus's fellow Samnite on the war council; even Silo refused, though he admitted the logic of it.

"It wouldn't be right" was the answer the Samnites kept getting, no matter how they pressed.

The massacre at Asculum Picentum made no impression either; Gaius Vidacilius of the Picentes refused to send a garrison force to the city to fend off Roman reprisals—Roman reprisals, he said, were proving long in coming, and might not come at all.

"We must march!" moaned Mutilus again and again. "The farmers are all saying it won't be much of a winter, so there's no reason to delay until spring! We *must* march!"

But no one wanted to march, and no one did march.

Thus it was that the first stirrings of revolt occurred among the Samnites. No one on either side considered Asculum Picentum evidence of revolt; the town had simply been tried beyond its endurance, and retaliated. Whereas, having simmered for generations, the huge Samnite population in Campania, inextricably mixed with Romans and Latins, began spontaneously to boil.

Servius Sulpicius Galba brought the first concrete news of it to Rome when he arrived, disheveled and minus his escort, during the month of February.

The new senior consul, Lucius Julius Caesar, summoned the Senate at once to listen to Galba's report.

"I've been a prisoner in Nola for six weeks," said Galba to a quiet House. "I had just sent off my note informing you that I was on my way home when I arrived in Nola. I hadn't originally intended to visit Nola, but since I was in the vicinity and Nola does have a large Samnite population, I decided at the last moment to go there. I stayed with an old lady who was my mother's best friend—a Roman, of course. And she informed me that there were peculiar things happening in Nola—all of a sudden, it was impossible for

Romans and Latins to obtain service, goods in the market, even food! Her servants were obliged to take a cart to Acerrae for staples. When I moved through the town with my lictors and troopers I was booed and hissed continuously—yet it was never possible to see which men or women were responsible."

Galba moved unhappily, aware that the tale of his adventures was not an inspiring one. "During the night after I arrived in Nola, the Samnites shut the city gates and took the place over completely. Every Roman and Latin was taken prisoner and held under restraint in their houses. Including my lictors, my troopers, and my clerks. I found myself locked into my hostess's house, with a Samnite guard at front door and back gate. And there I remained until three days ago, when my hostess managed to lure the guards at the back gate away for long enough to enable me to slip out. Dressed as a Samnite merchant, I escaped through the city gates before the hunt got up."

Scaurus leaned forward. "Did you see anyone of authority during your time as a prisoner, Servius Sulpicius?"

"No one," said Galba. "I had some conversation with the men on guard at the front door, that's all."

"What did they have to say?"

"Only that Samnium was in revolt, Marcus Aemilius. I had no way to ascertain the truth of this, so when I did manage to escape I wasted a whole day hiding from anyone I saw in the distance who looked like a Samnite. It was only when I reached Capua that I found no one knew of this revolt, at least in that part of Campania. In fact, it seems no one knew what was going on in Nola! During the day the Samnite Nolans kept one gate open and pretended nothing was wrong. So when I told those in Capua what had happened to me, they were amazed. And alarmed, I add! The *duumviri* of Capua have asked me to forward instructions to them from the Senate."

"Were you fed during your captivity? What about your hostess? Was she permitted to shop in Acerrae?" asked Scaurus.

"Of food, there was little. My hostess was allowed to shop in

Nola, but only for limited provisions at extortionate prices. No one Latin or Roman was allowed out of the town," said Galba.

This time the Senate was full; if the court of Varius had done nothing else, it had succeeded in uniting senatorial ranks—and driven the Senate to hunger for something dramatic enough to remove emphasis from the Varian Commission.

"May I speak?" asked Gaius Marius.

"*If* no one senior to you wants to speak," said the junior consul, Publius Rutilius Lupus, coldly; he held the *fasces* during February, and was no partisan of Marius's.

No one asked to speak ahead of Marius.

"If Nola has imprisoned its Roman and Latin citizens under circumstances of privation, then there can be no doubt of it—Nola is in revolt against Rome. Consider for a moment: in June of last year the Senate delegated two of its praetors to enquire into what our esteemed consular Quintus Lutatius called 'the Italian question.' Nearly three months ago the praetor Quintus Servilius was murdered in Asculum Picentum, along with every Roman citizen in the town. Nearly two months ago the praetor Servius Sulpicius was captured and imprisoned in Nola, along with every Roman citizen in the town.

"Two praetors, one north and one south, and two atrocious incidents, one north and one south. The *whole* of Italy—even in its most backward parts!—knows and understands the significance, the importance, of the Roman praetor. Yet, Conscript Fathers, in the one case, murder was done. In the other case, a long-term detention was enforced. That we do not know the ultimate outcome of Servius Sulpicius's detention is purely due to the lucky circumstance of his escaping. However, it would appear to me that Servius Sulpicius too would have died. Two praetors of Rome, each with a proconsular imperium! Attacked, it would seem, without fear of reprisal. And what does that tell me? Just one thing, my fellow senators! It tells me that Asculum Picentum and Nola were emboldened to do what they did feeling secure *against* reprisals! In other words, both Asculum Picentum and Nola are expecting a state of war to exist between Rome and their parts of Italy before Rome can retaliate."

The House was sitting up straight now, and hanging on Marius's every word. Pausing, he looked from one face to another, searching for particular men; Lucius Cornelius Sulla, for instance, whose eyes were glistening; and Quintus Lutatius Catulus Caesar, whose face registered a curious awe.

"I have been guilty of the same crime as the rest of you, Conscript Fathers. After Marcus Livius Drusus died I had no one to tell me there would be war. I began to think him wrong. When nothing more transpired after the march of the Marsian Silo upon Rome, I too began to deem it yet one more trick to gain the citizenship. When the Marsian delegate gave our Princeps Senatus a declaration of war, I dismissed it because it came from only one Italian nation, though eight nations were represented in the delegation. And—I admit it freely!—I could not believe in my heart that any Italian nation in this day and age would actually go to war against us."

He paced up the floor until he stood in front of the closed doors, where he could see the entire House. "What Servius Sulpicius has told us today changes everything, and sheds new light upon the events at Asculum Picentum as well. Asculum is a town of the Picentes. Nola is a town of the Campanian Samnites. Neither is a Roman or a Latin colony. I think we must now assume that the Marsi, the Picentes, and the Samnites are leagued together against Rome. It may be that all eight nations who sent us that deputation some time ago are party to this league. It may be, I think, that in giving our Leader of the House a formal declaration of war, the Marsi were warning us of that event. Whereas the other seven nations did not care enough about us to warn us. Marcus Livius Drusus said time and time again that the Italian Allies were on the brink of war. I now believe him—except that I think the Italian Allies have stepped over the brink."

"You do genuinely believe a state of war exists?" asked Ahenobarbus Pontifex Maximus.

"I do, Gnaeus Domitius."

"Continue, Gaius Marius," said Scaurus. "I would like to hear you out before I speak."

"I have little else to say, Marcus Aemilius. Except that we must mobilize, and very quickly. That we must endeavor to find out the extent of the league against us. That we must move whatever troops we have under arms to protect our roads and our access to Campania. That we must discover how the Latins feel about us, and how our colony towns in hostile regions are going to fare if war does commence. As you know, I have huge lands in Etruria, as does Quintus Caecilius Metellus Pius, and some others among the various Caecilii. Quintus Servilius Caepio has equally large amounts of land in Umbria. And Gnaeus Pompeius Strabo and Quintus Pompeius Rufus dominate northern Picenum. For that reason, I think we might hold Etruria, Umbria, and northern Picenum in our camp—*if* we move immediately to negotiate with their local leaders. In the matter of northern Picenum, however, their local leaders are sitting here in the House today."

Marius inclined his head toward Scaurus Princeps Senatus. "It goes without saying that I personally am Rome's to command."

Scaurus rose to his feet. "I agree absolutely with everything Gaius Marius has said, Conscript Fathers. We cannot afford to waste time. And though I am aware that this is the month of February, I move that the *fasces* be taken off the junior consul and given to the senior consul. It is the senior consul who must lead us in all matters as serious as this."

Rutilius Lupus sat up indignantly, but his popularity within the House was small; though he insisted upon a formal division, it went against him by a large majority. He was forced, fuming, to yield the place of first prominence to Lucius Julius Caesar, the senior consul. Lupus's friend Caepio was present, but his two other friends Philippus and Quintus Varius were not.

A delighted Lucius Julius Caesar soon demonstrated that the trust of the Leader of the House was not misplaced; within the space of that same day, the major decisions were taken. Both the consuls would take the field, leaving the urban praetor, Lucius Cornelius Cinna, to govern Rome. The provinces were got out of the way first, as this new crisis could not but alter the dispositions made earlier. As already arranged, Sentius would stay in Macedonia, and the Spanish governors too remained undisturbed. Lucius Lucilius would go to govern Asia Province. But, to give King Mithridates no opportunities while Rome was embroiled in a domestic furor, Publius Servilius Vatia was now sent to Cilicia to make sure that part of Anatolia stayed quiet. And—most important of all—the consular Gaius Coelius Caldus was given a special governorship, Gaul-across-the-Alps and Italian Gaul combined.

"For it is clear," said Lucius Julius Caesar, "that if Italy is in revolt, we will not find sufficient fresh troops among those in the peninsula who remain faithful to us. Italian Gaul has many Latin and a few Roman colonies. Gaius Coelius will quarter himself in Italian Gaul and recruit and train soldiers for us."

"If I might suggest," rumbled Gaius Marius, "I would like to see the quaestor Quintus Sertorius go with Gaius Coelius. His duties are fiscal this year, and he is not yet a member of the Senate. But, as I'm sure all of us present here know, Quintus Sertorius is a true Military Man. Let him have his experience of the *fiscus* in as military a fashion as he can."

"Agreed," said Lucius Caesar instantly.

There were of course enormous financial problems to struggle with. The Treasury was solvent and had resources beyond normal demand to hand, but—

"If this war is wider than we currently think, or more protracted than we currently think, we will need more money than we have," said Lucius Caesar. "I would rather we acted now than later. I suggest that we reimpose direct taxation upon all Roman citizens and holders of the Latin Rights."

That, of course, provoked furious opposition from many quarters of the House, but Antonius Orator delivered a very fine speech, as did Scaurus Princeps Senatus, and in the end the measure was agreed to. The *tributum* had never been levied constantly, only in times of need; after the conquest of Perseus of Macedonia by the great Aemilius Paullus, it had been abolished and replaced by a *tributum* levied upon non-Romans.

"If we are required to keep more than six legions in the field, our foreign income will not be enough," said the chief tribune of the Treasury. "The entire burden of arming them, feeding them, paying them, and keeping them in the field will now fall upon Rome and Rome's Treasury."

"Goodbye, Italian Allies!" said Catulus Caesar savagely.

"Given that we might have to keep—say, ten to fifteen legions in the field—what should the *tributum* be fixed at?" asked Lucius Caesar, disliking this part of his command.

The chief tribune of the Treasury and his clerical cohort went into a huddle which lasted for some time, then:

"One percent of a man's census worth" was the answer.

"The Head Count get out of it as usual!" shouted Caepio.

"The Head Count," said Marius with heavy irony, "are likely to be doing most of the fighting, Quintus Servilius!"

"While we are on financial matters," said Lucius Julius Caesar, ignoring this exchange, "we had best depute some of our more senior members to look after army supplies, particularly in the matter of armor and weapons. Normally the *praefectus fabrum* takes care of these things, but at this moment we have no real idea of how our legions will be distributed—nor how many we're likely to need. I think it necessary that the Senate look after army supplies, at least for the present. We have four veteran legions under arms in Capua, and two more legions being recruited and trained there. All were destined for service in the provinces, but that is now out of the question. Whatever troops the provinces have at the moment will have to suffice."

"Lucius Julius," said Caepio, "this is absolutely ridiculous! On no more evidence than two incidents in two cities, we're sitting here reimposing the *tributum*, talking about putting fifteen legions into the field, deputing senators to organize the buying of thousands upon thousands of mail-shirts and swords and all the rest, sending men to govern provinces we don't even officially call provinces—next, you'll be proposing to call up every male Roman or Latin citizen under thirty-five!"

"I will indeed," said Lucius Caesar cordially. "However, my

dear Quintus Servilius, you won't have to worry—you're well over thirty-five." He paused, then added, "In years, at least."

"It seems to me," said Catulus Caesar haughtily, "that Quintus Servilius *might*—I say only, might!—have a point. Surely we should content ourselves with what men we have under the eagles at the moment, and make further preparations as we go—and as the evidence of a massive insurrection materializes—or does *not*."

"When our soldiers are needed, Quintus Lutatius, they must be fit to fight as well as outfitted to fight!" said Scaurus testily. "They must be already trained." He turned his head to the man who sat on his right. "Gaius Marius, how long does it take to turn a raw recruit into a good soldier?"

"Fit to send into battle—one hundred days. At which point no man is a good soldier, Marcus Aemilius. It takes his first battle to make that of him," said Marius.

"Can it be done in less than one hundred days?"

"It can—if you have good raw material and better than average training centurions."

"Then we'd best find better than average training centurions," said Scaurus grimly.

"I suggest we get back to the matter in hand," said Lucius Caesar firmly. "We were talking about a senatorial *praefectus fabrum* to organize the equipping and outfitting of the legions we do not as yet possess. It would seem to me that we should nominate several names for the most senior job, then let the man elected choose his own staff—senatorial staff, I mean. I suggest we nominate only men who, for one reason or another, are not suited for the field. May I hear some names, please?"

The job went to the son of Gaius Cassius's senior legate, who had died at Burdigala in the German ambush—Lucius Calpurnius Piso Caesoninus. A victim of that strange disease which preyed upon children in summer, Piso had a badly wasted left leg, which negated military service. Married to the daughter of Publius Rutilius Rufus, now in exile in Smyrna, Piso was an intelligent man who had suffered greatly due to the premature death of his father, especially where money was concerned. At the news that he was to be in charge of all military purchasing, and could select his own staff, his eyes glistened. If he couldn't do a good job for Rome and fill his own empty purse at one and the same time, then he deserved to dwindle into obscurity! But, sitting smiling quietly, he was sure that he was equal to both tasks.

"Now we come to the commands and the dispositions," said Lucius Caesar; he was beginning to tire, but had no intention of concluding the meeting before this last subject was aired.

"How do we best organize ourselves?" he asked.

By rights he should have addressed that question directly to Gaius Marius. But he was no admirer of Marius, and felt, besides, that between his stroke and his age Marius was not the man he used to be. Marius had also taken the floor first; he had had his say, surely. Lucius Caesar's eyes roamed over the faces of the men on the tiers of either side, looking, wondering; and so, having asked how they might best organize themselves, he then put a second query too quickly on the heels of the first to permit Marius's answering.

"Lucius Cornelius cognominated Sulla, I would like to hear your opinion," said the senior consul, careful to speak clearly; the urban praetor was also a Lucius Cornelius, cog-nominated Cinna.

To be thus singled out startled Sulla, but he was ready to answer nonetheless. "If our enemies are the eight nations who sent that deputation to see us, then the chances are that we'll be assailed on two fronts—from the east along the Via Salaria and the Via Valeria with its two branches—and to our south, where Samnite influence crosses all the way from the Adriatic to the Tuscan at Crater Bay. To take the south first, if the Apuli, the Lucani, and the Venusini join the Samnites, the Hirpini, and the Frentani, then the south becomes a definite and ominous theater of war by itself. We can call the second theater of war by either of two names—a northern theater, meaning territories to the north and east of Rome, or a central theater, meaning territories to the north and east of Rome. The Marsi, the Paeligni, the Marrucini, the Vestini, and the Picentes are the nations involved in this central or northern theater. You will note that for the present moment I do not bring Etruria, Umbria, or northern Picenum into the discussion."

Sulla drew a breath, hurried on while it all glowed like crystal in his mind. "In the south, our enemies will do their utmost to cut us off from Brundisium, Tarentum, and Rhegium. In the center or north, our enemies will attempt to cut us off from Italian Gaul, certainly along the Via Flaminia, possibly also the Via Cassia. If they should succeed, then our only access to Italian Gaul would be along the Via Aurelia and the Via Aemilia Scauri to Dertona, and thence to Placentia."

Lucius Caesar interrupted. "Step down to the floor, Lucius Cornelius cognominated Sulla."

Down Sulla came, with a ghost of a wink for Marius; it gave him little joy to be filching this analysis from the Old Master. That he did so at all was a complicated matter—a combination of bitter resentment that Marius still had his son, umbrage that when he came back from Cilicia no one in the House including Marius had invited him to make a full report on his activities in the East, and a lightning understanding of the fact that if he spoke well at this moment, he would go very far, very fast. Too bad, Gaius Marius, he thought. I don't *want* to hurt you, but I'd do it every time anyway.

"I think," he went on from the floor, "that we'll need both consuls in the field, just as Lucius Julius suggested. One consul will have to go south because of Capua, which is vital to us. If we should lose Capua, then we lose our best training facilities as well as a town superbly experienced in aiding soldier-training and soldier-supplying. There will, of course, have to be a consular chief of training and recruiting in Capua itself, aside from the consul commanding in the field. Whoever the consul is to go south will have to take everything the Samnites and their allies throw at him. What the Samnites will attempt to do is to drive west through their old haunts around Acerrae and Nola toward the seaports on the south side of Crater Bay. Stabiae, Salernum, Surrentum, Pompeii, and Herculaneum. If they can capture any or all of those, then they have port facilities on the Tuscan Sea better by far than any ports on the Adriatic north of Brundisium. *And* they will have to cut us off from the far south."

Sulla was not a great speaker, for his training in rhetoric had been minimal, and his career in the House mostly spent out of it in one war or another. But this wasn't oratory. All this needed was good plain speaking.

"The northern or central theater is more difficult. We must presume that all the lands between northern Picenum and Apulia including the Apennine highlands are in enemy hands. Here, the Apennines themselves are our greatest obstacle. If we are to hold on to Etruria and Umbria, then we must make a good showing against these Italian peoples from the very start of our campaign. If we do not, Etruria and Umbria will go over to the enemy, we will lose our roads and Italian Gaul. One consul will have to command in this theater."

"Surely we should have one overall commander," said Scaurus.

"We cannot, Princeps Senatus. Our own lands separate the two theaters I have described," said Sulla firmly. "Latium is long and runs into northern Campania, which is the half of Campania we're more likely to find loyal to us. I doubt southern Campania will be loyal if the insurgents win any battles at all, it's too riddled with Samnites and Hirpini. Look at Nola, already. East of Latium, the Apennines are impossible, and we have the Pomptine Marshes besides. One overall commander would have to shuttle desperately between two widely separated areas of conflict, and he couldn't do it quickly enough to keep a proper eye on both. Truly, we will be fighting on two separate fronts! If not three. The south can possibly be run as one campaign because the Apennines are at their lowest where Samnium, Apulia, and Campania join. However, in the northern or central theater it's highly likely there will be both a northern *and* a central theater. Thank the Apennines for this, as they are at their highest. The lands of the Marsi, the Paeligni, and possibly the Marrucini form a separate theater from the Picentes and the Vestini. I don't see how we can contain all the Italians by fighting purely in the center. It's probably going to be necessary to send an army into the rebellious parts of Picenum through Umbria and northern Picenum, bringing it down on the Adriatic side of the mountains. In the meantime, we'll have to drive east of Rome into the lands of the Marsi and Paeligni."

Sulla paused; he couldn't help it, yet he hated himself for this weakness. How was Gaius Marius feeling? If he didn't like what Sulla was saying, then here was his opportunity to say so. And Gaius Marius spoke. Sulla tensed.

"Please go on, Lucius Cornelius," the Old Master said. "So far, I couldn't do better myself."

His pale eyes flashed, a faint smile grew at the corners of Sulla's mouth, then vanished. He shrugged. "I think that's all, really. And bear in mind that it's predicated on an insurrection involving at least eight Italian nations. I don't think it's my duty to indicate who goes where. However, I would say that I feel those who are sent to the north-central theater in particular ought to have many clients in the area. If, for instance, Gnaeus Pompeius Strabo were to maneuver in Picenum, he already has a base of power there, and thousands of clients. The same might be said of Quintus Pompeius Rufus, though on a lesser scale, I know. In Etruria, Gaius Marius is a great landowner, again with thousands of clients. As is true of the Caecilii Metelli. In Umbria, Quintus Servilius Caepio reigns supreme. If these men were connected to the northern or central theater, it would be a help."

Sulla bowed his head to Lucius Julius Caesar in the chair, and returned to his place amid murmurs of (he thought, anyway) admiration. He had been asked for his opinion ahead of anyone else in the House, and that, on such an occasion, was a huge leap into prominence. Unbelievable! Oh, was it possible he was on his way at last?

"We must all thank Lucius Cornelius Sulla for that very crisp and thoughtful statement of the facts," said Lucius Caesar, smiling at Sulla in a way that promised further distinction. "For myself, I agree with him. But how says the House? Does anyone have other or different ideas?"

It appeared no one had.

Scaurus Princeps Senatus cleared his throat gruffly. "You must make your dispositions, Lucius Julius," he said. "If it does not displease the Conscript Fathers, I would only say that I myself would prefer to remain in Rome."

"I think you will be needed in Rome, with both her consuls out of the city," said Lucius Caesar graciously. "The Leader of the House will prove immensely valuable to our good urban praetor, Lucius Cornelius cognominated Cinna." He glanced sideways at his colleague, Lupus. "Publius Rutilius Lupus, would you be willing to take the burden of command to the north and center of Rome?" he asked. "As senior consul, I think it essential that I command in the theater containing Capua."

Lupus glowed, swelled. "I will assume the burden with great pleasure, Lucius Julius."

"Then, if the House has no objections, I will command in Campania. As my chief legate, I choose Lucius Cornelius cognominated Sulla. To command in Capua itself and supervise all activity there, I appoint the consular Quintus Lutatius Catulus Caesar. As my other senior legates I will have Publius Licinius Crassus, Titus Didius, and Servius Sulpicius Galba," said Lucius Caesar. "My colleague Publius Rutilius Lupus, whom will you have?"

"Gnaeus Pompeius Strabo, Sextus Julius Caesar, Quintus Servilius Caepio, and Lucius Porcius Cato Licinianus," said Lupus loudly.

There was a sudden silence, not broken for what seemed an enormous length of time. *Someone* must break it! thought Sulla, and opened his mouth without meaning to, without wanting to.

"What about Gaius Marius?" he asked harshly.

Lucius Caesar blinked. "I must confess that I didn't choose Gaius Marius because, bearing in mind what you said, Lucius Sulla, I thought naturally that Publius Rutilius my colleague would want Gaius Marius!"

"Well, I don't want him!" said Lupus. "I'm not going to have him foisted on me, either! Let him stay in Rome with all the others of his age and infirmity. He's too old and sick for war."

At which point Sextus Julius Caesar rose to his feet. "May I speak, senior consul?" he asked.

"Please do, Sextus Julius."

"I am not old," said Sextus Caesar huskily, "but I am a sick man, as everyone in this House knows. I wheeze. I have had more than adequate military experience in my younger days, mostly with Gaius Marius in Africa and in the Gauls against the Germans. I also served at Arausio, where my malady undoubtedly saved my life. However, with winter coming on, I will prove of little use in an Apennine campaign. I am older, and my chest is weak. I will of course do my duty. I am a Roman of a great family. But in all of this, no one has yet mentioned cavalry. We will need cavalry. I would like to ask this House to excuse me duty as a commander in the field among the mountains. Instead, let me gather a fleet of transports and spend the colder months gathering cavalry from Numidia, from Gaul-across-the-Alps, and from Thrace. I can also enlist Roman citizens living abroad in our infantry. It is a job I feel myself fitted for. And then when I return, I will gladly take on any field command you might care to suggest." He cleared his throat, began slightly to wheeze. "To take my place as a legate, I would ask the House to consider Gaius Marius."

"Hoh! Brothers-in-law!" cried Lupus, jumping to his feet. "It won't work, Sextus Julius, it won't work! After listening to you for years, it seems to me that yours is a most convenient ailment! It comes and it goes on order! I can do it too—listen!" Lupus began to draw in noisy breaths.

"You may have grown tired of hearing me wheeze, Publius Lupus, but you haven't *listened*," said Sextus Caesar gently. "I don't make a noise when I inhale. I make it when I exhale."

"I don't care when you make your wretched noises!" shouted Lupus. "You're not avoiding your duty with me any more than I'll take Gaius Marius in your place!"

"One moment, if you please," said Scaurus Princeps Senatus, rising to his feet. "*I* have something to say about this." He looked at Lupus on the dais with much the same expression on his face as he had worn when Varius accused him of treason. "You are not one of my best-loved people, Publius Lupus! In fact, it pains me deeply that you happen to have the same name as my dear friend,

Publius Rutilius cognominated Rufus. Well, you may be relations, but there's absolutely no relationship between you! Rufus the Red was one of this House's chief adornments, very sorely missed. Lupus the Wolf is one of this House's most pernicious ulcers, very sore!"

"You're insulting me!" gasped Lupus. "You can't! I'm consul!"

"I am the Leader of the House, Publius Wolf Man, and I think at my age I have proved beyond a shadow of a doubt that I can do what I like—because when I do something, Publius Wolf Man, I have good reason and Rome's best interests at heart! Now, you miserable little worm, sit there and pull your head in! And I do not mean that part of your anatomy attached to your neck! Who *do* you think you are? You're only sitting in that particular chair because you had enough money to bribe the electorate!"

Purple with rage, Lupus opened his mouth.

"Don't do it, Lupus!" Scaurus snarled. "Sit there, be quiet!"

Scaurus turned then to Gaius Marius, who sat absolutely straight on his stool; how he felt about his name's being omitted no one present could tell. "Here is a very great man," said Scaurus. "Only the gods know how many times in my life I have cursed him! Only the gods know how many times in my life I have wished he never existed! Only the gods know how many times in my life I have been his worst enemy! But as time drips away faster and faster and wears my life ever thinner, ever frailer, I find myself remembering with affection fewer and fewer men. It is not merely a factor concerned with the increasing imminence of death and dying. It is an accumulation of experience which tells me who is *worth* remembering with affection—and who is not. Some of the men I have loved most, I feel nothing for now. Some of the men I have hated most, I feel everything for now."

Knowing very well that Marius was now looking at him with a twinkle in his eyes, Scaurus carefully avoided looking back; if he did, he knew he'd dissolve into fits of laughter, and this speech was coming from his very spirit as well as his heart. An acute sense of humor could be a wretched nuisance!

"Gaius Marius and I have been through a whole world together," he said, staring at the livid Lupus. "He and I have sat side by side in this House and glared at each other for more years than you, Wolf Man, have worn an adult's toga! We have fought and brawled, we have pushed and pulled. But we have fought together against the enemies of the Republic too. We have gazed down together upon the bodies of men who would have ruined Rome. We have stood shoulder to shoulder. We have laughed together—and we have wept together. I say again! Here is a very great man. A very great *Roman*."

Now Scaurus walked down the floor to the doors, and stood in front of them. "Like Gaius Marius, like Lucius Julius, like Lucius Cornelius Sulla, I am today convinced we face a terrible war. Yesterday I was not convinced. Why the change? Who knows, save the gods? When the established order of things tells us that matters are a certain way because they have been that same certain way for a very long time, we find it hard to alter what we feel, and our feelings cloud our intellects. But then in the smallest scrap of time the scales fall from our eyes, and we see clearly. That has happened to me today. It happened to Gaius Marius today. Probably it happened to most of us here in the House today. A thousand little signs are suddenly visible that yesterday we could not see.

"I elected to remain in Rome because I know I will be of best use to Rome within her body politic. But that is not true of Gaius Marius. Whether—like me!—you have disagreed with him far more often than you have agreed with him, or whether—like Sextus Julius!—you are tied to him by the double bond of fondness as well as marriage, all of you must admit—as I admit!—that in Gaius Marius we have a military talent of an excellence and a breadth of experience far greater than the rest of us put together. I would not care if Gaius Marius was ninety years old and had had *three* strokes! I would still be standing here saying what I am saying now—if the man can put words and ideas together the way he does, then we must use him where he shines the brightest—in the field! Confront your bigotry, Conscript Fathers! Gaius Marius is the same age as I am myself, a mere sixty-seven years, and the single stroke he suffered occurred ten years ago. As your Princeps

Senatus, I say to you adamantly, Gaius Marius must serve as chief legate to Publius Lupus, and put his multiple talents to best use."

No one spoke. No one, it seemed, breathed, even Sextus Caesar. Scaurus sat down beside Marius, with Catulus Caesar on his other side. Lucius Caesar looked at the three of them, then up along the same row toward the doors, where Sulla sat. His eyes met Sulla's; Lucius Caesar became conscious of an accelerated heartbeat. What did Sulla's eyes say? So many things it was not possible to tell.

"Publius Rutilius Lupus, I offer you the opportunity to accept voluntarily Gaius Marius as your senior legate. If you refuse, then I will put the matter to the House in a division."

"All right, all right!" cried Lupus. "But not as my sole senior legate! Let him share the post with Quintus Servilius Caepio!"

Marius threw back his head and roared with laughter. "Done!" he shouted. "The October Horse harnessed to a nag!"

Of course Julia was waiting for Marius, as anxious as only a politician's devoted wife could be. It always fascinated Marius that she seemed to know by instinct when something formidable was going to be discussed in the Senate. He hadn't honestly known himself before he set out for the Curia Hostilia today. Yet she knew!

"Is it war?" she asked.

"Yes."

"Very bad? Only the Marsi, or others as well?"

"I'd say about half of the Italian Allies, probably with more to join. I should have known it all along! But Scaurus was in the right of it. Emotions clouding facts. Drusus knew. Oh, if only he had lived, Julia! If he had lived the Italians would have got their citizenship. And war wouldn't be upon us."

"Marcus Livius died because there are some men who will not let the Italians have the franchise on any terms."

"Yes, you're right. Of course you're right." He changed the subject. "Do you think our cook will have an apoplexy if he's asked to make a sumptuous dinner for a tribe of people tomorrow?"

"I'd say he'll go into an ecstatic frenzy. He's always complaining we don't entertain enough."

"Good! Because I've invited a tribe to dinner tomorrow."

"Why, Gaius Marius?"

He shook his head, scowled. "Perhaps because I have an odd feeling that it will be the last time for many of us, *mea vita. Meum mel.* I love you, Julia."

"And I, you," she said tranquilly. "Now who's for dinner?"

"Quintus Mucius Scaevola, as I hope he's going to be our boy's father-in-law. Marcus Aemilius Scaurus. Lucius Cornelius Sulla. Sextus Julius Caesar. Gaius Julius Caesar. And Lucius Julius Caesar."

Julia was looking a little dismayed. "Wives too?"

"Yes, wives too."

"Oh, dear!"

"What's that for?"

"Scaurus's wife, Dalmatica! And Lucius Cornelius!"

"Oh, all that happened years ago," said Marius scornfully. "We'll put the men on the couches in strict order of rank, then you can put the women where they'll do the least harm. How's that?"

"Well, all right," said Julia, still looking doubtful. "I had better sit Dalmatica and Aurelia facing Lucius and Sextus Julius, Aelia and Licinia opposite the *lectus medius.* Claudia and I will sit looking at Gaius Julius and Lucius Cornelius." She giggled. "I don't *think* Lucius Cornelius has slept with Claudia!"

Marius's eyebrows danced wildly. "You mean to say he's slept with Aurelia after all?"

"No! Honestly, Gaius Marius, sometimes you are exasperating!"

"Sometimes you are," countered Marius. "In all this, where do you plan to put our son? He's nineteen, you know!"

Julia placed Young Marius on the *lectus imus* at its foot, the lowest place a man could occupy. Nor did Young Marius object; the next-lowest man had been an urban praetor, his uncle Gaius Julius, and beyond him was another urban praetor, his uncle Lucius Cornelius. The rest of the men were consulars, with his father holding two more consulships than the rest put together. That was a nice feeling for Young Marius—yet how could he hope to better his father's record? The only way was to become consul at a very early age, even younger than Scipio Africanus or Scipio Aemilianus had been.

Young Marius knew there was a marriage in the wind for him, with Scaevola's girl. He hadn't met Mucia, as she was too young to go to dinner parties, though he had heard she was very pretty. Not surprising; her mother, a Licinia, was still a very beautiful woman. Married now to Metellus Celer, son of Metellus Balearicus. Adultery. Little Mucia had two Caecilius Metellus half brothers. Scaevola had married a second Licinia, less beautiful; it was this Licinia who came with him to the party, and had a wonderful time.

Yet, wrote Lucius Cornelius Sulla to Publius Rutilius Rufus in Smyrna,

> I thought it was a dreadful affair. That it was not an appalling disaster was due entirely to Julia, who made sure every male was accommodated precisely according to protocol, then sat the ladies where they couldn't get into trouble. With the result that all I saw of Aurelia and Scaurus's wife, Dalmatica, was their backs.
>
> I know Scaurus is writing to you, because our letters are going with the same courier, so I won't repeat news of our imminent war with the Italians, nor give you a résumé of the speech Scaurus gave in the House in praise of Gaius Marius—I am quite sure Scaurus has sent you a copy! I will only say that I thought Lupus's action a disgrace, and couldn't sit there silent when I realized Lupus wasn't going to employ our Old Master. What galls me most is that a donkey like Lupus—no wolf, he!—will command a whole theater of war, while Gaius Marius is set to some menial task. The most intriguing factor is the affability with which Gaius Marius greeted the news that he would have to share his

duties as senior legate with Caepio. I wonder what the Arpinate fox plans for that particular donkey? Something nasty, I suspect.

But I have wandered away from the dinner party, and must get back to it, as Scaurus and I have agreed to, one, each write at length, and two, divide the subject matter between us. I inherited the gossip, which isn't at all fair. Scaurus is a bigger gossip than anyone I know except you, Publius Rutilius. Scaevola was there because Gaius Marius is busy arranging for Young Marius to marry Scaevola's daughter by the first of his two Licinias. Mucia (called Mucia Tertia to distinguish her from Scaevola the Augur's two elderly Mucias) is around thirteen now. I feel sorry for the girl. Young Marius is not one of my favorite people. An arrogant, conceited, ambitious pup. Whoever has to deal with him in times to come will have trouble on his hands. Not in the same league as *my* dear dead son.

Publius Rutilius, never having had much family life—as boy or as man, it seems to me—my son was infinitely precious. From the first time I saw him, a naked laughing tot in the nursery, I loved him with all my heart. In him, I found the perfect companion. No matter what I did, he thought it a wonder. On my journey to the East, he added a whole dimension of interest and enthusiasm. It didn't matter that he couldn't give me the advice or opinion a grown man of my own age would have. He always understood. He was always sympathetic. And then he died. So suddenly, so unexpectedly! If one could but have time. I said to myself, if one could but prepare . . . Yet what preparation can a father make for the death of his son?

Since he died, old friend, the world has greyed. I seem not to care the way I did. It is almost a year now, and in one way I suppose I have learned to cope with his absence. But in most ways I never will learn to cope. I am missing a part of the core of myself, there is an emptiness that never can be filled. I find myself, for instance, utterly unable to talk about him to anyone: I hide his name as if he had never been. Because the pain is just too much to bear. As I write of him now, I weep.

But I did not mean to write about my boy either. It is that wretched dinner party supposed to be engaging my pen! Perhaps what prompted thought of him (though I am never without them, I admit it) was the fact that *she* was there. Little Caecilia Metella Dalmatica, the wife of Scaurus. I imagine she is now about twenty-eight years old, or close to that. She married Scaurus at seventeen—at the beginning of the year we beat the Cimbri, as I remember. There is a girl aged ten, and a boy aged about five. Both Scaurus's beyond a shadow of doubt, for I have seen the poor little things—as plain as one of Cato the Censor's farmsteads. Scaurus is already talking about marrying the girl to the son of Scaevola the Augur's great friend, Manius Acilius Glabrio. Though they've been consular for long enough to escape any taint of the *homo novus,* it's not their bloodline is the lure. More the family wealth, almost up there with the Servilii Caepiones, I imagine. But I myself don't care for the Acilii Glabriones, even if this Manius Acilius Glabrio's granddad did side with Gaius Gracchus. Like the rest who sided with Gaius Gracchus, he died for it! Well now. I think that was quite a gossipy anecdote, don't you? You don't? Lamia take you, then!

She is a beautiful woman, Dalmatica. How she bedeviled me that first time I ran for praetor! Do you remember? Amazing to realize that is now almost ten years in the past. I am turned fifty, Publius Rutilius—and no nearer to being consul, it seems to me, than ever I was back in the days of the Subura. One is tempted to speculate what Scaurus did to her as a result of those idiocies nine years ago. But she hides it well. All I got from her when we met in the dining room was a cold *ave* and a frigid smile. She wouldn't meet my eyes. For which I do not blame her. I suppose she was terrified Scaurus would find her conduct reproachable, and acted accordingly. Certainly he could not have done anything other than approve, for once the greetings were over with she sat herself down in her chair with her back to me and never turned round once. Which is more than I can say about our dearest, darlingest Aurelia, who kept all of us dizzy with her turnings and twistings. Well, she's happy again because Gaius Julius is off on another expedition very shortly. He's accompanying his brother, Sextus Julius, on a mission to find Rome cavalry in Africa and far Gaul.

I'm not being malicious, though such is my reputation—and deservedly so, by and large. We both know this lady very well, and I can say nothing to you about her that would come as a surprise. There is considerable love between her and her husband, but it is not a happy or comfortable love. He cramps her style, and she resents that. Knowing he's off again for some months at least, last night she was animated, laughing, lifted out of her normal prosaic self. A mood which did not escape Gaius Julius, next to me on my couch! For, Publius Rutilius, when Aurelia is animated the whole male world is transfixed. Helen of Troy could not have held a candle to her. Imagine if you will the Princeps Senatus behaving like a silly adolescent! Not to mention Scaevola, and even Gaius Marius. Such is the effect she has. None of the other women were plain, several of them were downright beautiful. But even Julia and Dalmatica could not compete with her, a fact Gaius Julius was quick to note. I predict that when they arrived home, there was another quarrel.

Yes indeed, it was a very strange and awkward dinner party. Then why, I hear you ask, was the party given? I am not sure, though I did gain the distinct impression that Gaius Marius had been visited by a presentiment. To the effect that we would never meet again in similar circumstances, those of us in that room. He spoke sadly of you, mourned the fact we could not be complete without you. He spoke sadly of himself. He spoke sadly of Scaurus. Even, it struck me, of Young Marius! As for me—I seemed to inherit the bulk of his sorrow. Though we have moved apart steadily since the death of Julilla, I cannot quite understand this in him. We face what I think is going to be a very difficult war to win, which suggests to me that Gaius Marius and I will work together in all our old accord. The only conclusion I can arrive at with any logic is that he fears for *himself.* Fears he will not survive this war. Fears that, without the massive column of his presence to support us, all of us will suffer.

True to my bargain with Scaurus, I will not speak of the coming war. However, I do have one extremely interesting snippet to offer you that Scaurus can't. I had a visit the other day from Lucius Calpurnius Piso Caesoninus, who has been deputed to organize armaments and supplies for our new legions. Isn't he married to your daughter? Yes, the more I think of it, the more convinced I become that he is. Anyway, he had a curious tale to tell. It is a pity that the Apennines cut us off so completely from Italian Gaul, particularly at its Adriatic end. High time we organized Italian Gaul into a proper province and sent it a governor on a regular basis, and sent another governor regularly to Gaul-across-the-Alps. For the purposes of this war, we have sent a man to govern both the Gauls, but located him in Italian Gaul—the consular Gaius Coelius Caldus. Quintus Sertorius is his quaestor, a most reassuring appointment. There is astonishing military blood in the Marii, I am convinced of it, for Sertorius is a Marius on his mother's side. And a Sabine into the bargain.

But I am straying from my point. Piso Caesoninus made a quick trip to the north to commission arms and armor for Rome. He started in the customary places, Populonia and Pisae. But there he heard stories of new foundry towns in eastern Italian Gaul, run by a firm based in Placentia. So off he went to Placentia. And got nowhere! Oh, he found the company all right. But a closer-mouthed, more furtive lot you couldn't imagine. So he went east to Patavium and Aquileia, where he discovered that there's a whole new industry in that region. He also discovered that these foundry towns have been making arms and armor for the Italian Allies under an exclusive contract for almost *ten years!* Caesoninus thinks it innocent enough. The smiths were offered an exclusive contract, they were paid promptly, and so—they produced! Though the steelworks are all individually owned, the towns themselves were set up by a landlord who owns everything save the businesses. A landlord who, according to the locals, is a Roman senator! And to make the whole thing even murkier, it seems the smiths thought they had been making arms for Rome, and that the man who had put them under contract was a Roman *praefectus fabrum!* When Piso Caesoninus pressed them for a description of this mystery man, they painted a likeness of none other than Quintus Poppaedius Silo of the Marsi!

Now how would Silo have known where to go before we in Rome even knew of this eastern steel industry? And a curious answer has occurred to me—one I'll find difficult to prove, I suspect. Therefore I didn't mention it to Piso Caesoninus. Quintus Servilius Caepio lived with Marcus Livius Drusus for years, only left when his wife scampered off with Marcus Cato Salonianus. Now about the time that I was canvassing for my first try at the praetorship, Caepio went away—a long trip. You have assured me in earlier letters that the Gold of Tolosa is no longer in Smyrna, that Caepio appeared in Smyrna on this same absence from Rome and removed it, much to the sorrow of the local banks. Now Silo was in that house often. And far friendlier with Drusus than Drusus was with Caepio. What if he heard that Caepio was sinking some of his money into the establishment of foundry towns in eastern Italian Gaul? Silo could then have anticipated Rome, tied up those new towns making arms and armor for his own people before anyone in the area needed to tout for business.

I'm picking that Caepio is the Roman senator landlord, and that the company based in Placentia is his. But I doubt I'll manage to prove it, Publius Rutilius. Anyway, Piso Caesoninus put some pressure on the steelworkers of the area, with the result that they'll make no more arms and armor for the Italians. Instead, they will make for us.

Rome readies herself for war. But there is an eerie quality about the process, given who the enemy is. No one feels at ease fighting in Italy, including, I suspect, the enemy. Who could have marched on us three months ago, according to my intelligence reports. Oh, I have neglected to tell you that I am very busy putting together an intelligence network—if in no other way, I swear our information about their movements will be superior to their information about ours.

This section of my letter, by the way, is somewhat later in date than the first. Scaurus's courier didn't get away.

For the moment, we have secured Etruria and Umbria. Oh, there are rumbles, but the rumblers cannot gather enough clout to secede. Thanks in large measure to the *latifundia* economy. Gaius Marius is going everywhere, both recruiting and pacifying—and, to give Caepio his due, he's been very active in Umbria.

The Conscript Fathers flew into a fine old stew when my intelligence revealed that the Italians have as many as *twenty* legions already trained and under arms. Since I had evidence to back up my contention, they had to believe. And here are we with *six* legions! Luckily we have arms and armor for at least ten more legions, thanks to those thrifty fellows we depute to go around battlefields picking up stuff from our own and the enemy dead. As well as the enemy prisoners. It's stored in Capua in shed after shed after shed. But how we can recruit and train new troops in the time we have is more than anyone knows.

I should tell you that it was resolved in the House late in February that Asculum Picentum must be made an example of, in the mode of Numantia. So there is going to be a northern theater as well as a central theater. The command in the north was given to Pompey Strabo. Who was given his target—Asculum Picentum. And who was told he had to be ready to march on it by May. Still very early spring, as the seasons go at the moment, but at least this year our dilatory Pontifex Maximus has intercalated an extra twenty days at the end of February, which is why the date on this latter half of my letter is still March. I am now, by the way, writing a solo effort—Scaurus says he doesn't have time! As if I do! No, Publius Rutilius, it is *not* a burden. Many's the time in the past you've made the difference to me when I've been away. I render you no more than your due.

Lupus is the kind of commander who doesn't do anything he regards as beneath his dignity. So when it was agreed that he and Lucius Caesar would split the

four veteran legions of Titus Didius between them, and
each take one of the unblooded two legions as well,
Lupus didn't feel in the mood to leave Carseoli (where
he has established his headquarters for the central the-
ater campaign) in order to do the drudgery of going to
Capua and picking up his half of the troops. He sent
Pompey Strabo in his stead. He doesn't like Pompey
Strabo—well, who honestly does?

But Pompey Strabo paid him back! Having collected
the two veteran legions and the one unblooded legion
from Capua, he got as far as Rome. He had been ordered by Lupus to take the raw legion north with him
to Picenum, and deliver the two veteran legions to Lupus in Carseoli. Whereas what he did do had Scaurus
laughing for a week. He put the raw legion under the
command of Gaius Perperna and sent *it* to Lupus in
Carseoli, while he hied himself up the Via Flaminia
with the two veteran legions! Not only that, but when
Catulus Caesar got to Capua to take up command of
the place, he discovered that Pompey Strabo had also
rifled the sheds of stored arms and armor, and removed
enough to equip four legions! Scaurus is still laughing.
However, I can't. For what can we do about it now?
Nothing! Pompey Strabo bears watching. There's too
much Gaul in him—how's that for a pun?

When Lupus realized how neatly he'd been tricked,
he demanded that Lucius Caesar give him one of *his*
two veteran legions! Naturally Lucius Caesar said no,
in words to the effect that if Lupus couldn't control his
own legates, then he'd better not come crying to the senior consul about it. Unfortunately Lupus is taking it
out on Marius and Caepio, by flogging them to recruit
and train with redoubled vigor. He himself sits in Carseoli and sulks.

Coelius and Sertorius in Italian Gaul are moving
mountains to ship arms and armor and troops, and every

little steelyard and foundry in Roman territory any-where in the world is busier than a lone Sardinian cap-turing a convoy. So I suppose it doesn't really matter that Caepio's towns worked for the Italians all those years. We wouldn't have been bright enough to find work for them anyway. Now they are working for us, and that's as much as one can hope for.

Somehow before May we have to get sixteen legions into the field. That is, we have to produce ten legions we do not at the moment have. Oh, we'll do it! If there is one thing Rome excels at, it's getting the job done when the odds are against her. Volunteers are coming from everywhere and every class, and the Latin Rights peo-ple have proven staunch to us. Due to our haste, there has been no attempt to segregate the Latin volunteers from the Roman, so it looks as if some sort of hege-mony has been visited upon us involuntarily. What I am trying to say is, there will be no auxiliary legions in this war. They'll all be classified and numbered as Roman.

Lucius Julius Caesar and I leave for Campania at the start of April, about eight days away. Quintus Lutatius Catulus Caesar is already installed as the commandant of Capua, a job I consider he will do well. I am pro-foundly glad he won't be leading any armies. Our le-gion of raw recruits will be split into two units of five cohorts each—Lucius Caesar and I think it will be nec-essary to garrison both Nola and Aesernia. These troops can do that, they don't have to be crown-winners. Aeser-nia is a real outpost in enemy territory, of course, but it remains loyal to us, that we know. Scipio Asiagenes and Lucius Acilius—both junior legates (and both rather poor quality)—are taking five cohorts to Aesernia at once. The praetor Lucius Postumius is taking the other five cohorts to Nola. For a Postumius, he is a fairly steady sort of fellow. I like him. Is it because he's not an Albinus, would you say?

And that, dear Publius Rutilius, is all for the moment. Scaurus's courier is just about knocking on my door. When I have an opportunity I'll write again, but I fear you'll have to rely upon your women correspondents for the most regular news. Julia has promised she will write often.

Sulla laid down his pen with a sigh. A very long letter, but something of a catharsis too. Worth the effort, even if it did mean scant sleep. He was aware to whom he was writing, never forgot it, yet he found himself able to say things on his paper that he could never have said to Publius Rutilius Rufus in person. Of course that was because Publius Rutilius Rufus was too far away to represent a threat of any kind.

However, he hadn't mentioned his sudden elevation in the Senate by Lucius Julius Caesar. That was too new and too delicately poised to risk offending Fortune by talking about it as if it were an established fact. Mere accident had provoked it, of that Sulla was sure; disliking Gaius Marius, Lucius Caesar had looked for someone else to ask. By rights he should have asked Titus Didius or Publius Crassus, or some other *triumphator*. But his eye had lighted upon Sulla, and his mind decided Sulla would do. Of course he hadn't expected such a grasp of the situation, but when he got it, Lucius Caesar did a not unusual thing; he singled Sulla out as his in-House expert. To have to consult a Marius or a Crassus did the consul no good—it made the consul look like a tyro having to ask the masters all the time. Whereas to ask a relative nobody like Sulla looked like consular genius. Lucius Caesar could claim to have "discovered" Sulla. And when he leaned upon Sulla, it appeared to be a kind of patronage.

For the moment Sulla was content to have it so. As long as he behaved nicely and deferentially to Lucius Caesar, he would get the commands and the jobs he needed in order to eclipse Lucius Caesar. Who, as Sulla was rapidly discovering, had a streak of morbid pessimism in him, and was not as confidently competent as he had seemed in the beginning. When the two departed for

Campania early in April, Sulla left the military decisions and dispositions to Lucius Caesar, while he threw himself with praiseworthy energy and enthusiasm into recruiting and training new legions. There were plenty among the centurions of the two veteran legions in Capua who had served under Sulla somewhere or other, and even more among the retired centurions who had re-enlisted to train troops. The word got around, and Sulla's reputation grew. Now all he needed was for Lucius Caesar to make a few mistakes, or else become so bogged down in one section of the coming campaign that he had no choice but to give Sulla a free rein. On one point, Sulla was absolutely set; when his chances came, he wouldn't be making any mistakes at all.

Better prepared than any of the other commanders, Pompey Strabo equipped two new legions from the people on his own vast estates in northern Picenum; with the centurions of the two veteran legions he had stolen helping him, he got his new troops into fair condition in fifty days. During the second week in April he set off from Cingulum with four legions—two veteran, two raw. A good proportion. Though his military career had not been particularly distinguished, he had the requisite experience for command, and had made himself a reputation as a very hard man.

An incident which happened when he was a thirty-year-old quaestor in Sardinia had unfortunately contributed much toward his contempt for and isolation from his fellow members of the Senate. Pompey Strabo had written from Sardinia to the Senate requesting that he be allowed to impeach his superior, the governor Titus Annius Albucius, and that he himself be empowered to prosecute Titus Albucius upon their return to Rome. Led by Scaurus, the Senate had responded with a scathing letter from the praetor Gaius Memmius, who had included in it a copy of Scaurus's speech—in which he had called Pompey Strabo everything from a noxious mushroom to crass, bovine, ill-mannered, presumptuous, stupid, and under-bred. To Pompey Strabo, he had done the correct thing in demanding that he bring his superior to trial; to Scaurus and the other leaders of the House at that time, what

Pompey Strabo had done was unpardonable. No one indicted his superior! But, having indicted his superior, no one pressed for the job of prosecuting him! Then Lucius Marcius Philippus had turned the absent Pompey Strabo into a laughingstock by suggesting that the Senate should substitute a different cross-eyed prosecutor for the trial Titus Albucius now had to face, and nominated Caesar Strabo.

There was a lot of the Celtic king in Pompey Strabo, in spite of the fact that he claimed to be completely Roman. His chief defense of his Romanness was his tribe, Clustumina, a moderately elderly rural tribe whose citizens lived in the eastern Tiber valley. But few of the Romans who mattered doubted for one moment that the Pompeii had been in Picenum far longer than the date of Roman conquest of the area. The tribe created for the new Picentine citizens was Velina, and most of the vassals who lived on Pompeian lands in northern Picenum and eastern Umbria were of the tribe Velina. The interpretation among those who mattered in Rome was that the Pompeii were Picentines and owned vassals long before Roman influence in that part of Italy, and had bought themselves membership in a better tribe than Velina. It was an area of Italy where Gauls had settled in large numbers after the failed invasion of central Italy and Rome by the first King Brennus three hundred years earlier. And as Pompeian looks were Celtic in the extreme, those who mattered in Rome deemed them Gauls.

Be that as it may, some seventy years ago a Pompeius had finally taken the inevitable journey down the Via Flaminia to Rome, and by unscrupulously bribing the electors, got himself voted in as consul twenty years later. At first this Pompeius—who was more closely related to Quintus Pompeius Rufus than to Pompey Strabo—had found himself at loggerheads with the great Metellus Macedonicus, but they had patched up their differences, and eventually shared the censorship. All of which meant that the Pompeii were on their Roman way.

The first Pompeius of Strabo's branch to make the trip south had been Pompey Strabo's father, who had procured himself a seat in the Senate and married none other than the sister of the famous Latin language satirist, Gaius Lucilius. The Lucilii were Campanians who had been Roman citizens for generations; they were quite rich, and had consuls in the family. A temporary shortage of cash had transformed Pompey Strabo's father into desirable husband material—especially when Lucilia's abysmal unattractiveness was added to the Lucilian debit account. Unfortunately Strabo's father had died before he could attain a senior magistracy—but not before Lucilia had produced her cross-eyed little Gnaeus Pompeius, immediately cognominated Strabo. She had produced another boy, called Sextus, much younger than Pompey Strabo, and of much poorer quality. Thus it was Pompey Strabo who became the family's hope for great things.

Strabo was not by nature a student, let alone a scholar; though he was educated in Rome by a series of excellent tutors, he achieved little in the way of learning. Presented with the great Greek ideas and ideals, the boy Pompey Strabo had dismissed them as idle waffle and complete impracticality. He liked the warlords and international meddlers who liberally dotted Roman history. As a *contubernalis*—cadet—serving under various commanders, Pompey Strabo had not been popular with his peers—men like Lucius Caesar, Sextus Caesar, his middling cousin Pompeius Rufus, Cato Licinianus, Lucius Cornelius Cinna. They had used him as a butt because of his atrociously crossed eyes, certainly, but also because he had an innate uncouthness no amount of Roman polish ever managed to conceal. His early years in the army had been miserable, and his service as a tribune of the soldiers hardly less so. No one *liked* Pompey Strabo!

All of this he was later to tell his own son, a violent partisan of his father's. That son (now aged fifteen) and a daughter, Pompeia, were the products of another Lucilian marriage; following the precedent set by his father, Pompey Strabo also espoused an ugly Lucilia, this one the daughter of the famous satirist's elder brother, Gaius Lucilius Hirrus. Luckily the Pompeian blood was capable of overcoming Lucilian homeliness, for neither Strabo nor his son was homely, save for Strabo's cross-eyes. Like generations of

Pompeii before them, they were fair of face and coloring, blue-eyed, very snub of nose. In the Rufus branch of the family the hair ran to red; the Strabo branch ran to gold.

When Strabo marched his four legions south through Picenum, he left his son behind in Rome with his mother, there to further his education. But the son was no intellectual either—and very much shaped by his father into the bargain—so he packed up his trunk and headed home to northern Picenum, there to mingle with the centurions left behind to keep on training Pompeian clients as legionaries, and subject himself to a rigorous program of military training well before he could assume the toga of manhood. Unlike his father in this respect, Young Pompey was universally adored. He called himself plain Gnaeus Pompeius, no cognomen. None of that branch owned a cognomen save for Young Pompey's father, and Strabo was a name he could not adopt because he didn't have cross-eyes. Young Pompey's eyes were very large, very wide, very blue, and quite perfect. The eyes, said his doting mother, of a poet.

While Young Pompey kicked his heels at home, Pompey Strabo continued his march south. Then as he was crossing the Tinna River near Falernum, he was ambushed by six legions of Picentes under Gaius Vidacilius, and was obliged to fight a waterlogged defensive action which gave him no room to maneuver. To make his predicament worse, Titus Lafrenius came up with two legions of Vestini—and Publius Vettius Scato arrived with two legions of Marsi! Everyone Italian wanted to have a piece of the first action in the war.

The battle was a credit to neither side. Enormously outnumbered, Pompey Strabo managed to extricate himself almost intact from the river and hustled his precious army to the coastal city of Firmum Picenum, where he shut himself up and prepared to withstand a long siege. By rights the Italians should have annihilated him, but they hadn't yet absorbed the lesson of the one unfailing Roman military characteristic—speed. In that respect—and it turned out to be the vital respect—Pompey Strabo was the winner, even if the battle had to be awarded to the Italians.

Vidacilius left Titus Lafrenius outside the walls of Firmum Picenum to keep the Romans inside and took himself off with Scato to do mischief elsewhere, while Pompey Strabo sent a message to Coelius in Italian Gaul asking for relief to be sent as soon as possible. His plight was not desperate; he had access to the sea, and to a small Roman Adriatic fleet no one had remembered was based there. Firmum Picenum was a Latin Rights colony, and loyal.

 As soon as the Italians heard that Pompey Strabo was marching, honor was satisfied; Rome was the aggressor. Mutilus and Silo in the grand council now got all the support they wanted. While Silo remained in Italica and sent Vidacilius, Lafrenius, and Scato north to deal with Pompey Strabo, Gaius Papius Mutilus led six legions to Aesernia. No Latin outpost would mar the autonomy of Italia! Aesernia must fall.

The caliber of Lucius Caesar's two junior legates became embarrassingly obvious at once; Scipio Asiagenes and Lucius Acilius disguised themselves as slaves and fled the city before the Samnites arrived. Their defection dismayed Aesernia not at all. Formidably fortified and very well provisioned, the city shut its gates and manned its walls with the five cohorts of recruits the junior legates had left behind, so anxious were they to escape. Mutilus saw at once that the siege would be a prolonged one, so he left Aesernia under heavy attack by two of his legions and moved on with the other four toward the Volturnus River, which bisected Campania east to west.

When the news came that the Samnites were marching, Lucius Caesar shifted himself from Capua to Nola, where Lucius Postumius's five cohorts had tamed the town's insurrection.

"Until I find out what Mutilus plans to do, I think it best to garrison Nola with both our veteran legions as well," he said to Sulla as he prepared to leave Capua. "Keep up the work. We are frightfully outnumbered. As soon as you can, send some troops to Venafrum with Marcellus."

"It's already done," said Sulla laconically. "Campania has always been the favorite place for veterans to settle after they retire, and they're flocking to join. All they need is a helmet on the head, a mail-shirt, a sword by the side, and a shield. As fast as I can equip them and sort out the most experienced to serve as centurions, I'm sending them out to the places you want garrisoned. Publius Crassus and his two oldest sons went to Lucania yesterday with one legion of retired veterans."

"You should tell me!" said Lucius Caesar a little peevishly.

"No, Lucius Julius, I should not," said Sulla firmly, his calm unimpaired. "I am here to implement your plans. Once you tell me who is to go where with what, it's my job to see your orders carried out. You don't need to ask, any more than I need to tell."

"Whom did I send to Beneventum, then?" Lucius Caesar asked, aware that his weaknesses were beginning to show; the demands of generaling were too vast.

But not too vast for Sulla, who didn't permit his satisfaction to show. Sooner or later things would become too much for Lucius Caesar—and then it would be his turn. He let Lucius Caesar move to Nola, knowing it would be as temporary as it was futile. Sure enough, when word came of the investment of Aesernia, Lucius Caesar marched back to Capua, then decided his best move would be to march to the relief of Aesernia. But the central areas of Campania around the Volturnus were in open revolt, Samnite legions were everywhere, and it was rumored Mutilus had taken himself off in the direction of Beneventum.

Northern Campania was still safe, its allegiance more Roman; Lucius Caesar moved his two veteran legions through Teanum Sidicinum and Interamna in order to approach Aesernia across friendly ground. What he didn't know was that Publius Vettius Scato of the Marsi had detached himself from the siege of Pompey Strabo in Firmum Picenum and marched around the western foreshores of Lake Fucinus, also heading for Aesernia. He came down the watershed of the Liris, skirted Sora, and met Lucius Caesar between Atina and Casinum.

Neither side had expected it. Both sides fell into accidental battle complicated by the gorge in which they encountered each other, and Lucius Caesar lost. He retreated back to Teanum Sidicinum, leaving two thousand precious veteran soldiers dead on the field and Scato pushing on unimpeded toward Aesernia. This time the Italians could claim a solid victory, and did.

Never wholly reconciled to Roman rule, the towns of southern Campania declared one after the other for Italia, including Nola and Venafrum. Marcus Claudius Marcellus extricated himself and his troops from Venafrum ahead of the approaching Samnite army; but instead of retreating to a safely Roman place like Capua, Marcellus and his men elected to go to Aesernia. They found the Italians completely surrounding it, Scato and his Marsi on one side, Samnites on the other. But Italian guard duty was lax, and Marcellus was quick to take advantage of it. All the Romans managed to get inside the town during the night. Aesernia now possessed a brave and capable commandant, and ten cohorts of Roman legionaries.

Licking his wounds in Teanum Sidicinum as sullenly as an old dog losing its first fight, a depressed and dismayed Lucius Julius Caesar was bombarded with one piece of bad news after another; Venafrum gone, Aesernia heavily invested, Nola holding two thousand Roman soldiers prisoner including the praetor Lucius Postumius, and Publius Crassus and his two sons driven inside Grumentum by the Lucani, now also in revolt, and very ably led by Marcus Lamponius. To cap everything else, Sulla's intelligence was reporting that the Apuli and the Venusini were about to declare for Italia.

But all that was as nothing compared to the plight of Publius Rutilius Lupus just east of Rome. It had started when Gaius Perperna arrived with one legion of raw recruits instead of two legions of veterans during the intercalated February; after that, things went from bad to worse. While Marius threw himself into the work of enlisting and arming men and Caepio did the same, Lupus engaged himself in a battle of the pen with the Senate in Rome. There were elements of insurrection within his own forces

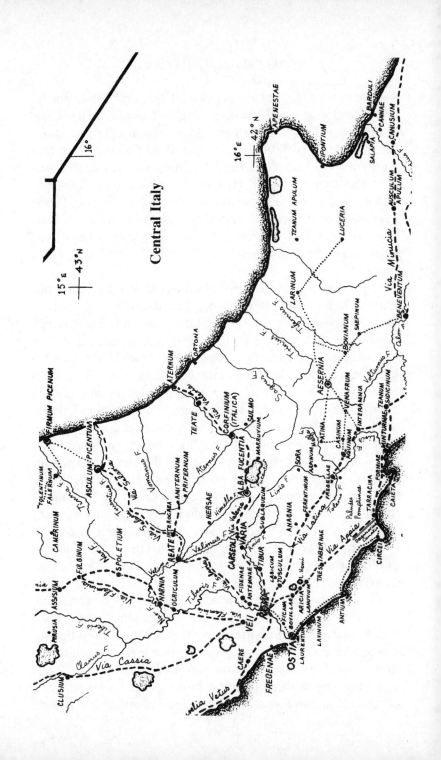

Central Italy

and even within the ranks of his own legates, scribbled Lupus furiously, and what was the Senate going to do about it? How could he be expected to conduct a war when his own people were inimical? Did Rome or did Rome not want Alba Fucentia protected? And how could he do that when he had not one experienced legionary? And when was something going to be done to recall Pompey Strabo? And when was someone going to move that Pompey Strabo be prosecuted for treason? And when was the Senate going to get his two legions of veterans back from Pompey Strabo? And when was he going to be relieved of that intolerable insect, Gaius Marius?

Lupus and Marius were encamped on the Via Valeria outside Carseoli in a very well-fortified way—thanks to Marius, who simply went ahead and got the recruits digging—to strengthen their muscles, he said innocently whenever Lupus complained that the men were digging when they ought to be drilling. Caepio lay behind them, also on the Via Valeria, outside the town of Varia. In one respect Lupus was not wrong; no one would see anyone else's point of view. Caepio kept himself absolutely away from Carseoli and his general because, he said, he couldn't bear the acrimonious atmosphere in the command tent. And Marius—who had a fair idea that his general would march against the Marsi as soon as he counted enough soldiers in the parades—never let up carping. The troops were hopelessly inexperienced, he said, they would need the full hundred days of training before they could cope with any sort of battle, a lot of the equipment was substandard, Lupus had better settle down and accept things for what they were instead of dwelling endlessly upon Pompey Strabo and the stolen veteran legions.

But if Lucius Caesar was indecisive, Lupus was downright incompetent. His military experience was minimal, and he belonged to that school of armchair general who believed that the moment an enemy set eyes upon a Roman legion, the fight was over—in Rome's favor. He also despised Italians, considering every last one of them a bucolic knave. As far as he was concerned, the moment Marius had gathered and armed four legions, they could move. However, he reckoned without Marius. Marius clung doggedly to his standpoint: that the soldiers must be kept out of action until they were properly trained. On the one occasion when he issued a direct order to Marius to march for Alba Fucentia, Marius flatly refused. And when Marius refused, so did the more junior legates.

Off went more letters to Rome, now accusing his legates of mutiny rather than insubordination. It was Gaius Marius at the bottom of it, always Gaius Marius.

Thus it was that Lupus made no move until the end of May, when he called a council and instructed Gaius Perperna to take the Capuan legion of recruits and the next-best legion, and advance through the western pass along the Via Valeria into the lands of the Marsi. His objective was Alba Fucentia, which he was to relieve should the Marsi have besieged it, or else garrison it against a Marsic attack. Once again Marius objected, but this time he was overridden; the recruits, said Lupus with truth, had had their training period. Perperna and his two legions set off up the Via Valeria.

The western pass was a rocky gorge lying at four thousand feet, and the snows of winter had not yet entirely melted. The troops muttered and complained of the cold, so Perperna failed to post as many lookouts on the high points as he should have, more concerned to keep everyone happy than everyone alive. Publius Praesenteius attacked his column just as it became completely enclosed by the ravine, leading four legions of Paeligni hungry for a victory. They had their victory, as complete as it was sweet. Four thousand of Perperna's soldiers lay dead in the pass to yield up their arms and armor to Praesenteius; the Paeligni also got the armor of the six thousand men who survived, as they had abandoned it in order to run away faster. Perperna himself was among the fastest runners.

In Carseoli, Lupus stripped Perperna of his rank and sent him to Rome in disgrace.

"That's stupidity, Lupus," said Marius, who had long given up according the general the courtesy of Publius Rutilius; it hurt to speak that beloved name to someone so unworthy of it. "You can't blame it all on Perperna, he's an amateur. The fault is yours, and nobody else's. I told you—the men weren't ready. And they ought to have been led by someone who understands green troops—*me*."

"Mind your own business!" snapped Lupus. "And try to remember that your chief business is to say yes to me!"

"I wouldn't say yes to you, Lupus, if you presented me with your bare arse," said Marius, eyebrows matted together across the bridge of his nose, and looking doubly fierce because of them. "You are a totally incompetent idiot!"

"I shall send you back to Rome!" cried Lupus.

"You couldn't send your grandmother ten paces down the road," said Marius scornfully. "Four thousand men dead who might one day have turned into decent soldiers, and six thousand naked survivors who ought to be scourged! Don't blame Gaius Perperna, blame no one but yourself!" He shook his head, slapped his flaccid left cheek. "Oh, I feel as if someone's sent me back twenty years! You're doing the same as all the rest of the senatorial fools, killing good men!"

Lupus drew himself up to his full height, which was not very imposing. "I am not only the consul, I am the commander-in-chief in this theater of war," he said haughtily. "In exactly eight days— today, I remind you, are the Kalends of June—you and I will march for Nersae and approach the lands of the Marsi from the north. We will proceed in two columns, each of two legions, and cross the Velinus separately. There are only two bridges between here and Reate, and neither is wide enough to take eight men abreast. Which is why we will proceed in two columns. Otherwise it will take too long to cross. I will use the bridge closer to Carse-oli, you will use the one closer to Cliterna. We will reunite on the Himella beyond Nersae and join the Via Valeria just before Anti-num. Is that understood, Marius?"

"It's understood," said Marius. "It's stupid! But it's understood. What you don't seem to realize, Lupus, is that there are very likely to be Italian legions west of the Marsic lands."

"There are no Italian legions west of Marsic lands," said Lupus. "The Paeligni who ambushed Perperna have gone east again."

Marius shrugged. "Have it your own way. But don't say I didn't warn you."

They moved out eight days later, Lupus taking the lead with his two legions, Marius following on until it came time to continue north alone, leaving Lupus with a shorter march to his bridge across the swift and icy Velinus, swollen with melted snows. The moment Lupus's column was out of sight, Marius led his troops into a nearby forest and ordered them to make smokeless camp.

"We're following the Velinus toward Reate, and on the far side of it are formidable heights," he said to his senior legate, Aulus Plotius. "If I were a canny Italian planning to beat Rome in a war—*and* I'd had a taste of our abysmal mettle—I'd have my longest-sighted men sitting on top of that ridge watching for troop movements on this side of the river. The Italians must know Lupus has been squatting at Carseoli for months, so why shouldn't they be expecting him to move, and watching out for him? They annihilated his last little effort. They're watching for his next, mark my words. So we are going to stay here in this nice thick wood until dark, then we'll march as best we can until daylight, when we'll hide in another nice thick wood. I am not going to expose my men until they're tramping across that bridge on the double."

Plotius of course was young, but more than old enough to have seen service as a junior tribune against the Cimbri in Italian Gaul; he had been attached to Catulus Caesar, but—as everybody did who served in that campaign—he knew where the real credit lay. And as he listened to Marius, he was profoundly glad that it had been his luck to be seconded to Marius's column, rather than to Lupus's. Before they had left Carseoli he had jokingly commiserated with Lupus's legate, Marcus Valerius Messala, who had also wanted to march with Marius.

Gaius Marius finally reached his bridge on the twelfth day of June, having proceeded at a painfully slow pace because the nights were moonless and the terrain roadless save for a meandering track he had preferred not to follow. He made his dispositions carefully, and in the secure knowledge that no one watched from the heights on the far side—he had had them scoured. The two legions were cheerful and willing to do anything Marius wanted them to do; they were exactly the same sort of men who had marched with Perperna through the western pass grumbling about the cold and unhappy to be there, they came from the same towns in the same lands. Yet these soldiers felt confident, fit for anything including battle, and obeyed their instructions to the letter as they commenced pouring across the little bridge. It is because, thought Aulus Plotius, they are Marius's men—even if that means they must also be Marius's mules. For, as always, Marius was marching light. Lupus, on the other hand, had insisted upon a proper baggage train.

Plotius strolled down to the stream south of the bridge, wanting to find a vantage point from which he could watch those fine stout fellows making the bridge timbers jingle and shudder as they jogged across. The river was up and roaring, but—due to the fact that Plotius had deliberately made for a small promontory jutting into the straight course of the stream—on the south side of the land where he stood there was a little bay full of eddies and bodies. At first he registered the bodies idly, not comprehending, then stared with growing horror. They were the bodies of soldiers! Two or three dozen of them! And judging from the plumes on their helmets, they were Roman.

He ran at once for Marius, who took one look and understood.

"Lupus," he said grimly. "He's been brought to battle on the far side of his bridge. Here, help me."

Plotius scrambled down the bank in Marius's wake and assisted him to bring one of the bodies in against the shore, where Marius turned it over and gazed down into the chalk-white, terrified face.

"It happened yesterday," he said, and let the body go. "I'd like to stop and attend to these poor fellows, but there isn't the time, Aulus Plotius. Assemble the troops on the far side of the bridge in battle marching order. I'll address them the moment you're ready. And make it quick! I'd say the Italians don't know we're here. So we might have a chance to make up for this in a small way."

Publius Vettius Scato, leading two legions of Marsi, had left the vicinity of Aesernia a month before. He headed for Alba Fucentia to find Quintus Poppaedius Silo, who was besieging that Latin Rights city, strongly fortified and determined to hold out. Silo himself had elected to remain within Marsic territory to keep the war effort at its peak, but intelligence had long informed him that the Romans were training troops at Carseoli and Varia.

"Go and have a look," he said to Scato.

Encountering Praesenteius and his Paeligni near Antinum, he received a full report upon the rout of Perperna in the western pass; Praesenteius was going east again to donate his spoils to the Paeligni recruitment campaign. Scato went west and did precisely what Marius had guessed a canny Italian would do; he put long-sighted men on top of the ridge beyond the eastern side of the Velinus. In the meantime he built a camp on the east bank of the river halfway between the two bridges, and was just beginning to think he ought to penetrate closer to Carseoli when a messenger came running in to tell him there was a Roman army crossing the more southerly of the two bridges.

With incredulous delight Scato himself watched Lupus get his soldiers from one side of the river to the other, committing every mistake possible. Before they even approached the bridge he allowed them to break ranks, and left them to mill in disorder on the far bank after they crossed. Lupus's own energies were devoted to the baggage train; he was standing at the bridge clad only in a tunic when Scato and the Marsi fell upon his army. Eight thousand Roman legionaries died upon the field, including Publius Rutilius Lupus and his legate, Marcus Valerius Messala. Perhaps two thousand managed to escape by dragging the ox-wagons off the bridge, shedding their mail-shirts, helmets and swords, and running for Carseoli. It was the eleventh day of June.

The battle—if such it could be called—took place in the late afternoon. Scato decided to stay where he was rather than send his men back to their camp for the night. At dawn on the morrow they would commence to pick the corpses clean, pile up the naked bodies and burn them, drive the abandoned ox-wagons and mule-carts across to the eastern bank. They would undoubtedly contain wheat and other rations. They would also do to carry the captured armaments. A wonderful haul! Beating Romans, Scato thought complacently, was as easy as beating a baby. They didn't even know how to protect themselves when on maneuvers in enemy country! And that was very odd. How had they ever managed to conquer half the world and keep the other half in a perpetual dither?

He was about to find out. Marius was on the move, and it was Scato's turn to be attacked with his own men in complete disorder.

Marius had encountered the Marsic camp first, utterly deserted. He romped through it taking everything it contained—baggage, food aplenty, money aplenty too. But not in a disorderly fashion. Rather, he left most of his noncombatants behind to do the gathering up and sorting out, while he pressed on with his legions. At about noon he reached yesterday's battlefield to find the Marsic troops going about stripping the armor from corpses.

"Oh, very nice!" he roared to Aulus Plotius. "My men are blooded in the best way—a rout! Gives them all sorts of confidence! They're veterans before they know it!"

It was indeed a rout. Scato took to his heels into the mountains leaving two thousand Marsic dead behind him as well as everything he owned. But the honors, Marius thought grimly, had still to be awarded to the Italians, who had had by far the best of things in terms of soldier dead. All those months of recruiting and training gone for nothing. Eight thousand good men dead because—as seemed inevitable—they were led by a fool.

They found the bodies of Lupus and Messala by the bridge.

"I'm sorry for Marcus Valerius; I think he would have turned out well," said Marius to Plotius. "But I am profoundly glad that Fortune saw fit to turn her face away from Lupus! If he had lived, we'd lose yet more men."

To which there was no reply. Plotius made none.

Marius sent the bodies of the consul and his legate back to Rome under the escort of his only cavalry squadron, his letter of explanation traveling with the cortege. Time, thought Gaius

Marius sourly, that Rome was given a thorough fright. Otherwise no one living there was going to believe there really was a war going on in Italy—and no one would believe the Italians were formidable.

Scaurus Princeps Senatus sent two replies, one on behalf of the Senate, the other on his own behalf.

I am truly sorry the official report says what it does, Gaius Marius. It was not my doing, I can assure you. But the trouble is, old man, that I just do not have the necessary reserves of energy one needs to swing a body of three hundred men around single-handedly. I did it over twenty years ago in the matter of Jugurtha— but it is the last twenty years are the ones which count. Not that there are three hundred in the Senate these days. More like one hundred. Those senators under thirty-five are all doing some sort of military service— and so are quite a few of the ancients, including a certain fellow named Gaius Marius.

When your little funeral train arrived in Rome it created a sensation. The whole city fell about screaming and tearing out hunks of hair, not to mention lacerating its breast. All of a sudden, the war was *real.* Perhaps nothing else could have taught them that particular lesson. Morale plummeted. In an instant, in less time than it takes a bolt of lightning to strike. Until the body of the consul arrived in the Forum, I think everyone in Rome—including senators and knights!— regarded this war as a sinecure. But there lay Lupus, stone dead, killed by an Italian on a battlefield not more than a few miles from Rome herself. A frightful instant, that one when we spilled out of the Curia Hostilia and stood gaping at Lupus and Messala—did you tell the escort to uncover them before they reached the Forum? I'll bet you did!

Anyway, all Rome has gone into mourning, it's dark

and dreary clothes wherever you go. All men left in the Senate are wearing the *sagum* instead of the toga, and a knight's narrow stripe on their tunics rather than the *latus clavus*. The curule magistrates have doffed their insignia of office, even to sitting on plain wooden stools in the Curia and on their tribunals. Sumptuary laws are being hinted at regarding purple and pepper and panoply. From total unconcern Rome has gone to the opposite extreme. Everywhere I go, people are audibly wondering if we are actually going to lose?

As you will see, the official reply is upon two separate matters. The first I personally deplore, but I was howled down in the name of "national emergency." To wit: in future all and any war casualties from the lowest ranker to the general will be given a funeral and all possible obsequies in the field. No one is to be returned to Rome for fear of what it might do to morale. Rubbish, rubbish, rubbish! But they wanted it so.

The second is far worse, Gaius Marius. Knowing you, you have taken this to read ahead of officialdom. So I had better tell you without further ado that the House refused to give you the supreme command. They didn't *precisely* pass you over—that they weren't quite courageous enough to do. Instead, they have given the command jointly to you and Caepio. A more asinine, stupid, futile decision they could not possibly have made. Even to have appointed Caepio above you on his own would have been smarter. But I suppose you will deal with it in your own inimitable way.

Oh, I was angry! But the trouble is that those who are left in the House are by and large the dried-up, rattly bits of shit hanging around the sheep's arse. The decent wool is in the field—or else, like me, had a job to do in Rome—but there are only a handful of us compared to the rattly bits. At the moment I feel as if I am quite superfluous. Philippus is running the place.

Can you truly imagine that? It was bad enough having to deal with him as consul in those awful days leading up to the murder of Marcus Livius, but now he's worse. And the knights in the Comitia eat out of his greasy palm. I wrote to Lucius Julius asking that he return to Rome and pick a consul *suffectus* in place of Lupus, but he wrote back saying we'd have to muddle along as we were because he's too tied up to leave Campania for so much as one day. I do what I can, but I tell you, Gaius Marius, I am getting very old.

Of course Caepio will be insufferable when he hears the news. I have tried to arrange the couriers so that you know ahead of him. It will give you time to decide how you will handle him when he struts up to peacock in front of you. I can only offer you one piece of advice. Deal with it your own way.

But in the end Fortune dealt with it—brilliantly, finally, ironically. Caepio accepted his joint command with extreme confidence, as he had beaten back a raiding legion of Marsi at Varia while Marius had been dealing with Scato along the river Velinus. Equating this small success with Marius's victory, he notified the Senate that *he* had won the first victory of the war, as it had happened on the tenth day of June, whereas Marius's victory was two days later. And in between there had been an appalling defeat, for which Caepio managed to blame Marius rather than Lupus.

To his chagrin, Marius seemed not to care who got the credit or what Caepio wanted in Varia. When Caepio directed him to return to Carseoli, Marius ignored him. He had taken over Scato's camp along the Velinus, fortified it heavily, and put every man he had at his disposal into it, there to drill and re-drill his troops while the days dripped on and Caepio chafed at being denied the chance to invade the lands of the Marsi. As well as inheriting what men of Lupus's had survived, some five cohorts, Marius had two thirds of the six thousand men who had fled from Praesenteius in the western pass; he had now re-equipped the lot. Which gave him a total of three over-strength legions. Before he moved an inch, he said by letter, they would be ready to *his* satisfaction, not some cretin's who didn't know his vanguard from his wings.

Caepio had about a legion and a half of troops which he had redistributed to form two under-strength units, and was not confident enough to move at all. So while Marius relentlessly drilled his men miles away to the northeast, Caepio sat in Varia and fumed. June turned into Quinctilis and still Marius drilled his men, still Caepio sat in Varia and fumed. Like Lupus before him, a good deal of Caepio's time was occupied in writing complaining letters to the Senate, where Scaurus and Ahenobarbus Pontifex Maximus and Quintus Mucius Scaevola and a few other stalwarts kept the slavering Lucius Marcius Philippus at bay every time he proposed that Gaius Marius be stripped of his command.

About the middle of Quinctilis, Caepio received a visitor. None other than Quintus Poppaedius Silo of the Marsi.

Silo arrived in Caepio's camp with two terrified-looking slaves, one heavily laden donkey, and two babies, apparently twins. Summoned, Caepio strolled out into the camp forum, where Silo stood wearing full armor, his little entourage behind him. The babes, held by the female slave, were wrapped in purple blankets embroidered with gold.

When he saw Caepio, Silo's face lit up. "Quintus Servilius, how good it is to see you!" he cried, walking forward with his right hand outstretched.

Conscious that they were the center of much attention, Caepio drew himself up haughtily and ignored the hand.

"What do you want?" he asked disdainfully.

Silo dropped his hand, managing to make the gesture independent and free from humiliation. "I seek Rome's shelter and protection," he said, "and for the sake of Marcus Livius Drusus, I preferred to give myself up to you rather than to Gaius Marius."

Mollified a little by this reply—and consumed with curiosity besides—Caepio hesitated. "Why do you need Rome's protection?" he asked, eyes moving from Silo to the purple-wrapped babes, then to the male slave and his charge, the overloaded donkey.

"As you know, Quintus Servilius, the Marsi gave Rome a formal declaration of war," said Silo. "What you do not know is that it was thanks to the Marsi that the Italian nations delayed their offensive for so long after that declaration of war. In the councils in Corfinium—the city now called Italica—I kept pleading for time and secretly hoping that no blows would be struck. For I regard this war as pointless, hideous, wasteful. Italy *cannot* beat Rome! Some among the council began to accuse me of harboring Roman sympathies, which I denied. Then Publius Vettius Scato—my own praetor!—came back to Corfinium after his clash with Lupus the consul and his subsequent clash with Gaius Marius. Whereupon the whole thing came to boiling point. Scato accused me of collusion with Gaius Marius, and everyone believed him. Suddenly I found myself an outcast. That I was not killed in Corfinium was due to the size of the jury—all five hundred Italian councillors. While they deliberated I left the city and hurried to my own city of Marruvium. I reached it ahead of pursuit—but with Scato leading the hunt, I knew I wouldn't be safe among the Marsi. So I took my twin sons, Italicus and Marsicus, and decided to flee to Rome for protection."

"What makes you think we'd want to protect you?" Caepio asked, nostrils flaring. Such an odd smell! "You've done nothing for Rome."

"Oh, but I have, Quintus Servilius!" Silo said, and pointed to the donkey. "I stole the contents of the Marsic treasury and would offer it to Rome. There on the ass is a little of it. Only a very little! Some miles behind me, well hidden in a secret valley behind a hill, there are thirty more asses, all laden with at least as much gold as this one carries."

Gold! *That* was what Caepio could smell! Everyone was always insisting gold was odorless; but Caepio knew better, just as his father before him had known better. Not a Quintus Servilius Caepio ever born could not smell gold.

"Give me a look," he said curtly, moving to the donkey.

Its panniers were well hidden by a hide cover which Silo now stripped off. And there it was. Gold. Five rough-cast round sows of it nestling in each pannier, glittering in the sun. Every sow stamped with the Marsic snake.

"About three talents," said Silo, covering the panniers again with anxious looks all about to see who might be watching. Having tied the thongs which held the cover on securely, Silo paused and gazed at Caepio out of those remarkable yellow-green eyes, little flames leaping in them, it seemed to the dazzled Caepio. "This ass is yours," he said, "and perhaps two or three more might be yours if you extend me your personal protection as well as Rome's."

"You have it," said Caepio instantly, and smiled an avaricious smile. "I'll take five asses, though."

"As you wish, Quintus Servilius." Silo sighed deeply. "Oh, I am tired! I've been running for three days."

"Then rest," said Caepio. "Tomorrow you can lead me to the secret valley. I want to *see* all this gold!"

"It might be wise to bring your army," said Silo as they moved off toward the general's tent, the female slave following with the babies. Good babies; they didn't cry or wriggle. "By now they'll know what I've done, and who knows what they'll send after me? I imagine they'll guess I've appealed to Rome for asylum."

"Let them guess!" said Caepio gleefully. "My two legions are a match for the Marsi!" He held open the tent flap, but preceded his suppliant inside. "Ah—of course I must ask that you leave your sons in this camp while we're away."

"I understand," said Silo with dignity.

"They look like you," said Caepio when the slave girl put the babies down upon a couch preparatory to changing their diapers. And they did indeed; both had Silo's eyes. Caepio shivered. "Stop, girl!" he said to the slave. "There'll be no baby-cack in here! You'll have to wait until I organize accommodation for your master, then you can do whatever it is you have to do."

Thus it was that when Caepio led his two legions out of their camp the next morning, Silo's slave girl remained behind with the royal twins; the gold remained behind too, safely unloaded from the donkey and hidden in Caepio's tent.

"Did you know, Quintus Servilius, that Gaius Marius is, at this very moment, beleaguered by ten legions of Picentes, Paeligni, and Marrucini?" asked Silo.

"No!" gasped Caepio, riding beside Silo at the head of his army. "*Ten* legions? Will he win?"

"Gaius Marius always wins," said Silo smoothly.

"Humph," said Caepio.

They rode until the sun was overhead in the sky, having left the Via Valeria almost immediately to head southwest along the Anio in the direction of Sublaqueum. Silo insisted on setting a pace which enabled the infantry to keep up, though Caepio was so eager to see the rest of the gold that he resented dawdling.

"It's safe, it isn't going anywhere," said Silo soothingly. "I would much rather that your troops be with us and not breathing hard when we get there, Quintus Servilius—for both our sakes."

The country was rugged but negotiable; the miles went by until, not far short of Sublaqueum, Silo halted.

"There!" he said, pointing to a hill on the far side of the Anio. "Behind that is the secret valley. There's a good bridge not far from here. We can cross safely."

It was a good bridge, wide and made of stone; Caepio ordered his army across at full march, but remained in the lead. The road came up from Anagnia on the Via Latina to Sublaqueum, traversed the Anio at this point, and ended in Carseoli. Once the troops crossed the bridge they had a good road to walk on and stretched out in stride, quite enjoying their outing. Caepio's mood had told them long since that this was some sort of jaunt, no martial foray, so they kept their shields across their backs and used their spears as staves to ease the weight of their mail-shirts. Time was dragging on, they might have to camp in the rough and without food that night, but it was worth it not to be burdened by packs, and the general's attitude said some sort of reward was imminent.

With the two legions strung out around the base of the hill as the road curved on its way northeast, Silo turned in his saddle to talk to Caepio.

"I'll ride on ahead, Quintus Servilius," he said, "just to make sure everything is all right. I don't want anyone frightened into trying to bolt."

Easing his own pace, Caepio watched as Silo kicked his horse into a canter and dwindled quickly in size; several hundred paces further up the road Silo turned off it and disappeared behind a small cliff.

The Marsi fell upon Caepio's column from everywhere—from the front, where Silo had vanished—from the rear—from behind every rock and stone and bank on both sides of the road. No one had a chance. Before shields could be stripped of their hide covers and swung to the front, before swords could be properly drawn and helms fitted upon heads, four legions of Marsi were amid the column in their thousands, laying about them as if engaged upon an exercise. Caepio's army perished to the very last man but one, and that one was Caepio himself, taken prisoner at the beginning of the attack, and forced to watch his troops die.

When it was all over, when not a Roman soldier moved on the road and all around it, Quintus Poppaedius Silo rode back into Caepio's view, surrounded by his legates, including Scato and Fraucus. He was smiling widely.

"Well, Quintus Servilius, what say you now?"

White-faced and trembling, Caepio summoned every reserve. "You forget, Quintus Poppaedius," he said, "that I still hold your babies as my hostages."

Silo burst out laughing. "*My* babies? No! They're the children of the slave couple you still hold. But I'll get them back—and my ass. There's no one left in your camp to gainsay me." The eerie eyes glowed coldly, goldly. "But I won't bother to remove the ass's cargo. You can have that."

"It's *gold*!" said Caepio, aghast.

"No, Quintus Servilius, it is not gold. It's lead covered with the thinnest possible skin of gold. If you'd scraped it, you would have discovered the trick. But I knew my Caepio better than that! You couldn't bring yourself to put a scratch in a chunk of gold if your life depended upon it—and your life did." He drew his sword, dismounted, strolled toward Caepio.

Fraucus and Scato moved to Caepio's horse and pulled him from the saddle. Without saying a word, they divested him of cuirass and hardened leather under-dress. Understanding, Caepio began to weep desolately.

"I would like to hear you beg for your life, Quintus Servilius Caepio," Silo said as he moved within striking distance.

But that Caepio found himself unable to do. At Arausio he had run away, and never since had he found himself in a genuinely perilous situation, even when the Marsic raiding party had attacked his camp. Now he saw why they had attacked; they had lost a handful of men, but they had regarded their losses as worth it. Silo had seen the lay of the land, and laid his plans accordingly. Had Caepio searched his mind about this present ordeal, he might have concluded that he would indeed beg for his life. Now that the ordeal was happening, he found he could not. A Quintus Servilius Caepio might not be the bravest of Roman men, but he was nonetheless a Roman, and a Roman of high degree—a patrician, a nobleman. A Quintus Servilius Caepio might weep, and who knew how much he wept for the cessation of his life, and how much for that lovely lost gold? But a Quintus Servilius Caepio could not beg.

Caepio lifted his chin, drew a veil down across his gaze, and stared into nothing.

"This is for Drusus," said Silo. "You had him killed."

"I did not," said Caepio from a great distance. "I would have. But it wasn't necessary. Quintus Varius organized it. And a good thing too. If Drusus hadn't been killed, you and all your dirty friends would be citizens of Rome. But you're not. And you never will be. There are many like me in Rome."

Silo raised the sword until his hand holding the hilt was slightly higher than his shoulder. "For Drusus," he said. Down came the sword into the side of Caepio's neck where it started to curve out into the shoulder; a huge piece of bone flew and struck Fraucus on the cheek, cutting it. But not so deeply as Silo's cut, down to the top of the sternum, through veins and arteries and nerves. Blood sprayed everywhere. But Silo was not finished, and Caepio did not fall. Silo moved a little, raised his arm a second time, and repeated the blow to the other side of Caepio's neck. Down he went with Silo following to deliver the third stroke, which severed the head. Scato picked it up and rammed it crudely through the gullet onto a spear. When Silo was in the saddle again, Scato handed him the spear. The army of the Marsi moved off down the road toward the Via Valeria, Caepio's head sailing before them, seeing nothing.

The rest of Caepio the Marsi left behind with Caepio's army; this was Roman territory, let the Romans clean up the mess. More important to make a getaway before Gaius Marius discovered what had happened. Of course the story Silo had told Caepio about a ten-legion attack upon Marius had been a fabrication—he had just wanted to see how Caepio reacted. Silo did send to the deserted camp outside Varia, however, and brought his slaves away together with their royally clad twin sons. And his donkey. But not the "gold." When that was unearthed inside Caepio's tent, everyone deemed it a part of the Gold of Tolosa, and wondered where the rest of it was. Until Mamercus came forward, and someone scraped the surface of the "gold" to bare the lead beneath, thus proving the truth of Mamercus's strange tale.

For it was necessary that Silo inform someone what had really happened. Not for his own sake. For the sake of Drusus. So he had written to Drusus's brother, Mamercus.

> Quintus Servilius Caepio is dead. Yesterday I led him and his army into a trap on the road between Carseoli and Sublaqueum, having lured him out of Varia with a tall story—how I had deserted the Marsi and stolen the contents of the Marsic treasury. I had an ass with me, loaded down with lead sows skinned to look like gold. You know the weakness of the Servilii Caepiones! Dangle gold under their noses, and all else is utterly forgotten.

Every single Roman soldier belonging to Caepio is dead. But Caepio I took alive, and killed him myself. I cut his head off and carried it before my army on a spear. For Drusus. For Drusus, Mamercus Aemilius. And for Caepio's children, who will now inherit the Gold of Tolosa, with the lion's share going to the red-haired cuckoo in the Caepio nest. Some justice. If Caepio had lived until the children were grown he would have found a way to disinherit them. As it is, they now inherit everything. I am pleased to do this for Drusus because it would have pleased Drusus mightily. For Drusus. Long may his memory live in the minds of all good men, Roman and Italian.

Because in that poor family nothing was dulled, or blunted, or rendered mercifully, Silo's letter arrived scant hours after Cornelia Scipionis had collapsed and died, compounding the frightful problem Mamercus faced. With the deaths of Cornelia Scipionis and Quintus Servilius Caepio, the last threads of stability for the six children who lived in Drusus's house were irrevocably broken. They were now absolute orphans, not a parent or a grandparent between them. Uncle Mamercus was their last living relative.

By rights that should have meant he would take them into his own house and complete their upbringing himself; they would have been company for his baby daughter Aemilia Lepida, just toddling. Over the months since the death of Drusus, Mamercus had become fond of all the children, even the dreadful Young Cato, whose unyielding character Mamercus found pitiable, and whose love for his brother, Young Caepio, Mamercus found touching to the point of tears. So it never occurred to him that he would not be taking the children home—until he went home after seeing to his mother's funeral arrangements and told his wife. They had not been married more than five years, and Mamercus was very much in love with her. Not needing to marry money, he had chosen a bride for love, under the fond delusion that she too was marrying for love. One of the lesser Claudias, impoverished and desperate,

Mamercus's wife had grabbed at him. But she didn't love him. And she didn't love children. Even her own daughter she found boring, and left in the company of the nurserymaids, so that little Aemilia Lepida was more spoiled than disciplined.

"They're not coming here!" Claudia Mamercus snapped, before he had quite finished his tale.

"But they have to come here! They have nowhere else to go!" he said, shocked anew; his mother's death was so recent he had not yet emerged from that shock.

"They have that huge gorgeous house to live in—we should be so lucky! There's more money than anyone knows what to do with—hire them an army of minders and tutors and leave them right where they are." Her mouth went hard, its corners turned down. "Get it out of your head, Mamercus! They are *not* coming here."

This was of course the first crack in his idol, something she did not understand. Mamercus stood looking at his wife with wonder in his eyes, his own mouth hard. "I insist," he said.

She raised her brows. "You can insist until water turns into wine, husband! It makes no difference. They are *not* coming here. Or put it this way: if they come, I go."

"Claudia, have some pity! They're so alone!"

"Why should I pity them? They're not going to starve or lack education. There's not one of them knows what having a parent was like anyway," said Claudia Mamercus. "The two Servilias are as catty as they are snobbish, Drusus Nero is an oaf, and the rest are the descendants of a slave. Leave them where they are."

"They must have a proper home," said Mamercus.

"They already have a proper home."

That Mamercus gave in was not evidence of weakness, simply that he was a practical man and saw the inadvisability of overruling Claudia. Did he bring them home after this declaration of war, their plight would be worse. He couldn't be inside his house all day every day, and Claudia's reaction indicated that she would make it her business to take out her resentment at being saddled with them on them at every opportunity.

He went to see Marcus Aemilius Scaurus Princeps Senatus, who was admittedly not an Aemilius Lepidus, but was the senior Aemilius in the whole *gens*. Scaurus was also co-executor of Drusus's will, and sole executor of Caepio's will. Therefore it was Scaurus's duty to do what he could about the children. Mamercus felt wretched. The death of his mother was a colossal blow to him, for he had always known her, always lived with her until she went to Drusus—which she had done, come to think of it just after he had married his Claudia and brought her home! Not one word of disparagement of Claudia had she ever uttered. But, looking back, how glad Cornelia Scipionis must have been to have a perfect excuse to move out.

By the time Mamercus reached the house of Marcus Aemilius Scaurus he had fallen out of love with Claudia Mamercus and would never replace that emotion with a friendlier, more comfortable kind of love. Until today he would have deemed it impossible to fall out of love so quickly, so thoroughly; yet—here he was, knocking on Scaurus's door, devastated by the loss of his mother and out of love with his wife.

It therefore cost Mamercus nothing to explain his predicament to Scaurus in the bleakest terms.

"What should I do, Marcus Aemilius?"

Scaurus Princeps Senatus sat back in his chair, lucent green eyes fixed upon this Livian face, with its beaky nose, dark eyes, prominent bones. The last of two families, was Mamercus. He must be cherished and assisted in every way possible.

"Certainly I think you must accommodate the wishes of your wife, Mamercus. Which means you will have to leave the children in Marcus Livius Drusus's house. And that in turn means you must find someone noble to live there with them."

"*Who?*"

"Leave it with me, Mamercus," said Scaurus briskly. "I'll think of somebody."

Think of somebody Scaurus did, two days later. Very pleased with himself, he sent for Mamercus.

"Do you remember that particular Quintus Servilius Caepio

who was consul two years before our illustrious relative Aemilius Paullus fought Perseus of Macedonia at Pydna?" asked Scaurus.

Mamercus grinned. "Not *personally,* Marcus Aemilius! But I do know who you mean."

"Good," said Scaurus, grinning back. "That particular Quintus Servilius Caepio had three sons. The oldest was adopted out to the Fabii Maximi, with bitter results—Eburnus and his unfortunate son." Scaurus was enjoying this; he was one of Rome's greatest experts in noble genealogy and could trace the ramifications in the family tree of anyone who mattered. "The youngest son, Quintus, sired the consul Caepio who stole the Gold of Tolosa and lost the battle of Arausio. He also sired a girl, Servilia, who married our esteemed consular Quintus Lutatius Catulus Caesar. From Caepio the consul there came that Caepio who was killed the other day by the Marsian Silo, and the girl who married your brother, Drusus."

"You've left out the middle son," said Mamercus.

"On purpose, Mamercus, on purpose! He's the one I'm really interested in today. His name was Gnaeus. However, he married much later than his younger brother, Quintus, so that *his* son, a Gnaeus of course, was only old enough to be a quaestor while his first cousin was already a consular and busy losing the battle of Arausio. Young Gnaeus was quaestor in Asia Province. He had recently married a Porcia Liciniana—not a well-dowered girl, but Gnaeus didn't need a well-dowered girl. He was, as are all the Servilii Caepiones, a very wealthy man. When Gnaeus the quaestor left for Asia Province he had produced one child—a girl I shall call Servilia Gnaea to distinguish her from all the other Servilias. Now the sex of his and Porcia Liciniana's child, Servilia Gnaea, was most unfortunate."

Scaurus paused for breath, beaming. "Isn't it wonderful, my dear Mamercus, how tortuously interconnected all our families are?"

"Daunting, I'd rather call it," said Mamercus.

"Getting back to the two-year-old girl, Servilia Gnaea," said Scaurus, sinking pleasurably into his chair, "I used the word 'unfortunate' with good reason. Gnaeus Caepio had prudently made his will before he left for Asia Province and his quaestorship, but I imagine he never dreamed for a moment that it would be executed. Under the *lex Voconia de mulierum hereditatibus,* Servilia Gnaea—a girl!—could not inherit. His will left his very large fortune to his first cousin, Caepio who lost the battle of Arausio and stole the Gold of Tolosa."

"I notice, Marcus Aemilius, that you're very frank about the fate of the Gold of Tolosa," said Mamercus. "Everyone always says he did steal it, but I've never heard someone of your *auctoritas* say so unequivocally before."

Scaurus flapped an impatient hand. "Oh, we all know he took it, Mamercus, so why not say so? You've never struck me as a chatty individual, so I think I'm safe in saying it to you."

"You are."

"The understanding, of course, was that Caepio of Arausio and the Gold of Tolosa would return the fortune to Servilia Gnaea if he inherited it. Naturally Gnaeus Caepio had provided for the girl to the full extent the law allowed in his will—a pittance compared to the entire fortune. And off he went as quaestor to Asia Province. On the way back, his ship was wrecked and he was drowned. Caepio of Arausio and the Gold of Tolosa inherited. But he did not give the fortune back to the little girl. He simply added it to his own already astronomical fortune, though he needed it not at all. And in the fullness of time, poor Servilia Gnaea's inheritance passed to the Caepio killed the other day by Silo."

"That's disgusting," said Mamercus, scowling.

"I agree. But it's also life," said Scaurus.

"What happened to Servilia Gnaea? And her mother?"

"Oh, they've survived, of course. They live very modestly in Gnaeus Caepio's house, which Caepio the consul and then in turn his son did permit the two women to keep. Not legally, just as a domicile. When the will of the last Quintus Caepio is probated—I am in the middle of that task now—the house will be documented in it. As you know, everything Caepio had with the exception of lavish dowries for his two girls goes to the little boy, Caepio of the red hair, ha ha! Much to my surprise, I was named sole executor! I had thought someone like Philippus would be named, but I ought to have known better. No Caepio ever lived who did not cultivate his fortune assiduously. Our recently deceased Caepio must have decided that if Philippus or Varius were executor, too much might go missing. A wise decision! Philippus would have behaved like a pig in acorns."

"All this is fascinating, Marcus Aemilius," said Mamercus, experiencing the stirrings of an interest in genealogy, "but I am as yet unenlightened."

"Patience, patience, Mamercus, I'm getting there!" said Scaurus.

"I imagine, by the way," said Mamercus, remembering what his brother Drusus had said, "that one of the reasons you were appointed executor was due to my brother, Drusus. He had, it seemed, certain information about Caepio that he threatened to disclose if Caepio didn't leave his children properly cared for in his will. It may be that Drusus stipulated the executor. Caepio was very much afraid of whatever information Drusus had."

"The Gold of Tolosa again," said Scaurus complacently. "It has to be, you know. My investigations into Caepio's affairs, though only two or three days old, are already fascinating. So much money! The two girls have been left dowries of two hundred talents each—yet that doesn't even begin to reach the limits of what they could have inherited, even under the *lex Voconia*. Red-haired Young Caepio is the richest man in Rome."

"Please, Marcus Aemilius! Finish the story!"

"Oh, yes, yes! The impatience of youth! Under our laws, given that the beneficiary is a minor, I am obliged to take into my consideration even such petty things as the house in which Servilia Gnaea— now aged seventeen—and her mother Porcia Liciniana still live. Now I have no idea what kind of man red-haired Young Caepio will turn out to be, and I have no wish to leave my own son testamentary headaches. It is not impossible that Young Caepio on reaching manhood will demand to know why I went on allowing Servilia Gnaea and her mother to live rent-free in that house. The original ownership by the time that Young Caepio is a man will be so far in the past that he may never know it. Legally, it is his house."

"I do see where you're going, Marcus Aemilius," said Mamercus. "Go on, do! I'm fascinated."

Scaurus leaned forward. "I would suggest, Mamercus, that you offer Servilia Gnaea—*not* her mother!—a job. The poor girl has absolutely no dowry. It has taken all of her slender inheritance to afford her and her mother comfortable living in the fifteen years since the father died. The Porcii Liciniani are not in any position to help, I add. Or will not help, which amounts to the same thing. Between our first talk and this one, I popped round to see Servilia Gnaea and Porcia Liciniana, ostensibly as the executor of Caepio's will. And after I had explained my own predicament, they became quite frantic as to what the future might hold for them. I explained, you see, that I thought I must sell the house so that its lack of earning rent over the past fifteen years need not appear in the estate accounts."

"That's clever enough and devious enough to allow you to qualify for the job of High Chamberlain to King Ptolemy of Egypt," said Mamercus, laughing.

"True!" said Scaurus, and drew a breath. "Servilia Gnaea is now seventeen, as I have said. That means she will reach normal marriageable age in about a year's time. But, alas, she is not a beauty. In fact she's extremely plain, poor thing. Without a dowry—and she has no dowry—she'll never get a husband of remotely her own class. Her mother is a true Cato Licinianus, not impressed by the idea of a rich but vulgar knight or a rich but bucolic farmer for *her* daughter. However, needs must when there is no dowry!"

How convoluted he is! thought Mamercus, looking attentive.

"What I suggest you do is this, Mamercus. Having received a worrisome visit from me already, the ladies will be in a mood to listen to you. I suggest that you propose that Servilia Gnaea—and her mother, but only as her guest!—accept a commission from you to look after the six children of Marcus Livius Drusus. Live in Drusus's house. Enjoy a generous allowance for upkeep, living expenses, and maintenance. *On the condition* that Servilia Gnaea remains single until the last child is well and truly of age. The last child is Young Cato, now three. Three from sixteen is thirteen.

Therefore Servilia Gnaea will have to remain single for the next thirteen to fourteen years. That would make her about thirty when her contract with you is worked out. Not an impossible age for marriage! Particularly if you offer to present her with a dowry the same size as the dowries of her young cousins—the two girls she will be looking after—when she finishes her task. The Caepio fortune can well afford to donate her two hundred talents, Mamercus, believe me. And to make absolutely sure—I am, after all, no longer a young man—I will peel off those two hundred talents now, and invest them in Servilia Gnaea's name. In trust until her thirty-first birthday. Provided she has acquitted herself to your and my satisfaction."

A wicked grin spread across Scaurus's face. "She is not pretty, Mamercus! But I guarantee that when Servilia Gnaea turns thirty-one she will find herself able to pick and choose between a dozen hopeful men of her own class. Two hundred talents are irresistible!" He fiddled with his pen for a moment, then looked directly into Mamercus's eyes, his own beautiful orbs stern. "I am *not* a young man. And I am the only Scaurus left among the Aemilii. I have a young wife, a daughter just turned eleven, and a son five years old. I am now the sole executor of Rome's greatest private fortune. Should anything happen to me before my son is mature, to whom do I trust the fortunes of my own loved ones, and the fortunes of those three Servilian children? You and I are the joint executors of Drusus's estate, which means we share the care of the three Porcian children already. Would you be willing to act as trustee and executor for me and mine after my death? You are a Livius by birth, but an Aemilius by adoption. I would rest easier, Mamercus, if you said yes to me. I need the reassurance of an honest man at my back."

Mamercus did not hesitate. "I say yes, Marcus Aemilius."

Which concluded their discussion. From Scaurus's house Mamercus went immediately to see Servilia Gnaea and her mother. They lived in an excellent location on the Circus Maximus side of the Palatine, but Mamercus was quick to note that, while Caepio might have permitted the ladies to live in the place, he had not been generous with funds for its upkeep. The paint on the stuccoed walls was flaking badly and the atrium ceiling was marred by several huge patches of damp and mildew; in one corner the leak was evidently so bad that the plaster had fallen away, exposing the hair and slats beneath. The murals had once been very attractive, but time and neglect had both faded and obscured them. However, a glance into the peristyle-garden while he waited to be received indicated that the ladies were not lazy, for it was carefully kept, full of flowers, minus weeds.

He had asked to see both of them, and both of them came, Porcia more curious than anything else. Of course she knew he was married; no noble Roman mother with a daughter needing a husband left any youngish man of her own class uninvestigated.

Both women were dark, Servilia Gnaea darker than her mother, however. And plainer, despite the fact that the mother had a true Catonian nose, hugely aquiline, whereas the daughter's nose was small. For one thing, Servilia Gnaea suffered dreadfully from acne; her eyes were set too close together and were slightly piggy, and her mouth was unfashionably wide and thin-lipped. The mother looked very proud and haughty. The daughter simply looked dour; she had that humorless kind of character flatness which had the power to daunt many a more courageous man than Mamercus, who did not lack courage in the least.

"We are related, Mamercus Aemilius," said the mother graciously. "My grandmother was Aemilia Tertia, daughter of Paullus."

"Of course," said Mamercus, and sat where indicated.

"We are also related through the Livii," she pursued as she sat on a couch opposite him, her daughter beside her mumchance.

"I know," said Mamercus, finding it difficult to think of a good way to introduce the reason for his call.

"What do you want?" asked Porcia, solving his dilemma bluntly.

So he stated his case with equal bluntness; Mamercus was not a man of easy words, for all that his mother had been a Cornelia of the Scipiones. Porcia and Servilia Gnaea sat and listened most attentively, but without giving away their thoughts.

"You would require us to live in the house of Marcus Livius Drusus for the next thirteen to fourteen years, is that right?" asked Porcia when he finished.

"Yes."

"After which my daughter, dowered with two hundred talents, would be free to marry?"

"Yes."

"And what about me?"

Mamercus blinked. He always thought of mothers continuing to live in the house of the *paterfamilias*—but of course that was this house, which Scaurus intended to sell. And it would be a brave man who asked this particular mother-in-law to live with him! thought Mamercus, smiling inwardly.

"Would you be willing to accept the life tenancy of a seaside villa at Misenum or Cumae, together with a competency adequate for the needs of a retired lady?" he asked.

"I would," said Porcia instantly.

"Then if all this is agreed to by legal and binding contract, may I assume both of you are willing to take on this burden, look after the children?"

"You may." Porcia looked down her amazing nose. "Have the children a pedagogue?"

"No. The oldest boy is just about ten years old, and has been going to school. Young Caepio is not yet seven, and Young Cato only three," said Mamercus.

"Nevertheless, Mamercus Aemilius, I think it vitally important that you find a good man to live in as tutor to all six children," announced Porcia. "We will have no male in the house. While this is not a danger physically, for the children's sake I feel there *must* be a man of authority who does not have slave status resident in the house. A pedagogue would be ideal."

"You are absolutely correct, Porcia. I shall see to it at once," said Mamercus, taking his leave.

"We will come tomorrow," said Porcia, escorting him out.

"So soon? I'm very pleased, but don't you have things to do, things to arrange?"

"My daughter and I own nothing, Mamercus Aemilius, beyond some clothes. Even the servants here belong to the estate of Quintus Servilius Caepio." She held open the door. "Good day. And thank you, Mamercus Aemilius. You have rescued us from worse penury."

Well, thought Mamercus as he hastened to the establishment in the Basilica Sempronia where he expected to find a pedagogue for sale, I'm glad I'm not one of those six poor children! Still, it will be a better life for them than living with my Claudia!

"We have quite a few suitable men on our books, Mamercus Aemilius," said Lucius Duronius Postumus, the owner of one of Rome's two best agencies for pedagogues.

"What's the going price for a superior pedagogue these days?" Mamercus asked, never having had this particular duty to do before.

Duronius pursed his lips. "Anywhere between one hundred and three hundred thousand sesterces—even more if the product is the very best anywhere."

"Phew!" whistled Mamercus. "Cato the Censor would not have been amused!"

"Cato the Censor was a parsimonious old fart," said Duronius. "Even in his day, a good pedagogue cost a lot more than a miserable six thousand."

"But I'm buying a tutor for three of his direct descendants!"

"Take it or leave it," said Duronius, looking bored.

Mamercus stifled a sigh. Looking after these six children was proving to be an expensive business! "Oh, all right, all right, I suppose I'll have to take it. When can I see the candidates?"

"Since I board all my readily marketable slaves within Rome, I'll send them round to your house in the morning. What's your absolute upper limit?"

"I don't know! What's a few more hundred thousand sesterces?" cried Mamercus, throwing his hands in the air. "Do your worst, Duronius! But if you send me a dunce or a cuckoo, I'll castrate you with great pleasure!"

He did not mention to Duronius that he planned to free the man he bought; that would only have increased the price even more. No, whoever it was would be manumitted privately and taken into Mamercus's own clientele. Which meant whoever it was could liberate himself no more easily from his employment than if he had still been a slave. A freedman client belonged to his ex-master.

In the end there was only one suitable man—and of course he was the most expensive. Duronius knew his business. Given that there would be two adult women in the house without a *paterfamilias* to supervise them, the tutor had to be of great moral integrity as well as a pleasant, understanding man. The successful candidate was named Sarpedon, and he hailed from Lycia in the south of the Roman Asia Province. Like most of his kind, he had sold himself voluntarily into slavery, deeming his chances of a comfortable, well-fed old age considerably better if he spent the years between in service to a Roman of high degree. Either he would earn his freedom, or he would be looked after. So he had taken himself off to the Smyrna offices of Lucius Duronius Postumius, and been accepted. This would be his first post—that is, his first time of purchase. He was twenty-five years old, extremely well read in both Greek and Latin; his spoken Greek was the purest Attic, and his spoken Latin so good he might have been a genuine Roman. But none of that was responsible for his getting the job. He got the job because he was appallingly ugly—so short he came only to Mamercus's chest, thin to the point of emaciation, and badly scarred from a fire in his childhood. His voice, however, was beautiful, and out of his maimed face there looked two very lovely, kind eyes. When informed he was to be freed immediately and that his name would henceforth be Mamercus Aemilius Sarpedon, he knew himself the most fortunate of men; his wage would be much higher and his citizenship Roman. One day he would be able to retire to his home town of Xanthus and live like a potentate.

"It's an expensive exercise," said Mamercus to Scaurus as he dropped a roll of paper on Scaurus's desk. "And, I warn you, as executor for the Servilius Caepio side of things, you're not going to get off any lighter than the two of us are as Drusus's executors. Here's the bill so far. I suggest we split it down the middle between the two estates."

Scaurus picked up the paper and unfurled it. "Tutor . . . *Four hundred thousand?*"

"You go and talk to Duronius!" snapped Mamercus. "I've done all the work, you've issued all the directives! There are going to be two Roman noblewomen in that house whose virtue has to be ensured, so there can be no handsome tutors living there as well. The new pedagogue is repellently ugly."

Scaurus giggled. "All right, all right, I'll take your word for it! Ye gods, what prices we endure today!" He perused further. "Dowry for Servilia Gnaea, two hundred talents—well, I can't grizzle about that, can I, when I suggested it? House expenses per annum not including repairs and maintenance, one hundred thousand sesterces . . . Yes, that's modest enough . . . Da da, da dee . . . Villa at Misenum or Cumae? What on earth for?"

"For Porcia, when Servilia Gnaea is free to marry."

"Oh, *merda*! I never thought of that! Of course you're right. No husband would take *her* on as well as marry a lump like Servilia Gnaea. . . . Yes, yes, you've got a deal! We'll split it right down the middle."

They grinned at each other. Scaurus got to his feet. "A cup of wine, Mamercus, I think! What a pity your wife wouldn't co-operate! It would have saved both of us—in our capacity as executors of the estates—a great deal of money."

"Since it isn't coming out of our own purses and the estates can well afford to bear the cost, Marcus Aemilius, why should we care? Domestic peace is worth any price." He took the wine. "I'm leaving Rome in any case. It's time I did my military duty."

"I understand," said Scaurus, sitting down again.

"Until my mother died I had thought it my principal duty to stay in Rome and help her with the children. She hadn't been well since Drusus died. Broke her heart. But now the children are properly organized, I've no excuse. So I'm going."

"Who to?"

"Lucius Cornelius Sulla."

"Good choice," said Scaurus, nodding. "He's the coming man."

"Do you think so? Isn't he a little old?"

"So was Gaius Marius. And face it, Mamercus—who else is there? Rome is thin of great men at the moment. If it wasn't for Gaius Marius we wouldn't have one victory under our belts—and as he rightly says in his report, it was very Pyrrhic at that. He won. But Lupus had lost in a far worse way the day before."

"True. I'm disappointed in Lucius Julius, however. I would have deemed him capable of great things."

"He's too highly strung, Mamercus."

"I hear the Senate is now calling this the Marsic War."

"Yes, the Marsic War is how it will go down in the history books, it seems." Scaurus looked impish. "After all, you know, we can't call it the *Italian* War! That would send everyone in Rome into a flat panic—they might think we were actually fighting all of Italy! And the Marsi did send us a formal declaration of war. By calling it the Marsic War, it looks smaller, less important."

Mamercus stared, astonished. "Who thought of that?"

"Philippus, of course."

"Oh, I'm glad I'm going!" said Mamercus, getting up. "If I stayed, who knows? I might get inducted into the Senate!"

"You must be of an age to stand for quaestor, surely."

"I am. But I'm not standing. I shall wait for the censors," said Mamercus Aemilius Lepidus Livianus.

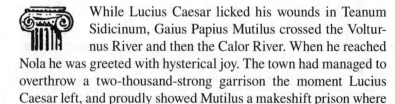 While Lucius Caesar licked his wounds in Teanum Sidicinum, Gaius Papius Mutilus crossed the Volturnus River and then the Calor River. When he reached Nola he was greeted with hysterical joy. The town had managed to overthrow a two-thousand-strong garrison the moment Lucius Caesar left, and proudly showed Mutilus a makeshift prison where

the Roman cohorts had been put. It was a small paddock inside
the walls where sheep and pigs had been kept before slaughter,
now fenced in by a very high stone barricade topped with broken
sherds, and patrolled constantly. To keep the Romans docile, said
the Nolans, they were only being fed once every eight days, and
watered every third day.

"Good!" said Mutilus, pleased. "I'll address them myself."

To deliver his speech he used the wooden platform from which
the Nolans threw bread and water to the captives in the mire below. "My name," he shouted, "is Gaius Papius Mutilus! I am a
Samnite. And by the end of the year I will be ruling all Italy, including Rome! You don't stand a chance against us. You're weak,
worn out, used up. Townspeople overcame you! Now here you are,
penned up like the animals which used to be kept in the same
place, but crowded in worse than those animals were. Two thousand of you in a paddock that used to hold two hundred pigs. Uncomfortable, isn't it? You're sick. You're hungry. You're thirsty.
And I'm here to tell you it's going to get worse. From now on you
don't get fed at all, and you'll get water every five days. There is an
alternative, however. You can enlist in the legions of Italia. Think
it over."

"There's nothing to think over!" cried Lucius Postumius, the
garrison commander. "Here we stay!"

Papius climbed down, smiling. "I'll give them sixteen days," he
said. "They'll surrender."

Things were going very well for Italia. Gaius Vidacilius had in-
vaded Apulia and found himself in a bloodless theater of war—
Larinum, Teanum Apulum, Luceria and Ausculum all joined the
Italian cause, their men flocking to enlist in the Italian legions.
And when Mutilus reached the coast at Crater Bay, the seaports of
Stabiae, Salernum and Surrentum declared for Italy, as well as the
river port of Pompeii.

Finding himself the owner of four fleets of warships, Mutilus
decided to carry the campaign onto the water by launching an attack upon Neapolis. But Rome had had a great deal more experience at sea. The Roman admiral, Otacilius, successfully beat the

Italian ships back to their home ports. Determined not to yield, the Neapolitans stoically beat out the fires caused by Mutilus's bombardment of the waterfront warehouses with oil-soaked, blazing missiles.

In every town where the Italian populace had succeeded in forging an alliance with Italia, the Roman populace was put to death. Among those towns was Nola; Servius Sulpicius Galba's courageous hostess perished with the rest. Even when apprised of this, the starving garrison of Nola held out until Lucius Postumius called a meeting, not a difficult thing to do; two thousand men in a compound designed for two hundred pigs meant a degree of crowding that made it hard for the men to lie down.

"I think all the rankers should surrender," Postumius said, looking with tired eyes at tired faces. "The Italians are going to kill us, of that we may be sure. And I for one must defy them until I am dead. Because I am the commander. It is my duty. Whereas you rankers owe Rome a different kind of duty. You must stay alive to fight in other wars—foreign wars. So join the Italians, I beg of you! If you can desert to your own side after joining, do so. But at all costs stay alive. Stay alive for Rome." He paused to rest. "The centurions must surrender too. Without her centurions, Rome is lost. As for my officers, if you wish to capitulate, I will understand. If you do not, I will understand."

It took Lucius Postumius a long time to persuade the soldiers to do as he asked. Everyone wanted to die, if only to show the Italians they couldn't cow genuine Romans. But in the end Postumius won, and the legionaries did surrender. However, talk though he did, try though he did, he couldn't persuade the centurions. Nor did his four military tribunes want to give in. They all died—centurions, military tribunes, and Lucius Postumius himself.

Before the last man in the Nolan pigpen was dead, Herculaneum declared for the Italian cause and murdered its Roman citizens. Now jubilant, sure of himself, Mutilus stepped up his sea war. Lightning raids were launched against Neapolis for a second time, Puteoli, Cumae, and Tarracina; this brought Latium's coast into the conflict and exacerbated already festering resentments between Romans, Latins, and the Italians of Latium. Admiral Otacilius fought back doggedly, and with sufficient success to prevent the Italians taking any port beyond Herculaneum; though many a waterfront burned, and men died.

When it became clear that all of the peninsula south of northern Campania was Italian territory, Lucius Julius Caesar conferred with his senior legate, Lucius Cornelius Sulla.

"We're completely cut off from Brundisium, Tarentum, and Rhegium, there can be no doubt of it," said Lucius Caesar gloomily.

"If we are, then let's forget about them," said Sulla cheerily. "I'd rather we concentrated upon northern Campania. Mutilus has laid siege to Acerrae, which means he's moving toward Capua. If Acerrae surrenders, Capua will go—its livelihood is Roman, but its heart is with Italia."

Lucius Caesar sat up, affronted. "How can you be so—so merry when we can't contain Mutilus or Vidacilius?" he demanded.

"Because we will win," said Sulla strongly. "Believe me, Lucius Julius, *we will win*! This isn't an election, you know. In an election, the early vote reflects the outcome. But in war, victory eventually goes to the side that doesn't give in. The Italians are fighting for their freedom, they say. Now on cursory inspection that might seem like the best of all motives. But it isn't. It's an intangible. A concept, Lucius Julius, nothing more. Whereas Rome is fighting for her life. And that is why Rome will win. The Italians aren't fighting for life in the same way at all. They already know a life they've been used to for generations upon generations. It may not be ideal, it may not be what they want. But it is tangible. You wait, Lucius Julius! When the Italian people grow tired of fighting for a dream, the balance will tip against Italia. They're not an *entity*. They don't have a history and a tradition like ours. They lack the *mos maiorum*! Rome is real. Italia is not."

Apparently Lucius Caesar's mind was deaf, even if his ears were not. "If we can't keep the Italians out of Latium, we're done for. And I don't think we'll keep them out of Latium."

"We *will* keep them out of Latium!" Sulla insisted, not losing one iota of his confidence.

"How?" asked the morbid man in the general's chair.

"For one thing, Lucius Julius, I am the bearer of good tidings. Your cousin Sextus Julius and his brother Gaius Julius have landed in Puteoli. Their ships contain two thousand Numidian cavalry and twenty thousand infantrymen. Most of the foot soldiers are veterans into the bargain. Africa yielded up thousands of Gaius Marius's old troops—a bit grizzled round the temples, but determined to fight for the homeland. By now they should all be in Capua, being outfitted and undergoing retraining. Four legions, Quintus Lutatius feels, rather than five under-strength legions, and I agree with him. With your permission, I'll send two legions to Gaius Marius in the north now that he's commander-in-chief, and we'll keep the other two here in Campania." Sulla sighed, grinned jubilantly.

"It would be better to keep all four here in Campania," said Lucius Caesar.

"I don't think we can do that," said Sulla gently but very firmly. "The troop losses in the north have been far greater than ours, and the only two battle-hardened legions are shut up in Firmum Picenum with Pompey Strabo."

"I suppose you're right." Lucius Caesar smothered his disappointment. "Much and all as I detest Gaius Marius, I have to admit I rest far easier now he's in full command. Things might improve in the north."

"*And* they will here too!" Sulla chirped brightly, smothering, not disappointment, but exasperation—ye gods, did any second-in-command ever have such a negative general to deal with? He leaned forward across Lucius Caesar's desk, face suddenly stern. "We have to draw Mutilus off from Acerrae until the new troops are ready, and I have a plan how to do that."

"What?"

"Let me take the two best legions we have, march for Aesernia."

"Are you sure?"

"Trust me, Lucius Julius, trust me!"

"Well . . ."

"We *must* draw Mutilus off Acerrae! A feint at Aesernia is the best way. Trust me, Lucius Julius! I'll do it, and I won't lose my men doing it either."

"How will you go?" Lucius Caesar asked, remembering the debacle in the defile near Atina when he met Scato.

"The same way you did. Up the Via Latina to Aquinum, then through the Melfa Gorge."

"You'll be ambushed."

"Don't worry, I'll be ready," said Sulla blithely, finding that the deeper went Lucius Caesar's depressions, the higher were his own flights of fancy.

However, to the Samnite leader Duilius, the two trim-looking legions which appeared on the road from Aquinum seemed far from ready to tackle an ambush. By late afternoon the head of the Roman column was marching jauntily into the maw of the defile, and he could distinctly hear the centurions and tribunes shouting among the ranks that they'd better be all inside and camped before darkness, or there'd be punishment duties for everyone.

Duilius stared down from the top of the crags, frowning, unconsciously chewing his nails. Was this Roman brashness the height of idiocy, or some brilliant ploy? As soon as the Roman front ranks had become properly visible, he knew who was leading them—and leading them on foot at that—Lucius Cornelius Sulla, unmistakable in his big floppy headgear. And Sulla had no reputation for idiocy, even though his activities in the field so far had been minimal. It seemed from the look of the scurrying figures that Sulla was setting about making a very strongly fortified camp, which suggested that his plan was to hang on to the gorge, eject the Samnite garrison.

"He can't succeed," said Duilius at last, still frowning. "Still, we'll do what we can tonight. It's too late to attack him—but I can make it impossible for him to retreat tomorrow when I do attack. Tribune, get a legion on the road in his rear, and do it quietly, understand?"

Sulla stood with his second-in-command on the floor of the gorge watching the intensely busy legionaries.

"I hope this works," said his second-in-command, none other than Quintus Caecilius Metellus Pius the Piglet.

Since the death of his father, Numidicus Piggle-wiggle, the Piglet's affection for Sulla had grown rather than diminished. He had gone south to Capua with Catulus Caesar and spent the early months of the war helping to put Capua on a war footing. This posting to Sulla was his first genuinely martial commission since the Germans, and he burned to excel, yet was determined too that Sulla should have no grounds to complain about his conduct; whatever the orders were, he intended to follow them to the letter.

Up went Sulla's fine brows, undarkened these days. "It will work," he said serenely.

"Wouldn't it just be better to stay here and throw the Samnites out of the gorge? That way, we'd have permanent access to the east," said the Piglet, looking eager.

"It wouldn't work, Quintus Caecilius. Yes, we could free the gorge. But we don't have the two spare legions it would take to hold the gorge in perpetuity. Which means the Samnites would move back into it the moment we left. They have the spare legions. So it's more important to show them that what seems an impregnable position isn't necessarily so." Sulla grunted, a contented sound. "Good, it's dark enough. Have the torches kindled—and make it look convincing."

Metellus Pius made it look convincing; to the watchers on the heights it appeared all through the hours of night that the fortification of Sulla's camp went on at frantic pace.

"They've decided to take the gorge off us, no doubt of it," said Duilius. "Fools! They're shut in here for the duration." He too sounded contented.

But the rising of the sun showed Duilius his mistake. Behind the huge mounds of rock and earth thrown up against the sides of the cliffs, there were no soldiers at all; having baited the Samnite bull, the Roman wolf had slunk away. To the east, not to the west. From his vantage point Duilius could see the rear of Sulla's column dwindling to a pall of dust on the road to Aesernia. And there was nothing he could do about it, for his orders were explicit; he was to garrison the Melfa Gorge, not pursue a formidable little force down onto the shelterless plains. The best he could do in this situation was to send a warning to Aesernia.

Even that recourse proved useless. Sulla punched a hole in the lines of the besiegers and got his expedition inside the city with scarcely a casualty.

"He's too good," was the next Italian message, this time from Gaius Trebatius, commanding the Samnite siege, to Gaius Papius Mutilus, attacking Acerrae. "Aesernia is too sprawling to enclose with the number of men I have; I couldn't spread myself out enough to prevent his getting in, nor compress myself enough to keep him from spreading his invaders. Nor do I think I can prevent his getting out if he decides he wants to."

The beleaguered city, Sulla soon discovered, was cheerful and undistressed; there were ten cohorts of good soldiers inside, those deserted by Scipio Asiagenes and Acilius having been joined by refugees from Venafrum and then Beneventum. The city also had a competent commander in the person of Marcus Claudius Marcellus.

"The supplies and extra arms you've brought us are welcome," said Marcellus. "We will survive here for many moons to come."

"Do you plan to stay here yourself, then?"

Marcellus nodded, grinned fiercely. "Of course! Having been driven out of Venafrum, I am determined I will not budge from Latin Aesernia." His smile faded. "All the Roman citizens of Venafrum and Beneventum are dead, killed by the townsfolk. How much they hate us, the Italians! Especially the Samnites."

"Not without reason, Marcus Claudius." Sulla shrugged. "But that's in the past and for the future. All which concerns *us* is victory in the field—and holding on to those towns which are defiant Roman outposts in a sea of Italians." He leaned forward. "This is a war of the spirit too. The Italians must be taught that Rome and Romans are inviolate. I sacked every settlement between the Melfa Gorge and Aesernia, even if it was only a pair of cottages. Why?

To demonstrate to the Italians that Rome can operate behind enemy lines and take the fruits of Italian soil to revictual places like
Aesernia. If you can hold out here, my dear Marcus Claudius, you
too will teach the Italians a lesson."

"While ever I can, I will hold Aesernia," said Marcellus, meaning every word.

Thus when Sulla quit the city he left in a mood of quiet confidence; Aesernia would continue to withstand its siege. He marched
through Italian territory in the open, trusting to his luck, that
magical bond he had with the goddess Fortune, for he had no idea
of the whereabouts of every Samnite or Picentine army. And his
luck held, even when he marched past towns like Venafrum, where
he actively encouraged his soldiers to shout and gesture insults up
at the watchers on the walls. When his troops strolled through the
gates of Capua they were singing, and the whole of Capua turned
out to cheer.

Lucius Caesar, Sulla was informed, had marched to Acerrae
the moment Mutilus pulled some of his troops out to follow what
had seemed like a major deployment against the siege of Aesernia;
but—as luck would have it—Mutilus himself had remained at
Acerrae. Leaving Catulus Caesar to ensure that his men enjoyed a
well-earned rest, Sulla straddled a mule and trotted off to locate
his general.

He found him in an ill humor, and bereft of the Numidian cavalry Sextus Caesar had transported across the seas.

"Do you know what Mutilus did?" demanded Lucius Caesar
the moment he set eyes upon Sulla.

"No," said Sulla, leaning casually against a pillar made of captured enemy spears and resigning himself to a litany of complaints.

"When Venusia capitulated and the Venusini joined Italia,
the Picentine Gaius Vidacilius found an enemy hostage living in
Venusia—I'd completely forgotten he was there, and so I suppose
had everyone else. Oxyntas, one of the sons of King Jugurtha of
Numidia. So Vidacilius sent the Numidian here to Acerrae. When

I attacked, I used my Numidian cavalry as an advance guard. And do you know what Mutilus did? He put a purple robe and a diadem on Oxyntas, and paraded him! The next thing I knew, there were my two thousand horse-troopers on their knees to an enemy of Rome!" Lucius Caesar's hands clawed at the air. "To think what it *cost* to bring them all this way! A futile exercise, futile!"

"What did you do?"

"I rounded them up, force-marched them to Puteoli, and sent them home to Numidia. Let their king deal with them!"

Sulla straightened. "That was good thinking, Lucius Julius," he said sincerely, turning to stroke the column of captured spears. "Come now, obviously you haven't suffered a military disaster, despite the appearance of Oxyntas! You've won a battle here."

Natural pessimism began to thaw, though Lucius Caesar could not quite summon up a smile. "Yes, I won a battle—for what it's worth. Mutilus attacked three days ago, I presume after he got word of your successful penetration through the besiegers at Aesernia. I tricked him by leading my forces out the back gate of my camp, and we killed six thousand Samnites."

"And Mutilus?"

"Withdrew immediately. For the moment, Capua is safe."

"Excellent, Lucius Julius!"

"I wish I thought so," said Lucius Caesar dolefully.

Suppressing a sigh, Sulla asked, "What else has happened?"

"Publius Crassus has lost his oldest boy before Grumentum, and was shut up inside the town for a long while. But the Lucanians are as fickle as they are lacking in discipline, luckily for Publius Crassus and his middle boy. Lamponius drew his men off to somewhere else, and Publius and Lucius Crassus got out." The commander-in-chief heaved an enormous sigh. "Those fools in Rome wanted me to drop everything and appear in Rome for no better reason than to supervise the choosing of a consul *suffectus* to replace Lupus until the elections. I told them where to go, and recommended that they rely upon their urban praetor—there's nothing in Rome Cinna can't deal with." He sighed yet again, sniffed, bethought himself of something else. "Gaius Coelius in

Italian Gaul has dispatched a beautiful little army under Publius Sulpicius to assist Pompey Strabo in getting his conceited Picentine arse out of Firmum Picenum. I wish Publius Sulpicius good luck in dealing with that cross-eyed semi-barbarian! I must say, however, Lucius Cornelius, that you and Gaius Marius were right about young Quintus Sertorius. At the moment he's governing Italian Gaul completely on his own, and doing better than Gaius Coelius. Coelius has gone off to Gaul-across-the-Alps in a hurry."

"What's going on there?"

"The Salluvii have gone on a headhunting spree." Lucius Caesar grimaced. "What hope have we ever got of civilizing these people when several hundred years of exposure to Greeks and Romans haven't even made an impression? The moment they thought we weren't looking, back came the old barbarian habits. *Headhunting!* I sent Gaius Coelius a personal message instructing him to be utterly merciless. We can't afford a major uprising in Gaul-across-the-Alps."

"So young Quintus Sertorius is holding the fort in Italian Gaul," said Sulla. An extraordinary expression of mingled weariness, impatience, and bitterness settled on his face. "Well, what else could one expect? The Grass Crown before he was thirty."

"Jealous?" asked Lucius Caesar slyly.

Sulla twisted. "No, I'm not jealous! Good luck to him, and may he prosper! I *like* that young man. I've known him since he was a cadet with Marius in Africa."

Lucius Caesar made an inarticulate noise and slumped back into his gloom.

"Has anything else happened?" prompted Sulla.

"Sextus Julius Caesar took his half of the troops he brought back from overseas and headed up the Via Appia to Rome, where I gather he intends to spend the winter." Lucius Caesar did not care very much for his cousin. "He's sick, as usual. Luckily he's got his brother Gaius with him—between them they make one decent man."

"Ah! So my friend Aurelia will have a husband for a little while," said Sulla, smiling tenderly.

"You know, Lucius Cornelius, you're odd! What on earth does that matter?"

"It matters not at all. But you are right nonetheless, Lucius Julius. I *am* odd!"

Lucius Caesar saw something in Sulla's face that made him decide to change the subject. "You and I are off again very soon."

"Are we? Upon what deed? To where?"

"Your move on Aesernia convinced me that Aesernia is the key to this whole theater of war. Mutilus is heading there himself, having lost here—or so your intelligence system tells me. I think we must head there too. It mustn't fall."

"Oh, Lucius Julius!" cried Sulla in despair. "Aesernia is no more than a spiritual thorn in the Italian paw! While ever it holds out, the Italians must doubt their ability to win this war. But beyond that, Aesernia has *no* importance! Besides which, it is very well provisioned, and it has a very capable and determined commandant in Marcus Claudius Marcellus. Let it sit there thumbing its nose at the besiegers and don't worry about it! The only route available if Mutilus has withdrawn into the interior is the Melfa Gorge. Why risk our precious soldiers in that trap?"

Lucius Caesar reddened. "*You* got through!"

"Yes, I did. I tricked them. It can't work a second time."

"I will get through," said Lucius Caesar stiffly.

"How many legions?"

"All we have. Eight."

"Oh, Lucius Julius, forget this scheme!" Sulla pleaded. "It would be smarter and wiser to concentrate upon driving the Samnites out of western Campania for good! With eight legions working as one unit, we can take all the ports off Mutilus, reinforce Acerrae, and take Nola. Nola to the Italians is more important than Aesernia is to us!"

The general's lips thinned in displeasure. "*I* am in the command tent, Lucius Cornelius, not you! And *I* say, Aesernia."

Sulla shrugged, gave up. "As you say, of course."

Seven days later Lucius Julius Caesar and Lucius Cornelius

Sulla moved out toward Teanum Sidicinum with eight legions, the entire force available in the southern theater. Every atom of superstition Sulla had in him was screaming in alarm, but he had no choice save to do as he was told. Lucius Caesar was the general. More's the pity, thought Sulla as he walked at the head of his two legions—the same he had taken to Aesernia—and surveyed the great column ahead of him snaking up and down the low hills. Lucius Caesar had placed Sulla at the tail of the march, far enough away from himself to ensure that Sulla could not share his bivouacs or his conversations. Metellus Pius the Piglet was now elevated to share Lucius Caesar's bivouacs and conversations, a promotion which had not pleased him in the least. He wanted to stay with Sulla.

At Aquinum the general sent for Sulla, and threw him a letter rather contemptuously. How have the mighty fallen! thought Sulla, remembering how in Rome at the beginning of all this, it had been he to whom Lucius Caesar had turned for advice, it had been he who became Lucius Caesar's "expert." Now Lucius Caesar regarded himself as the expert.

"Read that," said Lucius Caesar curtly. "It's just come in from Gaius Marius."

Courtesy normally prompted the man who had received a letter to read it out to those with whom he shared it later on; aware of this, Sulla smiled wryly to himself and laboriously worked his way through Marius's communication.

> As the northern commander-in-chief, Lucius Julius, I believe the time has come to inform you of my plans. I write this on the Kalends of Sextilis, in camp near Reate.
>
> It is my intention to invade the lands of the Marsi. My army is finally in peak condition, and I am absolutely confident it will acquit itself in the same magnificent fashion as all my armies in the past have done, for the sake of Rome and the sake of their general.

Oho! thought Sulla, hackles rising. I've never heard the old boy express himself in quite those terms before! "For the sake of Rome *and the sake of their general.*" Now what gnat is whining round in his mind? Why is he linking himself personally to Rome? *My* army! Not Rome's army, but *my* army! I wouldn't have noticed it—we all say it—except for his reference to himself as their general. This communication will go into the archives of the war. And in it, Gaius Marius is putting himself on an equal footing with Rome!

Quickly Sulla lifted his head, glanced at Lucius Caesar; but if the southern commander-in-chief had spotted the phrase, he was pretending he had not. And so much subtlety, decided Sulla, Lucius Caesar did not have. He went back to deciphering Marius's letter.

> I think you will agree with me, Lucius Julius, that we need a victory—a complete and decisive victory—in my theater. Rome has called our war against the Italians the Marsic War, so we must defeat the Marsi in the field, if at all possible break the Marsi beyond recovery.
>
> Now I can do that, my dear Lucius Julius, but in order to do it, I need the services of my old friend and colleague, Lucius Cornelius Sulla. Plus two more legions. I understand completely that you can ill afford to lose Lucius Cornelius—not to mention two legions. If I did not consider it imperative that I ask, I would not ask this favor of you. Nor, I assure you, is this transfer of personnel a permanent one. Call it a loan, not a gift. Two months is all I need.
>
> If you can see your way clear to granting my petition, Rome will fare the better for your kindness to me. If you cannot see your way clear, then I must sit down again in Reate and think of something else.

Sulla raised his head and stared at Lucius Caesar, his brows climbing. "Well?" he asked, putting the letter down on Lucius Caesar's desk carefully.

"By all means go to him, Lucius Cornelius," said Lucius Caesar indifferently. "I can deal with Aesernia without you. Gaius Marius is right. We need a decisive victory in the field against the Marsi. This southern theater is a shambles anyway. It's quite impossible to contain the Samnites and their allies or get enough of them together in one place to inflict a decisive defeat upon them. All I can do here is engage in demonstrations of Roman strength and persistence. There will be no decisive battle in the south, ever. It is in the north that must happen."

Up went Sulla's hackles yet again. One of the two generals was thinking of himself in the same breath as Rome, the other was in a permanent slough of despond, incapable of seeing any light in east or west or south. Lucky perhaps that he could see a little glow in the north! How can we succeed in Campania with a man like Lucius Caesar in command? asked Sulla of himself. Ye gods, why is it that I am never quite senior enough? I'm better than Lucius Caesar! I may well be better than Gaius Marius! Since I entered the Senate I have spent my life serving lesser men—even Gaius Marius is a lesser man because he isn't a patrician Cornelius. Metellus Piggle-wiggle, Gaius Marius, Catulus Caesar, Titus Didius, and now *this* chronically depressed scion of an ancient house! And who is it goes from strength to strength, wins the Grass Crown, and ends up governing a whole province at the ripe old age of thirty? Quintus Sertorius. A Sabine nobody. *Marius's* cousin!

"Lucius Caesar, we will win!" said Sulla very seriously. "I tell you, I can hear the wings of Victory in the air all around us! We'll grind the Italians down to so much powder. Beat us in a battle or two the Italians may, but beat us in a war, they cannot! No one can! Rome is Rome, mighty and eternal. I *believe* in Rome!"

"Oh, so do I, Lucius Cornelius, so do I!" said Lucius Caesar testily. "Now go away! Make yourself useful to Gaius Marius, for I swear you are not very useful to me!"

Sulla got to his feet, and was actually as far as the outer doorway of the house Lucius Caesar had commandeered when he turned back. So intent had he been upon the letter that Lucius Caesar's physical appearance hadn't had the power to deflect his attention away from Gaius Marius. Now a fresh fear filled him. The general was sallow, lethargic, shivering, sweating.

"Lucius Julius, are you well?" Sulla demanded.

"Yes, yes!"

Sulla sat down again. "You're not, you know."

"I am well enough, Lucius Cornelius."

"See a physician!"

"In this village? It would be some filthy old woman prescribing decoctions of pig manure and poultices of pounded spiders."

"I'll be going past Rome. I'll send you the Sicilian."

"Then send him to Aesernia, Lucius Cornelius, because that is where he'll find me." Lucius Caesar's brow shone with sweat. "You are dismissed."

Sulla lifted his shoulders, got up. "Be it on your own head. You've got the ague."

And that, he reflected, going through the door onto the street without turning back this time, was that. Lucius Caesar was going to enter the Melfa Gorge in no fit state to organize a harvest dance. He was going to be ambushed, and he was going to have to retire to Teanum Sidicinum a second time to lick his wounds, with too many precious men lying dead in the bottom of that treacherous defile. Oh, why were they always so pigheaded, so obtuse?

Not very far down the street he encountered the Piglet, looking equally grim.

"You've got a sick man in there," said Sulla, jerking his head toward the house.

"Don't rub it in!" cried Metellus Pius. "At the best of times he's quite impossible to cheer up, but in the grip of an ague—I despair! What did you do to make him stiffen up and ignore you?"

"Told him to forget Aesernia and concentrate on driving the Samnites out of western Campania."

"Yes, that would account for it, with our commander-in-chief in his present state," said the Piglet, finding a smile.

The Piglet's stammer had always fascinated Sulla, who said now, "Your stammer's pretty good these days."

"Oh, why did you have to suh-suh-say that, Lucius Cornelius? It's only all ruh-ruh-right as long as I don't think about it, cuh-cuh-curse you!"

"Really? That's interesting. You didn't stammer before—when? Arausio, wasn't it?"

"Yes. It's a puh-puh-puh-*pain* in the arse!" Metellus Pius drew a deep breath and endeavored to dismiss the thought of his speech impediment from consciousness. "In your pruh-pruh-present state of odium, I don't suppose he tuh-tuh-told you what he's planning to do when he gets back to Rome?"

"No. What is he planning to do?"

"Grant the citizenship to every Italian who hasn't so far lifted a finger against us."

"You're joking!"

"Not I, Lucius Cornelius! In *his* company? I've forgotten what a joke is. It's true, I swear it's true. As soon as things run down here—well, they always do when autumn gets old—he's putting off his general's suit and putting on his purple-bordered tuh-tuh-toga. His last act as consul, he says, will be to grant the citizenship to every Italian who hasn't gone to war against us."

"But that's treason! Do you mean to say that he and the rest of the inadequate idiots in command have lost thousands of men for the sake of something they haven't even got the stomach to see through?" Sulla was trembling. "Do you mean to say he's leading six legions into the Melfa Gorge *knowing* every life he loses in the process is worthless? *Knowing* that he intends to open Rome's back door to every last Italian in the peninsula? Because that is what will happen, you know. They'll *all* get the franchise, from Silo and Mutilus down to the last freedman Silo and Mutilus have in their clientele! Oh, he can't!"

"There's no use shouting at me, Lucius Cornelius! I'll be one of those fighting the franchise to the bitter end."

"You won't even get the chance to fight it, Quintus Caecilius. You'll be in the field, not in the Senate. Only Scaurus will be there to fight it, and he's too old." Lips thin, Sulla stared sightlessly down the busy street. "It's Philippus and the rest of the *saltatrices tonsae* will vote. And they'll vote yes. As will the Comitia."

"You'll be in the field too, Lucius Cornelius," said the Piglet gloomily. "I huh-huh-hear you've been seconded to duty with Gaius Marius, the fat old Italian turnip! *He* won't disapprove of Lucius Julius's law, I'll bet!"

"I'm not so sure," said Sulla, and sighed. "One thing you have to admit about Gaius Marius, Quintus Caecilius—he's first and last and foremost a soldier. Before *his* days in the field are over, there'll be a few Marsi too dead to apply for the citizenship."

"Let us hope so, Lucius Cornelius. Because on the day that Gaius Marius enters a Senate half full of Italians, he'll be the First Man in Rome again. *And* consul a seventh time."

"Not if I have anything to do with it," said Sulla.

The next day Sulla detached his two legions from the tail of Lucius Caesar's column when it wheeled right ahead of him onto the road leading up the Melfa River. He himself kept to the Via Latina, crossing the Melfa en route to the old ruined township of Fregellae, reduced to rubble by Lucius Opimius after its rebellion thirty-five years before. His legions halted outside the curiously peaceful, flower-filled dells created by Fregellae's fallen walls and towers. In no mood to supervise his tribunes and centurions doing something as fundamental as pitching fortified camp, Sulla himself walked on alone into the deserted town.

Here it lies, he thought, everything we're currently fighting about. Here it lies the way those asses in the Senate assured us it would be by the time we put this new Italy-wide revolution down. We've given our time, our taxes, our very lives to turn Italy into one vast Fregellae. We said every Italian life would be forfeit. Crimson poppies would grow in ground crimson with Italian blood. We said Italian skulls would bleach to the color of those white roses, and the yellow eyes of daisies would stare blindly up at the sun out of their empty orbits. What are we doing this for, if it is all to go for nothing? Why have we died and why are we still dying if it is all for nothing? He will legislate the citizenship for the half-rebels in Umbria and Etruria. After that, he cannot stop. Or someone else will pick up the wand of imperium he drops. They will all get the citizenship, their hands still red with our blood. What are we doing this for if it is all to go for nothing? We, the heirs of the Trojans, who therefore should well know the feeling of traitors within the gates. We, who are Roman, not Italian. And he will see *them* become Roman. Between him and those in his like, they will destroy everything Rome stands for. Their Rome will not be the Rome of their ancestors, nor my Rome. This ruined Italian garden here at Fregellae is my Rome, the Rome of my ancestors—strong enough and sure enough to grow flowers in rebellious streets, free them for the hum and twitter of bees and birds.

He wasn't sure how much of the shimmer in front of his eyes was a part of his grief, how much a part of the blistering cobbles beneath his feet. But through its rivulets in the air he began to discern an approaching shape, blue and bulky—a Roman general walking toward a Roman general. Now more black than blue, then a shining glitter off cuirass and helm. Gaius Marius! Gaius Marius the Italian.

The breath Sulla drew in sobbed, the heart within his chest tripped and stammered. He stopped in his tracks, waited for Marius.

"Lucius Cornelius."

"Gaius Marius."

Neither man moved to touch the other. Then Marius turned and ranged himself alongside Sulla and the two of them walked on, silent as the tomb. It was Marius who finally cleared his throat, Marius who could not bear these unspoken emotions.

He said, "I suppose Lucius Julius is on his way to Aesernia?"

"Yes."

"He ought to be on Crater Bay taking back Pompeii and Stabiae. Otacilius is building a nice little navy now he's getting a few more recruits. The navy is always a bad last in the Senate's order of preference. However, I hear the Senate is going to induct all of Rome's able-bodied freedmen into a special force to garrison and protect the coasts of upper Campania and lower Latium. So Otacilius will be able to take all the current coastal militia into his navy."

Sulla grunted. "Huh! And when do the Conscript Fathers intend to get around to decreeing this?"

"Who knows? At least they've started talking about it."

"Wonder of wonders!"

"You sound incredibly bitter. Lucius Julius getting on your nerves? I'm not surprised."

"Yes, Gaius Marius, I am indeed bitter," said Sulla calmly. "I've been walking up this beautiful road thinking about the fate of Fregellae, and the prospective fate of our present crop of enemy Italians. You see, Lucius Julius intends to legislate the Roman citizenship for all Italians who have remained peacefully inclined toward Rome. Isn't that nice?"

Marius's step faltered for a moment, then resumed its rather ponderous rhythm. "*Does* he now? When? Before or after he dashes himself on the rocks of Aesernia?"

"After."

"Makes you implore the gods to tell you what all the fighting is about, doesn't it?" asked Marius, unconsciously echoing Sulla's thoughts. A rumble of laughter came. "Still. I love to soldier, and that's the truth. Hopefully there's a battle or two left before the Senate and People of Rome completely crumble in their resolve! What a turnabout! And would that we might raise Marcus Livius Drusus from the dead. Then none of it need have happened. The Treasury would be full instead of emptier than a fool's head, and the peninsula would be peacefully, happily, contentedly stuffed with legal Romans."

"Yes."

They fell silent, walked on into the shell of the Fregellae forum, where occasional columns and flights of steps leading up to nothing reared above the grass and flowers.

"I have a job for you," said Marius, sitting down on a block of stone. "Here, stand in the shade or sit down with me, Lucius Cornelius, do! Then take off that wretched hat so I can see what those eyes of yours contain."

Sulla moved into the shade obediently and obediently doffed his hat, but did not sit down, and did not speak.

"No doubt you're wondering why I've come to Fregellae to see you instead of waiting in Reate."

"I presume you don't want me in Reate."

A laugh boomed. "Always up to my tricks, Lucius Cornelius, aren't you? Quite right. I don't want you in Reate." The lingering grin disappeared. "But nor did I want to set my plans down in a letter. The fewer people who know what you're going to be up to, the better. Not that I have any reason to assume there's a spy in Lucius Julius's command tent—just that I'm prudent."

"The only way to keep a secret is not to tell anybody."

"True, true." Marius huffed so deeply that the straps and buckles of his cuirass groaned. "You, Lucius Cornelius, will leave the Via Latina here. You'll head up the Liris toward Sora, where you will turn with the Liris and follow it to its sources. In other words, I want you on the southern side of the watershed, some few miles from the Via Valeria."

"So far I understand my part. What about yours?"

"While you're moving up the Liris, I'll be marching from Reate toward the western pass on the Via Valeria. I intend to broach the road itself beyond Carseoli. That town is in ruins, and garrisoned by the enemy—Marrucini, my scouts tell me, commanded by Herius Asinius himself. If possible I'll force a battle with him for possession of the Via Valeria before it enters the pass. At that stage I want you level with me—but *south* of the watershed."

"South of the watershed without the enemy's knowledge," said Sulla, beginning to lose his coolness.

"Precisely. That means you'll kill everyone you see. It's so well known that I lie to the north of the Via Valeria that I'm hoping it won't occur to either the Marrucini or the Marsi that there might be an army coming up on the southern flank. I'll try to focus all their attention on my own movements." Marius smiled. "You, of course, are with Lucius Julius on your way to Aesernia."

"You haven't lost the gift of generaling, Gaius Marius."

The fierce brown eyes flashed. "I hope not! Because, Lucius Cornelius, I tell you plainly—if *I* lose the gift of generaling, there'll be no one in this benighted conflagration to take my place. We'll end in granting the citizenship on the battlefield to those in arms against us."

Part of Sulla wanted to pursue the citizenship tack, but the dominant part had other ideas. "What about me?" he blurted. "I can general."

"Yes, yes, of course you can," said Marius in soothing tones. "I don't deny that for a moment. But generaling isn't in your very bones, Lucius Cornelius."

"Good generaling can be learned," Sulla said stubbornly.

"Good generaling can indeed be learned. As you have done. But if it isn't in your very bones, Lucius Cornelius, you can never rise above mere good generaling," said Marius, utterly oblivious to the fact that what he was saying was derogatory. "Sometimes mere good generaling isn't good enough. *Inspired* generaling is called for. And that's either in the bones, or absent."

"One day," said Sulla pensively, "Rome will find herself without you, Gaius Marius. And then—why, we shall see! *I'll* be holding the high command."

Still Marius failed to understand, still he didn't divine what lay in Sulla's thoughts. Instead, he chortled merrily. "Well, Lucius Cornelius, we'll just have to hope that when that day comes, all Rome will need is a good general. Won't we?"

"Whatever you say," said Lucius Cornelius Sulla.

The galling factor was that—of course!—Marius's plan was perfect. Sulla and his two legions penetrated as far as Sora without encountering any enemy at all, then—in what amounted to no more than a skirmish—he defeated a small force of Picentes under Titus Herennius. From Sora to the sources of the Liris he met only Latin and Sabine farmers who greeted his appearance with such transparent joy that he refrained from carrying out Marius's orders and killing them. Those Picentes who had escaped at Sora were more likely by far to report his presence, but he had given them the impression that his was a mission to Sora given to him by Lucius Caesar, and that he was marching then to join Lucius Caesar east of the Melfa Gorge. Hopefully the remnants of Titus Herennius's Picentes and the Paeligni were lying in wait for Sulla in quite the wrong place.

Marius, Sulla knew from constant communication, had done as he promised and broached the Via Valeria beyond Carseoli. Herius Asinius and his Marrucini had contested the road on the spot, and gone down to crushing defeat after Marius tricked them into thinking he didn't want a battle there. Herius Asinius himself perished, as did most of his army. Thus Marius marched into the western pass under no threat at all, now heading for Alba Fucentia with four legions comprised of men sure of victory—how could they possibly lose with the old Arpinate fox in their lead? They were blooded, and blooded well.

Sulla and his two legions shadowed Marius along the Via Valeria until the watershed separating them flattened out into the Marsic upland basin around Lake Fucinus; but even then Sulla kept ten miles between himself and Marius, skulking in a surprisingly easy concealment. For this fact, he had cause to be grateful to the Marsians' love of making their own wine, despite the handicaps of the area. South of the Via Valeria the country was solid vineyard, a vast expanse of grapes grown inside small high-walled enclosures to protect them from the bitter winds which swept off the mountains at just that time of year when the tender grape florets were forming and the insects needed calm air to pollinate. Now Sulla did kill as he went, women and children in the main; all save the oldest men had gone from the lakeside hamlets and farms to serve in the army.

He knew the very moment when Marius joined battle with the Marsi, for the wind that day was blowing from the north, and carried the sounds across the walled vineyards so clearly that Sulla's men fancied the fight was actually going on among the grapes. A courier had come at dawn to tell Sulla it was probably going to be today; so Sulla put his forces in an eight-deep line beneath the ten-foot fences of the vineyards, and waited.

Sure enough, fleeing Marsi began tumbling over the stone ramparts perhaps four hours after the sounds began—and tumbled straight onto the drawn swords of Sulla's legionaries, thirsty for a share of the action. In some places there was hard fighting—these were despairing men—but nowhere did Sulla stand in any danger.

As usual I am Gaius Marius's skilled lackey, Sulla thought, standing on high ground to watch. His was the mind conceived the strategy, his the hand directed the tactics, his the will finished it successfully. And here am I on the wrong side of some wretched wall, picking up his leavings like the hungry man I am. How well he knows himself—and how well he knows me.

Wishing he didn't have to rejoice, Sulla mounted his mule after his share of the fighting was over and rode the long way round to inform Gaius Marius on the Via Valeria that all had gone exactly as planned, that the Marsi involved were virtually extinct.

"I faced none other than Silo himself!" said Marius in his customary post-battle roar, clapping Sulla on the back and leading him into the command tent with an arm about his valued lieutenant's shoulders. "Mind you, they were napping," he said gleefully, "I suppose because this to them is home. I burst on them like a thunderclap, Lucius Cornelius! It seems they never dreamed Asinius might lose! No one came to tell them he had; all they knew was that he was moving because I had moved from Reate at last. So there I was coming round a sharp corner, straight into their faces. They were marching to reinforce Asinius. I fetched up just too far away to be obliged to join battle, formed my men into square, and looked as if I was prepared to fight defensively, but not to attack.

"'If you're such a great general, Gaius Marius, come and fight me!' shouted Silo, sitting on a horse.

"'If you're such a great general, Quintus Poppaedius, make me!' I shouted back.

"We'll never know what he might have intended to do after that, because his men took the bit between their teeth and charged without his giving the command. Well, they made it easy for me. I know what to do, Lucius Cornelius. But Silo doesn't. I say doesn't, as he got away unharmed. When his men broke in panic he turned his horse to face east and galloped off. I doubt he'll stop until he reaches Mutilus. Anyway, I forced the Marsi to retreat in one direction only—through the vineyards. Knowing you were there to finish them off on the other side. And that was that."

"It was very well done, Gaius Marius," said Sulla with complete sincerity.

And so they settled to a victory feast, Marius and Sulla and their deputies—and Young Marius, glowing with pride in his father, whom he now served as a cadet. Oh, there's a pup bears watching! thought Sulla, and refused to watch him.

The battle was fought all over again, almost at greater length in time; but eventually, as the level in the wine amphorae grew ever lower, the talk turned inevitably to politics. The projected legislation of Lucius Caesar was the subject, coming as a shock to Marius's juniors; he hadn't told them of his conversation with Sulla in Fregellae. Reactions were mixed, yet against this huge concession. These were the soldiers, these were men who had been fighting now for six months, seen thousands of their comrades perish—and felt besides that the dodderers and cravens in Rome hadn't given them a good chance to get into stride, to start winning. Those safe in Rome were apostrophized as a gaggle of dried-up old Vestal Virgins, with Philippus coming in for the strongest criticism, Lucius Caesar not far behind.

"The Julii Caesares are all over-bred bundles of nerves," said Marius, face purple-red. "A pity we've had a Julius Caesar as senior consul in this crisis. I knew he'd break."

"You sound, Gaius Marius, as if you'd rather we conceded absolutely nothing to the Italians," said Sulla.

"I *would* rather we didn't," Marius said. "Until it came to open war it was different. But once a people declares itself an enemy of Rome's, it's an enemy of mine too. Forever."

"So I feel," said Sulla. "However, if Lucius Julius does succeed in convincing Senate and People to pass his law, it will decrease the chance of Etruria's and Umbria's going over. I'd heard there were fresh rumblings in both places."

"Indeed. Which is why Lucius Cato Licinianus and Aulus Plotius have peeled Sextus Julius's troops away from him and gone—Plotius to Umbria and Cato Licinianus to Etruria," said Marius.

"What's Sextus Julius doing, then?"

Young Marius answered, very loudly. "He's recuperating in Rome. 'A very nasty chest' was how my mother put it in her last letter."

Sulla's look should have squashed him, yet didn't. Even when the commander-in-chief was one's father, one didn't butt into the conversation if one was only a *contubernalis*!

"No doubt the Etrurian campaign will do Cato Licinianus's chances of winning a consulship for next year the world of good," said Sulla. "Providing he does well. I imagine he will."

"So do I," said Marius, belching. "It's a pea-sized undertaking— suitable for a pea like Cato Licinianus."

Sulla grinned. "What, Gaius Marius, not impressed?"

Marius blinked. "Are you?"

"Anything but." He had had more than enough wine; Sulla switched to water. "In the meantime, what do we do with ourselves? September is a market interval old, and I'll be due to go back to Campania fairly soon. I'd like to make the most of what time I have left, if that's possible."

"I can't *believe* Lucius Julius let Egnatius fool him in the Melfa Gorge!" Young Marius interrupted.

"You're not old enough, my boy, to comprehend the extent of men's idiocy," said Marius, approving of the comment rather than disapproving of its maker making it. He turned then to Sulla. "We can't hope for anything from Lucius Julius now that he's back in Teanum Sidicinum a second time with a quarter of his army dead, so why return in a hurry, Lucius Cornelius? To hold Lucius Julius's hand? I imagine there are plenty doing that already. I suggest we go on together to Alba Fucentia," he said, ending with a peculiar sound somewhere between a laugh and a retch.

Sulla stiffened. "Are you all right?" he asked sharply.

For a moment Marius's color went from puce to ashes. Then he recovered; the laugh was all a laugh should be. "After such a day, perfect, Lucius Cornelius! Now as I was saying, we'll go on to relieve Alba Fucentia, after which—well, I fancy a stroll down through Samnium, don't you? We'll leave Sextus Julius to invest Asculum Picentum while we bait the Samnite bull. Investing cities is a bore, not my style." He giggled tipsily. "Wouldn't it be nice to show up in Teanum Sidicinum with Aesernia in the sinus of your toga as a present for Lucius Julius? How *grateful* he'd be!"

"How grateful indeed, Gaius Marius."

The party broke up. Sulla and Young Marius helped Marius to his bed, settled him on it without fussing. Then Young Marius escaped with a vindictive look for Sulla, who had lingered to examine the limp mountain on the couch more closely.

"Lucius Cornelius," said Marius, slurring his words, "come on your own in the morning to wake me, would you? I want some private talk with you. Can't tonight. Oh, the wine!"

"Sleep well, Gaius Marius. In the morning it shall be."

But in the morning it was not to be. When Sulla—none too well himself—ventured into the back compartment of the command tent, he found the mountain on the bed exactly as it had been the night before. Frowning, he approached quickly, feeling the beginnings of a horrible prickling. No, not fear that Marius was dead; the noise of his breathing had been audible from the front section of the tent. Now, gazing down, Sulla saw the right hand feebly plucking, picking at the sheet, and saw too Marius's goggling eyes alive with a terror so profound it imitated madness. From slumped cheek to flaccid foot his left side was stilled, felled, immobile. Down had come the forest giant without a murmur, powerless to fend off a blow not seen or felt until the deed was over.

"Stroke," mumbled Marius.

Sulla's hand went out of its own volition to caress the sweat-soaked hair; now he could be loved. Now he was no more. "Oh, my poor old fellow!" Sulla lowered his cheek against Marius's, turning his lips into the wet trickle of Marius's tears. "My poor old one! You're done for at last."

Out came the words immediately, hideously distorted, yet quite distinct enough to hear with faces pressed together.

"Not—done—yet . . . Seven—times."

Sulla reared back as if Marius had risen from the couch and struck him. Then, even as he scrubbed his palm across his own tears, he uttered a shrill little paroxysm of laughter, laughter ending as abruptly as it had begun. "If *I* have anything to do with it, Gaius Marius, you're done for!"

"Not—done for," said Marius, his still intelligent eyes no longer terrified; now they were angry. "Seven—times."

In one stride Sulla arrived at the flap dividing front room from back, calling for help as if the Hound of Hades was snapping many-headed at his heels.

Only after every last army surgeon had come and gone and Marius had been made as comfortable as possible did Sulla call a meeting of those who milled outside the tent, barred from entering it by Young Marius, weeping desolately.

He held his conference in the camp forum, deeming it wiser to let the ranks see that something was being done; the news of Marius's catastrophe had spread, and Young Marius was not the only one who wept.

"I am assuming command," said Sulla evenly to the dozen men who clustered around him.

No one protested.

"We return to Latium at once, before the news of this can reach Silo or Mutilus."

Now came the protest, from a Marcus Caecilius of the branch cognominated Cornutus. "That's ridiculous!" he said indignantly. "Here we are not twenty miles from Alba Fucentia, and you're saying we have to turn around and go back?"

Lips thin, Sulla gestured widely with his arm, encompassing the many groups of soldiers who stood watching and weeping. "Look at them, you fool!" he snapped. "Go on into the enemy heartlands with *them*? They've lost the stomach for it! We have to gentle them along until we're safely inside our own frontiers, Cornutus—then we have to find them another general they can love a tenth as well!"

Cornutus opened his mouth to say something further, then shut it, shrugged helplessly.

"Anyone else got anything to say?" asked Sulla.

It appeared no one had.

"All right, then. Strike camp on the double. I've sent word to my own legions on the far side of the vineyards already. They'll be waiting for us down the road."

"What about Gaius Marius?" asked a very young Licinius. "He might die if we move him."

Sulla's bark of laughter shocked them rigid. *"Gaius Marius? You couldn't kill him with a sacrificial axe, boy!"* Seeing their reaction, he brought his emotions very carefully under control before he went on. "Never fear, gentlemen, Gaius Marius assured me himself not two hours ago that I haven't seen the last of him yet. And I believed him! So we will take him with us. There will be no scarcity of volunteers to carry his litter."

"Are we all going to Rome?" asked the young Licinius timidly.

Only now that he had himself in hand did Sulla perceive how badly frightened and rudderless they all were; but they were Roman nobles, and that meant they questioned everything, weighed everything in terms of their own positions. By rights he ought to be treating them as delicately as newborn kittens.

"No, we are *not* all going to Rome," said Sulla without a trace of delicacy in voice or manner. "When we reach Carseoli, you, Marcus Caecilius Cornutus, will assume command of the army. You will put it into its camp outside Reate. His son and I will take Gaius Marius to Rome, with five cohorts of troops as his honor guard."

"Very well, Lucius Cornelius, if that's how you wish it done, I suppose that's how it will have to be done," said Cornutus.

The look he got from those strange light eyes set what felt like a thousand maggots crawling inside his jaws.

"You are not mistaken, Marcus Caecilius, in thinking that it must be done the way I wish it done," said Sulla softly, a caress in his voice. "And if it isn't done precisely as I wish, I'll grant *you* a wish—that you'd never been born! Is that quite clear? Good! Now move out."

PART VI

YOUNG POMPEY

When news of Lucius Caesar's defeat of Mutilus at Acerrae had reached Rome, senatorial spirits had temporarily lifted. A proclamation was issued to the effect that it was no longer necessary for Roman citizens to wear the *sagum*. Then when news came of Lucius Caesar's defeat in the Melfa Gorge for the second time, together with casualty figures almost exactly equaling enemy losses at Acerrae, no one in the Senate had moved to order the proclamation reversed; that would have pointed up the new defeat.

"Futile," Marcus Aemilius Princeps Senatus had said to the few senators who turned up to debate the issue. His lip trembled, was resolutely quelled. "What we have to face is a far more serious fact—that we are losing this war."

Philippus wasn't present to argue. Nor was Quintus Varius, still busy prosecuting minor lights for treason; now that he had abandoned quarry like Antonius Orator and Scaurus Princeps Senatus, the victims of his special court were mounting.

Thus, deprived of the stimulus of opposition, Scaurus found himself without the will to go on, and sat down heavily upon his stool. I am too old, he thought—how can Marius cope with a whole theater of war when he's the same age I am?

That question was answered at the end of Sextilis, when a courier came to inform the Senate that Gaius Marius and his troops had beaten Herius Asinius with the loss of seven thousand Marrucine lives, including Herius Asinius's. But such was the depth of the depression within the city that no one thought it wise to celebrate; instead, the city waited for the next few days to bring news of an equivalent defeat. Sure enough, some days later another courier arrived and presented himself to the Senate, whose members sat, stony-faced and stiff-backed, to hear the bad tidings. Only Scaurus had come among the consulars.

Gaius Marius takes great pleasure in informing the Senate and People of Rome that, on this day, he and his armies did inflict a crushing defeat upon Quintus Poppaedius Silo and the men of the Marsi. Fifteen thousand

Marsians lie dead, and five thousand more are taken prisoner.

Gaius Marius wishes to commend the invaluable contribution of Lucius Cornelius Sulla to this victory, and begs to be excused a full account of events until such time as he can inform the Senate and People of Rome that Alba Fucentia has been relieved. Long live Rome!

At first reading, no one believed it. A stir passed along the thinned white ranks, too sparse upon the tiers to look impressive. Scaurus read the letter out again, voice shaking. And finally the cheers started. Within an hour, all of Rome was cheering. Gaius Marius had done it! Gaius Marius had reversed Rome's fortunes! Gaius Marius, Gaius Marius, Gaius Marius!

"He's everybody's hero yet again," said Scaurus to the *flamen Dialis,* Lucius Cornelius Merula, who hadn't missed one meeting of the Senate since the war had begun, despite the huge number of taboos which hedged the *flamen Dialis* round. Alone among his peers, the *flamen Dialis* could never don a toga; instead, he was enveloped by a double-layered heavy woolen cape, the *laena,* which was cut on a full circle, and on his head he wore a close-fitting ivory helm adorned with the symbols of Jupiter and topped with a hard disc of wool pierced by an ivory spike. Alone among his peers he was hirsute, for this *flamen Dialis* had elected to leave his hair hanging down his back and his beard straggling down his chest rather than endure the torture of being barbered by bone or bronze. The *flamen Dialis* could not come into bodily contact with iron of any kind—which meant he could have no contact with war. Thwarted in doing his military duty to his country, Lucius Cornelius Merula had taken to attending the Senate assiduously.

Merula sighed. "Well, Marcus Aemilius, patricians though we may be, I think it's high time we admitted to ourselves that our bloodlines are so attenuated we can no longer produce a popular hero."

"Nonsense!" snapped Scaurus. "Gaius Marius is a freak!"

"Without him, where would we be?"

"In Rome, and true Romans!"

"You don't approve of his victory?"

"Of course I approve! I just wish the name at the bottom of the letter had been Lucius Cornelius Sulla's!"

"He was a good *praetor urbanus,* I know, but I never heard he was a Marius upon the battlefield," said Merula.

"Until Gaius Marius quits the battlefield, how can we know? Lucius Cornelius Sulla has been with Gaius Marius since—oh, the war against Jugurtha. And has always made a large contribution to Gaius Marius's victories. Marius takes the credit."

"Be fair, Marcus Aemilius! Gaius Marius's letter made specific mention of Lucius Sulla! I for one thought the praise ungrudging. Nor can I hear a word of disparagement about the man who has finally answered my prayers," said Merula.

"A man answers your prayers, *flamen Dialis*? That's an odd way of putting it, surely."

"Our gods do not answer us directly, Princeps Senatus. If they are displeased they present us with some sort of phenomenon, and when they act they do so through the agency of men."

"I am as aware of that as you are!" cried Scaurus, goaded. "I love Gaius Marius as much as I hate him. But I could still wish that the name on the bottom of the letter had been another's!"

One of the Senate clerks entered the chamber, deserted now save for Scaurus and Merula, who had fallen behind.

"Princeps Senatus, an urgent communication has just come from Lucius Cornelius Sulla."

Merula giggled. "There you are, an answer to your prayers! A letter with Lucius Sulla's name on its bottom!"

A scathing look was Merula's answer; Scaurus took the tiny roll and spread it between his hands. It contained, he saw in utter astonishment, two scant lines, carefully printed in big characters, and having dots between the words. Sulla wanted no misinterpretation.

GAIUS · MARIUS · FELLED · BY · STROKE · ARMY ·
MOVED · TO · REATE · AM · RETURNING · TO ·
ROME · AT · ONCE · BEARING · MARIUS · SULLA

Bereft of speech, Scaurus Princeps Senatus gave the sheet to
Merula and stumbled to a seat on the bare bottom tier.

"*Edepol!*" Merula too sat down. "Oh, is nothing ever going to
go right in this war? Is Gaius Marius dead, do you think? Is that
what Lucius Sulla means?"

"I think he lives but is incapable of command, and that his troops
know it," said Scaurus. He drew a breath, bellowed, "Clerk!"

Hovering in the doorway, the scribe returned immediately to
stand before Scaurus; he was bursting with curiosity.

"Call out the heralds. Have them proclaim the news that Gaius
Marius has had a stroke, and is being returned to Rome by his legate Lucius Cornelius Sulla."

The scribe gasped, blanched, hurried off.

"Was that wise, Marcus Aemilius?" asked Merula.

"Only the Great God knows, *flamen Dialis*. I do not. All *I*
know is that if I called the Senate to discuss this first, they'd vote
to suppress the news. And that I cannot condone," said Scaurus
strongly. He got up. "Walk with me. I have to tell Julia before the
heralds start braying from the rostra."

Thus it was that when the five cohorts of troops escorting Gaius
Marius's litter came through the Colline Gate, their spears wreathed
in cypress, their swords and daggers reversed, they entered a marketplace festooned with garlands of flowers and thronged with silent people—a feast and a funeral at one, it seemed. And so it was
all the way to the Forum Romanum, where again flowers hung everywhere, but the crowds were still and voiceless. The flowers had
been put out to celebrate Gaius Marius's great victory; his defeat by
illness had caused the silence.

When the closely curtained litter appeared behind the soldiers,
a great whisper spread:

"He must be alive! He must be alive!"

Sulla and his cohorts halted in the lower Forum alongside the rostra, while Gaius Marius was carried up the Clivus Argentarius to his house. Marcus Aemilius Scaurus Princeps Senatus climbed alone to the top of the rostra.

"The Third Founder of Rome lives, *Quirites!*" Scaurus thundered. "As always, he has turned the course of war in Rome's favor, and Rome cannot be grateful enough. Make offerings for his well-being, though it may be that it is time for Gaius Marius to leave us. His condition is grave. But thanks to him, *Quirites,* our condition has improved immeasurably."

No one cheered. No one wept either. Weeping would be saved for his funeral, for a moment without hope. Then Scaurus came down off the rostra and the people began to disperse.

"He won't die," said Sulla, looking very tired.

Scaurus snorted. "I never thought he would. He hasn't been consul seven times yet, so he can't let himself die."

"That is exactly how *he* put it."

"What, he's still able to speak?"

"A little. There's no lack of words, just clumsiness getting them out. Our army surgeon says it's because his left side bore the blow, not his right—though why that should be, I don't know. Nor does the army surgeon. He simply insists that's the usual pattern field surgeons see when heads are damaged. If the paralysis of the body is on the right, speech is obliterated. If the paralysis is on the left, speech is retained."

"How extraordinary! Why doesn't one hear this from our city physicians?" asked Scaurus.

"I suppose they don't see enough broken heads."

"True." Scaurus took Sulla by the arm warmly. "Come home with me, Lucius Cornelius. Take a little wine and tell me absolutely everything that's happened. I had thought you still with Lucius Julius in Campania."

Not with every ounce of will could Sulla suppress his complete withdrawal. "I'd rather we went to my house, Marcus Aemilius. I am still in armor, and it's hot."

Scaurus sighed. "It is time we both forgot what happened so

many years ago," he said sincerely. "My wife is older, more settled, and much occupied with her children."

"Then—your house it shall be."

She was waiting in the atrium to receive them, as anxious to know the condition of Gaius Marius as everyone else in Rome. Now twenty-eight years of age, she knew the felicitude of an increasing rather than a fading beauty; a brown beauty as rich as a fur pelt, though the eyes she lifted to rest on Sulla's face were the grey of the sea on a cloudy day.

It did not escape Sulla that, though Scaurus beamed upon her with genuine and obviously unquestioning affection, she was afraid of her husband, and did not see how he felt.

"Welcome, Lucius Cornelius," she said colorlessly.

"I thank you, Caecilia Dalmatica."

"There are refreshments laid out in your study, husband," she said to Scaurus colorlessly. "Is Gaius Marius going to die?"

Sulla answered her, smiling easily now the first moment was gone; this was very different from seeing her in Marius's house at a dinner party. "No, Caecilia Dalmatica. We haven't seen the last of Gaius Marius yet, so much I can promise you."

She sighed in simple relief. "Then I will leave you."

The two men stood in the atrium until she disappeared, after which Scaurus conducted Sulla to his *tablinum*.

"Do you want command of the Marsic theater?" Scaurus asked, handing Sulla wine.

"I doubt the Senate would give it to me, Princeps Senatus."

"Frankly, so do I. But do you want it?"

"No, I don't. My career throughout the year of this war has been based in Campania aside from this special exercise with Gaius Marius, and I'd prefer to stay in the theater I know. Lucius Julius is expecting me back," Sulla said, well aware what he intended to do when the new consuls were in office, but having no wish to make Scaurus a party to his plans.

"Are they your troops in Marius's escort?"

"Yes. The other fifteen cohorts I sent directly to Campania. I'll take the rest myself tomorrow."

"Oh, I wish you were standing for consul!" said Scaurus. "It is the most miserable field in half a generation!"

"I'm standing with Quintus Pompeius Rufus at the end of next year," said Sulla firmly.

"So I had heard. A pity."

"I couldn't win an election this year, Marcus Aemilius."

"You could—if I threw my weight behind you."

Sulla grinned sourly. "The offer comes too late. I'll be too busy in Campania to don the *toga candida*. Besides, I'd have to take pot luck with my colleague, whereas Quintus Pompeius and I will run as a team. My daughter is to marry his son."

"Then I withdraw my offer. You are right. Rome will just have to muddle through this coming year. It will be a great pleasure to have relatives as consuls the following year. Harmony in the chair is a wonderful thing. And you'll dominate Quintus Pompeius as easily as he'll accept your domination."

"So I think, Princeps Senatus. Election time is really the only time Lucius Julius can spare me, as he intends to wind hostilities down in order to return to Rome himself. I think I'll marry my daughter to Quintus Pompeius's son this December, even though she won't be eighteen. She's looking forward to it very much," lied Sulla blandly, knowing perfectly well that he still had a most unwilling child on his hands, but trusting to Fortune.

His understanding of Cornelia Sulla's attitude was reinforced when he came home some two hours later. Aelia greeted him with the news that Cornelia Sulla had tried to run away from home.

"Luckily her girl was too frightened not to report to me," Aelia ended mournfully, for she loved her stepdaughter dearly, and for her stepdaughter's sake wished she could have the marriage of her heart—a match with Young Marius.

"Just what did she think she was going to do, wandering around the war-torn countryside?" asked Sulla.

"I have no idea, Lucius Cornelius. I don't think she had either. It was an impulse, is my guess."

"Then the sooner she's married to young Quintus Pompeius, the better," said Sulla grimly. "I'll see her now."

"Here? In your study?"

"Here, Aelia. In my study."

Knowing he didn't appreciate her—nor appreciate her sympathy for Cornelia Sulla—Aelia gazed at her husband in mingled fear and pity. "Please, Lucius Cornelius, try not to be too hard on her!"

A petition Sulla ignored by turning his back.

Cornelia Sulla was brought to him looking much like a prisoner, placed as she was between two male household slaves.

"You can go," he said curtly to her guardians, and let his cold gaze rest upon his daughter's mutinous face, so exquisite with its mixture of his coloring and her mother's beauty, save that her eyes were all her own, very large and vividly blue.

"And what have you got to say for yourself, girl?"

"I'm ready this time, Father. You can hit me until you kill me—I don't care! Because I am *not* marrying Quintus Pompeius, and you can't make me!"

"If I have to tie you and drug you, my girl, you will marry Quintus Pompeius," said Sulla in those soft tones which preceded maximum violence.

But, for all her tears and tantrums, she was far more Sulla's child than she was Julilla's. Visibly she settled on her feet as if to ward off some frightful blow, and put sapphire glitters in her eyes. "I will not marry Quintus Pompeius!"

"By all the gods, Cornelia, you will!"

"I will not!"

Normally so much defiance would have produced an uncontrollable rage in Sulla; but now, perhaps because he saw something belonging to his dead son in her face, he found himself unable to be truly angry. He blew through his nose ominously. "Daughter, do you know who Pietas is?" he asked.

"Of course I know," said Cornelia Sulla warily. "She's Duty."

"Enlarge on that definition, Cornelia."

"She's the goddess of Duty."

"What kind of duty?"

"All kinds."

"Including the duty children owe their parents, is that not so?" asked Sulla sweetly.

"Yes," said Cornelia Sulla.

"To defy the *paterfamilias* is a frightful thing, Cornelia. Not only does it offend Pietas, but under the law you must obey the head of your family. I am the *paterfamilias,*" said Sulla sternly.

"My first duty is to myself," she said heroically.

Sulla's lips began to quiver. "It is not, daughter. Your first duty is to me. You are in *my* hand."

"Hand or no hand, Father, I will not betray myself!"

The lips stopped trembling, opened; Sulla burst into a huge roar of laughter. "Oh, go away!" he said when he could, and yelled after her, still laughing, "You'll do your duty or I'll sell you into slavery! I can, there's nothing to stop me!"

"I'm already a slave!" she called back.

What a soldier she would have made! When his amusement allowed it, Sulla sat down to write to that Greek citizen of Smyrna, Publius Rutilius Rufus.

> And that is exactly what happened, Publius Rutilius. The impudent little rubbish rolled me up! And has left me with no alternative than to carry out threats which cannot advance my intention to have myself elected consul in alliance with Quintus Pompeius. The girl is no use to me dead or a slave—and no use to young Quintus Pompeius if I have to tie her up and drug her in order to bring her before the marriage celebrant! So what *do* I do? I am asking you very seriously, and very desperately—what do I do? I remember the legend that it was you solved Marcus Aurelius Cotta's dilemma when he had to choose a husband for Aurelia. So here's another marital dilemma for you to solve, O admired and esteemed counselor.
>
> I admit that things here are in such a state that, were it not for my inability to marry my daughter off where I need to marry her off, I would not have stopped to

write to you. But now I've begun and—provided, that is, that you have a solution for my dilemma!—I may as well tell you what's happening.

Our Princeps Senatus I left beginning a letter of his own to you, so I don't need to apprise you of Gaius Marius's awful catastrophe. I shall confine myself to airing my hopes and fears for the future, and can at least look forward to being able to wear my *toga praetexta* and sit on my ivory curule chair when I'm consul, as the Senate has instructed its curule magistrates to don their full regalia following Gaius Marius's—and my!—victory over Silo's Marsians. Hopefully this means we've seen the last of these silly, empty gestures of mourning and alarm.

It seems highly likely at the moment that next year's consuls will be Lucius Porcius Cato Licinianus and— what a horrible thought!—Gnaeus Pompeius Strabo. What a terrible pair! A puckered-up cat's anus and an arrogant barbarian who can only look at the bridge of his own nose. I confess myself utterly at a loss to understand how or why some men come to the consulship. Clearly it is not enough to have been a good urban or foreign praetor. Or have a war record as long and illustrious as King Ptolemy's pedigree. I am fast coming to the conclusion that the only really important factor is getting on side with the Ordo Equester. If the knights don't like you, Publius Rutilius, you could be Romulus himself and not stand a chance in the consular elections. The knights put Gaius Marius in the consul's chair six times, three of them *in absentia*. And they still like him! He's good for business. Oh, they like a man to have ancestors too—but not enough to vote for him unless he's either opened his moneybags very wide, or he's offered them all sorts of added inducements like an easier loan market or inside news on everything the Senate contemplates doing.

I should have been consul years ago. If I had been a praetor years ago. And, yes, it was the Princeps Senatus who foiled me. But he did it by enlisting the knights, whole flocks of whom follow him, bleating like little lambs. So, you might say, I am coming to dislike the Ordo Equester more and more. Wouldn't it be wonderful, I ask myself, to be in a position to do with them what I willed? Oh, I'd make them suffer, Publius Rutilius! On your behalf too.

Speaking of Pompey Strabo, he's been very busy telling everyone in Rome how he's covered himself in glory in Picenum. The real author of his relatively minor success, in my opinion, is Publius Sulpicius, who brought him an army from Italian Gaul and inflicted a nasty defeat upon a combined force of Picentes and Paeligni before ever he made contact with Pompey Strabo. Our cross-eyed friend, rot him, summered extremely comfortably locked up in Firmum Picenum. Anyway, now he's out of his summer residence, Pompey Strabo is claiming *all* the credit for the victory over Titus Lafrenius, who died along with his men. Of Publius Sulpicius (who was there, and did most of the work), not a mention. And as if that were not enough, Pompey Strabo's agents in Rome are making his battle sound a lot more significant than Gaius Marius's actions against Marrucini and Marsi.

The war *is* on the turn. I know it in my bones.

I am sure I don't have to detail the new enfranchisement law Lucius Julius Caesar intends to promulgate in December. Scaurus's letter is full of it, I imagine. I gave the Princeps Senatus the news of this law scant hours ago, thinking he'd begin to roar in outrage. Instead, he was quite pleased. He thinks the idea of dangling the citizenship has a lot of merit, provided it isn't extended to those in arms against us. Etruria and Umbria prey upon him; he feels the trouble in both areas would die down the moment all Etrurians and Umbrians were given the vote. Try though I did, I couldn't persuade him that Lucius Julius's law would only be the beginning—that before too long *every* Italian would be a Roman citizen, no matter how much and how fresh the Roman blood on his sword. I ask you, Publius Rutilius—*what* have we been fighting for?

Write back at once, tell me how to deal with *girls*.

Sulla included his letter to Rutilius Rufus in the packet the Princeps Senatus sent to Smyrna by special courier. That meant Rutilius Rufus would probably receive the packet within a month, and his answer would be carried back by the same courier over a similar period of time.

In fact, Sulla had his answer by the end of November. He was still in Campania, shoring up the convalescent Lucius Caesar, who had been awarded a triumph by the sycophantic Senate for his victory over Mutilus at Acerrae; that the two armies had returned to Acerrae and at the time of the decree were actively engaged in fresh hostilities was something the Senate preferred to ignore. The reason for the awarding of this triumph and no other, said the Senate, was that Lucius Caesar's troops had hailed him imperator on the field. When Pompey Strabo heard about it his agents created such a fuss that the Senate then had to decree a triumph for Pompey Strabo as well. How low are we descended? asked Sulla of himself. To triumph over Italians is no triumph.

This signal honor had no power to excite Lucius Caesar. When Sulla asked him how he wished his triumph organized, he simply looked surprised, then said,

"Since there are no spoils, it will require no organization. I shall lead my army through Rome, that's all."

The winter hiatus had opened, and Acerrae it seemed was not much inconvenienced by the presence of two large armies outside its gates. While Lucius Caesar wrestled with the early drafts of his enfranchisement law, Sulla went to Capua to help Catulus Caesar and Metellus Pius the Piglet reorder the legions more than decimated by the second action in the Melfa Gorge; it was there in Capua that Rutilius Rufus's letter found him.

My dear Lucius Cornelius, why is it that fathers can never seem to find the right way to handle their daughters? I despair! Not, mind you, that I had any trouble with *my* girl. When I married her to Lucius Calpurnius Piso, she was in raptures. This was undoubtedly because she was such a plain little thing, and not well dowered; her chief worry was that her *tata* wouldn't manage to find her a husband at all. If I had brought her home that repellent son of Sextus Perquitienus's, she would have swooned. As it was, when I conjured Lucius Piso up, she deemed him a gift straight from the gods, and has not stopped thanking me since. And so happy has the union been, in fact, that it seems the next generation plans to do the same—my son's daughter is to marry my daughter's son when they are old enough. Yes, yes, I know what old Caesar Grandfather used to say, but these will be the first lot of first cousins to marry on either side. They will litter excellent pups.

The answer to your dilemma, Lucius Cornelius, is really ridiculously simple. All it requires is the connivance of Aelia, for you yourself must appear to have no part in it. Let Aelia commence by dropping the girl some heavy hints that you are changing your mind about the marriage, that you are thinking of looking elsewhere. Aelia must drop a few names too—names of absolutely repulsive fellows, like the son of Sextus Perquitienus. The girl will find all this most unwelcome.

Gaius Marius's moribund condition is—pardon the pun, do!—a stroke of good luck, for Young Marius can enter into no marriage while the *paterfamilias* is incapacitated. You see, it is essential that Cornelia Sulla be given the chance to meet privately with Young Marius.

After she learns that her husband may be worse by far than young Quintus Pompeius. Have Aelia take the girl with her to visit Julia at a time when Young Marius is home, and let no impediment prevent their meeting—you had better make sure Julia understands what is afoot!

Now Young Marius is a very spoiled and self-centered sort of fellow. Believe me, Lucius Cornelius, he will do or say nothing to endear himself to your lovesick child. Aside from his father's illness, the chief thing on his mind at the moment is who is going to have the honor of enduring him as a staff cadet. He is quite intelligent enough to know that whoever it is won't let him get away with a tenth as much as his father did—but some commanders are more lenient than others. I gather from Scaurus's letter that no one wants him, no one is willing to ask for him personally, and that his fate rests entirely upon the whim of the *contubernalis* committee. My little network of informants tells me Young Marius is dabbling heavily in Women and Wine, not necessarily in that order. Yet one more reason why Young Marius won't fall into an ecstatic transport at seeing Cornelia Sulla, relic of his childhood—for whom, when he was fifteen or sixteen, he cherished tender thoughts—and probably used her good nature then in ways she never noticed. He is not much different now than he was then. The difference is that he thinks he is, and she thinks he's not. Believe me, Lucius Cornelius, he will commit every possible blunder, and she will irritate him into the bargain.

Once the girl has had her interview with Young Marius, tell Aelia to harp a little harder on the fact that she thinks you're veering away from the Pompeius Rufus alliance—that you need the backing of a very rich knight.

And now I shall tell you an invaluable secret about women, Lucius Cornelius. A woman may have decided adamantly that she doesn't want some suitor—yet if that suitor should suddenly withdraw for reasons other than her spurning of his suit, a woman inevitably decides to take a closer look at the catch which is busy swimming away. After all, your girl has never even *seen* her fish! Aelia must produce some impressive reason why Cornelia Sulla must attend a dinner at the house of Quintus Pompeius Rufus—the father is in Rome on furlough, or the mother is sick, or anything. Could dear Cornelia Sulla possibly see her way to swallowing her dislike just enough to eat one meal in the presence of her despised fish? I guarantee you, Lucius Cornelius, that she will agree. And—since I *have* seen her fish—I am absolutely confident your girl will change her mind. He is exactly the sort to appeal to her. She'll always be cleverer than he, and have no trouble establishing herself as the head of the household. Irresistible! She is so like you. In some ways.

Sulla put the letter down, head spinning. *Simple?* How could Publius Rutilius concoct such a tortuous scheme as this, yet have the gall to term it simple? Military maneuvers were less complex! However, it was worth a try. Anything was worth a try. So he resumed his reading in a slightly happier frame of mind, anxious to see what else Rutilius Rufus had to say.

Matters in my small corner of our vast world are not good. I suppose no one in Rome these days has the time or the interest to follow events in Asia Minor. But somewhere, no doubt, there is a report lying in the Senate offices which by now our Princeps Senatus will have seen. He will also see the letter I have sent to him by the same courier as this one.

There is a Pontic puppet on the throne of Bithynia. Yes, the moment he was sure Rome's back was turned, King Mithridates invaded Bithynia! Ostensibly the leader of the invasion was Socrates, the younger brother of King Nicomedes the Third—which accounts for the fact that Bithynia is still calling itself a free country, having exchanged King Nicomedes for King Socrates. It seems a contradiction in terms to call a king Socrates, doesn't it? Can you imagine Socrates of Athens permitting himself to be crowned a king? However, no one in Asia Province is under any delusion that Bithynia is "free." In all save name, Bithynia is now the fief of Mithridates of Pontus—who must, incidentally, be fuming at the dilatory conduct of King Socrates! For King Socrates let King Nicomedes get away. Despite his accumulation of years, Nicomedes skipped across the Hellespont as nimbly as a goat; rumor here in Smyrna has it that he is en route for Rome, there to complain about the loss of the throne the Senate and People of Rome graciously let him sit on. You'll see him in Rome before the end of the year, burdened down with a large part of the contents of the Bithynian treasury.

And—as if one wasn't bad enough!—there is now a Pontic puppet upon the throne of Cappadocia. Mithridates and Tigranes rode in tandem to Eusebeia Mazaca and installed yet another son of Mithridates on the throne. This one is another Ariarathes, but probably not the Ariarathes whom Gaius Marius interviewed. However, King Ariobarzanes was just as nimble as King Nicomedes of Bithynia. He skipped off too, well ahead of his pursuers. And he will reach Rome with a petition in his hands not long after Nicomedes. Alas, he is much poorer!

Lucius Cornelius, there is sore trouble brewing for our Asia Province, I am convinced of it. And there are many in Asia Province who have not forgotten the heyday of the *publicani*. Many who loathe the word Rome. Thus is King Mithridates being actively wooed in some quarters here. I very much fear that if—or more likely when—he makes a move to steal our Asia Province, he will be welcomed with open arms.

All this is not your problem, I know. It will fall to Scaurus. Who is not very well, he tells me.

By now you will be hard at your war games in Campania. I agree with you, the course is turning. The poor, poor Italians! Citizenship or not, they will remain unforgiven for many generations to come.

Do let me know how things turn out for your girl. I predict that Love will take its course.

Rather than try to explain Publius Rutilius Rufus's ploy to his wife, Sulla simply sent that section of the letter to Aelia in Rome with an accompanying note advising her to do exactly as Rutilius Rufus directed—provided she could make head from tail of it.

Apparently Aelia had no trouble understanding her orders. When Sulla arrived in Rome with Lucius Caesar, he found his house redolent with domestic harmony, a beaming and affectionate daughter, and wedding plans.

"It all turned out exactly as Publius Rutilius said it would," said Aelia happily. "Young Marius was a brute to her when she saw him. Poor little thing! She went with me to Gaius Marius's house consumed with love and pity and sure Young Marius would fall onto her breast to cry upon her shoulder. Instead, she found him furious because he had been ordered by the cadet committee of the Senate to remain on the staff of his old command. Presumably the general replacing Gaius Marius will be one of the new consuls, and Young Marius hates both of them. I believe he tried to get himself posted to you, but got a very cold refusal from the committee."

"Not as cold as his welcome would have been had he come to me," said Sulla grimly.

"I think what was making him angriest was the fact that no one wanted him. Of course he's blaming his father's unpopularity for that, but in his heart I rather think he suspects it's due to his own shortcomings." Aelia jigged in a small triumph. "He didn't want Cornelia's sympathy and he didn't want adolescent adoration. So he was—if I am to believe Cornelia—utterly vile to her."

"So she decided to marry young Quintus Pompeius."

"Not at once, Lucius Cornelius! I let her weep for two days first. Then I said that, since it seemed there would be no pressure from you about marriage to young Quintus Pompeius, she might like to go to dinner at his house. Just to see what he was like. Just to satisfy her curiosity."

Sulla was grinning. "What happened?"

"They looked at each other and liked what they saw. At dinner they were opposite each other, and talked away like old friends." So delighted was she that Aelia took her husband's hand, squeezed it. "You were wise not to let Quintus Pompeius know our daughter was an unwilling bride. The whole family was delighted with her."

Sulla snatched his hand away. "The wedding's set?"

Face clouding, Aelia nodded. "As soon as the elections are over." She gazed up at Sulla with big sad eyes. "Dear Lucius Cornelius, why don't you like me? I try so hard!"

His expression darkened, he moved away. "Frankly, Aelia, for no other reason than you bore me."

And he was gone. She stood quite still, conscious only of a troubled joy; he hadn't said he wanted to divorce her. Stale bread was definitely preferable to no bread.

The news that Aesernia had finally surrendered to the Samnites came not long after Lucius Caesar and Sulla arrived in Rome. The city had literally starved, reduced to eating every dog, cat, mule, donkey, horse, sheep and goat it owned before capitulating. Marcus Claudius Marcellus had handed Aesernia over personally, then disappeared, no one knew where. Except the Samnites.

"He's dead," said Lucius Caesar.

"You're probably right," said Sulla.

Lucius Caesar, of course, would not be returning to the field. His term as consul was drawing to an end and he was hoping to stand for censor in the spring, so had no ambition to continue as a legate to the new commander-in-chief of the southern theater.

The incoming tribunes of the plebs were somewhat stronger than of recent years, perhaps because all Rome was now talking about the enfranchisement law Lucius Caesar was rumored to be going to introduce; they were, however, on the progressive side, and mostly in favor of lenient treatment for the Italians. The President of the College was a Lucius Calpurnius Piso who had a second cognomen, Frugi, to distinguish his part of the Calpurnius Piso clan from the Calpurnii Pisones who had allied themselves in marriage with Publius Rutilius Rufus, and bore the second cognomen Caesoninus. A forceful man of pronounced conservative leanings, Piso Frugi had already announced that he would on principle oppose the two most radical tribunes of the plebs, Gaius Papirius Carbo and Marcus Plautius Silvanus, if they tried to ignore the limitations of Lucius Caesar's bill and give the citizenship to Italians actively engaged in war as well; that he had agreed not to oppose Lucius Caesar's bill was thanks to the persuasive talking of Scaurus and others he respected. Thus interest in Forum doings, almost nonexistent since the beginning of the war, started to revive; the coming year promised to contain interesting political contention.

More depressing by far were the Centuriate elections, at least at the consular level. The two leading contenders had been accepted for two months as the winners, and now came in the winners; that Gnaeus Pompeius Strabo was senior consul and Lucius Porcius Cato Licinianus his junior everyone attributed to the fact that Pompey Strabo celebrated a triumph scant days before the elections.

"These triumphs are pathetic," said Scaurus Princeps Senatus to Lucius Cornelius Sulla. "First Lucius Julius, now Gnaeus Pompeius, if you please! I feel *very* old."

He also looked very old, thought Sulla, and experienced a frisson of alarm; if the lack of Gaius Marius promised torpid and unimaginative activity on the battlefield, what would the lack of Marcus Aemilius Scaurus do to that other battlefield, the Forum

Romanum? Who for instance would look after those minuscule yet ultimately very important foreign matters Rome always found herself embroiled in? Who would put conceited fools like Philippus and arrogant upstarts like Quintus Varius in their places? Who would face up to whatever came so fearlessly, so sure of his own ability and superiority? The truth was that ever since Gaius Marius's stroke Scaurus had visibly diminished; scrap and snarl though they had for over forty years, they needed each other.

"Marcus Aemilius, look after yourself!" said Sulla with sudden urgency, visited by a premonition.

The green eyes twinkled. "We all have to go some time!"

"True. But in your case, not yet. Rome needs you. Otherwise we'll be left to the tender mercies of Lucius Julius Caesar and Lucius Marcius Philippus—what a fate!"

Scaurus started to laugh. "Is that the worst fate can befall Rome?" he asked, and put his head to one side like a skinny, ancient, plucked fowl. "In some ways I approve of you tremendously, Lucius Cornelius. Yet in other ways I have a feeling Rome might fare worse at your hands than at Philippus's." He wiggled the fingers of one hand. "You may not be a natural Military Man, but most of your years in the Senate have been spent in the army. And I have noticed that many years of military service make autocrats out of senators. Like Gaius Marius. When they attain high political office, they become impatient of the normal political restraints."

They were standing outside the Sosius bookshop on the Argiletum, where one of Rome's best food stalls had been sitting for decades. So as they talked they were eating tarts filled with raisins and honeyed custard; a bright-eyed urchin watched them closely, ready to be ready with an offer of a basin of warm water and a cloth—the tarts were juicy and sticky.

"When my time comes, Marcus Aemilius, how Rome fares at my hands depends upon what sort of Rome she is. One thing I can promise you—I will not see Rome disgrace our ancestors. Nor will I see Rome dominated by the likes of a Saturninus," said Sulla harshly.

Scaurus finished his food, demonstrating to the urchin that he was aware of his presence by snapping sticky fingers before the urchin could rush forward unsolicited. Paying strict attention to the process, he washed and dried his hands, and gave the boy a whole sestertius. Then, while Sulla followed suit (and gave the boy a much smaller coin), he resumed talking.

"Once I had a son," he said without a tremor, "but that son was unsatisfactory. A weakling and a coward, for all he was in nature a nice young man. Now I have another son, too young to know what stuff he's made of. Yet my first experience taught me one thing, Lucius Cornelius. No matter how illustrious our ancestors might have been, in the end we still come to depend upon our progeny."

Sulla's face twisted. "My son is dead too, but I have no other," he said.

"In which case, it was meant."

"Do you not think it is all random, Princeps Senatus?"

"No, I do not. I have been here to contain Gaius Marius. Rome needed me to do that—and here I was, Rome's to command. These days I see *you* more as a Marius than as a Scaurus, somehow. And there is no one I can see on the horizon to contain you. Which might prove more dangerous to the *mos maiorum* than a thousand like Saturninus," said Scaurus.

"I promise you, Marcus Aemilius, that Rome stands in no danger from me." Sulla thought about that statement, and qualified it. "*Your* Rome, I mean. Not Saturninus's."

"I sincerely hope so, Lucius Cornelius."

They moved off in the direction of the Senate.

"I gather Cato Licinianus has elected to run things in Campania," said Scaurus. "He's a more difficult man to deal with than Lucius Julius Caesar—just as insecure, but more overbearing."

"He won't trouble me," said Sulla tranquilly. "Gaius Marius called him a pea, and his campaign in Etruria peasized. I know how to deal with a pea."

"How?"

"Squash it."

"They won't give you the command, you know. I did try."

"It doesn't matter in the least," said Sulla, smiling. "I'll take the command when I squash the pea."

From another man it might have sounded vainglorious; Scaurus would have whooped with laughter. From Sulla it sounded ominously prescient; Scaurus shuddered instead.

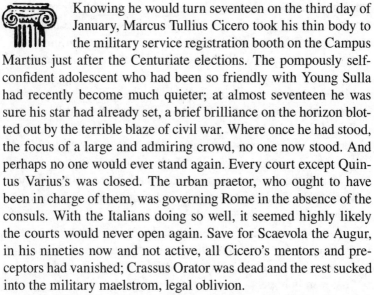

Knowing he would turn seventeen on the third day of January, Marcus Tullius Cicero took his thin body to the military service registration booth on the Campus Martius just after the Centuriate elections. The pompously self-confident adolescent who had been so friendly with Young Sulla had recently become much quieter; at almost seventeen he was sure his star had already set, a brief brilliance on the horizon blotted out by the terrible blaze of civil war. Where once he had stood, the focus of a large and admiring crowd, no one now stood. And perhaps no one would ever stand again. Every court except Quintus Varius's was closed. The urban praetor, who ought to have been in charge of them, was governing Rome in the absence of the consuls. With the Italians doing so well, it seemed highly likely the courts would never open again. Save for Scaevola the Augur, in his nineties now and not active, all Cicero's mentors and preceptors had vanished; Crassus Orator was dead and the rest sucked into the military maelstrom, legal oblivion.

What frightened Cicero most was that no one seemed a scrap interested in him or his fate. The few great men he knew who were still living in Rome were just too busy to bother—oh, he had indeed bothered them, considering his plight and his self unique— but he hadn't succeeded in securing an interview with anyone from Scaurus Princeps Senatus to Lucius Caesar. He was too small a fish after all, a flashy Forum freak not yet seventeen years old. Why indeed should the great men be interested in him? As his father (now the client of a dead man) had said, forget about a special posting, go without complaint to do whatever comes.

When he arrived at the booth on the Via Lata side of the Campus Martius he saw not one face he knew; these were elderly backbencher senators conscripted to do a job as onerous as important, a job they clearly didn't enjoy. The chairman of the group was the only one to look up when Cicero's turn came—the rest were busy with huge rolls of paper—and he eyed Cicero's under-developed physique (which always looked odder because of that huge, gourd-shaped head) without a scrap of enthusiasm.

"First name and family name?"

"Marcus Tullius."

"Father's first name and family name?"

"Marcus Tullius."

"Grandfather's first name and family name?"

"Marcus Tullius."

"Tribe?"

"Cornelia."

"Cognomen, if any?"

"Cicero."

"Class?"

"First—*eques*."

"Father got the Public Horse?"

"No."

"Can you afford to buy your own gear?"

"Of course."

"Read and write?"

"Of course!"

"Your tribe is rural. What district?"

"Arpinum."

"Oh, Gaius Marius country! Who's your father's patron?"

"Lucius Licinius Crassus Orator."

"No one at the moment?"

"Not at the moment, no."

"Done any preliminary military training?"

"No."

"Tell one end of a sword from the other?"

"If by that you mean can I use one, no."

"Ride a horse?"

"Yes."

The chairman finished making his notes, then looked up again with a sour smile. "Come back two days before the Nones of January, Marcus Tullius, and you will be given your military duty."

And that was that. He had been ordered to report back on his birthday, of all days. Cicero got himself away from the booth, utterly humiliated. They hadn't even realized who he was! *Surely* they had seen or heard his feats in the Forum! But if they had they hid it perfectly. Obviously they intended he should do military work. To have begged for clerical duties would have branded him a coward in their eyes, he was more than intelligent enough to see that. So he had kept silent, wanting no black mark against his name some rival candidate for the consulship could dredge up years later.

Attracted as he was to friends older than himself, there was no one he could seek out to confide in. They were all on military service somewhere outside Rome, from Titus Pomponius to various nephews and great-nephews of his deceased patron and his own cousins. Young Sulla, the only friend he might have hoped to find, was dead. Nowhere to go save home. He turned his feet in the direction of the Vicus Cuprius and began to plod toward his father's house on the Carinae, looking—and feeling—the epitome of despair.

Every male Roman citizen at seventeen was required to register for his campaign duty—even, these days, the Head Count—but, until the war with the Italians had broken out, it had not occurred to Cicero that he would ever actually be called upon to do any genuine soldiering; he had intended to use his Forum preceptors to secure for him an appointment where his literary talents would shine, and he would never need to don a mail-shirt or sword except on parade. But he did not have the luck, so much was clear now, and he knew in his slight bones that he was going to be subjected to a regimen he detested. That he would die.

Never really happy or comfortable in Rome, his father had gone back to Arpinum to ready his extensive lands for the winter. He would not, Cicero knew, be back in Rome until after his elder son was inducted into the army. Cicero's younger brother, Quintus, now eight years old, had gone home with his father; he lacked Marcus's brilliance and secretly preferred life in the country. Thus it was Cicero's mother, Helvia, who had been obliged to stay behind in Rome to keep the house there going for her son, and she resented it.

"You're nothing but a nuisance!" she said to him when he came in, lonely and unhappy enough to seek her out in the hope that she would lend him a sympathetic ear. "If it wasn't for you I'd be at home with your father and we wouldn't have to pay for this ridiculously expensive house. There's not a slave in this entire city who isn't a thief and a rogue, with the result that what time I don't spend checking their accounts books I have to spend watching their every move. They water the wine, bill me for the best olives, then only serve the worst, buy half the amount of bread and oil we're charged for, and eat and drink far too much themselves. I shall have to do all the shopping myself." She paused for breath. "It's all your fault, Marcus! These insane ambitions! Know your place, that's what I always say. Not that anyone listens to *me*. You deliberately encourage your father to waste far too much of our precious money on your fancy education—you'll never be another Gaius Marius, you know! A clumsier boy I've never met—and what's the use of Homer and Hesiod, tell me that? You can't make a meal out of paper. And you can't make a career out of paper either. Yet here I'm stuck, all because—"

He didn't wait to hear more. Marcus Tullius Cicero fled, hands over his ears, to his study.

That he owned a study was thanks to his father, who had given over what should have been his room for the exclusive use of his brilliant, extraordinarily promising son. Originally it had been the father possessed the ambition, though he had soon passed it on to the son. Keep such a prodigy at home in Arpinum? Never! Until the birth of Cicero, Gaius Marius had been Arpinum's only famous man, and the Tullii Cicerones regarded themselves as a distinct cut above the Marii because the Marii were not as intelligent.

Therefore let the Marii produce a man of war, of action—the Tullii Cicerones would produce a man of thought. Men of action came and went. Men of thought lasted forever.

The embryonic man of thought shut his study door and bolted it against his mother, then burst into tears.

On his birthday Cicero returned to the booth on the Campus Martius, knees shaking, and underwent a much shorter version of the original questioning.

"Whole name including cognomen?"

"Marcus Tullius Cicero Junior."

"Tribe?"

"Cornelia."

"Class?"

"First."

The scrolls of orders for those reporting today were told over and his scroll found; it would be given to him to present to his commanding officer. The practical Roman mind did not overlook the possibility that verbal orders might be ignored. A copy would already be on its way to the recruitment officers in Capua.

The chairman of the committee laboriously read the fairly extensive remarks written on Cicero's orders, then looked up coldly.

"Well, Marcus Tullius Cicero Junior, there's been a timely intercession on your behalf," said the chairman. "Originally we had placed you for service as a legionary and you would have gone to Capua. However, a special request has come from the Princeps Senatus that you be seconded to staff duties with one of the consuls. Accordingly, you have been posted to the staff of Gnaeus Pompeius Strabo. Report to him at his house at dawn tomorrow for his instructions. This committee notes that you have undergone no sort of preliminary training, and suggests therefore that you put in all your time until you take up your duties on the exercise fields of the Campus Martius. That is all. You are dismissed."

Cicero's knees shook even harder as the relief flooded through him. He took the precious scroll and hurried off. Staff duties! Oh, all the gods favor you, Marcus Aemilius Scaurus Princeps Senatus! Thank you, thank you! I will prove myself invaluable to Gnaeus Pompeius—I'll act as his army historian or compose his speeches and I'll never need to draw a sword!

He had no intention of attending any training exercises on the Campus Martius, for he had tried that in his sixteenth year, only to discover that he lacked neatness of foot, dexterity of hand, quickness of eye, presence of mind. Within a short time of being set to learn the drill with his wooden sword, he had found himself the focus of everybody's attention. But not—as in the Forum—an admiring, awestruck circle—his antics on the Campus Martius made his audience laugh itself sore in the sides. And as time went on he became every other boy's butt. His high shrill voice was mocked, his whinnying laugh was copied, his erudition thought beyond a joke, his elderliness worthy of the starring role in a farce. Marcus Tullius Cicero abandoned his military training, vowing never to resume it. No fifteen-year-old enjoys being a laughingstock, but this fifteen-year-old had already basked in the glow of grown men's approval, and considered himself a special case in every way.

Some men, he had told himself ever since, were not constructed to be soldiers. And he was such a one. It was *not* cowardice! It was rather an abysmal lack of physical prowess. It couldn't be marked against him as a weakness of innate character. Boys his own age were stupid, little better than animals, they prized their bodies but never their minds. Didn't they understand that their minds would be adornments long after their bodies began to creak? Didn't they want to be different? What was truly so desirable about being able to plug a spear into the exact middle of a target, or whack the head off a straw man? For Cicero was clever enough to see that targets and straw men were a far cry from the battlefield, and that many of these juvenile killers of symbols would loathe the reality.

At dawn the next morning he presented himself, wrapped in his *toga virilis,* at the house of Gnaeus Pompeius Strabo on the Forum side of the Palatine, wishing his father was with him for company when he saw how many hundreds of men were gathered there. A few recognized him as the rhetorical prodigy, but no one made any attempt to draw him into a conversation; he found himself gradually pushed into the most obscure corner of Pompey Strabo's vast atrium. There he waited for hours watching the crowd thin and waiting for someone to ask him his business. The new senior consul was Rome's most important man of the moment and all of Rome wanted a word with him or a favor from him. He also had a veritable army of clients, Picentines all, though Cicero had had no idea how many of these clients were resident in Rome until he experienced the enormous throng in Pompey Strabo's house.

Perhaps a hundred men were left and Cicero was beginning to hope he would catch the eye of one of the seven secretaries when a lad of his own age or thereabouts sidled up to him and leaned against the wall to look him over. The eyes which flicked up and down were cool, dispassionate, and quite the most beautiful the brown-eyed Cicero had ever seen. So widely opened they seemed permanently to contain an expression of surprise, their color was a pure rich sky blue, vivid enough to deserve the term unique. A tumbled mass of bright gold hair owned two peculiarities; one was the quiff which stood up from the broad brow, the other a peak which grew down into the middle of the broad brow. Beneath this interesting mop there resided a fresh, rather perky face that had nothing Roman about it at all. The mouth was thin-lipped, the cheekbones broad, the nose short and snubbed, the chin dented, the skin pinkish and faintly freckled, the brows and lashes as gold as the hair. It was, however, a most likable face, and its owner after that initial examination of Cicero produced a smile so attractive that Cicero was won over.

"Who might you be?" the lad asked.

"Marcus Tullius Cicero Junior. Who might you be?"

"I'm Gnaeus Pompeius Junior."

"Strabo?"

Young Pompey laughed without resentment. "Do I look cross-eyed, Marcus Tullius?"

"No. But isn't it usual to adopt one's father's cognomen anyway?" asked Cicero.

"Not in *my* case," said Pompey. "I intend to earn a cognomen for myself. I already know what it's going to be."

"What?"

"Magnus."

Cicero emitted one of his neighing laughs. "That's a bit much, isn't it? 'Great'? Besides, you can't give yourself a cognomen. Other people give it to you."

"I know. But they will."

No stranger to self-confidence, Pompey's degree of it took Cicero's breath away. "I wish you luck," he said.

"What are you here for?"

"I've been posted to your father's staff as a cadet."

Pompey whistled. "Oh, *Edepol!* He won't like you!"

"Why?"

The eyes lost their friendly gleam, became emotionless again. "You're a weed."

"I may be a weed, Gnaeus Pompeius, but what I own by way of intelligence is better than anyone else's!" snapped Cicero.

"That won't impress *my* father," said the son, looking down complacently at his own well-knit, broad-shouldered body.

His answer reduced Cicero to miserable silence; the depression which from time to time haunted him more mercilessly than it did most people four times his age began to descend. He swallowed, looked at the floor, willed Pompey to go away and leave him alone.

"There's no point in getting down in the dumps about it," said Pompey briskly. "For all he or I know, you might be a lion with sword and buckler! *That's* the way to his heart!"

"I am not a lion with sword and buckler," said Cicero, voice squeaking. "I am not a mouse either, you understand. The truth is that I'm absolutely useless with my hands and feet, and it isn't anything I can control or improve."

"You're all right when you're posturing up and down the Forum," said Pompey.

Cicero gasped. "You know who I am?"

"Certainly." The dense lashes fanned down demurely over the

lustrous eyes. "I'm no good at that speechifying stuff, and that too is the truth. My tutors have been beating me senseless for years and got nowhere. To me it's just a waste of time. I can't be bothered learning the difference between *sententia* and *epigramma,* let alone fiddle with *color* and *descriptio!*"

"But how can you hope to be cognominated Great if you don't know how to speak?" asked Cicero.

"How can *you* hope to be called great if you can't use a sword?"

"Oh, I see! You're going to become another Gaius Marius."

But the comparison did not please Pompey, who scowled. "*Not* another Gaius Marius!" he snarled. "I shall be myself. And I'll make Gaius Marius look like a tyro!"

Cicero giggled, his heavy-lidded dark eyes suddenly sparkling. "Oh, Gnaeus Pompeius, I'd like that!" he exclaimed.

A presence loomed; both lads looked round. And there stood Gnaeus Pompeius Strabo, so strongly built he looked square, though he lacked imposing height. In looks he was not unlike his son, save that his eyes were not so blue, and were so badly crossed they did indeed seem to see nothing except the bridge of his own nose. They gave him an enigmatic as well as an ugly quality, for no one could assess what lay in them, so odd and off-putting was their configuration.

"Who's this?" he asked his son.

And Young Pompey did something so wonderful that Cicero was never, never able to forget it or cease to be grateful for it—he threw his muscular arm around Cicero's shoulders, and squeezed them.

And he said cheerfully, as if it were of no consequence, "This is my friend Marcus Tullius Cicero Junior. He's been posted to your staff, Father, but you needn't worry about him in the least. I'll look after him."

"Huh!" grunted Pompey Strabo. "Who wished *you* on me?"

"Marcus Aemilius Scaurus Princeps Senatus," said Cicero in a very small voice.

The senior consul nodded. "Oh, he would, the sarcastic *cunnus!* Sitting at home laughing his head off, I'll bet." He turned away indifferently. "As well for you, *citocacia,* that you're a friend of my son's. Otherwise I'd feed you to my pigs."

Cicero's face burned. He came from a family which had always deplored salty language, his father deeming it unacceptably vulgar; to hear the senior consul say such words was a rude shock.

"You really are a lady, Marcus Tullius, aren't you?" asked Pompey, grinning.

"There are better and more picturesque ways of using our great Latin tongue than coarse imprecations," said Cicero with dignity.

But his new friend stiffened dangerously. "Are you actually criticizing my father?" he demanded.

Cicero retreated hastily. "No, Gnaeus Pompeius, no! I was reacting to your calling me a lady!"

Pompey relaxed, began to smile again. "Just as well for you! I don't like anyone finding fault with my father." He glanced at Cicero curiously. "Bad language is everywhere, Marcus Tullius. Even our poets use it from time to time. It's written on the city's buildings, especially around the brothels and the public latrines. And if a general doesn't call the troops *cunni* and *mentulae*—and a lot worse!—they think he's a stuck-up Vestal."

"I shut my eyes and my ears," said Cicero, then changed the subject. "Thank you for offering me your protection."

"Think nothing of it, Marcus Tullius! Between us we make a decent pair, I think. You help me with my reports and letters, and I'll help you with your sword and buckler."

"It's a deal," said Cicero, lingering in the same spot.

Pompey, who had begun to move away, turned back. "*Now* what?"

"I haven't given your father my orders."

"Throw them away," said Pompey casually. "From today you belong to me. My father won't even notice you."

This time Cicero followed him when he strolled off in the direction of the peristyle-garden. They found a seat in the chilly sun, and Pompey proceeded to demonstrate that though he disavowed any liking for rhetoric, he was yet a talker—and a gossip.

"Did you hear about Gaius Vettienus?"

"No," said Cicero.

"He chopped off the fingers of his right hand to avoid doing his military duty. The urban praetor Cinna sentenced him to lifelong residence as a servant in the Capuan barracks."

A shiver ran down Cicero's spine. "A peculiar sentence, don't you think?" he asked, his forensic interest stirred.

"Well, they had to make some sort of example of him! He could not be let escape with an exile and a fine. We're not like eastern kings, we don't throw people into prison until they die or they grow old. We don't even throw people into prison for a month! I thought Cinna's solution was quite neat, actually," said Pompey with a grin. "Those fellows in Capua will make Vettienus's life a misery for absolutely ever!"

"I daresay they will," said Cicero, gulping.

"Well, come on, it's your turn!"

"My turn to what?"

"Say something."

"I can't think of anything, Gnaeus Pompeius."

"What's the name of Appius Claudius Pulcher's wife?"

Cicero blinked. "I don't know."

"For such a brain, you don't know anything, do you? I suppose I'll have to tell you. Caecilia Metella Balearica. Isn't *that* a mouthful of a name?"

"It's a very august family."

"Not as famous as my family will be!"

"What about her?" Cicero asked.

"She died the other day."

"Oh."

"She had a dream just after Lucius Julius returned to Rome to hold the elections," Pompey went on chattily, "and she went to Lucius Julius the next morning, told him Juno Sospita appeared to her and complained about the disgusting mess in her temple. Some woman apparently crawled in there and died in childbirth, and all they did was take her body away, they didn't wash the floor. So Lucius Julius and Caecilia Metella Balearica got some rags and buckets and went and scrubbed the temple out on their hands and knees. Can you imagine it? Lucius Julius got his toga filthy because he wouldn't remove it, he said he must do the goddess full honor. Then he went straight to the Curia Hostilia and promulgated his law about the Italians—and gave the House a nasty tongue-lashing about neglecting the temples and how did Rome expect to win the war when the gods weren't receiving their proper measure of respect? So the next day the whole House went off with rags and buckets and cleaned all the temples." Pompey stopped. "What's the matter?"

"How *do* you know all this, Gnaeus Pompeius?"

"I listen when people talk, even slaves. What do you do all day, read Homer?" Pompey countered.

"I finished with Homer years ago," said Cicero complacently. "Nowadays I read the great orators."

"And don't have an idea what's going on in the city."

"Now I know you, I'm sure I'm going to learn. I take it that, having had her dream and cleaned up the temple of Juno Sospita, Appius Claudius Pulcher's wife drove home the lesson by expiring?"

"Died very suddenly. A great disaster, Lucius Julius thinks. She was one of Rome's most honored matrons—six children, all a year apart in age, and the youngest just a year old."

"Seven *is* a lucky number," said Cicero, who had a sharp wit.

"Not for her," said Pompey, the irony escaping him. "No one can understand it, after six safe childbirths. Lucius Julius says the gods are angry."

"Does he think his new law will appease divine displeasure?"

Pompey shrugged. "I don't know. Nor does anybody else. All I know is that my father's in favor, so I'm in favor. My father intends to legislate the full citizenship for every Latin Rights community in Italian Gaul."

"And Marcus Plautius Silvanus will soon legislate to extend the citizenship to any man with his name on an Italian municipal roll if he applies in person to a praetor inside Rome within sixty days of the passing of the law," said Cicero.

"Silvanus, yes. But together with his friend Gaius Papirius Carbo," Pompey corrected.

"Now this is more like it!" beamed Cicero, looking animated. "Laws and lawmaking—I *love* them!"

"I'm glad someone does," said Pompey. "I think laws are a nuisance myself. They're always leveled at superior men of superior ability distinguishing themselves, especially at an early age."

"Men cannot live without a system of laws!"

"Superior men can."

Pompey Strabo made no attempt to leave Rome, though he kept telling people that they wouldn't miss him or Lucius Cato because the urban praetor, Aulus Sempronius Asellio, was a very capable man. It soon became apparent, however, that the real reason he lingered was to keep an eye on the spate of legislation which followed the *lex Julia*. Lucius Porcius Cato Licinianus, the junior consul, left Pompey Strabo to it; this was one pair of consuls who were not amicable. Off Lucius Cato went to Campania, only to change his mind and locate himself in the central theater after all. Pompey Strabo had made no secret of his intention to continue the war in Picenum; yet it was Sextus Julius Caesar he sent to the siege of Asculum Picentum, though Sextus Caesar's chest was bad and the winter was the coldest anyone could remember. News came not long after Sextus Caesar set out that he had killed eight thousand rebel Picentines he caught changing from a fouled camp to a fresh one outside Camerinum. Pompey Strabo huffed, but remained in Rome.

His *lex Pompeia* was going through the Comitia uneventfully. It granted the full Roman citizenship to every Latin Rights town south of the Padus River in Italian Gaul, and gave the Latin Rights to the towns of Aquileia, Patavium, and Mediolanum north of the Padus. All the people of these many large and prosperous communities now entered into his clientele, the reason why he had legislated in the first place. No true champion of citizen rights, Pompey Strabo then permitted Piso Frugi to handicap those benefiting from the three enfranchisement laws. At first Piso Frugi enacted a bill creating two new tribes into which all the new citizens everywhere would be placed, keeping the thirty-five tribes exclusively for old Romans. But when Etruria and Umbria began to rumble at the unfairness of being treated no better than Roman freedmen, Piso Frugi altered his law to put all the new citizens into eight of the old tribes plus the two freshly invented ones.

The senior consul then held the censors' elections; Lucius Julius Caesar and Publius Licinius Crassus became censors. Even before he let the sacerdotal contracts, Lucius Caesar announced that in honor of his ancestor Aeneas he would remit all taxes levied upon the town of Troy, his beloved Ilium. As Troy was no more than a small village, he was let have his way without opposition. Scaurus Princeps Senatus—who might have objected—was being driven to distraction by the two refugee kings, Nicomedes of Bithynia and Ariobarzanes of Cappadocia, who wailed and bribed with equal fervor, finding it impossible to understand why Rome was more concerned with her war against the Italians than the coming war with Mithridates.

The chief opponent of Lucius Caesar's enfranchisement bill had been Quintus Varius, fearing that he would turn out to be the law's first victim. The new tribunes of the plebs fell on him like wolves, Marcus Plautius Silvanus in the lead; a quick *lex Plautia,* and the Varian Commission—hitherto prosecuting all those who had supported citizenship for the Italians—became the Plautian Commission, prosecuting all those who had tried to stop citizenship for the Italians. It was Lucius Caesar's younger brother, the cross-eyed Caesar Strabo, who drew the lucky straw and prepared the first case in the Plautian Commission—the prosecution of Quintus Varius Severus Hybrida Sucronensis.

Caesar Strabo's technique was—as always—brilliant. The verdict was a foregone conclusion long before the last day of Quintus Varius's trial, especially because the *lex Plautia* had taken the Commission off the knights and given it to citizens of all and any classes across the thirty-five tribes. Quintus Varius elected not to wait for the verdict. Much to the grief and chagrin of his close friends, Lucius Marcius Philippus and young Gaius Flavius Fimbria, Quintus Varius took poison. Unfortunately he chose his medicine badly, and lingered in agony for several days before expiring. Only his few friends came to his funeral, during which Fimbria swore an oath that he would revenge himself upon Caesar Strabo.

"Ask me if I'm frightened," said Caesar Strabo to his brothers, Quintus Lutatius Catulus Caesar and Lucius Julius Caesar, who had not attended the funeral, but had lingered with Scaurus Princeps Senatus on the Senate steps to see what happened.

"You'd dare Hercules or Hades," said Scaurus, eyes dancing.

"I tell you what I would dare—to run for consul without first being praetor," said Caesar Strabo quickly.

"Now why would you want to do that?" asked Scaurus.

"To test a point of law."

"Aaaaah, you advocates!" cried Catulus Caesar. "You're all the same. You'd test a point of law on what constitutes virginity in a Vestal, I swear you would."

"I think we have already!" laughed Caesar Strabo.

"Well," said Scaurus, "I'm off to see how Gaius Marius is, then I'm going home to work on my speech." He looked at Catulus Caesar. "When are you leaving for Capua?"

"Tomorrow."

"Don't, Quintus Lutatius, I beg of you! Stay until the end of the market interval and hear my speech! It's probably the most important one of my career."

"Now that is saying something," said Catulus Caesar, who had come up from Capua to witness his brother Lucius Caesar's lifting of the tribute from Troy. "May I ask the subject?"

"Oh, certainly. Readying ourselves for war with King Mithridates of Pontus," said Scaurus affably.

All the Caesars stared.

"I see none of you believes it will come either. It will, gentlemen, I promise you it will!" And off went Scaurus toward the Clivus Argentarius.

He found Julia with her sister-in-law Aurelia. So lovely, so quintessentially Roman did both women look, that he was moved to kiss their hands, an unusual homage from Scaurus.

"Not feeling well, Marcus Aemilius?" asked Julia with a smile and a glance at Aurelia.

"Feeling very tired, Julia, but never too tired to appreciate beauty." Scaurus inclined his head toward the study door. "And how is the Great Man today?"

"In a more cheerful mood, thanks to Aurelia," said the Great Man's wife.

"Oh?"

"He's been given a companion."

"Oh?"

"My son, Young Caesar," said Aurelia.

"A *boy*?"

Julia laughed as she led the way to the study. "At not quite eleven years of age, I suppose he is a boy. But in every other way, Marcus Aemilius, Young Caesar is at least as old as you. Gaius Marius is beginning to improve dramatically. However, he's bored. The paralysis makes it difficult for him to get about, yet he loathes being bedridden." She opened the door and said, "Here is Marcus Aemilius come to call, husband."

Marius was lying on a couch beneath a window opening on to the peristyle-garden, his useless left side propped up upon pillows, and the couch turned so that his right side was nearest to the room. On a stool at his feet sat Aurelia's son—or so, at least, Scaurus assumed, for he had never met the boy.

A true Caesar, he thought, having just left the company of three of them. Tall, fair, handsome. This one, rising to his feet, had a look of Aurelia as well.

"Princeps Senatus, this is Gaius Julius," said Julia.

"Sit down, lad," said Scaurus, leaning across to grasp Marius by the right hand. "And how goes it, Gaius Marius?"

"Slowly," said Marius, his speech still clumsy. "As you see, the women have given me a watch-dog. My own Cerberus."

"A watch-pup, more like." Scaurus sat down on the chair Young Caesar positioned for him before returning to the stool. "And what precisely are your duties, young man?"

"I don't know yet," said Young Caesar without evidence of shyness. "My mother only brought me today."

"I think the women think I need someone to read to me," said Marius. "What do you think, Young Caesar?"

"I'd rather talk to Gaius Marius than read to him," said Young Caesar, unabashed. "Uncle Marius doesn't write books, but I've often wished he did. I want to hear all about the Germans."

"He asks good questions," said Marius, starting to flounder as he tried to move.

The boy was up at once, slipping his entire arm under Marius's right arm, and giving his uncle sufficient impetus to complete his change of position. It was done without fuss or fluster, and it indicated a remarkable degree of strength for one so young.

"Better!" panted Marius, now able to look more comfortably into Scaurus's face. "I'm going to do well with my watch-pup."

Scaurus stayed for an hour, more fascinated with Young Caesar than with Marius's malady. Though the boy didn't put himself forward, he answered the questions put to him with an adult grace and dignity, and listened eagerly while Marius and Scaurus discussed the incursions of Mithridates into Bithynia and Cappadocia.

"You're well read for a ten-year-old, Young Caesar," Scaurus said when he rose to go. "Do you know a boy named Marcus Tullius Cicero, by any chance?"

"Only by repute, Princeps Senatus. They say he will be the finest advocate Rome has ever produced."

"Perhaps so. Perhaps not," said Scaurus, walking to the door. "For the moment Marcus Cicero is confined to duties military. I shall see you in two or three days, Gaius Marius. Since you can't come to the Senate to hear me speak, I shall try my speech out on you here—and on Young Caesar."

Scaurus set out to walk home to the Palatine, feeling very tired, and more distressed by Marius's condition than he cared to admit to himself. Nearly six months, and still the Great Man had not got any further than a couch in his *tablinum*. Perhaps the stimulus of the boy—a good idea, that!—would prod him on. But Scaurus doubted that his old friend and enemy would ever improve sufficiently to attend meetings of the Senate.

The long tramp up the Vestal Steps quite exhausted him: he was obliged to stop on the Clivus Victoriae and rest before plodding the last paces home. Mind preoccupied with the difficulties he knew he was going to have in impressing the Conscript Fathers with the urgency of matters in Asia Minor, he tapped on his street door, and was admitted by his wife rather than his porter.

How wonderful she was! thought Scaurus, looking with pure delight into her face. All those old troubles had faded long since, she was the woman of his heart. Thank you for that gift, Quintus Caecilius, he thought, fondly remembering his dead friend Metellus Numidicus Piggle-wiggle. It had been Metellus Numidicus who had given him Caecilia Metella Dalmatica.

Scaurus reached out to touch her face, then tipped his head forward to rest it against her breast and pillowed his cheek against her smooth young skin. His eyes closed. He sighed.

"Marcus Aemilius?" she asked, suddenly taking all his weight, and staggering a little. "Marcus Aemilius?"

Her arms went round him and she screamed until the servants came running, took his limp body from her. "What is it? What is it?" she kept asking.

The steward answered her at last, rising from his knees beside the couch where Marcus Aemilius Scaurus Princeps Senatus lay. "He is dead, *domina*. Marcus Aemilius is dead."

At almost the same moment as the news of the death of Scaurus Princeps Senatus flew around the city came the news that Sextus Julius Caesar had died of a chest inflammation while besieging Asculum Picentum. Having digested the contents of the letter from Sextus Caesar's legate, Gaius Baebius, Pompey Strabo made up his mind. As soon as the State funeral for Scaurus was over, he would proceed to Asculum Picentum himself.

It was extremely rare for the Senate to vote State funds for a funeral, but even in times as hard as these it was unthinkable that Scaurus not be given a State funeral. The whole of Rome had adored him, and the whole of Rome turned out to pay him their last respects. Nothing could ever be the same again without Marcus Aemilius's bald pate reflecting the sun like a mirror, without Marcus Aemilius's beautiful green eyes keeping a close watch on Rome's highborn villains, without Marcus Aemilius's wit and humor and courage. Long would he be missed.

To Marcus Tullius Cicero, the fact that he left a Rome draped in cypress branches was an omen; so too was he dead to all he held dear—Forum and books, law and rhetoric. His mother was busy arranging tenants for the house on the Carinae, her boxes already packed for her return to Arpinum, though she did no packing for Cicero and was not there when the time came for him to bid her farewell. He slipped out into the street and let himself be tossed into the saddle of the horse his father had sent from the country, as the family did not possess the honor of the Public Horse. His belongings were bestowed upon a mule; what didn't fit had to be left behind. Pompey Strabo ran a thin army, didn't tolerate baggage-hindered staff. That Cicero knew this was thanks to his new friend Pompey, whom he met outside the city on the Via Lata an hour later.

The weather was bitterly cold, the wind blustery, the icicles hanging from balconies and tree branches unmelted as Pompey Strabo's small staff began their journey north into the teeth of winter. Some of the general's army had been bivouacked upon the Campus Martius because they had marched in his triumph, and were already on the move ahead of his staff. The rest of Pompey Strabo's six legions waited for him outside Veii, not far from Rome. Here they camped overnight, and Cicero found himself sharing a tent with the other cadets attached to the general's staff, some eight young men aged from Pompey, the youngest at sixteen, through to Lucius Volumnius, the oldest at twenty-three. The day's journey had been neither time nor place to become acquainted with the other cadets, so Cicero faced this ordeal when they pitched camp. He had no idea how to erect a tent, nor what was required of him, and hung back miserably until Pompey thrust a cord into his hand and told him to hold on to it without moving.

Looking back on that first evening in the cadets' tent from the vantage point of age and distance years later, what amazed Cicero was how deftly and inconspicuously Pompey helped him, let it be known without actually saying so that Cicero was his protégé, not to be tormented because of appearance or physical incompetence. The general's son was undeniably the tent boss—but not because he was the general's son. Bookish or learned he was not, yet Pompey's intelligence was remarkable, and his self-confidence without a single flaw; he was a natural autocrat, impatient of restraint, intolerant of fools. Which might have been why he had conceived a liking for Cicero, never a fool, and in no position to apply restraints.

"Your gear's not adequate," he said to Cicero, casting his eyes over the jumble of possessions Cicero had carted in from his mule.

"No one told me what to bring," Cicero said, teeth chattering and face blue with cold.

"Haven't you got a mother or a sister? They always know what to pack," said Pompey.

"A mother, but no sister." He couldn't stop shivering. "My mother doesn't like me."

"Have you no breeches? No mittens? No double-layered woolen tunics? No thick socks? No woolen caps?"

"Only what's here. I didn't think. All that sort of thing is at home in Arpinum anyway."

What seventeen-year-old boy ever does think of warm clothing? asked Cicero of himself all those years later, still able to feel the cheer that spread through him when Pompey, without asking anyone's permission, made everyone donate Cicero something warm.

"Don't whine, you've got enough," Pompey said to the others. "Marcus Tullius may be an idiot in some respects, but he's also cleverer than the rest of us put together. And he's my friend. Just thank your lucky stars you've all got mothers and sisters who know what to pack. Volumnius, you don't need six pairs of socks, you never change them anyway! And hand over those mittens,

Titus Pompeius. Aebutius, a tunic. Teideius, a tunic. Fundilius, a cap. Maianius, you've got so much you can give up one of everything. So can I, easily."

The army struggled into the mountains through blizzards and feet of snow, a warmer Cicero tagging along helplessly, ignorant of what might happen if they encountered the enemy, or what he ought to do. As it happened, the encounter when it came was accidental and unexpected; they had just crossed the frozen river at Fulginum when Pompey Strabo's army became entangled with four raggle-taggle legions of Picentes coming over the ranges from southern Picenum, apparently en route to stir up trouble in Etruria. The engagement was a debacle. It did not involve Cicero personally because he was traveling in the rear with the baggage train, Young Pompey having decided he ought to keep an eye on the bulkier cadet possessions. This, Cicero was well aware, freed Pompey from concern about his welfare and whereabouts as they marched through enemy country.

"Marvelous!" said Pompey as he cleaned his sword in the cadet tent that night. "We slaughtered them! When they wanted to surrender, my father laughed. So we drove them into the peaks without their baggage train—such as it was. If they don't die of the cold, they'll soon starve." He held the blade up to the lamplight to make sure every part of it gleamed.

"Couldn't we have taken them prisoner?" asked Cicero.

"With *my* father in the general's tent?" Pompey laughed. "He doesn't believe in letting enemy live."

Since he was not without courage, Cicero persisted. "But they're Italians, not a foreign enemy. Mightn't we need them for our legions later, after this war is over?"

Pompey thought this over. "I agree we might, Marcus Tullius. But it's too late to worry about this lot now! My father was annoyed with them—and when he is annoyed he gives no quarter to anyone." The blue eyes stared into Cicero's brown ones. "I shall be the same."

It was months before Cicero ceased to dream of them, those Picentine farm workers, subsiding frozen into the snow, or scrabbling feverishly under oaks for acorns, all the food the mountains offered; just one more nightmarish aspect of war to one who found he loathed war.

By the time that Pompey Strabo reached the Adriatic at Fanum Fortunae, Cicero had learned ways of making himself useful, and had even grown used to wearing a mail-shirt and a sword. In the cadet tent he kept house, did the cooking and cleaning up, and in the general's tent he took over the literate chores which Pompey Strabo's Picentine clerks and secretaries found beyond their limited talents—reports to the Senate, letters to the Senate, accounts of battles and skirmishes. When Pompey Strabo perused Cicero's first effort, a letter to the urban praetor Asellio, he glared at the skinny lad with those eerie eyes of his trying to say something.

"Not bad, Marcus Tullius. Maybe there's some reason for my son's attachment to you. Couldn't see what it was—but he's always right, you know. That's why I let him have his way."

"Thank you, Gnaeus Pompeius."

The general swept a hand through the air, indicating a cluttered desk. "See what you can make of that, boy."

They came finally to rest some miles outside Asculum Picentum; since the dead Sextus Caesar's army was still lying before the city, Pompey Strabo decided to put himself down farther away.

Quite often the general and his son would march out to raid, taking however many troops they thought necessary, and staying away for some days. At such times the general would leave his younger brother, Sextus Pompey, in charge of the base, with Cicero left behind to supervise the ongoing paperwork. These periods of relative freedom should have been a joy to Cicero, but they were not. Young Pompey wasn't there to shield him, and Sextus Pompey despised him to the point of casual abuse—cuffs across the ear, boots up the backside, a foot to trip him up as he hurried about.

While the ground was still frozen hard and the spring thaw still a promise, the general and his son took a small force toward the coast in search of enemy troop movements. Shortly after dawn the next day as Cicero stood outside the command tent rubbing his sore buttocks, a troop of Marsic cavalry rode into the camp as if they owned it. So calm and confident was their demeanor that no one ran to arms; the only Roman response came from Pompey Strabo's brother Sextus, who strolled forward and lifted a casual hand in greeting as the troop halted outside the command tent.

"Publius Vettius Scato of the Marsi," said the leader, sliding off his horse.

"Sextus Pompeius, brother of the general, in temporary command during the general's absence."

Scato pulled a face. "That's a pity. I came to see if I could treat with Gnaeus Pompeius."

"He'll be back, if you care to wait," said Sextus Pompey.

"How long?"

"Anywhere between three and six days."

"Can you feed my men and horses?"

"Certainly."

It fell to Cicero, the only *contubernalis* left in the camp, to organize accommodation and provender for Scato and his troop; much to his surprise, the same men who had driven the Picentines into the mountains to freeze and starve now behaved toward the enemy in their midst with great hospitality, from Sextus Pompey down to the most insignificant noncombatant. I do not even begin to understand this phenomenon called war, thought Cicero as he watched Sextus Pompey and Scato walking together with what looked like great affection, or going off to hunt the wild pigs which winter had driven down in search of food. And when Pompey Strabo returned from his raiding expedition, he fell upon Scato's neck as if Scato was his dearest friend.

The treating went on over a great feast; with wondering eyes Cicero witnessed the Pompeys as he imagined they behaved in the fastnesses of their great estates in northern Picenum—huge boars roasting on spits, platters heaped high, everyone seated on benches at tables rather than reclining, servants scurrying with more wine than water. To a Roman of the Latin heartlands like Cicero, the spectacle in the command tent was barbarian. Not so did the men of Arpinum hold a feast, even a Gaius Marius. Of course it didn't occur to Cicero that an army camp giving a banquet for a hundred and more men could not run to couches or dainties.

"You won't get inside Asculum in a hurry," said Scato.

Pompey Strabo said nothing for a moment, too busy crunching through a slice of crisply bubbled pigskin; he finished, wiped his hands on his tunic, and grinned. "It makes no difference to me how long it takes," he said. "Sooner or later Asculum Picentum will fall. And I'll be there to make them wish they'd never laid a hand on a Roman praetor."

"The provocation was great," said Scato easily.

"Great or small makes no difference to me," said Pompey Strabo. "Vidacilius got in, I hear. The Asculans will be pushed to feed yet more mouths."

"There are no Vidacilian mouths to feed in Asculum," said Scato in an odd voice.

Pompey Strabo looked up, face greasy with pig. "Oh?"

"Vidacilius went mad, as far as we can tell," said Scato, a more delicate eater than his host.

Sensing a story, the whole tent fell silent to listen.

"He appeared before Asculum with twenty thousand men not long before Sextus Julius died," said Scato, "apparently with the intention of acting in concert with the people inside the city. His idea was that when he attacked Sextus Julius, the Asculans were to issue out and fall on the Roman rear. A good plan. It might have worked. But when Vidacilius attacked, the Asculans did nothing. Sextus Julius opened his lines and let Vidacilius and his men through, which left Asculum with no choice except to open its gates and let Vidacilius in."

"I didn't think Sextus Julius had so much military skill," said Pompey Strabo.

Scato shrugged. "Could have been an accident. I doubt it."

"I take it the Asculans were not delighted at the prospect of feeding another twenty thousand mouths?"

"They were dancing with rage!" said Scato, grinning. "Vidacilius was not greeted with open arms, but with closed minds. So

Vidacilius went to the forum, got up on the tribunal, and told the city just what he thought of people who didn't obey orders. Had they done as he had asked, Sextus Julius Caesar's army would be dead. And that is possibly true. Be that as it may, the Asculans were not prepared to admit it. The chief magistrate got onto the tribunal and told Vidacilius what *he* thought—didn't he understand there wasn't enough food to feed the army Vidacilius had brought inside?"

"I'm glad to know there's such lack of concord between various sections of the enemy," said Pompey Strabo.

"Don't assume I'm telling you this for any other reason than to demonstrate to you how determined Asculum is to hold out," said Scato, no edge to his voice. "You're bound to hear about it, and I'd rather you heard the real story."

"So what happened? A fight in the forum?"

"Correct. Vidacilius, it became clear, was quite mad. He called the townspeople secret Roman sympathizers and had his soldiers kill a number of them. Then the Asculans found their weapons and retaliated. Luckily most of Vidacilius's troops saw for themselves that he was insane, and left the forum. As soon as darkness fell the gates were opened and over nineteen thousand men sneaked away between the Roman lines—Sextus Julius had died, and his men were more interested in mourning him than keeping watch."

"Huh!" said Pompey Strabo. "Go on."

"Vidacilius took over the forum. He had brought a great deal of food with him, and that he now took and prepared a great feast from it. Perhaps seven or eight hundred men were left to him to help him eat it. He also had a massive funeral pyre built. When the feast was at its height he drank a cup of poison, climbed to the top of the pyre, and had it set alight. While his men roistered, he burned! They tell me it was appalling."

"Mad as a Gallic headhunter," said Pompey Strabo.

"Indeed," said Scato.

"So the city fights on, is what you're saying."

"It will fight until every last Asculan is dead."

"One thing I can promise you, Publius Vettius—if there are

any Asculans left alive when I take Asculum Picentum, they'll wish they were dead," said Pompey Strabo. He threw down his bone, wiped his hands on his tunic again. "You know what they call me, don't you?" he asked in polite tones.

"I don't think I do."

"*Carnifex*. The Butcher. Now I happen to be proud of that name, Publius Vettius," said Pompey Strabo. "I've had more than my share of nicknames during my lifetime. The Strabo is self-explanatory, of course. But when I was just a bit older than my son is now, I was serving as a *contubernalis* with Lucius Cinna, Publius Lupus, my cousin Lucius Lucilius, and my good friend Gnaeus Octavius Ruso here. We were with Carbo on that terrible expedition against the Germans in Noricum. And I wasn't very well liked by my fellow cadets. All except Gnaeus Octavius Ruso here, I add. If *he* hadn't liked me, he wouldn't be with me as one of my senior legates today! Anyway, my fellow cadets tacked another nickname onto the Strabo. Menoeces. We'd visited my home on the way to Noricum, you see, and they found out that my mother's cook was cross-eyed. His name was Menoeces. And that witty bastard Lucilius—no family feeling, my mother was his aunt!—called me Gnaeus Pompeius Strabo Menoeces, implying that my father was the cook." He sighed, a deadly little sound. "I wore that one for years. But nowadays they call me Gnaeus Pompeius Strabo Carnifex. It has a better ring. Strabo the Butcher."

Scato looked bored rather than afraid. "Well, what's in a name?" he asked. "I'm not called Scato because I was born on top of a nice spring of water, you know. They used to say I gushed."

Pompey Strabo grinned, but briefly. "And what brings you to see me, Publius Vettius the Gusher?"

"Terms."

"Tired of fighting?"

"Candidly, yes. I'm not unwilling to fight on—and I will fight on if I have to!—but I think Italia is finished. If Rome were a foreign enemy I wouldn't be here. But I'm a Marsic Italian, and Rome has been in Italy as long as the Marsi. I think it's time both sides salvaged what they can out of this mess, Gnaeus Pompeius. The *lex*

Julia de civitate Latinis et sociis danda makes a big difference. Although it doesn't extend to those in arms against Rome, I note that there's nothing in the *lex Plautia Papiria* to prevent my applying for the Roman citizenship if I cease hostilities and present myself in person to a praetor in Rome. The same holds true for my men."

"What terms are you asking, Publius Vettius?"

"Safe conduct for my army through Roman lines, both here and before Asculum Picentum. Between Asculum and Interocrea we will disband, throw our armor and weapons into the Avens. From Interocrea I will need a safe conduct for myself and my men all the way to Rome and the praetor's tribunal. I also ask that you give me a letter for the praetor, confirming my story and giving your approval for my own enfranchisement and that of every man with me."

Silence fell. Watching from a far corner, Cicero and Pompey looked from one man's face to the other's.

"My father won't agree," whispered Pompey.

"Why not?"

"He fancies a big battle."

And is it truly on such whims and fancies that the fate of peoples and nations depend? wondered Cicero.

"I see why you're asking, Publius Vettius," Pompey Strabo said finally, "but I cannot agree. Too much Roman blood has been shed by your sword and the swords of your men. If you want to get through our lines to present yourselves to the praetors in Rome, you'll have to fight every inch of the way."

Scato got up, slapping hands on thighs. "Well, it was worth a try," he said. "I thank you for your hospitality, Gnaeus Pompeius, but it's high time I went back to my army."

The Marsic troop left in the dark; no sooner had they ridden out of earshot than Pompey Strabo sounded his trumpets. The camp fell into an ordered activity.

"They'll attack tomorrow, probably on two fronts," said Pompey, shaving the crystal-colored hairs off one forearm with his sword. "It will be a good battle."

"What shall I do?" asked Cicero miserably.

Pompey sheathed his weapon and prepared to lie down on his camp bed; the other cadets had been posted to prebattle duties elsewhere, so they were alone.

"Put on your mail-shirt and your helmet, your sword and your dagger, and stack your shield and spear outside the command tent," said Pompey cheerfully. "If the Marsi break through, Marcus Tullius, you'll have to fight the last-ditch stand!"

The Marsi did not break through. Cicero heard the cries and thunder of far-off battle, but saw nothing until Pompey Strabo rode in with his son. Both were disheveled and bloodstained, but both were smiling broadly.

"Scato's legate Fraucus is dead," said Pompey to Cicero. "We rolled the Marsi up—and a force of Picentes too. Scato got away with a few of his men, but we've cut off all access to the roads. If they want to go home to Marruvium they'll have to do it the hard way—across the mountains without food or shelter."

Cicero swallowed. "Letting men die of cold and hunger seems to be one of your father's specialties," he said, quite heroically, he thought, knees trembling.

"Turns you sick, doesn't it, poor Marcus Tullius?" Pompey asked, laughing, then patted Cicero affectionately on the back. "War is war, that's all. They'd do the same to us, you know. You can't help it if it turns you sick. That's your nature. Maybe if a man is as intelligent as you are, he loses his appetite for war. Lucky for me! I wouldn't like to pit myself against a warlike man as intelligent as you are. It's as well for Rome that there are a lot more men like my father and me than there are like you. Rome got where she is by fighting. But someone has to run things in the Forum—and that, Marcus Tullius, is *your* arena."

 It was an arena quite as stormy as any theater of war that spring, for Aulus Sempronius Asellio ran foul of the moneylenders. The finances of Rome, both public and private, were in a worse condition even than during the second Punic war, when Hannibal had occupied Italy and isolated Rome. Money was hiding throughout the business community, the Treasury was virtually empty, and little was coming in. Even the parts of Campania still in Roman hands were too chaotic to permit the orderly collecting of rents; the quaestors were finding it hard to make anyone pay customs duties and port dues, while one of the two biggest ports, Brundisium, was completely cut off; the Italians were now nonpaying insurgents; pleading King Mithridates as an excuse, Asia Province was proving dilatory in returning its contracted incomes to Rome; Bithynia was paying nothing at all; and the incomes from Africa and Sicily were eaten up in extra purchases of wheat before they left Africa or Sicily. To make matters worse, Rome was actually in debt to one of her own provinces, Italian Gaul, from which area most of her weapons and armaments were coming. The one-in-eight plated silver denarius issue of Marcus Livius Drusus had given everyone an extreme mistrust of coined money, and too many sesterces were minted in an attempt to get around this difficulty. Borrowing was rife among those of middle and upper income, and the lending interest rate was higher than in history.

Having a good business head, Aulus Sempronius Asellio decided that the best way to improve matters was to act to relieve debt. His technique was attractive *and* legal; he invoked an ancient statute which forbade charging a fee for lending money. In other words, said Asellio, it was illegal to levy interest on loans. That the antique law had been ignored for centuries and that usury was a thriving business among a large group of knight-financiers was just too bad. The fact was, announced Asellio, that far more knight-financiers were in the business of *borrowing* money than lending it. Until their distress was relieved, no one in Rome could begin to recover. The number of unrepaid loans was escalating daily, debtors were at their wits' end, and—as the bankruptcy courts were closed along with all the other courts—creditors were resorting to violent means in order to collect their debts.

Before Asellio could enforce his revival of that old law, the moneylenders heard of his intention and petitioned him to reopen the bankruptcy courts.

"*Tat?*" he cried. "What? Here is Rome devastated by the most serious crisis since Hannibal, and the men I see in front of my tribunal are actually petitioning me to make matters worse? As far as I'm concerned, you are a small number of repellently avaricious men, and so I take leave to tell you! Go away! If you don't, you'll get a court reopened, all right! A court specially convened to prosecute *you* for lending money with interest!"

From this stand Asellio refused to be budged. If he could do no more for Rome's debtors than to insist that interest was illegal, he was nonetheless lightening the burden of debt enormously, *and* in a perfectly legal way. Let the capital be repaid, by all means. But not the interest. The Sempronii, Asellio's family, had a tradition of protecting the distressed; burning to follow in his family's tradition, Asellio espoused his mission with all the fervor of a fanatic, dismissing his enemies as impotent in the face of the law.

What he failed to take into account was that not all his enemies were knights. There were also senators in the moneylending business, despite the fact that membership in the Senate forbade any purely commercial activity—especially one as unspeakably sordid as usury. Included among the senatorial moneylenders was Lucius Cassius, a tribune of the plebs. At the outbreak of war he had gone into the business because his senatorial census income was barely enough; but as Rome's chances of winning deteriorated, Cassius found himself with everything he had lent outstanding, no payments coming in, and the prospect of scrutiny by the new censors looming ever closer. Though Lucius Cassius was by no means the biggest moneylender in the Senate, he was the youngest, he was desperate to the point of panic, and by nature he was a rather lawless individual. Cassius acted, not only on his own behalf; he engaged himself to act for all the usurers.

Asellio was an augur. As he was also the urban praetor, he inspected the omens on behalf of the city regularly from the podium of the temple of Castor and Pollux. A few days after his confrontation with the moneylenders he was already taking the auspices when he noticed that the crowd in the Forum below him was much larger than the usual gathering to witness an augury.

As he lifted a bowl to pour out a libation, someone threw a stone at him. It struck him just above the left brow, spinning him around, and the bowl flew from his hands to bounce down the temple steps in a series of ringing clatters, sacred water splashing everywhere. Then came more stones, storms of them; crouching low and pulling his particolored toga further over his head, Asellio ran down the steps and headed instinctively for the temple of Vesta. But the good elements in the crowd fled the moment they realized what was afoot, and the irate moneylenders who were his assailants positioned themselves between Asellio and sanctuary at Vesta's holy hearth.

There was only one way left for him to go, through the narrow passage called the Clivus Vestae and up the Vestal Steps onto the Via Nova, scant feet above the floor of the Forum. With the usurers in full cry after him, Asellio ran for his life into the Via Nova, a street of taverns serving Forum Romanum and Palatine both. Screaming for help, he burst into the establishment belonging to Publius Cloatius.

No help was forthcoming. While two men held Cloatius and two more his assistant, the rest of the crowd picked Asellio up bodily and stretched him out across a table in much the same way as an augur's acolytes dealt with the sacrificial victim. Someone cut his throat with such gusto that the knife scraped on the column of bones behind it, and there across the table Asellio died in a fountain of blood, while Publius Cloatius wept and vowed, shrieking, that he knew no one in that crowd, *no one!*

Nor, it appeared, did anyone else in Rome. Appalled by the sacrilegious aspects of the deed as much as by the murder itself, the Senate offered a reward of ten thousand denarii for information leading to the apprehension of the assassins, publicly deploring the killing of an augur clad in full regalia and in the midst of an official ceremony. When not a whisper surfaced during the ensuing eight days, the Senate added more incentives to its reward—pardon for an accomplice, manumission for a slave of either sex, promotion to a rural tribe for a freedman or freed-woman. Still not a whisper.

"What can you expect?" asked Gaius Marius of Young Caesar as they shuffled round the peristyle-garden. "The moneylenders covered it up, of course."

"So Lucius Decumius says."

Marius stopped. "How much congress do you have with that arch-villain, Young Caesar?" he demanded.

"A lot, Gaius Marius. He's a thousand paces deep in all sorts of information."

"Not fit for your ears, most of it, I'll bet."

Young Caesar grinned. "My ears grew, along with the rest of me, in the Subura. I doubt there's much can mortify them."

"Cheeky!" The massive right hand came out in a gentle cuff to the boy's head.

"This garden is too small for us, Gaius Marius. If you want to get any real use back in your left side, we're going to have to walk farther and faster." It was said with firmness and authority, in a tone which brooked no argument.

He got it anyway. "I am not permitting Rome to see me like this!" roared Gaius Marius.

Young Caesar deliberately relinquished his grasp of Marius's left arm and let the Great Man totter unsupported. When the prospect of a fall seemed inevitable, the boy moved back and propped Marius up with deceptive ease. It never failed to amaze Marius how much strength that slight frame contained, nor had it failed to register upon Marius that Young Caesar used his strength with an uncanny instinct as to where and how it would prove of maximum effect.

"Gaius Marius, I stopped calling you Uncle when I came to you after your stroke because I thought your stroke put us on much the same level. Your *dignitas* is diminished, mine is enhanced. We are equals. But in some things I am definitely your superior," said the boy fearlessly. "As a favor to my mother—and because I thought I could be of help to a great man—I gave up my free time to keep you company and get you walking again. You declined to lie on your couch and have me read to you, and the mine of stories you had to tell me are all told. I know every flower and every shrub and every weed in this whole garden! And I say to you straight, it has outlived its purpose. Tomorrow we're going out the door into the Clivus Argentarius. I don't care whether we go up it and onto the Campus Martius, or whether we go down it through the Porta Fontinalis. But tomorrow we go out!"

Fierce brown eyes glared down into rather chilly blue ones; no matter how Marius disciplined himself to ignore it, Young Caesar's eyes always reminded him of Sulla's. Like encountering some huge cat on a hunting expedition, and discovering that the orbs which ought to be yellow were instead a pale blue ringed round with midnight. Such cats were considered visitors from the Underworld; perhaps too were such men?

The duel of gazes continued unabated.

"I won't go," said Marius.

"You will go."

"The gods rot you, Young Caesar! I *cannot* give in to a boy! Haven't you some more diplomatic way of putting things?"

Pure amusement flooded into those unsettling eyes, gave them a life and attractiveness quite alien to Sulla's. "When dealing with you, Gaius Marius, there is no such thing as diplomacy," said Young Caesar. "Diplomatic language is the prerogative of diplomats. You are not a diplomat, which is a mercy. One always knows where one stands with Gaius Marius. And that I like as much as I like you."

"You're not going to take no for an answer, are you, boy?" Marius asked, feeling his will crumble. First the steel, then the fur mitten. What a technique!

"You're right, I will not take no for an answer."

"Well then, sit me down over there, boy. If we are to go out tomorrow, I'm going to need a rest now." A rumble came up through his throat. "How about we go outside with me in a litter, all the way to the Via Recta? Then I could hop out and we could walk to your heart's content."

"When we get as far as the Via Recta, Gaius Marius, it will be as the result of our own efforts."

For a while they sat in silence, Young Caesar keeping himself perfectly still; it had not taken him long to realize that Marius detested fidgeting, and when he had said so to his mother, she had simply observed that if such was the case, learning not to fidget would be very good training. He might have discovered how to get the best of Gaius Marius, but he couldn't get the best of his mother!

What had been required of him was, of course, not what any lad of ten wanted to do, or liked doing. Every single day after lessons with Marcus Antonius Gnipho finished, he had to abandon all his ideas of wandering off with his friend Gaius Matius from the other ground-floor apartment, and go instead to Marius's house to keep him company. There was no time left for himself because his mother refused to allow him to skip a day, an hour, a moment.

"It is your duty," she would say upon the rare occasions when he would beg to be permitted to go with Gaius Matius to the Campus Martius to witness some very special event—the choosing of the war-horses to run in the October race, or a team of gladiators hired for a funeral on the following day strutting through their paces.

"But I will never not have duty of some kind!" he would say. "Is there to be no moment when I can forget it?"

And she would answer, "No, Gaius Julius. Duty is with you in every moment of your life, in every breath you draw, and duty cannot be ignored to pander to yourself."

So off he would go to the house of Gaius Marius, no falter in his step, no slowing of his pace, remembering to smile and say hello to this one and that as he hurried through the busy Suburan streets, forcing himself to go a little faster as he passed by the bookshops of the Argiletum in case he succumbed to the lure of going inside. All the product of his mother's cool yet remorseless teaching—never dawdle, never look as if you have time to spare, never indulge yourself even when it comes to books, always smile and say hello to anyone who knows you, and many who don't.

Sometimes before he knocked on Gaius Marius's door he would run up the steps of the Fontinalis tower and stand atop it to gaze down on the Campus Martius, longing to be there with the other boys—to cut and thrust and parry with a wooden sword, to pound some idiot bully's head into the grass, to steal radishes from the fields along the Via Recta, to be a part of the rough-and-tumble. But then—long before his eyes could grow tired of the scene—he would turn away, lope down the tower steps and be at Gaius Marius's door before anyone could realize he was a few moments late.

He loved his Aunt Julia, who usually answered the door to him in person; she always had a special smile for him and a kiss too. How wonderful to be kissed! His mother did not approve of the habit, she said it had a corrupting influence, it was too Greek to be moral. Luckily his Aunt Julia didn't feel the same. When she leaned forward to plant that kiss upon his lips—she never, never turned her head aside to aim for cheek or chin—he would lower his lids and breathe in as deeply as he could, just to catch every last morsel of her essence in his nostrils. For years after she had passed from the world, the aging Gaius Julius Caesar would scent a faint tendril of her perfume stealing off some woman's skin, and the tears would spring to his eyes before he could control them.

She always gave him the day's report then and there: "He's very cross today," or, "He's had a visit from a friend and it's put him in an excellent mood," or, "He thinks the paralysis is becoming worse, so he's very down."

The routine was that she fed him his dinner in the midafternoon, sending him off to snatch a respite from his duties with Gaius Marius while she fed Gaius Marius his dinner herself. He would curl up on the couch in her workroom and read a book as he ate—something he would never have been allowed to do at home—and bury himself in the doings of heroes, or the verses of a poet. Words enchanted him. They could make his heart soar or stumble or gallop; there were times when, as with Homer, they painted for him a world more real than the one he lived in.

"Death can find nothing to expose in him that is not beautiful," he would say over and over to himself, picturing the young warrior dead—so brave, so noble, so *perfect* that, be he Achilles or Hector or Patroclus, he triumphed even over his own passing.

But then he would hear his aunt calling, or a servant would come to knock on the workroom door and tell him he was wanted again, and down would go the book immediately, his burden shouldered once more. Without resentment or frustration.

Gaius Marius was a heavy burden. Old—thin and fat and then thin again—his skin hanging in sloppy folds and wattles—that frightful fleshly landslide down the left side of his face—and the look in those terrible eyes. He drooled from the left side of his mouth without seeming to know he drooled, so that the gobbet hung until it made contact with his tunic and soaked into a permanently wet patch. Sometimes he ranted, mostly at his hapless watch-pup, the only person who was tethered to him for long enough to use as a verbal vent for all that ire; sometimes he would weep until tears joined the spittle, and his nose ran disgustingly too; sometimes he would laugh at some private joke until the very rafters shook and Aunt Julia would come drifting in with her smile plastered in place, and gently shoo Young Caesar home.

At first the child felt helpless, not knowing what to do or how to do it. But he was a creature of infinite resource, so in time he found out how to handle Gaius Marius. It was either that, or fail in the task his mother had given him—a thought so unthinkable he could not begin to imagine the consequences. He also discovered the flaws in his own nature. He lacked patience, for one thing, though his mother's training enabled him to conceal this shortcoming under mountains of what genuinely seemed like patience, and in the end he came not to know the difference between real patience and assumed patience. Being of strong stomach he came not to notice the drooling, and being of strong mind he came to know what must be done. No one ever told him, for no one ever understood save he; even the physicians. Gaius Marius must be made to move. Gaius Marius must be made to exercise. Gaius Marius must be made to see that he would live again as a normal man.

"And what else have you learned from Lucius Decumius, or some other Suburan ruffian?" Marius asked.

The lad jumped, so sudden was the question, so aimless and faraway his own thoughts. "Well, I've pieced something together—if I'm right. I think I am."

"What?"

"The reason behind Cato the Consul's decision to leave Samnium and Campania to Lucius Cornelius and transfer himself to your old command against the Marsi."

"Oho! Tell me your theory, Young Caesar."

"It's about the kind of man I think Lucius Cornelius has to be," said Young Caesar seriously.

"What kind of man is that?"

"A man who can make other men very afraid."

"He can that!"

"He must have known he would never be given the southern command. It belongs to the consul. So he didn't bother to argue. He just waited for Lucius Cato the Consul to arrive in Capua, and then he cast a spell that frightened Cato the Consul so badly that Cato the Consul decided to put as big a distance between himself and Campania as he possibly could."

"How did you piece that hypothesis together?"

"From Lucius Decumius. And from my mother."

"*She'd* know," said Marius cryptically.

Frowning, Young Caesar glanced sideways at him, then shrugged. "Once Lucius Cornelius has the top command and no one stupid to hamper him, he has to do well. I think he's a very good general."

"Not as good as me." Marius sighed, half a sob.

The boy pounced immediately. "Now don't you start to feel sorry for yourself, Gaius Marius! You'll be fit to command again, especially once we get out of this silly garden."

Not up to this attack, Marius changed the subject. "And has your Suburan grapevine told you how Cato the Consul is doing against the Marsi?" he asked, and snorted. "No one ever tells *me* what's going on—they think it might upset me! What upsets me, however, is not knowing what goes on. If I didn't hear from you, I'd explode!"

Young Caesar grinned. "My grapevine has it that the consul got into trouble the moment he arrived in Tibur. Pompey Strabo took your old troops—he's very good at that!—so Lucius Cato the Consul is left with none save raw recruits—farm boys newly enfranchised, from Umbria and Etruria. Not only is *he* at a loss how to train them, but his legates don't know either. So he commenced his training program by calling an assembly of the whole army. He harangued them without pity. You know the sort of thing—they were idiots and yokels, cretins and barbarians, a miserable lot of worms, he was used to far better, they'd all be dead if they didn't smarten up, and so forth."

"Shades of Lupus and Caepio!" cried Marius incredulously.

"Anyway, one of the men assembled at Tibur to hear all this rubbish is a friend of Lucius Decumius's. Name of Titus Titinius. By profession Titus Titinius is a retired veteran centurion whom you gave a bit of your Etrurian land to after Vercellae. He says he did you a good turn once."

"Yes, I remember him very well," said Marius, trying to smile and dribbling copiously.

Out came Young Caesar's "Marius handkerchief" as he called it; the saliva was wiped neatly away. "He comes to Rome to stay with Lucius Decumius regularly because he likes to hear the goings-on in the Forum. But when the war broke out he enlisted as a training centurion. He was based in Capua for a long time, but he was sent to help Cato the Consul at the beginning of this year."

"I presume Titus Titinius and the other training centurions hadn't had a chance to begin to train when Cato the Consul delivered his harangue at Tibur?"

"Exactly. But he didn't exclude them from the harangue. And *that* was how he got into trouble. Titus Titinius became so angry as he listened to Cato the Consul abuse everybody that he finally bent down and picked up a big clod of earth. And he threw it at Cato the Consul! The next thing, *everyone* was bombarding Cato the Consul with clods of earth! He ended knee-deep in them, with his army on the verge of mutiny." Finding inspiration, the boy chuckled. "Marred, mired, muzzled!"

"Stop fiddling around with words and get on with it!"

"Sorry, Gaius Marius."

"So?"

"He wasn't hurt at all, but Cato the Consul felt that his *dignitas* and *auctoritas* had suffered intolerably. Instead of just forgetting the incident, he clapped Titus Titinius in chains and sent him to Rome with a letter asking that the Senate try him for inciting a mutiny. He arrived this morning, and he's sitting in the Lautumiae cells."

Marius began to struggle to his feet. "Well, that settles our destination tomorrow morning, Young Caesar!" he said, sounding quite lighthearted.

"We're going to see what will happen to Titus Titinius?"

"If it's in the Senate, boy, I am, anyway. You can wait in the vestibule."

Young Caesar hauled Marius up and moved automatically to his left side to take the weight of the useless limbs. "I won't need to do that, Gaius Marius. He's being brought before the Plebeian Assembly. The Senate wants nothing to do with it."

"You're a patrician, you can't stand in the Comitia when the Plebs are meeting. But in my state, I can't either. So we will find a good spot on top of the Senate steps and watch the circus from there," said Marius. "Oh, I needed this! A Forum circus is far better than anything the aediles can ever think to put in the games!"

If Gaius Marius had ever doubted the depth of the love the people of Rome bore him, those fears would have been laid to rest the following morning when he emerged from his house and turned to negotiate the steep slope of the Clivus Argentarius as it plunged down through the Fontinalis Gate to end in the lower Forum. In his right hand he had a stick, on his left side he had the boy Gaius Julius Caesar—and soon, to right and to left of him, in front and behind him, he had every man and woman in the vicinity. He was cheered, he was wept over; with every grotesque step, the out-thrust of his right leg and the terrible dragging of his left leg twisting his hip, those who clustered around urged him on. Soon the word was going on ahead of him, so glad, so uplifted:

"Gaius Marius! Gaius Marius!"

When he entered the lower Forum the cheers were deafening. Sweat standing on his brow, leaning more heavily on Young Caesar than anyone there knew save he and Young Caesar, he hauled himself around the lip of the Comitia. Two dozen senators rushed to lift him to the top of the Curia Hostilia podium, but he held them at bay and struggled, step by dreadful step, all the way up. A curule chair was brought, he got himself down onto it with no help from anyone except the boy.

"Left leg," he said, chest heaving.

Young Caesar understood at once, got down on his knees and pulled the useless member forward until it rested ahead of the right in the classic pose, then took the inanimate left arm and laid it across Marius's lap, hiding the stiff clumped fingers of the hand beneath a fold of toga.

Gaius Marius sat then more regally than any king, bowing his head to acknowledge the cheers while the sweat rolled down his face and his chest labored like a gigantic bellows. The Plebs were already convoked, but every last man in the well of the Comitia turned to face the Senate steps and cheered, after which the ten tribunes of the plebs on the rostra called for three vast hurrahs.

The boy stood beside the curule chair and looked down at the crowd, this his first experience of the extraordinary euphoria so many united people could generate, feeling the adulation brush his cheek because he stood so close to its source, and understanding what it must be like to be the First Man in Rome. And as the cheers eventually died down his sharp ears caught the murmured whispers,

"Who *is* that beautiful child?"

He was well aware of his beauty, and aware too of the effect it had on others; since he liked to be liked, he also liked being beautiful. If he forgot what he was there for, however, his mother would be angry, and he hated vexing her. A bead of drool was forming in the flaccid corner of Marius's mouth, it must be wiped away. He took the Marius handkerchief from the sinus of his purple-bordered child's toga, and while the whole crowd sighed in tender admiration, he dabbed the sweat from Marius's face and at the same time whisked the gobbet away before anyone could notice it.

"Conduct your meeting, tribunes!" Marius cried loudly when he could find the breath.

"Bring the prisoner Titus Titinius!" ordered Piso Frugi, the President of the College. "Members of the Plebs gathered here in your tribes, we meet to decide the fate of one Titus Titinius, *pilus prior* centurion in the legions of the consul Lucius Porcius Cato Licinianus. His case has been referred to us, his peers, by the Senate of Rome after due consideration. The consul Lucius Porcius Cato Licinianus alleges that Titus Titinius did strive to incite a mutiny, and demands that we deal with him as severely as the law allows. As mutiny is treason, we are here to decide if Titus Titinius should live or die."

Piso Frugi paused while the prisoner, a big man in his early fifties clad only in a tunic, chains attached to manacles about his wrists and ankles, was led onto the rostra and made to stand at the front, to one side of Piso Frugi.

"Members of the Plebs, the consul Lucius Porcius Cato Licinianus states in a letter that he did call an assembly of all the legions of his army, and that while he was addressing this legally convoked assembly, Titus Titinius, the prisoner here on display, did strike him with a missile thrown from the shoulder, and that Titus Titinius did then incite all the men around him to do the same. The letter bears the consul's seal."

Piso Frugi turned to the prisoner. "Titus Titinius, how answer you?"

"That it's true, tribune. I did indeed strike the consul with a missile thrown from the shoulder." The centurion paused, then said, "A clod of soft earth, tribune, that was my missile. And when I threw it, everyone around me did the same."

"A clod of soft earth," said Piso Frugi slowly. "What made you hurl such a missile at your commander?"

"He called us yokels, miserable worms, stupid upcountry fools, impossible material to work with, and more besides!" shouted Titus Titinius in his parade voice. "Now I wouldn't have minded if he'd called us *mentulae* and *cunni*, tribune—that's good talk between a general and his men." He drew in a breath and thundered, "If there had been rotten eggs to hand, I'd rather have thrown rotten eggs! But a ball of soft earth is the next best thing, and there was plenty of that to hand! I don't care if you strangle me, I don't care if you throw me off the Tarpeian Rock! Because if I ever see Lucius Cato again, he'll get more of the same from me, and that's a fact!"

Titinius turned to face the Senate steps and pointed at Gaius Marius, chains clanking. "Now *there's* a general! I served Gaius Marius as a legionary in Numidia and I served him again in Gaul—but as a centurion! When I retired he gave me a bit of land in Etruria off his own estates. And I tell you, members of the Plebs, that Gaius Marius wouldn't have got himself buried by clods of earth! Gaius Marius *loved* his soldiers! He didn't hold them in contempt like Lucius Cato! Nor would Gaius Marius have clapped a man in chains and sent him to be judged by a lot of civilians in Rome just because that man lobbed *anything* at him! The general would have rubbed that man's face in whatever it was he threw! I tell you, Lucius Cato is no general and Rome will get no victories from him! A general cleans up his own messes. He doesn't give that job to the tribes in a gathering!"

A profound silence had fallen. When Titus Titinius ceased to speak, not one voice broke it.

Piso Frugi sighed. "Gaius Marius, what would you do with this man?" he asked.

"He's a centurion, Lucius Calpurnius Piso Frugi. And I do know him, as he says. Too good a man to waste. But he buried his general in clods of earth, and that is a military offense no matter what the provocation. He can't go back to the consul Lucius Porcius Cato. That would be to insult the consul, who dismissed this man from his service by sending him to us. I think we can best serve the interests of Rome by sending Titus Titinius to some other general. Might I suggest he return to Capua and take up his old duties there?"

"How say my fellow tribunes?" asked Piso Frugi.

"I say, let it be as Gaius Marius suggests," said Silvanus.

"And I," said Carbo.

The other seven followed suit.

"How says the *concilium plebis*? Do I need to call for a formal vote, or will you show your hands?"

Every hand shot up.

"Titus Titinius, this Assembly orders you to report to Quintus Lutatius Catulus in Capua," said Piso Frugi, allowing no smile to appear on his face. "Lictors, strike off his chains. He is free."

But he refused to go until he had been brought to Gaius Marius, whereupon he fell to his knees and wept.

"Train your Capuan recruits well, Titus Titinius," said Marius, his shoulders sagging in exhaustion. "And now, if I may be excused, I think it's time I walked home."

Lucius Decumius popped out from behind a pillar, face creased into smiles, his hand extended to Titus Titinius, but his gaze upon Gaius Marius. "There's a litter for you, Gaius Marius."

"I am not riding home in a litter when my feet got me this far!" said Gaius Marius. "Boy, help me up." His huge right hand ate into Young Caesar's thin arm until the flesh below its vise glowed dark red, but no expression save concern crossed Young Caesar's face. He bent to the task of getting the Great Man to his feet as if it were no trouble. Once standing, Marius took his stick, the boy moved to support his left side, and down the steps they went like two conjoined crabs. Half of Rome, it seemed, escorted them up the hill, cheering Marius's every effort.

The servants fought for the honor of escorting the grey-hued Marius to his room; no one noticed Young Caesar lag behind. When he thought himself alone he sank to a huddle in the passageway between door and atrium and lay motionless, eyes closed. Julia found him there some time later. Fear twisting her heart, she knelt beside him, oddly reluctant to call for help.

"Gaius Julius, Gaius Julius! What is it?"

As she took him into her arms he fell against her, his skin drained of color, his chest hardly moving. She drew his hand into hers to feel for a pulse and saw the livid bruise in the shape of Marius's fingers upon the child's upper arm.

"Gaius Julius, Gaius Julius!"

The eyes opened, he sighed and smiled, and the color came stealing back into his face. "Did I get him home?"

"Oh yes, Gaius Julius, you got him home magnificently," said Julia, close to tears. "It's worn you out more than it has him! These outside walks are going to be too much for you."

"No, Aunt Julia, I can manage, truly. He won't go with anyone else, you know that," he said, getting to his feet.

"Yes, unfortunately I do. Thank you, Gaius Julius! Thank you more than I can say." She studied the bruise. "He's hurt you. I shall put something on it to make it feel better."

The eyes filled with life and light, the mouth curved into the smile which melted Julia's heart. "I know what will make it better, Aunt Julia."

"What?"

"A kiss. One of your kisses, please."

Kisses he got aplenty, and every kind of food he liked, and a book, and the couch in her workroom to rest upon; she would not let him go home until Lucius Decumius came to fetch him.

As the seasons wore on in that year which saw the course of the war turn in Rome's favor at last, Gaius Marius and Young Caesar became one of Rome's fixtures, the boy helping the man, the man slowly becoming more able to help himself. After that first day they turned their feet toward the Campus Martius, where the crowds were far less and their progress eventually provoked scant interest. As Marius grew stronger they walked further, culminating in the triumphant day they reached the Tiber at the end of the Via Recta; after a long rest, Gaius Marius swam in the Trigarium.

Once he began to swim regularly his progress accelerated. So did his fascination with the martial and equine exercises they encountered along their way; Marius had decided that it was high time Young Caesar started his military education. At last! At last Gaius Julius Caesar received the rudiments of skills he had longed to acquire. He was tossed into the saddle of a rather mettlesome pony and demonstrated that he was a born rider; he and Marius dueled with wooden swords until even Marius couldn't fault the boy, and graduated him to the real thing; he was shown how to throw the *pilum,* and plugged the target every time; he learned to swim once Marius felt confident enough in the water to keep him out of trouble; and he listened to a new kind of story from Marius—the reminiscences of a general on the subject of generaling.

"Most commanders lose the battle before they ever get onto the field to fight," said Marius to Young Caesar as they sat side by side on the river bank, wrapped in linen shrouds.

"How, Gaius Marius?"

"In one of two ways, mostly. Some understand the art of command so little that they actually think all they have to do is point the enemy out to the legions, then stand back to watch the legions do their stuff. But others have their heads so full of manuals and hints from the generals of their cadet days that they go by the book when to go by the book is to beg for defeat. Every enemy— every campaign—every battle, Gaius Julius!—is unique. It must be approached with the respect due to the unique. By all means plan what you're going to do the night before on a sheet of parchment in the command tent, but don't regard that plan as cut-and-dried. You wait to form the true plan until you see the enemy, the lay of the land on the morning of the engagement, how the enemy is drawn up, and where his weaknesses are. *Then* you decide! Preconceptions are almost always fatal to your chances. And things can change even as the battle progresses, because every *moment* is unique! Your men's mood might change—or the site mud up faster than you thought it would—or dust might rise to obscure every sector of the field—or the enemy general spring a real surprise—or flaws and weaknesses show up in your own plans or the plans of the enemy," said Marius, quite carried away.

"Is it never possible for a battle to go exactly as it was planned the night before?" asked Young Caesar, eyes shining.

"It *has* happened! But about as frequently as hens grow teeth, Young Caesar. Always remember—whatever you've planned and no matter how complex your plan might be—be prepared to alter it in the twinkling of an eye! And here's another pearl of wisdom, boy. Keep your plan as simple as possible. Simple plans always work better than tactical monstrosities, if for no other reason than you, the general, cannot implement your plan without using the chain of command. And the chain of command gets vaguer the lower down and the farther away from the general it gets."

"It would seem that a general must have a very well-trained staff and an army drilled to perfection," said the boy pensively.

"Absolutely!" cried Marius. "That's why a good general always makes sure he addresses his troops before the battle. Not to boost morale, Young Caesar. But to let the rankers know what he plans to do. If they know what he plans to do, they can interpret the orders they get from the bottom of the chain of command."

"It pays to know your soldiers, doesn't it?"

"Indeed it does. It also pays to make sure they know you. And make sure they *like* you. If men like their general, they'll work harder and take bigger risks for him. Don't ever forget what Titus Titinius said from the rostra. Call the men every name under the sun, but *never* give them reason to suppose you despise them. If you know your ranker soldiers and they know you, twenty thousand Roman legionaries can beat a hundred thousand barbarians."

"You were a soldier before you were a general."

"I was. An advantage you'll never really have, Young Caesar, because you're a patrician Roman nobleman. And yet I say that if you're not a soldier before you're a general, you can never be a general in the true sense." Marius leaned forward, eyes looking at something far beyond the Trigarium and the neat sward of the Vatican plain. "The best generals were always soldiers first. Look at Cato the Censor. When you're old enough to be a cadet, don't skulk behind the lines making yourself useful to your commander—get out in the front line and *fight*! Ignore your nobility. Every time there's a battle, turn yourself into a ranker. If your general objects and wants you to ride around the field bearing messages, tell him you'd rather fight. He'll let you because he doesn't hear it very often from his own kind. You must fight as an ordinary soldier, Young Caesar. How else when you come to command can you understand what your soldiers in the front line are going through? How can you know what frightens them—what puts them off—what cheers them up—what makes them charge like bulls? And I'll tell you something else too, boy!"

"What?" asked Young Caesar eagerly, drinking in every word with bated breath.

"It's time we went home!" said Marius, laughing. Until he saw the look on Young Caesar's face. "Now don't get on your high horse with me, boy!" he barked, annoyed because his joke had fallen flat and Young Caesar was furious.

"Don't you *dare* tease me about something so important!" the child said, his voice as soft and gentle as Sulla's could be in a like moment. "This is serious, Gaius Marius! You're not here to entertain me! I want to know everything you know before I'm old enough to be a cadet—then I can go on learning from a more solid base than anyone else. I will *never* stop learning! So cut out your unfunny jokes and treat me like a man!"

"You're not a man," said Marius feebly, staggered at the storm he had raised and not sure how to deal with it.

"When it comes to learning I'm more a man than any man I know, including you!" Young Caesar's voice was growing louder; several nearby wet and shivering faces turned his way. Even in the midst of this towering rage, however, there was still presence of mind; he glanced at their neighbors and got abruptly to his feet, nostrils pinched, lips set hard. "I don't mind being a child when Aunt Julia treats me like a child," he said, quietly now, "but when you treat me like a child, Gaius Marius, I—am—*mortally* insulted! I tell you, I won't have it!" Out went one hand to pull

Marius up. "Come on, let's go home. I'm out of patience with you today."

Marius grasped the hand and went home without a murmur.

Which was just as well, as things turned out. When they came through the door they found Julia waiting for them anxiously, the marks of tears on her face.

"Oh, Gaius Marius, something dreadful!" she cried, quite forgetting he ought not to be upset; even now in his illness, when disaster struck Julia turned to Marius as to a savior.

"What is it, *meum mel?*"

"Young Marius!" Seeing her husband's look of stunned shock, she blundered on frantically. "No, no, he's not dead, my love! He isn't injured either! I'm sorry, I'm sorry, I shouldn't be giving you such frights—but I don't know where I am, or what to do!"

"Then sit down over there, Julia, and compose yourself. I will sit on one side of you and Gaius Julius will sit on the other side, and you can tell both of us—calmly, clearly, and without gushing like a fountain."

Julia sat down. Marius and Young Caesar ranged themselves on either side of her. Each took one of her hands and patted it.

"Now begin," said Marius.

"There's been a great battle against Quintus Poppaedius Silo and the Marsi. Somewhere near Alba Fucentia, I think. The Marsi won. But our army managed to retreat without losing a huge number of men," said Julia.

"Well, I suppose that's an improvement," said Marius heavily. "Go on. I presume there's more."

"Lucius Cato the Consul was killed shortly before our son ordered the retreat."

"Our *son* ordered the retreat?"

"Yes." Tears threatened, were resolutely suppressed.

"How do you know all this, Julia?"

"Quintus Lutatius called to see you earlier today. He's been on some sort of official visit to the Marsic theater, I gather to do with Lucius Cato's chronic troop troubles. I don't know—I'm not honestly sure," said Julia, taking the hand Young Caesar held from him and lifting it to her head.

"We won't worry about why Quintus Lutatius was visiting the Marsic theater," said Marius sternly. "I take it he was an observer of this battle Cato lost?"

"No, he was at Tibur. That's where our army retreated to after the battle. It was a debacle, apparently. The soldiers weren't led at all. The only one who preserved his reason was our son, it seems. That's why it was he sounded the retreat. On the way to Tibur he tried to restore order among the soldiers, but he didn't get anywhere. The poor fellows were quite demented."

"Then why—what is so wrong, Julia?"

"There was a praetor waiting at Tibur. A new legate posted to Lucius Cato. Lucius Cornelius Cinna . . . I'm sure that's the name Quintus Lutatius said. So when the army reached Tibur, Lucius Cinna took over from Young Marius, and everything seemed all right. Lucius Cinna even commended our son for his good sense." Julia plucked both hands from their keepers and wrung them together.

"*Seemed* all right. What happened then?"

"Lucius Cinna called a meeting to find out what went wrong. There were only a few tribunes and cadets to question—all the legates apparently were killed, for there were none got back to Tibur," said Julia, trying desperately to be lucid. "Then when Lucius Cinna came to the circumstances surrounding the death of Lucius Cato the Consul—one of the other cadets accused *our son* of murdering him!"

"I see," said Marius calmly, looking unperturbed. "Well, Julia, you know the story, I don't. Continue."

"This other cadet said Young Marius tried to persuade Lucius Cato to order the retreat. But Lucius Cato rounded on him and called him the son of an Italian traitor. He refused to order the retreat, he said it was better every Roman man on the field died than to live in dishonor. He turned his back on Young Marius in contempt. And the other cadet says *our son* stuck his sword up to the hilt in Lucius Cato's back! Then our son took over the command, and ordered the retreat." Julia was weeping.

"Couldn't Quintus Lutatius have waited to tell me rather than burdening you with this news?" asked Marius harshly.

"He truly didn't have the time, Gaius Marius." She wiped her eyes, tried to compose herself. "He is sent for urgently from Capua, he had to travel on at once. In fact he said he ought not have delayed to visit Rome and see us, so we must be grateful to him. He said you would know what to do. And when Quintus Lutatius said that, I knew he believed our son *did* kill Lucius Cato! Oh, Gaius Marius, what will you do? What can you do? What did Quintus Lutatius mean, you would know?"

"I must journey to Tibur with my friend Gaius Julius here," said Marius, getting to his feet.

"You can't!" gasped Julia.

"Indeed I can. Now calm yourself, wife, and tell Strophantes to send to Aurelia and ask for Lucius Decumius. He can look after me during the journey, and save the boy's energy." As he spoke Marius held on to Young Caesar's shoulder tightly—not as if he needed support, more as if he was signaling the boy to silence.

"Let Lucius Decumius take you alone, Gaius Marius," said Julia. "Gaius Julius should go home to his mother."

"Yes, you're right," said Marius. "Home you go, Young Caesar."

Young Caesar spoke up. "My mother placed me at your side to use, Gaius Marius," he said sternly. "If I were to desert you in this, my mother would be very angry."

Marius would have insisted; it was Julia, knowing Aurelia, who backed down. "He is right, Gaius Marius. Take him."

Thus it was that one long summer hour later a four-mule gig carried Gaius Marius, Young Caesar, and Lucius Decumius out of Rome through the Esquiline Gate. A good driver, Lucius Decumius kept his team to a brisk trot, a pace the mules could sustain all the way to Tibur without becoming exhausted.

Squeezed between Marius and Decumius, a delighted Young Caesar watched the countryside pass by until darkness fell, never called upon before to take a journey in such urgent circumstances, but secretly harboring a passion for swift travel.

Though they were nine years apart in age, Young Caesar knew his first cousin well, for he carried many more memories out of infancy and early childhood with him than other children, and he had no cause to love or like Young Marius. Not that Young Marius had ever mistreated him, or even derided him. No, it was the others whom Young Marius had mistreated and derided had turned Young Caesar against him. During the perpetual rivalry between Young Marius and Young Sulla, it was always the younger boy he had felt was in the right. And Young Marius had worn two faces for Cornelia Sulla—the charming one when she was present, the spiteful one when she was not—nor did he confine his mockery of her to his cousins, he aired it to his friends as well. Therefore the prospect of Young Marius's disgrace did not worry Young Caesar on a personal level at all. But because of Gaius Marius and Aunt Julia it worried him sick.

When darkness came down the road was lit by a half-moon overhead, though Lucius Decumius cut the mules back to a walk. The boy promptly fell asleep with his head pillowed in Marius's lap, his body disposed in that limp abandonment seen only in children and animals.

"Well, Lucius Decumius, we had better talk," said Marius.

"Good idea," said Lucius Decumius cheerfully.

"My son is in grave trouble."

"Tch, tch!" said Lucius Decumius, clicking his tongue. "Now we can't possibly have *that,* Gaius Marius."

"He's charged with the murder of Cato the Consul."

"From what I've heard about Cato the Consul, they ought to award Young Marius the Grass Crown for saving an army."

Marius shook with laughter. "I couldn't agree more. If I can believe my wife, such indeed are the circumstances. That fool Cato engineered a defeat for himself! I imagine his two legates were dead by then, and I can only assume that his tribunes were off carrying messages around the field—the wrong messages, probably. Certainly the only staff Cato the Consul had with him were cadets. And it was left to my son the cadet to advise the general that he must retreat. Cato said no, and called Young Marius the son of an Italian traitor. Whereupon—according to another cadet—Young Marius put two feet of good Roman sword into the consul's back, and ordered the retreat."

"Oh, well done, Gaius Marius!"

"So *I* think—in one way. In another, I'm sorry that he did it while Cato's back was turned. But I know my son. Temper, not lack of a sense of honor. I wasn't home enough when he was little to drub the temper out of him. Besides, he was too smart to show *me* his temper. Or show his mother."

"How many witnesses, Gaius Marius?"

"Only the one, as far as I can gather. But I won't know until I see Lucius Cornelius Cinna, who is now in command. Naturally Young Marius must answer charges. If the witness sticks to his story, then my son will face flogging and beheading. To kill the consul is not merely murder. It's sacrilege too."

"Tch, tch," said Lucius Decumius, and said no more.

Of course he knew why he had been asked along on this journey to sort out a hideous confusion. What fascinated him was that Gaius Marius had sent for him. Gaius Marius! The straightest, the most honorable man Lucius Decumius knew. What had Lucius Sulla said years ago? That even when he took a crooked path, Gaius Marius trod it straightly. Yet tonight it looked very much as if Gaius Marius had elected to walk a crooked path crookedly. Not in character. There were other ways. Ways he would have thought Gaius Marius would at least try first.

Then Lucius Decumius shrugged. Gaius Marius was a father, after all. Only had one chick. Very precious. Not a bad boy either, once one got beneath the cocksure arrogance. It must be hard to be the son of a Great Man. Especially for one who didn't have the sinews. Oh, he was brave enough. Had a mind too. But he'd never be a truly Great Man. That needed a hard life. Harder than the one Young Marius had experienced. Such a lovely mother! Now if he'd had a mother like Young Caesar's mother—it might be different. *She'd* made absolutely sure Young Caesar had a hard life. Never allowed him a whisker of latitude. Nor was there much money in that family.

Flat until now, the land began suddenly to rise steeply, and the tired mules wanted to halt. Lucius Decumius touched them with his whip, called them a few frightful names and forced them onward, his wrists steel.

Fifteen years ago Lucius Decumius had appointed himself the protector of Young Caesar's mother, Aurelia. At about the same time he had also found himself an additional source of income. By birth he was a true Roman, by tribe a member of urban Palatina, by census a member of the Fourth Class, and by profession the caretaker of a crossroads college located within Aurelia's apartment building. A smallish man of indeterminate coloring and anonymous features, his unprepossessing exterior and lack of erudition hid an unshakable faith in his own intelligence and strength of mind; he ran his sodality like a general.

Officially sanctioned by the urban praetor, the duties of the college involved care of the crossroads outside its premises, from sweeping and cleaning the area, through making sure the shrine to the Lares of the Crossroads was duly honored and the huge fountain supplying water to the district flowed constantly into a pristine basin, to supervising the festivities of the annual Compitalia. Membership in the college ran the full gamut of the local male residents, from Second Class to Head Count among the Romans, and from foreigners like Jews and Syrians to Greek freedmen and slaves; the Second and Third Classes, however, made no contribution to the college beyond donatives generous enough to avoid attendance. Those who patronized the surprisingly clean premises of the college were workingmen who spent their day off sitting talking and drinking cheap wine. Every workingman—free or slave—had each eighth day off work, though not all on the same day; a man's day off was the eighth day after he had commenced his job. Thus the men inside the college on any particular day would be a different lot from those present on other days. Whenever Lucius Decumius announced there was something to be done, every man present would down his wine and obey the orders of the college caretaker.

The brotherhood under the aegis of Lucius Decumius had activities quite divorced from care of the crossroads. When Aurelia's uncle and stepfather, Marcus Aurelius Cotta, had bought her an insula as a means of fruitfully investing her dowry, that redoubtable young woman had soon discovered that she housed a group of men who preyed upon the local shopkeepers and businessfolk by selling them protection from vandalism and violence. She had soon put a stop to that—or rather, Lucius Decumius and his brothers had shifted their protection agency further afield to areas where Aurelia neither knew the victims nor traversed the neighborhood.

At about the same time as Aurelia had acquired her insula, Lucius Decumius had found an avocation which suited his nature as much as it did his purse: he became an assassin. Though his deeds were rumored rather than recounted, those who knew him believed implicitly that he had been responsible for many political and commercial deaths, foreign and domestic. That no one ever bothered him—let alone apprehended him—was due to his skill and daring. There was never any evidence. Yet the nature of this lucrative avocation was common knowledge in the Subura; as Lucius Decumius said himself, if no one knew you were an assassin no one ever offered you any jobs. Some deeds he disclaimed, and again he was implicitly believed. The murder of Asellio, he had been heard to say, was the work of a bungling amateur who had put Rome in peril by killing an augur in the midst of his duties and while wearing his sacerdotal regalia. And though it was his considered opinion that Metellus Numidicus Piggle-wiggle *had* been poisoned, Lucius Decumius announced to all and sundry that poison was a woman's tool, beneath his notice.

He had fallen in love with Aurelia on first meeting—not in a romantic or fleshly way, he insisted—more the instinctive recognition of a kindred spirit, as determined and courageous and intelligent as he was himself. Aurelia became his to cherish and protect. As her children came along they too were gathered under Lucius Decumius's vulturine wing. He idolized Young Caesar, loving him, if the truth were known, far more than he did his own two sons, both almost men now and already being trained in the ways of the crossroads college. For years he had guarded the boy, spent hours in his company, filled him with an oddly honest appraisal of the boy's world and its people, shown him how the protection agency worked, and how a good assassin worked. There was nothing about Lucius Decumius that Young Caesar did not know. And nothing Young Caesar did not understand; the behavior appropriate for a patrician Roman nobleman was not at all appropriate for a Roman of the Fourth Class who was the caretaker of a crossroads college. Each to his own. But that did not negate their being friends. Or loving each other.

"We're villains, us Roman lowly," Lucius Decumius had explained to Young Caesar. "Can't not be if we're to eat and drink well, have three or four nice slaves and one of them with a *cunnus* worth lifting a skirt for. Even if we was clever in business—which we mostly isn't—where would we find the capital, I asks you? No, a man cuts his tunic to suit its cloth, I always says, and that's that." He laid his right forefinger against the side of his nose and grinned to display dirty teeth. "But not a word, Gaius Julius! Not a word to anyone! Especially your dear mother."

The secrets were kept and were to go on being kept, including from Aurelia. Young Caesar's education was broader by far than she remotely suspected.

By midnight the gig and its sweating mules had reached the army camp just beyond the small village of Tibur. Gaius Marius roused the ex-praetor Lucius Cornelius Cinna from his bed without the slightest compunction.

They knew each other only slightly, for there were almost thirty years of age between them, but Cinna was known from his speeches in the House to be an admirer of Marius's. He had been a good *praetor urbanus*—the first of Rome's wartime governors because of the absence of both consuls—but the confrontation with Italia had ruined his chances of swelling his private fortune during a term governing one of the provinces.

Now two years later he found himself without the means to dower either of his daughters, and was even in some doubt as to whether he could assure his son's senatorial career beyond the back benches. A letter from the Senate promoting him to the full command in the Marsic theater following upon the death of Cato the Consul had no power to thrill him; all it really meant was a great deal of work shoring up a structure rendered shaky by a man who had been as incompetent as he was arrogant. Oh, where was that fruitful province?

A stocky man with a weatherbeaten face and a maloccluded jaw, his looks had not prevented his making a notable marriage to an heiress, Annia from a rich plebeian family which had been consular for two hundred years. Cinna and Annia had three children—a girl now fifteen, a boy of seven, and a second girl, aged five. Though not a beauty, Annia was nevertheless a striking woman, red-haired and green-eyed; the older daughter had inherited her coloring, whereas the two younger children were as dark as their father. None of this had been important until Gnaeus Domitius Ahenobarbus Pontifex Maximus had visited Cinna and asked for the hand of the older daughter on behalf of his older son, Gnaeus.

"We like red-haired wives, we Domitii Ahenobarbi," the Pontifex Maximus had said bluntly. "Your girl, Cornelia Cinna, fulfills all the criteria I want in my son's wife—she's the right age, she's a patrician, and she's red-haired. Originally I had my eye on Lucius Sulla's girl. But she's to marry Quintus Pompeius Rufus's son, which is a shame. However, your girl will do just as well. Same *gens*—and, I imagine, a bigger dowry?"

Cinna had swallowed, offered up a silent prayer to Juno Sospita and to Ops, and put his faith in his future as the governor of a fruitful province. "By the time my daughter is old enough to marry, Gnaeus Domitius, she will be dowered with fifty talents. I cannot make it more. Is that satisfactory?"

"Oh, quite!" said Ahenobarbus. "Gnaeus is my principal heir, so your girl will be doing very well indeed. I believe I am among the five or six richest men in Rome, and I have thousands of clients. Could we go ahead and conduct the betrothal ceremony?"

All this had happened the year before Cinna was praetor, and at a time when he could be pardoned for assuming he would find the money to dower his older daughter at the time she would be given in marriage to Gnaeus Domitius Ahenobarbus Junior. If Annia's fortune were not so wretchedly tied up matters would have been easier, but Annia's father kept control of her money, and at her death it could not pass to her children.

When Gaius Marius roused him from sleep as the half-moon was sinking into the western sky, Cinna had no idea of the eventual consequences of this visit; rather, he pulled on a tunic and shoes with a heavy heart and prepared himself to say unpleasant things to the father of one who had seemed a most promising boy.

The Great Man entered the command tent with a peculiar escort in tow—a very common-looking man of perhaps a little under fifty years, and a very beautiful boy. The boy it was who did most of the work, and in a manner suggesting he was well accustomed to the task. Cinna would have deemed him a slave except that he wore the *bulla* around his neck and comported himself like a patrician of a better family than Cornelius. When Marius was seated the boy stood on his left side and the middle-aged man behind him.

"Lucius Cornelius Cinna, this is my nephew Gaius Julius Caesar Junior, and my friend Lucius Decumius. You may be absolutely frank in front of them." Marius used his right hand to dispose his left hand in his lap, seeming less tired than Cinna had expected, and more in command of his faculties than news from Rome—old news, come to think of it—had implied. Obviously still a formidable man. But hopefully not a formidable opponent, thought Cinna.

"A tragic business, Gaius Marius."

The wide-awake eyes roamed around the tent to ascertain who might be about, and when they found no one, swung to Cinna.

"Are we alone, Lucius Cinna?"

"Completely."

"Good." Marius settled more comfortably into his chair. "My source of information was secondhand. Quintus Lutatius called to see me and found me not at home. He gave the story to my wife, who in turn reported it to me. I take it that my son is charged with the murder of Lucius Cato the Consul during a battle, and that there is a witness—or some witnesses. Is this the correct story?"

"I am afraid so, yes."

"How many witnesses?"

"Just the one."

"And who is he? A man of integrity?"

"Beyond reproach, Gaius Marius. A *contubernalis* named Publius Claudius Pulcher," said Cinna.

Marius grunted. "Oh, that family! It's one notorious for harboring grudges and being difficult to get on with. It's also as poor as an Apulian shepherd. How therefore can you state unequivocally that the witness is beyond reproach?"

"Because this particular Claudius is not typical of that family," said Cinna, determined to depress Marius's hopes. "His reputation within the *contubernalis* tent and throughout the late Lucius Cato's staff is superlative. You will understand better when you meet him. He has a high degree of loyalty toward his fellow cadets—he is the oldest of them—and much genuine affection for your son. Also much sympathy for your son's action, I add. Lucius Cato was not popular with any of his staff, let alone his army."

"Yet Publius Claudius has accused my son."

"He felt it his duty."

"Oh, I see! A sanctimonious prig."

But Cinna disputed this. "No, Gaius Marius, he is not! Think for a moment as a commander, I beg you, not as a father! The young man Pulcher is the finest kind of Roman, as conscious of his duty as of his family. He did his duty, little though he liked it. And that is the simple truth."

When Marius struggled to rise it was more apparent that he was tired; clearly he had become accustomed to performing this deed unaided, yet now he could not move without Young Caesar. The commoner Lucius Decumius slid round to stand at Marius's right shoulder, and cleared his throat. The eyes staring at Cinna were trying to speak volumes, some sort of message.

"You wish to say something?" asked Cinna.

"Lucius Cinna, begging your pardon and all, must the hearing of the case against young Gaius Marius be tomorrow?"

Cinna blinked, surprised. "No. It can be the day after."

"Then if you don't mind, let it be the day after. When Gaius Marius gets up tomorrow—and that isn't going to be early—he will need exercise. He's just spent far too long sitting cramped up in a gig, you see." Decumius spoke slowly, concentrating on his grammar. "At the moment his exercise is riding, three hours a day. Tomorrow he has to ride, you see. He also has to be given the opportunity to inspect this Publius Claudius cadet for himself. Young Gaius Marius stands accused of a capital crime, and a man of Gaius Marius's importance has to satisfy himself, do he not? Now it might be a good idea if Gaius Marius was to meet this Publius Claudius cadet in a—a—a more *informal* way than in this tent. None of us wants—want—things to be more horrible than they need—needs—to be. So I think it would be a good idea if you organized a riding party for tomorrow afternoon and have all the cadets along on it. Including Publius Claudius."

Cinna was frowning, suspecting that he was being maneuvered into something he would regret. The boy to Marius's left gave Cinna a bewitching smile, and winked at him.

"Please forgive Lucius Decumius," said Young Caesar. "He is my uncle's most devoted client. And he's a tyrant too! The only way to keep him happy is to humor him."

"I cannot permit Gaius Marius to have private speech with Publius Claudius before the hearing," said Cinna miserably.

Marius had stood looking utterly outraged throughout this exchange; he now turned in such a patently genuine temper upon Lucius Decumius and Young Caesar that Cinna feared he would push himself into a fresh apoplexy.

"What is all this nonsense?" Marius roared. "I don't need to meet this paragon of youth and duty Publius Claudius under *any* circumstances! All I want to do is see my son and be present at his hearing!"

"Now, now, Gaius Marius, don't work yourself into a twitter," said Lucius Decumius in an oily voice. "After a nice little ride tomorrow afternoon, you'll feel more up to the hearing."

"Oh, preserve me from coddling idiots!" cried Marius, stumping out of the tent without assistance. "Where is my son?"

Young Caesar lingered while Lucius Decumius chased after the irate Marius.

"Don't take any notice, Lucius Cinna," he said, producing that wonderful smile again. "They squabble incessantly, but Lucius Decumius is right. Tomorrow Gaius Marius needs to rest and take his proper exercise. This is a very worrying business for him. All we are really concerned about is that it not affect Gaius Marius's recovery process too severely."

"Yes, I understand that," said Cinna, patting the boy paternally on his shoulder; he was too tall to pat on the head. "Now I had better take Gaius Marius to see his son." He took a spitting torch from its stand and walked out toward Marius's looming bulk. "Your son is this way, Gaius Marius. For the sake of appearances I have confined him to a tent on his own until the hearing. He is under guard and is allowed to have congress with nobody."

"You realize, of course, that your hearing is not a final one," said Marius as they passed between two rows of tents. "If its outcome is unfavorable toward my son, I will insist that he be tried by his peers in Rome."

"Quite so," said Cinna colorlessly.

When father and son confronted each other, Young Marius stared at Marius a little wildly, but looked to be in control of himself. Until he took in Lucius Decumius and Young Caesar.

"What have you got this sorry lot along for?" he demanded.

"Because I couldn't make the journey alone," said Marius, nodded a brusque dismissal to Cinna, and allowed himself to be lowered into the small tent's only chair. "So, my son, your temper has got you into boiling water at last," he said, not sounding very sympathetic or interested in hearing what his son had to say.

Young Marius gazed at him in apparent bewilderment, seeming to search for some signal his father was not semaphoring. Then he heaved a sobbing sigh and said, "I didn't do it!"

"Good," said Marius cordially. "Stick to that, Young Marius, and all will be well."

"Will it, Father? How can it? Publius Claudius will swear I did do it."

Marius rose suddenly, a bitterly disappointed man. "If you maintain your innocence, my son, I can promise you that nothing will happen to you. Nothing at all."

Relief spread over Young Marius's face; he thought he was receiving the signal. "You're going to fix it, aren't you?"

"I can fix many things, Gaius Marius Junior, but not an official army hearing conducted by a man of honor," said Marius wearily. "Any fixing will have to be for your trial in Rome. Now follow my example, and sleep. I'll see you late tomorrow afternoon."

"Not until then? Isn't the hearing tomorrow?"

"Not until then. The hearing is postponed a day because I have to have my proper exercise—otherwise I'll never be fit enough to stand for consul a seventh time." He turned in the tent entrance to smile at his son with grotesque mockery. "I have to ride, this sorry lot tell me. And I will be presented to your accuser. But not to persuade him to change his story, my son. I have been forbidden any private congress with him." He caught his breath. "I, Gaius Marius, to be instructed by *a mere praetor* as to the proper way to conduct myself! I can forgive you for killing a military bungler about to permit his army to be annihilated, Young Marius, but I cannot forgive you for putting me in the position of a potential panderer!"

When the riding party assembled the following afternoon, Gaius Marius was punctiliously correct in his manner toward Publius Claudius Pulcher, a dark and rather hangdog-looking young man who obviously wished he was anywhere but where he was. As the men moved out Marius fell in alongside Cinna, with

Cinna's legate Marcus Caecilius Cornutus riding behind them with Young Caesar, and the cadets bringing up the rear. After he established the fact that none of the others knew the area very well, Lucius Decumius took the lead.

"There's a magnificent view of Rome about a mile away," he said, "just the right distance for Gaius Marius to ride."

"How do you know Tibur so well?" asked Marius.

"My mother's father came from Tibur," said the leader of the expedition as its members strung themselves out along a narrow path winding steadily and steeply upward.

"I wouldn't have thought you had a rural bone in your whole disreputable body, Lucius Decumius."

"Actually I don't, Gaius Marius," said Decumius cheerfully over his shoulder. "But you knows what women are like! My mother used to drag us up here every summer."

The day was fine and the sun hot, but a cool breeze blew in the riders' faces and they could hear the tumbling Anio in its gorge, now louder, now dying to a whisper. Lucius Decumius set a slow pace and the time went by almost imperceptibly, only Marius's evident enjoyment making the rest of the party feel this activity was at all worthwhile. Deeming the ordeal of meeting Young Marius's father intolerable before it had actually happened, Publius Claudius Pulcher gradually relaxed enough to converse with the other two cadets, while Cinna, escorting Marius, wondered if Marius would try to make overtures to his son's accuser. For that, Cinna was convinced, was the true purpose of this ride. A father himself, he knew he would have tried every ploy he could think of if his son ever got into such trouble.

"There!" said Lucius Decumius proudly, reining his steed back out of the way so that the rest of the party could precede him. "A view worth the ride, isn't it?"

It was indeed. The riders found themselves on a small shelf in the side of a mountain, at a place where some massive cataclysm had pared a great slice of the flank away and a cliff fell sheer to the plains far below. They could trace the hurrying, white-flecked waters of the Anio all the way to its confluence with the Tiber, a blue and snaky stream coming down from the north. And there beyond the point where the two rivers joined lay Rome, a vivid sprawl of colored paints and brick-red roofs, the statues atop her temples glittering, and the clear air permitting even a glimpse of the Tuscan Sea on the knifelike edge of the horizon.

"We're much higher than Tibur here," said Lucius Decumius from behind them; he slid off his horse.

"How minute the city is from so far away!" said Cinna in wonder.

Everyone was pressing forward to see except Lucius Decumius, and the riders intermingled. Determined Marius was not going to get a chance to talk to Publius Claudius, Cinna pushed both of their mounts away as the cadets approached.

"Oh, look!" cried Young Caesar, kicking his horse hard when it balked. "There's the Anio aqueduct! Isn't it like a toy? And isn't it beautiful?" He directed his questions at Publius Claudius, who seemed quite as entranced by the view as Young Caesar, and just as eager to sample its delights.

The two of them edged as close to the brink as their horses were prepared to take them and gazed out to Rome, smiling at each other after their eyes were sated.

Since it truly was a magnificent view, the whole party save for Lucius Decumius directed all their attention, forward. Thus no one noticed Lucius Decumius withdraw a small, Y-shaped object from the purse tethered to the belt of his tunic, nor saw him slip a wicked little metal spike into a slot in the middle of a band of soft, stretchy kid connected between the open ends of the Y-shaped piece of wood. As casually and openly as he might have yawned or scratched himself, he raised the wooden object to eye level, stretched the kid to its utmost, sighted carefully, and let the leather go.

Publius Claudius's horse screamed, reared up, its front legs flailing; Publius Claudius clutched instinctively at its mane to stay on its back. Oblivious to his own danger, Young Caesar came forward of his saddle onto his horse's neck and grabbed for the other animal's bridle. It all happened so quickly that no one afterward could be sure of more than one glaring fact—that Young Caesar acted with a cool bravery far beyond his years. His mount panicked and reared too, cannoned broadside into Publius Claudius, and found its front legs coming down on nothing. Both horses and both riders went over the cliff, but somehow Young Caesar, even in the act of falling, had balanced upright on the tilting edge of his saddle and leaped for the shelf. He landed more on it than off it and scrabbled like a cat to safety.

Everyone was clustered on the ground at the brink of the precipice, faces white, eyes goggling, only concerned at first to see that Young Caesar was all right. Then, Young Caesar in the lead (breathing more easily than any of the rest), they looked over the edge. There far below lay the disjointed heaps of two horses. And Publius Claudius Pulcher. A silence fell. Straining to hear a cry for help, they heard only the sighing of the wind. Nothing moved, even a hawk in midair.

"Here, you come away!" said a new voice. Lucius Decumius took Young Caesar by the shoulder and yanked him further away from the cliff. On his knees, he shakily patted the boy all over to make sure there were no broken bones. "Why did you have to do that?" he whispered too softly for anyone but Young Caesar to hear.

"I had to make it look convincing," came an answering whisper. "For a moment I didn't think his horse was going to go. It was best to be sure. I knew I'd be safe."

"How did you know what I was going to do? You weren't even looking my way!"

Young Caesar heaved a sigh of exasperation. "Oh, Lucius Decumius! I know *you*! And I knew why Gaius Marius sent for you the instant he did. Personally I don't care much what happens to my cousin, but I won't have Gaius Marius and our own family disgraced. Rumor is one thing. A witness is quite another."

Cheek against the bright gold hair, Lucius Decumius let his eyes close in an exasperation easily the equal of Young Caesar's. "But you risked your *life*!"

"Don't worry about my life. I can look after it. When I let it go, it will be because I have no further use for it." The boy extricated himself from Lucius Decumius's embrace and went to make sure that Gaius Marius was all right.

Shaken and confused, Lucius Cornelius Cinna poured wine for himself and Gaius Marius the moment they reached his tent. Lucius Decumius had taken Young Caesar off to fish in the Anio cascades, and the rest of the party was regrouping to form another party—one deputed to bring the remains of the cadet Publius Claudius Pulcher back for his own funeral.

"I must say that as far as my son and I are concerned, that was a very timely accident," said Marius bluntly, taking a deep draft of his wine. "Without Publius Claudius you have no case, my friend."

"It was an accident," said Cinna in the tones of a man most preoccupied with convincing himself. "It *couldn't* have been anything except an accident!"

"Quite right. It couldn't have been *anything* else. I nearly lost a better boy than my son."

"I didn't think the lad had a hope."

"I think that particular lad is hope personified," said Marius with a purr in his voice. "I'll have to keep my eye on him in the future. Or he'll be eclipsing me."

"Oh, what a mess!" sighed Cinna.

"Not an auspicious omen for a man just promoted to the general's tent, I agree," said Marius affably.

"I shall acquit myself better than Lucius Cato did!"

Marius grinned. "It would be hard to do worse. However, I do sincerely think you will acquit yourself well, Lucius Cinna. And I am very grateful for your forbearance. *Very* grateful!"

Somewhere in the back of his mind Cinna could hear the tinkling cascade of coins—or was it the Anio, where that extraordinary boy was happily fishing as if nothing ever banished his composure?

"What is one's first duty, Gaius Marius?" Cinna asked suddenly.

"One's first duty, Lucius Cinna, is to one's family."

"Not to Rome?"

"What else is our Rome, than her families?"

"Yes . . . Yes, I suppose that's true. And those of us who are born to it—or have risen to find our children born to it—must strive to ensure that our families remain in a position to rule."

"Quite so," said Gaius Marius.

PART VII

LUCIUS CORNELIUS SULLA

Once Lucius Cornelius Sulla had cast his spell (as Young Caesar had put it) upon Cato the Consul and banished him to fight the Marsi, Sulla proceeded to take steps to recover all Rome's territories from the Italians. Though officially he still ranked as a legate, he was now in effect the commander-in-chief of the southern theater, and he knew there would be no interference from Senate or consuls—provided, that is, he produced results. Italia was tired; one of its two leaders, the Marsian Silo, might even have contemplated surrender were it not for the other one; Gaius Papius Mutilus the Samnite, Sulla knew, would never give up; therefore he had to be shown that his cause was lost.

Sulla's initial move was as secret as it was extraordinary, but he had the right man for a job he couldn't do himself. If his scheme succeeded, it would spell the beginning of the end for the Samnites and their allies of the south. Without telling Catulus Caesar in Capua why he was detaching the two best legions from Campanian service, Sulla loaded then at night aboard a fleet of transports moored in Puteoli harbor.

Their commander was his legate Gaius Cosconius, whose orders were explicit. He was to sail with these two legions right around the foot of the peninsula and land on the eastern coast somewhere near Apenestae, in Apulia. The first third of the voyage—down the west coast—didn't need to be out of sight of land, as any observer in Lucania might suppose the fleet to be going to Sicily, where there were rumors of uprisings. During the middle third the fleet could hug the coast and put in to revictual in places like Croton and Tarentum and Brundisium, where the tale would be that they were going to put down trouble in Asia Minor—a tale the troops themselves had been given to believe. And when the fleet sailed out of Brundisium on the last third of the voyage—the shortest third—all Brundisium had to be convinced it was on its way across the Adriatic to Apollonia in western Macedonia.

"Beyond Brundisium," said Sulla to Cosconius, "you dare not make a landfall until you reach your final destination. The decision as to exactly where you come ashore I leave to you. Just pick a quiet place, and don't strike until you're absolutely ready. Your task is to free up the Via Minucia south of Larinum and the Via Appia south of Auscutum Apulium. After that, concentrate on eastern Samnium. By the time you're doing that, I should be driving east to meet you."

Excited because he had been singled out for this vital mission and confident he and his men were formed of the right stuff to make a success of it, Cosconius concealed his elation and listened gravely.

"Remember, Gaius Cosconius, take your time while you're at sea," Sulla cautioned. "I want no more than twenty-five miles a day from you on most days. It's now the end of March. You must land somewhere to the south of Apenestae fifty days hence. Land too soon, and I won't have time to complete my half of the pincer. I need these fifty days to take back all the ports on Crater Bay and drive Mutilus out of western Campania. Then I can move east—but not until then."

"Since successful passage around the foot of Italy is very rare, Lucius Cornelius, I'm glad to have fifty days," said Cosconius.

"If you have to row, then row," said Sulla.

"I will be where I am supposed to be in fifty days. You can count on it, Lucius Cornelius."

"Without the loss of a man, let alone a ship."

"Every ship has a fine captain and an even finer pilot, and the logistics of the voyage encompass every possibility any of us can think of. I won't let you down. We'll get to Brundisium as quickly as we can and we'll wait there as long as we have to—not one day more, nor one day less," said Cosconius.

"Good! And remember one thing, Gaius Cosconius—your most reliable ally is Fortune. Offer to her every single day. If she loves you as much as she loves me, all will go well."

The fleet bearing Cosconius and his two crack legions left Puteoli the next day to brave the elements and lean most heavily upon one particular element—luck. No sooner had it gone than Sulla returned to Capua and marched then for Pompeii. This was to be a combined land and sea attack, as Pompeii had superb port facilities on the Sarnus near its mouth; Sulla intended to bombard the city with flaming missiles launched from his ships anchored in the river.

One doubt huddled in the back of his mind, though it was nothing he could rectify; his flotilla was under the command of a man he neither liked nor trusted to follow orders—none other than Aulus Postumius Albinus. Twenty years before, it had been the same Aulus Postumius Albinus who had provoked the war against King Jugurtha of Numidia. And he hadn't changed.

Sent orders from Sulla to bring up his ships from Neapolis to Pompeii, Aulus Albinus decided he should first let his crews and his marines know who was in charge—and what would happen to them if they didn't jump smartly to attention whenever he snapped his fingers. But the crews and the marines were all of Campanian Greek descent, and found the things Aulus Albinus said to them intolerable insults. Like Cato the Consul, he was buried under a storm of missiles—but these were stones, not clods of earth. Aulus Postumius Albinus died.

Fortunately Sulla wasn't far down the road when news of the murder was brought to him; leaving his troops to continue their march under the command of Titus Didius, Sulla rode on his mule to Neapolis, there to meet the leaders of the mutiny. With him he took Metellus Pius the Piglet, his other legate. Calm unimpaired, he listened to passionate reasons and excuses from the mutineers, then said coldly,

"I am afraid you are going to have to be the best sailors and marines in the history of Roman naval warfare. Otherwise, how can I forget you murdered Aulus Albinus?"

He then appointed Publius Gabinius admiral of the fleet, and that was the end of the mutiny.

Metellus Pius the Piglet held his tongue until he and Sulla were on their way to rejoin the army, at which time his burning question found voice: "Lucius Cornelius, do you not intend to give them *any* kind of punishment?"

Sulla deliberately tipped the brim of his hat back from his brow to show the Piglet a pair of coolly amused eyes. "No, Quintus Caecilius, I do not."

"You should have stripped them of their citizenship and then flogged them!"

"Yes, that is what most commanders would have done—more fool they. However, since you are undoubtedly one such foolish commander, I shall explain why I acted as I did. You ought to be able to see it for yourself, you know."

Holding up his right hand, Sulla told off the points one by one. "First of all, we can't afford to lose those men. They trained under Otacilius, and they're experienced. Secondly, I admire their eminent good sense in getting rid of a man who would have led them very poorly—and perhaps would have led them to their deaths. Three, *I* didn't want Aulus Albinus! But he's a consular and he couldn't be passed over or ignored."

Three fingers up, Sulla turned in the saddle to glare at the hapless Piglet. "I am going to tell you something, Quintus Caecilius. If I had my way, there would be no place—*no* place!—on my staff for men as inept and contentious as Aulus Albinus, the late unlamented consul Lupus, and our present consul Cato Licinianus. I gave Aulus Albinus a naval command because I thought he could do us the least harm on the sea. So how could I punish men for doing what I would have done in similar circumstances?"

Up went another finger. "Fourthly, those men have put themselves in a position where, if they don't do well, I can indeed strip them of their citizenship and flog them—which means that they have no choice but to fight like wildcats. And fifthly"—he had to use his thumb—"I don't care how many thieves and murderers I have in my forces—*provided* they fight like wildcats." Down went the hand, chopping through the defenseless air like a barbarian's axe.

Metellus Pius opened his mouth, thought better of what he had been going to say, and wisely said nothing at all.

At the point where the road to Pompeii divided, one branch going to the Vesuvian Gate, the other to the Herculanean Gate, Sulla put his troops into a strongly fortified camp. By the time he was settled in behind his entrenchments and ramparts, his flotilla had arrived and was busy firing blazing bundles over the walls into the midst of Pompeian buildings faster than the oldest and most experienced centurion had ever seen; frightened faces looking down from the walls revealed that this was one kind of warfare nobody had counted on, and one which made everyone very uneasy. Fire was worst.

That the Samnites of Pompeii had sent frantic messages for help became clear the next day when a Samnite army larger than Sulla's by a good ten thousand men arrived, and proceeded to halt not more than three hundred paces from the front of Sulla's camp. A third of Sulla's twenty thousand soldiers were absent on foraging excursions, and were now cut off from him. Looking his ugliest, Sulla stood on his ramparts with Metellus Pius and Titus Didius listening to the jeers and catcalls borne on the wind from the city's walls—noises he did not appreciate any more than he did the advent of a Samnite army.

"Sound the call to arms," he said to his legates.

Titus Didius was turning to leave when Metellus Pius reached out to grasp Didius by the arm, and detained him.

"Lucius Cornelius, we can't go out to fight that lot!" the Piglet cried. "We'd be cut to pieces!"

"We can't not go out and fight," said Sulla, curtly enough to indicate his anger at being questioned. "That's Lucius Cluentius out there, and he intends to stay. If I let him build a camp as strong as ours it will be Acerrae all over again. And I am *not* going to tie up four good legions in a place like this for months—nor do I need Pompeii's showing the rest of these rebel seaports that Rome can't take them back! And if *that* isn't sufficient reason to attack right now, Quintus Caecilius, then consider the fact that when our foraging parties return, they're going to trip over a Samnite army with no word of warning—and no chance to survive!"

Didius gave Metellus Pius a contemptuous look. "I'll sound the call to arms," he said, and wrenched his arm away.

Crowned with a helmet rather than his usual hat, Sulla climbed to the top of the camp forum tribunal to address the almost thirteen thousand men he had available.

"You all know what's waiting for you!" he shouted. "A pack of Samnites who outnumber us by nearly three to one! But Sulla is tired of Rome's being beaten by a pack of Samnites, and Sulla is tired of Samnites owning Roman towns! What good is it being a living Roman if Rome has to lie down before Samnites like a fawning bitch? Well, not *this* Roman! Not Sulla! If I have to go out and fight alone, I am going! Am I going alone? Am I? Or are you coming with me because you're Romans too, and just as tired of Samnites as I am?"

The army answered him with a mighty cheer. He stood without moving until they were done, for he was not done.

"They go!" he sang out, even louder. "Every last one of them must go! Pompeii is *our* town! The Samnites within its gates murdered a thousand Romans, and now those same Samnites are up there on Pompeii's walls thinking themselves safe and sound, booing and hissing us because they think we're too afraid to clean up a pack of dirty Samnites! Well, we're going to show them they're wrong! We're going to take everything the Samnites can dish out until our foraging parties return, and when they do return, *our* war cries will guide them to the battle! Hear me? We hold the Samnites until our foragers return to fall on their rear like the Romans they are!"

There came a second mighty cheer, but Sulla was already off the tribunal, sword in hand; three ordered columns of soldiers moved at a run through the front and both side gates, Sulla leading the middle column himself.

So swift was the Roman deployment that Cluentius, not expecting a battle, barely had time to ready his troops for the Roman charge. A cool and daring commander, he stood his ground and remained among his own front ranks. Undermanned, the Roman assault began to falter when it failed to break the Samnite line. But Sulla, still leading, refused to move back an inch, and his men refused to leave him there alone. For an hour Romans and Samnites fought a hand-to-hand engagement without let, mercy, retreat. Of truly confrontational battles there had been few; both sides understood that the outcome of this one must inevitably affect the outcome of the war.

Too many good legionaries fell in that hour marking noon, but just as it seemed Sulla must order his troops to fall back or see them die where they stood, the Samnite line trembled, shook, began to fold in on itself. The Roman foraging parties had returned, and were attacking from the rear. Shrieking that Rome was invincible, Sulla led his men back into the fray with renewed vigor. Even so Cluentius gave ground slowly. For a further hour he managed to hold his army together. Then when he saw that all was lost, he rallied his troops and fought his way through the Romans in his rear to retreat on the double toward Nola.

Regarding itself as the talisman of Italian defiance in the south—and knowing Rome was aware it had starved Roman soldiers to death—Nola could not afford to jeopardize its safety. So when Cluentius and over twenty thousand Samnite soldiers reached its walls a scant mile ahead of the pursuing Sulla, they found themselves locked out. Leaning over those lofty, smooth, stoutly reinforced stone bastions, the city magistrates of Nola looked down on Lucius Cluentius and their fellow Samnites, and refused to open the gates. Finally, as the Roman front ranks approached the Samnite rear and prepared to charge, the gate below which Cluentius himself stood—not one of the city's bigger gates—swung wide. But more than that one minor gate the magistrates would not open, plead though the floundering Samnite soldiers did.

Before Pompeii it had been a battle. Before Nola it was a rout. Stunned at Nolan treachery, panic-stricken because it found itself enclosed by the out-thrust corners of Nola's northern section of walls, the Samnite army went down to utter defeat, and died almost to the last man. Sulla himself killed Cluentius, who refused to seek shelter within Nola when only a handful of his men could do the same.

It was the greatest day of Sulla's life. Fifty-one years of age, a general in complete charge of a theater of war at last, he had won his first great battle as commander-in-chief. And what a victory! Covered so copiously in the blood of other men that he dripped it, his sword glued by gore to his right hand, reeking of sweat and death, Lucius Cornelius Sulla surveyed the field, snatched the helmet from his head and threw it into the air with a scream of sheer jubilation. In his ears was a gigantic noise drowning out the howls and moans of dying Samnites, a noise inexorably swelling, revealing itself as a chant:

"*Im-per-a-tor! Im-per-a-tor! Im-per-a-tor!*"

Over and over and over his soldiers roared it, the final accolade, the ultimate triumph, the victor hailed imperator on the field. Or so he thought, grinning broadly with sword above his head, his sweat-soaked thatch of brilliant hair drying in the dying sun, his heart so full he could not have said a word in return, had there been a word to say. I, Lucius Cornelius Sulla, have proven beyond a shadow of a doubt that a man as able as I am *can* learn what isn't in his bones—and win the hardest battle of this or any other war! Oh, Gaius Marius, just wait! Crippled hulk that you are, don't die until I can get back to Rome and show you how wrong your judgment was! I *am* your equal! And in the years to come I will surpass you. My name will tower over yours. As it should do. For I am a patrician Cornelius and you no more than a rustic from the Latin hills.

But there was work to be done, and he was a patrician Roman. To him came Titus Didius and Metellus Pius, curiously subdued, their bright eyes looking upon him with awe, with a shining adoration Sulla had only seen before in the eyes of Julilla and Dalmatica as they had gazed at him. But these are *men,* Lucius Cornelius Sulla! Men of worth and repute—Didius the victor over Spain, Metellus Pius the heir of a great and noble house. Women were unimportant fools. Men mattered. Especially men like Titus Didius and Metellus Pius. Never in all the years I served Gaius Marius did I see any man look at him with so much adoration! Today I have won more than a mere victory. Today I have won the vindication of my life, today I have justified Stichus, Nicopolis, Clitumna, Hercules Atlas, Metellus Numidicus Piggle-wiggle. Today I have proven that every life I have taken in order to stand here on the field at Nola was a lesser life than my own. Today I begin to understand the Nabopolassar from Chaldaea—I *am* the greatest man in the world, from Oceanus Atlanticus all the way to the River Indus!

"We work through the night," he said crisply to Didius and Metellus Pius, "so that by dawn the Samnite corpses are stripped and heaped together, and our own dead prepared for the pyre. I know it's been an exhausting day, but it isn't over yet. Until it is over, no one can rest. Quintus Caecilius, find a few reasonably fit men and ride back to Pompeii as fast as you can. Bring back bread and wine enough for everyone here, and bring up the noncombatants and set them to finding wood, oil. We have a veritable mountain of bodies to burn."

"But there are no horses, Lucius Cornelius!" said the Piglet faintly. "We *marched* to Nola! Twenty miles in four hours!"

"Then find horses," said Sulla, manner at its coldest. "I want you back here by dawn." He turned to Didius. "Titus Didius, go among the men and find out who should be decorated for deeds in the field. As soon as we burn our dead and the enemy dead we return to Pompeii, but I want one legion from Capua posted here before the walls of Nola. And have the heralds announce to the inhabitants of Nola that Lucius Cornelius Sulla has made a vow to Mars and Bellona—that Nola will look down to see Roman troops sitting before it until it surrenders, be that a month of days from now, or a month of months from now, or a month of years from now."

Before Didius or Metellus Pius could depart, the tribune of the soldiers Lucius Licinius Lucullus appeared at the head of a deputation of centurions; eight senior men, *primi pili* and *pili priores*. They walked gravely, solemnly, like priests in a sacred procession or consuls going to their inauguration on New Year's Day.

"Lucius Cornelius Sulla, your army wishes to give you a token of its gratitude and thanks. Without you, the army would have been defeated, and its soldiers dead. You fought in the front rank and showed the rest of us the way. You never flagged on the march to Nola. To you and you alone is due this greatest victory by far of the whole war. You have saved more than your army. You have saved Rome. Lucius Cornelius, we honor you," said Lucullus, stepping back to make way for the centurions.

The man in their midst, most senior centurion of them all, lifted both arms and held them out to Sulla. In his hands lay a very drab and tattered circlet made of grass runners plucked from the field of battle and braided together haphazardly, roots and earth and blades and blood. *Corona graminea. Corona obsidionalis.* The Grass Crown. And Sulla stretched out his own arms instinctively, then dropped them, utterly ignorant as to what the ritual should be. Did he take it and put it on his own head, or did the *primus pilus* Marcus Canuleius crown him with it on behalf of the army?

He stood then without moving while Canuleius, a tall man, raised the Grass Crown in both hands and placed it upon that red-gold head.

No further word was spoken. Titus Didius, Metellus Pius, Lucullus and the centurions saluted Sulla reverently, gave him shy smiles, and got themselves away. He was left alone to face the setting sun, the Grass Crown so insubstantial he scarcely felt its weight, the tears pouring down his bloodstained face, and no room inside himself for anything beyond an exaltation he wondered if he had steel enough to live through. For what was on its other side? What could life possibly offer him now? And he remembered his dead son. Before he had had time to truly relish the infinite extent of that joy it was vanished. All he had left was a grief so profound he fell to his knees and wept desolately.

Someone helped him to his feet, wiped the muck and the tears from his face, put an arm about his waist and helped him walk to a block of stone beside the Nola road. There he was lowered gently until he sat upon it, then his rescuer sat alongside him; Lucius Licinius Lucullus, the senior tribune of the soldiers.

The sun had set into the Tuscan Sea. The greatest day of Sulla's life was coming to its end in darkness. He dangled his arms down between his legs limply, drew in great breaths, and came to ask himself the old, old question: Why am I never happy?

"I have no wine to offer you, Lucius Cornelius. Nor water, for that matter," said Lucullus. "We ran from Pompeii without a thought for anything except catching Cluentius."

Sulla heaved an enormous sigh, straightened himself. "I'll live, Lucius Lucullus. As a woman friend of mine says, there is always work to do."

"We can do the work. You rest."

"No. I am the commander. I can't rest while my men work. A moment more, and I'll be right. I *was* right until I thought of my son. He died, you know." The tears came back, were suppressed.

Lucullus said nothing, just sat quietly.

Of this young man Sulla had seen little so far; elected a tribune of the soldiers last December, he had gone first to Capua and only been posted to command his legion days before it marched for Pompeii. Yet though he had changed enormously—grown from a stripling to a fine specimen of man—Sulla recognized him.

"You and your brother Varro Lucullus prosecuted Servilius the Augur in the Forum ten years ago, am I not right?" he asked.

"Yes, Lucius Cornelius. The Augur was responsible for the disgrace and death of our father, and the loss of our family fortune. But he paid," said Lucullus, his long homely face growing brighter, his humorous mouth turning up at the corners.

"The Sicilian slave war. Servilius the Augur took your father's place as governor of Sicily. And later prosecuted him."

"That is so."

Sulla got up, extended his right hand to take the right hand of Lucius Licinius Lucullus. "Well, Lucius Licinius, I must thank you. Was the Grass Crown your idea?"

"Oh no, Lucius Cornelius. Blame the centurions! They informed me that the Grass Crown has to come from the army's professionals, not the army's elected magistrates. They brought me along because one of the army's elected magistrates must be a witness." Lucullus smiled, then laughed. "I suspect too that addressing the general formally isn't quite in their line! So I got the job."

Two days later Sulla's army was back inside its camp before Pompeii. Everyone was so exhausted even decent food had no lure, and for twenty-four hours a complete silence reigned as the men and their officers slept like the dead they had burned against the walls of Nola, an insult to the nostrils of the flesh-famished inhabitants.

The Grass Crown now resided within a wooden box Sulla's servants had produced; when Sulla had the time, it would be put in the hair of the wax mask of himself he was now entitled to commission. He had distinguished himself highly enough to join the *imagines* of his ancestors, even though he had not yet been consul. And his statue would go into the Forum Romanum wearing a Grass Crown, erected in memory of the greatest hero of the war against the Italians. All of which hardly seemed real; but there in its box lay the Grass Crown, a testament to reality.

When, rested and refreshed, the army went on parade for the awarding of battle decorations, Sulla put his Grass Crown upon his head and was greeted with prolonged and deafening cheers as he climbed upon the camp tribunal. The task of organizing the ceremony had been given to Lucullus, just as Marius had once given the same task to Quintus Sertorius.

But as he stood there acknowledging the army's adulation, a thought occurred to Sulla that he didn't think had ever crossed the mind of Marius during those years in Numidia and Gaul—though perhaps it had while he commanded against the Italians. A sea of faces in parade order, parade dress—a sea of men who belonged to him, to Lucius Cornelius Sulla. These are *my* legions! They belong to me before they belong to Rome. I crafted them, I led them, I have given them the greatest victory of this war—and I will have to find their retirement gratuity. When they gave me the Grass Crown, they also gave me a far more significant gift—they gave me themselves. If I wanted to, I could lead them anywhere. I could even lead them against Rome. A ridiculous idea; but it was born in Sulla's mind at that moment on the tribunal. And it curled itself up beneath consciousness, and waited.

Pompeii surrendered the day after its citizens watched Sulla's decoration ceremony from their walls; Sulla's heralds had shouted the news of the defeat of Lucius Cluentius before the walls of Nola, and word had come confirming it. Still being relentlessly bombarded with flaming missiles from the ships in the river, the city was suffering badly. Every fiery breath of wind seemed to carry the message that the Italian and Samnite ascendancy was crumbling, that defeat was inevitable.

From Pompeii, Sulla moved with two of his legions against Stabiae, while Titus Didius took the other two to Herculaneum. On the last day of April Stabiae capitulated, and shortly afterward so too did Surrentum. As May reached its middle, Sulla was on the move again, this time heading east. Catulus Caesar had bestowed fresh legions upon Titus Didius before Herculaneum, so Sulla's own two legions were returned to him. Though it had held out the longest against joining the Italian insurrection, Herculaneum now demonstrated that it understood only too well what would happen if it surrendered to Rome; whole streets burning as the result of a naval bombardment, it continued to defy Titus Didius long after the other Italian-held seaports had given in.

Sulla moved his four legions past Nola without a sideways glance, though he sent Metellus Pius the Piglet to the commander of the legion sitting before it with a message to the effect that the praetor Appius Claudius Pulcher was not to shift himself for any reason short of Nola's complete submission. A dour man—and recently widowed—Appius Claudius merely nodded.

At the end of the third week in May, Sulla arrived at the Hirpini town of Aeclanum, which lay on the Via Appia. The Hirpini had begun to mass there, his intelligence sources had informed him; but it was not Sulla's intention to allow any further concentrations among the insurgents of the south. One look at the defenses of Aeclanum caused Sulla to smile his deadliest smile, long canines on full display—the town walls, though high and well built, were wooden.

Well aware that the Hirpini had already sent to the Lucanian Marcus Lamponius for help, Sulla sat his forces down without bothering to put them into a camp. Instead, he sent Lucullus to the main gate to demand Aeclanum's surrender. The town's answer came in the form of a question: please, would Lucius Cornelius Sulla give Aeclanum one day to think things over and come to a decision?

"They're playing for time in the hope that Lamponius will send them reinforcements tomorrow," said Sulla to Metellus Pius the Piglet and Lucullus. "I'll have to think about Lamponius, he can't be allowed to run rampant in Lucania any longer." Sulla shrugged, looked brisk, got back to the business of the moment. "Lucius Licinius, take the town my answer. They may have one hour, not more. Quintus Caecilius, take as many men as you need and scour every farm around the town for firewood and oil. Pile the wood and oil-soaked rags along the walls on either side of the main gates. And have our four pieces of artillery positioned in four different places. As soon as you can, set fire to the walls and start lobbing flaming missiles into the town. I'll bet everything inside is made of wood too. Aeclanum will go up like tinder."

"What if I'm ready to start burning in less than an hour?" asked the Piglet.

"Then start burning," said Sulla. "The Hirpini aren't being honorable. Why should I be?"

As the wood of which they were composed was aged and dry, Aeclanum's fortifications burned fiercely, as did the buildings inside. All the gates were thrown open in a panic and the people streamed out crying surrender.

"Kill them all and sack the place," said Sulla. "It's time the Italians understood they'll get no mercy from me."

"Women and children too?" asked Quintus Hortensius, the other senior tribune of the soldiers.

"What, not got the stomach for it, Forum advocate?" Sulla enquired with a mocking look.

"You mistake the intent of my question, Lucius Cornelius," said Hortensius evenly in his beautiful voice. "I have no feelings to spare for Hirpini brats. But like any other Forum advocate, I like everything clarified. Then I know where I stand."

"No one must survive," said Sulla. "However, tell the men to use the women first. Then they can kill them."

"You're not interested in taking prisoners to sell as slaves?" asked the Piglet, practical as always.

"Italians are not foreign enemies. Even when I sack their towns, there will be no slaves. I'd rather see them dead."

From Aeclanum, Sulla turned south on the Via Appia and marched his contented troops to Compsa, the second Hirpini stronghold. Like its sister town, its walls were made of wood. But news of the fate of Aeclanum had spread faster than Sulla had moved; when he arrived, Compsa was waiting with all its gates open and the magistrates outside. This time Sulla was inclined to be merciful. Compsa was spared a sack.

From Compsa the general sent a letter back to Catulus Caesar in Capua and told him to send two legions under the brothers Aulus and Publius Gabinius into Lucania. Their orders were to take every town off Marcus Lamponius and free up the Via Popillia all the way to Rhegium. Then Sulla bethought himself of another useful man, and added a post scriptum that Catulus Caesar should include the junior legate Gnaeus Papirius Carbo in the Lucanian expedition.

In Compsa, Sulla received two messages. One informed him that Herculaneum had finally fallen during a strongly contested attack two days before the Ides of June, but that Titus Didius had been killed during the fighting.

"Make Herculaneum pay," wrote Sulla to Catulus Caesar.

Sulla's second message came across country from Apulia, and was from Gaius Cosconius.

> After a remarkably easy and uneventful voyage, I landed my legions in an area of salt lagoons near the fishing village of Salapia exactly fifty days after leaving Puteoli. All went precisely as planned. We disembarked at night in complete secrecy, attacked Salapia at dawn and burned it to the ground. I made sure every person in the vicinity was killed so that no one could send news of our arrival to the Samnites.
>
> From Salapia I marched to Cannae and took it without

a fight, after which I forded the Aufidius River and advanced on Canusium. Not more than ten miles further on, I met a large Samnite host led by Gaius Trebatius. Battle could not be avoided. Since I was very much outnumbered and the ground was not favorable to me, the engagement was a bloody one, and costly to me. But costly to Trebatius as well. I decided to fall back on Cannae before I lost more men than I could afford, got my soldiers into good order and recrossed the Aufidius with Trebatius on my tail. Then I saw what my ploy should be, pretended we were in a panic, and hid behind a hill on the Cannae bank of the river. The trick worked. Sure of himself, Trebatius began to ford the Aufidius with his troops in some disarray. My men were calm and eager to continue the fight. I wheeled them at a run through a full circle, and we fell on Trebatius while he was still in the river. The result was a complete victory for Rome. I have the honor to inform you that fifteen thousand Samnites died at the Aufidius crossing. Trebatius and the few survivors fled to Canusium, which has prepared for a siege. I have obliged it.

I left five cohorts of my men, including the wounded, in front of Canusium under the command of Lucius Lucceius, then took the fifteen cohorts remaining to me and headed north toward Frentani country. Ausculum Apulium surrendered without a fight. So did Larinum.

As I write this report, I have just received news from Lucius Lucceius that Canusium has capitulated. Following his orders from me, Lucius Lucceius has sacked the town and killed everyone, though it would appear Gaius Trebatius himself escaped. As we have no facilities to cope with prisoners and I cannot afford to have enemy soldiers running loose in my rear, the destruction of all in Canusium was my only alternative. I trust

this does not displease you. From Larinum I shall continue to advance toward the Frentani, awaiting news of
your own movements and further orders.

Sulla laid the letter down with great satisfaction and shouted for
Metellus Pius and his two senior tribunes of the soldiers, as both
these young men were proving excellent.

Having given them Cosconius's news and listened with what
patience he could muster to their marveling (he had told no one of
Cosconius's voyage), Sulla proceeded to issue new orders.

"It's time we contained Mutilus himself," he said. "If we do
not, he'll fall on Gaius Cosconius in such numbers not one Roman man will be left alive, and that's scant reward for a brave
campaign. My sources of information tell me that at the moment
Mutilus is waiting to see what I do before he decides whether to
go after me or Gaius Cosconius. What Mutilus hopes is that I
turn south on the Via Appia and concentrate my efforts around
Venusia—which is strong enough to occupy all my attention for a
considerable length of time. Once he hears positive confirmation
of this, he'll look for Gaius Cosconius. So today we pull up stakes
and we set off to the south. However, with darkness we reverse the
direction of our march and leave the road completely. It's rough
and hilly country between here and the upper Volturnus, but that's
the way we're going. The Samnite army has been encamped halfway between Venafrum and Aesernia for far too long, but Mutilus
shows no sign of moving. We have almost a hundred and fifty
miles of very difficult marching before we reach him. Nevertheless, gentlemen, we're going to be there in eight days, and fit to
fight."

No one attempted to argue; Sulla always pushed his army unmercifully, but such was its morale since Nola that it felt itself—and
Sulla—equal to anything. The sack of Aeclanum had done wonders for the soldiers too, as Sulla had held nothing back out of the
meager spoils for himself or his officers save a few women, and
not the best women at that.

The march to Mutilus, however, took twenty-one days, not the original estimate of eight. Of roads there were none, and the hills were crags which often had to be skirted tortuously. Though inwardly Sulla fretted, he was wise enough to turn a cheerful and considerate face toward legionaries and officers both, and made sure his army maintained a certain degree of comfort. In certain ways the winning of his Grass Crown had made a tenderer man of Sulla, ways all aimed at his ownership of his army. If the terrain had been as easy as he had thought it was going to be, he would have pushed them; as it was, he could see the necessity of keeping them in good spirits and accepting the inevitable. If Fortune still favored him, he would find Mutilus where he expected to find him; and Sulla thought Fortune was still on his side.

Thus it was the end of Quinctilis when Lucullus rode into Sulla's camp, face eager.

"He's there!" cried Lucullus without ceremony.

"Good!" said Sulla, smiling. "That means his luck has run out, Lucius Licinius—because mine hasn't. You can pass that message on to the troops. Does Mutilus look as if he's planning to move soon?"

"He looks more as if he's giving his men a long holiday."

"They're fed up with this war, and Mutilus knows it," said Sulla contentedly. "Besides which, he's a worried man. He's been sitting in the same camp for over sixty days, and every fresh piece of news he gets only makes his decision as to where to go next more difficult. He's lost western Campania, and he's in the process of losing Apulia."

"So what do we do?" asked Lucullus, who had a natural martial streak and was loving his learning from Sulla.

"We make smokeless camp on the wrong side of the last ridge leading down to the Volturnus, and there we wait. Keeping very quiet," said Sulla. "I'd like to strike as he's preparing to move. He must move soon, or lose the war without another fight. If he were Silo, he might elect that course. But Mutilus? He's a Samnite. He hates us."

Six days later Mutilus decided to move. What Sulla couldn't know was that the Samnite leader had just received word of a terrible battle outside Larinum between Gaius Cosconius and Marius Egnatius. Though he had kept his own army idle, Mutilus hadn't permitted Cosconius to use northern Apulia like a parade ground. He had sent a big and experienced army of Samnites and Frentani under Marius Egnatius to contain Cosconius. But the little Roman force was in high fettle, trusted its leader completely, and had got into the habit of deeming itself unconquerable. Marius Egnatius had gone down in defeat and died on the field together with most of his men, appalling news for Mutilus.

Not long after dawn Sulla's four legions issued out of the concealing ridge and fell on Mutilus. Caught with his camp half dismantled and his troops in disorder, the Samnite stood no chance. Badly wounded himself, he fled with the remnants of his army to Aesernia, and shut himself up inside. Once more this beleaguered city girded itself to withstand a siege—only now it was Rome on the outside, Samnium within.

While he was still dealing with the aftermath of the rout, Sulla was informed of the victory against Marius Egnatius by letter from Cosconius himself, and looked exultant. No matter how many pockets of resistance remained, the war was over. And Mutilus had known it for over sixty days.

Leaving a few cohorts at Aesernia under the command of Lucullus to keep Mutilus locked up, Sulla himself marched to the old Samnite capital of Bovianum. This was a formidably fortified town, possessing three separate citadels connected by mighty walls. Each citadel faced in a different direction, built to watch one of the three roads at the junction of which Bovianum sat, deeming itself invulnerable.

"You know," said Sulla to Metellus Pius and Hortensius, "one thing I always noticed about Gaius Marius in the field—he was never enamored of the mechanics behind taking towns. To him, nothing mattered except pitched battle. Whereas I find taking towns quite fascinating. If you look at Bovianum, it appears impregnable. But make no mistake—it will fall today."

He made his word good by tricking the town into thinking his entire army was sitting below the citadel facing the road from

Aesernia; in the meantime, one legion sneaked through the hills and attacked the citadel looking south to Saepinum. When Sulla saw the huge column of smoke arising from the Saepinum tower—his prearranged signal—he attacked the Aesernia tower. Less than three hours later Bovianum submitted.

Sulla quartered his soldiers inside Bovianum instead of putting them into camp and used the town as his base while he scoured the countryside for miles around to make sure southern Samnium was properly subdued—and incapable of raising fresh troops.

Then, leaving Aesemia besieged by men sent from Capua, and with his own four legions reunited, Sulla conferred with Gaius Cosconius. It was the end of September.

"The east is yours, Gaius Cosconius!" he said cheerfully. "I want the Via Appia and the Via Minucia completely freed up. Use Bovianum as your headquarters, it makes a superb garrison. And be as merciless or as merciful as you see fit. The most important thing is to keep Mutilus penned up inside Aesernia and prevent any reinforcements from reaching him."

"How are things to the north of us?" asked Cosconius, who had heard virtually nothing since he had sailed from Puteoli in March.

"Excellent! Servius Sulpicius Galba has cleaned up most of the Marrucini, Marsi and Vestini. He says Silo was on the field, but escaped. Cinna and Cornutus have occupied all the Marsic lands, and Alba Fucentia is ours again. The consul Gnaeus Pompeius Strabo has reduced the Picentes and the rebel parts of Umbria to ruins. However, Publius Sulpicius and Gaius Baebius are still sitting in front of Asculum Picentum—which must surely be at death's door from starvation, but continues to hold out."

"Then we *have* won!" said Cosconius in tones of awe.

"Oh, yes. We had to win! An Italy without Rome in total command? The gods wouldn't countenance *that*," said Sulla.

Six days after the beginning of October he arrived in Capua to see Catulus Caesar and make the necessary arrangements for the wintering of his armies. Traffic was flowing once more down the Via Appia and the Via Minucia, though the town of Venusia held out stubbornly, powerless to do more than watch Roman activity on the great road running alongside it. The Via Popillia was safe for the passage of armies and convoys from Campania to Rhegium, but was still unsafe for small parties of travelers, as Marcus Lamponius clung to the mountains still, concentrating his energies now upon sorties little more impressive than brigand attacks.

"However," said Sulla to a happy Catulus Caesar as he prepared to leave for Rome at the end of November, "by and large, I think we can safely say the peninsula is ours again."

"I'd prefer to wait until Asculum Picentum is ours before I say that," said Catulus Caesar, who had worked indefatigably for two years in a thankless job. "The whole business started there, Lucius Cornelius. And it's still holding out."

"Don't forget Nola," said Sulla, and snarled.

 But the days of Asculum Picentum were numbered. Riding his Public Horse, Pompey Strabo brought his army to join that of Publius Sulpicius Rufus in October, and spread a wall of Roman soldiers all the way around the city; not even a rope let down from the ramparts could now go undetected. His next move was to sever the city from its water supply—an enormous undertaking, since the water was led off the gravel beneath the bed of the Truentius River at hundreds of different points. But Pompey Strabo displayed considerable engineering skill, and took pleasure in supervising the work himself.

In attendance upon the consul Strabo was his most despised cadet, Marcus Tullius Cicero; as Cicero could draw quite well and took a self-invented shorthand with extreme accuracy and rapidity, the consul Strabo found him very useful in situations like the one gradually depriving Asculum Picentum of water. As terrified of his commander as he was appalled at his commander's utter indifference to the plight of those within the city, Cicero did as he was told and remained dumb.

In November the magistrates of Asculum Picentum opened the main gates and crept out to tender the city's submission to Gnaeus Pompeius Strabo.

"Our home is now yours," said the chief magistrate with great dignity. "All we ask is that you give us back our water."

Pompey Strabo threw back his grizzled yellowish head and roared with laughter. "What for?" he asked ingenuously. "There won't be anyone left to drink it!"

"We are thirsty, Gnaeus Pompeius!"

"Then stay thirsty," said Pompey Strabo.

He rode into Asculum Picentum on his Public Horse at the head of a party comprising his legates—Lucius Gellius Poplicola, Gnaeus Octavius Ruso, and Lucius Junius Brutus Damasippus—plus his tribunes of the soldiers, his cadets, and a picked contingent of troops five cohorts strong.

While the soldiers immediately spread out through the town with smooth discipline to round up every inhabitant and inspect every house, the consul Strabo proceeded to the forum-marketplace. It still bore the scars of the time when Gaius Vidacilius had occupied it; where the magistrates' tribunal had once stood there now lay a tumbledown pile of charred log fragments, the remains of the pyre Vidacilius had climbed upon to burn himself to death.

Chewing the vicious little switch he used to chastise his Public Horse, the consul Strabo looked about him carefully, then jerked his head at Brutus Damasippus.

"Put a platform on top of that pyre—and make it quick," he said to Damasippus curtly.

Within a very short time a group of soldiers had torn down doors and beams from the buildings closest by and Pompey Strabo had his platform, complete with a set of steps. Upon it was placed his ivory curule chair and a stool for his scribe.

"You, come with me," he said to Cicero, mounted the steps and seated himself on his curule chair, still wearing his general's cuirass and helm, but with a purple cloak depending from his shoulders instead of his red general's cloak. Hands full of wax tablets, Cicero hastily put them on the deck next to his stool and huddled himself upon it, one tablet open on his lap, his bone stylus ready. This was, he presumed, to be an official hearing.

"Poplicola, Ruso, Damasippus, Gnaeus Pompeius Junior—join me," said the consul with his customary abruptness.

His heart slowing a little, Cicero's fright evaporated sufficiently for him to take in the scene while he waited to write his first official words down. Obviously the town had taken some precautions before opening its gates, for a great mound of swords, mail-shirts, spears, daggers, and any other objects which might be deemed weapons reared itself outside the city meeting hall.

The magistrates were brought forward and made to stand just beneath the makeshift tribunal. Pompey Strabo began his hearing, which consisted of his saying,

"You are all guilty of treason and murder. You are not Roman citizens. You will be flogged and beheaded. Think yourselves lucky I do not give you a slaves' fate, and crucify you."

Every sentence was carried out then and there at the foot of the tribunal, while the horrified Cicero, controlling his rising gorge by fixing his eyes rigidly on the tablet in his lap, made meaningless squiggles in the wax.

The magistrates disposed of, the consul Strabo proceeded to pronounce the same sentence upon every male between eighty and thirteen his soldiers could find. To expedite matters he set fifty soldiers to flog and fifty soldiers to decapitate. Other men were set to comb the mound of weaponry outside the meeting hall in search of suitable axes, but in the meantime the executioners were directed to use their swords; with practice they became so good at beheading their maimed and exhausted victims with swords that they refused the axes. However, at the end of an hour only three hundred Asculans had been dispatched, their heads fixed on spears and nailed to the battlements, their bodies tossed into a pile at one side of the forum.

"You'll have to improve your performance," said Pompey Strabo to his officers and men. "I want this done *today,* not eight days from now! Set two hundred men to flogging and two hundred more to beheading. And be quick about it. You have no teamwork and very little system. If you don't develop both, you might find yourselves on the receiving end."

"It would be much easier to starve them to death," said the consul's son, observing the carnage dispassionately.

"Easier by far. But not legal," said his father.

Over five thousand Asculan males perished that day, a slaughter which was to live on in the memory of every Roman present, though none voiced disapproval, and none said a word against it afterward. The square was literally awash with blood; the peculiar stench of it—warm, sweetish, foetid, ferrous—rose like a mist into the sunny mountain air.

At sunset the consul rose, stretching, from his curule chair. "Back to camp, everyone," he said laconically. "We'll deal with the women and children tomorrow. There's no need to set a guard inside. Just lock the gates and patrol outside." He gave no orders as to disposal of the bodies or cleaning the blood away, so both were left to lie undisturbed.

On the morrow the consul returned to his tribunal, unmoved by the prospect he viewed, while his soldiers held those still alive in groups just outside the perimeter of the forum. His sentence was the same for all:

"Leave this place immediately, taking only what you wear with you. No food, no money, no valuables, no keepsakes."

Two years of siege had left Asculum Picentum a pitifully poor place; of money there was little, of valuables less. But before the banished were allowed to leave the city they were searched, and none was permitted to return to her home from whence she had been shepherded; each group of women and children was simply driven through the gates like sheep and pushed then through the lines of Pompey Strabo's army into lands stripped completely bare by occupying legions. No cry for help, no weeping crone or howling child was succored; Pompey Strabo's troops knew better than that. Those women of beauty went to the officers and centurions, those women with any kind of appeal went to the soldiers; and when they were finished with, those who still lived were driven out into the devastated countryside a day or two behind their mothers and children.

"There's nothing worth taking to Rome for my triumph," said the consul when it was all done and he could get up from his curule chair. "Give what there is to my men."

Cicero followed his general down off the tribunal and gazed gape-mouthed at what seemed the world's vastest slaughteryard, beyond nausea now, beyond compassion, beyond all feeling. If this is war, he thought, may I never know another one. And yet his friend Pompey, whom he adored and knew to be so kind, could toss his beautiful mane of yellow hair unconcernedly back from his temples and whistle happily through his teeth as he picked his way between the deep congealed pools of flyblown blood in the square, his beautiful blue eyes containing nothing save approval as they roamed across the literal hills of headless bodies all around him.

"I had Poplicola save two very delectable women for us cadets," said Pompey as he fell behind to make sure Cicero didn't trip into a bath of blood. "Oh, we'll have a good time! Have you ever watched anyone do it? Well, if you haven't, tonight's the night!"

Cicero drew in a sobbing breath. "Gnaeus Pompeius, I do not lack backbone," he said heroically, "but I have neither the stomach nor the heart for war. After witnessing what's happened here during the past two days, I couldn't become excited if I watched Paris doing it to Helen! As for Asculan women—just leave me out of the whole thing, please! I'll sleep in a tree."

Pompey laughed, threw his arm about his friend's thin bent shoulders. "Oh, Marcus Tullius, you are the most desiccated old Vestal I've ever met!" he said, still chuckling. "The enemy is the enemy! You can't possibly feel sorry for people who not only defied Rome, but murdered a Roman praetor and hundreds of other Roman men and women and children by tearing them apart! Literally! However, go and sleep in your tree if you must. I'll take your poke myself."

They passed out of the square and walked down a short wide

street to the main gates. And there it all was again. A row of grisly trophies with tattered necks and bird-pecked faces that marched across the battlements as far as the eye could see in either direction. Cicero gagged, but had acquired so much experience in keeping from disgracing himself forever in the eyes of the consul Strabo that he did not now disgrace himself in front of his friend, who rattled on, oblivious.

"There was nothing here worth displaying in a triumph," Pompey was saying, "but I found a really splendid net for trapping wild game birds. And my father gave me several buckets of books—an edition of my great-uncle Lucilius neither of us has ever seen. We think it must be the work of a local copyist, which makes it well worth having. Quite beautiful."

"They have no food and no warm clothes," said Cicero.

"Who?"

"The women and children banished from this place."

"I should hope not!"

"And what happens to that mess inside?"

"The bodies, you mean?"

"Yes, I mean the bodies. And the blood. And the heads."

"They'll rot away in time."

"And bring disease."

"Disease to whom? When my father has the gates nailed shut forever, there won't be a single living person left inside Asculum Picentum. If any of the women and children sneak back after we leave, they won't be able to get in. Asculum Picentum is finished. No one will ever live in it again," said Pompey.

"I see why they call your father The Butcher," said Cicero, beyond caring whether what he said offended.

Pompey actually took it as a compliment; he had odd gaps in his intelligence where his personal beliefs were too strong to tickle, let alone undermine. "Good name, isn't it?" he said gruffly, afraid that the strength of his love for his father was becoming a weakness. He picked up his pace. "Please, Marcus Tullius, do get a move on! I don't want those other *cunni* starting without me when it was I had the clout to get us the women in the first place."

Cicero hurried. But hadn't finished. "Gnaeus Pompeius, I have something to tell you," he said, beginning to pant.

"Oh, yes?" asked Pompey, mind clearly elsewhere.

"I applied for a transfer to Capua, where I think my talents will prove of better use in the winding up of this war. I wrote to Quintus Lutatius, and I've had an answer. He says he will be very glad of my services. Or Lucius Cornelius Sulla will."

Pompey had stopped, staring at Cicero in amazement. "What did you want to do that for?" he demanded.

"The staff of Gnaeus Pompeius Strabo is soldierly, Gnaeus Pompeius. I am not soldierly." His brown eyes gazed with great earnestness and softness into the face of his puzzled mentor, who was not quite sure whether to laugh or lose his temper. "Please, let me go! I shall always be grateful to you, and I shall never forget how much you've helped me. But you're not a fool, Gnaeus Pompeius. The staff of your father isn't the right place for me."

The storm clouds cleared, Pompey's blue eyes glittered happily. "Have it your own way, Marcus Tullius!" he said. Then sighed. "Do you know, I shall miss you?"

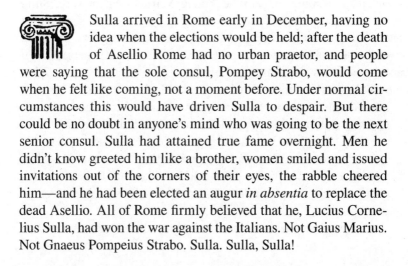 Sulla arrived in Rome early in December, having no idea when the elections would be held; after the death of Asellio Rome had no urban praetor, and people were saying that the sole consul, Pompey Strabo, would come when he felt like coming, not a moment before. Under normal circumstances this would have driven Sulla to despair. But there could be no doubt in anyone's mind who was going to be the next senior consul. Sulla had attained true fame overnight. Men he didn't know greeted him like a brother, women smiled and issued invitations out of the corners of their eyes, the rabble cheered him—and he had been elected an augur *in absentia* to replace the dead Asellio. All of Rome firmly believed that he, Lucius Cornelius Sulla, had won the war against the Italians. Not Gaius Marius. Not Gnaeus Pompeius Strabo. Sulla. Sulla, Sulla!

The Senate had never got around to formally appointing him commander-in-chief of the southern theater after Cato the Consul died; everything he had done, he had done as the legate of a dead man. However, he would shortly be the new senior consul—and *then* the Senate would have to give him whatever command he asked for. The embarrassment of certain senatorial leaders like Lucius Marcius Philippus at this legatal oversight quite amused Sulla when he met them. Clearly they had considered him a lightweight, incapable of performing miracles. Now he was everybody's hero.

One of the first visits he paid after returning to Rome was to Gaius Marius, whom he found so much improved he was astonished. With the old man was the eleven-year-old Gaius Julius Caesar Junior, now very nearly Sulla's height, though not yet pronouncedly pubescent. Just as striking, just as intelligent, and more of everything else than the boy had been during those past visits Sulla had paid Aurelia. He had been looking after Marius for a year, and he had listened with the keen ears of a wild creature to every word the Master had said. Heard it all, forgotten nothing.

Sulla learned from Marius of the near-downfall of Young Marius, still on duty with Cinna and Cornutus against the Marsi, a quieter and more responsible Young Marius than of yore. Sulla also learned of the near-fall of Young Caesar, who sat as the story was told smiling gently and looking into nothing. The presence of Lucius Decumius as a part of the episode had alerted Sulla immediately—and surprised him. Not like Gaius Marius! What was the world coming to when Gaius Marius stooped to hiring a professional assassin? So patently, blatantly accidental had the death of Publius Claudius Pulcher been that Sulla knew it was no accident. Only how had the deed been done? And how did Young Caesar fit into it? Was it really possible that this—this *child* had gambled his own life to push Publius Claudius Pulcher over a cliff? No! Not even a Sulla had so much confidence when it came to murder.

Bending his unsettling gaze on the boy while Marius prattled on (clearly *he* believed the intervention of Lucius Decumius had not been necessary), Sulla concentrated upon putting fear into Young Caesar. But the boy, feeling those sunless rays, simply looked up and across at Sulla, no trace of fear in his eyes. Not even faint apprehension. Nor was there a smile; Young Caesar stared at Sulla with an acute and sober interest. He knows me for what I am! said Sulla to himself—but, Young Caesar, I know you for what you are too! And may the Great God preserve Rome from both of us.

A generous man, Marius experienced nothing but joy at Sulla's success. Even the winning of the Grass Crown—the only military decoration which had escaped Marius's net—was applauded without resentment or envy.

"What have you to say now about generalship of the learned variety?" asked Sulla provocatively.

"I say, Lucius Cornelius, that I was wrong. Oh, not about learned generalship! No, I was wrong to think you don't have it in your bones. You do, you do. To send Gaius Cosconius by water to Apulia was inspired, and your pincer action was handled in a way no man—however superbly tutored!—could have, were he not a born general from the inside of his very marrow."

An answer which should have made Lucius Cornelius Sulla absolutely happy and completely vindicated. Yet it didn't. For Sulla understood that Marius still considered himself the better general, was convinced he could have subdued southern Italy faster and better. What do I have to do to make this stubborn old donkey see that he's met his match? cried Sulla within himself, betraying his thoughts in no external way. And felt his hackles stir, and looked at Young Caesar, and read in his eyes the knowledge of that unvoiced question.

"What do you think, Young Caesar?" asked Sulla.

"I am consumed with admiration, Lucius Cornelius."

"A soft answer."

"An honest one."

"Come on, young man, I'll take you home."

They walked at first in silence, Sulla wearing his stark white candidate's toga, the boy his purple-bordered child's toga, with his *bulla*-amulet to ward off evil on a thong about his neck. And at first Sulla thought all the smiles and nods were for himself, so famous had he become, until it was borne upon him that a good many of them were actually aimed at the boy.

"How does everyone know you, Young Caesar?"

"Only reflected glory, Lucius Cornelius. I go everywhere with Gaius Marius, you see."

"Not at all for yourself?"

"This close to the Forum I am simply Gaius Marius's boy. Once we enter the Subura, I'm known for myself."

"Is your father at home?"

"No, he's still with Publius Sulpicius and Gaius Baebius before Asculum Picentum," said the boy.

"Then he'll be home very soon. That army's marched."

"I suppose he will."

"Not looking forward to seeing your father?"

"Yes, of course I am," said Young Caesar easily.

"Do you remember your cousin—my son?"

The boy's face lit up; now the enthusiasm was genuine. "How could I ever forget him? He was so *nice*! When he died I wrote him a poem."

"What did it say? Can you recite it to me?"

Young Caesar shook his head. "I wasn't very good in those days, so I won't recite it if you don't mind. One day I'll write him a better one and then I'll give you a copy for yourself."

How stupid, to be led into reopening the wound because he was finding it awkward to make conversation with an eleven-year-old boy! Sulla fell silent, fighting tears.

As usual Aurelia was busy at her desk, but she came the moment Eutychus told her who had brought her son home. When they settled in the reception room Young Caesar remained with them, watching his mother closely. Now what gnat is flying round in his mind? wondered Sulla, irked because the boy's presence prevented his quizzing Aurelia about the things he wanted to. Luckily she perceived his irritation and soon dismissed her son, who went with reluctance.

"What's the matter with him?"

"I suspect Gaius Marius has said something or other to give Gaius Julius an erroneous idea about my friendship with you, Lucius Cornelius," Aurelia said calmly.

"Ye gods!—the old villain! How dare he!"

The beautiful Aurelia laughed merrily. "Oh, I've grown past letting things like that worry me," she said. "I know for a fact that when my uncle Publius Rutilius wrote to Gaius Marius in Asia Minor with the news that his niece had just been divorced by her husband after producing a red-haired son, Julia and Gaius Marius jumped to the conclusion that the niece was me—and the baby yours."

Now it was Sulla's turn to laugh. "Do they know so little about you? Your defenses are harder to break down than Nola's."

"True. Not that you haven't tried."

"I'm a man, built like any other."

"I disagree. You should have hay tied to *that* horn!"

Listening from his secret hiding place above the study's false ceiling, Young Caesar was conscious of an enormous relief—his mother was a virtuous woman after all. But then that emotion was chased out of his mind by another, much harder to deal with—why did she never show this side of herself to *him*? There she sat—laughing—relaxed—engaged in a kind of banter he was old enough to label as adultly worldly. *Liking* that repellent man! Saying things to him that indicated a very old and enduring friendship. Sulla's lover she might not be, but there was an intimacy between them that Young Caesar knew she did not share with her husband. His father. Dashing his tears away impatiently, he settled stealthily to lie full length and disciplined his mind to the detachment he could summon these days when he tried very hard. Forget she is your mother, Gaius Julius Caesar Junior! Forget how much you detest her friend Sulla! Listen to them and learn.

"You will be consul very soon," she was saying.

"At fifty-two. Older than Gaius Marius was."

"And a grandfather! Have you seen the baby yet?"

"Oh, Aurelia, please! Sooner or later I suppose I'll have to go around to Quintus Pompeius's house with Aelia on my arm—and have dinner—and chuck the child under the chin. But why should I care enough about the birth of a daughter to a daughter to want to rush round and see the sprog at once?"

"Little Pompeia is absolutely beautiful."

"Then may she wreak as much havoc as Helen of Troy!"

"Don't say that! I've always thought poor Helen led a most unhappy life. A chattel. A bed-toy," said Aurelia strongly.

"Women *are* chattels," said Sulla, smiling.

"*I* am not! I have my own property and my own activities."

Sulla's tone changed. "The siege of Asculum Picentum is no more. Gaius Julius will be home any day. And then what happens to all this brave talk?"

"Don't, Lucius Cornelius! Though I love him dearly, I dread his walking through the door. He will find fault with everything from the children to my role as landlady, and I will try desperately to please him until he issues some order I cannot countenance!"

"At which point, my poor Aurelia, you will tell him he's wrong, and the unpleasantness will start," said Sulla tenderly.

"Would *you* put up with me?" she demanded fiercely.

"Not if you were the last woman left alive, Aurelia."

"Whereas Gaius Julius does put up with me."

"Huh! What a world!"

"Oh, stop being flippant!" she snapped.

"Then I'll change the subject," said Sulla, and leaned back on both hands. "How is Scaurus's widow?"

The purple eyes glistened. "*Ecastor!* Still interested?"

"Definitely."

"I believe she's under the guardianship of a relatively young man—Livius Drusus's brother, Mamercus Aemilius Lepidus Livianus."

"I know him. He assists Quintus Lutatius in Capua, but he fought with Titus Didius at Herculaneum and he went to Lucania with the Gabinii. A sturdy sort of fellow—the kind who is thought the salt of the earth by everybody." He sat up, looking suddenly as alert as a cat sighting prey. "Is *that* how the wind lies? Is she going to marry Lepidus Livianus?"

Aurelia laughed. "I doubt it! He's married to a rather nasty woman who keeps her foot on him all the time. The Claudia who is a sister of Appius Claudius Pulcher—you know, his wife made Lucius Julius clean out the temple of Juno Sospita in his toga. She died in childbirth two months later."

"She's my Dalmatica's cousin—the dead Balearica, I mean," said Sulla with a grin.

"Everyone's her cousin," said Aurelia.

Sulla looked brisk. "Do you think my Dalmatica would be interested in me these days?"

Aurelia shook her head. "I have no idea! That is an honest answer, Lucius Cornelius. I have no contact with my woman peers whatsoever beyond my immediate family."

"Then perhaps you should cultivate her acquaintance when your husband comes home. You'll definitely have more spare time," said Sulla slyly.

"Enough, Lucius Cornelius! You can go home for that."

They walked to the door together. As soon as their forms had disappeared from the scope of Young Caesar's spyhole, he came down from the ceiling and was gone.

"Will you cultivate Dalmatica for me?" Sulla asked as his hostess held open the front door.

"No, I will not," said Aurelia. "If you're so interested, *you* cultivate her. Though I can tell you that a divorce from Aelia will make you a very unpopular man."

"I've been unpopular before. *Vale.*"

The tribal elections were held without the presence of the consul after the Senate conferred the task of scrutineer upon Metellus Pius the Piglet, who was a praetor and had come to Rome with Sulla. That the tribunes of the plebs were going to be a conservative lot was obvious when none other than Publius Sulpicius Rufus came in first and Publius Antistius not far behind him. Sulpicius had secured his release from Pompey Strabo; having made an excellent reputation in the field as a commander against the Picentes, Sulpicius now wished to make a political reputation. Rhetorical and forensic reputations he already possessed, having had a brilliant Forum career as a youth. Known as far and away the most promising orator among the younger men, like the dead Crassus Orator he affected the Asianic style, and was as gracefully calculated in his gestures as he was golden of voice, language, and rhetorical devices. His most famous case had been his prosecution of Gaius Norbanus for illegally convicting Caepio the Consul of Gold of Tolosa fame; that he had lost had not harmed his reputation in the least. A great friend of Marcus Livius Drusus's—though he did not support enfranchisement for the Italians—he had since Drusus's death drawn close to Quintus Pompeius Rufus, Sulla's running mate in the coming consular elections. That he was now the President of the College of Tribunes of the Plebs did not bode well for tribunician antics of demagogue kind. And, in fact, it looked as if not one of the ten who were elected was of the demagogue kind, nor was the election of the college followed by a spate of controversial new legislation. More promising was the installation of Quintus Caecilius Metellus Celer as a plebeian aedile; very rich, he was rumored to be planning wonderful games for the war-weary city.

With the Piglet presiding again, the Centuries met on the Campus Martius to hear the consular and the praetorian candidates declare themselves. When Sulla and his colleague Quintus Pompeius Rufus announced a joint candidacy, the cheers were deafening. But when Gaius Julius Caesar Strabo Vopiscus Sesquiculus announced *his* intention to contest the consular elections, there was a stunned silence.

"You can't!" said Metellus Pius in a winded voice. "You haven't been praetor yet!"

"It is my contention that there is nothing on the tablets to prevent a man's seeking the consulship before he is praetor," said Caesar Strabo, and produced a screed so long that the audience groaned. "I have here a dissertation which I shall read from beginning to end to prove my contention beyond all argument."

"Roll it up and don't bother, Gaius Julius Strabo!" called the new tribune of the plebs Sulpicius from the crowd below the candidates' platform. "I interpose my veto! You may not run."

"Oh, come, Publius Sulpicius! Let us try the law for once instead of using it to try people!" cried Caesar Strabo.

"I veto your candidacy, Gaius Julius Strabo. Come down from there and join your peers," said Sulpicius firmly.

"Then I declare my candidacy for praetor!"

"Not this year," Sulpicius said. "I veto that too."

Sometimes the younger brother of Quintus Lutatius Catulus Caesar and Lucius Julius Caesar the censor could be vicious and his temper lead him into difficulties, but today Caesar Strabo merely shrugged, grinned, and walked down quite happily to stand with Sulpicius.

"Fool! Why did you do that?" asked Sulpicius.

"It might have worked if you hadn't been here."

"I would have killed you first," said a new voice.

Caesar Strabo turned, saw that the voice belonged to the young man Gaius Flavius Fimbria, and sneered. "Pull your head in! *You* couldn't kill a fly, you money-hungry cretin!"

"No, no!" said Sulpicius quickly, putting himself between them. "Go away, Gaius Flavius! Go on, go away! Shoo! Leave the governing of Rome to your seniors—and your betters."

Caesar Strabo laughed, Fimbria slunk away.

"He's a nasty piece of work, young and all though he may be," said Sulpicius. "He's never forgiven you for prosecuting Varius."

"I'm not surprised," said Caesar Strabo. "When Varius died, he lost his only visible means of support."

There were to be no more surprises; once all the nominations for consul and praetor were in, everyone went home to wait with what patience he could muster for the appearance of the consul, Gnaeus Pompeius Strabo.

He did not return to Rome until almost the end of December, then insisted upon celebrating his triumph before he held any elections. That he had delayed his appearance in Rome was due to a brilliant idea he had conceived after the capture of Asculum Picentum. His triumphal parade (of course he was triumphing) would be a poor sort of affair; no spoils to display, no fascinatingly exotic floats depicting tableaux of sights and peoples alien to the inhabitants of Rome. At which point he had his brilliant idea. He would display thousands of male Italian children in his parade! His troops were put to scouring the countryside, and in time several thousand Italian boys aged between four and twelve were rounded up. So when he rode in his triumphal chariot along the prescribed route through the streets of Rome, he was preceded by a legion of little lads shuffling along; the sight was awesome, if only because it indicated how many Italian men had lost their lives through the agency of Gnaeus Pompeius Strabo.

The curule elections were held a scant three days before the New Year. Lucius Cornelius Sulla was returned as senior consul, with his friend Quintus Pompeius Rufus as his junior colleague. Two men with red hair from opposite ends of the Roman nobleman spectrum. Rome looked forward to having a team in office for a change, and hoped that some of the damage due to the war would be repaired.

It was to be a six-praetor year, which meant that most of the governors of overseas provinces were prorogued: Gaius Sentius and his legate Quintus Bruttius Sura in Macedonia; Publius Servilius Vatia and his legates Gaius Coelius and Quintus Sertorius in the Gauls; Gaius Cassius in Asia Province; Quintus Oppius in Cilicia; Gaius Valerius Flaccus in Spain; the new praetor Gaius Norbanus was sent to Sicily, and another new praetor, Publius Sextilius, was sent to Africa. The urban praetor was a very elderly man, Marcus Junius Brutus. He had a son just admitted to the Senate, but he had announced himself a candidate for praetor despite lifelong ill health because, he said, Rome needed decent men in office when so many decent men were in the field and unavailable. The *praetor peregrinus* was a plebeian Servilius of the Augur's family.

New Year's Day dawned bright and blue, and the omens of the night watch had been auspicious. It was perhaps not surprising that, after two years of dread and fear, all of Rome decided to turn out to watch the new consuls inaugurated. Everyone could see complete victory against the Italians looming, and there were many who hoped the new consuls would find the time now to deal with the city's appalling financial troubles.

Returned to his house from the night watch, Lucius Cornelius Sulla had his purple-bordered toga draped around him, and with his own hands put on his Grass Crown. He sallied forth from his house to relish the novelty of walking behind no less than twelve togate lictors who carried on their shoulders the bundle of rods ritually bound with red leather thongs. Ahead of him went the knights who had chosen to escort him rather than his colleague, and behind him walked the senators, including his dear friend the Piglet.

This is *my* day, he told himself as the huge crowd sighed and then voiced its approval at sight of the Grass Crown. For the first time in my life I have no rivals and no peers. I am the senior consul, I have won the war against the Italians, I wear the Grass Crown. I am greater than a king.

The two processions originating at the houses of the new consuls joined up at the foot of the Clivus Palatinus where the old Porta Mugonia still stood, a relic of the days when Romulus had walled his Palatine city. From there, six thousand men wended their way in solemn order across the Velia and down the Clivus Sacer into the lower Forum, most of them knights with the narrow stripe—the *angustus clavus*—on their tunics, a thinned Senate following behind the consuls and their lictors. And everywhere spectators cheered; they were perched on the front walls of the Forum houses, the arcade and upper roofs of the basilicas, the roofs of those temples offering a view, every set of steps leading up onto the Palatine, all the temple vestibules and steps, the roofs of the Via Nova taverns and shops, the loggias of the great houses of Palatine and Capitol facing the Forum. People. People everywhere. Cheering the man wearing the Grass Crown, a wreath most of them had never seen.

Sulla walked with a regal dignity he had not owned before,

acknowledging the admiration by inclining his head very slightly only, no smile touching his lips, no smugness or glee in his eyes. This was the dream made real; this was *his* day. One of the things he found fascinating was that he actually saw individual people in the vast crowds—a beautiful woman, an old man, a child perched on someone's shoulders, some outlandish foreigner—and Metrobius. Almost he stopped, forced himself onward. Just a face in the crowd. Loyal and discreet as always. No sign of a special relationship showed on his darkly handsome face, save perhaps in his eyes, though no one except Sulla could have known it. Sad eyes. And then he was gone, he was behind. He was in the past.

As the knights reached the area bordering the well of the Comitia and turned left to walk between the temple of Saturn and the vaulted arcade opposite housing the Twelve Gods, they paused, stopped, swung their heads toward the Clivus Argentarius and began to cheer in an acclamation far louder than that they had accorded Sulla. He heard but couldn't see, and was conscious of sweat crawling between his shoulder blades. Someone was stealing his crowd! For the crowd too had turned from every rooftop and tier of steps toward the same place, their cheers swelling amid a swaying sea of hands like water weeds.

No greater effort had Sulla ever had cause to make than the one he made now—no change in his expression, no diminution in the royal inclinations of his head, not even a flicker of feeling in his eyes. The procession started to move again; across the lower Forum he walked behind his lictors, never once craning his neck to verify what awaited him at the bottom of the Clivus Argentarius. What had stolen his crowd. Was stealing his day. *His* day!

And there he was. Gaius Marius. Accompanied by the boy. Clad in *toga praetexta*. Waiting to join the ranks of the curule senators who immediately followed Sulla and Pompeius Rufus. Back in action again. Going to attend the inauguration of the new consuls, attend the meeting of the Senate afterward in the temple of Jupiter Optimus Maximus atop the Capitol, attend the feast in the same temple. Gaius Marius. Gaius Marius the military genius. Gaius Marius the hero.

When Sulla drew opposite him, Gaius Marius bowed. Body filled with a howling rage he couldn't permit one single person to see—even Gaius Marius—Sulla turned and bowed to him. Whereupon the adulation reached fever pitch, the people screamed and shrieked with joy, every face was wet with tears. Then after Sulla turned to the left to walk beside the temple of Saturn and ascend the Capitol hill, Gaius Marius took his place among the men with purple-bordered togas, the boy at his side. So much had he improved that he hardly dragged his left foot, could display his left hand holding up all those heavy folds of toga and let the people see that it was no longer clumped and deformed; as for his face—he could afford to ignore the grimace his smile had become by not smiling.

I will ruin you for this, Gaius Marius, thought Sulla. You *knew* this was my day! Yet you couldn't resist showing me that Rome still belongs to you. That I—a patrician Cornelius!—am less than the dust compared to you, an Italian hayseed with no Greek. That I do not have the love of the people. That I can never rise to your heights. Well, maybe all this is really so, Gaius Marius. But I will ruin you. You yielded to the temptation of showing me on *my* day. If you had chosen to return to public life tomorrow—or the day after—or any other day—the rest of your life would be very different from the agony I will make it. For I will ruin you. Not by poison. Not by knife. I will make it impossible for your descendants ever to exhibit your *imago* in a family funeral procession, I will mar your reputation for all time.

Somehow it got itself over and done with, that awful day. Looking pleased and proud, the new senior consul stood to one side in the temple of Jupiter Optimus Maximus, the same hugely mindless grin on his face that the statue of the Great God wore, allowing the senators to pay homage to Gaius Marius just as if most of them didn't loathe him. When the realization dawned upon Sulla that Marius had done what he had done in all innocence—that he hadn't stopped to think he might be stealing Sulla's day, only thought what a splendid day today would be to make his reappearance in the Senate—the realization had no power to mollify Sulla's rage or soften his vow to ruin this terrible old man. Rather, the sheer thoughtlessness of it made Marius's action more intolerable still; in Marius's mind, Sulla mattered so little he never so much as loomed in the background of Marius's mirror of self. And for that, Marius would pay bitterly.

"Huh-huh-how *dared* he!" whispered Metellus Pius to Sulla as the meeting concluded and the public slaves began to bring in the feast. "He duh-duh-did it deliberately!"

"Oh yes, he did it deliberately," lied Sulla.

"Are you guh-guh-going to let him geh-geh-get away with it?" Metellus Pius demanded, almost weeping.

"Calm down, Piglet, you're stuttering," said Sulla, using that detested name, but in a manner the Piglet couldn't find detestable. "I refuse to let any of these fools see how I feel. Let them—and him!—think I approve wholeheartedly. I'm the consul, Piglet. He isn't. He's just a sick old man trying to snatch back an ascendancy he can never know again."

"Quintus Lutatius is livid about it," said Metellus Pius, concentrating on his stammer. "See him over there? He just gave Marius a piece of his mind, and the old hypocrite tried to pretend he never meant it that way, would you believe it?"

"I missed that," said Sulla, looking to where Catulus Caesar was talking with obviously furious hauteur to his brother the censor and to Quintus Mucius Scaevola, who looked unhappy. Sulla grinned. "He's picked the wrong audience in Quintus Mucius if he's saying insulting things about Gaius Marius."

"Why?" asked the Piglet, curiosity getting the better of rage and indignation.

"There's a marriage in the wind. Quintus Mucius is giving his daughter to Young Marius as soon as she's of age."

"Ye gods! He can do much better than that!"

Sulla lifted one brow. "Can he really, Piglet dear? Think of all that money!"

When Sulla went home he declined all company save Catulus Caesar and Metellus Pius, though when the three of them reached his house he entered it alone, with a wave of farewell for his escort. The house was quiet and his wife not in evidence, for which Sulla was enormously glad; he didn't think he could have faced all that wretched *niceness* without murdering her. Hurrying to his study, he bolted its doors, pulled the shutters of the colonnade window closed. The toga fell to the floor in a milky puddle around his feet and was kicked aside indifferently; face now displaying what he felt, he crossed to the long console table upon which rested six miniature temples in perfect condition, paintwork fresh and bright, gilding rich. The five belonging to his ancestors he had paid to have refurbished just after he had entered the Senate; the sixth housed his own likeness, and had been delivered from the workshop of Magius of the Velabrum only the day before.

Its catch was cunningly concealed behind the entablature of the front row of columns; when it was released, the columns divided in the midline as two opening doors. Inside he saw himself, a life-sized face and jaw connected to the anterior half of a neck, the whole complete with Sulla's ears; behind the ears were strings which held the mask in place while it was being worn, and which were hidden by the wig.

Made of beeswax, the *imago* was brilliantly done, its skin tinted as white as Sulla's own, the brows and lashes—both real—of the exact brown he colored them upon occasions like meetings of the Senate or dinner parties within Rome. The beautifully shaped lips were slightly parted because Sulla always breathed through his mouth, and the eyes were uncanny replicas of his own; however, minute inspection revealed that the pupils were actually holes through which the actor donning the mask could see just about well enough to walk if he was guided. Only when it came to the wig had Magius of the Velabrum fallen down on exact verisimilitude, for nowhere could he find hair of the correct color. Rome was plentifully endowed with wigmakers and false hair, and various shades of blond or red were by far the most popular hues; the original owners of the hair were barbarians of Gallic or German blood forced to part with their locks by slave-dealers or masters in need of extra money. The best Magius had been able to do was definitely redder than Sulla's thatch, but the luxuriance and the style were perfect.

For a long time Sulla stared at himself, not yet recovered from the amazement of discovering what he looked like to other people. The most flawless silver mirror gave no idea compared to this *imago*. I shall have Magius's team of sculptors do some portrait busts and a full-length statue in armor, he decided, quite delighted with how he looked to other people. Finally his mind returned to Marius's perfidy, and his gaze became abstracted; then he gave a little jump, hooked his forefingers around two horns on the front of the temple's floor. The head of Lucius Cornelius Sulla glided forward and out of the interior on the movable floor and sat, ready for someone to lift off its wig and lever the mask away from a base which was a clay mould of Sulla's face. Anchored to contours in its own image, shut away from the depredations of light and dust in its dark and airless temple home, the mask would last for generations after generations.

Sulla put his hands to the head atop his own shoulders and took off his Grass Crown, placed it upon the image's wig. Even on the day the runners had been torn from the soil of Nola they had been browned and bedraggled, for they came from a field of battle and had been bruised, trodden, ground down. Nor had the fingers which had woven them into a twisted braid been skilled and dainty florist's fingers; they had belonged to the *primus pilus* centurion Marcus Canuleius, and were more used to wrapping themselves about a gnarled vine *clava*. Now, seven months later, the Grass Crown had withered to spindling strings sprouting hair-like roots, and the few blades left were dry, shrunken. But you're tough, my beautiful Grass Crown, thought Sulla, adjusting it upon the wig until it framed the face and hairline as it ought, back from the brow like a woman's tiara. Yes, you're tough. You were made of Italian grass and crafted by a Roman soldier. You will endure. Just as I will endure. And together we will make a ruin of Gaius Marius.

The Senate met again the day after its consuls were inducted into office, summoned by Sulla. A new Princeps Senatus existed at last, appointed during the New Year's Day ceremonies. He was

Lucius Valerius Flaccus, Marius's "man of straw" junior consul during that momentous year when Marius had been consul a sixth time, had his first stroke, and had been helpless to prevent Saturninus's running amok. It was not a particularly popular appointment, but there were so many restrictions and precedents and regulations that only Lucius Valerius Flaccus had qualified—he was a patrician, the leader of his group of senators, a consular, a censor, and an *interrex* more times than any other patrician senator. No one had any illusions that he would fill the shoes of Marcus Aemilius Scaurus gracefully or formidably. Including Flaccus himself.

Before the meeting was formally convened he had come to Sulla and begun to ramble on about problems in Asia Minor, but so muddled was his presentation and so incoherent his sentences that Sulla put him firmly aside and indicated that the auspices might be taken. Himself an augur now, he presided over the ceremonies in conjunction with Ahenobarbus Pontifex Maximus. And there's another doesn't look well, thought Sulla, sighing; the Senate was in a sorry state.

Not all of Sulla's time since he had arrived in Rome at the beginning of December had been taken up in visits to friends, sittings for Magius of the Velabrum, idle chatter, a boring wife, and Gaius Marius. Knowing he would be consul, he had spent most of his time talking to those among the knights whom he respected or knew to be most able, in talking to senators who had remained in Rome throughout the war (like the new urban praetor Marcus Junius Brutus), and in talking to men like Lucius Decumius, member of the Fourth Class and caretaker of a crossroads college.

Now he rose to his feet and proceeded to demonstrate to the House that he, Lucius Cornelius Sulla, was a leader who would not brook defiance.

"Princeps Senatus, Conscript Fathers, I am not an orator," he said, standing absolutely still in front of his curule chair, "so you will get no fine speeches from me. What you will get is a plain statement of the facts, followed by an outline of the measures I intend to take to remedy matters. You may debate the issues—*if* you feel you must—but I take leave to remind you that the war is not yet satisfactorily concluded. Therefore I do not want to spend any more time in Rome than I must. I also warn you that I will deal harshly with members of this august body who attempt to hinder me for vainglorious or self-interested motives. We are not in a position to suffer the kind of antics performed by Lucius Marcius Philippus during the days before the death of Marcus Livius Drusus—I hope you are listening, Lucius Marcius?"

"My ears are absolutely *flappingly* wide open, Lucius Cornelius," drawled Philippus.

A different man might have chosen to flatten Philippus with a well-chosen phrase or two; Lucius Cornelius Sulla did it with his eyes. Even as the titters broke out, those eerie pale orbs were roaming the tiers searching for culprits. Expectation of a verbal exchange was stifled at birth, the laughter ceased abruptly, and everyone discovered valid reasons for leaning forward and looking intensely interested.

"None of us can be unaware how straitened the financial affairs of Rome are, both public and private. The urban quaestors have reported to me that the Treasury is empty, and the tribunes of the Treasury have given me a figure for the debt Rome owes to various institutions and individuals in Italian Gaul. The figure is in excess of three thousand silver talents and is increasing every day for two reasons: the first because Rome is still forced to buy from these institutions and individuals; the second because the principal outstanding remains unpaid, the interest remains unpaid, and we are not always able to pay the interest upon the unpaid interest. Businesses are foundering. Those who have lent money in the private sector cannot collect either debts or interest or interest upon unpaid interest. And those who have borrowed money are in worse condition still."

His eyes rested reflectively upon Pompey Strabo, who sat in the right-hand front row near Gaius Marius, looking in apparent unconcern at his own nose; here, Sulla's eyes seemed to be saying to the rest of the House, is a man who should have taken a little time off from his martial activities to do something about Rome's spiraling financial crisis, especially after his urban praetor died.

"I therefore request that this House send a *senatus consultum* to the Assembly of the Whole People in their tribes, patrician and plebeian, asking for a *lex Cornelia* to the following effect: that all debtors, Roman citizens or no, be obliged to pay simple interest only—that is, interest upon the principal only—at the rate agreed to by both parties at the time the loan was made. The levying of compound interest is forbidden, and the levying of simple interest at a higher rate than originally agreed to is forbidden."

There were murmurs now, particularly from those who had been lending money, but that invisible menace Sulla radiated kept the murmurs low. He was undeniably Roman all the way back to the very beginning. He had the will of a Gaius Marius. But he had the air of a Marcus Aemilius Scaurus. And somehow nobody, even Lucius Cassius, contemplated for one moment treating Lucius Cornelius Sulla in the way Aulus Sempronius Asellio had been treated. He just wasn't the kind of person other men speculated about murdering.

"No one wins in a civil war," said Sulla levelly. "The war we are currently concluding is a civil war. It is my personal view that no Italian can ever be a Roman. But I am Roman enough to respect those laws which have recently been enacted to make Romans out of Italians. There will be no booty, there will be no compensation paid to Rome of sufficient magnitude to put so much as one layer of silver sows upon the bare floor of the temple of Saturn."

"*Edepol!* Does he think that's oratory?" asked Philippus of anyone in hearing.

"*Tace!*" growled Marius.

"The Italian treasuries are as empty as ours," Sulla went on, ignoring the little exchange below him. "The new citizens who will appear on our rolls are as debt-ridden and impoverished as genuine Romans. At such a time, a new start has to be made somewhere. To promulgate a general cancellation of debts is unthinkable.

But nor can debtors be squeezed until they die from it. In other words, it is only fair and equitable that both sides of the lending equation be accommodated. And that is what my *lex Cornelia* will attempt."

"What about Rome's debt to Italian Gaul?" asked Marius. "Is the *lex Cornelia* to cover this as well?"

"Most definitely, Gaius Marius," said Sulla pleasantly. "We all know Italian Gaul is very rich. The war in the peninsula didn't touch it, and it has made a great deal of money out of the war in the peninsula. Therefore it and its businessmen can well afford to abandon measures like compound interest. Thanks to Gnaeus Pompeius Strabo, all of Italian Gaul south of the Padus is now fully Roman, and the major centers north of the river have been endowed with the Latin Rights. I think it only fair that Italian Gaul be treated like every other group of Romans and Latins."

"They won't be so happy to call themselves Pompey Strabo's clients after they hear about this *lex Cornelia* in Italian Gaul," whispered Sulpicius to Antistius with a grin.

But the House approved with an outburst of ayes.

"You are introducing a good law, Lucius Cornelius," said Marcus Junius Brutus suddenly, "but it doesn't go far enough. What about those cases where litigation is inevitable, yet one or both parties in litigation have not the money to lodge *sponsio* with the urban praetor? Though the bankruptcy courts are closed, there are many cases the urban praetor is empowered to decide without the encumbrances of a proper hearing. If, that is, the sum in question has been lodged in his keeping. But as the law stands at the moment, if the sum in question is not lodged, the urban praetor's hands are tied, he cannot hear the case nor give a finding. Might I suggest a second *lex Cornelia* waiving lodgment of *sponsio* in cases of debt?"

Sulla laughed, clapped his hands together. "Now that is the sort of thing I want to hear, *praetor urbanus*! Sensible solutions to vexing questions! By all means let us promulgate a law waiving *sponsio* at the discretion of the urban praetor!"

"Well, if you're going to go that far, why not just reopen the bankruptcy courts?" asked Philippus, very much afraid of any law to do with debt collection; he was perpetually in debt, and one of Rome's worst payers.

"For two reasons, Lucius Marcius," said Sulla, answering as if he thought Philippus's remark had been serious rather than ironic. "The first is that we do not yet have sufficient magistrates to staff the courts and the Senate is so thin of members that special judges would be hard to find, given that they must have a praetor's knowledge of the law. The second is that bankruptcy is a civil procedure, and the so-called bankruptcy courts are entirely staffed by special judges appointed at the discretion of the urban praetor. Which goes straight back to reason number one, does it not? If we cannot staff the criminal courts, how can we hope to staff the more flexible and discretionary hearings of civil offenses?"

"So succinctly put! Thank you, Lucius Cornelius," said Philippus.

"Don't mention it, Lucius Marcius—and I mean, *don't* mention it. Again. Understood?"

There was further debate, of course; Sulla had not expected to see his recommendations adopted without argument. But even among the senatorial moneylenders opposition was halfhearted, as everyone could appreciate that collecting some money was better than collecting none, and Sulla had not attempted to abolish interest entirely.

"I will see a division," said Sulla when he thought they had talked enough and he was tired of further time-wasting.

The division went his way by a very large majority; the House prepared a *senatus consultum* commending both Sulla's new laws to the Assembly of the People, a body to which the consul could present his case himself, patrician though he was.

The praetor Lucius Licinius Murena, a man more famous for his breeding of freshwater eels for the banquet table than his political activity, then proposed that the House consider the recall of those sent into exile by the Varian Commission when it had been under the aegis of Quintus Varius.

"Here we are awarding the citizenship to half of Italy, while the men condemned for supporting this enfranchisement are still without

their citizenships!" cried Murena passionately. "It's time they came
home, they're exactly the Romans we need!"

Publius Sulpicius bounced off the tribunician bench and faced
the consul's chair. "May I speak, Lucius Cornelius?"

"Speak, Publius Sulpicius."

"I was a very good friend of Marcus Livius Drusus's, though I
was never keen on the enfranchisement of Italy. However, I deplored
the way Quintus Varius conducted his court, and all of us must ask
ourselves how many of his victims were his victims for no other
reason than that he disliked them personally. But the fact remains
that his court was legally created and conducted its actual proceedings according to the law. At this present moment the same court is
still functioning, albeit in the opposite manner. It is the only court
open. Therefore we must conclude that it is a legally constituted
body, and that its findings must stand. I hereby notify this House
that if any attempt is made to recall *any* persons sentenced by the
Varian Commission, I will interpose my veto," said Sulpicius.

"As will I," said Publius Antistius.

"Sit down, Lucius Licinius Murena," said Sulla gently.

Murena sat down, crushed, and shortly afterward the House
ended its first ordinary sitting with the consul Sulla in the chair.

As he was making his way out of the chamber, Sulla found
himself detained by Pompey Strabo.

"A private word in your ear, Lucius Cornelius."

"Certainly," said Sulla heartily, resolving to prolong the conversation; he had seen Marius lurking in wait for him and wanted
nothing to do with Marius, yet knew he couldn't ignore him without good excuse.

"As soon as you've regulated Rome's financial affairs to your
satisfaction," said Pompey Strabo in that toneless yet menacing
voice of his, "I suppose you'll get round to dealing with who gets
what command in the war."

"Yes, Gnaeus Pompeius, I do expect to get round to that," said
Sulla easily. "I suppose it ought by rights to have been discussed
yesterday when the House ratified all the provincial governor-

ships, but—as you've probably gathered from my speech today—I look on this conflict as a civil war, and would rather see the commands debated in a regular meeting."

"Oh well, yes, I see your point," said Pompey Strabo, not in the manner of one abashed by the crassness of his question, but rather in the manner of one who had no idea of protocol.

"In which case?" asked Sulla politely, noticing out of the corner of his eye that Marius had dragged himself off in the company of Young Caesar, who must have waited patiently outside the doors.

"If I include the troops Publius Sulpicius brought from Italian Gaul the year before last—as well as the troops Sextus Julius brought from Africa—I have ten full legions in the field," said Pompey Strabo. "As I'm sure you'll appreciate, Lucius Cornelius— since I imagine you're in similar circumstances yourself—most of my legions haven't been paid in a year."

Down went the corners of Sulla's mouth in a rueful smile. "I do indeed know what you mean, Gnaeus Pompeius!"

"Now to some extent I've canceled that debt out, Lucius Cornelius. The soldiers got everything Asculum Picentum had to offer, from furniture to bronze coins. Clothes. Women's trinkets. Paltry, down to the last Priapus lamp. But it made them happy, as did the other occasions when I was able to give them whatever was there to be had. Paltry stuff. But enough for common soldiers. So that's one way I was able to cancel the debt." He paused, then said, "But the other way affects me personally."

"Indeed?"

"Four of those ten legions are *mine*. They were raised among the men of my own estates in northern Picenum and southern Umbria, and to the last soldier they're my clients. So they don't expect to be paid any more than they expect Rome to pay them. They're content with whatever pickings they can glean."

Sulla was looking alert. "Do go on!"

"Now," said Pompey Strabo reflectively, rubbing his chin with his big right hand, "I'm quite happy with things the way they are. Though *some* things will change because I'm not consul anymore."

"Things like, Gnaeus Pompeius?"

"I'll need a proconsular imperium, for one thing. And my command in the north confirmed." The hand which had caressed his jaw now swept in a wide circle. "You can have all the rest, Lucius Cornelius. I don't want it. All I want is my own corner of our lovely Roman world. Picenum and Umbria."

"In return for which, you won't send the Treasury a wages bill for four of your ten legions, and will reduce the bill you send in on behalf of the other six?"

"You're wide awake on all counts, Lucius Cornelius."

Out went Sulla's hand. "You've got a deal, Gnaeus Pompeius! I'd give Picenum and Umbria to Saturninus if it meant Rome didn't have to find the full wages for ten legions."

"Oh, not to Saturninus, even if his family did originally come from Picenum! I'll look after them better than he would."

"I'm sure you will, Gnaeus Pompeius."

Thus it was that when the question of apportioning out the various commands for the concluding operations of the war against the Italians came up in the House, Pompey Strabo got what he wanted without opposition from the consul with the Grass Crown. Or opposition from anyone else. Sulla had lobbied strenuously. Though Pompey Strabo was not a man of Sulla's kind—he utterly lacked subtlety or sophistication—he was known to be as dangerous as a bear at bay and as ruthless as an oriental potentate, to both of which he bore a strong resemblance. The tale of his doings in Asculum Picentum had filtered back to Rome through a medium as novel as it was unexpected; an eighteen-year-old *contubernalis* named Marcus Tullius Cicero had written an account of them in a letter to one of his only two living preceptors, Quintus Mucius Scaevola, and Scaevola had not been silent, though his loquaciousness was more because of the literary merit in the letter than Pompey Strabo's vile and monstrous behavior.

"Brilliant!" was Scaevola's verdict on the letter, and, "What else can one expect from such a blood-and-guts butcher?" on the letter's contents.

Though Sulla retained supreme command in the southern and

the central theaters, actual command in the south went to Metellus Pius the Piglet; Gaius Cosconius had sustained a minor wound which turned septic, and had retired from active service. The Piglet's second-in-command was Mamercus Aemilius Lepidus Livianus, who had relented and got himself elected a quaestor. As Publius Gabinius was dead and his younger brother, Aulus, was too young to be given a senior command, Lucania went to Gnaeus Papirius Carbo, generally felt to be an excellent choice.

In the midst of this debate—rendered more enjoyable by the knowledge that Rome had basically won the war already—Gnaeus Domitius Ahenobarbus Pontifex Maximus died. This meant proceedings had to be suspended in House and Comitia and the money found for a State funeral for one who was, at the time of his death, far richer than Rome's Treasury. Sulla conducted the election for his successor and for his priesthood in a mood of bitter resentment, for when he had assumed the consul's curule chair he had also assumed the largest part of the responsibility for Rome's fiscal problems, and it angered him to pay out good money for one in no need of it. Nor, before Ahenobarbus Pontifex Maximus, had there been any need to stand the expense of an election; he it was as a tribune of the plebs who carried the *lex Domitia de sacerdotiis,* the law changing the manner of appointing priests and augurs from an internal co-optation to an external election. Quintus Mucius Scaevola—already a priest—became the new Pontifex Maximus, which meant that Ahenobarbus's priesthood went to a new member of the College of Pontifices, Quintus Caecilius Metellus Pius the Piglet. At least in that respect, thought Sulla, some justice was done. When Metellus Piggle-wiggle had died, his priesthood had been voted to the young Gaius Aurelius Cotta, a fine example of how election to office could destroy a family's right to offices which had always been hereditary.

The obsequies over, business resumed in Senate and Comitia. Pompey Strabo asked for—and got—his legates Poplicola and Brutus Damasippus, though his other legate, Gnaeus Octavius Ruso, announced himself better able to serve Rome within Rome, a statement which everyone took to mean he would seek the consulship at the end of the year. Cinna and Cornutus were left to continue their operations in the lands of the Marsi, and Servius Sulpicius Galba remained in the field against the Marrucini, the Vestini, and the Paeligni.

"All in all, a good assortment," said Sulla to his consular colleague, Quintus Pompeius Rufus.

The occasion was a family dinner at the Pompeius Rufus mansion to celebrate the fact that Cornelia Sulla was pregnant again. This news had not smitten Sulla with the joy it obviously did Aelia and all the Pompeii Rufi, but it did resign him to family duties like finally setting eyes on his granddaughter, who—according to her other grandfather, his fellow consul—was the most exquisitely perfect baby ever born.

Now five months old, Pompeia was certainly beautiful, Sulla had to admit to himself. She had masses of dark red curls, black brows and black lashes so long and thick they were like fans, and enormous swamp-green eyes. Her skin was creamy, her mouth a sweet red bow, and when she smiled she displayed a dimple in one rosy cheek. Though Sulla admitted that he was no expert on babies, to him Pompeia seemed a very sluggish and stupid sort of child who only became animated when something gold and glittery was dangled under her nose. An omen, thought Sulla, chuckling silently.

His daughter was happy, so much was evident; on a far distant plane this quite pleased Sulla, who didn't love her, but was prone to like her when she didn't do anything to annoy him. And sometimes in her face he would catch an echo of her dead brother, some swift expression or lifting of her eyes, and then he would remember that her brother had loved her very much. How unfair life was! Why did it have to be Cornelia Sulla, a useless girl, who grew up in the bloom of health, and Young Sulla die untimely? It ought to have been the other way around. In a properly ordered world, the *paterfamilias* would have been offered a choice.

He never dredged his two German sons sired when he had lived among the Germans out of the back of his mind, never longed to see them or thought of them in any way as replacements for that beloved dead son of Julilla's. For they were not Roman, and their mother was a barbarian. Always it was Young Sulla, always an emptiness impossible to fill. And there she was under his nose, the daughter he would have given over to death in less than one beat of his heart, could he only have Young Sulla back.

"How delightful to see everything turn out so well," said Aelia to him as they walked home, unattended by a servant escort.

Because Sulla's thoughts were still revolving around life's unfairness in taking his son from him and leaving him only a useless girl, poor Aelia could not have made an unwiser remark.

He struck back instantly, with total venom. "Consider yourself divorced as of this moment!" he hissed.

She stopped in her tracks. "Oh, Lucius Cornelius, I beg of you, think again!" she cried, stunned at this thunderbolt.

"Find another home. You don't belong in mine." And Sulla turned to walk off toward the Forum, leaving Aelia standing on the Clivus Victoriae completely alone.

When she recovered sufficiently from the blow to be able to think, she too turned around, but not to walk to the Forum. She went back to the house of Quintus Pompeius Rufus.

"Please, may I see my daughter?" she asked the slave on door duty, who looked at her in bewilderment. Scant moments before he had let out a lovely woman wrapped in a glow of content—now here she was again looking as if she was going to die, so grey and blighted was her face.

When he offered to take her to his master, she asked if she might go to Cornelia Sulla's sitting room instead, see her daughter in private and without disturbing anyone else.

"What is it, Mama?" Cornelia Sulla asked lightly as she came through the door. And stopped at sight of that terrible face, and asked again, but in a very different tone, "What is it, Mama? Oh, what *is* it?"

"He's divorced me," said Aelia dully. "He told me I didn't belong in his home, so I didn't dare go home. He meant it."

"Mama! Why? When? *Where?*"

"Just now, on the street."

Cornelia Sulla sat down limply beside her stepmother, the only mother she had ever known beyond vague memories of a thin complaining wisp who was more attached to her wine cup than her children. Of course there had been nearly two years of Grandmother Marcia, but Grandmother Marcia hadn't wanted to be a mother again and had reigned over the nursery harshly, without love. So when Aelia had come to live with them, both Young Sulla and Cornelia Sulla had thought her utterly wonderful and loved her as a mother.

Taking Aelia's cold hand, Cornelia Sulla looked into the vortex of her father's mind, those frightful and stunningly quick changes of mood, the violence which could come leaping out of him like lava out of a volcano, the coldness which gave no hope or light to human heart. "Oh, he is a monster!" said his daughter between her teeth.

"No," said Aelia tiredly, "just a man who has never been happy. He doesn't know who he is, and he doesn't know what he wants. Or perhaps he does know, but dare not be it and want it. I've always known he'd end in divorcing me. Yet I did think he'd give me some warning—a change in his manner or—or *something*! You see, he was finished with me inside his mind before ever anything could begin. So when the years went by, I started to hope—it doesn't matter. All considered, I've had a longer run than I expected to."

"Cry, Mama! You'll feel better."

But what came out was a humorless laugh. "Oh no. I cried too much after our boy died. That was when *he* died too."

"He's not going to give you anything, Mama. I know him! He's a miser. He won't give you a thing."

"Yes, I am aware of that."

"But you do have a dowry."

"I gave him that a long time ago."

Cornelia Sulla drew herself up with great dignity. "You will live with me, Mama. I refuse to desert you. Quintus Pompeius will see the justice of it."

"No, Cornelia. Two women in a single house is one too many,

and you already have the second one in the person of your mother-in-law. A very nice woman. She loves you. But she won't thank you for wishing a third woman on her."

"But what can you do?" the young woman cried.

"I can stay here tonight in your sitting room, and think about my next step tomorrow," said Aelia calmly. "Don't tell your father-in-law yet, please. This will be a very awkward situation for him, you know. If you must, tell your husband. I must write Lucius Cornelius a note to say where I am. Could you have someone take it round straight away?"

"Of course, Mama." The daughter of any other man might have added words to the effect that in the morning he was sure to change his mind, but not Sulla's daughter; she knew her father better.

With the dawn came an answer from Sulla. Aelia broke its seal with steady hands.

"What does he say?" asked Cornelia Sulla tensely.

" 'I divorce you on the grounds of barrenness.' "

"Oh, Mama, how unfair! He married you *because* you were barren!"

"You know, Cornelia, he's very clever," said Aelia with some admiration. "Since he has chosen to divorce me on those grounds, I have no redress at law. I can't claim my dowry, I can't ask for a pension. I've been married to him for twelve years. When I married him I was still of an age to bear children. But I had none with my first husband, and none with him. No court would uphold me."

"Then you *must* live with me," said Cornelia Sulla in determined tones. "Last night I told Quintus Pompeius what had happened. He thinks it would work out well if you were to live here. If you were not so nice, perhaps it wouldn't. But it will work out. I know it!"

"Your poor husband!" said Aelia, smiling. "What else could he say? What else can his poor father say when he is told? They're both good men, and generous ones. But I know what I'm going to do, Cornelia, and it's by far the best thing."

"*Mama!* Not—"

Aelia managed a laugh. "No, no, of course I wouldn't do that, Cornelia! You'd be haunted by it for the rest of your life! I so much want you to have a wonderful life, dearest girl of mine." She sat up straighter, looked purposeful. "I'm going to your grandmother Marcia, at Cumae."

"Grandmother? Oh no, she's such a *stick!*"

"Nonsense! I stayed with her for three months last summer, and I had a most pleasant time. She writes to me often these days, mostly because she's lonely, Cornelia. At sixty-seven, she's afraid of being completely abandoned. It is a terrible fate to have no one there but slaves when you die. Sextus Julius didn't visit her often, yet when he died she felt it keenly. I don't think Gaius Julius has seen her in four or five years, and she doesn't get on with Aurelia or Claudia. Or her grandchildren."

"That's what I mean, Mama. She's so crotchety and hard to please. I know! She looked after us until you came."

"As a matter of fact, she and I get along together very well. We always did. And we were friends long before I married your father. It was she who recommended me to your father as a suitable wife. So she owes me a favor. If I go to live with her, I will be wanted, I will have a useful job to do, and I will be under no sort of obligation to her. Once I'm over the shock of this divorce, I think I'll enjoy both the life and her company," said Aelia firmly.

This perfect solution plucked out of what had seemed to be an empty bag was received with genuine gratitude by the consul Pompeius Rufus and his family. Though no member of his family would have denied Aelia a permanent home, they could now offer her a temporary one with honest pleasure.

"I don't understand Lucius Cornelius!" said the consul Pompeius Rufus to Aelia a day later. "When I saw him I tried to bring the matter of this divorce up, if only to explain why it was that I am sheltering you. And he—he turned on me with such a look on his face! I dried up! I tell you, I dried up. Terrible! I thought I knew him. The trouble is, I must continue to like him for the sake of our joint office. We promised the electors we'd work together in close harmony, and I can't go back on that promise."

"Of course you can't," said Aelia warmly. "Quintus Pompeius, it has never been my intention to turn you against Lucius Cornelius, believe me! What happens between husband and wife is a very private thing, and to all outside eyes it must seem inexplicable when a marriage terminates for no apparent reason. There are always reasons, and usually they're adequate. Who knows? Lucius Cornelius might genuinely wish for other children. His only son is dead, he has no heir. And he really doesn't have much money, you know, so I understand the dowry. I will be all right. If you could arrange to have someone carry this letter to Cumae for me and wait for a reply from Marcia, we'll know very soon what arrangements I can make."

Quintus Pompeius looked at the ground, face redder than his hair. "Lucius Cornelius has sent round your clothes and belongings, Aelia. I am very sorry."

"Well, that's good news!" said Aelia, maintaining her calm. "I was beginning to think he'd thrown them away."

"All of Rome is talking."

She lifted her eyes to his. "About what?"

"This divorce. His cruelty to you. It isn't being received well." Quintus Pompeius Rufus cleared his throat. "You happen to be one of the most liked and respected women in Rome. The story is everywhere, including your penniless state. In the Forum this morning he was booed and hissed."

"Oh, poor Lucius Cornelius!" she said sadly. "He would have hated that."

"If he did, he didn't show it. He just walked on as if nothing was happening." Quintus Pompeius sighed. "Why, Aelia? Why?" He shook his head. "After so many years, it doesn't make sense! If he wanted another son, why didn't he divorce you after Young Sulla died? That's three years ago now."

The answer to Pompeius Rufus's question came to Aelia's ears before she received the letter from Marcia bidding her come to Cumae.

This time it was the younger Quintus Pompeius who brought the news home, so out of breath he could hardly speak.

"What is it?" asked Aelia when Cornelia Sulla would not.

"Lucius—Cornelius! He's married—Scaurus's widow!"

Cornelia Sulla did not look surprised. "Then he can afford to pay you back your dowry, Mama," she said, tight-lipped. "She's as rich as Croesus."

Young Pompeius Rufus accepted a cup of water, drained it, and began to speak more coherently. "It happened late this morning. No one knew of it except Quintus Metellus Pius and Mamercus Lepidus Livianus. I suppose they had to know! Quintus Metellus Pius is her first cousin, and Mamercus Lepidus Livianus is the executor of Marcus Aemilius Scaurus's will."

"Her name! I can't remember her name!" said Aelia in wonder.

"Caecilia Metella Dalmatica. But everyone just calls her Dalmatica, I was told. They're saying that years ago—not long after Saturninus died—she was so much in love with Lucius Cornelius that she made a complete fool of herself—and of Marcus Aemilius Scaurus. They say Lucius Cornelius wouldn't look at her. Then her husband shut her away completely, and no one seems to have seen anything of her since."

"Oh yes, I remember the incident well," said Aelia. "I just couldn't remember her name. Not that Lucius Cornelius ever discussed it with me. But until Marcus Aemilius Scaurus did shut her away, I was not allowed to be out of our house if Lucius Cornelius was at home. He took enormous care that Marcus Aemilius Scaurus should know there was no impropriety on his part." Aelia sighed. "Not that it made any difference. Marcus Aemilius Scaurus still made sure he lost in the praetorian elections."

"She'll have no joy from my father," said Cornelia Sulla grimly. "No woman ever has had joy from him."

"Don't say such things, Cornelia!"

"Oh, Mama, I'm not a child anymore! I have a child of my own! And I know him better than you do because I don't love him the way you do! I'm blood of his blood—and sometimes that thought makes me so *afraid*! My father is a monster. And women bring out the worst in him. My real mother committed suicide—and no one will ever convince me that it wasn't over something my father did to her!"

"You'll never know, Cornelia, so don't think about it," said young Quintus Pompeius sternly.

Aelia looked suddenly surprised. "How odd! If you had asked me whom he might have married, I would have said, Aurelia!"

Cornelia Sulla nodded. "So would I. They've always been as chummy as two harpies on a rock. Different feathers. Same birds." She shrugged, said it. "Birds, nothing! Monsters, both of them."

"I don't think I've ever met Caecilia Metella Dalmatica," said Aelia, anxious to draw Cornelia Sulla away from dangerous statements, "even when she was following my husband around."

"Not your husband anymore, Mama! *Her* husband."

"Hardly anyone knows her," said young Pompeius Rufus, also anxious to pacify Cornelia Sulla. "Marcus Scaurus kept her in total isolation after that one indiscretion, innocent though it was. There are two children, a girl and a boy, but no one knows them. Or her. And since Marcus Scaurus died, she's been more invisible than ever. That's why the whole city is buzzing." He held out his cup for more water. "Today is the first day after her period of mourning. And that's yet another reason why all of Rome is buzzing."

"He must love her very much," said Aelia.

"Rubbish!" said Cornelia Sulla. "He doesn't love anyone."

After the white anger in which he had left Aelia standing on the Clivus Victoriae alone, Sulla underwent his usual plummet into black depression during the hours following. Partly to twist the knife in the colossal wound he knew he had inflicted upon the too-nice, too-boring Aelia, he went the next morning to the house of Metellus Pius. His interest in the Widow Scaurus was as old and cold as his mood; what he wanted was to make Aelia suffer. Divorce was not enough. He must find some better way to twist the knife. And what better way than to marry someone else immediately, make it look as if that was why he had divorced her?

These women, he thought as he walked to the house of Metellus Pius, they have driven me mad since I was a very young man. Since I gave up selling myself to men because I was stupid enough to think women easier victims. But I have been the victim. *Their* victim. I killed Nicopolis and Clitumna. And, thank every god there is, Julilla killed herself. But it's too dangerous to kill Aelia. And divorce *isn't* enough. She's been expecting that for years.

He found the Piglet deeply immersed in conversation with his new quaestor, Mamercus Aemilius Lepidus Livianus. A stroke of truly wonderful luck to find both of them together—but wasn't he always Fortune's favorite?

It was quite understandable that Mamercus and the Piglet should be closeted together, yet such was the aura around Sulla in one of his darker moods that the pair of them found themselves greeting him with the nervous agitation of a couple discovered in the act of making love to each other.

Good officers both, they sat down only after he was seated, then stared at him without finding a single thing to say.

"Had your tongues cut out?" asked Sulla.

Metellus Pius jumped, startled. "No, Lucius Cornelius! No! Forgive me, my thoughts were muh-muh-miles away."

"Yours too, Mamercus?" asked Sulla.

But Mamercus, slow and steady and trusty, discovered a smile buried in his courage. "Actually, yes," he said.

"Then I'll give them another direction entirely—and that goes for both of you," said Sulla with his most feral grin.

They said nothing, just waited.

"I want to marry Caecilia Metella Dalmatica."

"Jupiter!" squeaked Metellus Pius.

"That's not very original, Piglet," said Sulla. He got up, moved to the door of Metellus Pius's study and looked back, one brow raised. "I want to marry her tomorrow," he said. "I ask both of you to think about it and let me have your answer by dinnertime. Since I want a son, I've divorced my wife for barrenness. But I do not want to replace her with a young and silly girl. I'm too old for adolescent antics. I want a mature woman who has proven her fertility by already having had two children, including a boy. I thought of Dalmatica because she seems—or seemed, years ago—to have a soft spot for me."

With that he was gone, leaving Metellus Pius and Mamercus looking at each other, jaws hanging.

"Jupiter!" said Metellus Pius again, more feebly.

"It's certainly a surprise," said Mamercus, who was far less surprised than the Piglet because he didn't know Sulla one hundredth as well as the Piglet did.

The Piglet now scratched his head, shook it. "Why *her*? Except in passing when Marcus Aemilius died, I haven't thought of Dalmatica in years. She might be my first cousin, but after that business with Lucius Cornelius—how extraordinary!—she was locked up in her house under better security by far than the cells of the Lautumiae." He stared at Mamercus. "As executor of the will, you must surely have seen her during the last few months."

"To answer your first question first—why her?—I imagine her money won't go astray," said Mamercus. "As for your second question, I've seen her several times since Marcus Aemilius died, though not as often as I ought. I was already in the field at the time of his death, but I saw her then because I had to return to Rome to tidy up Marcus Aemilius's affairs. And if you want an honest opinion, I'd say she wasn't mourning the old man much at all. She seemed far more concerned with her children. Still, I found that absolutely reasonable. What was the age difference? Forty years?"

"All of that, I think. I remember when she married I felt sorry for her just a little. She was supposed to marry the son, but he suicided. My father gave her to Marcus Aemilius instead."

"The thing which struck me was her timidity," said Mamercus. "Or it could be that her confidence is gone. She's afraid to go out of the house, even though I told her she might. She has no friends at all."

"How could she have friends? I was quite serious when I said Marcus Aemilius locked her up," said Metellus Pius.

"After he died," said Mamercus reflectively, "she was of course alone in his house except for her children and a rather small group of slaves, considering the size of the establishment. But when I suggested this aunt or that cousin as a resident chaperone, she grew very upset. Wouldn't hear of any of them. In the end I was obliged to hire a Roman couple of good stock and reputation to live with her. She said she understood the conventions had to be observed, especially considering that old indiscretion, but she preferred to live with strangers than relatives. It is pathetic, Quintus Caecilius! How old was she at the time of that indiscretion? Nineteen? And married to a man of sixty!"

The Piglet shrugged. "That's marital luck, Mamercus. Look at me. Married to the younger daughter of Lucius Crassus Orator, whose older daughter has three sons already. Whereas *my* Licinia is still childless—and not for the want of trying, believe me! So we think we'll ask for one of the nephews to adopt."

Mamercus wrinkled his forehead, looked suddenly inspired. "I suggest *you* do what Lucius Cornelius wants to do! Divorce Licinia Minor for barrenness, and marry Dalmatica yourself."

"No, Mamercus, I couldn't. I'm very fond of my wife," said the Piglet gruffly.

"Then ought we think seriously about Lucius Cornelius's offer?"

"Oh, definitely. He's not a wealthy man, but he has something better, you know. He's a great man. My cousin Dalmatica has been married to a great man, so she's accustomed to it. Lucius Cornelius is going to go far, Mamercus. I don't know why I'm so utterly convinced of it, because I don't see any way in which he *can* go much further. But he will! I know he will. He's not a Marius. Nor is he a Scaurus. Yet I believe he will eclipse them both."

Mamercus rose to his feet. "Then we'd better go round and see what Dalmatica has to say. There's no possibility of a marriage tomorrow, however."

"Why not? She can't still be in mourning, surely!"

"No. Oddly enough, her mourning period finishes today. Which is why," said Mamercus, "it would look suspicious if she was to marry tomorrow. In a few weeks, I think."

"No, it must be tomorrow," said Metellus Pius strongly. "You don't know Lucius Cornelius the way I do. No man lives whom I esteem and respect more. But you *do not* gainsay him, Mamercus! If we agree they can marry, then it's tomorrow."

"I've just remembered something, Quintus Caecilius. The last time I saw Dalmatica—it would be two or three market intervals ago—she asked after Lucius Cornelius. But she's never asked after any other person, even you, her closest relative."

"Well, she was in love with him when she was nineteen. Maybe she's still in love with him. Women are peculiar, they do things like that," said the Piglet in tones of great experience.

When the two men arrived at Marcus Aemilius Scaurus's house and confronted Caecilia Metella Dalmatica, Metellus Pius saw what Mamercus had meant when he described her as timid. A mouse, was his verdict. A very attractive mouse, however, and sweet-natured. It did not occur to him to wonder how he might have felt had he been given in marriage at the age of seventeen to a woman almost sixty; women did as they were told, and a male sexagenarian had more to offer in every way than any female over forty-five. He launched into speech, as it had been decided that he—her closest relative—was technically in the position of *paterfamilias*.

"Dalmatica, today we have received an offer of marriage on your behalf. We strongly recommend that you accept, though we do feel you should have the right to decline should you wish," said Metellus Pius very formally. "You are the widow of the Princeps Senatus and the mother of his children. However, we think no better offer of marriage is likely to come your way."

"Who has offered for me, Quintus Caecilius?" Dalmatica asked, voice very small.

"The consul Lucius Cornelius Sulla."

An expression of incredulous joy suffused her face, the grey of her eyes shone silver; two rather ungainly hands came out, almost met in a clap.

"I accept!" she gasped.

Both men blinked, having expected to do some persuasive talking before Dalmatica could be made to agree.

"He wants to marry you tomorrow," said Mamercus.

"Today, if he wants!"

What could they say? What did one say?

Mamercus tried. "You are a very wealthy woman, Dalmatica. We have had no discussions with Lucius Cornelius regarding settlements and a dowry. In his mind, I think they are secondary considerations in that he knows you're rich, and isn't bothered beyond knowing you're rich. He said he had divorced his wife for barrenness and didn't want to marry a young girl, but rather a woman of sense still able to have children—and preferably a woman who already has children to establish her fertility."

This ponderous explanation drove some of the light out of her face, but she nodded as if she understood, though she said nothing.

Mamercus plodded on into the mire of financial matters. "You will not be able to continue living here, of course. This house is now the property of your young son and must remain in my custody. I suggest you ask your chaperones if they would mind continuing to live here until your son is of an age to assume responsibility. Those slaves you do not wish to take with you to your new establishment can remain here with the caretakers. However, the house of Lucius Cornelius is a very small one compared to this house. I think you would find it *claustra*."

"I find this one *claustra*," said Dalmatica with a flicker of—irony? Truly?

"A new beginning should mean a new house," said Metellus Pius, taking over when Mamercus bogged down. "If Lucius Cornelius agrees, the settlement could be a *domus* of this size in a location fitting for people of your status. Your dowry consists of the money left to you by your father, my uncle Dalmaticus. You also have a large sum left to you by Marcus Aemilius that cannot properly constitute a part of your dowry. However, for your own safety Mamercus and I will make sure that it is tied up in such a way that it remains yours. I do not think it wise to let Lucius Cornelius have access to your money."

"Anything you like," said Dalmatica.

"Then provided Lucius Cornelius agrees to these terms, the marriage can take place here tomorrow at the sixth hour of daylight. Until we can find a new house, you will live with Lucius Cornelius in his house," said Mamercus.

Since Lucius Cornelius agreed expressionlessly to every condition, he and Caecilia Metella Dalmatica were married at the sixth hour of the following day, with Metellus Pius officiating and Mamercus acting as witness. The usual trappings had been dispensed with; after the brief ceremony—not *confarreatio*—was over, the bride and groom walked to Sulla's house in the company of the bride's two children, Metellus Pius, Mamercus, and three slaves the bride had requested she take with her.

When Sulla picked her up to carry her over his threshold she stiffened in shock, so easily and competently was it done. Mamercus and Metellus Pius came in to drink a cup of wine, but left so quickly that the new steward, Chrysogonus, was still absent showing the children and their tutor where their new quarters were, and the two other slaves were still standing looking utterly lost in a corner of the peristyle-garden.

The bride and groom were alone in the atrium.

"Well, wife," said Sulla flatly, "you've married another old man, and no doubt you'll be widowed a second time."

That seemed such an outrageous statement to Dalmatica that she gaped at him, had to search for words.

"You're not *old*, Lucius Cornelius!"

"Fifty-two. That's not young compared to almost thirty."

"Compared to Marcus Aemilius, you're a youth!"

Sulla threw back his head and laughed. "There's only one place where that remark can be proven," he said, and picked her up again. "No dinner for you today, wife! It's bedtime."

"But the children! A new home for them—!"

"I bought a new steward yesterday after I divorced Aelia, and he's a very efficient sort of fellow. Name's Chrysogonus. An oily Greek of the worst kind. They make the best stewards once they're aware that the master is awake to every trick and quite capable of crucifying them." Sulla lifted his lip. "Your children will be looked after magnificently. Chrysogonus needs to ingratiate himself."

The kind of marriage Dalmatica had experienced with Scaurus became far more obvious when Sulla put his new wife down on his bed, for she scuttled off it, opened the chest sent on ahead to Sulla's house, and from it plucked a primly neat linen nightgown. While Sulla watched, fascinated, she turned her back to him, loosened her pretty cream wool dress but held it under her arms firmly, and managed thus to get the nightgown over her head and modestly hanging before she abandoned her clothes; one moment she was clad for day, the next moment she was clad for night. And never a glimpse of flesh!

"Take that wretched thing off," said Sulla from behind her.

She turned round quickly and felt the breath leave her body. Sulla was naked, skin whiter than snow, the curling hair of chest and groin reflecting the mop on his head, a man without a sag to his midriff, without the crepey folds of true old age, a man compact and muscular.

It had taken Scaurus what had seemed hours of fumbling beneath her robe, pinching at her nipples and feeling between her legs, before anything happened to his penis—the only male member she had known, though she had never actually *seen* it. Scaurus had been an old-fashioned Roman, kept his sexual activities as modest as he felt his wife should be. That when availing himself of a less modest female than his wife, his sexual activity was very different, his wife could not know.

Yet there was Sulla, as noble and aristocratic as her dead husband, shamelessly exhibiting himself to her, his penis seeming as huge and erect as the one Priapus displayed upon his bronze statue in Scaurus's study. She was not unfamiliar with the sexual anatomy of male and female, for both were everywhere in every house; the genitalia upon the herms, the lamps, the pedestals of tables, even some of the paintings on the walls. None of which had ever seemed remotely related to married life. They were simply a part of the furniture. Married life had been a husband who had never shown himself to her—who, despite the production of two children, as far as she knew could have been quite differently constructed from Priapus or the furniture and decorations.

When she had first met Sulla at that dinner party so many years ago, he had dazzled her. She had never seen a man so beautiful, so hard and strong yet so—so—womanish? What she had felt for him then (and during the time when she had spied on him as he went about Rome canvassing for the praetorian elections) was not consciously of the flesh, for she was a married woman with experience of the flesh, and dismissed it as the most unimportant and least appealing aspect of love. Her passion for Sulla was literally a schoolgirl crush—something of air and wind, not fire and fluid. From behind pillars and awnings she had feasted on him with her eyes, dreamed of his kisses rather than his penis, yearned for him in the most lavishly romantic way. What she wanted was a conquest, his enslavement, her own sweet victory as he knelt at her feet and wept for love of her.

Her husband had confronted her in the end, and everything to do with her life changed. But not her love for Sulla.

"You have made yourself ridiculous, Caecilia Metella Dalmatica," Scaurus had said to her evenly and coldly. "But—and this is far worse—you have made *me* ridiculous. The whole of the city is laughing at *me*, the First Man in Rome. And that must stop. You have mooned and sighed and gushed in the stupidest way over a man who has not noticed you or encouraged you, who does not want your attentions, and whom I have been obliged to punish in order to preserve my own reputation. Had you not embarrassed him and me, he would be a praetor—as he deserves to be. You have therefore spoiled the lives of *two* men—one your husband, the other impeccably blameless. That I do not call myself blameless is due to my weakness in allowing this mortifying business to continue so long. But I had hoped that you would see the error of your ways for yourself, and thus prove to Rome that you are, after all, a worthy wife for the Princeps Senatus. However, time has proven you a worthless idiot. And there is only one way to deal with a worthless idiot. You will never leave this house again for any purpose whatsoever. Not for funerals or for weddings, for lady-friends or shopping. Nor may you have lady-friends visit you here, as I cannot trust your prudence. I must tell you that you are a silly and empty vessel, an unsuitable wife for a man of my *auctoritas* and *dignitas*. Now go."

Of course this monumental disapproval did not prevent Scaurus's seeking his wife's body, but he was old and growing older, and these occasions grew further and further apart. When she produced his son she regained some slight measure of his approval, but Scaurus refused to relax the terms of her imprisonment. And in her dreams, in her isolation when time hung like a lead sow around her neck, still she thought of Sulla, still she loved him. Immaturely, from out of an adolescent heart.

Looking on the naked Sulla now provoked no sexual desire in her, just a winded amazement at his beauty and virility and a winded realization that the difference between Sulla and Scaurus was minimal after all. Beauty. Virility. They were the real differences. Sulla wasn't going to kneel at her feet and weep for love of her! She had not conquered him! He was going to conquer her. With his ram battering down her gates.

"Take that thing off, Dalmatica," he said.

She took her nightgown off with the alacrity of a child caught out in some sin, while he smiled and nodded.

"You're lovely," he said, a purr in his voice, stepped up to her, slid his erection between her legs, and gathered her close. Then he kissed her, and Dalmatica found herself in the midst of more sensations than she had ever known existed—the feel of his skin, his lips, his penis, his hands—the smell of him clean and sweet, like her children after their baths.

And so, waking up, growing up, she discovered dimensions which had nothing to do with dreams or fantasies and everything to do with living, conjoined bodies. And from love she fell into adoration, physical enslavement.

To Sulla she manifested the bewitchment he had first known with Julilla, yet magically mixed with echoes of Metrobius; he soared into an ecstatic delirium he hadn't experienced in almost twenty years. I am starved too, he thought in wonder, and I didn't even know it! This is so important, so vital to me! And I had lost all sight of it.

Little wonder then that nothing from that first incredible day of marriage to Dalmatica had the power to wound him deeply—not the boos and hisses he still experienced from those in the Forum who deplored his treatment of Aelia, not the malicious innuendo of men like Philippus who only saw Dalmatica's money, not the crippled form of Gaius Marius leaning on his boy, not the nudges and winks of Lucius Decumius nor the sniggers of those who deemed Sulla a satyr and Scaurus's widow an innocent, not even the bitter little note of congratulations Metrobius sent round with a bouquet of pansies.

Less than two weeks after the marriage they moved into a huge mansion on the Palatine overlooking the Circus Maximus and not far from the temple of Magna Mater. It had frescoes better than those in the house of Marcus Livius Drusus, pillars of solid marble, the best mosaic floors in Rome, and furniture of an opulence more suited to an eastern king than a Roman senator. Sulla and Dalmatica even boasted a citrus-wood table, its priceless peacock-grained surface supported by a gold-inlaid ivory pedestal in the form of interlocked dolphins; a wedding gift from Metellus Pius the Piglet.

Leaving the house in which he had lived for twenty-five years was another much-needed emancipation. Gone the memories of awful old Clitumna and her even more awful nephew, Stichus; gone the memories of Nicopolis, Julilla, Marcia, Aelia. And if the memories of his son were not gone, he had at least removed himself from the pain of seeing and feeling things his son had seen and felt, could no longer look in through the vacant nursery door and have an image of a laughing, naked little boy leap at him from nowhere. With Dalmatica he would start anew.

It was Rome's good fortune that Sulla lingered in the city far longer than he would have did Dalmatica not exist; he was there to supervise his program of debt relief and think of ways to put money in the Treasury. Shifting mightily and snatching income at every conceivable opportunity, he managed to pay the legions (Pompey Strabo kept his word and sent in a very light wages bill) and even a little of the debt to Italian Gaul, and saw with satisfaction that business in the city seemed on the verge of a slight recovery.

In March, however, he had seriously to think of tearing himself away from his wife's body. Metellus Pius was already in the south with Mamercus; Cinna and Cornutus were scouring the lands of the Marsi; and Pompey Strabo—complete with son but without the letter-writing prodigy Cicero—skulked somewhere in Umbria.

But there was one thing left to do. Sulla did it on the day before his departure, as it did not require the passage of a law. It lay in the province of the censors. This pair had been dilatory in the matter of the census, even though Piso Frugi's law had confined the new citizens to eight of the rural tribes and two new tribes, a distribution which could not destroy the tribal electoral status quo. They had provided themselves with a technical illegality in case the temperature of censorial waters grew too hot for their thin skins to bear and discretion dictated that they should resign their office; when directed by the augurs to conduct a very small and obscure ceremony, they had deliberately neglected to do so.

"Princeps Senatus, Conscript Fathers, the Senate is facing its own crisis," said Sulla, remaining without moving beside his own chair, as was his habit. He held out his right hand, in which reposed a scroll of paper. "I have here a list of those senators who will never attend this House again. They are dead. Just a little over one hundred of them. Now the largest part of the one hundred names on this list belongs to the *pedarii,* backbenchers who craved no special distinction in this House, did not speak, knew no more law than any senator must. However, there are other names—names of men we already miss acutely, for they were the stuff of court presidents, special judges and adjudicators and arbitrators, legal draftsmen, legislators, magistrates. And they have not been replaced! Nor do I see a move to replace them!

"I mention: the censor and Princeps Senatus, Marcus Aemilius Scaurus; the censor and Pontifex Maximus, Gnaeus Domitius Ahenobarbus; the consular Sextus Julius Caesar; the consular Titus Didius; the consul Lucius Porcius Cato Licinianus; the consul Publius Rutilius Lupus; the consular Aulus Postumius Albinus; the praetor Quintus Servilius Caepio; the praetor Lucius Postumius; the praetor Gaius Cosconius; the praetor Quintus Servilius; the praetor Publius Gabinius; the praetor Marcus Porcius Cato Salonianus; the praetor Aulus Sempronius Asellio; the aedile Marcus Claudius Marcellus; the tribune of the plebs Marcus Livius Drusus; the tribune of the plebs Marcus Fonteius; the tribune of the plebs Quintus Varius Severus Hybrida Sucronensis; the legate Publius Licinius Crassus Junior; the legate Marcus Valerius Messala."

Sulla paused, satisfied; every face was shocked.

"Yes, I know," he said gently. "Not until the list is read out can we fully appreciate how many of the great or the promising are gone. Seven consuls and seven praetors. Fourteen men eminently qualified to sit in judgment, comment upon laws and customs, guard the *mos maiorum*. Not to mention the six other names of men who would have led in time or joined the ranks of the leaders very soon. There are other names besides—names I have not read out, but which include tribunes of the plebs who made lesser reputations during their terms, yet were nonetheless experienced men."

"Oh, Lucius Cornelius, it is a tragedy!" said Flaccus Princeps Senatus, a catch in his voice.

"Yes, Lucius Valerius, it is that," Sulla agreed. "There are many names not on this list because they are not dead, but who are absent from this House for various reasons—on duty overseas, on duty elsewhere in Italy than Rome. Even in the winter hiatus of this war I have not managed to count more than one hundred men assembled in this body politic, though no senators resident in Rome are absent in this time of need. There is also a considerable list of senators at present in exile due to the activities of the Varian Commission or the Plautian Commission. And men like Publius Rutilius Rufus.

"Therefore, honored censors Publius Licinius and Lucius Julius, I ask you most earnestly to do everything in your power to fill our seats. Give the opportunity to men of substance and ambition in the city to join the disastrously thinned ranks of the Senate of Rome. And also appoint from among the *pedarii* those men who should be advanced to give their opinions and urged to take on more senior office. All too often there are not enough men present to make a quorum. How can the Senate of Rome purport to be the senior body in government if it cannot make a quorum?"

And that, concluded Sulla, was that. He had done what he could to keep Rome going, and given an inert pair of censors a public kick up the backside to do their duty. Now it was time to finish the war against the Italians.

PART VIII

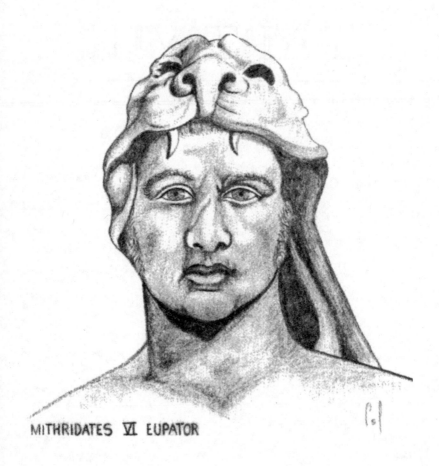

MITHRIDATES VI EUPATOR

The one aspect of government Sulla had completely overlooked had been invisible to everybody since the death of the much-missed Marcus Aemilius Scaurus; his successor, Lucius Valerius Flaccus, had made a halfhearted attempt to draw it to Sulla's attention, but quite lacked the forceful personality to do so. Nor could Sulla be blamed for his oversight. Italy had become the focus of the entire Roman world, and those physically embroiled in the mess could see no further than it.

One of the last duties Scaurus had attended to concerned the two dethroned kings, Nicomedes of Bithynia and Ariobarzanes of Cappadocia; the doughty old Princeps Senatus had sent a commission to Asia Minor to investigate the situation anent King Mithridates of Pontus. The delegation's leader was Manius Aquillius, he who had been Gaius Marius's valued legate at the battle of Aquae Sextiae, Marius's colleague in the fifth of his consulships, and victor of the Sicilian slave war. With Aquillius went two other commissioners, Titus Manlius Mancinus and Gaius Mallius Maltinus—and the two kings, Nicomedes and Ariobarzanes. The duty of the commission had been clearly delineated by Scaurus: it was to reinstate both sovereigns and warn Mithridates to remain behind his own borders.

Manius Aquillius had courted Scaurus strenuously to get the commission, as his finances were in desperate straits due to bad losses he had taken when the war against Italia had broken out. His governorship in Sicily ten years earlier had yielded him nothing but a prosecution upon his return; though acquitted, his reputation had rather undeservedly suffered. The gold his father had received from the fifth King Mithridates in return for the cession of most of Phrygia to Pontus had long gone, yet the odium of that deed continued to cling leechlike to the son. Scaurus, a firm adherent to the custom of hereditary posts—and understanding that the father would have talked about the area to the son—deemed it good sense to give Manius Aquillius the job of reinstating the two kings, and allowed him the additional privilege of choosing his own colleagues.

The result was a deputation dedicated more to avarice than to justice, the acquisition of money than the welfare of foreign peoples.

Before the first travel arrangements were made to get the commission to Asia Minor, Manius Aquillius had already concluded a highly satisfactory bargain with the seventy-year-old King Nicomedes, and a hundred talents of Bithynian gold had magically appeared at Manius Aquillius's bank. Had it not, so distressed were Aquillius's finances that he would have found himself under an injunction not to leave Rome, as all senators were obliged to seek formal permission to leave Italy. No chance to slip off undetected by banks and bankers, who kept a stern eye on the lists posted at rostra and Regia.

Having elected to sail rather than go overland on the Via Egnatia, the commission arrived at Pergamum in June of the previous year. It was received in some state by the governor of Asia Province, Gaius Cassius Longinus.

In Gaius Cassius the commissioner Manius Aquillius met his match when it came to greed and unscrupulousness; as each quickly discerned with considerable pleasure. Thus a plot was hatched that hot and sunny June in Pergamum at about the same time as Titus Didius was killed attacking Herculaneum. The object of the plot was to see how much gold the commissioners and the governor could squeeze out of the situation, and in particular squeeze out of territories bordering Pontus but not actually under the authority of Rome—namely Paphlagonia and Phrygia.

The Senate's letters to Mithridates of Pontus and Tigranes of Armenia commanding that they withdraw from Bithynia and Cappadocia were sent off from Pergamum by courier. No sooner had the bearers of the letters disappeared than Gaius Cassius ordered extra training and discipline for his one legion of auxiliaries, and called up the militia from one end of Asia Province to the other. Then, escorted by a small detachment of soldiers, the commissioners Aquillius, Manlius, and Mallius went off to Bithynia with King Nicomedes, while King Ariobarzanes remained in Pergamum with a suddenly very busy governor.

The power of Rome still worked. King Socrates found himself without a throne and took himself back to Pontus, King Nicomedes ascended that same throne, and King Ariobarzanes was bidden return to rule in Cappadocia. The three commissioners stayed in Nicomedia to while away the rest of the summer and firm their plan for an invasion of Paphlagonia, that strip of territory which separated Bithynia from Pontus along the shores of the Euxine Sea. The temples in Paphlagonia were rich in gold—which the disappointed commissioners had discovered Nicomedes was not. When the old man had fled to Rome the year before he had taken most of the contents of his treasury with him; it had all ended in the bank accounts of various Romans, from Marcus Aemilius Scaurus (not above accepting a little gift) to Manius Aquillius, with plenty of other greedy hands in between.

The discovery that Nicomedes lacked gold had led to some rancor among the three commissioners, Manlius and Mallius feeling they had been cheated, and Aquillius feeling he must bestir himself to find enough extra gold to satisfy them without breaking into his nest egg in Rome. Of course it was King Nicomedes who suffered. Three Roman noblemen badgered him incessantly to invade Paphlagonia, and threatened him with the loss of his throne if he failed to obey orders. Messages from Gaius Cassius in Pergamum reinforced the commission's stand, with the result that Nicomedes gave in and mobilized his modest but well-equipped army.

At the end of September the commissioners and old King Nicomedes marched into Paphlagonia, Aquillius leading the army, the King little better than an unwilling campaign guest. Burning to rub salt into the wounds of King Mithridates, Aquillius forced Nicomedes to issue certain instructions to the naval garrisons and fleets of Bithynia manning the Thracian Bosporus and the Hellespont; no vessel of Pontus was to pass between the Euxine Sea and the Aegean Sea. Defy Rome if you dare, King Mithridates! was the message implicit in this.

Everything fell out exactly as Manius Aquillius had planned. The Bithynian army marched along the coast of Paphlagonia taking towns and looting temples, the pile of golden artifacts and treasure grew, the big port of Amastris capitulated; and Pylaemenes, the ruler of inland Paphlagonia, joined his forces to those of the Roman invaders. At Amastris the three commissioners decided it was time for them to return to Pergamum, leaving the poor old King and his army to spend the winter somewhere between Amastris and Sinope, dangerously close to the border of Pontus.

It was in Pergamum halfway through November that the Romans received an embassage from King Mithridates, who so far had said nothing and done nothing. The chief ambassador was one Pelopidas, a cousin of the King's.

"My cousin King Mithridates humbly beseeches the proconsul Manius Aquillius to order King Nicomedes and his army to return to Bithynia forthwith," said Pelopidas, who was dressed in the attire of a Greek civilian, and had come to Pergamum without any kind of armed escort.

"That is impossible, Pelopidas," said Manius Aquillius, seated in his curule chair holding his ivory rod of power and surrounded by a dozen crimson-clad lictors bearing the axes in their *fasces*. "Bithynia is a sovereign state—Friend and Ally of the Roman People, admittedly, but fully in control of its own destiny. I cannot *order* King Nicomedes to do anything."

"Then, proconsul, my cousin King Mithridates humbly begs that you give him permission to defend himself and his realm against the depredations of Bithynia," said Pelopidas.

"Neither King Nicomedes nor the army of Bithynia is within Pontic territory," said Manius Aquillius. "I therefore strictly forbid your cousin King Mithridates to lift so much as one finger against King Nicomedes and his army. Under *no* circumstances—tell your King that, Pelopidas! Under *no* circumstances whatsoever."

Pelopidas sighed, hoisted his shoulders up and spread his hands wide in a gesture not Roman, and said, "Then the last thing I was instructed to tell you, proconsul, is that under the circumstances my cousin King Mithridates says the following: 'Even a man who knows he must lose will fight back!' "

"If your cousin the King fights back, he *will* lose," said Aquillius, and nodded to his lictors to show Pelopidas out.

A silence fell after the Pontic nobleman left, broken by a frowning Gaius Cassius when he said, "One of the Pontic barons with

Pelopidas told me that Mithridates intends to send a letter of protest directly to Rome."

Aquillius lifted an eyebrow. "What good will that do him?" he asked. "There's no one in Rome with time to listen."

But those in Pergamum were obliged to listen a month later, when Pelopidas returned.

"My cousin King Mithridates has sent me to repeat his plea that he be allowed to defend his country," said Pelopidas.

"His country isn't threatened, Pelopidas; therefore my answer is still no," said Manius Aquillius.

"Then my cousin the King has no choice except to go over your head, proconsul. He will formally complain to the Senate and People of Rome that Rome's commissioners in Asia Minor are supporting Bithynia in an act of aggression, and are simultaneously denying Pontus the right to fight back," said Pelopidas.

"Your cousin the precious King had better not, do you hear?" snapped Aquillius nastily. "As far as Pontus and the whole of Asia Minor are concerned, *I* am the Senate and People of Rome! Now take yourself off and don't come back!"

Pelopidas lingered in Pergamum for some time to find out what he could about the mysterious troop movements Gaius Cassius had put in train. While he was still there, news came that both Mithridates of Pontus and Tigranes of Armenia had broken the borders of Cappadocia, and that a son of Mithridates named Ariarathes—no one knew which of the several sons named Ariarathes this was—was once more trying to ascend the Cappadocian throne. Manius Aquillius immediately sent for Pelopidas and told him to instruct both Pontus and Armenia to withdraw from Cappadocia.

"They'll do as they're told because they're terrified of Roman reprisals," said Aquillius to Cassius complacently, and shivered. "It's *cold* in here, Gaius Cassius! Don't you think the resources of Asia Province will extend to a fire or two in the palace?"

By February, confidence in the governor's residence at Pergamum had risen so high that Aquillius and Cassius conceived an even bolder plan: why stop at the borders of Pontus? Why not teach the King of Pontus a much-needed lesson by invading Pontus itself? The legion of Asia Province was in fine fettle, the militia was encamped between Smyrna and Pergamum and was also in fine fettle, and Gaius Cassius had had yet another brilliant idea.

"We can add two more legions to our task force if we bring Quintus Oppius of Cilicia into it," he said to Manius Aquillius. "I shall send to Tarsus and command Quintus Oppius to come to Pergamum for a conference about the fate of Cappadocia. Oppius's imperium is only propraetorian, mine is proconsular. He *has* to obey me. I shall tell him that we plan to contain Mithridates by nipping him from behind rather than by invading Cappadocia."

"They say," said Aquillius dreamily, "that in Armenia Parva there are over seventy strongholds stuffed to the tops of their walls with gold belonging to Mithridates."

But Cassius, a warlike man from a warlike family, was not to be diverted. "We'll invade Pontus in four different places along the course of the river Halys," he said eagerly. "The Bithynian army can deal with Sinope and Amisus on the Euxine, then march inland along the Halys—that will give them plenty of forage, since they have the most cavalry and baggage animals. Aquillius, you will take my one legion of auxiliaries and strike at the Halys in Galatia. I'll lead the militia up the river Maeander and into Phrygia. Quintus Oppius can land in Attaleia and drive up through Pisidia. He and I will arrive on the Halys between you and the Bithynians. With four separate armies on his river roadway, we'll drive Mithridates to distraction. He won't know where he is—or what to do for the best. He's a petty king, my dear Manius Aquillius! More gold than soldiers."

"He won't stand a chance," said Aquillius, smiling, and still dreaming of seventy strongholds stuffed with gold.

Cassius cleared his throat ostentatiously. "There's only one thing we'll have to be careful of," he said in a different voice.

Manius Aquillius looked alert. "Oh?"

"Quintus Oppius is one of the old brigade—Rome forever, honor above all, perish the thought of making a little money from slightly suspicious extracurricular activities. We cannot do or say *anything* which might lead him to think the object of the exercise is not to see justice done in Cappadocia."

Aquillius giggled. "All the more for us!"

"So I think," said Gaius Cassius contentedly.

Pelopidas tried to ignore the sweat rolling from his scalp onto his brow and into his eyes, tried to position his hands so that their tremor would not be visible from the throne. "Thus, Great King, the proconsul Aquillius dismissed me from his presence," he concluded.

The King did not move so much as his lashes, and the look upon his face remained what it had been throughout the audience; impassive, expressionless, bland almost. At forty years of age, having held his throne now for twenty-three years, the sixth King Mithridates, called Eupator, had learned to conceal all save his mightiest displeasures. Not that the news Pelopidas had brought had not provoked a mighty displeasure; rather, it was news he had expected.

For two years he had been living in an accelerated atmosphere of hope, hope generated the day that he heard Rome was at war with her Italian Allies. Instinct had told him this was his chance, and he had gone so far as to write to Tigranes at the time, warn his son-in-law to be ready. When he received word that Tigranes was with him in anything he cared to do, he decided that the first thing he must do was to make the war in Italy as difficult for Rome as he could. So he had sent an embassage to the Italians Quintus Poppaedius Silo and Gaius Papius Mutilus in the new capital of Italica, and offered them money, arms, ships, even troops to augment their own. But to his astonishment, his ambassadors returned with empty hands. Silo and Mutilus refused the Pontic offer with outrage and contempt.

"Tell King Mithridates that Italia's quarrel with Rome is none of his business! Italia will do nothing to assist any foreign king make mischief against Rome" was their answer.

Like a prodded snail the King of Pontus had withdrawn into himself and sent Tigranes of Armenia an order to wait because the time was not right. Wondering if there would ever be a right time when even Italia, desperately in need of aid to win her battle for freedom and independence, could bite so savagely at the Pontic hand extended in friendship and dripping military largesse.

He dithered, just that little bit too apprehensive to make a firm decision and stick to it. One moment he was sure now was the time to declare outright war on Rome, the next moment he was not sure. Worrying, fretting, he kept all of this within himself; the King of Pontus could have no confidants and advisers extraordinary, even a son-in-law who was himself a great king. His court existed in a vacuum, no one able to say with certainty how the King felt, what his next move might be, whether there was a chance of war. All would welcome it, none wanted it.

Foiled in his overtures to the Italians, Mithridates then bethought himself of Macedonia, where the Roman province held an uneasy frontier a thousand miles long against the barbarian tribes to the north. Stir up trouble along that frontier, and Rome's full attention would become occupied with it. So Pontic agents were sent to water the seeds of an ever-present hatred of Rome among the Bessi and the Scordisci and the other tribes of Moesia and Thrace, with the result that Macedonia began to endure the worst outbreak of barbarian raids and incursions in many years. In the initial rush to do damage, the Scordisci got as far as Dodona in Epirus. As luck would have it, however, Roman Macedonia was blessed with a superb and incorrupt governor in Gaius Sentius, who was reinforced by a legate, Quintus Bruttius Sura, of even more formidable sinew.

When the barbarian unrest failed to prod Sentius and Bruttius Sura into sending to Rome for additional help, Mithridates turned his attention toward stirring up trouble within the province as well. Shortly after the King decided upon this course, there ap-

peared in Macedonia one Euphenes, who purported to be a direct
descendant of Alexander the Great (to whom he bore a startling
resemblance), and laid claim to the ancient and defunct throne of
Macedonia. The inhabitants of sophisticated places like Thessalonica and Pella saw through him at once, but the upcountry folk
espoused his cause ardently; alas for Mithridates, Euphenes proved
to lack a true martial spirit and any talent to organize his adherents into an army. Sentius and Bruttius Sura dealt with Euphenes
on a purely internal level and did not send urgently to Rome for
money and additional troops—the aim of the whole Pontic exercise.

So here he was, two years down the road from the outbreak of
war between Rome and her Italian Allies, no further toward ful-
filling his own ambitions. Dithering. Vacillating. Making life miserable for himself and his court. Fending off Tigranes, a more
aggressive man, if less intelligent. Wondering. Unable to confide
in anyone.

The King moved suddenly on his throne, and every courtier in
the room jumped. "What else did you discover during your
second—and very long—visit to Pergamum?" he asked Pelopidas.

"That Gaius Cassius the governor has placed his legion of Roman auxiliaries on a war footing and has been training and equipping two legions of militia as well, O Mighty One." Pelopidas
licked his lips, anxious to demonstrate that, though his mission
had been a failure, his zeal for his King's cause remained suitably
fanatical. "I have an agent now within the governor's palace at
Pergamum, Great King. Just before I left he told me that he thinks
Gaius Cassius and Manius Aquillius are planning to invade Pontus in the spring, in conjunction with Nicomedes of Bithynia and
his ally Pylaemenes of Paphlagonia. And also, it seems likely, in
conjunction with the governor of Cilicia, Quintus Oppius, who
came to Pergamum to confer with Gaius Cassius."

"Do you know if this projected invasion has the official sanction of the Senate and People of Rome?" asked the King.

"Gossip in the governor's palace says not, O Great One."

"Of Manius Aquillius I would expect it, if the pup is of the same kind as the dog was in the days of my father. Greed for gold. *My* gold." The full, very red lips stretched back to reveal large yellow teeth. "It seems the governor of the Roman Asian province is of like mind. And Quintus Oppius of Cilicia. A gold-hungry trio!"

"As to the governor of Cilicia, it would appear not, O Mighty King," said Pelopidas. "They are careful to give him to think that this is an operation mounted against our presence in Cappadocia. I gather Quintus Oppius is what the Romans call an honorable man."

The King lapsed into silence, lips working in and out like a fish, eyes looking into nothing. It makes a difference when they threaten one's own lands, thought King Mithridates. I am forced to stand with my back pressed hard against my frontiers, I am supposed to lay down my arms and allow these so-called rulers of the world to rape my country. The country which harbored me when I was a fugitive child, the country I love more than life itself. The country I want to see rule the world.

"They shall not do it!" he said aloud, very strongly.

Every head came up, but the King said nothing more; in and out went the lips, in and out, in and out.

The time is here. It has finally come, thought King Mithridates. My court has listened to this telling of the news from Pergamum, and the court is making a judgment. Not on the Romans. A judgment on me. If I lie down tamely while these gold-hungry Roman commissioners prate that *they* are the Senate and People of Rome—and talk of broaching my borders—my subjects will despise me. My reputation will suffer so badly that I will cease to make them fear me. And then some of my blood-relatives will deem me ripe for replacement as King of Pontus. I have sons of an age to rule now, each one supported by a mother just dying for power, and there are my cousins of the blood royal—Pelopidas, Archelaus, Neoptolemus, Leonippus. If I lie down under this like the cur the Romans think I am, I will not be King of Pontus any longer. I will be dead.

So it is war against Rome. The time has finally come. Not by my choice, and probably not by theirs. Conjured out of nothing by three gold-hungry Roman commissioners. My mind is made up. I will go to war against Rome.

And, having made his decision, Mithridates felt an enormous weight lift from him, a vast shadow suddenly vanish from the back of his mind; he sat on his throne and seemed to swell like a great golden toad, eyes glittering. Pontus was going to war. Pontus was going to make an example of Manius Aquillius and Gaius Cassius. Pontus was going to own the Roman Asian province. And Pontus was going to cross the Hellespont into eastern Macedonia, march down the Via Egnatia into the west. Pontus would sail out of the Euxine into the Aegean, spread ever westward. Until Italy and Rome herself lay before those Pontic armies and fleets. The King of Pontus would also be the King of Rome. The King of Pontus would be the mightiest sovereign in the history of the world, a greater by far than Alexander the Great. His sons would rule in places as remote as Spain and Mauretania, his daughters would be queens of every land from Armenia to Numidia to Farthest Gaul. All the treasures of the world would belong to the King of the World, all the beautiful women, all the lands *everywhere*! Then he remembered his son-in-law Tigranes, and smiled. Let Tigranes have the Kingdom of the Parthians, spread eastward to India and the misty countries beyond.

But the King didn't say he was going to war against Rome. He opened his mouth and said, "Send for Aristion."

A tenseness had entered into the court, though none knew exactly what was happening to the awesome presence upon the gem-studded throne. Just that something was happening.

There came into the audience chamber a tall and remarkably handsome Greek in tunic and *chlamys* wrap; without awkwardness or self-consciousness he prostrated himself before the King.

"Rise, Aristion. I have work for you."

The Greek rose to stand looking attentively adoring; it was a pose he practised in front of the mirror King Mithridates had most thoughtfully placed in his luxurious room, and Aristion flattered himself he had managed to poise himself on the exact line between a sycophancy the King would despise and an independence the King would condemn. For almost a year he had dwelt at the Pontic court in Sinope, having fetched up so far from his home in Athens because he was by trade a Peripatetic, a wandering philosopher of the school founded by the successors of Aristotle, and had thought to find fatter pickings in lands less well endowed with such as he than Greece, Rome, Alexandria. By sheer luck he had found the King of Pontus in need of his services, for the King had been uncomfortably aware of his educational shortcomings ever since his visit to Asia Province ten years earlier.

Careful to couch his instruction in purely conversational terms, Aristion filled the King's ears with his tales of the vanished might of Greece and then Macedonia, the repulsive and unwelcome might of Rome, the conditions which applied in business and commerce, the geography and history of the world. And eventually Aristion had come to think of himself as the King's arbiter of elegance and sophistication rather than as the King's pedagogue.

"The thought that I can be of some use to you fills me with delight, O Mighty Mithridates," said Aristion in mellifluous tones.

The King then proceeded to demonstrate that—while he may have *feared* to war against Rome—he had been thinking for years about exactly *how* he was going to war against Rome.

"Are you wellborn enough to cultivate political power in Athens?" asked the King unexpectedly.

Aristion didn't betray his surprise; he just looked charming. "I am, O Great One," he lied.

In actual fact he was the son of a slave, but all that had been a long time ago. No one remembered it, even in Athens. Appearance was all. And his appearance was impressively aristocratic.

"Then I require you to return to Athens at once and begin to amass political power there," said the King. "I need a loyal agent in Greece with sufficient clout to stir up Greek resentment against Rome. How you do it, I do not care. But when the armies and fleets of Pontus invade the lands on both sides of the Aegean Sea, I want Athens—and Greece!—in the palm of my hand."

A gasp and a murmur rippled through those present in the throne room, followed by a thrill of excitement, of martial fervor—the King was not going to lie down under the foot of Rome after all!

"We are with you, my King!" cried Archelaus, beaming.

"Your sons thank you, Great One!" cried Pharnaces, senior son.

Mithridates swelled up even more, so deep was his flush of pleasure. Why hadn't he seen earlier how dangerously close to rebellion and extinction he had come? These his subjects and blood relatives were *hungry* for war against Rome! And he was ready. He had been ready for years.

"We do not march until the Roman commissioners and the governors of Asia Province and Cilicia have marched," he said. "The moment our borders are breached, we retaliate. I want the fleets armed and manned, I want the armies in train to move. If the Romans think to take Pontus, I think to take Bithynia and Asia Province. Cappadocia is already mine, and will remain mine because I have armies enough to leave my son Ariarathes with his forces." The slightly bulging green eyes rested upon Aristion. "What are you waiting for, philosopher? Go to Athens with gold from my treasury to help your cause. But take heed! No one must know you are my agent."

"I understand, O Mighty King, I do understand!" cried Aristion loudly, and backed from the room.

"Pharnaces, Machares, Young Mithridates, Young Ariarathes, Archelaus, Pelopidas, Neoptolemus, Leonippus, remain here with me," said the King curtly. "The rest of you can go."

In April of the year Lucius Cornelius Sulla and Quintus Pompeius Rufus were consuls, the Roman invasion of Galatia and Pontus began. While the third Nicomedes wept and wrung his hands together and pleaded to be allowed to return to Bithynia, the Paphlagonian prince Pylaemenes ordered the army of Nicomedes to advance on Sinope. Manius Aquillius took the field at the head of the one legion of Roman auxiliaries present in Asia

Province and marched from Pergamum overland through Phrygia, intending to broach the Pontic border to the north of the great salt lake, Tatta. There was a trade route on this line, which meant Aquillius was able to move fairly quickly. Gaius Cassius picked up his two legions of militia outside Smyrna and took them up the valley of the Maeander into Phrygia on a line heading for the tiny trading settlement of Prymnessus. In the meantime Quintus Oppius had sailed from Tarsus to Attaleia and marched his two legions into Pisidia on a line which led him just to the west of Lake Limnae.

At the very beginning of May the Bithynian army crossed into Pontus and reached the Amnias, a tributary of the Halys flowing inland but parallel to the coast around Sinope. The strategy Pylaemenes had adopted consisted of a march from the junction of the Amnias and the Halys northward to the sea, where he intended to divide his forces to attack Sinope and Amisus simultaneously. Unfortunately the army of Bithynia encountered a huge Pontic army under the brothers Archelaus and Neoptolemus on the Amnias before it could reach the wider valley of the Halys, and went down to a crushing defeat. Camp, baggage, troops, arms, everything was lost. Except old King Nicomedes. He had taken a party of barons and slaves he could trust and left his army to its inevitable fate, pointing his own unerring nose toward Rome.

At almost the same moment in time as the Bithynian army met the brothers Archelaus and Neoptolemus, Manius Aquillius and his legion came over a ridge and looked down upon Lake Tatta in the distant south. But the vista had no power to charm Aquillius. Below him on the plain he saw an army vaster than the lake, equipment glittering, ranks betraying to an expert eye all the signs of superb discipline and confidence. No barbarian horde of Germans, this! One hundred thousand Pontic infantry and cavalry waiting for him to fall into their jaws. With the lightning rapidity only a Roman general truly understood, Aquillius turned his meager little force around and made a run for it. As he neared the Sangarius River not far from Pessinus—all that gold and he couldn't tarry to take it!—the Pontic army caught up with his rear and began to swallow him whole. Like King Nicomedes, Aquillius abandoned his army to its inevitable fate and fled with his senior officers and two fellow commissioners across the Mysian mountains.

King Mithridates himself went after Gaius Cassius, but his insecurity got the better of him; he began to dither, with the result that Cassius heard about the defeats of the Bithynians and Aquillius before Mithridates reached him. The governor of Asia Province picked up his army and retreated southward and eastward to the big trade route crossroads town of Apameia, where he went to earth behind its strong fortifications. South and west of Cassius again, Quintus Oppius also heard the news of defeat and elected to stand at Laodiceia, right in the path of Mithridates as he came down the Maeander.

Thus the Pontic army personally commanded by the King came across Quintus Oppius before it located Cassius. Himself wanting to withstand a siege, Oppius soon discovered that the Laodiceians were not of the same mind. The townspeople opened the gates to the King of Pontus strewing flower petals in his tracks, and handed Quintus Oppius over to him as a special gift. The Cilician troops were bidden go home by the same route as they had come, but the King detained their governor, who was tethered to a post in the agora of Laodiceia. Roaring with laughter, the King himself urged the populace to pelt Quintus Oppius with filth, rotten eggs, decaying vegetables, anything soft and noisome. No stones, no pieces of wood. For the King had remembered that Pelopidas had described Quintus Oppius as an honorable man. After two days Oppius was released more or less unharmed, and sent back under a Pontic escort to Tarsus. On foot, a very long walk.

When Gaius Cassius learned of the fate which had befallen Quintus Oppius, he abandoned his militia in Apameia and fled on a sorry horse toward the coast at Miletus, keeping the Maeander River between himself and Mithridates, and traveling completely alone. He succeeded in avoiding the Pontic net around Laodiceia, but his identity was discovered in the town of Nysa and he was haled before its

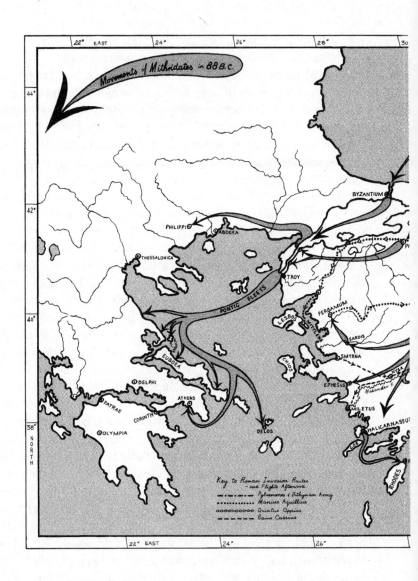

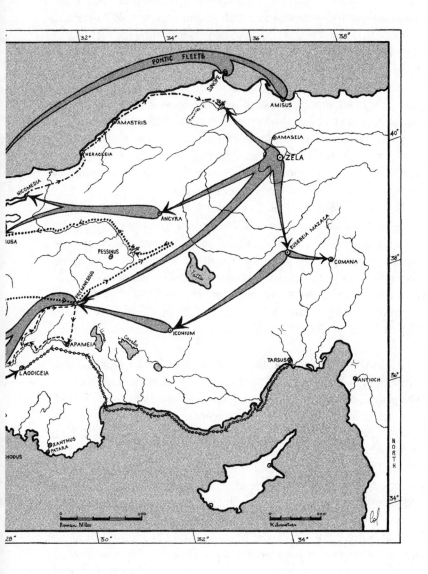

ethnarch, one Chaeremon. Gasping from fear turned to delight, Cassius found Chaeremon to be an ardent adherent of Rome and anxious to do anything he could to help. Bemoaning the fact that he dared not tarry, Cassius snatched a good meal and mounted a fresh horse, then rode at the gallop to Miletus, where he located a fast ship willing to take him to Rhodes. Safely arrived in Rhodes, he faced the most appalling task of all—the composition of a letter to the Senate and People of Rome that would manage to convince them of the seriousness of the Asian situation without highlighting his own frailties. Naturally enough this Herculean task was not completed in a day—or even in a month. Terrified of betraying his guilt, Gaius Cassius Longinus procrastinated.

By the end of June all Bithynia and Asia Province had fallen to King Mithridates, save for a few scattered intrepid communities which trusted to their fortifications, their inaccessibility, and the might of Rome. A quarter of a million soldiers of Pontus sat themselves down in lush green pastures from Nicomedia to Mylasa. Since the bulk of them were northern barbarians—Cimmerians, Scythians, Sarmatians, Roxolani, and Caucasians—only their healthy fear of King Mithridates prevented them from running amok.

The various Ionian, Aeolian, and Dorian Greek cities and sea-ports of Asia Province made absolutely sure they treated this eastern potentate with all the obsequious prostrations his sort desired. Hatred of forty years of Roman occupation now became an immense asset to King Mithridates, who encouraged anti-Roman sentiment by proclaiming that no taxes, tithes, or duties would be levied that year, nor for the five years to follow. Those who owed money to Roman or Italian lenders were absolved of their debts. As a result, Asia Province was inspired to hope that life under Pontus would be better than life under Rome.

The King came down the Maeander and headed north along the coast for one of his favorite cities, Ephesus. Here he took up temporary residence and dispensed justice, further endearing himself to the local people of Asia Province by proclaiming that any detachments of militia surrendering to him would not only be

forgiven and freed, but also given money to go home. Those who
hated Rome the most—or at least the most loudly—were elevated
to the senior ranks of citizens in every town, city, district. Lists of
people known to be Roman sympathizers or employees grew rapidly; the informers were thriving.

Beneath all the rejoicing and the fawning attentions, however,
lay the terror of those who understood only too well the complete
cruelty and capriciousness of eastern kings, how superficial was
any apparent kindness. High in favor one moment, head separated from body the next. And no one could tell when the balance
would tip.

At the end of June in Ephesus the King of Pontus issued three
orders: all were secret, but the third one was most secret of all.

How much he enjoyed everything about those orders! Who was to
go where, who was to do what—oh, the merry dances his dolls
would caper! Let other, lesser beings define and refine the details—to
him alone must the credit go for masterminding the vast and inter-
locking design. What a design! Humming and whistling, he bustled
around the palace driving several hundred co-opted scribes to the
writing of those orders, the sealing of them, a huge labor done in the
space of one day. And when the last packet for the last courier was
sealed, he shepherded the scribes into the palace courtyard and had
his bodyguard cut their throats. Dead men kept the best secrets!

The first order was sent to Archelaus, not in great favor with
Mithridates at the moment; he had tried to take the city of Magnesia-
under-Sipylus by frontal assault, was soundly trounced, and himself wounded. However, Archelaus was still his best general, so to
him was the first order sent. One packet only. It instructed him to
take command of all the Pontic fleets and sail out of the Euxine
into the Aegean at the end of Gamelion, a month hence; Gamelion
was Roman Quinctilis.

The second order was also a single packet. It was sent to the
King's son Young Ariarathes (a different son from that Ariara-
thes who was King of Cappadocia), and instructed him to lead a
Pontic army one hundred thousand strong across the Hellespont

and into eastern Macedonia at the end of Gamelion, a month hence.

The third order was distributed through several hundred packets sent to every town, city, district or community from Nicomedia in Bithynia to Cnidus in Caria to Apameia in Phrygia, and was addressed in each case to the chief magistrate. It decreed that every single Roman, Latin, and Italian citizen in Asia Minor—men, women, children—must be put to death together with their slaves at the end of Gamelion, a month hence.

The third one was his favorite order, the one which caused the King to hug himself and chuckle with glee, to give an occasional skip as he walked about Ephesus smiling from ear to ear. After the end of Gamelion there would be no Roman presence in Asia Minor. And when he was finished with Rome and the Romans, every last one from the Pillars of Hercules to the First Cataract on the Nilus would be dead. Rome would be no more.

At the beginning of Gamelion, hugging his secrets, the King of Pontus left Ephesus and journeyed north to Pergamum, where a special treat was in store for him.

The two other commissioners and all Manius Aquillius's officers elected to flee to Pergamum, but Manius Aquillius himself went to Mytilene on the island of Lesbos, intending there to take ship for Rhodes, where a message had informed him Gaius Cassius was lying low. But no sooner did he land on Lesbos than Manius Aquillius became ill with an enteric fever, and could not travel further. When the Lesbians heard of the fall of Asia Province (of which they were officially a part), they thoughtfully shipped the Roman proconsul to King Mithridates as a special token of their regard.

Arrived in the little port of Atarneus, opposite Mytilene, Manius Aquillius was chained to the saddlebow of a huge Bastarnian horseman and dragged all the way to Pergamum, at which city the King was now waiting eagerly for his treat. Constantly stumbling and falling, pelted with filth, jeered at, derided, reviled, Aquillius actually lived to complete the journey, sick though he was. But when Mithridates inspected him in Pergamum he saw at once that if this treatment were to be continued, Aquillius would die. And that would spoil some particularly delicious plans Mithridates had devised for Manius Aquillius!

So the Roman proconsul was tied into the saddle of an ass looking backward over its rump and driven mercilessly up and down the entire area around Pergamum to show the citizens of this erstwhile Roman capital how the King of Pontus felt about a Roman proconsul, and how little he feared retribution.

Finally, caked in filth and reduced to the merest shadow of a man, Manius Aquillius was led before the author of his torments. Sitting in state upon a golden throne mounted on a costly dais in the middle of the Pergamum agora, the King gazed down upon the man who had refused to send the army of Bithynia away, refused to let Mithridates defend his realm, refused to allow Mithridates to go over his head and complain directly to the Senate and People of Rome.

It was in that moment when he looked upon the bent and putrid form of Manius Aquillius that King Mithridates of Pontus lost the last vestige of his fear of Rome. What *had* he been frightened of? Why *had* he backed down before this ludicrous manifest weakling? He, Mithridates of Pontus, was far mightier than Rome! Four little armies, less than twenty thousand men! It was Manius Aquillius who personified Rome—not Gaius Marius, not Lucius Cornelius Sulla. The King's concept of Rome had been a myth perpetuated by two utterly atypical Roman men! The real Rome stood here at his feet.

"Proconsul!" cried the King sharply.

Aquillius looked up, but had not the energy to speak.

"Proconsul of Rome, I have decided to give you the gold you coveted from me."

Up onto the dais his guards drove Manius Aquillius and forced him down onto a low stool placed some distance to the front and left of the King. His arms from shoulders to hands were bound tightly against his body with broad straps, then one guard took hold of the straps on his right side and another took hold of the straps on his left side, giving him no opportunity to move.

There came a smith bearing a red-hot crucible in a pair of tongs. It was of a size to contain several cups of molten metal, and smoke rose from it, and an acrid, scorching smell.

A third guard went round behind Aquillius, took a fistful of his hair, and pulled his head back; the guard then took his nose between the fingers of the other hand, and pinched his nostrils cruelly shut. The reflex to breathe could not be disobeyed; Manius Aquillius opened his mouth and gasped. Instantly a beautiful turgid glittering river of liquid gold was poured down his air-hungry throat, more and more as he screamed and threshed and tried vainly to rise from his stool, until at last he died, mouth and chin and chest a frozen cascade of solidified gold.

"Cut him open and get every last drop of it back," said King Mithridates, and watched intently while all the gold was meticulously scraped from the inside and the outside of Manius Aquillius.

"Throw his carcass to the dogs," said King Mithridates, got up from his throne, came down to the level of the dais and stepped unconcernedly across the twisted and mangled remains of Manius Aquillius, proconsul of Rome.

Everything was going splendidly! No one knew that better than King Mithridates as he strolled the wind-cooled terraces of Pergamum atop its mountain and waited for the end of the month of Gamelion, which was Roman Quinctilis. Word had come from Aristion in Athens that he too had been successful.

> Nothing will stop us now, O Mighty Mithridates, for Athens will show Greece the way. I started my campaign by speaking about the old pre-eminence and wealth of Athens, for it is my opinion that a people past its prime looks back to the days of glory with exquisitely keen nostalgia, and is therefore easy to seduce with promises of a return to those days of glory. Thus did I speak in the Agora for six months, slowly grind-

ing down my opposition and gathering adherents. I even persuaded my audience that Carthage had allied itself with you against Rome, and my audience believed me! So much for the old saw that Athenians are the best educated men in the world. Not one of them knew that Carthage was obliterated by Rome nearly fifty years ago. Amazing.

I write because I have the pleasure to tell you that I have just been elected military leader of Athens—the time as I write is halfway through normal Poseideon. I was also given the power to choose my own colleagues. Naturally I have chosen men who firmly believe that the salvation of our Greek world is in your hands, Great King, and who cannot wait for the day when you crush Rome beneath your lion-booted heel.

Athens is now completely mine, including the Piraeus. Unfortunately the Roman elements and my avowed enemies fled before I could lay hands on them, but those who were foolish enough to stay—mostly rich Athenians who could not be brought to believe they stood in danger—have perished. I have confiscated all property belonging to the exiled and the dead, and put it into a fund to finance our war against the Romans.

What I promised my voters I would do, I have to do, but it will not inconvenience your own campaign, O Great King. I promised to take the island of Delos back from the Romans who now run it. Wonderfully profitable emporium that it is, the income from it was what kept Athens so affluent at the height of her power. At the beginning of Gamelion, my friend Apellicon (an excellent admiral and a skilled general) will mount an expedition against Delos. A rotten apple, the island will have no chance against us.

And that is all for the present, my Lord and Master. The city of Athens is yours and the port of the

Piraeus is open for your ships when and if you need them.

The King did need them, the Piraeus and the city of Athens behind it, connected by the Long Walls. For at the end of Quinctilis—Gamelion to the Greeks—the fleets of Archelaus issued out of the Hellespont and spilled down the western side of the Aegean Sea. They numbered three hundred decked war galleys of three or more banks, over one hundred undecked two-banker biremes, and fifteen hundred transports stuffed with troops and marines. Archelaus wasted no thought for the Asia Province littoral, as it was already in the hands of his King. He was intent upon establishing the Pontic presence in Greece so that the body of Macedonia would be crushed between two Pontic armies—his own in Greece and that of Young Ariarathes in the eastern part of Macedonia.

Young Ariarathes had also kept to the timetable given to him by his father, the King. At the end of Quinctilis he transported his hundred thousand men across the Hellespont and began to march along the narrow coastal strip of Thracian Macedonia, using the Roman engineered and built Via Egnatia. He found himself completely unopposed, set up permanent bases at Abdera on the sea and Philippi slightly inland, and continued westward toward the first formidable Roman settlement, the governor's city of Thessalonica.

And at the end of Quinctilis the Roman, Latin and Italian citizens resident in Bithynia, Asia Province, Phrygia and Pisidia were murdered down to the last man, woman, child, slave. In this most secret of his three orders Mithridates had displayed great cunning. For instead of using his own men to implement it, the King had directed that each local community of Aeolian or Ionian or Dorian Greeks should do the killing. Many areas hailed the decree with joy and experienced no difficulty assembling a force of volunteers eager to kill their Roman oppressors. But other areas were aghast and found it impossible to persuade anyone to kill Romans. In Tralles, the *ethnarch* was obliged to hire a band of Phrygian mercenaries to do murder on behalf of Tralles; other reluctant districts followed suit, hoping thus to transfer the guilt to the shoulders of strangers.

Eighty thousand Roman, Latin and Italian citizens and their families died in one single day, and seventy thousand slaves. The slaughter went on from Nicomedia in Bithynia all the way to Cnidus in Caria and as far inland as Apameia. No one was spared; nor was anyone hidden and assisted to flee; terror of King Mithridates far outweighed human compassion. Had Mithridates used his own soldiers to carry out the massacre, the blame for it would have rested with Mithridates entirely; but by forcing the Greek communities to do his dirty work for him, he ensured that they too would bear the blame. And the Greeks understood the King's reasoning perfectly. Life with King Mithridates of Pontus suddenly didn't seem any better than life with Rome, despite the remission of taxes.

Many of the persecuted sought asylum in temples, only to find no asylum was offered; they were carried out and dispatched still crying to this god or that god for refuge. Refusing to leave go of altars or statues and continuing to cling with fingers made superhuman by terror, some had their hands chopped off before being dragged away from holy ground and put to death.

Worst of all was the concluding clause of the general order of execution personally sealed by King Mithridates: no Roman or Latin or Italian or slave of Roman or Latin or Italian was to be burned or buried. The corpses were taken as far from human habitation as possible and left to rot in ravines, closed valleys, on the tops of mountains, and at the bottom of the sea. Eighty thousand Romans and Latins and Italians and seventy thousand slaves. One hundred and fifty thousand people. The birds of the air and the scavengers of earth and water dined well that Sextilis, for not one community dared to disobey and bury its victims; King Mithridates took great pleasure in journeying from place to place to view the enormous heaps of dead.

Just a very few Romans did escape death. These were the exiles, stripped of their citizenships and sentenced not to return to Rome. And among them they included one Publius Rutilius Rufus, friend of the Roman great, currently citizen of Smyrna held in honor and respect, producer of scurrilous pen portraits of men like Catulus Caesar and Metellus Numidicus Piggle-wiggle.

All in all, thought King Mithridates at the beginning of the month of Anthesterion, which was Sextilis to the Romans, things could not have looked better. His satraps were ensconced in the seats of government from Miletus to Andramyttium in Asia Province, and across the border in Bithynia. No more kings would be forthcoming for Bithynia. The only candidate Mithridates might have permitted to ascend the throne was dead. After Socrates returned to Pontus he irritated the King by whining incessantly, and was put to death to shut him up. The whole of Anatolia north of Lycia, Pamphylia and Cilicia now belonged to Pontus, and the rest would be his very soon.

Nothing, however, pleased the King quite as much as did the massacre of the Romans and Latins and Italians. Every time he came across another place where thousands of bodies had been dumped to rot, he beamed, he laughed, he rejoiced. He had made no distinction between Roman and Italian, despite the fact that he knew Rome and Italy were at war. A phenomenon no one was better able to understand than Mithridates—it was brother against brother, with power the prize.

Yes, everything was going splendidly. His son Young Mithridates was regent in Pontus (though the prudent King had taken his son's wife and children along on his march to Asia Province just to make sure Young Mithridates behaved himself); his son Ariarathes was King of Cappadocia; Phrygia, Bithynia, Galatia, and Paphlagonia were all royal satrapies under the personal rule of some of his elder sons; and his son-in-law Tigranes of Armenia was at liberty to do as he pleased east of Cappadocia as long as he didn't tread on the Pontic toes. Let Tigranes conquer Syria and Egypt; it would keep him busy. Mithridates frowned. In Egypt the populace would tolerate no foreign king. Which meant a puppet Ptolemy. If such a personage could be found. But certainly the queens of Egypt would be descendants of Mithridates; no daughter of Tigranes could be allowed to usurp a position destined for a daughter of Mithridates.

Most impressive of all was the success of the King's fleets—if, that is, he ignored the miserable failure of Aristion and his "excellent admiral and skilled general" Apellicon; the Athenian invasion of Delos had turned into a fiasco. But having taken the islands of the Cyclades, Archelaus's admiral Metrophanes went on to take Delos and put another twenty thousand Romans, Latins, and Italians to death there. The Pontic general then bestowed Delos upon Athens to make sure that Aristion stayed in power; the Pontic fleets needed the Piraeus as their western base.

All Euboea was now in Pontic hands, as was the island of Sciathos and a great deal of Thessaly around the Bay of Pagasae, including the vital ports of Demetrias and Methone. Because of their northern Greek conquests, Pontic forces were able to block the roads from Thessaly into central Greece, a discomfort which decided most of the rest of Greece to declare for Mithridates. The Peloponnese, Boeotia, Laconia, and all of Attica now hailed the King of Pontus fervently as their deliverer from the Romans—and sat back, pure spectators, to watch the armies and fleets of Mithridates crush Macedonia like a boot on a beetle.

But the crushing of Macedonia proved—for the time being, anyway—an impossibility. Caught between a suddenly antagonistic Greece and the advancing Pontic land forces on the Via Egnatia, Gaius Sentius and Quintus Bruttius Sura didn't panic, didn't concede defeat. They hustled to call up as many auxiliaries as they could, and put them into camp alongside the two Roman legions which were all Macedonia had to counter Mithridates. Pontus would not take Macedonia without paying a bitter price.

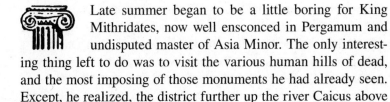 Late summer began to be a little boring for King Mithridates, now well ensconced in Pergamum and undisputed master of Asia Minor. The only interesting thing left to do was to visit the various human hills of dead, and the most imposing of those monuments he had already seen. Except, he realized, the district further up the river Caicus above

which Pergamum sat. There were two towns in Asia Province named Stratoniceia. The greater of them, situated in Caria, was still stubbornly holding out against a Pontic besieging force. The lesser Stratoniceia lay further inland than Pergamum upon the Caicus, and vowed itself completely loyal to Mithridates. So when the King rode into the town, its people turned out en masse to cheer him and throw flower petals before his triumphant progress.

In the crowd he set eyes upon a Greek girl called Monima, and had her brought to him immediately. So pale was her coloring that her hair seemed white and her brows and lashes invisible, which endowed her with an oddly bald kind of beauty; one close look, and the King added her to his wives, so rare and strange was she, with her lustrous dark pink eyes. He encountered no opposition from her father, Philopoemon, especially after he took Philopoemon south with him (and Monima) to Ephesus, where the King installed his father-in-law as satrap of the region.

Enjoying the diversions Ephesus was famous for—and enjoying his albino bride too—the King devoted enough time to business to send a laconic message to Rhodes demanding that it surrender itself and the refugee governor, Gaius Cassius Longinus. The answer, swiftly delivered, was a firm no to both requests; Rhodes was a Friend and Ally of the Roman People, and would honor its commitment to the death if necessary.

For the first time since he had set his campaign in motion, Mithridates had a temper tantrum. While his Pontic court and the more enterprising of the Ephesian sycophants cowered, the King ranted up and down his audience chamber until his rage blew out and he subsided to a glowering mass upon his throne, chin in hand, lips pouting, the marks of tears upon his fleshy cheeks.

From that moment he lost interest in every other enterprise he had started; he bent his energies exclusively upon securing the submission of Rhodes. How dared it say no to *him*! Did such a little place as Rhodes think it could hold out against the might of Pontus? Well, soon it would find out it didn't stand a chance.

His own fleets were too heavily involved in maneuvers on the western side of the Aegean to tap into their numbers for such an insignificant campaign as the one against little island Rhodes; so instead the King demanded that Smyrna, Ephesus, Priene, Miletus, Halicarnassus and the islands of Chios and Samos donate him all the ships he needed. Of land troops he had plenty, as he had kept two armies in Asia Province; but thanks to the dogged resistance of Lycian Patara and Termessus, he could not get those troops to the logical place from which to launch a land invasion of Rhodes—namely the beaches and coves of Lycia. The Rhodian navy was deservedly formidable of reputation, and was concentrated upon the western side of Rhodes overlooking that sea which washed down from Halicarnassus and Cnidus. But, unable to use Lycia, down these sea-lanes must the invasion forces of Mithridates pass.

He demanded transports by the hundreds and as many war galleys as Asia Province could find, ordering that they congregate in Halicarnassus—to which city, so beloved of Gaius Marius, he brought one of his armies for embarkation. And at the end of September he sailed, his own gigantic completely enclosed "sixteener" in the midst of the crowd, easily distinguished by the gold and purple throne erected under a canopy on the poop. Here he sat, master of all he surveyed, and reveling in it.

Cumbersome and slow though the biggest of the warships were, still any armed galley moved faster than the transports, a motley collection of all kinds of coastal cargo boats never designed to do more than hug the contours of bays and headlands. Thus by the time the forerunners of the fleet rounded the tip of the Cnidan peninsula and faced the open water of the Carpathian Sea, the enormous number of vessels was strung out all the way back to Halicarnassus, where the last of the transports were even then just leaving harbor, packed with terrified Pontic soldiers.

Manning light and very fast trireme galleys which were only partially decked, the Rhodian navy appeared on the horizon and headed straight for the makeshift Pontic fleet. It was no part of Rhodian sea tactics to employ the kind of heavy "sixteener" in which King Mithridates himself sat. These capital ships carried vast numbers of marines and many pieces of artillery; but the Rhodians despised the efficacy of artillery in sea battles and didn't keep still for long enough to allow their ships to be boarded by marines. The Rhodian navy's reputation had been won because of the speed and the extreme maneuverability of its vessels, able to dart at will between lumbering capital ships; the crews could stroke so strongly on a ramming charge that sheer speed more than compensated for lack of weight, and the bronze-reinforced oaken beak of a Rhodian trireme could drive deeply into the side of the heftiest "sixteener." Holing the enemy's ships was the only way to win decisively at sea, said the Rhodians.

When the Pontic fleet sighted the Rhodian navy, all was readied for a mighty battle. But it appeared Rhodes was only attempting a sally, for after making the Pontic galleys dizzy at the speed of their gyrations, the Rhodians turned and made off without doing more than stoving in the sides of two particularly inept five-bankers. However, before the Rhodians did depart the scene, they succeeded in giving King Mithridates the fright of his life. This was actually his first engagement at sea; he had done all his sailing within the Euxine, where not even the sauciest pirate would have dared to attack a ship of the Pontic navy.

Excited and fascinated, the King sat upon his gold and purple throne with his eyes trying to go everywhere at once; it did not occur to him that he himself stood in any danger. He had swiveled to his extreme left to watch the antics of a superbly sailed Rhodian galley some distance off his stem when his own huge ship lurched, groaned, shuddered convulsively, and the sounds of many oars snapping off like twigs became intermingled with cries of dismay and alarm.

His sudden and utterly overwhelming panic was over almost before it began; but not quickly enough. In the midst of his brief yet total terror, the King of Pontus shat himself. It went everywhere, solid faeces mixed with what seemed an incredible amount of more liquid bowel contents, a stinking brown mess all over the gold-encrusted purple cloth of his cushion, trickling down the legs of his throne, running down his own legs into the manes of the golden lions upon the flaps of his boots, pooling and plopping on the deck around his feet when he jumped up. *And there was nowhere to go!* He could not conceal it from the amazed eyes of his attendants and officers, he could not conceal it from the sailors below amidships who had looked up instinctively to make sure their King was safe.

Then he discovered that his ship had not been rammed at all. One of his own vessels, a big and clumsy "sixteener" from the isle of Chios, had blundered broadside into his own ship's beam and shorn off every oar down one side of each galley.

Was that amazement in their eyes? Or was it amusement? The King's bulging orbs glared with frightful fury from one face to the next and watched every face flush red, then pale like a transparent goblet suddenly emptied of wine.

"I'm ill!" he shouted. "There's something wrong, I'm ill! Help me, you fools!"

The stillness broke. People rushed at him from every side, cloths seemed to pop into existence from nowhere; two really quick thinkers found buckets and doused the King with seawater. It was when the cold contents of those pails slapped against his legs that the King bethought him of a better way to deal with this ghastly situation; he threw back his head and roared with laughter.

"Come on, you fools, get me clean!"

The King lifted up his skirts of golden *pteryges*, the kilt of golden mail beneath and the purple tunic under that again, displaying powerful thighs, firm buttocks—and, in front, a mighty engine which had sired half a hundred lusty sons. When the worst was washed from his nether regions to the deck, he doffed every item of clothing he wore and stood naked upon the high stern of his ship, showing his dazzled crew what a magnificent specimen was their King. He still laughed, still joked, and occasionally clutched at his belly and groaned for extra effect.

But later, when the Rhodian fleet had gone and the two Pontic "sixteeners" had been disentangled—and a clean cushion sat on his thoroughly scrubbed throne—the freshly garbed King beckoned his ship's captain to his side.

"The lookout and pilot of this ship, captain. I want their tongues torn out, their testicles cut off, their eyes put out, and their hands cut off. Then set them loose with begging bowls," said Mithridates. "On the Chian ship, I want the same punishment meted out to the lookout, the pilot, *and* the captain. Every other man on board the Chian ship is to be killed. And never, never, never let me go again within spitting distance of a Chian, or that vile island called Chios! Do you begin to understand, captain?"

The captain swallowed, closed his eyes. "Yes, O Great One. I understand." He cleared his spasmed throat, launched heroically into the question he had no choice but to ask, "Mighty King, I must put in somewhere to pick up more oars. I do not have enough spares on board. We cannot go on as we are."

It seemed as if the King took this news very well. He asked in a fairly mild voice, "Whereabouts do you suggest we put in?"

"Either Cnidus or Cos. Not anywhere to the south."

An expression of interest in something other than his public humiliation came into the King's eyes. "Cos!" he exclaimed. "Make it Cos! I have a bone to pick with the priests of the Asklepeion. They granted asylum to Romans. And I would like to see how much treasure they have. And gold. Yes, go to Cos, captain."

"Prince Pelopidas wishes to see you, O Great One."

"If he wants to see me, what is he waiting for?"

He was still dangerous, never more dangerous than when he laughed but was not amused. Anything might set him off—a wrong word, a wrong look, a wrong guess. When Pelopidas appeared before the throne in the time it would have taken the King to snap his fingers, he was terrified; but took enormous care not to show it.

"Well, what is it?"

"Great One, I heard you order this ship to Cos for repairs. May I transfer myself to another vessel and go on to Rhodes? I presume that you will want me there when our troops land—unless you plan to transfer yourself to another ship, in which case if you wish it I will remain here to see to things. Please instruct me, Mighty King."

"You go to Rhodes. I leave the choice of a landing place up to you. Not so far from Rhodus City as to tire the army on the march. Put the men into a camp, and wait for me to arrive."

When the "sixteener" hove to in the harbor of the city of Cos on the island of Cos, King Mithridates left the captain to deal with his oar troubles, and himself went ashore in a sleek and well-rowed lighter. He proceeded immediately with his guard to the precinct of the god of healing, Asklepios, which lay on the outskirts of the city; so rapidly had he moved that his identity was unknown when he strode into the forecourt of the sanctuary and bellowed to see whoever was in charge—a typical Mithridatic insult, as the King knew perfectly well the man in charge would be the high priest.

"Who is this arrogant upstart?" demanded one priest of another within the King's hearing.

"I am Mithridates of Pontus, and you are dead men."

Thus it was that by the time the high priest arrived, two of his servitors lay headless between him and his visitor. A very subtle and intelligent man, the high priest had guessed who his unknown visitor was the moment he had been informed a big gold and purple ape was shouting for him.

"Welcome to the precinct of Asklepios on Cos, King Mithridates," said the high priest calmly, displaying no fear.

"I hear that's what you say to Romans."

"I say it to everyone."

"Not to Romans I had ordered killed."

"Were you to come here yourself crying for asylum, it would be granted to you in like measure, King Mithridates. The God Asklepios plays no favorites, and *all* men need him at one time or another. A fact it is wise to remember. He is a god of life, not of death."

"All right, consider them your punishment," said the King, pointing to the two dead priests.

"A punishment two times greater than it ought to be."

"Don't try my temper too far, high priest! Now show me your books—and not the set you keep for the Roman governor."

The Asklepeion of Cos was the greatest banking institution in the world apart from Egypt's state bank, and had grown to be so because of the careful acumen of a long succession of priestly administrators who had come into being under the aegis of the Ptolemies of Egypt—Cos had once been an Egyptian possession. Therefore its development as an institute devoted to the care of money was a logical offshoot of the Egyptian banking system. At first the temple had been a more typical sanctuary, akin to those in other places. Consecrated to healing and to hygiene, the Asklepeion of Cos was the brainchild of some disciples of Hippocrates, and had originally practised the art of incubation—the sleep-cure of dreams and their interpretation as still practised in the precincts at Epidaurus and Pergamum. But with the passing of the generations on Cos and its occupation by the Ptolemies of Egypt, money had replaced cures as the staple income of the temple, and the priests had become more soaked in things Egyptian than in things Greek.

It was a huge precinct, its buildings scattered among parklands beautifully gardened—gymnasium, agora, shops, baths, library, a priestly training college, facilities for scholars in residence, houses and slave quarters, a palace for the high priest, a necropolis on special ground, circles of subterranean sleep cubicles, a hospital, the great complex devoted to banking, and the temple to the god himself contained within a sacred grove of plane trees.

His statue was neither chryselephantine nor gold, but made of white Parian marble by Praxiteles, and showed a bearded, rather Zeus-like deity standing leaning upon a tall staff around which a serpent was entwined. His right hand was extended and held a tablet, at his feet was a large and supine dog. The whole had been painted by Nicias in such a lifelike way that the statue seemed in the shadowy light to stir its garments from the minute and natural movements of its muscles; the god's eyes, a bright blue, sparkled with human and unmajestic joyousness.

None of which enchanted the King, who put up with the grand tour of the sanctuary for just long enough to decide that the statue in the god's temple was a poor thing, not worth looting. Then he got down to the books, and informed the high priest what he intended to confiscate. All Roman gold on deposit, of course; some eight hundred talents of gold on long-term deposit from the Great Temple in Jerusalem, whose synod was canny enough to keep an emergency nest egg safe from the depredations of the Seleucids and the Ptolemies; and the three thousand talents of gold brought to the temple some fourteen years earlier by the old Queen Cleopatra of Egypt.

"I see that the Queen of Egypt also gave three boys into your safekeeping," said Mithridates.

But the high priest was more concerned about his gold, and said in tones he tried to keep cool rather than angry, "King Mithridates, we do not keep our gold here in its entirety—we lend it!"

"I haven't *asked* you for all of it," said the King, voice ugly. "I've asked you for—yes, I make it five thousand talents of Roman gold, three thousand talents of Egyptian gold, and eight hundred talents of Jewish gold. A small percentage of what you carry on your books, high priest."

"But to give you almost nine thousand talents of gold would leave us completely without reserves!"

"How sad," said the King, getting up from the desk where he had been examining the temple records. "Hand it over, high priest, or watch your precinct reduced to dust before you bite the dust yourself. Now show me the three Egyptian boys."

The high priest yielded to the inevitable. "You will have the gold, King Mithridates," he said colorlessly. "Shall I send the Egyptian princes to you here?"

"No. I'd rather see them in daylight."

Of course he was looking for his puppet Ptolemy; Mithridates waited impatiently until they were brought to him at the spot where he strolled beneath the shady boughs of pines and cedars.

"Stand the three of them over there," said Mithridates, pointing to

a place twenty feet away, "and you, high priest, come here to me."
These directives fulfilled, the King asked, "Who is that?" indicating
the oldest-looking of the trio, a young man wearing a floating dress.

"That is the legitimate son of King Ptolemy Alexander of Egypt,
and next heir to the throne."

"Why is he here instead of in Alexandria?"

"His grandmother, who brought him here, feared for his life.
She made us promise we would keep him until he inherited the
throne."

"How old is he?"

"Twenty-five."

"Who was his mother?"

The Egyptian influence at work in the Asklepeion of Cos showed
in the awed tones the high priest used to answer; clearly he thought
the House of Ptolemy far more august than the House of Mithridates. "His mother was the fourth Cleopatra."

"The one who brought him here?"

"No, that was the third Cleopatra, his grandmother. His mother
was her daughter and the daughter of King Ptolemy Gross Belly."

"Married to their *younger* son, Alexander?"

"Later. She was married to the older son first, and had a daughter by him."

"That makes more sense. The oldest daughter always marries
the oldest son, as I hear it."

"That is so, but not necessary constitutionally. The old Queen
loathed both her oldest son *and* her oldest daughter. So she forced
them to divorce. Young Cleopatra fled to Cyprus, where she married her younger brother and bore him this young man."

"What happened to her?" asked the King, keenly interested.

"The old Queen forced Alexander to divorce her, so she fled to
Syria, where she married Antiochus Cyzicenus, who was warring
with his first cousin, Antiochus Grypus. When Cyzicenus was
defeated, she was hacked to death on the altar of Apollo at Daphne.
The author of her murder was her own sister, wife of Grypus."

"Sounds just like my family," said Mithridates, grinning.

The high priest did not think it a matter for humor, so went on

as if he hadn't heard this remark. "The old Queen finally succeeded in ejecting her older son from Egypt, and brought Alexander, this young man's father, to rule with her as King. This young
man went to Egypt with him. However, Alexander was afraid of
his mother, and hated her. Perhaps she knew what was in store for
her, I don't know. But certainly she arrived in Cos fourteen years
ago with several ships full of gold and three male grandchildren,
asking us to care for them. Not long after she returned to Egypt,
King Ptolemy Alexander murdered her." The high priest sighed;
clearly he had liked old Queen Cleopatra, the third of that name.
"Alexander then married his niece Berenice, the daughter of his
older brother Soter and the young Cleopatra who had been wife to
them both."

"So King Ptolemy Alexander rules in Egypt with his niece
Queen Berenice, this young man's aunt as well as his half sister?"

"Alas, no! His subjects deposed him six months ago. He died in
a sea battle trying to regain his throne."

"Then this young man should be King in Egypt right now!"

"No," said the high priest, trying to conceal his pleasure at confusing his unwelcome guest. "King Ptolemy Alexander's older
brother, Soter, is still alive. When the people deposed Alexander,
they brought Ptolemy Soter back to rule instead. Which he is doing right at this moment, with his daughter, Berenice, as his
queen—though he cannot marry her, of course. The Ptolemies
can only marry sisters, nieces, or cousins."

"Didn't Soter have another wife after the old Queen forced him
to divorce the young Cleopatra? Didn't he have more children?"

"Yes, he did marry again. His youngest sister, Cleopatra Selene.
They had two sons."

"Yet you say this young man is the next heir?"

"He is. When King Ptolemy Soter dies, he will inherit."

"Well, well!" said Mithridates, rubbing his hands together in
glee. "I see I will have to take him into *my* safekeeping, high priest!
And make sure he marries one of my own daughters."

"You may try," said the high priest dryly.

"What do you mean, try?"

"He doesn't like women and he won't have anything to do with women under any circumstances."

Mithridates made a noise of slightly anguished irritation, shrugged. "No heirs from him, then! But I'll take him anyway." He pointed to the two others, mere youths. "These then I take it are the sons of Soter and his second sister-wife, Cleopatra Selene?"

"No," said the high priest. "The sons of Soter and Cleopatra Selene *were* brought here by the old Queen, but they died not long afterward of the children's summer sickness. These boys are younger."

"Then who *have* we got here?" cried Mithridates, exasperated.

"These are the sons of Soter and his royal concubine, Princess Arsinoe of Nabataea. They were born in Syria during Soter's wars there against his mother, the old Queen, and his cousin Antiochus Grypus. When Soter left Syria, he didn't take these boys or their mother with him—he left them in the care of his Syrian ally, his cousin Antiochus Cyzicenus. Thus they spent their early childhood in Syria. Then eight years ago Grypus was assassinated and Cyzicenus became sole King of Syria. Grypus's wife at that time was Cleopatra Selene—he had married her as a replacement for his first wife, the middle Ptolemy sister, who died—ahem!—rather dreadfully."

"How dreadfully did she die?" asked the King, keeping it all straight because his own family history was somewhat similar, if not endowed with the glamor always attached to the Ptolemies of Egypt.

"She had murdered the young Cleopatra, as I have told you. On the altar of Apollo at Daphne. But Cyzicenus captured her and put her to death very, very slowly. A tooth at a time, so to speak."

"So the youngest sister, Cleopatra Selene, didn't stay a widow long after the death of Grypus. She married Cyzicenus."

"Correct, King Mithridates. However, she disliked these two boys. Something to do with her original marriage to Soter, whom she loathed. It was *she* who sent them here to us five years ago."

"After the death of Cyzicenus, no doubt. She married his son. And still reigns as Queen Cleopatra Selene of Syria. Remarkable!"

The high priest raised his brows. "I see you know the history of the House of Seleucus well enough."

"A little. I'm related to it myself," said the King. "How old are these boys and what are their names?"

"The elder of the two is properly Ptolemy Philadelphus, but we gave him the nickname Auletes because at the time he came to us he had a piping, flutelike voice. I am pleased to say that with maturity and our training, he no longer musically squeaks. He is now aged sixteen. The younger boy is fifteen. We just call him by his only name, Ptolemy. A nice lad, but indolent." The high priest sighed in the manner of a patient yet disappointed father. "It is his nature to be indolent, we fear."

"So it's really these two younger boys who are the future of Egypt," said Mithridates thoughtfully. "The trouble is, they're bastards. I presume that means they can't inherit."

"The bloodline is not absolutely pure, that is true," said the high priest, "yet if their cousin Alexander fails to reproduce himself— as seems certain—they are the only Ptolemies left. I have had a letter from their father, King Ptolemy Soter, asking that they be sent to him at once. Now he's King again—but without a queen he can marry—he wants to show them to his subjects, who have indicated that they are willing to accept these lads as the heirs."

"He's out of luck," said Mithridates casually. "I'm taking them with me. That way, I'll be sure they marry daughters of mine. Their children will be my grandchildren." His voice changed. "What happened to their mother, Arsinoe?"

"I don't know. I *think* Cleopatra Selene had her killed at the time she sent the sons to us here on Cos. The lads aren't sure, but they fear it," said the high priest.

"What's Arsinoe's bloodline like? Is it good enough?"

"Arsinoe was the oldest daughter of old King Aretas of Nabataea and his queen. It has always been Nabataean policy to send its most perfect daughter as a concubine to the King of Egypt. What more honorable alliance is there for one of the minor Semitic royal houses? The mother of old King Aretas was a Seleucid of the Syrian royal house. His wife—Arsinoe's mother—was a daughter of

King Demetrias Nicanor of Syria and the Princess Rhodogune of the Parthians—Seleucid again, with Arsacid for good measure. I would call Arsinoe's lineage quite splendid," said the high priest.

"Oh, yes, I've got one of those among my wives!" said the King of Pontus heartily. "Nice little thing named Antiochis—the daughter of Demetrias Nicanor and Rhodogune. I have three excellent sons from her, and two daughters. The girls will be perfect wives for these boys, perfect! Reconcentrates the bloodline nicely."

"I think King Ptolemy Soter plans to marry Ptolemy Auletes to his half sister and aunt, Queen Berenice," said the high priest firmly. "As far as the Egyptians are concerned, that would reconcentrate the bloodline far more acceptably."

"Too bad for the Egyptians," said Mithridates, and turned upon the high priest savagely. "Let no one forget that Ptolemy Soter of Egypt and I have the same Seleucid blood! My great-great-aunt Laodice married Antiochus the Great, and *their* daughter Laodice married my grandfather, the fourth Mithridates! That makes Soter my cousin, and my daughters Cleopatra Tryphaena and Berenice Nyssa also his cousins—and cousins twice over to his sons by Arsinoe of Nabataea because their mother is the daughter of Demetrias Nicanor and Rhodogune, and so is Arsinoe's mother!"

The King drew a deep breath. "You may write to King Ptolemy Soter and tell him that *I* will be looking after his sons. Tell Soter that since there are no women left of suitable age in the House of Ptolemy—Berenice must be almost forty now—his sons will marry the daughters of Mithridates of Pontus and Antiochis of Syria. And you may thank your god with the snake-staff that I need you to write that letter! Otherwise I'd have you killed, old man. I find you singularly lacking in respect."

The King strode across to where the three young men were still standing, looking as much bewildered as apprehensive. "You're going to Pontus to live, young Ptolemies," he said to them curtly. "Now follow me, and make it quick!"

Thus it was that when the mighty galley of King Mithridates put out to sea again, it shepherded several smaller ships and made sure they turned north of Cnidus on their way to Ephesus; aboard them were almost nine thousand talents of gold and the three heirs to the throne of Egypt. Cos had proven a profitable haven in time of need. And provided the King of Pontus with his puppet Ptolemy.

When the King arrived at the place Pelopidas had chosen for his landing on Rhodes, he found that very few soldier transports had turned up. He was therefore not able to assault the city of Rhodus until, as Pelopidas said,

"—we can organize the shipping of another army, Great King. The Rhodian admiral Damagoras attacked our transports on two different occasions, and has sent over half of them to the bottom of the sea. Of those which survived, some came on to join us here, but most turned back to Halicarnassus. The next time we will have to surround the transports with war galleys instead of leaving them to follow at their own pace and without any protection."

Of course this news could not please the King, but as he had arrived safely himself, had done well on Cos, and was indifferent to the fate of his Pontic soldiers, he accepted the fact that he must wait for reinforcements, and occupied himself in writing to his regent in Pontus, Young Mithridates, regarding the young heirs to the throne of Egypt.

They all seem well educated, but they are completely ignorant of the importance of Pontus in the world, my son, and that will have to be rectified. My daughters by Antiochis, Cleopatra Tryphaena and Berenice Nyssa, are to be betrothed at once to the two younger fellows. Cleopatra Tryphaena will go to Ptolemy Philadelphus, Berenice Nyssa to Ptolemy No Other Name. The marriages can take place when each girl becomes fifteen.

As to the effeminate one, Ptolemy Alexander, he must be broken of this love for men. The Egyptians would clearly prefer him as their next king because he is legitimate. Therefore he will learn to like women if he likes his head on his shoulders. I leave it to you to enforce this edict.

Setting pen to paper was an ordeal for the King, who normally used scribes, but he wanted to write this letter himself; it took him many days to compose in full, and many burned drafts.

By the end of October the letter was on its way and the King of Pontus felt himself strong enough at last to attack Rhodus. He mounted his assault at night, and concentrated upon the land perimeter of the city because the Rhodian navy was berthed in the harbor. But no one in the Pontic command chain had the necessary knowledge or skill to storm a city as large and well fortified as Rhodus, so the attack was a dismal failure. Unfortunately the King lacked the patience to subject Rhodus to a long-term blockade—the only sure way to conquer it. Frontal assault it must be. But this time the Rhodian navy would be lured outside the harbor and sent chasing off after a decoy, as the main thrust of the Pontic attack would come from the water, spearheaded by a *sambuca*.

What thrilled the King most was that the idea of the *sambuca* was entirely his, and had been greeted in council by Pelopidas and his other generals as a brilliant ploy, sure to work. Flushed with happiness, Mithridates decided to build the *sambuca* himself—that is, to design it personally and supervise its construction.

He took two identical and immense "sixteeners" built in the same shipyard and lashed them together amidships; it was here that the King's inadequacies as an engineer ill served his *sambuca*. What he should have done was to lash them together from their far sides, thus distributing the weight they would be called upon to carry evenly over the entire structure; instead, he lashed them together along their near sides, where they touched each other. Over the two ships he put a deck so large that parts of it overhung the water, but made no attempt to secure the deck to its substrate in any but the most superficial way. On top of this deck two towers went up in the midline, one situated above the gap between the two prows and one on top of the sterns, which were in closer proximity. Between the two towers a wide bridge was built so that it could be raised and lowered on a system of pulleys and winches from a resting position flat on the deck all the way up to the top of the towers. Inside each tower were huge treadmills operated by hundreds of slaves whose job it was to push the bridge from bottom to top. A tall fence of heavy planks was attached by hinges to one side of the bridge right along its length from prow tower to stern tower; while the bridge was being raised the fence formed a protection against missiles, and when the bridge attained its maximum altitude of just a little more than the immense seawall of Rhodus port, the fence could then be dropped onto the top of the seawall to form a gangplank.

The attack began on a calm day toward the end of November, two hours after the Rhodian navy was lured away to the north. The Pontic army assaulted the landward walls at their weakest points as the Pontic navy rowed into Rhodus harbor, its outer flank deployed to keep the Rhodian fleet on its periphery when the Rhodian fleet saw through the trick and returned. In the midst of the huge Pontic flotilla reared the mighty *sambuca,* towed by dozens of lighters and followed closely by transports loaded with troops.

Amid shrieks of alarm and frantic activity along the Rhodian battlements, with great dexterity the lightermen berthed the *sambuca* side-on to the vast seawall behind which lay the temple of Isis; the moment the maneuver was over, the troop transports crowded round it. Relatively unharmed by the frenzied hurling of stones and arrows and spears, the Pontic soldiers poured onto the *sambuca,* where they were packed densely onto the bridge, lying flat on the deck. Then the winch operators flogged their slaves to start walking the treadmills. Amid an horrific squealing and groaning, the bridge between the towers began to rise into the air bearing its load of soldiers. Hundreds of helmeted Rhodian heads popped up along the battlements to watch in mingled fascination and terror; Mithridates watched too, from his "sixteener" in the middle of the packed Pontic ships, waiting until the *sambuca* concentrated all Rhodian resistance to the temple of Isis section of the seawall. Once the *sambuca* was the center of attention, the other ships could draw up alongside the rest of the seawall and send troops up ladders with impunity. Pontic soldiers would be atop the fortifications all the way around the harbor.

It cannot fail! I've got them this time! thought the King to himself as he allowed his eyes to dwell lovingly upon his *sambuca* and its slowly rising bridge between the two towers. Soon the bridge would come level with the top of the seawall, magically the protective fence would drop on its hinges to form a gangway across which the soldiers would pour in among the Rhodian defenders. There were enough men aboard the bridge to hold the Rhodians at bay until the apparatus was lowered back to the deck to load another contingent and winch them to the top. There is no doubt about it, thought King Mithridates, I am the best at everything!

But as the center of gravity rose along with the *sambuca* bridge, the distribution of weight changed. The host ships lashed together began to split apart. Ropes snapped with little explosions, the towers began to totter, the deck to heave and buckle, the ascending bridge to sway like a dancer's scarf. Then the two ships bearing all of this began to capsize toward the midline. Decking, towers, bridge, soldiers, sailors, artificers, and treadmill slaves fell into the water between the rolling vessels amid a cacophony of screams, grinding crunches, roars—and hysterical cheers from the jubilant Rhodians atop their walls—cheers soon changing into paroxysms of mocking laughter.

"I never want to hear the name of Rhodes mentioned again!" said the King as his mighty galley bore him back to Halicarnassus. "It's too close to winter to continue this petty campaign against a pack of idiots and fools. My armies marching into Macedonia and my fleets along the coast of Greece need my closer attention. I also want every engineer who had anything to do with the design of that ridiculous *sambuca* dead—no, not dead! Tongues out, eyes out, hands off, balls off, and begging bowls!"

So furious was the King at this humiliation that he visited Lycia with an army and attempted to besiege Patara. But when he felled a grove of trees sacred to Latona, the mother of Apollo and Artemis came to him in a dream and warned him to stop. Next day the King handed over the investment to his underlings—the hapless Pelopidas was placed in command—and took his fascinating albino bride Monima to Hierapolis. There, cavorting and frolicking in the hot mineral pools amid petrified crystal waterfalls tumbling down the cliffs, he succeeded in forgetting all about the laughter of Rhodes—and Chian ships which gave him the fright of his life.

PART IX

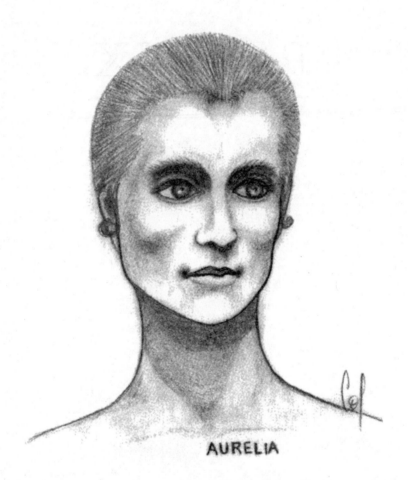

AURELIA

The news of the massacre of Asia Province's Roman and Latin and Italian residents reached Rome ahead of the news that Mithridates had invaded the province— and reached Rome in record time. Just nine days after the last day of Quinctilis, the Princeps Senatus Lucius Valerius Flaccus was convening the House in the temple of Bellona outside the *pomerium* because this was to do with a foreign war. To those present he read out a letter from Publius Rutilius Rufus in Smyrna.

I am sending this by a specially commissioned fast ship to Corinth, and onward to Brundisium by another just as fast, trusting that the rebellion in Greece does not prevent its passage. The courier has been instructed to ride from Brundisium to Rome at the gallop, night and day. The large sum of money this is costing has been given to me by my friend Miltiades, the *ethnarch* of Smyrna, who begs only that the Senate and People of Rome remember his service to them when, as must happen, Asia Province belongs to Rome again.

It may be that you do not know as yet of the invasion of King Mithridates of Pontus, who now rules both Bithynia and our Roman Asian province. Manius Aquillius is dead under the most hideous circumstances, and Gaius Cassius is fled I know not where. A quarter of a million Pontic soldiers are west of the Taurus, the Aegean is completely covered by Pontic fleets, and Greece has allied itself with Pontus against Rome. I very much fear that Macedonia is totally isolated.

But that is not the worst of it. On the last day of Quinctilis, every Roman and Latin and Italian in the Asia Province, Bithynia, Pisidia, and Phrygia was massacred by order of King Mithridates of Pontus. Their slaves were also massacred. The number of dead, I believe, is something like eighty thousand citizens and seventy thousand slaves—one hundred and fifty thousand altogether. That I did not suffer the same fate is due to my non-citizen status, though I believe the King issued a warning that I—by name!—was not to be touched. A nice sop to the hound of Hades. What can the sparing of my old life do to offset the brutal hacking into pieces of Roman women and little babies? They were torn from altars still crying on the gods and their bodies lie rotting unburied, again by order of the King of Pontus. This barbarian monstrosity now fancies himself the king of the world, and is boasting that he will be on Italian soil before the year is out.

No one is left east of Italy to gainsay his boast save our people in Macedonia. But I despair of Macedonia. Though I have not been able to confirm it, there is news that King Mithridates has mounted a land expedition against Thessalonica which has already penetrated west of Philippi without a shred of opposition. I know more about activities in Greece, where a Pontic agent named Aristion has snatched all power in Athens and persuaded most of Greece to declare for Mithridates. The isles of the Aegean are in Pontic hands, the fleets are gigantic. When Delos fell, another twenty thousand of our people were put to death.

Please, I beg of you, regard my letter as deliberately brief and understated, and do what you can to prevent this frightful barbarian Mithridates crowning himself the King of Rome. It is that serious.

"Oh, we don't need this!" said Lucius Caesar to his brother Catulus Caesar.

"We may not need it, but we've got it," said Gaius Marius, eyes sparkling. "A war against Mithridates! I knew it had to come. Surprising, really, that it's been so long."

"Lucius Cornelius is on his way to Rome," said the other censor, Publius Licinius Crassus. "I'll breathe easier then."

"Why?" demanded Marius fiercely. "We shouldn't have summoned him! Let him finish the Italian war."

"He is the senior consul," said Catulus Caesar. "The Senate cannot make far-reaching decisions without his presence in the chair."

"Tchah!" said Marius, and lumbered away.

"What's the matter with him?" asked Flaccus Princeps Senatus.

"What do you think, Lucius Valerius? He's an old warhorse snuffing the scent of just the right kind of war—a foreign one," said Catulus Caesar.

"But surely he can't think he's going to it," said Publius Crassus the censor. "He's too old and sick!"

"Of course he thinks he's going," said Catulus Caesar.

The war in Italy was over. Though the Marsi never did formally surrender, among all the peoples who had taken up arms against Rome they were the most devastated; hardly a Marsian male was left alive. In February, Quintus Poppaedius Silo fled to Samnium, and joined Mutilus within Aesernia. Mutilus he found so severely wounded that he was incapable ever again of leading an army. He was paralyzed from the waist down.

"I must pass the leadership of Samnium on to you, Quintus Poppaedius," Mutilus said.

"No!" cried Silo. "I don't have your way with troops—especially Samnite troops—nor do I have your skill as a general."

"There's no one else. My Samnites have elected to follow you."

"Do the Samnites really want to continue the war?"

"Yes," said Mutilus. "But in the name of Samnium, not Italia."

"I can understand that. But surely there is *one* Samnite left to lead them!"

"Not one, Quintus Poppaedius. It has to be you."

"Very well, then," said Silo, sighing.

What neither of them discussed was the ruin of their hopes for independent Italia. Nor did they discuss what both of them knew—that if Italia was finished, Samnium could not possibly win.

In May the last rebel army sallied out of Aesernia under the command of Quintus Poppaedius Silo. It numbered thirty thousand infantry and a thousand horse, and was further augmented by a force of twenty thousand manumitted slaves. Most of the infantry had been wounded in one battle or another and fetched up in Aesernia because it was the only secure place left to go; Silo had brought the cavalry with him and managed to get through the Roman lines around the city. All of which made this sally inevitable; Aesernia could not long continue to feed so many mouths.

As every marching man knew, it was a last-ditch stand; no one really expected to win. The most they could hope for was to make every death count. But then when Silo's soldiers took Bovianum and killed the Roman garrison there, they began to feel better. Perhaps there was a chance after all? Metellus Pius and his army were sitting before Venusia on the Via Appia, so to Venusia they would go.

And there outside Venusia the last battle of the war took place, a curious rounding out of the events which had started with the death of Marcus Livius Drusus. For on the field of Venusia there met in single combat the two men who had loved Drusus best—his friend Silo and his brother Mamercus. While the Samnites died in thousands, no match for the fit and experienced Romans, Silo and Mamercus slogged hand to hand until Silo fell. Mamercus stood looking down at the Marsian with tears in his eyes, sword raised. He hesitated.

"Finish me, Mamercus!" gasped Quintus Poppaedius Silo. "You owe me that for killing Caepio. I will walk in no triumph held by the Piglet!"

"For killing Caepio," said Mamercus, and finished him. Then wept desolately for Drusus, Silo, and the bitterness of victory.

"It's done," said Metellus Pius the Piglet to Lucius Cornelius Sulla, who had come to Venusia the moment he heard of the battle. "Venusia capitulated yesterday."

"No, it is not done," said Sulla grimly. "It won't be done until Aesernia and Nola submit."

"Have you considered," ventured the Piglet rather timidly, "that if we were to lift the sieges at Aesernia and Nola, life in those two places would go back to normal and everyone would probably pretend nothing had ever happened?"

"I'm sure you're right," said Sulla, "which is why we will *not* lift the siege at either place. Why should they get away with it? Pompey Strabo didn't let Asculum Picentum get away with it. No, Piglet, Aesernia and Nola stay the way they are. For all eternity if necessary."

"I hear Scato is dead, and the Paeligni surrendered."

"Correct, except that you have it the wrong way round," said Sulla with a grin. "Pompey Strabo accepted the surrender of the Paeligni. Scato fell on his sword rather than be a part of it."

"So it really is the end!" said Metellus Pius in wonder.

"Not until Aesernia and Nola submit."

The news of the massacre of the Romans and Latins and Italians of Asia Province reached Sulla in Capua, which town he had made his base, thus releasing Catulus Caesar to go back to Rome for a well-deserved rest; he had besides inherited Catulus Caesar's secretary, the prodigy Marcus Tullius Cicero, and found Cicero so efficient that Catulus Caesar wasn't necessary.

Cicero found Sulla as terrifying as he had found Pompey Strabo, though for different reasons. And missed Catulus Caesar acutely.

"Lucius Cornelius, will it be possible for me to have my discharge toward the end of the year?" Cicero asked. "Though I will have served in time not quite two years, I have added up my campaigns, and will have served in ten."

"I'll see," said Sulla, who felt about Cicero as a person much as Pompey Strabo had felt. "For the moment I can't spare you. No one else knows as much about the place as you, now that Quintus Lutatius has gone to Rome to rest."

But there never is a rest, thought Sulla, galloping to Rome in a four-mule gig. No sooner do we put one conflagration out than another bursts into flames. And this will make the war against Italy look like two twigs smoldering.

Every senior senator converged upon Rome for the Senate hearing on Asia Province, even Pompey Strabo; perhaps a hundred and fifty men gathered in the temple of Bellona outside the *pomerium* on the Campus Martius.

"Well, we know Manius Aquillius is dead. Presumably that means his two fellow commissioners are dead," said Sulla to the House in conversational tones. "However, it seems Gaius Cassius escaped, though we've heard nothing from him. What I can't understand is why we've heard not one squeak from Quintus Oppius in Cilicia. Presumably Cilicia too is lost. It is a sad business when Rome has to depend upon a civilian exile for news like this."

"I imagine it means Mithridates struck like lightning," said Catulus Caesar, brow furrowed.

"Or else," said Marius shrewdly, "there's been funny business going on between all our official representatives."

That provoked no replies, but a great deal of thought; some certain loyalty united the body at all times, but it was not possible to mix as consistently as members of the Senate did without everyone's knowing what everyone else was really like. And everyone knew what Gaius Cassius and the three commissioners were really like.

"Then Quintus Oppius at least should have been in contact," said Sulla, echoing everyone else's thoughts. "He's a man of great honor, he wouldn't let Rome go in ignorance a moment longer than he could help. I think we *must* presume Cilicia too is lost."

"We'll have to get word to Publius Rutilius somehow, and ask for more information," said Marius.

"I imagine that if any of our people survived, they'll start to reach Rome by the end of Sextilis," said Sulla. "We'll get more information then."

"I interpret Publius Rutilius's letter as meaning no one at all survived," said Sulpicius from the tribunician bench. He groaned, clenched his fists. "Mithridates made absolutely no distinction between an Italian and a Roman!"

"Mithridates is a barbarian," said Catulus Caesar.

But that answer was too pat for Sulpicius, who had seemed for many moments to have turned to stone when Flaccus Princeps Senatus had read Rutilius Rufus's letter out two days before.

"He made no distinction," Sulpicius said again. "*Why* he made no distinction is beside the point! Irrelevant! The Italians of Asia Province paid the same price as the Romans and the Latins of Asia Province. They're just as dead. Their women and children and slaves are just as dead. *He made no distinction!*"

"Oh, pull your head in, Sulpicius!" cried Pompey Strabo, who wanted to get down to business. "You're becoming a wheel in a rut."

"I will have order," said Sulla pleasantly. "We are not here in Bellona to investigate reasons or distinctions. We're here to decide what to do."

"War!" said Pompey Strabo instantly.

"Is that how everyone feels, or only some?" asked Sulla.

The House cried out unanimously for war.

"We have sufficient legions in the field," said Metellus Pius, "and they're properly equipped. At least in that respect we're better prepared than we usually are. We can ship twenty legions to the east tomorrow."

"We can't, you know," said Sulla levelly. "In fact, I doubt if we can ship *one* legion, let alone twenty."

The House fell silent.

"Conscript Fathers, where are we to find the money? With the war against Italy over, we have no choice except to disband our legions. *Because we can't afford to pay them a moment longer!* While Rome was imperiled within Italy, every man of Roman or Latin ancestry was obliged to take the field. We can say that the same holds true for a foreign war, especially as Asia Province is already swallowed by the aggressor and eighty thousand of our people are dead. But the fact remains that at this moment the Homeland is not directly under threat. And the men in our armies are tired. They've been paid at last—but it took everything we own to pay them. Which means they must be demobilized, sent home. *Because we do not have even the prospect of enough money to pay them for another campaign!"*

Sulla's words sank into the silence, intensified it.

Then Catulus Caesar sighed. "Let us put considerations of money to one side for a moment," he said. "More important by far is the fact that we *have* to stop Mithridates!"

"Quintus Lutatius, you haven't listened!" cried Sulla. "There is no money for a campaign!"

Catulus Caesar assumed his haughtiest look, and said, "I move that Lucius Cornelius Sulla be given the command against Mithridates. Once the matter of command is attended to, we can attend to money."

"And I give notice that I will move that Lucius Cornelius Sulla *not* be given the command against Mithridates!" roared Gaius Marius. "Let Lucius Cornelius Sulla remain in Rome to worry about money! *Money!* As if it is time to worry about money when Rome faces certain extinction! The money will be found. It always is. And King Mithridates has plenty of it, so it's he will wind up paying in the long run. Conscript Fathers, we cannot give the command in this campaign to a man who worries about money! You must give this campaign to me!"

"You are not well enough, Gaius Marius," said Sulla without any expression on his face or in his voice.

"I'm well enough to know that money is of no moment!" snapped Marius. "Pontus is the German threat all over again! And who won against the Germans? Gaius Marius! Fellow members of this august body, you *must* give the command in this war to me! I am the only man here who can win it!"

Up from his seat rose Flaccus Princeps Senatus, a mild man not famous for his courage. "If you were young enough and well enough, Gaius Marius, no more fervent adherent would you have than I. But Lucius Cornelius is right. You are not well enough. You are too old. You have had two strokes. We cannot give the command in this war to a man who is likely to be felled again at just the moment when his talents are likely to be most needed. We do not know what causes a stroke, Gaius Marius, but we do know that a man who has had one stroke will go on to have more. As you have. As you will! No, Conscript Fathers, as your Princeps Senatus I say that we cannot even consider Gaius Marius to lead this campaign. I second the motion that the command be given to our senior consul, Lucius Cornelius."

"Fortune will see me through," said Marius stubbornly.

"Gaius Marius, accept the opinion of the Princeps Senatus in the spirit in which it was tendered," said Sulla calmly. "No one holds you lightly, least of all me. But facts are facts. This House *cannot* run the risk of entrusting the conduct of *any* war to one who has had two strokes and is now seventy years old."

Marius subsided, but it was plain he had not reconciled himself to the House opinion; he sat with both hands grappled around his knees and the right corner of his mouth turned down to match the left.

"Lucius Cornelius, will you take the command?" asked Quintus Lutatius Catulus Caesar.

"Only if the House gives it to me by a clear majority, Quintus Lutatius. Not otherwise," said Sulla.

"Then let there be a division," said Flaccus Princeps Senatus.

Only three men stood in opposition when the senators trooped from their makeshift places in this makeshift meeting chamber— Gaius Marius, Lucius Cornelius Cinna, and the tribune of the plebs Publius Sulpicius Rufus.

"I don't believe it!" muttered the censor Crassus to his colleague, Lucius Caesar. *"Sulpicius?"*

"He's been acting most peculiarly ever since the news of the massacre came," said Lucius Caesar. "Keeps saying—well, you've heard him!—that Mithridates made no distinction between Romans and Italians. I imagine he's now regretting the fact that he was one who never wanted to see the Italians enfranchised."

"Why should that prompt him to stand with Gaius Marius?"

Lucius Caesar shrugged. "I don't know, Publius Licinius! I really don't know."

Sulpicius stood with Marius and Cinna because they stood against the Senate. For no other reason. When he had heard the news from Rutilius Rufus in Smyrna, Sulpicius had undergone a profound change, and had not managed since to live without pain. Without guilt. Without an agonized confusion of mind that could get little further than one fact: a foreign king had made no distinction between the men of Rome and the men of Italy. And if a foreign king lumped Romans and Italians together, then in the eyes of the rest of the world there was no difference between them. The nature and activities of the one were the same as the other.

An ardent patriot and intensely conservative, when the war against the Italians had broken out Sulpicius had espoused the Roman cause with all his considerable heart. A quaestor in the year Drusus had died, he had found himself entrusted with increasingly responsible duties—and had acquitted himself brilliantly. Thanks to his own efforts, many Italians had died. Thanks to his consenting to it, the inhabitants of Asculum Picentum had suffered more terribly than barbarians deserved to suffer. Those thousands of little Italian boys who had walked in Pompey Strabo's triumphal parade, and then been ejected from the city without food, clothing, or money, to live or to die according to the strength of will in their immature bodies. Who did Rome think she was, to inflict such terrible punishment upon people who were kinsfolk? How did Rome truly differ from the King of Pontus? His attitude at least was unequivocal! He at least had not shrouded his motives in righteousness and superiority. Nor for that matter had Pompey Strabo. It was the Senate had equivocated.

Oh, what was right? Who was right? If one Italian man, one Italian woman, one Italian child had managed to survive the massacre and turned up in Rome, how could he, Publius Sulpicius Rufus, ever look that poor survivor in the face? How did he, Publius Sulpicius Rufus, truly differ from King Mithridates? Had he not killed many thousands of Italians? Had he not been a legate under Pompey Strabo, and consented to that man's atrocities?

But amid all this pain and confusion inside Sulpicius's mind there were also coherent thoughts—or rather, thoughts *he* felt were coherent, valid, logical.

Rome was not really to blame. The Senate was. The men of his own class, including himself. In the Senate—in himself!—lay the wellsprings of Roman exclusivity. The Senate had murdered his friend Marcus Livius Drusus. The Senate had stopped giving out the Roman citizenship in the aftermath of the war against Hannibal. The Senate authorized the destruction of Fregellae. The Senate, the Senate, the Senate . . . The men of his own class. Including himself.

Well, they would now have to pay. Including himself. It was time, decided Sulpicius, that the Senate of Rome ceased to be. No more ancient ruling families, no more wealth and power concentrated in the hands of so few that injustices as monumental as the Italian injustice could be perpetrated to an ultimate end. We are wrong, he thought. We must pay. The Senate has to go. Rome must be handed over to the People, who are our pawns, for all that we insist they are sovereign. Sovereign? Not while there's a Senate! While there is ever a Senate, the People's sovereignty is in name only. Not the Head Count, of course. The *People.* The men of the Second and Third and Fourth Classes, who are by far the largest bulk of Romans, yet have the least power. The truly wealthy and powerful knights of the First Class are indistinguishable from the Senate in every way. So they too must go.

Standing with Marius and Cinna (Why was *Cinna* in opposition? What tied him to Gaius Marius all of a sudden?), Sulpicius looked at the packed mass of senators facing him. There stood his good friends Gaius Aurelius Cotta (appointed a senator at twenty-eight because the censors had taken Sulla's words to heart and were trying to fill that exclusive body, the Senate, with appropriate men) and the junior consul, Quintus Pompeius Rufus, dutifully clustered with the rest—couldn't they *see* their guilt? Why did they stare at *him* as if he were the guilty one? But he was! He was! He knew it. They had absolutely no idea.

And if *they* do not understand, thought Sulpicius, then I will bide my time until this new war—oh, why are we always at war?—is organized. Men like Quintus Lutatius and Lucius Cornelius Sulla will be a part of it, they will not be in Rome to oppose me. I will wait. I will bide my time. And kill the Senate. Kill the First Class.

"Lucius Cornelius Sulla," said Flaccus Princeps Senatus, "take command of the war against Mithridates in the name of the Senate and the People of Rome."

"Only where are we to find the money?" asked Sulla later over dinner in his new house.

With him were the Brothers Caesar, the *flamen Dialis* Lucius Cornelius Merula, the censor Publius Licinius Crassus, the banker and merchant Titus Pomponius, the banker Gaius Oppius, Quintus Mucius Scaevola Pontifex Maximus, and Marcus Antonius Orator, just returned to the Senate after a protracted illness. Sulla's guest list was designed to answer his question—if it could be answered at all.

"Is there nothing in the Treasury?" asked Antonius Orator, unable to believe this. "I mean, we all know how the urban quaestors and the tribunes of the Treasury behave—they're forever insisting that the place is empty when there's actually plenty."

"Believe it, Marcus Antonius, there is nothing," said Sulla firmly. "I've been to the Treasury myself several times—and I've been very careful not to let anyone know I was coming."

"What about the temple of Ops?" asked Catulus Caesar.

"Empty too."

"Well," said Scaevola Pontifex Maximus, "there *is* the gold hoarded by the Kings of Rome against just such an emergency."

"What gold?" asked several in chorus, including Sulla.

"I didn't know about it myself until I became Pontifex Maximus, honestly!" said Scaevola defensively. "It's in the basement of the temple of Jupiter Optimus Maximus—about—oh, something under two hundred talents."

"Wonderful!" said Sulla ironically. "No doubt when Servius Tullius was King of Rome, that was enough to fund the war to end all wars. Nowadays it's about enough to keep four legions in the field for six months. I'd better hurry!"

"It's a start," said Titus Pomponius comfortably.

"Why can't you bankers lend the State a couple of thousand talents?" asked Crassus Censor, who loved money dearly, but had not nearly as much of it as he wanted—just the tin concessions across Spain, and he'd been too busy to police those as closely as they needed.

"Because we don't have it to lend," said Oppius patiently.

"Also, most of us use banks in Asia Province for housing our surplus reserves—which means, I have no doubt, that Mithridates is now the owner of our reserves," said Titus Pomponius, and sighed.

"You must have money here!" said Crassus Censor, snorting.

"We do. But not enough to lend the State," maintained Oppius.

"*Res facta* or *res ficta*?"

"Fact, Publius Licinius, truly."

"Does everyone here agree that this present crisis is even more serious than the Italian crisis?" asked Lucius Cornelius Merula, priest of Jupiter.

"Yes, yes!" snapped Sulla. "Having interviewed the man in person once, *flamen Dialis,* I can assure you that if Mithridates is not stopped, he will crown himself King of Rome!"

"Then since we would never get permission from the People to sell off the *ager publicus,* there's only one more way to raise money short of imposing new taxes," said Merula.

"What?"

"We can sell all the property the State still owns in the vicinity of the Forum Romanum. We don't have to go to the People to do that."

An appalled silence descended.

"We couldn't be selling the State's assets at a worse time," said Titus Pomponius mournfully. "It's a buyer's market."

"I'm afraid I don't even know what land the State owns around the Forum except for the priests' houses," said Sulla, "and we can't possibly sell them."

"I agree, to sell them would be *nefas,*" said Merula, who lived in one of the State Houses. "However, there is other property. The slopes of the Capitol inside the Fontinalis Gate, and also facing the Velabrum. Prime land for big houses. There is also a large tract which includes the general market and the Macellum Cuppedenis. Both areas could be subdivided."

"I refuse to countenance the sale of everything," said Sulla strongly. "The market areas, yes. They're just markets and a playing field for the College of Lictors. Some of the Capitol—facing the Velabrum west of the Clivus Capitolinus—and from the Fontinalis Gate down as far as the Lautumiae. But *nothing* on the Forum itself, and nothing on the Capitol facing the Forum itself."

"I'll buy the markets," said Gaius Oppius.

"Only if no one offers more," said Pomponius, whose mind had been running the same way. "To be fair about it—and to get the best price—everything will have to be auctioned."

"Perhaps we should try to keep the general market area and sell only the Cuppedenis market," said Sulla, who found himself loathing the need to auction off such wonderful assets.

"I think you're right, Lucius Sulla," said Catulus Caesar.

"I agree with that," said Lucius Caesar.

"If we sell the Cuppedenis, I suppose that will mean increased rents for the spice and flower merchants," said Antonius Orator. "They won't thank us!"

But Sulla had thought of another alternative. "How about we *borrow* the money?" he asked.

"Where?" asked Merula suspiciously.

"From the temples of Rome. Pay them back out of the spoils. Juno Lucina, Venus Libitina, Juventas, Ceres, Juno Moneta, Magna Mater, Castor and Pollux, both Jupiter Stators, Diana, Hercules Musarum, Hercules Olivarius—they're all rich."

"No!" cried Scaevola and Merula together.

A quick glance from face to face told Sulla he would get no support from anyone. "All right, then, if you won't let Rome's temples pay for my campaign, would you object to the temples of Greece?" he asked.

Scaevola frowned. *"Nefas* is *nefas*, Lucius Sulla. The gods are the gods, in Greece or in Rome."

"Yes, but Greece's gods are not Rome's gods, now are they?"

"Temples are sacrosanct," said Merula stubbornly.

Out leaped the other creature inside Sulla; it was the first time some of those present had seen it, and it terrified them. "Listen," he said, teeth showing, "you can't have it all ways, and that goes for the gods too! I'll grant you the gods of Rome, but there's not one man here who doesn't understand how much it costs to keep legions in the field! If we can scrape two hundred talents of gold together, I can get six legions as far as Greece. That's a pretty paltry force to pit against a quarter of a million Pontic soldiers—and I would remind you that a Pontic soldier is *not* a naked German barbarian! I've seen the troops of Mithridates, and they are armed and trained much like Roman legionaries. Not as good, I imagine, but far better than naked German barbarians if only because they are protected by armor and trained to discipline. Like Gaius Marius in the field, I intend to keep my men alive. And that means money for forage and money for the upkeep of all equipment. Money we don't have—money you won't allow the gods of Rome to give me. So I am warning you—and I mean every word!—when I reach Greece, I take the money I need from Olympia, Dodona, Delphi, and anywhere else I can find it. Which means, *flamen Dialis*, Pontifex Maximus, that you'd better put in some hard work with our Roman gods, and hope that these days they have more clout than the Greek gods!"

No one said a word.

The creature disappeared. "Good!" said Sulla cheerfully. "Now I have more happy news for you, just in case you think that's the end of it."

Catulus Caesar sighed. "I am all agog, Lucius Cornelius. Pray tell us."

"I shall take my own four legions with me, plus two of the legions Gaius Marius trained and Lucius Cinna is presently using. The Marsi are a spent force, Cinna doesn't need troops. Gnaeus Pompeius Strabo will do whatever he wants to do, and as long as he refrains from sending in wages bills, I for one do not intend to waste time arguing with him. That means there are still some ten legions to demobilize—and pay out. With money we certainly will not have," said Sulla. "For that reason, I intend to legislate to pay out these soldiers with land in Italian areas whose populations we have virtually extirpated. Pompeii. Faesulae. Hadria. Telesia. Grumentum. Bovianum. Six empty towns surrounded by reasonable farming land. Districts which will belong to the ten legions I have to discharge."

"But that's *ager publicus!*" cried Lucius Caesar.

"Not yet, it isn't. Nor is it going to become public land," said Sulla. "It's going to the soldiers. Unless, that is, you intend to change your pious and devout minds about the temples of Rome?" he asked sweetly.

"We cannot," said Scaevola Pontifex Maximus.

"Then when my legislation is promulgated you had better swing both the Senate and the People on my side," said Sulla.

"We will uphold you," said Antonius Orator.

"And, while we're on the subject of *ager publicus,*" Sulla went on, "don't start declaring it while I'm away. When I come back with my legions, I will want more deserted Italian districts to settle them on."

In the end, Rome's finances did not stretch to six legions. Sulla's army was determined at five legions and two thousand horse, not a man or an animal more. When all the gold was put together it weighed nine thousand pounds—not even two hundred talents. A pittance indeed, but the best a bankrupt Rome could do. Sulla's war chest didn't even extend to the commissioning of one single fighting galley; it would barely cover the cost of hiring transports to get his men to Greece, the destination he thought he would prefer to western Macedonia. Not, however, that he intended to make settled plans until he heard more about the situation in Asia Minor and Greece. His mind inclined the way it did because in Greece lay the richest temples.

And at the end of September, Sulla was finally able to leave Rome to join his legions in Capua. He had interviewed his trusted and devoted military tribune, Lucius Licinius Lucullus, and asked him if he would be willing to stand for election as a quaestor if Sulla asked for his services by name. Delighted, Lucullus indicated that he would, whereupon Sulla sent him ahead to Capua as his deputy until he could come himself. Mired down in auctioning State property and in organizing his six soldier colonies, it seemed throughout the month of September that Sulla would never manage to get away. That he did was due to iron will and ruthless driving of his senatorial colleagues, all of whom were fascinated; somehow Sulla had always escaped their attention as a potential high leader.

"Overshadowed by Marius and Scaurus," said Antonius Orator.

"No, he just didn't have a reputation," said Lucius Caesar.

"And whose fault was that?" sneered Catulus Caesar.

"Mostly Gaius Marius's, I suppose," said his brother.

"He certainly knows what he wants," said Antonius Orator.

"That he does," said Scaevola, and shivered. "I would hate to get on the wrong side of him!"

Which was exactly what Young Caesar was thinking as he lay in his ceiling hiding place and watched and listened to his mother and Lucius Cornelius Sulla talking.

"I'm off tomorrow, Aurelia, and I don't like going away without seeing you," he said.

"I don't like your going without seeing me," she answered.

"No Gaius Julius?"

"He's off with Lucius Cinna among the Marsi."

"Picking up the pieces," nodded Sulla.

"You're looking very well, Lucius Cornelius, in spite of all your difficulties. I take it this marriage is turning out happily."

"Either that, or I'm becoming more uxorious."

"Rubbish! You'll never be uxorious."

"How is Gaius Marius taking his defeat?"

Aurelia pursed her lips. "Not without much grumbling to the family," she said. "You are not terribly popular with him."

"I didn't expect to be. But he surely admits that I acted in a temperate way, didn't chase after the command with slavering tongue and frenzied lobbying."

"You didn't need to," said Aurelia, "and that's why he's so upset. He isn't used to Rome's having an alternative war leader. Until you won the Grass Crown, he was always the only one. Oh, his enemies in the Senate were very powerful and thwarted him most of the time, but he *knew* he was the only one. He knew in the end they would have to use him. Now he's old and sick, and there's you. He's afraid you'll take away his support among the knights."

"Aurelia, he's finished! Not without honor, not without great fame. But it's over for him. Why can't he see that?"

"I suppose were he younger and in better mental condition, he would see it. The trouble is that his strokes have affected his mind—or so Julia thinks."

"She'd know more surely and sooner than anyone else," said Sulla, and rose to go. "How is your family?"

"Very well."

"Your boy?"

"Irrepressible. Unquenchable. Indomitable. I try to keep his feet on the earth, but it's very difficult," said Aurelia.

But my feet are on the ground, Mama! thought Young Caesar, wriggling out of his nest as soon as Sulla and Aurelia disappeared. Why is it that you always think me a feather, a crystal dandelion ball floating in the wind?

Thinking that Sulla would not waste time getting himself and his troops across the Adriatic ahead of winter's unfavorable winds, Publius Sulpicius struck his first blow against the established order of things halfway through October. Of preparation he had little save within his own mind; for someone without love for demagogues, it was impossible to cultivate the art of the demagogue. He had, however, taken the precaution of seeking an interview with Gaius Marius and asking for Marius's support. No lover of the Senate, Gaius Marius! Nor was Sulpicius disappointed in his reception. After listening to what Sulpicius proposed to do, Marius nodded.

"You may rest assured I will lend you my full support, Publius Sulpicius," the Great Man said. For a moment he said nothing more, then he added, apparently as an afterthought, "However, I will ask one favor of you—that you legislate to give *me* the command in the war against Mithridates."

It seemed like a small price to pay; Sulpicius smiled. "I agree, Gaius Marius. You shall have your command," he said.

Sulpicius convoked the Plebeian Assembly, and in *contio* put two prospective laws before it as separate bills. One called for the expulsion from the Senate of every member who was in debt to the tune of more than eight thousand sesterces; the other called for the return of all those men exiled by the Varian Commission in the days when Varius himself had prosecuted those he alleged had been in favor of the citizenship for Italy.

Silver-tongued, golden-voiced, Sulpicius found exactly the right note. "Who do they think they are to sit in the Senate and make the decisions *this* body should be making, when hardly one of them isn't a poor man and hopelessly in debt?" he cried. "For all of you who are in debt, there is no relief—no way of hiding behind senatorial exclusivity, no easing of your burdens by understanding moneylenders who do not think it politic to push you too far! Yet for them inside the Curia Hostilia, trifling little matters like debts can be ignored until better times! I know because I am a senator—I hear what they say to each other, I see the favors done here and there for moneylenders! I even know who among those in the Senate *lend* money! Well, it is all going to stop! No man who owes money should have a seat in the Senate! No man ought to be able to call himself a member of that haughty and exclusive club if he is no better than the rest of Rome!"

Shocked, the Senate sat up straight, astounded because it was Sulpicius acting like a demagogue. *Sulpicius!* The most conservative and valuable of men! It had been he who vetoed the recall of the Varian exiles back before the beginning of the year! Now here he was, recalling them! What had happened?

Two days later Sulpicius reconvened the Plebeian Assembly and promulgated a third law. All the new Italian citizens and many thousands of Rome's freedman citizens were to be distributed evenly across the whole thirty-five tribes. Piso Frugi's two new tribes were to be abandoned.

"Thirty-five is the proper number of tribes, there can be no more!" shouted Sulpicius. "Nor is it right that some tribes can hold as few as three or four thousand citizens, yet still have the same voting power in tribal assemblies as tribes like Esquilina and Suburana, each with more than a hundred thousand citizen members! *Everything* in Roman government is designed to protect the almighty Senate and the First Class! Do senators or knights belong to Esquilina or Suburana? Of course not! They belong to Fabia, to Cornelia, to Romilia! Well, let them continue to belong to Fabia, to Cornelia, to Romilia, I say! But let them share Fabia and Cornelia and Romilia with men from Prifernum, Buca, Vibinium—and let them share Fabia and Cornelia and Romilia with freedmen from Esquilina and Suburana!"

This was greeted with hysterical cheers, having the full approval of all strata save the uppermost and the lowliest; the uppermost because it would lose power, the lowliest because its situation would not be changed in the least.

"I don't understand!" gasped Antonius Orator to Titus Pomponius as they stood in the well of the Comitia surrounded by screaming, howling supporters of Sulpicius. "He's a nobleman! He hasn't had time to gather so many adherents! He's not a Saturninus! I—do—not—understand!"

"Oh, I understand," said Titus Pomponius sourly. "He's attacked the Senate for debt. What this crowd here today is hoping for is simple. They think if they pass whatever laws Sulpicius asks them to pass, as a reward he'll legislate for the cancellation of debts."

"But he can't do that if he's busy throwing men out of the Senate for being in debt for eight thousand sesterces! *Eight thousand sesterces!* It's a pittance! There's hardly a man in the whole city isn't in debt for at least that much!"

"In trouble, Marcus Antonius?" asked Titus Pomponius.

"No, of course not! But that can't be said for more than a handful—even men like Quintus Ancharius, Publius Cornelius Lentulus, Gaius Baebius, Gaius Atilius Serranus—ye gods, the best men on earth, Titus Pomponius! But who hasn't had trouble finding cash these past two years? Look at the Porcii Catones, with all that land in Lucania—not a sestertius of income thanks to the war.

And the Lucilii too—southern landowners again." Marcus Antonius paused for breath, then asked, "Why should he legislate for the cancellation of debts when he's throwing men out of the Senate for debt?"

"He hasn't any intention of cancelling debts," said Pomponius. "The Second and Third Classes are just hoping he will, that's all."

"Has he promised them anything?"

"He doesn't have to. Hope is the only sun in their sky, Marcus Antonius. They see a man who hates the Senate and the First Class as much as Saturninus did. So they hope for another Saturninus. But Sulpicius is vastly different."

"Why?" wailed Antonius Orator.

"I have absolutely no idea what maggot's in his mind," said Titus Pomponius. "Let's get out of this crowd before it turns on us and rends us limb from limb."

On the Senate steps they met the junior consul, who was accompanied by his very excited son, just back from military duty in Lucania and still in a martial mood.

"It's Saturninus all over again!" cried young Pompeius Rufus loudly. "Well, this time we will be ready for him—we're not going to let him get control of the crowds the way Saturninus did! Now that almost everybody is back from the war it's easy to get a trusty gang together and stop him—and that's what I'm going to do! The next *contio* he calls will turn out very differently, I promise you!"

Titus Pomponius ignored the son in order to concentrate upon the father and other senators in hearing. "Sulpicius is not remotely another Saturninus," he said doggedly. "The times are different and Sulpicius's motives are different. Then, it was shortage of food. Now, it's the prevalence of debt. But Sulpicius doesn't want to be King of Rome. He wants *them* to rule Rome"—finger pointing at the Second and Third Classes jammed into the Comitia— "and that is very different indeed."

"I've sent for Lucius Cornelius," said the junior consul to Titus Pomponius, Antonius Orator and Catulus Caesar, who had heard what Pomponius said and drifted over.

"Don't you think you can control what's happening, Quintus Pompeius?" asked Pomponius, who was adept at asking awkward questions.

"No, I don't," said Pompeius Rufus frankly.

"What about Gaius Marius?" asked Antonius Orator. "He can control any crowd within Rome."

"Not this time," said Catulus Caesar contemptuously. "In this instance, he's backing the rebellious tribune of the plebs. Yes, Marcus Antonius, it's Gaius Marius who has put Publius Sulpicius up to this!"

"Oh, I don't believe that," said Antonius Orator.

"I tell you, Gaius Marius is backing him!"

"If that is really true," said Titus Pomponius, "then I would say a fourth law will appear on Sulpicius's agenda."

"A fourth law?" asked Catulus Caesar, frowning.

"He will legislate to remove the command of the war against Mithridates from Lucius Sulla. Then give it to Gaius Marius."

"Sulpicius wouldn't dare!" cried Pompeius Rufus.

"Why not?" Titus Pomponius stared at the junior consul. "I am glad you've sent for the senior consul. When will he be here?"

"Tomorrow or the day after."

Sulla arrived well before dawn the next morning, having driven to Rome the moment Pompeius Rufus's letter found him. Did any consul ever have so much bad news? asked Sulla of himself—first the massacre in Asia Province, now another Saturninus. My country is bankrupt, I have just put down one revolution, and against my name in the *fasti* will go the odium of having sold off State property. Not that any of it matters provided I can deal with it. And I can deal with it.

"Is there a *contio* today?" he asked Pompeius Rufus, to whose house he had gone immediately.

"Yes. Titus Pomponius says Sulpicius is going to put a law forward to strip you of the command in the war against Mithridates and give it to Gaius Marius."

All outward movement in Sulla stilled, even his eyes. "I am the consul, and the war was given to me legally," he said. "If Gaius

Marius was well enough, he could have it gladly. But he isn't well enough. And he can't have it." He blew through his nose. "I suppose this means Gaius Marius is backing Sulpicius."

"So everyone thinks. Marius hasn't appeared at any of the *contiones* yet, but it is true that I've seen some of his minions at work in the crowd among the lower Classes. Like that frightful fellow who leads a gang of Suburan roughnecks," said Pompeius Rufus.

"Lucius Decumius?"

"Yes, that's him."

"Well, well!" said Sulla. "This is a new aspect of Gaius Marius, Quintus Pompeius! I didn't think he'd stoop to using tools like Lucius Decumius. Yet I very much fear that having his old age and his poor health pointed out to him so resoundingly in the House has given him to understand he's finished. But he doesn't want to be finished. He wants to go to war against Mithridates. And if that means he must turn himself into a Saturninus, he will."

"There's going to be trouble, Lucius Cornelius."

"I know that!"

"No, I mean that my son and a lot of other sons of senators and knights are assembling a force to expel Sulpicius from the Forum," said Pompeius Rufus.

"Then you and I had better be in the Forum when Sulpicius convenes the Plebeian Assembly."

"Armed?"

"Definitely not. We must try to contain this legally."

When Sulpicius arrived in the Forum shortly after dawn, it was apparent that he had heard rumors of the band led by the junior consul's son, for he appeared in the midst of a huge escort of young men of the Second and Third Classes, all armed with clubs and small wooden shields; and to protect this inner escort he had surrounded them with a mass of men from what seemed the Fifth Class and the Head Count—ex-gladiators and crossroads college members. So huge was the "bodyguard" that young Quintus Pompeius Rufus's little army was dwarfed to the size of impotence.

"The People," cried Sulpicius to a Comitia half filled by his "bodyguard" alone, "are sovereign! That is, the People are *said* to be sovereign! It's a convenient phrase trotted out by the members of the Senate and the leading knights whenever they need your votes. But it means absolutely nothing! It is hollow, it is a mockery! What responsibilities do you truly have in government? You are at the mercy of the men who call you together, the tribunes of the plebs! *You* don't formulate laws and promulgate them in this Assembly—you are simply here to *vote* on laws formulated and promulgated by the tribunes of the plebs! And with very few exceptions, who own the tribunes of the plebs? Why, the Senate and the Ordo Equester! And what happens to those tribunes of the plebs who declare themselves the servants of the sovereign People? I'll tell you what happens to them! They are penned up in the Curia Hostilia and smashed into pulp by tiles off the Curia Hostilia roof!"

Sulla twisted his shoulders. "Well, that's a declaration of war, isn't it? He's going to make Saturninus a hero."

"He's going to make himself a hero," said Catulus Caesar.

"Listen!" said Merula *flamen Dialis* sharply.

"It is time," Sulpicius was saying, "that the Senate and the Ordo Equester were shown once and for all who is sovereign in Rome! That is why I stand here before you—your champion—your protector—your *servant*! You are just emerging from three frightful years, years during which you were required to shoulder the bulk of the burden of taxes and land deprivation. You gave Rome most of the money to fund a civil war. But did anyone in the Senate ask you what you thought about war against your brothers, the Italian Allies?"

"We certainly did ask!" said Scaevola Pontifex Maximus grimly. "They were more passionately for war than the Senate was!"

"They're not about to remember that now," said Sulla.

"No, they didn't ask you!" shouted Sulpicius. "They denied your brothers the Italians *their* citizenship, not yours! Yours is a mere shadow. Theirs is the substance ruling Rome! They couldn't allow the addition of thousands of new members into their exclusive little rural tribes—that would have given their inferiors too much power! So even after the franchise was granted to the Italians they made sure the new citizens were contained within too few tribes to affect electoral outcomes! But all of that ends, sovereign People, the moment you ratify my law to distribute the new citizens and the freedmen of Rome across the whole thirty-five tribes!"

A wave of cheering broke out so loudly that Sulpicius was obliged to stop; he stood, smiling broadly, a handsome man in his middle thirties with a patrician look to him despite his plebeian rank—fine boned, fair in coloring.

"There are also other ways in which you have been cheated, thanks to the Senate and the Ordo Equester," Sulpicius went on when the noise died down. "It is more than time that the prerogative—and it is no more than prerogative, for it is *not* law!—of conferring all military commands and directing all wars was removed from the Senate and the Senate's secret masters of the Ordo Equester! It is time that you—the backbone, the basis of everything truly Roman!—were given the tasks you should have under the law. Among those tasks is the right to decide whether or not Rome should go to war—and if it is to be war, *who* should command."

"Here it comes," said Catulus Caesar.

Sulpicius turned to level his finger at Sulla, who stood in the forefront of the crowd atop the Senate steps, his looks singling him out. "There is the senior consul! Elected senior consul by *his* peers, not yours! How long is it since even the Third Class was needed to cast a ballot in the consular elections?"

Seeming to realize that he was in danger of drifting from his point, Sulpicius paused, came back to it. "The senior consul was given the command in a war so vital to the future of Rome that if that war is not conducted by the best man in Rome, Rome may well cease to exist. So who gave the command of the war against King Mithridates of Pontus to the senior consul? Who decided he was the best man in Rome to do the job? Why, the Senate and their secret masters of the Ordo Equester! Putting up their own, as always! Willing to jeopardize Rome in order to see a patrician nobleman put on the trappings of the general! For who *is* this Lucius Cornelius Sulla? What wars has he won? Do *you* know him, sovereign

People? Well, I can tell you who he is! Lucius Cornelius Sulla stands there because he rode on Gaius Marius's back! Everything he has achieved he achieved by riding on Gaius Marius's back! He is *said* to have won the war against the Italians! But we all know that it was Gaius Marius dealt the first and hardest blows—had Gaius Marius not, then this man Sulla couldn't have gone on to victory!"

"How *dare* he!" gasped Crassus Censor. "It was you and no one but you, Lucius Cornelius! You won the Grass Crown! You brought the Italians to their knees!" He drew in a great breath to shout this at Sulpicius, but shut his mouth when Sulla twisted his arm.

"Leave be, Publius Licinius! If we start shouting at them, they'll turn on us and lynch us. I want this mess cleared up in a legal and peaceful way," said Sulla.

Sulpicius was still hammering his point home. "Can this Lucius Cornelius Sulla address you, sovereign People? Of course he can't! He's a patrician! Too good for the likes of you! In order to give this precious patrician the command of the war against Mithridates, the Senate and the Ordo Equester passed over a far more qualified and able man! *They passed over none other than Gaius Marius!* Saying he was sick, saying he was old! But I ask you, sovereign People!—who have you seen every single day for the past two years walking through this city forcing himself to get well? Exercising, looking better every day? Gaius Marius! Who might be old, but is no longer sick! Gaius Marius! Who might be old, but is still the best man in Rome!"

The cheering had broken out again, but not for Sulpicius. The crowd parted to reveal Gaius Marius walking down to the bottom of the Comitia well, briskly and on his own; Gaius Marius no longer needed to lean on his boy, who was not with him.

"Sovereign People of Rome, I ask you to approve of a fourth law in my program of legislation!" Sulpicius shouted, beaming at Gaius Marius. "I propose that the command of the war against King Mithridates of Pontus be stripped away from the haughty patrician Lucius Cornelius Sulla, and given to your own Gaius Marius!"

Sulla waited to hear no more. Asking that Scaevola Pontifex

Maximus and Merula *flamen Dialis* accompany him, he walked home.

Ensconced in his study, Sulla looked at them. "Well, what do we do?" he asked.

"Why Lucius Merula and me?" was Scaevola's answer.

"You're the heads of our religion," said Sulla, "and you know the law as well. Find me a way to prolong Sulpicius's campaign in the Comitia until the crowd gets tired of it—and him."

"Something soft," said Merula thoughtfully.

"Soft as kitten's fur," said Sulla, tossing back a cup of unwatered wine. "If it came to a pitched battle in the Forum, he'd win. He's no Saturninus! Sulpicius is a much cleverer man. He beat us to the violent alternatives. I did a rough count of the number in his guard, and came up with a figure not much short of four thousand. And they're armed. Clubs on the surface, but I suspect swords underneath. We can't field a civilian force capable of teaching them a lesson in a space as confined as the Forum Romanum." Sulla stopped, grimaced as if he tasted something sour and bitter; his pale cold eyes looked into nothing. "If I have to, Pontifex Maximus, *flamen Dialis,* I will pile Pelion on top of Ossa before I see our rightful privileges overturned! Including my own position! But let us first see if we can't defeat Sulpicius with his own weapon—the People."

"Then," said Scaevola, "the only thing to do is to declare all the Comitial days between now and whenever you wish as *feriae.*"

"Oh, that's a good idea!" said Merula, face lightening.

Sulla frowned. "Is it legal?"

"Most definitely. The consuls, the Pontifex Maximus, and the Colleges of Pontifices are at complete liberty to set days of rest and holiday during which the Assemblies cannot meet."

"Then post the declaration of *feriae* this afternoon on rostra and Regia, and have the heralds proclaim days of rest and holiday between now and the Ides of December." Sulla grinned nastily. "His term as a tribune of the plebs finishes three days before that. And the moment he's out of office, I'll have Sulpicius up on charges of treason and inciting violence."

"You'll have to try him quietly," said Scaevola, shivering.

"Oh, for Jupiter's sake, Quintus Mucius! How can it be done *quietly*?" asked Sulla. "I shall haul him up and try him, that's all! If he can't woo the crowds with lovely words, he'll be helpless enough. I'll drug him."

Two pairs of startled eyes flew to Sulla's face; it was when he said things like drugging a man that he was most alien, least able to be understood.

Sulla convened the Senate next morning and announced that the consuls and pontifices had declared a period of *feriae* during which no meetings in the Comitia could be held. It fetched a round of quiet cheers, as Gaius Marius was not in the House to object.

Catulus Caesar walked out of the chamber afterward with Sulla. "How dared Gaius Marius place the State in jeopardy, all for the sake of a command he's not fit to take up?" demanded Catulus Caesar.

"Oh, because he's old, he's afraid, his mind's not what it was, and he wants to be consul of Rome seven times," said Sulla wearily.

Scaevola Pontifex Maximus, who had left ahead of Sulla and Catulus Caesar, suddenly came running back. "Sulpicius!" he cried. "He's ignoring the proclamation of *feriae,* he's calling it a ploy devised by the Senate and going ahead in *contio!*"

Sulla didn't look surprised. "I imagined that was what he would do," he said.

"Then what was the point of it?" asked Scaevola indignantly.

"It puts us in the position of being able to declare any laws he discusses or passes during the period of *feriae* invalid," said Sulla. "That's the only virtue *feriae* has."

"If he passes his law expelling everyone in debt from the Senate," said Catulus Caesar, "we'll never be able to declare his laws invalid. There won't be enough senators left to make a quorum. And that means the Senate will cease to exist as a political force."

"Then I suggest that we get together with Titus Pomponius,

Gaius Oppius, and other bankers and arrange for the cancellation of all senatorial debts—unofficially, of course."

"We can't!" wailed Scaevola. "The senatorial creditors are insisting on their money, and there *isn't* any money! No senator borrows from respectable lenders like Pomponius and Oppius! They're too public! The censors would get to know!"

"Then I'll charge Gaius Marius with treason and take the money from his estates," said Sulla, looking ugly.

"Oh, Lucius Cornelius, you can't!" moaned Scaevola. "The 'sovereign People' would tear us apart!"

"Then I'll open my war chest and pay the Senate's debts with that!" said Sulla through his teeth.

"You can't, Lucius Cornelius!"

"I am getting very tired of being told I can't," said Sulla. "Let myself be beaten by Sulpicius and a pack of gullible fools who think he's going to cancel *their* debts? I won't! Pelion on top of Ossa, Quintus Mucius! I will do whatever I have to do!"

"A fund," said Catulus Caesar. "A fund set up by those of us not in debt to salvage those who face expulsion."

"To do that, we would have needed to see into the future," said Scaevola miserably. "It would take at least a month. I'm not in debt, Quintus Lutatius. Nor are you, I imagine. Nor Lucius Cornelius. But ready money? I don't have any! Do you? Can you scrape up more than a thousand sesterces without selling property?"

"I can, but only just," said Catulus Caesar.

"I can't," said Sulla.

"I think we should put a fund together," said Scaevola, "but it will require the sale of property. Which means it will come too late. Those senators in debt will have been expelled. However, as soon as they're out of debt, the censors can reinstall them."

"You don't think Sulpicius will permit that, do you?" asked Sulla. "He'll do some more legislating."

"Oh, I hope I get a chance to lay my hands on Sulpicius some dark night!" said Catulus Caesar savagely. "How can he dare to do all this at a time when we can't even fund a war we *have* to win?"

"Because Publius Sulpicius is clever and committed," said Sulla. "And I suspect Gaius Marius put him up to it."

"They'll pay," said Catulus Caesar.

"Be careful, Quintus Lutatius. It's they might make you pay," said Sulla. "Still, they fear us. And with good reason."

Seventeen days had to elapse between the first *contio* at which a law was discussed and the meeting of the Assembly voting that law into being; Publius Sulpicius Rufus continued to hold his *contiones* while the days dripped away and the time for ratification came ever closer, seemed more inevitable.

On the day before the first pair of Sulpicius's laws were to be put to the vote, young Quintus Pompeius Rufus and his friends who were the sons of senators and knights of the First Class decided to put a stop to Sulpicius in the only way now possible—by force. Without the knowledge of their fathers or of the curule magistrates, young Pompeius Rufus and some others gathered over a thousand men aged between seventeen and thirty. They all owned armor and arms, they had all until very recently been in the field against the Italians. As Sulpicius conducted the *contio* applying the finishing touches to the actual drafting of his first pair of laws, a thousand heavily armed young men of the First Class marched into the Forum Romanum and immediately attacked the men attending Sulpicius's meeting.

The invasion caught Sulla completely unprepared; one moment he and his colleague Quintus Pompeius Rufus were observing Sulpicius from the top of the Senate steps, surrounded by other senior senators, and the next moment the whole of the lower Forum was a battlefield. He could see young Quintus Pompeius Rufus wreaking havoc with a sword, heard the father standing beside him cry out in anguish, and held the father's arm so strongly he couldn't move.

"Leave it, Quintus Pompeius. There's nothing you can do," said Sulla curtly. "You'd never even get to his side."

Unfortunately the crowd was so large it extended far beyond the actual Comitia well. No general, young Pompeius Rufus had deployed his men thinly spread out rather than kept them in a wedge. Had he done so, he might have driven through the middle of the pack; as it was, Sulpicius's guard had no difficulty in uniting.

Fighting bravely, young Pompeius Rufus himself succeeded in working his way around the rim of the Comitia well and reached the rostra. Intent upon Sulpicius as he scrambled up to the rostra platform, he never even saw the burly middle-aged fellow who had obviously retired from the gladiatorial ring until his sword was wrenched down. Young Pompeius Rufus tumbled from the rostra into Sulpicius's guard below, and was clubbed to death.

Sulla heard the father's scream, felt rather than saw several senators drag him away, and himself realized that the guard, now victorious over the ranks of the young elite, would turn next to the Senate steps. Like an eel he wriggled through the throng of panicked senators and dropped off the edge of the Senate House podium into the pandemonium below, his *toga praetexta* abandoned. A deft twist of his hand plucked a *chlamys* cloak from some Greek freedman trapped by the fight; Sulla threw it over his telltale head and pretended he too was a Greek freedman only intent upon removing himself from the turmoil. He ducked beneath the colonnade of the Basilica Porcia, where frantic merchants were trying to disassemble their stalls, and worked his way into the Clivus Argentarius. The crowd grew less, the fighting nonexistent; Sulla headed up the hill and through the Porta Fontinalis.

He knew exactly where he was going. To see the prime mover in all this. To see Gaius Marius, who wanted to command a war and get himself elected consul a seventh time.

He threw the *chlamys* away and knocked on Marius's door clad only in his tunic. "I want to see Gaius Marius," he said to the porter in tones which implied he was clad in all his regalia.

Unwilling to deny entry to a man he knew so well, the porter held the door open and admitted Sulla to the house.

But it was Julia who came, not Gaius Marius.

"Oh, Lucius Cornelius, this is terrible!" she said, and turned to a servant. "Bring wine."

"I want to see Gaius Marius," said Sulla through his teeth.

"You can't, Lucius Cornelius. He's asleep."

"Then wake him, Julia. If you don't, I swear I will!"

Again she turned to a servant. "Please ask Strophantes to wake Gaius Marius and tell him Lucius Cornelius Sulla is here to see him on urgent business."

"Has he gone completely mad?" asked Sulla, reaching for the water flagon; he was too thirsty to drink wine.

"I don't know what you mean!" cried Julia, looking defensive.

"Oh, come, Julia! You're the Great Man's wife! If you don't know him, no one does!" snarled Sulla. "He's deliberately engineered a series of events he thinks will bring him the command against Mithridates, he's cultivated the lawless career of a man who is determined to tear down the *mos maiorum,* he's turned the Forum into a shambles and caused the death of the son of the consul Pompeius Rufus—not to mention the deaths of hundreds of others!"

Julia closed her eyes. "I cannot control him," she said.

"His mind is gone," said Sulla.

"No! Lucius Cornelius, he *is* sane!"

"Then he's not the man I thought he was."

"He just wants to fight Mithridates!"

"Do you approve?"

Again Julia closed her eyes. "I think he should stay at home and leave the war to you."

They could hear the Great Man coming, and fell silent.

"What's amiss?" asked Marius as he entered the room. "What brings you here, Lucius Cornelius?"

"A battle in the Forum," said Sulla.

"That was imprudent," said Marius.

"Sulpicius *is* imprudent. He's given the Senate nowhere to go except to fight for its existence in the only way left—with the sword. Young Quintus Pompeius is dead."

Marius smiled, not a pretty sight. "That's too bad! I don't imagine his side won."

"You're right, it didn't win. Which means that at the end of a long and bitter war—and facing yet another long and bitter war!—Rome is the poorer by a hundred or so of her best young men," said Sulla harshly.

"Yet another long and bitter war? Nonsense, Lucius Cornelius! I'll beat Mithridates in a single season," said Marius complacently.

Sulla tried. "Gaius Marius, why can't you get it through your head that Rome has no money? Rome is bankrupt! Rome cannot afford to field twenty legions! The war against the Italians has put Rome into hopeless debt! The Treasury is empty! And even the great Gaius Marius cannot win against a power as strong as Pontus in one single season if he has only five legions to work with!"

"I can pay for several legions myself," said Marius.

Sulla scowled. "Like Pompey Strabo? But when you pay them yourself, Gaius Marius, they belong to you, not to Rome."

"Rubbish! It means no more than that I place my own resources at the disposal of Rome."

"Rubbish! It means you place Rome's resources at your disposal," Sulla countered sharply. "You'll lead *your* legions!"

"Go home and calm down, Lucius Cornelius. You're upset at the loss of your command."

"I haven't lost my command yet," said Sulla. He looked at Julia. "You know your duty, Julia of the Julii Caesares. Do it! To Rome, not to Gaius Marius."

She walked with him toward the door, face impassive. "Please don't say any more, Lucius Cornelius. I can't have my husband upset."

"To Rome, Julia! To Rome!"

"I am Gaius Marius's wife," she said as she held open the door. "My first duty is to him."

Well, Lucius Cornelius, you lost that one! said Sulla to himself as he walked down onto the Campus Martius. He's as mad as a Pisidian seer in a prophetic frenzy, but no one will admit it, and no one will stop him. Unless I do.

Taking the long way round, he went not to his own house but to the house of the junior consul. His daughter was now a widow with a newborn boy and a year-old girl.

"I have asked my younger son to take the name of Quintus," said the junior consul, tears rolling unchecked down his face. "And of course we have my dear Quintus's own little son, who will perpetuate the senior branch."

Of Cornelia Sulla there was no sign.

"How is my daughter?" Sulla asked.

"Heartbroken, Lucius Cornelius! But she has her children, and that is some consolation."

"Well, sad as this is, Quintus Pompeius, I'm not here to mourn," said Sulla crisply. "We must call a conference. It goes without saying that at a time like this a man wants nothing to do with the outside world—I speak feelingly, having lost a son myself. But the outside world will not go away. I must ask you to come to my house at dawn tomorrow."

Exhausted, Lucius Cornelius Sulla then plodded across the brow of the Palatine to his own elegant new house and his anxious new wife, who burst into tears of joy at seeing him unharmed.

"Never worry about me, Dalmatica," he said. "My time isn't yet. I haven't fulfilled my destiny."

"Our world is coming to an end!" she cried.

"Not while I live," said Sulla.

He slept long and dreamlessly, the repose of a man much younger than he, and woke before the dawn with no idea exactly what he ought to do. This rudderless state of mind did not worry him in the least; I do best when I act as Fortune dictates on the moment, he thought, and found himself actually looking forward to the day.

"As far as I can estimate, the moment Sulpicius's senatorial debt law is passed this morning, the number in the Senate will drop to forty. Not enough for a quorum," said Catulus Caesar gloomily.

"We still have censors, do we not?" asked Sulla.

"Yes," said Scaevola Pontifex Maximus. "Neither Lucius Julius nor Publius Licinius is in debt."

"Then we must act on the assumption that it has not occurred to Publius Sulpicius that the censors might have the courage to add to the Senate," said Sulla. "When it does occur to him, he'll bring in some other law, nothing is more certain. In the meantime, we can try to get our expelled colleagues out of debt."

"I agree, Lucius Cornelius," said Metellus Pius, who had made the trip from Aesernia the moment he heard what Sulpicius was doing in Rome, and had been talking with Catulus Caesar and Scaevola as they walked to Sulla's house. He threw out his hands irritably. "If the fools had only borrowed money from men of their own kind, they might have secured a dispensation for their debts, at least for the time being! But we're caught in our own trap. A senator needing to borrow money has to be very quiet about it if he can't secure a loan from a fellow senator. So he goes to the worst kind of usurer."

"I still don't understand why Sulpicius has turned on us like this!" said Antonius Orator fretfully.

"Tace!" said every other voice, goaded.

"Marcus Antonius, we may never know why," said Sulla with more patience than he was known for. "At this time it's even irrelevant why. *What* is far more important."

"So how do we go about getting the expelled senators out of debt?" asked the Piglet.

"A fund, as agreed to. There will have to be a committee to handle it. Quintus Lutatius, you can be the chairman. There's no senator in debt would have the gall to conceal his true circumstances from you," said Sulla.

Merula *flamen Dialis* giggled, clapped a guilty hand over his mouth. "I apologize for my levity," he said, lips quivering. "It just occurred to me that if we were sensible, we'd avoid seeking to pull Lucius Marcius Philippus out of the mire! Not only will his debts more than equal the combined total of everyone else's, but we could then lose him permanently from the Senate. After all, he's only one man. His omission won't make any difference except in the amount of peace and quiet."

"I think that's a terrifically good idea," said Sulla blandly.

"The trouble with you, Lucius Cornelius, is that you are politically nonchalant," said Catulus Caesar, scandalized. "It makes no difference what we think of Lucius Marcius—the fact remains that his is an old and particularly illustrious family. His tenure in the Senate must be preserved. The son is a far different man."

"You're right, of course," sighed Merula.

"Very well, that's decided," said Sulla, smiling faintly. "For the rest, we can do no more than wait upon events. Except that I think it's time to terminate the period of *feriae*. According to the religious regulations, Sulpicius's laws are more than effectively invalidated. And I have an idea that it behooves us to allow Gaius Marius and Sulpicius to think they've won, that we're powerless."

"We *are* powerless," said Antonius Orator.

"I'm not convinced of that," said Sulla. He turned to the junior consul, very silent and morose. "Quintus Pompeius, you have every excuse to leave Rome. I suggest you take your whole family down to the seashore. Make no secret of your going."

"What about the rest of us?" asked Merula fearfully.

"You're in no danger. If Sulpicius had wanted to eliminate the Senate by killing its members, he could have done that yesterday. Luckily for us, he's preferred to use more constitutional means. Is our urban praetor clear of debt? Not that it matters, I suppose. A curule magistrate can't be ejected from his office, even if he has been ejected from the Senate," said Sulla.

"Marcus Junius is clear of debt," said Merula.

"Good, it's unequivocal. He's going to have to govern Rome in the absence of the consuls."

"Both consuls? Don't tell me you intend to leave Rome too, Lucius Cornelius!" said Catulus Caesar, aghast.

"I have five legions of infantry and two thousand horse sitting in Capua waiting for their general," said Sulla. "After my precipitate departure the rumors will be flying. I must settle everyone down."

"You really are politically nonchalant! Lucius Cornelius, in a situation as serious as this, one of the consuls *must* remain in Rome!"

"Why?" asked Sulla, raising a brow. "Rome isn't under the administration of the consuls at the moment, Quintus Lutatius. Rome belongs to Sulpicius. And I intend that he be convinced it does."

From that stand Sulla refused to be budged, so the meeting broke up soon afterward, and Sulla left for Campania.

He took his time upon the journey, riding upon a mule without an escort of any kind, his hat on his head, and his head down. All along the way people were talking; the news of Sulpicius and the demise of the Senate had spread almost as quickly as the news of the massacre in Asia Province. As he chose to travel on the Via Latina, Sulla passed through loyally Roman countryside the whole way, and learned that many of the local people considered Sulpicius an Italian agent, that some thought him the agent of Mithridates, and that no one was in favor of a Rome without the Senate. Even though the magical name of Gaius Marius was also being bruited about, the innate conservatism of countryfolk tended toward skepticism of his fitness to command in this new war. Unrecognized, Sulla quite enjoyed these conversations in the various hostelries he patronized along the way, for he had left his lictors in Capua and was dressed like any ordinary traveler.

And on the road he thought in time to the jogging of his mule, leisurely thoughts which whirled and swirled, inchoate almost—but not quite. Not quite. Of one thing he was sure. He had done the right thing in electing to return to his legions. For they *were* his legions—or four of them were. He had led them himself for close to two years, they had given him his Grass Crown. The fifth legion was another Campanian one, under the command of Lucius Caesar first, then of Titus Didius, then of Metellus Pius. Somehow when it had come time to select a fifth legion to go east with him against Mithridates, he found himself turned against his original idea, which had been to second a Marian legion from service with Cinna and Cornutus. And now I am very glad indeed that I have no Marian legion in Capua, thought Lucius Cornelius Sulla.

"That's the problem with being a senator," said Sulla's loyal assistant Lucullus. "Custom dictates that all a senator's money be tied up in land and property, and who is going to leave money idle? So it becomes impossible to lay one's hands on sufficient cash when a senator suddenly needs it. We've got into the habit of borrowing."

"Are you in debt?" asked Sulla, not having thought of it; like Gaius Aurelius Cotta, Lucius Licinius Lucullus had been hustled into the Senate after Sulla had given the censors a public kick up the backside. He was twenty-eight years old.

"I am in debt to the amount of ten thousand sesterces, Lucius Cornelius," said Lucullus levelly. "However, my brother Varro will have seen to it, I imagine, with things in Rome the way they are. He's the one with the money these days. I struggle. But thanks to my uncle Metellus Numidicus and my cousin Pius, I do manage to meet the senatorial census."

"Well, be of good cheer, Lucius Licinius! When we get to the east we'll have the gold of Mithridates to play with."

"What do you intend to do?" asked Lucullus. "If we move very quickly, we can probably sail before Sulpicius's laws are enforced."

"No, I think I must remain to see what happens," said Sulla. "It would be foolish to sail with my command in doubt." He sighed. "Actually I think it's time I wrote to Pompey Strabo."

Lucullus's clear grey eyes rested upon his general with a big question in their depths, but in the end he said nothing. If any man had ever looked in control of a situation, that man was Sulla.

Six days later a letter came from Flaccus Princeps Senatus, not officially couriered; Sulla broke it open and scanned its short contents carefully.

"Well," he said to Lucullus, who had brought the note, "it seems there are only about forty senators left in the Senate. The Varian exiles are being recalled—but if in debt are no longer to be members of the Senate, and of course all of them are in debt. The Italian citizens and the freedman citizens are to be distributed across all thirty-five tribes. And—last but not least!—Lucius Cornelius Sulla has been relieved of his command and replaced by Gaius Marius in a special enactment of the sovereign People."

"Oh," said Lucullus, flattened.

Sulla threw the paper down and snapped his fingers to a servant. "My cuirass and sword," he said to the man, and then, to Lucullus, "Summon the whole army to an assembly."

An hour later Sulla ascended the camp forum speaker's platform in full military dress save for the fact that he wore his hat, not a helmet. Look familiar, Lucius Cornelius, he told himself— look like *their* Sulla.

"Well, men," he said in a clear, carrying voice, but without shouting, "it looks as if we're not going to fight Mithridates after all! You've been sitting here kicking your heels until those in power in Rome—and they are not the consuls!—made up their minds. They have now made up their minds. The command in the war against King Mithridates of Pontus is to go to Gaius Marius by order of the Plebeian Assembly. The Senate of Rome is no more, as there are not enough senators left to constitute a quorum. Therefore all decisions about matters martial and military have been assumed by the Plebs—under the guidance of their tribune, Publius Sulpicius Rufus."

He paused to let the soldiers murmur among themselves and transmit his words to those too far away to hear, then began to speak again in that deceptively normal voice (Metrobius had taught him to project it years ago).

"Of course," he said, "the fact of the matter is that I *am* the legally elected senior consul—that the choice of any command should by rights be mine—and that the Senate of Rome conferred a proconsular imperium upon me for the duration of the war against King Mithridates of Pontus. And—as is my right!—I chose the legions who would go with me. I chose *you*. My men through thick and thin, through one grueling campaign after another. Why would I not choose you? You know me and I know you. I don't love you, though I believe Gaius Marius loves his men. I hope you don't love me, though I believe Gaius Marius's men love him. But then, I have never thought it necessary for men to love other men in order to get the job done. I mean, why should I love you? You're a pack of smelly rascals out of every hole in every sewer inside or outside Rome! But—ye gods, how I *respect* you! Time and time again I've asked you to give me your best—and by all the gods, you've always given it!"

Someone started to cheer, then everyone was cheering. Except the small group who stood directly in front of the platform. The tribunes of the soldiers, elected magistrates who commanded the consul's legions. Last year's men, who had included Lucullus and Hortensius, had liked working under Sulla. This year's men loathed Sulla, thought him a harsh master, overly demanding. One eye on them, Sulla let his soldiers cheer.

"So there we were, men, all going off to fight Mithridates across the sea in Greece and Asia Minor! Not trampling down the crops of our beloved Italy, not raping Italian women. Oh, what a campaign it would have been! Do you *know* how much gold Mithridates has? Mountains of it! Over seventy strongholds in Lesser Armenia alone crammed to the tops of their walls with gold! Gold that might have been ours. Oh, I don't mean to imply that Rome would not have got her share—and more than her share! There's so much gold we could have bathed in it! Rome—and us! Not to mention lush Asian women. Slaves galore. Knacky items of no use to anyone but a soldier."

He shrugged, lifted his shoulders, held out his hands with their palms up and empty. "It is not to be, men. We've been relieved of our commission by the Plebeian Assembly. *Not* a body any Roman expects to be telling him who's to fight, or who's to command. But it's legal. So I'm told. Though I cannot help but ask myself if it is legal to cancel the imperium of the senior consul in the year of his consulship! I am Rome's servant. So are all of you. Better say goodbye to your dreams of gold and foreign women. Because when Gaius Marius goes east to fight King Mithridates of Pontus, he'll be leading his own legions. He won't want to lead mine."

Down from the platform came Sulla, walked through the ranks of his twenty-four tribunes of the soldiers without looking at a single one and disappeared into his tent, leaving Lucullus to dismiss the men.

"That," said Lucullus when he reported to the general's tent, "was masterly. You don't have the reputation of an orator, and I daresay you don't obey the rules of rhetoric. But you certainly know how to get your message across, Lucius Cornelius."

"Why, thank you, Lucius Licinius," said Sulla cheerfully as he divested himself of cuirass and *pteryges*. "I think I do too."

"What happens now?"

"I wait to be formally relieved of my command."

"Would you *really* do it, Lucius Cornelius?"

"Do what?"

"March on Rome."

Sulla's eyes opened wide. "My dear Lucius Licinius! How could you even think to ask such a thing?"

"That," said Lucullus, "is not a straight answer."

"It's the only one you'll get," said Sulla.

The blow fell two days later. The ex-praetors Quintus Calidius and Publius Claudius arrived in Capua bearing an officially sealed letter from Publius Sulpicius Rufus, the new master of Rome.

"You can't give it to me in private," objected Sulla, "it has to be handed to me in the presence of my army."

Once again Lucullus was directed to parade the legions, once again Sulla climbed upon the speaker's platform—but this time he was not alone. The two ex-praetors came with him.

"Men, here are Quintus Calidius and Publius Claudius from Rome," said Sulla casually. "I believe they have an official document for me. I've called you here as witnesses."

A man who took himself very seriously, Calidius made a great show of ensuring that Sulla acknowledge the seal upon the letter before he broke it. He then began to read it out.

"From the *concilium plebis* of the People of Rome to Lucius Cornelius Sulla. By order of this body, you are hereby relieved of your command of the war against King Mithridates of Pontus. You will disband your army and return to—"

He got no further. A superbly aimed stone struck him on the

temple and felled him. Almost immediately a second superbly aimed stone struck Claudius, who tottered; while Sulla stood unconcernedly not three feet away, several more stones followed until Claudius too subsided to the floor of the platform.

The stones ceased. Sulla bent over each man, got to his feet. "They're dead," he announced, and sighed loudly. "Well, men, this has definitely put the oil on the fire! In the eyes of the Plebeian Assembly I am afraid we are all now *personae non gratae*. We have killed the official envoys of the Plebs. And that," he said, still in conversational tones, "leaves us with but two choices. We can stay here and wait to be put on trial for treason—or we can go to Rome and show the Plebs what the loyal soldier servants of the People of Rome think about a law and a directive they find as intolerable as it is unconstitutional. I'm going to Rome, anyway, and I'm taking these two dead men with me. And I'm going to give them to the Plebs in person. In the Forum Romanum. Under the eyes of that stern guardian of the People's rights, Publius Sulpicius Rufus. This is all *his* doing! Not Rome's!"

He paused, drew a breath. "Now when it comes to going into the Forum Romanum, I need no company. But if there's any man here who feels he'd like to take a stroll to Rome with me, I'd be *very* glad of his company! That way, when I cross the sacred boundary into the city I can feel sure I've got company on the Campus Martius to watch my back. Otherwise I might suffer the same fate as the son of my colleague in the consulship, Quintus Pompeius Rufus."

They were with him, of course.

"But the tribunes of the soldiers won't march with you," said Lucullus to Sulla in his command tent. "They've not got enough gumption to see you in person, so they've deputed me to speak for them. They say they cannot condone an army's marching on Rome, that Rome is a city without military protection because the only armies in Italy belong to Rome. And with the single exception of a triumphing army, no Roman army is ever garrisoned anywhere near Rome. Therefore, they say, you are marching with an army on your homeland, and your homeland has no army to repel you. They condemn your action and will try to persuade your army to change its mind about accompanying you."

"Wish them luck," said Sulla, preparing to vacate his quarters. "They can stay here and weep that an army is marching on defenseless Rome. However, I think I'll lock them up. Just to ensure their own safety." His eyes rested upon Lucullus. "And what about you, Lucius Licinius? Are you with me?"

"I am, Lucius Cornelius. To the death. The People have usurped the rights and duties of the Senate. Therefore the Rome of our ancestors no longer exists. Therefore I find it no crime to march upon a Rome I would not want to see my unborn sons inherit."

"Oh, well said!" Sulla strapped on his sword and put his hat upon his head. "Then let us begin to make history."

Lucullus stopped. "You're right!" he breathed. "This is the making of history. No Roman army has ever marched upon Rome."

"No Roman army was ever so provoked," said Sulla.

Five legions of Roman soldiers set off along the Via Latina to Rome with Sulla and his legate riding at their head and a mule-cart carrying the bodies of Calidius and Claudius at the rear. A courier had been sent at the gallop to Quintus Pompeius Rufus in Cumae; by the time that Sulla reached Teanum Sidicinum, Pompeius Rufus was there waiting for him.

"Oh, I don't like this!" said the junior consul miserably. "I can't like it! You are marching on Rome! A defenseless city!"

"*We* are marching on Rome," said Sulla calmly. "Don't worry, Quintus Pompeius. It won't be necessary to invade the defenseless city, you know. I am simply bringing my army along for company on the way. Discipline has never been so strictly enforced—I've got over two hundred and fifty centurions under orders that there's not to be so much as one turnip stolen from a field. The men have a full month's rations with them, and they understand."

"We don't need your army for company."

"What, two consuls without a proper escort?"

"We have our lictors."

"Yes, that's an interesting thing. The lictors decided to go with us whereas the tribunes of the soldiers decided not to go with us," said Sulla. "Elected office obviously makes a difference to a man's attitude about who runs what in Rome."

"Why are you so *happy*?" cried Pompeius Rufus in despair.

"I don't quite know," said Sulla, concealing his exasperation beneath a show of surprise. Time to smooth some soothing cream on the soft hide of his sentimental and doubting colleague. "If I'm happy for any reason, I suppose it's that I've had enough of Forum idiocies, of men who think they know better than the *mos maiorum* and want to destroy what our ancestors built up so carefully and patiently. All I want is Rome the way Rome was designed to be. Fathered and guided by the Senate above all other bodies. A place where men who seek office as tribunes of the plebs are harnessed, not let run amok. There comes a time, Quintus Pompeius, when it is not possible to stand by and watch other men change Rome for the worse. Men like Saturninus and Sulpicius. But most of all, men like Gaius Marius."

"Gaius Marius will fight," said Pompeius Rufus dolefully.

"Fight with what? There's not a legion closer to Rome than Alba Fucentia. Oh, I imagine Gaius Marius will try to summon Cinna and his troops—Cinna's in his pocket, of that I'm sure. But two things will prevent him, Quintus Pompeius. One is the natural tendency of all other men in Rome to doubt my sincerity in leading my army to Rome—it will be deemed a ploy, no one will believe I'll carry this intent through to its bitter end. The second thing is the fact that Gaius Marius is a *privatus*. He has neither office nor imperium. If he calls to Cinna for troops, he has to do it as a plea to a friend, not as consul or proconsul. And I very much doubt that Sulpicius will condone any such action by Gaius Marius. Because Sulpicius is one who will think my action a ploy."

The junior consul was gazing now at his senior colleague in utter dismay—fine words! Correct words. Words which told Quintus Pompeius Rufus that Sulla had every intention of invading Rome.

Twice upon the way—once at Aquinum and once at Ferentinum—Sulla's army encountered envoys athwart its path; news that Sulla was marching to Rome must have flown like an eagle. Twice did envoys order Sulla to lay down his command in the name of the People and send his army back to Capua; twice did Sulla refuse, though on the second occasion he added,

"Tell Gaius Marius, Publius Sulpicius, and what remains of the Senate that I will meet them on the Campus Martius."

An offer the envoys did not believe, nor Sulla mean.

Then at Tusculum Sulla found the *praetor urbanus,* Marcus Junius Brutus, waiting in the middle of the Via Latina with another praetor for moral support. Their twelve lictors—six apiece—were huddled together on the side of the road trying to hide the fact that the *fasces* they carried contained the axes.

"Lucius Cornelius Sulla, I am sent by the Senate and the People of Rome to forbid your army to advance one foot closer to Rome than this spot," said Brutus. "Your legions are under arms, not en route to a triumph. I forbid them to go further."

Sulla said not a word, just sat his mule stony-faced. The two praetors were shoved roughly off the roadway into the midst of their terrified lictors, and the march to Rome continued. Where the Via Latina encountered the first of the *diverticulum* roads which ringed Rome round, Sulla halted and divided his forces; if anyone believed his story that the army would remain on the Campus Martius, that man now had to accept the fact that Sulla was bent upon invasion.

"Quintus Pompeius, take the Fourth Legion and go to the Colline Gate," said Sulla, privately wondering whether his colleague had the steel to carry this enterprise through. "You will not enter the city," he said gently, "so there is no need to worry. Your task is to prevent anyone's bringing legions down the Via Salaria. Put your men into camp and wait for word from me. If you see troops

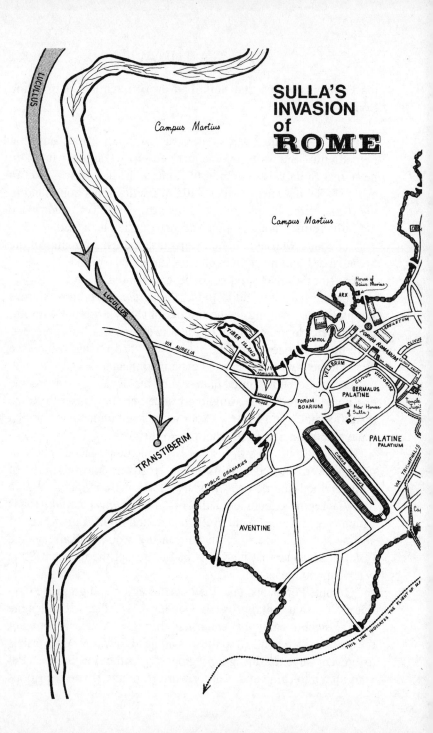

SULLA'S
INVASION
of
ROME

Campus Martius

Campus Martius

LUCULLUS

LUCULLUS

VIA AURELIA

TIBER ISLAND

AEMILIUS

WOODEN BRIDGE

TRANSTIBERIM

FORUM BOARIUM

PUBLIC GRANARIES

AVENTINE

House of Gaius Marius

ARX

CAPITOL

ARGILETUM

FORUM ROMANUM

CLIVUS

VELABRUM

CLIVUS VICTORIAE

GERMALUS PALATINE

New House of Sulla

Temple of Jupiter

PALATINE
PALATIUM

CIRCUS MAXIMUS

VIA TRIUMPHALIS

THIS LINE INDICATES THE FLIGHT OF MA

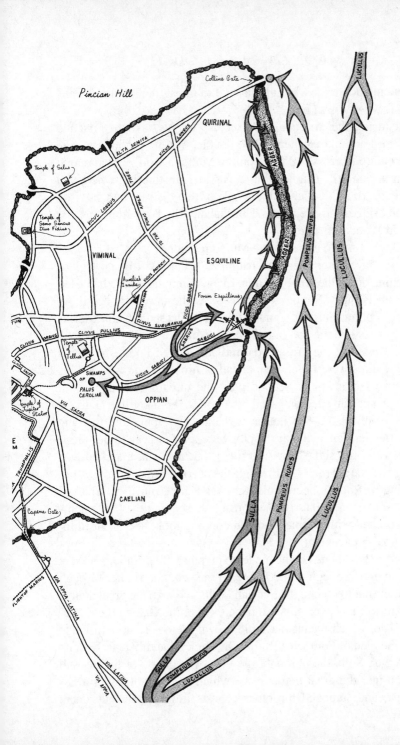

advancing down the Via Salaria send to me at the Esquiline Gate. That is where I will be."

He turned then to Lucullus: "Lucius Licinius, take the First and the Third and march them at the double. You have a long way to go. You are to cross the Tiber on the Mulvian Bridge, then march down through the Campus Vaticanus to Transtiberim, where you will halt. You will occupy the whole of that district, and garrison all the bridges—those across Tiber Island, the Pons Aemilius and the old Wooden Bridge."

"Ought I not to garrison the Mulvian Bridge?"

Sulla gave a fierce grin of triumph. "There will be no legions marching down the Via Flaminia, Lucius Licinius. I have had a letter from Pompey Strabo—who *deplores* the unconstitutional actions of Publius Sulpicius, and will be very pleased if Gaius Marius does not assume the command against Mithridates."

He waited at the crossroads until he judged Pompeius Rufus and Lucullus were far enough ahead of him, then he wheeled his own two legions—the Second plus one unnumbered because it was not a consul's legion—and led them to the Esquiline Gate. At the junction of the Via Latina with the Via Appia and the ring road, the Servian Walls of the city were too far away to be sure if there were any sightseers atop them, but as Sulla marched east along the road which led through the serried ranks of tombs belonging to Rome's necropolis, the walls grew much closer. And every soldier in Sulla's two legions could see that the battlements were packed with people who had come to look, to cry out in incredulous amazement.

At the Esquiline Gate he made no pretense of hesitation. He sent his unnumbered legion into Rome on the run, not to filter through its streets but to ascend the Servian Walls and man the great double rampart of the Agger; this ran from the Colline Gate to the Esquiline Gate, which meant that Sulla's own men were now in touch with the men of Pompeius Rufus. One legion handily placed along the Agger, Sulla then brought the first two cohorts of the Second Legion into the great marketplace which lay inside the Porta Esquilina, and stationed the other cohorts immediately outside it.

Rome was contained. It now depended upon Publius Sulpicius and Gaius Marius as to what would happen next.

The Esquiline Mount was not a suitable place for military maneuvers. The streets leading into the Forum Esquilinum were narrow, perpetually congested, any widening stuffed with booths, stalls, carts, wagons; and the great marketplace was home to merchants, idlers, washerwomen, slaves fetching water, people eating and drinking, ox-carts, panniered asses, peddlers, low-cost schools and a forest of stalls. There were lanes and alleys aplenty leading into the Forum Esquilinum, but two big streets also terminated here—the Clivus Suburanus coming uphill from the Subura, and the Vicus Sabuci coming uphill from the area of manufactories and workshops south and east of the swamp called Palus Ceroliae. Yet here on this unsuitable ground was the battle for Rome fought, about an hour after Sulla entered the city.

The Esquiline Forum itself had been ruthlessly cleared, of course; where the markets had been there now stood still and watchful lines of soldiers at easy attention. Clad in full armor, Sulla sat his mule to one side of his army's *vexillum* and the standards of the consul's Second Legion. At the end of an hour a curious hum began to drown out the cries and noises emanating from the streets leading to the square, growing louder and louder as its source approached, until it could be distinguished as the yells of a great body of men spoiling for a fight.

They erupted into the Esquiline Forum from the mouth of every alley and lane, the spearhead of Sulpicius's "bodyguard" plus the slaves and freedmen Gaius Marius and his son had rounded up, largely through the efforts of Lucius Decumius and the other leaders of the crossroads colleges which dotted Rome. And stopped short at the sight of rank upon rank of Roman legionaries, their silver standards flashing, drummers and trumpeters clustered beside their general waiting—quite placidly, it seemed—for his orders.

"Trumpeter, play, swords out and shields to the front," said Sulla in a clear calm voice.

A single trumpet brayed; it was followed immediately by the soft screech of a thousand swords being drawn from their scabbards, the thump of shields brought round and engaged.

"Drummers, play, hold ranks and wait to be attacked," said Sulla, his voice carrying easily to the unruly crowd of defenders.

The drums began, a hollow rattle that went on and on and on, more unsettling by far to the mob which faced the soldiers than the sound of war cries would have been.

Then the mob parted. Out in front stepped Gaius Marius, sword in hand, helmet on head, a scarlet general's cape streaming behind his shoulders; beside him was Sulpicius, behind him Young Marius.

"Charge!" roared Marius, and emitted a shrill whoop.

His men tried to obey, but could not gain sufficient impetus in that restricted space to budge Sulla's front line, which fended them off contemptuously with shields alone, keeping swords by sides.

"Trumpeters, play, engage the enemy," said Sulla, leaned in his saddle sideways and himself grasped the silver eagle of the Second.

With an enormous effort of will and only to please their general—for no man now the time had come truly wanted to draw blood—the soldiers of Sulla lifted their swords and fought back.

No tactics or maneuvers were possible. The Forum Esquilinum became a struggling mass of tightly packed men who slogged without direction or control. Within minutes the First Cohort had forced its way into the Clivus Suburanus and the Vicus Sabuci, the Second Cohort followed suit, and more cohorts were streaming in disciplined files through the Esquiline Gate, sheer weight and training pushing back the civilians fighting for Marius and Sulpicius. Sulla on his mule moved forward to see what if anything he could do, the only person present with sufficient height to see above the masses of bobbing heads. And discovered that in every street and lane the residents of the tall buildings leaning over them were raining missiles down upon his soldiers—clay pots, logs of wood, bricks, stools. Some, thought the Sulla who had once lived in just such an insula, were genuinely angry at the invasion of their city; but others simply couldn't resist the temptation to chuck things from on high into the wonderful free-for-all below.

"Find me some lighted torches," he said to the *aquilifer* who ought to have been carrying his legion's silver eagle.

The torches came very quickly, robbed from the square.

"Sound every trumpet and drum, top volume," said Sulla.

In this confined space overhung with insulae the noise was maddening; activity stopped for the precious moments Sulla needed.

"If one more object is thrown, I will fire this city!" he screamed at the top of his voice, took a torch and hurled it high into the air. It dropped neatly through a window, and was followed by more torches. Every head disappeared, the missiles ceased.

Satisfied, he returned his attention to the fight, sure there would be no further bombardment. The insula dwellers now understood this was no circus, it was serious. A fight was one thing—a fire quite another. Everyone feared fire more than war.

He called up a cohort not yet engaged and sent it off into the Vicus Sabuci under orders to turn right into the Vicus Sobrius and right again into the Clivus Suburanus, there to take the city mob in the rear.

This proved the turning point; the undisciplined rabble flagged, stopped, then panicked, leaving Marius shouting that any slave who continued to fight would be freed, and Sulpicius—no coward—still fighting a rearguard action with Young Marius inside the Esquiline Forum. But soon Marius, Sulpicius and Young Marius too turned and fled, heading down the Clivus Pullius with Sulla's troops in hot pursuit, Sulla at their head with the silver eagle in his hand.

At the temple of Tellus on the Carinae—where there was a precinct, therefore some space—Marius attempted to halt his polyglot force and rally it to return to the fight. But it refused to behave professionally, its members weeping, flinging swords and clubs away before running off toward the Capitol. Even within the streets of a city, soldiers were better.

When Marius, Young Marius, and Sulpicius suddenly disappeared, the fighting stopped completely. Sulla rode his mule down the Vicus Sandalarius to the great common land of the swamps below the Carinae, where the Via Sacra met the Via Triumphalis. There he halted and had his trumpeters and drummers call the Second to its standards. And there a few soldiers caught in the act of looting were brought before Sulla by their centurions.

"You were well warned—not so much as a turnip from a field," he said to them. "No legionary of Rome plunders Rome."

He then had the guilty men executed on the spot, a salutary lesson for the watching ranks.

"Send for Quintus Pompeius and Lucius Lucullus," he said after the soldiers had been dismissed to an ordered ease.

Neither Pompeius Rufus nor Lucullus had had to do any work, and certainly no fighting.

"That's good," said Sulla to them. "I am the senior consul, it is purely my responsibility. If mine was the only force engaged, then the blame is firmly at my door."

He could be so fair, thought Lucullus, looking at him in wonder; and then he could turn around and invade Rome. A complex man. No, that wasn't quite the right word. Sulla was a man of mood changes so opposite and so strong that one never knew how he was going to react. Nor did one ever know what might set him off. Except, suspected Lucullus, Sulla himself.

"Lucius Licinius, leave seven cohorts of the First across the river to keep Transtiberim quiet. Send three cohorts of the First to guard the granaries of the Aventine and the Vicus Tuscus against citizen looting. The Third will garrison all the most sensitive points along the river. Put one cohort at the Port of Rome, the Campus Lanatarius, the Piscinae Publicae, the Porta Capena, the Circus Maximus, the Forum Boarium, the Forum Holitorium, the Velabrum, the Circus Flaminius, and the Campus Martius. Yes, that's ten places for ten cohorts."

He turned to the junior consul. "Quintus Pompeius, keep the Fourth outside the Colline Gate and make sure they continue to watch for any legions which might come down the Via Salaria. Bring my other legion down off the Agger and disperse its cohorts among the northern and eastern hills—Quirinal, Viminal, Esquiline. And put two cohorts in the Subura."

"Do we garrison the Forum Romanum and the Capitol?"

Sulla shook his head emphatically. "Most definitely not, Lucius Licinius. I'll not copy Saturninus and Sulpicius. The Second can stand duty below the Capitol slopes and around the Forum—but out of sight of either place. I want the People to feel they're safe when I call a meeting."

"Do you remain here?" asked Pompeius Rufus.

"Yes. Lucius Licinius, another job for you. Have some heralds go through the city proclaiming that any missile thrown from an insula will be treated as an act of war against the lawful consuls, and the insula will be fired on the spot. Have other heralds follow the first lot to proclaim that a meeting for all the People will be held in the Forum at the second hour of day." Sulla paused to think if that was all, decided it was, and said, "As soon as you have everything in train, both of you will report back to me here."

The *primus pilus* centurion of the Second, Marcus Canuleius, appeared and stood in the background where Sulla could see him, looking perfectly content; that's a splendid sign, thought Sulla, relieved. It means my soldiers are still *my* soldiers.

"Any sign of them, Marcus Canuleius?" he asked.

The centurion shook his head, its great sideways plume of bright red horsehair riding his helmet like a fan. "No, Lucius Cornelius. Publius Sulpicius was seen crossing the Tiber in a boat, which may mean he's heading for a port somewhere in Etruria. Gaius Marius and his son are thought to be heading for Ostia. The urban praetor, Marcus Junius Brutus, has also fled."

"The fools!" exclaimed Lucullus, surprised. "If they genuinely felt they had the law on their side, they ought to have remained in Rome. Surely they know their chances are better if they debate you in the Forum!"

"You're quite right, Lucius Licinius," said Sulla, pleased that his legate had interpreted events in this way. "Panic, I think," he said. "If either Marius or Sulpicius had stopped to reason his course properly, he would have seen the wisdom of staying in Rome. But I am always lucky, you know. Luckily for me they chose to leave the city." Luck, nothing, he thought to himself. Both Marius and Sulpicius knew that if they had remained, I would have had no choice other than to have them secretly killed. If there's one thing I cannot afford, it is to debate either of them in the Forum. They're the popular heroes, not me. Still, their flight is a two-edged sword. It means I don't have to find a way to kill them in an apparently blameless manner—but it does mean I will have to incur the odium of procuring a sentence of exile on them.

All through the night wakeful soldiers patrolled the streets and open spaces of Rome, campfires burning in any small spot where one could be kindled, the tramp of hobnailed *caligae* a sound which no sleepless Roman had ever heard beneath his windows. But the city pretended to sleep, and got up shivering in a chilly dawn to the sounds of heralds crying that Rome was at peace in the custody of her lawfully elected consuls, and that at the second hour of daylight the consuls would hold a meeting from the rostra.

The meeting was surprisingly well attended, even by the many supporters of Marius and Sulpicius in the Second and Third and Fourth Classes. The First Class was there in entirety while the Head Count stayed away; the Fifth Class also stayed away.

"Ten, fifteen thousand," said Sulla to Lucullus and Pompeius Rufus as he walked down the slope of the Clivus Sacer from the Velia. He was clad in his purple-bordered toga, as was Pompeius Rufus, and Lucullus wore his plain white toga with the senator's broad stripe on the right shoulder of his tunic; there was to be no hint of armed might, nor any soldier on display. "It's vital that every word I say be heard by every man present, so make sure that heralds are properly stationed to relay my words out to the periphery of the crowd."

Preceded by their lictors, the consuls cleaved their way through the throng and mounted the rostra, where Flaccus Princeps Senatus and Scaevola Pontifex Maximus waited. To Sulla, this was a confrontation of enormous importance, for as yet he had seen no member of the skeletal Senate, nor had any idea whether men like Catulus Caesar, the censors, the *flamen Dialis,* or the two on the rostra would be with him now he had asserted the ascendancy of the army over peaceful institutions of government.

They weren't happy, so much was plain. Both were tied in some measure to Marius, Scaevola because he had a daughter affianced to Young Marius, Flaccus because he had only attained the consulship and the censorship thanks to Marius's support at the polls. Now was not the time to have a prolonged conversation with them, but he couldn't not say anything to them either.

"Are you with me?" he asked curtly.

Scaevola drew a quivering breath. "Yes, Lucius Cornelius."

"Then listen to what I have to say to the crowd. It will answer all your questions and doubts too." He looked toward the Senate steps and podium, where Catulus Caesar stood with the censors, Antonius Orator, and Merula *flamen Dialis.* Catulus Caesar gave him a ghost of a wink. "Listen well!" Sulla called.

He turned then to face the lower Forum—which meant his back was to the Senate House—and began to speak. His appearance had been greeted with no cheers, but no boos or hisses either. Which meant he faced an audience prepared to listen, and not entirely because in every side street and piece of vacant ground stood his soldiers.

"People of Rome, no one is more conscious of the gravity of my actions than I am," he said in his clear and carrying voice. "Nor must you think that the presence of an army within Rome is due to anyone's intent save my own. I am the senior consul, legally elected and legally put in command of my army. *I* brought that army to Rome, no one else. My colleagues acted under my orders, as they are obliged to do, including my junior consul, Quintus Pompeius Rufus—though I would remind you that his son was murdered here in our sacred Forum Romanum by some of the Sulpician rabble."

He was speaking slowly in order that the heralds could relay his words outward, and now he paused until the last shouts in the distance ceased.

"For far too long, People of Rome, the right of the Senate and the consuls to organize the affairs and laws of Rome has been ignored—and of recent years even trampled underfoot by a very few power-crazed, self-seeking demagogues calling themselves tribunes of the plebs. These unscrupulous crowd-pleasers seek election as the guardians of the rights of the People, then proceed to abuse that hallowed trust in a completely irresponsible manner. Their excuse is always the same—that they are acting on behalf of the 'sovereign People'! Whereas the truth is, People of Rome, that they are acting in their own interests entirely. You are lured on by promises of largesse or privilege which it is quite beyond the power of this State to grant—especially when you consider that these men usually arise at a time when this State is least able to grant largesse or privilege. That is why they succeed! They play upon your desires and your fears! But they do not mean you well. What they promise, they cannot deliver. For example, did Saturninus ever provide that free grain? Of course he did not! Because there was no grain available. If it had been, your consuls and the Senate would have provided it. When the grain did come, it was your consul, Gaius Marius, who distributed it—not free of charge, but at a very reasonable price."

He stopped again until the heralds caught up.

"Do you really believe that Sulpicius would have legislated to cancel your debts? Of course he would not! Even had I and my army not stepped in, it was beyond his power to do so. No man can evict a whole class from its rightful place—as Sulpicius did the Senate!—on grounds of indebtedness, then turn around and cancel all debt! If you examine his conduct, you will see all this for yourselves—Sulpicius wanted to destroy the Senate, found a way of doing so, and allowed you to think he would treat you in exactly the opposite manner to the way he treated men he had convinced you were your enemies. Always dangling a bait. That he could secure a general cancellation of debt. But he used you, People of Rome. Never once did he say in a public assembly that he would seek a general cancellation of debt! Instead, he sent his agents among you to whisper of it in private. Doesn't that tell you how insincere he was? If he intended to cancel debt, he would have announced it from the rostra. He never did. He used you with utter indifference to your plight. Whereas I as your consul did secure as much relief from the burden of debt as is possible without undermining the whole structure of money—and I did it for *every* Roman, from highest to lowest. I even did it for those who are not Roman! I enacted a general law limiting the payment of interest to interest on the capital only, and at the original agreed rate. So, you might say, it is I who helped relieve debt. Not Sulpicius!"

He rotated through a full circle, pretending that he was peering this way and that into the crowd. After repeating this several times, he turned back to face the crowd again and shrugged, lifting his hands in a gesture of futile appeal.

"Where is Publius Sulpicius?" he asked, seeming amazed. "Whom have I killed since I brought my army into Rome? A few slaves and freedmen, a few ex-gladiators. Rabble. Not respectable Romans. Why then isn't Publius Sulpicius here to speak to you, to refute what I am telling you? I call upon Publius Sulpicius to come forward and refute me in decent and honorable debate—not inside the Curia Hostilia, but out here in full view of his 'sovereign People'!" He cupped his hands around his mouth and roared, "Publius Sulpicius, tribune of the plebs, I demand that you come forward to answer me!"

But his only answer was the crowd's silence.

"He is not here to answer, People of Rome, because when I— the legally elected consul!—entered this city accompanied by my only friends, my soldiers, to seek justice for myself and for them, Publius Sulpicius ran away. But why did he run away? Did he fear for his life? Why should he do that? Have I tried to kill any elected magistrate, or even any ordinary respectable resident of Rome? Do I stand here in full armor holding a dripping sword in my right hand? No! I stand here in the purple-bordered toga of my high office, and my only friends, my soldiers, are not present to hear what I am saying to you. They do not need to be present! I am their legally elected representative as much as I am your legally elected representative. Yet Sulpicius is not here! Why is he not here? Do you truly believe he is fearful for his life? If he is, People of Rome, then he is because he *knows* what he did was illegal and treasonous. For myself, I would rather give him the benefit of the doubt, and wish with all my heart that he was here today!"

Time to stop again, time to peer into the crowd, to pretend to hope Sulpicius was present. Sulla cupped his hands around his mouth and roared, "Publius Sulpicius, tribune of the plebs, I demand that you stand forth to answer me!"

No one appeared.

"He is gone, People of Rome. He fled in the company of the man who duped him as surely as he duped you—Gaius Marius!" cried Sulla.

And now the crowd began to stir, to murmur; that was one name no member of the People of Rome liked to hear spoken of in tones of condemnation.

"Yes, I know," said Sulla very slowly and carefully, making sure his exact words were relayed outward, "Gaius Marius is everybody's hero. He saved Rome from Jugurtha of Numidia. He saved Rome and Rome's world from the Germans. He went to Cappadocia and single-handedly ordered King Mithridates to go home—you didn't know that, did you? Yet I stand here willing to tell you another of Gaius Marius's great deeds! Many of his greatest deeds *are* unsung. I know of them because I was his loyal legate in his campaigns against Jugurtha and the Germans. I was his right-hand man. It is the fate of right-hand men not to be known, not to be famous. And I do not grudge Gaius Marius one tittle of his glorious reputation. It is *deserved*! But I too have been Rome's loyal servant. I too went to the east and single-handedly ordered King Mithridates to go home. I led the first Roman army across the river Euphrates into unknown lands."

He stopped again, seeing with pleasure that the crowd was now settling down, that he had at least managed to convince it of his absolute earnestness.

"I have been Gaius Marius's friend as well as his right-hand man. For many years I was his brother-in-law—until my wife, who was the sister of his wife, died. I did not divorce her. There was no kind of animosity between us. His son and my daughter are first cousins. When some days ago the henchmen of Publius Sulpicius murdered many young men of fine family and great potential, including the son of my colleague Quintus Pompeius—a young man who happened to be my son-in-law, the husband of Gaius Marius's niece—I was obliged to flee for my life from the Forum. And where did I choose to go, sure my life was sacrosanct there? Why, I went to the house of Gaius Marius, and was sheltered by him."

Yes, the crowd was definitely settling down well. He had introduced the subject of Gaius Marius in the right way.

"When Gaius Marius won his great victory against the Marsi, I acted as his right-hand man yet again. And when my army—the army I led to Rome—awarded me the Grass Crown for saving it from certain death at the hands of the Samnites, Gaius Marius rejoiced that I, his unsung assistant, had at last won a reputation for myself upon the battlefield. In terms of importance and the number of enemy lives taken, my victory was a greater one than his, but did that affect him? Of course it did not! He rejoiced for me! And did he not choose to make his reappearance in the Senate on the day of my inauguration as consul? Did his presence not enhance my standing?"

They were completely absorbed now, and no one spoke; Sulla pushed on toward his peroration.

"However, People of Rome, all of us—you—me—Gaius Marius—must from time to time face and deal with very unpleasant facts. One such fact concerns Gaius Marius. He is neither young enough nor well enough to conduct a huge foreign war. His mind is damaged. That apparatus, as all of you know, does not seem to recover as does the body it inhabits recover. The man you have seen for the last two years walking, swimming, exercising, curing his *body* of its severe affliction, cannot cure his *mind*. It is that mental malady I blame for his actions of late. I excuse his excesses in the name of the love I bear him. As must you. Rome is facing a worse conflagration than the one from which she is currently emerging. A greater and far more dangerous power than the Germans has arisen in the person of an eastern king with properly trained and properly equipped armies whose men he numbers in the hundreds of thousands. A man with fleets of hundreds of decked war galleys. A man who has succeeded in obtaining the collaboration of foreign peoples Rome has sheltered and protected—and now give us no thanks. How can I, People of Rome, continue to stand by while you in your ignorance convey the command in this war from me—a man in my prime!—to him—a man past his prime?"

No lover of public speaking, he was feeling the strain. But when he stopped to allow the heralds to catch up he managed to stand as if he wasn't thirsty, as if his knees weren't trembling, as if he didn't care how the crowd reacted.

"Even had I been willing to give up my lawfully conferred command of the war against King Mithridates of Pontus in favor of Gaius Marius, People of Rome, the five legions comprising my army were not willing. I stand here not only as the legally elected senior consul, but as the legally appointed representative of Rome's soldiers. It was they who elected to march to Rome—not to conquer Rome, not to use Romans like enemies!—but to show the People of Rome how they feel about an illegal law extracted from an assembly of civilians by a tongue far more gifted than mine, and at the instigation of a sick old man who happens to be a hero. Yet before they were allowed an opportunity to have audience with you, my soldiers were forced to deal with gangs of armed ruffians who refused them peaceful entry. Gangs of armed ruffians got together from out of the ranks of slaves and freedmen by Gaius Marius and Publius Sulpicius. That my soldiers were not refused entry by the respectable citizens of Rome is manifest—the respectable citizens of Rome are here today to listen to me as I put forward my case and the case of my soldiers. I and they ask only one thing. That we be allowed to do what we were legally and validly appointed to do—fight King Mithridates."

He drew a breath, and when next he spoke produced a voice as loud and brazen as a trumpet call.

"I go to the East in the knowledge that no man enjoys better health, that I have suffered no cerebral catastrophes, that I am in a position to give Rome what Rome must have—victory against the evil foreign king who wants to crown himself King of Rome, who killed eighty thousand of our men and women and children as they clung to altars crying on the gods to protect them! My command is fully according to the law. In other words, the gods of Rome have given this task to *me*. The gods of Rome repose their trust in *me*."

He had won. As he stepped aside for a much greater orator to take his place in the person of Quintus Mucius Scaevola Pontifex Maximus, he knew he had won. For in spite of their susceptibility to those of silver tongue and golden voice, the men of Rome were sane and sensible, and could understand common sense when it was put to them as reasonably as it was forcibly.

"I could wish you had found some other way to assert yourself, Lucius Cornelius," said Catulus Caesar to him as the meeting finally broke up, "but I must support you."

"What other way did he have?" demanded Antonius Orator. "Go on, Quintus Lutatius, give me another way!"

It was the brother, Lucius Caesar, who answered. "One way was for Lucius Cornelius to stay in Campania with his legions and refuse to give up his command."

Crassus the Censor snorted. "Oh, certainly! And then after Sulpicius and Marius gathered the rest of the legions in Italy together, what do you suppose would have happened? If neither side stepped down, it would have been *real* civil war, not war against mere Italians, Lucius Julius! At least by coming to Rome, Lucius Cornelius did the only thing which could have avoided armed confrontation between Romans. The very fact that there are no legions in Rome was his greatest guarantee of success!"

"You're right, Publius Licinius," said Antonius Orator.

And thus it was left; everybody deplored Sulla's tactics, but no one could think of an alternative.

For ten more days Sulla and the leaders of the Senate continued to speak daily in the Forum Romanum, gradually winning the People over with a remorseless campaign aimed at discrediting Sulpicius and gently dismissing Gaius Marius as a sick old man who ought to be content to rest on his laurels.

After those summary executions for looting, Sulla's legions behaved impeccably, and found themselves taken to the hearts of many civilian residents, fed and pampered a little—especially once the news got round that this was the fabled army of Nola, that this was the army had *really* won the war against the Italians. Sulla was careful, however, to provision his troops without placing additional strain on the city's food supplies, and left the pampering up to free choice. But there were those among the populace who eyed the troops skeptically, and remembered that they had marched on Rome of their own volition; therefore if these soldiers were defied or annoyed, a mass slaughter might take place for all their general's fine words in the Forum. After all, he had not sent them back to Campania. He was keeping them within Rome. Not the act of one who would refuse to use them should the occasion arise.

"I don't trust the People," said Sulla to the leaders of the Senate, a body so small now that only its leaders were left. "The moment I'm safely overseas, a new Sulpicius is likely to appear. So I intend to pass legislation which will make that impossible."

He had entered Rome on the Ides of November, dangerously late in the year for a massive program of new laws. Since the *lex Caecilia Didia* had stipulated that three market days must elapse between the first *contio* addressing a new law and its ratification, there was every chance that Sulla's term as consul would be over before he had succeeded in his aims. To make matters worse, the other *lex Caecilia Didia* forbade the tacking together of unrelated items in one law. And the one way legally open to him to get his program finished in time was perhaps the most perilous course of all; to present every one of his new laws to the Whole People in one *contio,* and have them discussed together. Thus enabling everyone to see his ultimate design from the beginning.

It was Caesar Strabo who solved Sulla's dilemma. "Easy," said that cross-eyed worthy when applied to. "Add another law to your list, and promulgate it first of the lot. Namely, a law waiving the provisions of the *lex Caecilia Didia prima* for your laws only."

"The Comitia would never pass it," said Sulla.

"Oh, they will—if they see enough soldiers!" said Caesar Strabo cheerfully.

He was quite right. When Sulla convoked the Assembly of the Whole People—which contained patricians as well as plebeians— he discovered it was very willing to legislate on his behalf. Thus the first law presented to it was one waiving the provisions of the *lex Caecilia Didia prima* in the case of his laws alone; since it covered itself as well, the first *lex Cornelia* of Sulla's program was promulgated and passed on one and the same day. The time was now getting toward the end of November.

One by one, Sulla introduced six more laws, their order of presentation extremely carefully worked out; it was vital that the People not see his ultimate design until it was too late for the People to do anything about unraveling it. And during all this he strove assiduously to avoid any hint of confrontation between his army and the residents of Rome, understanding very well that the People mistrusted him because of those soldiers.

However, since he cared not a jot for the love of the People, only that they obey him, he decided that it would do no harm to institute a whispering campaign within Rome—if his laws were not passed, the city would undergo a bloodbath of epic proportions. For when his own neck was at stake Sulla would stop at nothing. As long as the People did as they were told, they were at complete liberty to hate Sulla as passionately as he had come to hate them. What he could not allow to happen, of course, was that bloodbath; did it happen, his career would be over forever. But, understanding the mechanics of fear, Sulla foresaw no bloodbath. And he was right.

His second *lex Cornelia* seemed innocuous enough. It commanded that three hundred new members be added to the Senate, which contained only forty men. Its wording was deliberately designed to avoid the stigma attached to laws recalling expelled or exiled senators, for the new senators were to be appointed by the censors in the normal way; the censors were not directed to reinstall any senator expelled for debt. As the fund to get the expelled senators out of debt was working as smoothly under Catulus Caesar as Capua had for the duration of the war, there could be no impediment to the censors' reinstating expelled senators. Also, the inroads made upon the Senate by the deaths of so many members would finally be properly repaired. Catulus Caesar had been given the unofficial job of keeping pressure upon the censors, which meant that the Senate would be better than full strength very soon, Sulla was sure. Catulus Caesar was a formidable man.

The third *lex Cornelia* began to reveal Sulla's fist clenched and menacing. It repealed the *lex Hortensia,* a law which had been on the tablets for a full two hundred years. Under the provisions of Sulla's new law, nothing could be brought before the tribal assemblies unless it had first received the stamp of the Senate's approval. This not only muzzled the tribunes of the plebs, it muzzled the consuls and praetors as well; if the Senate did not issue a *senatus consultum,* neither the Plebeian Assembly nor the Assembly of the Whole People could legislate. Nor could the tribal assemblies alter the wording of any *senatus consultum.*

Sulla's fourth *lex Cornelia* came down from the Senate to the Assembly of the Whole People as a *senatus consultum.* It strengthened the top-heaviness of the Centuries by removing the modifications to this body which it had undergone during the early days of the Republic. The *comitia centuriata* was now returned to the form it had enjoyed during the reign of King Servius Tullius, when its votes were skewed to give the First Class very nearly fifty percent of the power. Under Sulla's new law, the Senate and the knights were henceforward to be as strong as ever they were during the time of the kings.

The fifth *lex Cornelia* showed Sulla's sword out and ready. It was the last one in his program to be promulgated and passed in the Assembly of the Whole People. In future no discussion or voting on laws could take place in the tribal assemblies. All legislation had to be discussed and passed by Sulla's new top-heavy Centuriate Assembly, where the Senate and the Ordo Equester could control everything, particularly when they were closely united—as they always were in opposition to radical change or the conveyance of privileges to the lower Classes. From now on, the tribes possessed virtually no power, either in the Assembly of the Whole People or in the Plebeian Assembly. And the Assembly of the Whole People passed this fifth *lex Cornelia* knowing it was passing a sentence of extinction upon itself; it could elect those magistrates it was empowered to elect, but could do nothing else. To conduct a trial in a tribal assembly required the passage of a law first.

All the laws of Sulpicius were still on the tablets, still nominally valid. But of what use were they? What did it matter if the new citizens of Italy and Italian Gaul and the freedman citizens of the two urban tribes were to be distributed across the entire thirty-five tribes? The tribal assemblies could not pass laws, could not conduct trials.

There was a weakness, and Sulla was aware of it. Had he not been anxious to leave for the East he could have worked to overcome it, but it wasn't something he could achieve in the time he had at his disposal. It concerned the tribunes of the plebs. He had managed to draw their teeth; they couldn't legislate, they couldn't put men on trial. But he could not manage to pull out their claws—oh, such claws! They still had the powers the Plebs had invested upon them when they were first created. And among those powers was the power of the veto. In all his legislation, Sulla had been careful not to direct any of it at the magistrates themselves, only at the institutions in which the magistrates functioned. Technically he had done nothing overtly treasonous. But to remove the power of the veto from the tribunes of the plebs could be construed as treasonous. As going against the *mos maiorum*. Tribunician powers were almost as old as the Republic. They were sacred.

In the meantime, the program of laws concluded itself. Not in the Forum Romanum, where the People were accustomed to present themselves and where the People saw what was going on. The sixth and the seventh *leges Corneliae* were presented to the Centuriate Assembly on the Campus Martius—surrounded by Sulla's army, now encamped there.

The sixth law did what Sulla would have found difficult to do in the Forum; it repealed all of Sulpicius's legislation on the grounds that it had been passed *per vim*—with violence—and during lawfully declared *feriae*—religious holidays.

The last law was actually a trial process. It indicted twenty men on charges of treason. Not the new treasons of Saturninus's *quaestio de maiestate,* but the far older and more inflexible treason of the Centuries, *perduellio.* Gaius Marius, Young Marius, Publius Sulpicius Rufus, Marcus Junius Brutus the urban praetor, Publius Cornelius Cethegus, the Brothers Granii, Publius Albinovanus, Marcus Laetorius, and some twelve others were named. The Centuriate Assembly condemned them all. And *perduellio* carried the death sentence; exile was not enough for the Centuries. Even worse, death could be meted out at the moment of apprehension, it did not require formality.

 From none of his friends and from none of the leaders of the Senate did Sulla encounter opposition—except, that is, from the junior consul. Quintus Pompeius Rufus just kept getting more and more depressed, and ended in saying flatly that he could not countenance the execution of men like Gaius Marius and Publius Sulpicius.

Knowing that he had no intention of executing Marius—though Sulpicius would have to go—Sulla tried at first to jolly Pompeius Rufus out of his megrims. When that didn't work, he harped upon the death of young Quintus Pompeius at the hands of Sulpicius's mob. But the harder Sulla talked, the more obstinate Pompeius Rufus became. It was vital to Sulla that no one see a rift in the concord of those in power and so busily legislating the tribal assemblies out of existence. Therefore, he decided, Pompeius Rufus would have to be removed from Rome and from the sight of those soldiers who so offended his fragile sensitivities.

One of the most fascinating changes at work within Sulla concerned this new exposure to supreme power; it was a change he recognized for what it was, and relished it, cherished it. Namely, that he was able to find more satisfaction and release from inner torment by enacting laws to ruin people than ever in the days when he had had to resort to murder. To manipulate the State into ruining Gaius Marius was infinitely more enjoyable than administering a dose of the slowest poison to Gaius Marius, better even than holding Gaius Marius's hand while he died; this new aspect of statecraft set Sulla on a different plane, shot him up into heights so rarefied and exclusive that he could feel himself looking a long way down at the frantic gyrations of his puppets, a god upon Olympus, as free from moral as from ethical restraints.

And so he set out to dispose of Quintus Pompeius Rufus in a completely new and subtle way, a way which exercised his mental faculties and spared him a great deal of anxiety. Why run the risk of getting caught murdering when it was possible to have other people murder on your behalf?

"My dear Quintus Pompeius, you need a spell in the field," said Sulla to his junior colleague with great earnestness and warmth. "It has not escaped me that ever since the death of our dear boy you've been morose, too easily upset. You've lost your ability to be detached, to see the enormity of the design we weave upon the loom of government. The smallest things cast you down! But I don't think a holiday is the answer. What you need is a spell of hard work."

The rather faded eyes rested upon Sulla's face with a huge and genuine affection; how could he not be grateful that his term as consul had allied him to one of history's outstanding men? Who could have guessed it in the days when their alliance had been formed? "I know you're right, Lucius Cornelius," he said. "Probably about everything. But it's very hard for me to reconcile myself to what has happened. And is still happening. If you feel there is some job I can do usefully, I'd be very glad to do it."

"There's one extremely important thing you can do—a job only the consul can succeed in doing," said Sulla eagerly.

"What?"

"You can relieve Pompey Strabo of his command."

An unpleasant shiver attacked the junior consul, who now looked at Sulla apprehensively. "But I don't think Pompey Strabo wants to lose his command any more than you did!"

"On the contrary, my dear Quintus Pompeius. I had a letter from him the other day. In it he asked if it could be arranged that he be relieved of his command. And he specifically asked that his relief be you. Fellow Picentine and all the rest of it—you know! His troops don't like generals who aren't Picentines," said Sulla, watching the gladness spread over the junior consul's face. "Your chief job will be to see to their discharge, actually. All resistance in the north is at an end, there's no further need for an army up there, and certainly Rome can't afford to continue paying for one." Sulla adopted a serious mien. "This is not a sinecure I'm offering you, Quintus Pompeius. I know why Pompey Strabo wants to be replaced all of a sudden. He doesn't want the odium of discharging his men. So let another Pompeius do it!"

"That I don't mind, Lucius Cornelius." Pompeius Rufus squared his shoulders. "I'd be grateful for the work."

The Senate issued a *senatus consultum* the next day to the effect that Gnaeus Pompeius Strabo was to be relieved of his command and replaced by Quintus Pompeius Rufus. Whereupon Quintus Pompeius Rufus left Rome immediately, secure in the knowledge that none of the condemned fugitives had yet been apprehended; he would not be contaminated by the foulness of it after all.

"You may as well act as your own courier," said Sulla, handing him the Senate's order. "Just do me one favor, Quintus Pompeius— before you give Pompey Strabo the Senate's document, give him this letter from me and ask him to read it first."

Since Pompey Strabo at that time was in Umbria in the company of his own legions and encamped outside Ariminum, the junior consul traveled on the Via Flaminia, the great north road which crossed the watershed of the Apennines between Assisium and Cales. Though it was not yet winter, the weather at those heights was freezingly cold, so Pompeius Rufus journeyed warmly inside a closed *carpentum,* and with sufficient luggage to fill a mule-drawn cart. As he knew he was going to a military posting, his only escorts were his lictors and a party of his own slaves. As the Via Flaminia was one of the roads home, he had no need to avail himself of hostelries along the way. He knew all the owners of large houses en route, and stayed with them.

In Assisium his host, an old acquaintance, was obliged to apologize for the standard of accommodation he offered.

"Times have changed, Quintus Pompeius!" he sighed. "I have had to sell so much! And then—as if I didn't already have too many troubles!—I am invaded by a plague of mice!"

Thus Quintus Pompeius Rufus went to bed in a room he remembered as being more richly furnished than it now was, and colder than of yore due to the pillaging of its window shutters by a passing army in need of firewood. For a long time he lay sleepless listening to the scurryings and squeakings, thinking of what was going on in Rome and full of fear because he couldn't help but feel Lucius Cornelius had gone too far. Far too far. There was going to be a reckoning. Too many generations of tribunes of the plebs had strutted up and down the Forum Romanum for the Plebs to lie down under this insult Sulla was offering them. The moment the senior consul was safely abroad all his laws would tumble. And men like himself, Quintus Pompeius Rufus, would bear the blame—and the prosecutions.

His breath clouding the icy air, he got up at dawn and sought his clothes, shivering, teeth chattering. A pair of breeches to cover himself from waist to knees, a long-sleeved warm shirt he could tuck inside the breeches, two warm tunics over the top of that; and two tubes of greasy wool, nether ends sealed, to cover his feet and his legs up to the knees.

But when he picked up his socks and sat on the edge of the bed to draw them on, he discovered that during the night the mice had eaten the richly smelly nether ends of the socks completely away. Flesh crawling, he held them up to the grey light of the unshuttered window and gazed at them sightlessly, filled with horror. For he was a superstitious Picentine, he knew what this meant. Mice were the harbingers of death, and mice had eaten off his feet. He would fall. He would die. It was a prophecy.

His body servant found him another pair of socks and knelt to smooth them up over Pompeius Rufus's legs, alarmed at the still and voiceless effigy sitting on the edge of the bed. The man understood the omen well, prayed it was untrue.

"*Domine,* it is nothing to worry about," he said.

"I am going to die," said Pompeius Rufus.

"Nonsense!" said the slave heartily, helping his master to his feet. "*I'm* the Greek! I know more about the gods of the Underworld than any Roman! Apollo Smintheus is a god of life and light and healing, yet mice are sacred to him! No, I think the omen means you will heal the north of its troubles."

"It means I will die," said Pompeius Rufus, and from that interpretation he would not be budged.

He rode into Pompey Strabo's camp three days later more or less reconciled to his fate, and found his remote cousin living in some state in a big farmhouse.

"Well, this is a surprise!" said Pompey Strabo genially, holding out his right hand. "Come in, come in!"

"I have two letters with me," said Pompeius Rufus, sitting in a chair and accepting the best wine he had sampled since leaving Rome. He extended the little rolls of paper. "Lucius Cornelius asked if you would read his letter first. The other is from the Senate."

A change came over Pompey Strabo the moment the junior consul mentioned the Senate, but he said nothing, nor produced an expression which might have illuminated his feelings. He broke Sulla's seal.

> It pains me, Gnaeus Pompeius, to be obliged by the Senate to send your cousin Rufus to you under these circumstances. No one is more appreciative than I of

the many, many services you have done Rome. And no one will be more appreciative than I if you can do Rome yet one more service—one of considerable import to all our future careers.

Our mutual colleague Quintus Pompeius is a sadly shattered man. From the moment of his son's death—my own son-in-law, and father of my two grandchildren—our poor dear friend has been suffering an alarming decline. As his presence is a grave embarrassment, it has become necessary for me to remove him. You see, he cannot find it in himself to approve of the measures I have been forced—I repeat, forced—to take in order to preserve the *mos maiorum.*

Now I know, Gnaeus Pompeius, that you fully approve of these measures of mine, as I have kept you properly informed and you have communicated with me regularly yourself. It is my considered opinion that the good Quintus Pompeius is in urgent and desperate need of a very long rest. It is my hope that he will find this rest with you in Umbria.

I do hope you will forgive me for my telling Quintus Pompeius about your anxiety to be rid of your command before your troops are discharged from service. It relieved his mind greatly to know that you will welcome him gladly.

Pompey Strabo laid Sulla's piece of paper down and broke the official Senate seal. What he thought as he read did not appear on his face. Finished deciphering it—like Sulla's note, he kept his voice too low and slurred for Pompeius Rufus to hear—he put it on his desk, looked at Pompeius Rufus, and smiled broadly.

"Well, Quintus Pompeius, yours is indeed a welcome presence!" he said. "It will be a pleasure to shed my duties."

Expecting rage, frustration, indignation, despite Sulla's assurances, Pompeius Rufus gaped. "You mean Lucius Cornelius was right? You don't mind? Honestly?"

"Mind? Why should I mind? I am delighted," said Pompey Strabo. "My purse is feeling the pinch."

"Your purse?"

"I have ten legions in the field, Quintus Pompeius, and I'm paying more than half of them myself."

"*Are* you?"

"Well, Rome can't." Pompey Strabo got up from his desk. "It's time the men who aren't my own were discharged, and it's a task *I* don't want. I like to fight, not write things. Haven't got good enough eyesight, for one. Though I did have a cadet in my service who could write superbly. Actually loved doing it! Takes all sorts, I suppose." Pompey Strabo's arm went round Pompeius Rufus's shoulders. "Now come and meet my legates and my tribunes. All men who've served under me for a long time, so take no notice if they seem upset. I haven't told them of my intentions."

The astonishment and chagrin Pompey Strabo hadn't shown was clearly written on the faces of Brutus Damasippus and Gellius Poplicola when Pompey Strabo gave them the news.

"No, no, boys, it's excellent!" cried Pompey Strabo. "It will also do my son good to serve some other man than his father. We all get far too complacent when there are no changes in wind direction. This will freshen everybody up."

That afternoon Pompey Strabo paraded his army and permitted the new general to inspect it.

"Only four legions here—my own men," said Pompey Strabo as he accompanied Pompeius Rufus down the ranks. "The other six are all over the place, mostly mopping up or loafing. One in Camerinum, one in Fanum Fortunae, one in Ancona, one in Iguvium, one in Arretium, and one in Cingulum. You'll have quite a lot of traveling to do as you discharge them. There doesn't seem much point in bringing them all together just to give them their papers."

"I won't mind the traveling," said Pompeius Rufus, who was feeling somewhat better. Perhaps his body servant was in the right of it, perhaps the omen didn't indicate his death.

That night Pompey Strabo held a small banquet in his warm and commodious farmhouse. His very attractive young son was present, as were the other cadets, the legates Lucius Junius Brutus Damasippus and Lucius Gellius Poplicola, and four unelected military tribunes.

"Glad I'm not consul anymore and have to put up with those fellows," said Pompey Strabo, meaning the elected tribunes of the soldiers. "Heard they refused to go to Rome with Lucius Cornelius. Typical. Stupid oafs! All got inflated ideas of their importance."

"Do you *really* approve of the march on Rome?" asked Pompeius Rufus a little incredulously.

"Definitely. What else could Lucius Cornelius do?"

"Accept the decision of the People."

"An unconstitutional spilling of the consul's imperium? Oh, come now, Quintus Pompeius! It wasn't Lucius Cornelius acted illegally, it was the Plebeian Assembly and that traitorous *cunnus* Sulpicius. And Gaius Marius. Greedy old grunt. He's past it, but he hasn't even got the sense left to realize that. Why should he be allowed to act unconstitutionally without anyone's saying a word against him, while poor Lucius Cornelius stands up for the constitution and gets shit thrown at him from every direction?"

"The People never have loved Lucius Cornelius, but they most certainly don't love him now."

"Does that worry him?" asked Pompey Strabo.

"I don't think so. I also think it ought to worry him."

"Rubbish! And cheer up, cousin! You're out of it now. When they find Marius and Sulpicius and all the rest, you won't be blamed for their execution," said Pompey Strabo. "Have some more wine."

The next morning the junior consul decided to stroll about the camp, familiarize himself with its layout. The suggestion he do so had come from Pompey Strabo, who declined to keep him company.

"Better if the men see you on your own," he said.

Still astonished at the warmth of his reception, Pompeius Rufus walked wherever he liked, finding himself greeted by everyone from centurions to rankers in a most friendly manner. His opinion was asked about this or that, he was flattered and deferred to.

However, he was intelligent enough to keep his most condemnatory thoughts to himself until such time as Pompey Strabo was gone and his own command an established thing. Among these unfavorable reactions was shock at the lack of hygiene in the camp's sanitary arrangements; the cesspits and latrines were neglected, and far too close to the well from which the men were drawing water. This was typical of genuine landsmen, thought Pompeius Rufus. Once they considered a place was fouled, they just picked up and moved somewhere else.

When the junior consul saw a large group of soldiers coming toward him he felt no fear, no premonition, for they all wore smiles and all seemed eager for a conference. His spirits lifted; perhaps he could tell them what he thought about camp hygiene. So as they clustered thickly about him he smiled on them pleasantly, and hardly felt the first sword blade as it sheared through his leather under-dress, slid between two ribs, and kept on going. Other swords followed, many and quick. He didn't even cry out, didn't have time to think about the mice and his socks. He was dead before he fell to earth. The men melted away.

"What a *sad* business!" exclaimed Pompey Strabo to his son as he got up from his knees. "Stone dead, poor fellow! Must have been wounded thirty times. All mortal too. Good sword work—must have been good men."

"But who?" asked another cadet when Young Pompey didn't answer.

"Soldiers, obviously," said Pompey Strabo. "I imagine the men didn't want a change of general. I had heard something to that effect from Damasippus, but I didn't take it too seriously."

"What will you do, Father?" asked Young Pompey.

"Send him back to Rome."

"Isn't that illegal? Casualties in the war are supposed to be given a funeral on the spot."

"The war's over, and this is the consul," said Pompey Strabo. "I think the Senate should see his body. Young Gnaeus, my son, you can make all the arrangements. Damasippus can escort the body."

It was done with maximum effect. Pompey Strabo sent a courier to summon a meeting of the Senate, then delivered Quintus Pompeius Rufus to the door of the Curia Hostilia. No explanation was tendered beyond what Damasippus had to say in person—and that was simply that the army of Pompey Strabo refused to have a different commander. The Senate got the message. Gnaeus Pompeius Strabo was humbly asked if—considering that his delegated successor was dead—he would mind keeping his command in the north.

Sulla read his personal letter from Pompey Strabo in private.

Well, Lucius Cornelius, isn't this a sorry business? I'm afraid my army isn't saying who did it, and I'm not about to punish four good legions for something only thirty or forty men took it upon themselves to do. My centurions are baffled. So is my son, who stands on excellent terms with the rankers and can usually find out what's going on. It's my fault, really. I just didn't realize how much my men loved me. After all, Quintus Pompeius was a Picentine. I didn't think they'd mind him one little bit.

Anyway, I hope the Senate sees its way clear to keeping me on as commander-in-chief in the north. If the men wouldn't countenance a Picentine, they certainly wouldn't countenance a stranger, now would they? We're a rough lot, we northerners.

I would like to wish you very well in all your own endeavors, Lucius Cornelius. You are a champion of the old ways, but you do have an interesting new style. A man might learn from you. Please understand that you have my wholehearted support, and don't hesitate to let me know if there is any other way in which I can help you.

Sulla laughed, then burned the letter, one of the few reassuring pieces of news he had received. That Rome wasn't happy with the Sullan alterations to the constitution he now knew beyond a shadow of a doubt, for the Plebeian Assembly had met and elected ten new tribunes of the plebs. Every man voted in was an opponent of Sulla and a supporter of Sulpicius; among them were Gaius Milonius, Gaius Papirius Carbo Arvina, Publius Magius, Marcus Vergilius, Marcus Marius Gratidianus (the adopted nephew of Gaius Marius), and none other than Quintus Sertorius. When Sulla had heard that Quintus Sertorius was putting himself up as a candidate, he had sent a warning to Sertorius not to stand if he knew what was good for him. A warning Sertorius had chosen to ignore, saying steadily that it could now make little difference to the State who was elected a tribune of the plebs.

This signal defeat gave Sulla to understand that he must ensure the election of strongly conservative curule magistrates; both the consuls and all six praetors would have to be staunch proponents of the *leges Corneliae*. The quaestors were easy. They were all either reinstated senators or young men from senatorial families who could be relied upon to shore up the power of the Senate. Among them was Lucius Licinius Lucullus, who was seconded to Sulla's service.

Of course one of the consular candidates would have to be Sulla's own nephew, Lucius Nonius, who had been a praetor two years before, and would not offend his uncle if elected a consul. The pity of it was that he was a rather insipid man who had done nothing so far to distinguish himself, and was therefore not going to be someone the electors fancied. But his choice as a candidate would please Sulla's sister, whom Sulla had almost forgotten, so little family feeling did he have. When she came to Rome to stay—as she did periodically—he never bothered to see her. *That* would have to change! Luckily Dalmatica was anxious to do what she could, and was an hospitable, patient kind of wife; she could look after his sister and the dreary Lucius Nonius, hopefully soon to be consul.

Two other consular candidates were welcome. The erstwhile legate of Pompey Strabo, Gnaeus Octavius Ruso, was definitely for Sulla and the old ways; he probably also had orders from Pompey Strabo. The second promising candidate was Publius Servilius Vatia—a plebeian Servilius but from a fine old family, and highly thought of among the First Class. Into the bargain, he had a very formidable war record, always an electoral asset.

However, there was one candidate who worried Sulla greatly, chiefly because he would appear on the surface to the First Class as just the right kind of consular material, sure to uphold senatorial privilege and bolster knightly prerogatives, no matter how unwritten. Lucius Cornelius Cinna was a patrician of Sulla's own *gens,* he was married to an Annia, possessed of a luminous war record, and well known as an orator and advocate. But Sulla knew he had tied himself in some way to Gaius Marius—probably Marius had bought him. Like so many senators, a few months ago his finances were well known to be shaky—yet when the senators were expelled for debt, Cinna was discovered to be very plump in the purse. Yes, bought, thought Sulla gloomily. How clever of Gaius Marius! Of course it was to do with Young Marius and the accusation that he had murdered Cato the Consul. In normal times, Sulla doubted if Cinna could have been bought; he didn't seem that sort of man—one reason why he was going to appeal to the electors of the First Class. Yet when times were hard and ruin loomed of a scale to affect a man's sons as well as his own future, many a highly principled man might allow himself to be bought. Particularly if that highly principled man didn't think his altered status would lead him to alter his principles.

As if the curule elections were not worrying enough, Sulla was also aware that his army was tired of occupying Rome. It wanted to go east to fight Mithridates, and of course did not fully understand the reasons why its general kept lingering inside Rome. It was also beginning to experience increased resistance to its residence within the city; not that the number of free meals and free beds and free women had decreased, more that those who had never condoned its presence now were emboldened to retaliate by chucking the contents of their chamber pots out their windows onto hapless soldier heads.

Had Sulla only been willing to bribe heavily, he might have ensured success in the curule elections, as the climate was exactly right for bountiful bribery. But for nothing and nobody would Sulla consent to part with his little hoard of gold. Let Pompey Strabo pay legions out of his own purse if he chose and let Gaius Marius say he was prepared to do the same; Lucius Cornelius Sulla regarded it as Rome's duty to foot the bill. If Pompeius Rufus had still been alive, Sulla might have secured the money from the wealthy Picentine; but he hadn't thought of that before he sent the wealthy Picentine north to his death.

My plans are good but their execution is precarious, he thought. This wretched city is too full of men with opinions of their own, all determined to get what *they* want. Why is it that they can't see how sensible and proper my plans are? And how can any man draw sufficient power unto himself to ensure his plans remain undisturbed? Men of ideals and principles are the ruin of the world!

And so toward the end of December he sent his army back to Capua under the command of the good faithful Lucullus, now officially his quaestor. Having done that, he threw caution to the winds and his chances into the lap of Fortune by holding the elections.

Though he was convinced he had not underestimated the strength of the resentment against him in every stratum of Roman society, the truth was that Sulla did not grasp the depth and the extent of that animosity. No one said a word, no one looked at him awry; but beneath this lip service the whole of Rome was finding it impossible to forget or forgive Sulla's bringing an army into Rome—or Sulla's army holding its allegiance to Sulla ahead of its allegiance to Rome.

This seething resentment ran from the highest echelons all the way down into the very gutter. Even men as inescapably committed to him and to the supremacy of the Senate as the Brothers Caesar and the Brothers Scipio Nasica wished desperately that Sulla could have lit upon some other way of solving the Senate's dilemma than using his army. And below the First Class there were two additional ulcerations festering inside men's minds; that a tribune of the plebs had been condemned to death during his year in office, and that the old and crippled Gaius Marius had been hounded out of home, family, position—and condemned to death.

Some hint of all this rankling dissatisfaction became apparent as the new curule magistrates were returned. Gnaeus Octavius Ruso was the senior consul, but the junior consul was Lucius Cornelius Cinna. The praetors were an independent lot, among whom were none Sulla could really count on.

But it was the election of the tribunes of the soldiers in the Assembly of the Whole People that troubled Sulla most of all. They were uniformly ugly men, and included wolfs-heads like Gaius Flavius Fimbria, Publius Annius, and Gaius Marcius Censorinus. Ripe to ride roughshod over their generals, thought Sulla—let any general with this lot in his legions try to march on Rome! They'd kill him with as little scruple as Young Marius did Cato the Consul. I am very glad I am passing out of my consulship and won't have them in *my* legions. Every last one of them is a potential Saturninus.

Despite the disappointing electoral results, Sulla was not a wholly unhappy man as the old year wore away to its end. If the delay had done nothing else, it had given his agents in Asia Province, Bithynia, and Greece time to apprise him what the true situation was. Definitely his wisest course was to go to Greece, worry about Asia Minor later. He had not the troops to attempt a flanking maneuver; it would have to be a straight effort to roll Mithridates back and out of Greece and Macedonia. Not that the Pontic invasion of Macedonia had gone according to plan; Gaius Sentius and Quintus Bruttius Sura had proven yet again that might was not always enough when the enemy was Roman. They had wrought great deeds with their tiny armies. But they couldn't possibly keep going.

His most urgent consideration was therefore to get himself and his troops out of Italy. Only by defeating King Mithridates and plundering the East would he inherit Gaius Marius's unparalleled reputation. Only by bringing home the gold of Mithridates would he pull Rome out of her financial crisis. Only if he did all this would Rome forgive him for marching against her. Only then would the Plebs forgive him for turning their precious assembly into a place best suited for playing dice and twiddling thumbs.

On his last day as consul, Sulla called the Senate to a special meeting and spoke to them with genuine sincerity; he believed implicitly in himself and in his new measures.

"If it were not for me, Conscript Fathers, you would not now exist. I can say that in truth, and I do say it. Had the laws of Publius Sulpicius Rufus remained on the tablets, the Plebs—not even the People!—would now be ruling Rome without any kind of check or balance. The Senate would be just another vestigial relic staffed by too few men to form a quorum. No recommendations to Plebs or People could be made, nor any decisions be taken about matters we regard as purely senatorial business. So before you start weeping and wailing about the fate of the Plebs and the People, before you start wallowing in an excess of undeserved pity for the Plebs and the People, I suggest that you remember what this august body would be at this moment were it not for *me*."

"Here, here!" cried Catulus Caesar, very pleased because his son, one of the new slightly-too-young senators, had finally come back from his war duties and was sitting in the Senate; he had been anxious that Catulus should see Sulla act as consul.

"Remember too," said Sulla, "that if you wish to retain the right to guide and regulate Rome's government, you must uphold my laws. Before you contemplate any upheavals, think of Rome! For Rome's sake, there must be peace in Italy. For Rome's sake, you must make a strenuous effort to find a way around our financial troubles and give Rome back her old prosperity. We cannot afford the luxury of seeing tribunes of the plebs run riot. The status quo as I have set it up *must* be maintained! Only then will Rome recover. We *cannot* permit Sulpician idiocies!"

He looked directly at the consuls-elect. "Tomorrow, Gnaeus Octavius and Lucius Cinna, you will inherit my office and the office of my dead colleague, Quintus Pompeius. I shall have become a consular. Gnaeus Octavius, will you give me your solemn word that you will uphold my laws?"

Octavius didn't hesitate. "I will, Lucius Sulla. You have my solemn word on it."

"Lucius Cornelius of the branch cognominated Cinna, will you give me your word that you will uphold my laws?"

Cinna stared at Sulla fearlessly. "That all depends, Lucius Cornelius of the branch cognominated Sulla. I will uphold your laws *if* they prove to be a workable way of governing. At the moment I am not sure they will. The machinery is so incredibly antique, so manifestly unwieldy, and the rights of a large part of our Roman community have been—I can find no other word for it—annulled. I am very sorry to inconvenience you, but as things stand, I must withhold my promise."

An extraordinary change came over Sulla's face; like some other people of late, the Senate was now privileged to catch a glimpse of that naked clawed creature which dwelt inside Lucius Cornelius Sulla. And like all others, the senators never forgot that glimpse. And in the years to come, would shiver at the memory as they waited for the reckoning.

Before Sulla could open his mouth to answer, Scaevola Pontifex Maximus interjected.

"Lucius Cinna, leave well enough alone!" he cried; he was remembering that after his first glimpse of Sulla's beast, Sulla had marched on Rome. "I implore you, give the consul your promise!"

Then came the voice of Antonius Orator. "If this is the sort of attitude you intend to adopt, Cinna, then I suggest you watch your back! Our consul Lucius Cato neglected to do so, and he died."

The House was murmuring, new senators as well as old, and most of the words were of exasperation and fear at Cinna's stand. Oh, why couldn't all these consular men leave ambition and posturing aside? Didn't they see how desperately Rome needed peace, internal stability?

"Order!" said Sulla, just the once, and not very loudly. But as he still wore that look, silence fell immediately.

"Senior consul, may I speak?" asked Catulus Caesar, who was remembering that his first experience of Sulla's look had been followed by a retreat from Tridentum.

"Speak, Quintus Lutatius."

"First of all, I wish to pass a comment about Lucius Cinna," said Catulus Caesar coldly. "I think he bears watching. I deplore his election to an office I do not think he will fill meritoriously. Lucius Cinna may have a magnificent war record, but his political understanding and his ideas as to how Rome ought to be governed are minimal. When he was urban praetor none of the measures which ought to have been taken were taken. Both the consuls were in the field, yet Lucius Cinna—virtually in charge of the governance of Rome!—made no attempt to stave off her terrible economic afflictions. Had he done at that early stage, Rome might now be better off. Yet here today we have Lucius Cinna, now consul-elect, demurring at giving a far more intelligent and able man a promise which was asked of him in the true spirit of senatorial government."

"You haven't said a word to make me change my mind, Quintus Lutatius *Servilis*," said Cinna harshly, calling Catulus Caesar servile.

"I am aware of that," said Catulus Caesar, at his haughtiest. "In fact, it is my considered opinion that nothing any one of us—or all of us!—could say would influence you to change your mind. Your mind is closed fast, like your purse upon the money Gaius Marius gave you to whiten the reputation of his murdering son!"

Cinna flushed; it was an affliction he loathed, yet could not seem to cure, and it always betrayed him.

"There is one way, however, in which we Conscript Fathers can make sure Lucius Cinna upholds the measures our senior consul has taken with such care," said Catulus Caesar. "I suggest that a most solemn and binding oath be required of both Gnaeus Octavius and Lucius Cinna. To the effect that they will swear to uphold our present system of government, as laid down on the tablets by Lucius Sulla."

"I agree," said Scaevola Pontifex Maximus.

"And I," said Flaccus Princeps Senatus.

"And I," said Antonius Orator.

"And I," said Lucius Caesar the censor.

"And I," said Crassus the censor.

"And I," said Quintus Ancharius.

"And I," said Publius Servilius Vatia.

"And I," said Lucius Cornelius Sulla, turning to Scaevola. "High priest, will you administer this oath to the consuls-elect?"

"I will."

"And I will take it," said Cinna loudly, "if I see the House divide in a clear majority."

"Let the House divide," said Sulla instantly. "Those in favor of the oath, please stand to my right. Those not in favor, please stand to my left."

Only a very few senators stood to Sulla's left, but the first to get there was Quintus Sertorius, his muscular frame exuding anger.

"The House has divided and shown its wishes conclusively," said Sulla, the look vanished completely from his face. "Quintus Mucius, you are the Pontifex Maximus. How do you say this oath should be administered?"

"Legally," said Scaevola promptly. "The first phase involves the whole House going with me to the temple of Jupiter Optimus Maximus, where the *flamen Dialis* and I will sacrifice a victim to the Great God. It will be a two-year-old sheep, and the Priests of the Two Teeth will attend us."

"How convenient!" said Sertorius loudly. "I'll bet that when we get to the top of the Capitol, all the requisite men and animals will be waiting for us!"

Scaevola carried on as if no one had spoken. "After the sacrifice I will ask Lucius Domitius—who is son of the late Pontifex Maximus and not directly involved in this business—to take the auspices from the liver of the victim. If the omens are suitably propitious, I will then lead the House to the temple of Semo Sancus Dius Fidius, the god of Divine Good Faith. There—under the open sky, as is required of all oath-takers—I will charge the consuls-elect to uphold the *leges Corneliae*."

Sulla rose from his curule chair. "Then by all means let us do it, Pontifex Maximus."

The omens were propitious, made the more so on the walk from the Capitol to the temple of Semo Sancus Dius Fidius when an eagle was seen to be flying from left to right across the Porta Sanqualis by the whole Senate in procession.

But Cinna had no intention of allowing himself to be bound by an oath to uphold Sulla's constitution, and he knew exactly how he was going to render his oath no oath. As the senators wended their way up the hill to the temple of the Great God on the Capitol, he deliberately fell in with Quintus Sertorius, and without letting anyone see him speak—let alone hear what he said—he asked Quintus Sertorius to find him a certain kind of stone. Then as the senators wended their way from one temple to the other, Sertorius dropped the stone unnoticed within the folds of Cinna's toga. To work it to a place where he could close the fingers of his left hand around it was easy; for it was a small stone, smooth and oval.

From early childhood he, like every other Roman boy, had known that he must go outside into the open air before he could take one of the splendidly juicy oaths so loved by little boys—oaths of friendship and enmity, fear and fury, daring and delusion. For the swearing of an oath had to be witnessed by the gods of the sky; if they did not witness it, then it was not a true and binding oath. Like all his boyhood companions, Cinna had taken the ritual with total seriousness. But he had once met a fellow—the son of the knight Sextus Perquitienus—who, having been brought up in that hideous house, had abrogated every oath he ever swore. The two were much of an age, though the son of Sextus Perquitienus did not mix with the sons of senators. The encounter had been a chance one, and it had involved the taking of an oath.

"All you do," had said the son of Sextus Perquitienus, "is hold on to the bones of Mother Earth. And to do that, you just keep a stone in your hand as you swear. You have put yourself in the care of the gods of the Underworld because the Underworld is built of the bones of Mother Earth. Stone, Lucius Cornelius. Stone is bone!"

So when Lucius Cornelius Cinna swore his oath to uphold Sulla's laws, he held his stone tightly clenched in his left hand. Finished, he bent down quickly to the floor of the temple—which, being devoid of a roof, was littered by leaves, little stones, pebbles, twigs—and pretended to pick up his stone.

"And if I break my oath," he said in a clear and carrying voice, "may I be hurled from the Tarpeian Rock even as I hurl this stone away from me!"

The stone flew through the air, clattered against the grubby, peeling wall, and fell back to the bosom of its mother, Earth. No one seemed to grasp the significance of his action; Cinna released his breath in a huge gasp. Obviously the secret known to the son of Sextus Perquitienus was not known to Roman senators. Now when he was accused of breaking his oath, Cinna could explain why it did not bind him. The whole Senate had seen him throw his stone away, he had provided himself with a hundred impeccable witnesses. It was a trick could never work again—oh, but how Metellus Piggle-wiggle might have benefited had he only known of it!

Though he went to see the new consuls inaugurated, Sulla did not stay for the feast, pleading as his excuse that he had to ready himself to leave for Capua on the morrow. However, he was present at the Senate's first official meeting of the New Year in the temple of Jupiter Optimus Maximus, so he heard Cinna's short, ominous speech.

"I shall grace my office, not disgrace it," Cinna said. "If I have any misgiving, it is to see the outgoing senior consul lead an army to the East that should have been led by Gaius Marius. Even putting the illegal prosecution and condemnation of Gaius Marius aside, it is still my opinion that the outgoing senior consul ought to remain in Rome to answer charges."

Charges of what? No one quite knew, though the majority of the senators deduced that the charges would be treason, the basis of the charges Sulla's leading his army on Rome. Sulla sighed, resigned to the inevitable. A man without scruples himself, he knew that had he taken that oath, he would have broken it did the need arise. Of Cinna, he hadn't thought the man owned such metal. Now it seemed the man did. What a nuisance!

When he left the Capitol he headed in the direction of Aurelia's insula in the Subura, pondering as he walked how best to deal with Cinna. By the time he arrived he had an answer, so it was with a broad smile on his face that he entered when Eutychus held the door.

The smile faded, however, when he saw Aurelia's face; it was grim and the eyes held no affection.

"Not you too?" he asked, casting himself down on a couch.

"I too." Aurelia sat in a chair facing him. "You ought not to be here, Lucius Cornelius."

"Oh, I'm safe enough," he said casually. "Gaius Julius was settling himself in a cozy corner to enjoy the feast when I left."

"Nor would it worry you if he walked in at this moment," she said. "Well, I had better be adequately chaperoned—for my sake, if not for yours." She raised her voice. "Please come and join us, Lucius Decumius!"

The little man emerged from her workroom, face flinty.

"Oh, not you!" said Sulla, disgusted. "If it were not for the likes of you, Lucius Decumius, I would not have needed to lead an army on Rome! How could you fall for all that piffle about Gaius Marius's being fit? He's not fit to lead an army as far as Veii, let alone Asia Province."

"Gaius Marius is cured," said Lucius Decumius, defiant yet defensive. Sulla was not only the one friend of Aurelia's whom he couldn't like, he was also the one man of his own acquaintance whom he feared. There were many things he knew about Sulla that Aurelia did not; but the more he discovered, the less urge he experienced to say a word to anyone about them. It takes one to know one, he had thought to himself a thousand times, and I swear Lucius Cornelius Sulla is as big a villain as I am. Only he has bigger chances to do bigger villainies. And I know he does them too.

"It's not Lucius Decumius to blame for this mess, it's you!" said Aurelia snappishly.

"Rubbish!" said Sulla roundly. "*I* didn't start this mess! I was minding my own business in Capua and planning to leave for Greece. It's fools like Lucius Decumius to blame—meddling in things they know nothing about, deluding themselves their heroes are made from superior metal than the rest of us! Your friend here recruited a large number of Sulpicius's bully-boys to stuff the Forum and make my daughter a widow—and he mustered more of the same when I entered the Forum Esquilinum wanting nothing more badly than I did peace! *I* didn't stir up the trouble! I just had to pay for it!"

Angry now, Lucius Decumius stood stiffly, every hackle up. "I believe in the People!" he said, out of his depth and not used to being at someone else's mercy.

"You see? There you go, mouthing idiocies as empty as your Fourth Class mind!" snarled Sulla. " 'I believe in the People' indeed! You'd do better to believe in your betters!"

"Lucius Cornelius, please!" said Aurelia, heart thudding, legs trembling. "If you're Lucius Decumius's better, then act like it!"

"Yes!" cried Lucius Decumius, collecting himself because his beloved Aurelia was fighting for him—and wanting to look courageous in her eyes. But Sulla was no Marius. His nature made Lucius Decumius feel the screech of nails being dragged down something smooth and stony. Yet he tried. For Aurelia. "You don't mind yourself, Big Important Consular Sulla, you just might get a knife in your back!"

The pale eyes glazed, Sulla's lips peeled back from his teeth; he got up from the couch wrapped in an almost tangible aura of menace and advanced on Lucius Decumius.

Lucius Decumius backed away—not from cowardice, rather from a superstitious man's contact with something as mysterious as it was terrible.

"I could stamp on you the way an elephant stamps on a dog," said Sulla pleasantly. "The only reason I don't is this lady here. She values you, and you serve her well. You may have taken many a knife to many a man, Lucius Decumius, but don't ever delude yourself you will to me! Even in your dreams. Stay out of my arena, content yourself with commanding in your own. Now be off!"

"Go, Lucius Decumius," said Aurelia. *"Please!"*

"Not when he's in a mood like this!"

"I will be better on my own. Please go."

Lucius Decumius went.

"There was no need to be so hard on him," she said, nostrils pinched. "He doesn't know how to deal with you, and he has his loyalties, for all he is what he is. His devotion to Gaius Marius is on behalf of my son."

Sulla perched on the edge of the couch, not sure whether to go or to stay. "Don't be angry with me, Aurelia. If you are, then I'll become angry with you. I agree, he's a poor target. But he helped Gaius Marius put me in a situation I didn't want, didn't ask for, didn't deserve!"

She drew a huge breath, exhaled slowly. "Yes, I can understand your feelings," she said. "As far as it goes, you have some right." Her head began to nod rhythmically. "I know that. I know that. I know you tried in every way possible to contain things legally, peacefully. But don't blame Gaius Marius. It was Publius Sulpicius."

"That's specious," said Sulla, beginning to relax. "You're a consul's daughter and a praetor's wife, Aurelia. You're more aware than most that Sulpicius couldn't have got his program started had he not been backed by someone a great deal more influential than he was. Gaius Marius."

"Was?" she asked sharply, eyes dilating.

"Sulpicius is dead. He was caught two days ago."

Her hands went to her mouth. "And Gaius Marius?"

"Oh, Gaius Marius, Gaius Marius, always Gaius Marius! Think, Aurelia, *think!* Why would I want Gaius Marius dead? Kill the People's hero? I'm not so big a fool! Hopefully I've given him a scare which will keep him out of Italy until I've got myself out of Italy. And not only for my own sake, woman. For Rome's sake too. He can't be allowed to fight Mithridates!" He shifted sideways on the couch, hands held like an advocate attempting to convince an antipathetic jury. "Aurelia, surely you've noticed that since he came back into public life exactly a year ago he's tied himself to men he wouldn't have said *ave* to in the old days? We all use minions we'd rather not use, we're all obliged to suck up to men we'd rather spit on. But since that second stroke, Gaius Marius has resorted to tools and ploys he wouldn't have touched on pain of death in the old days! I know what I am. I know what I'm capable of doing. And it's no lie for me to say that I'm a more dishonest, unscrupulous man by far than Gaius Marius. Not only thanks to the life I've led. Thanks to the kind of man I am too. But he was *never* like that! He, to employ the likes of Lucius Decumius to get rid of a cadet who accused his precious son of murder? He, to employ the likes of Lucius Decumius to procure bully-boys and rabble? Think, Aurelia, think! The second stroke affected his mind."

"You should never have marched on Rome," she said.

"What other choice did I have, tell me that? If I could have found *any* other way, I would have! Unless you would rather have seen me continue to sit at Capua until Rome had a second civil war on her hands—Sulla versus Marius?"

Her color fled. "It could never have come to that!"

"Oh, there was a third alternative! That I lie down tamely under the feet of a maniac tribune of the plebs and a demented old man! Allow Gaius Marius to do to me what he did to Metellus Numidicus, use the Plebs to take away my lawful command? When he did that to Metellus Numidicus, Metellus Numidicus was no longer consul! I was *consul*, Aurelia! No one takes the command off a consul still in office. No one!"

"Yes, I see your point," she said, color returning. Her eyes filled with tears. "They will never forgive you, Lucius Cornelius. You led an army on Rome."

He groaned. "Oh, for the sake of all the gods, don't cry! I have never seen you cry! Not even at my boy's funeral! If you couldn't cry for him, then you can't cry for Rome!"

Her head was bent; the tears didn't run down her cheeks, they splashed into her lap, and the light caught glitters off her wet black lashes. "When I am most moved, I cannot cry," she said, and wiped her nose with the side of her hand.

"I don't believe that," he said, throat hard and aching.

She looked up. The tears ran down her cheeks. "I'm not crying for Rome," she said huskily, and wiped her nose again. "I am crying for you."

He got off the couch, gave her his handkerchief, and stood behind her chair with one hand pressed into her shoulder. Best she should not see his face.

"I will love you forever for that," he said, put his other hand in front of her face and took some of the tears from her lashes, then licked them from his palm. "It's Fortune," he said. "I was given the hardest consulship a man has ever had. Just as I was given the hardest life a man has ever had. I'm not the kind to surrender, and I'm not the kind to care how I win. There are plenty of eggs in the cups and plenty of dolphins down. But the race won't be over until I'm dead." He squeezed her shoulder. "I have taken your tears into me. Once I dropped an emerald quizzing-glass down a drain because it had no value to me. But I will never lose your tears."

His hand left her, he left the house. Walking very proudly, enriched and uplifted. All the tears those other women had shed over him were selfish tears, shed for the sake of their own broken hearts. Not for his. Yet she who never wept had wept for *him*.

Perhaps another man would have softened, reconsidered. Not Sulla. By the time he reached his house, a long walk, that private exaltation was tucked away below conscious thought; he dined very pleasantly with Dalmatica, took her to bed and made love to her, then slept his normal dreamless ten hours—or if he dreamed, he did not remember. An hour before dawn he woke and rose without disturbing his wife, took some crisp, freshly baked bread and cheese in his study and stared abstractedly as he ate at a box about the size of one of his ancestral temples. It sat on the far corner of his desk, and it held the head of Publius Sulpicius Rufus.

The rest of the condemned had escaped; only Sulla and a few of his colleagues knew that no exhaustive attempts to apprehend them had been mounted. Sulpicius, however, had to go. Therefore to catch him was imperative.

The boat across the Tiber had been a ruse. Further downstream Sulpicius crossed back again, but bypassed Ostia in favor of the little harbor town of Laurentum, some few miles down the coast. Here the fugitive had tried to engage a ship—and here, with the aid of one of his own servants, he was run to earth. Sulla's hirelings had killed him on the spot, but knew Sulla better than to ask for money without furnishing proof. So they cut off Sulpicius's head, put it in a waterproofed box, and brought it to Sulla's house in Rome. They were then paid. And Sulla had the head, still fairly fresh; it had only left its owner's shoulders two days earlier.

On his way out of Rome on that second day of January, Sulla summoned Cinna to the Forum. And there, stapled to the wall of the rostra, was a tall spear carrying Sulpicius's head. Sulla took Cinna ungently by the arm.

"Look well," he said. "Remember what you see. Remember the expression on its face. They say that when a man's head is taken, his eyes still have sight. If you did not believe that in the past, you will in the future. That's a man who watched his own head hit the dust. Remember well, Lucius Cinna. I do not intend to die in the East. And that means I will return to Rome. If you tamper with my remedies for Rome's current diseases, you too will watch your own head hit the dust."

His answer was a look of scorn and contempt, but Cinna may as well have saved himself the effort. For the moment he finished speaking Sulla hauled his mule's head around and trotted off up the Forum Romanum without a backward glance, his wide-brimmed hat upon his head. Not anyone's picture of the successful general. But Cinna's private picture of Nemesis.

He turned then to look up at the head, its eyes wide, its jaw sagging. Dawn had barely broken; if it was removed now, no one would see it.

"No," said Cinna aloud. "It should stay there. Let all of Rome see how far the man who invaded Rome is prepared to go."

 In Capua, Sulla closeted himself with Lucullus and got down to the logistics of transferring his soldiers to Brundisium. It had been Sulla's original intention to sail from Tarentum until he learned it did not possess sufficient transport ships. Brundisium it must be.

"You will go first, taking all the cavalry and two of the five legions," Sulla said to Lucullus. "I'll follow with the other three. However, don't look for me on the other side of the Ionian Sea. As soon as you land in Elatria or Buchetium, march for Dodona. Strip every temple in Epirus and Acarnania—they won't yield you a big fortune, but I suspect they'll yield you enough. A pity the Scordisci plundered Dodona so recently. However, never forget that Greek and Epirote priests are canny, Lucius Licinius. It may be that Dodona managed to hide quite a lot from a collection of barbarians."

"They won't hide anything from me," said Lucullus, smiling.

"Good! March your men overland to Delphi, and do what you have to do. Until I reach you, it's your theater of war."

"What about you, Lucius Cornelius?" Lucullus asked.

"I'll have to wait at Brundisium until your transports return, but before that I'll have to wait in Capua until I'm sure things are quiet in Rome. I don't trust Cinna, and I don't trust Sertorius."

As three thousand horses and a thousand mules were not popular residents around Capua, Lucullus marched for Brundisium by the middle of January, though winter was fast approaching and both Lucullus and Sulla doubted that Lucullus would sail much before March or April. Despite his urgent need to leave Capua, Sulla still hesitated; the reports from Rome were not promising.

First he heard that the tribune of the plebs Marcus Vergilius had made a magnificent speech to the Forum crowd from the rostra, and had avoided infringing Sulla's laws by refusing to call it a meeting. Vergilius had advocated that Sulla—no longer consul—be stripped of his imperium and brought to Rome—by force if necessary—to answer charges of treason for the murder of Sulpicius and the unlawful proscription of Gaius Marius and eighteen others, still at large.

Nothing came of the speech, but Sulla then heard that Cinna was actively lobbying many of the backbenchers for their support when Vergilius and another tribune of the plebs, Publius Magius, submitted a motion to the Senate to recommend to the Centuriate Assembly that Sulla be stripped of his imperium and made to answer charges of treason and murder. The House refused steadfastly to countenance any of these ploys, but Sulla knew they boded no good; they all knew he was still in Capua with three legions, so they had obviously decided he would not have the courage to march on Rome a second time. They felt they could defy him with impunity.

At the end of January a letter came to Sulla from his daughter, Cornelia Sulla.

> Father, my position is desperate. With my husband and my father-in-law both dead, the new *paterfamilias*—my brother-in-law who now calls himself Quintus—is behaving abominably toward me. He has a wife who dislikes me intensely. While my husband and my father-in-law were alive, there could be no trouble. Now, however, the new Quintus and his dreadful wife are living with my mother-in-law and me. By rights the house belongs to my son, but that seems to have been forgotten. My mother-in-law—naturally, I suppose—has transferred her allegiance to her living son. And they have all taken to blaming you for Rome's troubles as well as their own. They even talk that you deliberately

sent my father-in-law to his death in Umbria. As a result of all this, my children and I find ourselves without servants, we are given the same food to eat as the servants, and we are poorly housed. When I complain, I am told that technically I am your responsibility! Just as if I had not borne my late husband a son who is actually the heir to most of his grandfather's fortune! That too is a great source of resentment. Dalmatica is beseeching me to live with her in your house, but I feel I cannot do that until I obtain your permission.

What I would ask of you ahead of providing a home for me in your own house, Father (if in the midst of your own troubles you have time to think of me), is that you find me another husband. There are still seven months of my mourning period left. If you will give your consent I would like to spend them in your house under the protection and chaperonage of your wife. But I do not want to impose upon Dalmatica any longer than that. I must have my own home.

I am not like Aurelia, I do not want to live on my own. Nor can I face the kind of life Aelia seems genuinely to enjoy, Marcia's tyrannies notwithstanding. Please, Father, if you can find me a husband I would so much appreciate it! Marriage to the worst of men is infinitely preferable to invading the house of another woman. I say it with feeling.

In myself I am quite well, though plagued by a cough due to the coldness of my room. As are the children. It has not escaped me that there would be little grief in this house if something were to happen to my son.

Considered dispassionately, Cornelia Sulla's plaint was the smallest particle of aggravation; yet it was the particle which tipped the balance in Sulla's unsettled mind. Until he received it he hadn't known which was his best course. Now he knew. That course had nothing to do with Cornelia Sulla. But he had an idea about her poor little life too. How dare some jumped-up Picentine lout imperil the health and happiness of *his* daughter! And her son!

He sent off two letters, one to Metellus Pius the Piglet ordering him to come to Capua from Aesernia and bring Mamercus with him, the other to Pompey Strabo. The Piglet's letter consisted of two bald sentences. Pompey Strabo received more.

No doubt, Gnaeus Pompeius, you are aware of the goings-on in Rome—the imprudent actions of Lucius Cinna, not to mention his tamed pack of tribunes of the plebs. I think, my friend and colleague in the north, that you and I know each other well enough, at least by reputation—and I regret that our careers have not permitted us a closer friendship—to understand that our aims and intentions are of like kind. I find in you a conservatism and respect for the old ways similar to my own, and I know you bear Gaius Marius no affection. Or Cinna, I strongly suspect.

If you truly feel that Rome would be better served by sending Gaius Marius and his legions to fight King Mithridates, then tear this up as of now. But if you prefer to see me and my legions go to fight King Mithridates, read on.

As things stand in Rome at the present time, I am helpless to commence the venture I ought to have commenced last year well before my consulship expired. Instead of setting off for the East, I am obliged to remain in Capua with three of my legions to ensure that I am not stripped of my imperium, arrested, and made to stand trial for no worse crime than strengthening the *mos maiorum*. Cinna, Sertorius, Vergilius, Magius, and the rest talk of treason and murder, of course.

Leaving aside my legions here in Capua and the two before Aesernia plus the one before Nola, yours are the only legions left in Italy. I can rely upon Quintus

Caecilius at Aesernia and Appius Claudius at Nola to uphold me and my deeds while consul; what I am writing to ask is whether I can also rely upon you and your legions. It may be that after I leave Italy nothing will stop Cinna and his friends. I am happy to face the consequences of that eventuality when the time comes. I can assure you that if I return from the East victorious. I will make my enemies pay.

What concerns me is my present position. I need to be guaranteed sufficient time to depart from Italy, and (as you well know) that could mean as long as four or five more months. Winds across the Adriatic and the Ionian at this season are notoriously capricious, and storms frequent. I cannot afford to take any risks with troops Rome will need desperately.

Gnaeus Pompeius, would you undertake on my behalf the task of informing Cinna and his confederates that I am legally commissioned to go to this eastern war? That if they attempt to hinder my departure, it will go ill with them? That for the moment, at least, they must cease and desist this badgering?

Please consider me your friend and colleague in every regard if you feel you can answer me in the affirmative. I await your reply most anxiously.

Pompey Strabo's reply actually reached Sulla before his legates arrived from Aesernia. It was written in his own atrocious hand, and consisted of one brief, laconic sentence:

"Don't worry, I'll fix everything."

So when the Piglet and Mamercus finally presented themselves at Sulla's rented house in Capua, they found Sulla more genial and relaxed than their own informants in Rome had led them to believe remotely possible.

"Don't worry, everything's fixed," said Sulla, grinning.

"How can that be?" gasped Metellus Pius. "I hear there are charges looming—murder, treason!"

"I wrote to my very good friend Gnaeus Pompeius Strabo and poured out my troubles to him. He says he'll fix everything."

"He will too," said Mamercus, a slow smile dawning.

"Oh, Lucius Cornelius, I'm so glad!" cried the Piglet. "It isn't fair, the way they're treating you! They were far kinder to Saturninus! The way they're carrying on at the moment, anyone would think Sulpicius was a demigod, not a demagogue!" He paused, struck by his own inadvertent verbal cleverness. "I say, that was quite well put, wasn't it?"

"Save it for the Forum when you run for consul," said Sulla. "It's wasted on me. My schooling never went beyond the elementary."

Remarks like that puzzled Mamercus, who now resolved to sit the Piglet down and make him tell everything he knew or suspected about the life of Lucius Cornelius Sulla. Oh, there were always Forum stories circulating about anyone unusual or excessively talented or notorious in some way, but Mamercus didn't listen to Forum stories, deeming them the exaggerations and embellishments of idle minds.

"They'll kill your laws as soon as you leave Italy. What are you going to do when you come home again?" asked Mamercus.

"Deal with it when it arrives, not a whisker before."

"*Can* you deal with it, Lucius Cornelius? I would think it will be an impossible situation."

"There are always ways, Mamercus, but you may believe me when I say that I won't be spending my leisure during this campaign on wine and women!" laughed Sulla, who did not appear anxious. "I am one of Fortune's beloved, you see. Fortune *always* looks after me."

They settled down then to discuss the remnants of the war in Italy, and the doggedness with which the Samnites hung on; they still controlled most of the territory between Aesernia and Corfinium, as well as the cities of Aesernia and Nola.

"They've hated Rome for centuries, and they're the best haters in the world," said Sulla, and sighed. "I had hoped that by the time I left for Greece, Aesernia and Nola would have capitulated. As it is, they may well be waiting for me when I come home."

"Not if we can help it," said the Piglet.

A servant scratched, murmured that dinner was ready if Lucius Cornelius was.

Lucius Cornelius was. He got to his feet and led the way into the dining room. While the food was on the table and the servants scurried in and out, Sulla kept the conversation light and inconsequential; they enjoyed the luxury permitted only to old friends, of each having a couch to himself.

"Do you never entertain women, Lucius Cornelius?" asked Mamercus when the servants had been dismissed.

Sulla shrugged, grimaced. "On campaign, away from the wife, all that, you mean?"

"Yes."

"Women are too much trouble, Mamercus, so the answer is no." Sulla laughed. "If that was asked because of your custodial duty toward Dalmatica, then you've got an honest answer."

"As a matter of fact, it wasn't asked for any reason outside of sheer vulgar curiosity," said Mamercus, unabashed.

Sulla put his cup down and stared across at the couch opposite his own, where Mamercus reclined; he now studied this guest more carefully than he had in the past. No Paris or Adonis or Memmius, certainly. Dark hair very closely cropped, an indication it had no curl and his barber despaired of it; a bumpy face with a broken, rather flattened nose; dark eyes deeply set; good brown skin with a sheen to it, his best feature. A healthy man, Mamercus Aemilius Lepidus Livianus. Fit enough to have killed Silo in single combat—he had been awarded the *corona civica* for that. Therefore he was brave. Not so brilliant that he'd ever be a danger to the State, but no fool, either. According to the Piglet, he was steady and reliable in every emergency, and confident in command situations. Scaurus had loved him dearly, made him executor of his will.

Of course Mamercus knew perfectly well that he was suddenly being subjected to a minute examination; why did he feel as if he was being assessed by a prospective lover?

"Mamercus, you're married, aren't you?" Sulla asked.

That jolted him into blinking. "Yes, Lucius Cornelius."

"Any children?"

"A girl, now aged four."

"Attached to your wife?"

"No. She's an awful woman."

"Ever think of divorce?"

"Constantly while ever I'm in Rome. Out of Rome, I try not to think of her for any reason."

"What's her name? Her family?"

"Claudia. She's one of the sisters of the Appius Claudius Pulcher at present besieging Nola."

"Oh, not a wise choice, Mamercus! That's a queer family."

"*Queer?* I'd call them downright strange."

Metellus Pius had quite forgotten to recline; he was sitting bolt upright, eyes wide, and fixed on Sulla.

"My daughter is now a widow. She's not quite twenty years old. She has two children, a girl and a boy. Have you ever seen her?"

"No," said Mamercus calmly, "I don't believe I ever have."

"I'm her father, so in her case I'm no judge. But they tell me she's lovely," said Sulla, picking up his wine cup.

"Oh, she is, Lucius Cornelius! Absolutely ravishing!" said the Piglet, beaming fatuously.

"There you are, there's an outside opinion." Sulla looked into his cup, then flicked the lees expertly onto an empty platter. "Fives!" he exclaimed, delighted. "Fives are lucky for me." The eyes gazed directly at Mamercus. "I am looking for a good husband for my poor girl, whose in-laws are making her very miserable. She has a forty-talent dowry—which is more than most girls have—she has proven her fertility, she has one boy, she is still young, she is a patrician on both sides—her mother was a Julia—and she has what I'd call a nice nature. I don't mean she's the sort who will lie down and let you wipe your boots all over her, but she gets on with most people. Her late husband, the younger Quintus Pompeius Rufus, seemed quite besotted by her. So what do you say? Interested?"

"It all depends," said Mamercus cautiously. "What color are her eyes?"

"I don't know," said the father.

"A beautiful brilliant blue," said the Piglet.

"What color is her hair?"

"Red—brown—auburn? I don't know," said the father.

"It's the color of the sky after the sun has just disappeared," said the Piglet.

"Is she tall?"

"I don't know," said the father.

"She'd come to the tip of your nose," said the Piglet.

"What sort of skin does she have?"

"I don't know," said the father.

"Like a creamy-white flower, with six little gold freckles across her nose," said the Piglet.

Both Sulla and Mamercus turned to stare at the suddenly scarlet and shrinking occupant of the middle couch.

"Sounds like *you* want to marry her, Quintus Caecilius," said the father.

"No, no!" cried the Piglet. "But a man can look, Lucius Cornelius! She's absolutely adorable."

"Then I'd better have her," said Mamercus, smiling at his good friend the Piglet. "I admire your taste in women, Quintus Caecilius. So I thank you, Lucius Cornelius. Consider your girl betrothed to me."

"Her mourning period still has seven months to run, so there's no hurry," said Sulla. "Until it ends, she'll be living with Dalmatica. Go and see her, Mamercus. I'll write to her."

Four days later Sulla set off for Brundisium with three very happy legions. They arrived to find Lucullus still encamped outside the city and having no trouble locating grazing for the cavalry's horses and the army's mules, since much of the land was Italian, and the season early winter. It was wet and blustery weather and continued wet and blustery, no ideal conditions for a long sojourn; the men became bored and spent too much of their time gambling. When Sulla arrived in person, however, they settled down. It was Lucullus they couldn't stomach, not Sulla. He had no understanding of the legionary, Lucullus, and was not interested to understand any man so far beneath him on the social scale.

In calendar March, Lucullus set sail for Corcyra, his two legions and two thousand cavalry taking every ship the busy port could find. Which meant that Sulla had no choice but to wait for the return of the transports before he could sail himself. But at the beginning of May—he had very little left by then out of his two hundred talents of gold—Sulla finally crossed the Adriatic with three legions and a thousand army mules.

A good sailor, he leaned on the railing of his ship's stern, gazing back across the faint wake at the smudge on the horizon that was Italy. And then Italy was gone. He was free. At fifty-three years of age he was finally going to a war he could win honorably, against a genuinely foreign foe. Glory, booty, battles, blood.

And so much for you, Gaius Marius! he thought exultantly. This is one war you cannot steal away from me. This war is *mine*!

PART X

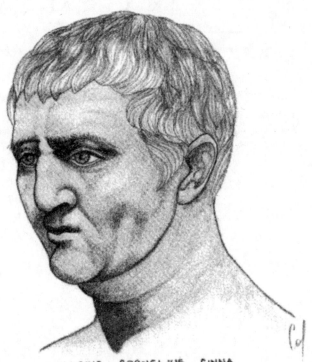

LUCIUS CORNELIUS CINNA

It was Young Marius and Lucius Decumius who got Gaius Marius away from the temple of Tellus and hid him within the *cella* of the temple of Jupiter Stator on the Velia; it was Young Marius and Lucius Decumius who then searched for Publius Sulpicius, Marcus Laetorius, and the other noblemen who had buckled on a sword to defend Rome against the army of Lucius Cornelius Sulla; and it was Young Marius and Lucius Decumius who shepherded Sulpicius and nine others into the temple of Jupiter Stator not very long afterward.

"This is all we could find, Father," said Young Marius, sitting down on the floor nearby. "I heard that Marcus Laetorius, Publius Cethegus, and Publius Albinovanus were seen slipping through the Capena Gate not long ago. But of the Brothers Granii I can find no sign. Hopefully that means they left the city even earlier."

"What an irony," said Marius bitterly to no one in particular, "to go to earth inside an establishment dedicated to the god who halts soldiers in retreat. Mine wouldn't stand and fight, no matter what I promised them."

"They weren't Roman soldiers," Young Marius pointed out.

"I know *that*!"

"I never thought Sulla would go through with it," said Sulpicius, breathing as if he had been running for hours.

"I did—after I met him on the Via Latina at Tusculum," said the urban praetor, Marcus Junius Brutus.

"Well, Sulla owns Rome now," said Young Marius. "Father, what are we going to do?"

Sulpicius answered, detesting the way everyone deferred to Gaius Marius, who might have been consul six times and been of great help to a tribune of the plebs bent on destroying the Senate, but at this moment was merely a *privatus*. "We go to our homes and we behave as if nothing has happened," he said firmly.

Marius turned his head to look at Sulpicius incredulously, more tired than he had ever been in his life, and horribly aware that his left hand, arm and jaw were needled with numbness. "*You* can if you like," he said, rolling his tongue in his mouth because it felt funny. "I know Sulla. And I know what I'm going to do. Run for my life."

"I think I agree with you," said Brutus, the blue tinge to his lips darker than usual, his chest laboring to pull in more air. "If we stay, he'll kill us. I saw his face at Tusculum."

"He cannot kill us!" said Sulpicius positively; a much younger man, he was recovering his wits along with his breath. "No one will be more aware than Sulla that he's *nefas*. He'll bend over backwards to make sure everything he does from now on is legal."

"Rubbish!" said Marius scornfully. "What do you think he's going to do, shoo his men back to Campania tomorrow? Of course he won't! He'll occupy Rome and do whatever he wants."

"He'd never dare," said Sulpicius, realizing that, in similar case to many others in the Senate, he didn't know Sulla well.

Marius found it in him to laugh. "Dare? Lucius Cornelius Sulla, dare? Grow up, Publius Sulpicius! Sulla would dare anything. And in the past he has. What's worse, he dares *after* he thinks. Oh, he won't try us for treason in some trumped-up court! That big a fool he's not. He'll just smuggle us off somewhere secret, kill us, and give out that we died in the battle."

"That's what I thinks too, Gaius Marius," said Lucius Decumius. "He'd as soon kill his mother, that one." He shivered, held up his right hand clenched into a fist, except that the index and the little fingers stuck up stiffly like two horns—the sign to ward off the Evil Eye. "He isn't like other men."

The nine lesser lights sat on the temple floor where they could watch the leaders debate, none of them important men in Senate or Ordo Equester, though all were members of one or the other. It had seemed a cause worth fighting for, to keep a Roman army out of Rome, but now that they had failed so miserably, each of them had arrived at that point where he deemed himself a fool for trying. Tomorrow their spines would stiffen again, as they all believed Rome worth dying for; but in the temple of Jupiter Stator, exhausted and disillusioned, they all hoped Marius would prevail over Sulpicius.

"If you go, Gaius Marius, I cannot stay," said Sulpicius.

"Better to go, believe me. I certainly am," said Marius.

"What about you, Lucius Decumius?" asked Young Marius.

Lucius Decumius shook his head. "No, I can't leave. But—lucky for me!—I isn't important. I have to look after Aurelia and Young Caesar—their *tata* is with Lucius Cinna at Alba Fucentia these days. I'll keep an eye on Julia for you, Gaius Marius."

"Whatever of my property Sulla can lay his hands on will be confiscated," said Marius, and grinned smugly. "Isn't it fortunate I have money buried everywhere?"

Marcus Junius Brutus hauled himself to his feet. "I'll have to go home and bring away what I can." He looked not to Sulpicius but to Marius. "Where are we going? Are we going our own ways, or is it better to go all together?"

"We'll have to leave Italy," said Marius, holding out his right hand to his son and his left to Lucius Decumius; he came to a standing position fairly easily. "I think we should leave Rome separately and stay separated until we're well clear of Rome. Then it will be better if we stick together. I suggest we rendezvous on the island of Aenaria in one month's time—the Ides of December. I won't have any trouble locating Gnaeus and Quintus Granius to make sure they're at the meeting place, and hopefully they'll know where Cethegus, Albinovanus, and Laetorius are. After we reach Aenaria, leave it to me. I'll procure a ship. From Aenaria we'll sail to Sicily, I think. Norbanus is my client, and he's the governor."

"But why Aenaria?" asked Sulpicius, still unhappy at the decision to quit Rome.

"Because it's an island, it's off the beaten track, and it's not very far from Puteoli. I have many relatives and a lot of money in Puteoli," said Marius, flapping his left hand around as if it annoyed him. "My second cousin Marcus Granius—he's the cousin of Gnaeus and Quintus, they'll go to him—is a banker. He has the use of a large part of my cash fortune. While we all make our separate ways to Aenaria, Lucius Decumius here will go to Puteoli with a letter from me to Marcus Granius. Granius will send sufficient funds from Puteoli to Aenaria to enable all twenty of us to live decently while we're away." He tucked the offending hand into his general's sash. "Lucius Decumius will also look for the others. We will be twenty, I assure you. It costs money to be an exile. But don't worry. I have money. Sulla won't stay in Rome forever. He'll go to fight Mithridates. Curse him! And when he's too committed to that war to contemplate a return to Italy, we'll all come home again. My client Lucius Cinna will be consul in the New Year, and he'll make sure we return."

Sulpicius looked astonished. "Your client?"

"I have clients everywhere, Publius Sulpicius, even among the great patrician families," said Gaius Marius complacently; he was beginning to feel better—or rather, the numbness had settled down. Moving toward the temple entrance, he turned to the others and said, "Keep your courage up! It was prophesied that I would be consul of Rome seven times, so this absence is purely a temporary one. And when I am consul a seventh time, you will all be rewarded greatly."

"I need no reward, Gaius Marius," said Sulpicius stiffly. "I do this for Rome alone."

"That's true of everyone here, Publius Sulpicius. In the meantime, we'd better get a move on. I give Sulla until darkness to garrison all the gates. Our best alternative is the Capena—but be careful, all of you."

Sulpicius and the other nine disappeared at a run up the Clivus Palatinus, but when Marius started to walk along the Velia toward the Forum and his house, Lucius Decumius detained him.

"Gaius Marius, you and I are going to the Capena Gate at once," said the little man from the Subura. "Young Marius can dash home and pick up a bit of ready money, he's the youngest and fittest. If he finds the Capena Gate garrisoned, he can find some other way out, even if he has to go over the walls. He can write that letter to your cousin, and your wife can add a bit to convince him."

"Julia!" said Marius desolately.

"You'll see her again, just like you said. The prophecy, eh? Seven times consul. You'll be back. She'll worry a lot less if she knows you're already on your way. Young Marius, your *tata* and I will wait among the tombs just beyond the gate. We'll try to keep an eye out for you, but if we can't, then look for us there."

While Young Marius turned in the direction of home, his father and Lucius Decumius walked up the Clivus Palatinus. Just inside the Porta Mugonia they entered the narrow street which ran to the old meeting houses above the Via Triumphalis, where a flight of steps led down off the Palatium. Noises in the distance told them that Sulla and his troops were moving from the Esquiline down into the Palus Ceroliae, but when Marius and Decumius hurried through the huge Capena Gate, no one garbed like a soldier was anywhere near it. They walked a short distance down the road before placing themselves behind a tomb from which they could see the gate comfortably. Many people came through Capena during the next two hours; not everyone wanted to remain in a Rome held by a Roman army.

Then they saw Young Marius. He was leading the donkey kept for fetching large loads from the marketplace or firewood from the hill of the Janiculum. With him walked a woman muffled closely in a dark mantle.

"Julia!" cried Marius, not caring who saw him emerge from his hiding place.

Her pace quickened, she met him and snuggled against him, eyes closing as his arms went round her. "Oh, Gaius Marius, I was sure I had missed you!" she said, and lifted her face to receive his kiss, and another, and another.

How many years had they been married? Yet it was still a deep pleasure to kiss, even in the grief and anxiety pressing upon them at that moment.

"Oh, I shall miss you!" she said, trying not to weep.

"I won't be away so very long, Julia."

"I can't believe Lucius Cornelius has done this!"

"If I were in his boots, Julia, I'd have done the same."

"You'd never lead an army on Rome!"

"I'm not so sure. In all fairness to him, the provocation was overmastering. If he hadn't done this, he'd be finished. And men like Lucius Cornelius and I can't accept that fate, we just can't. The luck of it was that he had the army and the magistracy. I didn't. But if our places had been reversed—I think I would have done what he did. It was a brilliant move, you know. And in all the history of Rome, there are only two men with the courage to have done it—Lucius Cornelius and me." He kissed her again, then released her. "Go home now, Julia, and wait for me. If Lucius Cornelius takes our house away, go to your mother in Cumae. Marcus Granius has more money of mine by far than I've asked him for, so apply to him if you're in need. In Rome, apply to Titus Pomponius." He thrust her away. "Now go, Julia, go!"

She went, looking back over her shoulder; but Marius had turned to speak to Lucius Decumius, and wasn't watching. Her heart swelled with pride. That was how it should be! When important things needed to be done in a hurry, a man ought not to waste his time looking longingly after his wife. Strophantes and six strong servants were hovering near the gate to escort her home; Julia looked where she was going, and stepped out purposefully.

"Lucius Decumius, you'll have to hire horses for us. I don't ride comfortably these days, but a gig would be too noticeable," Marius was saying. He looked at his son. "Did you get the bag of gold I save for emergencies?"

"Yes. And a bag of silver denarii. I have the letter to Marcus Granius for you, Lucius Decumius."

"Good. Give Lucius Decumius some of the silver too."

And so did Gaius Marius escape from Rome, he and his son riding hired horses, and leading an ass.

"Why not a boat across the river and a port in Etruria?" asked Young Marius.

"No, I think that's the way Publius Sulpicius will go. I'd rather head for Ostia, it's closest," said Marius, a little easier in himself because that awful pricking numbness was not so pronounced—or was it that he was getting used to it?

It was not yet fully dark when they rode into the outskirts of Ostia and saw the town walls looming ahead of them.

"No gate guards, Father," said Young Marius, whose vision these days was better than Marius's.

"Then we'll get ourselves inside before orders come to post some, my son. We'll go down to the dockside and see what's what."

Marius selected a prosperous-looking wharf tavern, and left Young Marius minding the horses and the ass in the darkest shadows while he went to hire a ship.

Obviously Ostia had not yet heard the news that Rome had fallen, though everyone was talking about Sulla's historic march; the whole complement of the inn recognized Marius as soon as he walked through the door, but no one acted as if he was a known fugitive.

"I have to get away to Sicily in a hurry," said Marius, paying for wine for everybody. "Any chance of a good ship ready to sail?"

"You can have mine for a price," said one salty-looking man, leaning forward. "Publius Murcius at your service, Gaius Marius."

"If we can sail tonight, Publius Murcius, it's a deal."

"I can up anchor just before midnight," said Murcius.

"Excellent!"

"I'll need to be paid in advance."

Young Marius came in shortly after his father had concluded his bargain; Marius rose to his feet, smiled around the room, and said, "My son!" before drawing Young Marius outside onto the docks.

"You're not coming with me," he said as soon as they were alone. "I want you to find your own way to Aenaria. The risk to you if you come with me is far greater. Take the ass and both horses and ride for Tarracina."

"Father, why not come with me? Tarracina would be safer."

"I'm too infirm to ride so far, Young Marius. I'll take ship from here and hope the winds behave." He kissed his son, a mere peck. "Take the gold. Leave me the silver."

"Half and half, Father, or none at all."

Marius sighed. "Gaius Marius Junior, why couldn't you have told me you killed Cato the Consul? Why did you deny it?"

His son stared, flabbergasted. "You'd ask me that? At a time like this? Is it so important?"

"To me it is. If Fortune has deserted me, we may never meet again. Why did you lie to me?"

Young Marius smiled ruefully, looking the image of Julia. "Oh, Father! One never knows what you want to hear! It's as simple as that. We all try to tell you what we think you want to hear. That's the penalty you pay for being a Great Man! It seemed more sensible to me to deny it in case you were in one of those moods when you insist upon doing the proper, ethical thing. In which instance, you wouldn't have wanted me to admit the deed—it would have meant you would have had no choice but to indict me. If I guessed wrongly, I'm sorry. You didn't give me any help, you know, you were closed up tighter than a snail in dry weather."

"I thought you were behaving like a spoiled child!"

"Oh, Father!" Young Marius shook his head, tears shining in his eyes. "No child is spoiled who is the son of a Great Man. Think what I have to measure up to! You stride across our world like a Titan and we all scurry about between your feet wondering what you want, how best to please you. None of those around you is your equal, in brains or competence. And that includes me. Your son."

"Then kiss me again, and go now." The embrace this time was heartfelt; Marius had never thought to like Young Marius so much. "You were absolutely right, by the way."

"Right about what?"

"To kill Cato the Consul."

Young Marius waved his hand about in deprecation. "I know *that*! I'll see you on Aenaria by the Ides of December."

"Gaius Marius! Gaius Marius!" called a fretful voice.

Marius turned back toward the tavern.

"If you're ready, we'll go out to my ship now," said Publius Murcius, still in that fretful voice.

Marius sighed. Clearly his instincts were right to tell him this voyage was somehow doomed; the salty-looking character was a wet fish, not a lusty pirate.

The ship, however, was reasonable in that it was well built and seaworthy, though how it would perform in the open waters between Sicily and Africa if the worst came to the worst and they had to go further than Sicily, Gaius Marius didn't know. The ship's chief disadvantage was undoubtedly its captain, Murcius, who did nothing save complain. But they put out across the mud flats and sandbars of that unsuitable harbor just before midnight and turned to follow a stiff northeasterly breeze, just right for sailing down the coast. Creaking and wallowing because Murcius hadn't loaded enough ballast in lieu of a cargo, the ship crept along about two miles offshore. The crew at least was cheerful: nobody needed to man the very few oars, and the two big unwieldy rudder oars lay in a following sea.

Then as dawn broke the wind veered through half a circle and came from the southwest at half gale force.

"Wouldn't it?" demanded Murcius peevishly of his passenger. "We'll be blown straight back to Ostia."

"There's gold says you won't, Publius Murcius. And there's more gold says you'll make for Aenaria."

Murcius's only answer was a suspicious glance, but the lure of gold was too much to resist; so the sailors, suddenly as full of woes as their master, took up the oars as soon as the big square sail was reefed in.

Sextus Lucilius—who happened to be the first cousin of Pompey Strabo—was hoping to be elected a tribune of the plebs for the coming year. As conservative as his family's traditions demanded, he looked forward with pleasure to vetoing any and all of those radical fellows sure also to be elected. But when Sulla marched into Rome and took up residence adjacent to the swamps of the Palus Ceroliae, Sextus Lucilius was one of the many men who wondered how it would change his own plans. Not that he objected to Sulla's action; as far as he was concerned, Marius and Sulpicius deserved to be strangled in the bottom chamber of the Tullianum—or, even better, to be hurled from the Tarpeian Rock. What a sight that would be, to watch Gaius Marius's bulky body go flapping down onto the needle rocks below! One either loved or hated the old *mentula,* and Sextus Lucilius hated him. Had he been pressed as to why he hated him, he would have answered that without Gaius Marius there could have been no Saturninus and—more recent crime by far—no Sulpicius.

Of course he sought out the busy consul Sulla and pledged his support enthusiastically, including his services as a tribune of the plebs for the coming year. Then Sulla rendered the Plebeian Assembly a hollow thing; the hopes of Sextus Lucilius were temporarily dashed. The fugitives were condemned, however, which made him feel a little better—until he discovered that, with the single exception of Sulpicius, absolutely no attempt was being made to apprehend them. Including Gaius Marius, bigger miscreant by far than Sulpicius! When Lucilius complained to Scaevola Pontifex Maximus, he got a cold stare.

"Try not to be stupid, Sextus Lucilius!" said Scaevola. "It was necessary to remove Gaius Marius from Rome, but how can you even imagine Lucius Cornelius wants *that* death on his hands? If we have all deplored his leading an army against Rome, how do you think the vast majority of people in Rome would react to his killing Gaius Marius, death sentence or not? The death sentence is there because Lucius Cornelius had no choice but try the fugitives *perduellio* in the Centuries, and conviction for *perduellio* automatically carries the death sentence. All Lucius Cornelius wants is a Rome without the presence of Gaius Marius in it! Gaius Marius is an institution, and no one in his right senses kills an institution. Now go away, Sextus Lucilius, and don't bother plaguing the consul with such utter foolishness!"

Sextus Lucilius went away. He didn't bother trying to see Sulla. He even understood what Scaevola had said; no one in Sulla's position would want to be responsible for executing Gaius Marius. But the fact remained that Gaius Marius had been convicted of *perduellio* by the Centuries, and was at large when he ought to be hunted down and killed. Apparently with impunity! To get away free! Provided he didn't enter Rome or any large Roman town, he could do precisely what he wanted. Secure in the knowledge that no one executed an institution!

Well, thought Sextus Lucilius, you have reckoned without me,

Gaius Marius! I am happy to go down in the history books as the man who terminated your nefarious career.

With that, Sextus Lucilius went out and hired fifty ex-cavalry troopers in need of a little money—not a difficult thing to do in a time when everyone was short of money. He then commissioned them to search out Gaius Marius. When they found him, they were to kill him on the spot. *Perduellio.*

In the meantime, the Plebeian Assembly went ahead and elected its tribunes of the plebs. Sextus Lucilius stood as a candidate and was voted in, as the Plebs always liked to have one or two extremely conservative tribunes; the sparks would fly.

Emboldened by his election, impotent though his new office was, Sextus Lucilius called in the leader of his troopers and gave him a little talk.

"I'm one of the few men in this city who isn't hard up," he said, "and I am willing to put up an additional sum of one thousand denarii if you bring me the head of Gaius Marius. Just his head!"

The troop leader—who would cheerfully have decapitated his whole family for a thousand denarii—saluted with alacrity. "I will definitely do my best, Sextus Lucilius," he said. "I know the old man isn't north of the Tiber, so I'll start searching to the south."

Sixteen days after leaving Ostia, the ship captained by Publius Murcius gave up its uneven battle against the elements and put in to port at Circei, a scant fifty miles down the coast from Ostia. The sailors were exhausted, water was low.

"Sorry, Gaius Marius, but it has to be done," said Publius Murcius. "We can't go on battling a sou'wester."

There seemed little point in protesting; Gaius Marius nodded. "If you must, you must. I'll stay on board."

This answer seemed a most peculiar one to Publius Murcius, and made him scratch his head. Once on shore, he understood. All of Circei was talking about the events in Rome and the *perduellio* condemnation of Gaius Marius; outside Rome, names like Sulpicius were hardly known, but Gaius Marius was famous everywhere. The captain returned to his ship quickly.

Looking wretched but determined, Murcius faced his passenger. "I'm sorry, Gaius Marius, I'm a respectable man with a ship to keep up and a business to run. Never in my life have I smuggled a cargo, and I'm not going to start now. I've paid my port dues and my excise taxes, there's no one in Ostia or Puteoli can say otherwise. And I can't help but think there's a message from the gods for me in this awful unseasonable wind. Get your things and I'll help you into the skiff. You'll just have to find another ship. I didn't say a word about your being on board, but sooner or later my sailors will talk. If you get going now and don't try to hire another ship here, you'll be all right. Go to Tarracina or Caieta, try there."

"I thank you for your consideration in not betraying me, Publius Murcius," said Marius graciously. "How much do I owe you for my journey this far?"

Additional remuneration Murcius refused. "What you gave me in Ostia is enough," he said. "Now please go!"

Between Murcius and the two slaves left on board, Marius managed to get over the side of the ship into the skiff, where he sat looking very old and defeated. He had brought no slave or attendant with him, and Publius Murcius fancied that over the sixteen days he had been a passenger, Marius's limp had worsened. A complaining man of flat moods though he was, the captain found himself unable to land Marius where he might be apprehended, so they beached the skiff well to the south of Circei and waited several hours until one of the two slaves came back with a hired horse and a parcel of food.

"I am really sorry," said Publius Murcius dolefully after he and both slaves had exhausted themselves getting Marius up into the saddle. "I'd like to help you further, Gaius Marius, but I dare not." He hesitated, then blurted it out. "You've been convicted of Great Treason, you see. When you're caught, you have to be killed."

Marius looked winded. "Great Treason? *Perduellio?*"

"You and all your friends were tried in the Centuries, and the Centuries convicted you."

"The Centuries!" Marius shook his head, dazed.

"You'd better go," said Murcius. "Good luck."

"You'll have better luck yourself now you're rid of the cause of your misfortunes," said Marius. He kicked his horse in the ribs and trotted off into a grove of trees.

I was right to leave Rome, he thought. The Centuries! He is determined to see me dead. Whereas for the last twelve days at least I have been deeming myself a fool to have left Rome. Sulpicius was right, I had become convinced of it. Too late to turn back now, I kept telling myself. Now I learn *I* was right all along! I wasn't dreaming of trials in the Centuries! I just knew Sulla, and I thought he'd have us done to death secretly. I didn't think him so great a fool as to try me! What does he know that I do not know?

As soon as he was clear of habitation Marius got down from his horse and began to walk; his malady made riding an ordeal, but the animal was useful for carrying his little hoard of gold and coins. How far to Minturnae? Thirty-five miles or thereabouts if he kept clear of the Via Appia. Swampy country alive with mosquitoes, but fairly deserted. Knowing Young Marius was going there, Tarracina he decided to avoid. Minturnae would do nicely—large, placid, prosperous, and almost untouched by the Italian war.

The journey took him four days, four days during which he ate very little once the parcel of food was gone; only a bowl of pulse porridge from an old woman living alone, and some bread and hard cheese he shared with a vagabond Samnite who volunteered to do the shopping if Marius provided the money. Neither the old woman nor the Samnite had cause to regret their charity, as Marius left a little gold with each of them.

Left side feeling like a lead weight he had to drag everywhere with him, he plodded on until the walls of Minturnae appeared at last in the distance. But as he drew closer, approaching from the wooded countryside, he saw a troop of fifty armed men trotting down the Via Appia. Concealed among some pines, he watched as they passed through the gate into the town. Luckily Minturnae's port lay outside the fortifications, so Marius was able to bypass the walls and reach the dockside area undetected.

Time to get rid of the horse; he untied his moneybag from the saddle, slapped the beast sharply, and watched it frisk away. Then he entered a small but prosperous-looking tavern nearby.

"I am Gaius Marius. I am condemned to death for Great Treason. I am more tired than I have ever been in my life. And I need wine," said Marius, voice booming.

Only six or seven men were inside. Every face turned to look, every mouth dropped open. Then chairs and stools scraped, he was surrounded by men who wanted to touch him for luck, not in anger.

"Sit down, sit down!" said the proprietor, beaming. "Are you *really* Gaius Marius?"

"Don't I fit the general description? Only half a face and older than Cronus, I know, but don't tell me you don't know Gaius Marius when you see him!"

"I know Gaius Marius when I see him," said one of the drinkers, "and you are Gaius Marius. I was there in the Forum Romanum when you spoke up for Titus Titinius."

"Wine. I need wine," said Gaius Marius.

He was given it, then more when he drained his cup in a single gulp. After that came food; while he ate he regaled the men with the story of Sulla's invasion of Rome and his own flight. Of the implications of *perduellio* conviction he did not need to speak; be he Roman, Latin, or Italian, every man in the peninsula knew about Great Treason. By rights those who listened should have been hustling him to the town magistrates for execution—or doing it themselves. Instead, they heard the weary Marius out and then helped him up a rickety ladder to a bed. The fugitive fell upon it and slept for ten hours.

When he woke he discovered that someone had laundered his tunic and his cloak, washed his boots inside and out; feeling better than he had since leaving Murcius's ship, Marius scrambled down the ladder to find the tavern crammed.

"They're all here to see you, Gaius Marius," said the proprietor, coming forward to take his hand. "What an honor you do us!"

"I am a condemned man, innkeeper, and there must be half a

hundred parties of troopers looking for me. I saw one such ride through the gates of your town yesterday."

"Yes, they're in the forum with the *duumviri* right at this moment, Gaius Marius. Like you, they've had a sleep, and now they're busy throwing their weight around. Half Minturnae knows you're here, but you needn't worry. We won't give you up. Nor will we tell the *duumviri*, who are both the sort of man adheres to the letter of the law. Best they don't know. If they did, they'd probably decide you ought to be executed, little though they'd relish the task."

"I thank you," said Marius warmly.

A short, plump little man who had not been present eleven hours earlier came up to Marius, hand outstretched. "I am Aulus Belaeus, and I am a merchant of Minturnae. I own a few ships. You tell me what you need, Gaius Marius, and you will have it."

"I need a ship prepared to take me out of Italy and sail to wherever in the world I can find asylum," said Marius.

"That's not a difficulty," said Belaeus promptly. "I have just the right lady sitting at her moorings in the bay. As soon as you've eaten, I'll take you out to her."

"Are you sure, Aulus Belaeus? It's my life they're after. If you help me, your own life might be forfeit."

"I'm ready to take that risk," said Belaeus tranquilly.

An hour later Marius was rowed out to a stout grain-carrier more used by far to adverse winds and heavy seas than Publius Murcius's little coastal trader.

"She's fresh from a refit after discharging her African grain cargo in Puteoli. I was intending to return her to Africa as soon as the winds were right," said Belaeus, assisting his guest on board via a stout wooden stern ladder more like a set of steps. "Her holds are full of Falernian wine for the African luxury market, she's in good ballast, and she's well provisioned. I always keep my ships ready—one never knows about winds and weather." This was said with a singularly affectionate smile for Gaius Marius.

"I don't know how to thank you, except to pay you well."

"This is an honor, Gaius Marius. Don't strip me of it by trying to pay me, I beg you. I shall dine for the rest of my days on this story—how I, a merchant from Minturnae, helped the great Gaius Marius elude his pursuers."

"And I shall not cease to be grateful, Aulus Belaeus."

Belaeus descended to his skiff, waved goodbye, and had himself rowed the short distance to shore.

Even as he landed at the jetty closest to his ship, the fifty troopers who had been enquiring through the town came riding onto the dockside. Ignoring Belaeus—whom they did not at first connect with the ship at that moment hauling anchor—the hirelings of Sextus Lucilius looked across the water at the men leaning over the vessel's side, and saw the unmistakable face of Gaius Marius.

The leading trooper spurred forward, cupped his hands round his mouth and shouted, "Gaius Marius, you are under arrest! Captain, you are harboring a fugitive from Roman justice! In the name of the Senate and People of Rome, I order you to put about and deliver Gaius Marius to me!"

On the ship, these hollered words were dismissed with a snort; the captain went placidly on with his preparations to sail. But Marius, looking back to see the good Belaeus taken by the troopers, swallowed painfully.

"Captain, stop!" he cried. "Your employer is now in the custody of men who really want me. I must go back!"

"It isn't necessary, Gaius Marius," said the captain. "Aulus Belaeus can look after himself. He gave you into my charge and told me to get you away. I must do as he says."

"You will do as *I* say, captain. Put about!"

"If I did that, Gaius Marius, I'd never command another ship. Aulus Belaeus would use my guts for rigging."

"Put about and put me in a boat, captain. I insist! If you won't return me to the dockside, then row me ashore in some place where I have a chance to get away." Marius stared fiercely, scowled. "Do it, captain! I insist!"

Much against his better judgment, the captain obeyed; there was something about Marius when he said he insisted that told all men this was a general used to being obeyed.

"I'll set you ashore in the thick of the marshes, then," said the unhappy captain. "I know the area well. There's a safe path will take you back into Minturnae, where I suggest you hide until the troopers pass on. Then I'll bring you on board again."

Over the side once more, into yet another rowboat; this time, however, the fugitive departed from the far side of the vessel and used it to conceal his movements from the troopers, still calling across the water that Gaius Marius must be returned.

Alas for Marius, the leader of the troop was a very farsighted man; as the lighter came into view heading into the southern distance, he recognized Marius's head between the six rowers bent to their task.

"Quick!" he shouted. "On your horses, men! Leave that stupid fellow, he's not important. We're going to follow that boat by land."

It proved easy to do so, for a well-used track outlined the contour of the bay through the salt marshes which festered around the mouth of the Liris River; the troopers actually gained ground on the lighter rapidly, only losing sight of it when it disappeared into the rushes and reeds growing on the Liris mud flats.

"Keep going, we'll find the old villain!"

Sextus Lucilius's hirelings did indeed find him, two hours later, and just in time. Marius had abandoned his clothes and was floundering waist-deep in a patch of gluey black mud, exhausted and sinking. To pull him out wasn't easy, but there were plenty of hands to help, and eventually the sucking mud parted reluctantly with its victim. One of the men took off his cloak and went to wrap it about Marius, but the leader stopped him.

"Let the old cripple go naked. Minturnae should see what a fine fellow the great Gaius Marius is! The whole town knew he was here. They'll suffer for sheltering him."

So the old cripple walked naked in the midst of the troopers, stumbling, limping, falling, all the way back to Minturnae; and the troopers didn't care how long it took to make the journey. As they neared the town and houses began to cluster along the track, the leader called loudly to everyone to come and see the captured fugitive Gaius Marius, who would soon lose his head in the Minturnae forum. "Come one, come all!" the leader shouted.

At midafternoon the troopers rode into the forum with most of the town accompanying them, too stunned, too amazed to protest at the way the great Gaius Marius was being treated, and aware he was condemned for Great Treason. Yet a slow dull anger grew in the backs of their minds—surely *Gaius Marius* could not commit Great Treason!

The two chief magistrates were waiting at the foot of the meeting-hall steps surrounded by a guard of town beadles, hastily called up to let these arrogant Roman officials see that Minturnae was not entirely at their mercy, that if necessary Minturnae could fight back.

"We caught Gaius Marius about to sail away in a Minturnaean ship," said the leader of the troop ominously. "Minturnae knew he was here, and Minturnae helped him."

"Minturnae cannot be held responsible for the actions of a few Minturnaeans," said the senior town magistrate stiffly. "However, you now have your prisoner. Take him and go."

"Oh, I don't want *all* of him!" said the leader, grinning. "I just want his head. You can keep the rest. There's a nice stone bench over there will do the job. We'll just lean him against it, and his head will be off in a trice."

The crowd gasped, growled; the two magistrates looked grim, their beadles restless.

"On whose authority do you presume to execute in the forum of Minturnae a man who has been consul of Rome six times—a hero?" asked the senior *duumvir*. He looked the leader up and down, the troop up and down, determined to make them feel a tittle of what he had felt when they had accosted him so arrogantly shortly after dawn. "You don't seem like Roman cavalry. How do I know you are who you say you are?"

"We've been hired specifically to do this job," said the leader, growing steadily more uneasy as he saw the faces in the crowd and the beadles shifting their scabbards to come at their swords.

"Hired by whom? The Senate and People of Rome?" asked the *duumvir* in the manner of an advocate.

"That's right."

"I do not believe you. Show me proof."

"This man is condemned of *perduellio*! You know what that means, *duumvir*. His life is forfeit in every Roman and Latin community. I'm not authorized to bring the whole man back to Rome alive. I'm authorized to bring back his head."

"Then," said the senior magistrate calmly, "you will have to fight Minturnae to get that head. Here in our town we are not common barbarians. A Roman citizen of Gaius Marius's standing is not decapitated like a slave or a *peregrinus*."

"Strictly speaking he's not a Roman citizen!" said the leader savagely. "However, if you want the job done nicely, then I suggest you do it yourselves! I'm off to Rome to bring you back all the proof you need, *duumvir*! I'll be back in three days. Gaius Marius had better be dead, otherwise this whole town will have to answer to the Senate and People of Rome. And in three days I will take the head from Gaius Marius's dead body, according to my orders."

Throughout all this, Marius had been standing swaying in the midst of the troopers, a ghastly apparition whose plight had moved many to tears. Angry at being cheated, one of the troopers drew his sword to cut Marius down, but the crowd was suddenly all among the horses, hands reaching for the fugitive to draw him out of reach of swords, ready to fight. As were the beadles.

"Minturnae will pay!" snarled the leader.

"Minturnae will execute the prisoner according to his *dignitas* and *auctoritas,*" said the senior magistrate. "Now leave!"

"Just one moment!" roared a hoarse voice. Gaius Marius came forward among a host of Minturnaean men. "You may have fooled these good country people, but you don't fool me! Rome has no cavalry to hunt condemned men down—neither Senate nor People hires it, only individuals. Who hired you?"

So evocative of old times under the standards was the power in Marius's voice that the leader's tongue had answered before his prudence could prevent it. "Sextus Lucilius," he said.

"Thank you!" said Marius. "I will remember."

"I piss on you, old man!" said the leader scornfully, and pulled his horse's head around with a vicious jerk. "You have given me your word, magistrate! When I return I expect Gaius Marius to be a dead man and his head ready for lopping!"

The moment the troop had ridden off, the *duumvir* nodded to his beadles. "Put Gaius Marius in confinement," he said.

The magistrate's men plucked Marius from the middle of the crowd and escorted him gently to a single cell beneath the podium of the temple of Jupiter Optimus Maximus, normally only used to shut up a violent drunkard for the night, or imprison someone gone mad until more permanent arrangements could be made.

As soon as Marius had been led away the crowd knotted into clusters suddenly talking urgently, none going any further than the taverns around the perimeter of the square. And here Aulus Belaeus, who had witnessed the whole incident, began to move among the groups, himself talking urgently.

Minturnae owned several public slaves, but among them was one extremely useful fellow whom the town had bought from an itinerant dealer two years before, and never regretted paying the hefty price of five thousand denarii asked. Then eighteen years old, now twenty, he was a gigantic German of the Cimbric nation, by name of Burgundus. He stood a full head higher than the few men of six feet Minturnae owned, and his thews were mighty, his strength of that breathtaking kind undamped by brilliance of intellect or oversensitivity of spirit—not surprising in one who had been six years old when he was taken after the battle of Vercellae and subjected ever since to the life of the enslaved barbarian. Not for him, the privileges and emoluments of the polished Greek who sold himself into slavery because it increased his chances of prosperity; Burgundus was paid a pittance, lived in a dilapidated wooden hut on the edge of town, and thought he had been visited by the magic wagon of the goddess Nerthus when some woman sought him out, curious to see what sort of lover a barbarian giant made. It never occurred to Burgundus to escape, nor did he find his lot an unhappy one; on the contrary, he had enjoyed his two years in Minturnae, where he felt quite important and knew himself valued. In time, he had been given to understand, his *stips* would be increased and he would be allowed to marry, to have children. And if he continued to work well, his children would be deemed free.

The other public slaves were put to weeding and sweeping, painting, washing down buildings and other kinds of maintenance, but Burgundus alone inherited the jobs requiring heavy labor or more than normal human strength. It was Burgundus who cleared the Minturnaean drains and sewers when they blocked after floods, Burgundus who removed a flyblown carcass of horse or ass or other big animal from an inconvenient place, Burgundus who took down trees considered dangerous, Burgundus who went after a savage dog, Burgundus who dug ditches single-handed. Like all huge creatures, the German was a gentle and docile man, aware of his own strength and in no need to prove it to anyone; aware too that if he aimed a playful blow at someone, that someone could well die as the result of it. He had therefore developed a technique to handle drunken sailors and overly aggressive little men determined to conquer him, and sported a few scars because of his forbearance—but also sported a kindly enough reputation in the town.

Having been maneuvered into the unenviable task of executing Gaius Marius and determined they would do their duty in as Roman a way as possible (and also aware that this duty would not be popular with the inhabitants of the town), the magistrates sent for Burgundus the handyman at once.

He, in ignorance of the events in Minturnae that day, had been piling huge stones in a heap below the walls on the Via Appia side of town, preparatory to beginning some repairs. And, fetched by a fellow slave, walked in the direction of the forum with his long, deceptively slow strides while the other public servant half-ran to keep up with him.

The senior magistrate was waiting for him in a lane outside the forum, a lane which backed onto the meeting hall and the temple of Jupiter Optimus Maximus; if the job was to be done without incurring a riot it would have to be done at once, and without the knowledge of the crowd in the forum.

"Ah, Burgundus, just the man I need!" said the *duumvir* (whose colleague, a less forceful man, had mysteriously disappeared). "In the *cella* below our capitol is a prisoner." He turned away and threw the rest over his shoulder in a casual, unconcerned manner. "You will strangle him. He's a traitor under sentence of death."

The German stood quite still, then lifted his hands and looked at their vastness in wonder; never before had he been called upon to kill a man. Kill a man with those hands. It would be as easy for him as for any other man to wring a chicken's neck. Of course he had to do as he was told, that went without saying; but suddenly the sense of comfortable well-being he had enjoyed in Minturnae blew away in a lonely wind. He was to become the town executioner as well as being made to do everything else unpalatable. Filled with horror, his usually placid blue eyes took in the back of the capitol, the temple of Jupiter Optimus Maximus. Where the prisoner he had been told to strangle was located. A very important prisoner, it seemed. One of the Italian leaders in the war?

Burgundus drew in a deep breath, then plodded toward the far side of the temple's podium, where the door to the little labyrinth beneath was located. To enter, he had not only to dip his head, but to bend almost double. He found himself inside a narrow stone hall, off which several doors opened on either side; at its far end an iron grille covered a slit made to let in light. In this gloomy place were kept the town's records and archives, local laws and statutes, the treasury, and, behind the first door to the left, the rare man or woman the *duumviri* had ordered detained until whatever troubled them had passed and they could be released.

Made of oak three fingers thick, this door was an even smaller one than the entranceway; Burgundus pulled back the bolt, crouched, and squeezed himself into the cell. Like the hall the room was illuminated by a barred opening, this one high up on the back wall of the temple base, where noises emanating from within were least liable to be heard from the forum. It gave barely enough light to see, especially because the eyes of Burgundus were not yet accustomed to the dimness.

Straightening as much as possible, the German giant distinguished a greyish-black lump, vaguely man-shaped; whoever it was rose to his feet and faced his executioner.

"What do you want?" the prisoner demanded loudly, his voice full of authority.

"I have been told to strangle you," said Burgundus simply.

"You're a German!" said the prisoner sharply. "Which tribe? Come on, *answer me,* you great gawk!"

This last was uttered even more sharply, for Burgundus was now beginning to see more clearly, and what had caused him to hesitate over his reply was the sight of a pair of fierce fiery eyes.

"I am from the Cimbri, *domine.*"

The large and naked man with the terrible eyes seemed visibly to swell. "What? A slave—and one whom I conquered into the bargain!—presumes to kill *Gaius Marius?*"

Burgundus flinched and whimpered, threw his arms up to cover his head, cowered away.

"Get out!" thundered Gaius Marius. "I'll not meet my death in any mean dungeon at the hands of any German!"

Wailing, Burgundus fled, leaving cell door and outer door ajar, and erupted into the open space of the forum.

"No, no!" he cried to those in the square, tears falling down his face in rivers. "I cannot kill Gaius Marius! I cannot kill Gaius Marius! I cannot kill Gaius Marius!"

Aulus Belaeus came striding across from the opposite side of the forum, took the giant's writhing hands gently. "It's all right, Burgundus, that won't be asked of you. Stop crying now, there's the good boy! Enough!"

"I can't kill Gaius Marius!" Burgundus said again, wiping his runny nose on his arm because Belaeus still held his hands. "And I can't let anyone else kill Gaius Marius either!"

"No one is going to kill Gaius Marius," said Belaeus firmly. "It's all a misunderstanding. Now calm yourself, and make yourself useful. Go across to Marcus Furius and take the wine and the robe he's holding. Offer Gaius Marius both. Then you may take Gaius Marius to my house and wait there with him."

Like a child the giant quietened, beamed upon Aulus Belaeus, and lolloped off to do as he was told.

Belaeus turned to face the crowd, gathering again; his eyes were fixed upon the *duumviri*, both rushing from the meeting hall, and his stance was aggressive.

"Well, citizens of Minturnae, are you going to allow our lovely town to inherit the detestable task of killing Gaius Marius?"

"Aulus Belaeus, we have to do this!" said the senior magistrate, arriving breathless. "It is Great Treason!"

"I don't care if it's every crime on the statutes!" said Aulus Belaeus. "Minturnae cannot execute Gaius Marius!"

The crowd was yelling its heartfelt support for Aulus Belaeus, so the magistrates convened a meeting then and there to discuss the matter. The result was a foregone conclusion; Gaius Marius was to go free. Minturnae could not possibly make itself responsible for the death of a man who had been consul of Rome six times and saved Italy from the Germans.

"So," said Aulus Belaeus contentedly to Gaius Marius a little later, "I am pleased to be able to tell you that I will put you back on my ship with the best wishes of all Minturnae, including our silly hidebound magistrates. And this time your ship will sail without your being dragged back to shore, I promise you."

Bathed and fed, Marius was feeling much better. "I have received much kindness since I fled Rome, Aulus Belaeus, but none so great as the kindness Minturnae has shown me. I shall never forget this place." He turned to give the hovering Burgundus the best smile his poor paralyzed face could produce. "Nor will I forget that I was spared by a German. Thank you."

Belaeus rose to his feet. "I'd like to permit my house the honor of having you stay, Gaius Marius, but I won't rest easy until I see your ship sailing out of the bay. Let me escort you to the docks immediately. You can sleep on board."

When they came out of the street door to Belaeus's house, most of Minturnae was waiting to walk with them to the harbor; a cheer went up for Gaius Marius, who stood acknowledging it with regal dignity. Then everyone proceeded to the shore with lighter hearts and more importance than in years. On the jetty Marius embraced Aulus Belaeus publicly.

"Your money is still on board," said Belaeus, tears in his eyes. "I have sent extra clothing out for you—and a much better brand of wine than my captain normally drinks! I am also sending the slave Burgundus with you, since you have no attendants. The town is afraid to keep him in case the troopers come back and some local fool talks. He doesn't deserve to die, so I bought him for your use."

"I accept Burgundus with pleasure, Aulus Belaeus, but on no account worry about those fellows. I know who hired them—a man with no authority and no clout, trying to win a reputation for himself. At first I suspected Lucius Sulla, and that would have been far more serious. But if the consul has troopers out looking for me, they haven't reached Minturnae yet. That lot were commissioned by a glory-seeking *privatus*." The breath hissed between Marius's teeth. "He'll keep, Sextus Lucilius!"

"My ship is yours until you can come home again," said Belaeus, smiling. "The captain knows. Luckily his cargo is Falernian, so it will only improve until he can unload it. We wish you well."

"And I wish you well, Aulus Belaeus. I will never forget you," said Gaius Marius.

And finally the day of excitement was over; the men and women of Minturnae stood on the docks and waved until the ship dropped below the horizon, then trooped home feeling as if they had won a great war. Aulus Belaeus walked home last of all, smiling to himself in the dying light; he had conceived a wonderful idea. He would find the greatest painter of murals in all the peninsula and instruct him to trace the story of Gaius Marius in Minturnae through a series of magnificent pictures. They would adorn the new temple of Marica in its lovely grove of trees. After all, she was the sea-goddess who gave birth to Latinus—whose daughter Lavinia married Aeneas and produced Iulus—so she had a special significance for Gaius Marius, married to a Julia. Marica was also the patroness of the town. No greater deed had Minturnae done than to decline to kill Gaius Marius; and in the years to come, all of Italy would know of it because of the frescoes in the temple of Marica.

From that time onward Gaius Marius was never in danger, though long and wearisome were his travels. In Aenaria nineteen of the fugitives were reunited, and waited then in vain for Publius Sulpicius. After eight days they decided sorrowfully that he would never come, and sailed without him. From Aenaria they braved the open waters of the Tuscan Sea and saw no land until they came to the northwestern cape of Sicily, where they put in at the fishing port of Erycina.

There in Sicily Marius had hoped to remain, not wanting to venture any further from Italy than he needed; though his physical health was remarkably good considering all that had befallen him, even he himself was aware that all was not well inside his mind. He forgot things, and sometimes every word said to him sounded like the bar-bars of Scythians or Sarmatians; he smelled unidentifiable yet repellent odors, and endured fishing-nets coming down across his eyes to mar his vision, or would grow unbearably hot, or wonder where he was; his temper frayed, he imagined slights and insults.

"Whatever it is inside of us that makes us think, be it in our chests as some say, or in our heads as Hippocrates says—and I believe it must be inside our heads because I think with my eyes and ears and nose, so why should they be as far away from the source of thought as they are from heart or liver?" he rambled one day to his son while they waited in Erycina to hear from the governor. His voice trailed away, he knitted his huge brows in a fierce frown, pulled at them constantly. "Let me start again. . . . Something is chewing my mind away a little bit at a time, Young Marius. I know whole books still, and when I force myself to it, I *can* think straight—I can conduct meetings, I can do anything I ever could in the past. But not always. And it's changing in ways I don't understand. At times I'm not even conscious of the changes. . . .

You must allow me these vaguenesses and crotchets. I have to conserve my mental strength because one day soon I will be consul for the seventh time. Martha said I would be, and she was never wrong. Never wrong . . . I told you that, didn't I?"

Young Marius swallowed, forced the lump in his throat away. "Yes, Father, you did. Many times."

"Did I ever tell you she prophesied something else?"

The grey eyes came round to rest upon the father's battered and twisted face, very high in its color these days. Young Marius sighed softly, wondering whether Marius's mind was rambling again, or if this was still a lucid period. "No, Father."

"Well, she did. She said I wasn't going to be the greatest man Rome would ever produce. Do you know who she said would be the very greatest Roman of them all?"

"No, Father. But I'd like to know." Not even a ray of hope stole into Young Marius's heart; he knew it would not be he. The son of a Great Man is all too aware of his own deficiencies.

"She said it would be Young Caesar."

"Edepol!"

Marius wriggled, giggled, suddenly chillingly eldritch. "Oh, don't worry, my son! He won't be! I refuse to let anyone be greater than I am! That's why I'm going to nail Young Caesar's star to the bottom of the deepest sea."

His son got to his feet. "You're tired, Father. I've noticed that these moods and difficulties you have are much worse when you're tired. Come and sleep."

The governor of Sicily was Gaius Marius's client Gaius Norbanus, who was in Messana dealing with an attempted invasion of Sicily by Marcus Lamponius and a force of rebel Lucanians and Bruttians. Sent as quickly as possible down the Via Valeria to Messana, Marius's messenger came back with the governor's answer in thirteen days.

> Though I am acutely aware of my cliental obligations
> to you, Gaius Marius, I am also governor *propraetore*

of a Roman province, and I am honor bound to observe
my duty to Rome ahead of my duty to my patron. Your
letter arrived after I had received an official directive
from the Senate notifying me that I can offer you and
the other fugitives no kind of succor. I am actually instructed to hunt you down and kill you if possible. That
of course I cannot do; what I can do is to order your
ship to leave Sicilian waters.

Privately I wish you well, and hope that somewhere
you find shelter and safety, though I doubt you will find
it in any Roman territory. I should tell you that Publius
Sulpicius was apprehended in Laurentum. His head
adorns the rostra in Rome. A vile deed. But you will
understand my position better when I tell you that the
head of Sulpicius was fixed to the rostra by none other
than Lucius Cornelius Sulla himself. No, not an order.
He did the deed personally.

"Poor Sulpicius!" said Marius, blinking away easy tears. Then
he squared his shoulders and said, "Very well, on we go! We'll see
how we are received in the African province."

But there too they were permitted no entry; the governor Publius Sextilius had also received orders, and could do no more for
the fugitives than to advise them to go somewhere else before duty
prompted him to hunt them down and kill them.

On they went to Rusicade, the port serving Cirta, capital of
Numidia. King Hiempsal now ruled Numidia; the son of Gauda,
he was a better man by far. When the King got Marius's letter he
was at his court in Cirta, not far from Rusicade. Impaled on the
horns of the biggest dilemma his tenure of the kingdom had yet
given him, he dithered for some time—Gaius Marius had put his
father on the throne, yet Gaius Marius might also be the man who
put the son off it. For Lucius Cornelius Sulla also had some claim
to pre-eminence in Numidia.

After some days of cogitation, he moved himself and part of

his court to Icosium, far west of Roman presence, and bade Gaius Marius and his colleagues sail to join him there. The King allowed them to move ashore, placing several comfortable villas at their disposal. He also entertained them frequently in his own house, large enough to be called a small palace, though not nearly as commodious as his establishment in Cirta. As a consequence of this restricted space, the King left some of his wives and all of his concubines behind, taking with him to Icosium only his queen, Sophonisba, and two minor wives, Salammbo and Anno. An educated individual in the best traditions of Hellenistic monarchs, he kept no sort of oriental state, but rather allowed his guests to mingle freely among all the members of his household— sons, daughters, wives. Which unfortunately led to complications.

Young Marius was now twenty-one years of age, and finding his feet as a man. Very fair and very handsome, he was also a fine physical specimen; too restless to settle himself to any mental task, he sought release in hunting, something King Hiempsal did not enjoy. However, his junior wife Salammbo did. The African plains teemed with wildlife—elephants and lions, ostrich and gazelle, antelope and bear, panther and gnu—and Young Marius spent his days out learning how to hunt animals he had never seen before. With Princess Salammbo as his guide and preceptress.

Perhaps thinking the public nature of these expeditions and the number of people involved in staffing them were sufficient protection to ensure the virtue of his junior wife, King Hiempsal saw no harm in sending Salammbo out with Young Marius; perhaps too he was grateful to have this overactive creature off his hands for days at a time. Himself closeted with Marius (who had markedly improved in his thinking since coming to Icosium), talking over old times, learning the stories of those campaigns in Numidia and Africa against Jugurtha, Hiempsal took copious notes for the archives of his family, and made bold to dream of an era when one of his sons or grandsons might actually be deemed grand enough to marry a Roman noblewoman. He had no illusions, Hiempsal; call himself royal he might, rule a big rich land he might, but in the eyes of the Roman nobility, he and his were less than the dust.

Of course the secret was not kept. One of the King's minions reported to him that the days Salammbo spent with Young Marius were innocent enough, but the nights an entirely different matter. This revelation threw the King into a panic; on the one hand he could not ignore the unchastity of his wife, but on the other hand he could not do what he would normally have done—execute the cuckolder. So he salvaged what dignity he could out of the affair by informing Gaius Marius that the situation was too delicate to allow the fugitives to stay any longer, and asking Marius to sail as soon as his ship was properly provisioned.

"Young fool!" said Marius as they walked down to the harbor. "Weren't there enough ordinary women available? Did you have to pilfer one of Hiempsal's wives?"

Young Marius grinned, tried to look contrite, and failed. "I'm sorry, Father, but she really was delicious. Besides, I didn't seduce her—she seduced me."

"You could have turned her down, you know."

"I could have," said Young Marius impenitently, "but I didn't. She really was delicious."

"You're using the correct tense, my son. *Was* is right. The stupid woman has parted company with her head because of you."

Knowing perfectly well that Marius was only annoyed because they were now obliged to move on, that otherwise he would have been pleased his boy could lure a foreign queen into indiscretion, Young Marius continued to grin. Salammbo's fate worried neither of them; she knew the penalty for being caught would be on her own head.

"That's too bad," said Young Marius. "She really was—"

"Don't say it!" his father interrupted sharply. "If you were smaller or I could balance on one leg, I'd put my boot so far up your arse I kicked your teeth out! We were *comfortable*!"

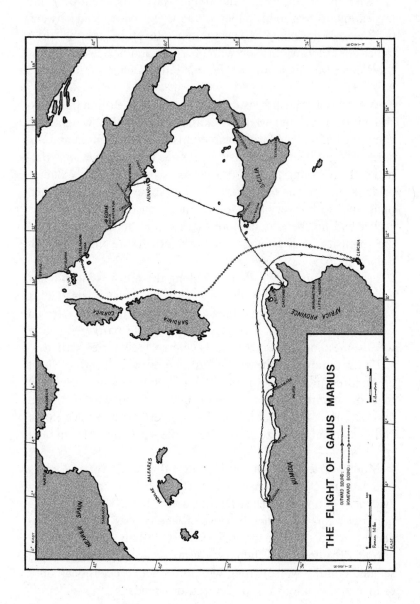

THE FLIGHT OF GAIUS MARIUS

OUTWARD BOUND: ———
HOMEWARD BOUND: +++++

"Kick me if you like," said Young Marius, bending over and presenting his rear to his father jokingly, legs wide, head between his knees. Why should he fear to do it? His crime was the sort a father could forgive his son with pleasure; and besides, in all his life Young Marius had never felt his father's hand, let alone his foot.

Whereupon Marius gestured to the faithful Burgundus, who slid his arm around Marius's waist and took his weight. Up came the right leg; Marius planted his heavy boot hard and accurately right inside the sensitive crevice between the son's buttocks. That Young Marius did not pass out was purely due to pride; the pain was truly frightful. For some days he remained in agony, talking very hard to persuade himself that his father's action had not been deliberate malice, that he had misgauged the intensity of his father's feelings about the incident with Salammbo.

From Icosium they sailed east along the north African coast and made no inhabited landfalls between Icosium and Gaius Marius's new destination—the island of Cercina, in the African Lesser Syrtis. Here at last they did find safe harbor, for here were some thousands of Marius's veteran legionaries settled to a life far removed from war. A little bored with farming wheat on hundred-*iugera* allotments, the grizzled veterans welcomed their old commander with open arms, made much of him and his son, and vowed that it would take every army Sulla's Rome could marshal to prize loose their hold on Gaius Marius and freedom.

More worried about his father since that kick, Young Marius watched him closely; consumed with grief, he now saw many tiny evidences of a crumbling mentality, and marveled at the way his father was forgiven much because of who he was, or would suddenly summon up an enormous effort of will and seem perfectly normal. To those who didn't see him often or intimately, there seemed nothing worse wrong with him than an occasional lapse of memory, or a look of puzzlement, or a tendency to wander off the subject if it failed to hold his interest. But could he hold a seventh consulship? Young Marius doubted it.

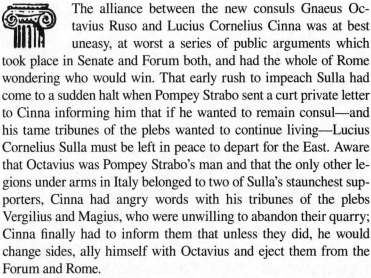

The alliance between the new consuls Gnaeus Octavius Ruso and Lucius Cornelius Cinna was at best uneasy, at worst a series of public arguments which took place in Senate and Forum both, and had the whole of Rome wondering who would win. That early rush to impeach Sulla had come to a sudden halt when Pompey Strabo sent a curt private letter to Cinna informing him that if he wanted to remain consul—and his tame tribunes of the plebs wanted to continue living—Lucius Cornelius Sulla must be left in peace to depart for the East. Aware that Octavius was Pompey Strabo's man and that the only other legions under arms in Italy belonged to two of Sulla's staunchest supporters, Cinna had angry words with his tribunes of the plebs Vergilius and Magius, who were unwilling to abandon their quarry; Cinna finally had to inform them that unless they did, he would change sides, ally himself with Octavius and eject them from the Forum and Rome.

During their first eight months in office, there were more than enough problems within Rome and Italy to occupy Octavius and Cinna; not only was the Treasury still empty and money still shy in coming into the open, but Sicily and Africa were enduring a second year of drought. Their governors, Norbanus and Sextilius, had been sent out while still praetors to do what they could to increase grain shipments to the capital, even if they had to buy in wheat with promissory notes enforced by their soldiers. Not for any consideration or any wheat growers' lobby would the consuls and the Senate see a repetition of the events which had led to that brief hour of glory Saturninus had enjoyed because the Head Count of Rome was hungry; the Head Count *must* be fed. Discovering some of the hideous difficulties Sulla had known during his year as consul, Cinna seized upon every source of revenue he could find, and sent letters to the two governors in the Spains instructing them to squeeze their provinces dry. The governor of the Gauls, Publius Servilius Vatia, was instructed to get what he could by walking the Gaul-across-the-Alps barbarian tightrope, while simultaneously balancing the creditors of Italian Gaul on the end of his nose. When the outraged replies came in, Cinna burned them after he read the opening columns, wishing for two inaccessible things; one, that Octavius would concern himself more with the hard parts of governing, and the other, that Rome still had the incomes from Asia Province.

Rome was also under duress from the newly enfranchised Italians, who resented their tribal status bitterly, even though under the *leges Corneliae* their tribal votes were nonexistent. The laws of Publius Sulpicius had whetted their appetite, they resented the invalidation of those laws. Even after more than two years of war there were still important men left among the Allies; they now inundated the Senate with letters of complaint on behalf of themselves and their less privileged Italian brothers. Cinna would gladly have obliged them by legislating to distribute all the new citizens equally across the thirty-five tribes, but neither the Senate nor the faction led by the senior consul Octavius would cooperate. And the Sullan constitution handicapped Cinna severely.

However, in Sextilis he saw his first ray of hope; word had come that Sulla was fully occupied in Greece, could not possibly contemplate a sudden return to Rome to shore up his constitution or pander to his supporters. Time, thought Cinna, to sort out his differences with Pompey Strabo, still lurking in Umbria and Picenum with four legions. Without telling anyone where he was going—including his wife—Cinna journeyed to see what Pompey Strabo had to say now that Sulla was totally committed to the war with Mithridates.

"I'm prepared to make the same bargain with you that I made with the other Lucius Cornelius," said the cross-eyed lord of Picenum, who had not been warm in his welcome, but had not indicated unwillingness to listen either. "You leave me and mine alone in my corner of our great big Roman world, and I won't bother you in the mighty city."

"So that was it!" exclaimed Cinna.

"That was it."

"I need to rectify many of the alterations the other Lucius Cornelius made to our systems of government," said Cinna, keeping his voice dispassionate. "I also want to distribute the new citizens equally across the whole thirty-five tribes, and I like the idea of distributing the Roman freedmen across the tribes." He smothered his outrage at needing to obtain permission from this Picentine butcher to do what had to be done, and continued smoothly. "How do *you* feel about all this, Gnaeus Pompeius?"

"Do whatever you like," said Pompey Strabo indifferently, "as long as you leave me alone."

"I give you my word I'll leave you alone."

"Is your word as valuable as your oaths, Lucius Cinna?"

Cinna blushed deep red. "I did not swear that oath," he said with great dignity. "I held a stone in my hand throughout, which invalidated it."

Pompey Strabo threw back his head and demonstrated that when he laughed, he neighed. "Oh, a proper little Forum lawyer, aren't we?" he asked when he was able.

"The oath did not bind me!" Cinna insisted, face still red.

"Then you are a far greater fool than the other Lucius Cornelius. Once he comes back, you won't last longer than a snowflake in a fire."

"If you believe that, why let me do what I want to do?"

"The other Lucius Cornelius and I understand each other, that's why," said Pompey Strabo. "He won't blame *me* for whatever happens—he'll blame you."

"Perhaps the other Lucius Cornelius won't come back."

That provoked another whinny of amusement. "Don't count on it, Lucius Cinna! The other Lucius Cornelius is definitely Fortune's prime favorite. He leads a charmed life."

Cinna journeyed back to Rome without staying in Pompey Strabo's fief a moment longer than their brief interview; he preferred to sleep in a house where his host was less unnerving. Consequently he had to listen to his host in Assisium recount the tale of how the mice ate the socks of Quintus Pompeius Rufus and thus foretold his death. All in all, thought Cinna when he finally got back to Rome, I do not like those northern people! They're too basic, too close to the old gods.

Early in September the greatest games of the year, the *ludi Romani,* were held in Rome. For three years they had been as small and inexpensive as possible, thanks to the war in Italy and the lack of those huge sums the curule aediles normally felt it worthwhile to dig out of their own purses. Great things had been hoped of last year's aedile, Metellus Celer, yet nothing had come of that. But this year's pair were both fabulously rich, and by Sextilis there was concrete evidence that they would honor their word and give great games. So the rumor went up and down the peninsula—the games were going to be spectacular! As a result, everyone who could afford to make the trip suddenly decided that the best cure for wartime woes and malaise was a holiday to Rome to see the *ludi Romani.* Thousands of Italians, newly enfranchised and smarting about the shabby way in which they had been treated, began to arrive in Rome toward the end of Sextilis. Theater lovers, chariot-racing lovers, wild-beast-hunt lovers, spectacle lovers—everyone who could come, came. The theater lovers especially knew themselves in for a treat; old Accius had been persuaded to leave his home in Umbria to produce his new play personally.

And Cinna decided he would act at last. His ally the tribune of the plebs Marcus Vergilius convened an "unofficial" meeting of the Plebeian Assembly, and announced to the crowd (among whom were many of the Italian visitors) that he intended to press the Senate to distribute the new citizens properly. This meeting was held purely to attract the attention of those interested to the subject, for Marcus Vergilius could not promulgate legislation in a body no longer permitted to legislate.

Vergilius then brought his proposition to the Senate, and was firmly told that the Conscript Fathers would not debate the issue now any more than they had done in January. Vergilius shrugged and sat down on the tribunician bench alongside Sertorius and the others. He had done what Cinna had required of him; find out how the House felt. The rest was up to Cinna.

"All right," said Cinna to his confederates, "we go to work. We promise the whole world that if our laws to remake the constitution in its old form and deal with the new citizens are passed in the Centuriate Assembly, we will legislate for a general cancellation of debts. Sulpicius's promises were suspect because he legislated in favor of creditors in the matter of the Senate, but we have no such handicap. We'll be believed."

The activity which followed was not secret, though it was not aired in the hearing of those bound to be against a general cancellation of debts. And so desperate was the position of the majority—even in the First Class—that opinion and support suddenly veered very much Cinna's way; for every knight and senator who didn't owe money or was involved in the lending of it, there were six or seven knights and senators who were in debt, many deeply.

"We're in trouble," said the senior consul Gnaeus Octavius Ruso to his colleagues Antonius Orator and the Brothers Caesar. "Waving a bait like a general cancellation of debts under so many greedy or needy noses will get Cinna what he wants, even from the First Class and the Centuries."

"Give him his due, he's clever enough not to try to convene the Plebs or the Whole People and force his measures through there," said Lucius Caesar fretfully. "If he passes his laws in the Centuries, they're legal under Lucius Cornelius's present constitution. And with the *fiscus* the way it is and private money in even worse case, the Centuries from their top to as far down as is necessary will vote to please Lucius Cinna."

"And the Head Count will run riot," said Antonius Orator.

But Octavius shook his head; he was by far the acutest business man among them. "No, not the *capite censi*, Marcus Antonius!" he said impatiently, as he was an impatient man. "The lowly are never in debt—they just don't have any money. It's those in the middle and upper Classes who borrow. Mostly they have to borrow in order to keep moving upward—or quite often to stay where they presently are. No moneylender obliges those with no real collateral. So the higher up you go, the better your chances of finding men who have borrowed."

"I take it you are convinced that the Centuries will vote to pass all this unacceptable rubbish, then?" asked Catulus Caesar.

"Aren't you, Quintus Lutatius?"

"Yes, I very much fear that I am."

"Then what can we do?" asked Lucius Caesar.

"Oh, I know what to do," said Octavius, scowling. "However, I shall do it without telling anyone, including you."

"What do you think he intends to do?" asked Antonius Orator after Octavius had gone off toward the Argiletum.

Catulus Caesar shook his head. "I haven't the faintest idea." He frowned. "Oh, I wish he had one-tenth the brains and ability of Lucius Sulla! But he doesn't. He's a Pompey Strabo man."

Brother Lucius Caesar shivered suddenly. "I have a nasty feeling," he said. "Whatever he means to do won't be what ought to be done. Oh, dear!"

Antonius Orator looked brisk. "I think I shall spend the next ten days out of Rome," he said.

In the end they all decided this was the wisest thing to do.

Sure of himself, Cinna now eagerly set the date for his *contio* in the Centuriate Assembly; the sixth day before the Ides of September, which was two days after the *ludi Romani* commenced. How prevalent was debt, how eager the debtors were to be relieved of their burdens was patent at dawn on that day, when some twenty thousand men turned up on the Campus Martius to hear Cinna's *contio*. Every one of them wished he could vote that day, which Cinna had explained firmly was impossible—that would mean his first law would have had to set aside the *lex Caecilia Didia prima* (as Sulla had done) to hustle the measures through. No, said Cinna, adamant, the customary waiting period of three *nundinae* would have to be observed. However, he did promise that he would introduce more laws at other *contiones* well before the voting time for this first law came round. That statement calmed everyone down, gave everyone a strong feeling that the general cancellation of debts would go through long before Cinna stepped down from his office.

There were actually two laws Cinna intended to discuss on this first day; the distribution of the new citizens across the tribes, and the pardon and recall of the nineteen fugitives. All of them, from Gaius Marius to the humblest of the knights, retained their property; Sulla had made no move to confiscate it during the last days of his consulship, and the new tribunes of the plebs—who could still exercise their vetos within the Senate—made it clear that anyone who tried to move for confiscation would be vetoed.

So when the twenty thousand members of the Classes gathered on the open grassy space of the Campus Martius, they looked forward to hearing about *one* law they could approve of, the recall of the fugitives; no one looked forward to distributing the new citizens across the tribes because it would dilute his own power in the tribal assemblies, and everyone knew this law was but a prelude to giving legislative powers back to the tribal assemblies. Cinna and his tribunes of the plebs were there before the crowds, moving among the growing throng answering questions and placating those who still had very grave doubts about the Italians. Most soothing of all, of course, was the promise of a general cancellation of debts.

So busy was the vast assembly talking among itself, yawning, listlessly getting ready to listen to Cinna because he and his tame tribunes of the plebs had ascended the speaker's platform, that no one found anything odd about a sudden large influx of new arrivals. They were togate, they were quiet, they looked like members of the Third and Fourth Classes.

Gnaeus Octavius Ruso had not served as a senior legate to Pompey Strabo for nothing; his remedy for the ills assailing the State was superbly organized and properly instructed. The thousand army veterans he had hired (with money provided by Pompey Strabo and Antonius Orator) had surrounded the crowd and actually had dropped their togas to stand in full armor before a single man in that huge number noticed anything amiss. A shrill whistling began, then the hirelings waded into the mass of men from all sides, swinging their swords. Hundreds and then thousands were cut down, but many more fell under the trampling feet of panicked electors. Driven in on themselves by the encircling wall of assailants, it was some time before any man in the crowd collected himself enough to attempt to run the gauntlet of swords and flee the field.

Cinna and his six tribunes of the plebs were not trapped as was the gathering; they came down off the speaker's platform and ran for their lives. Only some two thirds of those below were so fortunate. When Octavius came to view his handiwork, several thousand members of the upper Classes of the Centuriate Assembly lay dead on the Field of Mars. Octavius was angry, as he had wanted Cinna and his tribunes of the plebs killed first; but even men who hired themselves out to murder defenseless victims had a code, and deemed it too perilous to assassinate magistrates in office.

Quintus Lutatius Catulus Caesar and his brother Lucius Julius Caesar were staying together at Lanuvium. They heard of the massacre all Rome was calling Octavius's Day scant hours after it happened, and came hurrying back to Rome to confront Octavius.

"How could you?" asked Lucius Caesar, weeping.

"Appalling! Disgusting!" said Catulus Caesar.

"Don't give me that sanctimonious claptrap! You knew what I was going to do," said Gnaeus Octavius scornfully. "You even agreed it was necessary. And—provided you didn't have to be an actual part of it!—you gave your tacit consent. So don't come whining to me! I procured you what you wanted—tame Centuries. The survivors won't vote for Cinna's laws now, no matter what inducements he tries to hold out to them."

Shaken to the core, Catulus Caesar glared at Octavius. "Never in my life have I condoned violence as a political technique, Gnaeus Octavius! Nor do I admit I gave any kind of consent for this, *tacit* or otherwise! If you construed consent out of anything my brother or I said, you were mistaken. Violence is bad enough—but this! A *massacre*! Absolute anathema!"

"My brother is right," said Lucius Caesar, wiping away his tears. "We are branded, Gnaeus Octavius. The most conservative of men are now no better than Saturninus or Sulpicius."

Seeing that nothing he could say would convince this disciple of Pompey Strabo that he had acted wrongly, Catulus Caesar drew himself together with what dignity he could muster. "I hear the Campus Martius has been a field of horror for two days, senior consul. Relatives trying to identify bodies and take them for last rites, your minions scooping bodies up before any relatives have had a chance to see them, throwing them into a vast lime pit between the leeks and lettuces of the Via Recta—tchah! You have turned us into a breed of men worse than mere barbarians, for we know better than barbarians! I find myself becoming more and more unwilling to live."

Octavius sneered. "Then I suggest you go and open your veins, Quintus Lutatius! This isn't the Rome of your august ancestors, you know. It's the Rome of the Brothers Gracchi, Gaius Marius, Saturninus, Sulpicius, Lucius Sulla and Lucius Cinna! We've got ourselves into such a chaotic mess that nothing works anymore—if it did, there would be no need for massacres like Octavius's Day."

Stunned, the Brothers Caesar understood that Gnaeus Octavius Ruso was actually proud of that name.

"Who gave you the money to hire your assassins, Gnaeus Octavius? Was it Marcus Antonius?" Lucius Caesar asked.

"He contributed heavily, yes. *He* has no regrets."

"He wouldn't! He's an Antonius when all is said and done!" snapped Catulus Caesar. He got to his feet, slapping his hands against his thighs. "Well, it's over, and we'll never live it down. But I want no part of it, Gnaeus Octavius. I feel too much like Pandora after she opened her box."

Lucius Caesar asked a question. "What's happened to Lucius Cinna and the tribunes of the plebs?"

"Gone," said Octavius laconically. "They'll be proscribed, of course. Hopefully very soon."

Catulus Caesar stopped at the door of Octavius's study to look back sternly. "You cannot deprive a consul in office of his consular imperium, Gnaeus Octavius. This whole thing started in the first place because the opposition tried to remove Lucius Sulla's consular right to command Rome's armies from him. *That* cannot be done! But no one tried to deprive him of his office as consul. It can't be done. There is nothing in Roman law, constitution, or precedent that can give any magistrate—or governing body—or comitia—the authority to prosecute or discharge a curule magistrate ahead of the end of his term. You can sack a tribune of the plebs if you go about it in the right way, you can sack a quaestor if he's delinquent in his duty, you can expel them from the Senate or deprive them of their census. But you *cannot* sack a consul or any other curule magistrate during his term of office, Gnaeus Octavius."

Gnaeus Octavius looked smug. "Now I've found the secret of success, Quintus Lutatius, I can do anything I want." As Lucius Caesar followed his brother to the door, Octavius called after them, "There's a meeting of the Senate tomorrow. I suggest you be there."

No Jerusalem or Antioch, Rome had little patience or truck with prophets and soothsayers; the augurs conducted the rites of auspication in the true Roman spirit, knowing full well that they possessed no insight for the future course of events—strictly according to the books and charts.

There was, however, one genuinely Roman specimen of the prophet, a patrician of the *gens* Cornelia, and named Publius Cornelius Culleolus. Quite how he had earned his unfortunate nickname nobody remembered, as Culleolus was an ancient who had always seemed an ancient. He lived precariously on a small income derived from his Scipionic family, and was commonly to be seen in the Forum sitting on top of the two steps which led up into the tiny round temple of Venus Cloacina, older than the Basilica Aemilia, and incorporated into it when it was built. Neither a Cassandra nor a religious zealot, Culleolus confined his forecasts to the outcome of important political and State events; he never predicted the end of the world, nor the coming of some new and infinitely more powerful god. But he had predicted the war against Jugurtha, the coming of the Germans, Saturninus, the Italian war, and the war in the East against Mithridates—which last, he asserted, would go on for a full generation. Because of these successes, he now enjoyed a reputation which was almost great enough to offset the ridiculousness of his cognomen; Culleolus meant Little Ball-sack.

At dawn on the morning after the Brothers Caesar returned to Rome, the Senate met for the first time since the massacre of Octavius's Day, its members dreading this session more than any in living memory. Until now, the worst outrages perpetrated in the name of Rome had been the work of individuals or the Forum crowd; but the massacre of Octavius's Day came uncomfortably close to being labeled as the work of the Senate.

Sitting on the top step of the temple of Venus Cloacina, Publius Cornelius Culleolus was such a fixture that none of the Conscript Fathers hurrying by noticed him—though he noticed them, and rubbed his hands gleefully together. If he did what Gnaeus Octavius Ruso had paid him lavishly to do—and did it successfully— he would never have to sit on those hard steps again, he could retire at last from the prophesying business.

The senators lingered in the Curia Hostilia portico, a collection of small groups all talking about Octavius's Day and audibly wondering how it could possibly be dealt with in debate. A shrill screech brought all heads around; all eyes became riveted upon Culleolus, who had risen onto his toes, spine arched, arms outstretched, fingers knotted, foam bubbling from between his contorted lips. As Culleolus did not prophesy in a frenzy, everyone assumed he was having a fit. Some of the senators and most of the Forum frequenters continued to watch, fascinated, while a few went to the seer's aid and tried to lower him to the ground. He fought them blindly with teeth and nails, mouth opening ever wider, and then he cried out a second time. Not a noise. Words.

"Cinna! Cinna! Cinna! Cinna! Cinna!" he howled.

Suddenly Culleolus had a very intent audience.

"Unless Cinna and his six tribunes of the plebs are sent into exile, Rome will fall!" he shrieked, twisting and tottering, then shrieked it again, and again, and again, until he collapsed to the ground and was carried away, inanimate.

The startled senators then discovered that the consul Octavius had been trying for some time to convene his meeting, and hurried into the Curia Hostilia.

However the senior consul might have been going to explain the hideous events on the Campus Martius would never now be known; Gnaeus Octavius Ruso chose instead to focus his attention (and the attention of the House) upon the extraordinary possession of Culleolus—and upon what Culleolus had cried out for all the Forum to hear.

"Unless the junior consul and six of the tribunes of the plebs are banished, Rome will fall," said Octavius thoughtfully. "Pontifex Maximus, *flamen Dialis,* what do you have to say about this amazing business of Culleolus?"

Scaevola Pontifex Maximus shook his head. "I think that I must decline to comment, Gnaeus Octavius."

Mouth open to insist, Octavius saw something in Scaevola's eyes that caused him to change his mind; this was a man whose innate conservatism led him to condone much, but also a man not easily intimidated or hoodwinked. On more than one occasion in the House he had roundly condemned the conviction of Gaius Marius, Publius Sulpicius and the rest, and asked for their pardon and recall. No, best not antagonize the Pontifex Maximus; Octavius knew he had a far more gullible witness in the *flamen Dialis,* and had besides provided that innocent worthy with a fearful omen.

"Flamen Dialis?" asked Octavius solemnly.

Looking extremely perturbed, Lucius Cornelius Merula the *flamen Dialis* rose to his feet. "Lucius Valerius Flaccus Princeps Senatus, Gnaeus Octavius, curule magistrates, consulars, Conscript Fathers. Before I comment upon the words of the seer Culleolus, I must first tell you of a happening in the temple of the Great God yesterday. I was ritually cleansing his *cella* when I found a tiny pool of blood upon the floor behind the plinth of the Great God's statue. Beside it was the head of a bird—a *merula,* a blackbird! My own namesake! And I, who am forbidden under our most ancient and reverenced laws to be in the presence of death, was looking upon—I don't know! My own death? The Great God's death? I did not know how to interpret the omen, so I consulted the Pontifex Maximus. He did not know either. We therefore summoned the *decemviri sacris faciundis* and asked them to consult the Sibylline Books, which had nothing to say of any help."

Wrapped as he was in the double-layered circular cape of his calling, it was perhaps not illogical that Merula should visibly be sweating, except that he did not normally do so; his round smooth face beneath the spiked ivory helmet he wore shone with sweat. He swallowed, went on. "But I have got ahead of myself. When I first found the head of the blackbird I looked for the rest of its body, and discovered that the creature had made a nest for itself in a crevice beneath the golden robe of the Great God's statue. And there in the nest were six baby blackbirds, all dead. As far as I can tell, a cat must have got in, caught the mother bird and eaten it—all save the head, that is. But the cat could not reach the baby birds, which died of starvation."

The *flamen Dialis* shivered. "I am polluted. After this session of the House I must continue the ceremonies which will resanctify my own person and the temple of Jupiter Optimus Maximus. That I am here is as a result of my cogitations upon the omen—not so much the death of the *merula* as the entire phenomenon. It was not, however, until I heard Publius Cornelius Culleolus say what he said in the midst of his truly extraordinary prophetic frenzy that I understood the proper meaning."

The House was absolutely hushed, every face turned to see the priest of Jupiter, so well known as an honest—almost naïve—man, that what he said had to be taken very seriously.

"Now Cinna," the *flamen Dialis* went on, "does not mean blackbird. But it does mean ashes, and that is what I reduced the dead bird's head and the bodies of its six children to—ashes. I burned them in accordance with the ritual of purification. Amateur interpreter though I am, to me at this moment the omen uncannily resembles a personification of Lucius Cornelius Cinna and his six tribunes of the plebs. They have defiled the Great God of Rome, who stands in much danger because of them. The blood means that more strife and public turmoil will ensue because of the consul Lucius Cinna and those six tribunes of the plebs. I am in no doubt of it."

The House began to buzz, thinking Merula was finished, but quietened when he began to speak again.

"One more thing, Conscript Fathers. While I stood in the temple waiting for the Pontifex Maximus, I looked up for consolation into the smiling face of the Great God's statue. And it was *frowning!*" He shuddered, white-faced. "I fled into the open air, I could not bring myself to continue to wait within."

Everyone shuddered. The buzzing began again.

Gnaeus Octavius Ruso rose to his feet, looking to the Brothers Caesar and Scaevola Pontifex Maximus much as the cat must have looked after it devoured the *merula* in the temple. "I think, members of this House, that we must repair outside to the Forum, and from the rostra tell everyone what has happened. And ask for opinions. After which, the House will sit again."

So the tale of Merula's phenomenon in the temple and Culleolus's prophecy were told from the rostra; those who had gathered to hear looked awed and afraid, especially after Merula gave his interpretation and Octavius announced that he would seek the dismissal of Cinna and the six tribunes of the plebs. Not one man present objected.

In the House again shortly afterward, Gnaeus Octavius Ruso repeated his opinion that Cinna and the tribunes of the plebs must go.

Then Scaevola Pontifex Maximus rose to speak. "Princeps Senatus, Gnaeus Octavius, Conscript Fathers. As all of you are aware, I am one of the greatest ever exponents of the Roman constitution and the laws which compose it. In my opinion, there is no legal way to dismiss a consul from office before his term is ended. However, it may be that approximately the same effect can be achieved *religiously*. We cannot doubt that Jupiter Optimus Maximus has indicated his concern in two separate ways—through the medium of his own *flamen*, and through the medium of an old man whom we all know to be a worthy seer. In consideration of these two almost concurrent events, I suggest that the consul Lucius Cornelius Cinna be pronounced *nefas*. This does not strip him of his office as consul, but—as it renders him religiously odious—it disbars him from carrying out his duties as consul. The same is true of the tribunes of the plebs."

Octavius was scowling now, but knew better than to interrupt; it seemed Scaevola was going to work something out. Something, however, which made it impossible to secure a death sentence for Cinna—this being Octavius's aim. Cinna *must* be put out of action!

"It was the *flamen Dialis* who witnessed the events in the temple of Jupiter Optimus Maximus. He is also the Great God's personal priest, and his office is so old it pre-dates the Kings. He can conduct no wars, nor come into the presence of death, nor touch the substance from which weapons of war are made. Therefore I suggest that we appoint Lucius Cornelius Merula the *flamen Dialis* a suffect consul—not to take Lucius Cinna's place, but rather to caretake that place. In this way, the senior consul Gnaeus Octavius will not be governing as a consul without a colleague. Except during the war against the Italians, when circumstances prevented proper consular practices, *no* man can be allowed to be consul without a colleague."

Deciding to put a good face on it, Octavius nodded. "I agree to that, Quintus Mucius. Let the *flamen Dialis* sit in the curule chair of Lucius Cinna as its custodian! I will now see the House divide upon two intimately connected issues. Those in favor of recommending to the Centuriate Assembly that—number one, the consul Lucius Cinna and the six tribunes of the plebs be declared *nefas* and banished from Rome and all Roman lands—and, number two, that the *flamen Dialis* be appointed consul in custody, please stand to my right. Those opposed, please stand to my left. Now divide, please."

The House passed its dual recommendation without a single negative vote, and a Centuriate Assembly consisting almost solely of senators met on the Aventine outside the *pomerium* but inside the walls—no one could bear to meet on the blood-soaked ground of the *saepta*. The measures were passed into law.

The senior consul Octavius pronounced himself satisfied, and the business of governing Rome proceeded without Cinna. But Gnaeus Octavius did nothing to shore up his position, nor to protect Rome from the officially sacrilegious fugitives. He gathered no legions, he did not write to his master, Pompey Strabo. The truth of the matter was that Octavius blindly assumed Cinna and his six tribunes of the plebs would flee as quickly as possible to join Gaius Marius and eighteen other fugitives on the African island of Cercina.

 Cinna, however, had no intention of leaving Italy. Nor did his six tribunes of the plebs. After they fled from the slaughter on the Campus Martius, they gathered money and a few belongings and then met at the milestone on the Via Appia just outside Bovillae. Here they decided what to do.

"I'll take Quintus Sertorius and Marcus Gratidianus to Nola with me," said Cinna briskly. "There's a legion under arms at Nola, suffering a commander the men detest in Appius Claudius Pulcher. I intend to remove that legion from Appius Claudius and take my example from my namesake Sulla—I shall lead it on Rome. But not before we have gathered many more adherents. Vergilius, Milonius, Arvina, Magius, I want you to journey among the Italians and drum up support wherever you can. You will tell everybody the same thing—that the Senate of Rome has ejected its legally elected consul because he tried to get the new citizens properly distributed across the tribes, and because Gnaeus Octavius has massacred thousands of decent, law-abiding Roman men gathered at a legally convoked assembly." He found a wry smile. "It's as well we've been so heavily at war within the peninsula! Cornutus and I took thousands of sets of arms and armor off the Marsi and the rest. They're stored in Alba Fucentia. Milonius, you will get them and distribute them. After I take the legion off Appius Claudius, I'll pillage the warehouses in Capua."

Thus four of the tribunes of the plebs popped up in places like Praeneste, Tibur, Reate, Corfinium, Venafrum, Interamnia, and Sora, pleading for a hearing—and granted it gladly. The war-weary Italians even gave every coin they could possibly spare to this new campaign. Slowly the forces grew, slowly the net around Rome closed.

Cinna himself had no difficulty in causing the defection of Appius Claudius Pulcher's legion sitting outside Nola. A dour and aloof man who still secretly grieved over the death of his wife and the fate of his six motherless children, Appius Claudius yielded up his command without attempting to woo his soldiers back. He climbed upon his horse and rode to join Metellus Pius at Aesernia.

It had been a stroke of great good fortune to bring Quintus Sertorius with him, Cinna realized after he reached Nola. A born Military Man, Sertorius had a reputation among ranker soldiers that went back almost twenty years; he had won the Grass Crown in Spain, a dozen lesser crowns in campaigns against Numidians and Germans, he was the cousin of Gaius Marius, and this legion had been recruited by him in Italian Gaul three years before. Its men knew him well, and loved him dearly. They did not love Appius Claudius.

Cinna, Sertorius, Marcus Marius Gratidianus and the legion set off for Rome. The moment they did, Nola threw open its gates and a host of heavily armed Samnites pursued them up the Via Popillia—not to attack them, but to join them. And then when they reached the junction of this road with the Via Appia at Capua, every raw recruit, gladiator and drill centurion also flocked to their eagle. The army of Cinna now numbered twenty thousand. And between Capua and the little town of Labicum on the Via Latina, the four tribunes of the plebs who had gone elsewhere met up with Cinna, and gave him another ten thousand useful men.

It was now October, and Rome was only scant miles away. Cinna's agents reported to him that the city was in a panic—that Octavius had written to Pompey Strabo beseeching him to come to the aid of his country—and that, wonder of wonders, none other than Gaius Marius had landed on the Etrurian coast at the township of Telamon, adjacent to his own vast estates. This last item of news threw Cinna into transports of delight, especially when his agents followed it up with the intelligence that men from Etruria and Umbria were flocking to join Marius, who was marching down the Via Aurelia Vetus in the direction of Rome.

"This is the best news!" Cinna said to Quintus Sertorius. "Now Gaius Marius is back in Italy, this business will be over in a matter of days. Since you know him better than the rest of us do, find him and inform him of our dispositions. Discover what his own plans are too. Is he going to take Ostia or bypass it in favor of Rome? Make sure you tell him that if I can, I would rather keep our armies—and any hostilities!—on the Vatican side of the river. I hate the thought of bringing troops anywhere near the *pomerium,* and I have no wish to end in emulating Lucius Sulla. Find him, Quintus Sertorius, and tell him how glad I am that he's in Italy again!" Cinna thought of something else. "Tell him too that I'll send every spare item of armor I have to him before he reaches Ostia."

Sertorius located Marius near the little township of Fregenae, some miles north of Ostia; if his cross-country ride to Fregenae had been fast, his cross-country gallop back to Cinna at Labicum was at record pace. He erupted into the small house where Cinna had set up a temporary headquarters, and launched into speech before the astonished Cinna could open his mouth.

"Lucius Cinna, I beg of you, write to Gaius Marius and order him to disband his men or transfer them to your service!" Sertorius said, face drawn and set. "Order him to behave like the *privatus* he is—order him to disband his army—order him to return to his estates and wait like any *privatus* until the issue is decided."

"What on earth is the matter with you?" asked Cinna, hardly able to believe his ears. "How can you of all people say such things? Gaius Marius is essential for our cause! If he stands in our forefront, we can't lose."

"Lucius Cinna, it is *Marius* can't lose!" cried Sertorius. "I tell you straight—if you allow Gaius Marius to participate in this struggle, you will rue the day. For it won't be Lucius Cinna victorious and placed at the head of Rome's government—it will be Gaius Marius! I have just seen him, I have just spoken to him. He is old, he is bitter, and his mind has given way. Order him to go to his estates as a *privatus*, please!"

"What do you mean, his mind has given way?"

"Just that. He's mad."

"Well, that's not what my agents who are with him are saying, Quintus Sertorius. According to them, he's as superbly organized as he ever was, he's marching toward Ostia with a good sound plan in his head—why do you say his mind has given way? Is he gibbering? Is he ranting and raving? My agents are not as privy to him as you are, but they would surely have seen signs," said Cinna with obvious skepticism.

"He's not gibbering. He's not ranting and raving. Nor has he forgotten how to control or maneuver an army. But I have known Gaius Marius since I was seventeen years old, and I tell you in all sincerity, this is *not* the Gaius Marius I know! He's old and he's bitter. Thirsting for revenge. Quite obsessed with himself and his prophesied destiny. You cannot trust him, Lucius Cinna! He will end in taking Rome away from you and running it to suit his own purposes." Sertorius drew a breath, tried again. "Young Marius sends the same message to you, Lucius Cinna. Don't give his father any kind of authority! He's mad."

"I think you're both overreacting," said Cinna.

"I am not. Young Marius is not."

Cinna shook his head, drew a sheet of paper toward him. "Look, Quintus Sertorius, I *need* Gaius Marius! If he's as old and mentally disturbed as you say he is, then how can he be a threat to me—or to Rome? I shall confer a proconsular imperium upon him—I can have the Senate ratify it later—and use him to cover me on the west."

"You'll rue the day!"

"Nonsense," said Cinna, beginning to write.

Sertorius stood looking at his bent head for a moment, clawed at the air with his hands, then left the house.

Having received Marius's assurances that he would take care of Ostia and come up the Tiber on the Campus Vaticanus bank, Cinna split his own forces into three divisions of ten thousand men each, and marched from Labicum.

The first division—ordered to occupy the Vatican Plain—was under the command of Gnaeus Papirius Carbo, cousin of the tribune of the plebs Carbo Arvina, and victor over Lucania; the second division—ordered to occupy the Campus Martius (it was the only section of Cinna's army on the city side of the river)—was under the command of Quintus Sertorius; and the third division—commanded by Cinna himself—sat itself down on the northern flank of the Janiculan hill. When Marius arrived, he was to come up on the south side of the Janiculum.

However, there was an impediment. The middle section and the heights of the Janiculum had always been a Roman garrison, and Gnaeus Octavius had retained sufficient sense to gather what volunteers he could inside the city and send them to occupy and strengthen the Janiculan fortress. So between Cinna's army (which had crossed the river on the Mulvian Bridge) and whatever force Marius would bring from the direction of Ostia lay this formidable stronghold, filled with several thousand defenders, and extremely well fortified thanks to a program of repairs at the time the Germans had seemed likely to overrun Italy.

As if the presence of an impregnable garrison on the far side of the Tiber was not enough, Pompey Strabo unexpectedly arrived with his four legions of Picentine soldiers and took up a position just outside the Colline Gate. Save for the legion from Nola (which had gone to Sertorius), Pompey Strabo's army was the only fully trained one on the field, and therefore represented a major focus of power. Only the Pincian hill with its gardens and orchards separated Pompey Strabo from Sertorius.

The Siege of Rome

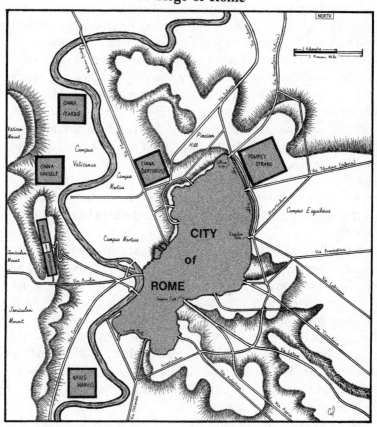

For sixteen days Cinna sat behind the entrenched palisades of three separate camps waiting for Pompey Strabo to attack; he had automatically assumed Pompey Strabo would make his move before Gaius Marius arrived. Quintus Sertorius, who would bear the initial shock, had dug himself in deeply on the Campus Martius. But no one moved. Nothing whatsoever happened.

In the meantime, Marius had encountered no resistance. At the instigation of its quaestor, Ostia opened its gates the moment Marius and his army came into sight, wild with joy and ready to welcome its hero with open arms. But its hero behaved with brutal indifference and allowed his army—largely composed of slaves and ex-slaves, one of the factors most perturbing to Sertorius when he had visited his old commander—to sack the town, which suffered terribly. As if blind and deaf, Marius made no attempt to curtail the insanities and atrocities of his motley troops; he bent his attention and his energies upon throwing a barrage across the mouth of the Tiber, effectively preventing the grain barges from going upriver to supply Rome. Even when he prepared to march up the Via Campana toward the city, he did nothing to succor Ostia's distress.

It had been a dry year in central Italy, and the snows of the previous winter atop the Apennines had been unusually scanty. So the Tiber was running low, and many of the little streams which fed its course dried up long before summer was over. The end of October in that year was actually the border between summer and autumn, so the weather was still very hot when all these small armies put themselves down in a three-quarters circle around the city of Rome. The African and Sicilian harvests were in, but the ships bringing the wheat were just beginning to arrive in Ostia; Rome's granaries were at their lowest.

Disease broke out not long after Pompey Strabo arrived at the Colline Gate, and spread quickly among the men of his legions as well as within the city itself. The various enteric fevers made their dreaded appearances, for the waters Pompey Strabo's soldiers were drinking were fouled by the same kind of careless sanitary arrangements Quintus Pompeius Rufus had noticed in the camp at

Ariminum. When the springs inside the city on the Viminal and Quirinal became contaminated, some of the people from the area went to see Pompey Strabo and begged him to deal with his cesspits properly; Pompey Strabo being Pompey Strabo sent them away with a series of crude remarks about what they might like to do with their own excrements. To make matters worse, from the Mulvian Bridge well above the Trigarium all the way to the sea the Tiber stank of human ordure and was unfit for any purpose save to spread disease; Cinna's three camps as well as the city were now using the Tiber as a sewer outflow.

Gnaeus Octavius and his custodial consular colleague Merula *flamen Dialis* saw October slip into the past without any change in the dispositions of the armies, and despaired. Whenever they managed to gain an audience with Pompey Strabo, he had some reason why he couldn't fight; Octavius and Merula were eventually forced to come to the conclusion that the real reason was that he preferred to outnumber his opponent in a battle situation, whereas in fact Cinna outnumbered him.

When the city learned that Marius owned Ostia and there would be no grain barges coming up the river with the new harvest, gloom rather than a fresh panic ensued. The consuls saw into a terrible future, and wondered how long they could last if Pompey Strabo continued to refuse to engage the enemy.

Finally Octavius and Merula decided to recruit among the Italians, and had the Senate recommend to the Centuries that those Italians who supported the "true" government of Rome be awarded full citizen status across the tribes. Once the law was passed, heralds were sent out to proclaim it throughout Italy, and call for soldier volunteers.

Hardly any came, chiefly because Cinna's tribunes of the plebs had beaten the "true" government of Rome to all the available men more than two months before.

Then Pompey Strabo hinted that if Metellus Pius brought his two legions from Aesernia, together they would defeat Cinna and Marius. So Octavius and Merula sent a deputation to see the Piglet before Aesernia, beg him to conclude a peace treaty with the be-leaguered Samnites and come to Rome as quickly as he could.

Torn between his duty to reduce Aesernia and the critical situa-tion within Rome, the Piglet rode out to treat with a paralyzed Gaius Papius Mutilus, who was—of course—completely aware of what was going on around Rome.

"I am willing to conclude a peace with you, Quintus Caecilius," said Mutilus from his litter, "on the following terms: give back to the Samnites all you have taken from them—return the Samnite deserters and prisoners of war in your custody to us unharmed—renounce all claim to the booty the Samnites have taken off you—and bestow the full citizenship of Rome upon every free man in the nation of Samnium."

Metellus Pius reared back, outraged. "Yes, certainly!" he said sarcastically. "Why not just require us to pass under the yoke, Gaius Papius, as the Samnites did after the battle of the Caudine Forks two hundred years ago?" he asked. "Your terms are absolutely im-possible! Good day to you."

Head up and spine straight, he rode back to his camp and icily informed the delegation from Octavius and Merula that there would be no peace treaty, and that in consequence he would not be able to go to Rome's assistance.

The Samnite Mutilus returned in his litter to Aesernia feeling a great deal happier than the Piglet; he had been visited by a bril-liant idea. After nightfall his courier sneaked through the Roman lines bearing a letter from Mutilus to Gaius Marius asking Marius if he was interested in concluding a peace treaty with Samnium. Though he was well aware that Cinna was the rebel consul and Marius only a rebel *privatus*, it never even occurred to Mutilus to send his letter to Cinna. In any enterprise involving Gaius Marius, he would be the leader, the man with the clout.

With Marius, now approaching Rome, was the tribune of the soldiers Gaius Flavius Fimbria; he had been with the legion at Nola, and like his colleagues Publius Annius and Gaius Marcius Censorinus, elected to follow Cinna. But the moment Fimbria heard of the advent of Marius in Etruria, he transferred immediately to Marius, who was delighted to see him.

"No point in making you a tribune of the soldiers here," Marius said. "My army has few Roman legionaries, it's mostly servile. So I'll give you the command of my Numidian cavalry—brought them from Africa with me."

When Marius received Mutilus's letter, he sent for Fimbria. "Go and see Mutilus in the Melfa Gorge, which is where he says he'll be." Marius snorted contemptuously. "No doubt he wants to remind us how many times we were beaten in that selfsame spot. However, for the time being we'll ignore his impudence. Meet him, Gaius Flavius, and agree to whatever he asks, be it rule over all Italy or a trip to the land of the Hyperboreans. We'll cut Mutilus and the Samnites down to size later."

While this was going on, a second delegation from Rome arrived to see Metellus Pius before Aesernia. It comprised much stronger men; Catulus Caesar and his son Catulus, and Publius Crassus the censor and his son Lucius.

"I beg you, Quintus Caecilius," said Catulus Caesar to the Piglet and his legate, Mamercus, "leave as small a force as you can to contain Aesernia, and come to Rome yourself! Otherwise you will have no purpose besieging Aesernia anyway. Rome and all Rome stands for will be finished."

So Metellus Pius agreed. He left Marcus Plautius Silvanus behind with a paltry five cohorts of suddenly very frightened men to contain the Samnites, but no sooner had the other fifteen cohorts disappeared in the direction of Rome than the Samnites issued out of Aesernia. They trounced Silvanus's skeleton force, and then overran all of Roman-held Samnium. Those Samnites who had not gone to Rome with Cinna now overran all southwestern Campania almost as far as Capua; the little town of Abella was sacked and burned, after which a second Samnite army went off to join the insurgents. These Italians gave Cinna no thought whatsoever—they went directly to Gaius Marius and offered *him* their services.

With Metellus Pius were Mamercus and Appius Claudius Pulcher.

The fifteen cohorts they brought from Aesernia were put into the Janiculan garrison; Appius Claudius was appointed garrison commander. Unfortunately Octavius insisted upon retaining the title of chief garrison commander for himself, which Appius Claudius took as a monumental insult. Why should he do all the work and get none of the glory? Smoldering, Appius Claudius contemplated changing sides.

Word had also been sent by the Senate to Publius Servilius Vatia in Italian Gaul, where two legions of trainees had been kept under arms; one lay in Placentia with the legate Gaius Coelius, and one in Aquileia with Vatia, far to the east. These two forces were purely intended to intimidate the Italian Gauls, as Vatia feared the accumulating resentment of Rome's unpaid war debts, particularly in the steel towns near Aquileia. When he got the Senate's letter Vatia notified Coelius to march his legion from Placentia to the east, and himself set off for Rome with his own legion the moment Coelius assured him it was safe to do so.

Unfortunately for the "true" government of Rome, when Vatia reached Ariminum he encountered the outlawed tribune of the plebs Marcus Marius Gratidianus, who had been sent north on the Via Flaminia with every spare cohort Cinna could provide, just in case the governor of Italian Gaul should try to send reinforcements. After his unblooded recruits gave a very poor account of themselves, Vatia crossed back into his own province and abandoned all ideas of trying to relieve Rome. Hearing a garbled version of what had happened at Ariminum, Gaius Coelius, a very depressed man, decided all was lost for the "true" government of Rome, and killed himself.

Octavius, Merula, and the rest of the "true" government of Rome watched their position worsen almost hour by hour. Gaius Marius came prancing up the Via Campana and set his troops down just to the south of the Janiculan garrison, whereupon the resentful Appius Claudius secretly collaborated with Marius and allowed him to penetrate the Janiculan fortress's outer stockade and defenses. That the citadel did not fall was thanks to Pompey Strabo, who deflected Cinna's attention from Marius by marching

over the Pincian hill and engaging Sertorius. At the same time
Octavius and the censor Publius Crassus led a fresh force of volunteers across the Wooden Bridge and relieved the citadel just in
time to prevent its being overwhelmed. Hampered by the lack of
discipline among his slave soldiers, Marius was forced to withdraw; the tribune of the plebs Gaius Milonius was killed trying to
help him. Publius Crassus and his son Lucius were put permanently inside the Janiculan citadel to keep an eye on Appius Claudius, who had changed his mind again and now felt the "true"
government would win. And Pompey Strabo, informed the fortress was safe, disengaged his legions from those belonging to
Sertorius and marched back to his camp on the Colline Gate side
of the Pincian hill.

To give him his due, all was far from well with Pompey Strabo.
As ever by his side, his son no sooner got his father back to their
camp than he ordered Pompey Strabo to bed. Fever and dysentery
had struck while the battle was going on, and though Pompey
Strabo continued to command in person, it was clear to his son
and his legates that he was in no condition to follow up his partial
success on the Campus Martius. Too young yet to enjoy the full
confidence of the Picentine troops, Young Pompey elected not to
try to assume the command, especially in the midst of heavy
fighting.

For three days the lord of northern Picenum and adjacent Umbria lay in his house a prey to the worst ravages of enteric fever,
while Young Pompey and his friend Marcus Tullius Cicero nursed
him devotedly and the troops waited to see what would happen. In
the early hours of the fourth day, Pompey Strabo, so strong and
vigorous, died of dehydration and physical exhaustion.

Supported by Cicero, his weeping son walked down the Vicus
Sub Aggere below the double rampart of the Agger, heading for Venus Libitina to arrange for his father's funeral. Had this been held in
Picenum on Pompey Strabo's enormous estates, it would have been
almost as large as the parade of a triumphing general, but the son
was as shrewd as he was capable, and understood that the obsequies

must be kept as simple as possible given the circumstances; the men were upset enough, and the inhabitants of the Quirinal, Viminal, and upper Esquiline hated the dead leader intensely, blaming his camp for the diseases currently decimating them.

"What will you do?" asked Cicero as the grove of cypresses sheltering the booths of the Guild of Undertakers came into view.

"I'm going home to Picenum," said Pompey amid terrible heaves of chest and shoulders, eyes and nose running. "My father was wrong to come—I *told* him not to come! Let Rome perish, I said! But he wouldn't listen. He said he had to protect *my* birthright, he had to make sure Rome was still Rome against the day when it would be my turn to be consul."

"Come into the city with me and stay for a while in my house," said Cicero, in tears himself; much though he had loathed and feared Pompey Strabo, he was not proof against the son's desolation. "Gnaeus Pompeius, I've met Accius! He came to Rome to produce his new play for the *ludi Romani*, and then when the trouble arose between Lucius Cinna and Gnaeus Octavius, he said he was too old to make the journey back to Umbria while there was so much unrest. I suspect he likes the present atmosphere of high drama is closer to the truth! Please, come and stay with me for a while. You're closely related to the great Lucilius—you'd so much enjoy Accius. And it would take your mind off all this chaotic horror."

"No," said Pompey, still weeping. "I'm going home."

"With your army?"

"It was my father's army. Rome can have it."

The two young men were some hours on their doleful errand, so did not return to the villa just outside the Colline Gate wherein Pompey Strabo had taken up residence until well after noon. No one—least of all the grief-stricken Pompey—had thought to mount a guard within the spacious grounds; the general was dead, there was nothing of value within. Of servants there were few thanks to the inroads of disease, but when son and friend had left, they had already laid Pompey Strabo out upon his bed, two female slaves keeping vigil.

Now Pompey and Cicero found the place utterly deserted—still, silent, seemingly untenanted. And when they entered the room wherein Pompey Strabo lay, they discovered him gone.

Pompey whooped triumphantly. "He's alive!" he cried, face suffused with incredulous joy.

"Gnaeus Pompeius, your father is dead," said Cicero, whose emotions were not engaged upon the father's account at all, and who therefore retained his good sense. "Come, calm yourself! You know he was dead when we left. We washed him, we dressed him. He was *dead*!"

The joy died, but not to be replaced by a new outbreak of tears. Instead, the fresh young face hardened to stone. "What is it then? Where is my father?"

"The servants are gone, even those who were ill, I think," said Cicero. "The first thing we had better do is search the place."

The search revealed nothing, yielded no clues as to where the body of Gnaeus Pompeius Strabo had gone. The one growing ever stonier, the other ever more bewildered, Pompey and Cicero left the villa to gather its silence fast around it, and stood outside on the Via Nomentana looking both ways.

"Do we go to the camp or the gate?" asked Cicero.

Both lay within scant paces. Pompey wrinkled his brow as he thought, then made up his mind.

"We'll go to the general's tent. Perhaps the men removed him to lie in state there," he said.

They had turned and were walking campward when someone shouted.

"Gnaeus Pompeius! Gnaeus Pompeius!"

Back they swung toward the gate, to see a disheveled Brutus Damasippus waving at them as he ran.

"Your father!" he panted, reaching Pompey.

"What about my father?" Pompey asked, very cool, very calm.

"The people of Rome stole his body saying they were going to drag it behind an ass through every street in the city!" said Brutus Damasippus. "One of the women keeping vigil came to tell me, and like a fool I just ran! I suppose thinking I'd catch them. Luckily

I saw you—otherwise they'd probably be dragging me as well." He looked at Pompey with as much respect as he would have accorded the father. "What do you want me to do?" he asked.

"Bring two cohorts of soldiers to me here at once," Pompey said curtly. "Then we'll go inside and look for him."

Cicero didn't ask why, nor did Pompey say a word while they waited. The ultimate insult had been done Pompey Strabo, and there could be no doubt why; it was the only way left to the people of the northeastern city to express their contempt and disgust for one they deemed the author of their woes. The more crowded parts of Rome all received their water from the aqueducts, but the upper Esquiline, Viminal and Quirinal, less populous, relied heavily on local spring water.

When Pompey led his cohorts through the Colline Gate and into its very large marketplace, he found the whole area deserted. Nor was a soul on the streets beyond, even in the meanest alley leading to the lower Esquiline. One by one the narrow thoroughfares were combed, Damasippus taking a cohort toward the Agger, the two young men working in the opposite direction. Three hours later Pompey's contingent found their dead general sprawled on the lower Alta Semita outside the temple of Salus.

Well, thought Cicero to himself, the place they chose to leave him says everything. Outside the temple of Good Health.

"I shall not forget," said Pompey, looking down at the naked and mangled body of his father. "When I am consul and embark upon my building program, *nothing* will I give to the Quirinal!"

When Cinna heard of the death of Pompey Strabo, he breathed a sigh of relief. Then when he heard how the body of Pompey Strabo had been dragged through the streets of the city, he whistled softly. So all was not happy within Rome! Nor apparently were Rome's military defenders popular with the ordinary people. Happily he settled to wait for the surrender he now expected would come within hours.

But it did not come. Seemingly Octavius had decided that only if the ordinary people boiled into open revolt would he surrender.

Quintus Sertorius came to report late on that same day, his left eye covered by a blood-soaked bandage.

"What's happened to you?" demanded Cinna, dismayed.

"Lost my eye," said Sertorius briefly.

"Ye gods!"

"Lucky for me it's my left one," said Sertorius stoically. "I can still see on my sword side, so it shouldn't inconvenience me much in a battle."

"Sit down," said Cinna, pouring wine. He watched his legate closely, deciding there was little in this life capable of throwing Quintus Sertorius off balance. Then, when Sertorius was settled, Cinna sat down himself, sighing. "You know, Quintus Sertorius, you were quite right," he said slowly.

"About Gaius Marius, you mean?"

"Yes." Cinna turned the cup between his hands. "I am no longer in total command. Oh, I'm respected among the senior ranks! I mean the men. The soldiers. The Samnite and other Italian volunteers. It's Gaius Marius they follow, not me."

"It was bound to happen. In the old days it wouldn't have mattered a rush. No fairer-minded, more farsighted man than Gaius Marius ever lived. But this isn't *that* Gaius Marius," said Sertorius. A bloody tear slid from beneath his bandage, and was wiped away. "No worse thing could have happened to him at his age and in his infirmity than this exile. I've seen enough of him to know that he's simply counterfeiting an interest in the job—what he's really interested in is his revenge on those who exiled him. He's surrounded himself with the worst specimens of legate I've seen in years—*Fimbria*! A complete wolfshead. As for his personal legion—he calls it his bodyguard and refuses to admit it's an official part of his army—it's composed of as vicious and rapacious a collection of slaves and ex-slaves as any Sicilian slave rebel leader might hope for. But he's not lost his mental acuteness, Lucius Cinna, so much as he's lost his moral acuteness. He *knows* he owns your armies! And I very much fear he intends to use them for his personal advancement, not Rome's welfare. I am only here with you and your forces for one big reason, Lucius Cinna—I cannot condone the illegal dismissal of a consul during his year in office. But I cannot condone what I suspect Gaius Marius is planning to do, so it may well be that you and I will have to part company."

Cinna's hackles were rising; he stared at Sertorius in dawning horror. "You mean he's set on a bloodbath?"

"I believe so. Nor do I think anyone can stop him."

"But he can't *do* that! It is absolutely essential that I enter Rome as rightful consul—restore peace—prevent further shedding of blood—and try to get our poor Rome on her feet again."

"The best of luck," said Sertorius dryly, and stood up. "I'll be on the Campus Martius, Lucius Cinna, and I intend to stay there. My men will follow *me,* so much you can count on. And I support the reinstallation of the legally elected consul! I do not support any faction led by Gaius Marius."

"Stay on the Campus Martius, by all means. But please, I beg you, come to whatever negotiations ensue!"

"Don't worry, I wouldn't miss that fiasco for anything," said Sertorius, and departed, still wiping his left cheek.

The next day, however, Marius packed up his camp and led his legions away from Rome toward the Latin plains. The death of Pompey Strabo had brought home a lesson; that so many men temporarily crowded around such a large city bred frightful disease. Better, Marius decided, to draw his men into the fresh air and unpolluted water of the countryside, and there pillage the grain and other foodstuffs they needed from the various granaries and barns dotted all over the Latin plains. Aricia, Bovillae, Lanuvium, Antium, Ficana, and Laurentum all fell, though none had offered resistance.

Hearing of Marius's departure, Quintus Sertorius privately wondered whether the real reason behind Marius's withdrawal was a reflexive movement to safeguard himself and his men from *Cinna.* Mad he might be, but a fool he was not.

It was now the end of November. Everyone on both sides—or all three sides might have been a more accurate assessment—knew that Gnaeus Octavius Ruso's "true" government of Rome was doomed. The dead Pompey Strabo's army had flatly refused to accept Metellus Pius as its new commander, then marched over the Mulvian Bridge to offer its services to Gaius Marius. Not to Lucius Cinna.

The death toll from disease now stood at over eighteen thousand people, many of them from the ranks of Pompey Strabo's legions. And the granaries within Rome were now completely empty. Sensing the beginning of the end, Marius brought his five-thousand-strong bodyguard of slaves and ex-slaves back to the southern flank of the Janiculum. Significantly, he did not bring the rest of his army with him, neither the Samnites, the Italians nor the remnants of Pompey Strabo's forces. Thus ensuring his own safety? wondered Quintus Sertorius. Yes, it very much looked as if Marius was deliberately keeping the bulk of his own men in reserve.

On the third day of December a treating party crossed the Tiber via the two bridges connecting through Tiber Island. It consisted of Metellus Pius the Piglet (who was its official leader), the censor Publius Crassus, and the Brothers Caesar. Waiting for them at the end of the second bridge was Lucius Cinna. And Gaius Marius.

"Greetings, Lucius Cinna," said Metellus Pius, outraged to see Marius present, especially as he was attended by that vile wretch Fimbria, and a gigantic German in ostentatious golden armor.

"Do you address me as the consul or as a private citizen, Quintus Caecilius?" asked Cinna coldly.

As Cinna said this, Marius rounded on him furiously and snarled, "Weakling! Spineless idiot!"

Metellus Pius swallowed. "As consul, Lucius Cinna," he said.

Whereupon Catulus Caesar rounded on the Piglet furiously and snarled, "Traitor!"

"That man is not consul! He is guilty of sacrilege!" cried the censor Crassus.

"He doesn't need to be consul, he's the victor!" shouted Marius.

Clapping his hands over his ears to shut out the heated exchanges between all present save himself and Cinna, Metellus Pius turned on his heel in anger and stalked back across the bridges into Rome.

When he reported what had happened to Octavius, Octavius too flew at the hapless Piglet. "How dared you admit he's consul? He is not consul! Cinna is *nefas!*" snapped Octavius.

"The man is consul, Gnaeus Octavius, and will continue to be consul until the end of this month," said Metellus Pius coldly.

"A fine negotiator you turned out to be! Don't you even understand that the worst thing any of us can do is to acknowledge Lucius Cinna as true consul?" asked Octavius, wagging one finger at the Piglet much as a schoolmaster might chastise a student.

The Piglet lost his temper. "Then *you* go and do better!" he said tightly. "And don't you point your finger at me! You're little better than a jumped-up nobody! I am a Caecilius Metellus, and not Romulus himself points a finger at me! Whether it suits your ideas or not, Lucius Cinna *is* consul. If I go back again and he asks me the same question again, I will give him the same answer!"

His unhappiness and discomfort, present since the very beginning of his tenure of the curule chair, now became intolerable; the *flamen Dialis* and suffect consul Merula drew himself up and faced his colleague Octavius and the enraged Metellus Pius with all the dignity he could muster. "Gnaeus Octavius, I must resign as consul *suffectus*," he said quietly. "It is not fitting that the priest of Jupiter be a curule magistrate. The Senate, yes. Imperium, no."

Speechless, the rest of the group watched Merula leave the lower Forum—where this exchange had taken place—and walk up the Via Sacra toward his State House.

Catulus Caesar then looked at Metellus Pius. "Quintus Caecilius, would you assume the military high command?" he asked. "If we made your appointment official, perhaps both our men and our city might take on a new lease of life."

But Metellus Pius shook his head firmly. "No, Quintus Lutatius, I will not. Our men and our city have no heart for this cause, between disease and hunger. And—though it gives me no joy to say it—their uncertainty as to who is in the right. I hope none of us wants another battle through the streets of Rome—Lucius Sulla's was one too many. We *must* come to terms! But with Lucius Cinna. *Not* with Gaius Marius."

Octavius looked around the faces of his treating party, lifted his shoulders, shrugged, sighed in defeat. "All right then, Quintus Caecilius. All right. Go back and see Lucius Cinna again."

Back went the Piglet, accompanied only by Catulus Caesar and his son, Catulus. It was now the fifth day of December.

This time they were received in greater state. Cinna had set up a high platform and sat atop it in his curule chair while the treating party stood below and were forced to look up at him. With him on the dais—though unseated and standing behind him—was Gaius Marius.

"First of all, Quintus Caecilius," said Cinna loudly, "I bid you welcome. Secondly, I assure you that Gaius Marius's status is that of an observer only. He understands that he is a *privatus,* and cannot speak during formal negotiations."

"I thank you, Lucius Cinna," said the Piglet with equally stiff formality, "and inform you that I am authorized to treat only with you, not with Gaius Marius. What are your conditions?"

"That I enter Rome as Rome's consul."

"Agreed. The *flamen Dialis* has already stepped down."

"No future retaliations will be tolerated."

"None will be made," said Metellus Pius.

"The new citizens from Italy and Italian Gaul will be given tribal status across the full thirty-five."

"Agreed absolutely."

"The slaves who deserted from service under Roman owners to enlist in my armies are to be guaranteed their freedom and the full citizenship," said Cinna.

The Piglet froze. "Impossible!" he snapped. *"Impossible!"*

"It is a condition, Quintus Caecilius. It must be agreed to along with the rest," Cinna maintained.

"I will *never* consent to free and enfranchise slaves who deserted their legal masters!"

Catulus Caesar stepped forward. "A word with you in private, Quintus Caecilius?" he asked delicately.

It took Catulus Caesar and his son a long time to persuade the Piglet this particular condition must be met; that in the end Metellus Pius yielded was only because he too could see Cinna was adamant—though he wondered on whose behalf, his own or Marius's? There were few slaves in Cinna's forces, but Marius's were riddled with them, according to reports.

"All right, I agree to that stupidity about the slaves," said the Piglet ungraciously. "However, there is one point on which *I* must set the terms."

"Oh?" from Cinna.

"There can be no bloodshed," said the Piglet strongly. "No disenfranchisements, no proscriptions, no banishments, no trials for treason, no executions. In this business, all men have done as their principles and convictions have dictated. No man ought to be penalized for adhering to his principles and convictions, no matter how repugnant they may seem. That goes as much for those who have followed you, Lucius Cinna, as it does for those who followed Gnaeus Octavius."

Cinna nodded. "I agree with you wholeheartedly, Quintus Caecilius. There must be no revenge."

"Will you swear to that?" asked the Piglet slyly.

Cinna shook his head, blushing. "I cannot, Quintus Caecilius. The most I can guarantee is that I will do my personal utmost to see that there are no treason trials, no bloodshed, no confiscations of men's property."

Metellus Pius turned his head slightly to look directly at the silent Gaius Marius. "Are you implying, Lucius Cinna, that you—the consul!—cannot control your own faction?"

Cinna flinched, but said steadily, "I can control it."

"Then will you swear?"

"No, I will not swear," said Cinna with great dignity, red face betraying his discomfort. He rose from his chair to signify that the meeting was over, and accompanied Metellus Pius down to the Tiber Island bridge. For a few precious moments he and the Piglet were alone. "Quintus Caecilius," he said urgently, "I *can* control my faction! Just the same, I would rest easier if Gnaeus Octavius is kept out of the Forum—kept completely out of sight! In case. A remote possibility. I *can* control my faction! But I would rather Gnaeus Octavius was not on display. Tell him!"

"I will," said Metellus Pius.

Marius caught up to them at a hobbling run, so anxious was he to cut this private conversation short. He looked, the Piglet thought, quite grotesque. There was something new and horribly simian about him, and a diminishing in that awesome air of power he had always radiated, even in the days when the Piglet's father had been his commander in Numidia, and the Piglet a mere cadet.

"When do you and Gaius Marius plan to enter the city?" asked Catulus Caesar of Cinna as the two parties prepared to go their separate ways.

Before Cinna could answer, Gaius Marius broke his silence with a contemptuous snort. "Lucius Cinna can enter as the lawful consul any time he likes," said Marius, "but I am waiting here with the army until the convictions against me and my friends have been legally quashed."

Cinna could hardly wait for Metellus Pius and his escort to start walking away down the Tiber Island bridge before he said to Marius sharply, "What do you mean, you'll stay with the army until your conviction is quashed?"

The old man stood there looking more inhuman than human; like Mormolyce or Lamia, a monstrous, wickedly intelligent tormentor from the Underworld. He was smiling, his eyes glittering through the tangled curtain of his brows, bushier than of yore because he had developed a habit of pulling at them.

"My dear Lucius Cinna, it's Gaius Marius the army follows, not you! Were it not for me, the desertions would have been all the other way, and Octavius would have won. Think on that! If I enter the city still inscribed on the tablets as an outlaw under sentence of death, what's to stop you and Octavius agreeing to patch up your differences and carry out the sentence on me? What a pickle for *me* to be in! There I'd be, standing around with my cap of liberty in my hand, a *privatus* waiting for the consuls and the Senate—a body I no longer belong to!—to absolve me of my nonexistent crimes. Now I ask you—is that a fitting stance for Gaius Marius?" He patted Cinna patronizingly on the shoulder. "No, Lucius Cinna, you have your little moment of glory all to yourself! You enter Rome alone. I'll stay where I am. With the army *I* own. Because you don't."

Cinna writhed. "Are you saying you'd use the army—*my* army!—against me? The lawful consul?"

"Cheer up, it won't get as far as that," said Marius with a laugh. "Say, rather, that the army will be most concerned to see Gaius Marius gets his due."

"And what exactly *is* Gaius Marius's due?"

"On the Kalends of January, I will be the new senior consul. You of course will be my junior colleague."

"But I can't be consul again!" gasped Cinna, horrified.

"Rubbish! Of course you can! Now go away, do!" said Marius in the same tone he would have used to an importunate child.

Cinna went to seek out Sertorius and Carbo, who had been present at the negotiations, and told them what Marius had said.

"Don't say you weren't warned," said Sertorius grimly.

"What can we do?" wailed Cinna, despairing. "He's right, the army belongs to him!"

"Not my two legions," said Sertorius.

"Insufficient to pit against him," said Carbo.

"What can we do?" wailed Cinna again.

"For the moment, nothing. Let the old man have his day—and his precious seventh consulship," said Carbo, teeth set hard together. "We'll worry about him after Rome is ours."

Sertorius made no further comment; he was too busy trying to decide what his own future course ought to be. Somehow every last one of them was sounding meaner, nastier, smaller, more selfish, more grasping. They've caught the disease from Gaius Marius, and they're busy giving it to each other. As for myself, he thought, I am not sure I want to be a part of this sordid and unspeakable conspiracy for power. *Rome* is sovereign. But thanks to

Lucius Cornelius Sulla, men have now got the idea that they can be sovereign over Rome.

When Metellus Pius reported the gist of Cinna's advice about Octavius's staying out of sight to Octavius and the rest, every last one of them knew what was in the wind. This was one of the few conferences at which Scaevola Pontifex Maximus was present; it had not escaped notice that he was withdrawing as unobtrusively as possible into the background. Probably, thought Metellus Pius, because he can see victory for Gaius Marius looming, and remembers that his daughter is still affianced to Young Marius.

Catulus Caesar sighed. "Well, I suggest that all the younger men quit Rome before Lucius Cinna enters. We will need all our younger *boni* for the future—these awful creatures like Cinna and Marius will not last forever. And one day Lucius Sulla is going to come home." He paused, then added, "I think we old fellows are better off staying in Rome and taking our chances. I for one have no desire to emulate Gaius Marius's odyssey, even were I guaranteed no Liris swamps."

The Piglet looked at Mamercus. "What do you say?"

Mamercus considered. "I think it imperative you should go, Quintus Caecilius, I really do. But for the moment I shall stay. I'm not such a big fish in Rome's pond."

"Very well, I will go," said Metellus Pius with decision.

"And *I* will go," said the senior consul Octavius loudly.

Everyone turned to look at him, puzzled.

"I will set myself up on a tribunal in the Janiculan garrison," Octavius said, "and wait there for whatever comes. That way, if they are determined to spill my blood, it will not pollute the air or the stones of Rome."

No one bothered to argue. The massacre of Octavius's Day made this course inevitable.

The following day at dawn Lucius Cornelius Cinna, in his *toga praetexta* and preceded by his twelve lictors, entered the city of Rome on foot across the bridges linking Tiber Island with either bank of the Tiber River.

But, having heard where Gnaeus Octavius Ruso had gone from a friend in the confidence of those inside Rome, Gaius Marcius Censorinus gathered a troop of Numidian cavalry and rode for the fortress on the Janiculum. No one had authorized this sortie—indeed, no one knew of it, least of all Cinna. That Censorinus had taken it upon himself to do what he intended to do was Cinna's fault; those of wolfish disposition among Cinna's officers had come to the conclusion that once he entered the city, Cinna would knuckle under to men like Catulus Caesar and Scaevola Pontifex Maximus. That the whole campaign to return Cinna to authority in Rome would end as a dry and bloodless exercise. But Octavius at least would not escape, vowed Censorinus.

Finding his entry to the stronghold uncontested (Octavius had dismissed the garrison), Censorinus rode into the outer stockade at the head of his five-hundred-strong troop.

And there on the tribunal in the citadel forum sat Gnaeus Octavius Ruso, shaking his head adamantly in response to his chief lictor's pleas that he leave. Hearing the sound of many hooves, Octavius turned and arranged himself properly upon his curule chair, his lictors white-faced in fear.

Gaius Marcius Censorinus ignored the attendants. Sword drawn, he came down from his horse, bounded up the tribunal steps, walked to where Octavius sat calmly, and fastened the fingers of his left hand in Octavius's hair. One powerful yank, and the senior consul—who did not fight back—came to his knees. While the terrified lictors looked on helplessly, Censorinus raised his sword in both hands and brought it down with all the force he could summon upon Octavius's bared neck.

Two of the troopers took the dripping head, its face curiously peaceful, and fixed it upon a spear. Censorinus took it himself, then dismissed the squadron back to camp on the Vatican plain; on one point he was not prepared to disobey orders, and that concerned Cinna's edict that no soldiers of any kind were to cross the *pomerium*. Tossing his sword, helmet, and cuirass to his servant, he mounted his horse clad in his leather under-dress and rode straight to the Forum Romanum, carrying the shaft before him like a lance. Without a word he raised the spear on high and presented the head of Octavius to the unsuspecting Cinna.

The consul's initial reaction was naked horror; he recoiled physically, both hands up with palms outward to fend this appalling gift off. Then he thought of Marius waiting across the river, and of all those eyes upon him and his known lieutenant Censorinus. He drew a sobbing breath, closed his eyes in pain, and faced the hideous consequences of his march upon Rome.

"Fix it to the rostra," he said to Censorinus. Turning to the silent crowd, he shouted, "This is the only act of violence I condone! I vowed that Gnaeus Octavius Ruso would not live to see me resume my place as consul. He it was—together with Lucius Sulla!—who began this custom! They put the head of my friend Publius Sulpicius where this head is now. It is fitting that Octavius should continue the custom—as will Lucius Sulla when *he* returns! Look well on Gnaeus Octavius, People of Rome! Look well on the head of the man who brought all this pain and hunger and suffering into being when he slaughtered over six thousand men upon the Campus Martius in the midst of a legally convened assembly. Rome is avenged! There will be no more bloodshed! Nor was the blood of Gnaeus Octavius shed within the *pomerium*."

Not quite the truth; but it would serve.

Within the space of seven days the laws of Lucius Cornelius Sulla came tumbling down. A pale shadow of its old self, the Centuriate Assembly took its example from Sulla by legislating to pass the measures in a bigger hurry than the *lex Caecilia Didia prima* permitted. Its former powers restored, the Plebeian Assembly then met to elect new tribunes of the plebs, as they were already overdue. A spate of new legislation followed: the Italian and Italian Gallic citizens (but not the freedmen of Rome—Cinna had decided not to risk that) were distributed across the thirty-five tribes without let or hindrance or special provisos; Gaius Marius and his fellow fugitives were restored to their rightful positions and ranks; a proconsular imperium was now officially bestowed upon Gaius Marius; the two new tribes of Piso Frugi were abolished; all the men exiled under the original Varian Commission were recalled; and—last but not least—Gaius Marius was formally given command of the war in the East against King Mithridates of Pontus and his allies.

The elections for the plebeian aediles were held in the Plebeian Assembly, after which the Assembly of the Whole People was convoked to elect curule aediles, quaestors, tribunes of the soldiers. Though they were three to four years off their thirtieth birthdays, Gaius Flavius Fimbria, Publius Annius and Gaius Marcius Censorinus were all elected quaestors and appointed immediately to the Senate, neither censor thinking it wise to protest.

In an odor of extreme sanctity, Cinna ordered the Centuries to assemble to elect the curule magistrates; he convened his meeting on the Aventine outside the *pomerium,* as Sertorius was still sitting on the Campus Martius with two legions. A sad gathering of no more than six hundred men of the Classes, most of them senators and very senior knights, dutifully returned as consuls the only two names put up as candidates—Lucius Cornelius Cinna, and Gaius Marius *in absentia.* The form had been observed, the election was legal. Gaius Marius was now consul of Rome for the seventh time, and the fourth time *in absentia.* The prophecy was fulfilled.

Cinna had his little moment of revenge nonetheless; when the consuls were elected, it was he who occupied the senior position, Gaius Marius the junior. Then came the praetorian elections. Only six names were put up to fill six positions, but again the form was observed, the vote could be said to be legal. Rome had her proper array of magistrates, even if there had been a dearth of candidates. Cinna could now concentrate upon trying to rectify the damage of the past few months—damage Rome could ill afford to sustain after the long war against the Italians and the loss of the East.

Like an animal backed into a corner, the city remained still and vigilant during the remainder of December, while the armies packed around her shifted and redistributed. The Samnite contingents went back to Aesernia and Nola, the latter to lock themselves in again; for Gaius Marius had graciously given Appius Claudius

Pulcher permission to remove himself and his old legion back to the siege of Nola. Though Sertorius had the legion, he persuaded its men to go back to work for a commander they despised, and saw it march for Campania without regret. Many of the veterans who had enlisted to help their old general now also returned to their homes, including the two cohorts who had sailed from Cercina with Marius the moment Marius had heard Cinna was moving.

Reduced to one legion, Sertorius lay on the Campus Martius like a cat feigning deep sleep. He kept himself aloof from Gaius Marius, who had elected to keep his five-thousand-strong body-guard of slaves and ex-slaves. What are you up to, you dreadful old man? asked Sertorius of himself. You have deliberately sent every decent element away, and retained that element which is committed to follow you into any atrocity.

 Gaius Marius entered Rome at last on New Year's Day as her lawfully elected consul, riding a pure white horse, clad in a purple-bordered toga, and wearing an oak-leaf crown. At his side rode the hulking Cimbric slave Burgundus in beautiful golden armor, girt with a sword, and mounted upon a Bastarnian horse so big its hooves were the size of buckets. And behind him walked five thousand slaves and ex-slaves, all clad in reinforced leather, and wearing swords—not quite soldiers, but not civilians either.

Consul seven times! The prophecy was fulfilled. Nothing else lived inside Gaius Marius's head but those words as he rode between walls of cheering, weeping people; what did it really matter whether he was the senior or the junior consul, when the people welcomed their hero so passionately, so blindly? Did they care that he rode instead of walked? Did they care that he came from across the Tiber rather than from his house? Did they care that he hadn't stood the night watch for omens in the temple of Jupiter Optimus Maximus? Not one iota! He was Gaius Marius. What was required for other, lesser men was not required for Gaius Marius.

Moving inexorably toward his fate, he arrived in the lower Forum Romanum and there found Lucius Cornelius Cinna waiting for him at the head of a procession comprising senators and a very few senior knights. Burgundus got Marius down from the pure white horse with a minimum of fuss, adjusted the folds of his master's toga—and, when Marius took the place in front of Cinna, stood beside him.

"Come on, Lucius Cinna, let's get it over!" snapped Marius in loud tones, starting to walk. "I've done this six times before and you've done it once, so let's not turn it into a triumphal parade!"

"Just a moment!" shouted the ex-praetor Quintus Ancharius, stepping out of his place among the men in purple-bordered togas who followed Cinna, and moving quickly to plant himself firmly in front of Gaius Marius. "You are in the wrong order, consuls. Gaius Marius, you are *junior* consul. You go after Lucius Cinna, not ahead of him. I also demand that you get rid of this great barbarian brute from our solemn deputation to the Great God, and order your bodyguard to leave the city or remove their swords."

For a moment Marius looked as if he would strike Ancharius, or perhaps order his German giant to set the expraetor aside; then the old man shrugged, repositioned himself behind Cinna. But the slave Burgundus remained alongside him, and he had spoken no word commanding his bodyguard to leave.

"On the first issue, Quintus Ancharius, you have a point of law," said Marius fiercely, "but on the second and third issues I will not yield. My life has been imperiled enough of late years. And I am infirm. Therefore my slave will remain by my side. My Bardyaei will remain in the Forum and wait to escort me after the ceremonies are over."

Quintus Ancharius looked mutinous, but finally nodded and went back to his place; a praetor in the same year Sulla had been consul, he was an inveterate Marius-hater, and proud of it. Not unless he had been tied down would he have allowed Marius to get away with walking ahead of Cinna in the procession, especially after it dawned upon him that Cinna was going to accept this monumental insult. That he went back to his place was in reaction to the look of piteous appeal Cinna gave him; his gorge rose. Why should he fight a weak man's battles? Oh, prayed Quintus Ancharius, finish that war and come home soon, Lucius Sulla!

The hundred-odd knights who led the procession had moved off the moment Marius commanded Cinna to walk, and had reached the temple of Saturn before realizing the two consuls and the Senate were still halted, apparently in argument. Thus the start of that pilgrimage to the home of the Great God on the Capitol was as ill-concerted as it was ill-omened. No one, including Cinna, had had the courage to point out that Gaius Marius had not kept watch through the night, as the new consuls were obliged to do; and Cinna said nothing to anyone about the dense black shape of some webbed and taloned creature he had seen fly across the wan sky as he stood his watch.

Never had a New Year's Day consular inauguration been so quickly completed as that one, either, even the famous one when Marius had wanted to commence the consular ceremonies still garbed as a triumphing general. Less than four shortish daylight hours later, everything was over—sacrifices, the meeting of the Senate within the temple of the Great God, the feast which followed. Nor had any group of men in the past ever been so anxious to escape afterward. As the procession came down off the Capitol, every man saw the head of Gnaeus Octavius Ruso still rotting on its spear at the edge of the rostra, bird-tattered face turned to gaze up at the temple of Jupiter Optimus Maximus—with empty sockets. A terrible omen. Terrible!

Emerging from the alleyway between the temple of Saturn and the Capitol hillside, Gaius Marius spied Quintus Ancharius ahead of him, and hastened to catch up. When he put his hand upon Ancharius's arm the ex-praetor looked around, his startled surprise changing to revulsion when he saw who accosted him.

"Burgundus, your sword," said Marius calmly.

The sword was in his right hand even as he finished speaking; his right hand flashed up, and down. Quintus Ancharius fell dead, his face cloven from hairline to chin.

No one tried to protest. As their shock dissipated, senators and knights scattered, running. Marius's legion of slaves and ex-slaves—still standing in the lower Forum—went in hot pursuit the moment the old man snapped his fingers.

"Do what you like with the *cunni*, boys!" roared Marius, beaming. "Only do try to distinguish between my friends and my enemies!"

Horrified, Cinna stood watching his world disintegrate, utterly powerless to intervene. His soldiers were either on their way home or still in their camp on the Vatican plain; Marius's "Bardyaei"— as he called his slave followers because so many of them were from this Dalmatian tribe of Illyrians—now owned the city of Rome. And, owning it, treated it more pitilessly than a crazed drunkard the wife he hates. Men were cut down for no reason, houses invaded and robbed, women defiled, children murdered. A lot of it was senseless, causeless; but there were other instances too—men whom Marius hungered to see dead, or perhaps merely fancied he would like to see dead—the Bardyaei were not clever at distinguishing between Marius's various moods.

For the rest of the day and far into the night, Rome screamed and howled, and many died or wished they could die. In some places huge flames leaped skyward, screams turned to high and maddened shrieks.

Publius Annius, who loathed Antonius Orator above all others, led a troop of cavalry to Tusculum, where the Antonii had an estate, and took great pleasure in hunting down Antonius Orator and killing him. The head was brought back to Rome amid great jubilation, and planted on the rostra.

Fimbria chose to take his squadron of horsemen up onto the Palatine, looking first for the censor Publius Licinius Crassus and his son Lucius. It was the son Fimbria spied as he sped up the narrow street toward the safety of home; spurring his horse, Fimbria came alongside him and, bending in the saddle, ran his sword through Lucius Crassus's back. Seeing it happen and powerless to prevent the same fate happening to him, the father drew a dagger from the recesses of his toga and killed himself. Luckily Fimbria had no idea which door in that alleyway of windowless walls belonged to the Licinii Crassi, so the third son, Marcus—not yet of an age to be a senator—was spared.

Leaving his men to decapitate Publius and Lucius Crassus, Fimbria took a few troopers and went looking for the Brothers Caesar. Two of them he found in the one house, Lucius Julius and his younger brother, Caesar Strabo. The heads of course were kept for the rostra, but Fimbria dragged the trunk and limbs of Caesar Strabo out to the tomb of Quintus Varius, and there "killed" him all over again as an offering for the man Caesar Strabo had prosecuted, and who had taken his own life so slowly, so painfully. After that he went looking for the oldest brother, Catulus Caesar, but was found by a messenger from Marius before he found his quarry; Catulus Caesar was to be spared to stand his trial.

In the next morning's light the rostra bristled with heads on spears—Ancharius, Antonius Orator, Publius and Lucius Crassus, Lucius Caesar, Caesar Strabo, the ancient Scaevola Augur, Gaius Atilius Serranus, Publius Cornelius Lentulus, Gaius Nemetorius, Gaius Baebius, and Octavius. Bodies littered the streets, a pile of unimportant heads lay against the angle where the tiny temple of Venus Cloacina tucked itself into the Basilica Aemilia, and Rome stank of coagulating blood.

Indifferent to all save the pursuit of his revenge, Marius walked to the well of the Comitia to hear his own newly elected tribune of the plebs, Publius Popillius Laenas, convene the Plebeian Assembly. Of course no one came to attend, but the meeting went ahead anyway after the Bardyaei chose rural tribes for themselves as part of their new citizenship package. Quintus Lutatius Catulus Caesar and Lucius Cornelius Merula *flamen Dialis* were immediately indicted for treason.

"But I shall not wait for the verdict," said Catulus Caesar, eyes red from weeping at the fate of his brothers and so many of his friends.

He said this to Mamercus, whom he had summoned urgently to his house. "Take Lucius Cornelius Sulla's wife and daughter and flee at once, Mamercus, I beg of you! The next to be indicted will be Lucius Sulla, and everyone even remotely attached to him will die—or worse, in Dalmatica's case—and in the case of your own wife, Cornelia Sulla."

"I had thought to remain," said Mamercus, looking exhausted. "Rome will need men untouched by this horror, Quintus Lutatius."

"Yes, Rome will. But she won't find them among those who stay, Mamercus. I do not intend to live a moment longer than I have to. Promise me you'll bundle up Dalmatica, Cornelia Sulla, all the various children, and send them to safety in Greece. With yourself as their escort. Then I can get on and do what I have to do."

So Mamercus promised, heavyhearted, and did much that day to safeguard the mobile and monetary property of Sulla, Scaurus, Drusus, the Servilii Caepiones, Dalmatica, Cornelia Sulla, and himself. By nightfall he and the women and children were through the Porta Sanqualis, least popular of Rome's gates, and heading for the Via Salaria; it seemed a safer way to go than south to Brundisium.

As for Catulus Caesar, he sent little notes to Merula the *flamen Dialis,* and to Scaevola Pontifex Maximus. Then he had his slaves light every brazier his house possessed and put them in his principal guest suite, so newly plastered its walls exuded the pungent odor of fresh lime. Having sealed every crack and opening with rags, Catulus Caesar sat himself down in a comfortable chair and opened a scroll which contained the last books of the *Iliad,* his favorite literature. When Marius's men broke down the door, they found him still sitting upright and naturally in his chair, the scroll tidily in his lap; the room was choked with noxious fumes, and the corpse of Catulus Caesar was quite cold.

Lucius Cornelius Merula never saw his note from Catulus Caesar, as it found him already dead. After reverently placing his *apex* and his *laena* in a tidily folded bundle beneath the statue of the Great God in his temple, Merula went home, got into a hot bath, and opened his veins with a bone knife.

Scaevola Pontifex Maximus read his note.

I know, Quintus Mucius, that you have elected to throw in your lot with Lucius Cinna and Gaius Marius. I can even begin to understand why. Your girl is pledged to Young Marius, and that is a tidy fortune to toss away. But you are wrong. Gaius Marius is diseased of mind, and the men who follow him are little better than barbarians. I do not mean his slaves. I mean men like Fimbria, Annius, and Censorinus. Cinna is a good enough fellow in many ways, but he cannot possibly control Gaius Marius. Nor can you.

By the time you get this, I will be dead. It seems to me infinitely preferable to die than to live out the rest of my life as an exile—or, briefly, as one of Gaius Marius's many victims. My poor, poor brothers! It pleases me to choose my own time, place and method of dying. Did I wait until tomorrow, none of those would be mine.

I have finished my memoirs, and I freely admit that it pains me not to be present to hear the comments when they are published. However, *they* will live, though I do not. To safeguard them—they are anything but complimentary to Gaius Marius!—I have sent them with Mamercus to Lucius Cornelius Sulla in Greece. When Mamercus comes back in better days, he has undertaken to publish them. And to send a copy to Publius Rutilius Rufus in Smyrna, to pay him back for being so venomous about me in his own writings.

Look after yourself, Quintus Mucius. It would be most interesting to see how you manage to reconcile your principles with necessity. I could not. But then, my children are safely married.

Tears in his eyes, Scaevola screwed the small sheet of paper up into a ball and thrust it into the middle of a brazier, for it was cold and he was old enough now to feel the cold. Fancy killing his old uncle the Augur! Harmless. They could talk until they were black in the face that it was all a terrible mistake. Nothing that had happened in Rome since New Year's Day was a mistake. Warming his hands and sniffling his tears away, Scaevola stared at the glowing coals contained within the bronze tripod, having no idea that Catulus Caesar's last impressions of life were much the same.

The heads of Catulus Caesar and Merula *flamen Dialis* were added to the rostra's mounting collection before dawn of the third day of Gaius Marius's seventh consulship; Marius himself spent long moments contemplating Catulus Caesar's head—still handsome and haughty—before allowing Popillius Laenas to convene another Plebeian Assembly.

This meeting directed its spleen at Sulla, who was condemned and voted a public enemy; all his property was confiscated, but not for the greater good of Rome. Marius let his Bardyaei loot Sulla's magnificent new house overlooking the Circus Maximus, then let them burn it to the ground. The property of Antonius Orator suffered a similar fate. However, neither man left any indication as to where his money was secreted, and none ever turned up in a Roman bank, at least recognizably. Thus the slave legion did very well out of Sulla and Antonius Orator, whereas Rome did no good at all. So angry was Popillius Laenas that he sent a party of public slaves to sift through the ashes of Sulla's house after they cooled, looking for hidden treasure. The image cupboards containing Sulla and his ancestors had not been in the house when the Bardyaei plundered it; nor had the priceless citrus-wood table. Mamercus was very efficient. So was Sulla's new steward, Chrysogonus. Between the two of them and a small army of slaves under strict instructions not to appear either furtive or guilty, they stripped the best out of half a dozen of Rome's most beautiful houses in less than a day and put the best into hiding in places no one would dream of looking.

During the first days of Marius's seventh consulship he never went home to his house, nor set eyes upon Julia; even Young Marius had been sent out of the city before New Year's Day and put to work discharging the men Marius felt he would no longer need. At the beginning he seemed to fear that Julia would seek him out, and hedged himself behind his Bardyaei, under strict orders to escort his wife home should she appear in the Forum. But when three days went by without a sign of her, he relaxed somewhat, the only evidence of his state of mind the endless letters he kept writing to his son adjuring him to stay where he was, not to come to Rome.

"He's quite mad, but he's also quite sane—he knows he could never look Julia in the face after that bloodbath," said Cinna to his friend Gaius Julius Caesar, that moment returned to Rome from Ariminum, where he had been helping Marius Gratidianus keep Servilius Vatia inside Italian Gaul.

"Where is he living, then?" asked Marius's ashen brother-in-law, maintaining a steady voice by sheer willpower.

"In a tent, if you'd believe that. There it is, see? Pitched alongside the Pool of Curtius, in which he has his bath. But he never seems to sleep anyway. When he isn't carousing with the worst of his slaves and that monster Fimbria, he's walking, walking, walking, nosing into this and that for all the world like one of those little old grannies who poke their walking sticks through everything they see. Nothing is sacred!" Cinna shivered. "I can't control him. I have no idea what's in his mind—or what he's likely to do next. I doubt he knows himself."

The rumors of insanities within Rome had started to impinge upon Caesar's journey when he reached Veii, but so strange and muddled were the stories that he took no credence in them beyond altering his route. Instead of proceeding across the Campus Martius and calling in to say hello to his cousin-by-marriage Sertorius, Caesar took a *diverticulum* the moment he crossed the Mulvian Bridge and headed for the Colline Gate; his information about recent events in Rome was current enough for him to know that Pompey Strabo's army was no longer encamped there, and he knew Pompey Strabo was dead. At Veii he had discovered Marius and Cinna were consuls, one reason why he paid little attention to the rumors of unbelievable violence in the city. But when he reached the Colline Gate he found it occupied by a century of soldiers.

"Gaius Julius Caesar?" asked the centurion, who knew the legates of Gaius Marius quite well.

"Yes," said Caesar, growing anxious.

"I have a message from the consul Lucius Cinna that you are to go straight to his offices in the temple of Castor."

Caesar frowned. "I will be happy to do that, centurion, but I would prefer to go home first."

"The message is, at once, Lucius Julius," said the centurion, managing to make it sound both courteous and an order.

Stifling his anxiety, Caesar rode straight down the Vicus Longus heading for the Forum.

The smoke which had marred the perfect blue of a cloudless sky from as far away as the Mulvian Bridge was now a pall, and cinders floated on the air; in growing horror his eyes took in the sight of dead bodies—men, women, children—sprawled here and there on the sides of this wide straight thoroughfare. By the time he reached the Fauces Suburae his heart was thudding, and every part of him wanted to turn uphill, ride at the gallop to his home to make sure his family was unharmed. But instinct said he would do better by his family to go where he had been ordered to go. Clearly there had been war in the streets of Rome, and in the far distance toward the jumbled insulae of the Esquiline he could hear shouts, screams, howls. Not a single living person could he see looking down the Argiletum; he turned instead into the Vicus Sandalarius and came into the Forum at its middle, where he could skirt the buildings and arrive at the temple of Castor and Pollux without entering the lower Forum.

Cinna he found at the foot of the temple steps, and from him learned what had happened.

"What do you want of me, Lucius Cinna?" he asked, having seen the big tent sprawled by the Pool of Curtius.

"I don't want anything of you, Gaius Julius," said Cinna.

"Then let me go home! There are fires everywhere, I must see that my family is all right!"

"*I* didn't send for you, Gaius Julius. Gaius Marius himself did. I simply told the gate guards to make sure you came to me first because I thought you'd be in ignorance of what's happening."

"What does Gaius Marius want me for?" asked Caesar, trembling.

"Let's ask him," said Cinna, starting to walk.

The bodies now were headless; almost fainting, Caesar saw the rostra and its decorations.

"Oh, they're *friends*!" he cried, tears springing to his eyes. "My cousins! My colleagues!"

"Keep your manner calm, Lucius Julius," said Cinna tonelessly. "If you value your life, don't cry, don't pass out. His brother-in-law you may be, but since New Year's Day I wouldn't put it past him to order the execution of his wife or his son."

And there he stood about halfway between the tent and the rostra, talking to his German giant, Burgundus. And to Caesar's thirteen-year-old son.

"Gaius Julius, how good to see you!" rumbled Marius, clasping Caesar in his arms and kissing him with ostentatious affection; the boy, Cinna noticed, winced.

"Gaius Marius," said Caesar, croaking.

"You were always efficient, Gaius Julius. Your letter said you'd be here today, and here you are. Home in Rome. Ho ro, ho ro!" Marius said. He nodded to Burgundus, who stepped away quickly.

But Caesar's eyes were on his son, who stood amid the bloody shambles as if he didn't see any of it, his color normal, his face composed, his eyelids down.

"Does your mother know you're here?" Caesar blurted, looking for Lucius Decumius and finding him lurking in the lee of the tent.

"Yes, Father, she knows," said Young Caesar, voice deep.

"Your boy's really growing up, isn't he?" asked Marius.

"Yes," said Caesar, trying to appear collected. "Yes, he is."

"His balls are dropping, wouldn't you say?"

Caesar reddened. His son, however, displayed no embarrassment, merely glanced at Marius as if deploring his crassness. Not an atom of fear in him, Caesar noted, proud in spite of his own fear.

"Well now, I have a few things to discuss with both of you," Marius said affably, including Cinna in his statement. "Young Caesar, wait with Burgundus and Lucius Decumius while I talk to your *tata*." He watched until he was sure the lad was out of hearing distance, then turned to Cinna and Caesar with a gleeful look on his face. "I suppose you're all agog, wondering what business I could have that concerns you both?"

"Indeed," said Caesar.

"Well now," he said—this phrase had become one of his favorites, and was uttered regularly—"I probably know Young Caesar better than you do, Gaius Julius. I've certainly seen more of him these last few years. A remarkable boy," said Marius, voice becoming thoughtful, eyes now holding something slyly malicious. "Yes indeed, a truly extraordinary boy! Brilliant, you know. More intelligent than any fellow I've ever met. Writes poetry and plays, you know. But just as good at mathematics. Brilliant. Brilliant. Strong-willed too. Got quite a temper when he's provoked. And he's not afraid of trouble—or making trouble, for that matter."

The malicious gleam increased, the right corner of Marius's mouth turned up a little. "Well now, I said to myself after I became consul for the seventh time and fulfilled that old woman's prophecy about me—I am very fond of this lad! Fond enough of him to want to see him lead a more tranquil and even kind of life than I for one have led. He's a terrific scholar, you know. So, I asked myself, why not ensure him the position he will need in order to study? Why subject the dear little fellow to the ordeals of—oh, *war*—the Forum—politics?"

Feeling as if they trod on the crumbling lip of a volcano, Cinna and Caesar stood listening, having no idea where Gaius Marius was leading them.

"Well now," Marius went on, "our *flamen Dialis* is dead. But Rome can't do without the special priest of the Great God, now can she, eh? And here we have this perfect child, Gaius Julius Caesar Junior. Patrician. Both parents still living. Therefore the ideal candidate for *flamen Dialis*. Except that he isn't married, of course. However, Lucius Cinna, you have an unbetrothed girl-child who is a patrician and has both parents still living. If you married her to Young Caesar, every criterion would be met. What a wonderfully ideal *flamen* and *flaminica Dialis* they would make! No need to worry about finding the money to see your boy climb the *cursus honorum,* Gaius Julius, and no need to worry about finding the money to dower your girl, Lucius Cinna. Their income is provided by the State, they are housed at the expense of the State, and their future is as august as it is assured." He stopped, beamed upon the two transfixed fathers, held out his right hand. "What do you say?"

"But my daughter is only seven!" said Cinna, aghast.

"That's no impediment," said Marius. "She'll grow up. They can continue to live in their own homes until they're old enough to set up house together in their State House. Naturally the marriage can't be consummated until little Cornelia Cinna Minor is older. But there is nothing in the law to stop their marrying, you know." He jigged a little. "So what do you say?"

"Well, it's certainly all right by me," said Cinna, enormously relieved that this was all Marius had wanted to see him about. "I admit I'll find it difficult to dower a second daughter after my older girl cost me so much."

"Gaius Julius, what do you say?"

Caesar looked sidelong at Cinna, receiving his unspoken message clearly; agree, or things will not go well for you and yours. "It's all right by me too, Gaius Marius."

"Splendid!" cried Marius, and did a little dance of joy. He turned toward Young Caesar and snapped his fingers—yet another recent habit. "Here, boy!"

What a striking lad he is! thought Cinna, who remembered him vividly from the time when Young Marius had been accused of murdering Cato the Consul. So handsome! But why don't I like his eyes? They unsettle me, they remind me . . . He couldn't remember.

"Yes, Gaius Marius?" asked Young Caesar, whose gaze came to rest a little warily upon Marius's face; he had known, of course, that he was the subject of the conversation he had not been allowed to listen to.

"We have your future all mapped out for you," said Marius with bland contentment. "You are to marry Lucius Cinna's younger daughter at once, and become our new *flamen Dialis*."

Nothing did Young Caesar say. Not a muscle of his face did he move. Yet as he heard Marius say it, he changed profoundly, though none watching could guess in what way.

"Well now, Young Caesar, what do you say?" asked Marius.

A question greeted with silence; the boy's eyes had fallen away from Marius the moment the announcement was made, and now rested firmly on his own feet.

"What do you say?" Marius repeated, beginning to look angry.

The pale eyes, quite expressionless, lifted to rest upon his father's face. "I thought, Father, that I was committed to marry the daughter of the rich Gaius Cossutius?"

Caesar flushed, tightened his lips. "A marriage with Cossutia was discussed, yes. But no permanent arrangements have been made, and I much prefer this marriage for you. And this future for you."

"Let me see," said Young Caesar in a musing voice, "as *flamen Dialis* I can see no human corpse. I can touch nothing made of iron or steel, from a pair of scissors and a razor to a sword and a spear. I can have no knot upon my person. I can touch no goat, no horse, no dog, no ivy. I can eat no raw meat, no wheat, no leavened bread, no beans. I can touch no leather taken from a beast specially killed to provide it. I have many interesting and important duties. For instance, I announce the vintage at the Vinalia. I lead the sheep in a *suovetaurilia* procession. I sweep out the temple of the Great God Jupiter. I arrange for the purification of a house after someone has died in it. Yes, many interesting, important things!"

The three men listened, unable to tell from Young Caesar's tone whether he was being sarcastic or naïve.

"What do you say?" demanded Marius for the third time.

The blue eyes lifted to his face, so like Sulla's that for an uncanny moment Marius fancied it was Sulla stood there, and groped instinctively for his sword.

"I say . . . Thank you, Gaius Marius! How thoughtful and how considerate of you to take the time to arrange my future so neatly," said the boy, voice devoid of any feeling, yet not in an offensive way. "I understand exactly why you have visited such care upon my humble fate, Uncle. Nothing is hidden from the *flamen Dialis*! But I tell you also, Uncle, that nothing can alter any man's fate, or prevent his being what he is meant to be."

"Ah, but you can't get around the provisions of the priest of Jupiter!" cried Marius, growing angrier; he had wanted desperately to see the boy flinch, beg, weep, throw himself down.

"I should hope not!" said Young Caesar, shocked. "You quite mistake my meaning, Uncle. I thank you most sincerely for this new and truly Herculean task you have given me." He looked at his father. "I am going home now," he said. "Do you want to walk with me? Or do you have further business here?"

"No, I'll come," said Caesar, startled, then lifted a brow at Gaius Marius. "Is that all right, consul?"

"Certainly," said Marius, accompanying father and son as they started to walk across the lower Forum.

"Lucius Cinna, we will meet later," said Caesar, lifting a hand in farewell. "My thanks for everything. The horse—it belongs to Gratidianus's legion, and I have no stable for it."

"Don't worry, Gaius Julius, I'll have one of my men take care of it," said Cinna, heading for the temple of Castor and Pollux in a far better mood than he had suffered as he went to see Marius.

"I think," said Marius when these civilities were concluded, "that we will tie our children up tomorrow. The marriage can be celebrated at the house of Lucius Cinna at dawn. The Pontifex Maximus, the College of Pontifices, the College of Augurs and all the minor priestly colleges will gather afterward in the temple of the Great God to inaugurate our new *flamen* and *flaminica Dialis*. Consecration will have to wait until after you don the toga of manhood, Young Caesar, but inauguration fulfills all the legal obligations anyway."

"I thank you again, Uncle," Young Caesar said.

They were passing the rostra. Marius stopped to throw his arm toward the dozens of grisly trophies ringing the speaker's platform around. "Look at that!" he cried happily. "Isn't that a sight?"

"Yes," said Caesar. "It certainly is."

The son strode out at a great pace; hardly conscious, thought the father, that anyone strode alongside him. Turning his head to look back, the father noted that Lucius Decumius was following at a discreet distance. Young Caesar hadn't needed to come alone to that frightful place; for all Caesar himself disliked Lucius Decumius, it was a comfort to know he was there.

"How long has he been consul?" the boy suddenly demanded. "A whole four days? Oh, it seems like an eternity! I have never seen my mother cry before. Dead men everywhere—children sobbing—half of the Esquiline burning—heads fencing the rostra round—blood everywhere—his Bardyaei as he calls them hard put to choose between pinching at women's breasts and guzzling wine! What a glorious seventh consulship is this! Homer must be wandering the ditch along the edge of the Elysian Fields craving a huge drink of blood so he can hymn the deeds of Gaius Marius's seventh consulship! Well, Rome can certainly spare Homer the blood!"

How did one answer a diatribe like that? Never home, having no real understanding of his son, Caesar didn't know, so said nothing.

When the boy erupted into his own home, his father trying to keep up with him, he stood in the middle of the reception room and bellowed, *"Mother!"*

Caesar heard the clatter of a reed pen being dropped, then she came hurrying out of her workroom, face terrified. Of her normal beauty there was scarcely a relic left; she was thin, there were black crescents beneath her eyes, her face was puffy, her lips bitten to shreds.

Her attention was focused on Young Caesar; as soon as she saw him apparently unharmed her whole body sagged. Then she saw who was with him, and her knees gave way. "Gaius Julius!"

He caught her before she could fall, holding her very closely.

"Oh, I am so glad you're back!" she said into the horsey folds of his riding cloak. "It is a nightmare!"

"When you've *quite* finished!" snapped Young Caesar.

His parents turned to look at him.

"I have something to tell you, Mother," he said, not concerned with anything save his own monumental trouble.

"What is it?" she asked distractedly, still recovering from the double shock of seeing her son unharmed and her husband home.

"Do you know what he's done to me?"

"Who? Your father?"

Young Caesar dismissed his father with a lavish gesture. "No, not him! No! *He* just fell in with it, and I expected that. I mean dear, kind, thoughtful Uncle Gaius Marius!"

"What has Gaius Marius done?" she asked calmly, quaking inside.

"He's appointed me *flamen Dialis*! I am to marry the seven-year-old daughter of Lucius Cinna at dawn tomorrow, and then be inaugurated as *flamen Dialis* straight afterward," said Young Caesar through clenched teeth.

Aurelia gasped, could find no words to say; her immediate reaction was of profound relief, so afraid had she been when the summons came that Gaius Marius wanted Young Caesar in the lower Forum. All the time he had been away she had worked upon the same column of figures in her ledger without arriving at the same total twice, her mind filled with visions of what she had only heard described and her son must now see—the heads on the rostra, the dead bodies. The crazy old man.

Young Caesar grew tired of waiting for an answer, and launched into his own answer. "I am never to go to war and rival him there. I am never to stand for the consulship and rival him there. I am never to have the opportunity to be called the Fourth Founder of Rome. Instead, I am to spend the rest of my days muttering prayers in a language none of us understands anymore—sweeping out the temple—making myself available to every Lucius Tiddlypuss in need of having his house purified—wearing ridiculous clothes!" Square of palm and long of finger, beautiful in a masculine way, the hands were lifted to grope at the air, clench upon it impotently. "That old man has stripped me of my birthright, all to safeguard his own wretched status in the history books!"

Neither of them had much insight into how Young Caesar's mind worked, nor had either of them been privileged to listen to his dreams for his own future; as they stood listening to this passionate speech, both of them searched for a way to make Young Caesar understand that what had happened, what had been decided, was now inevitable. He must be made to see that the best thing he could do in the circumstances was to accept his fate with a good grace.

His father chose to be stern, disapproving. "Don't be so ridiculous!" he said.

His mother followed suit because this was how she always handled the boy—duty, obedience, humility, self-effacement—all the Roman virtues he did not possess. So she too said, "Don't be ridiculous!" But she added, "Do you seriously think you could ever rival Gaius Marius? No man can!"

"*Rival* Gaius Marius?" asked their son, rearing back. "I will outstrip him in brilliance as the sun does the moon!"

"If that is how you see this great privilege, Gaius Junior," she said, "then Gaius Marius was right to give you this task. It is an anchor you badly need. Your position in Rome is assured."

"I don't *want* an assured position!" cried the boy. "I want to *fight* for my position! I want my position to be the consequence of my own efforts! What satisfaction is there in a position older than Rome herself, a position visited upon me by someone who dowers me with it to save his own reputation?"

Caesar looked forbidding. "You are ungrateful," he said.

"Oh, *Father*! How can you be so obtuse? It isn't I at fault, it's Gaius Marius! I am what I have always been! *Not* ungrateful! In giving me this burden I shall have to find a way to rid myself of, Gaius Marius has done not one thing to earn gratitude from me! His motives are as impure as they are selfish."

"Will you stop overrating your own importance?" cried Aurelia in despairing tones. "My son, I have been telling you since you were so small I had to carry you that your ideas are too grand, your ambitions too overweening!"

"What does that matter?" asked the boy, his tones more despairing still. "Mother, *I* am the only one who can make that judgment! And it is one I can make only at the end of my life—not before it has begun! Now it cannot begin at all!"

Caesar thought it time to try a different tack. "Gaius Junior, we have no choice in the matter," he said. "You've been in the Forum, you know what's happened. If Lucius Cinna, who is the senior consul, thinks it prudent to agree to whatever Gaius Marius says, I cannot stand against him! I have not only to think about you, but to think about your mother and the girls. Gaius Marius is not his old self. His mind is diseased. But he has the power."

"Yes, I see that," said Young Caesar, calming a little. "In that one respect I have no desire to surpass him—or even to emulate him. I will never cause blood to flow in the streets of Rome."

As insensitive as she was practical, Aurelia deemed the crisis over. She nodded. "There, that's better, my son. Like it or not, you are going to be *flamen Dialis*."

Lips hard, eyes bleak, Young Caesar looked from his mother's haggardly beautiful face to his father's tiredly handsome one and saw no true sympathy; worse by far, he thought he saw no true understanding. What he didn't realize was that he himself lacked understanding of his parents' predicament.

"May I please go?" he asked.

"Provided you avoid any Bardyaei and don't go further than Lucius Decimius's," Aurelia said.

"I'm only going to find Gaius Matius."

He walked off to the door which led into the garden at the bottom of the insula's light-well, taller than his mother now and slim rather than thin, with shoulders seeming too broad for his width.

"Poor boy," said Caesar, who did understand some of it.

"He's permanently anchored now," said Aurelia tightly. "I fear for him, Gaius Julius. He has no brakes."

Gaius Matius was the son of the knight Gaius Matius, and was almost exactly the same age as Young Caesar; they had been born on opposite sides of the courtyard separating the apartments of their parents, and had grown up together. Their futures had always been different, just as their childish hopes were, but they knew each other as well as brothers did, and liked each other very much more than brothers usually did.

A smaller child than Young Caesar, Gaius Matius was fairish in coloring, with hazel eyes; he had a pleasantly good-looking face and a gentle mouth, and was his father's son in every way—he was already attracted to commerce and commercial law, and most happy that his manhood would be spent in them; he also loved to garden, and had eight green fingers and two green thumbs.

Digging happily in "his" corner of the courtyard, he saw his friend come through the door and knew immediately that something serious was wrong. So he put his trowel down and got to his feet, flicking soil from his tunic because his mother didn't like his bringing dirt inside, then ruining the effect by wiping his grubby paws on its front.

"What's the matter with you?" he asked placidly.

"Congratulate me, Pustula!" said Young Caesar in ringing tones. "I am the new *flamen Dialis*!"

"Oh, dear," said Matius, whom Young Caesar had called Pimple since early childhood because he was always much smaller. He squatted down again, resumed his digging. "That is a shame, Pavo," he said, putting just enough sympathy into his voice. He had called Young Caesar a peacock for as long as he had been called a pimple; their mothers had taken them and their sisters on a picnic treat out to the Pincian hill, where peacocks strutted and fanned out their tails to complement the froth of almond blossoms and the carpet of narcissus. Just so did the toddler Caesar strut, just so did he plume himself. And Pavo the peacock it had been ever since.

Young Caesar squatted beside Gaius Matius and concentrated upon keeping his tears at bay, for he was losing his anger and discovering grief instead. "I was going to win the Grass Crown even younger than Quintus Sertorius," he said now. "I was going to be the greatest general in the history of the world—greater even than *Alexander*! I was going to be consul more times than Gaius Marius. My *dignitas* was going to be enormous!"

"You'll have great *dignitas* as *flamen Dialis*."

"Not for myself, I won't. People respect the position, not the holder of it."

Matius sighed, put his trowel down again. "Let's go and see Lucius Decumius," he said.

That being exactly the right suggestion, Young Caesar rose with alacrity. "Yes, let's," he said.

They emerged into the Subura Minor through the Matius apartment and walked up the side of the building to the big crossroads junction between the Subura Minor and the Vicus Patricius. Here in the apex of Aurelia's triangular insula was located the premises of the local crossroads college, and here inside the crossroads college had Lucius Decumius reigned for over twenty years.

He was there, of course. Since New Year's Day he hadn't gone anywhere unless to guard Aurelia or her children.

"Well, if it isn't the peacock and the pimple!" he said cheerfully from his table at the back. "A little wine in your water, eh?"

But neither Young Caesar nor Matius had a taste for wine, so they shook their heads and slid onto the bench opposite Lucius Decumius as he filled two cups with water.

"You look glum. I wondered what was going on with Gaius Marius. What's the matter?" Lucius Decumius asked Young Caesar, shrewd eyes filled with love.

"Gaius Marius has appointed me *flamen Dialis*."

And at last the boy got the reaction he had wanted so badly; Lucius Decumius looked stunned, then angry.

"The vindictive old shit!"

"Yes, isn't he?"

"When you looked after him all those months, Pavo, he got to know you too well. Give him this—he's no fool, even if his head is cracked from the inside out."

"What am I going to do, Lucius Decumius?"

For a long moment the caretaker of the crossroads college did not reply, chewing his lip thoughtfully. Then his bright gaze rested upon Young Caesar's face, and he smiled. "You don't know that now, Pavo, but you will!" he said chirpily. "What's all this down in the dumps for? Nobody can plot and scheme better than you when you needs to. You're farsighted about your future—but you isn't *afraid* of your future! Why so frightened now? Shock, boy, that's all. I knows you better than Gaius Marius do. And I thinks you'll find a way around it. After all, Young Caesar, this is Rome, not Alexandria. There's always a legal loophole in Rome."

Gaius Matius Pustula sat listening, but said nothing. His father was in the business of drawing up contracts and deeds, so no one knew better than he how accurate that statement was. And yet . . . That was all very well for contracts and laws. Whereas the priesthood of Jupiter was beyond all legal loopholes because it was older even than the Twelve Tables, as Pavo Caesar was certainly intelligent and well-read enough to know.

So too did Lucius Decumius definitely know. But, more sensitive than Young Caesar's parents, Lucius Decumius understood that it was vital to give Young Caesar hope. Otherwise he was just as likely to fall on the sword he was now forbidden to touch. As Gaius Marius surely knew, Young Caesar was not the type suited to holding a flaminate. The boy was inordinately superstitious, but religion bored him. To be so confined, to be so hedged around with rules and regulations, would kill him. Even if he had to kill himself to escape.

"I am to be married tomorrow morning before I am inaugurated," said Young Caesar, pulling a face.

"What, to Cossutia?"

"No, not her. She's not good enough to be *flaminica Dialis,* Lucius Decumius. I was only marrying her for her money. As *flamen Dialis* I have to marry a patrician. So they're going to give me Lucius Cinna's daughter. She's seven."

"Well, that don't matter either then, do it? Better seven than eighteen, little peacock."

"I suppose so." The boy folded his lips together, nodded. "You are right, Lucius Decumius. I *will* find a way!"

But the events of the next day made that vow seem hollow, as Young Caesar came to understand how brilliantly Gaius Marius had trapped him. Everyone had dreaded the walk from the Subura to the Palatine, but during the previous eighteen hours a massive cleanup had taken place, as Lucius Decumius was able to inform the anxious Caesar when he debated how far around the city's center they ought to walk, not so much for the sake of Young Caesar—who had been exposed to the worst of it already—but for the sake of his mother and his two sisters.

"Your boy's is not the only wedding this morning, the Bardyaei tell me," said Lucius Decumius. "Gaius Marius brought Young Marius back to Rome last night for *his* wedding. He don't mind who sees the mess. Except for Young Marius. We can walk across the Forum. The heads is all gone. Blood's washed away. Bodies dumped. As if the poor young fellow don't know what his father's gone and done!"

Caesar eyed the little man with awe. "Do you actually stand on speaking terms with those terrible men?" he asked.

"Course I does!" said Lucius Decumius scornfully. "Six of them was—well, is, I suppose—members of my own brotherhood."

"I see," said Caesar dryly. "Well, let us go, then."

The wedding ceremony at the house of Lucius Cornelius Cinna was *confarreatio,* and therefore a union for life. The tiny bride— tiny even for her age—was neither bright nor precocious. Incongruously tricked out in flame and saffron, hung about with wool and talismans, she went through the ceremonies with the animation and enthusiasm of a doll. When the veil was lifted from her face, Young Caesar found it dimpled, flowerlike, and endowed with an enormous pair of soft dark eyes. So, feeling sorry for her, he smiled at her with that conscious charm of his, and was rewarded with a display of the dimples and a gleam of adoration.

Married at an age when most noble Roman parents had done no more than toy with possible candidates for betrothal, the child newlyweds were then escorted by both families up onto the Capitol and into the temple of Jupiter Optimus Maximus, whose statue smiled down on them fatuously.

There were other newlyweds present. Cinnilla's older sister, who was properly Cornelia Cinna, had been hastily married the day before to Gnaeus Domitius Ahenobarbus. The haste was not due to the usual reason. Rather, Gnaeus Domitius Ahenobarbus thought it prudent to safeguard his head by marrying Gaius Marius's colleague's daughter, to whom he was promised anyway. Young Marius, arriving after dark the day before, at dawn had married Scaevola Pontifex Maximus's daughter, called Mucia Tertia to distinguish her from her two elderly cousins. Neither couple looked in the least happy, but particularly was this true of Young Marius and Mucia Tertia, who had never met and would not have an opportunity to consummate their union, as Young Marius had been ordered back to duty the moment the last of the day's formalities was over.

Of course Young Marius knew of his father's atrocities, and had expected to know their extent when he reached Rome. Marius saw him at his camp in the Forum, a very brief interview.

"Report to the house of Quintus Mucius Scaevola at dawn for your wedding," he was told. "Sorry I won't be there, too busy. You and your wife will attend the inauguration of the new *flamen Dialis*—that's a very big occasion, they tell me—and then go to the feast at the house of the new *flamen Dialis* afterward. The moment that's finished, you go back to duty in Etruria."

"What, don't I get an opportunity to consummate my marriage?" asked Young Marius, trying to be light.

"Sorry, my son, that will have to wait until things are tidier," said Marius. "Straight back to work!"

Something in the old man's face made him hesitate to ask the question he had to ask; Young Marius drew in a breath and asked it. "Father, may I go now to see my mother? May I sleep there?"

Grief, pain, anguish; all three flared in Gaius Marius's eyes. His lips quivered. Then he said, "Yes," and turned away.

The moment in which he met his mother was the most awful of all Young Marius's life. Her eyes! How old she looked! How beaten. How sad. She was completely closed in upon herself, and reluctant to discuss what had happened.

"I want to know, Mama! What did he do?"

"What no man does in his right mind, little Gaius."

"I have known he was mad since Africa, but I didn't know how bad it was. Oh, Mama, how can we repair the damage?"

"We cannot." She lifted one hand to her head, frowned. "My son, let us not speak of it!" She wet her lips. "How does he look?"

"You mean it's true?"

"What is true?"

"That you haven't seen him at all?"

"I haven't seen him at all, little Gaius. I never will again."

And the way she said it, Young Marius didn't know whether she meant it from her own side, or divined it from a presentiment of the future, or thought that was how his father wanted it.

"He looks unwell, Mama. Not himself. He says he won't be at my wedding. Will you come?"

"Yes, little Gaius, I'll come."

After the wedding—what an interesting-looking girl Mucia Tertia was!—Julia accompanied the party to Young Caesar's ceremonies in the temple of Jupiter Optimus Maximus because Gaius Marius was not present. They had found the city scrubbed and polished, so Young Marius still did not know the extent of his father's atrocities. And being the Great Man's son, could not ask a soul.

The rituals in the temple were enormously long and unbelievably boring. Stripped to his ungirt tunic, Young Caesar was invested with the garments of his new office—the hideously uncomfortable and stuffy circular cape made of two layers of heavy wool widely striped in red and purple, the close-fitting spiked ivory helmet with its impaled disc of wool, the special shoes without knot or buckle. How could he possibly endure to wear all this every single day of his life? Used to feeling his waist cinched with a neat leather belt Lucius Decumius had given him together with a beautiful little dagger in a sheath attached to the belt, Young Caesar's midriff felt peculiar without it, and the ivory helmet—made for a man with a much smaller head—did not come down to encircle his ears as it should, but sat perched ridiculously atop his ivory-colored hair. That was all right, Scaevola Pontifex Maximus assured him; Gaius Marius was donating him a new *apex*, and the maker would come round to his mother's apartment to measure his head for it on the morrow.

When the boy set eyes on his Aunt Julia, his heart smote him. Now, while the various priests droned on and on and on, he watched her fixedly, willing her to look at him. She could feel that will, of course, but she would not look. Suddenly she was so much older than her forty years; all her beauty retreated before a wall of worry she couldn't see over or around. But at the end of the ceremonies, when everybody clustered round to greet the new *flamen Dialis* and his doll like *flaminica,* Young Caesar saw Julia's eyes at last, and wished he had not. She kissed him on the lips as she always did, and leaned her head onto his shoulder to weep a little.

"I am so sorry, Young Caesar," she whispered. "An unkinder thing he could not have done. He is so busy hurting everyone, even those he ought not to hurt. But he isn't himself, please see that!"

"I do see that, Aunt Julia," the boy said too softly for anyone else to hear. "Don't worry about me. I will deal with everything."

Finally, it being sunset, the departures were permitted. The new *flamen Dialis*—carrying his too-small *apex* but clad in his suffocating *laena,* his shoes slopping because they could not be made to fit well by laces or straps—walked home with his parents, his unusually solemn sisters, his Aunt Julia, and Young Marius and his bride. Cinnilla the new *flaminica Dialis*—now also robed without knot or buckle in stifling heavy wool—went home with her parents, her brother, her sister Cornelia Cinna, and Gnaeus Ahenobarbus.

"So Cinnilla will remain with her own family until she's eighteen," said Aurelia brightly to Julia, intentionally making small talk as she got everyone settled in the dining room to enjoy a late and festive dinner. "Eleven years into the future! At that age it seems such a long time. At my age, it is too short."

"Yes, I agree," said Julia colorlessly, sitting down between Mucia Tertia and Aurelia.

"What a lot of weddings!" said Caesar cheerfully, terribly aware of his sister's blighted face. He was reclining on the *lectus medius* in the host's normal place, and had given the place of honor alongside him to the new *flamen Dialis*, who had never been allowed to recline in his life, and now found it as strange and uncomfortable as everything else was on this tumultuous day.

"Why didn't Gaius Marius come?" asked Aurelia tactlessly.

Julia flushed, shrugged. "He's too busy."

Wishing she could bite off her tongue, Aurelia subsided without commenting, and looked rather wildly toward her husband for rescue. But rescue didn't come; instead, Young Caesar made things worse.

"Rubbish! Gaius Marius didn't come because he didn't dare come," said the new *flamen Dialis,* suddenly sitting, bolt upright on the couch and removing his *laena*, which was dumped unceremoniously on the floor beside the special shoes. "There, that's better. The wretched thing! I hate it, I hate it!"

Seizing upon this as a way out of her own dilemma, Aurelia frowned at her son. "Don't be impious," she said.

"Even if I speak the truth?" asked Young Caesar, subsiding onto his left elbow and looking defiant.

At that moment the first course came in—crusty white bread, olives, eggs, celery, several lettuce salads.

Finding himself very hungry—the rituals had permitted him no food—the new *flamen Dialis* reached out for the bread.

"Don't!" said Aurelia sharply, color fading in fear.

The lad froze, staring at her. "Why not?" he asked.

"You are forbidden to touch wheaten or leavened bread," said his mother. "Here is your bread now."

And in came a platter which was set in front of the new *flamen Dialis;* a platter containing some thin, flat, utterly unappetizing slabs of a grey-hued substance.

"What is it?" Young Caesar asked, gazing at it with loathing. *"Mola salsa?"*

"Mola salsa is made from spelt, which is wheat," said Aurelia, knowing very well that he knew it. "This is barley."

"Unleavened barley bread," said Young Caesar tonelessly. "Even Egyptian peasants live better than this! I think I will eat ordinary bread. This stuff would make me sick."

"Young Caesar, this is the day of your inauguration," said the father. "The omens were auspicious. You are now the *flamen Dialis*. On this day above all other days, everything must be scrupulously observed. You are Rome's direct link to the Great God. Whatever you do affects Rome's relations with the Great God. You're hungry, I know. And it is pretty awful stuff, I agree. But you cannot think of self ahead of Rome from this day forward. Eat your own bread."

The boy's eyes traveled from face to face. He drew a breath, and said what had to be said. No adult could say it, they had too many years and too many fears for this and that and everything.

"This is not a time for rejoicing. How can any of us feel glad? How can I feel glad?" He reached out for the fresh crisp white bread, took a piece, broke it, dipped it in olive oil, and thrust some into his mouth. "No one bothered to ask me seriously whether I wanted this unmanly job," he said, chewing with relish. "Oh yes, Gaius Marius asked me three times, I know! But what choice did I have, tell me that? The answer is, none. Gaius Marius is mad. We all know that, though we don't say it openly among ourselves as dinnertime conversation. He did this to me deliberately, and his reasons were not pious, not concerned with the welfare of Rome, religious or otherwise." He swallowed the bread. "I am not yet a man. Until I am, I will not wear that frightful gear. I will put on my belt and my *toga praetexta* and decently comfortable footwear. I will eat whatever I like. I will go to the Campus Martius to perform my drills, practise my swordplay, ride my horse, handle my shield, throw my *pilum*. When I am a man and my bride is my wife, we shall see. Until then, I will not act as *flamen Dialis* inside the bosom of my family or when it interferes with the normal duties of a noble Roman boy."

Complete silence followed this declaration of independence. The mature members of the family tried to find the right response, feeling for the first time some of the helplessness the crippled, incapacitated Gaius Marius had felt when he came up against that will of iron. What could one do? wondered the father, who shrank from locking the boy in his sleeping cubicle until he changed his mind, for he did not think the treatment would work. More determined by far, Aurelia seriously contemplated the same course of action, but knew much better than her husband that it would not work. The wife and son of the man who had generated all this unhappiness were too aware of the truth to be angry, too aware of their own inability to change things to be righteous. Mucia Tertia, awed at the size and good looks of her new husband, unused to a family circle which spoke frankly, gazed at her knees. And Young Caesar's sisters, older than he and therefore used to him since his infancy, looked at each other ruefully.

Julia broke the silence by saying peacefully, "I think you are quite right, Young Caesar. At half past thirteen, the most sensible things you can do are to eat good food and keep exercising vigorously. After all, Rome may need your health and skills one day, even if you are the *flamen Dialis.* Look at poor old Lucius Merula. I'm sure he never expected to have to act as consul. But when he had to, he did. No one deemed him less the priest of Jupiter, or impious."

The senior in age among the women, Julia was allowed to have her way—if for no other reason that it presented the boy's parents with an attitude which prevented a permanent breach between them and their difficult son.

Young Caesar ate wheaten leavened bread and eggs and olives and chicken until his hunger pangs vanished, then patted his belly, replete. He was not a poor eater, but food interested him little, and he knew perfectly well that he could have gone without the crusty white bread, could have satisfied himself with the other. But it was better that his family understood from the beginning how he felt about his new career, and how he intended to approach it. If Aunt Julia and Young Marius were rendered unhappy and guilty by his words, that was too bad. Vital to the well-being of Rome the priest of Jupiter might be, yet the appointment was not of his choosing, and Young Caesar knew in his heart that the Great God had other things for him to do than sweep out the temple.

Dietary crisis aside, declaration of independence aside, it was a bitter meal. So much unsaid, so much which had to remain unsaid. For everybody's sake. Perhaps Young Caesar's candidness had saved the dinner; it drew the focus of everyone's thoughts away from the atrocities of Gaius Marius, the madness of Gaius Marius.

"I'm glad today is over," said Aurelia to Caesar as they went to their bedroom.

"I never want another such," said Caesar with feeling.

Before she removed her clothes Aurelia sat on the edge of the bed and looked up at her husband. He seemed fatigued—but then, he always did. How old was he? Almost forty-five. The consulship was passing him by, and he was no Marius, no Sulla. Gazing at him now, Aurelia knew suddenly that he would never be consul. A great deal of the blame for that, she thought, must be laid at my feet. If he had a less busy and independent wife, he would have spent more time at home this last decade, and made more of a reputation for himself in the Forum. He's not a fighter, my husband. And how can he go to a madman to ask for the funds to mount a serious campaign to be elected consul? He won't do it. Not from fear. From pride. The money is sticky with blood now. No decent man would want to use it. And he is the most decent of men, my husband.

"Gaius Julius," she said, "what can we do about our son and his flaminate? He hates it so!"

"Understandably. However," he said with a sigh, "I will never be consul now. And that means he would have a very difficult time of it becoming consul himself. With this war in Italy, our money has dwindled. You may as well say I've lost the thousand *iugera* of land I bought in Lucania because it was so cheap. It's too far from a town ever to be safe, I suspect. After Gaius Norbanus turned the Lucanians back from Sicily last year, the insurgents have gone to earth in places like my land. And Rome will not have the time, the men or the money to chase them out, even in our son's lifetime. So all that remains is my original endowment, the six hundred *iugera* Gaius Marius bought for me near Bovillae. Enough for the back benches of the Senate, not the *cursus honorum*. You might say

Gaius Marius took the land back again. His troops have ruined it in these last months while they roamed Latium."

"I know," said Aurelia sadly. "Our poor son will have to be content with his flaminate, won't he?"

"I fear so."

"He's so convinced Gaius Marius did it on purpose!"

"Oh, I think he did," said Caesar. "I was there in the Forum. He was—*indecently* pleased with himself."

"Then my son has received scant thanks for all the time he gave Gaius Marius after his second stroke."

"Gaius Marius has no gratitude left. What frightened me was the fear in Lucius Cinna. He told me that no one was safe, even Julia and Young Marius. After seeing Gaius Marius, I believe him."

Caesar had removed his clothes, and Aurelia saw with faint alarm that he had lost weight; his ribs and hipbones were showing, his thighs were farther apart.

"Gaius Julius, are you well?" she asked abruptly.

He looked surprised. "I think so! A little tired, perhaps, but not ill. It's probably that sojourn in Ariminum. After three years of Pompey Strabo's marching up and down, there's very little left to feed legions with anywhere in Umbria or Picenum. So we had short commons, Marcus Gratidianus and I, and if one cannot feed the men well, one cannot eat well oneself. I seemed to spend most of my time riding all over the place looking for supplies."

"Then I shall feed you nothing but the very best food," she said, one of her rare smiles lighting up her drawn face. "Oh, I wish I thought things were going to get better! But I have a horrible feeling they're going to get worse." She stood up and began to divest herself of her gown.

"I share your feeling, *meum mel*," he said, sitting on his side of the bed and swinging his legs onto it. Sighing luxuriously, he tucked his hands behind his head on the pillow, and smiled. "However, while we live at all, this is one thing cannot be taken from us."

She crawled in beside him and snuggled her face into his

shoulder; his left arm came down and encircled her. "A very nice thing," she said gruffly. "I love you, Gaius Julius."

When the sixth day of Gaius Marius's seventh consulship dawned, he had his tribune of the plebs Publius Popillius Laenas convene yet another Plebeian Assembly. Only Marius's Bardyaei were present in the well of the Comitia to hear the proceedings. For almost two days they had been under orders to behave, had had to clean the city and disappear from sight. But Young Marius was gone to Etruria, and the rostra was bristling again with all those heads. Only three people stood on the rostra—Marius himself, Popillius Laenas, and a prisoner cast in chains.

"This man," shouted Marius, "tried to procure my death! When I—old and infirm!—was fleeing from Italy, the town of Minturnae gave me solace. Until a troop of hired assassins forced the magistrates of Minturnae to order my execution. Do you see my good friend Burgundus? It was Burgundus deputed to strangle me as I lay in a cell beneath the Minturnaean capitol! All alone and covered in mud. Naked! I, Gaius Marius! The greatest man in the history of Rome! The greatest man Rome will ever produce! A greater man than Alexander of Macedon! Great, great, great!" He ran down, looked bewildered, sought for memory, then grinned. "Burgundus refused to strangle me. And, taking their example from a simple German slave, the whole town of Minturnae refused to see me killed. But before the hired assassins—a paltry lot, they wouldn't even do the deed themselves!—left Minturnae, I asked their leader who had hired them. 'Sextus Lucilius,' he said."

Marius grinned again, spread his feet and stamped them in what apparently he fancied was a little dance. "When I became consul for the seventh time—what other man has been consul of Rome seven times?—it pleased me to allow Sextus Lucilius to think no one knew he hired those men. For five days he was foolish enough to remain in Rome, deeming himself safe. But this morning before it was light and he was out of his bed, I sent my lictors to arrest him. The charge is treason. He tried to procure the death of Gaius Marius!"

No trial was ever shorter, no vote was ever taken more cavalierly; without counsel, without witnesses, without due form and procedure, the Bardyaei in the well of the Comitia pronounced Sextus Lucilius guilty of treason. Then they voted to have him cast down from the Tarpeian Rock.

"Burgundus, I give the task of casting this man from the rock to you," said Marius to his hulking servant.

"I will do so gladly, Gaius Marius," rumbled Burgundus.

The whole assemblage then moved to a better place from which to view the execution; Marius himself, however, remained on the rostra with Popillius Laenas, its height affording it a superb outlook toward the Velabrum. Sextus Lucilius, who had said nothing in his defense nor allowed any expression on his face save contempt, went to his death gallantly. When Burgundus, a great golden glitter in the distance, led Lucilius to the end of the Tarpeian overhang, he didn't wait to be picked up and tossed away; instead, he leaped of his own accord and almost brought the German down as well, for Burgundus had not let go of his chains.

This defiant independence and the risk to Burgundus angered Marius terribly; dark red in the face, he choked and spluttered, began to roar his outrage at the dismayed Popillius Laenas.

The weak little light still illuminating his mind was snuffed out in a torrent of blood. Gaius Marius fell to the floor of the rostra as if poleaxed, lictors clustering about him, Popillius Laenas calling frantically for a stretcher or a litter. And all those heads of old rivals, old enemies, ringed Marius's inert body round, teeth beginning to show in the skull's grin because the birds had feasted.

Cinna, Carbo, Marcus Gratidianus, Magius, and Vergilius came down from the Senate steps at a run, displacing the lictors as they gathered about the fallen form of Gaius Marius.

"He's still breathing," said his adopted nephew, Gratidianus.

"Too bad," said Carbo under his breath.

"Get him home," said Cinna.

By this time the members of Marius's slave bodyguard had learned of the disaster and had crowded round the base of the rostra, all weeping, some wailing outlandishly.

Cinna turned to his own chief lictor. "Send to the Campus Martius and summon Quintus Sertorius here to me urgently," he said. "You may tell him what has happened."

While Marius's lictors carried him off on a stretcher and the Bardyaei followed up the hill, still wailing, Cinna, Carbo, Marius Gratidianus, Magius, Vergilius and Popillius Laenas came down off the rostra and waited at its base for Quintus Sertorius; they sat on the top tier of the Comitia well, trying to regain their senses.

"I can't believe he's still alive!" said Cinna in wonder.

"I think he'd get up and walk if someone stuck two feet of good Roman sword under his ribs," said Vergilius, scowling.

"What do you intend to do, Lucius Cinna?" asked Marius's adopted nephew, who agreed with everyone's attitude but could not admit it, and so preferred to change the subject.

"I'm not sure," said Cinna, frowning. "That's why I'm waiting for Quintus Sertorius. I value his counsel."

An hour later Sertorius arrived.

"It's the best thing could have happened," he said to all of them, but particularly to Marius Gratidianus. "Don't feel disloyal, Marcus Marius. You're adopted, you have less Marian blood in you than I do. But, Marian though my mother is, I can say it without fear or guilt. His exile drove him mad. He is not the Gaius Marius we used to know."

"What should we do, Quintus Sertorius?" asked Cinna.

Sertorius looked astonished. "About what? *You* are the consul, Lucius Cinna! It's up to you to say, not to me."

Flushing scarlet, Cinna waved his hand. "About the duties of the consul, Quintus Sertorius, I am in no doubt!" he snapped. "What I called you here for was to ask you how best we can rid ourselves of the Bardyaei."

"Oh, I see," said Sertorius slowly. He was still wearing a bandage about his left eye, but the discharge seemed to have dried up, and he looked comfortable enough with his handicap.

"Until the Bardyaei are disbanded, Rome still belongs to Marius," said Cinna. "The thing is, I doubt they'll want to be disbanded.

They've had a taste of terrorizing a great city. Why should they stop because Gaius Marius is incapacitated?"

"They can be stopped," said Sertorius, smiling nastily. "I can kill them."

Carbo looked overjoyed. "Good!" he said. "I'll go and fetch whatever men are left across the river."

"No, no!" cried Cinna, horrified. "Another battle in the streets of Rome? We don't dare after the past six days!"

"I *know* what to do!" said Sertorius, impatient at these silly interruptions. "Lucius Cinna, tomorrow at dawn you must summon the leaders of the Bardyaei to you here at the rostra. You must tell them that even in extremis Gaius Marius thought of them, and gave you the money to pay them. That will mean you must be seen to enter Gaius Marius's house today, and stay there long enough to make it look as if you could have talked to him."

"Why do I need to go to his house?" asked Cinna, shrinking at the thought.

"Because the Bardyaei will spend the whole of today and tonight in the street outside Gaius Marius's door, waiting for news."

"Yes, of course they will," said Cinna. "I'm sorry, Quintus Sertorius, I'm not thinking very well. What then?"

"Tell the leaders that you have arranged for the whole of the Bardyaei to receive their pay at the Villa Publica on the Campus Martius at the second hour of day," said Sertorius, showing his teeth. "I'll be waiting with my men. And that will truly be the end of Gaius Marius's reign of terror."

When Gaius Marius was carried into his house Julia looked down at him with terrible grief, infinite compassion. He lay with eyes closed, breathing stertorously.

"It is the end," she said to his lictors. "Go home, good servants of the People. I will see to him now."

She bathed him herself, shaved a six-day stubble from his cheeks and chin, clothed him in a fresh white tunic with the help of Strophantes, and had him put into his bed. She didn't weep.

"Send for my son and for the whole family," she said to the steward when Marius was ready. "He will not die for some time, but he will die." Sitting in a chair beside the Great Man's bed, she gave Strophantes further instructions against the background horror of that snoring, bubbling respiration—the guest chambers were to be readied, sufficient food was to be prepared, the house must look its best. And Strophantes should send for the best undertaker. "I do not know a single name!" she said, finding that strange. "In all the time I have been married to Gaius Marius, the only death in this house was that of our little second son, and Grandfather Caesar was still alive, so he looked after things."

"Perhaps he will recover, *domina,*" said the weeping steward, grown middle-aged in Gaius Marius's service.

Julia shook her head. "No, Strophantes, he will not."

Her brother Gaius Julius Caesar, his wife, Aurelia, their son, Young Caesar, and their daughters Lia and Ju-ju arrived at noon; having much further to travel, Young Marius did not arrive until after nightfall. Claudia, the widow of Julia's other brother, declined to come, but sent her young son—another Sextus Caesar—to represent his branch of the family. Marius's brother, Marcus, had been dead for some years, but his adopted son, Gratidianus, was present. As was Quintus Mucius Scaevola Pontifex Maximus and his second wife, a second Licinia; his daughter, Mucia Tertia, was of course already in Marius's house.

Of visitors there were many, but not nearly as many as there would have been a month earlier. Catulus Caesar, Lucius Caesar, Antonius Orator, Caesar Strabo, Crassus the censor—their tongues could no longer speak, their eyes no longer see. Lucius Cinna came to call several times, the first time tendering the apologies of Quintus Sertorius.

"He can't leave his legion at the moment."

Julia glanced at him shrewdly, but said only, "Tell dear Quintus Sertorius that I understand completely—and agree with him."

This woman understands everything! thought Cinna, flesh creeping. He took his leave as quickly as he could, given that he had to stay long enough to make it look as if he might have spoken to Marius.

The vigil was continuous, each member of the family taking a turn to sit with the dying man, Julia in her chair beside him. But when his turn came, Young Caesar refused to enter that room.

"I may not be in the presence of death," he said, face smooth, eyes innocent.

"But Gaius Marius is not dead," said Aurelia, glancing at Scaevola and his wife.

"He might die while I was there. I couldn't allow that," said the boy firmly. "After he is dead and his body removed, I will sweep out his room in the purification rites."

The trace of derision in his blue gaze was so slight only his mother saw it. Saw it and felt a numbness crawling through her jaw, for in it she recognized a perfect hate—not too hot, not too cold, not at all devoid of cerebration.

When Julia finally emerged to rest—Young Marius having removed her physically from her husband's side—it was Young Caesar who went to her and took her away to her sitting room. On the point of getting up, Aurelia read a different message in her son's eyes, and subsided immediately. She had lost all her control of him, he was free.

"You must eat," said the boy to his beloved aunt, settling her full length on her couch. "Strophantes is coming."

"Truly, I am not hungry!" she said in a whisper, face as white as the bleached linen cover the steward had spread on the couch for her to rest upon; her own bed was the one she shared with Gaius Marius, she had no other in that house.

"Hungry or not, I intend to feed you a little hot soup," Young Caesar said in that voice even Marius had not argued against. "It's necessary, Aunt Julia. This could go on for many days. He won't leave go of life easily."

The soup came, together with some cubes of stale bread; Young Caesar made her drink soup and sippets, sitting on the edge of the couch and coaxing softly, gently, inexorably. Only when the bowl was empty did he desist, and then took most of the pillows away, covered her, smoothed back the hair from her brow tenderly.

"How good you are to me, little Gaius Julius," she said, eyes clouding with sleep.

"Only to those I love," he said, paused, and added, "Only to those I love. You. My mother. No one else." He bent over and kissed her on the lips.

While she slept—which she did for several hours—he sat curled in a chair watching her, his own eyelids heavy, though he would not let them fall. Drinking her in tirelessly, piling up a massive memory; never again would she belong to him in the way she did sleeping there.

Sure enough, her waking dispelled the mood. At first she tried to panic, calming when he assured her Gaius Marius's condition had not changed in the least.

"Go and have a bath," her nurse said sternly, "and when you come back, I'll have some bread and honey for you. Gaius Marius does not know whether you're with him or not."

Finding herself hungry after sleeping and bathing, she ate the bread and honey; Young Caesar remained curled in his chair, frowning, until she rose to her feet.

"I'll take you back," he said, "but I cannot enter."

"No, of course you can't. You're *flamen Dialis* now. I'm so sorry you hate it!"

"Don't worry about me, Aunt Julia. I'll solve it."

She took his face between her hands and kissed him. "I thank you for all your help, Young Caesar. You're such a comfort."

"I only do it for you, Aunt Julia. For you, I would give my life." He smiled. "Perhaps it's not far from the truth to say I already have."

Gaius Marius died in the hour before dawn, when life is at its ebbing point and dogs and cockerels cry. It was the seventh day of his coma, and the thirteenth day of his seventh consulship.

"An unlucky number," said Scaevola Pontifex Maximus, shivering and rubbing his hands together.

Unlucky for him but lucky for Rome, was the thought in almost every head when he said it.

"He must have a public funeral," said Cinna the moment he arrived, this time accompanied by his wife, Annia, and his younger daughter, Cinnilla, who was the wife of the *flamen Dialis*.

But Julia, dry-eyed and calm, shook her head adamantly. "No, Lucius Cinna, there will be no State funeral," she said. "Gaius Marius is wealthy enough to pay for his own funeral expenses. Rome is in no condition to argue about finances. Nor do I want a huge affair. Just the family. And that means I want no word of Gaius Marius's death to leave this house until after his funeral is over." She shuddered, grimaced. "Is there any way we can get rid of those dreadful slaves he enlisted at the last?" she asked.

"That was all taken care of six days ago," said Cinna, going red; he never could conceal his discomfort. "Quintus Sertorius paid them off on the Campus Martius and ordered them to leave Rome."

"Oh, of course! I forgot for the moment," said the widow. "How kind of Quintus Sertorius to solve our troubles!" No one there knew whether or not she was being ironic. She looked across to her brother, Caesar. "Have you fetched Gaius Marius's will from the Vestals, Gaius Julius?"

"I have it here," he said.

"Then let it be read. Quintus Mucius, would you do that for us?" she asked of Scaevola.

It was a short testament, and turned out to be very recent; Marius had made it, apparently, while he lay with his army to the south of the Janiculum. The bulk of his estate went to his son, Young Marius, with the maximum he could allow left to Julia in her own right. A tenth of the estate he bequeathed to his adopted nephew, Marcus Marius Gratidianus, which meant Gratidianus was suddenly a very wealthy man; the estate of Gaius Marius was enormous. And to Young Caesar he left his German slave, Burgundus, as thanks for all the precious time out of his boyhood Young Caesar had given up to help an old man recover the use of his left side.

Now why did you do that, Gaius Marius? asked the boy silently of himself. Not for the reason you say! Perhaps to ensure the cessation of my career should I manage to deflaminate myself? Is he to kill me when I pursue the public career you do not want me to have? Well, old man, two days from now you'll be ashes. But I will not do what a prudent man ought to do—kill the Cimbric lump.

He loved you, just as once I loved you. It is a poor reward for love to be done to death—be that death of the body or the spirit. So I will keep Burgundus. And make him love *me*.

The *flamen Dialis* turned to Lucius Decumius. "I am in the way here," he said. "Will you walk home with me?"

"You're going? Good!" said Cinna. "Take Cinnilla home for me, would you? She's had enough."

The *flamen Dialis* looked at his seven-year-old *flaminica*. "Come, Cinnilla," he said, giving her the smile he was well aware worked woman-magic. "Does your cook make good cakes?"

Shepherded by Lucius Decumius, the two children emerged into the Clivus Argentarius and walked down the hill toward the Forum Romanum. The sun was risen, but its rays were not yet high enough to illuminate the bottom of the damp gulch wherein lay the whole reason for Rome's being.

"Well, look at that! The heads are gone again! I wonder, Lucius Decumius," the *flamen Dialis* mused as his foot touched the first flagstone at the rim of the Comitia well, "if one sweeps the dead presence out of the place where he died with an ordinary broom, or if one has to use a special broom?" He gave a skip, and reached for his wife's hand. "There's nothing for it, I'm afraid! I shall have to find the books and read them. It would be dreadful to get one iota of the ritual wrong for my benefactor Gaius Marius! If I do nothing else, I must rid us of *all* of Gaius Marius."

Lucius Decumius was moved to prophesy, not because he had the second sight, but because he loved. "You'll be a far greater man than Gaius Marius," he said.

"I know," said Young Caesar. "I know, Lucius Decumius, I know!"

FINIS

AUTHOR'S NOTE

The First Man in Rome, which was the initial book in this projected series of novels, laid in the backdrop of an alien world. After it, I am obliged by the sheer length of this project to restrict my detail to what is necessary to advance characters and plot—both of which, being history, are in one sense already established.

Wherever possible, anachronisms are avoided; but sometimes an anachronistic word or phrase is the only way to get one's point across. There are not many. What I would like my readers to know is that each one of them has been carefully considered before being resorted to. I am, after all, writing in English for an audience separated by two thousand years from the people and events which make up these books; even the greatest of the modern scholars on the period has occasionally to resort to anachronisms.

The Glossary that follows has been rewritten. Some items have been removed, others inserted. There are now entries under: Arausio, Battle of; Saturninus; the Gold of Tolosa: all events or people featuring in *The First Man in Rome,* now become part of history as far as events and people in *The Grass Crown* are concerned.

Some of the drawings are repeated, as these characters are still important. Others have been added. The likenesses of Marius, Sulla, King Mithridates, and Young Pompey are authentic, the others taken from anonymous (that is, unidentified) portrait busts of Republican date. As no portrait busts of famous Republican Romans are known to have been taken in their youth, the drawing of Young Pompey is the first I have "youthened." It is the famous bust of Pompey in his fifties with the weight of middle age removed and the lines of living taken out of the face. I did this because Pultarch assures us that the Young Pompey was striking and beautiful enough to remind his contemporaries of Alexander the Great—*very* difficult to see in the likeness of the middle-aged man! However, once the extra thirty-odd pounds are removed, one can discern a very attractive young man.

The style of the maps has changed somewhat. One learns by experience and actually has the opportunity to mend earlier style mistakes, a luxury open to me because I am writing sequentially.

A word about the bibliography. For those who have written to me (care of the publisher) requesting a copy—do not despair! It is coming, if it has not already arrived. The trouble is that I have produced two novels—each over 400,000 words in length and drafted several times—within twelve months of each other. Spare time is not something I have had, and the formal compilation of a bibliography is a daunting task. Hopefully now done with.

I must thank a few people by name, and others too numerous to single out by name. My classical editor, Dr. Alanna Nobbs of Macquarie University, Sydney. Miss Sheelah Hidden. My agent, Frederick T. Mason. My editors, Carolyn Reidy and Adrian Zackheim. My husband, Ric Robinson. Kaye Pendleton, Ria Howell, Joe Nobbs, and the staff.

LIST OF CONSULS

99 (655 A.U.C.)[*]
 Marcus Antonius Orator (censor 97)
 Aulus Postumius Albinus

98 (656 A.U.C.)
 Quintus Caecilius Metellus Nepos
 Titus Didius

97 (657 A.U.C.)
 Gnaeus Cornelius Lentulus
 Publius Licinius Crassus (censor 89)

96 (658 A.U.C.)
 Gnaeus Domitius Ahenobarbus (Pontifex Maximus, censor 92)
 Gaius Cassius Longinus

95 (659 A.U.C.)
 Lucius Licinius Crassus Orator (censor 92)
 Quintus Mucius Scaevola (Pontifex Maximus 89)

94 (660 A.U.C.)
 Gaius Coelius Caldus
 Lucius Domitius Ahenobarbus

---

[*]A.U.C.: *Ab Urbe Condita* (years from founding of Rome in 753)

93 (661 A.U.C.)
   Gaius Valerius Flaccus
   Marcus Herennius

92 (662 A.U.C.)
   Gaius Claudius Pulcher
   Marcus Perperna (censor 86)

91 (663 A.U.C.)
   Sextus Julius Caesar
   Lucius Marcius Philippus (censor 86)

90 (664 A.U.C.)
   Lucius Julius Caesar (censor 89)
   Publius Rutilius Lupus

89 (665 A.U.C.)
   Gnaeus Pompeius Strabo
   Lucius Porcius Cato Licinianus

88 (666 A.U.C.)
   Lucius Cornelius Sulla
   Quintus Pompeius Rufus

87 (667 A.U.C.)
   Gnaeus Octavius Ruso
   Lucius Cornelius Cinna
   Lucius Cornelius Merula (*flamen Dialis,* consul *suffectus*)

86 (668 A.U.C.)
   Lucius Cornelius Cinna (second term)
   Gaius Marius (seventh term)
   Lucius Valerius Flaccus (consul *suffectus*)

GLOSSARY

ABSOLVO   The term employed by a jury when voting for the acquittal of the accused. It was used in the courts, not in the Assemblies.

advocate   The term generally used by modem scholars to describe a man active in the Roman law courts. "Lawyer" is considered too modern, hence is not used in this book.

aedile   There were four Roman magistrates called aediles; two were called plebeian aediles, two were called curule aediles. Their duties were confined to the city of Rome. The plebeian aediles were created first (in 493 B.C.) to assist the tribunes of the plebs in their duties, but, more particularly, to guard the rights of the plebs in relation to their headquarters, the temple of Ceres in the Forum Boarium. Elected by the Plebeian Assembly, the plebeian aediles soon inherited supervision of the city's buildings as a whole, as well as archival custody of laws (plebiscites) passed in the Plebeian Assembly, together with any senatorial decrees (*consulta*) directing the passage of plebiscites. In 367 B.C. two curule aediles were created to give the patricians a share in custody of public buildings and archives; they were elected by the Assembly of the People in their tribes. Very soon, however, the curule aediles were as likely to be plebeians as patricians by status. From the third century B.C. onward, all four were responsible for the care of Rome's streets, water supply, drains and sewers, traffic, public buildings, monuments and facilities, markets, weights and measures (standard sets of these were housed in the basement of the temple of Castor and Pollux), games, and the public grain supply. They had the power to fine citizens and noncitizens alike for infringements of any regulations connected to any of the above, and deposited the monies in their coffers to help fund the games. Aedile—plebeian or curule—was not a part of the *cursus honorum,* but because of the games was a valuable magistracy for a praetorian hopeful to hold.

Aeneas   Prince of Dardania, in the Troad. He was the son of King Anchises and the goddess Aphrodite (Venus to the Romans). When Troy fell to the forces of Agamemnon, he fled the burning city with his aged father perched on his shoulders and the Palladium under one arm. After many adventures, he arrived in Latium and founded the race from whom true Romans were descended. His son, Iulus, was the direct ancestor of the Julian family; therefore the identity of Iulus's mother was of some import. Virgil says Iulus was actually Ascanius, the son of Aeneas by his Trojan wife, Creusa, Aeneas having brought the boy with him from Troy (Ilium to the Romans). On the other hand, Livy says Iulus was the son of Aeneas by his Latin wife, Lavinia. What the Julian family of Caesar's day believed is not known. I shall go with Livy, who seems on the whole a more reliable source than Virgil.

Aesernia   A small city in northwestern Samnium. It was given the Latin Rights in 263 B.C. to encourage its people to be loyal to Rome rather than to Samnium, the traditional Italian enemy of Rome.

Africa   During the Roman Republic, the word "Africa" referred to that part of the North African coast around Carthage—modern Tunisia.

Africa Province   That part of Africa which physically belonged to Rome. In size it was quite small—basically, the out-thrust of land which contained Carthage and Utica. This Roman territory was surrounded by the much larger Numidia.

ager publicus   Land vested in Roman public ownership, most of it acquired by right of conquest or taken off its original owners as a punishment for disloyalty. This latter was particularly true of *ager publicus* in the Italian peninsula. The censors leased it out on behalf of the State in a manner favoring large estates. There was Roman *ager publicus* in every overseas province, in Italian Gaul, and in the Italian peninsula. The most famous and contentious of all the many pieces of *ager publicus* was the *ager Campanus,* extremely rich land which had once belonged to the city of Capua, and was confiscated by Rome after several Capuan insurrections.

Agger A part of the Servian Walls of Rome, the Agger protected the city on its most vulnerable side, the Campus Esquilinus. The Agger consisted of a double rampart bearing formidable fortifications.

Allies of Rome Quite early in the history of the Roman Republic, its magistrates began to issue the title "Friend and Ally of the Roman People" to peoples and/or nations who had assisted Rome in an hour of need; the most usual form of assistance was military. The first Allies were located in the Italian peninsula, and as time went on toward the later Republic, those Italian peoples not enfranchised as full Roman citizens nor possessed of the Latin Rights were deemed the Italian Allies. Rome assured them military protection and gave them some other concessions, but in return they were expected to give Rome troops whenever she asked, and to support those troops in the field without financial assistance from Rome. Abroad, peoples and/or nations began to earn the title too; for instance, the Aedui of Gallia Comata and the Kingdom of Bithynia were formally deemed Allies. The Italian nations were mostly called "the Allies," while overseas nations were accorded the full title "Friend and Ally of the Roman People."

Amor Literally, "love." Because it is "Roma" spelled backward, the Romans of the Republic commonly believed it was Rome's vital secret name.

amphora Plural, amphorae. A pottery vessel, bulbous in shape, the amphora had a narrow neck and two handles connecting the shoulders with the upper neck; its bottom was pointed or conical, rather than flat, which meant it could not be stood upright on level ground. It was used for the bulk transport (usually maritime) of wheat and other grains, wine, oil, and other pourable substances. Its pointed bottom enabled it to be fitted easily into the sawdust which filled the ship's hold or the cart's interior, so that it was cushioned and protected during its journey. This pointed bottom also enabled it to be dragged across level ground with considerable ease when being loaded and unloaded. The customary sized amphora held about twenty-five liters (six American gallons), which made it too heavy and awkward to be shouldered.

Anatolia Roughly, modern Asian Turkey. It extended from the south coast of the Euxine Sea (the Black Sea) to the north coast of the Mediterranean, and from the Aegean Sea in the west to modern Russian Armenia, Iran, Iraq, and Syria in the east. The Taurus and Anti-taurus mountains made its interior and much of its coastline very rugged, but it was then, as now, fertile and arable. The climate of the interior was continental.

Antiochus The generic name of many of the Kings of Syria and other, smaller kingdoms in that part of the East.

Apulia That part of southeastern Italy extending from Samnium in the north to ancient Calabria in the south (the back of the Italian leg). Fertile enough when there was water, the region has always suffered greatly from a sparse rainfall. Its people, the Apuli, were considered very poor and backward. The major towns were Luceria, Venusia, Barium, and Canusium.

aquilifer Presumably a creation of Gaius Marius's at the time he gave the legions their silver eagles. The best man in the legion, the *aquilifer* was chosen to carry the legion's silver eagle, and was expected never to surrender it to the enemy. As a mark of his distinction, he wore a wolf skin or a lion skin over his head and shoulders, and all his decorations for valor.

Arausio, Battle of On October 6, 105 B.C., the three Germanic peoples (Cimbri, Teutones, and Tigurini/Marcomanni/Cherusci) who had been trying to migrate for fifteen years met Rome in battle outside the town of Arausio, in the valley of the Rhodanus (the Rhone). Due to a complete lack of co-operation between the two Roman commanders, Gnaeus Mallius Maximus and Quintus Servilius Caepio, the Roman forces were both separated from each other and hopelessly positioned; the result was the worst defeat in the history of the Republic. Eighty thousand Roman soldiers died.

Arpinum A town in Latium not far from the border of Samnium, and probably originally populated by Volsci. Together with Formiae Fundi, it was the last Latin Rights community to receive the full Roman citizenship (in 188 B.C.), but it did not enjoy proper municipal status during the late Republic. Arpinum's chief claim to fame was as the birthplace and homeland of two very distinguished men, Gaius Marius and Marcus Tullius Cicero.

artillery Before the employment of gunpowder, these were military machines, usually spring-driven or spring-loaded, capable of launching projectiles—boulders, rocks, stones, darts, canister, grape, or bolts. Among the various kinds of Roman artillery were the *ballista,* the *catapultus,* and the *onager.*

Arx The Capitoline Mount of the city of Rome was divided into two humps by a declivity called the Asylum; the Arx was the more northern of the two humps, and contained the temple of Juno Moneta.

as The smallest in value of the coins issued by Rome; ten of them equaled one denarius. They were bronze. I have avoided all mention of the *as* in this book because of (a) its relative unimportance, and (b) its identical spelling to the English language adverb and/or conjunction "as"—most confusing!

Asia Minor Basically, modern Turkey, Syria, Iran, Iraq, and Armenia. So little was known by the ancients about Arabia that its inclusion in Asia Minor was ephemeral; the Black Sea and the Caucasus formed the northern boundary of Asia Minor.

Asia Province The Roman province left to Rome in the will of King Attalus III of Pergamum. It consisted of the west coast and hinterland of what is now Turkey, from the Troad and Mysia in the north to the Cnidan peninsula in the south; thus it included Caria, but not Lycia. Its capital in Republican times was Pergamum, but Smyrna, Ephesus, and Halicarnassus rivaled the seat of the governor in importance. The islands lying off its coast—Lesbos, Lemnos, Samos, Chios, et cetera—were a part of the province. Its people were sophisticated and highly commercial in outlook, and were the descendants of successive waves of Greek colonization—Aeolian, Dorian, Ionian. It was not centralized in the modern sense, but was administered by Rome as a series of separate communities which were largely self-governing and gave tribute to Rome.

Assembly (*comitia*) Any gathering of the Roman People convoked to deal with governmental, legislative, judicial, or electoral matters. In the time of Marius and Sulla there were three true Assemblies—of the Centuries, the Whole People, and the Plebs.

The **Centuriate Assembly** (*comitia centuriata*) marshaled the People, patrician and plebeian, in their Classes, which were filled by a means test and were economic in nature. As this was originally a military assembly, each Class gathered in the form of Centuries (which by the time of Marius and Sulla numbered far in excess of one hundred men per century, as it had been decided to keep the number of Centuries in each Class the same). The Centuriate Assembly met to elect consuls, praetors, and (every five years) censors. It also met to hear trials involving a charge of major treason, and could pass laws. Because of the unwieldy nature of the Centuriate Assembly, which had to meet outside the *pomerium* on the Campus Martius at a place called the *saepta,* it was in normal times not convoked to pass laws or hear trials.

The **Assembly of the People** (*comitia populi tributa*) allowed the full participation of patricians, and was tribal in nature. It was convoked in the thirty-five tribes into which all Roman citizens were placed. When speaking of this Assembly throughout the book, I have mostly chosen to call it the Whole People to avoid confusion. It was called together by a consul or praetor, and elected the quaestors, the curule aediles, and the tribunes of the soldiers. It could formulate laws and conduct trials. The normal meeting place was in the lower Forum Romanum, in the Well of the Comitia.

The **Plebeian Assembly** (*comitia plebis tributa* or *concilium plebis*) did not allow the participation of patricians, and met in the thirty-five tribes. The only magistrate empowered to convoke it was the tribune of the plebs. It had the right to enact laws (strictly, plebiscites) and conduct trials. Its members elected the plebeian aediles and the tribunes of the plebs. The normal meeting place was in the Well of the Comitia.

In no Roman Assembly could the vote of one individual be credited directly to his wants; in the Centuriate Assembly his vote was incorporated into the vote of his Century in his Class, his Century's majority vote then being cast as a single vote; in the two tribal Assemblies his vote was incorporated into the vote of his tribe, the majority vote of the tribe then being cast as one single vote.

atrium The main reception room of a Roman *domus* or private house; it contained a rectangular opening in the roof (the *compluvium*), below which was a pool (the *impluvium*). Originally the purpose of the pool was to provide a reservoir of water for household use, but by the late Republic the pool was usually purely ornamental.

Attalus III The last King of Pergamum, and ruler of most of the Aegean coast of western Anatolia as well as inland Phrygia. In 133 B.C. he died at a relatively early age, and without heirs closer than a collection of cousins. His will bequeathed his kingdom to Rome, much to the chagrin of the cousins, who promptly went to war against Rome. The insurrection was put down by Manius Aquillius in 129 and 128 B.C., after which Aquillius settled to organize the bequest as the Roman province of Asia. While going about this task, Aquillius sold most of Phrygia to the fifth King Mithridates of Pontus for a sum of gold which he put into his own purse. Discovered by those in Rome, this deed of greed permanently crippled the reputation of the family Aquillius.

Attic helmet An ornate helmet worn by Roman officers above the rank of centurion. It is the kind of helmet commonly worn by the stars of Hollywood Roman epic movies—though I very much doubt that any Attic helmet of Republican times was crested with ostrich feathers! There were ostrich feathers available, but their employment would have been deemed decadent, to say the least.

auctoritas A very difficult Latin term to translate, as it meant far more than the English word "authority" implies. It carried nuances of pre-eminence, clout, leadership, public importance, and—above all—the ability to influence events through sheer public reputation. All the magistracies possessed *auctoritas* as a part of their very nature, but *auctoritas* was not confined to those who held magistracies; the Princeps Senatus, Pontifex Maximus, consulars, and even some private individuals outside the Senate could also own *auctoritas*. Where the term occurs in the book, I have left it untranslated.

augur   A priest whose duties concerned divination rather than prognostication. He and his fellow augurs comprised the College of Augurs, an official State body, and at the time of this book numbered twelve, six patricians and six plebeians. Until 104 B.C., when Gnaeus Domitius Ahenobarbus passed his *lex Domitia de sacerdotiis,* new augurs had been co-opted by those already in the College; after that law, augurs had to be elected by an Assembly of seventeen tribes chosen by lot. The augur did not predict the future, nor did he pursue his auguries at his own whim; he inspected the proper objects or signs to ascertain whether or not the projected undertaking was one having the approval of the gods, be the undertaking a meeting, a war, a proposed new law, or any other State business, including elections. There was a standard manual of interpretation to which the augur referred; augurs "went by the book." The augur wore the *toga trabea* (see that entry), and carried a curved staff called the *lituus.*

auxiliary   A legion of non-citizens incorporated into a Roman army was called an auxiliary legion; its soldiers were also called auxiliaries, and the term extended to cavalry as well. In the time of Marius and Sulla, most auxiliary infantry was Italian in origin, whereas most auxiliary cavalry was Numidian, Gallic, or Thracian, all lands where the soldiers habitually rode horses. The Roman soldier (and the Italian soldier) was not enamored of horses.

barbarian   Derived from a Greek word having strong onomatopoeic overtones; on first hearing these peoples speak, the Greeks thought they sounded "bar-bar," like animals barking. The word "barbarian" was used to describe races and nations deemed uncivilized, lacking in any admirable or desirable culture. Gauls, Germans, Scythians, Sarmatians, and Dacians were considered barbarian.

basilica   A large building devoted to public activities such as courts of law, and also to commercial activities in shops and offices. The basilica was two-storeyed and clerestory-lit, and incorporated an arcade of shops under what we might call verandah extensions along either side. During the Republic it was erected at the expense of some civic-minded Roman nobleman, usually of consular status, often censorial as well. The first basilica was built by Cato the Censor on the Clivus Argentarius next door to the Senate House, and was known as the Basilica Porcia; as well as accommodating banking institutions, it was also the headquarters of the College of Tribunes of the Plebs. At the time of this book, there also existed the Basilica Aemilia, the Basilica Sempronia, and the Basilica Opimia, all on the fringes of the lower Forum Romanum.

Bellona The Roman goddess of war. Her temple lay outside the *pomerium* or sacred boundary of the city on the Campus Martius, and was vowed in 296 B.C. by the great Appius Claudius Caecus. A group of special priests called *fetiales* conducted her rituals. A large vacant piece of land lay in front of the temple of Bellona, and was known as Enemy Territory.

Bithynia A kingdom flanking the Propontis (the modern Sea of Marmara) on its Asian side, extending east to Paphlagonia and Galatia, south to Phrygia, and southwest to Mysia. It was fertile and prosperous, and was ruled by a series of kings of Thracian origin—the first two were named Prusias, the rest Nicomedes. The traditional enemy of Bithynia was Pontus. From the time of Prusias II, Bithynia enjoyed the status Friend and Ally of the Roman People.

boni Literally, "the Good Men." First mentioned in a play by Plautus called *The Captives,* the term came into political use during the days of Gaius Gracchus. He used it to describe his followers—but so also did his enemies Opimius and Drusus. It then passed gradually into general use, indicating men of intensely conservative political inclination; the "true" government of Rome in this book—that is, the faction led by the consul Gnaeus Octavius Ruso—would have described its members as *boni.*

Brennus A king of the Gauls (or Celts) during the third century B.C. Leading a large confraternity of Celtic tribes, Brennus invaded Macedonia and Thessaly in 279 B.C., turned the Greek defense at the pass of Thermopylae and sacked Delphi, in which battle he was badly wounded. He then penetrated into Epirus and sacked the enormously rich oracular precinct of Zeus at Dodona; and went on to sack the richest precinct in the world, that of Zeus at Olympia in the Greek Peloponnese. Retreating before a determined Greek guerrilla resistance, Brennus returned to Macedonia, where he died of his wound. Without Brennus to hold them together, his Gauls were rudderless. Some of them (the Tolistobogii, the Trocmi, and a segment of the Volcae Tectosages) crossed the Hellespont into Asia Minor and settled in a land thereafter called Galatia. Those Volcae Tectosages who did not go to Asia Minor returned to their homeland around Tolosa in southwestern Gaul; with them they carried the entire loot of Brennus's campaign, holding it in trust against the return of the rest of the tribes to Gaul. Apparently they melted the gold and silver down (turning the silver into gigantic millstones) before hiding it in various sacred lakes within the precinct of Herakles in Tolosa. The gold amounted to fifteen thousand talents. See also **Gold of Tolosa**.

Burdigala   Modern Bordeaux, in southwestern France. A great Gallic *oppidum* (fortress) belonging to the Aquitani, it lay on the south bank of the Garumna River (the modern Garonne) near its mouth. In 107 B.C. it was the scene of a debacle, when a combined force of Germans and Aquitani annihilated the Roman army of Lucius Cassius Longinus, consul (with Gaius Marius) in that year. Lucius Calpurnius Piso Caesoninus was killed, as was Cassius himself. Only Gaius Popillius Laenas and a handful of men survived.

Calabria   Confusing for those who know modern Italy better than they do ancient Italy! Nowadays Calabria is the toe of the boot, but in ancient times Calabria was the heel. Brundisium was its most important city, followed by Tarentum. The region was not mightily involved in the Marsic War, though its people, the Calabri, were sympathetic to the Italian cause.

Campania   A fabulously rich and fertile basin, volcanic in origin and soil, Campania lay between the Apennines of Samnium and the Tuscan Sea, and extended from Tarracina in the north to a point well south of the modern Bay of Naples. Watered by the Liris, Volturnus/Calor, Clanius, and Sarnus rivers, it grew bigger, better, and more of everything than any other region in Italy, even Italian Gaul of the Padus. Colonized during the seventh century B.C. by the Greeks, it fell under Etruscan domination, then affiliated itself to the Samnites (of whom there was a large element in its population), and eventually became subject to Rome. Because of the Greek and

Samnite population, it was always an area prone to insurrection, and lost much of its best countryside to Rome as Roman **ager publicus**. The towns of Capua, Teanum Sidicinum, Venafrum, Acerrae, Nola, and Interamna were important inland centers, while the ports of Puteoli, Neapolis, Herculaneum, Pompeii, Surrentum, Stabiae, and Salemum constituted the best on Italy's west coast. Puteoli was the largest and busiest port in all of Italy. The Viae Campana, Appia, and Latina passed through it.

campus   Plural, *campi*. A plain, or a flat expanse of ground.

Campus Esquilinus   The area of flat ground outside the Servian Walls and the double rampart of the Agger, between the Querquetulan Gate and the Colline Gate. Here lay Rome's necropolis.

Campus Martius   Situated to the north and northwest of the Servian Walls of Rome, the Campus Martius was bounded by the Capitol to its south and the Pincian Hill on its east; the rest of it was enclosed by a huge bend in the Tiber River. On the Campus Martius armies awaiting their general's triumph were bivouacked, military exercises and the training of the young went on, the stables and exercise tracks for horses engaged in chariot racing were situated, assemblies of the *comitia centuriata* took place, and market gardening vied with public parklands. The Tiber swimming hole of the Trigarium lay at the apex of the bend, and just to the north of that were medicinal mineral hot springs called the Tarentum. The Via Lata (Via Flaminia) crossed the Campus Martius on its way to the Mulvian Bridge, and the Via Recta bisected it at right angles to the Via Lata.

Campus Vaticanus   Situated on the opposite (north) bank of the Tiber from the Campus Martius, the Campus Vaticanus was an area of market gardening and had no importance in the Rome of Marius and Sulla.

Cannae   An Apulian town on the Aufidius River in southeastern Italy. Here in 216 B.C., Hannibal and his Punic army (allied with the Samnites) met a Roman army commanded by Lucius Aemilius Paullus and Gaius Terentius Varro. The Roman army was annihilated; until the Battle of Arausio in 106 B.C., it ranked as Rome's worst military disaster. Somewhere between 30,000 and 60,000 men died. The survivors were made to pass beneath the yoke (see **yoke**).

Capena Gate   Porta Capena. This was one of the two most strategic gates in Rome's Servian Walls (the other was the Colline Gate). It lay south of the Circus Maximus, and outside it was the common road which branched into the Via Appia and the Via Latina about half a mile from the gate itself.

capite censi   Literally, "Head Count." The *capite censi* were those full Roman citizens too poor to belong to one of the five economic classes, and so were unable to vote in the Centuriate Assembly at all. As most *capite censi* were urban in origin as well as in residence, they largely belonged to urban tribes, which numbered only four out of the total thirty-five tribes; this meant they had little influence in either of the tribal Assemblies, People or Plebs (see also **Head Count,** *proletarii*).

Cappadocia   A kingdom located in central Anatolia (it is still known today as Cappadocia). Lying at high altitude, the land was created by the outpourings of many volcanos, the most notable of which was Mount Argaeus; Cappadocia's only township, Eusebeia Mazaca, lay on the lower flanks of this mighty cone. Bountifully watered and rich of soil, Cappadocia was perpetually coveted by the more powerful kings to its north (Pontus) and south (Syria). However, Cappadocia maintained its own line of kings, who usually went by the title Ariarathes. The people were akin to the people of Pontus. The temple-state of Ma at Comana, rich enough to keep 6,000 temple slaves, was reserved as a fief for the reigning king's brother, who functioned as its high priest.

Capua   The most important inland town in Campania. A history of broken pledges of loyalty to Rome led to Roman reprisals which stripped Capua of its extensive and extremely valuable public lands; these became the nucleus of the *ager Campanus,* and included, for instance, the fabulous vineyards which produced Falernian wines. By the time of Marius and Sulla, Capua's economic well-being depended upon the many military training camps, gladiatorial schools, and slave camps for bulk-lot prisoners that lay on the town's outskirts; the people of Capua made their livings from supplying and servicing these huge institutions.

Carinae   One of Rome's more exclusive addresses. The Carinae (which incorporated the Fagutal) was the northern tip of the Oppian Mount on its western side; it extended between the Velia and the Clivus Pullius. Its outlook was southwestern, across the swamps of the Palus Ceroliae toward the Aventine.

Carthage   Capital and chief center of the trading empire founded by Phoenician colonists in central North Africa (modern Tunisia). Situated on one of the finest harbors in the Mediterranean, Carthage's port facilities were enhanced by massive man-made improvements. After Scipio Aemilianus terminated the activities of the Carthaginians in the Third Punic War, Carthage itself virtually ceased to exist.

Caudine Forks   In 321 B.C. a Roman army was trapped in a gulch known as the Caudine Forks, somewhere near the Samnite town of Beneventum. It surrendered to the Samnite Gavius Pontius, who forced its soldiers to pass beneath the yoke, a terrible disgrace.

Celtiberian   The name given to the members of that segment of the Celtic race which crossed the Pyrenees into Spain and settled in its central, northwestern, and northeastern regions. By the time of Marius and Sulla the Celtiberians were so well ensconced that they were generally regarded as indigenous to Spain.

Celts   More the modern than the ancient term for a barbarian race which emerged from north-central Europe during the early centuries of the first millennium B.C. From about 500 B.C. onward, the Celts attempted to invade the lands of the European Mediterranean; in Spain and Gaul they succeeded, whereas in Italy, Macedonia, and Greece they failed. However, in Italian Gaul, Umbria, and Picenum in Italy (as well as in Macedonia, Thessaly, Illyricum, and Moesia) they seeded whole populations which gradually admixed with older local stock. Racially the Celts were different from, yet akin to, the later Germans; they considered themselves a discrete people, and had a more complex religious culture than the Germans. Their languages were similar in some ways to Latin. A Roman rarely if ever used the word "Celt"; he said "Gaul."

censor   The censor was the most senior of all Roman magistrates, though he lacked imperium and was not therefore escorted by lictors. No man who had not already been consul could seek election as censor, and only those consulars owning tremendous *auctoritas* and *dignitas* normally bothered to stand. To be elected censor (by the Centuriate Assembly) was a complete vindication of a man's political career, as it told Rome he was one of the very top men. Two censors were elected to serve together for a period of five years called the *lustrum,* though the censors were active in their duties only for about the first eighteen months. The censors inspected and regulated membership in the Senate, the Ordo Equester (the knights), the holders of the Public Horse (the 1,800 most senior knights), and conducted a general census of Roman citizens throughout the Roman world. They also applied the means test. State contracts and various public works and buildings were in the domain of the censors.

census Every five years the **censors** brought the roll of the citizens of Rome up to date. The name of every Roman citizen male was entered on these rolls, together with information about each man's tribe, his economic class, his property and means, and his family. Neither women nor children were formally registered as being Roman citizens, though there are cases documented in the ancient sources in which a woman was awarded the Roman citizenship in her own right. The city of Rome's census was taken on the Campus Martius at a special station erected for the purpose; those living elsewhere in Italy had to report to the authorities at the nearest municipal registry, and those living abroad to the provincial governor. There is some evidence, however, that the censors of 97 B.C., Lucius Valerius Flaccus and Marcus Antonius Orator, changed the manner by which citizens living outside Rome but inside Italy were enrolled.

Centuriate Assembly See **Assembly**.

centurion The regular officer of both Roman citizen and auxiliary legions. It is a mistake to equate him with the modern noncommissioned officer; centurions were complete professionals enjoying a status uncomplicated by our modern social distinctions. A defeated Roman general hardly turned a hair if he lost military tribunes, but tore his hair out in clumps if he lost centurions. Centurion rank was graduated; the most junior *centurio* (plural, *centuriones*) commanded a group of eighty soldiers and twenty noncombatants called a century. In the Republican army as reorganized by Gaius Marius, each cohort had six centurions, with the most senior man—the *pilus prior*—commanding the senior century of his cohort as well as commanding his entire cohort. The ten men commanding the ten cohorts making up a legion were also ranked in seniority, with the legion's most senior centurion, the *primus pilus,* answering only to his legion's commander (either one of the elected tribunes of the soldiers, or one of the general's legates). Promotion during Republican times was up from the ranks.

chersonnese   The name the Greeks gave to a peninsula, though they used it somewhat more flexibly than modern geographers employ the term peninsula. Thus the Tauric Chersonnese, the Cimbrian Chersonnese, the Thracian Chersonnese, the Cnidan Chersonnese, et cetera.

Chios   A large island in the Aegean Sea, lying off the coast of Asia Minor (the Roman Asia Province) near Smyrna. Chios was chiefly famous for its wine, which had no peer. After an accident to his flagship caused by a Chian ship, King Mithridates VI of Pontus ever after harbored a huge grudge against Chios and Chians.

Cilicia   Cilicia was that part of southern Anatolia lying opposite the Cleides peninsula of Cyprus and extending westward as far as the further end of Cyprus, where it adjoined Pamphylia. Its eastern border lay along the Amanus mountains, which separated it from Syria. Western Cilicia was harsh, arid, and extremely mountainous, but eastern Cilicia (known as Cilicia Pedia) was a large and fertile plain watered by the Pyramus, the Sarus and the Cydnus rivers. Its capital was Tarsus, on the Cydnus. Modern scholars hold differing opinions as to when Cilicia was formally made a province of Rome, but there seems to me plenty of evidence to suggest that Marcus Antonius Orator annexed it during his campaign against the pirates in 101 B.C. Certainly Sulla was sent to govern Cilicia during the nineties, well before the Marsic War.

Cimbri   A very large confraternity of Germanic tribes who lived in the more northern half of the Cimbric Chersonnese (the modern

Jutland Peninsula) until about 120 B.C., when some natural disaster prompted them to migrate. Together with their southern neighbors, the Teutones, they began an epic trek to find a new homeland—a trek which lasted twenty years, took them thousands of miles, and finally brought them up against Rome—and Gaius Marius. They were virtually annihilated at the battle of Vercellae in 101 B.C.

citadel   Properly, a fortress atop a precipitous hill. Sometimes it lay within its own walls within a larger, more open fortress, as was the case with the Roman stronghold on the Janiculum.

citizenship   For the purposes of this book, the Roman citizenship. Possession of it entitled a man to vote in his tribe and his class (if he was economically qualified to belong to a class) in all Roman elections. He could not be flogged, he was entitled to the Roman trial process, and he had the right of appeal. At various times both his parents had to be Roman citizens, at other times only his father (hence the *cognomen* Hybrida); after the *lex Minicia* of 91 B.C., a Roman male marrying a non-Roman woman would have had to acquire *conubium* for his wife if the child was to be a Roman citizen. The male citizen became liable for military service on his seventeenth birthday, and had then to serve for ten campaigns or six years, whichever came first. Before Gaius Marius's army reforms, a citizen had to possess sufficient property to buy his own arms, armor, gear, and provisions if he was to serve in the legions; after Gaius Marius, legions contained both propertied men and men of the *capite censi,* the **Head Count**.

citocacia   A mild Latin profanity, meaning "stinkweed."

citrus wood   The most prized cabinet wood of the Roman world, seen at its very best during the last century of the Republic. Citrus wood was cut from vast galls on the root system of a cypresslike tree, *Callitris quadrivavis vent.*, which grew in the highlands of North Africa all the way from the Oasis of Ammonium, and Cyrenaica, to the far Atlas of Mauretania; it must be emphasized that the tree was no relation of orange or lemon, despite the name of its timber. Different trees produced different patterns in the grain, all of which had names—*tiger* had a long and rippling grain, *panther* a spiral grain, *peacock* had eyes like those in a peacock's tail, *parsley* a ruffled grain, and so on. In Republican times it was cut as solid wood rather than as a veneer (scarcity dictated veneer during the Empire), and always mounted upon an ivory leg or legs, usually inlaid with gold. Hence a special guild of tradesmen grew up, the *citrarii et eborarii,* combining citrus wood joiners with ivory carvers. Most citrus wood was reserved for making tabletops, where the beauty of its grain could really be displayed, but it was also turned as bowls. No tables have survived to modern times, but we do have a few bowls, and can see that citrus wood was certainly the most beautiful timber of all time.

classes These were five in number, and represented the economic divisions of property-owning or steady-income-earning Roman citizens. The members of the First Class were the richest, the members of the Fifth Class the poorest. The *capite censi* or Head Count did not have class status, and so could not vote in the Centuriate Assembly.

client In Latin, *cliens.* The term denoted a man of free or freed status (he did not have to be a Roman citizen, however) who pledged himself to a man he called his patron. In the most solemn and binding way, the client undertook to serve the interests and obey the wishes of his patron. In return he received certain favors—usually gifts of money, or a job, or legal assistance. The freed slave was automatically the client of his ex-master until discharged of this obligation—if he ever was. A kind of honor system governed the client's conduct in relation to his patron, and was remarkably consistently adhered to. To be a client did not necessarily mean a man could not be a patron; more that he could not be an ultimate patron, as technically his own clients were also the clients of his patron. During the Republic there were no formal laws concerning the client-patron relationship because they were not necessary—no man, client or patron, could hope to succeed in life were he known as dishonorable in this vital function. However, there were laws regulating the foreign client-patron relationship; foreign states or client-kingdoms acknowledging Rome as patron were legally obliged to find the ransom for any Roman citizen kidnapped in their territories, a fact that pirates relied on heavily for an additional source of income. Thus, not only individuals could become clients; whole towns and countries often were.

client-king   A foreign monarch might pledge himself as a client in the service of Rome as his patron, thereby entitling his kingdom to be called Friend and Ally of the Roman People. Sometimes, however, a foreign monarch pledged himself as the client of one Roman individual.

clivus   A street on an incline—that is, a hilly street. Rome, a city of hills, had many.

cognomen   Plural, *cognomina*. This was the last name of a Roman male anxious to distinguish himself from all his fellows possessed of an identical first and family name. In some families it became necessary to have more than one *cognomen:* for example, Quintus Caecilius Metellus Pius Scipio Nasica; Quintus was his first name (*praenomen*), Caecilius his family name (*nomen*), and Metellus Pius Scipio Nasica were all *cognomina*. The *cognomen* usually pointed up some physical characteristic or idiosyncrasy—jug ears, flat feet, hump back—or else commemorated some great feat—as in the Caecilii Metelli who were cognominated Dalmaticus, Balearicus, Numidicus, these being countries each man had conquered. Many *cognomina* were heavily sarcastic or extremely witty.

cohort   After the reforms Gaius Marius carried out upon the Roman legion, the cohort became the tactical unit of the legion. It comprised six centuries of troops; in normal circumstances, a legion owned ten cohorts. When discussing troop movements, it was customary to speak of tactical strength in terms of cohorts rather than legions—thus, twenty-five cohorts rather than two and a half legions, or five cohorts rather than half a legion.

college   A body or society of men having something in common. Thus, Rome owned priestly colleges (the College of Pontifices), political colleges (the College of Tribunes of the Plebs), religious colleges (the College of Lictors), and work-related colleges (the Guild of Undertakers). Certain groups of men from all walks of life, including slaves, banded together in what were called Crossroads Colleges to look after the city of Rome's crossroads and conduct the annual feast of the crossroads, the Compitalia.

colonnade   A roofed walkway flanked by one outer row of columns when attached to a building in the manner of a verandah, or two rows of columns, one on either side, if freestanding.

comitia   See **Assembly**.

Comitia   The large round well in which meetings of the *comitia* were held. It lay in the lower Forum Romanum adjacent to the steps of the Senate House and the Basilica Aemilia, and was formed of a series of tiers. When packed, perhaps three thousand men could be accommodated in it. The rostra, or speakers' platform, was attached to its side.

CONDEMNO   The word employed by a jury when delivering a verdict of "guilty." It was a term confined to the courts (see also *DAMNO*).

confarreatio   The oldest and the strictest of the three forms of Roman marriage. By the time of Marius and Sulla, only patricians still practised it—but by no means all patrician marriages were *confarreatio*, as it was not mandatory. The *confarreatio* bride passed from the hand of her father to the hand of her husband, thus preventing her acquiring any measure of independence; this was one reason why *confarreatio* was not a popular form of marriage, as the two easier forms allowed a woman more control over her dowry and business affairs. The other cause of its unpopularity lay in the extreme difficulty of dissolving it; divorce (*diffarreatio*) was a legally and religiously arduous business considered more trouble than it was worth unless the circumstances left no other alternative.

Conscript Fathers   When it was established by the kings of Rome, the Senate consisted of one hundred patricians titled *patres*—"fathers." Then, after the Republic was established and plebeians were also admitted to the Senate, and its membership had swelled to three hundred, and the censors were given the duty of appointing new senators, the word "conscript" came into use as well because the censors conscripted these new members. By the time of Marius and Sulla, the two terms had been run together and senators were addressed in the House as Conscript Fathers.

consul   The consul was the most senior Roman magistrate owning imperium, and the consulship (modern scholars do not refer to it as "the consulate" because a consulate is a modern diplomatic institution) was considered the top rung of the *cursus honorum*. Two consuls were elected each year by the Centuriate Assembly, and served for one year. The first day of the new consul's office was New Year's Day, January 1. The senior of the two consuls—who had polled his requisite number of centuries first—held the *fasces* for the month of January, which meant he officiated while his junior colleague looked on. Each consul was attended by twelve lictors, but only the lictors of the consul officiating during the month (it was the junior consul's turn in February, and they then alternated for the rest of the year) carried the *fasces* on their shoulders. By the first century B.C. consuls could be either patrician or plebeian, excepting only that two patricians could not hold office together. The proper age for a consul was forty-two, twelve years after entering the Senate at thirty. A consul's imperium knew no bounds; it operated not only in Rome, but throughout Italy and the overseas provinces as well, and overrode the imperium of a proconsular governor. The consul could command any army.

consular The name given to a man who had been consul. He was held in special esteem by the rest of the Senate, was asked to speak ahead of the junior magistrates, and might at any time be sent to govern a province should the Senate require the duty of him. He might also be asked to take on other duties, like caring for the grain supply.

consultum The proper term for a senatorial decree. It did not have the force of law. In order to become law, a *consultum* had to be presented by the Senate to any of the Assemblies, tribal or centuriate, which then voted it into law—*if* the members of the Assembly in question felt like voting it into law. However, many senatorial *consulta* (plural) were never submitted to an Assembly, nor voted into law, yet were accepted as law by all of Rome; such were senatorial decisions about who was going to govern a province—the declaration or pursuit of war—who has to command an army—and foreign affairs.

contio Plural, *contiones*. A preliminary meeting to discuss the promulgation of a law or any other comitial business. All three

Assemblies were required to debate a measure in *contio,* which, though no voting took place, was formally convoked by the magistrate so empowered in the particular Assembly concerned.

contubernalis A military cadet, a subaltern of lowest rank in the hierarchy of Roman legion officers, but excluding the centurions— no centurion was ever a cadet, he was an experienced soldier.

corona A crown. The word was usually confined to military decorations for the very highest valor. Those crowns mentioned in this book are:

corona graminea or ***obsidionalis*** The Grass Crown. Made of grass (or sometimes a cereal like wheat, if the battle took place in a field of grain) taken from the battlefield and awarded "on the spot," the Grass Crown was the rarest of all Roman military decorations. It was given only to a man who had by personal efforts saved a whole legion—or a whole army.

corona civica The Civic Crown. It was made of ordinary oak leaves. Awarded to a man who had saved the lives of fellow soldiers and held the ground on which he did this for the rest of the duration of a battle, it was not given unless the soldiers in question swore a formal oath before their general that such were the circumstances.

Crater Bay The name the Romans used when referring to what is today called the Bay of Naples. Though the ancient sources assure us that the eruption of Vesuvius in A.D. 79 was the first ever known, the name Crater Bay suggests that at some time during prehistory a much larger eruption of a volcano had created this huge bay.

cuirass The name for the armor which encased a man's upper body. It consisted of two plates of bronze or steel or hardened leather, one protecting the thorax and abdomen, the other his back from shoulders to lumbar spine. The plates were held together by straps or ties at the shoulders and along each side under the arms. Some cuirasses were exquisitely tailored to the contours of the torso, whereas others fitted all men of a certain size and physique. The men of highest rank—especially generals—wore cuirasses tooled in high relief and silver-plated (sometimes, though rarely, gold-plated). The general and his legates also wore a thin red sash around the cuirass about halfway between the nipples and the waist; this sash was ritually knotted and looped.

Cumae   This town was the first Greek colony in Italy, established early in the eighth century B.C. It lay on the Tuscan Sea side of Cape Misenum just to the north of Crater Bay, and was a very fashionable seaside resort for Republican Romans.

cunnus   A Latin obscenity of extremely offensive nature— "cunt." It meant the female genitalia.

Cuppedenis market   This area lay behind the upper Forum Romanum on its eastern side, between the Clivus Orbius and the edge of the Fagutal/Carinae. It was devoted to luxury and specialty items such as pepper, spices, incense, ointments and unguents and balms, and also served as the flower markets, where a Roman could buy anything from a bouquet to a garland to go round the neck or a wreath to go on the head. Until sold to finance Sulla's campaign against King Mithridates, the land belonged to the State.

Curia Hostilia   The Senate House. It was thought to have been built by Tullus Hostilius, the shadowy third of Rome's kings, hence its name ("meeting house of Hostilius").

cursus honorum   "The Way of Honor." If a man aspired to be consul, he had to take certain steps, collectively called the *cursus honorum*. First he was admitted to the Senate (in the time of Marius and Sulla, he was appointed by the censors or was elected a tribune of the plebs—the office of quaestor did not then automatically admit a man to the Senate); he had to serve as a quaestor, either before admission to the Senate or after it; a minimum of nine years after entering the Senate he had to be elected a praetor; and finally, two years after serving as a praetor, he could stand for the consulship. The four steps—senator, quaestor, praetor, consul—constituted the *cursus honorum*. All other magistracies, including the censorship, were independent of the *cursus honorum* and did not constitute a part of it.

curule chair   The *sella curulis* was the ivory chair reserved exclusively for magistrates owning imperium—a curule aedile sat in one, a plebeian aedile did not. In style, the curule chair was beautifully carved from ivory, with curved legs crossing in a broad X; it was equipped with low arms, but had no back.

custodes   These were the minor officials who took care of electoral procedures—tally clerks, keepers of the ballot tablets, et cetera.

DAMNO   This was the word used to deliver a verdict of condemnation (that is, "guilty") in a trial conducted by one of the Assemblies. It did not belong to the courts, which used *CONDEMNO*. The glossary entry in my first Roman book was not informative because I hadn't tracked the words down; when rereading Dr. L. R. Taylor's *Roman Voting Assemblies* during the writing of *The Grass Crown,* I discovered the information now tendered. Research never stops! Nor does one get everything out of a valuable book on first reading.

Delphi   The great sanctuary of the god Apollo, lying in the lap of Mount Parnassus, in central Greece. From very ancient times it was an important center of worship, though not of Apollo until about the seventh or sixth century B.C. The shrine contained an *omphalos* or navel stone (probably a meteorite), and Delphi itself was thought to be the center of the earth. An oracle of awesome fame resided at Delphi, its prophecies delivered by a crone in a state of ecstatic frenzy; she was known as Pythia, or the Pythoness. Fabulously rich due to the constant stream of costly gifts from grateful petitioners, Delphi was sacked and plundered several times during antiquity (see **Brennus**), but recovered quickly afterward, as the gifts never stopped coming in.

demagogue   Originally a Greek concept, meaning a politician whose chief appeal was to the crowds. The Roman demagogue preferred the arena of the Comitia well to the Senate House, but it was no part of his policy to "liberate the masses," nor on the whole were those who listened to him composed of the very lowly. The term was employed by ultra-conservative factions within the Senate to describe the more radical tribunes of the plebs.

denarius   Plural, denarii. Save for a very rare issue or two of gold coins, the denarius was the largest denomination of coin during the Roman Republic. Of pure silver, it contained about

3.5 grams of the metal, and was about the size of a dime—very small. There were 6,250 denarii in one silver talent.

diadem A thick white ribbon about one inch (25 mm) wide, each end embroidered, and often finished with a fringe. It was worn tied around the head, either across the forehead or behind the hairline, and was knotted at the back beneath the occiput; the ends trailed down onto the shoulders. Originally a mark of Persian royalty, the diadem became the symbol of the Hellenistic monarch after Alexander the Great removed it from the tiara of the Persian kings as being a more appropriately Greek understatement of kingship than either a crown or a tiara. It could be worn only by a reigning sovereign but was not confined to the male sex—women wore the diadem too.

dignitas A concept peculiar to Rome, *dignitas* cannot be translated to mean English "dignity." It was a man's personal share of public standing in the community, and involved his moral and ethical worth, his reputation, his entitlement to respect and proper treatment by his peers and by the history books. *Auctoritas* was public, *dignitas* personal, an accumulation of clout and standing stemming from a man's own personal qualities and achievements. Of all the assets a Roman nobleman possessed, *dignitas* was likely to be the one he was most touchy about; to defend it, he might be prepared to go to war or into exile, to commit suicide, or to execute his wife and son. I have elected to leave the term in my text untranslated.

diverticulum In the sense used in this book, a road connecting the main arterial roads which radiated out from the gates of Rome—in effect, a "ring road."

Dodona A temple and precinct sacred to Zeus. Located among the inland mountains of Epirus some ten miles to the south and west of Lake Pamboris, it was the home of a very famous oracle situated in a sacred oak tree which was also the home of doves. Like all the great oracular shrines, Dodona was the recipient of many gifts, and was in consequence extremely rich. It was sacked several times in antiquity: by the Aetolians in 219 B.C., by the Roman Aemilius Paullus in 167 B.C., and by the Scordisci in 90 B.C. On each occasion, the temple recovered quickly and accumulated more riches.

dominus Literally, "lord." *Domine,* the vocative case, was used in address. *Domina* meant "lady" and *dominilla* "little lady."

Ecastor! The exclamation of surprise or amazement considered polite and permissible for women to utter. Its root suggests it invoked Castor.

Edepol! The exclamation of surprise or amazement considered polite and permissible for men to utter when in the company of women. Its root suggests it invoked Pollux.

Elysian Fields Republican Romans had no real belief in the intact survival of the individual after death, though they did believe in an underworld and in "shades," which latter were rather mindless and characterless effigies of the dead. To both Greeks and Romans, however, certain men were considered by the gods to have lived lives of sufficient glory (rather than merit) to warrant their being preserved after death in a place called Elysium, or the Elysian Fields. Even so, these privileged shades were mere wraiths, and could only come to re-experience human emotions and appetites after drinking blood. The living human being requiring an audience with a dweller in the Elysian Fields had to dig a pit on the border, sacrifice his animal, and fill the pit with blood. After drinking, the shade could talk.

emporium This word had two meanings. It could denote a seaport whose commercial activities were tied up in maritime trade, as in the case of the island of Delos; or it could denote a large waterfront building where importers and exporters had their offices.

epulones Some of the religious holidays in the Republican year were celebrated by a feast, or a feast was a part of the day's festivities. The task of organizing these feasts was the responsibility of the College of Epulones, a minor priestly institution. If the feast involved only the Senate or a similarly small number of men, catering for it was easy; but some feasts involved the entire free population of Rome. Originally there had been only three *epulones,* but by the time of Marius and Sulla, there were eight or ten of them.

ergastula Singular, *ergastulum.* These were locked barracks for criminals or slaves. *Ergastula* became infamous when large-scale pastoralists increased in numbers from the time of the Brothers

Gracchi onward; such land leasers used chain-gang labor to run their *latifundia* (ranches) and locked them into *ergastula*.

ethnarch   The Greek word for a city or town magistrate.

Etruria   The Latin name for what had once been the kingdom of the Etruscans. It incorporated the wide coastal plains west of the Apennines, from the Tiber in the south to the Arnus in the north. During the late Republic its most important towns were Veii, Cosa, and Clusium. The Viae Aurelia, Clodia, and Cassia ran through it.

Euxine Sea   The modern Black Sea. It was extensively explored by the Greeks during the seventh and sixth centuries B.C., and several colonies of Greek traders were established on its shores. Because of the large number of mighty rivers which emptied into it, it was always less salty than other seas, and the current through the Thracian Bosporus and the Hellespont always flowed from the Euxine to the Aegean—a help leaving, a hindrance entering. By far the most powerful nation bordering it was Pontus; the Euxine shores were subdued and conquered by the sixth King Mithridates of Pontus. However, Bithynia controlled the Thracian Bosporus, the Propontis, and the Hellespont, and so made a large income from levying duty and passage fees upon ships passing through these bodies of water. Bithynia's ownership of the Euxine entrance undoubtedly accounted for the bitter enmity between Bithynia and Pontus.

extortion   See *repetundae*.

faction   This is the term usually applied to Republican Roman political groups by modern scholars. These groups could in no way be called political parties in the modern sense, as they were extremely flexible, with a constantly changing membership. Rather than form around an ideology, the Republican Roman faction formed around an individual owning enormous *auctoritas* or *dignitas*. I have completely avoided the terms "Optimate" and "Popularis" because I do not wish to give any impression that political parties existed.

fasces   The *fasces* were bundles of birch rods ritually tied together in a crisscross pattern by red leather thongs. Originally an emblem of the Etruscan kings, they passed into the customs of the emerging Rome, persisted in Roman public life throughout the

Republic, and on into the Empire. Carried by men called lictors, they preceded the curule magistrate (and the propraetor and proconsul as well) as the outward symbol of his imperium. Within the *pomerium,* only the rods went into the bundles, to signify that the curule magistrate had only the power to chastise; outside the *pomerium* axes were inserted into the bundles, to signify that the curule magistrate also had the power to execute. The number of *fasces* indicated the degree of imperium—a dictator had twenty-four, a consul (and proconsul) twelve, a praetor (and propraetor) six, and a curule aedile two.

fasti This Latin word actually meant days on which business could be transacted, but by the time of Marius and Sulla it had come to mean several other things: the calendar, lists relating to holidays and festivals, and the list of consuls (this last probably because Republican Romans did not reckon their years by number as much as by who had been consuls). The entry in the glossary to *The First Man in Rome* contains a fuller explanation of the calendar than space permits me here—under *fasti*, of course.

flamen Plural, *flamines.* A priest of a very special kind. There were fifteen *flamines,* three major and twelve minor. The three major *flamines* were the *flamen Dialis* (priest of Jupiter Optimus Maximus), the *flamen Martialis* (priest of Mars), and the *flamen Quirinalis* (priest of Quirinus). Save for the *flamen Dialis*, no *flamen* seemed to have very onerous duties, yet the three major priests at least received their housing and living at the expense of the State. They were probably Rome's most ancient pontifices.

Fortuna The Roman goddess of fortune, and one of the most fervently worshipped deities in the Roman pantheon. There were many temples to Fortuna, each dedicated to the goddess in a different guise or light. But the aspect of Fortuna who mattered most to politicians and generals was Fortuna Huiusque Diei—"The Fortune of This Present Day." Even men as formidably intelligent and able as Gaius Marius, Lucius Cornelius Sulla, and Gaius Julius Caesar the Dictator believed in the machinations of Fortuna implicitly, and courted her favor.

forum   An open-air meeting place for all kinds of business, public and private. Some fora (plural) were devoted to meat, others to vegetables, or fish, or grain, while others witnessed political assemblies and the business of government. Even an army camp had its forum, situated alongside the general's tent.

freedman   A manumitted slave. Though technically a free man (and, if his former master was a Roman citizen, a Roman citizen himself), the freedman remained in the patronage of his former master. At the time of Marius and Sulla he had little chance to exercise his right to vote in the tribal assemblies, as he belonged to one of two urban tribes—Esquilina and Suburana. If he was of superior ability or ruthlessness, he might, however, be able to vote in the classes of the Centuriate Assembly once he acquired sufficient wealth; freedmen capable of amassing a fortune usually bought their way into a rural tribe and so possessed the complete franchise.

free man   A man born free and never sold into slavery (except as a *nexus* or debt slave, which was rare among Roman citizens during the time of Marius and Sulla, though still prevalent among the Italian Allies).

Fregellae   This had been a Latin Rights community with an unblemished record of loyalty to Rome; then in 125 B.C. it revolted against Rome and was crushed by the praetor Lucius Opimius in circumstances of singular cruelty. Destroyed completely, the town never recovered. It was situated on the Via Latina and the Liris River just across the border in Samnium.

Further Spain   Hispania Ulterior. This was the further of Rome's two Spanish provinces—that is, it lay further away from Rome than the other province, called Nearer Spain. In the time of Marius and Sulla the border between Nearer and Further Spains was somewhat tenuous. By and large, the Further province encompassed the entire basins of the Baetis and Anas rivers, the ore-bearing mountains in which the Baetis and the Anas rose, the Atlantic littoral from the Pillars of Hercules to Olisippo at the mouth of the Tagus, and the Mediterranean littoral from the Pillars to the port of Abdera. The largest city by far was Gades, but the seat of the governor was Corduba. Strabo calls it the richest growing land in the world.

Gallia Comata   Long-haired Gaul. Having excluded the Roman province of Gaul-across-the-Alps, Gallia Comata incorporated modern France and Belgium, together with that part of Holland south of the Rhine. The Rhine throughout its length formed the border between Gaul and Germania. The inhabitants of all areas away from the Rhine were Druidical Celts; close to the Rhine the strains were mixed due to successive invasions of Germans. Long-haired Gaul was so called because its peoples wore their hair uncut.

games   In Latin, *ludi*. They were a Roman institution and pastime which went back at least as far as the very early Republic, and probably a lot further. At first they were celebrated only when a general triumphed, but in 336 B.C., the *ludi Romani* became an annual event held in honor of Jupiter Optimus Maximus, whose feast day occurred on September 13. At first the *ludi Romani* were over in a single day, but as the Republic aged they increased in length; at the time of Marius and Sulla they went on for ten days. Though there were a few rather half-hearted boxing and wrestling bouts, Roman games never possessed the athletic nature of Greek games. At first the games consisted mostly of chariot races, then gradually came to incorporate animal hunts, and plays performed in specially erected theaters. On the first day of every games, there was a spectacular religious procession through the Circus, after which came a chariot race or two, and then the boxing and wrestling, limited to this first day. The succeeding days were taken up with plays in the theater; tragedies were far less popular than comedies, and by the time of Marius and Sulla mimes were most popular of all. Then as the games drew to a close, chariot racing reigned supreme, with wild beast hunts to vary the program. Gladiatorial combats did *not* form a part of Republican games (they were put on by private individuals, usually as part of a funeral, in the Forum Romanum rather than in the Circus). The games were put on at the expense of the State, though men ambitious to make a name for themselves dug deep into their purses when serving as aediles to make "their" games more spectacular than the State allocation of funds permitted. Most of the big games were held in the Circus Maximus, some of the smaller ones in the Circus Flaminius. Free Roman citizen men and women could attend (there was no admission charge), with women segregated in the theater but not in the Circus; neither slaves nor freedmen were allowed admission, probably because even the Circus Maximus, which held perhaps 150,000 people, was not large enough to contain freedmen as well as free men.

Gaul-across-the-Alps   Gallia Transalpina. I have preferred to endow Gallia Transalpina with a more pedestrian name because of the hideous confusion nonclassical readers would experience if they had to deal with Cis and Trans. Gnaeus Domitius Ahenobarbus won the Roman Gallic province for Rome just before 120 B.C. to ensure that Rome would have a safe land route for her armies marching between Italy and Spain. The province consisted of a coastal strip all the way from Liguria to the Pyrenees, with two inland incursions—one to Tolosa in Aquitania, the other up the valley of the Rhodanus as far as the trading post of Lugdunum (Lyon).

gens   Plural, *gentes.* A Roman clan whose members all owned the same *nomen* or family name, also called the gentilicial name. Julius, Domitius, Cornelius, Aemilius, Servilius, Livius, Porcius, Junius and Licinius were all gentilicial names, for example. All the genuine members of the same *gens* (that is, excluding freed slaves who adopted their masters' names) could trace their line back to a common ancestor. The terms *gens* was feminine gender, hence *gens Julia, gens Cornelia, gens Servilia,* and so forth.

gig   A two-wheeled vehicle drawn by either two or four animals, more usually mules than horses. The gig was very lightly and flexibly built within the limitations of ancient vehicles—springs and shock absorbers did not exist—and was the vehicle of choice for a Roman in a hurry because it was easy for the animals to draw, therefore speedy. However, it was open to the elements. In Latin it was *cisia.* The two-wheeled closed-in carriage, a heavier and slower vehicle, was called the *carpentum.*

gladiator   A soldier of the sawdust, a professional warrior who performed his trade before an audience as a form of entertainment. An inheritance from the Etruscans, he always flourished throughout Italy, including Rome. During the Republic he was an honorable as well as an heroic figure, was well cared for and free to come and go. His origins were several: he might be a deserter from the legions, a condemned criminal, a slave, or a free man who voluntarily signed himself up. In Republican times he served for perhaps four to six years, and on an average fought perhaps five times in any one year; it was rare for him to die, and the Empire's "thumbs-up, thumbs-down" verdict was still far in the future. When he retired he was prone to hire himself out as a bodyguard or bouncer. To own a gladiatorial school was considered a smart investment for a Roman businessman.

Gold of Tolosa   Perhaps several years after 278 B.C., a segment of the tribe Volcae Tectosages returned from Macedonia to their homeland around Aquitanian Tolosa (modern Toulouse) bearing the accumulated spoils from many sacked temples (see **Brennus**). These were melted down and stored in the artificial lakes which dotted the precincts of Tolosa's temples; the gold was left lying undisturbed beneath the water, whereas the silver was regularly hauled out—it had been formed into gigantic millstones which were used to grind the wheat. In 106 B.C. the consul Quintus Servilius Caepio was ordered during his consulship to make war against migrating Germans who had taken up residence around Tolosa. When he arrived in the area he found the Germans gone, for they had quarreled with their hosts, the Volcae Tectosages, and been ordered away. Instead of fighting a battle, Caepio the Consul found a vast amount of gold and silver in the sacred lakes of Tolosa. The silver amounted to 10,000 talents (250 imperial tons) including the millstones, and the gold to 15,000 talents (370 imperial tons). The silver was transported to the port of Narbo and shipped to Rome, whereupon the wagons returned to Tolosa and were loaded with the gold; the wagon train was escorted by one cohort of Roman legionaries, some 520 men. Near the fortress of Carcasso the wagon train of gold was attacked by brigands, the soldier escort was slaughtered, and the wagon train disappeared, together with its precious cargo. It was never seen again.

At the time no suspicion attached to Caepio the Consul, but after the odium he incurred over his conduct at the battle of Arausio a year later, it began to be rumored that Caepio the Consul had organized the attack on the wagon train and deposited the gold in Smyrna in his own name. Though he was never tried for the Great Wagon Train Robbery, he was tried for the loss of his army, convicted, and sent into exile. He chose to spend his exile in Smyrna, where he died in 100 B.C. The story of the Gold of Tolosa is told in the ancient sources, which do not state categorically that Caepio the Consul stole it. However, it seems logical. And there is no doubt that the Servilii Caepiones who succeeded Caepio the Consul down to the time of Brutus (the last heir) were fabulously wealthy. Nor is there much doubt that most of Rome thought Caepio the Consul responsible for the disappearance of more gold than Rome had in the Treasury.

Good Men   See *boni*.

governor   A convenient English word to describe the consul or praetor, proconsul or propraetor, who—usually for the space of one year—ruled a Roman province in the name of the Senate and People of Rome. The degree of imperium the governor owned varied, as did the extent of his commission. However, no matter what his imperium, while in his province he was virtual king of it. He was responsible for its defense, administration, the gathering of its taxes and tithes, and all decisions pertaining to it. Provinces notoriously difficult to govern were generally given to consuls, peaceful backwaters to praetors.

The Gracchi   More generally known as the Brothers Gracchi. Cornelia, the daughter of Scipio Africanus and Aemilia Paulla, was married when eighteen years old to the forty-five-year-old Tiberius Sempronius Gracchus; the year was about 172 B.C., and Scipio Africanus had been dead for twelve years. Tiberius Sempronius Gracchus was consul in 177 B.C., censor in 169 B.C. and consul a second time in 163 B.C. By the time he died in 154 B.C. he was the father of twelve children. However, they were a universally sickly brood; only three of them did Cornelia manage to raise to adulthood, despite assiduous care. The oldest of these three was a girl,

Sempronia, who was married as soon as she was of age to her cousin Scipio Aemilianus. The two younger children were boys. Tiberius was born in 163 B.C., his brother Gaius not until the year of his father's death, 154 B.C. Thus both boys owed their upbringing to their mother, who by all accounts did a superlative job.

Both the Brothers Gracchi served under their mother's first cousin (and their own brother-in-law) Scipio Aemilianus—Tiberius during the Third Punic War, Gaius at Numantia—they were conspicuously brave. In 137 B.C. Tiberius was sent as quaestor to Nearer Spain, where he single-handedly negotiated a treaty to extricate the defeated Hostilius Mancinus from Numantia, thus saving Mancinus's army from annihilation; however, Scipio Aemilianus considered Tiberius's action disgraceful, and managed to persuade the Senate not to ratify the treaty. Tiberius never forgave his cousin and brother-in-law.

In 133 B.C. Tiberius was elected a tribune of the plebs and set out to right the wrongs the State was perpetrating in its leasing of the *ager publicus*. Against furious opposition, he passed an agrarian law which limited the amount of public land any one man might lease or own to 500 *iugera* (with an extra 250 *iugera* per son), and set up a commission to distribute the surplus land this limit produced among the civilian poor of Rome. His aim was not only to rid Rome of some of her less useful citizens, but also to ensure that future generations would be in a position to give Rome sons qualified at the means test to serve in the army. When the Senate chose to filibuster, Tiberius took his bill straight to the Plebeian Assembly— and stirred up a hornets' nest thereby, as this move ran counter to all established practice. One of his fellow tribunes of the plebs, his relative Marcus Octavius, vetoed the bill in the Plebeian Assembly, and was illegally deposed from office—yet another enormous offense against the *mos maiorum* (that is, established custom and practice). The legality of these ploys mattered less to Tiberius's opponents than did the fact that they contravened established practice, however unwritten that established practice might be.

When Attalus III of Pergamum died that year and was discovered to have bequeathed his kingdom to Rome, Tiberius ignored the

Senate's right to decide what ought to be done with this bequest, and legislated to have the lands used to resettle more of Rome's poor. Opposition in Senate and Comitia hardened day by day.

Then when 133 B.C. drew to a close without Tiberius's seeing a successful conclusion to his program, he flouted another established practice—the one which said a man might be a tribune of the plebs only once. Tiberius Gracchus ran for a second term. In a confrontation on the Capitol between his own faction and an ultra-conservative faction led by his cousin Scipio Nasica, Tiberius was clubbed to death, as were some of his followers. His cousin Scipio Aemilianus—though not yet returned from Numantia when this happened—publicly condoned the murder, alleging that Tiberius had wanted to make himself King of Rome.

Turmoil died down until ten years later, when Tiberius's little brother Gaius was elected a tribune of the plebs in 123 B.C. Gaius Sempronius Gracchus was the same kind of man as his elder brother, but he had learned from Tiberius's mistakes, and was besides the more able of the two. His reforms were far wider; they embraced not only agrarian laws, but also laws to provide very cheap grain for the urban lowly, to regulate service in the army, to found Roman citizen colonies abroad, to initiate public works throughout Italy, to remove the extortion court from the Senate and give it to the knights, to farm the taxes of Asia Province by public contracts let by the censors, and to give the full Roman citizenship to all those having the Latin Rights, and the Latin Rights to every Italian. His program was nowhere near completed when his term as a tribune of the plebs came to an end, so Gaius did the impossible—he ran for a second term, and got in. Amid mounting fury and obdurate enmity, he battled on to achieve his program of reform, which was still not completed when his second term expired. He stood a third time for the tribunate of the plebs. This time he was defeated, as was his friend and close colleague, Marcus Fulvius Flaccus.

When 121 B.C. dawned, Gaius saw his laws and policies attacked at once by the consul Lucius Opimius and the ex-tribune of the plebs Marcus Livius Drusus. Desperate to prevent everything he had done being torn down again, Gaius Sempronius Gracchus resorted to violence. The Senate responded by passing its first-ever "ultimate decree" to stop the escalating Forum war; Fulvius Flaccus and two of his sons were murdered and the fleeing Gaius Gracchus committed suicide in the Grove of Furrina on the flanks of the Janiculan hill. Roman politics could never be the same; the aged citadel of the *mos maiorum* was now irreparably breached.

The same thread of tragedy wove through the personal lives of the Brothers Gracchi also. Tiberius married a Claudia, the daughter of Appius Claudius Pulcher, consul in 143 B.C., an inveterate enemy of Scipio Aemilianus and as idiosyncratic as most Claudius Pulcher men tended to be. There were three sons of the marriage between Tiberius and Claudia, none of whom lived to achieve a public career. Gaius Gracchus also married the daughter of one of his stoutest supporters—Licinia, daughter of Publius Licinius Crassus Mucianus. They had one child only, a daughter, Sempronia, who married a Fulvius Flaccus Bambalio—*she* produced a daughter, Fulvia, who became in turn the wife of Publius Clodius Pulcher, Gaius Scribonius Curio, and Mark Antony.

grammaticus   *Not* a teacher of grammar! He taught the basic arts of rhetoric—public speaking (see **rhetoric**).

Greece   By the beginning of the first century B.C. Greece had been stripped of the territories of Macedonia and Epirus. It comprised Thessaly, Dolopia, Malis, Euboeia, Ocris, Phocis, Locris, Aetolia, Acarnania, Boeotia, Attica, Corinth, and the various states of the Peloponnese. Things Greek had fallen into almost complete decline; many of Greece's regions were bare of people, their towns ghost, their coffers empty. Only places like Athens continued in some way to thrive. Centuries of war—with foreign invaders, at the whim of would-be conquerors, and—most often of all—between Greek states, had impoverished the country and halved its population, many of whom (if fortunate enough to possess a good trade or education) voluntarily sold themselves into slavery.

Hannibal   The Carthaginian prince who led his country in the second of its three wars against Rome. Born in 247 B.C., the son of Hamilcar, Hannibal was taught to soldier in Spain as a mere child; he spent his youth in Spain, where his father was the Carthaginian governor. In 218 B.C. Hannibal invaded Italy, a shock tactic which confounded Rome; his crossing of the Alps (complete with elephants) through the Montgenèvre Pass was brilliantly done. For sixteen years he roamed at will through Italian Gaul and Italy, defeating Roman armies at Trebia, Trasimene, and finally Cannae. But Quintus Fabius Maximus Verrucosis Cunctator evolved a strategy which eventually wore Hannibal out; relentlessly he shadowed the Carthaginian army with an army of his own, yet never offered battle nor allowed his men to be trapped into battle—the so-called "Fabian tactics." Because Fabius Maximus was always in his vicinity somewhere, Hannibal never quite got up the courage to attack the city of Rome herself. Then his allies among the Italians began to flag; after his hold on Campania was broken, Fabius Maximus forced Hannibal further and further south in Italy. The Carthaginian lost the (verbal) battle for Tarentum at about the same time as his younger brother, Hasdrubal, was defeated at the Metaurus River in Umbria. Penned up in Bruttium, the very toe of Italy, he evacuated his undefeated army back to Carthage in 203 B.C. At Zama he was beaten by Scipio Africanus, after which, as the Head of State, he intrigued with Antiochus the Great of Syria against Rome. Roman pressure forced him to flee from Carthage and seek asylum with Antiochus in Syria; after Rome subdued the King, Hannibal had to move on. He is reputed to have wandered to Armenia, where he helped King Artaxias design and build his capital, Artaxata. So oriental a court could not please; Hannibal journeyed west across Anatolia and fetched up with King Prusias in Bithynia. Then in 182 B.C., Rome demanded that Prusias hand the Carthaginian over. Rather than fall into Roman hands, Hannibal committed suicide. An unrepentant enemy of Rome, he was always admired and respected by Rome.

"hay on his horn" Ancient oxen were endowed with most formidable horns, and not all ancient oxen were placid, despite their castrated state. A beast which gored was tagged in warning; hay was wrapped around the horn it gored with, or around both horns if it gored with both. Pedestrians scattered wildly on seeing an ox tagged in this manner. The saying "hay on his horn" came to be applied to a very large, good-natured, placid man after it was discovered that this same man could turn like lightning and strike with the ruthlessness of a born killer.

Head Count   This is the term I have used throughout the book to describe the lowliest of Roman citizens—those who were too poor to belong to one of the five economic Classes. All the censors did was to take a "head count" of them. I have preferred Head Count to "the proletariat" or "the masses" because of our modern post-Marxist attitudes—attitudes entirely misleading in the ancient context (see also *capite censi* and *proletarii*).

Hellenic   The term used to describe Greek culture outside Greece after Alexander the Great introduced a Greek element into the courts and kingdoms of Mediterranean and Asian rulers.

Herakles   The Greek form. In Latin, Hercules. A mortal man (though a son of Zeus), his sheer strength, indomitability and perseverance in adversity immortalized him for all time. After he died inside the poisoned shirt, Zeus also immortalized him. However, it was undoubtedly his human qualities which made him such an attractive object of worship; he held sway from one end of the Mediterranean to the other. His cult was exclusively male, and he was regarded as the embodiment of all traditional male virtues. His was the statue dressed in the raiment of the triumphing general. In Rome, he was also a god of merchant trading, particularly for vendors of olive oil. Some men thought themselves his descendants; this was true of Mithridates and the Roman Antonii.

Hyperboreans   Literally, the people beyond the home of Boreas, the North Wind. They were mythical, said to worship only the god Apollo, and to live an idyllic existence. The Land of the Hyperboreans was, however, definitely thought by the ancients to exist somewhere in the far north.

Ilium   The name the Romans gave to the city of **Troy**.

imago   Plural, *imagines*. This was the beautifully painted and bewigged, lifelike mask of a Roman family's consular (or perhaps also praetorian) ancestor. It was made out of beeswax and kept in a dust-free cupboard shaped like a miniature temple. The mask and its cupboard were the objects of enormous reverence. When a man of the family died, an actor was hired to don the mask and wig and impersonate the dead ancestor in the funeral procession. If a man became consul, his mask was added to the family collection. From time to time a man who was not consul did something so remarkable it was considered he deserved an *imago*.

imperator   Literally, the commander-in-chief or the general of a Roman army. However, the term gradually came to be given only to a general who won a great victory; his troops hailed him imperator on the field. In order to gain permission from the Senate to celebrate a triumph, a general had to prove that his men had indeed hailed him as imperator on the field. Imperator is the root of the word "emperor."

imperium   Imperium was the degree of authority vested in a curule magistrate or promagistrate. Imperium meant that a man owned the authority of his office, and could not be gainsaid (provided he was acting within the limits of his particular level of imperium and within the laws governing his conduct). It was conferred by a *lex Curiata*, and lasted for one year only; extensions had to be ratified by Senate and/or People in the case of promagistrates who had not completed their original commissions in the space of one year. Lictors bearing *fasces* indicated that a man possessed imperium, the higher the number, the higher the imperium (see also *fasces;* **lictor; magistrate**).

insula   Plural, insulae. Literally, "island." Because it was usually surrounded on all sides by streets or lanes or alleys, an apartment building became known as an insula. Roman insulae were very tall (up to one hundred feet—thirty meters—in height), and most were large enough to warrant the incorporation of an internal light-well; many were large enough to contain more than one internal light-well. Then, as now, Rome was a city of apartment dwellers. This in itself is a strong clue to the answer to the vexed question—how many people lived in Rome? We know the dimensions of the city within the Servian Walls: one-plus kilometers in width, two-plus kilometers in length. That meant the population of Rome at the time of Marius and Sulla had to have been at least one million, probably more. Otherwise the insulae would have been half empty and the city smothered in parks. Rome teemed with people, its insulae were multitudinous. Two million (including slaves) might be closer to the truth of the matter.

interrex   The word means "between the kings." It dates back to the kings of Rome, when the patrician Senate appointed one of its members to act after the death of one king and before the accession of a new king. After the establishment of the Republic the practice survived in cases where, due to death or other disaster, no consuls were left in office, and no elections had yet been held. The members of the Senate were divided into decuries of ten men, each decury being headed by a patrician senator; this was always so. But while Rome had no consuls, an *interrex* was chosen from among the patrician heads of the senatorial decuries. He could serve for five days only, then was succeeded by another patrician head of a decury; this went on until elections could be held and proper consuls take office. While in office the *interrex* was endowed with a full consular imperium, had the full complement of twelve lictors, and could perform all the fuctions of the consul. No man could be an *interrex* unless he was the patrician head of a senatorial decury. The first in a series of *interreges* (plural) was not allowed to hold consular elections.

Italia   For the purposes of this book, the word has two meanings. First of all, it refers to all of ancient peninsular Italy south of the Arnus and Rubico rivers. Secondly, it is used to refer to the rebel Italian nations which rose against Rome in 91 B.C. and fought the Marsic (later known as the Social) War.

Italian Allies   The peoples, tribes, or nations (they are variously described as all three) who lived in the Italian peninsula without enjoying either the full Roman citizenship or the Latin Rights were known as the Italian Allies, In return for military protection and in the interests of peaceful co-existence, they were required by Rome to furnish properly armed soldiers for the armies of Rome, and to pay for the upkeep of these soldiers. The Italian Allies also bore the brunt of general taxation within Italy at the time of Marius and Sulla, and in many instances had been obliged to yield part of their lands to swell the Roman *ager publicus*. Many of them had either risen against Rome (like the Samnites) or sided with Hannibal and others against Rome (like parts of Campania). To some extent, there was always some movement among the Italian Allies to throw off the Roman yoke, or to demand that Rome accord them the full citizenship; but until the last century of the Republic, Rome was sensitive enough to act before the grumbling grew too serious. After the joint enfranchisement of Formiae Fundi and Arpinum in 188 B.C., no more Italian Allied communities were rewarded with the citizenship or even the **Latin Rights**. The final straw which turned Italian Allied discontent into open revolt was the *lex Licinia Mucia* of 95 B.C., at the end of 91 B.C. war broke out. The regions of Italy which remained loyal to Rome were: Etruria, Umbria, Northern Picenum, Northern Campania, Latium, the Sabine country.

The nations which rose up against Rome were: Marsi (after whom the war was named, the Marsic War), Samnites, Frentani, Marrucini, Picentes south of the Flosis River, Paeligni, Vestini, Hirpini, all of whom rose up together, and were soon joined by: Lucani, Apuli, Venusini.

The two regions in the extreme south, Bruttium and Calabria, were sympathetic to the Italian cause, but took little part in hostilities. Quintus Poppaedius Silo of the Marsi and Gaius Papius Mutilus of the Samnites were the heads of the Italian Allied government.

Italian Gaul   Gallia Cisalpina—Gaul-on-this-side-of-the-Alps. In the interests of simplicity, I have elected to call it Italian Gaul. It incorporated all the lands north of the Arnus-Rubico border on the Italian side of the formidable semicircle of alps which cut Italy off from the rest of Europe. It was bisected from west to east by the Padus River (the modern Po). South of the river the people and towns were heavily Romanized, many of them possessing the Latin Rights. North of the river the peoples and towns were more Celtic than Roman; Latin was at best a second language, if spoken at all. The *lex Pompeia* promulgated by Pompey Strabo in 89 B.C. gave the full Roman citizenship to all the Latin Rights communities south of the Padus, and gave the Latin Rights to the towns of

Aquileia, Patavium, and Mediolanum to the north of the Padus. Politically Italian Gaul dwelt in a kind of limbo at the time of Marius and Sulla, for it had neither the status of a true province nor was it a part of Italia. The Marsic (Social) War saw for the first time the men of Italian Gaul drafted into Rome's armies—as auxiliaries before the *lex Pompeia*, as full Roman legions after that.

Italica   The capital of the new nation of Italia as dreamed of by the insurgents of the Marsic (Social) War. It was actually the city of Corfinium, and enjoyed the name Italica only while the war went on.

iugera   Singular, *iugerum*. The Roman unit of land measurement. In modern terms one *iugerum* was 0.623 (or five eighths) of an acre, or 0.252 (one quarter) of a hectare. The modern user of imperial measure will get close enough in acres by dividing the *iugera* in two; in metric measure, to divide by four will be very close in hectares.

ius Latii   See **Latin Rights**.

Janiculum   The Janiculan hill consisted of the heights behind the northwest bank of the Tiber, opposite the city of Rome. During the Republic there was a defensive fortress upon it; this was still kept up and was ready to be garrisoned during the time of Marius and Sulla. A flagpole stood atop the citadel inside the stronghold; if the red flag flying from it was pulled down, it was a signal that Rome lay under threat of attack.

Jugurtha   King of Numidia from 118 B.C. until his capture by Sulla in 105 B.C. An illegitimate son, he gained his throne by murdering those more legitimately entitled to the throne than himself, and he hung onto it grimly, despite great opposition from certain elements in the Roman Senate led by Marcus Aemilius Scaurus the Princeps Senatus. In 109 B.C. (after a disgraceful act of aggression by the young Aulus Postumius Albinus) Jugurtha went to war against Roman Africa; Quintus Caecilius Metellus the consul was sent to Africa to subjugate him, his legates being Gaius Marius and Publius Rutilius Rufus (both of whom had served as cadets with Jugurtha in Spain years before). Metellus (who earned the extra *cognomen* Numidicus from this campaign) and Marius could not get on, with the result that Marius ran for consul in 108 B.C. for 107 in office, and had the Plebeian Assembly take the command in the war off Metellus Numidicus, who never forgave him. Marius did well against the Numidian army, but Jugurtha himself constantly eluded capture until Sulla, then Marius's quaestor, persuaded King Bocchus of Mauretania to trick Jugurtha, who was captured and sent to Rome. He walked in Marius's triumphal parade on New Year's Day of 104 B.C., then was thrown into the lower chamber of the Tullianum and left there to starve to death.

Juno Moneta Juno of Warnings, or perhaps Reminders. Rome's highest goddess, Juno had many guises, including Juno Moneta. It was her gaggle of sacred geese which cackled so loudly they woke Marcus Manlius in time for him to dislodge the Gauls trying to scale the Capitol cliffs in 390 B.C. The mint was located inside the podium of her temple on the Arx of the Capitol; from this fact, we obtain our English word "money."

Jupiter Optimus Maximus Literally, "Jupiter Best and Greatest." He was the king of the Roman pantheon, Rome's Great God. He had a huge and magnificent temple on the Capitolium of the Capitol, and his own special priest, the *flamen Dialis.*

Jupiter Stator Jupiter the Stayer. It is a title having to do with military men and matters; Jupiter Stator was that aspect of Jupiter who arrested retreats, gave soldiers the courage to stand and fight, hold their ground. Two temples of Jupiter Stator existed, one very old establishment on the corner of the Via Sacra and the Velia adjacent to the Clivus Palatinus (it was here Gaius Marius hid after his defeat by Sulla in 88 B.C.), and the other Rome's first all-marble temple, on the Campus Martius adjacent to the Porticus Metelli.

Kingdom of the Parthians *Regnum Parthorum.* This is the way the ancients expressed the name of that vast area of western Asia under the domination of the King of the Parthians. It was *not* called Parthia; Parthia was a small nation to the northeast of the Caspian Sea, near Bactria, and was important only because it had produced the seven great Pahlavi families, and the Arsacid Parthian kings. By the time of Marius and Sulla the Arsacid Parthian kings held sway over all of the lands between the Euphrates River of Mesopotamia and the Indus River of modern Pakistan. The King of the Parthians did not live in Parthia itself, but ruled his domains from Seleuceia-on-Tigris in winter and Ecbatana in summer. Pahlavi satraps ruled the various regions into which the Kingdom of the Parthians was split up, but only as the King's designated representatives. Though government was loose and no genuine national feeling existed, the King of the Parthians held his empire together by military excellence. The army was purely cavalry, but of two different kinds: light-armed bowmen who delivered the "Parthian shot" twisted facing backward as they pretended to flee, and cataphracts who were clad from head to foot in chain mail, as were their horses. Thanks to Syrian Seleucid contacts, the Parthian court's oriental atmosphere was partially leavened by a little Hellenism.

knights   The *equites,* the members of the **Ordo Equester**. It had all started when the kings of Rome enrolled the city's top citizens as a special cavalry unit provided with horses paid for from the public purse. At that time, horses of good enough quality were both scarce and extremely costly. When the young Republic came into being there were 1,800 men so enrolled, grouped into eighteen centuries. As the Republic grew, so too did the number of knights, but all the extra knights were obliged to buy their own horses and maintain them at their own expense. However, by the second century B.C. Rome was no longer providing her own cavalry; the knights became a social and economic entity having little to do with military matters, though the State continued to provide the 1,800 senior knights with the **Public Horse**. The knights were now defined by the censors in economic terms; the original eighteen centuries holding the 1,800 senior knights remained at one hundred men each, but the rest of the knights' centuries (some seventy-one) swelled within themselves to contain many more than one hundred men. Thus all the men who qualified at the census as knights were accommodated within the First Class.

Until 123 B.C., all senators were knights as well; it was Gaius Sempronius Gracchus (see **The Gracchi**) who in that year split the Senate off as a separate body of three hundred men, and gave the knights the title Ordo Equester. The sons of senators and other

nonsenatorial members of senatorial families continued to be classified as knights. To qualify as a knight at the census (held on a
special tribunal in the lower Forum Romanum), a man had to have
property or assets giving him an income in excess of 400,000 sesterces. There was no restriction upon the nature of the activities
which brought him in his income, as there was on the senator.

From the time of Gaius Gracchus down to the end of the Republic, the knights either controlled or temporarily lost control of the
major courts which tried senators for minor treason or provincial
extortion; this meant the knights were often at loggerheads with
the Senate. There was nothing to stop a knight who qualified for
the senatorial means test becoming a senator if the censors agreed
upon a vacancy falling due; that by and large the knights did not
aspire to the Senate was purely because of the knightly love of
trade and commerce, both forbidden fruit for senators. The members of the Ordo Equester liked the thrills of the business forum
more than they craved the thrills of the political forum.

Lar   Plural, Lares. These were among the most Roman of all gods,
having no form, shape, sex, number, or mythology. They were *nu-
mina*. There were many different kinds of Lares, who might function as the protective spirits or forces of a locality (as with crossroads
and boundaries), a social group (as with the family's private Lar, the
Lar Familiaris), an activity such as voyaging (the Lares Permarini),
or a whole nation (as with Rome's public Lares, the Lares Praestites).
By the late Republic they had acquired both form and sex, and were
depicted (in the form of small statues) as two young men with a dog.
It is doubtful, however, whether a Roman actually believed by this
that there were only two of them, or that they owned this form and
sex; more perhaps that the increasing complexity of life made it convenient to tag them in a concrete way.

latifundia   Large tracts of public land leased by one person and
run as a single unit in the manner of a modem ranch. That is, the
activity was purely grazing, not farming. They were usually
staffed by slaves who increasingly became treated like chain-gang
prisoners and were locked at night in barracks called ***ergastula***.

Latin Rights   *Ius Latii*. They were an intermediate citizen status between the nadir of non-citizenship as suffered by the Italian Allies and the zenith of the full Roman citizenship. In other words, they were a typically Roman ploy to soothe ruffled non-citizen feelings without conceding the full citizenship. Those having the Latin Rights shared privileges in common with Roman citizens; booty was divided equally, contracts with full citizens could be entered into and legal protection sought for these contracts, marriage was allowed with full citizens, and there was the right to appeal against capital convictions. However, there was no *suffragium*—no right to vote in any Roman election. Nor the right to sit on a Roman jury. After the revolt of Fregellae in 125 B.C. (this was a Latin Rights town grown tired of waiting for the full citizenship), an unknown tribune of the plebs in 123 B.C. passed a law allowing the magistrates of Latin Rights communities to assume the full citizenship for themselves and their direct descendants in perpetuity—another typically Roman ploy, as it soothed the ruffled feelings of a town's important men, yet did nothing to enfranchise the ordinary residents.

Latium   The region of Italy in which Rome was situated; it received its name from the original inhabitants, called Latini. Its northern boundary was the Tiber, its southern a point extending inland from the seaport of Circei; on the east it bordered the lands of the Sabines and Marsi. When the Roman conquest of the Volsci and the Aequi was completed by 300 B.C., Latium became purely Roman.

Lautumiae   The ancient tufa-stone quarry in the base of the northeast cliffs of the Arx of the Capitol. The earliest of the buildings contained in the Forum Romanum of Marius and Sulla's day were made from stone quarried there. At some time a prison was built in the convenient quarry's lap, but as lengthy incarceration was not a Roman concept, the place was never rendered secure. The Lautumiae was a collection of holding cells—mostly used, it seems, to confine recalcitrant magistrates and politicians. As punishment for crime, the Romans preferred exile to imprisonment. It was much cheaper.

legate   *Legatus.* The most senior members of the Roman general's military staff were his legates. In order to be classified as a legate, a man had to be of senatorial rank, and often was a consular (it appears these elder statesmen occasionally hankered after a spell of army life, and volunteered their services to a general commanding some interesting campaign). Legates answered only to the general, and were senior to all types of military tribune.

legion *Legio.* This was the smallest Roman military unit capable of fighting a war on its own (though it was rarely called upon to do so). That is, it was complete within itself in terms of manpower, equipment, and facilities. By the time of Marius and Sulla, a Roman army engaged in any major campaign rarely consisted of fewer than four legions—though equally rarely of more than six legions. Single legions without prospect of reinforcement did garrison duty in places where rebellions or raids were small-scale. A legion contained something over five thousand soldiers divided into ten cohorts of six centuries each, and about one thousand men of noncombatant status; there was a modest cavalry squadron attached to the legion under normal circumstances. Each legion fielded its own **artillery** and matériel. If a legion was one of the consul's legions, it was commanded by up to six elected tribunes of the soldiers; if it belonged to a general not currently consul, it was commanded by a legate, or else by the general himself. Its regular officers were centurions, of which it possessed some sixty. Though the troops belonging to a legion camped together, they did not live together en masse; instead, they were divided into units of eight men who tented and messed together.

legionary This is the correct English word to describe an ordinary soldier (*miles gregarius*) in a Roman legion. "Legionnaire," which I have sometimes seen instead, is more properly the term applied to a member of the French Foreign Legion.

lex Plural, *leges.* A law. The word "*lex*" came to be applied also to a *plebiscitum* (plebiscite), which was a law passed in the Plebeian Assembly. A *lex* was not considered valid until it had been inscribed on bronze or stone and deposited in the vaults below the temple of Saturn. However, logic says the tablet's residence in the temple of Saturn must have been brief, as the vaults could not have contained anything like the number of tablets necessary to hold the body of Roman law at the time of Marius and Sulla—especially not when the Treasury also lay beneath the temple of Saturn. I imagine the tablets were whisked in and out to be stored permanently elsewhere.

leges Caecilia Didia I have called the first one *prima*, as it figures more prominently in the book than the second *lex Caecilia Didia*. The first of these two laws stipulated that three *nundinae* or market days must elapse between the first *contio* to promulgate a law in any of the Assemblies and the vote which passed a bill into law. There is some debate as to whether the waiting period was seventeen or twenty-four days; I have chosen the smaller wait because it seems more Roman. The second *lex Caecilia Didia* forbade the tacking of unrelated matters together to form one law. They were passed by the consuls of 98 B.C.

lex Calpurnia de civitate sociorum The law of Piso Frugi passed in 89 B.C. Originally it stipulated that all the new citizens of the *lex Julia* should be placed in two newly created tribes; when this caused a hugh outcry, Piso Frugi changed his law to admit the new citizens to his two new tribes plus eight existing tribes.

leges Corneliae The laws of Sulla, passed in 88 B.C., during his consulship. They fall into three lots, passed at different times. At the beginning of his consulship he passed two laws to regulate Rome's rocky finances; the first stipulated that all debtors were to pay simple interest only on loans at the rate agreed to by both parties at the time the loan was made. The second waived the lodgment of *sponsio* (that is, the sum in dispute) with the praetor in cases of debt, enabling the praetor to hear the case.

After the slaughter in Asia Province by Mithridates and before the laws of Sulpicius came Sulla's agrarian law. It gave the confiscated lands of the rebel towns Pompeii, Faesulae, Hadria, Telesia, Bovianum, and Grumentum to Sulla's veteran soldiers upon their retirement. The final batch of laws was passed after Sulla's march on Rome.

The first waived the waiting period of the *lex Caecilia Didia prima*.

The second added three hundred members to the Senate, to be appointed by the censors in the usual way.

The third repealed the *lex Hortensia* of 287 B.C. by stipulating that nothing could now be brought before the tribal Assemblies unless the Senate issued a *consultum*. The wording of the *consultum* could not be changed in the Assemblies.

The fourth returned the Centuriate Assembly to the form it had known under King Servius Tullius, thus giving the First Class of voters almost 50 percent of the voting power.

The fifth prohibited either discussion of or passing of laws in the tribal Assemblies. All laws in future were to be discussed and passed in the Centuriate Assembly only.

The sixth repealed all of the *leges Sulpiciae* because they had been passed with violence during legally declared religious holidays.

The seventh indicted twenty men on charges of high treason (*perduellio*)—and damned them—in the Centuriate Assembly. Gaius Marius, Young Marius, Sulpicius, Brutus the urban praetor, Cethegus, the Brothers Granii, Albinovanus, Laetorius, and eleven more were named.

lex Domitia de sacerdotiis   Passed in 104 B.C. by Gnaeus Domitius Ahenobarbus, later Pontifex Maximus. It required that future members of the College of Pontifices and College of Augurs be elected by a special tribal Assembly comprising seventeen tribes chosen by lot.

lex Julia de civitate Latinis et sociis danda   Passed by Lucius Julius Caesar at the end of his consulship in 90 B.C. It gave the Roman citizenship to all Italians who had not taken up arms against Rome during the Marsic War. Presumably it also fully enfranchised all Latin Rights communities in Italy.

lex Licinia Mucia   Passed by the consuls of 95 B.C. in response to an outcry about the number of spurious Roman citizens who appeared on the census rolls in 96 B.C. It legislated the creation of a number of special courts (*quaestiones*) to enquire into the credentials of all new names on the citizen register, and prescribed severe penalties for those found to have falsified citizenship.

*lex **Plautia iudiciaria*** Passed in the Plebeian Assembly in 89 B.C. It changed the frame of reference of the so-called Varian Commission to prosecute those who had opposed enfranchisement of the Italians. Further, it took the court off the knights and gave it to citizens of all and any Classes right across the thirty-five tribes.

*lex **Plautia Papiria*** Passed by the Plebeian Assembly in 89 B.C. It extended the full citizenship to any Italian with his name on an Italian municipal roll (if an insurgent, it required that he withdraw from all hostilities against Rome) provided the applicant lodged his case with the urban praetor inside Rome within sixty days of the passing of the law.

*lex **Pompeia*** Passed by the consul of 89 B.C., Pompey Strabo. This law gave the full citizenship to every Latin Rights community south of the Padus River in Italian Gaul, and gave the Latin Rights to Celtic tribes attached to the towns of Aquileia, Patavium, and Mediolanum north of the Padus River.

*leges **Sulpiciae*** There were four such, passed after the consul Sulla had been given command of the war against Mithridates in about September of 88 B.C. The first recalled all those exiled under the terms of the Varian Commission; the second provided that all the new Roman citizens should be distributed equally across the thirty-five tribes, and that the freedmen of Rome also be distributed across the thirty-five tribes; the third expelled all senators in debt for more than two thousand denarii from the Senate; and the fourth took the command of the war against Mithridates off Sulla and gave it to Marius. After Sulla's march on Rome, his laws were annulled.

*lex **Varia de maiestate*** Passed in the Plebeian Assembly by Quintus Varius Severus Hybrida Sucronensis in 90 B.C. It created a special court (thereafter always called the Varian Commission) to try those accused of attempting to secure the Roman citizenship for Italians.

*lex **Voconia de mulierum hereditatibus*** Passed in 169 B.C. This law severely curtailed the right of women to inherit from wills. Under no circumstances could she be designated the principal heir, even if she was the only child of her father; his nearest agnate relatives (that is, on the father's side) superseded her. Cicero quotes a case where it was argued that the *lex Voconia* did not apply because the dead man's property had not been assessed at a census; but the praetor (Gaius Verres) overruled the argument and refused to allow the girl in question to inherit. The law was certainly got around, for we know of several great heiresses; by securing a law waiving the *lex Voconia,* perhaps; or by dying intestate, in which case the old law prevailed, and children inherited irrespective of sex or close agnate relatives. Until Sulla as dictator established permanent *quaestiones* there does not appear to have been a court to hear testamentary disputes, which meant the urban praetor must have had the final say.

LIBERO   The verdict of acquittal in a trial conducted in one of the voting Assemblies.

licker-fish   A freshwater bass of the Tiber River. It was found only between the Wooden Bridge and the Pons Aemilius, where it lurked around the outflows of the great sewers and fed upon what the sewers disgorged. Apparently it was so well fed that it was notoriously difficult to catch—which may be why it was regarded as a great delicacy.

lictor   One of the few genuine public servants of Rome. There was a College of Lictors; how many it contained is uncertain, but enough certainly to provide the traditional single-file escort for all holders of imperium, both within and without the city, and to perform other duties as well. Two or three hundred lictors all told may not have been unlikely. A lictor had to be a full Roman citizen, but that he was lowly seems fairly sure, as his official wage was minimal; he relied heavily upon gratuities from those he escorted. Within the college the lictors were divided into groups of ten (decuries), each headed by a prefect; there were several presidents of the college as a whole. Inside Rome the lictor wore a plain white toga; outside Rome he wore a crimson tunic with a wide black belt heavily ornamented in brass; at funerals he wore a black toga. I have located the College of Lictors behind the temple of the Lares Praestites on the eastern side of the Forum Romanum adjacent to the great inn on the corner of the Clivus Orbius, but there is no factual evidence to support this location.

Long-haired Gaul   See **Gallia Comata**.

Lucania   Western peninsular Italy lying south of Campania and north of Bruttium—the front of the Italian ankle and foot. It was a wild and mountainous area and contained huge and magnificent forests of fir and pine. Its people—called Lucani—had strong ties with the Samnites, the Hirpini, and the Venusini, and bitterly resented Roman incursions into Lucania.

Lucius Tiddlypuss   See **Tiddlypuss, Lucius**.

ludi Romani   See **games**.

Lusitani   The people of the southwestern and western areas of the Iberian peninsula; they lay beyond the frontiers of the Roman province of Further Spain, and strenuously resisted all Roman attempts to penetrate their lands. They also regularly invaded Further Spain to annoy the Roman occupiers.

lustrum   This word came to mean two things, both connected with the office of censor. It meant the entire five-year term the censors served, but also meant the ceremony with which the censors concluded the census of the ordinary Roman People on the Campus Martius.

magistrates   The elected executives of the Senate and People of Rome. By the middle Republic, all the men who held magistracies were members of the Senate (elected quaestors, if not already senators, were normally approved as senators by the next pair of censors). This gave the Senate a distinct advantage over the People, until the People (in the person of the Plebs) took over the lawmaking. The magistrates represented the executive arm of government. In order of seniority, the most junior magistrate was the elected tribune of the soldiers, who was not old enough to be admitted to the Senate under the *lex Villia annalis*, yet was nonetheless a true magistrate. Then, in ascending order came the quaestor, the tribune of the plebs, the plebeian aedile, the curule aedile, the praetor, the consul, and the censor. Only the curule aedile, the praetor, and the consul held imperium. Only the quaestorship, praetorship, and consulship constituted the *cursus honorum*. Tribunes of the soldiers, quaestors, and curule aediles were elected by the Assembly of the People; tribunes of the plebs and plebeian aediles were elected by the Plebeian Assembly; and praetors, consuls, and censors were

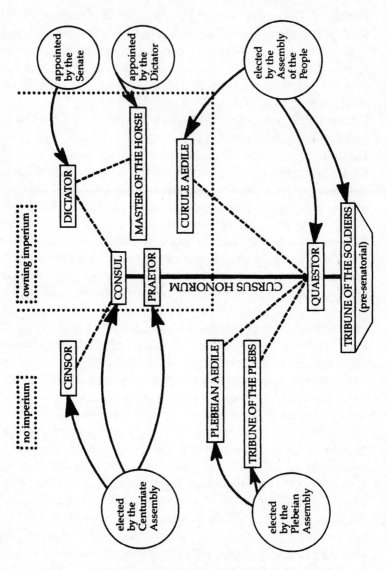

Roman Magistrates

elected by the Centuriate Assembly. In times of emergency, the Senate was empowered to create an extraordinary magistrate, the dictator, who served for six months only, and was indemnified against answering for his dictatorial actions after his term as dictator was over. The dictator himself appointed a Master of the Horse to function as his war leader and second-in-command. On the death or incapacitation of a consul, the Senate was also empowered to appoint a suffect consul without holding an election. Save for the censors, all magistrates served for one year only.

maiestas Treason. After Lucius Appuleius Saturninus first put *maiestas minuta* ("little treason") on the law tablets as a criminal charge, the old-style treason charge of *perduellio* (high treason) was virtually abandoned. Saturninus set up a special court or *quaestio* to hear charges of *maiestas minuta* during his first term as tribune of the plebs in 103 B.C.; it was staffed entirely by knights, though the men tried in it were usually senators.

manumission The act of freeing a slave (manumit, manumitted). When the slave's master was a Roman citizen, manumission automatically endowed the slave with the Roman citizenship. However, the freed slave, or freedman, had little opportunity to exercise his franchise, as he was placed in one of two of the four urban tribes—Esquilina or Suburana—and therefore found his vote worthless in tribal elections; his economic lowliness (though slaves occasionally did manage to make a lot of money) meant he was not made a member of one of the Five Classes, so he could not vote in the Centuriate Assembly either. The manumitted slave took the name of his old master as his new name, adding to it his original slave name as a *cognomen*. A slave might be manumitted in any one of several ways: by buying his freedom out of his earnings; as a special gesture of the master's on some great occasion like a coming-of-age birthday; after an agreed number of years in service; in a will. Though technically the freedman was the equal of his master, in actual fact he was obliged to remain in his old master's clientship, unless this was formally dispensed with. Despite this, most slaves found the Roman citizenship highly desirable, not so much for themselves as for their freeborn descendants. The freedman was obliged for the rest of his life to wear a slightly conical skullcap on the back of his head; this was the Cap of Liberty.

Marsi   One of the most important of the Italian peoples. The Marsi lived around the shores of the Fucine Lake, which belonged to them; their territory extended into the high Apennines. Their history indicates that they were always loyal to Rome until came the time of the Marsic War. They were affluent, martial, and populous, and had adopted Latin as their language fairly early. Their chief town was Marruvium; the larger and more important town of Alba Fucens was a Latin Rights colony seeded on Marsic territory by Rome. The Marsi worshipped snakes, and were famous snake charmers.

Martha   The Syrian prophetess who predicted that Gaius Marius would be consul of Rome seven times, and did this before he had been consul at all. She extracted a promise from Marius that he would bring her from Africa to Rome, where she lived in his house as his guest until she died, and regularly scandalized Rome's populace by appearing in a purple litter. My own novelist's license added the second part to her prophecy—that Marius would be eclipsed in greatness by his wife's nephew; I did this to make later events more logical.

mentula   Plural, *mentulae*. The Latin obscenity for the penis.

mentulam caco   "I shit on your prick!"

merda   A Latin obscenity referring more to the droppings of animals than to human excrement.

Metrobius   Plutarch attests to the existence of this beloved boyfriend of Sulla's, and gives us his name—Metrobius.

Middle Sea   The name I have given the Mediterranean Sea, which had not at the time of Marius and Sulla acquired its later name of Mare Nostrum—"Our Sea." Properly, at the time of Marius and Sulla it was called Mare Internum.

Military Man   *Vir militaris.* He was a man whose whole career revolved around the army, and who continued to serve in the army after his obligatory number of campaigns or years had expired. He entered the political arena relying upon his military reputation to recommend him to the electors. Many Military Men never bothered to enter the political arena at all, but if such a one wanted to general an army, he had to attain the rank of praetor, and that meant a political career. Gaius Marius, Quintus Sertorius, Titus Didius, Gaius Pomptinus, and Publius Ventidius were all Military Men; but Caesar the Dictator, the greatest military man of them all, was never a Military Man.

military tribune See **tribune, military**.

modius Plural, *modii*. The measure of grain in Rome. One *modius* weighed thirteen pounds, or six kilograms.

Mormolyce Also known as Mormo. A children's bogey, she appears to have been an historical figure, at least in myth. The queen of a race of cannibal giants, she lost her children, and ever afterward preyed upon the children of humankind.

mos maiorum The established order of things. Perhaps the best definition is to say that the *mos maiorum* was Rome's unwritten constitution. *Mos* meant established customs; *maiores* meant ancestors or forebears in this context. The *mos maiorum* was how things had always been done.

Nearer Spain Hispania Citerior. The territory of this Roman province embraced the Mediterranean coastal plain and the mountainous foothills beyond it all the way from the Pyrenees to just south of the seaport of New Carthage. The southern boundary splitting the Further province off from it was fairly tenuous, but seems to have run between the range of mountains called the Orospeda and the taller range behind Abdera called the Solorius. In the time of Marius and Sulla the largest settlement was New Carthage (modern Cartagena) because the Orospeda ranges behind this seaport were honeycombed with productive silver mines the Romans had taken over when Carthage fell. Only one other part of the province was of much interest to its Roman owners; the valley of the Iberus River (modern Ebro) and its tributaries, this area being very rich. The governor had two seats: New Carthage in the south and Tarraco in the north. Nearer Spain was never as economically important to Rome as the Further province; it was, however, the only land route to Further Spain, and therefore had to be kept subdued.

nefas Sacrilege.

nobleman *Nobilis.* A man and his descendants were described as noble once he had achieved his consulship. This was an artificial aristocracy invented by the plebeians in order to cut the patricians down to size, since more plebeians reached the consulship than did patricians once the first century of the Republic was over. By the time of Marius and Sulla, nobility mattered greatly. Some modern authorities extend the term *nobilis* to cover those men who reached the status of praetor without ever attaining the consulship. However, my feeling is that to have admitted praetors into the plebeian nobility would have demeaned the exclusivity of nobility too much. Therefore I have reserved the term nobleman for those men of proven consular family.

nomen The family, clan, or gentilicial name—the title of the *gens.* Cornelius, Julius, Domitius, Livius, Marius, Marcius, Junius, Sulpicius, et cetera, are all *nomina* (plural), gentilicial names. I have not used the word *gens* very much in this book, as it takes a feminine ending—*gens Julia, gens Aurelia,* et cetera—too confusing for non-Latinate readers.

Numidia A kingdom in ancient middle North Africa which always surrounded the limited lands owned by Carthage (lands which became the Roman African province). The original inhabitants were Berbers, and lived a semi-nomadic life. After the defeat of Carthage, Rome encouraged the establishment of a regal dynasty, the first member of which was King Masinissa. The capital of Numidia was Cirta.

October Horse On the Ides of October (this was about the time the old campaigning season used to finish), the best war-horses of that year were picked out and harnessed in pairs to chariots. They then raced on the sward of the Campus Martius, rather than in one of the circuses. The right-hand horse of the winning team was sacrificed to Mars on an altar specially erected to Mars adjacent to the course of the race. The animal was killed with a spear, after which its head was severed and piled over with little cakes, while its tail and genitals were rushed to the Regia in the Forum Romanum, and the blood dripped onto the Regia's altar. Once the ceremonies over the cake-decorated horse's head were ended, it was thrown at two crowds of people, one comprising the residents of the Subura, the other residents of the Via Sacra; they fought for possession of it. If the people of the Via Sacra won, they nailed the head to the outside wall of the Regia; if the people of the Subura won, they nailed it to the outside wall of the Turris Mamilia (the most conspicuous building in the Subura). What was the reason behind all this is not known; modern scholars tend to think it was concerned with the closing of the campaign season in much earlier times than the day of Marius and Sulla, by which era the Romans themselves may not have been sure of its origins. We do not know whether the warhorses involved in the race were Public Horses or not; one might presume they were Public Horses.

Odysseus To Romans, he was Ulysses. King of Ithaca in days of legend. One of the main characters in Homer's *Iliad,* he was the hero of Homer's *Odyssey.* By nature crafty, brilliant, and deceitful (deceit was not necessarily odious to the ancient Greeks), he was also a great warrior, strong enough to own a bow no other man could bend and string; physically he was red-haired, left-handed, grey-eyed, and so short in the legs that he looked "taller sitting than he did standing." Having fought for the whole ten years at Troy (Ilium) and survived, Odysseus set out for home when the war was over, bearing as his special prize old Queen Hekabe (Hecuba), widow of King Priam of Troy. But he soon abandoned her, disgusted at her weeping and wailing, and then became embroiled in a decade of amazing adventures which took him all over the Mediterranean. At the end of ten years (having been away for twenty) he arrived home in Ithaca, where his wife, Penelope, and his son, Telemachus, and his dog, Argus, had all waited for him faithfully. The first thing he did was to string his bow and shoot an arrow through the hollows in a series of axe heads, after which he turned his mighty weapon upon his wife's importunate suitors, and killed them all, his son helping. After that, he settled down with Penelope and lived happily ever after.

Ordo Equester See **knights.**

Oxyntas A son of King Jugurtha of Numidia, he walked with his brother Iampsas in Gaius Marius's triumphal parade of 104

B.C. His father was put to death immediately afterward, but Oxyntas was sent to the town of Venusia, where he remained until 89 B.C. What happened to him after the Marsic War is not known.

Parthia See **Kingdom of the Parthians**.

paterfamilias The head of the family unit. His right to do as he pleased with his family was rigidly protected at law.

patricians The original Roman aristocracy. Patricians were distinguished citizens before there were kings of Rome, and after the establishment of the Republic they kept the title of patrician, as well as a prestige unattainable by any plebeian—and this in spite of the nobility, the "new aristocracy" ennobled above mere plebeian status by having consuls in the family. However, as the Republic grew older and the power of the plebeians grew in pace with their wealth, the special rights and entitlements of the patricians were inexorably stripped from them, until by the time of Marius and Sulla they tended to be relatively impoverished compared to those of the plebeian nobility. Not all patrician clans were of equal antiquity; the Julii and the Fabii were some centuries older in their tenure of patrician status than the Claudii. Patricians married in a form called *confarreatio* which was virtually for life, and patrician women never were allowed the relative emancipation of their plebeian sisters. Certain priesthoods could be held only by patricians—the Rex Sacrorum and the *flamen Dialis*—and certain senatorial positions could only be held by patricians—head of a decury, *interrex*, Princeps Senatus. At the time of Marius and Sulla the following patrician families were still regularly producing senators (if not praetors and consuls): Aemilius, Claudius, Cornelius, Fabius (but through adoption only), Julius, Manlius, Pinarius, Postumius, Sergius, Servilius, Sulpicius, and Valerius.

patronage Roman Republican society was organized into a system of patronage and clientship (see also **client**). Though perhaps the smallest businessmen and the ordinary lowly workers of Rome were not always participants in the system, the system was nevertheless very prevalent at all levels of society, and not all patrons were from the uppermost levels of society. The patron undertook to offer protection and favors to those who acknowledged themselves his clients. Freed slaves were in the patronage of their ex-masters. No woman could be a patron. Many patrons were clients of more powerful patrons than themselves, which technically made their clients also the clients of their patron. Though at law the domestic system was not recognized, there was a very strong principle of honor involved, and it was a rare client who ignored or cheated his patron. The patron might do nothing for years to obtain help or support from a client, but one day the client would be called upon to do his patron a favor—vote for him, or lobby for him, or perform some special task. It was customary for the patron to see his clients at dawn on "business" days in the calendar; at these matinees the clients would ask for help or favor, or merely attend to show respect, or offer services. The patron, if he was rich or generous, often bestowed gifts of money upon his clients when they assembled at such times. If a man became the client of another man whom in earlier days he had hated to the point of implacable enmity, that client would thereafter serve his erstwhile enemy, now his patron, with complete fidelity, even to death (*vide* Caesar the Dictator and Curio the Younger).

pedagogue *Paedagogus.* A teacher of young children. He was the man who instilled rudimentary education—reading, writing, arithmetic. His status was usually that of a slave or freedman, he lived within the family unit as a particularly privileged servant, and his nationality was more often than not Greek; he was, however, required to teach in Latin as well as Greek.

pedarius Plural, *pedarii*. See **Senate**.

Penates The Di Penates, the gods of the storage cupboards. Among the oldest and most numinous of all Roman gods, the Di Penates were worshipped in every Roman house in conjunction with Vesta (spirit of the hearth) and the Lar Familiaris. Like the Lares, the Di Penates eventually acquired a form, shape and sex, and were depicted as two youths, usually bronze statuettes. The Roman State had its own Di Penates, called the Penates Publici—guardians of the State's well-being and solvency.

Penelope The wife of Odysseus, King of Ithaca (see **Odysseus**). He won her in a footrace her father, Icarius, staged among her suitors. When it was prophesied that if Odysseus went to the war against Troy (Ilium), he would be away for twenty years, Penelope and her infant son, Telemachus, settled down to wait for him. The succession to the throne of Ithaca must have been matrilineal, for, presuming Odysseus dead, a large number of suitors for Penelope's hand in marriage moved into the palace and stayed for the duration. She refused to marry anyone until she had finished weaving a shroud for her father-in-law, Laertes; every night she unraveled what she had woven the previous day. According to Homer, this ploy worked until Odysseus returned home and killed the suitors.

People of Rome   This term embraced every single Roman who was not a member of the Senate; it applied to patricians as well as to plebeians, and to the Head Count as well as to the First Class.

perduellio   High treason. Until the later Republic saw the introduction of the lesser form of treason called *maiestas* (see **Saturninus**), *perduellio* was the only form treason had in Roman law. Old enough to be mentioned in the Twelve Tables, it required a trial process in the Centuriate Assembly, cumbersome and glaringly public until the secret ballot was finally extended to trial in the centuries. It was, however, virtually impossible to persuade the centuries to convict a man of *perduellio* unless he stood there and openly admitted that he had conspired to make war upon Rome—and Roman political miscreants were not so stupid. It carried an automatic death penalty.

peristyle   An enclosed garden or courtyard which was surrounded by a colonnade and formed the outdoor segment of a house.

permutatio   A banking term. It meant that sums of money could be transferred between institutions inside and outside Rome, sometimes over very long distances, without the actual money changing hands.

Phrygia   This was one of the wilder and less populated parts of Anatolia, synonymous to the ancients with nymphs, dryads, satyrs, and other mythical woodland folk, as well as with peasants so naïve and defenseless they were ridiculously easy to enslave. Phrygia lay inland from Bithynia, south of Paphlagonia, and west of Galatia. Its southern boundary was with Pisidia. Mountainous and heavily forested, it was a part of the Attalid empire of Pergamum;

after settling the wars following the bequest of the Kingdom of Pergamum to Rome, the Roman proconsul Manius Aquillius literally sold most of Phrygia to the fifth King Mithridates of Pontus in return for a large sum of gold. Aquillius kept the gold for himself.

Picenum That part of the eastern Italian peninsula roughly occupying the area of the Italian leg's calf muscle. Its western boundary followed the ridge of the Apennines; to its north lay Umbria, and to its south Samnium. Since it possessed a good section of the Adriatic coast, it possessed several seaports, the most important of which were Ancona and Firmum Picenum. The main inland town and capital city was Asculum Picentum. The original inhabitants were of Italiote and Illyrian stock, but when the first King Brennus invaded Italy many of his Celtic tribesmen settled in Picenum, and intermarried with the earlier folk. There was also a tradition that Sabines from the other side of the Apennines had migrated to settle Picenum. Its people were referred to as Picentines or Picentes. The region fell more or less into two parts—northern Picenum, closely allied to southern Umbria, was under the sway of the great family called Pompeius, whereas Picenum south of the Flosis River was connected more closely to Samnium in the spiritual ties of its people.

pilum Plural, *pila*. The Roman infantry spear, especially as modified by Gaius Marius. It had a very small, wickedly barbed head of iron and an upper shaft of iron; this was joined to a shaped wooden stem which fitted the hand comfortably. Marius modified it by introducing a weakness into the junction between iron and wooden sections of the shaft; when the *pilum* lodged in a shield or enemy's body, it broke apart, and thus was of no use to enemy soldiers. The Roman legions, however, possessed craftsmen who could quickly mend *pila* after a battle.

Pisidia This region lay to the south of Phrygia, and was even wilder and more backward. Extremely mountainous and filled with lakes, its climate was held to be a very healthy one. Little industry or populous settlement existed; the countryside was heavily forested with magnificent pines. Its people apparently were an ancient and indigenous strain allied to the Thracians, and its language was unique. Those few Pisidians who came to the notice of Rome and Romans were famous for their bizarre religious beliefs.

Plautus His real name was Titus Maccius Plautus. An Umbrian, he lived during the third century B.C., and died at some date after 184 B.C. During his long career he wrote about 130 plays. He worked in the comedic form, and in Latin; though his plots were essentially borrowed from Greek comedy, he contributed an unmistakably Roman feel to his plays, shifting his locales from Greece to Rome, enhancing the importance of slave characters, and giving his Roman or Italian audiences a completely comfortable feeling that what they saw was taking place at home rather than in Greece. His dialogue (even in modern English translation) is remarkably free and extremely funny. Critically he failed to be faithful to his own plots and often succumbed to interpolated scenes having nothing to do with what had gone before or was yet to come—wit was all. Though no trace of the music has come down to us, his plays were larded with songs, some accompanied by a lyre (the *canticum*) or flute. The importance of music in Latin comedy relative to Greek comedy may perhaps have been a heritage from the Etruscans; the music in Latin plays may have been freer and more melodic in our present-day terms than Greek music.

plebeian, Plebs All Roman citizens who were not patricians were plebeians—that is, they belonged to the Plebs (the *e* is short, so *Pleb* rhymes with *Feb* of "February"). At the beginning of the Republic, no plebeian could be a priest, a curule magistrate, or even a senator. This situation lasted only a very short while; one by one the exclusively patrician institutions crumbled before the onslaught of the Plebs, that much larger class of citizens not being above threatening to secede. By the time of Marius and Sulla it could be said that the Plebs ran Rome, that there was little if any advantage in being patrician.

plebiscite *Plebiscitum.* A law passed in the Plebeian Assembly was more properly a *plebiscitum* than a *lex.* From very early in the Republic, plebiscites were regarded as legally binding, but the *lex Hortensia* of 287 B.C. made this an official fact. From then on, there was virtually no difference at law between a *plebiscitum* and a *lex*. By the time of Marius and Sulla almost all the legal clerks who were responsible for putting the laws on tablets and recording them for posterity neglected to mention whether the laws were *plebiscitum* or *lex*.

pomerium   The sacred boundary enclosing the city of Rome. Marked by stones called *cippi,* it was reputedly inaugurated by King Servius Tullius, and remained without alteration until the later years of Sulla's career. The *pomerium* did not exactly follow the Servian Walls, one good reason why it is doubtful that the Servian Walls were built by King Servius Tullius—who would surely have caused his walls to follow the same line as his *pomerium.* The whole of the ancient Palatine city of Romulus was enclosed by the *pomerium,* but the Aventine lay outside it, and so did the Capitol. Tradition held that the *pomerium* might be enlarged only by a man who significantly increased the size of Roman territory. In religious terms, Rome herself existed only within the *pomerium;* all outside it was merely Roman territory.

pons   A bridge.

pontifex   The Latin word for a priest; it has survived to be absorbed unchanged into most modern European languages. Many Latin etymologists consider that in very early Roman times the pontifex was a maker of bridges, and that the making of bridges was considered a mystical art, thus putting the maker in close touch with the gods. Be that as it may, by the time the Republic was flourishing the pontifex was a priest; incorporated into a special college, he served as an adviser to Rome's magistrates in religious matters—and inevitably would be a magistrate himself. At first all pontifices had to be patrician, but a *lex Ogulnia* of 300 B.C. stipulated that half of the College of Pontifices had to be plebeian.

Pontifex Maximus   The head of Rome's State-run religion, and most senior of all priests. He seems to have been an invention of the infant Republic, a typically masterly Roman way of getting around an obstacle without ruffling too many feelings; for in the time of the kings of Rome, the Rex Sacrorum had been the chief priest, this being a title held by the king. Probably because they considered it unwise to abolish the Rex Sacrorum, the rulers of the new Republic of Rome simply created a new pontifex whose role and status were superior to those of the Rex Sacrorum. This new priest was given the title Pontifex Maximus; to reinforce his states-manlike position, he was to be elected rather than co-opted (as the ordinary pontifices were). At first he was probably required to be a patrician (the Rex Sacrorum remained a patrician right through the Republic), but by the middle of the Republic he was more likely to be a plebeian. He supervised all the various members of the various priestly colleges—pontifices, augurs, *flamines*, fetials, and other minor priests—and the Vestal Virgins. In Republican times he occupied the most prestigious State-owned house, but shared it with the Vestal Virgins. His official headquarters had the status of a temple—the little old Regia in the Forum Romanum just outside his house.

Pontus   A large kingdom at the southeastern end of the Euxine Sea. In the west it bordered Paphlagonia at Sinope, in the east Colchis at Apsarus. Inland it bordered Armenia Magna on the east and Armenia Parva on the southeast; to proper south was Cappadocia, west of it was Galatia. Wild, untamed, beautiful, and mountainous, Pontus had a fertile littoral dotted with Greek colony cities like Sinope, Amisus and Trapezus. Some idea of the climate can be gained from the fact that Pontus was the original home of the cherry and the rhododendron. Because the interior of Pontus was divided by three ranges of very high peaks running parallel to the coastline, it was never in antiquity a truly combined entity; its kings took tribute rather than taxed, and allowed each district to run its affairs in the manner local terrain and sophistication dictated. Gemstones and much alluvial gold added to the wealth of its kings, the Mithridatidae, as did silver, tin and iron.

praefectus fabrum   "He who supervises the making." One of the most important men in a Roman Republican army, technically he was not even a part of it; he was a civilian appointed to the post of *praefectus fabrum* by the general. The *praefectus fabrum* was responsible for the equipping and supplying of the army in all respects, from its animals and their fodder to its men and their food. Because he let out the contracts to businessmen and manufacturers for equipment and supplies, he was a very powerful figure—and unless he was a man of superior integrity, in a perfect position to enrich himself.

praenomen The first name of a Roman man. There were very few of them in use—perhaps twenty at the time of Marius and Sulla, and half of that twenty were not common, or were confined to the men of one particular *gens*, as with Mamercus, confined to the Aemilii Lepidi. Each *gens* or clan favored certain *praenomina* only, which further reduced the number available. A modern scholar can often tell from a man's *praenomen* whether or not that man was a genuine member of the *gens;* the Julii, for instance, favored Sextus, Gaius and Lucius only, so a man called Marcus Julius was not a true Julian of the patrician *gens;* the Licinii favored Publius, Marcus and Lucius; the Pompeii favored Gnaeus, Sextus and Quintus; the Cornelii favored Publius, Lucius and Gnaeus; the Servilii of the patrician *gens* favored Quintus and Gnaeus. Appius belonged only to the Claudii. One of the great puzzles for modern scholars concerns that Lucius Claudius who was Rex Sacrorum during the late Republic; Lucius is not a Claudian *praenomen,* but as he was certainly a patrician, Lucius Claudius the Rex Sacrorum must have been a genuine Claudian. I have postulated that there was a branch of the Claudian *gens* bearing the *praenomen* Lucius which traditionally always held the priesthood of Rex Sacrorum.

praetor This was the second most senior position in the hierarchy of Roman magistrates (excluding the office of censor, a special case). At the very beginning of the Republic the two highest magistrates of all were called praetors. But by the end of the fourth century B.C. the word "consul" was being used to describe these highest magistrates. One praetor was the sole representative of this position for many decades thereafter; he was very obviously the *praetor urbanus,* as his duties were confined to the city of Rome, thus freeing up the two consuls for duty as war leaders away from Rome. In 242 B.C. a second praetor was created—the *praetor peregrinus.* There soon followed Rome's acquisition of overseas provinces requiring governance, so in 227 B.C. two more praetors were created, to deal with Sicily and Sardinia/Corsica. In 197 B.C. the number was increased from four to six praetors, to cope with governance of the two Spains. However, after that no more praetors were created; at the time of Marius and Sulla, six seems to have been the standard number, though in some years the Senate apparently felt it necessary to bring the number up to eight. There is, I add, modern argument about this; some scholars think it was Sulla as dictator who increased the praetors from six to eight, whereas others consider the number became eight during the time of Gaius Gracchus.

praetor peregrinus In English, I have chosen to describe the *praetor peregrinus* as the foreign praetor because he dealt only with legal matters and lawsuits involving one or more parties who were not Roman citizens. By the time of Marius and Sulla the foreign praetor's duties were confined to the dispensation of justice; he traveled all over Italy, and sometimes further afield than that. He also heard the cases involving non-citizens within the city of Rome.

praetor urbanus In English, the urban praetor. By the time of Marius and Sulla his duties were almost purely in litigation; he was responsible for the supervision of justice and the law courts within the city of Rome. His imperium did not extend beyond the fifth milestone from Rome, and he was not allowed to leave Rome for more than ten days at a time. If both the consuls were absent from Rome, he was its senior magistrate, therefore empowered to summon the Senate, make decisions about execution of government policies, even organize the defenses of the city if under threat of attack. It was his decision as to whether two litigants should proceed to court or to a formal hearing; in most cases he decided the matter there and then, without benefit of hearing or trial process.

primus pilus Later, *primipilus*. The centurion in command of the leading century of the leading cohort of a Roman legion, and therefore the chief centurion of that legion. He rose to this position by a serial promotion, and was considered the most able man in the legion. During the time of Marius and Sulla, the centuries in the leading cohort appear to have been the same size as all the other centuries.

Princeps Senatus The Leader of the House. He was chosen by the censors according to the rules of the *mos maiorum:* he had to be a patrician, the leader of his decury, an *interrex* more times than anyone else, be of unimpeachable moral integrity, and have more *auctoritas* and *dignitas* than any other patrician senator. The title of Princeps Senatus was not given for life, but was subject to review by each new pair of censors, who could remove a man from the post and substitute another man did the Princeps Senatus fail to measure up. Marcus Aemilius Scaurus was chosen Princeps Senatus at an early age, apparently during his consulship in 115 B.C. and long before his term as censor (109 B.C.); it was unusual for a man to be appointed Princeps Senatus before he had been censor. Scaurus's winning of the post was either a signal mark of honor for an extraordinary man, or else (as some modern scholars have suggested), in 115 B.C. Scaurus was the most senior patrician senator available for the job. Whatever the reason behind his appointment, Scaurus held the title Princeps Senatus until his death in 89 B.C. His successor was Lucius Valerius Flaccus, consul in 100 B.C. and censor in 97 B.C.

privatus   A private citizen. I use the term in this book to describe a man who was a member of the Senate but not serving as a magistrate.

proconsul   One serving with the imperium of a consul but not in office as consul. Proconsular imperium was normally given to a man who had just finished his year as consul and went to govern a province or command an army in the name of the Senate and People of Rome. A man's term as proconsul usually lasted for one year, but was commonly prorogued beyond that year if the man was engaged in a campaign against an enemy still unsubdued, or there was no one suitable to take his place. If a consular was not available to govern a province difficult enough to warrant a proconsul, one of the year's crop of praetors was sent to govern it, but endowed with proconsular imperium. Proconsular imperium was limited to the area of the proconsul's province or task, and was lost the moment he stepped across the *pomerium* into the city of Rome.

proletarii   Another name for the lowliest of all Roman citizens, the *capite censi* or Head Count. The word *proletarius* derived from *proles*, which meant progeny, offspring, children in an impersonal sense; the lowly were called *proletarii* because children were the only thing they were capable of producing. I have avoided using the word because of its Marxist connotations, connotations having absolutely no validity in ancient times.

propraetor   One serving with the imperium of a praetor but not in office as a praetor. It was an imperium given to a praetor after his year in office was over in order to empower him to govern a province and, if necessary, conduct a defensive war. Like the imperium of the proconsul, it was lost the moment its holder stepped over the *pomerium* into the city of Rome. In degree it was a lesser imperium than proconsul, and was normally given to the governor of a peaceful province. According to the rules, any war the propraetor engaged upon had to be forced upon him, he could not seek it out. However, that didn't stop propraetors like Gaius Marius making war in their provinces.

prorogue   To extend a man's tenure of magisterial office beyond its normal time span. It applied to governorships or military commands rather than to the magistracies themselves. That is, it affected proconsuls and propraetors. Metellus Numidicus was sent to Africa to fight Jugurtha while still consul, but had not got his campaign off the ground when his year as consul expired; his command in the war against Jugurtha was prorogued into the following year, and into the year following that. I include the word in this glossary because I have discovered that modern English language dictionaries of small and medium size neglect to give this meaning in treating the word "prorogue."

province   *Provincia.* Originally this meant the sphere of duty of a magistrate or promagistrate holding imperium, and therefore applied as much to consuls and praetors in office inside Rome as it did to those in the field. Then the word came to mean the place where the imperium was exercised by its holder, and finally was applied to that place as simply meaning it was in the ownership of Rome. By the time of Marius and Sulla, all of Rome's provinces were outside Italy and Italian Gaul.

publicani   Singular, *publicanus.* Tax-farmers. These were the great private companies run from Rome which "farmed" the taxes of various parts of Rome's growing empire. The whole activity of farming the taxes was let out on contract by the censors every five years. The employees of these companies who actually collected the taxes in the provinces were also called *publicani*.

Public Horse   A horse which belonged to the State—to the Senate and People of Rome. Going all the way back to the kings, it had been State policy to provide the 1,800 most senior knights of Rome with horses. Presumably when the practice began horses were both scarce and colossally expensive, otherwise the State of Rome, notoriously parsimonious, would not have spent its precious money; it would simply have required its knights to provide their own mounts, as happened during the Republic when the number of knights far exceeded 1,800.

By the time of Marius and Sulla, to own a Public Horse was a social cachet of no mean order; the animals were handed down from generation to generation in the same families, so to possess a Public Horse was tantamount to saying your family had been around since the beginning. That this was not so we know from the fact that Pompey possessed a Public Horse—presumably when a family died out, its Public Horse was passed to someone of newer origins but enormous influence. Cato the Censor, considered a peasant New Man, was very proud to say that his great-grandfather (who must have lived during the fourth century B.C.) had received from the Treasury of Rome the price of no less than five Public Horses killed under him in battle.

When Gaius Sempronius Gracchus (see **The Gracchi**) split the Senate off from the **knights**, there is no evidence that his law required that a senator give up his Public Horse because he was no longer a knight; on the contrary, those of senatorial family who had possessed the Public Horse continued to possess it, witness Pompey the Great, and presumably his father.

Though it was not always observed, some censors (including Cato the Censor) insisted that the 1,800 owners of the Public Horse parade themselves and their animals in order to make sure that these men were keeping themselves in shape and caring properly for their steeds. The parade of the Public Horse, when held, occurred perhaps on the Ides of July; the censors sat in state on a tribunal atop the steps of the temple of Castor and Pollux in the Forum Romanum and watched each holder of the Public Horse solemnly lead his mount in a kind of march-past. If the censors considered a man had let himself go to seed, they stripped him of his entitlement to the Public Horse.

Punic   The adjective applied to Carthage and its people, but particularly to the three wars fought between Carthage and Rome. The word is derived from the origin of the Carthaginians— Phoenicia.

quaestor   The lowest rung on the senatorial *cursus honorum.* At the time of Marius and Sulla, to be elected a quaestor did not mean a man was automatically a member of the Senate; however, it was the normal practice of the censors to admit quaestors to the Senate. Many who stood for election as quaestor were already in the Senate. The exact number of quaestors elected in any one year at this time is not known, but was perhaps twelve to sixteen. The age at which a man sought election as a quaestor was thirty, which was also the correct age for entering the Senate. A quaestor's chief duties were fiscal: he might be seconded to the Treasury in Rome, or to secondary treasuries, or to collecting customs and port dues (there were three such quaestors at this time, one in Ostia, one in Puteoli, and one who did the other ports), or to collecting Rome's rents from *ager publicus* at home and abroad, or to managing the finances of a province. A consul going to govern a province could ask by name for a particular man to serve as his quaestor—this was a great distinction for the man in question, and assured him of both election and a place in the Senate. Normally the quaestorship lasted for one year, but if a man was requested by name he was obliged to remain with his chief until his chief's term came to an end. Quaestors entered office on the fifth day of December.

Quirites   Literally, Roman citizens of civilian status. What we do not know is whether the word "*Quirites*" also implied that the citizens in question had never served as soldiers in Rome's armies; certain remarks of Caesar the Dictator might lead one to believe that this was so, for he addressed his mutinous soldiers as *Quir-*

ites, and in doing so heaped such scorn upon them that they immediately pleaded for his pardon. However, much changed between the time of Marius and Sulla and the time of Caesar the Dictator. I have chosen to assume that at the time of Marius and Sulla, to be hailed as *Quirites* was no insult.

quizzing-glass A magnifying lens on a stick. It had much the same connotations in the ancient world as a monocle during the early twentieth century—it was an affectation. It was also, however, of great good use to one suffering the presbyopia of encroaching age in an era before the invention of spectacles. It could not contain a lens specifically ground for the purpose of enlarging print, but some stones accidentally possessed lens properties, and were thus immensely valuable objects. We know the emperor Nero had an emerald quizzing-glass; having seen the wealth of emeralds which came from Asia Minor, it is logical to assume that the Kings of Pontus had free access to emeralds, and that an occasional stone was suited for use in a quizzing-glass.

repetundae Extortion. Until the time of Gaius Gracchus, it was not standard practice to prosecute provincial governors who used their power to enrich themselves; one or two special courts had been set up to prosecute specific men, but that was all. These early special courts were staffed entirely by senators, and quickly became a joke—senatorial juries would not convict their fellows. Then in 122 B.C. Manius Acilius Glabrio, boon companion of Gaius Gracchus, passed a *lex Acilia* providing a permanent court staffed by knights to hear cases of *repetundae,* and impaneled 450 named knights to act as a pool from which the juries would be drawn. In 106 B.C. Quintus Servilius Caepio, consul in that year, returned all courts to the Senate, including the extortion court. Then in 101 B.C. Gaius Servilius Glaucia gave the extortion court back to the knights, with many innovative refinements which were to become standard practice in all courts. The cases we know of were all concerned with governors of provinces, but it would seem that after the *lex Acilia* of 122 B.C., the extortion court was empowered to try any kind of case dealing with illegal enrichment. There were rewards offered to citizen informants, and non-citizens who successfully brought a prosecution before the court were rewarded with the citizenship.

Republic The word was originally two words—*res publica*—that is, the thing which constitutes the people as a whole—that is, its government. We use the word "republic" today to mean an elected government which does not acknowledge any monarch its superior, but it is doubtful if the Romans thought of it in quite that way, despite the fact that they founded their Republic as an alternative to kings.

rhetoric The art of oratory, something both the Greeks and the Romans turned into an approximation of science. A proper orator spoke according to carefully laid out rules and conventions which extended far beyond mere words; body language and movements were intrinsic parts of it. In the early and middle Republic teachers of Greek rhetoric were despised, and sometimes even outlawed from Rome; Cato the Censor was an avowed enemy of the Greek rhetor. However, the Graecophilia of Scipio Aemilianus's day broke down much of this Latin opposition, so that by the time of the Brothers Gracchi most young Roman noblemen were being taught by Greek rhetors. Whereupon the Latin rhetors fell into disfavor! There were different styles of rhetoric—Lucius Licinius Crassus Orator favored the Asianic style, more florid and dramatic than the Attic style. It must always be remembered that the audience which gathered to listen to public oration—be it concerned with politics or the law courts—was composed of connoisseurs of rhetoric. The audience watched and listened in a spirit of extreme criticism; it knew all the rules and techniques, and was not easy to please.

Roma The Latin name of Rome.

Romulus and Remus The twin sons of Rhea Silvia, daughter of the King of Alba Longa and the god Mars. Her uncle Amulius, who had usurped the throne, put the twins in a basket made of rushes and set them adrift on the Tiber. They were washed up beneath a fig tree at the base of the Palatine, found by a she-wolf, and suckled by her in her cave nearby. They were rescued by Faustulus and his wife Acca Larentia, who raised them to manhood. After deposing Amulius and putting their grandfather back on his throne, the twins founded a settlement on the Palatine. Once its walls were built, Remus jumped over them and was put to death by Romulus, apparently for sacrilege. Romulus then set out to acquire subjects to live in his town, which he did in respect of males by establishing an asylum in the depression between the two humps of the Capitol, there collecting refugees who seem to have been criminals. Female citizens he acquired by tricking the Sabines of the Quirinal into bringing their women to a feast and then kidnapping them as wives for his men. Romulus ruled for a long time. Then one day he went hunting in the Goat Swamps of the Campus Martius and was caught in a terrible storm; when he didn't come home, it was believed that he had been taken by the gods and made an immortal.

rostra The plural form of "*rostrum*," meaning a ship's bronze or reinforced oaken beak. This fierce object jutted well forward of the bows just below the level of the water, and was used to hole an enemy ship in the maneuver called "ramming." When in 338 B.C. the consul Gaius Maenius attacked the Volscian fleet in Antium harbor, he defeated it completely. To mark the end of the Volsci as a rival power to Rome, Maenius removed the beaks of the ships he had sent to the bottom or captured and fixed them to the Forum wall of the speaker's platform tucked into the well of the Comitia. Ever after, the speaker's platform was known as the rostra—the ships' beaks.

Rubico River Also known as the Rubicon, it was the river which formed the boundary between Italian Gaul and peninsular Italy on the eastern side of the Apennines (the Arnus did the same thing to the west). No one today is sure which modern river is the antique Rubico; scholarly opinion favors a very short and uninspiring stream now called the Rubicone. I beg to differ. Surely the Rubico was that river which had its source in closest proximity to the source of the Arnus? Ancient boundaries wherever possible were visible phenomena—otherwise, why have the border of Italian Gaul follow the contour of the huge loop in the Arnus? I contend that the Rubico was not a short little coastal stream, but a long river with its source high enough up in the Apennines to give it a respectable volume of water in its bed as well as the necessary proximity to the source of the Arnus. My pick is the modern Ronco, which enters the Adriatic between Ravenna and Rimini (Ariminum) and rises very close to the Arnus. Why would a people as sensible as the Romans choose a little coastal trickle as the boundary when a much larger and longer river was in the vicinity? Extensive drainage and canal work has been going on for so many centuries around Ravenna that no one can be sure.

saepta   "The sheepfold." In Republican times, this was simply an open area on the Campus Martius not far from the Via Lata, and in proximity to the Villa Publica; it possessed no permanent buildings. Here the *comitia centuriata* met in its centuries. As the Centuriate Assembly normally called for a voting procedure, the *saepta* was divided up for the occasion by temporary fences so that the Five Classes could vote in their Centuries.

sagum   The soldier's heavy-weather cape. It was made out of greasy wool to make it as waterproof as possible, cut on the full circle with a hole in its middle for the head to poke through, and came well down the body for maximum protection; it was capacious enough to cover the soldier's back-borne kit also. The best kind of *sagum* came from Liguria, where the wool was exactly right for it.

saltatrix tonsa   "Barbered dancing-girl." That is, a male homosexual who dressed as a woman and sold his sexual favors.

Samnium   The territory lying between Latium, Campania, Apulia, and Picenum. Most of Samnium was ruggedly mountainous and not particularly fertile; its towns tended to be poor and small, and numbered among them Bovianum, Caieta, and Aeclanum. Aesernia and Beneventum, the two biggest towns, were Latin Rights communities implanted in Samnite territory by Rome. The people of the general area called Samnium were of several different nations—the Paeligni, the Marrucini, the Vestini, and the Frentani each occupied a different part, and the Samnites the rest. Throughout their history the Samnites were implacable enemies of Rome, and several times during the early and middle Republic inflicted crushing defeats on Rome. However, they had neither the manpower nor the financial resources to throw off the Roman yoke permanently. About 180 B.C. the Samnites were sufficiently sapped of strength to prove incapable of refusing a foreign race of settlers; to lessen Roman troubles in the northwest, Rome shifted forty thousand Ligurians to Samnium. At the time it had seemed to Rome an excellent idea, but the new settlers were eventually fully absorbed into the Samnite nation—and harbored no more love for Rome than their Samnite hosts. Thus Samnite resistance grew afresh.

satrap The title given by the Persian kings to their provincial or territorial governors. Alexander the Great seized upon the term and employed it, as did the later Arsacid kings of Parthia. The region ruled by a satrap was called a satrapy.

Saturninus Lucius Appuleius Saturninus was born about 135 B.C., of a respectable family with close links to Picenum (his sister was married to the Picentine Titus Labienus, his colleague in his last tribunate of the plebs). Elected quaestor for 104 B.C., he was given the job of looking after the grain supply and the port of Ostia, only to be sacked from his position and expelled from the Senate when Marcus Aemilius Scaurus the Princeps Senatus blamed him for a premature increase in the price of grain. Saturninus didn't take this disgrace lying down; he stood for election as a tribune of the plebs for 103 B.C., and got in. During this first term as a tribune of the plebs Saturninus allied himself with Gaius Marius, and passed laws benefiting Marius, particularly one allocating land in Africa for Marius's Jugurthine War veterans. He also passed a law establishing a special court to try those accused of a crime he called *maiestas minuta*—"little treason."

In 102 and 101 B.C. Saturninus was out of office, but sufficiently obnoxious to irritate the censor Metellus Numidicus, who tried to expel him from the Senate; the result was a riot in which Metellus Numidicus was severely beaten about. He stood for a second term as tribune of the plebs for 100 B.C., and was elected, still in alliance with Marius. A second land bill, to settle Marius's veterans from the war against the Germans on land in Gaul-across-the-Alps, provoked huge fury in the Senate, but Saturninus went ahead and procured it. The members of the Senate were required to swear an oath to uphold the law; all swore except Metellus Numidicus, who elected to pay a heavy fine and go into exile. From there on, Saturninus became an increasing embarrassment for Marius, who sloughed him off, his own reputation having suffered greatly.

Saturninus then began to woo the Head Count with promises of grain; there was a famine at the time, and the Head Count was hungry. When the elections for tribunes of the plebs for 99 B.C. were held, Saturninus ran for a third term, and was defeated; his boon companion Gaius Servilius Glaucia conveniently arranged that one of the successful candidates be murdered, and Saturninus gained office to replace the dead man. Stirred to the point of revolution, the Forum crowds threatened the government of Rome sufficiently to spur Marius and Scaurus into an alliance which produced the Senate's Ultimate Decree. Saturninus and his friends were apprehended after Marius cut off the water supply to the Capitol, where the group had taken refuge. Put in the Senate House for safekeeping, they were stoned to death by a rain of roof tiles. All of Saturninus's laws were then annulled.

Scordisci   A tribal confederation of Celts admixed with Illyrians and Thracians, the Scordisci lived in Moesia between the valley of the Danubius and the Macedonian border. Powerful and warlike, they plagued the Roman governors of Macedonia perpetually.

Scythians   This people was probably of Germanic stock, and spoke an Indo-European language. They lived in the Asian steppelands to the east of the Tanais River, extending south as far as the Caucasus. They were well organized enough socially to have kings, and were fabled goldsmiths.

Senate   Properly, *Senatus*. The Romans believed that Romulus himself founded the Senate by collecting one hundred patrician men into an advisory body and giving them the title *patres* ("fathers"). However, it is more likely that the Senate was an advisory body set up by the later kings of Rome. When the Republic replaced the kings, the Senate was retained, now comprising three hundred patricians. Scant years later it contained plebeian senators also, though it took the plebeians somewhat longer to attain the senior magistracies.

Because of the Senate's antiquity, legal definition of its powers, rights, and duties were at best inadequate; it was an important constituent of the ***mos maiorum***. Membership of the Senate was for life, which predisposed it toward the oligarchy it soon became. Throughout its history, its members fought strenuously to preserve their—as they saw it—natural pre-eminence. Under the Republic, senators were appointed by (and could be expelled by) the censors. There were thirty decuries of ten senators each, the decury being led by a patrician—which meant that there always had to be a minimum of thirty patrician senators in the Senate. By the time of Marius and Sulla it was customary to demand that a senator have property bringing him in at least a million sesterces a year, though during the entire life of the Republic this was never a formal law. Like much else, it simply *was*.

Senators alone were entitled to wear the *latus clavus* or broad stripe on their tunics; they wore closed shoes of maroon leather, and a ring which had originally been made of iron, but came to be of gold. Meetings of the Senate had to be held in properly inaugurated premises. The Senate had its own meeting-house, the **Curia Hostilia**, but often chose to assemble elsewhere. The ceremonies and meeting of New Year's Day, for example, were held in the temple of Jupiter Optimus Maximus, while meetings to discuss war were held outside the *pomerium* in the temple of **Bellona**. Sessions could only go on between sunrise and sunset, and could not take place on days when any of the Comitia met, though could take place on a comitial day if no Comitia meeting was convoked.

There was a rigid hierarchy among those allowed to speak in senatorial meetings, with the Princeps Senatus at the top of the list at the time of Marius and Sulla; patricians always preceded plebeians of exactly the same status otherwise. Not all members of the House were allowed the privilege of speaking. The *senatores pedarii* (I have used a British parliamentary term, backbenchers, to describe them, as they sat behind those permitted to speak) were allowed to vote only, not to speak. No restrictions were placed upon a man's oration in terms of length of time or germane content—hence the popularity of the technique now called filibustering—talking a motion out. If the issue was unimportant or the response completely unanimous, voting could be by voice or a show of hands, but a formal vote took place by division of the House, meaning that the senators left their stations and grouped themselves to either side of the curule dais according to their yea or nay, and were then physically counted. An advisory rather than a true legislating body always, the Senate issued its *consulta* or decrees as requests to the various Comitia. If the issue was serious, a quorum had to be present before a vote could be taken, though we do not know the precise number of senators who constituted a quorum—perhaps a quarter? Certainly most meetings were not heavily attended, as there was no rule which said a senator had to attend meetings on a regular basis.

In certain areas the Senate traditionally reigned supreme, despite its lack of legislating power: the *fiscus* was controlled by the Senate, as it controlled the Treasury; foreign affairs were left to the Senate; war was the business of the Senate; and the appointment of provincial governors and the regulation of provincial affairs were left to the Senate to decide. After the time of Gaius Gracchus, in civil emergencies the Senate could override all other bodies in government by passing the *Senatus Consultum de republica defendenda*—its Ultimate Decree proclaiming its own sovereignty and the establishment of martial law. The Ultimate Decree, in other words, was a senatorial sidestep to prevent the appointment of a dictator.

Servian Walls *Murus Servii Tullii*. Republican Romans believed that the formidable walls enclosing the city of Rome had been erected in the time of King Servius Tullius. However, evidence suggests that they were built after Rome was sacked by the Gauls in 390 B.C. (see **Juno Moneta**). Down to the time of Caesar the Dictator they were scupulously kept up.

sesterces Latin singular, *sestertius*. The commonest of Roman coins. Roman accounting practices were expressed in sesterces, hence their prominence in Latin writings of Republican date. The name sestertius derives from *semis tertius*, meaning two and a half *as*es (see **as**). In Latin writing, it was abbreviated as *HS*. A small silver coin, the sestertius was worth a quarter of a denarius.

I have kept to the Latin when speaking of this coin in the singular, but have preferred to used the Anglicized form in the plural.

Sibylline Books   The Roman State possessed a series of prophecies written in Greek and called the Sibylline Books. They were acquired, it was believed, by King Tarquinius Priscus, at which date they were written on palm leaves; each time the King refused to buy them, one book was burned and the price for the rest went up until finally the King agreed to take the remainder. They were greatly revered and were in the care of a special college of minor priests called the *decemviri sacris faciundis;* in State crises they were solemnly consulted to see if there was a prophecy which fitted the situation.

sinus   A pronounced curve or fold. The term was used in many different ways, but for the purposes of this book, two only are of interest. One described the geographical feature we might call a gulf—Sinus Arabicus, et cetera. The second described the looping fold of toga as this garment emerged from under the right arm and was swept up over the left shoulder—the togate Roman's pocket.

Sosius   A name associated with the book trade in Rome. Two brothers Sosius published during the principate of Augustus. I have taken the name and extrapolated it backward in time; Roman businesses were often family businesses, and the book trade in Rome was already a flourishing one at the time of Marius and Sulla. Therefore, why not a Sosius?

spelt   A very fine, soft white flour. It was not suitable for making bread, but was excellent for making cakes. It was ground from the variety of wheat now known as *Triticum spelta.*

sponsio   In cases of civil litigation not calling for a hearing in a formal court of law (that is, cases which could be heard by the urban praetor), the urban praetor could only proceed to hear the case if a sum of money called *sponsio* was lodged in his keeping before the hearing began. This was either damages, or the sum of money in dispute. In bankruptcy complaints or nonpayment of debts, the sum owed was the *sponsio.* This meant that when the sum concerned could not be found by either the plaintiff or the defendant, the urban praetor was not empowered to hear the case.

In times of money shortage, it became a problem, hence the inclusion by Sulla in his law regulating debt of a provision waiving the lodgement of *sponsio* with the urban praetor.

steel The term Iron Age is rather misleading, as iron in itself is not a very usable metal. It only replaced bronze when ancient smiths discovered ways of steeling it; from then on, it was the metal of choice for tools, weapons, and other apparatus demanding a combination of hardness, durability and capacity to take an edge or point. Aristotle and Theophrastus, both writing in the Greece of the fourth century B.C., talk about steel, not about iron. However, the whole process of working iron into a usable metal evolved in total ignorance of the chemistry and metallurgy underlying it. The main ore used to extract iron was haematite; pyrites was little used because of the extreme toxicity of its sulphuric by-products. Strabo and Pliny the Elder both describe a method of roasting the ore in a hearth-type furnace (oxidation), and the shaft furnace (reduction). The shaft furnace was more efficient, could smelt larger quantities of ore, and was the method of choice. The carbon necessary for smelting was provided (as with bronze and other alloys) by charcoal. Most smelting works used both hearth and shaft furnaces side by side, and produced from the raw ore slag-contaminated "blooms" which were called sows (hence, presumably, our term "pig"). These sows were then reheated to above melting point and compelled to take up additional carbon from the charcoal by hammering (forging); this also drove out most of the contaminating slag, though ancient steels were never entirely free of slag. Roman smiths were fully conversant with the techniques of annealing, quenching, tempering, and cementation (this last forced yet more carbon into the iron). Each of these procedures changed the characteristics of the basic carbon steel in a different way, so that steels for various purposes could be made—razors, sword blades, knives, axes, saws, wood and stone chisels, cold chisels, nails, spikes, et cetera. So precious were the steels suitable for cutting edges that a thin piece of edge steel was welded (the Romans knew two methods of welding, pressure welding and fusion welding) onto a cheaper-quality base, as seen with ploughshares and axes. However, the Roman sword blade was made entirely from steel taking a cruelly sharp edge; it was produced by tempering at about 280°C. Tongs, anvils, hammers, bellows, crucibles, fire bricks, and the other tools in trade of a smith were known and universally used. Many of the ancient theories were quite wrong; it was thought, for instance, that the nature of the liquid used in quenching affected the quenching— urine was the quenching liquid of choice. And no one understood that the real reason why the iron mined in **Noricum** produced such superb steel lay in the fact that it naturally contained a small amount of manganese uncontaminated by phosphorus, arsenic, or sulphur, and therefore was modern manganese steel.

stibium   A black antimony-based powder soluble in water, *stibium* was used to dye or paint eyebrows and eyelashes, and to draw a line around the eyes.

stips   A wage. In the sense used in this book, the *stips* was the wage paid to a slave by his master. It was also called *peculium*.

Subura   The poorest and most densely populated part of the city of Rome. It lay to the east of the Forum Romanum in the declivity between the Oppian spur of the Esquiline Mount and the Viminal Hill. Its very long main street had three different names: at the bottom, where it was contiguous with the Argiletum, it was the Fauces Suburae; the next section was known as the Subura Major; and the final section, which scrambled up the steep flank of the Esquiline proper, was the Clivus Suburanus. The Subura Minor and the Vicus Patricii branched off the Subura Major in the direction of the Viminal. The Subura was an area composed entirely of insulae and contained only one prominent landmark, the Turris Mamilia, apparently some kind of tower. Its people were notoriously polyglot and independent of mind; many Jews lived in the Subura, which at the time of Marius and Sulla contained Rome's only synagogue. Suetonius says Caesar the Dictator lived in the Subura.

suffect consul   Consul *suffectus*. When an elected consul died in office or was in some other way rendered incapable of conducting the duties of his office, the Senate appointed a substitute called the *suffectus*. He was not elected. Sometimes the Senate would appoint a *suffectus* even when the consular year was just about over; at other times no substitute would be appointed even when the consular year was far from over. These discrepancies apparently reflected the mood of the House at the particular time. It seems too that the Senate needed the presence of the remaining consul to appoint a *suffectus*—witness senatorial helplessness when Cato the Consul was killed in 90 B.C. and the remaining consul, Lucius Julius Caesar, refused to come to Rome for the choosing of a *suffectus*. The name of the suffect consul was engraved upon the consular *fasti*, and he was entitled to call himself a consular after his period in office was over.

sumptuary law   A *lex sumptuaria*. These laws sought to regulate the amount of luxurious (that is, expensive) goods and/or foodstuffs a Roman might buy or have in his house, no matter how wealthy he was. Presumably the goods targeted were imported from abroad. During the Republic many sumptuary laws were leveled at women, forbidding them to wear more than a specified amount of jewelry, or ride in litters or carriages within the Servian Walls; as several magistrates found out, women so legislated against were inclined to turn nasty and become a force to be reckoned with.

suovetaurilia   This was a special sacrifice consisting of a pig (*su*), a sheep (*ove*), and an ox or bull (*taur*). It was offered to certain gods on critical occasions; Jupiter Optimus Maximus was one, Mars another. The ceremonies surrounding the *suovetaurilia* called for the sacrificial victims to be led in a solemn procession before being killed. Besides these special occasions of national crisis, there were two regular occasions on which a *suovetaurilia* was offered; the first occurred in late May when the land was purified by the twelve minor priests called the Arval Brethren; the second occurred at five-year intervals when the censors set up their booth on the Campus Martius and prepared to take the full census of Roman citizens.

tablinum   This room was the exclusive domain of the *paterfamilias* in a Roman family unit; unless too poor to have more than one or two rooms, he had his study, as I have chosen to call it.

talent   This ancient unit of weight was defined as the load a man could carry. Bullion and very large sums of money were expressed in talents, but the term was not confined to precious metals and money. In modem terms the talent weighed about fifty to fifty-five pounds (25 kilograms). A talent of gold weighed the same as a talent of silver, of course, but was far more valuable.

Tarpeian Rock Its precise location is still hotly debated, but it is known to have been quite visible from the lower Forum Romanum, and presumably was an overhang at the top of the Capitolium cliffs. Since the drop was not much more than eighty feet from the Tarpeian Rock to the bottom, the rock itself must have been located precisely above some sort of jagged outcrop—we have no evidence that anyone survived the fall. It was the traditional place of execution for Roman citizen traitors and murderers, who were either thrown from it or forced to jump from it. I have located it on a line from the temple of Ops.

tata The Latin diminutive for "father"—akin to our "daddy." I have, by the way, elected to use the almost universal "mama" as the diminutive for mother, but the Latin was *"mamma."*

Tellus The Roman earth goddess. Her worship became largely neglected after the importation of Magna Mater from Pessinus. Tellus had a big temple on the Carinae, in early days imposing; by the time of Marius and Sulla it was dilapidated.

Tiddlypuss, Lucius I needed a joke name of the kind people in all places at all times have used when they want to refer to a faceless yet representative person. In the USA it would be "Joe Blow," in the UK "Fred Bloggs." As I am writing in standard English for a largely non-Latinate readership, it was not possible to choose a properly Latin name to fulfill this function. I coined "Lucius Tiddlypuss" because it looks and sounds patently ridiculous, has an "uss" ending—and because of a mountain. This mountain was named in a Latin distortion after the villa of Augustus's infamous freedman, Publius Vedius Pollio, which lay on its flanks. The villa's name, a Greek one, was Pausilypon, whereas the Latin name of the mountain was Pausilypus—a clear indication of how much Pollio was loathed, for *pus* then meant exactly the same as "pus" does today in English. Speakers of Latin punned constantly, as we know. And that's how Lucius Tiddlypuss came into being, one of the few fictitious characters in this book.

toga The garment only a full citizen of Rome was permitted to wear. Made of lightweight wool, it was a most peculiar shape (which is why the togate "Romans" in Hollywood movies never look right). After exhaustive and brilliant experimentation, Dr. Lillian Wilson of Johns Hopkins worked out a size and shape which produce a perfect-looking toga. To fit a man five feet nine inches (175 cm) tall and having a waist of thirty-six inches (89.5 cm), the toga was about fifteen feet (4.6 m) wide, and seven feet six inches (2.25 m) long; the length measurement is draped on his height axis while the much bigger width measurement is wrapped around him. However, the shape was *not* a simple rectangle! It looked like this:

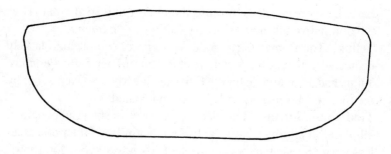

Unless the toga is cut as illustrated, it will absolutely refuse to drape the way it does on the togate men of the ancient statues. The Republican toga of Marius and Sulla's day was very large (the toga varied considerably in size between the time of the Kings of Rome and 500 A.D., a period of one thousand years). One final observation about the toga resulted from my own experimentation—I proved rather conclusively that the togate Republican Roman could not possibly have worn under-drawers or a loincloth. The toga itself disqualified the left hand from performing any task at groin level, as the left arm carried multiple folds and most of the weight of the garment. But when the toga is properly draped, the right hand can part it with astonishing ease, push up the hem of the tunic, and perform the act of urinating from a standing position—provided, that is, that there are no under-drawers or loincloth to fiddle with! I mention this interesting fact only because it is still said the Roman wore some sort of nether under-garment. Well, if he was wearing a toga, he couldn't have.

toga alba   Or *toga pura*, or *toga virilis*. This was the plain white toga of manhood as worn by an ordinary citizen. It was probably more cream or ecru than stark white.

toga candida   This was the specially whitened toga worn by those seeking office as an elected magistrate (our word "candidate" comes from the *toga candida*). The candidate wore his special toga on the day when he registered his candidacy, as he went about Rome canvassing, and on election day. Its stark whiteness was achieved by bleaching the garment in the sun for many days, and then working finely powdered chalk through it.

toga picta   The all-purple toga of the triumphing general, lavishly embroidered (presumably in gold) with pictures of people and events. The kings of Rome had worn the purple *toga picta*, and so too did the statue of Jupiter Optimus Maximus in his temple on the Capitol.

toga praetexta   The purple-bordered toga of the curule magistrate, it continued to be worn by these men after their term in office was over. It was also the garment worn by children of both sexes.

toga pulla   This was the toga of mourning, and was made of wool as close to black as possible. Senators in mourning also wore a knight's tunic bearing the *angustus clavus*, or "narrow stripe," on its shoulder.

toga trabea   Cicero's "particolored toga." It was the striped toga of the augur, and very likely the pontifex also. Like the *toga praetexta*, it had a purple border, but also was striped in alternate red and purple down its length.

togate   The correct English-language term to describe a man clad in his toga.

tribe   *Tribus*. By the beginning of the Republic, *tribus* to a Roman was not an ethnic grouping of his people, but a political grouping of service only to the State. There were thirty-five tribes altogether; thirty-one of these were rural, only four urban. The sixteen really old tribes bore the names of the various original patrician *gentes*, indicating that the citizens who belonged to these tribes were either members of the patrician families, or had once lived on land owned by the patrician families. During the early and middle Republic, when Roman-owned territory in the Italian peninsula began to expand, tribes were added to accommodate the new citizens within the Roman body politic. Full Roman citizen colonies also became the nuclei of fresh tribes. The four urban tribes were supposed to have been founded by King Servius Tullius, though the time of their actual foundation is more likely to have been during the early Republic. The last date of a tribal creation was 241 B.C. Every member of a tribe was entitled to register one vote in a tribal assembly; but his vote was not in itself significant. The votes in each tribe were counted first, then the tribe as a whole cast one single vote, the majority vote within the ranks of its members. This meant that in no tribal assembly could the huge number of citizens enrolled in the four urban tribes influence the outcome of a vote, as each of the thirty-one rural tribes had the exact same degree of voting power as each urban tribe. Members of rural tribes were not disbarred from living within the city of Rome, nor were their progeny forced into an urban tribe. Most senators and knights of the First Class belonged to rural tribes.

tribune *Tribunus.* An official representing the interests of a certain part of the Roman body politic. The name originally referred to those men who represented the tribes (*tribus—tribunus*), but, as the Republic got into its stride, the name came to mean an official representing various institutions not directly connected with the tribes per se.

tribune, military Those on the general's staff who were not elected tribunes of the soldiers, yet who ranked below legate but above cadet. If the general was not a consul currently in office, military tribunes might command his legions. Otherwise they did staff duties for the general. Military tribunes also served as commanders of cavalry units.

tribune of the plebs These magistrates came into being early in the Republic, when the Plebs was at complete loggerheads with the patricians. Elected by the tribal body of plebeians formed as the *concilium plebis* or *comitia plebis tributa* or Plebeian Assembly, they took an oath to defend the lives and property of members of the Plebs. By 450 B.C. there were ten tribunes of the plebs. By the time of Marius and Sulla these ten tribunes of the plebs had proven themselves a thorn in the side of the Senate rather than merely the patricians—and even though, by this time, they were themselves members of the Senate. A *lex Atinia de tribunis plebis in senatum legendis* of 149 B.C. had made tribunes of the plebs automatically members of the Senate upon election. Because they were not elected by the Whole People (that is, by patricians as well as plebeians), they had no power under Rome's unwritten constitution and were not magistrates in the same way as tribunes of the soldiers, quaestors, curule aediles, praetors, consuls, and censors; their magistracies were of the Plebs and their power in office resided in the oath the whole Plebs took to defend the sacrosanctity— the inviolability—of its elected tribunes. That the tribunes of the plebs were called tribunes was possibly due to the tribal organization of the Plebeian Assembly. The power of the tribunate of the plebs lay in the right of its officers to exercise a veto against almost any aspect of government: a tribune of the plebs could veto the actions or laws of his nine fellow tribunes, or any—or all!— other magistrates, including consuls and censors (witness how in 109 B.C. the censor Marcus Aemilius Scaurus, who had defied attempts to remove him from his office, yielded immediately when the tribune of the plebs Mamilius interposed his veto); he could veto the holding of an election; he could veto the passing of *lex* or *plebiscitum;* and he could veto decrees of the Senate, even in war and foreign affairs. Only a dictator (and perhaps an *interrex*) was not subject to the tribunician veto. Within his own Plebeian Assembly, the tribune of the plebs could even exercise the death penalty if his right to proceed in his duties was denied him.

During the early and middle years of the Republic, tribunes of the plebs were not members of the Senate. Then came the *lex*

Atinia of 149 B.C., which meant that election as a tribune of the plebs became a way of entering the Senate without being approved by the censors; from that time on, men who had been expelled from the Senate by the censors often sought election as tribunes of the plebs in order to get back in again. The tribune of the plebs had no imperium, and the authority vested in the office did not extend past the first milestone. Custom dictated that a man serve only one term as a tribune of the plebs, entering office on the tenth day of December for one year. But custom was not legally binding, as Gaius Sempronius Gracchus proved when he successfully sought a second term in 122 B.C. The real power of the office was vested in the *sacrosanctitas* (inviolability) of its holders, and *intercessio*, the right to interpose a veto. Tribunician contribution to government was in consequence more often obstructive than constructive.

tribune of the soldiers   Two dozen young men, aged between about twenty-five and twenty-nine years, were elected each year by the Assembly of the (whole) People to serve as *tribuni militum*, or military tribunes. As they were elected by the Whole People, they were true magistrates. They were the legally elected officers of the consul's legions (four legions belonged to the consuls in office), and were posted to command them, six per legion. At times when the consuls had more than six legions in the field (as at Arausio) the tribunes of the soldiers were rationed out between them, not always equally in numbers per legion.

tribune of the Treasury   *Tribuni aerarii*. There is a great deal of mystery about who the *tribuni aerarii* actually were. Originally they definitely were the army's paymasters, but by the middle of the Republic this task had been assumed by the quaestors. Yet at the time of Marius and Sulla, *tribuni aerarii* were numerous enough (and wealthy enough) to qualify for the Second Class in the Centuriate Assembly, having a census economic status not far inferior to the knights' minimum. Perhaps they were men descended from the original *tribuni aerarii* who simply clung to their old status to prove their antiquity. However, more likely, I think, that they were senior civil servants attached to the Treasury. Though the Senate and People of Rome frowned heavily upon bureaucracy and strenuously resisted any growth in numbers of public employees, there can be no doubt that once Rome's territorial possessions began to increase, one branch of the SPQR must have demanded more and more public officials of unelected nature. This branch was the Treasury (the *aerarium*). By the late Republic there must have been a fairly large number of senior civil servants administering the many departments and duties attached to the Treasury (and this increased dramatically after the time of Marius and Sulla). Money had to be exacted for many different taxes, at home and abroad; and money had to be found for everything from the purchase of public grain, to censors' building programs, to the army's pay, to minutiae like purchases of the urban praetor's pigs distributed throughout Rome at the Compitalia. While no doubt an elected magistrate issued orders about any or all of these items, he certainly did not concern himself with the mechanics implementing his orders. For these, there had to have been senior civil servants, men whose rank was distinctly higher than clerk or scribe; they probably came from respectable families and were probably well paid. The existence of a class of them can definitely be supposed at the time Cato Uticensis (in 64 B.C.) made such a nuisance of himself when appointed Treasury quaestor, for it was glaringly obvious that many years had elapsed since Treasury quaestors concerned themselves personally with the Treasury—and by 64 B.C. the Treasury was huge.

triclinium The dining room. By preference the family dining room was square in shape, and possessed three couches arranged to form a U. Standing in the doorway one looked into the hollow of the U; the couch on the left was called the *lectus summus*, the couch forming the middle or bottom of the U was the *lectus medius*, and the couch forming the right side was the *lectus imus*. Each couch was very broad, perhaps four or more feet (1.25 m), and at least twice that long. One end of the couch had a raised arm forming a head, the other end did not. In front of the couches, a little lower than the height of the couches, was a narrow table also forming a U. The male diners reclined on their left elbows, supported by bolsters; they were not shod, and could call for their feet to be washed. The host of the dinner reclined at the left end

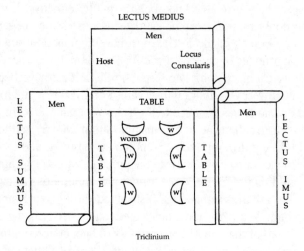

Triclinium

of the *lectus medius*, this being the bottom or armless end of it; the right-hand end of the same couch—its head—was the place where the most honored guest reclined, and was called the *locus consularis*. At the time of Marius and Sulla it was rare for women to recline alongside the men unless the dinner party was a men's party and the women invited of low virtue. The women of the family sat on upright chairs inside the double U of couches and table; they entered the room with the first course and left as soon as the last course was cleared away. Normally they drank only water, as women drinking wine were "loose."

triumph   The greatest of days for the successful general was the day upon which he triumphed. By the time of Marius and Sulla, a general had to have been hailed on the field as imperator by his troops, after which he was obliged to petition the Senate to grant him his triumph; only the Senate could sanction it, and sometimes—though not often—unjustifiably withheld it. The triumph itself was a most imposing parade consisting of musicians, dancers, wagons filled with spoils, floats depicting scenes from the campaign, the Senate in procession, prisoners and liberated Romans, and the army. The parade began in the Villa Publica on the Campus Martius, and followed a prescribed route thereafter—a special gate in the Servian Walls called the Porta Triumphalis, into the Velabrum, the Forum Boarium, and the Circus Maximus, after which it went down the Via Triumphalis and turned into the Via Sacra of the Forum Romanum. It terminated on the Capitol at the foot of the steps of the temple of Jupiter Optimus Maximus. The triumphing general and his lictors went into the temple and offered the god their laurels of victory, after which a triumphal feast was held in the temple.

triumphator The name given to the triumphing general.

tunic *Tunica.* The tunic was the basic item of clothing for almost all ancient Mediterranean peoples, including the Greeks and the Romans. As worn by a Roman of the time of Marius and Sulla, the tunic's body was rectangular in shape, without darts to confine it at the sides of the chest; the neck was probably cut on a curve for comfort rather than kept as a straight edge contiguous with the shoulders. The sleeves may have been woven as rectangular projections from the shoulders, or they may have been set in. It was not beyond the skill of ancient tailors to set in sleeves, and some people wore long sleeves, which had to be set in. The statues do not indicate that the tunics of men important enough to have statues were simply joined up the sides with a gap left at the top for the arms to go through. The sleeves of the tunics shown on statues of generals in particular look like proper short sleeves. The tunic was either belted with leather or girdled with a cord; the Roman tunic was always worn longer at the front than at the back by about three inches (75 mm). Those of the knight's census wore a narrow purple stripe down the right side of the tunic, those of the senator's census a wide purple stripe. The stripe may also have run down the left side of the tunic as well. I do not believe the stripe was a single one at mid-chest. A wall painting from Pompeii displaying a man wearing the *toga praetexta* shows a wide purple stripe going down the tunic from the right shoulder.

Tusculum A town on the Via Latina some fifteen miles from Rome. It was the first Latin town to receive the Roman citizenship, in 381 B.C., and was always unswervingly loyal to Rome. Cato the Censor came from Tusculum, where his family had possessed the Public Horse of Roman knighthood for at least three generations.

Vaticanus Both a plain, the Campus Vaticanus, and a hill, the Mons Vaticanus. They lay on the northern bank of the Tiber opposite the Campus Martius. At the time of Marius and Sulla, the plain was used for market gardening, the hill behind it for no published purpose.

Venus Libitina Goddess of the life force, Venus had many aspects. Venus Libitina was concerned with the extinction of the life force. An underworld deity of great importance in Rome, her temple was located outside the Servian Walls, more or less at the central point of Rome's vast necropolis on the Campus Esquilinus. Its exact location is not known, but since I had to site it somewhere, I put it at the crossroads where the Via Labicana intersected with two important *diverticula* (ring roads). The temple precinct was large for a Roman temple, and had a grove of trees, presumably cypresses (associated with death). In this precinct Rome's undertakers and funeral directors had their headquarters, presumably operating from stalls or booths. The temple itself contained a register of Roman citizen deaths and was rich, thanks to the accumulation of the coins which had to be paid to register a death. Should there be no consul to employ them, the *fasces* of the consul were deposited on a special couch inside the temple; the axes which were inserted into his *fasces* only when he left the city were also kept in the temple. I imagine that Rome's burial clubs, of which there were many, were connected in some way to Venus Libitina.

Vesta A very old Roman goddess of numinous nature, having no mythology and no image. She was the hearth, and so had particular importance within the family unit and the home, where she was worshipped alongside the Di Penates and the Lar Familiaris. Her official public cult was equally important, and was personally supervised by the Pontifex Maximus. Her temple in the Forum Romanum was very small, very old, and round in shape; it was adjacent to the Regia, the Well of Juturna and the residence of the

Pontifex Maximus. A fire burned in the temple permanently, and could not be allowed to go out.

Vestal Virgins Vesta had her own priesthood, the college of six women called the Vestal Virgins. They were inducted at about seven or eight years of age, took vows of complete chastity, and served the goddess for thirty years, after which they were released from their vows and sent back into the community at large. Their service over, they could marry if they wished—though few did, as it was thought unlucky. Their chastity was Rome's luck; that is, the luck of the State. When a Vestal was deemed unchaste she was not judged and punished out of hand, but was formally brought to trial in a specially convened court. Her alleged lovers were also tried, but in a different court. If convicted, she was cast into an underground chamber dug for the purpose; it was sealed over, and she was left there to die. In Republican times the Vestal Virgins lived in the same State house as the Pontifex Maximus, though sequestered from him.

vexillum A flag or banner.

via A main highway, road, or street.

villa A country residence, completely self-contained, and originally having an agricultural purpose—in other words, a farmstead. It was built around a peristyle or courtyard, had stables or farm buildings at its front, and the main dwelling at its back. Wealthy Romans of the late Republic began to build villas as vacation homes rather than as farmsteads, considerably changing the architectural nature (and grandeur) of the villa. Many holiday villas were on the seashore.

vir militaris See **Military Man**.

voting Roman voting was timocratic, in that the power of the vote was powerfully influenced by property status, and in that voting was not "one man, one vote" in style. Whether an individual voted in the Centuries or in the Tribes, his own personal vote could only influence the verdict of the Century or the Tribe in which he polled. Election outcomes were determined by the number of Century or Tribal votes going a particular way. Juridical voting was different. On a jury an individual did have a direct say in the outcome, as the jury contained an odd number of men and the decision was a majority one, not an unanimous one. It was timocratic, however, as a man of little property had little chance of jury duty.

Wooden Bridge   The name always given to the Pons Sublicius, the oldest of the bridges spanning the Tiber at the city of Rome.

yoke   The yoke was the crossbeam or tie which rested upon the necks of a pair of oxen or other animals in harness to draw a load. In human terms, it came to mean the mark of servility, of submission to the superiority and domination of others. There was a yoke for the young of both sexes to pass beneath inside the city of Rome, located somewhere on the Carinae; it was called the Tigillum, and perhaps signified submission to the seriousness of adult life. However, it was in military circumstances that the yoke came to have its greatest metaphorical significance. Very early Roman (or perhaps Etruscan) armies forced a defeated enemy to pass beneath the yoke; two spears were planted upright in the ground, and a third spear was placed from one top to the other to form a crosstie—the whole was too low for a man to pass beneath walking erect, he had to bend right over. Other peoples within Italy also adopted the custom, with the result that from time to time a Roman army was forced to pass beneath the yoke. To acquiesce to this was an intolerable humiliation; so much so, that the Senate and People back in Rome usually preferred to see an army stand and fight until the last man was dead, rather than sacrifice honor and *dignitas* by surrendering and passing beneath the yoke.

COLLEEN McCULLOUGH is the internationally acclaimed author of eighteen immensely successful novels. She lives on Norfolk Island in the South Pacific with her husband, Ric Robinson.

Colleen McCullough